THE COMPLETE GUIDE TO
TANKS
& ARMOURED FIGHTING VEHICLES

THE COMPLETE GUIDE TO
TANKS
& ARMOURED FIGHTING VEHICLES

OVER 400 VEHICLES AND 1200 WARTIME AND MODERN PHOTOGRAPHS

Features A–Z directories of tank destroyers, command versions, specialized tanks, armoured cars, armoured personnel carriers and self-propelled artillery

An illustrated history of the world's most important tanks and AFVs from the beginning of the 20th century to the present day

GEORGE FORTY & JACK LIVESEY

southwater

This edition is published by Southwater, an imprint of Anness Publishing Ltd, Blaby Road, Wigston, Leicestershire LE18 4SE; info@anness.com

www.southwaterbooks.com; www.annesspublishing.com

Anness Publishing has a new picture agency outlet for images for publishing, promotions or advertising. Please visit our website www.practicalpictures.com for more information.

Publisher: Joanna Lorenz
Managing Editor: Conor Kilgallon
Project Editor: Felicity Forster
Copy Editor and Indexer: Tim Ellerby
Cover Design: Dawn Young
Designer: Design Principals
Editorial Reader: Jay Thundercliffe
Production Manager: Steve Lang

Previously published as two separate volumes, *The Illustrated Guide to Tanks of the World* and *The Illustrated Guide to Armoured Fighting Vehicles of the World*

NOTE
The nationality of each vehicle is identified in the relevant specification box by the national flag that was current at the time of the vehicle's use.

PUBLISHER'S NOTE
Although the advice and information in this book are believed to be accurate and true at the time of going to press, neither the authors nor the publisher can accept any legal responsibility or liability for any errors or omissions that may have been made.

PAGE 1: **Challenger 1;** PAGE 2: **SA-8b "Gecko" SAM Vehicle;**
PAGE 3: **LVTP-7 Armoured Amphibious Assault Vehicle.**

Contents

A–Z of Modern Tanks: 1945 to the Present Day

ARMOURED FIGHTING VEHICLES

A–Z of Modern Armoured Fighting Vehicles: 1945 to the Present Day

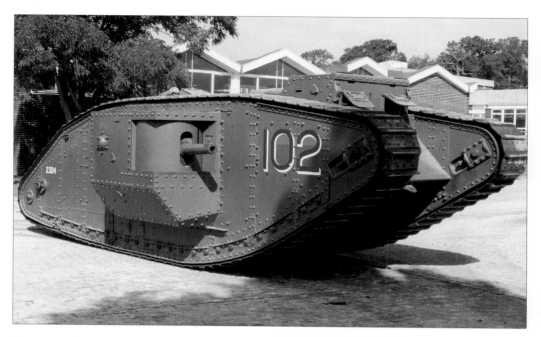

Introduction

The ability to transport weapon systems and men around the battlefield while protecting them from enemy fire has taxed military commanders and engineers alike for many centuries. The increasing availability, effectiveness and reliability of artillery, machine-guns and rifles at the end of the 19th century quickly made unprotected movement around the battlefield suicidal, as witnessed during the early engagements of World War I. There was no longer any place for cavalry, and infantry were quickly forced to become trench dwellers.

At the same time, the internal combustion engine was becoming a reliable and powerful technology and, together with the caterpillar track and rubber tyre, provided a less vulnerable replacement for the horse. The revolution in battleship contruction, which took place at the same time, produced high-quality steel plate, a technology that was transferred to vehicles. Thus the scene was set for the development of the modern armoured fighting vehicle.

Initially, it was the commercial motor car that provided the platform on which to mount machine-guns in a lightly armoured housing, and these "armoured cars" quickly demonstrated their usefulness in many of the traditional reconnaissance roles that had previously been fulfilled by light cavalry. They also proved themselves extremely adaptable and excelled on the hard-baked surfaces that were found in desert theatres such as Palestine. However, the cloying mud of the Western Front in World War I proved to be an insurmountable obstacle, and it

TOP: **The British Mark IV Heavy Tank was produced in greater numbers than any other model during World War I. This beautifully restored "male" carries two 6pdr guns mounted in sponsons on either side of the main body.** ABOVE: **Armoured cars saw action in virtually every theatre during World War I. This Austin Armoured Car is in Russian service, where the primitive roads added to the rate of attrition.**

was this lack of cross-country performance as well as limitations in the armour protection that led military engineers to consider alternatives to the standard wheeled vehicle.

By 1915, the stalemate of trench warfare on the Western Front and other theatres had become clear. The task now facing military leaders on both sides was to find a way of breaking the deadlock and transforming this static siege-like conflict into one of movement and manoeuvre. Initially, overwhelming force was thought to be the answer, and so huge

LEFT: The PzKpfw IV (together with the PzKpfw III) was the backbone of the Germany Panzer Division and spearhead of Blitzkrieg. This Ausf C carries a short-barrelled 7.5cm/2.95in L/24 low-velocity gun that was best suited to the infantry support role. BELOW: This vehicle made NATO commanders sit up and take notice. The Soviet BMP-1 Infantry Fighting Vehicle was highly innovative and posed a real threat to tactical thinking amongst the Western Allies at the time of its introduction in 1966.

quantities of men and munitions were deployed in set-piece frontal assaults on sections of the enemy line. However, the unprotected assaulting troops were bloodily repulsed by a virtually impregnable wall of machine-gun and rifle fire, together with pre-registered defensive artillery fire. The answer lay in the construction of the tank, a solution that was first developed by the British, although other combatant nations had also taken steps to design similar vehicles by the time the first units were deployed in autumn 1916.

At the same time, it was appreciated that if the much sought after breakthrough was achieved, then supplies and men would be needed to keep pace with the advance to clear enemy fortifications and strong-points. Tanks and artillery would need to be maintained with munitions and other materiel. Following the use of field-converted gun tanks to carry supplies, the "support tank" idea was developed. First a gun carrier was brought into service in 1917, and subsequently a supply or troop-carrying "tank" was built, although it was too late to see any action. At this time, the first tank destroyers and armoured engineer vehicles, which performed tasks such as mine-clearing and vehicle recovery, were also being developed and, even more remarkably, experiments were also underway to make tanks amphibious by attaching floats. Thus, by the end of World War I, many of the vehicle types that became vital components of the integrated armoured formations of later conflicts were already established or under development.

Tank and AFV development following the end of World War I was varied and chequered, with different nations taking radically different approaches based on their military philosophy, technological knowledge, financial resources and political approach to conflict resolution. By the outbreak of World War II, the military advantage clearly lay with German armoured technology and tactics, although their army still relied very heavily on horse-drawn transport. For the Allies, it was initially a case of playing catch-up and exploiting the advantages of much higher industrial production capacities. This period also saw an explosion in the numbers and types of AFVs, developing many of the early World War I experimental vehicle ideas and creating a whole host of specialized types. World War II also saw the first massed tanks battles and the dramatic rise in anti-tank technology with the introduction of dedicated anti-tank vehicles.

Since the end of World War II, AFV development has continued to take place in many countries around the globe, although it has been dominated by the USA and former Soviet Union. There has also been a dramatic shift in the direction of development. Specialized vehicles are now required for peacekeeping and internal security, and air-portability for rapid deployment is a major requirement. This period has also seen the development of the first true Infantry Fighting Vehicles (IFVs) and the rise of missile-carrying vehicles, as well as the introduction of an extraordinary number of electronic systems and protective technologies.

This book looks in detail at the development of the tank and other AFVs in both the historical context and through the examination of the most important examples of each vehicle type, from the earliest armoured cars through to the vehicles of today's modern armies.

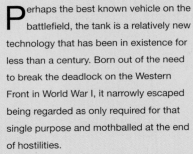

TANKS

Perhaps the best known vehicle on the battlefield, the tank is a relatively new technology that has been in existence for less than a century. Born out of the need to break the deadlock on the Western Front in World War I, it narrowly escaped being regarded as only required for that single purpose and mothballed at the end of hostilities.

World War II bore witness to the tank's true potential with the development of armoured formations and tactics that overwhelmed opponents and shocked the world. It was also during World War II that specialized armour proved its usefulness with armoured recovery vehicles, tank destroyers, command versions and other adapted vehicles being developed from the basic tank chassis.

Post World War II saw continued tank development as the Warsaw Pact and NATO anticipated vast tank formations engaging in Western Europe. Since the end of the Cold War, further development has transformed the tank into a truly modern weapons system, taking advantage of developments in electronics, protective systems and ballistics. In this way, it still maintains its position as "Queen of the Battlefield".

LEFT: **A34 Cruiser Tank Comet.**

Introducing tanks

What is a tank? Expressed in its simplest terms, a tank can be defined as a means of transporting firepower around the battlefield, with its weapon system and crew protected from direct enemy fire. This revolutionary weapon has been in existence for under a hundred years, and in that time it has become one of the most important and indispensable components of the battle-winning All Arms Team. The tank is just one of the many types of Armoured Fighting Vehicle (AFV) found on the modern battlefield. What makes it special is the careful blend of its three basic characteristics – firepower, protection and mobility – into a lethal mix that can bring instantaneous, accurate, direct fire to bear, whenever and wherever it is needed, day and night, whether on the move or stationary. These three characteristics can be blended together in differing amounts to produce very different results, as can be seen in the directory sections of this book.

Firepower is undoubtedly the most important characteristic because it is a tank's reason for being. The type and size of weapon system can vary enormously, and as this becomes larger and more sophisticated, the carrying vehicle invariably increases in both size and weight as there is more to protect.

If a tank is to achieve its mission, then an effective means of protection is vital. Although this can be achieved in a variety of ways, the basis is usually some form of armour plate composed of steel, aluminium, plastic-sandwich, ceramic, reactive or other materials, which inevitably increases the

TOP: **Firepower. Challenger MBTs of A Squadron, 1st Royal Tank Regiment, night-firing on Castlemartin Ranges, Pembrokeshire, Wales, 2001.**

ABOVE: **Protection. The massively thick, advanced Chobham type armour on the hull and turret of this Abrams M1A1 MBT gives protection against ATGWs (Anti-Tank Guided Weapons) and other battlefield weapons.**

tank's size and weight. Main Battle Tanks (MBTs) of today weigh around 60–70 tons, including much weighty armour. There are also other ways of providing protection, such as limiting size, lowering silhouette, camouflaging the tell-tale shape and using aids such as local smoke to help it "disappear". Inevitably as the tank's protection has become more and more sophisticated, so too have the anti-tank weapons ranged against it. Therefore its protection must be able to deal with all manner of attacks,

LEFT: **River Crossing. Royal Engineers have constructed this Class 80 ferry, to practise ferrying a Challenger 2 during training at Bovington, Dorset, England.** BELOW: **Mobility. A Challenger 2, belonging to the Armour Centre at Bovington, Dorset, England, powers its way effortlessly through thick mud on the training area.** BOTTOM: **Sea Movement. Challenger tanks being loaded at Zebrugge, Belgium, bound for the Middle East during the first Gulf War.**

from ground level – such as mines – through a vast range of hand-held/vehicle-borne guns and guided missiles that can attack at any level, to specific top-attack weapons. As far as possible, it must also now protect against nuclear, biological and chemical weapons. To all of this must be added a tank's deadliest foe – another tank, with its weapon system firing more and more sophisticated ammunition specifically designed to penetrate armour.

Mobility is the third vital characteristic, and again as the tank has become larger and heavier, increasingly more powerful powerplant, transmission and suspension are needed to move it over all types of terrain. Cross-country, the track clearly wins over the wheel, and good mobility is essential if the tank is to achieve its varying missions. Weight affects its portability, especially by air or over water. MBTs have probably now reached their ultimate size and weight, and so there is now a trend towards lighter, smaller, more portable tanks. However, this in turn puts the smaller tank at a distinct disadvantage in any tank versus tank engagements, when faced with a larger, better protected and better armed enemy, so tank development can be a vicious circle.

The first half of this book contains a wide selection of tanks through the ages. We have deliberately confined our coverage to the more important and interesting models worldwide, so while it is definitely not an exhaustive encyclopedia, it will give the reader a good indication of what the tank is all about.

The tank ended World War II in a pre-eminent position in the land battlefield and has lost none of its usefulness during the turbulent days that have followed. The last two conflicts in Iraq

have again shown that it is still a potent force, not yet superseded as "Queen of the Battlefield" by any other weapon system. In the hands of well-trained, highly professional soldiers, the awesome power of the tank still lives on and will continue to do so into the foreseeable future. FEAR NAUGHT!

The History of Tanks

The history of the tank has very largely been the history of 20th-century ground warfare, this revolutionary new weapon being conceived to help break the early battlefield stalemate of World War I. Later it had mixed fortunes in the years of peace following 1918, but came back into its own during World War II and has maintained its pre-eminent position ever since. Tanks have been produced in all shapes and sizes throughout their history. Nevertheless, without exception, they have all had the basic characteristics of firepower, protection and mobility. It is how these are balanced together that makes a critical difference to their effectiveness. During the tank's history some of its original roles have been taken over by other types of Armoured Fighting Vehicle (AFV). Nevertheless, the ability of the tank to carry firepower about on the battlefield with a protected crew and weapons has remained essential. We are now seeing a requirement for lighter AFVs to replace current Main Battle Tanks (MBTs), which poses the question of whether the tank as we currently know it will still be with us by the end of the 21st century.

LEFT: **The Type 61 MBT was the first tank produced by Japan after World War II. After almost a decade in development, it ended a long period when Japan had no armaments industry.**

Evolution of the tank

Since earliest times humankind has searched for bigger and better weapons with which to defend themselves and destroy their enemies. Without doubt each one must have initially appeared to be invincible on the battlefield, more fearsome than its predecessor. None has been more effective than the tank, a revolutionary weapon system, tracing its ancestry back partly to the war chariot, partly to the armoured war elephant and partly to a mechanical war machine in the fertile mind of Leonardo da Vinci. Not until the 20th century was it possible to propel a suitably armoured vehicle containing a crew and its weapons across all types of terrain. The invention of the internal combustion engine, modern methods of fabricating armour plate and the caterpillar track all combined to make this possible.

The stimulus for this new weapon came about in 1914, following the stalemate on the Western Front after the First Battle of Ypres. Neither side could advance because the defences of the other were too strong. The artillery shell, machine-gun, barbed wire and never-ending trenches stretching from the Belgian coast to Switzerland, had effectively brought war to a grinding halt. Until some way could be found of providing mobile, protected fire support for the attacker, this impasse could not be broken.

Before World War I there had been a number of designs proposed for bizarre-looking mechanical devices in both Britain and France, but all had been summarily discounted or pigeonholed. These included a tracked armoured vehicle using Diplock caterpillar tracks and another, the "Big Wheel", which was propelled along by three enormous wheels. Ad hoc armoured vehicles were also produced by bolting sheet armour plate on to early motor cars and were used to rescue downed British pilots from behind enemy lines and for light "cavalry" raids by the Belgian Army. Foremost of these

ABOVE: **Wooden model of the "War Machine" as taken from Leonardo da Vinci's notebook. The model was something of a guess as Leonardo never actually built it. Motive power was to be provided by a man inside turning a handle that can be seen connected to the axles, so its engine power was "one manpower"! This model was on show at the Israeli Tank Museum at Latrun, but has now been dismantled.** BELOW: **The "Big Wheel" project must have seemed like something out of H.G. Wells'** *War of the Worlds.* **It was designed to move an armoured vehicle forward on huge 12.2m/40ft diameter wheels, but was never completed. The man in the bowler hat is William Tritton, managing director of William Foster's who would build the first tanks.**

inventors was a British Royal Engineer officer, Ernest Swinton, whose proposal was for an armoured vehicle using American Holt farm-tractor caterpillar tracks for cross-country propulsion. Fortunately Swinton had the backing of Winston Churchill, then First Lord of the Admiralty, otherwise his "landship" might never have seen the light of day. Instead, a Landships

> "And the Lord was with Judah, and he drove out the inhabitants of the mountain, but he could not drive out the inhabitants of the valley, because they had chariots of iron."
> Judges, Chapter 1, Verses 19 and 20

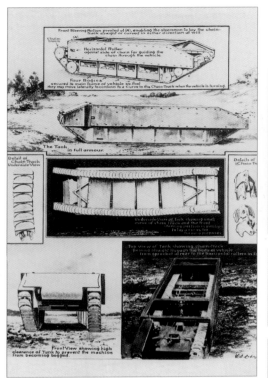

"The structure of the machine in its early stages being boxlike, some term conveying the idea of a box or container seemed appropriate. We rejected in turn — container — reservoir — cistern. The monosyllable TANK appealed to us as being likely to catch on and be remembered."
The Landships Committee

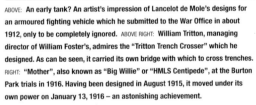

ABOVE: An early tank? An artist's impression of Lancelot de Mole's designs for an armoured fighting vehicle which he submitted to the War Office in about 1912, only to be completely ignored. ABOVE RIGHT: William Tritton, managing director of William Foster's, admires the "Tritton Trench Crosser" which he designed. As can be seen, it carried its own bridge with which to cross trenches. RIGHT: "Mother", also known as "Big Willie" or "HMLS Centipede", at the Burton Park trials in 1916. Having been designed in August 1915, it moved under its own power on January 13, 1916 – an astonishing achievement.

Committee was formed, chaired by Tennyson d'Eyncourt, Director of Naval Construction, and included remarkable men such as William Tritton, managing director of William Foster and Co. Ltd of Lincoln (the firm that would build the first tanks), Royal Naval Lieutenants Walter Gordon Wilson and Albert Stern, and of course Ernest Swinton.

Designed by Tritton and Wilson, the No. 1 Lincoln Machine (also called the "Tritton Machine"), and later, after a complete track redesign, given its more familiar name of "Little Willie", came into existence on September 18, 1915. Weighing 18 tons, it was to have had a centrally mounted turret although this was never fitted. This was almost immediately superseded by "Big Willie" also known as "HMLS Centipede" or more affectionately as "Mother", despite being a "Male" tank armed with two long-barrelled 6pdr guns ("Females" had only machine-guns). She was completed in January 1916, and

secretly moved to a trials area near Hatfield Park. Here, on February 2, 1916, "Mother" performed magnificently before a VIP audience and again six days later to His Majesty The King, who was also most impressed. One hundred Mark Is were ordered and given the nickname "Tank" because this was thought to be most likely to catch on and to be memorable.

Other nations were also coming to terms with the need for such a weapon system – first and foremost the French, once Colonel Estienne put forward plans to develop a land battleship, the *Cuirasse terrestre*, after witnessing British trials of the Holt tractor towing artillery guns. This led not only to the production of both the Schneider and St Chamond heavy tanks, but also the remarkably effective FT-17 light tank series. The Americans, Italians, Russians and surprisingly even the Germans would drag their heels somewhat, but eventually all the major nations would produce their own versions of the tank.

The tank crew

Like every other crew-served weapon system, a tank is only as good as its crew, which is at all times an integral and indispensable component. The first tanks had of necessity either large crews in heavy tanks – the German A7V topped the bill at eighteen, while the British Mark I and the French Saint Chamond had eight and nine respectively – or small crews of only two or three such as those in the tiny French FT-17 and British Whippet. The average-sized tank during World War II and after would have a crew of four men – a driver, a gunner, a loader/radio operator and a commander. They each had their allotted space in the driving or fighting compartment and were allocated personal hearing and vision devices.

The driver was seated at the front surrounded by his controls and instruments. Sometimes he operated a bow machine-gun, or there was a co-driver seated alongside to do so. The other three crewmen were in the turret/fighting compartment, normally with two on one side of the main armament (gunner in front of commander) and one (loader/operator) on the other. All were located close to their controls and had dedicated seats, vision and intercommunication devices and access/escape hatches.

Today's tank crew live, eat, sleep and fight in their tank throughout the 24-hour battlefield day, but can and do dismount when necessary. Modern tanks are equipped so that the crew can live on board – eating, sleeping and defecating within a filtered atmosphere so that they do not need to wear NBC

(nuclear, biological and chemical) clothing or respirators once inside and pressured up. In the early days, British tank crews wore chain-mail visors to protect against cuts from spawl (flakes of metal chipped off from bullet strikes outside), while heat, fumes and poisonous gas were other hazards they faced. Modern tanks are now designed to be fought closed down, very different to World War II when commanders normally had to have their heads out. The radio system in a tank provides both inter-communications between crewmen as well as long- and short-distance external communications.

"Volunteers are required for an exceedingly dangerous and hazardous duty of a secret nature. Officers who have been awarded decorations for bravery, and are experienced in the handling of men, and with an engineering background, should have their names submitted to this office."
War Office Secret and Confidential Memorandum

Although an individual tank can operate alone, it should never do so, and usually functions as part of a troop or platoon of three or four tanks, or in a larger subunit or unit. Furthermore, tank formations should not operate in isolation, needing infantry, engineer and other all-arms support, especially when holding ground by night, or when operating in urban areas.

Traditionally, tank crews have been all-male, although there were a few cases of women crew members serving in the Red Army during World War II, and there is now an increasing trend towards integration. In some cases, robotic accessories can also take the place of crew members – the most obvious being an automatic loader for the weapon system. While this usually works well, it does inevitably mean that there is one less person to carry out the many and varied other crew tasks such as replenishing ammunition, fuel and rations, gun cleaning, basic maintenance and even the simple yet essential tasks of mounting guard and radio watch, cooking and making the cups of tea or coffee, without which no tank crewman can survive!

"Tank aces" occur in any conflict; however, it is always difficult to single out an individual for special praise because a tank crew lives and fights as a team, and it is this teamwork that wins battles. However, there can be little doubt that the tank commander has the most difficult job, especially if he is commanding other tanks as well as his own, maybe at troop, squadron or regimental level. This requires him to listen constantly on the radio via his headphones (which are now built into his helmet), read a map, guide the driver, locate targets, give fire orders to the gunner, specify what type of ammunition to load, and a hundred and one other things – all at once!

ABOVE LEFT: **Map-reading is one of the many skills a tank commander has always required. Nowadays, an on-board Global Positioning System (GPS) helps.**
ABOVE: **Commander (in rear) and gunner use their vision devices to acquire targets in the turret of this closed-down Chieftain. The complexity and compactness of their controls is well evident.** BELOW: **Time for a brew! The crew of a Chieftain use their cooking stove to brew up a "cuppa" during training. The canned rations, known as Composite Packs ("Compo" for short) are ideal for tank crews and can be carried in the external bins.**

As warfare becomes more sophisticated, so inevitably do modern tanks, and consequently more skills are needed by all members of tank crews to enable them to survive and to fight effectively. The success of the American and British tank crews in the recent war in Iraq is testament to this continuing ability.

World War I

On August 13, 1916, the first detachment of British tanks left for France, the crews departing from Southampton but, because there was no crane there capable of loading them, the tanks left from Avonmouth. They then moved forward by train to the Somme where the great Allied offensive had opened on July 1, with horrendous casualties (British losses were 60,000 on the first day). The Commander-in-Chief of the British Expeditionary Force, General Sir Douglas Haig, was desperate to find a solution to the mounting casualties and seized on the handful of tanks as a panacea, despite the tanks being initially met with amused tolerance or contemptuous scepticism. Haig's plan was to deploy the available tanks (49 in total) over the entire front in twos and threes.

ABOVE: **Moving up for the Battle of Cambrai. British Mark IV heavy tanks, belonging to 4 Battalion, at the Plateau Railhead. Note that they have brushwood fascines (to help with trench crossing) on their fronts and unditching beams on their rears.** BELOW: **Into battle. A British Mark I heavy tank advances, with infantry on foot behind its tail-wheels. This was a device to help with steering but was soon discarded because the wheels fell into shell-holes or trenches, thus proving more a hindrance rather than a help.**

First tank action

On the morning of September 15, 1916, Zero Hour was at 06:20 hours, the tanks being on the move much earlier to reach the start line in time. Some broke down or were ditched moving forward, so where they did get into action, they were available only in ones or twos. Despite this, the effect upon the battle was out of all proportion to their number. Typical were the exploits of D 17 (Dinnaken) of 3 Section, D Company, which was reported in the British Press as "walking up the High Street of Flers with the British Army cheering behind!". German war correspondents were more dramatic: "One stared and stared as if one had lost the power of one's limbs," wrote one, "the monsters approached slowly, hobbling, rolling and rocking, but they approached. Nothing impeded them;

a supernatural force seemed to impel them on. Someone in the trenches said, 'The devil is coming,' and the word passed along the line like wildfire."

Cambrai

Unfortunately their very success worked against them and they continued to be deployed in small numbers for over a year, normally on appalling mud, the thick morass being so bad that tank officers took to carrying long ash sticks to test the depth

in front of their tanks. Eventually Haig allowed Brigadier Hugh Elles, who had taken over command of the Tank Corps from Swinton, to plan a battle on ground of his own choosing. The result was that on November 20, 1917, the entire Tank Corps of 476 tanks took part in the Battle of Cambrai, with Elles in the lead tank, flying the Tank Corps colours from his ash plant.

Zero Hour was 06:00 hours, and after ten hours the battle was won as far as the Tank Corps was concerned; the most rapid advance of the entire war had been achieved at minimal cost – only some 6,000 casualties instead of the anticipated 250,000 or more. Had the British been able to take advantage of this remarkable breakthrough, then a great victory might have been achieved – a remarkable feat by just 690 officers and 3,500 men of the Tank Corps. The Tank Corps had proved itself beyond all expectations, Haig writing in his dispatches that "the great value of the tanks had been conclusively proved".

Five months earlier, however, at Berry au Bac, Estienne's fledgling French tank arm had fought its first battle with 132 Schneiders taking part, but unfortunately involving a long approach march in full view of the enemy. The French tanks quickly encountered heavy artillery fire and many obstacles, 76 tanks being lost without much success. The Germans concluded that tanks were not very effective weapons – a conclusion they would live to regret! One of the main reasons for such heavy losses was the Schneider's vulnerability to the new German "K" anti-tank bullet, but this failure was to make the French concentrate their efforts on the highly successful light FT-17 two-man tanks.

Despite continuing British success, the Germans were slow in appreciating the potential of the new weapon system. However the Americans, who entered the war in April 1917, formed a special board to look into their employment, concluding that the tank was destined to become an important element in the war. They formed a separate tank corps, equipped with a mixture of British heavy and French light tanks. First to make his name in the new corps was a young cavalry captain, George S. Patton, Jnr, destined to become a famous tank commander in World War II.

TOP: **A battlefield scene showing American "doughboys" advancing across enemy trenches, with tank support from the ubiquitous FT-17s.** ABOVE: **A good rear view of a column of Medium Mark A Whippet tanks pausing on its way forward. No doubt the infantry who were passing would have liked a ride!** BELOW: **Two crew members of a British Mark V heavy tank talking to an infantryman. This is of course a modern-day re-enactment at the Tank Museum Bovington, Dorset, England, but the crew members are wearing authentic khaki overalls and the composite/leather crew helmets (affectionately known as "Dead Tortoises"), while their chain-mail face masks (to prevent cuts from spawl) are hanging around their necks.**

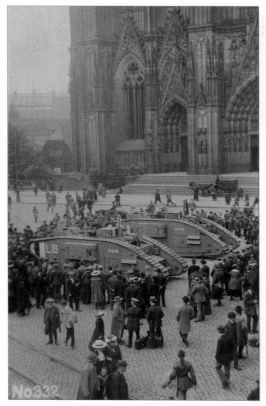

ABOVE: "Goodbye to boots and saddles!" An M2A4 light tank passes a column of horse-mounted cavalry during exercises in the USA during 1940. LEFT: British Army of Occupation in Germany. Taken in 1919, these two Mark V tanks of 12th Battalion Tank Corps are seen outside Cologne Cathedral, on their way to the station to welcome General Petain who was visiting that day. BELOW: "Thank God for the French Army!" French AMR 33 light tanks on parade in Paris on Bastille Day, June 14, 1935, when President Lebrun took the salute. France had more tanks than Germany at the start of World War II, but they were still deployed using the old fashioned infantry tactics and spread out in "penny packets", unable to stand up to the new German Blitzkrieg.

Between the wars

Between September 1916 and November 1918, British tanks took part in 3,060 separate engagements, French in 4,356 and American in 250, so it is not surprising that one German historian commented that they had been defeated "not by the genius of Marshal Foch, but by 'General Tank'". Despite their successes, the tanks were in for some lean years following World War I, principally due to cost, but also as a result of prejudice against all things mechanical. The British Tank Corps was reduced from 25 battalions when the Armistice was signed to five just a year later. Not until 1922 was a firm decision made to retain a permanent British Tank Corps, while the Americans abolished theirs completely and subjugated their tanks under infantry control. They fared a little better in France, where their tank arm was retained, but seen only as support for the all-powerful infantry, while the cavalry re-emerged, despite their proven battlefield vulnerability.

Apart from the tank element of the British Army of Occupation in Germany, the only exciting episode was the "Russian Stunt", when British tanks were sent to southern

> "The Germans were beaten ... not by the genius of Marshal Foch but by 'General Tank'."
> German historian Gen der Infanterie AWH von Zwehl

Russia to help fight against the Bolsheviks, the tank once again showing its prowess – a single tank capturing an entire city. Remarkably the city was Tsaritsin, renamed Stalingrad after the Revolution, which an entire German Army could not capture during World War II.

The 1920s was a great time for armoured theorists, especially in the UK, where Fuller and Liddell Hart produced a stream of books on the theory and practice of armoured warfare. Most remained ignored at home but were avidly read abroad, especially by the Germans. While British, American and French tank soldiers had to fight against the anti-armour prejudice pervading their respective armies, the Germans, despite the crippling restraints of the Versailles Treaty, secretly planned for the future, designing tanks and forming tank units to man them. In Britain prejudice was eventually overcome and mechanization began slowly in 1926, still to be incomplete at

ABOVE: **Hitler reviews his panzer troops. This scene is in pre-war Berlin, where any excuse for a military parade – such as Hitler's birthday, heroes' memorial days and foreign visitors – was snapped up. Here, Hitler is inspecting his big six-wheeled armoured cars and troop carriers, but on the other side of the Platz are the panzers and crews in their distinctive black uniforms.**

the outbreak of World War II. There was no shortage of able tank designers with men such as Martel in the UK designing cheap, small tanks ideal for training, and J. Walter Christie in the United States creating a revolutionary suspension which allowed high-speed cross-country movement.

The newly emerging Soviet Union did not take an interest in tank development until the start of their first "Five Year Plan" in 1929, thereafter building large numbers of poorly designed tanks. Stalin hindered their armoured development when he carried out his savage purges, removing many of those who had been advocating the theories of Fuller and Liddell Hart. Covertly the Soviets also helped the Germans by allowing them to send prototypes of their new tanks to the secret tank testing ground at Kazan.

When Hitler came to power he quickly realized the potential of the tank and by 1934, having thrown aside all pretence of obeying the Versailles Treaty, began tank-building on a large scale. He created the *Panzerwaffe* (Tank Arm), the first three panzer divisions being formed on October 15, 1935. Their organization bore a close resemblance to the British experimental armoured force of 1927. Officers and men of these divisions would gain useful combat experience as

"volunteers" in the German Condor Legion, fighting for General Franco during the Spanish Civil War. It was during this time that the new tactics of *Blitzkrieg* (Lightning War) were perfected, which soon came to revolutionize the battlefield, employing innovative elements such as air–ground support, with dive-bombers and tank formations working closely together. Much of their tactics and training was based on the teachings of General Heinz Guderian, the armoured guru, who had been the first to realize that the panzer division would be the weapon of decision in the new German Army. He visualized armoured forces which did not only contain tanks, but a mix of all fighting arms and services, thus differing from the "all-tank" theories of Fuller and from the policy of tying tanks to infantry as adopted by the French and Americans. His new panzer arm would be the primary striking force in the coming war, and not just a supporting player.

Blitzkrieg!

On September 1, 1939, two German Army Groups swept across the Polish frontier, spearheaded by two Panzer Corps, their aim being to encircle and destroy the Polish Army in a gigantic pincer movement. Germany knew the Poles would fight stubbornly, buoyed up by promises of British and French support. However, unbeknown to Poland and her allies, there was a Nazi–Soviet Pact in which Poland was to be divided in two, the Russians attacking from the rear.

The Germans unleashed a new tactical system on the Poles, perfected by Guderian, which pierced the enemy's front and then encircled and destroyed all or part of their forces. Its key elements were surprise, speed of manoeuvre, shock action from both ground and air, and the retention of battlefield initiative. It required that all commanders used their initiative to the full. Reconnaissance elements led, accompanied by Artillery Forward Observers and Luftwaffe Forward Air Controllers, who could quickly call for fire support. Having located the enemy main positions, the reconnaissance would bypass these strong-points and quickly press on to maintain momentum. They were in constant radio communication with the force commander who controlled the speed of advance, deciding whether the whole force should bypass enemy positions or engage them. The *Schwerpunkt* ("centre of gravity") of the assault was where the commander, being well forward, decided was the best point to attack. Overwhelming force was then concentrated against this point, as Guderian put it, "*Klotzen nicht Kleckern!*" ("Thump them hard, don't pat them!"). The aim of this initial attack was to punch a hole through their lines, to be immediately followed by another element of the force that would pass through and press on,

ABOVE: **At the Channel Coast. The date is May 20, 1940, the place Dunkirk, the tank a PzKpfw 38(t) built by the Czechs and "appropriated" by the Germans.** BELOW: **Blitzkrieg in action! In the suburbs of Warsaw, a column of German tanks, led by a PzKpfw II Ausf F, passes a 7.5cm/2.95in infantry gun as they batter their way into the city, September 1939.**

avoiding main enemy positions, creating havoc in their rear. Following this up would be motorized infantry, who would "mop up" any remaining resistance, ensuring that the gap was permanent. Such operations demanded teamwork, good communications, command and control, and where possible, surprise. There were no more massive build-ups, long artillery barrages or set-piece attacks which gave the enemy time to prepare. Instead, the overwhelmingly powerful attacking force would hit without warning, smashing through on a narrow front. No wonder Guderian's nickname was *Schnelle Heinz* ("Hurrying Heinz")!

Blitzkrieg was repeated on May 10, 1940, when the Germans invaded the Low Countries and then crossed the Meuse into France. The disorganized and demoralized French

FAR LEFT: **On into Russia! A column of PzKpfw III Ausf Es leaving a ruined Russian village as they head for the steppes.**
LEFT: **The prime architect of the German Blitzkrieg tactics was General Heinz Guderian, seen here during pre-war training.**
BELOW: **The All Arms team was one of the vital components of the German Blitzkrieg. The infantry had to work closely with tanks, as shown here, where they use a tank to get them nearer to the enemy. However, they will have to dismount once the action begins, so that the tank can traverse its turret and engage targets.**

had their armour spread out in "penny packets" and were no match for the German assault, while the British Expeditionary Force (BEF) soon struggled to escape over the Channel. However, a few important challenges to the German offensive occurred, most notably at Arras where a counter-attack by the 4th and 7th Royal Tank Regiments held up the panzers long enough to prevent the BEF from being cut off from their escape ports. By June 18, Paris had capitulated, followed by the complete surrender of France on June 24. The *Panzerwaffe* was in the ascendancy.

Operation "Barbarossa"

Just under a year later, on June 22, 1941, the Germans unleashed three massive army groups against their erstwhile Soviet ally. Similar to the campaigns in Poland and France, panzers spearheaded the German forces, with a front line extending 3,219km/2,000 miles from the Baltic to the Black Sea. The Red Army retreated everywhere, losing more than 3,000 tanks. By autumn the Germans had advanced 885km/

550 miles and occupied 1.3 million sq km/500,000sq miles of Soviet territory, inflicting 2.5 million casualties on the Red Army and capturing over a million prisoners.

On the other side of the world, the USA had begun to awaken, and its massive armaments and tank-building industry swung into action, anticipating its entry into the war. This would change the US Army into the most mechanized force in the world. The British were grateful to receive American tanks to boost their armoured divisions because they were still bedevilled with tank design problems, having too many models that were under-armoured, under-gunned and restricted by turret rings too small to take larger calibre weapons.

Elsewhere, other countries, such as Axis partners Italy and Japan, began increasing their tank-building programmes, but were never very successful. Commonwealth tank development also played its part, although the Allies were to rely on the industrial output of the USA to build the tanks they needed for their armoured forces. On every battlefield, the tank had begun to play a more pivotal role than ever before.

Tanks in other theatres

Of all the unlikely places for tanks to prove their abilities, the barren Western Desert of North Africa was probably the strangest. Yet despite problems caused by the extremes of heat and cold, combined with the effect of sand and grit on their engines and running gear (let alone on their crews), tanks once again proved themselves the dominant arm, this time in desert warfare. Initially it was British tanks against Italian that would capture the headlines, the Matilda II swiftly earning the title "Queen of the Desert". The Italian invasion of Egypt and their subsequent trouncing by a much smaller British and Commonwealth force culminated in the surrender of the entire 10th Italian Army at Beda Fomm, Libya, in February 1941. Here the British 7th Armoured Division (the "Desert Rats") took 20,000 prisoners, together with immense quantities of vehicles, arms and ammunition, for the loss of just nine killed, fifteen wounded and four tanks knocked out.

However, the British would not have it all their own way for long, once General Erwin Rommel and his *Deutsches Afrika Korps* (DAK) arrived. The "Desert Fox", as he was called by both sides, soon proved that he was in his element in the desert, leading from the front and dominating battles by his sheer personality. Hard-fought campaigns then took place

TOP: **"Queen of the Desert". The British Matilda Mark II was far superior to any of the Italian tanks in the Western Desert because its protection was far better.** ABOVE: **Across the steppes. Blasting their way through Russian defences, the panzers initially made good progress on the wide open steppes until winter set in.**

from one end of the Western Desert to the other between March 1941 and October 1942. The turning point came with the Battle of El Alamein, Egypt, which gave victory to General Montgomery and his British 8th Army. The DAK then fought a stubborn withdrawal action all the way back to Tunisia, where they were finally forced to surrender on May 12, 1943.

The Japanese bombed Pearl Harbor on December 7, 1941, and in so doing brought the USA into the war, switching their enormous armaments industry to full-scale production. Over 88,400 tanks were built during the war years, nearly four times the production of Germany or Britain. The American armed forces soon numbered over 12 million and a goodly proportion of these fought the Japanese in the Pacific "island-hopping" campaigns that saw tanks being used in a wide variety of new roles. In other parts of the Far East, British and Commonwealth armour fought in unlikely jungle settings, winning victories where tanks were not expected to be able to survive, let alone operate.

> "We have already reached our first objective which we weren't supposed to get to until the end of May ...
> You will understand that I can't sleep for happiness."
> Rommel in a letter home to his wife

From mid-1943, the tide had turned against the Axis powers in nearly every theatre of the war, nowhere more so than on the Russian steppes where the Red Army was able to employ its excellent new tanks – the T-34 and KV-1 – built in ever larger numbers at factories that had been moved safely eastwards. Soon they turned the tables on the overstretched Nazis and were pushing them inexorably back to the Fatherland, in the process winning some enormous tank battles such as the one at Kursk in July–August 1943.

In the Mediterranean theatre, tanks also played a major part in the conquest of Sicily and Italy. In north-west Europe, with the opening of the Second Front on D-Day, June 6, 1944, specialized armour in the form of the Funnies was used to great effect in these landings. Once a breakout from the beaches had been achieved, tanks led the way on all fronts with armoured commanders such as General Patton racing to go further and faster than his fellow generals, giving the Germans no opportunity to regroup.

Nevertheless, the Germans still had a surprise up their sleeve with their heavy armour playing a major role in a totally unexpected counter-attack through the Ardennes region in a conflict which became known as the "Battle of the Bulge".

TOP: *"Panzer Rollen in Afrika Vor!"* A PzKpfw IV belonging to the *Deutsches Afrika Korps* negotiates a sand dune in the North African desert.

ABOVE LEFT: The Red Army resists. Russian medium tanks pressing the Germans back towards Rostov during the autumn of 1942. ABOVE: A US Marine Corps Sherman M4A2 medium tank operating deep in the jungle of Cape Gloucester. Tanks proved their worth in jungles all over the Pacific theatre, being used to great effect by both the US Army and USMC.

This nearly succeeded in breaking through the Allied forces, but proved to be a last gasp, and Allied tanks were soon hammering on the gates of Berlin from all sides. Following Hitler's suicide, Germany sued for peace, surrendering unconditionally on May 7, 1945. Fighting in the Pacific would take a further three months to force Japan into a similar surrender on August 14, bringing World War II to a close.

Would the atom bomb, which had so dramatically heralded in the nuclear age, lead to the demise of the tank?

Wartime development

As World War II progressed, most major tank-building nations produced larger, more powerful, better armed and better armoured tanks. The UK, once the world leader, had been left woefully far behind by the others with tanks that were under-equipped and ill-prepared for the Blitzkrieg tactics of modern war. Their machine-gun armed light tanks were suitable only for peacetime training or possibly reconnaissance tasks, a role soon to be taken over by armoured cars. Likewise, the cruiser and infantry tanks mounted either a tiny 2pdr high velocity anti-tank gun or a 75mm/2.95in close support howitzer. The former was adequate in the anti-armour role but of little use firing High-Explosive (HE) in support of infantry. Unfortunately, the diameter of their turret rings was mainly too small to allow the mounting of larger-calibre weapons. German tanks did not suffer from this design fault. The PzKpfw IIIs and PzKpfw IVs, designed in the early 1930s and forming the backbone of the *Panzerwaffe*, were still in quantity production in the early 1940s, well able to be up-armoured and up-gunned.

The Americans had recognized the need for a dual-purpose main tank armament and the advantages of stabilizing the gun platform so as to hit targets on the move – in most tank versus tank battles the one who hit first usually won. The introduction of American Medium M3 Lee/Grants into British service in the North African desert was the first time they had had a tank gun of this size with dual capability since the naval 6pdr of the Heavy Mark V in World War I. Despite this advantage, the 75mm/2.95in gun remained in service far too long, not being replaced by the much improved 76mm/2.99in gun until later in the war. The British did not produce a real match-winner until the A34 Comet, with its excellent 77mm/3.03in gun, which entered service in March 1945.

ABOVE: **The backbone of the panzer divisions for many years was the PzKpfw IIIs and IVs. This interesting line-up shows (from left to right) Pz IV Ausf F, Pz III Ausf L/M, Pz III Ausf H and Pz IV Ausf F, taken in March 1944.**
BELOW LEFT: **The deeper the Germans penetrated into the Soviet Union, the farther east the Soviets had to move their tank-building factories, like this one that was producing their new heavy tank, the KV-1.**

Although the Germans mostly led the field in tank design – with obvious exceptions such as the Soviet T-34, probably the best all-round tank of the war – they could not match the Americans or the Russians in mass production output. Curiously, they squandered much of their precious production capacity on building ever larger tanks. They created behemoths such as the 68-ton King Tiger, 70-ton Jagdtiger and the last of which was too late to see combat, the 180-ton Maus. These tanks were very difficult to manoeuvre, slow, needed specially reinforced bridging and guzzled fuel, although they could see off every other tank they met with ease. Had they concentrated on producing the PzKpfw V Panther, things might have been different.

Protection became more of a problem as anti-tank weapons improved and the means of penetrating armour became more varied. In addition to conventional Kinetic Energy penetration by solid shot, a new method, High-Explosive Anti-Tank (HEAT) was introduced, which relied on the chemical energy generated

by a high-velocity, high-temperature jet of HE. This was fired at low velocity and was thus most accurate at shorter ranges in hand-held weapons such as the bazooka. This led to the fitting of "stand-off" armour to protect suspensions and turrets, while front glacis and turret frontal arcs became ever thicker. Other methods of protection included painting with anti-magnetic mine paste (*Zimmerit*) and fitting local smoke dischargers, which fired a pattern of local smoke allowing a tank to escape to cover. Internal protection was improved by not storing ammunition above the turret ring (apart from ready rounds) and by fitting ammunition bins with water jackets.

Engine and track performance also improved, but in many cases petrol engines still had to be used instead of the more robust (and less inflammable) diesels because the majority of diesel fuel was needed for the navies. "Duckbills" (track extensions) were fitted in some cases to improve traction in muddy conditions, while the ingenious Culin Hedgerow Cutter, a device that could cut its way through the thick *bocage* hedgerows of Normandy, won a medal for the American NCO who invented it.

Undoubtedly the biggest continual threat to tanks came from the air in the form of specialized "tank busters" or *Jabos* (*Jagdbombers*), constantly searching out and destroying tank columns, a particular problem for the Germans thanks to the Allies' almost complete air superiority.

TOP: **As well as tank crews, technicians had to learn about new tanks as they came into service – like these REME (Royal Electrical and Mechanical Engineers) craftsmen removing the 75mm/2.95in gun and mantlet from this US M24 Chaffee, the last of the American light tank line of World War II.** ABOVE: **Stand-off armour. As can be seen on this German PzKpfw III, side plates to protect the suspension and turret sides give the tank improved protection against HEAT (High-Explosive Anti-Tank) projectiles.** BELOW: **Light tanks had to be able to be carried in gliders to support airborne operations. Here a 7-ton British Light Tank Mark VII Tetrarch exits from the nose of a glider.**

The Funnies

Crucial to the success of the Allied armies landing on the Normandy beaches was the support they had from all manner of specialized armour. The driving force behind these strange devices – the product of many inventive minds – was one man, arguably the greatest trainer of British armoured soldiers: Major-General Percy Hobart. He had already proved his prowess before World War II on Salisbury Plain and then in Egypt where he turned the Cairo Mobile Division into the world-famous 7th Armoured Division – the original "Desert Rats" – and following this by forming and training the formidable 11th Armoured Division. However, the 79th Armoured Division, "Hobo's Funnies" (although he detested the nickname), was his crowning achievement.

Strange-looking tanks, fitted with deep-water wading screens, mine-clearing flails, portable bridges, flamethrowers or tank-borne searchlights, joined the more conventional armoured bulldozers and armoured engineers assault vehicles to provide the fire support and assist more conventional tanks over and through the natural and man-made beach obstacles. The Division went on playing an important role right up to and over the Rhine Crossing, when it had a strength of 21,000 all ranks and 1,566 tracked vehicles (compared with 14,000 men and 350 AFVs in a normal armoured division), but always operating in "penny packets" spread across the front line. "Hobo's eagle-eye" appeared to be everywhere, and his contribution to the Allied success was enormous.

As the photographs here and in the directory section show, the majority of Funnies were based upon either the highly adaptable American Sherman M4 Medium Tank or the equally versatile British A22 Churchill Infantry Tank Mark IV. Before the

TOP: **The Churchill "Crocodile" Flamethrower was a fearsome weapon that was still in service in the 1950s. In fact, a squadron's worth went to Korea with the Commonwealth Division as part of the United Nations force, but were only ever used as gun tanks.** ABOVE: **A Sherman DD enters the water during training before D-Day. Note the propellers on the rear (run off the engine and yet to be lowered) and the raised canvas screen which gives the tank the necessary buoyancy.**

LEFT: **The 79th Armoured Division, "Hobo's Funnies", took a bull's head as its insignia.**

formation and equipping of 79th Armoured Division, there had been some limited specialized armour, mainly used in the Middle East, such as Matilda and Valentine-based mine-sweeping tanks, the Matilda nightfighting searchlight (known as the Canal Defence Light) and the Valentine amphibious tank (using a collapsible screen and fitted with Duplex Drive propellers to enable it to swim). These clearly led on to the Sherman/Churchill derivatives that were much improved versions of the originals. Here are some of the most widely used Funnies.

Sherman DD (Duplex Drive)

First ashore with the leading troops was a Sherman gun tank fitted, like the Valentine, with DD propellers and a collapsible screen. Unfortunately, those on the American beaches were launched too far out and many sank before they could reach shore. However, on the British and Canadian beaches they landed successfully and proved invaluable.

LEFT: A Churchill gun tank uses a Churchill Great Eastern Ramp to surmount an extra high wall.
BELOW LEFT: One of the very few Sherman DDs left in existence is this one on show at the Tank Museum, Bovington, as part of the D-Day exhibits.
BELOW: A Churchill AVRE (Armoured Vehicle Royal Engineers) fitted with a fascine carrier and brushwood fascine ready to be dropped into any ditch or crater that blocked its way. BOTTOM: One of the most successful mine-clearing devices was the Sherman Flail (British designation: the Sherman Crab) that used flails attached to a front-mounted spinning drum to literally blast the mines out of the ground or set them off.

Sherman Crab

This was again a Sherman gun tank fitted with a flail mine-sweeping device which could sweep a safe lane through a minefield, wide enough to allow tanks and other vehicles to negotiate it in safety.

Churchill AVRE (Armoured Vehicle Royal Engineers)

These were Churchill Mark III or IV tanks, modified to mount a 290mm/11.42in spigot mortar, together with other devices such as various bridges, Bobbin "carpet-layers", fascines and mine exploders. The spigot mortar was used to destroy pill-boxes and was known as a "Flying Dustbin".

Churchill ARKs

A turret-less Churchill tank, modified to carry ramps for use in obstacle crossing. The Germans were completely surprised by these strange-looking vehicles which had no counterpart in the German Army. The Funnies accomplished many tasks on D-Day, including crossing sea walls and anti-tank ditches; breaching sea walls and other obstacles; knocking out gun

emplacements and defended buildings; filling ditches and craters with fascines or crossing them with tank bridges.

After D-Day other Funnies were brought into action, such as Churchill "Crocodile" Flamethrowers, "Kangaroo" armoured personnel carriers (based on Ram tanks) and other types of bridges, bulldozers, etc. No wonder they were called the "tactical key to victory".

On to victory!

Once the Rhine was crossed, with armour leading on all fronts, the Allied armies moved deeper and deeper into Germany. Now the lighter, faster American mediums and British cruisers really came into their own, their speed, reliability and overwhelming numbers counting for more in the end than the superior enemy firepower and protection. I remember being told of one German tank commander who, having boasted that one Tiger was better than ten Shermans, then smiled ruefully and said, "but you alvays haff eleven!" Nevertheless it was no easy ride, especially with the added danger from a proliferation of hand-held anti-tank weapons, such as the *Panzerfaust* and *Panzerschreck*. The once proud panzer divisions were by now a shadow of their former selves, yet single Tigers and Panthers still performed miracles until they were taken out by superior numbers or by the dreaded *Jabos*.

The Allies were also fielding better tanks, the American M26 General Pershing heavy tank, with its highly effective 90mm/3.54in M3 gun, had reached Europe in January 1945 and even saw action in the Pacific theatre before the war ended. The highly effective British Comet entered service at about the same time as the Pershing, but unfortunately its successor, the world-beating A41 Centurion, was not in prototype stage until January 1945 with the first six vehicles

ABOVE: **Brilliant British commander Field Marshal Bernard Montgomery always wore a Royal Tank Regiment black beret and badge on to which was sewn his General's badge. "Monty" had his own M3 Grant medium tank in the Western Desert, now in the Imperial War Museum, London.**

ABOVE: **One of the greatest German armoured commanders was Field Marshal Erwin Rommel, who commanded the *Deutsches Afrika Korps* in North Africa, then Army Group B on the Atlantic Wall and Channel Coast. Implicated in the bomb plot against Hitler, he was forced to commit suicide.**

being rushed to Germany for testing in combat conditions in May 1945. This gives a measure of how far behind the British were in the tank development race.

On the Eastern Front the Red Army "Steamroller" moved closer to Berlin, headed by the ubiquitous T-34 and the new JS-1, JS-2 and JS-3, with their 122mm/4.8in gun and thick armour. Particularly deadly was the JS-3 with its new ballistically shaped cast hull and smoothly curved turret, but all were more than a match for their aging opponents.

Tank destroyers

Before closing on World War II it is perhaps relevant to deal here with tank destroyers. All the major tank-building nations employed them because they were an ideal way of getting a

> "Armor, as the ground arm of mobility, emerged from World War II with a lion's share of the credit for the Allied victory. Indeed armor enthusiasts at that time regarded the tank as being the main weapon of the land army."
> US Army Lineage series *Armor-Cavalry*

more powerful anti-armour weapon into battle on a smaller, lighter or almost obsolescent tank chassis, thus prolonging its effective battlefield life. The Americans, however, viewed things slightly differently. Early in the war they had been heavily influenced by the way German tanks had sliced through the opposition in Poland, France and Russia, and this had a bad effect on American morale. They came to the conclusion that the answer was to have masses of fast-moving, high-velocity anti-tank guns whose primary task was to knock out enemy tanks. This led to the creation of Tank Destroyer Command (with their motto "Seek, Strike and Destroy!"), which at its peak in early 1943 contained 106 active tank destroyer battalions – only 13 less than the total number of US tank battalions. From then on, numbers started to decline, principally because the expected massed German tank formations were not used against the Americans, being needed more on the Eastern Front. Nevertheless, the M10 Wolverine, the M18 Hellcat and the M36 tank destroyers all gave useful service in the US Army, while both the British and the Germans made full use of their tank destroyers for many tasks, often in lieu of normal gun tanks. The British up-gunned some of their M10s by installing their 17pdr Mk V gun, the resulting highly effective tank destroyer being known as the "Achilles". Undoubtedly the German *Jagdpanther* was one of the best tank destroyers ever built, while *Jagdtiger* was the heaviest German AFV to go into active service. Smaller tank destroyers, like the Hetzer, which utilized well-proven

TOP LEFT: **One of the smallest number of tanks in any theatre were those of the composite squadron of Light Mark VI and Matilda Mark II on Malta. Note the strange camouflage to blend in with the hundreds of dry stone walls on the island.** TOP RIGHT: **America's most famous armoured general was General George S. Patton, Jr, whose flamboyant style made him instantly recognizable everywhere. This evocative statue of Patton stands at Ettelbruck, Luxembourg.** ABOVE: **Berlin at last! A column of Red Army JS-2 heavy tanks drives through the Brandenburg Gate, sealing the fate of the Third Reich.**

components of the Czech-built PzKpfw 38(t), continued to be used by the Swiss Army long after the end of the war.

"Armor, as the ground arm of mobility, emerged from World War II with a lion's share of the credit for the Allied victory. Indeed armor enthusiasts at that time regarded the tank as being the main weapon of the land army." That is how the US Army Lineage series *Armor-Cavalry* put it, and it would be hard to disagree. "General Tank" had done it again!

The Cold War

While there is no doubt that World War II had proved once again that tanks could win major battles, just as after World War I, the American and British armoured forces were reduced significantly to peacetime levels – 20 cavalry regiments and eight from the Royal Tank Regiment (RTR) respectively – the rest disbanded, despite worldwide commitments such as the dismantling of the British Empire. In addition, the spectre of nuclear war between the Super Powers hung over Europe, with NATO and the Warsaw Pact countries facing each other across the Iron Curtain. Bolstering up the Soviet threat to the West was a mass of armoured units that appeared ready to strike at any moment and whose purpose was to follow-up a pre-emptive nuclear strike. To guard against such an eventuality the US, UK and other NATO nations stationed many of their tank units in north-west Europe, or had complicated "Reforger" programmes in which the tanks were

ABOVE RIGHT: On the other side of the Iron Curtain, American M60s, belonging to their armoured regiments stationed in West Germany, got on with their training for battle. These three are firing on the open range. BELOW: The Cold War was certainly cold on the eastern side of the Iron Curtain. Here Red Army soldiers on manoeuvres in the early 1950s use a platoon of T-34/76s to help them move through thick snow.

kept in specially weatherproofed shelters in Europe while the crews were at home – ready to be flown out to man them at a moment's notice. Either way it was an expensive and time-consuming business, but the threat was real enough, both sides fearing that the other would strike first.

The "shield and sword" principle of NATO undoubtedly did much to prevent a third world war during the remainder of the 20th century. Had war occurred, tank battles would have been a major feature. Cracks in the Warsaw Pact were apparent from time to time, such as with the Hungarian uprising in October 1956, but these were savagely repressed,

LEFT: **Guns rear, a column of M60s return to their barracks after manoeuvres in southern Germany. They are passing another armoured column led by an M113 APC.** BELOW LEFT: **Driving home in the morning mist. A German Leopard 1 returning to barracks at the end of an exercise through mist-shrouded pine forests.** BELOW: **NBC (Nuclear, Biological, Chemical) warfare was yet another feature of the Cold War, which required tank soldiers to wear special uniforms, including respirators, and to decontaminate their tanks. Here a German crew practise decontamination drills, with suitable detergent sprays.**

slowly starting up their own tank-building industry once again, but this time with very different objectives. It was soon clear that German tank-building expertise was as good as ever, clearly demonstrated by the Leopard 1 and later Leopard 2 tanks. For anyone stationed in Germany during the 1940s to the 1970s, this was a time of considerable change, encompassing initially an era of massive free-wheeling exercises that saw tanks running on their tracks over much of the countryside, and then of tactical training becoming more and more restricted as costs increased and land became more precious.

The training expedients that had to evolve are dealt with later in this book, but it is worth noting that as the lethality of tank gun ammunition increased, so too did the size of army firing-range danger areas in order to safeguard the public; alternatively, other methods of training tank gunners would have to evolve. Nevertheless, the threat of armoured conflict was always present, making this type of training essential at all levels.

There was also an important shift in some countries, such as Great Britain, for their armies to change from conscripts to regular soldiers, causing considerable changes to the training cycle of tank crews. In general terms, after some teething problems, this was to produce a far more professional and well motivated tank crewman, whose expertise has been evidenced in the last two Gulf Wars. Tanks were also becoming ever more sophisticated, requiring that the training of tank crewmen also had to develop and improve continually.

using in this case over 1,000 tanks to crush it. At the same time the whole world was becoming "awash" with tanks – the highly successful Soviet T series, for example, being widely available and mirroring the similar worldwide availability of such small arms as the AK-47 Kalashnikov assault rifle. NATO countries favoured the American M47, M48, M60 series or the British Centurion, all of which were produced in large numbers both at home for export and under licence abroad. Additionally, other "sleeping giants" like China had also begun to develop their own tank-building industry.

The Armies of Occupation in Germany gradually became less "occupying forces" and more equal partners as the erstwhile enemies were welcomed back into the fold, even

Korea and Vietnam

On June 25, 1950, Blitzkrieg struck again, this time in the Far East where a two-pronged assault, spearheaded by tanks, raced south across the 38th Parallel dividing North Korea from South Korea. Their success was stunning, although the North Korean Peoples Army (NKPA) based their armoured tactics more on those of the Red Army than of the *Panzerwaffe*. The South Koreans and the Americans, who were there as an army of occupation, could muster just a handful of M24 Chaffee light tanks, which the NKPA T-34s dealt with easily. Somehow, the Americans managed to hold on and regroup, bring in some Pershings and Shermans from Japan, and then one battalion of more modern M46 Pattons. By the third week in August, there were over 500 US tanks in the Pusan perimeter, and by early September, US tanks outnumbered the NKPA by at least five to one.

The United Nations forces (the defending force was now approved by the UN) soon went on to the offensive, driving the North Koreans back over the 38th Parallel and into North Korea. By now there were small numbers of both British and French tanks in the UN command, the British Centurion proving conclusively to be the best tank of the campaign. The war looked like drawing to a victorious close, but on November 25, 1950,

TOP: **Invasion! On the morning of June 25, 1950, some 10,000 North Korean infantry supported by more than 50 tanks (Soviet-built T-34/85s) swept across the 38th Parallel, spearheading the invasion of South Korea. They were followed by more troops and more tanks, and swiftly over-ran most of the country.** ABOVE: **Shermans of 2nd US Infantry Division blast enemy positions during an assault on the Chinese Communist Forces on the East Central Front in Korea, September 1951.**

the Chinese launched a massive offensive, the front not being stabilized until early April, back along the 38th Parallel. Thereafter, although tanks had shown themselves well able to operate in the rugged terrain, the use of armour both in attack and defence was sidelined and the war lapsed into an uneasy truce.

Since those days, the NKVA has built up a massive army containing over 6,500 tanks, half of which are main battle tanks of Russian or Chinese manufacture. South Korea has some 4,650 tanks, of which some 2,330 are also main battle tanks. The latter is tasked to absorb and then defeat any Blitzkrieg-type assault with prompt support from the US Army.

LEFT: **Sweeping for mines. An M48 tank with an automatic mine-sweeper checks the road from Cam Lo to Mai Loc, Vietnam, in the northern I Corps area near the Demilitarized Zone (DMZ), September 16, 1970.**
BELOW: **An M155 Sheridan tank belonging to Troop "A" of the 1st Battalion, 1st Cavalry Regiment, American Division, pauses beneath some trees about 30.6km/19 miles north of Tam Ky, Vietnam, March 18, 1970.**

Indo-China and Vietnam

The French fought a guerrilla war here from 1951–54 against the Viet Minh, in the end suffering a humiliating defeat at Dien Bien Phu, Vietnam. They used American World War II armour, including less than 500 tanks and tank destroyers spread over an area of some 72,520sq km/28,000sq miles. By comparison, when it came to be the Americans' turn to fight there, they employed some 600 tanks and over 2,000 other AFVs in an area less than one-third that size. A terrain study carried out in Vietnam by a team of US tankers in 1967 showed that nearly half the country could be traversed by AFVs all year round. Nevertheless, in the difficult areas like the Mekong Delta and the Central Highlands the lightly equipped, fast-moving Vietcong were far more capable of carrying out full-scale mobile war.

While the main American AFV used was the M113 (almost in the role of a light tank), M41s and later M48s were introduced as the war escalated. From 1967–68 the Australians sent a

squadron of medium tanks (British-built Centurions), and they fought a number of successful actions before being withdrawn from 1971–72. New equipment arriving in the late 1960s included the Sheridan Light Tank, with its wholly inappropriate 152mm/5.98in anti-tank missile that was never used in anger. Tank versus tank combat took place only twice: once at Ben Het in March 1969 between two tanks of US 69th Armour and a number of North Vietnam Army (NVA) PT-76s, two of which were knocked out; and in Laos in March 1971, where South Vietnamese M41s clashed with NVA tanks.

In their spring offensive in 1972, Viet Cong Russian-built T-54s and their Chinese equivalent Type 59s fought it out with American M48A3s of the South Vietnamese 20th Tank Regiment. Unfortunately the South Vietnamese not only let the initiative pass to the enemy, but also used their armour in a static role, inviting piecemeal destruction. Thus, as in Indo-China, a seemingly unsophisticated "peasant" army had shown itself better able to handle armour than its far more armour-conscious opponent.

LEFT: **USMC flamethrowing M67s (developed from the M48), burning fields in Vietnam, near the 1st Battalion, 3rd Regiment command post, 3rd Marine Division, January 1966.**

The uneasy peace

In addition to the Korean and Vietnam Wars, the 20th century saw many other conflicts taking place all over the world, for example on the Indian subcontinent, in the ever-turbulent Middle East, and even on the "roof of the world" in Afghanistan. Tanks have been employed in all of these wars, as the following four examples demonstrate.

India–Pakistan

Following World War II, the British Army found itself responsible not only for occupation duties in Europe but also for "Imperial Policing" in the British Empire as trouble flared in Palestine, then Malaya, Cyprus, Aden, Borneo and elsewhere, as erstwhile colonies sought their independence. Those units involved in such activities were mostly armoured cars and scout cars, but on some occasions tanks were deployed. Indeed, it was the norm for British armoured regiments to serve tours in the armoured reconnaissance role, the lighter AFVs being more suitable for aid to the civil power and counter-insurgency operations.

Such disturbances also occurred on the Indian subcontinent, as both Hindus and Muslims sought self-government. Then on August 14, 1947, India and Pakistan became separate countries. This momentous event was sadly accompanied by widespread communal violence, which inevitably led to war between the two new nations – first of all over Kashmir in November 1947, then over the Rann of Kutch in January 1957.

The United Nations mediated and a ceasefire was effected, but not before a number of major tank battles had taken place, in which the Indian-manned, British-built Centurions took on and beat the more sophisticated American-built Pakistani M48 Pattons. In 1965 during the 22-day war, the largest tank battle ever fought in Asia took place, with over 1,500 tanks involved and many being knocked out. On January 10, 1966, the two countries signed an uneasy truce, but in 1971, the Awami League declared East Pakistan to be the independent republic of Bangladesh. This led to Pakistan attacking India from West Pakistan in the "Lightning War". India retaliated by sending some eight divisions, including over 700 tanks (more than 400 Soviet-built T-55s and 300 home-produced Vickers Vijayanta, plus a number of Centurions, French-built AMX-13s and

BELOW: **An Indian Commanding Officer issues orders to his squadron commanders on the eve of battle, April 13, 1948. The Stuart Light Tank behind them is now on a plinth at the Indian War Museum.**

Russian amphibious PT-76s), forcing the Pakistanis into a humiliating surrender. Since then no major conflicts have occurred and both countries now have their own main battle tanks under construction (with outside assistance).

Iran–Iraq

The Iran–Iraq conflict is often forgotten despite being one of the longest-running wars of the 20th century. On September 22, 1980, Saddam Hussein attacked Iran, anticipating a short three-week Blitzkrieg-type campaign, leading to victory using more than 3,000 mainly Soviet-built tanks. Instead the war lasted for eight years and resulted in over a million casualties. Western arms dealers were only too happy to supply both sides with weapons, especially Iran, whose tanks were in a parlous state after years of neglect following the deposing of the Shah, who had taken a great interest in all things military.

Russo–Afghan War

In December 1979, the USSR attempted to take over Afghanistan, invading it with more than 100,000 troops supported by large numbers of tanks, helicopters and jet fighters. For the next ten years they fought a bitter, bloody war against the Mujahedin, who were clandestinely aided by Western finance. Eventually the Soviets realized that they could not win and signed a peace agreement in April 1988, withdrawing troops in 1989. Fighting has continued there ever since, but with different protagonists.

The Balkans

Closer to Europe, the Balkans has been a potential and actual battleground throughout the 20th century. During his lifetime, Marshal Tito managed to hold the various ethnic components of Yugoslavia together – an explosive mixture of Serbs, Croats and Slovenes – and fought successfully against the Germans in World War II. However, following his death the situation deteriorated, with widespread ethnic violence, leading to UN intervention in which British and American main battle tanks were employed in peace-keeping operations.

Sadly, this handful of examples is only the tip of the iceberg, as shown only too often by the twisted hulks of burnt-out tanks found all over the world.

ABOVE LEFT: **Indo-Pakistan conflict. This Pakistani M48 Medium Tank was knocked out by Indian Centurions during the war in 1965.** ABOVE: **Some Indian tank commanders pose with one of their victorious Centurions.** BELOW: **Soviet tanks on the streets of Bratislava in 1968. A stone-throwing youth uses the leading Soviet T-62 to provide cover from the other Russian tanks in this failed uprising, August 1968.** BOTTOM: **War in the Falklands. A small number of British tanks were used in the Falklands War in 1982. Here a Scimitar CVR(t) gains extra protection by being dug in.**

TOP: **Patton tanks of Israel Defence Force (IDF) 7th Armoured Brigade breaking into Khan Younis on the morning of June 5, 1967, when the Six Day War began.** ABOVE: Yom Kippur. Israeli Patton tanks advancing across the desert in central Sinai, making for the Suez Canal.

The Arab-Israeli wars

It is ironic that after World War II the dashing image of the *Panzerwaffe* should have been taken over by Jewish tank commanders – the people the Nazis most reviled. The Israeli Armoured Corps was born in battle from small beginnings, yet rapidly became one of the most formidable armoured forces the world has known. Their commanders learned the hard way – on the battlefield – at all levels, putting lessons into practice immediately, instituting a rigorous system of discipline, yet without stifling individual initiative. The resulting potent mixture enabled them time and again to overcome the far larger, better-equipped forces of their Arab neighbours.

During the initial War of Independence in 1948, they had to organize effective armoured units while at the same time obtaining tanks from all over the world. Their first (and only) armoured brigade contained just one tank battalion comprising one company of smuggled in French Hotchkiss Light Tanks, manned by Russian immigrants who spoke little Yiddish, and one company of two Cromwells and one Sherman (stolen from the British), manned by British and South African volunteers. Nevertheless, they performed miracles.

1956 saw another upsurge in violence following the nationalization of the Suez Canal and the decision by Britain and France to send in troops to maintain free, open transit

through the canal. British Centurion tanks landed and took Port Said, but the major armoured effort came from two Israeli armoured brigades – part of their invasion force from Sinai. The Israeli 7th Armoured Brigade, for example, reached the Suez Canal in less than 100 hours, having travelled 241km/150 miles and having fought several fierce battles on the way.

A period of hasty reorganization followed, in which a number of new armoured brigades were formed, and in 1960 the Israelis took delivery of British Centurions, which soon proved their worth against Syrian tanks in border skirmishes. They were followed by more modern tanks, such as American M48A2 Pattons, fortunately in time for the Six Day War of 1967,

LEFT: **Paratroopers with armoured support (Sherman M4A1 Horizontal Volute Spring Suspension with 76mm/2.99in gun and wet stowage) break through to the American colony, north-west of the Old City wall of Jerusalem.** BELOW: **An excellent photograph of two Israeli Centurions churning through the sands of Sinai during the lightning campaign that lasted just six days.**

"The outcome of the war will depend on our performance ... If we fail the outcome will be disastrous for the whole campaign ... There will be heavy fire and the Egyptians will fight well, so keep moving ... fire from as far as possible, knocking out enemy tanks and anti-tank guns at long range."
General Israel Tal, then Director of the Israeli Armoured Corps to his tank commanders

ABOVE: **Part of a company of Merkava MBT in a Palestinian camp. The Israelis are probably the most experienced army in the world as far as street fighting is concerned.**

in which the Israeli armour did particularly well, the individual tank gunnery skills of their tank crews completely dominating their Egyptian and Syrian opponents.

Then followed the War of Yom Kippur in October 1973, when the Egyptians took the initiative, launching a surprise attack across the Suez Canal. The Bar Lev Line was heavily attacked by 280,000 troops and 2,000 tanks, and many defending Israeli tanks were knocked out by man-portable, Soviet-made "Sagger" guided missiles. By the morning of October 8, the Egyptian Army had achieved a tremendous success and had put five divisions across the Canal. Nevertheless, despite being taken by surprise, the Israeli

reservists were soon rushing to join their units, two armoured divisions reaching Sinai during the night of October 7–8. Instead of the expected Egyptian breakout, there followed a period when they merely held their positions and knocked out many of the counter-attacking Israeli tanks. Clearly the Israelis needed to regain the initiative, and so they decided to re-cross the Canal and infiltrate their armour behind the Egyptian lines. After some delay, this was achieved at dawn on October 15, and by October 19 they had the best part of three tank divisions across. They were soon threatening Port Tewfik and the Gulf of Suez, encircling the Egyptians and forcing them into a ceasefire by October 24. Success on the Golan against the Syrians soon followed.

Since then there has been much activity but no all-out war, although Israeli armour, in particular their remarkable Merkava tank (one of many home-grown armoured successes) has been in constant action along their disputed frontiers with the Palestinians. The Israelis have certainly become experts in the difficult art of urban warfare, using heavy armour effectively against short-range urban targets. This requires specialized ammunition for the main armament and the use of the tank's excellent target-acquisition capability coupled with on-board machine-guns to deal with snipers and other threats. Another highly successful weapon on the latest Merkava Mk IV is the remotely activated, internally mounted Soltam 60mm/2.36in mortar which is used most effectively against tank-hunting parties.

Improvements in basic characteristics

Following World War II, while the speed and quantity of tank-building worldwide has slowed down, there are still plenty of new tanks being built, with some new countries indulging in first-time manufacture or in the improvement of less modern tanks so that they are capable of holding their own in future battles. All three of the basic characteristics have seen improvements, as have many other, less vital features.

Regarding firepower, Main Battle Tanks (MBTs) now mount main guns of 120–122mm/4.72–4.80in calibre. However, the fitting of conventional rifled guns has been overtaken by smooth-bore weapons of similar calibre, the only exception among the latest MBTs being the British CR2. Both have a similar range of anti-armour projectiles, which now include fin-stabilized, long rod, DU (Depleted Uranium) penetrators. These are necessary to defeat new forms of armour like the British Chobham – the latest type being called "Dorchester",

which gives a significant increase in protection against both KE (Kinetic Energy) and CE (Chemical Energy) attack. In 1988 the USA announced a new version on the M1A1 with steel-encased depleted uranium armour, two and a half times the density of steel.

Gun performance has also been significantly improved by a wide variety of new vision and gun-laying devices designed to improve the chances of a first-round hit by day or night. For example, some of the fire-control equipment found in the US Army Abrams M1A1 MBT includes a laser rangefinder, a full solution solid-state digital computer and a stabilized day/thermal night sight. The stabilizer allows for accurate firing on the move, the gunner merely placing the reticule in his sight on to the target and using his laser rangefinder to measure the range. The computer then works out and applies the weapon sight offset angles necessary to hit the target, and the gunner

LEFT AND ABOVE: **In these two photographs taken inside the Challenger building plants at what was the Royal Ordnance Factory, Leeds (now closed), tank turrets are being fitted with Chobham armour for increased protection. Compare them with the normal Chieftain turrets alongside.**

opens fire. The gun has a muzzle reference system to measure any bend in the gun tube, while other sensors check wind speed, barrel temperature, ammunition temperature, etc, and automatically feed the results into the computer.

Added protection is afforded to many MBTs by the external fitting of reactive armour in the form of explosive-filled tiles. These detonate and explode outwards when struck by a shaped-charge projectile, thus disrupting the armour-piercing jet and negating its penetrative effect. Internally, sliding armoured doors and armour-protected boxes isolate crew members from on-board ammunition explosions, while automatic fire extinguishing systems will react to a fire and extinguish it.

Engines are now invariably run on diesel or are kerosene-based and despite being smaller in size are more powerful, having to deal with an MBT normally weighing between 60–70 tons. They are also generally simpler to maintain, the Abrams power pack (a Lycoming Textron AGT 1500 gas turbine), for example, being capable of removal and replacement in less than one hour (compared with four hours for the M60 series). Equally, modern-day suspensions give a smoother ride, not only benefiting the crew, but also making the weapon stabilization system more effective.

In addition to all these major new items, there are land-navigation and battlefield information systems, and better day/night viewing devices together with longer-range yet more compact radios. The inevitable result of all these improvements, however, has been a considerable increase in manufacturing costs. Thus, there has been a significant consolidation and specialization within the armaments industry, for example in the UK, first the acquisition of Vickers Defence Systems by Alvis plc in late 2002, and then the take-over of Alvis Vickers by BAe Systems. Building MBTs is clearly an expensive business.

ABOVE LEFT: **Even "bombing-up" a tank on the ranges and not under battlefield conditions is still a time-consuming job. Here crewmen load practice ammunition (note the colour is different from service rounds). In the photograph there are APDS (Armour-Piercing Discarding Sabot) and HESH (High-Explosive Squash-Head) practice rounds, plus bag charges, vent tubes (in the small can he is holding) and belts of machine-gun ammunition for the coaxial machine-gun.** ABOVE: **Modern tank ammunition includes Armour-Piercing Fin-Stabilized Discarding Sabot rounds such as these for a British 120mm/4.72in tank gun. The part that does the damage is the Long Rod Penetrator (two versions are on show here) to defeat Depleted Uranium armour.** BELOW: **Amphibious light tanks are still extremely useful for reconnaissance purposes. Here a number of Soviet PT-76s swim ashore during a training exercise.**

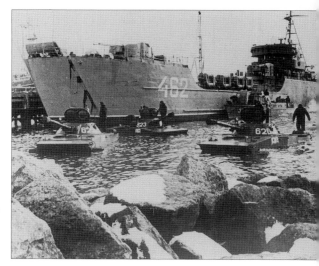

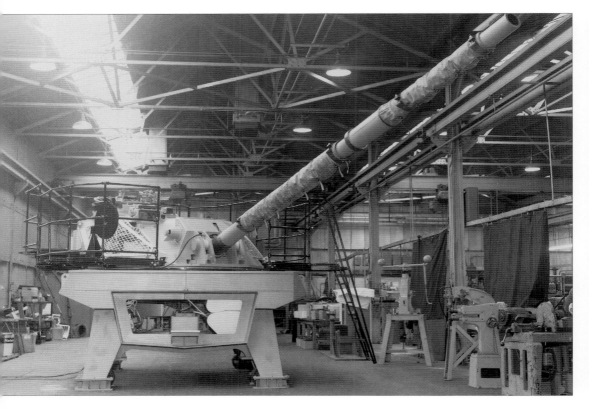

Training expedients

ABOVE: **Gunnery training simulators were essential to save both expensive training areas and equally expensive track mileage. This Classroom Armament Instructional Mounting for a Chieftain was used by the REME (Royal Electrical and Mechanical Engineers) to instruct gun-fitters.**

Immediately post-World War II, armoured training on both sides of the Iron Curtain was intensified at all levels, with major exercises being held by NATO and Warsaw Pact forces at varying levels of realism. However, it soon became clear that other cheaper and more sustainable methods of training had to be found if vast training damage bills were to be avoided – not to mention the wear and tear on AFVs. Nevertheless, tank crews still had to be kept at the right level of readiness so that they could go to war at a moment's notice.

Considerable work was therefore done on improving indoor static-training devices such as Classroom Simulators, especially for both tank driver/commander and tank gunner/loader/commander skills. While this could not entirely replace actual hands-on training in the AFV, it certainly could and did give all crew members good, basic training and made it easier to sustain follow-on training in regiments, so that tank crews could be kept at a suitable level of operational readiness. In military schools such as the Armor School at Fort Knox, USA, and the RAC (Royal Armoured Corps) Centre (now called the Armour Centre) in the UK and in training regiments, suites of

such training devices have been installed and are used extensively. In addition, it was realized that training a tank driver did not require an AFV with a vastly expensive fighting compartment (i.e. a turret), so now MBTs such as CR2 have a specially built turret-less Driver Trainer Tank (DTT).

Regular gunnery training periods on open ranges are still essential if crews are to become accustomed to live firing. However, the increased range and lethality of tank gun ammunition has made it necessary to invent new training rounds which have similar characteristics to service ammunition, but without the same range or lethality.

Another perennial problem for training at lower levels has been finding a suitable method of registering hits on two-sided exercises. Initially this could only be done by means of on-the-spot umpires, but this not only required manpower, but was in many cases ineffective. There are now training devices that can be fitted to tanks, anti-tank guns/missile launchers, and even to individual personal weapons, which give a realistic impression

both to the firer and at the target end. When an accurate hit by a suitable type of armour-piercing round is registered on the target vehicle, coloured smoke may be emitted, a siren sounded, or the vehicle engine or gun control computer may be shut down by means of suitably located detectors on board. However, this must be carefully controlled so that the "knocked-out" tank and its crew are not put at risk. The firer also gets a suitable reaction, even as far as reducing the amount of his on-board ammunition, so that in due course he must replenish if he is to continue to take part in the battle.

Restrictions on space in Europe have led to the British seeking training areas further afield. None has been more successful than the British Army Training Unit, Suffield (BATUS), in Alberta, Canada. Armoured units stationed in the UK and Germany now regularly train at BATUS against "live" enemy. In addition, the lowering of the Iron Curtain and the dismantling of the Berlin Wall has led to NATO and erstwhile Warsaw Pact armies exchanging training grounds and working together to deal with common problems.

Additionally, the mere fact that much of the equipment on a modern tank is computer-controlled means that built-in training devices are commonplace, allowing crews to practise their drills without even having to leave the tank hangar.

ABOVE: **Bale out! With a coloured smoke pyrotechnic belching smoke (for 30 seconds) denoting a "kill", the crew of this Chieftain bale out of their "knocked-out" tank.** BELOW: **Fording water obstacles is another part of tank training. Note the tall "conning tower" fixed to the commander's hatch of this Chieftain and the rubber sealing covers to prevent water from getting inside the tank.**

Wars in Iraq

In early August 1990, tiny oil-rich Kuwait was invaded by its neighbour Iraq, which boasted the fourth largest and supposedly most powerful army in the world. The Iraqis used thousands of Russian-built T-series tanks (such as T-62 and T-72 MBT) to spearhead their invasion in typical Blitzkrieg style. Fortunately, apart from a few "prophets of doom", Saddam Hussein found few allies, while the United Nations, with America leading the way, imposed an immediate naval blockade. This was swiftly followed by an impressive build-up of sea, land and air forces in Saudi Arabia, to back up the UN resolution ordering Iraq to withdraw. Operation "Desert Shield", as it was called, was followed by Operation "Desert Storm" in which first Coalition air forces and then ground troops were employed. The ground offensive, Operation "Desert Sabre", was launched on February 23, 1991. Meticulously planned and executed with élan, its speed and direction came as a complete surprise to the Iraqis. With armour to the fore – in particular the main battle tank playing a major role – it was yet another example of a highly successful all-arms team action. It was also fought on a 24-hour battlefield day, in which the vastly superior night-fighting capability of the British Challenger and the American Abrams tanks was in evidence from the outset.

The battle went so quickly that many observers could not believe what they saw on their television screens all over the world. Thousands of the enemy were killed, wounded or captured – out of all proportion to the small numbers of Coalition casualties. The much-vaunted Soviet tanks were a disaster, and in many cases dug in so deeply that they could not traverse their turrets, while their AFV batteries had been removed and used to light underground shelters rather than work their vehicle electrical systems! The fourth largest army in the world turned out to be a paper tiger thanks to the sheer professionalism of the Allied tank crews. Pentagon officials estimated that some 4,000 Iraqi tanks were destroyed in the 100-hour battle, which ended on February 28 when the Coalition forces cut the highway from Kuwait to Basra, thus preventing the bulk of the battered and defeated Iraqi Army from escaping.

ABOVE LEFT: **Operation "Desert Storm". Crews of British Challenger 1s carry out last-minute adjustments before going into battle.** ABOVE: **The detritus of war. In the foreground are the knocked-out blackened hulks of two Iraqi tanks during the aftermath of Operation "Desert Storm", barely recognizable as once combat-ready MBTs. A convoy of Coalition force vehicles can be seen in the background.** BELOW: **A British Challenger 1 advances to meet the enemy.**

The second Gulf War

World opinion prevented the Coalition forces from "finishing the job" and calling Saddam Hussein to account. Instead, for the next 14 years they vacillated, while Iraq threatened its neighbours with supposed "Weapons of Mass Destruction" and the Iraqi leader continued to oppress his own people. Eventually the Allies once again decided to act, although this time world opinion was not as solidly behind

BELOW: **Operation "Telic". Striking picture of the "business end" of a 2nd Royal Tank Regiment Challenger 2. Note the 7th Armoured Brigade "Desert Rat".** BOTTOM: **Gunner action! A CR2 belonging to the 2 RTR Battlegroup traverses on to a target.**

the USA and UK as it had been on the first occasion. Nevertheless, on March 20, 2003, the Allied armies invaded Iraq from Kuwait, the British elements targeting the southern city of Basra, while the Americans drove all-out for Baghdad. The success of the armour-led Allied columns was even more spectacular than in 1991, the war-fighting being over in a matter of just a few days. Once again the American and British main battle tanks had shown their complete

superiority – a testament to how effective tanks still are on the modern battlefield, provided they are manned by thoroughly professional, properly motivated, well-disciplined and well-trained tank crews. Operation "Iraqi Freedom", as it was known by the Americans, and Operation "Telic", as it was called by the British, showed once again that it is the all-arms team that wins battles and that the human element in the shape of the tank crew is still the most important ingredient.

The future

As must be evident from what has been covered already, the tank undoubtedly played a major part in securing victory in both World Wars and has gone on to prove itself time and time again ever since, being employed in most of the high-intensity conflicts that have occurred worldwide. There was also a large armoured presence on both sides of the Iron Curtain ready to take part in World War III if the unthinkable had ever happened and the world had descended into nuclear war. This led to increasingly large numbers of sophisticated Main Battle Tanks (MBTs) being built by both sides before the thaw in the Cold War started.

There is now, however, no doubt that things are changing, principally because the end of the Cold War has seen a downsizing of most European armies, leading to considerable over-capacity in tank-building and associated armaments industries, despite the continuing lucrative trade in the upgrading and modernization of older MBTs. However, this has not been the case worldwide where countries in the Far East, such as China, Japan and the Republic of Korea, now have their own tank-building industries, some even exporting to neighbours and further afield. In the West there has thus been a declining MBT market, especially as a number of countries, including the USA and UK, have started to favour a more balanced force composition. Therefore, as well as needing a "heavy" element based upon MBTs, infantry fighting vehicles and Self-Propelled (SP) artillery, they have now stated a requirement for a "light" element that can be air-transportable

TOP: **One of the obvious employments for British armour will be in peacekeeping operations on behalf of NATO and the UN, as in Kosovo. The photograph shows three elements of IFOR, including a Challenger 2 MBT and a CVR Scimitar Light Tank.** ABOVE: **Fitting old tanks with more powerful guns, power packs, etc, is now big business all over the world. Here an American-built M48 has been fitted with a more powerful diesel engine – the AVDS 1790 2C tank engine – by means of installing a TCM/GPD simplified dieselization kit.**

in medium-range transport aircraft, such as the C-130 Hercules. This challenges the armaments industry to produce a class of tank weighing about 16 tons – a very demanding requirement for any would-be manufacturer who must produce a new tank with firepower, protection and mobility on a par with the current 70-ton MBT, but weighing some 75 per cent less. This calls for considerable innovation, and consideration is now being given to lighter, smaller, wheeled AFVs as well as tracked vehicles. Miniaturization of components and the use of machinery to perform crew tasks (such as automatic loaders) so as to cut down on the space requirements also becomes a major issue.

LEFT: Added protection against HEAT (High-Explosive Anti-Tank) projectiles is achieved by the fitting of tiles of Explosive Reactive Armour (ERA), as on this Russian T-72 tank. BELOW: Testing new materials for the future. An early test model, developed in 2000 by the Defence Evaluation and Research Agency (DERA) in partnership with Vickers Defence Systems, to examine the trend towards smaller, lighter MBTs. It has a plastic/glass fibre composite hull rather than one made of conventional steel. It was known as the Advanced Composite Armoured Vehicle Platform (ACAVP), but christened by some the "Tupperware Tank"! Its basic purpose was for stress and strain analysis under field conditions.

In addition, the use of non-conventional, lighter, composite armour is also being studied. An example of such lighter systems is the much-debated American "Future Combat System". It is early days yet and, at least for the time being, MBTs will continue to rule.

Various MBTs and other AFVs are now being offered with a variety of alternative subsystems – such as varying power packs, fire-control systems and night/day vision devices – to suit all customers' needs. As mentioned before, the British CR2 is now the only top-grade MBT with a rifled gun. This could possibly change as consideration is currently being given to replacing it by one of a number of similar calibre smoothbore guns. New types of ammunition specifically for urban warfare have been developed, such as the American Multi-Purpose Anti-Tank round (MPAT) to create breaches in buildings for assault team access and the Israeli Anti-Personnel Anti-Material tank round (APAM) containing six sub-munitions with thousands of tungsten cubes for controlled fragmentation.

Suffice it to say that for the time being anyway, there is little chance of the MBT going out of fashion or being replaced by some other weapon system such as the armed helicopter. Although the balance of the "Firepower, Protection and Mobility" equation may alter and thus produce a more varied selection of the weapon system that we call the "Tank", their future place on the battlefield as an indispensable member of the battle-winning all-arms team still appears secure.

ABOVE: On guard at the edge of Podujevo during Operation "Agricola". A close-up of the CR2 belonging to the Commanding Officer of 2 RTR, 7th Armoured Brigade (note the "Desert Rat" emblem). LEFT: After many years without an armaments industry, Japan, like other Far Eastern countries, now makes its own tanks. These are Type 61 MBTs, the first home-produced tank since World War II.

A–Z of World War Tanks

1916–45

The size and shape of the first tanks of 1916 depended more upon the need to cross trenches and deal with machine-gun nests than any other factor. Improvements were then rapidly made, the "International" Mark VIII of 1918 being way ahead of the original Mark I, while the tiny French FT-17, which was the first tank with a fully traversing turret, was sought worldwide. From 1918 onwards, financial restrictions put paid to progress among the victors, leaving it to Germany to develop armoured warfare. Tanks like the Panzer III and IV stayed in production for most of World War II, while the Allies floundered, building a plethora of generally inferior models. In the end it was the remarkable transformation of American industry that saved the day, producing vast numbers of reliable, adaptable tanks like the Sherman. Towards the end of World War II, the Soviets also produced some excellent medium and heavy tanks, including perhaps the best Allied tank of all, the T-34. Nevertheless, ask anyone to name the outstanding tank of the war and they will invariably say the German Tiger I, whose dreaded 8.8cm/3.46in gun and thick armour made it feared everywhere.

LEFT: **This British Heavy Mark V of 1918 is still in full running order at the Tank Museum, Bovington, Dorset, despite having seen action on the battlefields of France during World War I.**

A7V Sturmpanzerwagen

At the start of World War I the Germans lacked anyone at ministerial level prepared to put their weight behind any tank projects; consequently no attempt was made to build one until after British tanks had already appeared. Ultimately only one German tank type took part in the war, the A7V, with 100 being ordered but less than a quarter of that number being built.

Weighing 30,480kg/30 tons, this leviathan consisted of a basic massive steel box superstructure built over a tractor chassis. It had a suitably enormous crew of 18, 12 of whom were machine-gunners, divided into pairs, with one team stationed at the rear and the rest along the sides. The main armament was a 5.7cm/2.24in gun mounted in the nose. The A7V's cross-country performance was poor, although it had a top road speed of 14kph/9mph. Despite this and its frightening appearance, it was remarkably ineffective, being both cumbersome and mechanically unreliable.

The first tank versus tank battle took place at Villers Bretonneux, France, on April 24, 1918, when three British tanks (two Female and one Male) met three A7Vs. Two of the enemy were too far away to be engaged, but the British Male, a Mark IV, opened up on the leading A7V. The British tank crews had been badly gassed the previous day, two of the Mark IV Male's crew being evacuated and the remainder still suffering from the effects of the mustard gas. This made it very difficult for the British tank gunners to see properly to engage their enemy.

TOP: **The only surviving A7V is in the Australian War Museum. However, the German Panzer Museum at Munster now has a full-scale replica which is seen here in a panorama setting in their museum.** LEFT: **A captured A7V arriving at Erin near Bermicourt, France, the location of the Tank Corps Central Workshops.**

ABOVE: **Two A7Vs in a village near Villers Bretonneux, France. The vehicles were "Hagen" and "Wotan".** RIGHT: **According to the chalk marking, this A7V was captured by the New Zealanders.** BELOW: **Thirteen of the eighteen-man crew are seen here riding on the outside of the tank – probably to escape from the heat, fumes and noise inside.**

A7V Sturmpanzerwagen

Entered service: 1917
Crew: 18
Weight: 30,480kg/30 tons
Dimensions: Length – 8m/26ft 3in
  Height (over turret hatch) – 3.4m/11ft 2in
  Width – 3.2m/10ft 6in
Armament: Main – 5.7cm/2.24in gun
  Secondary – 6 x 7.92mm/0.31in Maxim-Spandau 08/15 machine-guns
Armour: Maximum – 30mm/1.18in
Powerplant: 2 x Daimler-Benz 4-cylinder petrol, 74.5kW/100hp
Performance: Speed – 15kph/9mph
  Range – 60–70km/37–44 miles

Their first rounds missed, and the A7V quickly replied with armour-piercing machine-gun fire, causing "splash" and sparks inside the British tanks. The German tank engaged the two Female tanks, damaging both and forcing them to withdraw. The British commander of the Male, Second Lieutenant Frank Mitchell then halted his tank to give the gunner a steady shot. They were both delighted to see the A7V keel over, but it had simply run down a steep bank and overturned. This was nevertheless counted as the first tank kill.

A1E1 Independent

In December 1922, the War Office asked Vickers to design a new heavy tank to replace the World War I Mark V. The chosen design was for a tank with a main gun in an all-round traversing turret and machine-guns in four small separate turrets with limited traverse only. The "land warship" idea, pioneered by the British with this tank, would enjoy a brief European-wide popularity before its shortcomings became apparent and the practical problems of command, crew control, weight and size made it redundant.

However, as an experimental model it anticipated and influenced future tank design with various new developments, including: a self-cleaning drive sprocket; an aero-marine inertia starter; a

prototype intercom system using the laryngaphone and mechanical indicators; as well as better battle stations for increased crew comfort and safety.

The controls of the A1E1 were hydraulically operated by the driver at the front, with the engine at the rear and the tracks slung low with the hull between them. Main armament was a 3pdr in the main turret, with four Vickers machine-guns in the subsidiary turrets. Its 296.7kW/398bhp Armstrong-Siddeley V12 engine theoretically gave the A1E1 a road speed of 40kph/25mph, but in practice it was lower (32kph/20mph) because it consumed oil heavily. The engine was also notoriously difficult to start – hence the fitting of the aero-marine inertia starter.

TOP: **Built in 1926, this multi-turreted, heavily armed British tank was designed, as the name implies, for independent action. Its design was very advanced for the time, and it set a trend for similar tanks in France, Germany and Russia. The only A1E1 built still survives at the Tank Museum, in Dorset. During World War II it was taken out of the Museum and used to guard the approaches to Bovington.**
LEFT: **Internal photograph of the main armament of the Independent.**

With the weight at 32,514kg/32 tons, the engine, final drive, suspension, rubber tyres of the road wheels and the brakes all gave constant trouble because the tank was too heavy, out of proportion and too long for its width. This in turn made it difficult to steer, and caused serious problems at the rear where the track frames started to peel away from the hull. Eventually after an expensive but useful seven-year development cycle, the project was shelved after costing over £150,000 – a high price at that time.

A1E1 Independent

Entered service: This tank never entered service
Crew: 8
Weight: 32,514kg/32 tons
Dimensions: Length – 7.6m/24ft 11in
    Height (over turret hatch) – 2.72m/8ft 11 in
    Width – 2.67m/8ft 9in
Armament: Main – 3pdr QF (quick-firing) gun
    Secondary – 4 x Vickers machine-guns in
    subsidiary turrets
Armour: Maximum – 30mm/1.18in
Powerplant: Armstrong-Siddeley air-cooled V12,
    296.7kW/398bhp
Performance: Speed – 32kph/20mph
    Range – 150km/93 miles

A9 Cruiser Tank Mark I

Medium tanks lacked speed, while light tanks lacked both firepower and protection. This led to the design of a series of "Cruiser" tanks, the A9 being the first. Sir John Carden completed the design in 1934, trials started in 1936, and production in 1937. One hundred and twenty-five tanks were built in total, and saw service from 1938–41.

The weight of the A9 being relatively low allowed it to be powered by a commercially available 9.64 litre AEC bus engine, which gave it a top speed of 40kph/25mph. It also had a distinctive "slow-motion" suspension system with the triple-wheel bogies on springs mounted with Newton hydraulic shock absorbers.

It was armed with a 2pdr main gun and three machine-guns, one coaxial in the main turret and the other two in separate auxiliary turrets, and it was the first British tank with an hydraulic-powered turret traverse.

Combat experience in France in 1940 proved that the design had two critical drawbacks: the armour was too thin and

A9 Cruiser Tank Mk I

Entered service: 1938
Crew: 6
Weight: 12,190 kg/12 tons
Dimensions: Length – 5.79m/19ft
  Height (over turret hatch) – 2.54m/8ft 4in
  Width – 2.54m/8ft 4in
Armament: Main – 2pdr gun
  Secondary – 3 x Vickers 7.7mm/0.303in machine-guns (one coaxial, two in separate turrets)
Armour: Maximum – 10–14mm/0.39–0.55in
Powerplant: AEC Type A179 6-cylinder petrol, 111.9kW/150bhp
Performance: Speed – 40kph/25mph
  Range – 241km/150 miles

the speed too slow for the cruiser role. It also fought in the Western Desert in North Africa, where, although adequate against the Italian armour, it was just too slow and thinly armoured when confronted by contemporary German tanks.

A10 Cruiser Tank Mark IIA

The A10 shared various features with the A9, including the same designer, Sir John Carden. It had the same basic turret and hull shape but with the two secondary turrets removed and additional armour installed by simply bolting extra plates on to the outside of the hull and turret, making it the first British tank built in this composite fashion. One hundred and seventy-five vehicles were ordered and completed by September 1940. A10s were issued to units of the 1st Armoured Division, and were used in France in 1940 and in the Western Desert until late 1941. However, like its predecessor, it was too slow and lightly armoured when confronted by contemporary German tanks.

A10 Cruiser Tank Mk IIA

Entered service: 1940
Crew: 5
Weight: 13,970kg/13.75 tons
Dimensions: Length – 5.51m/18ft 1in
  Height (over turret hatch) – 2.59m/8ft 6in
  Width – 2.54m/8ft 4in
Armament: Main – 2pdr QFSA (quick-firing semi-automatic) L/52 gun
  Secondary – 2 x 7.92mm/0.31in Besa (one coaxial and one hull)
Armour: Maximum – 22–30mm/0.87–1.18in
Powerplant: AEC Type A179 6-cylinder petrol, 111.9kW/150bhp
Performance: Speed – 26kph/16.16mph
  Range – 161km/100 miles

LEFT: **Sir John Carden designed the A10 Cruiser Tank Mark II. It was more heavily armoured than its A9 predecessor, and replaced the two separate machine-gun turrets with a single Besa machine-gun. This model has been painted in the original British wartime desert camouflage pattern rather than that used in temperate climates.**

A11 Infantry Tank Mark I Matilda I

The first pilot model of the A11 was designed by Sir John Carden and produced by Vickers in 1936. It had a maximum speed of only 13kph/8mph because at the time it was considered that Infantry tanks were only required to keep up with the infantry as they advanced at a walking pace. It was armed with either a 7.7mm/0.303in or 12.7mm/0.5in machine-gun.

To keep costs to a minimum, the construction was kept very simple. A commercial Ford V8 engine and transmission were installed with the steering, brakes, clutches and suspension adapted from those used in the Vickers Light Tanks and Dragon gun tractors. The body was of an all-riveted construction, with the exception of the turret which was cast.

The first production order for 60 vehicles was placed in April 1937, and later increased to 140, all of which were completed by August 1940. Although they were cheap and reliable, they were soon obsolete – being outgunned from the start. Nevertheless, they did see action in the early days of World War II and thereafter were used for training purposes only.

There are a number of stories as to how the tank got its nickname Matilda, one being that when General Sir Hugh Elles saw the tank's comic, duck-like appearance and gait, he named it after a cartoon series of the day. In fact, the codeword "Matilda" appears on the original proposal for the A11 in John Carden's handwriting.

A11 Infantry Tank Mk I Matilda I

Entered service: 1938
Crew: 2
Weight: 11,160kg/11 tons
Dimensions: Length – 4.85m/15ft 11in
    Height (over turret hatch) –1.85m/6ft 1in
    Width – 2.29m/7ft 6in
Armament: 1 x 12.7mm/0.5in or 7.7mm/0.303in
    Vickers machine-gun
Armour: Maximum – 60mm/2.36in
Powerplant: Ford V8 petrol, 52.22kW/70bhp
Performance: Speed – 13kph/8mph
    Range – 129km/80 miles

TOP: **The small but heavily armoured A11 Infantry Tank Mark I Matilda I. It was invulnerable to anything but the largest enemy anti-tank guns because of its thick armour. However, it was only armed with a single machine-gun, and was very slow.**

LEFT: **A somewhat battle-scarred Matilda I – this model is the A11E1 prototype.**

A12 Infantry Tank Mark II Matilda II

In 1936, design began on the successor to the Matilda I, which was to mount a 2pdr main gun and have an increased road speed of around 16–24kph/10–15mph. It was hoped to modify the A11, but it soon became apparent that this would not be practical. Instead, the new design, designated the A12 Infantry Tank Mark II, would be based on the A7 Medium Tank, and built by the Vulcan Foundry of Warrington. Twin ganged AEC diesel engines and a Wilson epicyclic gear box were installed, and the tank was armed with a coaxially mounted 2pdr and 7.92mm/0.312in Besa machine-gun.

The powered turret could be traversed in 14 seconds using a system adapted from that fitted to the Vickers A9. The hull armour was cast and the tracks were protected by one-piece armour side skirts with five mud chutes.

The Matilda played its most important role in the early Western Desert campaigns. In Libya in 1940, its heavy armour was soon found to be almost immune to Italian anti-tank and tank fire. Until the appearance of the German 8.8cm/3.46in Flak gun in 1941, used in an anti-tank role, it was the most effective of the British tanks.

ABOVE: **The Bovington Tank Museum's A12 Infantry Tank Mark II Matilda. It is painted in the original Western Desert camouflage and named "Golden Miller" in honour of Major General Bob Foote's tank which he commanded when, as Commanding Officer of 7 RTR, he was awarded the Victoria Cross for outstanding courage and leadership over the period from May 27 to June 15, 1942.**

Unfortunately, as the Matilda turret could not fit the 6pdr due to the small size of its turret ring, its importance began to diminish. There were, however, many special purpose variants produced, including:
• Matilda CDL (Canal Defence Light): a powerful searchlight used to illuminate battlefields at night.
• Baron I, II, III and IIIA: flail mine-clearers.
• Matilda Scorpion: flail mine-clearer.
• Matilda with AMRA (Anti-Mine Roller Attachment): mine-clearer using rollers.
• Matilda with Carrot (Carrot demolition charge): 272kg/600lb HE (High-Explosive).
• Matilda Frog: flamethrower developed in Australia.
• Matilda Murray: flamethrower also developed in Australia.

ABOVE RIGHT: **Sandstorm approaching! A Matilda Mark II – the Commanding Officers's tank of 4 RTR – in the desert, alongside his heavy-utility staff car, as a *Khamseen* (dust storm) blows up behind them.**
LEFT: **A Matilda II in the shadow of St Paul's Cathedral, London.**

A12 Infantry Tank Mk II Matilda II

Entered service: 1939
Crew: 4
Weight: 26,924kg /26.5 tons
Dimensions: Length – 5.61m/18ft 5in
    Height (over turret hatch) – 2.52m/8ft 3in
    Width – 2.59m/8ft 6in
Armament: Main – 2pdr OQF (ordnance quick-firing) gun
    Secondary – 1 x coaxial 7.92mm/0.312in Besa machine-gun
Armour: Maximum – 78mm/3.07in
Powerplant: 2 x AEC 6-cylinder diesels, 64.8kW/87bhp
Performance: Speed – 13kph/8mph
    Range – 258km/160 miles

LEFT: Developed from the high-speed Christie-type BT tanks then in service with the Red Army, the A13 was based on a Christie model imported from the USA. It saw operational service both in France and the Western Desert.

A13 Cruiser Tank Mk III

Entered service: 1938
Crew: 4
Weight: 14,225kg/14 tons
Dimensions: Length – 6.02m/19ft 9in
  Height (over turret hatch) – 2.59m/8ft 6in
  Width – 2.54m/8ft 4in
Armament: Main – 2pdr QFSA (quick-firing
  semi-automatic) gun
  Secondary – 1 x coaxial Vickers 7.7mm/0.303in
  machine-gun
Armour: Maximum – 14mm/0.55in
Powerplant: Nuffield Liberty V12 petrol,
  253.64kW/340bhp
Performance: Speed – 48kph/30mph
  Range – 145km/90 miles

A13 Cruiser Tank Mark III

The A13 originated in late 1936 after British War Office observers had witnessed the high speed of the Russian Christie-type BT tanks in service with the Red Army. The Nuffield Company was asked to design a similar tank based on the Christie design as a high-speed replacement for the A9 and A10. The A13 was based on an actual Christie vehicle imported from the USA, developed in under two years and in service by 1938. It had the Christie suspension system, a high power-to-weight ratio, and a very high top speed of over 48kph/30mph. The engine could be started electrically or by using compressed air. The simple flat-sided turret gave the tank a distinctive appearance. It was used by the 1st Armoured Division in France 1940 and in small numbers with the 7th Armoured Division in the Western Desert in 1940–41, but was too lightly armoured and under-gunned when compared to its German contemporaries.

A13 Mark II Cruiser Tank Mark IV

The A13 Mark II was the up-armoured version of the A13 with extra armoured steel plates giving added protection and eliminating shot traps. Hollow "V"-sided plates were added to the original A13 type turret – some A13s were also upgraded to similar standards – and this gave the turret a very distinctive appearance with its faceted sides. Due to the high power-to-weight ratio of the Nuffield Liberty V12 petrol engine, the extra armour did not adversely affect the vehicle's performance. The A13 Mark II was in production in 1938, and used in France in 1940 and in the Western Desert in 1940–41. Features included Christie suspension and varied patterns of mantlet. Some 655 were built in total. Once more it was under-gunned, its 2pdr being a satisfactory anti-tank weapon but far too small when used with HE (High-Explosive) munitions.

A13 Mk II Cruiser Tank Mk IV

Entered service: 1940
Crew: 4
Weight: 15,040kg/14.8 tons
Dimensions: Length – 6m/19ft 9in
  Height (over turret hatch) – 2.59m/8ft 6in
  Width – 2.59m/8ft 6in
Armament: Main – 2pdr OQF (ordnance quick-firing)
  L/52 gun
  Mk IVCS (close-support) 94mm/3.7in howitzer
  Secondary – 1 x coaxial 7.7mm/0.303in or
  7.92mm/0.312in Besa or 7.7mm/0.303in Vickers
  machine-gun
Armour: Maximum – 30mm/1.18in
Powerplant: Nuffield Liberty V12 petrol,
  253.64kW/340bhp
Performance: Speed – 48kph/30mph
  Range – 145km/90 miles

LEFT: The A13 Mark II Cruiser Tank Mark IV was essentially an up-armoured version of the Cruiser Tank Mark III. The excellent power-to-weight ratio meant that the increase in armour had little effect upon its top speed.

A13 Mark III Cruiser Tank Mark V Covenanter

Built by the London, Midland and Scottish Railway Company, the Covenanter was based on the A13 Mark II and used many of its parts in order to keep costs down. It had a powerful purpose-built Meadows Flat-12 engine and a low-set Christie suspension. However, a design flaw of this vehicle was the positioning of the engine at the rear while the cooling radiator was placed at the front alongside the driver. As a result, the vehicle was plagued by overheating, causing continual mechanical problems.

It saw service from 1940–43, later versions having a better engine-cooling system, a different mantlet, and a number of other improvements.

However, the Covenanter's problems were never satisfactorily solved. As a result, the vehicle never saw action, but was used in a training role and in the development of variants, including:
• Covenanter CS: close-support version, armed with a 76.2mm/3in howitzer in place of the normal 2pdr.
• Covenanter with AMRA (Anti-Mine Roller Attachment): mine-clearing device pushed in front of the tank in order to set off mines by pressure.

TOP: **An excellent view of an A13 Mark III Cruiser Tank Mark V Covenanter taken during "Battle Day" at Bovington, Dorset. The ill-fated Covenanter was a failure due to engine overheating problems, and it never saw action.** ABOVE: **Despite its stylish appearance, the unhappy Covenanter was never a success and was plagued with mechanical problems. (The Tank Museum's model was dug up some years ago and restored to cosmetic order before going on show.)**

• Covenanter OP (Observation Post), Command: with extra radio equipment and a dummy gun.
• Covenanter Bridgelayer: bridgelayer with 10.36m/34ft bridge.

A13 Mk III Cruiser Tank Mk V Covenanter

Entered service: 1940
Crew: 4
Weight: 18,289kg/18 tons
Dimensions: Length – 5.8m/19ft
  Height (over turret hatch) – 2.24m/7ft 4in
  Width – 2.62m/8ft 7in
Armament: Main – 2pdr OQF (ordnance quick-firing) gun
  Secondary – 1 x coaxial 7.92mm/0.312in Besa machine-gun
Armour: Maximum – 40mm/1.57in
Powerplant: Meadows DAV1 12-cylinder petrol, 223.8kW/300bhp
Performance: Speed – 50kph/31mph
  Range – 161km/100 miles

A15 Cruiser Tank Mark VI Crusader

The Crusader was built by Nuffields utilizing a large number of components from the A13 series, including both the Christie suspension and Liberty engine of the original design, as always to keep down costs, production time and vehicle weight. It too had a riveted hull, welded turret and an extra outer layer of armour bolted on.

Ready by March 1940, production was then increased and a consortium produced 5,300 Crusaders by 1943 as it became the principal British tank from spring 1941 until the arrival of the American Sherman.

However, the Crusader always suffered from poor reliability, which reflected the urgency with which it had been rushed into production. It first saw action near Fort Capuzzo, Libya, in June 1941 and did well against Italian armour, but although the Germans respected its speed, it was no match for the PzKpfw III

or indeed the 5.5cm/2.17in, 7.5cm/2.95in and 8.8cm/3.46in anti-tank guns.

After withdrawal from front-line use in May 1943, it was mainly used for training, but also converted for special purposes, including:

• Crusader OP (Observation Post) and Crusader Command: vehicles modified with dummy gun and extra radio and communications equipment.
• Crusader III, AA (Anti-Aircraft) Marks I/II/III: Mark I – the turret was removed and replaced by single Bofors 40mm/1.57in Anti-Aircraft mount; Mark II – a new enclosed turret with twin 20mm/0.79in Oerlikon AA cannon; Mark III – similar to the AA Mark II but with radio equipment removed from turret and installed in hull.
• Crusader II, Gun Tractor Mk 1: open-topped box superstructure converted as a fast tractor for 17pdr anti-tank gun and its crew.

ABOVE LEFT: **This is the Tank Museum's Crusader III, the final production model, armed with a 6pdr instead of the original 2pdr gun.** ABOVE: **Tank crewmen hard at work. The crew of a Crusader III, belonging to the 16th/5th Royal Lancers cleaning their 6pdr gun in Tunisia, April 1943.**

• Crusader ARV (Armoured Recovery Vehicle): removal of turret and addition of recovery equipment.
• Crusader Dozer: turret removed, winch and jib fitted for working dozer blade.
• Crusader with AMRA (Anti-Mine Roller Attachment): mine-clearer.

LEFT: **Tanks in line! This mixed 8th Army tank column, photographed in the Western Desert, is being led by two Crusaders, the front one being a Crusader IICS (mounting the close-support 76.2mm/3in howitzer instead of a 2pdr). The Crusader was the best of the early cruisers.**

A15 Cruiser Tank Mk VI Crusader

Entered service: 1940
Crew: Mk VI – 5; Mk III – 3
Weight: Mk I/II – 19,255kg/18.95 tons
  Mk III – 20, 067kg/19.75 tons
Dimensions: Length – Mk I/II – 5.99m/19ft 8in
  Mk III – 6.3m/20ft 8in
  Height (over turret hatch) – 2.24m/7ft 4in
  Width – 2.64m/8ft 8in
  Mk III – 2.79m/9ft 2in
Armament: Main – Mk I/II – 2pdr OQF (ordnance
  quick-firing) L/52 gun
  Mk III – 6pdr OQF gun
  Secondary – 1 or 2 x 7.92mm/0.312in Besa
  machine-guns
Armour: Maximum – 51mm/2.01in
Powerplant: Nuffield Liberty Mk III/IV V12 petrol,
  253.64kW/340bhp
Performance: Speed – 44kph/27mph
  Range – 161km/100 miles

A17 Light Tank Mark VII Tetrarch

Following on from the light Mark VI family, Vickers built the Tetrarch (originally called Purdah) in 1937. It was accepted by the British Army in 1938, but production was delayed until 1940, by which time it was obsolescent, light tanks having been almost entirely replaced by armoured cars in the reconnaissance role. Eventually, however, about 180 were built, some being sent to the USSR (Lend-Lease),

while a squadron's worth saw action in Madagascar in May 1942. They proved unsuitable for the desert (due to inadequate cooling), but were given a new lease of life in 1943 when adopted for use as an air-portable tank to support airborne forces (the Hamilcar glider being specially designed to carry it). Some saw action on D-Day and others at the Rhine Crossing. A few were converted to perform a close-support role mounting

a 76.3mm/3in howitzer instead of the usual 2pdr. The Tetrarch's unique feature was its new suspension with large road wheels which could be partially skid-steered to improve turning.

LEFT: **Designed in 1937 as a private venture, the A17 Light Tank Mark VII Tetrarch came into its own with the development of airborne forces. An airborne reconnaissance regiment was specially formed as a part of 6th Airborne Division for the Normandy invasion. Tetrarchs remained in service until 1949 when the Hamilar glider, which had been designed to carry them, was withdrawn from service.**

A17 Light Tank Mk VII Tetrarch

Entered service: 1942
Crew: 3
Weight: 7,620kg/7.5 tons
Dimensions: Length – 4.11m/13ft 6in
  Height (over turret hatch) – 2.12m/6ft 11.5in
  Width – 2.31m/7ft 7in
Armament: Main – 2pdr QFSA (quick-firing semi-automatic) gun
  Secondary – 1 x coaxial 7.92mm/0.312in Besa machine-gun
Armour: Maximum – 14mm/0.55in
Powerplant: Meadows MAT 12-cylinder petrol, 123kW/165bhp
Performance: Speed – 64kph/40mph
  Range – 225km/140 miles

A25 Light Tank Mark VIII Harry Hopkins

Last of the Vickers Light series and originally known as Tank, Light Mark VII, revised, this model underwent two more changes in name – officially being called the Mark VIII but more colloquially Harry Hopkins after the American President Roosevelt's confidential advisor. Although there were improvements, including a revised faceted hull and

turret, thicker armour and hydraulically assisted steering, the Harry Hopkins was still small, unreliable and vulnerable when compared to the opposition. It was perhaps just as well that it was destined never to see action.

Instead, some were used as the basis for the Alecto dozer and other self-propelled gun projects mounting:

a 95mm/3.74in howitzer (Alecto I); a 6pdr (Alecto II); a 25pdr howitzer (Alecto III); and a 32pdr (Alecto IV) – although only the first two were actually built, and none entered service.

LEFT: **The A25 Light Tank Mark VIII Harry Hopkins was designed as a successor to the Tetrarch. Although some 100 were built in 1944, they were never used in action. The Alecto Dozer had a hydraulically operated dozer blade in place of the gun mount, so it was turretless.**

A25 Light Tank Mk VIII Harry Hopkins

Entered service: 1944
Crew: 3
Weight: 8,636kg/8.5 tons
Dimensions: Length – 4.27m/14ft
  Height (over turret hatch) – 2.11m/6ft 11in
  Width – 2.71m/8ft 10.5in
Armament: Main – 2pdr OQF (ordnance quick-firing) gun
  Secondary – 1 x 7.92mm/0.312in Besa machine-gun
Armour: Maximum – 38mm/1.5in
Powerplant: Meadows 12-cylinder petrol, 110.3kW/148bhp
Performance: Speed – 48kph/30mph
  Range – 201km/125 miles

A22 Infantry Tank Mark IV Churchill

The Churchill was the first British tank to be completely designed during World War II, and was in production throughout the conflict. The earliest model was built in 1941, armed with a 2pdr gun in the turret and a 76.2mm/3in close-support howitzer in its nose. With thick armour and a good cross-country performance (albeit slow), it was undoubtedly one of the best and most well-liked British tanks of the war. It was also the first British tank to mount the US 75mm/2.95in gun – the guns and mantlets being salvaged from knocked-out Shermans in Tunisia.

With less than 100 tanks in the UK after Dunkirk, the A22 was built hurriedly by a consortium of companies, and this rushed development programme led to frequent breakdowns and problems with the early Marks. Its size was limited by the British railway loading gauge restrictions, and it suffered from the same disadvantages of other contemporary British designs, namely that it was too narrow to take a larger turret needed for the 17pdr gun. Thus, by 1944–45 it was under-gunned by German standards, although this was offset by heavy armoured protection.

The other factor which made the Churchill one of the most important British tanks of 1939–45 was its adaptability to specialized armour roles (the Funnies) needed for the invasion of Europe in 1944, for example:
• Churchill Oke/Crocodile: flamethrowers.
• Churchill AVRE (Armoured Vehicle, Royal Engineers) Mark I and II: to carry and support assault engineers charged with breaching heavy defences. Fitted with demountable jibs, front and rear, earth spade at rear, and two-speed winch. Also a 290mm/11.42in spigot mortar for demolition tasks.
• Churchill Ark Mark I/II/III: bridge-carrying vehicles able to lay ramps across sea walls or span defence ditches and craters.
• Churchill AMRA (Anti-Mine Roller Attachment)/AMRCR (Anti-Mine Reconnaissance Castor Roller)/CIRD (Canadian Indestructible Roller Device)/Plough/Snake/Conger: mine-clearers using various systems, usually front-mounted to detonate mines.
• Churchill with Bobbin/Twin Bobbins: mat layers for use during beach landings.
• Churchill with mine plough (A–D, Bullshorn/Jeffries and Farmer Ploughs).

ABOVE: **An A22 Infantry Tank Mark IV Churchill. The Churchill Mark I mounted a 2pdr gun and had a 76.2mm/3in howitzer in the hull. From Churchill Mark III onwards its main armament was a 6pdr, and from Mark VIII a 75mm/2.95in gun.**

A22 Infantry Tank Mk IV Churchill (family)

Entered service: 1941
Crew: 5
Weight: Mks III–VI – 39,626kg/39 tons
Mks VII–VIII – 40,642kg/40 tons
Dimensions: Length – 7.44m/24ft 5in
   Height (over turret hatch) – 3.25m/10ft 8in
   Mks VII–VIII – 3.45m/11ft 4in
   Width – 2.74m/9ft
   Mks I–II – 2.49m/8ft 2in
Armament: Main – Mk I – 76.2mm/3in nose-mounted gun and 2pdr turret-mounted gun
   Mks III, IV – 6pdr OQF (ordnance quick-firing) Mk III or V gun
   Mks V, VIII – 95mm/3.74in gun
   Mks VI, VII – 75mm/2.95in L/40 gun
   Secondary – 1 or 2 x 7.92mm/0.312in Besa machine-guns, coaxial or hull-mounted
Armour: Maximum – 102mm/4.02in
   Mks VI–VIII: 152mm/5.98in
Powerplant: Beford 12-cylinder petrol, 261.1kW/350bhp
Performance: Speed – 25kph/15.5mph
   Range – 193km/120 miles

A43 Infantry Tank Black Prince

In December 1943, Allied tanks were still out-gunned and out-armoured by the Germans. Neither the Challenger A30 nor the Sherman Firefly, both of which mounted 17pdr guns, had adequate armoured protection to engage the German Panther and Tiger tanks on equal terms. It was therefore planned to put the 17pdr gun into the more heavily armoured Churchill. The design of the turret was to be governed by the size of the gun – although consideration had still to be given to the possibility of a later even larger calibre gun such as the 94mm/3.7in Mark VI, which had a penetration performance of 25 per cent better than that of the 17pdr.

Owing to the larger turret ring diameter required for the 17pdr gun, the standard Churchill hull was too narrow. An enlarged version was therefore designed, using as many Churchill A22 components as possible, and with the same thickness of armour.

Vauxhall built six pilot models designated A43 and known as Black Prince, with full production scheduled to start by the spring of 1945. Unfortunately, the combination of two other factors caused the project to be shelved. First, the standard 261kW/350hp Bedford engine was found not to be powerful enough for the A43 which weighed 50,802kg/ 50 tons (some 10 tons heavier than the Churchill). Secondly, by the time plans had been made to replace it with the 447.4kW/600hp Rolls-Royce Meteor engine, a decision had been taken to concentrate the future tank programme on one class of tank only, namely the world-beating Centurion, which was on the point of being built.

A43 Infantry Tank Black Prince

Entered service: 1945
Crew: 5
Weight: 50,802kg/50 tons
Dimensions: Length – 8.81m/28ft 11in
Height (over turret hatch) – 2.74m/9ft
Width – 3.43m/11ft 3in
Armament: Main – 17pdr gun
Secondary – 2 x 7.92mm/0.312in Besa machine-guns
Armour: Maximum – 152mm/5.98in
Powerplant: Bedford 12-cylinder petrol, 261kW/350hp
Performance: Speed – 18kph/11mph
Range – 161km/100 miles

BELOW: **The A43 Infantry Tank Black Prince or Super Churchill. It mounted a 17pdr gun, which required the redesign and widening of the hull. Six prototypes were built. However, the A41 Centurion proved to be a far superior tank, and Black Prince was scrapped.**

A24 Cruiser Tank Mark VII Cavalier

LEFT: The A24 Cruiser Tank Mark VII Cavalier was requested in late 1940 to overcome all the problems inherent in the earlier cruisers. Fitted with a Mark III or Mark V 6pdr gun, the latter was distinguishable from the prominent counterweight on the muzzle.

A24 Cruiser Tank Mk VII Cavalier

Entered service: 1941
Crew: 5
Weight: 26,925kg/26.5 tons
Dimensions: Length – 6.35m/20ft 10in
Height (over turret hatch) – 2.44m/8ft
Width –2.9m/9ft 6in
Armament: Main – 6pdr OQF (ordnance
quick-firing) gun
Secondary – 1 or 2 x 7.92mm/0.312in Besa
machine-guns
Armour: Maximum – 76mm/2.99in
Powerplant: Nuffield Liberty V12 petrol,
253.64kW/340bhp
Performance: Speed –39kph/24mph
Range – 266km/165 miles

Experience with Crusader and its predecessors in World War II led to the production of the first new wartime Cruiser, the Cavalier, which had thicker armour, a bigger gun (the 6pdr) and wider tracks. All this increased its weight by over an extra 5,080kg/5 tons more than the Crusader and consequently reduced its top speed because it used the same engine and power train despite improvements in its suspension.

Externally it was almost identical in appearance to both the Cromwell and Centaur. The Cavalier was only built in small numbers and was never used operationally as a gun tank. Some had the 6pdr gun replaced with a dummy barrel and were used for artillery OP (Observation Post), while others were converted to an ARV (Armoured Recovery Vehicle) role with the turret removed and a winch and a demountable A-frame jib fitted.

A27L Cruiser Tank Mark VIII Centaur

LEFT: The A27L Cruiser Tank Mark VIII Centaur. Like the Cavalier, it too was initially called Cromwell, but changed to Centaur. Nearly 1,000 were built, with 80 mounting the 95mm/3.74in close-support howitzer instead of the 6pdr gun.

A27L Cruiser Tank Mk VIII Centaur

Entered service: 1942
Crew: 5
Weight: 28,849kg/28.4 tons
Dimensions: Length – 6.35m/20ft 10in
Height (over turret hatch) – 2.49m/8ft 2in
Width – 2.9m/9ft 6in
Armament: Main – Mk I – 6pdr OQF (ordnance
quick-firing) gun
Mk IV – 95mm/3.74in howitzer
Secondary – 1 or 2 x 7.92mm/0.312in Besa
machine-guns
Armour: Maximum – 76mm/2.99in
Powerplant: Nuffield Liberty V12 petrol
Performance: Speed – 43.5kph/27mph
Range – 266km/165 miles

Next in the Cruiser line was the A27L Centaur, which was unfortunately compromised from the start by production shortages. The intention was to fit this tank with a new powerful Rolls-Royce Meteor engine. However, supplies were not available because all production was required for aircraft. Consequently the old Liberty V12 engine was fitted instead. Some Centaurs were later upgraded to Cromwells (the Mark X) with a Meteor engine retro-fit, while others had their existing engines up-rated, and were armed with a 95mm/3.74in howitzer to be used by the Royal Marines to give supporting fire from LCTs (Landing Craft Tanks) during the D-Day landings. A few were also converted for special-purpose roles, including AA (Anti-Aircraft) tanks, ARVs (Armoured Recovery Vehicles), OP (Observation Post) vehicles, and Dozers, all being used in the 1944–45 north-west Europe campaign.

A27M Cruiser Tank Mark VIII Cromwell

ABOVE: **An excellent photograph of an A27M Cruiser Tank Mark VIII Cromwell. Light, fast and armed with a 75mm/2.95in gun, initially it did not do well in Normandy but came into its own when the battle became more fluid.** BELOW: **A cutaway drawing of the Cromwell showing its main components, with the engine and transmission at the rear.**

Early Cromwells closely resembled the Cavalier and Centaur, except, of course, for the fitting of the Meteor engine – hence the letter "M" in their title. The Meteor engine was a 447.4kW/ 600hp V12, and made Cromwell the fastest Cruiser tank so far, with increased reliability. It went on to become the most used British cruiser tank of World War II, and formed the main equipment of British armoured divisions from 1944–45, together with the US-built Sherman M4.

Cromwell's hull and turret were of simple box shape and its construction composite – an inner skin with an outer layer of armour bolted on. An important difference between early and later models was the introduction of all-welded construction process in place of riveting, which further simplified the mass production of the vehicle.

Undoubtedly there were misgivings among many tank crews when they were converted from Sherman to Cromwell (the 7th Armoured Division was re-equipped with Cromwells when they returned to the UK from Italy to prepare for D-Day) because of its lack of firepower – it was armed with either a 75mm/2.95in or a 6pdr gun, neither of which was a real match for the German Tiger and Panther tanks. The narrowness of the Cromwell's hull prevented it from being further up-gunned until an

extensive redesign had been implemented, and it was not until after the end of World War II that this took place. Here is how one experienced 7th Armoured Division tank crewman summed up the Cromwell: "I think it was a useless tank – fast enough – but without adequate armour and under-gunned." To be fair, however, once the Normandy "bocage" country was left behind and speed became more important than tank versus tank battles, then the Cromwell did far better, although its basic faults remained.

The design was also flexible enough to be fitted with wider tracks and employed in specialist roles. These included:

• Cromwell ARV (Armoured Recovery Vehicle): vehicle with turret removed and winch and demountable A-frame jib fitted.
• Cromwell Command/OP (Observation Post): fitted with dummy gun and extra radio equipment.
• Cromwell CIRD (Canadian Indestructible Roller Device): vehicle fitted with CIRD mine-exploder.
• Cromwell Prong: standard vehicle fitted with Culin Hedgerow Cutting Device fitted to cut through "bocage" hedgerows.

A27M Cruiser Tank Mk VIII Cromwell

Entered service: 1943
Crew: 5
Weight: 27,941kg/27.5 tons
Dimensions: Length – 6.35m/20ft 10in
   Height (over turret hatch) – 2.49m/8ft 2in
   Width – 2.9m/9ft 6in
Armament: Main – Mk I–III – 6pdr gun
   Mks IV, V, VII 75mm/2.95in OQF (ordnance quick-firing) gun
   Mks VI, VII – 95mm/3.74in howitzer
   Secondary – 1 or 2 x 7.92mm/0.312in Besa machine-guns (one coaxial, one hull-mounted)
Armour: Maximum – 76mm/2.99in (101mm/3.98in with appliqué)
Powerplant: Rolls-Royce Meteor V12 petrol
Performance: Speed – Mk I–III – 64.4kph/40mph
   Mk IVs on – 52kph/32mph
   Range – 278km/173 miles

LEFT: **The A30 Cruiser Tank Challenger. This was an attempt to mount a more powerful gun into a cruiser tank, the gun being the British 17pdr which had already been mounted successfully in the Sherman Firefly.**

A30 Cruiser Tank Challenger

Entered service: 1943
Crew: 5
Weight: 33,022kg/32.5 tons
Dimensions: Length – 8.15m/26ft 8.75in
  Height (over turret hatch) – 2.77m/9ft 1.25in
  Width – 2.91m/9ft 6.5in
Armament: Main – 17pdr OQF (ordnance quick-firing) gun
  Secondary – 1 x 7.62mm/0.3in coaxial Browning machine-gun
Armour: Maximum – 101mm/3.98in
Powerplant: Rolls-Royce Meteor V12 petrol, 447.4kW/600bhp
Performance: Speed – 52kph/32mph
  Range – 193km/120 miles

A30 Cruiser Tank Challenger

The main drawback to Cromwell was its lack of firepower, thus it was logical to produce a tank packing a bigger punch, and so the Challenger was specifically designed to mount the British 17pdr gun which had been developed in 1941. This required a larger turret and led to the need to increase both the length and width of the Cromwell hull. A sixth road wheel was then also added to accommodate this change, and the all-up weight increased to 33,022kg/32.5 tons. Production of Challenger was much slower than the Sherman Firefly (also mounting the British 17pdr), and by September 1944 there were only enough to provide three armoured regiments with twelve apiece.

LEFT: **The A30 Tank Destroyer Avenger self-propelled gun was similar to the A30 Challenger, but its open-topped turret was nearly 0.6m/2ft lower and the overall battle weight about 1,524kg/1.5 tons lighter. The turret had a mild steel canopy to give the crew some protection. The Avenger was not designed to fire on the move, hence the absence of vision devices.**

A30 Tank Destroyer Avenger

Entered service: 1943–44
Crew: 4–5 (optional second loader)
Weight: 31,498kg/31 tons
Dimensions: Length – 8.71m/28ft 7in
  Height (over turret hatch) –2.21m/7ft 3in
  Width – 3.05m/10ft
Armament: Main – 17-pdr OQF (ordnance quick-firing) gun
  Secondary – 1 x 7.7mm/0.303in Bren machine-gun on an AA (anti-aircraft) mount
Armour: Maximum – 101mm/3.98in
Powerplant: Rolls-Royce Meteor V12 petrol, 447.4kW/600bhp
Performance: Speed – 52kph/32mph
  Range – 169km/105 miles

A30 Tank Destroyer Avenger

An alternative version of the A30 was also developed from 1943–44, namely an SP (Self-Propelled) anti-tank gun called the Avenger. This was a British attempt to produce a tank destroyer armed with a 17pdr gun and with an open-topped turret in order to reduce weight. The Avenger was a stopgap weapon while the Valentine Archer SP was being put into production and before the British began to receive supplies of the US M10. Unfortunately it was not ready for use operationally, and by the time the pilot model was completed it had been decided to switch production effort to the Comet instead.

A33 Heavy Assault Tank Excelsior

LEFT: **Only two pilot models of the A33 Heavy Assault Tank Excelsior were ever built. The requirement disappeared following the success of the Churchill in Tunisia and Italy, so there was no production order. The pilot model mounted a 6pdr gun, although a 75mm/2.95in had been originally proposed.**

A33 Heavy Assault Tank Excelsior

Entered service: 1943 (prototypes only)
Crew: 5
Weight: 45,722kg/45 tons
Dimensions: Length – 6.91m/22ft 8in
  Height (over turret hatch) – 2.41m/7ft 11in
  Width – 3.39m/11ft 1.5in
Armament: Main – 75mm/2.95in OQF (ordnance quick-firing) gun
  Secondary – 2 x 7.92mm/0.312in Besa machine-guns
Armour: Maximum – 114mm/4.49in
Powerplant: Rolls-Royce Meteor V12 petrol, 447.4kW/600bhp
Performance: Speed – 39kph/24mph
  Range – 209km/130 miles

Following the debacle of the raid on Dieppe, France, in August 1942, the poor performance of the early production Churchills forced the British to question its continuation and consider an alternative tank which combined the "cruiser" and "infantry" roles – the Excelsior. Based on the A27 hull and mounting a 75mm/2.95in dual-purpose gun – capable of firing both HE (High-Explosive) and AP (Armour-Piercing) ammunition – and with additional armour and wider tracks, it was an attempt to mount as large a gun as possible on an existing hull. It had an up-rated Meteor engine of 447.4kW/600bhp, giving it a top speed of 39kph/24mph – considerably faster than the Churchill. A second pilot model was built with widened, Cromwell-type tracks, known as the R/L Heavy Type.

In the end the Excelsior never went beyond the prototype stage. The Churchill's performance in North Africa redeemed its reputation, and the Excelsior project was quietly shelved with production effort being switched to the new all-purpose medium tank, the Comet.

A38 Infantry Tank Valiant

A38 Infantry Tank Valiant

Entered service: 1943–45 (prototypes only)
Crew: 4
Weight: 27,433kg/27 tons
Dimensions: Length – 5.36m/17ft 7in
  Height (over turret hatch) – 2.13m/7ft
  Width – 2.82m/9ft 3in
Armament: Main – 6pdr or 75mm/2.95in OQF (ordnance quick-firing) gun
  Secondary – 2 x 7.92mm/0.31in Besa machine-guns
Armour: Maximum – 114mm/4.49in
Powerplant: GMC diesel, 156.5kW/210bhp
Performance: Speed – 19kph/12mph
  Range – 129km/80 miles

LEFT: **The A38 Infantry Tank Valiant was an improved version of the Valentine with an up-rated diesel engine and other mechanical parts of its predecessor.**

Conceived as a successor to the Valentine, this small 27-ton tank was some 10,160kg/10 tons heavier than its predecessor. Design began in 1943, two pilot models being built, one with a GMC 156.5kW/210bhp engine and AEC gearbox, the other with a Rolls-Royce Meteor 261kW/350hp engine and gearbox. With a wider, longer turret than the Valentine, it could mount either a 6pdr or a 75mm/2.95in gun, as well as having space for three men – thus freeing the commander from having to load the gun. However the war ended, and in preference to other more successful types the project was shelved.

A34 Cruiser Tank Comet

The next logical development of the Centaur/Cromwell design was to produce a tank that really had the firepower, protection and mobility to match its German counterparts. This was to be the Comet, which, like the last Marks of Cromwell, was of an all-welded construction and at 35,560kg/ 35 tons was nearly 5,080kg/5 tons heavier than the last up-armoured version of the Cromwell series. It was to all intents and purposes an up-gunned, up-armoured Cromwell, retaining many similar features and components, as well as the same general layout. The initial Comet prototype was the last British cruiser to have the Christie suspension (the same as the Cromwell but with the top rollers) and it had a good cross-country performance and a top speed of 47kph/29mph.

Where it departed from its predecessor was in mounting a completely redesigned main gun, a 76.2mm/3in, known as the 77mm, which had just about the same performance as the 17pdr, but was smaller and lighter.

TOP: **Undoubtedly the best British tank of the war was the A34 Cruiser Tank Comet. Bearing the Black Bull divisional sign of 11th Armoured Division, this one was photographed at Bovington, Dorset. Comet was not available in sufficient numbers until after the Rhine Crossing in March 1945.** ABOVE: **Comets of the 1st Royal Tank Regiment on parade in Berlin, September 20, 1945, when they were inspected by Field Marshal Montgomery.**

Fast and reliable, the Comet was the best all-round British tank produced during World War II, but was introduced far too late to have much effect on tank versus tank combat. Production deliveries started late in 1944, but regiments did not receive issues until after the Rhine Crossing in March 1945. Fast and reliable, it was the first British tank to begin to match the German PzKpfw V Panther in all-round performance,

especially firepower. It would remain in service for the next 15 years, the last Comets not being withdrawn from British service until 1960. Its successor was the A41 Centurion.

Visually, Comet is quickly distinguishable from Cromwell by virtue of the four return rollers above the road wheels. Note also the prominent commander's all-round vision cupola, the forward-sloping turret roof and the large counterweight on the turret rear.

Comet was thus the last British tank to be developed during World War II and the last in the cruiser line, as its successor the A41 Centurion was classed as the first "universal" tank. Initially there was some criticism of Comet concerning the retention of the hull gunner and the thinness of the belly armour, as mines became more and more of a threat during the later stages of the campaigns of north-west Europe. However, these faults were deliberately ignored in order to get it into operational service.

A34 Cruiser Tank Comet

Entered service: 1945
Crew: 5
Weight: 35,560kg/35 tons
Dimensions: Length – 7.66m/25ft 1.5in
Height (over turret hatch) – 2.68m/8ft 9.5in
Width – 3.05m/10ft
Armament: Main – 77mm (76.2mm/3in) OQF (ordnance quick-firing) gun
Secondary – 2 x 7.92mm/0.312in Besa machine-guns (one coaxial and one hull-mounted)
Armour: Maximum – 101mm/3.98in
Powerplant: Rolls-Royce Meteor V12 petrol, 447.4kW/600bhp
Performance: Speed – 47kph/29mph
Range – 198km/123 miles

TOP: **Ready for battle! A Comet tank "bombed up" and ready for action.**

ABOVE LEFT AND ABOVE: **Views of the Comet during the war. Comet remained in British Army service for many years after the end of World War II. It was also in service with the Irish Army from 1950–70. It was the "end of the line" for British cruiser tanks, which had begun with the A9 and A10 in the early 1930s.**

LEFT: **The massive A39 Heavy Assault Tank Tortoise. Six pilot models were built from August 1945 onwards but were not trialled until 1946–47.**

A39 Heavy Assault Tank Tortoise

Entered service: 1946–47 (pilot models only)
Crew: 7
Weight: 79,252kg/78 tons
Dimensions: Length – 10.06m/33ft
　　　　　　 Height (over turret hatch) – 3.05m/10ft
　　　　　　 Width – 3.91m/12ft 10in
Armament: Main – 32pdr OQF (ordnance quick-firing) gun
　　　　　　 Secondary – 3 x Besa 7.92mm/0.312in machine-guns, 2 in AA (anti-aircraft) mount
Armour: Maximum – 225mm/8.86in
Powerplant: Rolls-Royce Meteor V12 petrol, 484.7kW/650bhp
Performance: Speed – 19kph/12mph
　　　　　　 Range – 81km/50 miles

A39 Heavy Assault Tank Tortoise

The last of the British attempts to produce a heavy tank during World War II was the equivalent of the Jagdtiger, a 79,252kg/78-ton monster, appropriately called Tortoise. With a 32pdr main gun having limited traverse,

it had armour up to 225mm/8.86in thick and a crew of seven. Although it was first designed in 1942, work progressed slowly until 1944, when the Jagdtiger appeared and the project received extra impetus; however, the pilot models were

not delivered until after the war had ended. In trials, performance and manoeuvrability were adequate, with a top speed of 19kph/12mph, but ultimately Tortoise was really too heavy to be a feasible proposition.

TOG 1 and TOG 2 Heavy Tanks

TOG Heavy Tank

Entered service: 1940 (prototypes only)
Crew: TOG 1 – 6; TOG 2 – 8
Weight: TOG 1 – 64,555kg/63.5 tons
　　　　　 TOG 2 – 81,284kg/80 tons
Dimensions: Length – 10.13m/33ft 3in
　　　　　　 Height (over turret hatch) – 3.05m/10ft
　　　　　　 Width – 3.12m/10ft 3in
Armament: Main – TOG 1 – 2pdr in turret and a 75mm/2.95in howitzer in nose
　　　　　　 TOG 2 – 6pdr (77mm/3.03in) or 17pdr OQF (ordnance quick-firing) gun
　　　　　　 Secondary – None fitted
Armour: Maximum – 75mm/2.95in
Powerplant: Paxman-Ricardo V12 diesel, 447.4kW/600bhp
Performance: Speed – 14kph/8.5mph
　　　　　　 Range – 81km/50 miles

LEFT: **TOG 2 after restoration. The massive tank then mounted a 17pdr gun in the large turret that would later be fitted to the A30 Challenger.**

The acronym TOG stands for "The Old Gang" and refers to the team set up on the outbreak of World War II to find solutions to UK tank needs. The members were all men who had been directly responsible for the very successful World War I tank programme: Stern, Wilson, Swinton, d'Eyncourt, Ricardo, Symes and Tritton. They now produced a very large, heavy tank, weighing some 81,284kg/80 tons, which was long enough to cross wide trenches

and well protected against anti-tank weapons. TOG 1 had a 75mm/2.95in howitzer in its nose and a 2pdr in a Matilda II-type turret above, and would probably have been ideal to fight the largely static battles of World War I but was entirely wrong for the Blitzkrieg of World War II.

The trials of TOG 1 revealed problems with the electric transmission, and so a hydraulic transmission was tried out on TOG 2, which also mounted a larger

turret and a 6pdr gun (later changed to a 17pdr). This was the heaviest British tank of World War II; however, during development the Churchill was produced, trialled and accepted, so interest in TOG waned. It became yet another failed design project, and TOG 2 (Revised) was never built.

BT Medium Tank series

This series of Soviet medium tanks owes its existence to the purchase of an American M1931 Christie tank by the Soviet Purchasing Commission. It had, like the original Christie tank, the ability to run either on its tracks or on its road wheels (four large road wheels on each side). The Soviets did their copying very thoroughly and the BT-1 was made to the same all-riveted construction as the American M1931, with a similar turret containing two machine-guns. Even the engine was a copy of the Liberty from the Christie model.

The BT-1 was only a limited production run, soon replaced by the BT-2 which had a new turret mounting a 37mm/1.46in gun and a machine-gun. This was the first major production model and weighed about a ton more than its predecessor.

The next model was the BT-3/BT-4, again very similar but with solid disc wheels rather than spoked wheels. It also had a 45mm/1.77in gun as its main armament. Production was limited, but there were conversion models: one (in 1939) which had a new turret mounting a flamethrower, while another had its gun removed and carried a folding wooden bridge – neither went into full production.

Then came the major production model, the BT-5, with a larger cylindrical turret mounting a 45mm/1.77in gun and coaxial machine-gun, better vision devices, a strengthened suspension and a new, more powerful engine. The BT-5A model was for close-support work and mounted a 76.2mm/3in howitzer instead of the 45mm/1.77in gun. There was also a command version which had an extensive frame aerial around the turret and a radio inside at the rear.

Next in line was the BT-7 which had a new conical turret (with a ball-mounted machine-gun in its rear) on all except the earliest vehicles. It was of an all-welded construction, with a new, more powerful engine, a new gearbox, more space for extra fuel and ammunition stowage and thicker frontal armour. This model was the main type in service from the beginning of World War II until the end of 1941. Like its predecessor, there was also both a close-support version (76.2mm/3in howitzer) and a command version (BT-7-1 (V)).

Drastic redesign then took place, the BT-7M model being considerably more streamlined with more room for the new V2 diesel engine, sloped front glacis plate rather than the distinctive "V" nose and the same turret as the T-28 medium tank. It was also known as the BT-8.

Final development was the BT-IS, which was only built as a prototype, but was significantly different in design, being the first Red Army tank to have sloping side armour and front glacis.

ABOVE AND LEFT: **The BT-7 Red Army Medium Tank was the direct descendant of the BT heritage that owes its origin to the Christie M1931 from which it was copied. All had the pointed front glacis and large roadwheels, which gave them high cross-country speed. Heavier than the BT-5, it had an improved conical turret, mounting a 45mm/1.77in gun and was the main tank in Russian service during 1940–41.**

BT Medium Tank series (1, 2, 5 and 7) family				
Entered service:	BT-1	BT-2	BT-5	BT-7
	1932	1933	1935	1936
Crew: 3				
Weight: kg	10,200	11,200	11,500	13,900
tons	10	11	11.3	13.7
Dimensions:				
Length m	5.49	5.49	5.49	5.66
ft in	18	18	18	18 / 7
Height m	1.93	1.93	2.21	2.41
ft in	6 / 4	6 / 4	7 / 3	7 / 11
Width m	2.24	2.24	2.24	2.43
ft in	7 / 4	7 / 4	7 / 4	7 / 11.5

Armament: Main – BT-1 – 2 x machine-guns; BT-2 – 1 x 37mm/1.46in gun; BT-5 and BT-7 – 1 x 45mm/1.77in gun
Secondary – All 1 x 7.62mm/0.3in DT machine-gun, except BT-7 2 x 7.62mm/0.3in DT machine-guns

Armour: Maximum – All 13mm/0.5in, except BT-7 – 22mm/0.87in

Powerplant: All Liberty Aero V12 petrol, 298.5kW/400bhp, except BT-7 – M-15T V12 petrol, 335.8kW/450bhp

Performance:
Speed tracks – All 65kph/40mph, except BT-7 – 72kph/45mph
Speed wheels – BT-1/2 – 105kph/65mph; BT-5 – 112kph/70mph
Range tracks – All c200km/124 miles, except BT-7 – c400km/249 miles
Range wheels – All c300km/186 miles, except BT-7 – c500km/311 miles

Carro Armato M11/39 Medium Tank

LEFT: The M11/39 Medium Tank directly evolved from the Carro Armato tank of 1935. A hundred were ordered following the Spanish Civil War which had revealed inadequacies in the small CV33 and CV35 tankettes. They proved to be no match for the British tanks in the early days of the desert war.

Carro Armato M11/39 Medium Tank

Entered service: 1939
Crew: 3
Weight: 11,000kg/10.8 tons
Dimensions: Length – 4.74m/15ft 6.5in
Height (over turret hatch) – 2.3m/7ft 6.5in
Width – 2.21m/7ft 3in
Armament: Main – 37mm/1.46in Vickers-Terni L/40 gun
Secondary – 2 x 8mm/0.315in Breda Model 38 machine-guns
Armour: Maximum – 30mm/1.18in
Powerplant: Fiat SPA 8T V8 diesel, 78.3kW/105bhp
Performance: Speed – 32kph/20mph
Range – 200km/124 miles

At almost 11 tons, this was the start of the Italian medium tank line and evolved from lighter versions. The main armament was a 37mm/1.46in hull-mounted gun, while the manually operated turret, offset to the left, contained twin 8mm/0.315in Breda machine-guns. Although it had an adequate diesel engine and a good sprung bogie suspension,

its riveted armour was very thin, giving minimal protection to its crew, so it was of very little use in battle and fell as easy prey to the British tanks when it went into action in Libya in 1940. Many were knocked out, while a few were captured and used by the Australians in the North African desert in early 1941. The M11/39 was soon withdrawn from service.

Carro Armato M13/40 Medium Tank

Developed in 1939, this tank was largely based upon the M11/39, although at almost 14 tons it was larger and had slightly thicker armour. Its main armament was a new high-velocity 47mm/1.85in gun and coaxial 8mm/0.315in Breda machine-gun, which was mounted in the turret, replacing the twin 8mm/0.315in Breda machine-guns which were now gimbal-mounted in the front hull.

It was probably the best and most widely used Italian tank of World War II, although it was still no match for its opponents. Initially in the desert it suffered from mechanical failure and had to be tropicalized (especially against the sand which got into everything mechanical), with the fitting of improved air and fuel filters. The M13/40 saw action during the first campaign in the North African desert, and despite its excellent gun, it soon proved easy meat for the British heavy infantry tanks

LEFT: Probably the most widely used Italian tank of the war, the M13/40 was still no match for the British Matilda II. It first saw action in December 1940 in Libya, but its armoured protection proved inadequate in battle, even in 1940. This one is at the Aberdeen Proving Ground in the USA.

Carro Armato M13/40 Medium Tank

Entered service: 1940
Crew: 4
Weight: 14,000kg/13.8 tons
Dimensions: Length – 4.90m/16ft 1in
Height (over turret hatch) – 2.39m/7ft 10in
Width – 2.21m/7ft 3in
Armament: Main – 47mm/1.85in Model 37 L/32 Ansaldo gun
Secondary – 3 x 8mm/0.315in Breda Model 38 machine-guns (one coaxial and two hull-mounted)
Armour: Maximum – 42mm/1.65in
Powerplant: SPA 8 TM40 V8 diesel, 93kW/125bhp
Performance: Speed – 32kph/20mph
Range – 200km/124 miles

(Matilda II). During the resounding defeat of the 10th Italian Army at Beda Fomm/ Sidi Saleh, Libya, in February 1941, over a hundred M13/40s were captured in pristine condition. These were used to equip both the British 6th Royal Tank Regiment and the Australian 6th Cavalry as a temporary, emergency measure.

Carro Veloce 33 Tankette

In 1929 the Italians purchased some Vickers Carden-Loyd Mark VI tankettes from Britain, and at the same time obtained permission to manufacture them in Italy. A total of 25 were built under the designation Carro Veloce 29 by Ansaldo, with automotive parts from Fiat. The CV33 was directly descended from the CV29, designed and built by Ansaldo from 1931–32. There were various models over the years of this little two-man tankette. The usual armament was either one or two Breda machine-guns; however, from 1940 some vehicles were re-armed with a 20mm/0.79in Solothurn anti-tank gun while all had a stronger suspension, new tracks and better vision devices for the driver.

LEFT: **The Carro Veloce 33 – this is an early production model – was armed with either a single 6.5mm/0.256in machine-gun or twin 8mm/0.315in machine-guns. A mass of these little tankettes looked most impressive but were no real use even against light tanks with thicker armour and bigger guns.**

Carro Veloce 33 Tankette

Entered service: 1933
Crew: 2
Weight: 3,200kg/3.2 tons
Dimensions: Length – 3.18m/10ft 5in
Height (over turret hatch) – 1.3m/4ft 3in
Width – 1.42m/4ft 8in
Armament: Main – 1 x 6.5mm/0.26in or
2 x 8mm/0.32in Breda machine-guns
Armour: Maximum – 14mm/0.55in
Powerplant: FIAT-SPA CV3 4-cylinder petrol,
31kW/42bhp
Performance: Speed – 42kph/26mph
Range – 125km/78 miles

Carro Veloce L35/Lf Flamethrower Tankette

LEFT: **The flamethrowing version of the small Italian tankette was the L35/Lf, which towed a trailer full of flame fluid (later models had the fuel tank mounted in the rear of the tankette above the engine). This model is on show at the Bovington Tank Museum, Dorset. Other L35s were fitted with eight bridges: L3/35(P) – *Passarella* (Gangway).**

Carro Veloce L35/Lf Flamethrower Tankette

Entered service: 1933
Crew: 2
Weight: 3,200kg/3.2 tons
Dimensions: Length – 3.18m/10ft 5in
Height (over turret hatch) – 1.3m/4ft 3in
Width – 1.42m/4ft 8in
Armament: Main – Lanciaflamme Flamethrower
Armour: Maximum – 14mm/0.55in
Powerplant: FIAT-SPA CV3 4-cylinder petrol,
31kW/42bhp
Performance: Speed – 42kph/26mph
Range – 125km/78 miles

The Carro Veloce L35/Lf (*Lanciaflamme*) was the flamethrower variant of the CV33 tankette. It had a long-barrelled hooded flamethrower instead of the usual machine-guns. A 500-litre/110-gallon armoured fuel trailer was towed behind the *carro d'assalto lanciafiamme*. On a later model the flamethrower fuel tank was mounted on the rear of the vehicle. The range of the flamethrower was about 100m/328ft.

Char d'Assault Schneider CA1 Heavy Tank

Char d'Assault Schneider CA1 Heavy Tank	
Entered service: 1916	
Crew: 7	
Weight: 12,500kg/12.3 tons	
Dimensions: Length – 6.32m/20ft 8in	
Height (over turret hatch) – 2.3m/7ft 6in	
Width – 2.05m/6ft 9in	
Armament: Main – 75mm/2.95in gun	
Secondary – 2 x 8mm/0.315in Hotchkiss machine-guns	
Armour: Maximum – 11mm/0.43in	
Powerplant: Schneider, 4-cylinder petrol, 41kW/55bhp	
Performance: Speed – 8.1kph/5mph	
Range – 80km/49.7 miles	

LEFT: **The Schneider CA1 was the first French tank to be designed in World War I. The first of the 400 to be built were delivered in September 1916, not long after the first British tanks made their appearance. It had vertically coiled spring suspension.**

The Schneider CA1 was the first French tank to be designed and, as with many designs of the time, it was based upon the Holt tractor chassis. The first of those built was delivered in September 1916, so the French were not very far behind the British in the design and production of this new type of weapon system. The driving force was Colonel (later General) Jean Baptiste Estienne, who is reputed to have said, "Whoever shall first be able to make land ironclads armed and equipped ... will have won the war." Designed by Eugene Brille of the Schneider Company, the Char d'Assault Schneider CA1 weighed 12,500kg/12.3 tons, mounted a 75mm/2.95in gun in a sponson on the right-hand side of the tank along with two 8mm/0.315in machine-guns, one on each side. It had a crew of seven men and rear main access doors. Note also the nosepiece which acted as a wire-cutter, important for cutting barbed wire.

RIGHT: **On the left side the sponson just contained a machine-gun. This is a late-production CA1 with improved roof ventilation and larger fuel tanks.**

The Schneider was first committed to battle at Berry-au-Bac on April 16, 1917. 132 Schneider's in eight companies were organized into two columns and reached their objectives but were then subjected to heavy enemy fire and many were lost – 76 in total – with 57 being completely destroyed by artillery. The other main reason for such heavy losses was the vulnerability of the Schneider's fuel tanks to the German "K" anti-tank bullet.

Late production models attempted to solve these problems with better-protected fuel tanks and more roof ventilation than the earlier model.

Schneider also built a prototype CA2 with a turret-mounted 47mm/1.85in main gun, but this was never put into production.

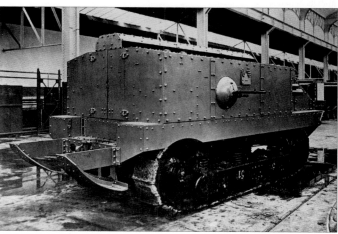

Char d'Assault Saint Chamond Heavy Tank

The second French heavy tank of World War I was the Saint Chamond, designed by a Colonel Rimailho and built in 1916 by the *Compagnie des Forges et Acieries de la Marine et d'Homércourt*, whose factory at Saint Chamond gave the tank its name. At almost 23 tons, it was heavier than the Schneider, had a large crew of nine, mounted a 75mm/2.95in gun in its nose, and also had four machine-guns, positioned two to each side of the vehicle. It was easily identified from its front hull and flat roof.

ABOVE: **Some 400 Saint Chamonds were built in 1916.** BELOW: **On later models of the St Chamond, the original gun was replaced by a regular Model 1897 field gun.**

The Saint Chamond had an electric transmission, with a 67.1kW/90bhp Panhard motor driving a dynamo which powered two electric motors – one per track, with a top speed of 12kph/7.45mph. Despite this, its cross-country performance was indifferent, as it tended to bury its nose when negotiating soft going.

By mid-range production of the vehicle, the two cylindrical cupolas were replaced by a flat pitched roof. Later models reinstalled a single, flat-topped cupola on the right for the driver, and replaced the original main gun with the regular 75mm/2.95in Model 1897 field gun.

A total of 400 Saint Chamonds were built, and the tank first saw action in early May 1917, but the design problem with the nose was insurmountable and the quest for a perfect heavy tank moved on.

Char d'Assault Saint Chamond Heavy Tank

Entered service: 1917
Crew: 9
Weight: 23,000kg/22.64 tons
Dimensions: Length – 8.83m/28ft 11.5in
  Height (over turret hatch) – 2.36m/7ft 9in
  Width – 2.67m/8ft 9in
Armament: Main – 75mm/2.95in 1897 Model field gun
  Secondary – 4 x 8mm/0.315in Hotchkiss machine-guns
Armour: Maximum – 17mm/0.67in
Powerplant: Panhard, 4-cylinder petrol 67.1kW/90bhp
Performance: Speed – 12kph/7.45mph
  Range – 60km/37.3 miles

LEFT: **Coming into service in 1935, with 40mm/1.57in of armour plate and a 75mm/2.95in gun in its belly, the Char B1 was one of the most formidable tanks in the world at that time. The Char B1-bis was even heavier, with a larger secondary armament in its turret and thicker armour. This Char B1 is on parade in Paris in 1936.**

Char B1 Heavy Tank

Entered service: 1931
Crew: 4
Weight: 30,480kg /30 tons
Dimensions: Length – 6.37m/20ft 11in
Height (over turret hatch) – 2.82m/9ft 3in
Width – 2.49m/8ft 2in
Armament: Main – 1 x 75mm/2.95in short gun in hull and 1 x 47mm/1.85in gun in turret
Secondary – 2 x 7.5mm/0.295in machine-guns (one in hull, one in turret)
Armour: Maximum – 40mm/1.57in
Powerplant: Renault, 6-cylinder petrol, 134.2kW/180bhp
Performance: Speed – 28kph/17.4mph
Range – 150km/93 miles

Char B1 Heavy Tank

The development of the Renault Char de Bataille B1 began in the 1920s when, at the request of General Estienne ("Father of the French Tank Corps"), a consortium of French companies designed a new tank under the codename *Tracteur 30*, with specifications for a vehicle with high mobility and heavy fire power. The result was the Char B1, a tank with considerable potential.

Armed with a short 75mm/2.95in gun carried in a front hull mounting, the sighting of the weapon was controlled by the driver, and corrections were made by moving the tank. The sophisticated Naeder Steering Unit, which allowed delicate and very accurate adjustment, had a double differential and hydrostatic drive, which gave the "infinitely variable steering" necessary to lay the 75mm/

2.95in gun. There was also a fixed 7.5mm/0.295in machine-gun controlled by the driver, both weapons being loaded by a crewman sitting beside him. In the turret there was a coaxially mounted 47mm/1.85in anti-tank gun and 7.5mm/0.295in machine-gun fired by the commander. This gun layout effectively halved the amount of ammunition the vehicle could carry.

Char B1-bis Heavy Tank

Char B1-bis Heavy Tank

Entered service: 1935
Crew: 4
Weight: 32,500kg/32 tons
Dimensions: Length – 6.52m/21ft 5in
Height (over turret hatch) – 2.79m/9ft 2in
Width – 2.5m/8ft 2in
Armament: Main – 1 x 75mm/2.95in short gun in hull and 1 x 47mm/1.85in gun in turret
Secondary – 2 x 7.5mm/0.295in machine-guns
Armour: Maximum – 60mm/2.36in
Powerplant: Renault, 6-cylinder petrol, 223.7kW/300bhp
Performance: Speed – 28kph/17.4mph
Range – 180km/111.8 miles

The B1-bis version evolved from the B1 and appeared in 1935. It had thicker armour, a larger gun in the turret (47mm/1.85in instead of 37mm/1.46in) and a more powerful 223.7kW/300bhp Renault aircraft engine. Again no traverse was possible for its nose-mounted 75mm/

ABOVE: **A Char B1-bis (Encore). Note the new AP x 4 turret and 47mm/1.85in gun.**

2.95in gun, so to lay in azimuth the tank had to be turned on its tracks. Of the 365 Char B1-bis built, large numbers were captured in a serviceable condition by

the Germans in France in 1940. Although one of the best armed and armoured tanks of its day, these captured B1s were not immediately issued to German fighting units, because of the limitations of the one-man turret and the tank's generally poor performance. Instead they were used as training vehicles or fitted with radio sets and used to equip second line units, mainly in the west.

Char 2C Heavy Tank

During World War I, the French had issued a specification for a heavy "breakthrough" tank, Char de Rupture C, at a weight of about 40 tons. Two prototypes, Chars 1A and 1B were produced from 1917–18. Further development then produced an even heavier tank of nearly 70 tons – and this was the Char 2C. Although it did not become operational during the war, ten were built, the last being delivered in 1922. In their day they were the most powerful tanks in the world, with a crew of twelve, a 75mm/2.95in gun in the front turret and four machine-guns (one in an auxiliary turret at the rear of the tank). One of them was converted to mount a 155mm/6.1in howitzer as well as the 75mm/2.95in gun and the four machine-guns, and this led some Intelligence circles to think that France was building large numbers of "super tanks". The Char 2C had two engines totalling 186.4kW/ 250bhp, driving electric generators to run a motor for each track, giving the tank a top speed of 12kph/7.5mph.

The last of these tanks were destroyed in 1940 by enemy air attack or captured, when they were being transported to the front by train.

TOP: **Ten Char 2C Heavy Tanks were produced before the end of the war in 1918, but did not see operational service until 1921. They were fitted with German engines provided as part of post-war reparations.** ABOVE: **The massive Char 2C Heavy Tank was designed by FCM and was selected as the "breakthrough" tank for the large scale offensive planned for 1919, but was never needed.** BELOW LEFT: **In 1940, the surviving six Char 2Cs were destroyed or captured by the Germans while still on railway flat cars. The 2C had a crew of 12 men. Here, one still on its flat car is under German guard.**

Char 2C Heavy Tank

Entered service: 1918
Crew: 12
Weight: 69,000kg/67.9 tons
Dimensions: Length – 10.26m/33ft 8in
Height (over turret hatch) – 4m/13ft 1in
Width – 2.95m/9ft 8in
Armament: Main – 75mm/2.95in
Secondary – 4 x 8mm/0.315in Hotchkiss machine-guns
Armour: Maximum – 45mm/1.77in
Powerplant: 2 x Daimler or Maybach, 6-cylinder petrol, 387.7kW/520bhp
Performance: Speed – 12kph/7.5mph
Range – 100km/62.1 miles

Elefant/Ferdinand Heavy Tank Destroyer

This 65,000kg/64-ton tank destroyer/ heavy assault gun mounted an 8.8cm/3.46in StuK 43/2 L/71 gun in a limited traverse mount. The monstrous Ferdinand (named in honour of its creator Ferdinand Porsche) was ideal when used as a long-range tank killer, but not nearly as effective as an assault gun because of its lack of traverse and the absence of any close-in defensive capability. At Kursk its performance was disappointing, and almost all were lost to determined Soviet tank-killer teams.

This problem was solved to a degree with the fitting of an MG34 (Maschinengewehr 34), but Elefant was really only at its best when fighting at long range – it is reputed to have knocked out a T-34 at a distance of 4.82km/3 miles. Another improvement to the superstructure of about half the Elefants built was the fitting of a cupola for the commander.

Elefant/Ferdinand Heavy TD

Entered service: 1942
Crew: 6
Weight: 65,000kg/64 tons
Dimensions: Length – 8.14m/26ft 8in
Height (over turret hatch) – 2.97m/9ft 9in
Width – 3.38m/11ft 1in
Armament: Main – 8.8cm/3.46in gun
Secondary – 7.92mm/0.312in machine-gun
Armour: Maximum – 200mm/7.87in
Powerplant: 2 x Maybach HL120TRM V12 petrol, each developing 223.7kW/300bhp
Performance: Speed – 30kph/18.6mph
Range – 150km/93.2 miles

LEFT: The *Sturmgeschutz mit 8.8cm(3.46in) PaK43/2 (Sd Kfz 184)*, to give its full title, was a heavy assault gun/tank destroyer, known as both Elefant and Ferdinand (the latter in honour of Dr Ferdinand Porsche). Only 90 of these massive vehicles were produced, and they first fought at Kursk, from July to August 1943.

Jagdpanzer IV Tank Destroyer

The PzKpfw IV chassis was used for a number of excellent tank destroyers, over 3,500 being produced and used to great effect in battle. The first Jagdpanzer IV replaced the StuG III in early 1944, weighing nearly 24 tons; with a 7.5cm/ 2.95in PaK39 L/48 gun and carrying 79 rounds, it was basically an improved version of its predecessor. The next development Jagdpanzer IV/70(V) and Jagdpanzer IV/70(A) followed later in the year, mounting the deadly new Vomag long-barrelled 7.5cm/2.95in PaK42 L/70 main gun, with a performance similar to that of Panther. The only difference between these two new Marks was the manufacturer – "V" for Vomag and "A" for Alkett.

Jagdpanzer IV TD

Entered service: 1943
Crew: 4
Weight: 24,000kg/23.6 tons
Dimensions: Length – 6.85m/22ft 6in
Height (over turret hatch) – 1.85m/6ft 1in
Width – 3.17m/10ft 5in
Armament: Main – 7.5cm/2.95in gun
Secondary – 1 or 2 x 7.92mm/0.312in machine-guns
Armour: Maximum – 100mm/3.94in
Powerplant: Maybach HL120TRM, V12 petrol, 522kW/700hp
Performance: Speed – 40kph/24.9mph
Range – 210km/130.5 miles

LEFT: The Panzer IV/70(V) (*Sd Kfz 162/1*) was another German tank destroyer. It was an improved version of the Jagdpanzer IV which itself had been an improved version of the StuG III. This one is at the Aberdeen Proving Ground in the USA.

E-100 Super Heavy Tank

LEFT, BELOW AND BOTTOM LEFT: **As well as producing the massive 191,000kg/188-ton Maus, the Germans also began a parallel development in 1943 of a super-heavy series known as the E-100 and weighing 140,000kg/137.8 tons. A year later Hitler put an end to such super-heavy development and the project continued at very low priority. At the end of the war just one chassis remained without its turret, as these three photographs show (note that the chassis in the bottom photograph is on a trailer).**

In May 1945 at the Henschel tank proving ground and development centre near Kassel, an enormous experimental heavy tank was discovered by the Allied forces. It weighed approximately 138 tons, with its external features resembling the Tiger Model B tank, but with increased length and width, heavier armour plate, wider tracks and a new suspension system.

The E-100 heavy tank that the Allies had found was the most advanced of an entirely new series of tanks which the German weapons procurement department had initiated in mid-1943. Known as the E-Series, its purpose

was ultimately to replace all the current tanks with a new group of standardized vehicles (E-10, E-25, E-50, E-100), incorporating all the improvements learned from five years AFV combat. However, by the end of the war only this prototype vehicle had been built.

The E-100 was to have been armed with the same weapons as Maus in the same Krupp turret, although one was never fitted. The tank was to have been powered by a Maybach 12-cylinder "V" type engine, developing 521.9kW/700hp, though for initial testing a normal Tiger B H1 230 P30 engine was fitted. With tracks nearly 102cm/40in wide, the

E-100 had a ground pressure of nearly 1.4kg/cm^2 (20psi), while its suspension comprised a series of overlapping steel road wheels, with MAN disc springs – so it did indeed look very like the Tiger B.

In fact, the E-100, like the Maus, was an absurd "wonder weapon" dreamed up to keep an insane Führer happy. It was doomed from the start by its weight.

E-100 Super Heavy Tank	

Entered service: 1945 (prototype only)
Crew: 5
Weight: 140,000kg/137.8 tons
Dimensions: Length – 10.27m/33ft 8in
   Height (over turret hatch) – 3.29m/10ft 10in
   Width – 4.48m/14ft 8in
Armament: Main – 17.2cm/6.77in gun
   Secondary – 7.5cm/2.95in gun and a
   7.92mm/0.312in machine-gun
Armour: Maximum – 240mm/9.45in
Powerplant: Maybach HL234, V12 petrol,
   521.9kW/700hp (for trials only)
Performance: Speed – 40kph/24.9mph
   Range – 120km/74.6 miles

FCM 36 Infantry Tank

The French FCM 36 was produced in 1936 as a light infantry support tank using welded armour. It was armed with a 37mm/1.46in low-velocity main gun and a 7.55mm/0.297in machine-gun in an octagonal turret, which had a non-rotating commander's position on the top. Powered by an 8.4-litre Berliet water-cooled diesel engine (the first French tank to be diesel powered), it had a top speed of 24kph/15mph and a radius of action of about 225km/140 miles. A distinctive feature of this vehicle was the skirting plates with mud chutes fitted over the upper half of the tracks.

When the manufacturers raised the unit price, the French Army curtailed their order to 100 vehicles, which were built between 1936–39 and saw action

between May and June 1940. Combat proved it to be severely under-gunned and many were captured by the Germans who, appreciating this vehicle's range, modified them into a gun carriage, mounting the Krupp 10.5cm/4.1in leFH18 gun in an armoured superstructure on top of the original chassis.

ABOVE: The Char FCM 36 was a French infantry support tank built in 1936, and mounting a 37mm/ 1.46in gun and machine-gun in an octagonal-shaped turret. It was the first French tank to be powered by a diesel engine. BELOW: These FCM 36s were on parade in Paris on July 14, 1939, the last Bastille Day before war came. BOTTOM LEFT: The diesel engine for this tank was made in France under licence from Ricardo, who had made engines for some of the first British tanks during World War I.

FCM 36 Infantry Tank

Entered service: 1936
Crew: 2
Weight: 12,350kg/12.15 tons
Dimensions: Length – 4.22m/13ft 10m
Height (over turret hatch) – 2.15m/7ft 0.61in
Width – 1.95m/6ft 4.75in
Armament: Main – 37mm/1.46in gun
Secondary – 7.55mm/0.297in machine-gun
Armour: Maximum – 40mm/1.57in
Powerplant: Berliet 8.4-litre, 4-cylinder diesel, 67.9kW/91hp
Performance: Speed – 24kph/15mph
Range – 225km/140 miles

LEFT: Although the Ford 3 Ton was designated as a "tank", it was designed as a machine-gun carrier. Only 15 of these tiny 3,150kg/3.1-ton tankettes were built before the Armistice cancelled further orders.

Ford 3 Ton Tank

Entered service: 1918
Crew: 2
Weight: 3,150kg/3.1 tons
Dimensions: Length – 4.17m/13ft 8in
Height (over turret hatch) – 1.60m/5ft 3in
Width – 1.68m/5ft 6in
Armament: Main – 7.62mm/0.3in machine-gun
Armour: Maximum – 13mm/0.51in
Powerplant: 2 x Ford Model T 4-cylinder petrol, 33.58kW/45hp
Performance: Speed – 13kph/8mph
Range – Unknown

Ford 3 Ton Tank

The US Army tank battalions that saw action in France during World War I were equipped with either British heavy tanks or French light tanks. In 1918, Ford built a two-man tank using the same characteristics and basic design of the highly successful French Renault FT-17. It was the cheapest and smallest tank built in the USA and undoubtedly the most successful. It was powered by two electrically started Model T Ford engines, producing 33.58kW/45hp between them, with the driver seated at the front and the steering being controlled through variation of the gear ratios of each engine. The gunner also was positioned at the front, armed with a 7.62mm/0.3in machine-gun in a limited-traverse mount. A prototype was sent to France and arrived in time to be tested and approved before the Armistice. Although over 15,000 were originally ordered, only 15 vehicles were actually ever built.

LEFT: The Ford 6 Ton Tank was an exact American copy of the French FT-17, although because of the difference between French and American engineering standards, they virtually had to be completely redesigned.

Ford 6 Ton Tank (M1917)

Entered service: 1917
Crew: 2
Weight: 6,574kg/6.47 tons
Dimensions: Length – 5.0m/16ft 5in
Height (over turret hatch) – 2.3m/7ft 7in
Width – 1.9m/6ft 3in
Armament: Main – 1 x 37mm/1.46in cannon or 1 x Colt 7.62mm/0.3in machine-gun
Armour: Maximum – 17mm/0.67in
Powerplant: Buda HU modified 4-cylinder petrol, 31.34kW/42hp
Performance: Speed – 9kph/5.6mph
Range – 48km/29.8 miles

Ford 6 Ton Tank (M1917)

Copied directly from the French Renault FT-17 tank, this vehicle's official name was the M1917, but was known initially as the 6 Ton Special Tractor for security reasons. Although nearly 1,000 of these tanks were built, only 64 had been finished before the end of the war, and of these only 10 reached France. There were numerous improvements over the French design, including replacing the steel-rimmed wooden idler wheels on the Renault with all-steel ones, fitting a self-starter to the 4-cylinder engine and constructing a bulkhead between the crew and the engine compartment.

They continued in service for many years, and like the Liberty tank (the British Mark VIII), they were given to Canada for training purposes in 1939.

Holt Gas-Electric Tank and other US experimental tanks

As soon as tanks had been used in combat and their exploits reported in the newspapers, designs for tanks of all shapes and sizes began to appear in the USA. All were private ventures, the first being the CLB 75 Tank, designed and built by the CL Best Agricultural Tractor Company and comprising one of their tractors with a simulated armoured body, surmounted by a revolving turret containing two light cannon. There were many others: the Holt's HA 36; the Holt's Gas and Electric Tank; the Steam Tank; the Skeleton Tank; the Studebaker Tank; and the One-Man Tank.

The HA 36, built by the Holt Tractor Factory in 1916, was a small one-man tank, closely resembling a British heavy tank in miniature. Powered by a motorcycle engine with link chain tracks and wooden track plates, it was "armed" with dummy guns. The Holt's Gas and Electric Tank was built by Holt's and General Electric, USA, and was based upon standard Holt tracks and suspension components. It was driven by a Holt 67.1kW/90hp engine which powered a General Electric generator that provided the current to drive two electric motors – one for each track. It was armed with a 75mm/2.95in mountain gun. The Steam Tank was produced by the US Engineer Corps in 1918, with the assistance once again of

TOP: **The Holt's Gas-Electric Tank weighed some 25,400kg/25 tons and was armed with a 75mm/2.95in howitzer. It was based upon standard Holt tracks and suspension components.** ABOVE: **The Holt's HA 36 Tank, a one-man machine, closely resembled a British heavy tank, only much smaller.**

Holt's, and had a very similar external appearance to a British Mark IV; however, the similarity ended there. Motive power was to be provided via two 2-cylinder steam engines, each with its own kerosene burning boiler. One can imagine what heat this

LEFT: **The Steam Tank, a 50,800kg/ 50-ton machine, had many of the characteristics of the British Mark IV Heavy Tank, but power was via two steam engines.** BELOW: **The smallest of the experimental tanks was this One-Man Tank which had an armoured body on top of a tractor.** BOTTOM: **The Skeleton Tank. With a crew of two men, this 9,144kg/ 9-ton vehicle was armed with just one machine-gun, but was light enough to have a good cross-country performance.**

would have generated inside the vehicle, and what would have happened to the crew if enemy fire had pierced a boiler! The Skeleton Tank was built by the Pioneer Tractor Company of Winona, and as its name implies, was built in skeleton form, with a two-man fighting compartment suspended between the track frames. The use of ordinary iron piping for the skeleton kept the weight down to less than 9,144kg/9 tons and resulted in a good cross-country performance. The Studebaker Supply Tank was of conventional design and was to have been ordered in large numbers for use in 1919, but the Armistice was signed and the contract cancelled. The One-Man Tank, as the name implies was a small track-based, lightly armoured vehicle, crewed by one man and armed with a single machine-gun.

None of these experimental models would be adopted, the US Army eventually equipping their fledgling armoured forces with British and French tanks instead.

Space does not allow for the detailed specifications of all these prototypes, so those for the Holt's Gas-Electric are included by way of example.

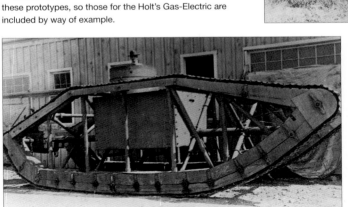

Holt Gas-Electric Tank

Entered service: 1918 (prototype only)
Crew: 6
Weight: 25,400kg/25 tons
Dimensions: Length – 5.03m/16ft 6in
Height (over turret hatch) – 2.38m/7ft 10in
Width – 2.77m/9ft 1in
Armament: Main – 75mm/2.95in Mountain Howitzer
Secondary – 2 x 7.62mm/0.3in machine-guns
Armour: Maximum – 15mm/0.59in
Powerplant: Holt 4-cylinder petrol, generating
67.1kW/90hp
Performance: Speed – 9.66kph/6mph
Range – Unknown

Hotchkiss H-35 Light Tank

LEFT: **The Hotchkiss H-35 was a *char leger* (cavalry tank) and thus considered by some French infantry as unsuitable. Nevertheless, it did come into service, many seeing action in France in 1940, with large numbers being captured and used by the Germans.**

Hotchkiss H-35 Light Tank	

Entered service: 1936
Crew: 2
Weight: 10,600kg/10.43 tons
Dimensions: Length – 4.22m/13ft 10in
    Height (over turret hatch) – 2.62m/8ft 7in
    Width – 1.96m/6ft 5in
Armament: Main – 37mm/1.46in gun
    Secondary – 7.5mm/0.295in machine-gun
Armour: Maximum – 40mm/1.58m
Powerplant: Hotchkiss 1935, 6-cylinder, 55.91kW/75hp
Performance: Speed – 27.4kph/17mph
    Range – 150km/93.2 miles

Following demands from the French Cavalry for a light tank, the Hotchkiss H-35 was designed in 1933 and entered service in 1936, at which time its role was expanded to that of an infantry support tank. In the end some 400 were manufactured, with three quarters allotted to the Cavalry and the remaining quarter to the Infantry.

However, with its short-barrelled 37mm/1.46in main gun and single machine-gun as armament and its poor speed, its combat performance was disappointing against German armour. Under-gunned and underpowered, its sole advantage was its thick cast armour in the hull and turret. Commandeered by the Germans, the remaining H-35s had their turrets removed and were used as "schleppers" – to haul artillery and munitions. The turrets were incorporated into static defence lines.

Hotchkiss H-39 Light Tank

LEFT: **A line of brand new H-39s being prepared for issue. This little light tank was a development of the H-35 but had a new engine and a long-barrelled 37mm/1.46in gun. Like the H-35, it was also captured and used by the Germans, both in Russia and the Mediterranean theatre. Some H-39s were still in use by the Israelis in 1956.**

Hotchkiss H-39 Light Tank	

Entered service: 1939
Crew: 2
Weight: 12,100kg/11.9 tons
Dimensions: Length – 4.23m/13ft 10in
    Height (over turret hatch) – 2.16m/7ft 1in
    Width – 1.96m/6ft 5in
Armament: Main – 37mm/1.46in gun
    Secondary – 7.5mm/0.295in machine-gun
Armour: Maximum – 40mm/1.57in
Powerplant: Hotchkiss 1938, 6-cylinder petrol, 89.5kW/120hp
Performance: Speed – 36.5kph/22.7mph
    Range – 150km/93.2 miles

Between the H-35 and H-39 there was an interim model, the H-38. It sported a new, more powerful 89.5kW/120hp petrol engine which improved its mobility but still had the same ineffectual 37mm/1.46in main gun. It was only in the final model of the series, the H-39, that the main armament, though remaining the same calibre, was upgraded to a long-barrelled variant.

This vehicle did not fare long or well against the Germans in 1940 who, as with its predecessors, removed the turret to use it as a tractor to haul artillery and munitions. Radio sets were fitted with a 2m/6ft 6in-long rod aerial mounted on a tripod on the front right-hand mudguard. It was used by the Germans both in the Russian and Mediterranean theatres.

LEFT: The first of the new breed of Soviet heavy tanks to replace the KV-1 was the Joseph Stalin 1, which mounted an 85mm/3.34in gun, although some were fitted with 100mm/3.94in guns. Here one fires at point-blank range at a German strongpoint in East Prussia, January 25, 1945.

JS-1 Heavy Tank

Entered service: 1943
Crew: 4
Weight: 46.000kg/45.3 tons
Dimensions: Length – 8.32m/27ft 3in
  Height (over turret hatch) – 2.9m/9ft 6in
  Width – 3.25m/10ft 8in
Armament: Main – 100mm/3.94in gun
  Secondary – 2 x 7.62mm/0.3in machine-guns
Armour: Maximum – 132mm/5.2in
Powerplant: V2-IS 12-cylinder diesel,
  382.8kW/510hp
Performance: Speed – 40kph/24.9mph
  Range – 250km/155 miles

JS-1 Heavy Tank

Hard on the heels of the KV-1, Russia began to develop a new tank in 1941, to cope with the new German tanks that had appeared in response to both it and the T-34 in the race for battlefield supremacy. At that time, the requirement was for a four-man tank with an 85mm/3.35in gun and sufficient armour to keep out the German 50mm/ 1.97in anti-tank gun round, but with no significant increase in weight over the KV-1 series. By the time the JS-1 appeared in 1943, the main armament had been changed from 85mm/3.34in to 100mm/3.94in. Basically an enlarged superstructure over a KV chassis enabled the fitting of a larger turret ring and turret to accommodate the larger main gun. This tank had a very good ballistic shape, a low silhouette and was very reliable. In late 1944 a small number had their 100mm/3.94in gun replaced with a 122mm/4.8in gun in a larger turret.

LEFT: Popularly known as the Victory Tank, the JS-2 was next in line, and mounted a 122mm/4.8in gun. Production began in January 1944.

JS-2 Heavy Tank

Entered service: 1944
Crew: 4
Weight: 46,000kg/45.3 tons
Dimensions: Length – 9.9m/32ft 6in
  Height (over turret hatch) – 2.73m/8ft 11in
  Width – 3.09m/10ft 2in
Armament: Main – 122mm/4.8in D-25 gun
  Secondary – 3 x 7.62mm/0.3in machine-guns
Armour: Maximum – 120mm/4.72in
Powerplant: V2-IS 12-cylinder diesel,
  382.8kW/513hp
Performance: Speed – 37kph/23mph
  Range – 240km/149 miles

JS-2 Heavy Tank

The next model in the JS series appeared in 1944, an improved model of the JS-1, but with little external difference other than the 122mm/4.8in main gun which now became standard. This made the JS-2 the most powerfully armed tank in the world at that time. It had a smaller cupola and some differences in the armour silhouette around the front hull. The JS-2 was known as the Victory Tank, and led on to the JS-3. It was undoubtedly the most advanced heavy tank of its time and had a major influence on Western tank design. The JS-2 was accepted for production at the end of December 1943, and by the beginning of 1944 some 100 were in operational service.

KV-1 Heavy Tank

The KV-1 Heavy Tank with which Russia entered World War II was, along with the T-34, the closest any Allied forces came to armour parity with the Germans at that time. It was basically a redesign of the T-100, with one its turrets eliminated. Named after the Russian defence commissar Marshal Klimenti Voroshilov, it first saw active service in the Russo-Finnish war. It was replaced a little later, in 1940, by the KV-1A, which mounted a better gun with a higher muzzle velocity and firing a larger round – the 76.2mm/3in L/41.5 Model 40. This firepower combined with thick armour stunned the Germans when they first encountered it. A special diagnostic team from Germany was rushed to the front to analyse both it and the T-34. However, it was let down by its unreliable transmission, and this, coupled with its weight, made it difficult to drive, slow and cumbersome. Production ceased in 1943.

LEFT: The KV-1 Heavy Tank gave the Germans a shock when they first encountered it during the opening weeks of their assault on the USSR because they had summarily discounted the Red Army's heavy tanks as being both old-fashioned and obsolete. This one, having been captured in the Russo-Finnish war, still has a Finnish swastika on its turret.

KV-1 Heavy Tank

Entered service: 1939
Crew: 5
Weight: 43,000kg/42.3 tons
Dimensions: Length – 6.68m/21ft 11in
  Height (over turret hatch) – 2.71m/8ft 11in
  Width – 3.32m/10ft 11in
Armament: Main – 76.2mm/3in L/41 ZiS-5 gun
  Secondary – up to 4 x 7.62mm/0.3in
  machine-guns
Armour: Maximum – 75mm/2.95in
Powerplant: V2K V12 diesel, 410kW/550bhp
Performance: Speed – 35kph/21.7mph
  Range – 150km/93 miles

KV-2 Heavy Tank

KV-2 Heavy Tank

Entered service: 1940
Crew: 6
Weight: 53,963kg/53.1 tons
Dimensions: Length – 6.79m/22ft 3in
  Height (over turret hatch) – 3.65m/12ft
  Width – 3.32m/10ft 11in
Armament: Main – 152mm/5.98in L/20 howitzer
  Secondary – 2 x 7.62mm/0.3in machine-guns
Armour: Maximum – 110mm/4.33in
Powerplant: V2K V12 diesel, 410kW/550bhp
Performance: Speed – 26kph/16mph
  Range – 150km/93 miles

LEFT: The close-support version of the KV-1 was known as the KV-2, and mounted a massive 152mm/5.98in howitzer in a large slab-sided turret. This captured KV-2 is being inspected by the Germans.

The KV-2 was a specialized tank developed to break through fortifications similar to the Funnies being developed in the Western theatre by the British. A huge 152mm/5.98in howitzer was mounted in a gargantuan turret and could fire a special dustbin-sized anti-concrete shell to destroy bastions and pillboxes. There was an extra crew member in the turret to help operate this weapon system, pushing the crew total up to six.

The chassis and engine were the same as that of the KV-1, which made it even slower and more vulnerable than its predecessor, and the Germans quickly learned to aim for its tracks to first immobilize and then destroy it.

The No. 1 Lincoln Machine "Little Willie"

Designed by William Tritton (later Sir), chief executive of William Foster and Co. Ltd of Lincoln, and Lt W. G. Wilson, then an RNAS (Royal Naval Air Service) armoured car officer, the "Tritton Machine", as it was sometimes called, was designed and constructed between August 2 and September 8, 1915. It weighed 18,290kg/18 tons, and above its rectangular hull was to have been a centrally mounted turret with a 2pdr gun; however, this was never fitted and a dummy turret of the correct weight was used when the machine was tested.

The machine had Bullock tracks, brought from America, where they had been developed commercially from an original British design. Tail wheels helped the cross-country performance and aided steering.

The first version prototype of the No. 1 Lincoln Machine suffered from track problems, through a lack of grip and an inclination for the tracks to come off when crossing trenches. Speed was between 3.2–4.8kph/2–3mph. It could just about cross a 1.2m/4ft wide trench and mount a 0.61m/2ft vertical step.

ABOVE: **The very first tank to be built in the world – "Little Willie", the No. 1 Lincoln Machine – which was designed and completed in 1915.** RIGHT: **This was the No. 1 Lincoln Machine as designed by Tritton and Wilson, utilizing Bullock tracks and a dummy turret. It was modified to become "Little Willie" by using different tracks. Note also the rear steering wheels.**

In order to meet new War Office revised requirements to cross a 1.52m/5ft trench and climb a 1.37m/4.5ft step, the No. 1 Lincoln Machine had to be rebuilt, using the original hull and engine (a 6-cylinder Daimler petrol engine, developing 78.29kW/105bhp), but with completely redesigned tracks. The new tracks had their frames increased in length and comprised cast steel plates riveted to links which had guides engaging with rails on the side of the track frames. This pattern of track construction was used for all British tanks up to 1918 to improve cross-country performance. The simulated turret was also removed, and "Little Willie" was completed early in December 1915. (Presumably the name had some ribald connection with Kaiser Wilhelm II.)

The No. 1 Lincoln Machine "Little Willie"

Entered service: 1915 (prototype only)
Crew: 4–6
Weight: 18,290kg/18 tons
Dimensions: Length – 5.53m/18ft 2in
Height (over turret hatch) – 3.1m/10ft 2in
Width – 2.85m/9ft 4in
Armament: Main – 2pdr (40mm/1.57in) gun
Secondary – 1 x 7.7mm/0.303in Maxim machine-gun and up to 3 x 7.7mm/0.303in Lewis machine-guns
Armour: Maximum – 6mm/0.24in
Powerplant: Daimler 6-cylinder petrol, generating 78.29kW/105bhp
Performance: Speed – 3.2kph/2mph
Range – Unknown

LK I Light Tank

LEFT: The LK I was a relatively simple tank, with a Daimler car chassis and axles for its suspension. It was only ever produced in prototype form in mid-1918.

LK I Light Tank

Entered service: 1918 (prototype only)
Crew: 3
Weight: 7,000kg/6.89 tons
Dimensions: Length – 5.49m/18ft
    Height (over turret hatch) – 2.48m/8ft 2in
    Width – 2m/6ft 7in
Armament: Main – 1 x 7.92mm/0.312in machine-gun
    Secondary – None
Armour: Maximum – 8mm/0.31in
Powerplant: 4-cylinder petrol, 44.7kW/60bhp
Performance: Speed – 13kph/8mph
    Range – 64km/40 miles

The German light tank LK I (*Leichte Kampfwagen I*) was designed in mid-1918 by Joseph Vollmer, who had also worked on the A7V. He advocated the use of simple, light tanks that were easy and cheap to produce in preference to large, heavy and expensive ones. The LK I only reached prototype stage before the Armistice. Using a Daimler car chassis as well as other automotive parts (such as axles for the sprocket and idler wheels), it followed the normal layout of an automobile, weighed nearly 7 tons, had a three-man crew and was armed with one 7.92mm/0.312in machine-gun.

LK II Light Tank

LEFT: The *Leichte Kampfwagen II* was produced from the LK I. It had thicker armour and a 57mm/2.24in gun, but was still a relatively simple tank. Two prototypes were built, but the subsequent order for 580 never materialized, because World War I ended. The design was passed to Sweden and used as the basis of their Strv M/21 Light Tank.

LK II Light Tank

Entered service: 1918
Crew: 3
Weight: 8,890kg/8.75 tons
Dimensions: Length – 5.1m/16ft 9in
    Height (over turret hatch) – 2.49m/8ft 2in
    Width – 1.98m/6ft 6in
Armament: Main – 1 x 57mm/2.24in gun or
    2 x 7.92mm/0.312in machine-guns
Armour: Maximum – 14mm/0.55in
Powerplant: Daimler-Benz, 4-cylinder petrol,
    44.7kW/60hp
Performance: Speed – 12kph/7.5mph
    Range – 64.4km/40 miles

An LK II was then designed from the LK I, mounting a larger 57mm/2.24in main gun and weighing almost 2,000kg/2 tons more due to its thicker armour, but otherwise being similar to its predecessor. It also did not get further than prototype stage. A variant carrying two 7.92mm/0.312in machine-guns in a traversing turret was also proposed but never built, for although two gun-armed LK II prototypes were manufactured, the planned production run of 580 was terminated by the Armistice of November 1918. After 1918, the LK II drawings were passed to Sweden and used to manufacture their Strv M/21 of 1921.

Medium B Whippet

The shape of the Medium B was more like that of the heavy tank than its predecessor, the Medium A Whippet, but with a large fixed turret mounted on top at the front of the hull. The Medium B weighed 18,289kg/18 tons and was longer and wider than the Medium A, but not so tall. The engine, a 6-cylinder 74.57kW/100hp Ricardo, was mounted in a separate compartment, with a bulkhead to divide it from the crew of four – the first tank ever to have this feature.

BELOW LEFT: **Built in 1918, the shape of the Medium B Whippet reverted back to the earlier rhomboidal design. The Armistice led to the cancellation of the order; however, 17 of the 45 built were sent to Russia in 1919, to support the White Russians against the Bolsheviks.**

Medium B Whippet

Entered service: 1918
Crew: 4
Weight: 18,289kg/18 tons
Dimensions: Length – 6.93m/22ft 9in
  Height (over turret hatch) – 2.59m/8ft 6in
  Width – 2.69m/8ft 10in
Armament: Main – 4 x 7.7mm/0.303in Hotchkiss
  machine-guns
Armour: Maximum – 14mm/0.55in
Powerplant: Ricardo 6-cylinder petrol,
  74.57kW/100hp
Performance: Speed – 12.7kph/7.9mph
  Range – Approximately 64km/40 miles

Medium C Hornet

Although it was designed in late 1917, none of the 45 Medium Cs built actually left the factory until after the Armistice. They remained in service until 1925, and proved to be remarkably effective tanks, with a better performance than any of the previous Mediums.

The Medium C had a fixed turret armed with four Hotchkiss 7.7mm/0.303in machine-guns, and a rotating commander's cupola. At 20,320kg/20 tons, its rear-mounted 111.8kW/150hp Ricardo engine gave it a power-to-weight ratio of 7.5, while its fuel tanks held 682 litres/150 gallons – over double that of the Medium A. Top speed was still only 12.9kph/8mph and its radius of action was 121km/75 miles.

The very last tank to be designed in World War I was the Medium Mark D, which never got further than the design stage. However, various modified models were produced after the war, the Johnson Light Infantry Tank being based on the Medium D design. It also had a fixed turret with three ball-mounted machine-guns sited ahead of the driver who sat at the rear above the gunners' stations, steering by means of a small conning tower. There was also a new wire rope suspension system to improve its speed.

LEFT: **Designed by Tritton in late 1917, the Hornet, as the Medium C was also called, resembled the Medium B (engine at rear), but incorporated all the wartime experience of the tank crews, so it was considerably improved.**

Medium C Hornet

Entered service: 1918
Crew: 4
Weight: 20,320kg/20 tons
Dimensions: Length – 7.92m/26ft
  Height (over turret hatch) – 3.00m/9ft 6in
  Width – 2.54m/8ft 4in
Armament: Main – 4 x 7.7mm/0.303in Hotchkiss
  machine-guns
Armour: Maximum – 14mm/0.55in
Powerplant: Ricardo 6-cylinder petrol,
  111.8kW/150hp
Performance: Speed – 12.9kph/8mph
  Range – 121km/75 miles

Medium A Whippet

Designed by Sir William Tritton in November 1916, the Medium A, also known as the Whippet or the Tritton Chaser, was the only British medium tank to see action during World War I. Construction began in December 1916 at William Foster's factory in Lincoln, and trials were held on February 11, 1917, after which an order was placed for 200 tanks four months later.

The tank ran on two 33.6kW/45hp 4-cylinder Tyler lorry engines – one for each track, with dual ignition. It also had twin four-speed gearboxes and clutches, making it very difficult to handle and seriously increasing servicing time. Gentle steering, such as on roads, was by means of a column which controlled the throttle on each engine – and thus each track, accelerating one and retarding the other automatically. For serious turning, especially on cross-country, the gearboxes had to be used.

Seventy gallons of fuel was carried, contained in a drum-shaped tank in the front of the machine (under armour-plating) and was fed to the engines by an autovac system. The tracks were half-round, like those on "Little Willie". There was no unditching beam, but instead there were two towing shackles, and oak spuds were provided. For observation, there were three rotary peephole covers and three periscope openings.

ABOVE: **The Tank Museum's Whippet. This was the tank, nicknamed Caesar, on which Lt Sewell won his Victoria Cross on April 29, 1918.** LEFT: **One of Sewell's No. 9 Section, 3rd (Light) Tank Battalion, which he commanded in 1918.**

The first Whippets to see action did so on March 26, 1918, at Hebuterne, during the Second Battle of the Somme. They continued to perform sterling work right up to the Armistice; indeed, one of the Tank Corps Victoria Crosses was awarded to Lieutenant Cecil Sewell while he was commanding his Whippet, Caesar II, A 253, which is now on show at the Tank Museum, Bovington, England.

The official account of his action says, "This officer displayed the greatest gallantry and initiative in getting out of his own tank and crossing open ground under heavy shell and machine-gun fire to rescue the crew of another Whippet of his section which had side-slipped into a large shell hole, overturned and taken fire." After releasing the crew, Sewell then dashed back across open ground to assist one of his own crew, and a few minutes later he was hit again, this time fatally, while dressing his driver's wounds. He showed "utter disregard for his own personal safety".

ABOVE LEFT: **Good view of the open rear door of a 3rd Battalion Whippet. Two hundred of these 14,225kg/14-ton tanks were built.** ABOVE: **A quartet of Medium A Whippets take part in the Armistice Day parade in Central London as part of a large tank column.** BELOW: **The lighter, faster Whippet was ideal for exploiting the successes of the heavy tanks – a sort of armoured cavalry.**

Medium A Whippet

Entered service: 1917

Crew: 3

Weight: 14,225kg/14 tons

Dimensions: Length – 6.10m/20ft
Height (over turret hatch) – 2.74m/9ft
Width – 2.62m/8ft 7in

Armament: 4 x 7.7mm/0.303 Hotchkiss machine-guns

Armour: Maximum – 14mm/0.55in

Powerplant: 2 x Taylor JB4 petrol, each developing 33.6kW/45hp

Performance: Speed – 12.9kph/8mph
Range – 64.4km/40 miles

Mark I Heavy Tank "Mother"

Even while "Little Willie" was being built, Tritton and Wilson were working on a new design, which had a much longer track length in order to improve its cross-country performance and – to be sure of meeting the new War Office requirements – to cross a 1.52m/5ft trench and climb a 1.22m/4ft step. It had been worked out that this could be achieved by a wheel 1.83m/6ft in diameter, so the length of the track on the ground and its shape had to be the same as the lower curve of a wheel of that size. This meant raising the height of the front horns, and gave

rise to the now familiar rhomboidal shape common to all of the British World War I heavy tanks. In order to keep the centre of gravity low, it was decided to mount the tank's main armament – two naval 6pdr guns – in side sponsons. During her life, "Mother" had various names such as "Big Willie" and "HMLS Centipede", but as the very first battle tank she was rightly called "Mother" – despite her Male armament (Female tanks had two extra machine-guns instead of 6pdrs so they were about a ton lighter).

ABOVE: "Clan Leslie" a British Heavy Tank Mark I (Male). Note the long-barrelled 6pdr naval gun in its side sponson. A total of 150 of these tanks were built, the basic design being exactly the same as for "Mother".

LEFT: Mark I Male tank D7 (No. 742) commanded by Lt Enoch pauses after the Flers Battle.

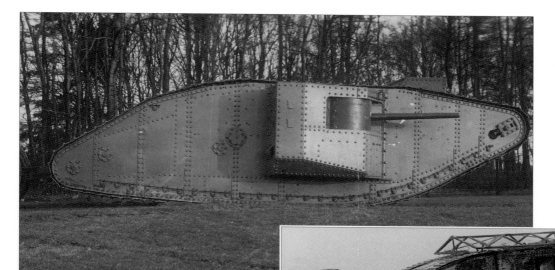

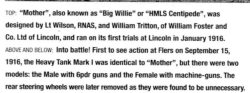

The building of the first batch of 100 Mark I tanks began in February 1916, following the same basic design as "Mother". They were called "tanks" for security reasons, to disguise their true purpose. Half of the first batch was Male tanks with 6pdr guns, the rest Female with two machine-guns in each sponson.

It was not until after the first tank versus tank engagement in April 1918 that the danger of having a tank with no effective weapon capable of penetrating an enemy tank was realized, and thereafter hermaphrodite tanks with one 6pdr sponson and one dual machine-gun sponson were introduced. The Mark I was recognizable by its tail wheels to assist with steering, the unshortened barrel on its ex-Naval 6pdr guns and the anti-grenade "roof" made of chicken wire.

TOP: **"Mother", also known as "Big Willie" or "HMLS Centipede", was designed by Lt Wilson, RNAS, and William Tritton, of William Foster and Co. Ltd of Lincoln, and ran on its first trials at Lincoln in January 1916.**
ABOVE AND BELOW: **Into battle! First to see action at Flers on September 15, 1916, the Heavy Tank Mark I was identical to "Mother", but there were two models: the Male with 6pdr guns and the Female with machine-guns. The rear steering wheels were later removed as they were found to be unnecessary.**

Mark I Heavy Tank "Mother" (Male)

Entered service: 1916
Crew: 8
Weight: 28,450kg/28 tons
Dimensions: Length – 9.9m/32ft 6in
    Height (over turret hatch) – 2.41m/7ft 11in
    Width – 4.19m/13ft 9in
Armament: Main – 2 x 6pdr (57mm/2.24in) guns
    Secondary – 7.7mm/0.303in Hotchkiss
    machine-gun
Armour: Maximum – 12mm/0.47in
Powerplant: Daimler 6-cylinder petrol,
    111.8kW/150bhp
Performance: Speed – 5.95kph/3.7mph
    Range – 35.4km/22 miles

Mark I Medium Tank

Following on from the Medium D, this Vickers-built 12,192kg/12-ton tank was originally called Light Tank Mark I and was the first British tank designed after World War I, with production models coming into service in 1924. It was later reclassified as Mark I Medium Tank and

was the first British tank to have all-round traverse capability and geared elevation for the main gun, a 3pdr (47mm/1.85in), a 94mm/3.7in howitzer being fitted in the close-support tanks. Two Vickers machine-guns were ball-mounted in the hull sides, while there were four Hotchkiss machine-guns carried in the turret for dismounted use. The crew was five (commander, driver, radio-operator and two gunners). Spring suspension enabled it to achieve a higher speed than previous designs, the 67.1kW/90hp air-cooled Armstrong Siddeley V8 engine giving it a top speed of 24kph/15mph. Production of the Mark I and II amounted to some 160 in total.

LEFT: **Mediums on training. The Mark I remained in operational service until 1938 and was thereafter only used for training.**

ABOVE: **The Mark I Medium Tank was the first British tank to be designed after World War I, and to reach production. It had a fully traversing turret and its main armament could be elevated. This rear view has the turret traversed rear and the rear door open.**

Mark I Medium Tank

Entered service: 1924
Crew: 5
Weight: 12,192kg/12 tons
Dimensions: Length – 5.33m/17ft 6in
  Height (over turret hatch) – 2.82m/9ft 3in
  Width – 2.79m/9ft 2in
Armament: Main – 3pdr (47mm/1.85in) gun
  Secondary – 2 x 7.7mm/0.303in Vickers machine-guns and 4 x Hotchkiss 7.7mm/0.303in machine-guns
Armour: Maximum – 8mm/0.315in
Powerplant: Armstrong-Siddeley V8 petrol, developing 67.1kW/90hp
Performance: Speed – 24kph/15mph
  Range – 241km/150 miles

LEFT: **The Tank Museum's Mark II Heavy Tank is a Female – note the machine-gun in the sponson and also the slot for the second machine-gun (not fitted).** BELOW: **The Mark II Heavy Tank was almost identical to the Mark I, except that no tail wheels were fitted and there was also a revised hatch on top.**

Mark II and Mark III Heavy Tanks

In all, some 150 Mark I Heavy Tanks were produced and delivered to the Army. As a result of their impact upon the battlefield, the Commander-in-Chief Field-Marshal Sir Douglas Haig ordered a further 1,000 tanks to be built. First of these were 50 Mark IIs – 25 Male and 25 Female. They were almost identical to the Mark I apart from minor alterations resulting from the limited battle experience of the Mark Is on the Somme.

The tail wheels were discarded, there was a revised hatch on top, and a wider track shoe at every sixth track link in order to improve traction. Armour on these early tanks had to be cut and drilled as soft steel and then hardened to inhibit hostile fire. The front plates were 10mm/0.394in thick, the sides 8mm/0.315in. The tank was built by riveting sheets of armour plate to butt straps and angle iron. Inevitably, there were gaps,

which allowed molten metal to penetrate inside when a joint was hit by small arms fire. This "splash", as it was called, meant that the crew had to wear small

steel masks with a chain-mail visor hanging down over the face, to reduce injury. However, they were uncomfortable to wear and made it much more difficult to observe, so the crews would hang blankets inside to absorb the splash.

The Mark III Heavy Tank was virtually identical to the Mark II except that it had slightly thicker armour. Fifty Mark IIIs (half of them Male and half Female) were built. The later Males were armed with the short-barrelled 6pdr gun because naval guns proved too long for land use, banging into trees or becoming buried in the mud. Guns could fire either High-Explosive or Armour-Piercing shot.

BELOW: **Apart from having slightly thicker armour, the Mark III was identical to the Mark II. Only 50 were built (half Male and half Female).**

Mark III Heavy Tank (Male)

Entered service: 1917
Crew: 8
Weight: 28,450kg/28 tons
Dimensions: Length – 9.9m/32ft 6in
  Height (over turret hatch) – 2.41m/7ft 11in
  Width – 4.19m/13ft 9in
Armament: Male – 2 x 6pdr (57mm/2.24in) guns
  Female – 2 x Hotchkiss 7.7mm/0.303in machine-guns
Armour: Maximum – 12mm/0.47in
Powerplant: Daimler 6-cylinder petrol, developing 111.8kW/150bhp
Performance: Speed – 5.95kph/3.7mph
  Range – 35.4km/22 miles

Mark II Medium Tank

The Mark II Medium Tank shared many features with the Mark I Medium, using the same basic chassis, engine and armament. They also both had the sprung "box bogie" suspension which gave the Mark II a speed of 40–48kph/25–30mph, far in advance of its theoretical design speed of around 29kph/18mph. However, the extra weight of the Mark II reduced the top speed to around 24kph/15mph. Armament comprised the 3pdr gun, plus two Vickers machine-guns in the hull sides and three Hotchkiss machine-guns projecting out around the turret.

There were other differences between the Marks. Externally, the Mark IIs appeared much bulkier, the armour was thicker, the superstructure was a little higher, and the driver's hood stood proud of the hull top. Also, the driver's glacis was steeper, the headlights larger and the Mark IIs had suspension skirts. The major mechanical difference was in the steering, with the Mark II having Rackham Steering, with an additional epicyclic gearbox between the main gearbox and the differential cum cross-shaft.

ABOVE: **A line of Mediums firing on the Gunnery School Ranges at Lulworth, Dorset. This is still the "home" of tank gunnery, now as part of the British Army Armour Centre.** BELOW: **The Tank Museum's Vickers Mark II* Medium Tank. Entering service in 1926, the Royal Tank Corps was pleased to receive these modern tanks, although they probably did not realize that they would stay in active service until after the beginning of World War II!**

In 1932, modifications were made to the Medium Mark II, resulting in the Marks II* and II**. In the former, the three Hotchkiss machine-guns in the turret were replaced by a single coaxial Vickers, while the commander's cupola was set further back in the turret roof. A lead counterweight was added at the back of the turret. In the latter, the wireless was placed in an armoured container and attached at the back of the turret.

A total of 160 Mark II Mediums were built and were used for training after war was declared, but never saw action. Latterly, some of those in Egypt were buried up to their turrets at Mersa Matruh as static pillboxes. The Tank Museum's Mark II* was restored to full running order by Vickers Defence Systems in the 1980s.

Mark II Medium Tank

Entered service: 1925
Crew: 5
Weight: 14,224kg/14 tons
Dimensions: Length – 5.33m/17ft 6in
Height (over turret hatch) – 2.69m/8ft 10in
Width – 2.79m/9ft 2in
Armament: Main – 3pdr (47mm/1.85in) gun
Secondary – 3 x 7.7mm/0.303 Vickers
machine-guns (1 x coaxial replacing 3 x Hotchkiss)
Armour: Maximum – 12mm/0.47in
Powerplant: Armstrong-Siddeley 8-cylinder petrol,
developing 67.1kW/90hp
Performance: Speed – 24kph/15mph
Range – 193km/120 miles

Mark II and Mark III Light Tanks

LEFT: Following on from the Mark I Light Tank came the Mark II, which appeared in 1931 and had the Horstmann coil spring suspension, which improved its cross-country performance.

mounting a single Vickers machine-gun, they were later enlarged into three-man light tanks armed with two machine-guns in a two-man turret. These light AFVs were perfect for patrolling the border provinces of the far-flung British Empire.

The Mark II was based on the Mark I, with the same hull, but having a larger rectangular turret, the No. 1 Mark I, and with a new, more powerful Rolls-Royce 6-cylinder engine replacing the Meadows of its predecessor. It was fitted with Horstmann spring coil suspension.

The next two Marks – the IIA and IIB – were fitted with the No. 1 Mark II turret, modified with air louvers on the sides for hot climates. A difference between the two was that the Mark IIA had an extra fuel tank fitted and the Mark IIB a single large-capacity tank of the same capacity as the Mark IIA. Entering service in 1933, the Mark III was the same as its predecessors other than having an extended rear superstructure to accommodate a modified Horstmann suspension system which had evolved from a two-pair to four-pair type.

British light and medium tank development began with the Whippet, which was created to provide a fast cavalry or pursuit tank to exploit any opportunity or breakthrough by the heavy tanks. Later, after the war, light tanks or tankettes were built to help mechanize the infantry. However, with the advent of these small, fast and low-silhouette vehicles, a new concept for their use was found, namely to provide reconnaissance for the heavier tanks. Turreted versions of the Carden-Loyd were developed and known as Patrol Tanks Marks I and II.

During the mid-1930s and after having taken over Carden-Loyd, Vickers-Armstrong spent much time and effort in the development of light tanks. Initially a series of two-man machines (Marks I–IV)

LEFT: Entering service in 1933, the Mark III Light Tank was similar in layout to the Mark II, but had its superstructure extended rearwards and was fitted with a modified Horstmann suspension.

Mark II Light Tank

Entered service: 1931
Crew: 2
Weight: 4572kg/4.5 tons
Dimensions: Length – 3.58m/11ft 9in
  Height (over turret hatch) – 2.01m/6ft 7in
  Width – 1.91m/6ft 3in
Armament: Main – 7.7mm/0.303in Vickers machine-gun
Armour: Maximum – 10mm/0.39in
Powerplant: Rolls-Royce 6-cylinder, 49.2kW/66bhp
Performance: Speed – 48.3kph/30mph
  Range – 209.2km/130 miles

Mark III Valentine Infantry Tank

The prototype of the Valentine was produced by Vickers on February 14, 1940, hence its name. Over 8,000 Valentines were built in 11 different Marks, as well as various specialized variants, and it remained in production until 1944, being supplied to Russia and built under licence in Canada. This accounts for approximately a quarter of all British wartime tank production.

Over the course of its service life the Valentine's construction changed from being riveted to welded, and its power source from petrol to diesel – the AEC petrol and diesel engines being finally replaced with the more reliable GMC two-stroke diesel. It also had a variety of main armaments, beginning with the 2pdr, giving way to the 6pdr and then to the 75mm/2.95in on the final model. The Valentine saw most of its active service in the North African theatre, where extra fuel tanks attached to the rear increased its range, although it was also used by Commonwealth troops in the Pacific and Asian theatres.

Variants included a bridgelayer, flail and snake explosive-charge mine-sweepers, self-propelled guns, a flame-thrower and also an amphibious version.

ABOVE: **A modern photograph of the Bovington Tank Museum's Infantry Tank Mark III Valentine in desert colours. Developed by Vickers, it proved to be both strong and reliable.** BELOW LEFT: **In April 2004 Ex Smash was held at Studland Bay in Dorset, during which Mr John Pearson's wonderfully restored Valentine DD (Duplex Drive) went into the water from a landing craft to commemorate the loss of six crewmen of 4/7 DG back in 1944. The DD was also on show at the Tank Museum's "Tankfest" on May 23, 2004.**

Mark III Valentine Infantry Tank

Entered service: 1940
Crew: 3
Weight: 17,272kg/17 tons
Dimensions: Length – 5.89m/19ft 4in
 Height (over turret hatch) – 2.29m/7ft 6in
 Width – 2.64m/8ft 8in
Armament: Main – 2pdr (40mm/1.58in) or 6pdr (57mm/2.24in) or 75mm/2.95in gun
 Secondary – 7.92mm/0.312in Besa machine-gun
Armour: Maximum – 65mm/2.56in
Powerplant: AEC 6-cylinder diesel, 97.73kW/131bhp; or AEC 6-cylinder petrol, 100kW/135bhp; or GMC diesel, 100kW/135bhp
Performance: Speed – 24kph/14.9mph
 Range – 145km/90 miles

Mark IV Light Tank

Mark IV Light Tank

Entered service: 1934
Crew: 2
Weight: 4,674kg/4.6 tons
Dimensions: Length – 3.40m/11ft 2in
Height (over turret hatch) – 2.13m/7ft
Width – 2.06m/6ft 9in
Armament: 1 x 7.7mm/0.303in and
1 x 12.7mm/0.5in machine-guns
Armour: Maximum – 12mm/0.47in
Powerplant: Meadows 6-cylinder petrol,
65.6kW/88bhp
Performance: Speed – 56kph/35mph
Range – 201km/125 miles

LEFT: **Built in the 1930s and based on the "Indian Pattern" light tanks, this Mark IV Light Tank now resides at the Tank Museum. The principal change to the Mark III was its suspension.**

The Mark IV Light Tank was based on the Vickers experimental "Indian Pattern" vehicles of 1933, being produced the following year. It was the first light tank that used the hull as a chassis, with its automotive parts then bolted on to it. The hull was lengthened, its armour thickened and it consequently had a higher superstructure with the turret set further back than other light tanks. The Horstmann suspension was modified to dispense with the idler wheel by re-spacing the bogies, which gave the vehicle a distinctive track path. The turret itself was similar to that of the Mark III Light Tank, but certain modifications were made, with a cupola variant for those vehicles bound for service in India.

Mark V Light Tank

Mark V Light Tank

Entered service: 1935
Crew: 3
Weight: 4,217kg/4.15 tons
Dimensions: Length – 3.68m/12ft 1in
Height (over turret hatch) – 2.21m/7ft 3in
Width – 2.06m/6ft 9in
Armament: 1 x 7.7mm/0.303in and
1 x 12.7mm/0.5in Vickers machine-guns
Armour: Maximum – 12mm/0.5in
Powerplant: Meadows 6-cylinder petrol, developing
65.6kW/88bhp
Performance: Speed – 51kph/32mph
Range – 200km/125 miles

LEFT: **This Mark V Light Tank is being inspected by a visiting German delegation during the 1930s. It was the first of the light series to have a three-man crew (two men in the turret).**

Entering service in 1935, the Mark V Light Tank had a longer hull than its predecessor in order to accommodate a turret ball-race and then a larger two-man turret – the first on a light tank – raising the crew total to three. It was armed with Vickers 7.7mm/0.303in and 12.7mm/0.5in coaxial machine-guns and had a circular commander's cupola. With its heavier weight of 4,217kg/ 4.15 tons, its handling and characteristics were a big improvement on earlier Marks.

However both the Mark IV and Mark V were obsolete at the start of World War II. A few remained, mostly used for training, though two chassis were used for experiments with anti-aircraft mounts in 1940.

Mark IV Heavy Tank

Designed in October 1916, the Mark IV was put into production between March and April 1917. More Mark IVs were built than any other model – a total of 1,220 – of which 205 were tank tenders with specially boosted 93.2kW/125bhp Daimler engines. The tenders were fitted with square box-like sponsons and used to carry tank supplies into battle.

The Mark IV had various improvements, including an armoured 273-litre/60-gallon petrol tank mounted outside the tank between the rear horns. This was much safer than the earlier internal tanks, which were located on either side of the driver. Sponsons were hinged so that they could be swung

TOP: **More Mark IV Heavy Tanks were built than any other model – a total of 1,220 in all. This is the Tank Museum's "HMS Excellent", which was restored to full running order in 1971 by 18 Command Workshop, REME.** ABOVE: **This Mark IV Heavy Tank bears the letters "WC" for "Wire Cutter", but is being used as an observation platform, having lost part of its right-hand track.** BELOW LEFT: **Male Tank No. 2341 bore the "Chinese Eye" on its sides as it was paid for by Mr Eu Tong Sen of the Malay States. This custom is still retained today by the tanks and other AFVs of 1 RTR.**

inside during rail journeys, instead of having to be removed and carried separately. The size of the sponsons was also reduced so that the lower edges were not so close to the ground. In both versions, the Vickers and Hotchkiss machine-guns were replaced by Lewis guns, but these proved a great disappointment and later had to be replaced with modified Hotchkiss machine-guns. Thicker steel was used in the construction of the Mark IV – 12mm/0.47in in front and on the sides, decreasing to 8mm/0.315in elsewhere. This made it bullet-proof against the German anti-tank rifle. The first Mark IVs went into action on June 7, 1917, at the Battle of Messines Ridge.

However, it would be during the Battle of Cambrai on November 20, 1917, that they really showed their prowess, many of the 476 tanks taking part being heavy Mark IVs, whose silhouette now forms an indispensable part of

both the RTR cap and arm badges, while November 20 is celebrated every year as the RTR Regimental Day.

Many of the tank crews fighting at Cambrai had been trained with the invaluable help of the Royal Navy Gunnery Training Establishment at Whale Island, Portsmouth, so Mark IV Heavy Tank No. 2324 was presented to HMS *Excellent* in recognition on May 1, 1919. Twenty years later it was restored to full serviceability and allocated to the RN defence battalion, patrolling Portsmouth during air raids, until it damaged a private car and had to be confined to barracks!

ABOVE: **"Any more for the Skylark?" A crowd of footsore infantrymen cadge a lift on this Mark IV (Female), those at the rear resting their feet on the unditching beam.** BELOW: **Without its weapons fitted, this Mark IV Heavy Tank is recognizable as a Female by its smaller sponsons. The steel plate was proof against German armour-piercing "K" rounds.**

In 1971 it was decided to hand back the historic old tank to the Army and before doing so, 18 Command Workshop, REME at Bovington, spent three years carefully restoring it to full running order.

Mark IV Heavy Tank (Male)

Entered service: 1917
Crew: 8
Weight: 28,450kg/28 tons
Dimensions: Length – 8.03m/26ft 4in
    Height (over turret hatch) – 2.49m/8ft 2in
    Width – 3.91m/12ft 10in
Armament: Main – 2 x 6pdr (57mm/2.24in) guns
    Secondary – 4 x 7.7mm/0.303in Lewis
    machine-guns
Armour: Maximum – 12mm/0.47in
Powerplant: Daimler 6-cylinder petrol, developing
    74.57kW/100bhp
Performance: Speed – 6kph/3.7mph
    Range – 40km/25 miles

Mark V Heavy Tank

The major step forward achieved with the Mark V, designed in August 1917 and in the hands of troops in May 1918, was that one man could drive the tank by himself. This was because it was fitted with a four-speed epicyclic gearbox designed by W. G. Wilson, replacing the change-speed gearing of earlier models. The engine was a purpose-built Ricardo, developing 111.85kW/150hp. The tank also had better observation and ventilation, while the 273 litres/60 gallons of petrol contained in armoured fuel tanks at the tail gave a radius of action of 72.4km/45 miles compared with 38.6km/24 miles of the early Marks and 40km/25 miles of the Mark IV. A total of 200 Males and 200 Females were built between December 1917 and June 1918. One device that could be fitted to the Mark IV or Mark V was the Tadpole Tail – a device which lengthened the tank by about 2.74m/9ft to improve its performance. However, this lacked both rigidity and lateral stability.

The most ideal solution came with the Mark VA, when an additional 1.83m/6ft of armour was added between the sponson opening and the epicyclic gear housing, allowing additional storage space to carry up to 25 men. As a result, the weight went up from 29,465kg/29 tons to 33,530kg/33 tons and, because the engine power was not increased, the tank was much less manoeuvrable and slower than the standard Mark V.

TOP: **The Mark V Heavy Tank, which is in immaculate running order, belonging to the Tank Museum. The major advance with the Mark V was the fact that it could be driven by one man and thus did not require secondary gearsmen to change gear.** ABOVE: **A Mark V Heavy Tank demonstrates how the unditching beam is used – attached to the tracks by chains, tracks then rotate, bringing the beam down until it can get some purchase so as to assist in egress.**

Mark V Heavy Tank No. 9199, now at the Tank Museum and still in full running order, was issued to the 8th Battalion, Tank Corps, in July 1918. They were the first battalion to receive the Mark V. Crew H 41 were the first to see action in 9199, the commander, Lt H. A. Whittenbury, writing afterwards, "8th August 1918. Commenced the attack at 8:20am preceding the infantry by about 100yds ... enemy gun flashes observed ... Drove on zig-zag course ... Both six pounders had picked up targets and were firing ... Drove down steep slope into ravine ... opened fire with both six pounders firing HE and case shot at 40yds range into trenches and dugouts. Also fired a good many rounds with front Hotchkiss and observed many casualties."

At 10:15am, after a fierce battle, H 41 returned unscathed, having expended 87 6pdr HE, 18 case shot and 1,960 Hotchkiss rounds. Whittenbury would be awarded a Military Cross for his gallant action.

The following month, with a different commander, H 41 preceeded an infantry attack on the village of Estrees and was hit by shellfire which damaged its left track, but they managed to get back to the rallying point before the track broke.

From 1918–19 No. 9199 was used for training at Bovington, then in 1921 it went to the 4th Battalion, Tank Corps at Wogret Camp near Wareham until 1925, when it returned to Bovington. During World War II it was used for towing and recovery by the Camp Workshops and the Driving and Maintenance School, then in 1949 it was donated to the Tank Museum.

ABOVE: **Mark V Heavy Tank No. 9199 at the Bovington Tank Museum, painted in its World War I colours. The white/red/white stripes on the nose were British tank recognition markings that were still being used at the start of World War II in the Western Desert.** LEFT: **This Mark V has really got itself stuck in a very deep hole and will need more than an unditching beam to free itself!** BELOW: **The Mark V* had an additional 1.82m/6ft of armour added between the sponson housing and the epicyclic gear housing. Not only did this improve its trench-crossing ability, it also gave much more storage room inside (e.g. it could carry 25 men or the equivalent weight in stores).**

Mark V Heavy Tank (Male)

Entered service: 1918
Crew: 8
Weight: 29,465kg/29 tons
Dimensions: Length – 8.03m/26.4ft in
　Height (over turret hatch) – 2.49m/8ft 2in
　Width – 3.91m/12ft 10in
Armament: Main – 2 x 6pdr (57mm/2.24in) gun
　Secondary – 4 x 7.7mm/0.303in Hotchkiss
　machine-guns
Armour: Maximum – 12mm/0.47in
Powerplant: Ricardo 6-cylinder petrol,
　111.85kW/150hp
Performance: Speed – 7.4kph/4.6mph
　Range – 72.4km/45 miles

Mark VI Light Tank

The Mark VI Light Tank was similar to the Mark V Light Tank, except for its turret which was redesigned to allow room for a wireless. This tank was produced in a number of versions, the main two being the Mark VIA and VIB. The Mark VIA had a single return roller removed from the top of the leading bogie and attached to the hull sides, and an octagonal cupola fitted with two lookouts.

The differences in the Mark VIB were to simplify production, and included a one-piece armoured louvre over the radiator (rather than two pieces) and a plain circular commander's cupola, replacing the faceted one of the Mark VIA, fitted with glass block lookouts.

The Light Tank Mk VI series entered production in 1936, and a thousand were in service worldwide with the British Army at the outbreak of World War II. In 1940, both in Europe and North Africa, the Light Mark VI formed a major part of the British tank strength. When the British Expeditionary Force (BEF) sailed for France in 1940, this tank was to be found in all divisional cavalry regiments and in the cavalry light tank regiments of 1st Armoured Division. Unfortunately, it was widely used in roles other than that for which it was designed (reconnaissance) and suffered heavy losses when used in a front-line role, especially when confronted by the better-armed and armoured German

TOP: **The immaculately restored Mark VIB Light Tank is in full running order at the Tank Museum, Bovington. It entered production in 1936, and over a thousand were in worldwide service when war began.** ABOVE: **Equipped with flotation gear, this Mark VI Light Tank carried out successful swimming trials.**

tanks. However, the Mark VI served with distinction not only in France, but in the Western Desert, Greece, Malta, Crete and Syria (with the Australians), and took part in the siege of Tobruk.

It was, however, woefully under-armoured (10mm/0.39in maximum armour thickness) and under-gunned (just machine-guns). In fact, some of the Light Mark VIs that were rushed

ABOVE: **Speeding across the training area at Bovington, Dorset, this Mark VIB Light Tank could reach a speed of 56kph/35mph on roads.** RIGHT: **The last of the series – the Mark VIC Light Tank had its Vickers machine-guns replaced by one 7.92mm/0.312in Besa and one 15mm/0.59in Besa air-cooled machine-gun. It also had wider suspension wheels and broader tracks.** BELOW: **Good photograph of a Vickers Mark VIA Light Tank. The commander wears the badge of the 3rd The King's Own Hussars who were part of 1st (Light) Armoured Brigade.**

over to France to support the BEF did not even have their machine-guns because they were still packed in grease in their crates on board ships that had yet to arrive! No wonder the commander of 1st Armoured Division, Maj Gen Roger Evans, would later write of it as: "this travesty of an armoured division". Thus, the tank crews had just their pistols as their tanks' only offensive weapons!

Mark VIB Light Tank

Entered service: 1937
Crew: 2
Weight: 5,080kg/5 tons
Dimensions: Length – 4.01m/13ft 2in
   Height (over turret hatch) – 2.26m/7ft 5in
   Width – 2.08m/6ft 10in
Armament: Main – 1 x 12.7mm/0.5in or
   1 x 15mm/0.59in machine-gun
   Secondary – 1 x 7.7mm/0.303in Vickers or
   1 x 7.92mm/0.312in Besa machine-gun
Armour: Maximum – 10mm/0.394in
Powerplant: Meadows 6-cylinder, 65.6kW/88bhp
Performance: Speed – 56kph/34.78mph
   Range – 200km/124.2 miles

Mark VIII Heavy Tank

Instead of just improving on existing Marks, the Mark VIII Heavy Tank was an entirely new design. The "International", as it was called, was the largest, heaviest and most powerful of all the British World War I heavy tanks. It had a Ricardo V12 (or Liberty V12) engine, producing 223.7kW/300hp at 1,250rpm. At 37,593kg/37 tons it was a good 9,144kg/9 tons heavier than the Mark I, with roughly double the power-to-weight ratio. This was to have been a joint Anglo-American venture to build in all some 4,450 tanks "to win the war in 1919", along with 2,000 Mark Xs which never reached a full design stage.

Before the war ended, the British sent one of the few Mark VIIIs they had constructed over to the USA so that they could replicate it – although the Americans decided to fit their own Liberty V12 engine in place of the British Ricardo.

However, the Armistice rapidly put paid to their grandiose ideas and, although about 100 Mark VIIIs were built by the Americans after the war, only five were ever completed by

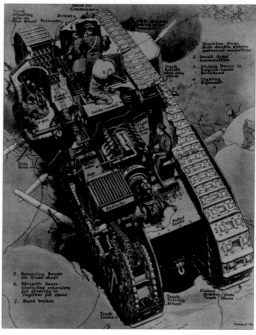

ABOVE: **Moving the Tank Museum's International. After spending many years outside in all weathers, the Mark VIII was moved under cover into the new "George Forty Hall", together with all the other priceless World War I exhibits, during the mid-1980s.** RIGHT: **Cutaway drawing of the Mark VIII, showing its main components.**

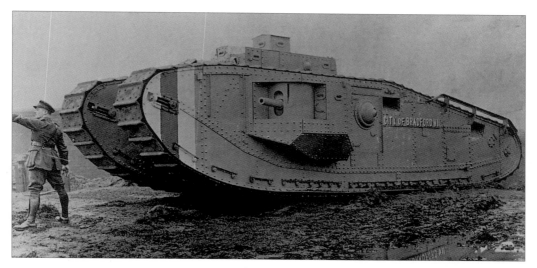

the British before the Armistice, and only three of these reached the troops. Armed with two 6pdrs, seven machine-guns, and a separate engine compartment (the first heavy tank to have one), it had great potential and would undoubtedly have been a battle-winner.

In 1940 the US Army sent some of the Mark VIIIs to Canada to help train the newly forming Canadian armoured units (they also sent a number of the Ford 6 Ton version of the Renault FT-17).

Not shown here, because it was a troop/cargo carrier rather than a tank, is the Mark IX, the very last British design of World War I to go into action. It had four large oval doors (two on each side) instead of gun sponsons, and could carry 10 tons of stores or 30 fully equipped infantrymen inside its capacious interior and thus under armour. One of its prototypes was even made amphibious by attaching large air drums to its sides, and was being tested on Armistice Day!

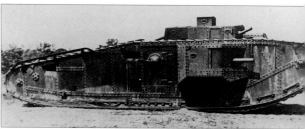

TOP, ABOVE AND BELOW: **This selection of all-round views of the Mark VIII give an excellent impression of the entirely new design of the International – so named because it was going to be built by Britain and the USA as a joint venture "to win the war in 1919". The Armistice put paid to that, with only some 100 of the proposed 4,500 being built. Only five were completed, and only three reached troops before the war ended.**

Mark VIII Heavy Tank

Entered service: 1918
Crew: 8
Weight: 37,593kg/37 tons
Dimensions: Length – 10.41m/34ft 2in
Height (over turret hatch) – 3.12m/10ft 3in
Width – 3.76m/12ft 4in
Armament: Main – 2 x 6pdr (57mm/2.24in) guns
Secondary – 7 x 7.7mm/0.303in machine-guns
Armour: Maximum – 16mm/0.63in
Powerplant: Ricardo or Liberty V12 petrol,
223.7kW/300bhp
Performance: Speed – 9.7kph/6mph
Range – 88km/55 miles

M1 and M2 Combat Cars

ABOVE: A close-up of M1 Combat Cars belonging to the 1st Cavalry Regiment. Here the commanders man their pintle-mounted anti-aircraft machine-guns with air-cooled barrels.

At the beginning of World War II, the United States had four closely related basic types of light AFV. The Infantry had Light Tanks M2A2 and M2A3, while the Cavalry, who were not allowed to have tanks, called theirs Combat Cars M1 and M2. The simplest way of telling them apart was that the light tanks had twin turrets, earning themselves the nickname of "Mae Wests" (for obvious anatomical reasons)!

The Combat Cars had single octagonal turrets with two machine-guns, one 12.7mm/0.5in and one 7.62mm/0.3in calibre, mounted coaxially. All had a second 7.62mm/0.3in machine-gun in the hull, and a third for anti-aircraft defence – the first recorded instance of this provision on any AFV.

Both the M1 and M2 had a crew of four, two in the turret and two in the hull. However, it must be said that both these vehicles were totally inadequate for operating on the modern battlefield of the time, except in a scouting role, and fortunately they never had to prove themselves in battle.

The Combat Car M2 was the first to be fitted with the distinctive trailing idler wheel, which increased the vehicle's footprint and aided traction and therefore

overall performance. It also had its power plant changed from a Continental petrol engine to a Guiberson diesel radial engine. In 1940, with the formation of the American Armored Force, the need for the "Combat Car" subterfuge became unnecessary and Combat Cars M1 and M2 became known as the M1A1 and M1A2 Light Tanks.

M1 Combat Car

Entered service: 1935
Crew: 4
Weight: 8,528kg/8.39 tons
Dimensions: Length – 4.14m/13ft 7in
Height (over turret hatch) – 2.36m/7ft 9in
Width – 2.39m/7ft 10in
Armament: Main – 12.7mm/0.5in machine-gun
Secondary – 3 x 7.62mm/0.3in machine-guns
Armour: Maximum – 16mm/0.63in
Powerplant: Continental W-670 7-cylinder petrol, 186.4kW/250hp
Performance: Speed – 72.4kph/45mph
Range – 161km/100 miles

LEFT: **A "Mae West" (so called because it had twin turrets!) fords a stream during training. Note that no armament is installed.** ABOVE: **This M2A4, the very first US-built tank to arrive in the UK, is seen here being inspected by General (later Field Marshal) Alexander.**

M2 Light Tank series

As World War II approached, the Americans still had four basic types of light armoured vehicle, all of which were closely related because all had been developed from the T2 tank series. The two infantry tanks were known as the M2A2 and M2A3. The M2A2 had numerous development models with a mixture of petrol and diesel engines, modified suspensions and other features. These were all of a similar size, weight, crew and armament, and all had twin turrets. The best was probably the M2A2E3, developed in 1938, which had a modified suspension with a trailing idler.

BELOW: **An M2A2 Light Tank being driven up a loading ramp onto a rail flat car. One turret contains a 12.7mm/0.5inch machine-gun, the other a 7.62mm/0.30 inch machine-gun.**

The M2A3 was an improved version of the M2A2, and appeared during 1938. Not only did it have slightly thicker frontal armour, better engine cooling and improved engine access, but it also had a longer track base, which necessitated repositioning the bogie units. Last of the development models of the M2A3s was the M2A3E3, which had a reworked suspension with a trailing idler wheel, giving it a better cross-country performance.

The M2A4 represented the last model of the M2 Light Tank series and was perhaps the most important and best of them all. For the first time it had a main armament larger than a machine-gun, the 37mm/1.46in M5 tank gun which had an armour-piercing capability. This was housed in a single turret with an all-round

manual traverse. One hundred and three rounds were carried on board for the gun which, even though it did not have much hitting power (it could only penetrate 25.4mm/1in of armour at 914m/1,000 yards), was just coming into service as the US Army's standard anti-tank gun.

The pilot model of the M2A4 was completed at Rock Island Arsenal in early 1939. The single turret had been found to be greatly superior to the twin "Mae Wests", while the tank had thicker armour on the front and hull sides (up to 25mm/0.98in), which increased the weight up to 12,193kg/12 tons and reduced its top speed accordingly. Nevertheless, the M2A4 was undoubtedly the best of the early American light tanks and would lead directly on to the M3 light – the famous Honey.

M2A4 Light Tank

Entered service: 1940

Crew: 4

Weight: 12,193k/12 tons

Dimensions: Length – 4.45m/14ft 7in
Height (over turret hatch) – 2.52m/8ft 3in
Width – 2.54m/8ft 4in

Armament: Main – 37mm/1.46m gun
Secondary – 4 x 7.62mm/0.3in machine-guns

Armour: Maximum – 25mm/0.98in

Powerplant: Continental 7-cylinder radial, 186.6kW/250hp

Performance: Speed – 54.7kph/34mph
Range – 209km/130 miles

M3 General Lee Medium Tank and variants

The British called the standard M3 the "General Lee", after the Civil War General Robert E. Lee. Its main armament was the sponson-mounted 75mm/2.95in gun which only had a limited traverse. In the fully rotating turret on the top of the tank was a 37mm/1.46in gun and coaxial machine-gun. There were up to three more machine-guns – one in the commander's cupola and either one or two fixed machine-guns firing through the front plate (the earlier production models had two).

M3 General Grant Medium Tank

The British version of the M3 was purchased under Lend-Lease by a special Tank Commission and modified for British Army service. It differed from the General Lee in having a larger turret with a bulge at the rear to take a radio set. This meant that the operator could also act as loader for the 37mm/1.46in gun, and one crew member fewer was needed to man the "General Grant", as the British version was called (after General

Ulysses S. Grant). The commander's cupola was also dispensed with, thus reducing the overall height by some 101mm/4in. The General Grant made a significant impact in the Western Desert and was later used in Europe and the Far East, where it did excellent work, "bunker-bashing" and supporting infantry.

The Lee had a seven-man crew – commander, 37mm/1.46in gunner, 37mm/1.46in loader, 75mm/2.95in

ABOVE: The American M3 Medium Tank, known to the British as the "General Lee". It was then specially modified for British service, their model being known as the "General Grant". This Lee belongs to the Budge Collection and was taking part in an Open Day at the Tank Museum, Bovington. There is no commander's cupola on this particular M3 Lee.

gunner, 75mm/2.95in loader, radio operator and driver. In the Grant, the 37mm/1.46in loader doubled up as a radio operator.

RIGHT: A British-crewed M3 Medium Grant is admired by some local boys in Tunisia. The Grant had no commander's cupola, so it was lower. It also had a larger turret with room for the radio in the bustle.

LEFT: **On show at the Bovington Tank Museum is this General Grant, as supplied to the British. It differs from the Lee by not having a commander's cupola, and with an enlarged turret bustle in the top turret for the wireless, thus saving one crewman.**

ABOVE: **This shows a T5 Phase III Medium Tank, photographed at the Rock Island arsenal in 1938. It was the prototype of the standard M2 Medium Tank and the forerunner of the M3.** ABOVE RIGHT: **This M3A1 is a Lee with the additional commander's cupola and a cast hull. Later production models had no side door or escape hatch in the floor.** RIGHT: **This is the M3A2, again a Lee, but with an all-welded hull.**

M3 in combat

The first M3s to see action were those sent with British Eighth Army in the Western Desert in 1942. Rommel wrote in his diary of them: "The advent of the new American tank has torn great holes in our ranks. Our entire force now stood in heavy and destructive combat with a superior enemy."

M3 Grant Canal Defence Light

When the M3 was replaced by the Sherman M4, a number of British Grants were fitted with a Canal Defence Light similar to that which had been previously installed in the Matilda CDL. The turret was removed and replaced with an armoured searchlight housing, sporting a dummy wooden gun, but also containing a machine-gun.

M3 General Grant Medium Tank

Entered service: 1941
Crew: 6 (7 on the Lee)
Weight: 27,219kg/26.7 tons
Dimensions: Length – 5.64m/18ft 6in
    Height (over turret hatch) – 3.12m/10ft 3in
    Width – 2.72m/8ft 11in
Armament: Main – 75mm/2.95in M2 or M3 gun
    Secondary – 37mm/1.46in M5 or M6 cannon,
    4 x 7.62mm/0.3in machine-guns
Armour: Maximum – 57mm/2.24in
Powerplant: Continental R-975-EC2 radial petrol,
    253.5kW/340hp
Performance: Speed – 42kph/26mph
    Range – 193km/120 miles

M4 Sherman Medium Tank

Of all the tanks ever built, the M4 Sherman was undoubtedly the most widely used by all the Allies, a staggering 49,234 Sherman guns tanks being produced in the USA, more than half the entire American wartime tank production and equal to the total combined wartime output of Great Britain and Germany! Add to this the vast number of variants and the figure becomes even more impressive.

The M4 Medium was the logical successor to the M3 Medium Tank Lee/Grant, and about the same time as the latter was first going into production, the Ordnance Committee directed that work should begin on its successor because they appreciated that the M3 was only a stopgap. This resulted in the construction of the Medium Tank T6 (the prototype M4) at the Aberdeen Proving Ground in early 1941. Clearly there was British and Canadian input into the design, which bore a striking resemblance to the Canadian Ram Medium Tank.

At about the same time, the Rock Island Arsenal built a second pilot model and, in September 1941, the new tank was quickly standardized, entering service on September 5, 1941, as the Medium Tank M4. Interestingly, one of the new tank factories to build the Sherman had first to be built from scratch near Detroit – in just three months from breaking earth to rolling out the first tank! Full-scale production would end in early 1944, by which time six basic models of the gun tank, designated M4 through to M4A6 (less M4A5), had been built.

The Sherman, as it was soon called, would first see active service with the British 8th Army in North Africa in October 1942. Two months later, it was first used in action by American troops in Tunisia in early December 1942. The M4 was an extremely robust and reliable tank which used the same basic chassis as the M3 Medium; it therefore had vertical volute spring suspension, a rear engine and front drive. There were six

TOP: **The Canadian-built "Grizzly I" is virtually identical to the M4 Sherman, apart from having different drive sprockets and tracks. Nearly 50,000 Shermans were built during World War II.** ABOVE: **This immaculate Sherman M4A1E8 (76) is privately owned by the Indiana Military Museum in Vincennes, USA. The "Easy Eight" had an improved suspension and mounted the 76mm/2.99in gun.**

basic Marks of Sherman produced in three main tank factories in the USA. Initially armed with the 75mm/2.95in gun, there were also two models with close-support 105mm/4.13in howitzers, four with the improved 76mm/2.99in gun and "Wet" stowage (ammunition in water-protected racks below the turret) and, finally, a heavily armoured assault version nicknamed "Jumbo".

The main change from the M3 Medium was the fact that Sherman had a fully rotating turret instead of its main gun being in a side sponson. Not only did this give the gun all-round traverse, but also meant that the crew could be reduced to five: three in the turret (commander, gunner and loader/operator) and two in the hull (driver and co-driver/hull gunner). The Sherman was a very user-friendly AFV, and well able to deal with most terrain. Unfortunately, however, it had a tendency to catch fire easily when struck by enemy shells – the Allies nicknamed it the "Ronson Lighter" because it was guaranteed to light first time, while the Germans called it the "Tommy Cooker" – hence the wet stowage arrangement when the tank was re-gunned, plus the addition of appliqué armour and even sandbags, to increase protection. A continuing shortage of the initial R-975 Continental air-cooled radial aircraft engine led to the forced adoption of no fewer than four further engines, both petrol and diesel, including the remarkable Chrysler multi-bank 30-cylinder petrol engine.

The Sherman was adapted to perform a wide range of specialized tasks with conversion to swimming tanks (the addition of a flotation screen in the highly secret Sherman DD swimming tank, used most effectively during the D-Day landings), engineer/dozer vehicles, tank recovery vehicles, beach recovery vehicles, armoured personnel carriers, assault bridge-carriers, flamethrower tanks, mine-clearing tanks (including flails, rollers and explosives – even a mine-resistant vehicle), self-propelled guns, howitzer, anti-aircraft gun and rocket platforms, and as tank destroyers to name but a few! The British had their own designations for the wide range of variants, which included the most effective Sherman to see wartime action – the Firefly, which mounted a highly effective 17pdr gun.

The Sherman's versatility was immense and did not end when war finished. After 1945, the Sherman was used by many armies worldwide, especially by the Israelis who, in their own inimitable way, adapted the tank for a wide variety of uses and prolonged its life as a gun tank by refitting with improved engine, main armament and armour.

RIGHT: **A Sherman fords a canal near Nancy, France, September 12, 1944. Note the foliage cut as camouflage to break up the tank's unmistakable outline, and also the heavy 12.7mm/0.5in Browning Heavy AA machine-gun on top of the turret.**

ABOVE: **This massive rocket array, mounted on top of a sandbagged Sherman, was known as the Rocket Launcher T 34 "Calliope". It consisted of 60 x 117mm/4.6in rocket tubes and saw limited combat during World War II.**
BELOW: **US Marines hitch a ride. Tank-borne infantry moving up to occupy Ghuta on Okinawa. There are at least 18 "passengers" hitching a ride, which is fine until the tank has to use its guns.**

M4 Sherman Medium Tank (mid-production)

Entered service: 1941
Crew: 5
Weight: 30,339kg/29.86 tons
Dimensions: Length – 5.88m/19ft 4in
    Height (over turret hatch) – 2.74m/ 9ft
    Width – 2.68m/8ft 10in
Armament: Main – 75mm/2.95in M3 gun
    Secondary – 2 x 7.62in/0.3in and
    1 x 12.7mm/0.5in AA (anti-aircraft) machine-guns
Armour: Maximum – 75mm/2.95in
Powerplant: Continental R-975C1 Petrol, 9-cylinder
    4-cycle radial, 298.5kW/400hp
Performance: Speed – 39kph/24.2mph
    Range – 192km/119.3 miles

M3 Light Tank series

The M2A4 was effectively a prototype for the next light tank, the M3, which had many of its features, such as the single rotating seven-sided turret and 37mm/1.46in gun. The M3 was designed in the spring of 1940, the main requirement being for thicker armour which increased the weight to 12,904kg/12.7 tons combat-loaded, and required stronger suspension. Nicknamed the Honey, the M3 first saw action with the British Army in the Western Desert, where it was officially known as the Stuart I in British Army nomenclature.

The first production models of the M3 were of a riveted construction, but they were soon followed in the series with increasing proportions with welded armour. There were also petrol and diesel engine variants. With the M3A1, the side sponson machine-guns were soon removed because they could not be properly aimed and must have wasted a great deal of ammunition. There was also now no commander's cupola; instead the turret had a basket and a power traverse.

The final model of the M3 series was the M3A3 (Stuart V in British parlance). It had a larger turret and no side sponsons, which created space for extra fuel tanks and ammunition stowage. An experimental model, which had twin Cadillac engines, a turret basket and other modifications, was the prototype for the M5 Light Tank.

ABOVE: **The M3A1 Light Tank was so well liked by its crews that they called it the Honey when it first came into British service in the Western Desert in 1941. Their experience led to modifications such as the removal of the two sponson machine-guns.**

M3A1 Light Tank Stuart Mk III

Entered service: 1940
Crew: 4
Weight: 12,904kg/12.7 tons
Dimensions: Length – 4.52m/14ft 10in
　　Height (over turret hatch) – 2.31m/7ft 7in
　　Width – 2.24m/7ft 4in
Armament: Main – 37mm/1.46in M6 gun
　　Secondary – 3 x 7.62mm/0.3in machine-guns
Armour: Maximum – 51mm/2.01in
Powerplant: Continental W-670, 7-cylinder radial petrol, 186.4kW/250hp
Performance: Speed – 58kph/36mph
　　Range – 113km/70 miles

M5 Light Tank

ABOVE: **The end of the Honey tank line was the M5 that came off the assembly line in March 1942. This beautifully restored M5A1 belongs to Judge Jim Osborne of the Indiana Military Museum, Vincennes, Indiana.**

The end of the Honey line was the M5 – they missed out the "M4" designation so as not to cause confusion with the M4 Sherman. It shared the same weapon systems as the M3, and first came off the assembly line in March 1942, with the British calling it the Stuart VI. It weighed 14,936kg/14.7 tons and was powered by two Cadillac engines, giving the vehicle a top speed of 60kph/37mph.

M5 Light Tank

Entered service: 1942
Crew: 4
Weight: 14,936kg/14.7 tons
Dimensions: Length – 4.34m/14ft 3in
　　Height (over turret hatch) – 2.31m/7ft 7in
　　Width – 2.26m/7ft 5in
Armament: Main – 37mm/1.46in M6 gun
　　Secondary – 3 x 7.62mm/0.3in machine-guns
Armour: Maximum – 64mm/2.52in
Powerplant: 2 x Cadillac Series 42 V8, each developing 82kW/110hp
Performance: Speed – 60kph/37mph
　　Range – 161km/100 miles

M6 Heavy Tank

Until the start of World War II the USA had shown little interest in heavy tanks, one major reason being the difficulty of transporting them, especially overseas. However, the success of German armour and the obvious vulnerability and lack of firepower of the standard light and medium tanks led to a recommendation to develop a heavy tank in the 50,800kg/50-ton class.

Designed in 1940, the M6 Heavy Tank weighed almost 45 tons and was armed with a 76.2mm/3in main gun, plus a 37mm/1.46in gun mounted coaxially, and a total of four machine-guns (two 12.7mm/0.5in and two 7.62mm/0.3in). Its armour was up to 133mm/5.24in thick and it had a top speed of 35kph/22mph. When it appeared in 1942 it was the most powerful tank in the world.

However, the Armored Force were not impressed with the new tank and, after testing, concluded that it was too heavy, did not have a large enough main armament and suffered from transmission problems. Some 40 vehicles were built, but they were only ever used for trial purposes.

LEFT: **This M6A2 Heavy Tank weighed 45,316kg/44.6 tons and was armed with a 76.2mm/3in gun. Originally designed as the heavy counterpart to the M3/M4 Mediums, only 40 were ever built of all models, and it never saw operational service.**

M6 Heavy Tank

Entered service: 1942
Crew: 5
Weight: 45,316kg/44.6 tons
Dimensions: Length – 8.43m/27ft 8in
   Height (over turret hatch) – 3.23m/10ft 7in
   Width – 3.23m/10ft 7in
Armament: Main – 1 x 76.2mm/3in gun and
   1 x 37mm/1.46in gun
   Secondary – 2 x 12.7mm/0.5in and
   2 x 7.62mm/0.3in machine-guns
Armour: Maximum – 133mm/5.24in
Powerplant: Wright Whirlwind G-200 9-cylinder
   radial, 690kW/925hp
Performance: Speed – 35kph/22mph
   Range – 161km/100 miles

M26 Pershing Heavy Tank

The M26 Pershing was developed from the T26 series – the outcome of reclassifying the T25 as a heavy tank in June 1944. Weighing about 41 tons, with a 90mm/3.54in main gun, 102.6mm/4in armour on the front of the turret and a top speed of 48kph/30mph, the new tank was just about a match for the German Tiger I, produced some years

earlier. There were also attempts to further upgrade the main armament, such as the T15E1 gun, and to increase the armour by welding extra plates on the front of the hull. It was the most powerful American tank to see combat in World War II. Wartime production of the M26 totalled 1,436. It went on to see service in the Korean War.

M26 Pershing Heavy Tank

Entered service: 1944
Crew: 5
Weight: 41,861kg/41.2 tons
Dimensions: Length – 8.61m/28ft 3in
   Height (over turret hatch) – 2.77m/9ft 1in
   Width – 3.51m/11ft 6in
Armament: Main – 90mm/3.54in M3 gun
   Secondary – 1 x 12.7mm/0.5in and
   2 x 7.62mm/0.31in machine-guns
Armour: Maximum – 102.6mm/4in
Powerplant: Ford GAF, 373kW/500hp
Performance: Speed – 48kph/30mph
   Range – 161km/100 miles

LEFT: **The M26 Pershing was the most powerful and best all-round American tank of World War II, but was only standardized and entered service in 1944. Its 90mm/3.54in main gun was almost on a par with the German 8.8cm/3.46in. It went on to do well following World War II, seeing service in the Korean War (1950–53).**

M10 Wolverine Tank Destroyer

This was the first really successful tank destroyer in the US Army. With a five-sided open topped turret it had a crew of five, a 76mm/2.99in main gun and could carry 54 rounds of ammunition. It had a top speed of 48kph/30mph and weighed 29,059kg/28.6 tons – with a counterweight needed to the rear of the turret to balance the gun. A total of 5,000 M10s were built between September 1942 and December 1943, initially using the Lee/Grant M3 standard chassis, then the M4 Sherman chassis.

ABOVE: **The M10 Wolverine was a well-liked and effective American tank destroyer, armed with a 76mm/2.99in M7 gun. The M10 was based on the M3 medium chassis, and the M10A1 was based on the M4 Sherman.**

M10 Achilles Tank Destroyer

The British up-gunned some of the M10s they received from America by fitting their highly lethal 17pdr. The result was known as "Achilles", with a similar open-topped turret to Wolverine and its counter-weight situated at the end of the gun barrel just behind the muzzle brake. Fast and hard-hitting, it was one of the best Allied tank killers of World War II.

M10 Wolverine TD		
Entered service: 1942		
Crew: 5		
Weight: 29,059kg/28.6 tons		
Dimensions: Length – 5.82m/19ft 1in		
Height (over turret hatch) – 2.49m/8ft 2in		
Width – 3.05m/10ft		
Armament: Main – 76mm/2.99in M7 gun		
Secondary – 12.7mm/0.5in machine-gun		
Armour: Maximum – 37mm/1.46in		
Powerplant: 2 x GMS6-71 diesel		
Performance: Speed 48kph/30mph		
Range – 322km/200 miles		

LEFT: **Most effective of the M10s was the British conversion, known as "Achilles", which mounted the Ordnance quick-firing 17pdr Mark 5 in place of the 76mm/2.99in gun. This was the same gun as mounted on the Sherman Firefly and the Challenger A30.**

M18 Hellcat TD

Entered service: 1943
Crew: 5
Weight: 18,187kg/17.9 tons
Dimensions: Length – 6.66m/21ft 10in
Height (over turret hatch) – 2.57m/8ft 5in
Width – 2.97m/9ft 9in
Armament: Main – 76mm/2.99in M1 gun
Secondary – 12.7mm/0.5in machine-gun
Armour: Maximum – 12mm/0.47in
Powerplant: Continental R-975, 9-cylinder radial, 298.5kW/400hp
Performance: Speed – 89kph/55mph
Range – 241km/150 miles

M18 Hellcat Tank Destroyer

The Hellcat was also very fast, with a top speed of 80–89kph/50–55mph. Its lower silhouette from a redesigned turret and good cross-country performance made it liked by its crews and an excellent hit-and-run hunter-killer. Similar to the Wolverine, it mounted a 76mm/2.99in main gun and a 12.7mm/0.5in machine-gun for close defence.

M36 Gun Motor Carriage

Most effective of all American tank destroyers was the M36, which mounted a 90mm/3.54in main gun that was the most powerful on the battlefield to date. The only problem was the weight of the new gun which necessitated the creation of a new rounded turret. Standardized in July 1944, the first of these new TDs arrived in Europe in August 1944 and were immediately in action.

Demand for the M36 Gun Motor Carriage increased enormously after the battles in Normandy which had shown that this was the best US weapon to deal with enemy tanks.

M36 Gun Motor Carriage

Entered service: 1944
Crew: 5
Weight: 28,145kg/27.7 tons
Dimensions: Length – 6.15m/20ft 2in
Height (over turret hatch) – 2.72m/8ft 11 in
Width – 3.05m/10ft
Armament: Main – 90mm/3.54in M3 gun
Secondary – 12.7mm/0.5in machine-gun
Armour: Maximum – 50mm/1.97in
Powerplant: Ford GAA V8, 373kW/500hp
Performance: Speed – 48kph/30mph
Range – 241km/150 miles

RIGHT: The M36 Gun Motor Carriage mounted a 90mm/3.54in gun in an attempt to be able to knock out the large, better-armed enemy tanks such as Tiger and Panther. Over 1,500 were built and reached north-west Europe in September 1944.

M22 Locust Light Tank

LEFT: Out of a total of just over 800 Locusts, the British took delivery of several hundred, issuing them to the 6th Airborne Armoured Reconnaissance Regiment to supplement the Tetrarchs carried in Hamilcar gliders. They saw action during the Rhine Crossing in March 1945. One M22 was rebuilt as the T10 Light Tractor (airborne) designed to carry five men, but this project was suspended in 1943.

M22 Locust Light Tank

Entered service: 1941
Crew: 3
Weight: 7,417kg/7.3 tons
Dimensions: Length – 3.94m/12ft 11in
    Height (over turret hatch) – 1.73m/5ft 8in
    Width – 2.24m/7ft 4in
Armament: Main – 37mm/1.46in M6 gun
    Secondary – 7.62mm/0.3in machine-gun
Armour: Maximum – 25mm/0.98in
Powerplant: Lycoming 0-435T 6-cylinder radial, 121kW/162hp
Performance: Speed – 64kph/40mph
    Range – 217km/135 miles

Designed as an airborne tank in 1941 by the charismatic J. Walter Christie, the M22 Locust only saw operational service with the British Army, who deployed it in small numbers with the 6th Airborne Reconnaissance Regiment during the Rhine Crossing. The Locust was transported by a Hamilcar glider, which had been specially designed to carry the British light airborne tank, the Tetrarch. The Locust was armed with a 37mm/1.46in gun and a coaxial machine-gun but it really proved too light to be of any great consequence on the battlefield.

M24 Chaffee Light Tank

Undoubtedly the best light tank of World War II was the M24 Chaffee, named after General Adna Chaffee, the "Father of the US Armored Force". It was a five-man tank, but was normally manned by only four men due to manpower shortages. The main armament was a powerful 75mm/2.95in gun which had been adapted from the heavy aircraft cannon as used in the B-25G Mitchell bomber. Although no match for the bigger German tanks, the M24 was remarkably effective against smaller targets. It remained the standard US light tank long after the end of the war and was modified to anti-aircraft and mortar carriage variants. The M24 Chaffee also saw service in Korea in the 1950s.

M24 Chaffee Light Tank

Entered service: 1944
Crew: 4 or 5
Weight: 18,289kg/18 tons
Dimensions: Length – 5.49m/18ft
    Height (over turret hatch) – 2.46m/8ft 1in
    Width – 2.95m/9ft 8in
Armament: Main – 75mm/2.95in M6 gun
    Secondary – 1 x 12.7mm/0.5in and
    2 x 7.62mm/0.3in machine-guns
Armour: Maximum – 38mm/1.5in
Powerplant: 2 x Cadillac 44T24 V8, each developing 82kW/110hp
Performance: Speed – 55kph/34mph
    Range – 282km/175 miles

LEFT: Named after the "Father" of the Armored Force, General Adna R. Chaffee, the M24 was not a great success as a gun tank either during World War II or in the early part of the Korean War, when it was outgunned by the North Korean T-34/85. Variants included the M19 GMC, an AA tank mounting twin 40mm/1.58in guns, and the M41 HMC, mounting a 155mm/6.1in M1 howitzer.

M1931 Christie

Tank development between the wars owed much to the brilliant, but unpredictable American engineer J. Walter Christie, who was the advocate of light, fast tanks that could move cross country at amazing speeds on his unique suspension system, or equally well without their tracks, just on their road wheels. His designs proved very influential in the burgeoning world of armour design beyond his native country, but closer to home in the USA he was regarded as a difficult man to deal with.

Based on his M1928 vehicle, the M1931 was modified to include a turret as well as various automotive improvements so that it was reputed to have had a top speed on its tracks of 74kph/46mph, while on its wheels on roads it could supposedly reach 113kph/70mph.

Although the US Army did not adopt his designs to a significant extent, other countries showed far more interest. Two of these tanks were purchased by the Russians and became the models for the BT series, while in the UK it was to influence British Cruiser tank development.

LEFT: **This is another of Christie's modern, streamlined tanks – the M1936 Airborne tank. Christie and his son are inside. Despite lack of interest in the USA, his revolutionary suspension was adopted by the British, the Poles and, most importantly, by the Soviet Union in their BT series.**

TOP: **Designed by the brilliant but irascible J. Walter Christie, the T3 Medium Tank was also called the Convertible and the 1928 Tank. It led on to the M1931 Medium Tank, which had a turret with a 37mm/1.46in gun.** ABOVE: **The M1931 tank could run on its tracks, as seen here, or on its wheels.**

M1931 Christie

Entered service: 1931 (prototype only)
Crew: 2
Weight: 10,668kg/10.5 tons
Dimensions: Length – 5.43m/17ft 10in
    Height (over turret hatch) – 2.21m/7ft 3in
    Width – 2.24m/7ft 4in
Armament: Main – 37mm/1.46in gun
    Secondary – 7.62mm/0.3in machine-gun
Armour: Maximum – 16mm/0.63in
Powerplant: Liberty, 12-cylinder petrol, 252kW/338hp
Performance: Speed – 64kph/40mph (tracks),
    113kph/70mph (wheels)
    Range – 274km/170 miles

Neubaufahrzeuge V and VI

Tank production developed very rapidly in pre-World War II Nazi Germany. In addition to light and medium tanks, some interest was also shown in designing a heavy tank to follow on from the Grosstraktor. This new vehicle was simply called *Neubaufahrzeuge* (NbFz)

(New Construction Vehicle) and weighed about 24,385kg/24 tons. Five prototypes were built by Krupp and Rheinmetall, the former building the Model A, armed with coaxial 7.5cm/2.95in and 3.7cm/1.46in

guns, and the latter the Model B, mounting a 10.5cm/4.13in howitzer and a 3.7cm/1.46in gun. Both Models also had a second subsidiary turret in front of the main one, mounting two coaxial 7.62mm/0.3in machine-guns.

Ordered in 1934–35, the tanks were originally designated PzKpfw V and VI, but, as neither was put into production, these designations were passed on to the Panther and Tiger tanks. The prototype NbFzs were initially located at the tank training school at Putlos until early in 1940, when three were used in Norway. One was destroyed there and the other two returned to Germany towards the end of that year, where they returned to the panzer training school to be used as parade ornaments in the camp.

ABOVE AND BELOW LEFT: **As a direct result of the experience gained from the *Grosstraktor* (cover name for a heavy tank secretly produced in the late 1920s), Krupp and Rheinmetall were each asked to produce prototype heavy tanks *Neubaufahrzeuge* (New Construction Vehicle) Model A (NbFz VI) and Model B (NbFz V) respectively. Both were multi-turreted. Three were sent to Oslo, Norway, in April 1940 and saw action there, one being destroyed and the other two returning to Germany.**

Neubaufahrzeuge V/VI

Entered service: 1934
Crew: 6
Weight: 24,385kg/24 tons
Dimensions: Length – 7.32m/24ft
    Height (over turret hatch) – 2.72m/8ft 11in
    Width – 3.05m/10ft
Armament: Main – 7.5cm/2.95in gun or
    10.5cm/4.13in howitzer and 1 x 3.7cm/1.46in
    coaxial gun
    Secondary – 3 x 7.92mm/0.312in machine-guns
    (2 x coaxial in subsidiary turret)
Armour: Maximum – 70mm/2.76in
Powerplant: 6-cylinder petrol, 372.9kW/500hp
Performance: Speed – 35.4kph/22mph
    Range – 140km/87 miles

PzKpfw Maus Super-Heavy Tank

Hitler's obsession with heavy tanks reached its zenith with the production of the super-heavies, of which only two models were actually ever built – Maus and the E-100 – although a number of others were talked about and some even reached the design stage. Clearly certain influential members of the German armaments industry shared Hitler's enthusiasm for super-heavy tanks, initially anyway, and foremost among them was Dr Porsche.

What is clear is that the time and energy spent on designing and producing these behemoths wasted a vast amount of precious design and

production effort, which Germany could ill afford to spare. Guderian described the Maus as "this gigantic offspring of the fantasy of Hitler and his advisers" which originally started life under the more appropriate codename of *Mammut* (Mammoth).

The heaviest tank ever built, Maus weighed an incredible 191,000kg/188 tons – too heavy to cross any bridge or move anywhere off level ground on its own. Only one Maus was completed to the stage where it had a turret and armament, consisting of one 12.8cm/5.04in L/55 gun and one coaxial 7.5cm/2.95in L/36.5 gun. It is now in the Russian Tank Museum.

ABOVE AND BELOW LEFT: **Super-Heavy German Tank, Maus, which at 191,000kg/188 tons was the largest and heaviest tank ever built during World War II. It was designed to out-gun and outperform all Allied AFVs. With a 12.8cm/5.04in gun and immensely thick frontal armour, two prototypes were constructed in late 1943, but although five more were ordered, they were never completed. Maus did at least have its turret fitted, unlike E100. The tank is crammed with complicated machinery so it would have been difficult to maintain. It was intended to be submersible to a depth of 8m/26ft!**

PzKpfw Maus Super-Heavy Tank

Entered service: 1945 (prototype only)
Crew: 5
Weight: Approximately 191,000kg/188 tons
Dimensions: Length – 10.09m/33ft 1in
  Height (over turret hatch) – 3.66m/12ft
  Width – 3.67m/12ft 0.5in
Armament: Main – 12.8cm/5.04in and
  7.5cm/2.95in coaxial gun
  Secondary – 7.92mm/0.312in machine-gun
Armour: Maximum – 200mm/7.87in
Powerplant: Mercedes-Benz MB509 V12 petrol,
  783kW/1,080hp
Performance: Speed – 20kph/12.4mph
  Range – 186km/115.6 miles

PzKpfw I Light Tank

The PzKpfw I Ausf A was the first German tank to go into mass production. It had the same hull and suspension as its predecessor, the PzKpfw I Ausf A *Ohne Aufbau* (literally "without turret") which had been produced without a turret and weapon system to bypass the Treaty of Versailles that prevented Germany from building tanks. Weighing just over 5 tons, with a crew of two and mounting two 7.92mm/0.312in machine-guns, it was soon outclassed on the battlefield and was withdrawn from active service in 1941. The Ausf B had a slightly longer chassis than the Ausf A (just under 0.5m/8in longer) and a more powerful engine.

The modification increased its weight to 5,893kg/5.8 tons. It was also phased out of service in 1941.

There was also a command version of the PzKpfw I, which was used at company, battalion, regimental and brigade level in the headquarters of panzer units from the mid-1930s up to the early war years. A radio transmitter was included in addition to the radio receiver normally only fitted in the PzKpfw I. The superstructure had to be raised in height to make room for the radio and its operator.

Some versions of the Ausf B had an odd-looking cable-operated arm which could drop a demolition charge over the

ABOVE: **The PzKpfw I Ausf B was the second production model and entered service in 1935, being slightly longer than the Ausf A. It was armed with two machine-guns.** BELOW LEFT: **The Tank Museum's Kleinerbefelswagen I, the command version of the PzKpfw IB. It has a fixed turret and was for use by unit commanders.**

rear end of the tank. This could be placed near obstacles and then set off remotely.

The final development of the PzKpfw I was a 21,337kg/21-ton infantry assault tank, which had very thick armour. Thirty were built in 1942, and a few were taken to Russia for combat testing. However, as a result of these tests, further orders were cancelled.

PzKpfw I Ausf B Light Tank

Entered service: 1934
Crew: 2
Weight: 5,893kg/5.8 tons
Dimensions: Length – 4.42m/14ft 6in
　　Height (over turret hatch) – 1.72m/5ft 8in
　　Width – 2.06m/6ft 9in
Armament: Main – 2 x 7.92mm/0.312in
　　machine-guns
Armour: Maximum – 13mm/0.51in
Powerplant: Maybach NL38TR, 6-cylinder petrol,
　　74.5kW/100hp
Performance: Speed – 40kph/24.9mph
　　Range – 153km/95.1 miles

PzKpfw II Light Tank

The next model in the German light tank family was the PzKpfw II, weighing nearly 10 tons, with a crew of three, mounting a 2cm/0.79in cannon capable of firing both high-explosive and armour-piercing ammunition, along with a coaxial MG34 machine-gun. First manufactured in 1936, it underwent an initial development cycle of three versions – A, B and C, by which time the suspension had changed from one very similar to the PzKpfw I to five independently sprung, larger roadwheels and four top rollers. The A version is distinguishable from later models by the periscope on the turret top placed centrally behind the guns. With the B and C models only minor variations were made, which included extra bolted-on armour plate, improvements in vision devices and the addition of a turret cupola.

The PzKpfw II series then continued up to the Ausf L, with its armament remaining the same but with constant changes to its chassis, superstructure and automotive systems, as well as increases in armour thickness. PzKpfw IIs

saw action in all theatres and were later modified into a number of variants, including having the turret removed to become an artillery and ammunition "Schlepper". There was also the "Flamingo" flamethrower variant, which had two flamethrowers mounted on the front corners of the tank's superstructure.

The final model of this series was the Panzerspahwagen II Light Recce tank, called the *Luchs* (Lynx) and was

ABOVE: **PzKpfw II Ausf F. This was the final model of the normal PzKpfw II series. The major difference was that the hull was made from one flat 35mm/ 1.38in plate.**

designed and developed as a reconnaissance tank. It had a crew of four and weighed 13,208kg/13 tons. Its main armament was a 2cm/0.79in KwK38 gun, with a coaxially mounted MG34. About 100 were built in late 1943 and saw service in both Russia and Europe.

BELOW: **PzKpfw II Ausf L was also known as the *Luchs*. It was a light reconnaissance tank with a crew of four and weighed 13,208kg/13 tons. This one is in the Tank Museum, Bovington.**

PzKpfw II Ausf F Light Tank	

Entered service: 1935 (Ausf A), 1941 (Ausf F)
Crew: 3
Weight: 9,650kg/9.5 tons
Dimensions: Length – 4.81m/15ft 9in
    Height (over turret hatch) – 2.15m/7ft 0.5in
    Width – 2.28m/7ft 8in
Armament: Main – 2cm/0.79in cannon
    Secondary – 7.92mm/0.315in machine-gun
Armour: Maximum – 35mm/1.38in
Powerplant: Maybach HL62TR, 6-cylinder petrol, 104.4kW/140hp
Performance: Speed – 40kph/24.9mph
    Range – 200km/124.3 miles

PzKpfw III Medium Tank

The backbone of the German Panzer Divisions was their medium tanks in the 15,240–20,320kg/15–20-ton range. Tracing its original development as far back as 1935, the PzKpfw III was a vital tank produced up until 1943. There were versions ranging from Ausf A–N (minus I and K), but with other variants including flamethrower, submersible, various command versions, and a turret-less ammunition carrier. The chassis was also the foundation of the StuG assault-gun series.

The early models mounted a KwK 3.7cm/1.46in gun, plus twin machine-guns in the turret and a third in the hull, manned by the radio operator. Ausf As were issued first in 1937, but withdrawn from service in early 1940 because their armour thickness, at only 15mm/0.59in, was found to be inadequate. By the time of the Ausf E, the tank still mounted the same armament, but its armour was now up to 30mm/1.18in and its weight had increased accordingly to over 19 tons.

The first model to mount the new KwK 5cm/1.97in gun (necessitating a turret redesign) was the Ausf F. First ordered in 1939, it saw service in Poland and France, when it was quickly realized that more armour and bigger guns were needed. The problem with the PzKpfw III was that it could not accept a gun larger than 5cm/1.97in because of the restrictive size of the turret ring. Six hundred Ausf G models were produced from April 1940 onwards, with their weight now just over 20,320kg/ 20 tons.

The Ausf L mounted the 5cm/1.97in KwK39 L/60 gun and once again had thicker armour on the front of the turret, now 57mm/2.24in. Ausf M came fitted with *Schürzen* (skirts) to protect from HEAT (High-Explosive Anti-Tank) weapons such as the bazooka and the PIAT.

TOP: **The Tank Museum's PzKpfw III Ausf L, which mounts a long-barrelled 5cm/1.97in KwK39 L/60 gun, the second model to do so. The Ausf L first saw action in USSR in 1942.** LEFT: **The Tank Museum's PzKpfw III going through its paces during a Tankfest. As can be seen, it is still in excellent running order.**

Variants included: a specially designed artillery OP tank (*Artillerie Panzerbeobachtungwagen*) to enable the Forward Observation Officer to accompany a panzer formation (the turret space normally taken up by the main armament being replaced by an artillery plotting board and extra radios); a command tank (*Panzerbefelswagen*); an armoured recovery vehicle (*Bergepanzer III*); a supply carrier (*Schlepper III*); and an engineer vehicle (*Pionerpanzer*). However, more remarkable was the *Tauchpanzer* (literally "diving tank") which was completely waterproofed so that it could operate at depths of 15m/50ft and remain submerged for up to 20 minutes. Designed for use in 1940 for the aborted invasion of England, they were later used to great effect for the crossing of the River Bug on June 22, 1941, at the start of the invasion of Russia.

TOP: **This well-camouflaged PzKpfw III has the long-barrelled 5cm/1.97in KwK39 L/60 gun fitted, unusually with a false muzzle brake.** ABOVE: **A column of PzKpfw III Ausf Js move through a Russian village. Over 1,500 of this model were produced between March 1941 and July 1942.** BELOW: **One way of getting a larger-calibre gun on to an existing tank chassis was via the *Sturmgescheutz* (assault gun/tank destroyer). This model mounted a 7.5cm/2.95in gun.**

PzKpfw III Ausf F Medium Tank

Entered service: 1937
Crew: 5
Weight: 19,500kg/19.2 tons
Dimensions: Length – 5.38m/17ft 8in
Height (over turret hatch) – 2.45m/8ft 0.5in
Width – 2.91m/9ft 7in
Armament: Main – 3.7cm/1.46in KwK gun (early models)
Secondary – 2 x 7.92mm/0.312in machine-guns
Armour: Maximum – 30mm/1.18in
Powerplant: Maybach HL120 TRM, V12 petrol, 223.7kW/300hp
Performance: Speed – 40kph/24.9mph
Range – 165km/102.5 miles

PzKpfw IV Medium Tank

Undoubtedly the best German medium tank was the PzKpfw IV, and it was the only German battle tank to remain in production throughout World War II, being constantly up-armoured and up-gunned. The PzKpfw IV was a well-made robust tank with a satisfactory cross-country performance and a large turret ring that enabled it to take more powerful guns.

The early models mounted a 7.5cm/2.95in L/24 low-velocity, short-barrelled gun in its role as an infantry support tank. Versions Ausf A–E had increased armour and therefore increased weight and the hull machine-gun, omitted on both the Ausf B and C, was again fitted from the Ausf D onwards.

In 1941 plans were laid to improve the firepower of PzKpfw IV by fitting a long-barrelled 7.5cm/2.95in gun. The Ausf F was the first to be so fitted, and stowage arrangements had to be modified to accept the larger rounds. When it first appeared in mid-1942, it was more than a match for any of the contemporary Allied tanks

The Ausf G was very like the Ausf F, with minor variations, including thicker side armour. More of the Ausf H was produced than any other model and had better transmission, thicker armour and a new idler. It was the penultimate model in the PzKpfw IV range.

Last of the line was the Ausf J, which weighed 25,401kg/ 25 tons, had a range of over 300km/186 miles and a top speed of 38kph/23.6mph. It was also fitted with *Schürzen* (skirts) to

TOP: **The Tank Museum's PzKpfw IV which, together with the PzKpfw III, was the backbone of the *Panzerwaffe*, remaining in quantity production from 1937 to 1945.** ABOVE: **A striking photograph of a PzKpfw IV Ausf C that appeared in *SIGNAL*, the German propaganda magazine.**

protect against HEAT (High-Explosive Anti-Tank) weapons and had extra "stand-off" armour around the turret. Its long-barrelled 7.5cm/2.95in gun had an excellent performance against enemy armour.

LEFT: **Early model PzKpfw IVs break through a wall into woodland during training prior to the invasion of the Low Countries in 1940.** BELOW LEFT: **A column of PzKpfw IV Ausf Hs make their way up to the Orel battle front in August 1943. Note the add-on "stand-off" armour around the turret to guard against bazooka-type weapons (also side plates to similarly protect the suspension).** BELOW: **These GIs of 35th US Infantry Division make their way carefully in this ruined town, skirting a knocked-out and abandoned PzKpfw IV.** BOTTOM: **An early model PzKpfw IV armed with the short-barrelled support 7.5cm/ 2.95in KwK37 L/24 gun waits to engage an enemy strongpoint while a Russian soldier crawls to safety – but was it staged for propaganda purposes?**

Like the PzKpfw III, the IV also had many variants in addition to the more obvious ones. There was a range of assault gun/ tank destroyers, including StuG IV, Jagdpanzer IV, Panzer IV 70(V) and Panzer IV 70(A), on up to *Hornisse* which mounted an 8.8cm/3.46in anti-tank gun. Then there was a range of AA guns (*Flakpanzer*) and numerous self-propelled howitzers and various types of bridges. However, probably the most unusual was the ammunition carrier for the SP heavy siege mortar *Karlgerät* that could carry four of its massive 60cm/23.61in rounds in specially designed racks above the engine compartment!

PzKpfw IV Ausf F2 Medium Tank

Entered service: 1942
Crew: 5
Weight: 22,350kg/22 tons
Dimensions: Length – 6.63m/21ft 9in
    Height (over turret hatch) – 2.68m/8ft 9.5in
    Width – 2.88m/9ft 5.5in
Armament: Main – 7.5cm/2.95in KwK40 L/43 gun
    Secondary – 2 x 7.92mm/0.312in machine-guns
Armour: Maximum – 50mm/1.97in
Powerplant: Maybach HL120 TRIM, V12 petrol, 223.7kW/300hp
Performance: Speed – 40kph/24.9mph
    Range – 209km/129.9 miles

PzKpfw V Panther Heavy Tank

As World War II progressed, the Germans maintained their tank superiority by bringing the PzKpfw V and VI heavy tanks into service in the 40,640–60,960kg/40–60 ton range, well ahead of the Allies. PzKpfw V, or Panther as it is more commonly known, owes much of its design to a detailed study undertaken of the Russian T-34 which had proved to be greatly superior to the PzKpfw III and IV. The Ausf D model Panther, appearing in 1943, weighed 43,690kg/43 tons, mounted a 7.5cm/2.95in KwK42 L/70 gun and had a crew

of five. With a top speed of about 45kph/28mph, and a radius of action of 200km/124.3 miles, it was a formidable opponent.

A total of 850 of the Ausf D model were built, and it was the first to go into service despite the fact that the next model following it was called Ausf A! Some 2,000 Ausf As were built between August 1943 and May 1944. It had various improvements over its predecessor, including better running gear, thicker armour and a new commander's cupola.

The Ausf G was produced as a result of combat experience with the Ausf D

ABOVE: **This Panther is in the show ring at the French Armour School, Saumur – still in good running order.** BELOW: **A peasant family in their ancient horse-drawn cart pass a knocked-out Panther Ausf G in an Italian village.**

and A. Over 3,000 Ausf Gs were built between March 1944 and April 1945. The hull was redesigned, now without the driver's vision visor – which must have been a vulnerable spot. Variants included command and observation tanks and also the ARV (Armoured Recovery Vehicle) Bergepanther.

PzKpfw V Ausf G Heavy Tank

Entered service: 1944
Crew: 5
Weight: 45,465kg/45.5 tons
Dimensions: Length – 8.87m/29ft 1in
Height (over turret hatch) – 2.97m/9ft 9in
Width – 3.43m/11ft 3in
Armament: Main – 7.5cm/2.95in KwK42 L/70 gun
Secondary – 2 x 7.92mm/0.312m machine-guns
Armour: Maximum – 100mm/3.94in
Powerplant: Maybach HL230P30 V12 petrol,
522kW/700hp
Performance: Speed – 46kph/28.75mph
Range – 200km/125 miles

Jagdpanther Heavy Tank Destroyer

O f the various special adaptations of Panther, the Jagdpanther Heavy Tank Destroyer was perhaps the most famous. It mounted an 8.8cm/3.46in PaK43/3 L/71 gun which could penetrate 182mm/7.17in of armour at 500m/1,640ft. It was a well-protected, fast (46kph/28.6mph) and effective tank destroyer.

According to the official German handbook, the Jagdpanther was designed as a *Schwerpunkt* (literally

"centre of gravity") weapon for the destruction of enemy tank attacks, and its employment as a complete battalion was considered to be the primary consideration towards achieving success. Production began in January 1944, and the first Jagdpanthers entered service in June 1944. Nearly 400 were built between January 1944 and March 1945. The Jagdpanther was undoubtedly the most important variant of the Panther.

ABOVE: **The Jagdpanther, sporting an unusual camouflage pattern. This tank destroyer mounted the fearsome 8.8cm/3.46in PaK43/3 L/71. Probably the largest concentration of Jagdpanthers was assembled for the Ardennes offensive in December 1944.** BELOW LEFT: **This abandoned Jagdpanther – note the unfired ammunition alongside the track – may well be badly damaged on the far side; certainly the idler wheel and track guard seem to have sustained a strike. 392 Jagdpanthers were built, the prototype being shown to Hitler in December 1943.**

Jagdpanther Heavy TD

Entered service: 1944
Crew: 5
Weight: 46,000kg/45.3 tons
Dimensions: Length – 9.9m/32ft 8in
 Height (over turret hatch) – 2.72m/8ft 11in
 Width – 3.42m/11ft 2.6in
Armament: Main – 8.8cm/3.46in anti-tank gun
 Secondary – 2 x 7.92mm/0.312in machine-guns
Armour: Maximum – 100mm/3.94in
Powerplant: Maybach HL230P30, V12 petrol, 522kW/700hp
Performance: Speed – 46kph/28.6mph
 Range – 160km/99.4 miles

PzKpfw VI Ausf E Tiger 1 Heavy Tank

The most famous of all German World War II tanks was the Tiger, although only approximately 1,360 were ever produced – compared with 6,000 Panthers. Tiger production began in July 1942 and first saw action in Russia in August 1942.

Weighing 56,900kg/56 tons, the Tiger's main armament was the dreaded 8.8cm/3.46in KwK36 L/56 gun that could penetrate 110mm/4.33in of armour at 2,000m/6,561ft. To the average Allied soldier, the Tiger became the symbol of the invincibility of German armour – to a degree which completely outweighed its true capabilities – although when introduced, it was undoubtedly the world's most powerful tank. It did have weak points, however, one of them being its very low-gear turret traverse, which made bringing the main gun to bear on a target very slow.

ABOVE: Probably the most famous tank of World War II was the German PzKpfw VI Ausf E, Tiger I. This was the first one ever captured complete by the British in North Africa, and is now in running order at the Tank Museum, Bovington. BELOW: Question: "When is a Tiger not a Tiger?" Answer: "When it has been specially made for the movies!". This excellent replica "Tiger I" was built using a T-34 chassis for the film *Saving Private Ryan*. It is seen here at a Bovington Tankfest in 2002. It is much smaller than the original but otherwise looks remarkably similar, apart from the running gear.

PzKpfw VI Ausf E Tiger 1 Heavy Tank

Entered service: 1942
Crew: 5
Weight: 56,900kg/56 tons
Dimensions: Length – 8.45m/27ft 8.5in
    Height (over turret hatch) – 3m/9ft 10in
    Width – 3.56m/11ft 8in
Armament: Main – 8.8cm/3.46m KwK36 L/56 gun
    Secondary – 2 or 3 x 7.92mm/0.312in
    machine-guns
Armour: Maximum – 100mm/3.94in
Powerplant: Maybach HL210P45 V12 petrol,
    522kW/700hp
Performance: Speed – 37kph/22.9mph
    Range – 195km/121 miles

PzKpfw VI Ausf B Tiger 2 Heavy Tank

The *Königstiger* (Royal or King Tiger) or Tiger 2, as it was called, was a formidable tank that could deal with any of its opponents on the battlefield with ease. It weighed over 69,090kg/68 tons, was armed with a long-barrelled 8.8cm/ 3.46in KwK43 L/71 gun which could penetrate 132mm/5.19in of armour at 2,000m/6,561ft. It was thus able to deal effortlessly with the heaviest Allied tanks. However, its sheer weight and bulk gave it a relatively poor cross-country performance and made for problems in maintenance and reliability. Only 489 King Tigers were built, and they were used mainly in the defensive battles as the Allies advanced deep into Germany.

RIGHT: **This King Tiger has the much more streamlined Porsche turret, and is on show at the Tank Museum, Bovington. The King Tiger mounted the more powerful, longer-barrelled KwK43 L/71 8.8cm/3.46in gun.**

PzKpfw VI Jagdtiger Heavy Tank Destroyer

This monster tank destroyer, weighing 70,000kg/68.9 tons, mounted a 12.8cm/5.04in PaK44 L/55 gun and was undoubtedly the largest and most powerful armoured fighting vehicle to see combat service in World War II, its gun out-ranging most others. The 77 Jagdtigers that were built saw service in the Ardennes and later in the defence of the German "Fatherland".

PzKpfw VI Jagdtiger Heavy TD

Entered service: 1944
Crew: 6
Weight: 70,000kg/68.9 tons
Dimensions: Length – 10.65m/34ft 11.5in
   Height (over turret hatch) – 2.95m/9ft 8in
   Width – 3.63m/11ft 11in
Armament: Main – 12.8cm/5.04in anti-tank gun
   Secondary – 2 x 7.92in/0.3in machine-guns
Armour: Maximum – 250mm/9.8in
Powerplant: Maybach HL230P30 V12 petrol,
   522kW/700hp
Performance: Speed – 38kph/23.6mph
   Range – 170km/105.6 miles

LEFT: **Largest and heaviest of the Tiger conversions was the Jagdtiger, which mounted a massive 12.8cm/ 5.04in PaK44 L/55 gun that could penetrate 157mm/ 6.18in of armour at 1,500m/4,921ft. I once saw a Jagdtiger that had knocked out nearly an entire regiment of Shermans, but had then been knocked out itself by a *Jabo* (fighter-bomber).**

131

Renault FT-17 Light Tank and derivatives

Designed by Louis Renault, with the support of the irrepressible General Estienne, the Char Mitrailleuse Renault FT-17 was a remarkable little tank, a true milestone in design which lasted right up to the outbreak of World War II, and was adapted and produced by many countries all over the world. The American Ford 6 Ton Tank, for example, was in essence an American-built Renault FT.

A very large number of FT-17s were built, in seven different models, including a cast turret version. One unique aspect of the tank was its fully revolving turret – the first tank in the world to have all-round traverse. Armed with an 8mm/0.315mm Hotchkiss machine-gun, the two-man tank weighed just over 6 tons, was powered by a 26.1kW/35hp Renault engine and had vertical coil suspension. Later the Hotchkiss was replaced with a new 7.5mm/0.295in machine-gun.

The Renault factory received its first order for 150 F-17s in March 1917 and the first tanks appeared on the battlefield on May 31, 1918, at the Forest of Retz.

FT-17 in American Service

Renault FT-17 tanks were used by the US Army to equip the 344th and 345th Light Tank Battalions. Armed with a 37mm/1.46in gun in the turret and a machine-gun in the hull, they first saw action on September 12, 1918, under the command of Lieutenant Colonel George S. Patton, in an attack against the St Mihiel Salient, France.

TOP: **The most important French tank of World War I was the FT-17, and it was later copied by many other nations, including the Americans, Russians and Italians.** LEFT: **Armed with an 8mm/0.315in Hotchkiss machine-gun, the tiny 6,604kg/6.5-ton Char Mitrailleuse Renault FT-17, to give its full title, was the first tank in the world to have a fully traversing turret.**

FT-17 in Russian Service

Although the Russians now claim that they invented the tank, the first Russian tanks were actually 32 British Mark Vs and Medium Cs, plus 100 French Renault FT-17s, bought in 1918 by the Imperial Government, many of which were later captured by the Bolsheviks. They then acquired even more when the small British force withdrew from Russia and had to leave its tanks behind. The first Russian-built tank was a copy of the Renault FT-17, the KS (*KrasnoSormova*), after the place where it was built, but was also called the Russki-Renault. It would set the pattern for Soviet tank development over the next decade.

RIGHT: **A later post-war derivative of the FT-17 was this Soviet-designed and built MS-2 Light Tank, which had an entirely new sprung suspension and transverse engine. It mounted both a 37mm/1.46in gun and two machine-guns.**

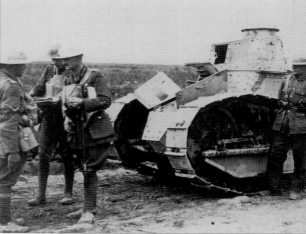

ABOVE: **Another version of the ubiquitous little French tank had a moulded turret. FT-17s were still in service at the start of World War II, and some were still being used by the Vichy French in North Africa against Operation "Torch" (November 1942).** RIGHT: **An FT-17 in British Army service. The British used these small tanks for command and liaison work, normally (as here) with the gun removed.**

LEFT: **This version of the FT-17 mounted a 37mm/ 1.46in Puteaux gun. Some 1,830 of this model were built and, as can be seen, many are still in existence as monuments.**

Renault FT-17 Light Tank

Entered service: 1917
Crew: 2
Weight: 6,604kg/6.5 tons
Dimensions: Length – 4.09m/13ft 5in
　　Height (over turret hatch) – 2.13m/7ft
　　Width – 1.70m/5ft 7in
Armament: Main – 8mm/0.315in machine-gun or 37mm/1.46 gun
Armour: Maximum – 22mm/0.87in
Powerplant: Renault 4-cylinder petrol, 26.1kW/35hp
Performance: Speed – 7.7kph/4.8mph
　　Range – 35km/21.7 miles

Ram Mark I Cruiser Tank

In early 1941 it was decided to produce a tank in Canada based largely on the US M3 Medium Tank, but better suited to Canadian needs. It was to have a Canadian-produced turret and main armament, together with a redesigned hull to avoid the excessively tall silhouette of the M3. The Ram I went into production in late 1941, mounting a 2pdr gun.

RIGHT: **The Tank Museum's Ram Mark II which mounts a 6pdr gun instead of the original 2pdr on the Ram Mark I. These Canadian-built medium tanks were mainly shipped to the UK during 1943 and used for training.**

Ram Mark II Cruiser Tank

After only 50 Ram Is had been produced, the main armament was changed to a 6pdr equipped with stabilization. More than 1,000 were produced and used for training in Canada and the UK. However, the only Rams to see action were those with their turrets removed and converted to Armoured Personnel Carriers (APCs) known as Ram Kangaroos. These were very successful in a variety of roles – hauling ammunition and artillery, as well as carrying troops and a variety of other weapon systems.

The arrival of the US Sherman M4 rendered the Ram unnecessary, as the new tank incorporated most of the features which had been found lacking in the M3.

Canada did go on to build their own version of the Sherman M4A1, known as the Grizzly, which had certain minor alterations to make it more suitable for UK and Canadian use.

ABOVE: **The earlier Ram 1 Cruiser Tank was armed with just a 2pdr. It incorporated all the latest American, British and Canadian ideas on firepower, protection and mobility, and was built ahead of the advent of the British 6pdr.** LEFT: **The British took the turrets off some of the Canadian Ram tanks, "gutted" them and used them as armoured personnel carriers for infantry sections. This one is badged for the 79th Armoured Division.**

Ram Mark II Cruiser Tank

Entered service: 1942
Crew: 5
Weight: 29,484kg/29 tons
Dimensions: Length – 5.79m/19ft
  Height (over turret hatch) – 2.67m/8ft 9in
  Width – 2.77m/9ft 1in
Armament: Main – 6pdr (57mm/2.24in) gun
  Secondary – 3 x 7.62mm/0.3in machine-guns
Armour: Maximum – 87mm/3.43in
Powerplant: Continental R-975 9-cylinder petrol, 298kW/400bhp
Performance: Speed – 40.2kph/25mph
  Range – 232km/144 miles

Renault Char D2 Infantry Tank

The D2 came in to service in 1934 and was essentially the same as the D1 but with thicker armour which increased the weight to 19,305kg/19 tons. To cope with the heavier weight, a bigger 6-cylinder 111.9kW/150hp engine was fitted and there were improvements to the transmission and suspension.

The armament remained the same. A distinctive feature of this vehicle was the large aerial mounted on the right of the rear deck behind the turret.

Renault began deliveries in 1934, but their D series was to lose out to the SOMUA Medium Tank, which was selected in preference by the French Army.

In the end only about 50 D2s were taken into service and their automotive unreliability and slow speed ensured a fairly dismal combat record. Most were deployed in North Africa as static defences and a few captured ones were incorporated into the Atlantic Wall by the Germans.

LEFT: **Orders for D2 were reduced in 1936 in preference for the Char S-35 SOMUA, but a number still saw action in May 1940. One major improvement over the Char D1B was far better ammunition stowage for its 47mm/ 1.85in main gun – from 35 to 108 rounds. In most other respects it was disappointing.**

Renault Char D2 Infantry Tank

Entered service: 1934
Crew: 3
Weight: 19,305kg/19 tons
Dimensions: Length – 4.81m/15ft 9.5in
　　Height (over turret hatch) – 2.4m/7ft 10.5in
　　Width – 2.16m/7ft 1in
Armament: Main – 47mm/1.85in SA34 gun
　　Secondary – 2 x 7.5mm/0.295in machine-guns
Armour: Maximum – 50mm/1.97in
Powerplant: Renault, 6-cylinder petrol, delivering 111.9kW/150hp
Performance: Speed – 22.5kph/14mph
　　Range – 90km/55.9 miles

Renault FT Kegresse-Hinstin M24/25 Light Tank

In 1924, the well-known French automotive engineer Adolphe Kegresse received financial backing from M. Hinstin to work on improving the highly successful little Renault FT-17 in order to produce a quieter, faster tank. His new running-gear employed a suspension comprising eight small road wheels plus a standard-sized sprocket and idler, both at ground level, together with rubber track bands (for

quietness). Additionally, there were more rollers on outriggers both at the front and rear, designed to assist in trench crossing. The French Army bought a number of these "wheel cum tracks" and shipped them over to Morocco in 1925 when the Riffs invaded, where they were used in combat. A number were also sold to overseas buyers, including the Americans, who bought them for evaluation.

In 1925, an improved version was produced, which modified the suspension, strengthened the rubber tracks with metal pads and did away with the front rollers, but retained those at the rear. Unfortunately, there were no buyers, and this innovative AFV was shelved.

LEFT: **A Renault FT M24/25 climbs a concrete step during trials with the US Army circa 1925, clearly showing its innovative suspension. Some of these interesting little tanks saw action in North Africa in 1925 against the Riffs in Morocco.**

Renault FT Kegresse-Hinstin M24/25 Light Tank

Entered service: 1924
Crew: 2
Weight: 6,600kg/6.5tons
Dimensions: Length – 5.00m/16ft 5in
　　Height (over turret hatch) – 2.14m/7ft
　　Width – 1.83m/6ft
Armament: Main – 37mm/1.46in gun or 8mm/0.315in machine-gun
Armour: Maximum – 22mm/0.866in
Powerplant: Renault 4-cylinder petrol, 26.1kW/35bhp
Performance: Speed: – 12kph/7.5mph
　　Range – 35km/21.7 miles

Renault R-35 Light Tank

Following on from the disappointing AMC 34, Renault produced their AMC 35 model, which was very similar, but with a more powerful liquid-cooled 4-cylinder engine, an upgraded bell-crank scissors suspension system and improved vision devices. The hull was of riveted construction made with rolled steel plates. The turret armament remained the short-barrelled high-velocity 47mm/1.85in main gun, although some of the late models were fitted with a long-barrelled 25mm/0.98in Hotchkiss anti-tank gun and had a crew of three. The R-35 was the most numerous of the

French tanks to fight in 1940, but fared badly because it was found to have a high fuel consumption which limited its range. It was also out-gunned by the German AFVs.

ABOVE: **Most numerous of the French tanks to fight in May/June 1940 were the light infantry support Renault R-35, armed with a short-barrelled 37mm/1.46in gun. This one is taking part in the annual demonstration at the French Armour School, Saumur.** LEFT: **On parade in Paris pre-war, the Char Leger R-35, Renault Type ZM Light Tank had a crew of only two, so the commander also had to act as gunner traversing the turret by hand.** BELOW LEFT: **A file of R-35 light infantry support tanks on training. Some 2,000 were built, many of which were exported to Poland, Turkey and Romania. The Germans also used captured R-35s and gave some to Italy.**

Renault R-35 Light Tank	

Entered service: 1935
Crew: 2 or 3
Weight: 14,500kg/14.3 tons
Dimensions: Length – 4.55m/14ft 11in
 Height (over turret hatch) – 2.3m/7ft 6.5in
 Width – 2.2m/7ft 2.5in
Armament: Main – 37mm/1.46in gun
 Secondary – 7.5mm/0.295in machine-gun
Armour: Maximum – 45mm/1.77in
Powerplant: Renault, 4-cylinder petrol,
 134.2kW/180hp
Performance: Speed – 42kph/26.1mph
 Range – 160km/99.4 miles

Sentinel AC1, AC2, AC3 and AC4 Cruiser Tank

In late 1940, given the fragile state of supply between Britain and its colonies, it was decided to design a tank which could be produced in Australia, using easily obtainable items, such as truck engines. The Sentinel, as the result was called, was a tremendous achievement for a nation with such a small industrial base. It was initially produced in two versions, the first of these being the AC1, the most striking feature of this model being the very large sleeve for the bow machine-gun which was situated in the

centre of the hull. It also mounted a 2pdr main gun and had two Vickers machine-guns. The cast hull and turret were mounted on a suspension system which resembled the French Hotchkiss design, while various parts such as the final drives and transmission were copied from the American M3 Medium Tank.

Production began in 1942, and more than 60 tanks were built. However, these were only ever used for training. The second Sentinel model, the AC2, was not developed, so the next Sentinel to

reach the prototype stage was the AC3, which mounted a 25pdr howitzer in a larger turret. The triple engines (three Cadillac V8s) were now given a single crankcase. The AC3 did not progress further than testing. The next Sentinel model to be produced, the AC4, mounted a 17pdr, and this prototype was completed in 1943. However, with ample supplies of American tanks now being available, no further Sentinel production was required.

TOP: **A remarkable achievement for the infant Australian tank industry was the production of the Sentinel Cruiser Tank in 1942, seen here at the Tank Museum, Bovington. The AC1 was armed with a 2pdr gun.** LEFT: **Some prototype Sentinels were fitted with twin 25pdrs in order to simulate the recoil of an even larger weapon, like the 17pdr which was then tried in AC4 but never went into production.**

Sentinel AC1 Cruiser Tank

Entered service: 1942
Crew: 5
Weight: 28,489kg/28 tons
Dimensions: Length – 6.32m/20ft 9in
 Height (over turret hatch) – 2.57m/8ft 5in
 Width – 2.77m/9ft 1in
Armament: Main – 2pdr (40mm/1.58in) or
 25pdr (AC3) or 17pdr (AC4)
 Secondary – 2 x 7.62mm/0.3in machine-guns
Armour: Maximum – 65mm/2.56in
Powerplant: 3 x Cadillac V8 petrol, 87kW/117bhp
Performance: Speed – 48.3kph/30mph
 Range – 319km/198 miles

137

7TP Light Tank

In addition to the Carden-Loyds, another British export was the ubiquitous Vickers-Armstrong 6 Ton Mark E model, which was bought and copied by the Poles, who then in turn produced the 7TP – a 9,550kg/9.4-ton plus twin-turreted light tank with thicker armour than its progenitor. It was crewed by three men – the driver and one man in each turret, each armed with a 7.92mm/0.312in machine-gun (various models – Maxim, Browning and Hotchkiss – were tried). It was powered by a Polish-built Swiss-patterned Saurer 82kW/110hp 6-cylinder diesel engine.

The twin turrets of the first model were soon replaced by a single-turret variant, 7TP 2, still mounting a Bofors 37mm/ 1.46in gun. The final model, 7TP 3, came into production in 1937, with about 160 being built. It had thicker welded armour and now weighed 11,177kg/11 tons, a new engine and also a new turret produced in Sweden, which overhung to the rear, mounting the 37mm/1.46in Bofors high-velocity anti-tank gun, along with a coaxial 7.92mm/0.312in machine-gun. This was certainly the best tank the Poles had in service when the Germans invaded, with a few being modified and pressed into service by the Germans following their capture. Its Bofors gun was widely used by both sides in the war.

TOP: **The Poles developed the British Vickers Armstrong 6 Ton Tank first as a twin-turreted model, but then as a single, mounting a 37mm/ 1.46in, which then went into production in 1937.**
LEFT: **The improved model of the 7TP Light Tank had better armour up to 40mm/1.58in thick and weighed 11,177kg/11 tons.**

7TP Light Tank

Entered service: 1937
Crew: 3
Weight: 9,550kg/9.4 tons
Dimensions: Length – 4.6m/15ft 1in
    Height (over turret hatch) – 2.02m/6ft 7.5in
    Width – 2.16m/7ft 1in
Armament: Main – 37mm/1.46in anti-tank gun
    Secondary – 1 or 2 x 7.92mm/0.312in
    machine-guns
Armour: Maximum – 17mm/0.67in
Powerplant: Saurer 6-cylinder diesel, 82kW/ 110hp
Performance: Speed – 32kph/19.9mph
    Range – 160km/99.4 miles

SMK Heavy Tank

Two multi-turreted heavy tanks were designed by leading Soviet tank designer Kotin in 1938, each with three turrets, which were later reduced to two. They were designated as the T-100 and the SMK (the latter initials standing for Sergei Mironovich Kirov). They were almost identical in appearance, both having a an upper central turret mounting a 76.2mm/3in gun with all-round traverse and a lower front turret mounting a 45mm/1.77in gun which had 180-degree traverse only.

ABOVE AND BELOW: The SMK (Sergei Mironovich Kirov) was another multi-turreted Soviet heavy tank that followed on after the T-35 and T-100. It closely resembled the T-100 and was used in the Russo-Finnish War, but proved to be lacking in both protection and firepower. It was abandoned in favour of the KV-1, which proved much more successful.

The SMK, which at 45,722kg/45 tons was 11,177kg/11 tons lighter than the T-100, had a new torsion bar suspension, with eight independently sprung, smallish road wheels on either side (with resilient rubber-bushed hubs) with four upper return rollers. The tracks were of a new design, with heavily spudded, small-pitch links. (Spuds are part of the metal track that juts out and provides traction.) The tank was constructed of cast armour, both on hull and turrets, that was designed to give protection against at least 37mm/1.46in anti-tank round at all ranges and was up to 60mm/2.36in thick.

A small number were used in Finland, but were not successful in combat, being difficult to manoeuvre and lacking both firepower and armour, so the project was abandoned in favour of the KV-1.

SMK Heavy Tank	
Entered service: 1939	
Crew: 7	
Weight: 45,722kg/45 tons	
Dimensions: Length – 9.66m/31ft 6in	
Height (over turret hatch) – 3.3m/10ft 10in	
Width – 3.45m/11ft 4in	
Armament: Main – 76.2mm/3in L11 and	
45mm/1.77in gun	
Secondary – 4 x 7.62mm/0.3in machine-guns	
Armour: Maximum – 60mm/2.36in	
Powerplant: AM-34 diesel	
Performance: Speed – 36kph/22.4mph	
Range – 150km/93.2 miles	

Skoda LT-35 Medium Tank

Developed in 1934 and in production the following year, the Skoda LT-35 was the main battle tank of the Czech Army during the years immediately preceding the German invasion, and was also sold to Romania. It had riveted armour, and its main 37mm/1.46in gun was developed from the Skoda anti-tank gun of the same calibre, renowned for its accuracy. There were also two 7.92mm/0.312in machine-guns, one mounted coaxially. Although generally reliable, it suffered from a few mechanical faults in its early life, which somewhat sullied its reputation. However, the proof of this vehicle's pedigree is that the Germans took over 200 into service, although they modified it and renamed it the PzKpfw 35(t).

They also continued to have it produced within Axis Europe until 1941, and it saw action in various theatres including Poland 1939, France 1940 and on the central Russian front up to 1941, where it reached the end of its front-line life and was thereafter relegated to secondary roles such as artillery tractor – *Artillerie Schlepper* 35(t).

BELOW: **The LT-35 in German service – now known as the PzKpfw 35(t).**

ABOVE: **This small Czech tank, the LT-35, was taken into service by the Germans and designated as the PzKpfw 35(t). Over 200 were acquired from the Czechs in March 1939. This model is at the Aberdeen Proving Ground in the USA.** LEFT: **The LT-35 was also in service with Romania and Slovakia pre-war, who purchased them in 1936–37 from the Czechs, as well as being in Czech service, as here.**

Skoda LT-35 Medium Tank

Entered service: 1935
Crew: 4
Weight: 10,670kg/10.5 tons
Dimensions: Length – 4.9m/16ft 1in
　　　　Height (over turret hatch) – 2.21m/7ft 3in
　　　　Width – 2.16m/7ft 1in
Armament: Main – 37mm/1.46in
　　　　Secondary – 2 x 7.92mm/0.312in machine-guns
Armour: Maximum – 25mm/0.98in
Powerplant: Skoda T11 6-cylinder petrol, 89.5kW/120bhp
Performance: Speed – 35kph/22mph
　　　　Range – 190km/118 miles

Skoda LT-38 Medium Tank

The Skoda LT-38 follows a similar history to that of the Skoda LT-35, although its quality was far superior to its predecessor, being reliable, hard-wearing and easy to maintain. Originally built for the export market by CKD, it was chosen by the Czech Army as the successor to the Skoda LT-35, with both companies co-producing the vehicle. The war then intervened, and the Germans were quick to pick up on the Skoda LT-38's value and pressed it into service for themselves.

By removing some of its ammunition and making room for a loader, they freed the vehicle's commander from that role and thereby still further improved the tank's overall performance. Later models had extra riveted armour, and following the vehicle's withdrawal from active service in 1942, the excellent chassis was used as the basis for both the Marder and Hetzer tank destroyers, as well as many others, one even mounting an 8.8cm/ 3.46in PaK43 (prototype only).

TOP: **Best of the Czech tanks "acquired" by the Germans was the LT-38 (CKD Praga TNHP) which had been chosen to equip the Czech Army after the CKD Skoda LT-35.** ABOVE: **The LT-38 chassis was also used by the Germans as the basis for a variety of SP anti-tank guns – such as this 7.5cm/2.95in PaK39 L/48 known as Hetzer.** BELOW LEFT: **Two of the excellent LT-38 Czech-built tanks, commandeered by the Germans and used to equip four of their panzer divisions (together with the LT-35).**

Skoda LT-38 Medium Tank

Entered service: 1938
Crew: 4
Weight: 9,400kg/9.25 tons
Dimensions: Length – 4.60m/15ft 1in
    Height (over turret hatch) – 2.4m/7ft 10in
    Width – 2.11m/6ft 11in
Armament: Main – 37mm/1.46in or 37mm/1.46in
    KwK L/40 or 37mm/1.46in L/45 gun
    Secondary – 2 x 7.92mm/0.312in machine-guns
Armour: Maximum – 25mm/0.98in
Powerplant: Praga EPA 16-cylinder petrol,
    93kW/125bhp
Performance: Speed – 42kph/26.1mph
    Range – 250km/155.3 miles

SOMUA S-35 Medium Tank

The SOMUA (its name an acronym of its producers: *Societe d'Outillage Mecanique d'Usinage d'Artillerie*) was the first tank with an all-cast construction of both hull and turret (which also had an electrically powered traverse), the thick armour providing excellent protection.

In the turret, the main armament was a long-barrelled high-velocity 47mm/1.85in gun, with a coaxial machine-gun alongside. The 141.7kW/190hp engine gave the S-35 a top speed of 40kph/25mph and a radius of action of 257km/160 miles. Fast and reliable, it was actually better armed and better armoured than its German opponents in 1940, but they were

not available in sufficient numbers, and, given the speed of the German attack, could not have made that much difference to the immediate outcome of events.

Some 500 of these 20-ton tanks were built and, like all contemporary French armour, were captured in large numbers

by the Germans and then pressed into their own service. As the tide of World War II turned, some came back once again into (Free) French hands, and they remained in service with the French Army for a considerable time after the end of the conflict.

ABOVE AND BELOW: **This French tank was probably one of the best medium tanks of the 1930s, with its 47mm/1.85in gun and 40mm/1.58in thick armour. This one belongs to the Bovington Tank Museum.** ABOVE LEFT: **SOMUA S-35s like these fought in France in the 1940s, and captured models were used by both the Germans and Italians.**

SOMUA S-35 Medium Tank

Entered service: 1935
Crew: 3
Weight: 19,500kg/19.2 tons
Dimensions: Length – 5.38m/17ft 7.8in
　　　　Height (over turret hatch) – 2.62m/8ft 7in
　　　　Width – 2.12m/6ft 11.5in
Armament: Main – 47mm/1.85in gun
　　　　Secondary – 7.5mm/0.295in machine-gun
Armour: Maximum – 40mm/1.58in
Powerplant: V8 petrol, 141.7kW/190hp
Performance: Speed – 40.7kph/25.3mph
　　　　Range – 257km/160 miles

Strv M/21 Light Tank

Entered service: 1920
Crew: 4
Weight: 9,850kg/9.7 tons
Dimensions: Length – 5.71m/18ft 9in
  Height (over turret hatch) – 2.51m/8ft 3in
  Width – 2.06m/6ft 9in
Armament: Main – 6.5mm/0.256in machine-gun
Armour: Maximum – 14mm/0.55in
Powerplant: Daimler 4-cylinder petrol,
  41.8kW/55hp
Performance: Speed – 16kph/9.9mph
  Range – 150km/93.2miles

Strv M/21 and M/29 Light Tanks

Despite the fact that Sweden has not taken part in any war since the beginning of the 20th century, they have still kept pace with the development of armoured fighting vehicles, having begun in 1921 with a copy of the German *Leichte Kampfwagen*. This is hardly surprising, as it was designed by Joseph Vollmer, the German engineer who designed and built the LK I and LK II and moved to Sweden after World War I. The Strv (*Stridsvagn* – "tank") M/21 was built in 1921 and was powered by a 4-cylinder 41.8kW/55hp Daimler engine. It had a crew of four and was armed with a single 6.5mm/0.256in machine-gun. The

Strv M/29, produced in 1929, underwent a rebuild, having a more powerful Scania-Vabis 6-cylinder 59.7kW/80hp engine and heavier armour fitted, though the armament remained the same.

Strv M/31 Light Tank

By the late 1920s the Swedes had, with German assistance, established their own tank factory, the AB Landsverk Company at Landskrons. Their first design, which appeared in 1931, was a wheeled and tracked vehicle, with duplicate running gear. Two years later they produced the Strv M/31, which had a design that was well ahead of other nations, the turret and hull both being of welded construction.

The main armament of this four-man tank was a rapid-fire high-velocity 37mm/1.46in gun housed in a two-man turret with a coaxial machine-gun. The driver operated a second machine-gun.

It had a German Bussing V6 petrol engine, two-way radio communications, high-quality optical, sighting and vision devices.

Strv M/31 Light Tank

Entered service: 1931
Crew: 4
Weight: 11,500kg/11.3 tons
Dimensions: Length – 5.18m/17ft
  Height (over turret hatch) – 2.23m/7ft 4in
  Width – 2.13m/7ft
Armament: Main – 37mm/1.46in gun
  Secondary – 2 x 6.5mm/0.256in machine-guns
Armour: Maximum – 9mm/0.35in
Powerplant: Bussing V6, petrol, 104.4kW/140hp
Performance: Speed – 40kph/24.9mph
  Range – 200km/124.3 miles

Strv M/40, M/41 and M/42 Light Tanks

The Strvs of the early 1940s were another series of well designed light tanks from the Swedish AB Landsverk Company that can trace their ancestry back to the original Czech design. The Strv M/40 was the first to be produced in quantity. It was powered by a Scania-Vabis 105.9kW/142hp 6-cylinder engine, giving it a speed of just under 48.3kph/30mph, had a crew of three, and was armed with a 37mm/1.46in gun with two coaxial 8mm/0.315in machine-guns.

The Strv M/41, though similarly armed, had slightly thicker armour than its predecessor. To cope with the inevitable increase in weight, it was powered by an uprated Scania-Vabis 108kW/145hp engine.

The M/41 continued in service with the Swedish Army until the 1950s, when many were modified for use as armoured personnel carriers. The Strv M/42 was the first Swedish tank to mount a 75mm/2.95in main gun. Entering service in 1944, it weighed 22,353kg/22 tons and had a four-man crew. In the late 1950s the M/42 was rebuilt as the Strv 74, with a more powerful gun and thicker armour.

ABOVE: **Built to the basic design of the L/60 Light Tank, the M/40 L was the first Swedish tank to reach quantity production. This model is held at the Tank Museum, Bovington Camp.** LEFT: **The Strv M/42. This extremely modern-looking tank was designed by the Swedes in 1941–42. It was the first Swedish tank to be armed with a 75mm/2.95in gun. In 1958–60 it was modernized and rebuilt as the Strv 74.**

Strv M/41 Light Tank

Entered service: 1942
Crew: 3
Weight: 10,500kg/10.3 tons
Dimensions: Length – 4.57m/15ft
　　　　　Height (over turret hatch) – 2.37m/7ft 9in
　　　　　Width – 2.13m/7ft
Armament: Main – 37mm/1.46in gun
　　　　　Secondary – 2 x 6.5mm/0.256 machine-guns
Armour: Maximum – 25mm/0.98in
Powerplant: Scania-Vabis 6-cylinder petrol, 108kW/145hp
Performance: Speed – 45kph/28mph
　　　　　Range – 200km/124.3 miles

LEFT: **In the early 1920s the Americans built a number of prototype medium tanks – the M1921, the M1922 and the T1 of 1925. The latest model of the 1925 series was the T1E2, seen here, which had a crew of four and mounted a 57mm/2.24in gun. However, none of these models were put into production due to the demise of the Tank Corps and the upper weight limit of 15,240kg/ 15 tons being applied. The T1E2 weighed 22,352kg/22 tons and had a speed of 22.53kph/14mph, so it was well over the upper weight limit of 15,240kg/15 tons imposed by the War Department.**

T1 and T2 Medium Tanks

Three prototype medium tanks were built by the USA in the early 1920s: the Medium A of 1921; the Medium A2 of 1922; and the T1 of 1925. The main armament of the T1 was either a 57mm/ 2.24in gun or a 75mm/2.95in gun. It also had two 7.62mm/0.3in machine-guns.

Further development continued, with the next medium tank – designated the T2 – appearing in 1930. This had a semi-automatic 47mm/1.85in gun and a 12.7mm/0.5in machine-gun in the turret, plus a 37mm/1.46in and a 7.62mm/0.3in machine-gun in the right front of the hull. This dual mounting was later replaced by a single 7.62mm/ 0.3in machine-gun.

The T1 had weighed nearly 20 tons. The T2, however, had to conform to the new weight limit of 15 tons, as laid down by the US War Department. It weighed just 14 tons combat-loaded and was powered by a 252kW/338hp Liberty engine. The armament included a semi-automatic 57mm/2.24in main gun with a coaxial 12.7mm/0.5in Browning machine-gun plus two 7.62mm/0.3in

machine-guns in sponsons. It had good cross-country performance and externally looked quite similar to the British Vickers Medium Mark II.

Three more prototypes were built – T3, T3E2 and T4 – all of which were based upon the designs of Walter Christie. They were all fast and reliable, but only lightly armoured, and none ever saw action.

T1 Medium Tank

Entered service: 1925
Crew: 4
Weight: 19,912kg/19.6 tons
Dimensions: Length – 6.55m/21ft 6in
  Height (over turret hatch) – 2.88m/9ft 5.5in
  Width – 2.44m/8ft
Armament: Main – Either 57mm/2.24in
  or 75mm/2.95in gun
  Secondary – 2 x 7.62mm/0.3in machine-guns
Armour: Maximum – 9.5mm/0.37in
Powerplant: Liberty V12 petrol, 252kW/338hp
Performance: Speed – 22.5kph/14mph
  Range – 56km/35 miles

ABOVE: **Next in line was the T2 Medium Tank, which bore a strong resemblance to the British Vickers Medium. It weighed only 14,225kg/14 tons, having been deliberately designed to conform with the US War Department's 15,240kg/15-ton weight limit.**

145

LEFT: **Yet another foreign tank based upon the British export Vickers 6 Ton Tank was the Soviet T-26 Light Tank series. This one (in Finnish colours) is the T-26B, which mounted a 37mm/1.46in high velocity gun.**

T-26-S Light Tank	
Entered service: 1935	
Crew: 3	
Weight: 10,460kg/10.3 tons	
Dimensions: Length – 4.8m/15ft 9in	
Height (over turret hatch) – 2.33m/7ft 7.5in	
Width – 2.39m/7ft 10in	
Armament: Main – 45mm/1.77in L/46 gun	
Secondary – 2 or 3 x 7.62mm/0.3in	
machine-guns	
Armour: Maximum – 25mm/0.98in	
Powerplant: GAZ t26 8-cylinder petrol, 67.9kW/91hp	
Performance: Speed – 28kph/17.4mph	
Range – 200km/124.3 miles	

T-26 Light Tank

The T-26 was a version of the Vickers 6 Ton Light Tank built under licence using an all-riveted construction and either a single or twin turrets mounting 7.62mm/0.3in machine-guns. Early versions were exact copies of the original Vickers design, apart from a progression of armament changes ranging from a 12.7mm/0.5in machine-gun to a 27mm/1.06in gun, and then a 37mm/1.46in long-barrelled gun in the right-hand turret. From 1933 onwards, production of the twin turret version ceased, and instead a single round turret version (T-26/B-1) was introduced, mounting firstly a 37mm/1.46in, then later a 47mm/1.85in main gun.

The early models in the series weighed in the region of 8,636kg/8.5 tons, had a crew of three, a top speed of 35.4kph/22mph and saw action in Spain during the Civil War, against the Japanese in Manchuria in 1939 and in the Russo-Finnish War of 1939–40. Disappointing reports from the first two of these wars prompted a redesign with thicker, better-sloped armour, a lower silhouette and a new semi-conical turret. Known as the T-26S and made of welded construction throughout, it weighed 10,460kg/10.3 tons and mounted a 45mm/1.77in main gun plus two 7.62mm/0.3in machine-guns.

T-28 Medium Tank

The T-28 weighed 28,509kg/28 tons, had a 76.2mm/3in gun in the main turret and two separate machine-guns in subsidiary turrets with a crew of six and was powered by a 373kW/500hp engine, allowing a top speed of 37kph/23mph. The T-28A was an improved production model with thicker front armour (30mm/1.18in), while most of the next model, the T-28B, were armed with the longer, more powerful, 76.2mm/3in L/26 gun, which also had a turret basket and better vision for the driver. The final model was the T-28C, which had thicker armour – up to 80mm/3.15in on the front of the tank and high armour screens around the turret which mounted a longer L/26 gun. The T-28C was first used against the *Panzerwaffe* in 1941.

T-28 Medium Tank	
Entered service: 1933	
Crew: 6	
Weight: 28,509kg/28 tons	
Dimensions: Length – 7.44m/24ft 5in	
Height (over turret hatch) – 2.82m/9ft 3in	
Width – 2.81 m/9ft 2.5in	
Armament: Main – 76mm/3in gun	
Secondary – 3 x 7.62mm/0.3in machine-guns	
Armour: Maximum – 30mm/1.18in	
Powerplant: M17 V12 petrol, 373kW/500hp	
Performance: Speed – 37kph/23mph	
Range – 190km/118.1 miles	

LEFT: **Another multi-turreted tank to appear in the Red Army was the Soviet T-28 (note that the machine-guns are missing out of the front auxiliary turrets).**

T-37 Amphibious Light Tank

The T-37 was based on the Carden Loyd amphibious tank, again bought from the British. However, it used a GAZ AA engine and an improved suspension derived from that of the French AMR Light Tank and floated with aid of flotation pontoons. It weighed 3,200kg/3.15 tons, had a crew of two and was armed with a single 7.62mm/0.3in machine-gun in its small cylindrical turret located on the right-hand side of the vehicle. Some T-37s had an all-welded turret like that used on the T-35 or T-28 instead of the usual type.

Finally, towards the end of the production run in 1936, the hull was redesigned, most noticeably in the driver's area, and the flotation pontoons on the side of the hull were dispensed with. A total of approximately 1,200 T-37s were manufactured between 1933 and 1936.

T-37 Amphibious Light Tank

Entered service: 1933
Crew: 2
Weight: 3,200kg/3.15 tons
Dimensions: Length – 3.75m/12ft 3.5in
  Height (over turret hatch) – 1.82m/5ft 11.5in
  Width – 2.1m/6ft 10.5in
Armament: Main – 7.62mm/0.3in machine-gun
Armour: Maximum – 4mm/0.157in
Powerplant: GAZ AA 4-cylinder, 48.5kW/65hp
Performance: Speed – 56.3kph/35mph
  Range – 185km/115 miles

LEFT: **T-37 Amphibious Light Tank. The Russians developed these small, light, amphibious tanks after purchasing a number of Carden-Loyd tankettes. They were designed purely for reconnaissance.**

T-40 Amphibious Light Tank

The T-40 was built as a replacement for the T-37. Main armament was still one machine-gun like its predecessor (although of a larger calibre), but the T-40 anticipated the later T-30 series in having flotation tanks built into its hull and in being powered in the water by a single, four-bladed propeller.

The first version had a squared-off blunt nose, but later models were more streamlined. There was also an attempt to redress the T-37's flaw – its thin armour. However, an increase in armour thickness was at the expense of the vehicle's amphibious capability – and so development soon left the T-40 behind.

T-40 Amphibious Light Tank

Entered service: 1941
Crew: 2
Weight: 5,900kg/5.8 tons
Dimensions: Length – 4.11/13ft 6in
  Height (over turret hatch) – 1.95m/6ft 5in
  Width – 2.33m/7ft 7.5in
Armament: Main – 12.7mm/0.5in machine-gun
Armour: Maximum – 14mm/0.55in
Powerplant: GAZ 202 6-cylinder petrol, 336kW/450hp
Performance: Speed – 65kph/40.4mph
  Range – 320km/198.8 miles

LEFT: **The T-40 amphibian was a replacement for the T-37 and other earlier models. The small 5,900kg/5.8-ton tank had a 12.7mm/0.5in machine-gun and a crew of two. The later T-40S had thicker armour, but had its rear propeller removed so it was non-amphibious. The photograph shows a T-40A, which had a streamlined, pointed nose and a folding trim vane.**

T-34/76A Medium Tank

One of the most unpleasant surprises experienced by the Germans in Russia came some five months after the launching of Operation "Barbarossa" in the shape of a new tank which inflicted heavy losses upon the PzKpfw IIIs and IVs. General Guderian was so impressed with the new Russian tank that he thought the quickest way for the Germans to deal with the situation would be to copy it! It was, of course, the T-34, one of the most important single elements in the eventual Russian victory.

Using a Christie-type suspension and mounting a 76.2mm/3in gun, the 31,390kg/30.9-ton tank had a crew of four and a top speed of 40kph/25mph. Well-armoured, robust and devoid of any frills, it was easily mass-produced – another vital factor in its favour. The next in the series, the T-34/76D, had a new hexagonal turret, with no overhang as on the previous models. This did away with the "bullet trap" which the overhang had created, and also made it more difficult for enemy soldiers who had climbed on to

the back to wedge Teller mines under the rear of the turret overhang. The T-34/76 was a critical tank at a critical time, and it helped the USSR stem and then turn the tide of World War II in their favour.

ABOVE: Undoubtedly one of the best tanks of World War II was the Soviet T-34/76 Medium Tank, based upon the earlier T-32. It became the main Russian medium tank of the war. BELOW LEFT: These T-34/76Ds are advancing through the forests of Byelorussia. Note the entirely new hexagonal turret on this much improved production model.

T-34/76A Medium Tank	
Entered service: 1940	
Crew: 4	
Weight: 31,390kg/30.9 tons	
Dimensions:	Length – 6.09m/20ft
	Height (over turret hatch) – 2.57m/8ft 5in
	Width – 2.88m/9ft 5.5in
Armament:	Main – 76.2mm/3in L41 gun
	Secondary – 2 x 7.62mm/0.3in machine-guns
Armour:	Maximum – 65mm/2.56in
Powerplant:	V234 V12 diesel, developing 373kW/500hp
Performance:	Speed – 40kph/25mph
	Range – 430km/267.2 miles

T-34/85 Medium Tank

Towards the end of 1943 the T-34 was made even more lethal by the fitting of a new 85mm/3.35in gun in an enlarged turret. The new gun had an effective range of 1,000m/3,281ft and could penetrate the frontal armour of both the Tiger and Panther at that range – or so the Russians claimed. The German MBTs probably had the edge over their Soviet counterparts, but in the end the Russian tanks were available in far larger numbers, and this would be the decisive factor – quantity to overwhelm all opposition.

ABOVE: **The T-34/85 was a much-improved model, giving it better firepower so as to match later German tanks. This one was photographed at Bovington.** ABOVE RIGHT: **The up-gunned version of the T-34 mounted the 85mm/3.35in gun in an enlarged turret. It is seen here at the Aberdeen Proving Ground in the USA.**

BELOW LEFT AND RIGHT: **Internal views of the T-34/85 at the Tank Museum. The first shows the driver's seat, instruments and one of his steering levers. The other shows the breech end of the main armament.**

T-34/85 Medium Tank

Entered service: 1944
Crew: 5
Weight: 32,000kg/31.5 tons
Dimensions: Length – 8.15m/26ft 9in
Height (over turret hatch) – 2.74m/9ft
Width – 2.99m/9ft 9.5in
Armament: Main – 85mm/3.35in ZiS S53 gun
Secondary – 2 x 7.62mm/0.3in machine-guns
Armour: Maximum – 90mm/3.54in
Powerplant: V234 12-cylinder diesel, 373kW/500hp
Performance: Speed – 55kph/34.2mph
Range – 300km/186.4 miles

Turan I and II Medium Tanks

The first tanks in Hungary were Italian CV33 tankette imports in the 1930s. When World War II broke out, the government then attempted to purchase tanks from Czechoslovakia, but with their total production taken up by Germany, the Czechs could not oblige. Instead, Hungary obtained the rights to one of the latest Skoda tanks – the T-21 – which it then modified to suit its own military and industrial requirements. Powered by a Hungarian 8-cylinder 194kW/260hp engine, equipped with leaf spring suspension and with the original two-man turret replaced with a three-man version equipped with radio communications, the Turan I mounted a Skoda 40mm/1.58in main gun and two 8mm/0.315in machine-guns – one of them coaxial and one in the hull – and had a crew of five. The Turan II had an upgraded 75mm/2.95in main gun mounted in a modified turret, but was otherwise the same as its predecessor.

Turan II Medium Tank

Entered service: 1943
Crew: 5
Weight: 18,500kg/18.2 tons
Dimensions: Length – 5.69m/18ft 8in
   Height (over turret hatch) – 2.33m/7ft 7.5in
   Width – 2.54m/8ft 4in
Armament: Main – 75mm/2.95in gun
   Secondary – 2 x 8mm/0.315in machine-guns
Armour: Maximum – 50mm/1.97in
Powerplant: Weiss V8 petrol, 194kW/260hp
Performance: Speed – 47kph/29.2mph
   Range – 165km/102.5 miles

Type 3 Ka-Chi Amphibious Tank

The Japanese had long been interested in amphibious armoured vehicles for use by their Imperial Navy. Based upon the Chi-He design, the Ka-Chi was of an all-welded construction and had two detachable floats, one at the bow and one at the stern, that gave the tank its buoyancy while in the water and once ashore could be discarded. It was driven through the water by means of two propellers

working off the main engine, while the commander steered via twin rudders which he operated from his turret. Powered by a 179kW/240hp V12 diesel engine and operated by a crew of seven, the Ka-Chi mounted a 47mm/1.85in main gun along with two 7.7mm/0.303in machine-guns – one of them mounted coaxially in a turret which was surmounted by a cylindrical chimney, providing an escape hatch for the crew.

Type 3 Ka-Chi Amphibious Tank

Entered service: 1942
Crew: 7
Weight: 28,700kg/28.3 tons
Dimensions: Length – 10.3m/33ft 9.5in
 Height (over turret hatch) – 3.82m/12ft 6.5in
 Width – 3m/9ft 10in
Armament: Main – 47mm/1.85in gun
 Secondary – 2 x 7.7mm/0.303in machine-guns
Armour: Maximum – mm/1.97in
Powerplant: Mitsubishi 100 V12 diesel, 179kW/240hp
Performance: Speed – 32kph/19.9mph
 Range – 319km/198.2 miles

LEFT: The Type 3 Ka-Chi Amphibious Tank, seen here out of the water after its capture by the Americans. Weighing 28,700kg/28.3 tons, mainly due to its large, detachable pontoons, it was developed by the Japanese Navy after the Army lost interest in amphibians. Note the submarine-type escape hatch on the top of the turret.

Type 5 To-Ku Amphibious Tank

Largest of the Japanese amphibious tanks was the Type 5 To-Ku, the increase in size enabling an increase in firepower. It mounted a 47mm/1.85in main gun and a machine-gun in the front

of its hull with a further 25mm/0.98in naval cannon and a coaxial machine-gun in its turret. However, the vehicle never reached full production before the end of World War II.

Type 5 To-Ku Amphibious Tank

Entered service: 1945
Crew: 7
Weight: 29,465kgkg/29 tons
Dimensions: Length – 10.81m/35ft 5.5in
 Height (over turret hatch) – 3.00m/9ft 10in
 Width – 3.38m/11ft 1 in
Armament: Main – 47mm/1.85in gun and 25mm/0.98in cannon
 Secondary – 2 x 7.7mm/0.303in machine-guns
Armour: Maximum – 50mm/1.97in
Powerplant: Type 100 V12 diesel, 179kW/240hp
Performance: Speed – 32kph/20mph
 Range – 319km/198 miles

LEFT: The Type 5 To-Ku Amphibious Tank was the largest of the Japanese amphibious tanks and mounted a 47mm/1.85in gun and a machine-gun in its front hull, while in the turret was a naval 25mm/0.98in cannon and another machine-gun. It weighed 29,465kg/29 tons with its pontoons. On this model the escape tower had been done away with.

Type 95 Ha-Go Light Tank

Speedy and reliable, the Ha-Go was one of the best tanks to be built by the Japanese, and it saw action in China and then throughout the Far East in World War II. It was powered by an advanced 6-cylinder 89.5kW/120hp diesel engine giving it a speed of 45kph/28mph, steered by the clutch and brake method with front drive sprockets and had a sliding transmission allowing four forward and one reverse gear. Its small turret was offset to the left and

mounted a 37mm/1.46in gun as its main armament, with another coaxial 7.7mm/0.303in machine-gun alongside. The somewhat bulbous superstructure protruded out over the tracks with an extra prominence for the bow 7.7mm/0.303in machine-gun.

The tank had a crew of three and suffered from the disadvantage of having the bow machine-gunner seated next to the driver in the hull leaving the commander to load, aim and fire the

ABOVE LEFT: **Undoubtedly the most-used small Japanese tank of the war. The Type 95 Ha-Go saw action in China and then throughout the Far East.** ABOVE: **An excellent photograph of a Japanese tank commander standing proudly in front of his three-man Ha-Go.** BELOW LEFT: **The main armament of the Ha-Go was a 37mm/1.46in gun, and it also had two machine-guns. With a crew of three, it had a top speed of 45kph/28mph.**

turret guns by himself. There was also an amphibious version based on the Ha-Go that was known as the Type 2 Ka-Mi and intended for Japanese Navy use. Some 1,350 Ha-Go were built between 1935–43.

Type 95 Ha-Go Light Tank	
Entered service: 1935	
Crew: 3	
Weight: 7,400kg/7.28 tons	
Dimensions: Length – 4.38m/14ft 4.5in	
Height (over turret hatch) – 2.18m/7ft 2in	
Width – 2.06m/6ft 9in	
Armament: Main – 37mm/1.46in gun	
Secondary – 2 x 7.7mm/0.303in machine-guns	
Armour: Maximum – 12mm/0.47in	
Powerplant: Mitsubishi NVD 6-cylinder diesel, 89.5kW/120hp	
Performance: Speed – 45kph/28mph	
Range – 242km/150.4 miles	

LEFT: **The Type 89 Ot-Su Medium Tank was developed from the British Vickers Medium. Its main armament was a 57mm/2.24in gun.**

Type 89B Ot-Su Medium Tank

Entered service: 1936 (designed in 1929)
Crew: 4
Weight: 13,000kg/12.8 tons
Dimensions: Length – 5.73m/18ft 9.5in
  Height (over turret hatch) – 2.56m/8ft 5in
  Width – 2.13m/7ft
Armament: Main – 57mm/2.24in gun
  Secondary – 2 x 6.5mm/0.256in machine-guns
Armour: Maximum – 17mm/0.67in
Powerplant: Mitsubishi 6-cylinder diesel, 89.5kW/120hp
Performance: Speed – 26kph/16.2mph
  Range – 170km/105.6 miles

Type 89B Ot-Su Medium Tank

Having obtained a Vickers Medium C from Britain, the Japanese Osaka Arsenal produced a modified version in the Type 89 Light Tank of just under 10,160kg/10 tons, mounting a 57mm/2.24in main gun and two machine-guns. They were so delighted with this design that they used it as the basis for a heavier medium tank (Type 89) which was standardized in 1929. From 1936, a diesel version of this tank, the Type 89B, was developed by Mitsubishi and remained in service during most of World War II.

There were two versions; the first had a one-piece front plate, the driver being located on the left. Main armament was a Type 90 57mm/2.24in gun and there was a 6.5mm/0.256in machine-gun at the rear of the turret, plus another one on the right of the front plate. The second model had the driver's position and machine-gun reversed, while the front plate was all in one piece. The skirting plates had also been redesigned, with four return rollers in place of the five girder-mounted return rollers of the previous model, while the armament remained the same.

Like most Japanese tanks, the Ot-Su fared badly against Allied armour such as the M4 Sherman because they were undergunned and underarmoured by comparison, due to the Japanese disinterest in tanks for most of the war.

Type 97 Chi-Ha Medium Tank

Probably the most successful of all Japanese tank designs, the Chi-Ha saw service throughout World War II, having been selected for mass production in 1937. However, its medium status could really only be considered in Japanese tank production, for in combat it was no match for the Sherman or other Allied medium tanks. It was essentially a scaled-up version of the Type 95 Ha-Go Light Tank fitted with a two-man turret and armed with a 57mm/2.24in short-barrelled main gun and two machine-guns, one of which was mounted at the turret rear. With a crew of four, this tank weighed nearly 15 tons, had a helical suspension system with clutch and brake steering, and was powered by a 126.8kW/170hp air-cooled diesel engine with a top speed of 39kph/24mph. As the war progressed and the Japanese came to realize just how under-developed their AFVs were when compared with the opposition, the demand grew for more powerful equipment. A later development (1942) was the Shinhoto Chi-Ha ("New Turret" Chi-Ha), an interim model Type 97 Chi-Ha fitted with a modified turret which mounted a long-barrelled, high-velocity 47mm/1.85in main gun.

LEFT: **This Chi-Ha was photographed at the Aberdeen Proving Ground in the USA. Unfortunately, most of their exhibits are outdoors, so they inevitably deteriorate.**

Type 97 Chi-Ha Medium Tank

Entered service: 1937
Crew: 4
Weight: 15,000kg/14.8 tons
Dimensions: Length – 5.5m/18ft 0.5in
  Height (over turret hatch) – 2.23m/7ft 4in
  Width – 2.33m/7ft 7.5in
Armament: Main – 57mm/2.24in gun
  Secondary – 2 x 7.7mm/0.303 machine-guns
Armour: Maximum – 25mm/0.98in
Powerplant: Mitsubishi 97 V12 diesel, 126.8kW/170hp
Performance: Speed – 39kph/24.2mph
  Range – 200km/124.3 miles

Vickers Commercial Dutchman Light Tank

Between the wars, Vickers Armstrong, having absorbed Carden-Loyd, became a major player in the international arms industry, building prototypes and exporting AFVs all over the world. The Commercial Dutchman was one such venture, sold to the Dutch East Indies and China. Some were still in the UK when war broke out and were pressed into service, although used only for training. This vehicle was to all intents and purposes mechanically the same as the Vickers Light Mark IV, the only major difference being its hexagonally shaped turret.

ABOVE: **A modern photograph of the Bovington Tank Museum's "Dutchman" in its striking pre-war camouflage. Mechanically similar to the Vickers Mark IV Light Tank, it was powered by a Meadows 65.6kW/88bhp engine.**

BELOW: **Sharing this colourful stand with the Vickers 6 Ton at the Bovington Tank Museum is the other Vickers export model, the Light Tank, Model 1936, also known as the "Dutchman" (it was sold to China and to the Dutch East Indies).**

Vickers Commercial Dutchman Light Tank

Entered service: 1936
Crew: 2
Weight: 3,860kg/3.8 tons
Dimensions: Length – 3.63m/11ft 11in
    Height (over turret hatch) – 2m/6ft 7in
    Width – 1.8m/5ft 11in
Armament: Main – Vickers 7.7mm/0.303in MG
Armour: Maximum – 10mm/0.39in
Powerplant: Meadows 6-cylinder, 65.6kW/88bhp
Performance: Speed – 65kph/40mph
    Range – 209.2km/130 miles

Vickers 6 Ton Tank

Although the British Army was not interested in purchasing the Vickers 6 Ton Tank, it became one of the bestsellers of its day – being exported to many countries, including the USSR, Poland, Bulgaria, Greece, Finland, Portugal, Bolivia, Thailand and China. The first versions had twin turrets with Vickers 7.7mm/0.303in machine-guns, and the later ones a 3pdr (47mm/1.85in) main gun and coaxial machine-gun in a single turret. The Vickers 6 Ton had a crew of three and featured some new features, including a "Laryngophone" system for internal communication, new improved suspension and had a fitted fireproof partition separating the engine from the fighting compartment. For some countries it was an influential design that

was copied (such as the Polish 7TP and Russian T-26), being mechanically straightforward and, for its size, well-armoured with good firepower.

Although rejected by the British, they established a formidable combat record in foreign service. For example, they saw action for the first time in the Gran Chaco War, when Bolivian 6 Tonners fought in the battle for Nanawa in August 1933. Later, in both the Spanish Civil War and the Winter War between Russia and Finland, 6 Tonners fought each other. It was also one of the principal tanks of the Polish armoured corps, so fought against the German invasion in 1939. The Chinese used theirs against the Japanese in Manchuria, and the Thais did the same in the 1940–41 war against Indo-China.

ABOVE: **Although it was called the Vickers 6 Ton Tank, it actually weighed 7,115kg/7 tons! It was sold (and copied) all over the world, but was not initially purchased by the British Army. They did eventually take over some of the undelivered overseas orders and used them for training purposes when World War II began in 1939.**

Vickers 6 Ton Tank	

Entered service: 1928
Crew: 3
Weight: 7,115kg/7 tons
Dimensions: Length – 4.57m/15ft
  Height (over turret hatch) – 2.08m/6ft 10in
  Width – 2.42m/7ft 11in
Armament: Main – 2 x 7.7mm/0.303in
  machine-guns (later, 1 x 3pdr and 1 machine-gun)
Armour: Maximum – 13mm/0.51in
Powerplant: Armstrong-Siddeley 4-cylinder petrol,
  64.8kW/87hp
Performance: Speed 32kph/20mph
  Range – 200km/124 miles

A–Z of Modern Tanks

1945 to the Present Day

The Cold War and the limited wars in such places as the Far and Middle East have ensured the continuing need for tanks. In particular, there has been a requirement for Main Battle Tanks (MBTs) with improved, more powerful weapons, sophisticated gun control and viewing equipment, more effective protection, and better engines and running gear. MBTs have grown larger and heavier, yet are faster and more manoeuvrable, with tanks like the Abrams and Challenger being far superior to their World War II equivalents. Major changes have also occurred among tank builders. In the last war it was really only the USA, USSR, Germany and the UK that produced tanks. Now there are some 30 nations either building their own MBT, a "cloned" replica of a major producer's tank, or an upgraded version of an older model. China is now a major producer, as are, once again, Germany and France. Even smaller nations like Israel and Japan build excellent MBTs. With the advent of global terrorism, there has also been a shift in requirement away from MBTs towards more strategically mobile AFVs, but mounting larger weapon systems than in the past.

LEFT: **Vastly superior to Leopard 1, the Leopard 2 is currently one of the best Main Battle Tanks in service in the world.**

A41 Centurion Medium Tank

The A41 Centurion is undoubtedly one of the major British successes in tank design and production. The mock-up was ready in May 1944, but troop trials did not begin until May 1945 (due to a Government ruling banning development work on all projects that could not be in service by 1944), so it never saw action during World War II. Twenty pilot models were ordered mounting a 17pdr gun as their main weapon and with a mixture of Polsten cannon (in a ball-mount) or Besa machine-gun as secondary armament, the first ten only having Polstens. The Mark II (A41A) incorporated numerous improvements including a cast turret, commander's vision cupola and a combined gunner's periscope and coaxial Besa machine-gun. This became the first production model, known thereafter as the Centurion 2.

Over 4,400 Centurions in 12 different models were produced, the most plentiful being over 2,800 Centurion 3s. This version incorporated numerous major improvements, including the more efficient 484.7kW/650bhp Rolls-Royce Meteor engine, the Ordnance Quick-Firing 20pdr main gun together and new gun control equipment. It was the first British tank that could fire accurately on the move thanks to its gyroscopic gun control system, while the policy of not storing ammunition above the turret ring greatly increased its chances of survival by limiting ammunition fires. Many other modifications and improvements were constantly being added as the years went by, the most important being the fitting of the 105mm/4.13in rifled gun. Centurions saw action in Korea,

TOP: **An early Centurion Mark 3 on the test track at the Fighting Vehicle Research and Development Establishment, Chertsey. Originally armed with a 17pdr, then 20pdr and finally 105mm/4.13in gun, the Centurion was one of Britain's most successful post-war main battle tanks and sold in large numbers worldwide.** ABOVE: **Sweden made an initial order for 88 Mark 3s (known as the Stridsvagn 81). Later they would purchase more, including Centurion Mark 10s (known as Stridsvagn 102), as seen here.**

Vietnam and numerous other wars, having been purchased by many nations, perhaps most notably by the Israelis who had over 1,000 Centurions in service at one time. At the beginning of the 21st century this excellent AFV is still to be found in use with some countries.

RIGHT: Sweden purchased two Marks of Centurion in the late 1950s, renaming them Stridsvagn 101 and 102. This is an up-armoured version of the Stridsvagn 102. BELOW RIGHT: The Israeli Army was at one time the largest user of the Centurion, with over 1,000 in service. This one is on show at the IDF Tank Museum at Latrun. Initially the Centurion had a poor reputation until General Israel Tal, a man of wide technical expertise and character, took a hand and instilled the essential gunnery discipline into his crews which swiftly showed the gun's inherent accuracy. BOTTOM: A Centurion Beach Armoured Recovery Vehicle, whose primary role was to rescue drowned vehicles to the shoreline and to keep exits from landing craft clear during beach landings. They went on serving in the British Army long after other Centurions, one each being manned by the Royal Marines on HMS *Fearless* and HMS *Intrepid* (Landing Platform Dock Ships).

In addition to gun tanks, there are Centurion Armoured Recovery Vehicles (ARVs), specialized Beach ARVs, Assault Engineer – Armoured Vehicle Royal Engineers (AVRE) and armoured bridgelayers – Armoured Vehicle Launched Bridge (AVLB).

In 2004 there were four major countries with significant numbers of Centurion gun tanks/variants in service, although Israel has converted most of its 1,000 to other roles. Jordan had 293 (called *Tariq*), which are now being replaced by Challenger 1 Main Battle Tanks. Singapore had between 12 and 63, based in Brunei and Taiwan. South Africa had 224, which are known as *Olifant*.

A41 Centurion Medium Tank

Entered service: 1945
Crew: 4
Weight: 43,182kg/42.5 tons
Dimensions: Length – 7.47m/24ft 6in
Height (over turret hatch) – 3.02m/9ft 11in
Width – 3.40m/11ft 2in
Armament: Main – 17pdr (76mm/2.99in) gun
Secondary – 7.92mm/0.312in Besa machine-gun
Armour: Maximum – 101.6mm/4in
Powerplant: Meteor V12 petrol, 484.7kW/650hp
Performance: Speed – 35.4kph/22mph
Range – 193.1km/120 miles

M1A1/M1A2 Abrams Main Battle Tank

The M1A1/2 Abrams Main Battle Tank is the prime weapon of the US armoured forces, and is manufactured by General Dynamics Land Systems. The first M1 tank came into service in 1978, the M1A1 in 1985, and the M1A2 in 1986. Since then, system enhancement packages have kept this AFV as a state-of-the-art weapons system, and undoubtedly one of the most formidable tanks in the world.

Built using steel-encased depleted uranium armour to protect against modern HEAT (High-Explosive Anti-Tank) weapons, the M1A1's main weapon is the 120mm/4.72in M256 smoothbore gun (the original M1 had a 105mm/4.13in gun), developed by Rheinmetall GmbH of Germany, with a 7.62mm/ 0.3in M240 machine-gun mounted coaxially on its right. The commander also has a 12.7mm/0.5in Browning M2 machine-gun and the loader a 7.62mm/0.3in M240 machine-gun.

Needless to say, the tank is crammed full of the most advanced electronic equipment. The commander's station is equipped with an independent stabilized day and night vision

TOP: The XM1 tank programme was begun in 1971, and five years later Chrysler was awarded a three-year contract to produce 11 pilot vehicles and spares at the Detroit Arsenal Tank Plant. In 1982, Chrysler sold its tank building subsidiary to General Motors. First-production MBT was completed in February 1980. It is anticipated that in total (up to and including the M1A2 MBT upgrades), the US Army will order over 1,000 such M1 upgrades, while sales to other countries (e.g. 555 to Egypt) were agreed and delivered in 1998. This photograph of a basic M1 gives a good impression of its power, speed and protection. RIGHT: A column of Abrams returning from training. With a combat weight of 57,154kg/56.3 tons and a maximum road speed of 67.6kph/42mph, the Abrams is a formidable sight to meet anywhere.

LEFT: **Three of the four-man crew are visible in this photograph of an M1A1, two of the turret crew manning secondary armament (both 7.62mm/0.3in machine-guns), while the driver's excellent central position is evident.** BELOW: **Excellent internal view of the M1A1 turret, looking at the gunner's station and the rear of the breech.**

device with a 360-degree view, automatic sector scanning, automatic target cueing of the gunner's sight and back-up fire control. The gunner's specially modified seat also locks him in position so that even on the move his eyes are unwaveringly locked in his sight.

The powerplant was originally diesel for the M1/M1A1 models, but the M1A2 is fitted with a new gas turbine engine which is more powerful but uses more fuel. However, like all of the most modern tanks, the Abrams is built in a modular fashion, whereby new feature "suites" or packages can replace any previous one. In this way, any of the main features of the tank – turret, armament, and power pack – can be constantly refined and upgraded.

The Abrams combat effectiveness has been proved in the recent conflicts in the Gulf, where it dominated the battlefield completely. It has also been sold to Egypt, Saudi Arabia, Kuwait and Australia. Those M1A1s in service with the USMC are fitted with a Deep Water Fording Kit (DWFK).

BELOW: **Three Abrams use the concrete test slopes at the factory to show off their paces. The MBT can deal with a 60 per cent gradient, a side slope of 30 per cent and a 0.914m/3ft vertical obstacle.** BOTTOM: **Operation "Desert Storm".** **Abrams manoeuvre in the Iraqi desert during Operation "Desert Storm", when the US Army had 1,956 M1A1 Abrams MBTs deployed with units in Saudi Arabia.**

M1A1 Abrams MBT

Entered service: 1985
Crew: 4
Weight: 57,154kg/56.3 tons
Dimensions: Length – 9.77m/32ft 0.5in
  Height (over turret hatch) – 2.44m/8ft
  Width – 3.66m/12ft
Armament: Main – 120mm/4.72in M256
  smoothbore gun
  Secondary – 1 x 7.62mm/0.3in coaxial machine-gun,
  plus 1 x 12.7mm/0.5in machine-gun (commander)
  and 1 x 7.62mm/0.3in machine-gun (loader)
Armour: Thickness unknown, depleted uranium,
  steel
Powerplant: AGT 1500 gas turbine,
  1,118.6kW/1,500hp
Performance: Speed – 67.6kph/42mph
  Range – 465.1km/289 miles

AAI Rapid Deployment Force Light Tank

Manufactured by the AAI Corporation in conjunction with the US Army's Tank-Automotive Research and Development Command Armored Combat Vehicle Technology (ACVT), the AAI AFV was an air-portable light tank designed to boost the firepower of Rapid Deployment Forces (RDFs). This tank was a development of the HSTV(L) project and was part of the continuing attempt to perfect air-transportable firepower

that began during World War II and is especially relevant to the war scenarios of today. The vehicle shares its main armament with the earlier AAI HSTV(L) – the ARES 75mm/2.95in hypervelocity automatic gun, with a range of over 12.1km/7.5 miles at maximum elevation. This weapon was so advanced that the ARES Corporation was forbidden by the US Government to sell it to anyone other than NATO member countries. The

prohibition effectively killed off the AAI RDF, although the company did try to rescue the vehicle by bringing out a heavier model mounting a 76mm/2.99in main gun in a newly designed turret. However, there was no sales interest generated and in 1985 the project was shelved.

AAI RDF Light Tank	

Entered service: 1983 (prototypes only)
Crew: 3
Weight: 13,200kg/13 tons
Dimensions: Length – 7.34m/24ft
    Height (over turret hatch) – 2.24m/7ft 4in
    Width – 2.54m/8ft 4in
Armament: Main – 75mm/2.95in ARES
    or 76mm/2.99in M32 gun
    Secondary – 7.62mm/0.3in machine-gun
Armour: Maximum – Unrevealed
Powerplant: General Motors 6V53T 6-cylinder
    diesel, 224kW/300hp
Performance: Speed – 64kph/39.9mph
    Range – 500km/310.6 miles

ABOVE AND LEFT: **Two views of the AAI Corporation's Rapid Deployment Force Light Tank (RDF/LT) which mounted the ARES Corporation 75mm/2.95in hypervelocity automatic gun with a range of some 12.1km/7.5 miles! Based upon an experimental AFV, it had export problems due to its experimental main armament. This meant it could not be exported outside NATO, so a 76mm/2.99in gun was offered as an alternative.**

Alan Degman Main Battle Tank

First revealed in the late 1990s, the Croatian Degman MBT traces its origins back to the Yugoslavian M-84A, itself a Russian T-72 derivative manufactured in Yugoslavia since the previous decade. Specifications for this vehicle are sketchy, but it is based closely upon its predecessor and weighs approximately 40,600kg/40 tons, and is powered by a new diesel engine with automatic transmission delivering a top speed of around 60kph/37mph with a range of about 600km/370 miles. The turret is of a new Croatian design and manufacture, and includes the fitting of ERA (Explosive Reactive Armour) modules that are formed in distinctive

long bands and are also positioned on the glacis plate and sides skirts. (Most Eastern European and ex-Soviet satellite states have been influenced by the Russian predilection for ERA.)

It mounts the up-rated D-81 125mm/4.92in smoothbore main gun, served by an automatic loader, thereby allowing a crew of just three, along with two machine-guns – one coaxial 7.62mm/0.3in and the other of 12.7mm/0.5in for anti-aircraft and close-quarter defence.

The vehicle's fire control is based on the Omega system designed and manufactured in Slovenia, and its communications systems have been sourced from the UK.

Other enhancements include NBC (Nuclear, Biological and Chemical) protection, navigation and safety systems. The Degman is currently in service with the Croatian Army and has also been sold to Kuwait. There are also command, ARV (Armoured Recovery Vehicle) and engineering variants.

Alan Degman MBT

Entered service: 1999
Crew: 3
Weight: Approximately 40,600kg/40 tons
Dimensions: Close to T-72 specifications
Armament: Main – 125mm/4.92in D-81 gun
  Secondary – 1 x 7.62mm/0.3in and
  1 x 12.7mm/0.5in machine-guns
Armour: Unspecified
Powerplant: Unspecified diesel generating around 745.7kW/1,000hp
Performance: Speed – Approximately 60kph/37mph
  Range – Approximately 600km/370 miles

LEFT AND BELOW: **The RH Alan Degman Croatian MBT that was first seen in 1999 is an enhanced version of the Yugoslavian T-84A MBT, which in turn was based on the Russian T-72 MBT. Although sometimes called the M95, it is very similar to the M-84/M-84A and is armed with a 125mm/4.92in smoothbore gun with an automatic loader.**

Alvis Scimitar Combat Vehicle Reconnaissance (Tracked)

LEFT: **The latest version of the original Alvis Combat Vehicle Reconnaissance Scimitar is the Alvis Sabre Reconnaissance Vehicle, which has the same original chassis as the Scimitar, but with the two-man operated Fox turret, mounting the L94 Hughes 7.62mm/0.3in chain gun and extra bins.**
BELOW: **A CVR(T) Scimitar on training. 165 rounds were carried (in clips of three) for the 30mm/1.18in Rarden cannon. Basically a single-shot weapon, it could fire short bursts of up to six rounds.**
BOTTOM LEFT: **A trio of Scimitars on training/ operations in the north of the NATO area.**

The Scimitar is the light reconnaissance version of the Combat Vehicle Reconnaissance (Tracked) – CVR(T) – series produced by Alvis of Coventry. It was primarily designed to deal with hostile Armoured Personnel Carriers (APCs) and other lightly armoured vehicles at ranges of about 1,000m/1,087yds or more, and also for close reconnaissance and internal security roles.

Like the Scorpion, its outstanding cross-country performance and low silhouette, combined with its small size, enabled the Scimitar to perform these tasks very well indeed. It was also ideal for the "shoot and scoot" tactics of fighting a delaying battle. The vehicle's hull and turret was built out of a newly developed aluminium-zinc-magnesium alloy and mounts a 30mm/1.18in Rarden gun as its main armament, along with a coaxial 7.62mm/0.3in machine-gun. Powered by a Jaguar XK J60, 4.2-litre 6-cylinder engine giving a top speed of 80.5kph/50mph, the Scimitar has a crew of three, with the driver in the hull and the other two in the turret side by side – each with a cupola.

A later 1993 upgrade of the Scimitar was the Sabre, equipped with a new turret, mounting the L49 Hughes 7.62mm/0.3in high velocity chain gun along with a Rarden 30mm/1.18in cannon. As with all the vehicles in this successful series, the Scimitar was sold abroad to various countries.

Alvis Scimitar CVR(T)

Entered service: 1973
Crew: 3
Weight: 7,900kg/7.8 tons
Dimensions: Length – 4.39m/14ft 4.5in
Height (over turret hatch) – 2.09m/6ft 10.5in
Width – 2.18m/7ft 2in
Armament: Main – 30mm/1.18in Rarden cannon
Secondary – 7.62mm/0.03in machine-gun
Armour: Unspecified
Powerplant: Jaguar 4.2 litre petrol, 141.7kW/190hp
Performance: Speed – 80.5kph/50mph
Range – 644km/400 miles

LEFT: One of the latest versions of this replacement for the ubiquitous Saladin armoured car was this Scorpion 90, which Alvis fitted with a 90mm/3.54in Cockerill Mark 3 gun, reducing its ammunition load from 40 rounds with the 76mm/2.99in to 34 with the 90mm/3.54in. Malaysia bought some 26 Scorpion 90s in the late 1980s and early 90s, as did Nigeria (33), and it is also believed that Venezuela bought an undisclosed number in the 1980s (possibly over 80).

BELOW: The first prototype appeared in 1969 (production three years later) and has been in service in various forms ever since as the lead AFV of the Combat Vehicle Reconnaissance (Tracked) family. Used in both low and high intensity warfare, Scorpion mounts a 76mm/2.99in gun and has a crew of three.

Alvis Scorpion Combat Vehicle Reconnaissance (Tracked)

Produced by Alvis of Coventry as a replacement for the ageing Saladin and Saracen wheeled vehicles, the Combat Vehicle Reconnaissance (Tracked) – CVR(T) – family comprised: Scorpion – Fire Support; Scimitar – Anti-APC (Armoured Personnel Carrier); Spartan – APC; Samson – ARV; Striker – Anti-Tank Guided Weapon (ATGW); Sultan – ACV (Armoured Combat Vehicle); and Samaritan – Ambulance.

All were deliberately compact enough to be air-transportable. The Scorpion, with its light but strong aluminium alloy armour weighed 7,800kg/7.67 tons and was fast, with a top speed of 80.5kph/

50mph. It had the same basic design, layout and crew numbers as the Scimitar, but was fitted with a more powerful main gun – the L23A1 76mm/2.99in – along with a coaxial 7.62mm/0.3in machine-gun.

The L23A1 fires four types of ammunition: HESH (High-Explosive Squash-Head) – capable of defeating medium armour at a range of up to 3,500m/11,500ft and also very effective against the tracks and side armour of most MBTs; HE (High-Explosive); Smoke – base ejection type; and Canister – a short-range anti-infantry round which produces 800 steel pellets to devastating

effect. The gun has a maximum range of 5,000m/16,400ft and a relatively low muzzle velocity which contributes to the accuracy by producing a light recoil and low barrel wear (each barrel can fire 3,000 HESH rounds). One of the latest versions is Scorpion 90, which is equipped with the 90mm/3.54in Cockerill Mark 3 main gun.

LEFT: Cutaway drawing of a Scorpion CVR(T), fitted with its flotation screen. It was built of aluminium alloy armour, which did produce some problems; however, it was certainly both light and fast. The original version is no longer in British Army service. However, as the other photographs show, a variety of other models are still available.

Alvis Scorpion CVR(T)

Entered service: 1973
Crew: 3
Weight: 7,800kg/7.67 tons
Dimensions: Length – 4.39m/14ft 5in
　Height (over turret hatch) – 2.08m/6ft 10in
　Width – 2.18m/7ft 2in
Armament: Main – 76mm/2.99in or 90mm/3.54in gun
　Secondary – 7.62mm/0.03in machine-gun
Armour: Maximum – Unspecified thickness, aluminium
Powerplant: Jaguar 4.2 petrol, 141.7kW/190hp
Performance: Speed – 80.5kph/50mph
　Range – 644km/400 miles

AMX-13 Light Tank

Designed just after World War II, the AMX-13 (the "13" in its name is its original designated weight in tonnes) was initially manufactured in 1950 by Atelier de Construction Roanne, then from the early 1960s by Mecanique Creusot-Loire, and finally by GIAT into the late 1980s, a lengthy period that saw it grow into a large family of successful variants.

The AMX-13 was manned by a crew of three and powered by a SOFAM 8-cylinder petrol engine, giving it a top speed of 60kph/37.3mph and a range of 400km/248.5 miles. Its most distinctive feature was the extraordinary rear-mounted, low-profile, oscillating turret.

Initially mounting a long-barrelled 75mm/2.95in self-loading main gun based on a pre-1945 German design, it was then upgraded to a 90mm/3.54in weapon and then in 1987 Creusot-Loire introduced a 105mm/4.13in low-recoil gun option. When the AMX-13 was sold abroad, some other countries also mounted their own weapons of choice.

All these main gun upgrades continued to be based on the original oscillating turret, which proved to be troublesome. The excellent tough chassis remained essentially the same, though there were changes of engine from petrol to diesel. Variants included an

ABOVE: The highly successful AMX-13, designed soon after the end of World War II by Atelier de Construction d'Issy les Moulineaux, the significance of the "13" being its original weight in tonnes. Production was subsequently moved to the Creusot-Loire factory at Chalon sur Saone, and over 7,700 AFVs were eventually built, including variants such as self-propelled artillery guns, anti-aircraft guns and infantry fighting vehicles. One feature of the original model was its oscillating FL-10 turret, containing a 75mm/2.95in gun and coaxial machine-gun.

armoured personnel carrier, a light recovery vehicle, an armoured bridgelayer, different calibres of self-propelled gun and an artillery rocket-system launch platform. Regular upgrade packages extended the AMX-13's service life, and almost 8,000 vehicles were manufactured.

ABOVE: Now on show at the Israeli Tank Museum at Latrun, Israel purchased a number of AMX-13s from France in 1956 and used them in the Six Day War. However, the gun, with its two revolver-type magazines (each 6 rounds), was ineffective against the front armour of Soviet-sourced tanks such as T-54/T-55, so it was phased out and sold elsewhere.

AMX-13 Light Tank

Entered service: 1950
Crew: 3
Weight: 15,000kg/14.8 tons
Dimensions: Length – 4.88m/16ft
    Height (over turret hatch) – 2.3m/7ft 6.5in
    Width – 2.51m/8ft 3in
Armament: Main – 75mm/2.95in or 90mm/3.54in
    or 105mm/4.13in
    Secondary – 2 x 7.5mm/0.295in or 7.62mm/0.3in
    machine-guns
Armour: Maximum – 25mm/0.98in
Powerplant: SOFAM 8Gxb petrol, 186.4kW/250hp
Performance: Speed – 60kph/37.3mph
    Range – 400km/248.5 miles

AMX-30 Main Battle Tank

Manufactured by Giat Industries, the AMX-30 Main Battle Tank was first produced in the mid-1960s as a lighter yet more powerfully armed replacement for the American-supplied M47. It had a crew of four and mounted one 105mm/4.13in main gun with a coaxial 20mm/0.79in cannon and a 7.62mm/0.3in machine-gun. It was powered by a Hispano-Suiza 12-cylinder multi-fuel engine that gave it a top speed of 65kph/40.4mph and a range of 450km/280 miles.

The AMX-30 B2 was an improved version of the AMX-30, some of them newly made and some with the B2 upgrade packages retrofitted to earlier models. The upgrade included an automatic fire-control system and NBC (Nuclear, Biological and Chemical warfare) proofing, enabling the AMX-30 to fight in a contaminated atmosphere. Over 3,500 of this vehicle were built, including variants such as self-propelled howitzers, anti-aircraft missile or gun systems and armoured recovery vehicles.

TOP: Good photograph of an AMX-30 in a Paris street. Like AMX-13 and others, the AMX-30 was designed post-war to replace the American M47s which had been supplied by the USA via the Mutual Defence Aid Programme. ABOVE: The AMX-30 D armoured recovery vehicle has a dozer blade mounted at the front of the hull, plus two winches and a hydraulic crane. LEFT: Most advanced of the AMX-30 models is the AMX-30 B2, which was the one in main French Army service. It incorporated many of the improvements, such as laser rangefinder, low-light TV and an integrated fire-control system. There is even an AMX-30 "Stealth" MBT fitted with radar-absorbing material and carefully shaped to reduce the radar signature.

AMX-30 MBT

Entered service: 1967
Crew: 4
Weight: 36,000kg/35.43 tons
Dimensions: Length – 9.48m/31ft 1in
　　Height (over turret hatch) – 2.29m/7ft 6in
　　Width – 3.1m/10ft 2in
Armament: Main – 105mm/4.13in smoothbore gun
　　Secondary – 1 x 20mm/0.79in cannon and
　　1 x 7.62mm/0.3in machine-gun
Armour: Maximum – 80mm/3.15in
Powerplant: Hispano-Suiza HS 110 multi-fuel,
　　522kW/700hp (for AMX-30 B2)
Performance: Speed – 65kph/40.4mph
　　Range – 450km/280 miles

AMX-32 Main Battle Tank

The AMX-32 was developed in 1975 as an export model of the AMX-30 and was available with either a 105mm/4.12in rifled main gun or a 120mm/4.72in smoothbore alternative, along with a coaxial 20mm/0.79in cannon and a 7.62mm/0.3in anti-aircraft machine-gun. The layout, weight, armour and crew numbers remained the same as its predecessor, but the engine was upgraded to the more recent Hispano-Suiza 110-S2R supercharged model developing 800hp, coupled with the ENC gearbox, with lock-up torque converter and hydrostatic steering. However, when no sales interest was generated, the project was dropped in favour of the AMX-40.

TOP: **The AMX-32 was the export model of the AMX-30, having a redesigned turret and thicker front hull armour to give better armoured protection. Weighing just over 38 tons and mounting a 120mm/4.72in smoothbore (second prototype) gun, it was much more powerful than the AMX-30, but had a marginally worse performance.** ABOVE: **Good side view of the AMX-32 export model.** BELOW LEFT: **Despite the improvements, including an all-welded turret in the second prototype, no purchasers materialized, and the AMX-32 was withdrawn.**

AMX-32 MBT

Entered service: 1979
Crew: 4
Weight: 39,000kg/38.38 tons
Dimensions: Length – 9.48m/31ft 1in
  Height (over turret hatch) – 2.29m/7ft 6in
  Width – 3.24m/10ft 7in
Armament: Main – 120mm/4.74in gun
  Secondary – 1 x 20mm/0.79in cannon and
  1 x 7.62mm/0.3in machine-gun
Armour: Maximum – 80mm/3.15in
Powerplant: Hispano-Suiza HS 110-S2R,
  596.6kW/800hp
Performance: Speed – 65kph/40.4mph
  Range – 530km/329 miles

AMX-40 Main Battle Tank

In the early 1980s came the next in the Giat manufactured, export-driven AMX series. As the AMX-32 had failed to attract any sales, the company decided to produce yet another upgrade, the AMX-40. This vehicle was based on the earlier AMX-32, with its essential design and layout remaining much the same, including the main 120mm/4.72in smoothbore main gun and the COTAC fire-control system.

The main improvements came in armour and mobility, the armour thickness being increased, especially on the frontal arc. A new engine was also installed, the Poyaud 12-cylinder diesel, with a top speed of 70kph/43.5mph and a range of 530km/329 miles. In order for the vehicle to make use of this additional power, an extra road wheel was added to each side, and wider tracks were fitted to reduce ground pressure and increase traction, all of which improved the overall performance of the vehicle.

Brought out in 1983, and despite three prototypes completed by late 1984, there was insufficient sales interest in the AMX-40, so it was withdrawn.

ABOVE, BELOW AND BOTTOM LEFT: **Another "hopeful" French export tank, the AMX-40 was designed by Giat Industries, using the AMX-32 as its model. It first appeared in 1983, and had a better overall performance and agility than its predecessor, although many of its basic characteristics remained unchanged. Sadly, it did not produce any buyers and was therefore withdrawn at prototype stage.**

AMX-40 MBT	
Entered service: 1983	
Crew: 4	
Weight: 43,700kg/43 tons	
Dimensions: Length – 10m/32ft 9.5in	
Height (over turret hatch) – 2.29m/7ft 6in	
Width – 3.3m/10ft 10in	
Armament: Main – 120mm/4.72in gun	
Secondary – 1 x 20mm/0.79in cannon and	
1 x 7.62mm/0.3in machine-gun	
Armour: Maximum – 100mm/4in	
Powerplant: Poyaud V12X diesel, 820.3kW/1,100hp	
Performance: Speed – 70kph/43.5mph	
Range – 530km/329 miles	

LEFT: **At 54,000kg/53.1 tons, with a 120mm/ 4.72in smoothbore gun and a speed in excess of 65kph/40.4mph, the Italian Ariete is a formidable second-generation MBT and well able to hold its own on the modern battlefield. Its Oto Breda 120mm/4.72in smoothbore gun can engage targets both by day and night, while it has a laser warning system for added protection (electrically operated smoke grenades being automatically launched when the MBT is lazed by the enemy).**

Ariete Main Battle Tank

The 1995 Consorzio Iveco Fiat and Oto Melara produced C1 Ariete, which is the latest Italian main battle tank. Weighing 54,000kg/53.1 tons and with a crew of four, it is powered by a Fiat V12 MTCA turbo-charged, 12-cylinder diesel engine, giving it a top speed in excess of 65kph/40.4mph and a range of 550km/342 miles. The turret, with crew of commander, gunner and loader, mounts the Oto Breda 120mm/4.72in smoothbore main gun and is also armed with a 7.62mm/0.3in machine-gun mounted coaxially and another 7.62mm/0.3in machine-gun fitted on the roof for air defence. The vehicle carries the latest optical and digital-imaging and fire-control systems, enabling it to fight day and night and to fire on the move. The tank is built in a modular fashion so that elements such as the power pack can be replaced swiftly and easily.

Ariete MBT

Entered service: 1988
Crew: 4
Weight: 54,000kg/53.1 tons
Dimensions: Length – 7.59m/24ft 11in
   Height (over turret hatch) – 2.5m/8ft 2in
   Width – 3.60m/11ft 9.5in
Armament: Main – 120mm/4.72in gun
   Secondary – 2 x 7.62mm/0.3in machine-guns
Armour: Unspecified
Powerplant: IVECO V12 MTCA diesel,
   970kW/1,300hp
Performance: Speed – 65kph/40.4mph
   Range – 550km/341.8 miles

Arjun Main Battle Tank

The Arjun Mark 1 is India's first indigenous main battle tank, designed to replace the Vickers Vijayanta. This project began in 1974 as an attempt at armour autonomy but production was delayed by various problems, and the Arjun was held up for many years before finally entering service at prototype stage in 1987. Built using composite armour, the vehicle is manned by a crew of four (commander, loader and gunner in the turret, and driver in the hull) and mounts a 120mm/4.72in stabilized main gun and also a 7.62mm/0.3in machine-gun in its turret, along with all the necessary modern additions of stabilization, digital fire control, optical and laser sighting and fire suppression. Powered by a MTU MB 838 Ka 501 water-cooled diesel engine delivering a top speed of 72kph/44.7mph and equipped with hydro-pneumatic suspension, the Arjun has a range of approximately 400km/248.5 miles.

LEFT: **In 1974, the Indian Combat Research and Development Establishment began work on a successor to the ageing Vijayanta. However, it was not until April 1987 that its successor, the Arjun, was unveiled. The new MBT has a crew of four and mounts a 120mm/4.72in rifled gun. It is anticipated that some 125 MBTs will be produced in "slow time" for "home" consumption.**

Arjun MBT

Entered service: 1987 (prototype)
Crew: 4
Weight: 58,000kg/57.1 tons
Dimensions: Length – 9.8m/32ft 2in
   Height (over turret hatch) – 2.43m/8ft
   Width – 3.17m/10ft 5in
Armament: Main – 120mm/4.72in gun
   Secondary – 1 x 12.7mm/0.5in and
   1 x 7.62mm/0.3in machine-guns
Armour: Unspecified
Powerplant: MTU MB 838 Ka 501 diesel,
   1,045kW/1,400hp
Performance: Speed – 72kph/44.7mph
   Range – 400km/248.5 miles

LEFT: Designed and developed as a private venture by Santa Barbara Sistemas of Spain and Steyr-Daimler-Puch of Austria, this is a combination of the ASCOD IFV chassis which is already in production in Austria, with a South African 105mm/4.13in Rooikat turret. To date, an order for 15 plus a command vehicle has been placed by the Royal Thai Army. The ASCOD 105 in this first colour photograph has an Oto Melara 105LRF turret fitted for trials.

BELOW AND BOTTOM LEFT: The chassis and hull are of all-welded steel armour which provides protection against small-arms fire and shell splinters, its total weight being 28,500kg/28 tons, with a four-man crew. The light tank is now ready for production, but to date the Thais are the only customers.

ASCOD 105 Light Tank

The ASCOD 105 Light Tank emerged in 1996, built as a private commercial venture by a consortium of Spanish and Austrian companies, Santa Barbara Sistemas of Spain and Styr-Daimler-Puch of Austria, who manufactured the vehicle between them and also purchased some of its parts internationally.

Known as the "Ulan" in Austria and in Spain as the "Pizarro", the ASCOD 105 is a light tank variant of the APC ASCOD already being built by the Austrian part of the consortium, Styr-Daimler-Puch. The tank uses the chassis of its sister vehicle, which can carry up to eight infantrymen in addition to the crew of three. The main difference between the two is in the turret and its main armament – the ASCOD 105 being fitted with South

African Denel turret, mounting a 105mm/4.13in GT7 main gun. Weighing 28,500kg/28 tons and fitted with torsion bar suspension, the ASCOD 105 is powered by a German MTU 8VTE22 V90 diesel engine, giving it a top speed of 70kph/43mph and a range of 500km/310 miles.

Alternative main armament mounts include a two-man South African Rooikat turret with a 20mm/0.79in Mauser cannon, an Italian turret fitted with a 25mm/0.98in cannon and two TOW ATGW (Tube-launched, Optically-tracked, Wire-guided Anti-Tank Guided Weapon) launchers and a lower, flatter American turret with just an externally mounted 105mm/4.13in main weapon that reduced the vehicle's profile considerably.

All turret configurations feature digital fire control, gun stabilization, as well as the latest night-vision, navigation and safety systems. As well as being deployed by both Austrian and Spanish armoured forces, the vehicle has also been sold to Thailand.

ASCOD 105 Light Tank

Entered service: 1996
Crew: 4
Weight: 28,500kg/28 tons
Dimensions: Length – 6.61m/21ft 8in
Height (over turret hatch) – 2.76m/9ft 0.5in
Width – 3.15m/10ft 4in
Armament: Main – 105mm/4.13in GT7 gun
Secondary – 2 x 7.62mm/0.3in machine-guns
Armour: Unspecified
Powerplant: MTU 8V183TE22 V90 diesel, 447.4kW/600hp
Performance: Speed – 70kph/43.5mph
Range – 500km/310.7 miles

ASU-57 TD	
Entered service: 1957	
Crew: 3	
Weight: 7,400kg/7.3 tons	
Dimensions: Length – 3.73/12ft 3in	
Height (over turret hatch) – 1.42m/4ft 8in	
Width – 2.2m/7ft 2.5in	
Armament: Main – 57mm/2.24in gun	
Secondary – 1 x 7.62mm/0.3in machine-gun	
Armour: Maximum – 15mm/0.59in	
Powerplant: ZIL-123 6-cylinder petrol, delivering 82kW/110hp	
Performance: Speed – 65kph/40.4mph	
Range – 320km/198.8 miles	

ASU-57 Tank Destroyer

The ASU-57 was part of the USSR's attempt to develop air-portable firepower for use by airborne forces in the years of the Cold War, entering service in 1957. Weighing 7,400kg/ 7.3 tons and manned by a crew of three, it mounted a 57mm/2.24in CH-51M gun around which the superstructure was built, which was set back and sloped to the front where the gun protruded. It also mounted a 7.62mm/0.3in machine-gun for anti-aircraft and close-quarter defence. Powered by a ZIL-123 6-cylinder petrol engine, the ASU-57 had a top speed of 65kph/40.4mph and a range of 320km/198.8 miles. The ASU-57 was used by Soviet forces and their satellite client states well into the 1980s, at which time it would have been beyond the capability of its gun to knock out the then current NATO MBTs, so it was used for other purposes such as LAA (light anti-aircraft).

ASU-85 Tank Destroyer

The ASU-85 was a continuation of the ASU series, emerging in 1962 and based upon a PT-76 chassis, though not required to be amphibious but rather air-portable. The main changes from the ASU-57 approach were to the superstructure, which was now completely enclosed, and in its armament, which was upgraded to an 85mm/3.35in D-70 gun in a fixed mount along with a coaxial 7.62mm/0.3in SGMT machine-gun and cupola-mounted 12.7mm/0.5in anti-aircraft machine-gun. At more than double the weight of its predecessor, the ASU-85 now required a new engine, and was fitted with a V6 diesel engine, giving it a speed of 45kph/28mph and a range of 260km/ 161 miles.

ASU-85 TD	
Entered service: 1962	
Crew: 4	
Weight: 15,500kg/15.26 tons	
Dimensions: Length – 6m/19ft 8in	
Height (over turret hatch) – 2.1m/6ft 10.5in	
Width – 2.8m/9ft 2in	
Armament: Main – 85mm/3.35in D-70 gun	
Secondary – 1 x 12.7mm/0.5in and 1 x 7.62mm/0.3in machine-guns	
Armour: Maximum – 40mm/1.58in	
Powerplant: V6 diesel, 179kW/240hp	
Performance: Speed – 45kph/28mph	
Range – 260km/161.5 miles	

LEFT: The US Army provided Brazil with a number of their M41 Light Tanks, which the Brazilians took into service and improved. For example, their M41B had its old petrol engine replaced by a 302kW/450hp diesel, while the M41C (seen here) had better vision equipment, additional armour plate and a new 90mm/3.54in gun.

Bernardini M41C Light Tank

Entered service: 1983
Crew: 4
Weight: 25,000kg/24.6 tons
Dimensions: Length – 8.21m/26ft 11in
Height (over turret hatch) – 2.76m/9ft 0.5in
Width – 3.2m/10ft 6in
Armament: Main – 90mm/3.54in gun
Secondary – 1 x 12.7mm/0.5in and
1 x 7.62mm/0.3in machine-guns
Armour: Unspecified
Powerplant: Scania DS14 diesel, 302kW/450hp
Performance: Speed – 70kph/43.5mph
Range – 600km/372.8 miles

Bernardini M41 Light Tank

A clever choice or sales pitch determined a useful future for the US-made M41 Walker Bulldog. After an upgrade package which combined items shopped for on the open market and indigenously produced parts which were then assembled locally, the Brazilian Government equipped their armoured forces with an AFV well suited for their requirements. The first drawback was the short operational range of the original M41 petrol engine. This was soon identified and quickly dealt with by replacement using a locally built Scania DS14 diesel engine, along with new cooling and electrical systems. The original 76mm/2.99in gun was also upgraded by being re-bored locally to 90mm/3.54in, and the final upgrade, the M41C, had additional armour and improved vision equipment. By March 1985, 386 M41s had been upgraded.

Bernardini X1A1 and X1A2 Light Tanks

The Bernardini X1A1 was another example of tank recycling for the US, who was able to sell on "obsolete" tanks, and helped Brazil in the development of their own armaments industry. It was based on the M3A1 Stuart Light Tank, combined with another indigenously put together upgrade package consisting of a new locally designed and built turret which mounted a French-bought 90mm/3.54in main gun.

This model, however, did not progress beyond the prototype stage and was followed by the X1A2, which had a completely redesigned chassis fitted with a new two-man turret in which to mount the 90mm/3.54in main gun. The X1A2 model that was accepted by the Brazilian Army weighed almost 19 tons, with its Saab-Scania 6-cylinder 224kW/300hp diesel engine giving it a top speed of 55kph/34mph and a range of 600km/372.8 miles.

LEFT: The Bernardini X1A2 Light Tank. Essentially its predecessor had been an upgraded US M3A1 Stuart Light Tank fitted with a locally produced 90mm/3.54in French gun. In due course it was replaced by the 100 per cent Brazilian-made X1A2 seen here, which had a brand-new two-man turret and 90mm/3.54in gun. This came into service in the Brazilian Army, but its successor, the X1A3, did not.

Bernardini X1A2 Light Tank

Entered service: 1978
Crew: 3
Weight: 19,000kg/18.7 tons
Dimensions: Length – 6.5m/21ft 4in
Height (over turret hatch) – 2.45m/8ft 0.5in
Width – 2.6m/8ft 6.5in
Armament: Main – 90mm/3.54in gun
Secondary – 1 x 12.7mm/0.5in and
1 x 7.62mm/0.3in machine-guns
Armour: Unspecified
Powerplant: Saab-Scania DS11 diesel,
224kW/300hp
Performance: Speed – 55kph/34.2mph
Range – 600km/372.8 miles

Challenger 1 Main Battle Tank

Manufactured by Vickers Defence Systems (VDS), the Challenger 1 is the last in the progression of British MBTs tracing their origin back to the Centurion through Chieftain. It is based on the Shir 2 – originally an updated Chieftain variant, designed as an export project for the Shah of Iran's armed forces, but accepted by the British Army under the re-designation "Challenger". Built using advanced Chobam composite armour and cast and rolled steel, the emphasis is on protection and firepower rather than mobility. The CR1 mounts a Royal Ordnance 120mm/4.72in L11A5 rifled main gun, fitted with

ABOVE: **Operation "Desert Storm". A CR1 moves up into position. Note the additional armour plates on its sides and fuel drums on its rear.** BELOW LEFT: **The "Chinese Eye" on the side of the turret denotes that this CR1 belongs to 1 RTR.**

a thermal sleeve, fume extractor and muzzle brake, and has two 7.62mm/0.3in machine-guns, one coaxial with the main gun. These weapons are operated by a three-man turret crew – commander, gunner and loader, with the aid of the latest digital and optical range-finding and fire-control equipment. It is powered by a Rolls-Royce CV12 engine, giving it a top speed of 57kph/35mph and a range of 450km/280 miles. Three different models of the CR1 have been developed, with upgrade suites fitted to ensure pre-eminence as one of the world's most formidable tanks.

In September 1978, the MOD had placed an order with the ROF Leeds to supply 243 Challenger 1s. Four years later, in December 1982, the MBT was accepted by the General Staff, by which time production was well under way. The first order was sufficient to equip four armoured regiments, and in July 1984 there was a further order for 64 more to equip a fifth regiment. In 1986, ROF Leeds was bought by Vickers Defence Systems and a new factory was built at Leeds, identical to the VDS Newcastle works. The new factory was operational by late 1987, when a further order for another 76 CR1s was placed by MOD. The last of the CR1s was delivered in mid-1990. Ten years later the last CR1 was phased out of British Army service (late 2000), being replaced by Challenger 2 MBT. Then in March

1999 it was agreed that 288 CR1s would be supplied to Jordan (renamed Al Hussein in Jordanian service).

In addition to the MBTs, the following variants were built: 17 Challenger Training Tanks and 30 Challenger Armoured Repair and Recovery Vehicles (CR ARRV).

The CR1 demonstrated its battle-winning capabilities with a highly successful combat record in the first Gulf War. It was heavily involved in Operation "Desert Storm", destroying some 300 Iraqi MBTs for the loss of no Challengers.

ABOVE AND BELOW: **Factory fresh. These remarkably crisp photographs were taken on "Roll-out" Day at ROF Leeds before it closed. They give excellent all-round views of CR1 No. 33KA 95.** BOTTOM LEFT: **This CR1 is part of IFOR on operational service in the Balkans.**

Challenger 1 MBT

Entered service: 1982
Crew: 4
Weight: 62,000kg/61.02 tons
Dimensions: Length – 8.33m/26ft 4in
Height (over turret hatch) – 2.5m/8ft 2.5in
Width – 3.52m/11ft 6.5in
Armament: Main – 120mm/4.72in L11A5 gun
Secondary – 2 x 7.62mm/0.3in machine-guns
Armour: Unspecified
Powerplant: Rolls-Royce CV12 diesel, 894.8kW/1,200bhp
Performance: Speed – 57kph/35.4mph
Range – 450km/279.6 miles

Challenger 2 Main Battle Tank

A logical development of the Vickers-built Challenger 1, the Challenger 2 shares its predecessor's hull and automotive parts but has many new and improved features, making it a vastly improved MBT. These include Chobham second-generation composite armour, an NBC (Nuclear, Biological and Chemical) protection suite, and, for the first time in any British tank, both a heating and a cooling system in the crew compartment.

The vehicle's armament consists of a gyrostabilized Royal Ordnance 120mm/4.72in rifled main gun designated the L30, along with a coaxial McDonnell Douglas Helicopter Systems 7.62mm/0.3in chain gun and a 7.62mm/0.3in anti-aircraft machine-gun. Its fire-control system is the latest generation in digital computer technology, as are its range-finding, sighting and fire-suppression systems.

The CR2 carries a crew of four. Power is supplied by a Rolls-Royce Perkins Condor CV12 894.8kW/1,200bhp engine and it is equipped with a Hydrogas variable spring suspension system.

The initial order placed by the MOD in June 1991 was for 127 CR2 MBTs, plus 13 Driver Training Tanks. First to be completed were the Driver Training Tanks (in 1993), so that training could commence before the gun tanks began to arrive.

Interestingly, CR2 was the first post-World War II British tank to be designed, developed and produced by a single manufacturer, VDS (now Alvis Vickers – part of BAe Systems). The first CR2 MBTs were formally accepted into service on May 16, 1994.

TOP AND ABOVE: **The British Army's latest MBT, Challenger 2 (CR2) is now battle-proven, having seen active service both in the Balkans and the Gulf War. As can be seen from these two photographs taken on training, the turret incorporates second-generation Chobham armour – known as "Dorchester", which gives significantly improved protection against both Kinetic and Chemical Energy attacks.**

Two months later, VDS were awarded a second contract to supply a further 259 CR2 MBTs and nine Training Tanks, together with the necessary training and logistic support. This was sufficient to maintain a total of six CR2 MBT-equipped armoured regiments each of 36 CR2s, of which the Royal Scots Dragoon Guards were the first to be so equipped in June 2000. Of course, events have moved on since then, and

RIGHT, BELOW RIGHT AND BOTTOM: **Three views of Britain's Challenger 2 Main Battle Tank on training and operations. This was originally a private venture begun in the 1980s by Vickers Defence Systems and eventually led to a firm production proposal in 1988. The MOD approved the building of nine prototypes (seven at Leeds and two at Newcastle), which led to a contract being awarded for 127 CR2s, plus 13 Driver Training Tanks. CR2 was the very first British Army tank to be completely developed by a single contractor, VDS (now Alvis Vickers – part of BAe Systems). The tank did exceptionally well in Operation "Telic" (the war in Iraq), being rated as one of the best MBTs in the world, along with Abrams, Merkava and Leopard 2.**

the CR2-equipped 7th Armoured Brigade has taken part in war fighting in Iraq, proving the excellence of both the MBT and its crewmen to the world. Sadly, its reward appears to have been a "restructuring" that will reduce the number of CR2s in front-line service. Presumably the rest will be "mothballed". It was at the end of February 2002 that the British Army took delivery of the last of its CR2s, the total being 386.

To date, there has been only one export success, namely to Oman. Their first order, placed in July 1993, was for 18 CR2s, four CR ARRVs and two Driver Training Tanks. This was followed in November 1997 by a further order for 20 CR2 MBTs, again for Oman.

Challenger 2E Main Battle Tank

In the early 1990s, VDS (now Alvis Vickers) embarked on the development of an enhanced export model of the CR2 MBT. It ran for the first time in 1994 and since that date has completed many trials in temperate and desert conditions. The aim has been to take it as the manufacturers have stated: "a generation ahead of current in service MBTs". Undoubtedly CR2 has proved itself to be a "Top Gun" among the world's leading MBTs.

Challenger 2 MBT	
Entered service: 1994	
Crew: 4	
Weight: 62,500kg/61.51 tons	
Dimensions: Length – 8.33m/27ft 4in	
Height (over turret hatch) – 2.49m/8ft 2in	
Width – 3.52m/11ft 6.5in	
Armament: Main – 120mm/4.72in L30A1 gun	
Secondary – 1 x 7.62mm/0.3in L94A1 chain gun	
and 1 x 7.62/0.3in L37A2 machine-gun	
Armour: Unspecified	
Powerplant: Perkins CV12 TCA Condor diesel, 894.8kW/1,200hp	
Performance: Speed – 60kph/37.3mph	
Range – 450km/279.6 miles	

177

Chieftain Main Battle Tank (FV 4202)

Britain's successor to their world-beating Centurion was originally designed in 1956 by Leyland Motors, Centurion's "design parents", who built three prototypes. Then in 1961–62, six more were completed and trials took place. The following year the tank was taken into British Army service and production continued at ROF Leeds and Vickers Defence Systems, Newcastle.

The first true British Main Battle Tank (Centurion was strictly a medium gun tank), the Chieftain had a somewhat chequered early career due to problems with its engine (cracking of cylinder liners, failure of lip seals and piston ring breakages), which meant that it had to be continually up-rated from 436.3kW/585bhp (Mark 4A), to 484.7kW/650bhp (Mark 5A), then to 536.9kW/720bhp (Mark 7A) and finally to 559.3kW/

TOP: **Chieftain on training. There were a total of 12 different Marks of Chieftain, the last (Mark 12) being a Mark 5 with IFCS, Stillbrew armour, TOGS and the No. 11 NBC system.** ABOVE: **A Chieftain MBT moves across the RAC Centre training area during the yearly "Open Day" that used to be held at Gallows Hill, north of Bovington – but sadly no longer.**

750bhp (Mark 8A). Designed as a multi-fuel engine, it was normally run on diesel and as such was extremely dirty. It also showed a tell-tale smoke plume when starting up, which could give away its position. Nevertheless, despite these early problems the Chieftain settled down to become a reliable and well-liked tank.

It was of conventional design with a forward driving compartment, central fighting compartment and a rear compartment for the engine, gearbox and transmission. The driver was centrally positioned in the hull and when closed down adopted a reclining position, which meant that the hull height could be reduced, thus lowering the overall height of the tank's silhouette. In the fighting compartment the loader/radio operator was on the left of the main armament, with the gunner and commander seated on the right. All had the necessary inter-communication equipment and all-round vision devices, both for day and night viewing.

The main armament was the highly effective 120mm/4.72in L11A5 rifled tank gun, which used the bagged charge system for the first time in a British tank, the projectile and charge being separately loaded, the latter being ignited by means of an electrically fired vent tube. This reduced loader fatigue and gave a maximum rate of fire of some eight to ten rounds in the first minute, then six rpm thereafter. Initially the system employed a Ranging machine-gun – a 12.7mm/0.50cal Browning Heavy machine-gun which fired flashing tipped trace ammunition, but this was later replaced by a Tank Laser Sight.

Apart from the Mark 1s, all Chieftains in British Army service were retro-fitted with the fully integrated Improved Fire-Control System (IFCS), which ensured a considerable degree of accurate, first round hits on static targets at up to 3,000m/9.843ft and on moving targets at up to 2,000m/6,562ft.

The Marconi Fighting Vehicle Control System gave four modes of control (stabilizer, power traverse, hand and emergency) and allowed targets to be engaged with reasonable accuracy while on the move. Other gunnery equipment included night IR/WL sights (used in conjunction with the IR/WL searchlight mounted on the left-hand side of the turret) and TOGS (Thermal Observation and Gunnery Sight).

The L60 engine was coupled to a TN 12 epicyclic gearbox, incorporating a Merrit-Wilson differential steering system and electrohydraulic gear selection, with six forward and two reverse gears, plus an emergency low reverse. In all, there were 12 Marks of Chieftain, with various armour configurations, including a passive armour package known as Stillbrew. Some 1,350 Chieftains were built, of which 450 were exported.

The Chieftain was phased out of British Army service in 1996, but may still be found in Iran, Iraq, Jordan, Oman and Kuwait (their Chieftains saw combat during the Iraqi invasion in 1990). The Chieftain was also used as a test bed for the Marconi Marksman twin anti-aircraft gun turret and the "Jagd Chieftain" which mounted a 120mm/4.72in gun in its hull, and was also used to develop the Shir 1 (Chieftain 800), Shir 2 (Chieftain 900) and Khalid (FV 4211). Additionally, there were three variants which are still serving in various parts of the world;

• Chieftain ARRV (Armoured Repair and Recovery Vehicle), which is basically a Chieftain ARV fitted with a powerful crane that can lift a complete CR1 power pack.

• Chieftain AVRE (Armoured Vehicle, Royal Engineers) which, unlike the Centurion AVRE, does not mount a 165mm/6.49in demolition gun but can carry out a variety of engineer tasks with its bulldozer blade (removing obstacles), plastic pipe fascines (filling ditches), plus mine-clearing (either with a mine plough fitted or by using its Giant Viper rocket-propelled system) and laying Class 60 trackway.

• Chieftain AVLB (Armoured Vehicle Launched Bridge), that can be fitted with a variety of single span, folding or "scissors-type" bridges.

TOP: **A Chieftain fitted with the Pearson Engineering track width mine plough system (as fitted to some Chieftain AVLBs during Operation "Desert Storm").**
ABOVE: **Chieftain 900, the Royal Ordnance Factory's private venture main battle tank completed in 1982. Its layout was basically the same as the Chieftain, but with the British-developed Chobham armour.** BELOW: **A Chieftain AVRE, carrying pipe fascines and towing a Giant Viper mine clearing rocket device.**

Chieftain Mark 5 MBT (FV 4201)

Entered service: 1963 (Mark 1)
Crew: 4
Weight: 55,000kg/54.13 tons (combat-loaded)
Dimensions: Length (gun forward) – 10.87m/35ft 8in
Width (including searchlight) – 3.66m/12ft
Height (overall) – 2.89m/12ft
Armament: Main – 120mm/4.72in L11A7 rifled gun
Secondary – 2 x 7.62mm/0.3in machine-guns, one coaxial and one on the commander's cupola
Armour: Not given
Powerplant: Leyland L60 petrol engine (Mark 7A), 536.9kW/720bhp
Performance: Speed – 48kph/30mph
Range – 400–500km/250–300 miles

179

Charioteer Tank Destroyer

The Charioteer was a post-World War II development that gave the Royal Armoured Corps a tank destroyer armed with a 20pdr main gun and replaced the aging A30 Avenger and Archer anti-tank weapons that had been manned by the Royal Artillery. This was achieved without any new vehicle having to be designed and was built using existing resources to fill the gap in requirements until something better could be sourced. A recycled Cromwell chassis was modified to take a new, larger turret mounting the same 20pdr main gun as that of the new Centurion tank. This created a powerful tank destroyer at a low unit cost. With a weight of 28,960kg/28.5 tons and powered by a Rolls-Royce Meteor V12 petrol engine, the Charioteer had a top speed of 50kph/31mph and a range of 266km/165 miles. When compared with the Centurion Main Battle Tank, however, its performance was poor, and after 1958, when the Centurion's main armament was upgraded with the 105mm/41.3in L7 gun, the Charioteer became obsolete.

ABOVE AND LEFT: **The FV 4101 Charioteer Tank Destroyer was a refurbished Cromwell on which was mounted a new, larger turret containing the 20pdr gun that was also fitted to the Centurion. These two photographs are of the Charioteer at the Bovington Tank Museum.**

Charioteer TD

Entered service: 1954
Crew: 4
Weight: 28,960kg/28.5 tons
Dimensions: Length – 6.43m/21ft 1in
　　Height (over turret hatch) – 2.44m/8ft
　　Width – 3.05m/10ft
Armament: Main – 20pdr (83.88mm/3.3in) QF (quick-firing) gun
Armour: Maximum – 60mm/2.36in
Powerplant: Rolls-Royce Meteor V12 petrol, 447.4kW/600hp
Performance: Speed – 50kph/31mph
　　Range – 266km/165 miles

Conqueror Heavy Tank

The appearance of the Russian JS-3 Heavy Tank, with its powerful 122mm/4.8in main gun and thick armour, established the need for heavier British main battle tanks. In 1946 it was therefore decided to produce a completely new range of tanks based on the FV200 Universal Tank, of which the FV201 was the basic gun tank.

Conqueror was developed from the original FV201 prototype, powered by a Rolls-Royce Meteor M120 V12 petrol engine with Merritt-Brown transmission

with a modified Horstman suspension. Its main armament, the 120mm/4.72in rifled L1 gun, mounted in a well-shaped turret, was derived from an American tank gun, which in turn was derived from an anti-aircraft gun.

The Conqueror was the first British tank in which the shell case and projectile were separate – and with the Conqueror this was not an advantage because a large brass shell case was used to hold the propellant rather than a bag charge, and this made it very heavy and

ABOVE: **The massive Conqueror Heavy Tank weighed 66,043kg/65 tons. While they were capable of dealing with the heavy Soviet tanks (like JS-3), Conqueror was sadly too large and too heavy, being withdrawn in the mid-1960s when the Centurion 105mm/4.13in gun came into service.** BELOW LEFT: **The Conqueror Heavy Tank on training.**

cumbersome to load, while the stowage was limited to 35 rounds in the turret. Throughout its career the Conqueror was plagued by various electrical and mechanical malfunctions, and while necessary to combat the threat of the Soviet heavy tanks, it proved difficult and cumbersome to use and was generally unpopular with the crews.

Conqueror Heavy Tank

Entered service: 1956
Crew: 4
Weight: 66,043kg/65 tons
Dimensions: Length – 11.58m/38ft
    Height (over turret hatch) – 3.35m/11ft
    Width – 3.96m/13ft
Armament: Main – 120mm/4.72in L1 gun
    Secondary – 2 x 7.7mm/0.303in machine-guns
Armour: Maximum – 178mm/7.01in
Powerplant: Rover Meteor M120 petrol,
    604kW/810hp
Performance: Speed – 34kph/21.1mph
    Range – 153km/95.1 miles

CV90-120-T Light Tank

The CV90-120-T is a light tank based on the latest CV90 infantry vehicle chassis fitted with a Hagglunds twin-hatch turret. Weighing almost 25 tons, the CV90-120 is powered by a Scania 4-cylinder 447.4kW/600hp diesel engine, giving it a top speed of 70kph/43.5mph and a range of 670km/416.3 miles. The main armament is a Swiss-manufactured, fully stabilized 120mm/4.72in high-pressure smoothbore CTG 120/L50 gun with a vertical sliding breech and a rate of fire of up to 14 rounds per minute. There is also a state-of-the-art fire-control system and a crew video network with displays at each crew station. Its Defensive Aids Suite (DAS) contains a laser, radar and missile approach warning system and a Multi-Spectral Aerosols (MSA) active countermeasure system equipped with top attack radar that can identify smart indirect munitions. The turret incorporates stealth characteristics.

Betraying its CV90 roots, it has a rear door entry in the hull and room inside for up to four extra men in addition to the crew of four.

CV90-120-T Light Tank

Entered service: 1998
Crew: 4
Weight: 25,000kg/24.6 tons
Dimensions: Length – 6.47m/21ft 2.5in
  Height (over turret hatch) – 2.90m/9ft 6in
  Width – 3.10m/10ft 2in
Armament: Main – 120mm/4.72in gun
  Secondary – 7.62mm/0.3in machine-gun
Armour: Unspecified
Powerplant: Scania diesel, generating
  447.4kW/600hp
Performance: Speed – 70kph/43.5mph
  Range – 670km/416.3 miles

LEFT: **Here is the CV90-120 on the Alvis Vickers stand at DSEi 1999.** BELOW: **The Swedish CV90-120 Light Tank is armed with the Swiss Ordnance Enterprise Corporation 120mm/4.72in Compact Tank Gun, weighs some 25,000kg/24.6 tons and has a crew of four. It was built by Hagglunds, now part of Alvis Vickers.**

EE T1 Osorio Main Battle Tank

The Osorio was the first indigenous MBT design of the growing Brazilian armaments industry, developed mainly for export by Engesa in the late 1980s, with help in the turret design and manufacture from Vickers. Weighing 43,690kg/43 tons and powered by a MWM TBD 234 12-cylinder diesel engine with automatic suspension, the Osorio had a top speed of 70kph/43.5mph and a range of 550km/341.8 miles.

It was armed at first with a Royal Ordnance 105mm/4.13in main gun, but later a French Giat 120mm/4.72in gun was mounted in a modified turret, along with a 7.62mm/0.3in machine-gun and a 12.7mm/0.5in anti-aircraft gun.

Despite initial interest and successful tests in Saudi Arabia, the Gulf War intervened and Saudi interest in the Osorio transferred rapidly to the now battle-proven Abrams.

TOP AND BELOW LEFT: **The Brazilians began to design and build their own MBT in the 1980s, in co-operation with Vickers Defence Systems. The EE T1 Osorio was the result, Engesa concentrating on the chassis and running gear, while VDS designed the three-man turret. In fact two turrets were eventually built – one mounting the ROF 105mm/4.13in gun, the other a French 120mm/4.72in built by Giat Industries.** ABOVE: **Loading the main armament on the Osorio. The makers stressed that the tank was designed for use by crews with a wide range of skill levels, simplicity of operation being the key.**

EE T1 Osorio MBT	
Entered service: 1985	
Crew: 4	
Weight: 43,690kg/43 tons	
Dimensions: Length – 7.13m/23ft 4.5in	
Height (over turret hatch) – 2.89m/9ft 6in	
Width – 3.26m/10ft 8.5in	
Armament: Main – 120mm/4.72in gun	
Secondary – 1 x 12.7mm/0.5in and	
1 x 7.62mm/0.3in machine-guns	
Armour: Unspecified	
Powerplant: MWM TBD 234 12-cylinder diesel,	
775.5kW/1,040hp	
Performance: Speed – 70kph/43.5mph	
Range – 550km/341.8 miles	

Hetzer G13 Tank Destroyer

Over 2,500 of the successful low-profile tank destroyers – the Hetzer (Hunter) – were produced by the Germans in World War II, using the basic components of the excellent Czech-built PzKpfw 38(t) and making use of the extensive Skoda works at Pilsen. The 38(t)'s hull was enlarged and the main 75mm/2.95in PaK39 L/48 gun mounted in a *Saukopf* (boarshead) mantlet on the right-hand side of the hull front.

Following the end of World War II, the Swiss Army purchased a number of Hetzers from Czechoslovakia, who continued to make this vehicle after the end of the hostilities, and modified them to suit their own needs.

This consisted primarily of relocating the machine-gun to the rear plate and fitting a commander's periscope in its place. It was renamed the Hetzer G13, and about 160 vehicles remained in service with the Swiss Army until the early 1970s. With a weight of just over 15 tons, the Hetzer had a speed of 42kph/26.1mph and a range of 180km/111.8 miles, and was manned by a crew of four.

ABOVE AND BELOW LEFT: **This wartime German tank destroyer was originally based upon the highly successful Skoda LT-38 Medium Tank. Over 1,500 were built and they were highly prized because they were small enough to hide with ease, yet could knock out most Allied tanks. Hetzer continued in service post-war with the Swiss Army, also becoming a firm favourite with AFV restorers.**

Hetzer G13 TD	
Entered service: 1947	
Crew: 4	
Weight: 15,750kg/15.5 tons	
Dimensions: Length – 6.38m/21ft	
Height (over turret hatch) – 2.17m/7ft 2in	
Width – 2.63m/8ft 8in	
Armament: Main – 75mm/2.95in L48 gun	
Secondary – 7.62mm/0.3in machine-gun	
Armour: Maximum – 60mm/2.36in	
Powerplant: Praga AC2 6-cylinder petrol, 197.6kW/265hp	
Performance: Speed – 42kph/26.1mph	
Range – 180km/111.8 miles	

LEFT: **Photographed at Yuma Proving Ground, Arizona, in 1979, the High Mobility Agility (HIMAG) Test Vehicle was part of the US Army's Tank Research and Development Command's attempt to combat the major increase in weight of MBTs. It was simply a test vehicle with a hydro-pneumatic suspension, which was armed with a 75mm/2.95in ARES gun on an exposed mounting. It was only ever built as a prototype.**

High Mobility Agility Test Vehicle

Designed by the US Army's Tank-Automotive Research and Development Command, the HIMAG (High Mobility Agility) Test Vehicle was part of an ongoing attempt to design an air-portable tank to add firepower to its airborne forces that must deploy rapidly far afield.

The HIMAG used a conventional tank hull and running gear and was powered by a Continental AVCR 1360 12-cylinder supercharged diesel engine with hydro-pneumatic suspension, delivering a top speed 96.6kpm/60mph and a range of 160km/100 miles. To keep its silhouette low, the vehicle did not have a turret – instead, the main armament was mounted on its own barbette with nothing else around it. This was the state-of-the-art ARES 75mm/2.95in hypervelocity automatic anti-armour cannon, linked to infrared search and computer fire-control systems.

In the end, although the HIMAG remained only a prototype, a great deal of useful information was accrued.

HIMAG	
Entered service: 1978 (prototypes only)	
Crew: 3	
Weight: 40,824kg/40.2 tons	
Dimensions: Length – 8.94m/29ft 4in	
Height (over turret hatch) – 3.67m/12ft 0.5in	
Width – 3.81m/12ft 6in	
Armament: Main – 75mm/2.95in ARES gun	
Armour: Unspecified	
Powerplant: Continental AVCR 1360 12-cylinder diesel, 1,118.6kg/1,500hp	
Performance: Speed – 96.6kph/60mph	
Range –160km/100 miles	

High Survivability Test Vehicle (Lightweight)

LEFT: **The HSTV(L) – the High Survivability Test Vehicle (Lightweight) – resembled in some ways the Swedish "S" tank, with a flat, very low profile turret in which was also mounted a 75mm/2.95in ARES gun. Trials took place in the early 1980s, some of the components being used in further development, so the work on HSTV(L) was most useful (compared to HIMAG).**

The second vehicle designed under the aegis of the US Army's ACVT (Armored Combat Vehicle Technology) programme was the High Survivability Test Vehicle (Lightweight) or HSTV(L). Looking more like a conventional tank, albeit with a very low-silhouette turret, the HSTV(L) had a crew of three, two seated semi-reclined in the hull, both equipped with driving controls and the commander, also semi-reclined, in a turret which mounted the same gun as the HIMAG – the ARES 75mm/2.95in hypervelocity cannon. All three crew members were equipped with sights and digital fire-control systems in order for anyone to be able to fire the gun. A camera mounted on the engine deck gave a rear view.

Elements of the HSTV(L) would also occur on the next vehicle – the AAI RDF Light Tank – as the research moved on, so much useful information was accrued.

HSTV(L)	
Entered service: 1980 (prototypes only)	
Crew: 3	
Weight: 20,450kg/20.13 tons	
Dimensions: Length – 8.53m/28ft	
Height (over turret hatch) – 2.41m/7ft 11in	
Width – 2.79m/9ft 2in	
Armament: Main – 75mm/2.95in ARES gun	
Armour: Maximum – 75mm/2.95in	
Powerplant: Avco Lycoming 650 gas turbine, 484.7kW/650hp	
Performance: Speed – 83kph/51.5mph	
Range – 160km/99.4 miles	

IKV-91 TD

Entered service: 1975
Crew: 4
Weight: Unknown
Dimensions: Length – 6.41m/21ft 0.5in
    Height (over turret hatch) – 2.32m/7ft 7.5in
    Width – 3m/9ft 10in
Armament: Main – 90mm/3.54in gun
    Secondary – 2 x 7.62mm/0.3in machine-guns
Armour: Unspecified
Powerplant: Volvo-Penta 6-cylinder diesel,
    268.4kW/360hp
Performance: Speed – 65kph/40.4mph
    Range – 550km/341.8 miles

IKV-91 Tank Destroyer

The IKV-91 was developed in the 1960s as a replacement for the Strv 74 and entered service with the Swedish Army in 1975. Moving away from the turretless fixed gun concept that emerged at the end of World War II, the IKV-91 managed to have a turret but still keep its profile fairly low through cunning design – the turret tapering down at the front. Powered by a Volvo-Penta 6-cylinder turbocharged diesel engine, the vehicle had a top speed of 65kph/ 40.4mph, a range of 550km/341.8 miles and mounted a 90mm/3.54in main gun with 60 rounds of ammunition.

Of the four crew, three – commander, gunner and loader – are positioned in the turret with the driver in the hull front left.

The IKV-91 is also fully amphibious, being propelled in the water by its tracks. There was also a trial version which had the three-man 90mm/3.54in armed turret

replaced by a Rheinmetall turret armed with the Rh 105-11 super-low recoil gun. This version was tested by both Sweden and India and proved effective over an arc of 90 degrees left and right. The IKV-91 served with the Swedish Army but was not sold abroad.

TOP, LEFT AND BELOW: **This Swedish tank destroyer was developed in the late 1960s/early 70s to replace earlier Swedish tank destroyers. Its powerful 90mm/3.54in main gun carried 60 rounds of ammunition (with one up the spout!) and it had a streamlined, all-welded hull and a crew of four, with three men in the turret.**

LEFT: **Now on show at the Israeli Tank Museum, Latrun, this Soviet-built JS-3 (Pike) was captured from the Arabs during one of the previous Arab-Israeli conflicts.** BELOW: **On September 7, 1945, Berlin echoed with the sounds of some 4,000 infantrymen and 200 tanks from the four Great Powers on parade in the Tiergarten. They included the latest Russian heavy tanks, the JS-3 seen here passing the saluting base.**

JS-3 Heavy Tank

Towards the end of 1944, Kotin designed the JS-3 Heavy Tank in conjunction with two other designers, Shashmurin and Rybin. Coming into service with Red Army tank troops in January 1945, it did not make its mark until after the end of World War II. The JS-3 retained all the advantages of its predecessors but had better armour, including a new front glacis plate and a new mushroom carapace-shaped turret, giving it an overall lower silhouette.

One immediately distinctive feature was its bow shape, which came to a point in the middle, earning it the nickname of the "Pike". The JS-3 weighed 46,250kg/45.52 tons, had a crew of four, was powered by a V2 IS diesel engine and was equipped with a torsion bar suspension system, giving it a top speed of 37kph/23mph and a range of around 209km/129.9 miles.

The main armament was the D-25 L/43 122mm/4.8in gun, a weapon that made this vehicle the most formidable tank in the world at that time, and far bigger than anything the opposing NATO forces could field (hence the decision to build Conqueror).

Secondary armament consisted of two 7.62mm/0.3in DT machine-guns and a single 12.7mm/0.5in anti-aircraft machine-gun fitted to the commander's cupola. Although the limitations of its main armament ammunition stowage remained a critical factor (it could only hold 28 rounds), it continued in service long after the end of World War II, serving in many Eastern Bloc armies and other armies all over the world.

Following the Korean War, the Red Army asked for the JS-3 to be modernized and this resulted in a new model, designated as the JS-4, which weighed slightly more, had a more powerful 514.5kW/690hp engine and thicker armour on its hull sides.

JS-3 Heavy Tank

Entered service: 1945
Crew: 4
Weight: 46,250kg/45.52 tons
Dimensions: Length – 6.81m/22ft 4in
Height (over turret hatch) – 2.93m/9ft 7.5in
Width – 3.44m/11ft 3.5in
Armament: Main – 122mm/4.8in D-25 gun
Secondary – 1 x 12.7mm/0.5in and
2 x 7.62mm/0.3in machine-guns
Armour: Maximum – 230mm/9.06in
Powerplant: V2 IS 12-cylinder diesel,
387.8kW/520hp
Performance: Speed – 37kph/23mph
Range – 209km/129.9 miles

LEFT: **JS-3 Red Army Heavy Tank, also known as the Pike. This new configuration was completed in November 1944, with thick, heavily rounded turret armour. The 46,250kg/45.52-ton tank, with its powerful 122mm/4.8in gun, became the standard Soviet heavy tank of the post-war period.**

Jagdpanzer Kanone TD

Entered service: 1965
Crew: 4
Weight: 25,700kg/25.3 tons
Dimensions: Length – 8.75m/28ft 6in
    Height (over turret hatch) – 2.05m/6ft 8.5in
    Width – 2.98m/9ft 9.5in
Armament: Main – 90mm/3.54in gun
    Secondary – 2 x 7.62mm/0.3in machine-guns
Armour: Maximum – 50mm/1.97in
Powerplant: Daimler-Benz MB837 8-cylinder diesel,
    372.9kW/500hp
Performance: Speed – 70kph/43.5mph
    Range – 400km/248.5 miles

LEFT AND BELOW: **Armed with a powerful 90mm/3.54in limited traverse gun, the Jagdpanzer Kanone was something of a hangover from the highly successful German wartime tank destroyers. One major advantage was that it could fire standard US Army 90mm/3.54in tank gun ammunition. It continued in service for many years, some being modified so as to carry and launch the TOW anti-tank guided missile.**

Jagdpanzer Kanone Tank Destroyer

The Jagdpanzer Kanone was a Cold War tank destroyer based on the Hetzer of World War II. The idea behind these vehicles was to use the defensive capacity of a low-silhouette chassis to mount larger fixed guns with limited traverse and elevation. This concept originated from German tank designers reacting to the desperate events at the end of the World War II when various chassis were used to develop tank destroyers.

Hidden away in barns or buildings, or in prepared hull-down positions, they were very effective in the last-ditch defence of the Nazi regime. The thinking remained essentially the same when faced with the massive forces of the Soviet Eastern Bloc, and so the Jagdpanzer Kanone was built.

It mounted a powerful Rheinmetall 90mm/3.54in limited traverse main gun and two 7.62mm/0.3in machine-guns. Power was provided by a Daimler-Benz 8-cylinder diesel engine, giving it a top speed of 70kph/43.5mph and a range of 400km/248.5 miles. However, no sooner had production been completed than the whole concept of a fixed gun tank

destroyer was brought into question and quickly fell out of fashion. Fortunately for the Jagdpanzer Kanone, its excellent chassis could be easily modified and converted to other uses.

With their guns removed and plated over, they morphed to become the Jagdpanzer Rakete Jaguar 2, mounting TOW (Tube-launched, Optically-tracked, Wire-guided) anti-tank guided missiles. A total of 750 Jagdpanzer Kanones were

built for the Germany Army between 1965 and 1967. Then, in late 1972 the Belgians ordered some 80 improved versions of the tank destroyer, which had the complete Renk transmission, final drives, suspension and tracks of the German Marder Mechanised Infantry Combat Vehicle, and gave it the Belgian Army designation of "JPK-90". None of these tank destroyers are now in front-line service with either army.

Jagdpanzer Rakete Jaguar Tank Destroyer

The Jagdpanzer Rakete Jaguar was developed from the Jagdpanzer Kanone, which it replaced. The first prototype was completed by Hanomag and was followed by a further six, three of which were built by Hanomag and three by Henschel from 1963 onwards.

Four years later the Jagdpanzer Rakete Jaguar had succeeded the Jagdpanzer Kanone in production, 370 being built by the following year, half by each of the manufacturers. The main difference between the two is in the main weapon system mounted, although there were also other modifications to the Jagdpanzer Kanone's chassis, hull and front superstructure in order to mount the new weapon system. This was the European manufactured long-range HOT (*Haute subsonique Optiquement Téléguidée*) anti-tank missile, fired from a single roof-mounted launcher equipped with a thermal sight for nightfighting.

Powered by the same Daimler-Benz 8-cylinder diesel engine, the Rakete Jaguar had the same speed and range as its predecessor. The second version of the Jagdpanzer Rakete was a retrofit to the Jagdpanzer Kanone itself, with its main gun removed and the hole plated over in order to mount the TOW (Tube-launched, Optically-tracked, Wire-guided) missile system.

ABOVE AND BELOW: **The Jaguar replaced the Jagdpanzer Kanone, and is based on its modified chassis, coming into production in the late 1960s. It mounted a long-range anti-tank guided missile, there being two models – Jaguar with the HOT missile and Jaguar 2 with TOW.**

A total of 162 Jagdpanzer Kanones were converted into TOW ATGW (Anti-Tank Guided Weapon) carriers from 1983–85. The system already had its Texas Instruments night sight, while the TOW missile flies faster than HOT but has an almost identical range (3,750m/12,303ft as compared with 4,000m/13,123ft).

Jagdpanzer Rakete Jaguar TD

Entered service: 1967
Crew: 4
Weight: 25,500kg/25.1 tons
Dimensions: Length – 6.77m/22ft 2.5in
  Height (over turret hatch) – 2.16m/7ft 1in
  Width – 2.95m/9ft 8in
Armament: Main – HOT missile launcher
  Secondary – 2 x 7.62mm/0.3in machine-guns
Armour: Maximum – 50mm/1.97in
Powerplant: Daimler-Benz MB837 8-cylinder diesel, 372.9kW/500hp
Performance: Speed – 70kph/43.5mph
  Range – 400km/248.5 miles

ABOVE: **Jagdpanzer Rakete Jaguar, mounting the HOT missile, which has both semi-automatic IR guidance and optical manual guidance, where the commands are transmitted via a wire which is immune to jamming. Missiles largely took over from guns in the post-war anti-tank role.**

LEFT: **Shir 1.** Originally built to fill an order from the Shah of Iran, the Shir 1 (Lion) was a combat-improved Chieftain (FV 4030) which incorporated all the new features, such as IFCS (Improved Fire-Control System), CV12 Rolls-Royce 894.8kW/1,200hp engine, automatic gearbox and new hydro-pneumatic suspension. The Shah was deposed and the Shir 1 was subsequently sold to Jordan, and is now known as the Khalid. BELOW AND BOTTOM: The **Shir 2** was essentially the same as the British Army Challenger 1, and so had the same basic layout as Chieftain.

Khalid Shir
Main Battle Tank

The Khalid Shir traces its development through the Chieftain series of vehicles. A late-production, combat-improved Chieftain called the Shir was designed by the UK's Royal Ordnance for the Shah of Iran, but the project was cancelled after the Iranian Revolution of 1979 toppled the Peacock Throne. It had been a massive order – 125 Shir I (FV 4030/2) and 1,225 Shir 2 (FV 4030/3), so its cancellation by the new Iranian Government in February 1979 was a considerable blow to the British Royal Ordnance, who had already begun production of Shir I, with the first

production tanks being scheduled for delivery in 1980.

Fortunately, however, they were able to switch to another Middle Eastern customer, namely Jordan, who in November 1979, placed an order with the UK for 270 "Khalid Shirs" (their name for the Shir I) for delivery from 1981. The two tanks were not completely identical, there having been some modifications, such as upgrading the fire-control systems. The Khalid Shir is therefore in essence a combat-improved Chieftain.

Powered by a Perkins Condor V12 diesel engine, the vehicle has a top speed of 48kph/29.9mph and a range of 400km/248.5 miles. With a crew of four (three in the turret and a driver in the hull), the Khalid Shir mounts the 120mm/4.72in L11A5 rifled bore main gun (the same as the Chieftain) with a digital fire-control system, along with two 7.62mm/0.3in machine-guns – one coaxial in its ergonomically shaped turret.

Khalid Shir MBT

Entered service: 1981
Crew: 4
Weight: 58,000kg/57.08 tons
Dimensions: Length – 8.39m/27ft 6.5in
    Height (over turret hatch) – 2.98m/9ft 9in
    Width – 3.52m/11ft 6.5in
Armament: Main – 120mm/4.72in L11A5 gun
    Secondary – 2 x 7.62mm/0.3in machine-guns
Armour: Unspecified
Powerplant: Perkins Condor V12 diesel,
    894.8kW/1,200hp
Performance: Speed – 48kph/29.9mph
    Range – 400km/248.5 miles

M8 Ridgeway Armoured Gun System

The M8 Ridgeway Armoured Gun System (AGS) was another US attempt in the never-ending quest to boost the firepower of RDF (Rapid Deployment Force) troops with an air-portable tank – and it reflects the size of that superpower that there is much more than one strand in their development programme.

Developed and manufactured by United Defense (formerly FMC), the M8 AGS comprises the XM35 105mm/4.13in rifled gun with an automatic loader, giving the gun a rate of fire of 12 rounds per minute. The vehicle's weight was kept down by employing variable suites of armour, including appliqué and ERA (Explosive Reactive Armour), so it was fully transportable in a C-130 Hercules transport aircraft.

Perhaps because the US Army's Tank-Automotive Research and Development Command Armored Combat Vehicle Technology (ACVT) was busy co-developing the HIMAG and HSTV airborne AFVs (also destined to be discontinued), the M8 was not pursued, which left the company to try to sell it elsewhere. Despite initial interest from Japan and Turkey, no orders materialized and the project was terminated.

ABOVE AND BELOW LEFT: **Developed in the early 1990s as a light tank to replace the M551 Sheridan, the M8 AGS reached production status in the mid-1990s, but the US Army then cancelled the programme. They have since tried to interest Turkey and Japan in the project, but without success. The light tank mounts a respectable 105mm/4.13in gun and weighs 23,590kg/23.2 tons.**

M8 Ridgeway AGS

Entered service: 1995
Crew: 3
Weight: 23,590kg/23.2 tons
Dimensions: Length – 8.97m/29ft 5in
Height (over turret hatch) – 2.55m/8ft 4.5in
Width – 2.69m/8ft 10in
Armament: Main – 105mm/4.13in M35 gun
Secondary – 1 x 7.62mm/0.3in machine-gun and
either 1 x 12.7mm/0.5in or 1 x 7.62mm/0.3in
machine-gun or 1 x 40mm/1.58in grenade launcher
Armour: Unspecified
Powerplant: Unspecified
Performance: Speed – 72kph/44.7mph
Range – 451km/280 miles

Leclerc Main Battle Tank

Stemming from an abandoned Franco-German MBT design project of the 1980s, the Leclerc (named after the World War II Free French liberator of Paris) entered service in 1992 and is the prime weapon of the French armoured forces. Built using welded rolled steel and composite armour, weighing 56,000kg/55.1 tons and fitted with a hydro-pneumatic suspension system, it is powered by a SACM V8X-1500 12-cylinder diesel engine, giving a top speed of 72kph/ 44.7mph and a range of 450km/279.6 miles.

The main armament is a 120mm/4.72in smoothbore gun served by an automatic loader capable of delivering 12 rounds per minute. There is also a 12.7mm/0.5in heavy machine-gun mounted coaxially and a 7.62mm/0.3in machine-gun for anti-aircraft and close quarter defence.

The Leclerc also carries all the latest digital optical, fire-control and battlefield management systems. Giat Industries have designed a new turret for the Leclerc which can accommodate a 140mm/5.51in smoothbore gun together with an automatic loader in the turret bustle, but currently there are no plans to replace the existing gun. There are plans for future improvements that include enhanced command and control systems, battlefield identification friend-or-foe, automatic target-tracking, a defensive aids suite, a new thermal imager and enhanced armour.

Leclerc variants include an ARV (Armoured Recovery Vehicle), an ARV with K2D mine-clearing equipment and an armoured engineer vehicle which is similar to the ARV but can be fitted with specialist engineering equipment (now in prototype stage).

In 2002 the French revealed that they were studying further upgrades to the Leclerc MBT in service with the French Army, aiming for 2015. These are likely to include mobility, lethality, survivability, command and control, communications and intelligence, and support. As far as survivability is concerned, Giat Industries are looking to incorporate several layers of protection, the first line of defence being stealth and the second a soft kill kit. They have built an AMX-30 Stealth demonstrator and are evaluating a version of the stealth kit for the Leclerc. The soft kill kit will probably be based upon

ABOVE: **The Giat Industries MBT – called the Leclerc from 1986 onwards – was first mooted in 1985 and made its first appearance just five years later in 1990 at the Satory defence exhibition. This photograph shows it in the ring at the French Armour School's annual demonstration at Saumur. So far, over 400 have been built and used to equip French tank regiments, while the United Arab Emirates have also purchased 436 tropicalized Leclercs.** LEFT: **A French Army Leclerc on operations in Kosovo.**

ABOVE: **A Close-up of the FINDERS Battle Management System as installed in a Leclerc MBT.**
RIGHT: **A pair of Leclercs on training. The 120mm/ 4.72in smoothbore gun is the same calibre as that fitted to Leopard 2 and has an automatic loader containing 22 ready-rounds.**

a basic countermeasures kit, to which will be added a system to detect and foil guided missiles and tank rounds. There will also be a third layer, namely a hard kill system capable of destroying incoming munitions.

Finally, it is worth noting that while the Leclerc has an impressive specification, it has yet to be tried in combat. As such, it has not achieved the "Top Gun" status of other MBTs such as the Abrams, Challenger 2 and Merkava. The vehicle has been purchased by the United Arab Emirates.

RIGHT: **This impressive gathering of tanks and men is probably part of a French armoured regiment while on training. Each French Army regiment equipped with the Leclerc MBT has a total of 40 tanks – one at RHQ and three squadrons of 13 each.** BELOW: **A Leclerc ARV pulls a Leclerc MBT during a training exercise in Qatar. The first of these ARVs was completed in Spring 1994. As well as recovering disabled tanks and towing them to safety, the ARV has the necessary equipment to carry out repairs in forward areas, such as power pack changes.**

Leclerc MBT

Entered service: 1992
Crew: 3
Weight: 56,000kg/55.1 tons
Dimensions: Length – 9.87m/32ft 4.5in
    Height (over turret hatch) – 2.53m/8ft 3.5in
    Width – 3.71m/12ft 2in
Armament: Main – 120mm/4.72in gun
    Secondary – 1 x 12.7mm/0.5in and
    1 x 7.62mm/0.3in machine-guns
Armour: Unspecified
Powerplant: SACM V8X-1500 12-cylinder diesel,
    1,118.6kW/1,500hp
Performance: Speed – 72kph/44.7mph
    Range – 450km/279.6 miles

Leopard 1 Main Battle Tank

Originating from an earlier development project shared by
Germany, France and Italy, the Leopard 1 was the German
vehicle that resulted when that programme failed. First
manufactured in 1963 by Krauss-Maffei of Munich, the initial
design was influenced by the French AMX-30, where the
armour was kept relatively light when compared with other
contemporary MBTs in order to gain on mobility (although it
was increased in later Marks).

With a weight of almost 40 tons and powered by a MTU MB
10-cylinder 618.9kW/830hp multi-fuel engine, it has a top
speed of 65kph/40.4mph and a range of 600km/373 miles.
The main armament is the British-made 105mm/4.13in rifled
gun fitted with a gyroscopic stabilizer for accurate firing on the
move. There are also two 7.62mm/0.3in machine-guns, one
mounted coaxially. The vehicle has a crew of four and is fitted
with automatic fire control, NBC (Nuclear, Biological and
Chemical) protection and night-vision equipment.

With its good design and all-round reliability, the Leopard 1
has had a successful commercial history, over 6,000 vehicles
being exported to nine NATO countries and also Australia, as
well as being made under licence in Italy. Over its long lifespan
the Leopard 1 has seen various extra armour upgrades and
variants appear, including a mine-clearer and bulldozer. Though
now replaced by Leopard 2 in the German Armed Forces, it is
still in service with many other armies.

ABOVE: **This Leopard 1 is on training in the south of Holland.** BELOW: **Following
rehabilitation, post-war German main battle tank development was initially a
tripartite programme between Germany, Italy and France. For the Germans this
resulted in Leopard 1, with Krauss-Maffei as prime contractor. Although it was
a satisfactory tank, Leopard 1 was really too light and it lacked armoured
protection. Nevertheless, it stayed in service up to the Leopard 1 A5 model at
the end of the century. It is still in service worldwide although some, in places
like Brazil and Chile, originate from other NATO countries rather than Germany.**

LEFT: **Excellent view of an Italian Leopard 1. They were not ordered until 1970, 720 being ordered and delivered. In addition MaK delivered a further 120 gun tanks, 69 ARVs and 12 AEVs.** ABOVE: **Leopard 1 could be fitted with a snorkel mast for deep wading.** BELOW: **As with Challenger, Leopard 1 had a driver training model where the turret was replaced by an observation cabin. German models still had the 105mm/4.13in gun barrel (Dutch and Belgian models did not).** BOTTOM LEFT: **Good internal view of a Leopard 1 turret.**

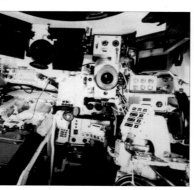

The first NATO country to place an order for Leopard 1 was Belgium (in 1967), and in all they have 334 gun tanks, plus a further 100 or more variants, of which 55 are the Gepard AA vehicle with twin 35mm/1.38in Oerlikon cannon. Next came the Netherlands, who ordered 468 Leopard 1s between 1968–70. Now, as well as the countries mentioned already, Canada, Denmark, Greece, Norway and Turkey have all purchased Leopard 1s from Germany, while Brazil has 87 from Belgium, and Chile has 200 from the Netherlands.

Kraus-Maffei Wegmann, who have factories in Munich and Kassel, still offer a wide range of modification kits for the Leopard 1 MBT which include: extra armour for the turret and mantlet; armoured skirts (side plates); automatic transmission; integral thermal imaging; snow grousers (plus stowage brackets on the glacis plate); a dozer blade (already adopted by Australia); additional external stowage boxes; tracks with replaceable track pads; and a fire-suppression system.

Leopard 1 MBT

Entered service: 1963
Crew: 4
Weight: 40,400kg/39.76 tons
Dimensions: Length – 9.54m/31ft 3.5in
Height (over turret hatch) – 2.76m/9ft 0.5in
Width – 3.41m/11ft 2.5in
Armament: Main – 105mm/4.13in gun
Secondary – 2 x 7.62mm/0.3in machine-guns
Armour: Maximum – 70mm/2.76in
Powerplant: MTU MB 828 M500 multi-fuel, 618.9kW/830hp
Performance: Speed – 65kph/40.4mph
Range – 600km/373 miles

Leopard 2 Main Battle Tank

TOP AND ABOVE: **Excellent views of the Leopard 2 Main Battle Tank. It was in 1970 that Germany decided to proceed with a new MBT – the Leopard 2. Numerous production lots have since been built and taken into service with the German, Greek, Spanish, Dutch, Austrian, Danish, Finnish, Norwegian, Polish, Swiss and Swedish armies. In total, well over 1,000 have been produced, all built by Krauss-Maffei Wegmann GmbH. Leopard 2 is one of the finest MBTs currently in world service, and in addition to the gun tank, there are AVLBs, ARVs and driver training vehicles, while the latest developments involve the fitting of a new gun.**

The Leopard 2 is produced by Krauss-Maffei of Munich – and like the Leopard 1, originated in another failed, shared AFV project, this time between Germany and the USA, and known as the MBT 70. Using many components designed for that project, Leopard 2 emerged in 1979, after a spate of prototypes and intensive trials. The all-round quality of the Leopard 2's performance is indicative of the meticulous development cycle this vehicle has undergone. With upgrade packages including improved spaced armour, main gun, stabilization, suspension, navigation and fire control, it is still very much a contemporary "Top Gun" MBT.

Leopard 2 weighs almost 59 tons and is powered by an MTU MB 873 12-cylinder diesel engine, giving it a top speed of 72kph/44.7mph and a range of 550km/310.7 miles. The main armament was initially the L4, a Rheinmetall 120mm/4.72in smoothbore gun, but this has more recently been upgraded to the longer-barrelled L55. There are also two 7.62mm/0.3in machine-guns, one mounted coaxially to the main armament.

Used and manufactured under licence by many NATO member countries, the Leopard 2 has spawned many indigenous variants, mounting different extra armour, weapons and fire-control systems, or otherwise modified for a specific purpose such as the ARV (Armoured Recovery Vehicle) and mine-clearer versions. The Swiss Army now has about 400 Leopard 2 (Pz 87 Leo) MBTs, 60–70 per cent of which were built in Switzerland.

The latest model is the Leopard 2A5/2A6 MBT, which is virtually identical to its predecessor but has the following improvements: commander's roof-mounted periscope now has a thermal sight whose image is transmitted to a monitor inside the turret; all-new electrical gun control equipment has replaced the earlier hydraulic system, now quieter, easier to maintain and uses less electrical energy; improved armour protection for the frontal arc of the turret, giving it a distinctive arrowhead shape; new driver's hatch that slides to the right; TV camera installed at the rear of the hull to allow for safer reversing (it has a 65-degree field of view both in horizontal and vertical planes); a hybrid navigation system enabling the commander to navigate in any operational environment; and modifications to the laser range data processor.

There have also been a number of improvements to the Swedish Leopard 2 (known as Strv 122), which include: more protection to the front and sides of the chassis similar to that for the turret; improved roof protection against bomblets; and an eye-safe laser range finder.

TOP: **This Leopard 2 Main Battle Tank is one of about 400 ordered by the Swiss Army, the first being operational by early 1988.** ABOVE: **Leopard 2 deep-wading at the factory.** BELOW: **The Leopard 2 moving cross-country.**

Leopard 2 MBT

Entered service: 1979
Crew: 4
Weight: 59,700kg/58.76tons
Dimensions: Length – 9.97m/32ft 8.5in
Height (over turret hatch) – 2.64m/8ft 8in
Width – 3.74m/12ft 3in
Armament: Main – 120mm/4.72in gun
Secondary – 2 x 7.62mm/0.3in machine-guns
Armour: Unspecified
Powerplant: MTU MB 873 Ka501 12-cylinder diesel, 1,118.5kW/1,500hp
Performance: Speed – 72kph/44.7mph
Range – 500km/310.7 miles

M41 Walker Bulldog Light Tank

Designed after the end of World War II to replace the M24 Chaffee, the M41 Walker Bulldog eventually surfaced in 1951 after an extensive period of prototype testing. With a weight of 23,495kg/23.1 tons, it was powered by a Continental AOS 95-3 6-cylinder supercharged petrol engine, delivering a top speed of 72.4kph/45mph, and had a range of 161km/ 100 miles. The main armament was a 76mm/2.99in main gun supplemented by two machine-guns, one of 12.7mm/ 0.5in and the other 7.62mm/0.3in.

The Walker Bulldog was fast and packed a powerful punch for its size. It saw action in Vietnam and served in many NATO member armies, as well as being exported to various countries in South America and Asia.

Some of these countries have carried out extensive modifications, as well as building "lookalikes" such as the Bernardini M41 manufactured in Brazil, while other extensive work was done in the 1980s by Spain to convert the M41 to an anti-tank role,

The Belgian company Cockerill successfully replaced the existing 76mm/2.99in main gun with a 90mm/3.54in, and that particular model was adopted by Uruguay.

Production of the Bulldog has long ceased, but the M41 is still to be found in service all over the world. Perhaps the strangest use for it was as a remote-controlled tank for testing air-to-ground missiles by the US Navy in the 1980s. It was also widely used for trial purposes by the USA, especially for work on the M551 Sheridan project. Modifications included a variety of weapons systems, including an Anti-Aircraft (AA) variant armed with twin 40mm/1.58in M2A1 Bofors AA guns.

ABOVE: American-built and widely sold overseas, more than 5,500 of these excellent little light tanks were built and exported, many fighting both in Korea and Vietnam, being one of the most effective weapons of the South Vietnamese. It mounted a 76mm/2.99in gun which had a good anti-armour performance. This M41 belonged to the New Zealand Armoured Corps. BELOW: The 23,495kg/ 23.1 ton M41 was a relatively easy transporter load, as is seen here. First production models appeared in 1951, there being three Marks (A1, A2 and A3), as well as the chassis being used for both AA and SP gun conversions.

ABOVE: **The M41 was exported worldwide. In Brazil it was upgraded to the Bernardini M41 and serves both with the Brazil and Uruguay armies, mounting a 90mm/3.54in Cockerill gun.** RIGHT: **A breech-end view inside the turret of an M41 Walker Bulldog.** BELOW: **Realistic training in the USA included anti-gas exercises with both the infantry and tank crews wearing respirators.**

Fifty years after it was rushed into service, the Walker Bulldog still remains "on the books" of eight countries, five of which are in South America. Largest holdings, however, are currently in Taiwan – estimated to be between 400 and 675. With a new engine, performance of the tank has been greatly increased; for example, a maximum road speed of 72kph/45mph and a range of 450km/280 miles. The Walker Bulldog lives on!

M41 Walker Bulldog Light Tank

Entered service: 1951
Crew: 4
Weight: 23,495kg/23.1 tons
Dimensions: Length – 8.21m/26ft 11in
Height (over turret hatch) – 2.72m/8ft 11in
Width – 3.2m/10ft 6in
Armament: Main – 76mm/2.99in gun
Secondary – 1 x 12.7mm/0.5in and
1 x 7.62mm/0.3in machine-guns
Armour: Maximum – 32mm/1.26in
Powerplant: Continental AOS 95-3 petrol,
372.9kW/500hp
Performance: Speed – 72.4kph/45mph
Range – 161km/100 miles

M47 Medium (Patton) Tank

Named after the famous US World War II General, George S. Patton, the M47 was the first truly post-war American tank to be produced, being rushed into production during the Korean crisis in 1952. Its interim predecessor, the M46, which was to all intents and purposes an improved M26 Pershing, did fight in Korea and was also known as the Patton.

The M47 was based on the M46 hull with a newly designed turret, and weighed 46,165kg/45.4 tons. Using a torsion bar suspension system and powered by a Continental AVDS

1790 5B 12-cylinder supercharged petrol engine, it had a top speed of 48kph/29.8mph and a range of 129km/80.1 miles. The new cast turret made the M47 easily identifiable, as it bulged out to the rear and tapered sharply to the front to a small mantlet mounting the M36 90mm/3.54in main gun. For the secondary armament there were two Browning machine-guns, one of 12.7mm/0.5in and the other 7.62mm/0.3in.

The M47 was the last American tank with a five-man crew and it did not have NBC (Nuclear, Biological and Chemical) protection, night-fighting or computerized fire-control systems, so it could not fire accurately while on the move. It proved to be a stopgap development soon invalidated by the advent of the M48.

Although it did not serve for long with US forces, it was exported extensively to her allies, including Taiwan, Greece, Iran, Italy, Japan, Jordan, Netherlands, Pakistan, Portugal, Saudi Arabia, South Korea, Spain, Turkey and Yugoslavia. A final upgrade programme began in the late 1960s, resulting in the M47M, using the engine and fire-control system from the M60A1 to further extend this vehicle's operational life.

There were some faults with the M47 that were recognized even before production began. Indeed, work had already

ABOVE AND LEFT: **First of the truly post-war American tanks was the 90mm/3.54in gun tank, designated as the M47, but popularly known as the Patton after the famous General George S. Patton, Jnr, who had been killed in a road accident in 1945. It would soon be replaced by the M48, also called the Patton.**

ABOVE: **Trials took place to fit the British 105mm/4.13in L7A1 tank gun into the M47s in service with the Italian Army, which proved to be very successful because the up-gunned result was much more stable. The M47s in Spanish service were fitted with the Rheinmetall 105mm/4.13in smoothbore gun (known as the M47-E2).** RIGHT: **This highly painted M46 is located at the Tank Museum, Bovington. The M47 used the same hull.** BELOW: **Part of a tank company of M47s on the firing line at the Armor School, Fort Knox, Kentucky, 1953.**

begun on its successor while it was being accepted by the US Army Equipment Review Board. For example, it was clear that turret protection was generally lower than that of the hull and that the fuel carried was insufficient to last through a normal battlefield day. It would never see action with the regular US Army and would soon be relegated to the National Guard (November 1953). In fact, it was a better training vehicle because its five-man crew (the M48 had only four) meant that 20 per cent more men could be trained in each training cycle.

M47 Medium (Patton) Tank

Entered service: 1952
Crew: 5
Weight: 46,165kg/45.4 tons
Dimensions: Length – 8.56m/28ft 1in
Height (over turret hatch) – 3.35m/11ft
Width – 3.2m/10ft 6in
Armament: Main – 90mm/3.54in M36 gun
Secondary – 1 x 12.7mm/0.5in and 1 x 7.62mm/0.3in machine-guns
Armour: Maximum – 115mm/4.53in
Powerplant: Continental AVDS 1790 5B V12 petrol, 604kW/810hp
Performance: Speed – 48kph/29.8mph
Range – 129km/80.1 miles

M48 Patton Main Battle Tank

The M48 Patton Main Battle Tank was another American tank to be rushed into production during the Korean crisis, and it initially suffered from teething problems as a consequence. However, it went on to have a long and distinguished service life, including combat with US forces in Vietnam.

It had a lower wider hull than the previous M47, along with a new, less bulging turret, with a visually distinctive and powerful searchlight just above the main gun. Weighing 48,987kg/48.2 tons, the M48 was powered by a Continental AVDS 1790 2 12-cylinder engine, giving it a top speed of 48kph/29.8mph and a range of 499km/310.1 miles.

The main armament of the M48 was a 90mm/3.54in gun, supplemented by a 7.62mm/0.3in coaxial machine-gun and a 12.7mm/0.5in anti-aircraft machine-gun mounted on the commander's cupola.

It was one of the first tanks to have an analogue mechanical fire-control system and saw various upgrades. These included different engines, suspension, fire-control and weapons systems, and main armament, which was upgraded to a 105mm/4.13in gun almost immediately. The M48 was very popular on the US export market, being supplied to many countries worldwide. Some of these customers modified it extensively for their own use, including Spain, Israel and Taiwan.

ABOVE AND BELOW: **The M48 Patton tank was originally armed with a 90mm/3.54in gun, later to be replaced by a 105mm/4.13in gun. Despite being rushed into service in 1952 and having some faults, the Patton was a popular tank, with large numbers being built (over 11,000). It was produced in five Marks (up to A5) and sold to Greece, Germany, South Korea, Spain, Taiwan, Turkey, Iran and Israel.**

Starting in 1958, the West German army was supplied with a total of 1,400 M48 series AFVs, including armoured recovery vehicles (M88), M55 SP howitzers and M48 AVLB as well as gun tanks. It is also most interesting to note that subsequently, after fruitless negotiations direct with the USA, Israel was able to obtain their first M48s from the Germans, a party of selected Israeli tank officers being trained on a crash course in great secrecy in Germany!

The Taiwanese M48H, also known as Brave Tiger, was produced in 1990 by combining M60 hulls with M48 turrets, mounting an indigenously built version of the 105mm/4.13in rifled main gun, along with other elements including digital fire control and sight stabilization from the Abrams M1.

TOP LEFT: **The Tank Museum's M48 in a display of NATO tanks.** ABOVE LEFT: **The M67 flamethrower version of the M48 is seen here in Vietnam in 1968 in the act of using its flamethrower. None of this model are still in service.** ABOVE: **The M48H, also known as Brave Tiger, was a modified M48 with a home-produced version of the British 105mm/4.13in gun. The tank actually uses the hulls of the US M60, M60A1, M60A3, as well as the M48A5 and South Korean K1. In addition, it is said that some Merkava Marks 1 and 2 are also employed, so it really is a hybrid!** LEFT: **An M48 moving into action in Vietnam. M48A1, A2 and A3 all saw active service there, as did the M48 AVLB and M88 recovery vehicle.**

M48 Patton MBT

Entered service: 1953
Crew: 4
Weight: 48,987kg/48.2 tons
Dimensions: Length – 9.31m/30ft 6.5in
   Height (over turret hatch) – 3.01m/9ft 10.5in
   Width – 3.63m/11ft 11in
Armament: Main – 105mm/4.13in L7 gun
   Secondary – 1 x 12.7mm/0.5in and 1 x
   7.62mm/0.3in machine-guns
Armour: Maximum – 180mm/7.07in
Powerplant: Continental AVDS 1790 2 12-cylinder
   diesel, 559.3kW/750hp
Performance: Speed – 48kph/29.8mph
   Range – 499km/310.1 miles

M50 Ontos Tank Destroyer

In the mid-1950s the USA developed the M50 Ontos (*Ontos* is Greek for "thing") as an early attempt to provide rapidly deployable air-portable firepower for airborne troops. It was based on the chassis of the T55/T56 series of experimental vehicles, combined with a new a distinctive pyramidal mini-turret which mounted six 106mm/4.17in M40A1 recoilless (RCR) rifles, three to a side, firing mainly HEAT (High-Explosive Anti-Tank) but also anti-personnel munitions. These weapons were aimed by using a Spotting Rifle fitted to the top tubes which was fired first to determine the range and bearing of the target, the six recoilless rifles then being discharged singly or en masse.

The Ontos weighed 8,641kg/8.5 tons, had a crew of three and was powered by a Chrysler V8 engine, giving it a speed of 48kph/30mph and a range of 241km/150 miles. This vehicle suffered from a number of serious disadvantages: the loader was vulnerable to enemy fire when reloading the weapons system because he had to get out of the vehicle; the recoilless rifles lacked any real accuracy; and there was a massive and dangerous back-blast from the rifle tubes when discharged.

The Ontos was really only a stopgap measure, with as few as 300 being made before it was discontinued. It saw action only briefly in Vietnam, where it was used by troops on the ground primarily in an artillery mode from prepared firebases. In 1966 the engine was upgraded to the Chrysler V8, generating 134.2kW/180hp, but the vehicle was soon superseded and withdrawn from service in 1970 to be replaced by other air-portable alternatives offering more firepower and protection.

ABOVE AND BELOW LEFT: **Designed in the mid-1950s as a small air-portable tank destroyer, Ontos (Greek for "thing") comprised six 106mm/4.17in recoilless rifles mounted on a modified APC chassis. While the US Army dropped the idea in preference for Jeep-mounted recoilless rifles, the USMC avidly seized on the proposal, and it went into production in 1955, some 300 being built. It saw action in Dominica and Vietnam and knocked out various light tanks (e.g. AMX-13). It was retired in the late 1960s. It was also used for experiments with titanium armour as the T55 Ontos APC, while another version proposed was a light assault vehicle, armed with four or eight machine-guns. Finally, there were three more proposals, all with various anti-tank guns. None were ever built.**

M50 Ontos TD

Entered service: 1955
Crew: 3
Weight: 8,641kg/8.5 tons
Dimensions: Length – 3.83m/12ft 7in
Height (over turret hatch) – 2.13m/7ft
Width – 2.60m/8ft 6.5in
Armament: Main – 6 x 106mm/4.17in recoilless rifles
Secondary – 7.62mm/0.3in machine-gun
Armour: Maximum – 13mm/0.51in
Powerplant: General Motors 302 V6 petrol, 108.1kW/145hp
Performance: Speed – 48kph/29.8mph
Range – 241km/149.8 miles

LEFT AND BELOW LEFT:
Another light airborne support weapon was the Scorpion 90mm/3.54in anti-tank gun mounted on an all aluminium hull and weighing a total of just 7,144kg/7 tons. Its major drawbacks were the lack of crew protection and a vulnerable petrol engine. It was soon replaced by the M551 Sheridan.

M56 Scorpion Tank Destroyer

Known officially as the M56 Self-Propelled Anti-Tank (SPAT), the M56 was another US attempt at developing air-portable firepower during the 1950s for use with rapidly deployable troops.

To save on weight, the vehicle had an aluminium hull and no turret, with only a small gun-shield for protection – an approach that didn't endear it to the troops that had to operate it. It was actually based on the unarmoured chassis of the M76 amphibious cargo carrier, the gun being on a low pedestal mount on top of the hull, which carried four road-wheels on either side suspended by torsion bars.

The engine, driver and his controls took up all of the remaining space in the hull, leaving the gun-layer to ride on top of the vehicle. Where the remaining two crewmen travelled is not clear, although logically they must have gone with any ammunition vehicle attached to the detachment. Presumably when the Scorpion went into action and they had to change position, they would simply hang on to the outside as best they could! At 7,144kg/7 tons, the M56 was powered by a Continental AOI-4025 6-cylinder petrol engine, giving it a top speed of 45kph/28mph and a range of 225km/139.8 miles. It mounted a 90mm/3.54in M54 main gun and saw action in Vietnam, where it tended to be used as a support weapon in a prepared position.

Under-armoured, under-powered and unpopular, it was soon replaced by the M551 Sheridan.

M56 Scorpion TD		
Entered service: 1953		
Crew: 4		
Weight: 7,144kg/7 tons		
Dimensions: Length – 5.84m/19ft 2in		
Height (over turret hatch) – 2.05m/6ft 8.5in		
Width – 2.57m/8ft 5in		
Armament: Main – 90mm/3.54in M54 gun		
Armour: None		
Powerplant: Continental AOI-4025 6-cylinder petrol, 149.kW/200hp		
Performance: Speed – 45kph/28mph		
Range – 225km/139.8 miles		

M60 Main Battle Tank

Manufactured by General Dynamics, the M60 is one of the world's most successful MBTs, with over 15,000 built. First entering service with the US Army in 1960, it went on to serve in the armies of at least 22 countries. The tank has provided excellent battlefield performance over four decades and has been continuously advanced and upgraded with appliqué armour, increasingly powerful engines, new guns and fire-control systems, ammunition and other features.

Weighing almost 52 tons and with a crew of four, the M60 is powered by a Continental AVDS 1790 2A V12 turbo-charged diesel engine, giving it a top speed of 48kph/29.8mph and a range of 500km/310.7 miles. The main armament is the 105mm/4.13in M68 rifled gun derived from the L7A1 105mm/4.13in gun of the British Centurion, along with two machine-guns – a coaxial 7.62mm/0.3in M240 and a 12.7mm/0.5in.

The M60A1, with a new turret and thicker armour, was manufactured from 1962 to 1980. The M60A2, with a new turret mounting a 152mm/5.98in gun and missile launcher, was produced in 1972. From 1978 to 1987 the M60A3, with improvements to its fire control, was the most successful and numerously produced of the series.

ABOVE AND LEFT: **Two views of the Tank Museum's M60 Main Battle Tank, including one of it going through a "wall of fire". The M60 was approved in the late 1950s and the contract awarded to Chrysler in 1959. Since then, over 5,400 have been built for the US forces and many thousands sold worldwide, the Israelis being the next largest user. The tank has a 105mm/4.13in gun and a very prominent searchlight.**

ABOVE: **An IDF (Israeli Defence Force) M60 moves into battle with some extra passengers.** LEFT: **Hard at work building M60 turrets in the Chrysler factory.** BELOW: **The M60A1 fitted with ERA (Explosive Reactive Armour). A small number of USMC M60A1s were used during Operation "Desert Storm" in 1991. The Israeli-invented ERA gives added protection to vulnerable areas such as the turret.**

Having such a long front-line life in so many countries, the M60 has seen many variants, modifications and enhancements, with Israel in particular upgrading M60s into their own types, including the Magach and the Sabra. With so many countries still fielding M60s, General Dynamics Land Systems (GDLS) has recently brought out the M60-2000 upgrade package, using the turret and 120mm/4.72in M256 smoothbore main gun of the M1 Abrams, along with a new up-rated engine, fire-control and safety systems. In this way the service life of this excellent MBT has been prolonged still further.

M60A1 MBT

Entered service: 1960
Crew: 4
Weight: 52,617kg/51.8 tons
Dimensions: Length – 9.44m/31ft
    Height (over turret hatch) – 3.27m/10ft 8.5in
    Width – 3.63m/11ft 11in
Armament: Main – 105mm/4.13in M68 gun
    Secondary – 1 x 12.7mm/0.5in and
    1 x 7.62mm/0.3in machine-guns
Armour: Maximum – 143mm/5.63in
Powerplant: Continental AVDS 1790 2A V12 diesel,
    559.3kW/750hp
Performance: Speed – 48kph/29.8mph
    Range – 500km/310.7 miles

LEFT: **A US Army M60 takes cover in a corn field during a NATO exercise in the 1960–70s, being totally ignored by the farmer and his wife!**

LEFT: The Sheridan Light Tank. Worried by the ever increasing size and weight of modern main battle tanks, the Sheridan was a US attempt to combine a gun and missile system in one 152mm/5.98in launcher. The 15,830kg/15.6-ton light tank had a crew of four and was developed in 1959.
BELOW: Good photograph of an anti-armour Shillelagh missile being launched. The Sheridan continued to serve until the 1990s.

M551 Sheridan Light Tank

The M551 Sheridan is yet another air-portable American light tank developed for its airborne divisions to replace the unsatisfactory M56 Scorpion. Entering service in 1968 with a weight of 15,830kg/15.6 tons and a crew of four, the Sheridan was powered by a Detroit Diesel 6V-53T 6-cylinder turbocharged engine, giving it a top speed of 72kph/44.7mph and a range of 600km/372.9 miles.

The main armament was the MGM-51 Shillelagh tube-launched, wire-guided missile system, which could also fire 152mm/5.98in shells, along with a 7.62mm/0.3in machine-gun for close-quarter protection. However, there were lots of problems with this weapons system, which held up the vehicle's entry into service and plagued it thereafter.

It was also lightly armoured with aluminium to save on weight, and as a consequence very vulnerable to a whole range of weapons. During combat in Vietnam the missile system was soon rejected in favour of more conventional munitions, but the Sheridan still did not perform well, being adversely affected by the moist conditions and, with little protection on its hull bottom, it was very vulnerable to mines. Nevertheless, the Sheridan continued in service until the 1990s; for example, 82 Airborne Division's Sheridans were among the first AFVs to arrive in the Persian Gulf in 1990.

M551 Sheridan Light Tank	

Entered service: 1968
Crew: 4
Weight: 15,830kg/15.6 tons
Dimensions: Length – 6.30m/20ft 8in
  Height (over turret hatch) – 2.95m/9ft 8in
  Width – 2.82m/9ft 3in
Armament: Main – 152mm/5.98in gun/
  missile system
  Secondary – 7.62mm/0.3in machine-gun
Armour: Unspecified
Powerplant: Detroit Diesel 6V-53T 6-cylinder diesel, 223.7kW/300hp
Performance: Speed – 72kph/44.7mph
  Range – 600km/372.9 miles

LEFT: The missile system was the 152mm/5.98in Shillelagh missile system, whose HEAT warhead could knock out any known tank. Sheridan was swiftly deployed in Vietnam. The missile guidance system was withdrawn and replaced by the "beehive" anti-personnel round, but this also led to many problems.

LEFT: **The Israeli name for their upgrade of the American M60 MBT was Magach, a Hebrew acronym for the Jewish letters: Mem and Chaf plus the middle letter "Gimel" which stands for "Germany", the first source of Israeli M48s. Latest of the continuing upgrades is Magach 7, which is fitted with passive armour to its hull and turret.** BELOW LEFT: **Another view of the M60 Magach. This was the first version specifically up-armoured for urban combat.**

Magach Main Battle Tank

The Magach is the Israeli Defence Force (IDF) name for what was the Patton M48/M60 MBT series of US tanks which have been in active service with the Israeli armoured forces for over 30 years. In that time they have undergone sustained indigenous modification and enhancement to keep the Magach as a state-of-the-art weapons system, continuously tried and tested in combat.

Armed with the original 90mm/3.54in main gun, they first saw action during the 1967 Six Day War and were then upgraded (Magach 3 and 5) with a new 105mm/4.13in M68 L7 gun (as carried by the Centurion) and used in the 1968 War of Attrition. Deployed in time for the 1973 Yom Kippur War, the M60 (Magach 6 and 7) models went on to become the mainstay of the IDF's armoured corps

for many years. These Magachs were upgraded with Explosive Reactive Armour (ERA), new engines, tracks and improved fire control and then used in the 1982 Israeli invasion of Lebanon.

The Magach 7 had further new upgrade suites, some of which could be retrofitted to earlier versions, including engine and transmission packs, passive armour, optical systems, ranging and new fire-control systems, NBC (Nuclear, Biological and Chemical) protection, fire suppression, navigation and weapons systems.

Magach MBT	

Entered service: 1970
Crew: 4
Weight: 54,857kg/54 tons
Dimensions: Length – 8.56m/28ft 1in
    Height (over turret hatch) – 3.35m/11ft
    Width – 3.2m/10ft 6in
Armament: Main – 90mm/3.54in and
    then 105mm/4.13in gun
    Secondary – 3 x 7.62mm/0.3in machine-guns, 1 x
    12.7mm/0.5in coaxial machine-gun above main gun
Armour: Maximum – 115mm/4.53in
Powerplant: General Dynamics AVDS 1790 A
    V12 diesel, 677.1kW/908hp
Performance: Speed – 48kph/29.8mph
    Range – 129km/80.6 miles

Merkava Main Battle Tank

The Merkava (Chariot) is an unusual MBT of innovative design, attributed to the Major General Israel Tal of the IDF's (Israeli Defence Force) Armoured Corps, which places special emphasis on crew protection. To further this aim, the engine is located in the front of the vehicle and special attention has been paid to the siting of extra-spaced armour on the frontal arc, the side skirts and track protectors, and the bulkheads between the crew and the fuel and ammunition. There is even a special protective umbrella for the tank

commander when his hatch is open. Another unusual feature is that the tank has rear doors in the hull, enabling it either to carry extra ammunition or a small squad of infantry.

The Merkava Mark 1 came into service in 1979, when 40 tanks were delivered to 7th Armoured Brigade. Weighing 60,963kg/60 tons and powered by a TCM diesel AVDS 1790 9AR engine delivering a top speed of 46kph/28.6mph and a range of 400km/248.5 miles, the Mark 1 mounted a 105mm/4.13in main gun along with a coaxial 7.62mm/0.3in machine-gun and a 12.7mm/0.5in commander's machine-gun. The Merkava Mark 2 had increased engine performance, which gave it a top speed of 55kph/34mph and a range 500km/310 miles. Merkava first saw action in Lebanon, between April and June 1982.

ABOVE: **No nation has more post-war armoured battle experience than the Israelis, who have been fighting almost non-stop since 1948. It was in 1967 after the Six Day War that they decided to design and build their own main battle tank, the revolutionary Merkava, test rigs being based on both the M48 and Centurion, under the expert eye of General Israel Tal. First production models appeared in 1978, but the MBT did not see action until 1982 in Lebanon. This photograph is of a Merkava Mark 2.** LEFT: **An impressive line-up of Merkava Mark 2s, which weighed over 60 tons and mounted a 105mm/4.13in rifled gun.**

ABOVE: **This Merkava Mark 2 was photographed in Lebanon during Operation "Peace for Galilee".** RIGHT: **An early Mark 1 on show at the IDF Tank Museum at Latrun.** BELOW: **A Mark 3, known as Baz (Hawk), which mounts a 120mm/ 4.72in smoothbore gun, a modular armour suite and an improved suspension.**

New suites covering the various elements of the tank are constantly being updated in the light of combat experience. For Merkava Mark 3 these included a new suspension system, a 894.8kW/1,200hp engine and new transmission, an upgraded 120mm/4.72in main gun developed by Israel Military Industries with a thermal sleeve to increase accuracy by preventing heat distortion, and ballistic protection provided by further special add-on armour modules. The Merkava Mark 4 has further improved night and remote vision devices, a new MTU 1,118.5kW/ 1,500hp diesel engine, an enhanced main gun package and increased modular passive armour.

Merkava Mark 3 MBT

Entered service: 1977 (Mark 1)
Crew: 4
Weight: 62,000kg/61.02 tons
Dimensions: Length – 7.6m/24ft 11in
Height (over turret hatch) – 2.64m/8ft 8in
Width – 3.7m/12ft 1.5in
Armament: Main – 120mm/4.72in gun
Secondary – 3 x 7.62mm/0.3in machine-guns
Armour: Unspecified
Powerplant: Teledyne AVDS 1790 9AR V12 diesel,
894.8kW/1,200hp
Performance: Speed – 55kph/34.2mph
Range – 500km/310.7 miles

211

Main Battle Tank 70

The MBT-70 was a joint US–German heavy tank project that was launched in the 1960s and formed the source vehicle for both the Abrams M1 and Leopard 2 main battle tanks. The MBT-70 incorporated some radical new design elements, including a main gun that could fire wire-guided missile munitions as well as conventional rounds, and a bustle-mounted automatic loading system for the main gun, thereby doing away with the need for a loader and reducing the crew to three.

Weighing 46,000kg/45.3 tons, equipped with hydro-pneumatic suspension and powered by a Continental AVCR 12-cylinder multi-fuel engine, the MBT-70 had a top speed of 70kph/43.5mph and a range of 650km/403.9 miles. The American model mounted the 152mm/5.98in gun/missile system – as later fitted to the Sheridan M551 – while the German version had a 120mm/4.72in smoothbore main armament – both with

ABOVE: In 1963, West Germany and the USA signed an agreement to build a main battle tank which they called MBT-70. While it had many innovative modern features, agreement on a standardized vehicle could not be reached, and the project was eventually cancelled in 1970. Nevertheless, numerous features were brought forward into the two nations' tank-building programmes for the Abrams and the Leopard 2. LEFT AND BELOW LEFT: Two photographs of MBT-70 pilot number two which shows the tank with the fire-control equipment installed.

a state-of-the-art digital fire-control and gun-stabilization system. However, in the end the two countries could not agree on a standardized vehicle, so in 1970 the project was cancelled and each partner went their own way to develop individual main battle tanks.

MBT-70

Entered service: 1967 (prototypes only)
Crew: 3
Weight: 46,000kg/45.3 tons
Dimensions: Length – 6.99m/22ft 11in
　　　Height (over turret hatch) – 2.59m/8ft 6in
　　　Width – 3.51m/11ft 6in
Armament: Main – 152mm/5.98in gun/missile
　　　system or 120mm/4.72in smoothbore main-gun
　　　Secondary – 7.62mm/0.3in machine-gun
Armour: Unspecified
Powerplant: Continental AVCR 12-cylinder multi-fuel,
　　　1,099.9kW/1,475hp
Performance: Speed – 70kph/43.5mph
　　　Range – 650km/403.9 miles

Olifant Medium Tank

The South African Olifant is a Centurion-derived medium tank which became the mainstay of the South African armoured forces for a long period of time. The Olifant was made in South Africa by Vickers OMC Company in conjunction with the larger British parent Vickers. Since its introduction in the 1980s it has undergone various upgrades and enhancements to maintain it as a viable battlefield weapons system.

Weighing over 55 tons and powered by a V12 diesel engine with a top speed of 45kph/28mph and a range of 500km/310.6 miles, the Olifant has a crew of four and mounts as its main armament either the LIW GT-7 105mm/4.13in, or a LIW proprietary 120mm/4.72in smoothbore tank gun. Either of these is fitted into a newly designed turret incorporating a bustle-mounted ammunition carousel and all the latest fire-control and safety features, including blow-off panels on the turret deck.

The latest model (Mark 1B) also boasts a new power pack, new torsion bar suspension, new electronic systems and modular add-on-armour packages.

In addition to the gun tank, there are ARV (Armoured Recovery Vehicle), AVLB (Armoured Vehicle Launched Bridge) and mine-clearing variants.

ABOVE AND RIGHT: **Designed in 1976 and based on the British Centurion, the South African Olifant (Elephant), weighs 56,000kg/55.1 tons, has a crew of four and mounts a 105mm/4.13in gun. The latest version (the Mark 1B) has numerous modern features. South Africa has a total of 224 Olifant Mark 1A and 1Bs in service.**

LEFT: **In addition to the gun tank, there are ARVs, AVLBs and mine-clearing vehicles. The ARV seen here is based upon an Olifant Mark 1A.**

Olifant Medium Tank

Entered service: 1980
Crew: 4
Weight: 56,000kg/55.1 tons
Dimensions: Length – 8.29m/27ft 2.5in
　　　　　Height (over turret hatch) – 2.94m/9ft 7.5in
　　　　　Width – 3.39m/11ft 1.5in
Armament: Main – 105mm/4.13in LIW GT-7
　　　　　or 120mm/4.72in LIW gun
　　　　　Secondary – 2 x 7.62mm/0.3in machine-guns
Armour: Unspecified
Powerplant: V12 diesel, delivering 708.4kW/950hp
Performance: Speed – 45kph/28mph
　　　　　Range – 500km/310.6 miles

213

OF-40 Main Battle Tank

First emerging in 1977, the Italian Oto Melara OF-40 was designed and manufactured by Oto Melara and Fiat, who provided the power pack. It was based on the German Leopard 1 A4 which it strongly resembled and was designed exclusively for export.

Weighing 45,000kg/44.3 tons and powered by a Fiat MTU 90 diesel engine, it had a speed of 60kph/37.3mph and a range of 600km/372.8 miles. The OF-40 had a crew of four and mounted an Oto Melara-designed 105mm/4.13in rifled main armament, along with secondary 7.62mm/0.3in and 12.7mm/0.5in machine-guns in its turret. It was also fitted with

a fire-control system combining a computer and a laser range finder. United Arab Emirates bought 18 OF-40 Mark 1s, the first being delivered in 1981. Since then they have taken delivery of a further 18 OF-40 Mark 2s and three ARVs (Armoured Recovery Vehicles), while the Mark 1s have been retrofitted up to Mark 2 standard, which essentially involves the fitting of a new fire-control and stabilization system. No other sales have materialized.

A later model was planned, along with an ARV and a self-propelled gun (Palmaria 155 howitzer), but following the dismal sales of the gun tank, this was not put into production and the OF-40 MBT is no longer being marketed.

The all-welded steel hull of the OF-40 is divided conventionally, the driver being at the front on the right, with three periscopes, the centre one of which can be replaced by an Image Intensification (II) periscope for night driving. To his left is the NBC pack and 42 rounds of ammunition, the other 15 being in the turret for immediate use.

Turret layout is normal: commander and gunner on the right; loader on the left. The commander has a circular hatch cover with eight periscopes, one of which can be replaced by an II periscope. He does not have a cupola, but mounted in the

ABOVE AND LEFT: Designed in 1977 by Oto Melara and Fiat (power pack), this 45,000kg/44.3-ton Italian MBT has a crew of four and mounts a 105mm/4.13in rifled gun. Offered (but not accepted) for local production in Spain and Greece, demonstrated in Thailand and Egypt, the OF-40 is also in service in Dubai.

OF-40 MBT

Entered service: 1977
Crew: 4
Weight: 45,000kg/44.3 tons
Dimensions: Length – 6.89m/22ft 7in
Height (over turret hatch) – 2.76/9ft 0.5in
Width – 3.35m/11ft
Armament: Main – 105mm/4.13in gun
Secondary – 1 x 7.62mm/0.3in and
1 x 12.7mm/0.5in machine-guns
Armour: Unspecified
Powerplant: MTU 90 diesel, 620.4kW/832hp
Performance: Speed – 60kph/37.3mph
Range – 600km/372.8 miles

ABOVE: **No longer being marketed, the OF-40 hull has been used to mount other weapon systems such as the Gepard anti-aircraft turret and as the basis of the Oto Melara Palmaria 105mm/4.13in SP howitzer.** LEFT: **The OF-40 MBT was designed by Oto Melara and Fiat for the export market, however despite being tested in Thailand, demonstrated in Egypt and offered for local production in Spain and Greece, the only purchasers have been UAE (Dubai).** BELOW: **Firing now! A well-trained crew can achieve a rate of fire of nine rounds per minute with their Oto Melara-designed 105mm/4.13in rifled gun.**

roof of his hatch is the Officine Galileo day/night sight, which is stabilized and fitted with II night-vision equipment. The gunner (seated in front of the commander) has a forward-facing roof-mounted periscope and an optical sight.

The Alenia C215 articulated x 8 magnification telescope is mounted coaxially with the 105mm/4.13in gun. The loader also has a circular hatch cover in front of which are two roof-mounted periscopes that give observation to the front and left side.

The 105mm/4.13in main armament has a falling wedge breechblock, concentric buffer and recuperator. It is fired electrically, but there is also a manually actuated impulse generator. There is a thermal sleeve on the barrel and a bore evacuator.

A well-trained crew can achieve a rate of fire of nine rounds per minute, the gun firing standard NATO ammunition, including APDS, canister, HEAT, HESH and smoke. The gun can be stabilized in both elevation and traverse. One machine-gun is coaxially mounted; the other on the turret roof for AA use.

Mounted on either side of the turret are banks of four electrically operated smoke grenade dischargers. The engine, transmission and cooling system are assembled to form the power pack, which can be removed by four men with a crane in under 45 minutes.

PT-76 Amphibious Light Tank

Having suspended light tank production, believing them to be of limited use, the USSR returned to the idea of a fast, lightly armoured all-terrain reconnaissance vehicle with the PT-76 in 1952. This 14,000kg/13.8-ton light tank had an extremely useful additional feature – it was amphibious. Water-borne propulsion was provided by a double hydro-jet system, which used water taken in at the front of the vehicle and pumped to the rear, where it was expelled at high pressure. Based on an arctic tractor chassis with a torsion bar suspension system and powered by a V6 6-cylinder diesel engine, the vehicle had a top speed of 45kph/28mph and a range of 280km/174 miles. The PT-76 was a robust little tank with a good all-round performance which made it popular with crews despite its light armour. The D056T 76.2mm/3in rifled main gun was mounted in an archetypal Soviet low silhouette turret with a slightly cylindrical top and a wide two-man elliptical cupola. Secondary armament was provided by two machine-guns, one 7.62mm/0.3in and one 12.7mm/0.5in in calibre.

The PT-76 was a successful light tank, with over 7,000 being built and exported widely to Soviet satellite and client states in the Cold War era, as well as being built under licence in China. It saw combat in the Vietnamese and Indo-Pakistan wars and various African conflicts. Production ceased in 1967.

ABOVE: Inevitably the PT-76 saw action in the Arab-Israeli wars, and this model is on show at the IDF Tank Museum at Latrun. LEFT: Light tanks went out of favour in the Red Army towards the end of World War II due to their vulnerability. However, post-war in the early 1950s the PT-76 Amphibious Light Tank came back into vogue. While its 76.2mm/3in gun is small, it is adequate for the job, and its light weight (14,000kg/13.8 tons) and reliability have made it a winner worldwide.

Upgraded PT-76

The Israeli company NIMDA offers a complete upgrade package which includes fitting a new power pack, a Detroit Diesel 6V-92T developing 223.7kW/300hp at 2,100rpm, coupled to the original transmission with a new clutch assembly. There is also a new alternator, new cooling and electrical systems and numerous other modifications to the exhaust, air inlet, hull and top deck.

The 76.2mm/3in gun is replaced by the new 90mm/3.54in Cockerill Mark III gun that fires a wide range of ammunition, including fin-stabilized APDS. The Russian coaxial machine-gun has been replaced by a Western one and another added on the turret roof for AA protection. There is a new solid state stabilization and power control system, together with a new fire-control system incorporating a new day/night sight and laser rangefinder. It is understood that part of the Indonesian PT-76 fleet have already been upgraded with this package.

ABOVE LEFT, ABOVE AND LEFT: **This adaptable tank is at home in water and on land. It has seen service in China and Vietnam, and also in the Indo-Pakistan wars.**

PT-76 Amphibious Light Tank

Entered service: 1952
Crew: 3
Weight: 14,000kg/13.8 tons
Dimensions: Length – 6.91m/22ft 8in
Height (over turret hatch) – 2.26m/7ft 5in
Width – 3.14m/10ft 3.5in
Armament: Main – 76.2mm/3in gun
Secondary – 1 x 7.62mm/0.3in and
1 x 12.7mm/0.5in machine-guns
Armour: Maximum – 17mm/0.67in
Powerplant: V6 6-cylinder diesel, 179kW/240hp
Performance: Speed – 45km/28mph
Range – 280km/174 miles

PT-91 Main Battle Tank

The Polish PT-91 was brought out in 1993 to replace the locally built version of that country's ageing Russian T-72 series of main battle tanks. Manufactured by Bumar-Labedy and weighing almost 45 tons, the PT-91 has a crew of three and is powered by a S12U V12 supercharged diesel engine delivering a top speed of 60kph/ 37.3mph and a range of 650km/ 403.9 miles. The main armament is the 125mm/4.92in gun, along with two secondary machine-guns, one of 7.62mm/0.3in and one of 12.7mm/0.5in. Other modern enhancements included digital fire control, night-vision and engine management systems, as well as the Explosive Reactive Armour (ERA) in which the vehicle was sheathed.

While still in use with the Polish armoured forces, production of the PT-91 has now ceased, although the manufacturers have developed an enhanced version for export.

ABOVE AND LEFT: **Also known as** *Twardy* **(Hard), the PT-91 is a development of the Russian-designed T-72M1 which had been built in Poland for a number of years. It has numerous modifications and has even been built as an enhanced version for export. The current PT-91 has a 125mm/ 4.92in smoothbore gun with an automatic loader, while a future model may well have a 120mm/4.72in NATO smoothbore gun.**

PT-91 MBT

Entered service: 1993
Crew: 3
Weight: 45,300kg/44.6 tons
Dimensions: Length – 9.67m/31ft 6in
  Height (over turret hatch) – 2.19m/7ft 2in
  Width – 3.59m/11ft 9.5in
Armament: Main – 125mm/4.92in gun
  Secondary – 1 x 7.62mm and 1 x 12.7mm/
  0.5in machine-guns
Armour: Unspecified
Powerplant: S12U V12 diesel, 633.8kW/850hp
Performance: Speed – 60kph/37.3mph
  Range – 650km/403.9 miles

Pz 61 Medium Tank

Switzerland had no tank-building capability until the 1950s, when it decided to build the Panzer 58, armed with a Swiss-produced 90mm/3.54in gun, to replace their ageing fleet of British Centurions. In the mid-1960s this MBT was replaced by the Panzer 61, armed with a British gun. Based on the previous Pz 58, itself a development of the American M48/M60 series, the Pz 61 was designed and built by RUAG Land Systems, its appearance resembling its predecessors.

With a single-cast hull and turret and weighing over 37 tons, it was powered by a MTU MB-837 V8 diesel engine delivering a top speed of 55kph/34.2mph, and had a range of 300km/186.4 miles. The Pz 61 mounted the British-designed L7 105mm/4.13in rifled main gun built under licence in Switzerland, and had two 7.62mm/0.3in secondary machine-guns.

It was replaced by the Pz 68, which went on in service until final replacement in 1999 by the Leopard 2.

Pz 61 Medium Tank	
Entered service: 1965	
Crew: 4	
Weight: 38,000kg/37.4 tons	
Dimensions: Length – 6.78m/22ft 3in	
Height (over turret hatch) – 2.72m/8ft 11in	
Width – 3.08m/10ft 1.5in	
Armament: Main – 105mm/4.13in gun	
Secondary – 2 x 7.62mm/0.3in machine-guns	
Armour: Maximum – 120mm/4.72in	
Powerplant: MTU MB-837 V8 diesel,	
469.8kW/630hp	
Performance: Speed – 55kph/34.2mph	
Range – 300km/186.4 miles	

RIGHT: **The Pz 61 Medium Tank. This and the Pz 68 certainly had a number of improvements but did not represent a major change in tank design and were very similar in outward appearance. The 105mm/4.13in gun has a fume extractor, thermal sleeve and muzzle reference system fitted, while there is the Bofors Lyran (illuminating rocket system) fitted at both the commander's and loader's stations which will launch an illuminating rocket out to 1,300m/4,265ft.**

Pz 68 Main Battle Tank

The Pz 68 was the next development in the Swiss-manufactured series derived from the US M48/M60, emerging in 1971 as the upgrade model of the Pz 61. Though still armed with the 105mm/4.13in main gun and two 7.62mm/0.3in secondary machine-guns, many of the tank's other subsystems were upgraded over a period of years. These included an up-rated MTU MB-837 diesel engine and a new gun stabilization and fire-control system, allowing it to engage targets while on the move. Wider tracks were also fitted to reduce ground pressure and improve overall vehicle performance.

Other enhancements have followed to maintain the vehicle's viability and service life, and a RUAG-designed 120mm/4.72in main gun replacement is also under development. A total of 390 Pz 68s were built and of these nearly 200 have been upgraded with the installation of a new fire-control system, the resulting upgraded tank being known as Pz 68/88. An ARV (Armoured Recovery Vehicle), Amoured Bridgelayer and Target Tank have also been produced. The Pz 68, like its predecessors, is only in service with the Swiss Army. It has now been joined by the Swiss-built Leopard 2 (Pz 87 Leo).

Pz 68 MBT	
Entered service: 1971	
Crew: 4	
Weight: 39,700kg/39.1 tons	
Dimensions: Length – 6.88m/22ft 7in	
Height (over turret hatch) – 2.75m/9ft	
Width – 3.14m/10ft 4in	
Armament: Main – 105mm/4.13in gun	
Secondary – 2 x 7.62mm/0.3in machine-guns	
Armour: Maximum – 120mm/4.72in	
Powerplant: MTU MB-837 V8 diesel,	
492.2kW/660hp	
Performance: Speed – 56kph/34.8mph	
Range – 350km/217.5 miles	

LEFT: **Approved for production in 1974, some 50 Pz 68 Mark 2s were delivered to the Swiss Army in 1977.**

LEFT AND BELOW: **The Sabra (literally "a native-born Israeli") was developed from the US M60A3 series by Israeli Military Industries. It is fitted with an IMI 120mm/4.72in smoothbore gun (the same as the Merkava Mark 3) and a hybrid armour package. The Sabra Mark II (most recent model) is being offered with either an up-rated General Dynamics AVDS V12 diesel engine which develops 894.8kW/1,200hp or a German 745.7kW/1,000bhp MTU diesel engine.** BOTTOM LEFT: **This Sabra photograph was taken at the Israeli Tank Museum at Latrun.**

Sabra Main Battle Tank

The Sabra Main Battle Tank is another AFV to come out of the Israeli "cauldron" of tank development, and is based upon the US M60A3 series which was originally purchased in the 1960s. The continuous warfare in which the state of Israel has been involved since its inception has resulted in the constant upgrading of all the AFVs they possess, including captured enemy vehicles, as well as the development of their indigenous arms industry.

Weighing 55,000kg/54.1 tons, and built with an eye for the export market, the Sabra MBT is powered by a General Dynamics AVDS 1790 5A diesel engine, giving it a top speed of 48kph/29.8mph and a range of 450km/279.6. Its main armament is a new 120mm/4.72in smoothbore gun cunningly developed to fit the relatively small turret dimensions

of the older M60s with no extra machining or welding necessary. Even within the turret there has been only minimal change – to the ammunition racking and the fire-control systems.

Combined with the new main weapon, add-on armour, engine, safety, navigation and fire-control system, regular enhancement packages keep the

Sabra in the front line and will do so for some time to come. In early 2002 Turkey negotiated a contract with Israel to upgrade 170 M60A3s to Sabra Mark III standard, with the Israeli 120mm/4.72in smoothbore gun, a new power pack and automatic transmission. The upgrade programme is underway at the Israeli Ordnance Corps Workshops at Tel Aviv.

Sabra MBT

Entered service: 1999
Crew: 4
Weight: 55,000kg/54.1 tons
Dimensions: Length – 8.26m/27ft 1in
Height (over turret hatch) – 3.05m/10ft
Width – 3.63m/11ft 11in
Armament: Main – 120mm/4.72in gun
Secondary – 3 x 7.62mm/0.3in machine-guns
Armour: Unspecified
Powerplant: General Dynamics AVDS 1790 5A
V12 diesel, 677.1kW/908hp
Performance: Speed – 48kph/29.8mph
Range – 450km/279.6 miles

LEFT AND BELOW LEFT: **Built by Steyr-Daimler-Puch in the mid-1960s, this neat little 17,700kg/17.2-ton Austrian SK 105 Light Tank is also known as the Kürassier. It was developed from the Saurer APC, mounts a 105mm/4.13in Giat gun and has a crew of three. In service with Austria (286) and six other countries, over 650 have been built. An upgrade package is also now being marketed.**

SK 105 Kürassier Light Tank

Based on the Saurer Armoured Personnel Carrier, the SK 105 Kürassier Light Tank was built by Steyr-Daimler-Puch and brought into service to improve the anti-tank capability of the Austrian armed forces. With a crew of three and weighing 17,700kg/17.2 tons, it was powered by a Steyr 7FA diesel engine and fitted with a torsion bar suspension system, providing a top speed of 65kph/40.4mph and a range of 300km/186.4 miles. In its two-man hydraulically powered turret the Kürassier mounts a French Giat

105mm/4.13in rifled gun as main armament, served by an autoloader with two rotating carousels in the turret bustle. There is also a coaxial 7.62mm/0.3in machine-gun.

Upgrades carried out over the last few years have further equipped the SK 105 with improved rangefinding, fire control, gun stabilization, communications and night-fighting systems, as well as add-on armour modules to the frontal arc, turret and vehicle sides. There is also an ARV (Armoured Recovery Vehicle) and engineer variant.

SK 105 Kürassier has been sold to Argentina, Bolivia, Brazil, Botswana, Morocco and Tunisia. The latest model is the SK 105 A2, which replaces the manual gear shift with a ZF6HP automatic transmission and features a new fully stabilized and partly oscillating turret fitted with upgraded armour and retaining the Giat 105mm/4.13in main gun and autoloader, but with improved night-vision equipment and a digital fire-control system.

SK 105 Kürassier Light Tank	

Entered service: 1965
Crew: 3
Weight: 17,700kg/17.2 tons
Dimensions: Length – 5.58m/18ft 3.5in
    Height (over turret hatch) – 2.53m/8ft 3.5in
    Width – 2.5m/8ft 2.5in
Armament: Main – 105mm/4.13in gun
    Secondary – 7.62mm/0.3in machine-gun
Armour: 40mm/1.58in
Powerplant: Steyr 7FA diesel, 238.6kW/320bhp
Performance: Speed – 65kph/40.4mph
    Range – 300km/186.4 miles

LEFT: The Stingray Light Tank was developed by Cadillac Gage in the 1980s as a private venture and was modernized with new armour and fire-control system ten years later. It mounts a 105mm/4.13in LRF gun. Layout of both models is similar. To date, the only overseas order has been for the Royal Thai Army in late 1987, who took delivery of 106 vehicles.

Stingray I Light Tank

Cadillac Gage Textron developed the US Stingray Light Tank for the export market in 1984. It was specifically manufactured using as many existing components of other American AFVs as possible in order to keep costs down.

With a weight of 21,205kg/20.9 tons, torsion bar suspension and a crew of four, the Stingray was powered by a Detroit Diesel 8V-92TA engine, giving it a top speed of 67.6kph/42mph and a range of 482.8km/300 miles.

The Stingray mounts a British-built Royal Ordnance 105mm/4.13in Low Recoil Force (LRF) main gun in the distinctive tapered-front three-man turret, along with digital fire control, stabilization and two machine-guns – one 7.62mm/0.3in coaxial and one 12.7mm/0.5in AA. The vehicle is also fitted with night-vision and thermal imaging equipment and was sold successfully to Thailand in 1988, leading to the development of the Stingray II.

Stingray I Light Tank	
Entered service: 1988	
Crew: 4	
Weight: 21,205kg/20.9 tons	
Dimensions: Length – 9.30m/30ft 6in	
Height (over turret hatch) – 2.55m/8ft 4.5in	
Width – 2.71m/8ft 10.5in	
Armament: Main – 105mm/4.13in LRF gun	
Secondary – 1 x 7.62mm/0.3in and	
1 x 12.7mm/0.5in machine-guns	
Armour: Unspecified	
Powerplant: Detroit Diesel 8V-92TA, 398.9kW/535hp	
Performance: Speed – 67.6kph/42mph	
Range – 482.8km/300miles	

Stingray II Light Tank

Also built by Cadillac Gage Textron, the Stingray II is an evolutionary progression of its predecessor, with a cascade of improvements ranging from new add-on appliqué, laminate and titanium armour suites, a new independent trailing arm suspension system, wider tracks, and new digital fire-control,

navigation, communication and safety systems added. The Stingray II can also mount the new Textron LAV-105 turret (still distinctively tapered into a diamond lozenge at the front), armed with the M35 105mm/4.13in main gun and fed by an automatic loader, thereby reducing the crew to three.

Stingray II Light Tank	
Entered service: 1996	
Crew: 4	
Weight: 22,600kg/22.2 tons	
Dimensions: Length – 9.35m/30ft 8in	
Height (over turret hatch) – 2.55m/8ft 4.5in	
Width – 2.8m/9ft 2in	
Armament: Main – 105mm/4.13in LRF gun	
Secondary – 1 x 7.62mm/0.3in and	
1 x 12.7mm/0.5in machine-guns	
Armour: Unspecified	
Powerplant: Detroit Diesel 8V-92TA generating 398.9kW/535hp	
Performance: Speed – 70kph/43.5mph	
Range – 525km/326.2 miles	

LEFT: The Stingray II is virtually identical to the Stingray I except for the new "2001" special high-hardness steel armour which gives added protection over the frontal arc. It will protect against small-arms fire up to 23mm/0.91in calibre. Studies have shown that it is possible to fit the Swiss RUAG 120mm/4.72in compact gun into Stingray II.

LEFT: **This dramatic photograph shows an Strv 74 being struck by a Bofors Bill top-attack ATGW (Anti-Tank Guided Weapon).** BELOW AND BOTTOM LEFT: **During World War II the Swedes built a series of light tanks such as the M/38 and M/41, which led to the post-war development of the Strv 74. It had a four-man crew and was armed with an effective 75mm/2.95in gun.**

Strv 74 Light Tank

The Strv 74's development path stretches back through the Strv M/40 and M/42 to the original 16,257kg/16-ton Lago tank, manufactured by the Swedish firm Landswerk for the Hungarian Army. The Strv 74 was therefore in essence a modernized version of the World War II M/42 tank which was itself an attempt to bring Swedish tanks up to the standard of the rest of war-torn Europe. It was most successful.

Produced in 1958, weighing 39,700kg/22.14 tons and powered by a Scania-Vabis 239kW/320.5hp diesel engine, the Strv 74 had a top speed of 45kph/28mph and a range of 200km/124.3 miles. With a crew of four, it mounted a 75mm/2.95in main gun and had three machine-guns in its updated turret, which was later further modified with a more sophisticated fire-control system and an upgrading of the main armament to increase its velocity.

Strv 74 Light Tank

Entered service: 1958
Crew: 4
Weight: 39,700kg/22.14 tons
Dimensions: Length – 4.9m/16ft 1in
    Height (over turret hatch) – 1.61m/5ft 3.5in
    Width – 2.2m/7ft 2.5in
Armament: Main – 75mm/2.95in gun
    Secondary – 2 x 7.62mm/0.3in and
    1 x 12.7mm/0.5in machine-guns
Armour: Maximum – 80mm/3.15in
    Minimum – 15mm/0.59in
Powerplant: Scania-Vabis diesel, 239kW/
    320.5hp
Performance: Speed – 45kph/28mph
    Range – 200km/124.3 miles

Strv 103 S Main Battle Tank

The Swedish Strv 103 S tank is another highly unusual MBT which was developed in response to a detailed study into the hits and injuries sustained by tanks and their crews in combat. This showed that there was a high percentage of disabled turrets and guns, but very few impacts below 1m/3ft in height. The Swedes therefore decided by to dispense with the turret entirely, mounting the main weapon directly on the chassis, which then had to be turned for the gun to be traversed. They also added a front-mounted dozer blade so that the tank could prepare its own hulldown positions and a flotation screen so that it could cope with the many waterways found in Sweden.

With a weight of almost 40 tons, hydro-pneumatic suspension and a crew of three, the S tank was powered by a Rolls-Royce K60 multi-fuel engine (sited in the front of the vehicle for added crew protection), giving a top speed of 50kph/31.1mph and a range of 390km/242.3 miles. There was also a second engine – a Boeing 553 gas turbine – to aid with cold-weather starting and to give the vehicle extra power when in combat or moving cross-country.

The main armament was the Royal Ordnance 105mm/4.13in L7 gun fitted with an automatic loader, along with two coaxial 7.62mm/0.3in machine-guns and another for anti-aircraft defence. 300 Strv 103s were built between 1967 and 1971, equipping three armoured brigades of 72 each and two independent tank battalions.

ABOVE AND LEFT: **Views of the Strv 103 S Tank from Sweden, now located at the Tank Museum, Bovington. The Stridsvagn 103 was a revolutionary Swedish main battle tank, designed in the 1960s to replace the fleet of 300 British Centurions that had been in service for many years. Weighing 39,700kg/ 39.07 tons and armed with a 105mm/4.13in gun in an external mounting, the tank had no turret to traverse so the crew had to "track" instead. However, its automatic loader allowed for a rate of fire of some 15 rounds per minute.**

Removing the traversing turret of an AFV undoubtedly reduces its offensive capability, but conversely increases its defensive ability. This AFV's design reflects the intelligent and essentially peaceful, but realistic intentions of the Swedes.

Early production models were not fitted with either the dozer blade or flotation screen, and were known as the Strv 103A, while later production models were fitted with both, and were known as the Strv 103B.

The former was carried folded under the nose of the tank and when required was swung forward and secured by two rods, then operated by adjusting the hydro-pneumatic suspension. The flotation screen was carried around the top of the hull and took about 15–20 minutes to erect. The tank was then propelled in the water by its tracks at a speed of 6kph/3.75mph. When afloat, the driver stood on top at the rear with a remote throttle control and steered by means of reins attached to the main tiller.

ABOVE, BELOW AND BOTTOM: **Three further views of the S Tank, which show exactly how low the tank can go, and some of its other technical innovations.**

Strv 103 S MBT

Entered service: 1966
Crew: 3
Weight: 39,700kg/39.07 tons
Dimensions: Length – 8.42m/27ft 7.5in
Height (over turret hatch) – 2.50m/8ft 2.5in
Width – 3.62m/11ft 10.5in
Armament: Main – 105mm/4.13in gun
Secondary – 2 x 7.62mm/0.3in and
1 x 12.7mm/0.5in
Armour: Unspecified
Powerplant: Rolls-Royce K60 multi-fuel, generating
365.4kW/490hp
Performance: Speed – 50kph/31.1mph
Range – 390km/242.3 miles

225

Israeli upgrades

Few states have seen as much continuous military action since their inception as that of Israel. As a result, any and all available armour that was bought, borrowed or captured was turned to good use, with nothing being wasted. The readily available M4A1 Sherman was soon selected by the Israeli Defence Force (IDF) for enhancement, including a new suspension system, sprockets and idlers, and a new mantlet to take the British 105mm/4.13in L7 main gun with new fire-control and later night-vision equipment.

The British Centurion was renamed Sh'ot (Scourge) by the Israelis and it proved to be just that as far as the Arabs were concerned. Israel bought many different variants over the years from a number of countries. The original Centurions were swiftly up-gunned with the British 105mm/4.13in L7, along with new fire-control and night-vision equipment. The vehicle's rear deck was raised so that a new larger diesel engine could be fitted, which more than doubled its operational range, and the armour was increased with a succession of add-on suites, including Blazer (Israeli explosive reactive armour).

The opposing forces lost hundreds of tanks and AFVs in their wars against Israel, the most common being the Soviet-made T-54 and T-55. These were swiftly re-engined, re-gunned with the standard 105mm/4.13in gun used in the Centurion, and renamed Tiran. When used in combat they could cause considerable confusion with the Arab forces.

ABOVE: **This M51 Super Sherman was pictured during the Six Day War of 1967. It had been refitted with a Cummings diesel engine and up-gunned with the 105mm/4.13in L44 gun.** BELOW: **This version of the Sherman served the IDF in many guises, but as a gun tank it was armed with the 105mm/4.13in French gun (from the later models of the AMX-13). The suspension is the more modern Horizontal Volute Spring Suspension (HVSS) rather than the original Vertical Volute type. It also had modified steering and a new turret bustle.**

With the advent of the US M48/M60 series, together with the other conversions becoming available, the Tirans were soon relegated – either to be given to allies such as the SLA (South Lebanon Army) militia, or converted into an APC (Armoured Personnel Carrier) called the Achzarit.

The Israeli Armoured Corps has come a long way since its beginnings in 1948, when their only heavy armour was just one derelict Sherman scheduled for the scrap heap and two elderly Cromwells "acquired" from the British Army in Palestine. Next to arrive was a company of French Hotchkiss light tanks that had been smuggled into Israel under the guise of "farm machinery".

These were its humble beginnings, but now, more than half a century later, Israel has one of the largest and best-equipped armoured forces in the world, with a tradition second to none. In addition, they are not only still prepared to modify constantly and enhance whatever tanks they have in service, but they have also joined the world's elite tank builders with their own revolutionary designs.

TOP: **The upgraded (captured) T-55/62, still with the original 115mm/4.53in gun and known as the T-62I.** ABOVE: **An Israeli-modified Centurion at Latrun: the Sh'ot (Scourge) version with an air-cooled diesel engine (this batch was purchased in the 1960s).** BELOW: **Another Israeli-modified Sherman photographed at the IDF Tank Museum, Latrun. Note the differing suspension and weapon system, namely the AMX-13 turret.**

M51 Sherman Medium Tank

Entered service: 1960
Crew: 5
Weight: 39,625kg/39 tons
Dimensions: Length – 5.89m/19ft 4in
Height (over turret hatch) – 2.75m/9ft
Width – 2.62m/8ft 7in
Armament: Main – French 105mm/4.13in
CN 105-F 1 gun
Secondary – 2 x 7.62mm/0.3in and
1 x 12.7mm/0.5in machine-guns
Armour: Maximum – 203mm/7.99in
Powerplant: Cummins diesel, 343kW/460hp
Performance: Speed – 45kph/28mph
Range – 270km/167.8 miles

Upgraded Centurion MBT

Entered service: 1967
Crew: 4
Weight: 53,500kg/52.7 tons
Dimensions: Length – 7.84m/25ft 8.5in
Height (over turret hatch) – 3.01m/9ft 10.5in
Width – 3.38m/11ft 1in
Armament: Main – 105mm/4.13in gun
Secondary – 3 x 7.62mm/0.3in
machine-guns
Armour: Maximum – 152mm/5.98in
Powerplant: General Dynamics AVDS 1790 2AC
diesel, 599.3kW/750hp
Performance: Speed – 50kph/31.1mph
Range – 500km/310.7 miles

LEFT: **It was the German company Rheinmetall who developed the TAM (*Tanque Argentino Mediano*) to meet the requirements of the Argentine Army, the first prototype being produced in 1976. The TAM had a crew of four, an all-up weight of 30,000kg/29.53 tons and mounted a 105mm/4.13in rifled gun. The original requirement was for 512 TAM medium tanks and tracked armoured personnel carriers, but for financial reasons only about 350 were built. Some recent reports, however, indicate that production may well have recommenced.**

TAMSE TAM Medium Tank

The TAM was initially designed and produced by the German arms company Rheinmetall and then by TAMSE in Argentina to replace Argentina's ageing fleet of M4 Shermans. A critical factor in the selection of this tank by the Argentines was meeting the weight restrictions imposed by the country's bridge and road infrastructure. Following on from prototype testing in the mid-1970s, the vehicle was accepted and production began in Argentina under licence. The TAM was first delivered to the Argentine amoured forces in the early 1980s, although none saw action in the Falklands War in 1982.

Weighing almost 30 tons and with a crew of four, the TAM is powered by a MTU 6-cylinder diesel engine, giving it a top speed of 75kph/46.6mph and a range of 940km/584.1 miles. The chassis of the vehicle was based on the Marder APC, which was also manufactured by Rheinmetall but with a newly designed three-man turret mounting a 105mm/4.13in rifled main gun and a 7.62mm/0.3in coaxial machine-gun, with another 7.62mm/0.3in gun mounted on the turret roof for anti-aircraft and close-quarter defence. The TAM also has modern gun stabilization, fire-control, communications and safety equipment, and variants so far produced include a self-propelled howitzer, an ARV (Armoured Recovery Vehicle) and a multiple-launch rocket system. However, it is no longer being marketed and the manufacturer TAMSE has gone out of business.

LEFT: **Other versions included the Israeli LAR 160 multiple rocket system, the original turret being replaced by two 18-round launcher pods. It is thought that a small number of these were delivered to the Argentine Army.** BELOW LEFT: **The TAM on trials in Thailand in 1978 when the potential export model was known as the TH 301.**

TAMSE TAM Medium Tank	
Entered service: 1976	
Crew: 4	
Weight: 30,000kg/29.53 tons	
Dimensions: Length – 6.77m/22ft 3in	
Height (over turret hatch) – 2.71m/8ft 10.5in	
Width – 3.92m/10ft 10.5in	
Armament: Main – 105mm/4.13in gun	
Secondary – 2 x 7.62mm/0.3in machine-guns	
Armour: Unspecified	
Powerplant: MTU MB 833 Ka500 diesel, 536.9kW/720hp	
Performance: Speed – 75kph/46.6mph	
Range – 940km/584.1 miles	

LEFT, BELOW AND BOTTOM LEFT:
The Lenin Heavy Tank was to all intents and purposes the last in the Soviet World War II heavy tank series, being a redesign of the JS-4 but incorporating lessons learned in the early post-war years. In fact, it was heavy, large and not as easy to move around the countryside as the more modern medium tanks such as the T-62, which replaced it in the mid-1960s.

T-10 Lenin Heavy Tank

Last in the KV and JS series of heavy tanks originating in the 1930s and being developed through World War II, the T-10 (also known as the Lenin) replaced the short-lived JS-4. Entering service in 1953, weighing 52,000kg/ 51.2 tons and fitted with torsion bar suspension, it was powered by the V12 diesel engine originally developed for the JS-4, providing a top speed of 42kph/26.1mph and a range of 250km/ 155.3 miles.

The T-10 was manned by a crew of four, protected by armour up to 270mm/ 10.63in thick on the frontal arc and armed with a D74 122mm/4.8in main gun in a classic Soviet "mushroom head" turret which was sited well forward on the hull. There were also two 14.55mm/ 0.57in machine-guns and an optional extra 12.7mm/0.5in anti-aircraft machine-gun mounted outside on the commander's cupola.

The main drawback of the Lenin was its very limited ammunition stowage capacity of fewer than 30 rounds, although this was increased later to 50. The reality was that the T-10 Lenin belonged to a previous generation of AFV made obsolete by new types of armour and ammunition that were enabling a new type of faster, lighter tank such as the T-62 to take on the role of the older classic heavies.

T-10 Lenin Heavy Tank

Entered service: 1953
Crew: 4
Weight: 52,000kg/51.2 tons
Dimensions: Length – 7.41m/24ft 3.5in
  Height (over turret hatch) – 2.43m/7ft 11.5in
  Width – 3.56m/11ft 8in
Armament: Main – 122mm/4.8in gun
  Secondary – 2 x 14.55mm/0.57in and
  1 x 12.7mm/0.3in machine-guns
Armour: Maximum – 270mm/10.63in
Powerplant: V2IS 12-cylinder diesel, 514.5kW/690hp
Performance: Speed – 42kph/26.1mph
  Range – 250km/155.3 miles

T-54/T-55 Medium Tank

This series of AFV ranks as one of the most prolific in terms of the sheer numbers produced, with some estimates as high as 60,000. It became the primary MBT of post-World War II Soviet tank forces and their satellite and client states all over the world for at least two decades. It was also built under licence in Czechoslovakia, Poland and China, and did not go out of production in the USSR until early in the 1990s.

The T-54 had a low-silhouette hull with a classic Soviet "mushroom dome" turret, weighed over 35 tons and was powered by a V54 V12 diesel engine, giving it a top speed of 48kph/29.8mph and a range 400km/248.5 miles. It was armed with a D10 100mm/3.94in rifled main gun, along with

ABOVE AND BELOW LEFT: **Following on from their highly successful wartime T-34/76 and T-34/85, the Soviets produced what must have been their most successful medium tanks ever – the T-54 and T-55 – with production starting in 1947. Estimates of the numbers produced since then must be in the region of 60,000, a staggering number, and even more than the wartime Sherman M4 Medium Tanks.**

a 7.62mm/0.3in coaxial machine-gun. Early versions also mounted a fixed 7.62mm/0.3in machine-gun in the bow, which was operated by the driver.

New models featured improvements as they came into service – beginning with night-vision equipment and an extra machine-gun for anti-aircraft defense, and going on to full-blown upgrade programmes with fire-control, navigation, communication and safety systems, as well as add-on armour suites. There were also the inevitably endless variants of an AFV whose use was so widespread and culturally diverse.

With the advent of the T-55 in the 1950s, the main flaw of the T54 – its automotive unreliability – was tackled with the fitting of a larger V255 V12 water-cooled diesel engine, thereby increasing the power, speed (50kph/31.1mph) and range (500km/310.7 miles) of the vehicle. There was also a new turret fitted – still a mushroom – without the loader's cupola or the prominent roof-top ventilator dome, and with two enlarged "D" roof panels. It also mounted an infrared gunner's searchlight above the main gun, but this was retrofitted to the T-54 and so is not a distinctive feature.

LEFT: **Many of these "rough and ready", highly reliable and easy-to-crew main battle tanks are still in service worldwide, with many having been sold off by European armies as they took on more sophisticated MBTs. The all-welded steel hull is divided into three compartments – driving at the front, fighting in the centre and engine at the rear.**
BELOW: **Russian tank crews working on their vehicles in their tank hangar.**

Again, improved models surfaced regularly, sporting an array of enhancements and variants, including further engine tweaks, NBC (Nuclear, Biological and Chemical) protection, add-on armour suites – especially ERA (Explosive Reactive Armour) – new main gun stabilization and fire-control systems.

Civilian conversions

Although the original production finished long ago, the T-54/T-55 is still in service with armies all over the world – a staggering 65 at last count – so it must be one of the most successful tanks ever built. Remarkably, the RFAS has also now started marketing a number of systems based on the T-54/T-55 MBT with purely civilian applications. These mainly centre around fire-fighting.

RIGHT AND BELOW: **The all-welded steel hull is divided into three compartments – driving at the front, fighting in the centre and engine at the rear. There are a wide variety of models of this 36,000kg/35.4-ton four-man tank, both T-54 and T-55 being armed with a 100mm/3.94in rifled gun.**

T-54/T-55 Medium Tank

Entered service: 1948
Crew: 4
Weight: 36,000kg/35.4 tons
Dimensions: Length – 6.45m/21ft 2in
Height (over turret hatch) – 2.4m/7ft 10.5in
Width – 3.27m/10ft 8.5in
Armament: Main – 100mm/3.94in gun
Secondary – 2 x 7.62mm/0.3in and
1 x 12.7mm/0.5in machine-guns
Armour: Maximum – 203mm/7.99in
Powerplant: V54 12-cylinder diesel, generating
387.8kW/520hp
Performance: Speed – 48kph/29.8mph
Range – 400km/248.5 miles

T-62 Main Battle Tank

The T-62 was the next progression in the Soviet development cycle based on the T-54/55 series, and featured an enlarged hull to fit a new turret carrying a larger bore main gun. This tank was destined to become the primary main battle tank of the Soviet amoured forces during the 1970s, with over 20,000 built.

Weighing almost 40 tons, the T-62 was powered by the same 432.5kW/580hp V12 water-cooled diesel engine as its predecessor, which provided a top speed of 50kph/31.1mph and a range of 650km/403.9 miles. Mounted centrally over the third road wheel, the new "mushroom dome" cast turret had a U-5T (2A20) Rapira 115mm/4.53in main gun with a longer, thinner barrel than the 100mm/3.94in of the T-54/55. An unusual feature of the new turret was the automatic shell ejector system, which worked from the recoil of the main gun, ejecting the spent shell casings through a port in the rear of the turret.

There was also a 7.62mm/0.3in coaxial machine-gun and a 12.7mm/0.5in anti-aircraft machine-gun mounted by the loader's hatch. A gunner's infrared searchlight was mounted on the right, above the main gun. Later models included the usual improvements – gun stabilization and fire control, NBC

(Nuclear, Biological and Chemical) protection, communication and safety systems, add-on armour suites (including ERA (Explosive Reactive Armour), appliqué and increased belly armour for mine protection). Although there were many variations on the T-54/55 chassis, there were surprisingly few on the T-62, although the gun tank was upgraded regularly.

Recent modifications to various Marks of T-62 have included the fitting of some or all of the following: the Sheksna laser beam riding missile system; the Volna fire-control system, which includes the KDT-2 laser rangefinder with a range of 4,000m/13,123ft; a 12.7mm/0.5in AA machine-gun; a thermal sleeve for the barrel of the main gun; auxiliary armour to hull,

ABOVE, LEFT AND BELOW: **Using the T-55 as the basis for its design but with a longer, wider hull and a new turret, the T-62 came into Red Army service in 1961, but was first seen in public at the Moscow May Day Parade in 1965. Production continued until 1975, by which time over 20,000 had been built, including a wide family of variants. The 40,000kg/39.4-ton MBT had a crew of four and mounted a 115mm/4.53in smoothbore gun (40 rounds carried). Numerous modifications have been incorporated since it was accepted into service, including a flamethrower version.**

LEFT: The "mushroom domed" turret is very clear on this uncluttered photograph, as are the rest of the tank's clean lines. The T-62 was first seen in public during a parade in Moscow in 1965. Over the next ten years some 20,000 T-62s would be built by the USSR. BELOW: Note the longer gun barrel of the 115mm/4.53in as compared with its predecessor. The tank carried 40 rounds of main gun ammunition, 16 in the forward part of the tank, 20 in the rear of the fighting compartment, two ready rounds in the turret and one more between the feet of both the gunner and loader! The spent shell ejection system was activated by the recoil of the gun – the empty case being ejected automatically through a trapdoor in the turret rear. The maximum rate of fire was four rounds per minute when at the halt. After firing, the gun automatically elevated to an angle of 3.5 degrees or more for reloading, and the turret could not be traversed while loading was in progress. BOTTOM: Columns of T-62 MBTs on training make a very impressive sight.

T-62 MBT

Entered service: 1961
Crew: 4
Weight: 40,000kg/39.4 tons
Dimensions: Length – 6.63m/21ft 9in
    Height (over turret hatch) – 2.39m/7ft 10in
    Width – 3.3m/10ft 10in
Armament: Main – 115mm/4.53in Rapira gun
    Secondary – 1 x 7.62mm/0.3in and
    1 x 12.7mm/0.5in machine-guns
Armour: Maximum – 242mm/9.53in
Powerplant: V55 12-cylinder diesel, delivering
    432.5kW/580hp
Performance: Speed – 50kph/31.1mph
    Range – 650km/403.9 miles (with additional fuel
    tank), 450km/280 miles (without)

turret and belly; ERA; side skirts; Napalm protection system; local smoke launchers; modernized suspension system; R-173 radio system; and V55U engine. The Sheksna missile, which is fired from the 115mm/4.53in gun, weighs some 28kg/61.72lb and has a range of 4,000m/13,123ft. Guidance is semi-automatic beam riding, so that all the operator has to do to ensure a hit is to keep the sight crosshairs on the target.

A conservative estimate of the number of T-62s built in the USSR and still in service worldwide is in excess of 8,000, spread among some 18 countries in Asia, the Middle and Far East, with North Korea having the largest holding (1,800) after Russia. Other T-62s were produced by the Czechs for export, while they were also once built in North Korea. The Russians are, therefore, currently offering a number of upgrades that will considerably improve the T-62's battlefield survivability.

T-72 Main Battle Tank

Developed as an alternative to the highly complicated and expensive T-64 and introduced in 1972, the T-72 has a crew of three, weighs 45,500kg/44.8 tons and is powered by a V12 diesel engine, delivering a top speed of 60kph/37.3mph and a range of 550km/341.8 miles. The classic low, rounded turret is centred on the hull and has two cupolas, one each for the gunner and commander. The main armament is a stabilized 125mm/4.92in 2A46 smoothbore gun fitted with a light alloy thermal sleeve and served by an automatic carousel fitted vertically on the floor and attached to the rear wall of the turret, carrying 28 projectiles. This gun has the ability to fire both the Songster-type wire-guided missile as well as normal main gun munitions. A 7.62mm/0.3in PKT machine-gun was also mounted coaxially to the right of the main armament and there was a 12.7mm/0.5in NSV machine-gun for anti-aircraft defence outside on the commander's cupola.

The tank also mounts a dozer blade under its nose, to clear obstacles and prepare fire positions, as well as having snorkelling equipment for deep wading. New versions had a cascade of improvements, including new engines (633.8kW/850hp, then 932.1kW/1,250hp), computerized fire-control systems, thermal and passive night-sights and fire detection and suppression systems. Variants included command, ARV, mine-clearer and bridgelayer models.

ABOVE AND LEFT: **Designed as a simpler alternative to the complicated and costly T-64, the T-72 has seen combat service in Iraq and Lebanon and is now serving with armies worldwide. Its main armament (on the T-72S) is the 125mm/4.92in smoothbore gun (45 rounds carried). The tank has recently been comprehensively upgraded and is in service with 30 different countries worldwide, the largest number (over 9,000) being in Russia. The T-72S weighs 1,000kg/2,204lb more than the T-72.**

ABOVE: **A captured Iraqi T-72 being dragged off during Operation "Desert Storm".** RIGHT: **During the 1970s the Soviets licensed the building of their T-72 to Yugoslavia, who adapted it to suit their own needs, putting in a different engine (a V12 diesel). Yugoslavia sold a number to Kuwait, and here are two of them, known as the M48A, flying Kuwaiti flags. These tanks saw combat during the first Gulf War.**

Like the T-54/55 series, the T-72 was built in massive numbers and supplied to client and satellite states, undergoing various modifications. They were also built under licence by seven other countries with their own model numbers, including the Czechoslovakian PSP T-72, the Polish PT-91 and the Yugoslavian M-84. There are even captured Arab-Israeli-modified versions.

RIGHT: **An internal view of part of the turret.** BELOW: **A T-72 with ERA on upgrade. The ERA bricks cover much of the vulnerable frontal area.**

T-72 MBT

Entered service: 1972
Crew: 3
Weight: 45,500kg/44.8 tons
Dimensions: Length – 9.53m/31ft 3in
Height (over turret hatch) – 2.22m/7ft 3in
Width – 3.59m/12ft 9in
Armament: Main – 125mm/4.92in gun
Secondary – 1 x 7.62mm/0.3in and
1 x 12.7mm/0.5in machine-guns
Armour: Maximum – 250mm/9.84in
Powerplant: V46 12-cylinder diesel, generating
581.6kW/780hp
Performance: Speed – 60kph/37.3mph
Range – 550km/341.8 miles (with long-range
tanks), 480km/300 miles (without)

LEFT: **Built both in Russia and the Ukraine, the T-64 MBT was the first Russian MBT to have a three-man crew, made possible by the installation of an automatic loader. The tank is only in service within armies of the Russian Federation and has never been offered for export.** BELOW: **Two T-64s being moved by tank train, a sensible way of preserving tank mileage. They are fitted with long-range fuel drums on the rear decks.** BOTTOM LEFT: **This T-64 MBT also has long-range fuel drums fitted above the rear engine deck. Its 125mm/4.92in smoothbore gun can fire the Songster ATGW (Anti-Tank Guided Weapon), taking 9–10 seconds to reach 4,000m/13,123ft.**

T-64 Main Battle Tank

Only ever in service with the Russian Federation and associate states, the T-64 MBT was never offered for export because it incorporated too many advanced features. The main differences between the T-64 and its predecessors were in its automotive and suspension systems, which consequently gave it a superior mobility. Weighing 42,000kg/ 41.3 tons, it was powered by a 5DTF 5-cylinder opposed-piston water-cooled diesel engine delivering a top speed of 75kph/46.6mph and a range of 400km/ 248.5 miles. Centred on the hull, the classic Soviet low-profile, rounded turret had two cupolas and mounted the 125mm/ 4.92in 2A26 Rapira 3 smoothbore main gun, fitted with a vertical ammunition stowage system and automatic loader, enabling the T-64 to be the first Soviet

tank operated by a crew of three. There was also a 7.62mm/0.3in coaxial machine-gun mounted to the right of the mantlet and an infrared searchlight on the left of the main armament, as well as an optional 12.7mm/0.5in anti-aircraft machine-gun.

Other improvements included new armour to protect against HEAT (High-Explosive Anti-Tank) attack, incorporating conventional steel with ceramic inserts and called laminate, and also gill-type panels which sprung outward to detonate projectiles off the main body of the tank. As other models were introduced, the usual add-on armour suites also included

ERA (Explosive Reactive Armour), passive and appliqué, as well as updates to the vehicle's gun stabilization and fire control, NBC (Nuclear, Biological and Chemical) protection, communication and safety systems. Variants included command, ARV (Armoured Recovery Vehicle) and Kobra missile-carrier models. Only about 8,000 T-64s were ever built, of which the largest number outside the Russian Federation are some 2,200 in service with the Ukrainian Army.

T-64 MBT

Entered service: 1972
Crew: 3
Weight: 42,000kg/41.3 tons
Dimensions: Length – 7.4m/24ft 3.5in
  Height (over turret hatch) – 2.2m/7ft 2.5in
  Width – 3.46m/11ft 4in
Armament: Main – 125mm/4.92in Rapira 3 gun
  Secondary – 1 x 7.62mm/0.3in and
  1 x 12.7mm/0.5in machine-guns
Armour: Maximum – 200mm/7.87in
Powerplant: 5DTF 5-cylinder diesel, 559.3kW/750hp
Performance: Speed – 75kph/46.6mph
  Range – 400km/248.5 miles

T-80 Main Battle Tank

The T-80 MBT was designed as an upgrade to replace the T-64, being produced at the Kirov Plant, Leningrad, and entering service in 1976. Initially only a small number were built and these were soon followed by the much improved T-80B.

Weighing 42,500kg/41.8 tons and fitted with torsion bar suspension, it was the first Soviet tank to have a gas-turbine engine – the GTD 1000 – which, coupled with a manual transmission, delivered a top speed of 70kph/43.5mph and a range of 335km/208.2 miles.

Unfortunately the engine proved a major stumbling block for the T-80, as it was very fuel-hungry and unreliable, necessitating changes to the hull shape in order to store more fuel as well as changes to the engine. The overall layout of the T-80 is similar to the T-64, but there are numerous differences in detail.

The wide flat turret is centred on the hull, with the commander's cupola on the right and the gunner's hatch on the left. It mounts a 125mm/4.92in 2A46 Rapira 3 smoothbore gun firing both ATGW (Anti-Tank Guided Weapon) missiles and normal main gun munitions, which is

served by a 28-projectile, horizontal automatic carousel loader, mounted on the floor and rear wall of the turret. A 7.62mm/0.3in coaxial machine-gun is mounted to the right of the mantlet and an infrared searchlight is mounted to the right of the main armament. The vehicle is also fitted with a dozer blade underneath the laminate armour glacis, as well as snorkelling equipment for deep wading.

The T-80B, which replaced the T-80 in 1978, had a modified up-armoured turret with an upgraded 125mm/4.92in main gun firing the new Kobra missile munition (known as Songster in US/NATO parlance) as well as a new fire-control system. Further upgrades include extensive extra frontal and ERA (Explosive, Reactive Armour) packages, a new, more powerful GTD-1250 turbine engine, a new laser-guided anti-tank main gun missile munition (Sniper), as well as an array of digital fire-control, navigation and safety systems.

Some 4,500 T-80s are in service in Russia, as well as a small number in four or five other countries, which surprisingly includes 41 in Cyprus.

TOP: **Similar to the T-64 series, the T-80 was accepted into service in 1976. It has a two-man turret and an automatic loader for its 125mm/4.92in smoothbore gun. A small number of T-80s have been purchased by Cyprus and Korea, as well as Pakistan, from the Ukraine factory. Note the large exhaust outlet at the rear.** ABOVE: **A Russian Federation T-80 firing on the ranges. It has a 125mm/4.92in 2A46M smoothbore gun, the same as that fitted to the T-72, and can fire either the Songster ATGW or 125mm/4.92in separate-loading ammunition (i.e. projectile-loaded first, then semi-combustible case, the stub base of which is the only part ejected).**

T-80 MBT

Entered service: 1976
Crew: 3
Weight: 42,500kg/41.8 tons
Dimensions: Length – 7.4m/24ft 3.5in
 Height (over turret hatch) – 2.2m/7ft 2.5in
 Width – 3.4m/11ft 2in
Armament: Main – 125mm/4.92in Rapira 3 gun
 Secondary – 1 x 7.62mm/0.3in and
 1 x 12.7mm/0.5in machine-guns
Armour: Unspecified
Powerplant: GTD 1000 12-cylinder gas-turbine,
 820.3kW/1,100hp
Performance: Speed – 70kph/43.5mph
 Range – 335km/208.2 miles

T-84 Main Battle Tank

The T-84 is a recent Ukrainian upgrade of the Russian T-80, with both being manufactured at the well-established Malyshev Plant at Kharkov in the Ukraine, and using as many locally produced components as possible. The main differences from its predecessor begin with a more powerful up-rated 6TD-2 diesel engine developing 894.8kW/1,200hp, which gave the vehicle a top speed of 65kph/40.4mph and a range of 540kph/335.5 miles. To handle this extra performance, new improved tracks were fitted.

Next, the turret mounted the Ukrainian-made 125mm/4.92in KBA3 smoothbore main gun, fitted with a

vertical carousel autoloader containing 28 rounds and an up-rated fire-control system including the French ALIS thermal sight. This armament fires both normal munitions and the Songster AT-11 Anti-Tank Guided Missile (ATGM).

Secondary armament consisted of two machine-guns – one of 7.62mm/0.3in and one of 12.7mm/0.5in. The T-84 also came equipped with an ARENA Active Protection System (APS) and the SHTORA-1 active IR (InfraRed) ATGM jammer – an electro-optical countermeasures system, along with Ukrainian-manufactured ERA (Explosive Reactive Armour) enhancements. Subsequent updates include improved

fire-control, communication, navigation and safety systems. There is also a later model mounting the NATO standard 120mm/4.72in main gun.

In 2001 the Ukrainian Army received two new T-84s – the first new main battle tanks delivered since the country became independent from Russia. As well as being accepted by the Ukrainian Army, this vehicle has been successfully sold to Pakistan and aroused the interest of other countries, including Turkey.

ABOVE AND LEFT: **Two views of the Ukranian-built T-84, some 8,000 having been built by the Malyshev plant for the Russian Army. Based upon the T-64 and designed jointly by the Leningrad Kirov plant and Malyshev, this MBT is now almost completely built in the Ukraine. It has a crew of three, weighs 46,000kg/45.3 tons and mounts a 125mm/4.92in smoothbore gun. These photographs were taken at an arms fair.**

T-84 MBT

Entered service: 1995
Crew: 3
Weight: 46,000kg/45.3 tons
Dimensions: Length – 7.08m/23ft 2.5in
    Height (over turret hatch) – 2.22m/7ft 3.5in
    Width – 3.56m/11ft 8in
Armament: Main – 125mm/4.92in KBA3 gun
    Secondary – 1 x 7.62mm/0.3in and
    1 x 12.7mm/0.5in machine-guns
Armour: Unspecified
Powerplant: 6TD-2 6-cylinder diesel, developing
    894.8kW/1,200hp
Performance: Speed – 65kph/40.4mph
    Range – 540km/335.5 miles

T-90 MBT	
Entered service: 1993	
Crew: 3	
Weight: 46,500kg/45.8 tons	
Dimensions: Length – 6.86m/22ft 6in	
Height (over turret hatch) – 2.23m/7ft 4in	
Width – 3.37m/11ft 1in	
Armament: Main – 125mm/4.92in Rapira 3 gun	
Secondary – 1 x 7.62mm/0.3in and	
1 x 12.7mm/0.5in machine-guns	
Armour: Unspecified	
Powerplant: V-84MS 12-cylinder diesel,	
626.4kW/840hp	
Performance: Speed – 60kph/37.3mph	
Range – 500km/310.7 miles	

T-90 Main Battle Tank

The T-90 traces its development back to the T-72BM MBT – the improved T-72B with built-in ERA (Explosive Reactive Armour) – and was first manufactured at the Uralvagon Plant in Nizhnyi-Tagil in the late 1980s.

Developed at the same time as the T-80, but with a less complex and therefore cheaper design ethos, the first major difference between the two was in the choice of power pack, which in the T-90 was a V84MS diesel engine, producing 626.4kW/840hp and providing a top speed of 60kph/37.3mph and a range of 500km/310.7 miles.

The classic Russian low-profile, rounded turret is centred on the hull and mounts the 125mm/4.92in 2A46 smoothbore main gun (the same as the T-72 and T-80) firing the AT-11 Sniper laser-guided ATGM (Anti-Tank Guided Missile), as well as normal main gun munitions.

There is a coaxial 7.62mm/0.3in machine-gun and a 12.7mm/0.5in heavy anti-aircraft machine-gun on the turret top by the gunner's hatch. The T-90 also mounts two infrared searchlights on either side of the main armament, which are part of the Shtora ATGM defence system, and the turret is covered with second-generation ERA on the frontal arc, making this one of the best protected of Russian main battle tanks. It is equipped with the latest fire-control, navigation and safety systems. There is also a T-90S MBT version, designed to meet the operational requirements of Asian countries – some 310 having been bought by India.

TOP AND ABOVE: **The T-90, which is yet another development of the T-72, first came to prominence in 1993 and is believed to have gone into small-scale production the following year. It has a crew of three, with a two-man turret with an automatic loader for its 125mm/4.92in gun. The photographs show a snorkel attached to the turret rear, but no long-range fuel tanks fitted on the rear. It made its first appearance outside Russia at Abu Dhabi in March 1997.** LEFT: **Standard equipment on the T-90S is the latest generation of Kontakt 5 Explosive Reactive Armour, as fitted in this photograph.**

239

TR-580 and TR-85 Main Battle Tanks

Both the TR-580 and TR-85 are Romanian variants of the Russian T-55 series, manufactured or modified at the Brashove factory in Romania, and the prime weapon of their armoured forces in the 1980s and 1990s.

The TR-580 was the first redesign, its alphanumeric name denoting the size of its 432.5kW/580hp engine, which necessitated a hull redesign. It was armed with the same weapons as the T-55 and its sister vehicle the TR-85, and weighed over 37 tons. It was fitted with a new torsion bar suspension system, the main visual difference between both of the Romanian vehicles and their T-55 predecessor being the sixth road wheel (the T-55 only had five).

The TR-85 also has a new German 641.3kW/860hp 8-cylinder diesel engine, providing a top speed of 60kph/38mph and a range of 310km/192.6 miles,

which required substantial modification of the rear hull and decking. In the turret the main armament mounted was the same 100mm/3.94in gun with a new fire-control system and two machine-guns – one of 7.62mm/0.3in and one of 12.7mm/0.5in.

One visual difference between the two tanks is the spoked road wheels of the TR-580. An upgrade currently under development ports additional passive armour, a new fire-control and gun-stabilization system, as well as night-vision and safety equipment updates.

LEFT: **The Romanian TR-85 MBT is a local Romanian design which is very similar to the Russian T-55. In the early 1990s the Romanians said that they had over 600 of these MBTs in service, but that figure has now dropped. The TR-85 is basically a T-55 with a fume extractor fitted to the end of the 100mm/ 3.94in rifled main armament and a thermal sleeve. There is also an upgrade mooted which has a new power pack (596.6kW/800hp diesel) and a fully automatic transmission. The TR-85M1 is the upgraded version of the TR-85, built in the 1970s with German help in chassis technology, the prime Romanian contractor being Arsenalul Armetel. Various foreign companies were also involved.**

TR-85 MBT

Entered service: 1987
Crew: 4
Weight: 50,000kg/49.2 tons
Dimensions: Length – 9.96m/32ft 8in
  Height (over turret hatch) – 3.10m/10ft 2in
  Width – 3.44m/11ft 3.5in
Armament: Main – 100mm/3.94in gun
  Secondary – 1 x 7.62mm/0.3in and
  1 x 12.7mm/0.5in machine-guns
Armour: Unspecified
Powerplant: MTU 8-cylinder diesel,
  641.3kW/860hp
Performance: Speed – 60kph/37.3mph
  Range – 310km/192.6 miles

RIGHT: **The other Romanian MBT is the TR-580, which is very similar to the TR-85 that it preceded in production. The main differences are that the gun does not have a thermal sleeve or laser rangefinder installed.**

TR-580 MBT

Entered service: 1982
Crew: 4
Weight: 38,200kg/37.6 tons
Dimensions: Length – 6.45m/21ft 2in
  Height (over turret hatch) – 2.4m/7ft 10.5in
  Width – 3.27m/10ft 8.5in
Armament: Main – 100mm/3.94in gun
  Secondary – 1 x 7.62mm/0.3in and
  1 x 12.7mm/0.5in machine-guns
Armour: Unspecified
Powerplant: Thought to be 12-cylinder diesel,
  432.5kW/580hp
Performance: Speed – 60kph/37.3mph
  Range – 300km/186.4 miles

LEFT: **Based upon the T-72, the TR-125 MBT is heavier (48,000kg/47.2 tons), with thicker armour and a larger engine. It can be recognized externally from the additional seventh roadwheel on either side. Armament is identical to the T-72.**

TR-125 MBT

Entered service: 1989
Crew: 4
Weight: 48,000kg/47.2 tons
Dimensions: Length – 6.9m/22ft 7.5in
 Height (over turret hatch) – 2.37m/7ft 9.5in
 Width – 3.60m/11ft 9.5in
Armament: Main – 125mm/4.92in gun
 Secondary – 1 x 7.62mm/0.3in and
 1 x 12.7mm/0.5in machine-guns
Armour: Unspecified
Powerplant: V12 diesel, 656.2kW/880hp
Performance: Speed – 60kph/37.3mph
 Range – 540km/335.5 miles

TR-125 Main Battle Tank

The TR-125 is a Romanian-built version of the Soviet T-72, manufactured at the end of the 1980s until the collapse of the USSR led to the cessation of production in favour of other vehicles. With considerably thicker armour, it was heavier than its predecessor, weighing 48,000kg/ 47.2 tons, with a crew of four. The TR-125 was powered by a V12 diesel engine, providing a top speed of 60kph/ 37.3mph and a range of 540km/335.5 miles. It was armed with a 125mm/4.92in main gun, with a coaxial 7.62mm/0.3in machine-gun and one of 12.7mm/ 0.5in for anti-aircraft defence. The main visual difference between it and other T-72 variants is in it having a seventh road wheel. It is still in service with the Romanian Army today.

TM-800 Main Battle Tank

The most recent of the Romanian-manufactured MBTs, the TM-800 first emerged in the mid-1990s as an upgraded version of the TR-580 – itself a T-55 derivative. With new laminate armour increasing its weight to 45,000kg/44.3 tons but giving it improved survivability on the battlefield, and powered by its 618.9kW/830hp diesel engine, the TM-800 has a top speed of 60kph/37.3mph and a range of 500km/310.7 miles. In its "mushroom head" two-hatched turret it mounts a 100mm/3.94in D10 series main gun with a computerized fire-control system and laser rangefinder, along with two machine-guns – one an internal coaxial of 7.62mm/0.3in and the other a heavier calibre 12.7mm/0.5in mounted on the outside of the turret for anti-aircraft (AA) defence.

LEFT: **The TM-800 is an up-rated TR-580 MBT, currently the most modern Romanian MBT. It appeared in service in 1994 and has not yet gone into full production.**

TM-800 MBT

Entered service: 1994
Crew: 4
Weight: 45,000kg/44.3 tons
Dimensions: Length – 6.74m/22ft 1.5in
 Height (over turret hatch) – 2.35m/7ft 8.5in
 Width – 3.30m/10ft 10in
Armament: Main – 100mm/3.94in gun
 Secondary – 1 x 7.62mm/0.3in and
 1 x 12.7mm/0.5in machine-guns
Armour: Unspecified
Powerplant: Diesel, 618.9kW/830hp
Performance: Speed – 60kph/37.3mph
 Range – 500km/310.7 miles

LEFT: **In the early 1950s the Soviet Union supplied China with a number of their T-54 Main Battle Tanks and afterwards, production of such MBTs was taken on by NORINCO (China North Industries Corporation) under the designation of Type 59. Later Type 59As were fitted with an IR searchlight above the 100mm/3.94in gun, while other retrofits have included a more powerful diesel and even an RO Defence 105mm/4.13in L7A3 rifled gun to improve the resulting package.** BELOW: **This Type 59 has been fitted with the British 105mm/4.13in L7A3 rifled gun, a private venture by UK Royal Ordnance (now BAe Systems). Note also the British pattern smoke dischargers.** BOTTOM: **A column of parked Chinese Type 59-IIs. They were a further development of the Type 59, and also had a number of improvements, such as stabilization for the main gun, a 432.5kW/580hp diesel engine and new radios.**

Type 59 Main Battle Tank

The Chinese Type 59 and its successor the Type 69 were both based upon the Soviet T-54 and it was the first Chinese tank built under licence at the inception of its own permanent armoured formations. With an identical layout to its Soviet predecessor, manned by the same number of crew and weighing 36,000kg/35.4 tons, its V12 diesel engine gave it a top speed of 50kph/31.1mph and a range of 420km/ 261 miles. Within its classic Russian "mushroom head" turret, it mounted a 100mm/3.94in rifled gun, together with two coaxial machine-guns, plus a 12.7mm/0.5in on top for anti-aircraft defence. At first the Type 59 had only the bare essentials, but later models have mounted infrared searchlights, laser rangefinders, night-vision equipment and armour enhancements.

Both Type 59s and Type 69s have been built in large numbers for the People's Liberation Army and for export, an estimate being that some 6,000 are still in service in China, while it has been sold to over a dozen countries, one of the largest numbers being about 1,200 in Pakistan, which now produces them locally and has exported to other countries in Asia and Africa.

Type 59 MBT

Entered service: 1959
Crew: 4
Weight: 36,000kg/35.4 tons
Dimensions: Length – 7.9m/25ft 11in
  Height (over turret hatch) – 2.59m/8ft 6in
  Width – 3.27m/10ft 8.5in
Armament: Main – 100mm/3.94in gun
  Secondary – 2 x 7.62mm/0.3in and
  1 x 12.7mm/0.5in machine-guns
Armour: Maximum – 203mm/7.99in
Powerplant: 12150L V12 diesel, generating
  320.7kW/430hp
Performance: Speed – 50kph/31.1mph
  Range – 420km/262.5 miles

Type 61 Main Battle Tank

Japan's first post-World War II attempt at MBT construction, The Type 61 emerged in 1962 after a development phase of almost a decade, looking very like the M48 Patton that it was so obviously based on.

Built using welded rolled steel and with a cast turret, the vehicle weighed 35,000kg/34.4 tons and was fitted with torsion bar suspension. It had a crew of four, and was powered by a Mitsubishi Type 12 HM 21 WT diesel engine delivering a top speed of 45kph/28mph and a range of 200km/124.3 miles. Mounted in the dome-shaped turret with its bulging rear was a newly designed

Type 61 90mm/3.54in main gun which was not fitted with stabilization and therefore could not fire accurately on the move. There were two machine-guns – one 7.62mm/0.3in internal coaxial and the other 12.7mm/0.5in for anti-aircraft defence.

There were also an ARV (Armoured Recovery Vehicle), AVLB (Armoured Vehicle Launched Bridge), Armoured Engineer and a Type 61 training tank.

Although it never saw action anywhere and was only in service with the Japanese Defence Force, it proved an important step in the return to indigenous tank production for the Japanese.

TOP AND ABOVE: **The first Japanese-built tank after World War II, the Type 61 was heavily influenced by the Americans. Over 500 were built of this 35,000kg/34.4-ton four-man MBT, which was armed with a 90mm/3.54in gun.**

LEFT: **Japan did not take much interest in tanks during World War II, so the Type 61 gave them a great deal of useful experience. Although it resembled the M48, it had no stabilization on its main armament. A small number are still in service.**

Type 61 MBT

Entered service: 1962
Crew: 4
Weight: 35,000kg/34.4 tons
Dimensions: Length – 8.19m/26ft 10.5in
  Height (over turret hatch) – 2.49m/8ft 2in
  Width – 2.95m/9ft 8in
Armament: Main – 90mm/3.54in Type 61 gun
  Secondary – 1 x 7.62mm/0.3in and
  1 x 12.7mm/0.5in machine-guns
Armour: Maximum – 64mm/2.52in
Powerplant: Mitsubishi HM21WT diesel,
  447.4kW/600hp
Performance: Speed – 45kph/28mph
  Range – 200km/124.3 miles

LEFT: The Type 62 Light Tank was a reduced-size version of their Type 59 MBT, which was a licensed copy of the Red Army T-59. It was the first "home-grown" light tank in Chinese service. Some 800 were built, and many still serve in training units.

Type 62 Light Tank

Entered service: China
Crew: 4
Weight: 21,000kg/20.7 tons
Dimensions: Length – 7.9m/25ft 11in (gun forward)
Height (over turret hatch) – 2.25m/7ft 4.5in
Width – 2.68m/8ft 9.5in
Armament: Main – 85mm/3.35in gun
Secondary – 2 x 7.62mm/0.3in and
1 x 12.7mm/0.5in machine-guns
Armour: Unspecified
Powerplant: Thought to be 12-cylinder diesel, 320.7kW/430hp
Performance: Speed – 60kph/37.3mph
Range – 500km/310.7 miles

Type 62 Light Tank

The Type 62 Chinese Light Tank is based on the previous Type 59 and was introduced in 1962 as an indigenous scaled-down version of its predecessor with a much lower ground pressure to cope with the specific environments of rough and soft terrain. Weighing 21,000kg/20.7 tons and with a crew of four, the Type 62 was powered by a 320.7kW/430hp diesel engine providing a top speed of 60kph/37.3mph and a range of 500km/310.7 miles. In its Russian-style "mushroom head" turret it mounted an 85mm/3.35in rifled main gun, along with a coaxial 7.62mm/0.3in machine-gun, and another of 12.7mm/0.5in for anti-aircraft defence located by the loader's hatch. There was also another 7.62mm/0.3in machine-gun in the bow operated by the driver. Approximately 800 are currently in Chinese service, and this AFV was widely exported to countries in Africa and Asia, especially Vietnam. The vehicle has been modified into ARV (Armoured Recovery Vehicle) and engineering variants, and there is also a tropicalized version.

Type 63 Light Amphibious Tank

The Type 63 is a light tank with amphibious capability and is of a similar size and weight to the Type 62. It also shares its turret and weapons systems, although its hull is based on the Type 77 APC. With a weight of over 18 tons, the Type 63 is powered by a 12150 LV12 diesel engine, giving a top speed of 64kph/39.8mph and a range of 370km/229.9 miles. Propulsion in the water is provided by hyrdro-jets located at the hull rear. It is estimated that some 1,200 are in service with the Chinese Army and Marine Corps, at least 500 of which have been upgraded to Type 63A standard, carrying a large three-man turret armed with a 105mm/4.13in rifled main gun. It is also in service with North Korea, Myanmar (Burma) and Vietnam.

RIGHT: The Type 63 was the Chinese improvement on the Red Army PT-76 Light Amphibious Tank, which combined the T-54/T-55 turret on to the Type 77 APC chassis. It will most probably be replaced by the Type 99 Light Tank when it comes into full production.

Type 63 Light Amphibious Tank

Entered service: 1963
Crew: 4
Weight: 18,400kg/18.1 tons
Dimensions: Length – 8.44m/27ft 8.5in
Height (over turret hatch) – 2.52m/8ft 3.5in
Width – 3.2m/10ft 6in
Armament: Main – 85mm/3.35in gun
Secondary – 1 x 7.62mm/0.3in and
1 x 12.7mm/0.5in machine-guns
Armour: Maximum – 14mm/0.55in
Powerplant: 12150LV 12-cylinder diesel, 298.3kW/400hp
Performance: Speed – 64kph/39.8mph
Range – 370km/229.9 miles

Type 69 Main Battle Tank

The first firm sighting of a Type 69 was on a Beijing parade in 1982. It entered service earlier – perhaps even as early as 1969, hence its name. Although it looks much like its predecessor, the Type 59, it has had a whole raft of new fire-control, stabilization, NBC (Nuclear, Biological and

BELOW: **These Type 69s are in Iraqi desert livery, having been captured by Coalition forces in the first Gulf War. Note the large 12.7mm/0.5in heavy anti-aircraft machine-gun on the top of the turret of the nearest one.**

Chemical) protection, navigation and safety systems installed. At one time British Royal Ordnance produced a Type 59 armed with a 105mm/4.13in L7 series rifled gun for the export market. The Type 69-I MBT is now armed with a 100mm/3.94in smoothbore gun, while the Type 69-II MBT has a 105mm/4.13in rifled gun (possibly derived from the L7) and fitted with a thermal sleeve. There are also command, ARV (Armoured Recovery Vehicle), mine-clearing and twin 57mm/2.24in anti-aircraft variants.

TOP: **Two Chinese Type 69-IIs (sold to Pakistan) on parade with the Pakistan Army. Note that they have been upgraded by fitting the 105mm/4.13in gun.** ABOVE: **Captured by Coalition forces during the first Gulf War, this Type 69-II has lost its laser rangefinder, which is usually externally mounted over the main armament.**

Type 69 MBT	
Entered service: 1980 (or perhaps as early as 1969)	
Crew: 4	
Weight: 36,700kg/36.1 tons	
Dimensions: Length – 6.24m/20ft 5.5in	
Height (over turret hatch) – 2.81m/9ft 2.5in	
Width – 3.3m/10ft 10in	
Armament: Main – 100mm/3.94in gun	
Secondary – 2 x 7.62mm/0.3in and	
1 x 12.7mm/0.5in machine-guns	
Armour: Maximum – 100mm/3.94in	
Powerplant: 1210L-7BW V12 diesel,	
432.5kW/580hp	
Performance: Speed – 50kph/31.1mph	
Range – 420km/261 miles	

245

Type 74 Main Battle Tank

ABOVE AND BELOW LEFT: Designed by Mitsubishi in the early 1960s, the Type 74 was completed in 1969 when it was known as the STB 1. However, it was not until 1973 that the final production model was completed. Another two more years elapsed before the production run of some 560 were built and it replaced the Type 61.

The Type 74 MBT was the next tank developed and produced by Japan to succeed the Type 61. Having tested two different prototypes – the primary difference between them being manual or automatic loading of the main gun – the manual version was chosen, with the vehicle being produced by Mitsubishi Heavy Industries and first appearing in 1975. Weighing 38,000kg/37.4 tons and fitted with a new vertically variable hydro-pneumatic suspension system, the Type 74 is powered by a Mitsubishi 10ZF22

WT 10-cylinder diesel engine, providing a top speed of 60kph/37.3mph and a range of 400km/248.5 miles. In the electrically powered turret – a sleeker looking version of the M47/48, but still with a rear bulge – the main armament is the British-designed 105mm/4.13in L7 type rifled tank gun, manufactured under licence in Japan. There is also one 7.62mm/0.3in coaxial machine-gun and one of 12.7mm/0.5in for Anti-Aircraft (AA) and close-quarter defence. Internally the vehicle is equipped with all the latest target and fire

control, gun stabilization, NBC (Nuclear, Biological and Chemical) protection, communication, navigation, night-vision and safety systems. Variants include an ARV (Armoured Recovery Vehicle) and a twin 35mm/1.38in AA gun version. Approximately 560 were built, but all have now been phased out of front-line service.

Type 74 MBT	
Entered service: 1975	
Crew: 4	
Weight: 38,000kg/37.4 tons	
Dimensions: Length – 9.42m/30ft 11in	
Height (over turret hatch) – 2.48m/8ft 1.5in	
Width – 3.18m/10ft 5in	
Armament: Main – 105mm/4.13in L7 gun	
Secondary – 1 x 7.62mm/0.3in and	
1 x 12.7mm/0.5in machine-guns	
Armour: Unspecified	
Powerplant: Mitsubishi 10ZF22 WT 10-cylinder	
diesel, 536.9kW/720hp	
Performance: Speed – 60kph/37.3mph	
Range – 400km/248.5 miles	

Type 80 Main Battle Tank

Development of the Chinese Type 80 MBT began in the early 1980s, and full production was achieved towards the end of that decade. Although based on the Type 59/69 series, it has a newly designed chassis and running gear, with six road wheels and a torsion bar suspension system. Weighing 38,500kg/ 37.9 tons and with a crew of four, the Type 80 is powered by a VR36 V12 diesel engine, providing a top speed of 60kph/ 37.3mph and a range of 430km/267.2 miles. The turret has a "mushroom head" profile similar to the Type 69 but with a distinctive open grill stowage basket wrapped around the back and sides.

The main armament is an L7 type 105mm/4.13in rifled main gun fitted with a fume extractor and a thermal sleeve. There is also a coaxial 7.62mm/0.3in machine-gun and a 12.7mm/0.5in anti-aircraft machine-gun mounted outside the loader's hatch. The Type 80 ports all the latest essential equipment, including a ballistics computer, a laser rangefinder integrated with stabilized sights, attack sensors and composite armour suites. To extend the operational range of the Type 80 MBT, two large drum fuel tanks (jettisonable) can be fitted at the rear.

Some 500 Type 80 Main Battle Tanks are in service with the Chinese army and a small number were exported to Myanmar (Burma).

Type 80 MBT

Entered service: 1988
Crew: 4
Weight: 38,500kg/37.9 tons
Dimensions: Length – 9.33m/30ft 7.5in
 Height (over turret hatch) – 2.29m/7ft 6in
 Width – 3.37m/11ft 0.5in
Armament: Main – 105mm/4.13in gun
 Secondary – 1 x 7.62mm/0.3in and
 1 x 12.7mm/0.5in machine-guns
Armour: Unspecified
Powerplant: VR36 V12 diesel, 544.4kW/730hp
Performance: Speed – 60kph/37.3mph
 Range – 430km/267.2 miles

Type 85-II Main Battle Tank

The Type 85-II Chinese MBT is an upgrade of the Type 80 with an improved chassis and a new, flatter welded turret, using the latest upgraded modular composite armour. Weighing just over 40 tons, it is powered by a V12 supercharged diesel engine, giving it a top speed of 62kph/39mph and a range of 450km/280 miles. Initially it mounted the same 105mm/4.13in main armament as its predecessor, but this has recently been upgraded to a larger, fully stabilized 125mm/4.92in smoothbore main gun served by an autoloader, thus reducing the crew to three. This weapon enables the Type 85 to fire accurately on the move – the first Chinese MBT to be able do so, which is a significant advantage.

ABOVE: **The Type 85-II initially had a 105mm/4.13in rifled gun, which has now been replaced by a 125mm/4.92in smoothbore gun with an automatic loader. In recent years China has exported more than 250 to Pakistan – known as the Type 85-IIAP, which is shown in this photograph.**

The most recent version, the Type 85-III is in service with the Chinese army and is built under licence in Pakistan, where its nomenclature is the Type 85-IIAP.

Variants

The Type 85-IIM, known in the People's Liberation Army as the Type 88C MBT, was first seen in 1999. It weighs 41,000kg/40.35 tons and is armoured with an automatic loader. It has the ISFCS 22 computerized fire-control system fitted. Some also appear to have been fitted with a laser-jamming device operated from inside the turret and mounted on the left side of the turret roof.

Type 85-II MBT	
Entered service: 1995	
Crew: 3	
Weight: 41,000kg/40.35 tons	
Dimensions: Length – 10.1m/33ft 1.5in	
Height (over turret hatch) – 2.37m/7ft 9.5in	
Width – 3.50m/11ft 6in	
Armament: Main – 125mm/4.92in gun	
Secondary – 1 x 7.62mm/0.3in and	
1 x 12.7mm/0.5in machine-guns	
Armour: Unspecified	
Powerplant: Perkins V12 diesel, 894.8kW/1,200hp	
Performance: Speed – 62kph/38.5mph	
Range – 450km/279.6 miles	

Type 88 K1 Main Battle Tank

Emerging in 1987 from a joint US–South Korean project begun in 1980, the Type 88 K1/K1A1 MBT is now entirely South Korean-built, with various parts manufactured under licence. It resembles the Abrams in appearance, with its flat faceted composite armoured turret. Weighing 51,100kg/50.3 tons and fitted with a hybrid suspension system combining hydro-pneumatic elements and torsion bar springs, the Type 88 K1 is powered by an MTU MB 871 Ka-501 turbocharged diesel engine, giving a top speed of 65kph/40.4mph and a range of 440km/273.4 miles.

Main armament in earlier models was the same as the M1, the 105mm/4.13in gun, along with three machine-guns, two of 7.62mm/0.3in and one of 12.7mm/ 0.5in. However, the latest version, the K1A1, mounts the M1A1's 120mm/4.72in smoothbore main gun. The vehicle also ports the latest target and fire control, gun stabilization, NBC (Nuclear,

Biological and Chemical) protection, communication, navigation, night-vision and safety systems.

There are also up-armour packages as well as ARV (Armoured Recovery Vehicle), mine-clearing vehicle and bridge-layer variants, all of which are currently being marketed to other countries, but to date without success.

TOP: **In early 1980 the Republic of South Korea chose the General Dynamics Company of the United States to design and build a new main battle tank for them. A few years later the Type 88 K1 appeared, which looks very like the Abrams M1 and mounts the same 105mm/4.13in gun.**
ABOVE: **Over 1,000 K1s have been built by Hyundai for the South Korean Army. Future developments may include a lighter model, that would include fitting ERA, to sell to other Far Eastern armies.**

Type 88 K1 MBT	

Entered service: 1987
Crew: 4
Weight: 51,100kg/50.3 tons
Dimensions: Length – 7.48m/24ft 6.5in
  Height (over turret hatch) – 2.25m/7ft 4.5in
  Width – 3.59m/11ft 9.5in
Armament: Main – 105mm/4.13in gun
  Secondary – 2 x 7.62mm/0.3in and
  1 x 12.7mm/0.5in machine-guns
Armour: Unspecified
Powerplant: MTU MB 871 Ka-501 diesel,
  984.8kW/1,200hp
Performance: Speed – 65kph/40.4mph
  Range – 440km/273.4 miles

Type 90 Main Battle Tank

ABOVE AND BELOW LEFT: **Mitsubishi was the prime contractor for this Japanese MBT that was first designed in 1976. Apart from its 120mm/4.72in smoothbore Rheinmetall gun, it was completely Japanese-designed and built. Later, two prototypes with Japanese 120mm/4.72in guns (firing Japanese ammunition) were also built. It is now in service with the Japanese Ground Self-Defence Force, and has never been offered on the export market.**

In 1976, development of the next indigenous Japanese tank was initiated as soon as the Type 74 had entered service and, in 1990, the Type 90 was produced by a consortium of Japanese companies headed by Mitsubushi Heavy Industries. Weighing 50,000kg/49.2 tons and fitted with a hybrid hydro-pneumatic and torsion bar suspension system, the Type 90 is powered by a Mitsubishi 10ZG 10-cylinder liquid-cooled diesel engine, giving it a speed of 70kph/43.5mph and a range of 400km/248.5 miles. The German Rheinmetall 120mm/4.72in smoothbore

main gun – the same armament as Leopard 2 – is mounted in a wide, flat turret resembling that of the Abrams M1A1 and is armoured with a combination of the latest composite and laminate packages. This weapon was chosen after extensive testing in preference over the original Japanese design, and it is served by an autoloader, thereby reducing the crew to three.

Secondary weaponry includes the normal 7.62mm/0.3in coaxial and 12.7mm/0.5in machine-guns. The vehicle is also equipped with the latest digital fire-control,

navigation, night-vision, communication and safety systems. The Type 90 is currently in Japanese service but has not been offered for export. There are the usual ARV (Armoured Recovery Vehicle), AVLB (Armoured Vehicle Launched Bridge) and mine-clearing variants.

Type 90 MBT	

Entered service: 1991
Crew: 3
Weight: 50,000kg/49.2 tons
Dimensions: Length – 9.76m/32ft
Height (over turret hatch) – 2.34m/7ft 8in
Width – 3.43m/11ft 3in
Armament: Main – 120mm/4.72in gun
Secondary – 1 x 7.62mm/0.3in and
1 x 12.7mm/0.5in machine-guns
Armour: Unspecified
Powerplant: Mitsubishi 10ZG 10-cylinder diesel,
1,118.6kW/1,500hp
Performance: Speed – 70kph/43.5mph
Range – 400km/248.5 miles

Type 90-II (MBT 2000) Main Battle Tank

The NORINCO Type 90-II MBT, also now known as MBT 2000, first emerged in 1991 and was a development of the Type 85 design, with the first model never reaching production stage. Having undergone armour, engine and main gun upgrades, the new improved model, Type 90-II, weighed over 47 tons and was powered by a Perkins V12 diesel engine, providing a top speed of 62kph/38.5mph and a range of 450km/279.6 miles. Mounted in a flat turret tapering at the front and fitted with a kind of composite armour, the 125mm/4.92in smoothbore main gun is served by an automatic loader, allowing the tank to be crewed by three men – commander, gunner and driver. Secondary armament consists of two machine-guns – one of 7.62mm/0.3in and one of 12.7mm/0.5in.

Internally, the digital fire-control system includes a stabilized laser rangefinder sight, passive thermal imaging and crosswind, tilt and angular velocity sensors, allowing the Type 90-II to engage targets accurately while on the move in day or night conditions.

Currently in Chinese service, this AFV has been marketed for export under the name of MBT 2000 and, following a further agreement, Pakistan has been licensed to produce the Type 90-II, renaming it the Al-Khalid.

LEFT: **The Type 90 appeared in the early 1990s, and had considerable improvements in firepower, protection and mobility over previous Chinese MBTs. The main armament of this 48,000kg/ 47.2-ton three-man tank is a 125mm/4.92in smoothbore gun with an automatic loader and Image Stabilized Fire-Control System. Additional fuel drums can be mounted on the rear.**

Type 90-II (MBT 2000) MBT

Entered service: 1995
Crew: 3
Weight: 48,000kg/47.2 tons
Dimensions: Length – 10.1m/33ft 1.5in
Height (over turret hatch) – 2.37m/7ft 9.5in
Width – 3.50m/11ft 6in
Armament: Main – 125mm/4.92in gun
Secondary – 1 x 7.62mm/0.3in and
1 x 12.7mm/0.5in machine-guns
Armour: Unspecified
Powerplant: Perkins V12 diesel, generating 894.8kW/1,200hp
Performance: Speed – 62kph/38.5mph
Range – 450km/279.6 miles

Type 98 Main Battle Tank

A little-seen upgrade development of the Type 90-II is the Type 98 MBT, first glimpsed in 1999 at the 50th Anniversary of the Chinese People's Republic. It is an upgrade of the Type 90-II, with the same armament mounted on a modified turret with a new modular armour package. Improvements will no doubt include substantial enhancement of its fire-control, navigation, NBC (Nuclear, Biological and Chemical) protection and safety systems. It is currently in production and has been deployed with the People's Liberation Army (PLA).

Development is continuing, and an improved Type 98 with a heavier combat weight (52,800kg/52 tons) has appeared. It retains the 125mm/4.92in smoothbore main gun and is said to be more reliable and better protected, possibly using the "arrowhead"-type armour as on the latest Leopard 2.

Type 98 MBT

Entered service: 1998
Crew: 35
Weight: 50,793kg/50 tons
Dimensions: Length – 11m/36ft
Height (over turret hatch) – approximately 2m/6ft 6in
Width – 3.4m/11ft 2in
Armament: Main – 125mm/4.92in gun
Secondary – 1 x 7.62mm/0.3in and
1 x 12.7mm/0.5in machine-guns
Armour: Not known
Powerplant: 894.8kW/1,200hp diesel
Performance: Speed – 65kph/40.6mph
Range – 450km/280 miles (600km/375 miles with external fuel tanks)

LEFT: **Yet another parade and another immaculate Chinese tank, this time a Type 98, one of their most modern tanks, clearly showing its 125mm/4.92in smoothbore gun.**

Vickers Mark 1 (Vijayanta) Main Battle Tank

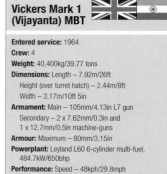

LEFT: It was in the late 1950s that Vickers began to consider producing a tank to its own design for overseas markets. First to be produced was the Mark 1 MBT which weighed 38,600kg/38 tons, had a crew of four and mounted a 105mm/4.13in gun. A total of 70 Mark 1s were sold to Kuwait.

Vickers Mark 1 (Vijayanta) MBT	
Entered service: 1964	
Crew: 4	
Weight: 40,400kg/39.77 tons	
Dimensions: Length – 7.92m/26ft	
Height (over turret hatch) – 2.44m/8ft	
Width – 3.17m/10ft 5in	
Armament: Main – 105mm/4.13in L7 gun	
Secondary – 2 x 7.62mm/0.3in and	
1 x 12.7mm/0.5in machine-guns	
Armour: Maximum – 80mm/3.15in	
Powerplant: Leyland L60 6-cylinder multi-fuel, 484.7kW/650bhp	
Performance: Speed – 48kph/29.8mph	
Range – 480km/298.3 miles	

The Vickers Mark 1 was based on the Chieftain MBT but produced in a lightly armoured configuration in 1964 for the Asian and Arab export market. This was a viable AFV, if not of NATO MBT quality, and was built using as many existing parts as possible. Weighing 38,600kg/38 tons, it was powered by a Leyland L60 Mk 4B 6-cylinder water-cooled multi-fuel engine which provided a top speed of 48kph/29.8mph and a range of 480km/298.3 miles. It was armed with the Royal Ordnance L7 105mm/4.13in main gun as well as two 7.62mm/0.3in and one 12.7mm/0.5in machine-guns. These were mounted in a turret that resembled the Centurion's in appearance, having an angular flat box shape with a rear stowage bustle, rather than the Chieftain's more ergonomic turret shape. The main customer of the Vickers Mark 1 was India, where a prototype had been sent in 1963. Accepted by India, it was renamed the Vijayanta (Victory), and local production was started in 1965 by an Vickers Indian subsidiary in Madras.

Local modifications were made over the years that followed, and these included a new engine, new fire-control, night-vision and navigation systems, and add-on suites of passive armour. In this way the life of the vehicle was extended until the Arjun came into service.

Some 2,200 Vijayantas were built before production ceased. Other countries who also bought the Vickers Mark 1 included Kuwait, who purchased 70 from 1970–72.

BELOW: In the late 1950s India was looking to replace their ageing Centurions, which had done so well in the Indo-Pakistan wars against the American-built Pakistani tanks, due mainly to their simpler fire-control systems. They decided upon the Vickers Mark 1, which they called Vijayanta (Victory). Vickers built the first 90 in order to meet the agreed production deadline, the rest of the order being manufactured in India at a new factory in Madras. Many of the 2,000 fleet remain in service, despite being supplemented or replaced by more modern Russian MBTs, some of which are locally built.

ABOVE: The Kartik AVLB is based upon the lengthened chassis of the Vijayanta, which is also used for the Catapult SP artillery system.

Vickers Mark 3 Main Battle Tank

An upgrade of the Mark 1 with changes to the hull, a new engine and a new turret, the Vickers Mark 3 MBT first appeared as an export model in 1977. Weighing 38,700kg/38.1 tons and fitted with a torsion bar suspension system, it was powered by a Detroit Diesel 12V-71T engine, giving it a top speed of 50kph/31.1mph and a range of 530km/329.3 miles. The vehicle's armament remained the same as its predecessor, the 105mm/4.13in L7A1 main gun and two 7.62mm/0.3in machine-guns (one coaxial), but mounted in a newly designed steel turret, with a reloading port on the left-hand side and a commander's cupola and hatch for the loader on the turret top. Fifty rounds of main gun ammunition were carried – 18 in the turret itself and a further 32 in the hull. Other changes included up-rated fire-control, night-vision, NBC (Nuclear, Biological and Chemical) protection, communication and safety systems, making the Mark 3 an infinitely more sophisticated weapon system than the Mark 1.

Another version developed for sale to Malaysia included an ERA (Explosive Reactive Armour) armour package and a GPS (Global Positioning System) Satellite Navigation (SatNav) system, as well as a range of further optional enhancement packages.

LEFT, ABOVE AND ABOVE RIGHT: **The next Vickers MBT was the Mark 3, of similar weight and size to the Mark 1, with a 105mm/4.13in gun, complete with laser rangefinder. The first Mark 3 production order was placed in 1977 by Kenya, followed by Nigeria. Sadly, others did not follow.**

Vickers Mark 3 MBT

Entered service: 1977
Crew: 4
Weight: 38,700kg/38.1 tons
Dimensions: Length – 7.56m/24ft 9.5in
Height (over turret hatch) – 2.48m/8ft 1.5in
Width – 3.17m/10ft 5in
Armament: Main – 105mm/4.13in L7A1 gun
Secondary – 2 x 7.62mm/0.3in and
1 x 12.7mm/0.5in machine-guns
Armour: Maximum – 80mm/3.15in
Powerplant: Detroit Diesel 12V-71T diesel,
536.9kW/720bhp
Performance: Speed – 50kph/31.1mph
Range – 530km/329.3 miles

Vickers VFM Mark 5 Light Tank

The VFM Mark 5 was first seen in 1986 at the British Army Equipment Exhibition (BAEE), and was another AFV developed by Vickers for the export market. The vehicle was developed in conjunction with an American company – FMC – using its Close Combat Vehicle (Light) or CCV(L) as the basis on which to mount a turret containing British armament. This produced a light tank with a considerable punch.

Weighing 19,750kg/19.4 tons with welded aluminium armour, the VFM was powered by a modular Detroit Diesel V6 turbocharged engine, delivering a top speed of 70kph/43.5mph and a range of 480km/298.3 miles. The power pack is housed in the distinctly raised rear hull and fitted with a ramp door to enable speedy access. The turret echoes the rising hull by also tapering at its rear, while mounting the L7 105mm/4.13in smoothbore main gun, along with two 7.62mm/0.3in machine-guns.

Designed to be air-portable in both the C130 Hercules and C141 Starlifter transport aircraft, it could also be dropped using the Low Altitude Parachute Extraction System (LAPES).

ABOVE LEFT, ABOVE AND BELOW LEFT: **The Vickers VFM 5 was a 19,750kg/19.4-ton light tank that was a joint venture between Vickers Defence Systems and the FMC Corporation of USA. The first prototype was on show at the 1986 BAEE, and a year later it had completed its firing and mobility trials. It was designed to be air-portable in both the C130 Hercules and the C141 Starlifter transport aircraft, and to be dropped by LAPES (Low Altitude Parachute Extraction System). It did not find a market, so never went into full production.**

Vickers VFM Mark 5 Light Tank

Entered service: 1987
Crew: 4
Weight: 19,750kg/19.4 tons
Dimensions: Length – 6.20m/20ft 4in
   Height (over turret hatch) – 2.62m/8ft 7in
   Width – 2.69m/8ft 10in
Armament: Main – 105mm/4.13in L7 gun
   Secondary – 2 x 7.62mm/0.3in machine-guns
Armour: Unspecified
Powerplant: Detroit Diesel V6, 739.9kW/992hp
Performance: Speed – 70kph/43.5mph
   Range – 480km/298.3 miles

Vickers Mark 7 Valiant Main Battle Tank

Originally developed as a technology demonstrator at the same time as the VFM Mark 5, the Vickers Mark 7 Valiant represented another strand in the dynamic export market push of the mid-1980s undertaken by Vickers. This time the development partner was Germany and the resulting Vickers Mark 7 was even more versatile than its Mark 5 predecessor in being able to port a wide variety of European-manufactured equipment. Using British composite armour (known as Chobham after the town where it was developed) and a British turret, combined with a German chassis, engine and running gear (essentially the bottom of the Kraus-Maffei-built Leopard 2), the Valiant could mount a variety of main guns. The first option was the British rifled 120mm/4.72in L11A5, the second a French Giat

CN 120-26 120mm/4.72in, and the third a German Rheinmetall smoothbore 120mm/4.72in.

The vehicle is also fitted with the Marconi Centaur integrated gun and fire control as well as navigation, NBC (Nuclear, Biological and Chemical) protection and fire-suppression systems. The Mark 7 Valiant was overtaken by events (the first

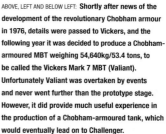

ABOVE, LEFT AND BELOW LEFT: **Shortly after news of the development of the revolutionary Chobham armour in 1976, details were passed to Vickers, and the following year it was decided to produce a Chobham-armoured MBT weighing 54,640kg/53.4 tons, to be called the Vickers Mark 7 MBT (Valiant). Unfortunately Valiant was overtaken by events and never went further than the prototype stage. However, it did provide much useful experience in the production of a Chobham-armoured tank, which would eventually lead on to Challenger.**

Gulf War of the early 1990s) and never went into production, but it did provide much useful experience, which led to the development of the Vickers Challenger 2 MBT.

Vickers Mark 7 Valiant MBT	

Entered service: 1985
Crew: 4
Weight: 54,640kg/53.4 tons
Dimensions: Length – 7.72m/25ft 4in
    Height (over turret hatch) – 2.54m/8ft 4in
    Width – 3.42m/11ft 2.5in
Armament: Main – 120mm/4.72in L11A5 gun
    Secondary – 2 x 7.62mm/0.3in machine-guns
Armour: Unspecified
Powerplant: MTU MB873 V12 diesel, delivering
    1,118.6kW/1,500hp
Performance: Speed – 72kph/44.7mph
    Range – 550km/343.75 miles

255

ARMOURED FIGHTING VEHICLES

The group of armoured fighting vehicles (AFVs) that excludes the tank represents a huge range of functionally diverse machines. This group includes the earliest modern armoured vehicle – the armoured car – as well as armoured personnel carriers, self-propelled artillery and anti-aircraft guns, infantry fighting vehicles, rocket launchers, prime movers and command vehicles. It also includes a range of traction mechanisms with fully-tracked, half-tracked and fully-wheeled vehicles.

Although the armoured car was the first AFV to see action in World War I, the necessity for battle-worthy vehicles to accompany tanks into action or provide specialized support was identified early on. As a result, gun carriers, mobile anti-aircraft guns and more latterly supply and personnel carriers were developed. Indeed, many of the specialized vehicles that were fully developed in World War II had already been identified during the earlier conflict.

Developments since World War II have produced a huge range of specialized vehicles. Some of these have taken over roles previously performed by the tank, particularly those of reconnaissance and peacekeeping, but also in the deployment of fast-moving offensive firepower.

LEFT: **Rolls-Royce Armoured Car.**

Introducing AFVs

Armoured Fighting Vehicles (AFVs) form one of the most complex groups of machines found on the modern battlefield. Excluding the tank, the AFV manifests itself in a wide and diverse variety of machines that can multi-task and are multi-functional. They form the core of the armoured division and can be found in greater numbers around the world than the tank, even replacing the tank in some armies.

Before the invention of the internal combustion engine, engineers had tried to devise various ways of using wagons as crude mobile fighting platforms. Some of these performed quite well but most were ill-conceived. After 1900, AFV use and development started to speed up, evolving into three main types. The armoured car was the first of the AFVs to be deployed by the armed forces, with the Self-Propelled Gun (SPG) and the Armoured Personnel Carrier (APC) following on more slowly.

The biggest debate surrounding the AFV is the choice of wheels or tracks to provide mobility. At first, wheeled vehicles had very poor cross-country ability compared with that of the tracked tank. However, today the wheeled vehicle has very good cross-country ability, is air-portable and can be used in an urban area far more easily than the tank, and has greater flexibility. The armoured car has always used wheels, but from time to time light tanks have been developed to be used in the same primary reconnaissance role. The SPG is usually mounted on tracks, but wheeled SPGs have also been developed on occasion, especially by the Russians.

TOP: **The Marksman SPAAG (Self-Propelled Anti-Aircraft Gun) was developed by BAe Systems for the British Army but it was not taken into service. As yet it has only been sold to Finland.** ABOVE: **Saloon car converted by the British Home Guard into an AFV by fitting armour to the windows and radiator.**

The APC started life as a battlefield taxi for the infantry, initially with a mix of wheels and tracks, and was known as the half-track. Being such a useful and versatile vehicle, it was very quickly adapted into other roles such as command, armoured ambulance and supply vehicle.

The armoured car has taken over from the cavalry as one of the main Armoured Reconnaissance Vehicles (ARVs) on the battlefield. The ARV has to be well armed and armoured, and capable of travelling at relatively high speed. The main work of this vehicle is to serve as the eyes of the army, well in advance of its own front line. It has to rely on speed and agility to get out of trouble if observed by the opposing forces. As the destructive power of anti-tank guns has increased, armoured cars have become much larger, surrendering speed for increased crew protection.

The APC has undergone a metamorphosis and emerged as the Infantry Fighting Vehicle (IFV). Starting life as an open-topped box for transporting infantry to the edge of the fighting, the infantry then had to leave the vehicle and attack the enemy position on foot with support from the vehicle. With the modern IFV, the infantry can attack from the safety of a vehicle that can fight its own way into the enemy position and then disgorge the troops.

The role of the SPG is to support tank attacks with high-explosive rounds. Early tanks did not have an adequate long-range gun which could fire a high-explosive round, making the SPG essential. In early SPGs, the gun was mounted in an open box on the top of a tracked vehicle, leaving the gun crew very exposed. Since then, the gun calibre has grown in size and the range of the gun has increased, becoming very sophisticated and accurate, and in some cases missiles are beginning to replace the gun on the battlefield. Crews are now much better protected from both the weather and enemy action.

This part of the book contains a wide selection of armoured fighting vehicles from around the world, dating from the early 20th century to the present day. The selection of machines is confined to those that are of primary interest and importance, and which particularly demonstrate the diversification of the armoured fighting vehicle. These will give a good insight into why the AFV plays such a crucial role in military forces around the world today.

ABOVE LEFT: **The Gepard Flakpanzer 1 emerged in the late 1960s as an indigenous SPAAG for the West German Army. The Contraves turret mounts twin 35mm/1.38in Oerlikon KDA cannon. The Gepard chassis is based on the Leopard 1 MBT.** TOP: **The Fox FV 721 armoured car entered service with the British Army in 1973 as a replacement for the Ferret armoured car. It is armed with a 30mm/1.18in RARDEN cannon which can destroy light armoured vehicles at 1,000m/3,281ft.** ABOVE: **The Commando M706 armoured car was built by Cadillac Gage for the US Army. Originally intended as an export vehicle for police forces around the world, it saw extensive service during the Vietnam War with both the South Vietnamese and US armies as a convoy escort vehicle.** BELOW: **The LAV-25 8x8 APC is a copy of the Swiss MOWAG Piranha, one of the world's most successful armoured personnel carriers. The LAV-25 is built by General Motors of Canada and has been sold to many countries around the world, including the USA.**

259

The History of Armoured Fighting Vehicles

In 100 years, the armoured fighting vehicle has undergone many transformations. The first vehicles were created by designers who were unsure of what it was that the army required, or indeed how to produce a machine that would usefully replace the horse. Once armies had acquired useful vehicles, they then spent the next 30 years learning how to use these new weapon systems. Men such as Sir Basil Henry Liddell Hart and Heinz Guderian would be fundamental in devising and developing the theory of mechanized warfare.

In 1914, armoured vehicles were improvised using boiler plate and this was quickly improved upon by introduction of armour plate. The modern vehicle is constructed from composite materials, making it very light and fast yet giving the crew adequate protection.

After 1945, the Cold War arms race started and new weapons, nuclear and chemical, made their debut on the modern battlefield. Armoured fighting vehicles would not only deliver these but would also have to protect their crews and infantry from these unseen threats. This is vital as it takes 20 days to produce a vehicle but 20 years to grow a soldier. The priority is clear.

LEFT: **The American DUKW served in many different theatres in World War II. Here "Pistol Packen Mama" takes US troops over the Rhine in 1945.**

LEFT: **In 1902, F. R. Simms designed and built a "war car" which had a crew of five. One man drove the vehicle while two operated the Maxim 1pdr "pom-pom" gun in the rear and two men operated the two forward machine-guns.**
BELOW: **One of the early development vehicles designed to act as an infantry fighting vehicle. Made from an old steam boiler, the cab and engine were also covered in boiler plate. The engine was not powerful enough to handle the weight of all this armour.**

Evolution

Probably the earliest significant use of the AFV was in 1125 when the army of the Sung dynasty halted the advance of the invading Tartar forces in Northern China using iron-plated armoured "cars" to break up the Tartar cavalry. The next time that AFVs make an appearance on the battlefield is between 1420 and 1431 during the peasant rebellion in Bohemia (the modern Czech Republic). Jan Zizka led a peasant army of 25,000 against the might of the 200,000-strong Imperial German army. Zizka came up with the idea of putting sheets of iron on some of his wagons. Inside were men armed with handguns, crossbows and large axes and could fire from the wagons through slits in the iron plates.

The AFV did not come into its own until the 20th century, with each type developing separately. First was the armoured car, followed by the Self-Propelled Gun (SPG) and finally the infantry carrier. Mr F. R. Simms, a British motoring enthusiast, came up with the idea of mounting a machine-gun on the front of a quadricycle and installing a small petrol engine at the rear. The Simms machine was widely publicized and spurred others on to design "war cars" of one sort or another, and even Henry Ford got in on the act and mounted a machine-gun on the front of a Model T. France produced a Charron armoured car in 1906 and a Hotchkiss car in 1909. These were basic touring cars with a sheet of armour bent around the tonneau. These early machines represent the first attempts to bring a new measure of speed and mobility to the battlefield.

SPGs made slow progress. The first ones to be developed were mobile anti-balloon guns such as the German Rheinmetall of 1909. The idea of these vehicles was to provide a highly mobile defensive force, capable of rapid deployment against a very mobile enemy. By December 1914, trenches ran from the Swiss border to the North Sea and siege warfare had started. In Britain there were no mobile Anti-Aircraft (AA) guns at the start of World War I, so a crash programme was put in place. The 5.9kg/13lb gun, weighing 457kg/9cwt was placed on Thornycroft and Peerless trucks as a makeshift response, but once established it built up a sound reputation. When the rains came to the Flanders area and the earth turned into a sea of mud, horse-drawn transport with its narrow steel-rimmed wheels ground to a halt. In particular, the movement of guns was almost impossible. After a successful attack, the infantry would be without close artillery support, as horse-drawn artillery could not cross the mud of No Man's Land. They needed this support to keep the momentum of the attack going. As a result, Gun Carrier Tanks were developed and an order for 48 units was placed. They arrived in France in 1917 but were only deployed a few times before being relegated to the supply role. The main problem was that these new vehicles did not fit the established way of handling guns in the British Army, namely, with horse teams.

For centuries, the infantry have had to march to the battlefield and then go into battle on foot. Railways were to change the face of warfare in Europe, by enabling armies to move over large distances very quickly and to arrive on the battlefield in good order. The Franco-Prussian War of 1870–71 was the first example of transportation by rail. In 1914, the French garrison of Paris was loaded into taxis and moved to the front to help stop the German advance. The British Army came up with the idea of moving troops to the front line by putting them into imported London buses, the sides of which were covered in heavy timber to give the troops some protection from shell splinters. In 1917, the British Army asked for a supply tank that could carry 10.16 tonnes/10 tons of supplies or 30 armed men. Being a converted tank, it could keep up with a tank assault and deliver the infantry into the German lines. The first of these machines did not arrive in France until October 1918, in readiness for the attacks planned for 1919, which were to prove to be unnecessary.

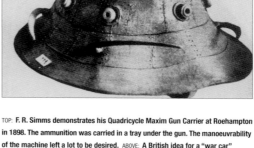

TOP: **F. R. Simms demonstrates his Quadricycle Maxim Gun Carrier at Roehampton in 1898. The ammunition was carried in a tray under the gun. The manoeuvrability of the machine left a lot to be desired.** ABOVE: **A British idea for a "war car" designed in 1855. Called the Cowen Battle-Car, it had several retractable scythes fitted to the sides of the vehicle.** BELOW: **The armoured traction engine of Fowler's Armoured Road Train. This was sent to South Africa in 1902 during the Boer War to pull armoured wagons full of British troops. The idea did not work as well as expected.**

ABOVE: **The Holzschuher car of 1558 was conceived as a mobile "war car" that would be pulled into position by a team of horses, unhitched and left to pour fire into the flanks of an enemy.**

> "Operations of war require 1,000 fast chariots, 1,000 four-horse wagons covered in leather and 100,000 mailed troops. Now when an army marches abroad the treasury will be empty at home."
> Sun Tzu, c.500–320 BC

Components of an Armoured Division

The basic components of an armoured division have not changed a great deal since 1934. These are armoured reconnaissance, tanks, motorized infantry, self-propelled artillery, engineer and signal units.

During World War I, there was no formal tank formation – a set number of tanks would be assigned to a particular attack. The infantry and the supporting artillery assigned to the attack might never have worked with tanks before. As a result of the lack of training with this new weapon there were large numbers of unnecessary infantry casualties that could have been avoided. Aerial photographs provided forward reconnaissance, as armoured cars could not breach the German trenches.

During World War I and until the formation of the integrated armoured force, the tank was felt to be purely an infantry support vehicle, with the French continuing to believe this until World War II. In 1926, the British government decided to establish an experimental armoured force consisting of an armoured reconnaissance battalion, made up of one company of light tanks and two companies of armoured cars, a medium tank battalion and an infantry battalion. Other supporting units were a towed motorized artillery detachment, a battery of SPGs, a machine-gun company, an engineering company and a signals company. This unit was the first complete armoured formation in the world and would be widely copied. Wound up in late 1928 having been led in a restricted and conventional way, the unit allowed the army to learn some very useful lessons in the detailed handling of armour and mechanized infantry. In 1931, the British had another go at an armoured formation by creating the 1st Armoured Brigade which remained in service and was sent to France with the British Expeditionary Force in 1939.

The theory had been developed in Britain by military theoreticians such as J. F. C. Fuller and Sir Basil Henry Liddell Hart, but the real father of the armoured division was Heinz Guderian. He had learnt the theory from the British and had built up practical experience at the German training school in Russia. A German armoured brigade was formed under his command in 1934, and one year later Germany would have three full armoured divisions.

The strength of a standard British armoured division in 1944 was 15,464 men and 3,464 vehicles, made up of 343 tanks, 261 tracked carriers, 100 armoured cars and 2,710 other vehicles. The large number of AFVs is significant; the roles they play were and are vital within the division's makeup.

> "Designed to convey, under the most trying conditions imaginable, accurate and balanced information to the general's battle map."
> Sir Arthur Bryant (on the armoured car), 1950

ABOVE: **In the foreground is an FV 432 armed with a single 7.62mm/0.3in machine-gun turret. Behind is a line-up of ten different types of the basic FV 432 vehicle, all of which were built by GKN Sankey.**
LEFT: **Part of the 7th Armoured Division before the start of the 1991 Gulf War. In the front is a CVR(T) while behind it are two Centurion AVRE tanks armed with the 165mm/6.5in demolition charge projector. On the left is an FV 434 engineer's vehicle.**

LEFT: **Part of a Soviet battle group. In the foreground are six ACRV M1974/1, in the middle are T-72 MBTs, while in the rear are a mixture of Zil and Ural trucks.**

ABOVE RIGHT: **A Black Hawk helicopter picking up a British Light 105mm/4.13in field gun during a combined exercise. Behind it is a Land Rover.** LEFT: **Two Willys Jeeps lead a Sexton SPG past a stationary convoy of British carriers, during the fighting in Normandy in June 1944. The leading Jeep has additional fuel in jerry-cans fixed on the bonnet.** BELOW: **A British Chieftain MBT passing an FV 432 APC during an exercise on Salisbury Plain. The Chieftain is fitted with Still Brew armour while the FV 432 has a 7.62mm/0.3in gun turret fitted to it.**

Tanks are the main offensive unit of the division and supply the armoured punch to smash through an enemy's defence. However, some tanks were converted into anti-aircraft vehicles (to give the division some protection from the air) and command vehicles.

The purpose of reconnaissance is to provide the commander with an accurate assessment of what the enemy is doing, its strength and position. Reconnaissance takes the form of aerial, ground and signals information and this intelligence helps the commander make tactical decisions. The armoured car performed the ground reconnaissance role for many years within the British Army until replaced by the light tank.

Motorized infantry specifically trained in the art of armoured warfare co-operate in action with the tanks. The job of the infantry is to attack enemy anti-tank guns and to clear infantry defensive positions that would normally stop the armour.

The SPGs give covering fire to the initial assault of the division. The bombardment must be short and not churn up the ground. Artillery can also give covering fire to engineers or infantry as they move forward. SPGs are essential as getting towed artillery into position is slow and very time consuming and they can easily become bogged down when off-road on difficult ground.

The engineers supply the bridging equipment, mine-field clearing and many other specific roles that now can be carried out from specialized AFVs. The British Army leads the world in this type of vehicle development.

Without signals or radio communications, the division could wander aimlessly over the battlefield as was the case in World War I. Now a divisional commander can keep control of 3,500 vehicles spread over many miles of the battlefield.

World War I

The story of the AFV in World War I is the story of the armoured car, and in particular its use by the British Royal Naval Air Service (RNAS). When the Germans overran Belgium in 1914, they came up against a few improvised armoured cars being used by the Belgian Army. These vehicles, the first AFVs to see action, were basic touring cars with boiler plate fitted to them and armed with one or two machine-guns. They did excellent work in slowing the German advance. The RNAS based at Dunkirk had 18 cars for aircraft support and downed-pilot rescue, and, on hearing about the Belgian success with armouring touring cars, armed two of their own and used them effectively against German cavalry.

The RNAS continued producing these home-made armoured cars and the Royal Naval Armoured Car Division (RNACD) was officially formed in October 1914, taking part in the land battles in Flanders over the next year. The Division would eventually consist of 15 armoured car squadrons and a Divisional HQ. Each armoured car squadron consisted of three sections, each with four cars. The Navy pushed on converting more and more vehicles including several trucks, but this led to problems with maintenance and spare parts. A basic armoured body with full body and overhead protection and mounting a turret with 360-degree traverse was developed so that it could be fitted to several makes of car. The two main chassis used were the Rolls-Royce and the Lanchester. The first of these new designs started arriving in France by Christmas 1914.

> "'The Chase' was the unit's especial type of war, and went into it with all the dash and efficiency that its long training had produced."
> **RNAS Armoured Car Section Commander, 1915**

TOP: **One of the British Gun Carriers developed to move heavy guns forward after a successful attack in World War I. The two-wheel trailer at the rear of the vehicle was to aid steering, but this idea was quickly dropped. The doors in the rear of the vehicle are the main entrance and exit for the gun crew.**
ABOVE: **A British RNAS Seabrook armoured car of 1915. This 10,160kg/10-ton vehicle had a crew of six and was armed with a 3pdr gun and a Vickers machine-gun. All these early RNAS vehicles were built as "one-offs". Most were later handed over to the British Army.**

Once the Western Front had settled into stagnant trench warfare, there was very little for the RNACD to do and in October 1915 the last section returned to Britain for re-assignment. RNACD squadrons Nos.3 and 4 were first redeployed to Gallipoli, where they did nothing, and then to Egypt, where the British Army reluctantly took charge of them and used them for patrolling the Suez Canal and in western desert operations. The army broke up the naval units and formed the Light Armoured Motor (LAM) Batteries of the Motor Machine Gun Corps, standardizing on the Rolls-Royce armoured car as it was very reliable. The British Army in

FAR LEFT: **London buses shipped over to France were used to move British troops up to the front line. At first they carried their London bus livery, but this was quickly removed along with all the window glass.**

ABOVE: **The front view of the British Gun Carrier. The driver's station is on the left and the vehicle commander's on the right, with the field gun in the middle, mounted on its carriage from which the wheels have been removed.** BELOW: **Senior British officers inspecting a line-up of Royal Naval mobile anti-aircraft guns. The guns mounted on these vehicles are French 75mm/2.95in AA guns.** BOTTOM: **British officers inspecting a Thornycroft mobile anti-aircraft gun. These vehicles were formed into mobile brigades and were moved around the battlefield to cover any major attack.**

general was not sure how to deploy the armoured car but individual officers discovered their worth and used them with imagination and panache. The desert proved to be an excellent operational area for the armoured car, but it also had significant success against German forces in German South West Africa and British East Africa. No.1 squadron RNACD, which was sent to Russia in June 1916 to help fight the Germans in that country, had covered 85,295km/53,000 miles from the White Sea to the Crimea in their operations by the time of their return to Britain after the Russian surrender in late 1917.

The armoured car also showed its value in India, particularly on the Northern Frontier, where demand for troops in other theatres had weakened the forces used for peacekeeping. Armoured vehicles of all types were found to be a very satisfactory substitute for both infantry and cavalry against marauding tribesmen. Armoured cars had speed and endurance, and could be adapted to suit local conditions. One was even fitted with a ten-barrelled Gatling gun, while others had pom-pom guns fitted. Some trucks were converted to the SPG role having 76mm/2.99in guns fitted to them.

Other AFV developments of World War I were comparatively minor. They included early SPGs – guns mounted on trucks for mobile Anti-Aircraft (AA) defence, such as the Thornycroft, or in the support role for armoured car operations. One tracked SPG was developed by the British but only used a few times, as it did not conform to standard army procedure. Infantry carriers were under development and if the war had gone on into 1919 would have been deployed in action against the Germans. All of these were minor developments compared to the armoured car, and it was undoubtedly due to the ingenuity of the RNAS that the armoured car played such an important role in World War I.

Between the wars

After the developments in armoured vehicles by France and Britain during World War I, many military men felt that the days of the horse were numbered, and between 1920 and 1939 there was a general move towards the mechanization of armed forces. Britain continued to build and experiment with more tanks, armoured cars and carriers than any other nation and would lead the world for many years in this development. French and British light tanks and armoured cars would be sold to many countries, becoming the nucleus of many virgin armoured units. In 1929 Britain made two significant developments in the use of the AFV: the fitting of short-range two-way radios to all AFVs, and the development and use of the smoke mortar, both of which would become standard equipment in practically all armies.

Under the Treaty of Versailles that ended World War I, Germany was not allowed to build any AFVs. They were allowed unarmed armoured cars for policing duties, and some of these were borrowed by the army for exercises. Nevertheless, some tanks and armoured cars were built secretly both in Germany and in a German-controlled factory in Sweden, and a German-Soviet pact enabled the Germans to open a testing establishment in Kazan in 1926. Heinz Guderian made the most of this test area and companies like Daimler-Benz, Rheinmetall and Bussing sent armoured cars and other AFVs for testing. By 1927–28 the Germans had developed a number of very good half-track vehicles for towing artillery. Although Guderian had most of the components of an armoured division either in place or under development by 1936, it would not be until the spring of 1939 that the armoured half-track Sd Kfz 251 infantry carrier would start to come into service.

TOP: **In 1928, Vickers Armstrong were experimenting with the idea of the wheel-cum-tracked vehicle. The vehicle in the picture has the tracks deployed and is armed with a single Vickers machine-gun. Only two machines were built.** ABOVE: **Two Birch Gun SPAAGs of 20 Battery deployed on the roadside during an exercise on Salisbury Plain. These vehicles were not very reliable and were quickly dropped by the British Army.**

Russia had bought a large number of British armoured cars during World War I and more were sent to aid the White Russians, but these early cars had great problems with the rough Russian roads and were badly maintained by the Russian peasants who used them. The Soviet Union developed several very good armoured cars and other AFVs in this period, but not armoured infantry carriers and SPGs. The Soviets felt that the infantry could travel on the outside of the tanks, as with almost unlimited manpower life was cheap – Mother Russia was all.

The Americans sat back and did practically no AFV development between 1919 and 1930. There was great debate between the cavalry and the infantry over what they wanted and how it was going to be used. However, between 1930 and 1939, development went into overdrive and 48 projects were

ABOVE: **A Light Tank Mk II fitted with collapsible pontoons. The exhaust pipe on the left has been raised and the driver's visor has been smeared with sealant. The man on the rear of the vehicle is operating the outboard motor, which was attached to the rear of the tank.**

on trials with the army, but only six would eventually see service. With the start of World War II, the Americans very quickly discovered that they had been left far behind by developments in Britain and Germany and so they swiftly set about improving the standard of the AFVs in service with the US Army.

Italy had undertaken some armoured car development during World War I, but this was now considerably increased by the Fiat Company. In addition, the Italians had bought several of the new Carden-Loyd small fast tanks from Britain.

By the end of World War I it was considered very desirable to have SPGs and they were under development in many countries but few would see service, like the Birch guns in the British Army. It would not be until 1940 that the first real SPG would appear. In the meantime the Portee was developed. This was a basic truck that the small field gun or anti-tank gun would be winched up on to. There was room for the gun crew on the vehicle, which would be driven to where the gun was required. The gun and crew would then leave the vehicle that would move off to a place of safety.

Many traditionally inclined army officers and men around the world had been greatly opposed to the introduction of mechanization and the loss of the horse, but nothing could withstand the power of the armoured formation which Guderian and his Panzer Divisions would demonstrate to the world with the invasion of Poland in 1939.

TOP: **An armoured Burford-Kegresse machine-gun carrier B11E5. It was based on the company's 1,524kg/30cwt half-track chassis. The gun-mounting could be removed and the vehicle turned into a personnel carrier.** ABOVE: **The Burford-Kegresse Half-track Portee vehicles of the 9th Light Battery. The 94mm/3.7in howitzers are carried complete on the rear of the vehicle. The loading ramps can also be seen on the rear deck.** BELOW: **An Indian Pattern armoured car and a Crossley Mk 1 on display at the Bovington Tank Museum. These large armoured cars were developed to help police the Empire, especially in areas such as the North West Frontier in India.**

> "The German system consists essentially of making a breach in the front with armour and aircraft, then to throw mechanized and motorized columns into the breach."
> General A. Armengaud (analysis of the Blitzkrieg on Poland), 1939

Dad's Army

After the withdrawal of British and French forces from Dunkirk in June 1940, there was a real threat that the Germans would invade Britain once France had been defeated. There was a great shortage of AFVs in Britain as the British Expeditionary Force (BEF) had left all its heavy equipment behind so an urgent programme of rearmament was started. In the meantime, a number of makeshift designs were used, based on standard civilian saloon cars and trucks.

Many Home Guard units produced their own armoured cars. Some were very good and would have performed well against the enemy, but most were death traps to their users and would have been all too easily brushed aside by the Germans. One unit based at Chiswick in London converted several buses, by removing the bus bodywork and replacing it with a steel shell that had several firing slits in it. These unorthodox armoured cars and trucks were officially discouraged by the high command as they did not fit into the designated role of the Home Guard and the use of these unsupported AFVs would have been a disaster. Two of the better armoured cars were the Beaverette and the Humberette, based on the standard Humber Super Snipe chassis, built at the insistence of Lord Beaverbrook (the Beaverette was named after him). Sir Malcolm Campbell, the land and water world speed record holder, was the provost company commander of the 56th London Division, Home Defence Force, and he designed and then built the prototype of the Dodge armoured car which was

unofficially known as the "Malcolm Campbell" car. Seventy of these were built by Briggs Motor Bodies of Dagenham and were ready by the end of August 1940. To increase the fire-power of these cars and trucks, the Home Guard would often fit captured German machine-guns from crashed bombers to their vehicles, the only problem being fresh supplies of ammunition! Some units managed to get hold of a few World War I 6pdr tank guns and fitted them to the Malcolm Campbell cars.

ABOVE: **Two 762kg/15cwt civilian vehicles converted for the use of the Home Defence Force in 1940. Each vehicle has a crew of three, one driver and two for the single machine-gun mounted in the open-topped rear.**
BELOW: **A Humber saloon car converted for the Home Guard. Six men could be carried in the vehicle. The windows have been removed and replaced with metal plates with a firing slit cut in them.**

"Armadillos" were a large group of AFVs designed and built by the London Midland and Scottish Railway (LMS) workshop at Wolverton. Several prototypes were developed using different types of boiler plate as armour, but these were rejected in favour of a wooden box structure. The wooden box armour was made up as a sandwich with 76mm/3in wooden planks front and back, with a 152mm/6in thick filling of gravel between the planks. The box had an open top with an AA machine-gun mount and all-round armoured firing slits in the sides, and was bolted to the flat bed of many different types of truck. It was proof against small arms fire but nothing else. The cab had the glass removed and mild steel plate inserted which gave the driver some protection but was not bullet-proof. Some 700 Armadillos of three different marks were built. Concrete was also used as armour on several types of truck, known as "Bison". These were bullet-proof and proof against small anti-tank rounds and were basically concrete pillboxes mounted on truck flat beds. The Beaver Eel, known to the RAF as "Tender, Armoured, Leyland Type C", was built by Leyland for the protection of aircraft factories and airfields. These vehicles were based on the Leyland Retriever 3-ton truck and by the end of September 1940, Leyland had produced 250 and LMS 86 of this type. The last major conversion type was the Bedford type OXA which was officially the "Lorry, 30cwt, Armoured Anti-Tank,

ABOVE LEFT: **A heavy truck chassis has been used for this large armoured infantry carrier. This conversion has been carried out by the LMS workshops. It carried a crew of two plus an infantry section of ten men.** ABOVE: **A civilian 1,524kg/30cwt truck converted into an armoured car in 1940. It has been named "Flossie" by the crew. The vehicle had a crew of eight and was armed with a single light machine-gun and small arms. Only the driver's position was equipped with a visor.**

Bedford". These had a custom-made armoured cab and body for the truck and were fitted with the Boys anti-tank rifle and several machine-guns. All these truck conversions could take up to five men in the fighting compartment and some of the larger conversions could take a full section of ten men.

By the summer of 1942 as the threat of invasion diminished and more conventional vehicles were available, all the truck conversions had reverted back to their normal role, and the light armoured cars were by now relegated to airfield defence, some even being passed over to the American 8th Air Force.

ABOVE: **A Humber Saloon car being used by the British Home Guard in 1940. This car has had a hatch cut in the roof above the passenger's seat and a larger removable hatch over the rear section so the men in the back could stand up and fire from the car.** RIGHT: **A Bedford 1,524kg/30cwt truck converted and issued to the British Army in 1940. This vehicle was called a Lorry Armoured Anti-Tank as the vehicle carried a Boys anti-tank rifle and light machine-guns.**

The coming of age of the Self-Propelled Gun

The SPG is a motorized or tracked artillery piece which unlike the tank does not have to be in visual range of its target. A number of countries had tried SPGs before World War II but nothing had come of it, either because they were not reliable or because they did not conform to basic army modes of operation. The rise of the SPG can be attributed to the impact of the tank on the battlefield, as demonstrated by Guderian's new formation that swarmed all over Poland, France, and later the Soviet Union. Supporting forces now had to move at the same speed as the tank and go where the tank went. Two distinct ideologies of how the SPG should be used in action came to the fore during World War II. One regarded the SPG as an extension of basic artillery doctrines, developing and using these guns as platforms to deliver indirect supporting fire in the usual way. The other school believed that the SPG should be used as a mobile gun to deliver close support to armour, and this theory, favoured by the Germans, led to the development of the Assault Gun.

Guderian knew he needed an SPG to support his tanks and infantry. The Germans started development in 1938 of the 15cm/5.91in sIG on a Panzer I chassis. This was an infantry

> "Unleash the God of War!"
> Marshal Zhukov's order to the Soviet artillery in front of Berlin, 1945

ABOVE: **A Churchill Mk 1 SPG armed with a 76.2mm/3in anti-aircraft gun. Originally 100 of these vehicles were ordered, but this was reduced to 50 with deliveries starting in July 1942. The vehicle had a crew of four and none of them saw active service. Later in the war some were converted into experimental Snake Demolition Carriers.**

gun mounted on top of the tank chassis with very basic protection and first saw action during the invasion of France in 1940. The Germans would go on to produce some very good SPG mounts and some extraordinary mounts that were just plain crazy. The largest production run was for the Sturmgeschutz III, often mistaken for a tank, as it very often had to fill the role of the tank. As the war turned against Germany there was a mad scramble to get more and more guns on self-propelled mounts.

By 1941 there was an urgent need for SPGs for the British forces, both for the Home Defence Forces and for the 8th Army in the deserts of North Africa. For the Home Forces, the Churchill 76.2mm/3in Gun Mk 1 was developed. An order for 100 vehicles was placed but only 24 were produced before the order was cancelled. They were very quickly transferred to the training role and did not see action. The Bishop was developed for the British 8th Army, with which it would see extensive service in North Africa and later in Sicily. These guns were very quickly phased out of service by the American M7, which in turn was replaced by the Sexton.

Like the Germans, the Italians very quickly took to the idea of the SPG and put it into production and service with the Italian Army. The majority of the Italian SPGs were known as Semovente. These were very good vehicles and were also used in large numbers by the Germans. They were used to equip several reformed Italian units after World War II.

The Japanese were well behind in the development of armour compared to the other combatants of World War II and even further behind in the development of the SPG. They did come up with a few designs but these were never produced in any large numbers. The most numerous type was the Type 4 HO-RO 150mm/5.91in SPG. These vehicles were hand-built and no production facility was ever set up. Very few records survive about these vehicles in action and deployment.

After the destruction of the Soviet armoured forces during the German invasion of the Soviet Union in June 1941 (Operation "Barbarossa"), the Russians had to start rebuilding their armoured formations almost from scratch. They took the idea of the SPG to heart and produced it in great numbers, concentrating on the assault gun types as these fitted into Soviet armed forces doctrine better than the indirect artillery support of Western design.

World War II would see the meteoric rise of the SPG both as an important weapon system in its own right and as part of the armoured formation, and would go on to replace the towed gun in many armed forces around the world.

TOP LEFT: **A British prototype SPG developed during World War II that never went into production. The chassis was from a Crusader tank and the gun was a 140mm/5.51in medium gun.** TOP RIGHT: **An Italian mobile anti-aircraft vehicle developed in 1915. A Lancia I Z lorry chassis was used with a 75/30 gun mounted on the rear. There was only room for the driver and gun commander on the vehicle, the rest of the crew travelling in a separate one.** ABOVE LEFT: **A Carden-Loyd Mk VI carrier armed with a 47mm/1.85in gun. Development started in 1927. However, the British Army preferred the machine-gun armed carrier, so the 47mm/1.85in version was only sold abroad.** ABOVE RIGHT: **An American prototype SPAAG vehicle. The T53E1 used the Sherman tank chassis and mounted a 90mm/3.54in anti-aircraft gun. The top of the turret was open to allow for maximum elevation of the gun and the vehicle had four stabilizers fitted to the running gear.** BELOW: **The rear of the AMX GCT 155mm/6.1in SPG. The chassis of this vehicle is the AMX-30 MBT. The rear ammunition bins hold 42 mixed rounds, which can be reloaded in about 30 minutes. It has a crew of four.**

LEFT: **A DUKW, usually pronounced "Duck", emerging from the water on to an Italian beach. It has its trim vane raised on the front of the vehicle. Derived from the GMC 6x6 2,540kg/2.5-ton truck, but fitted with a boat-shaped hull, a total of 21,000 of these vehicles were built.** BELOW: **A DUKW on shore in hostile territory. This vehicle has been fitted with a machine-gun mount above the co-driver's position. Operating the machine-gun was very dangerous as there was no protection for the gunner.**

Amphibious Infantry Assault Vehicles

There are several ways for a vehicle to cross a water obstacle such as a river; it can go over a bridge, be ferried across by boat, swim across under its own power or drive across the river bed fully submerged and out the other side. For amphibious landings on an enemy coastline, vehicles have to swim ashore under their own power or be landed by special landing craft.

Amphibious vehicles did not make an appearance until World War II, but since then great strides have taken place in many armoured forces around the world. During World War II there were many variations on a theme, some vehicles being designed to carry loads from ship to shore while others were designed to take a section of 35 men and put them on a beach. A British idea for producing an amphibious tank involved using a flotation screen, which was also used on several post war vehicles. At first the DD (Duplex Drive) Sherman tank (as these first models were known) were not liked by the Navy and it took the intervention of General Eisenhower himself to get the project moving. Eventually, some 300 of these tanks were built to take part in the D-Day invasion.

The Americans were to produce two of the best and most numerous amphibious vehicles of the war, both of which would soldier on for many years after it finished. The first was the DUKW amphibious truck based on the GMC 6x6 2,540kg/ 2.5-ton truck – one of the most important weapons of World War II as far as General (later President) Eisenhower was

concerned. The letters DUKW (pronounced "Duck") explain the vehicle's specification. D stands for a 1942 vehicle, U is for amphibious, K indicates that it is all-wheel drive and W denotes that it has twin rear axles. Most of these vehicles were not armoured, but some were converted into special support vehicles, like the rocket-firing version known as the Scorpion, while others had field guns firing from the cargo area. The second vehicle was the Landing Vehicle Tracked (LVT) which was to play a very important role in the island-hopping campaign in the Pacific and in the crossing of the last great water barrier in Europe: "The Rhine Crossing". The LVT was to be found in many different variations from the basic troop transport and cargo carrier to vehicles fitted with tank turrets

LEFT: **A DUKW entering the Rhine and about to take American troops over into Germany. The DUKW had a central tyre inflation system so the driver could raise or lower tyre pressures from the driving position.** ABOVE: **An LVT (A) 1 demonstrating its full firepower during a night exercise. The vehicle had a crew of six and was armed with one 37mm/1.46in gun, one 12.7mm/50cal machine-gun in a turret and two 7.62mm/30cal machine-guns in pits behind the turret.**

giving close support to the invading forces. These vehicles would remain in service with armed forces around the world until the 1970s.

The Germans and the Japanese both dabbled in developing amphibious vehicles, the Germans with greater success. They produced a very effective amphibious version of the Kubelwagen called the *Schwimwagen* which proved to be a very useful vehicle. They also tried to give tanks like the Panzer III *Tauchpanzer* a snorkel device and converted some 168 vehicles, which were used once in 1941 at the crossing of the river Bug in Soviet Russia. The Japanese went for amphibious tanks such as the Type 2 Ka-Mi light tank developed by the Japanese Navy. Used several times very successfully, the big problem, as with all Japanese armour, was the lack of numbers, and so these were used in penny packets. Most ended their life as dug-in pillboxes on various Pacific islands.

During the "Cold War", NATO forces went for specialized armoured vehicles to bridge water obstacles, while the Soviet forces concentrated on amphibious vehicles. The Soviets designed and produced vehicles such as the BMP-1, BTR-60, 2S1 and the SA8 – a whole family of amphibious vehicles that used a water jet propulsion system when in the water. The main battle tanks use the snorkel system and take a large amount of time to ready for the water crossing, but once ready are driven into the river and the crew and engine draw air into the vehicle down the snorkel tube. The largest amphibious force in the world is the US Marine Corps which performs spearhead-style operations for the American Army but also act as an independent force when required.

ABOVE: **The LVT was also used by the British Army where it was known as the Buffalo. These two Buffalos are being loaded with Universal Carriers.**
BELOW: **Seven British LVT Buffalos are being readied for an operation to cross the Rhine. These vehicles are armed with three machine-guns and a single 20mm/0.79in cannon, and had a crew of four.**

275

TOP: **A Morris Commercial C9/B portee armed with a 40mm/1.58in Bofors AA gun. The seats and windscreen could be folded forward to give the gun a full 360-degree traverse. It had a crew of four.**

ABOVE: **A 6pdr (57mm) anti-tank gun portee. This vehicle was a conversion of a Bedford truck. It is passing a burnt-out Panzer IV in North Africa during a British advance in 1942.**

Wartime developments

Great strides in AFV design and development were taken during World War II. The SPG went from a makeshift development into a sophisticated weapon system in the Allied armies, while the Axis forces scrambled to place as many guns as possible on to tracked or wheeled chassis. The British Army ended World War II with the medium 25pdr Sexton and the M40 155mm/6.1in heavy gun as the main SPGs and these would remain in service until the early 1960s. The Americans had several new designs in development at the end of the war that came into service during the 1950s.

The infantry carrier started as a lightly armed and armoured vehicle and was only capable of taking troops to the edge of the fighting. The British and Canadians came up with the idea of using the redundant SPG Priest vehicles in this role – by removing the gun and plating over the opening 12 men could be carried in safety. These were known as "unfrocked Priests" and were first used by the Canadians during their attack on Caen in 1944. The British also used a redundant tank chassis as an armoured infantry carrier. The Kangaroo, as it was called,

> "Behind this armoured and mechanized onslaught came a number of German divisions in lorries."
> Winston Churchill (description of Blitzkrieg in France), June 1940

was a conversion of the Canadian Ram tank; by removing the turret and the internal fittings there was room for ten men. Two regiments were kitted out with this vehicle and some 300 of these were used in north-west Europe by the Allies. In Italy, the Allies converted a further 177 vehicles. The one big disadvantage was that the infantry had to disembark over the top of the vehicle leaving them very exposed to enemy fire; this and other faults would be rectified in post-war development. The Russians did not develop any form of Armoured Personnel Carrier (APC) during World War II, feeling that the infantry could ride on the outside of the tank, and it would not be until the 1950s that they would start to develop APCs. The Americans looked at the Kangaroo and could see its shortcomings so stayed with the half-track infantry carrier until the mid-1950s.

The armoured car had started World War II for the Allies as a small vehicle that was fast but poorly armed and armoured. They learnt quickly, and bigger and better cars did come into service by the war's end. In Britain they came up with the idea of making a wheeled version of the Sherman tank called the Boarhound. This was an eight-wheeled monster, 6.1m/20ft long and weighing 26,416kg/26 tons, which never went into service. The Germans went down the road of developing their eight-wheeled armoured car even further and putting larger and larger guns on the same chassis. In America the M6 and M8 armoured cars had been developed and saw extensive service during the war and further development post-war until replaced by modern armoured cars in the 1960s.

The rocket was beginning to make a name on the battlefield with many armies during World War II, and a number of special vehicles were developed to carry this new weapon. The main players in the rocket weapon system were the Germans, Russians and the Americans. The Germans put several different types of rockets on various half-tracks, but the biggest was the Sturmmörser. The Russians developed the Katyusha rocket system and would go on to develop several other systems post-war. The Americans also developed several systems, one being the T34 Calliope mounted on the Sherman tank. They also developed the artillery rocket further and designed several new vehicles post-war.

One of the most important vehicles to be developed was the armoured command truck or tank. These were often only lightly armed with just machine-guns, but would carry several extra radio sets so that commanders could keep in touch with their fighting units in the front line. These vehicles were developed further post-war and now are even more important on the battlefield. The story of the AFV in World War II clearly demonstrates the principle that the pace of development of new weapons and vehicles is very fast during a time of war while in times of peace it is long and slow.

ABOVE: **A German Sd Kfz 263 heavy armoured radio car. Above it is the large frame aerial that on later vehicles was replaced by a rod aerial. It carried a long-range radio transmitter and receiver and had a crew of five. The turret was fixed and had a machine-gun fitted in the front.**

ABOVE MIDDLE: **Two British LVT Buffalos entering the Rhine. These vehicles were operated by the 79th Armoured Division. The rear machine-gun positions have gun shields to protect the gunners from enemy fire.** ABOVE: **Two DD (Duplex Drive) tanks being readied to take to the water as part of a training exercise. One of the flotation screens has been fully inflated while the other is about half-raised.** LEFT: **A German RSO fitted with a PaK40 75mm/2.95in anti-tank gun. Designed and built by Steyr, the gun was directly mounted without its wheels and trails on to the wooden body at the rear of the vehicle.**

> "Divisional reconnaissance units should be armoured and preferably contain 2-pounder guns."
> General Bartholomew, July 1940

The adaptation of soft-skin vehicles

The average soldier around the world is very good at adapting to local terrain and conditions, and at adapting his vehicles to do the same. This has gone on since motorized vehicles first appeared on the battlefield. The RNAS armoured car section was one of the first units to do this and were very good at this type of conversion. They did a number of local conversions of cars and trucks, and would scrounge, beg or borrow weapons which they would fit to whatever vehicle was suitable, for example, 6-pound naval guns fitted to Peerless trucks to give the armoured cars better support.

During World War II, there was wholesale conversion of vehicles, which started with the British forces after the withdrawal from France in 1940. The shortage of vehicles made the troops very ingenious at adapting what they could, and turning them into some form of AFV. The Home Defence forces and the Home Guard made many local conversions of vehicles, which were frowned upon and openly discouraged by high command but not stopped. The British 8th Army in North Africa became real experts in the local adaptation of soft-skin vehicles into AFVs. With the constant advance and retreat by opposing forces, large numbers of enemy vehicles fell into each other's hands. One unit in particular would make its name from its vehicle conversions: the Long Range Desert Group (LRDG). This group took vehicles such as the Chevrolet truck and the Jeep and fitted them with a large number of cannon and machine-guns. The Jeeps carried up to five heavy machine-

> "Very largely the story of mechanization is the story of adaptation of commercial motoring to military purposes."
> Professor A. W. Low (in *Modern Armaments*), 1939

guns, while the trucks had the heavier weapons such as 20mm/0.79in cannon and several heavy machine-guns fitted. They then took these vehicles far behind the German lines and created havoc in the German supply routes. The LRDG worked very closely with another new unit called the Special Air Service (SAS), who would take their converted Jeeps into Sicily, Italy and finally into north-west Europe where they continued to work deep behind the German front line.

The Germans were better known for their conversion of captured enemy armour, but they did do a number of conversions to their half-tracks and other soft-skin vehicles, mounting various different types of captured field guns on them. A large number of these vehicles were used by the German *Afrika Korps* in the fast flowing mobile warfare conducted in the deserts of North Africa.

The Americans were and still are great innovators and converters of soft-skin vehicles. During World War II, they converted the Jeep from a light utility vehicle into a heavily armed AFV by fitting armour plate and numerous heavy machine-guns to the vehicle. Some were fitted with rocket launchers. During the Battle of the Bulge, the American paratroopers surrounded at Bastogne turned a number of Jeeps into armoured cars and used them as a mobile fire-fighting unit rushed to any position under great pressure from

ABOVE: **A British AEC 10,160kg/ 10-ton truck that has been converted into an SPG in 1940. A number of these vehicles were built to help bolster the coastal defences of Britain. They were armed with a range of obsolete naval guns.**
RIGHT: **An American pick-up truck has been converted into an AFV by fitting a single Lewis gun in the rear cargo area. The standard road wheels have been replaced with railway wheels so the vehicle can be used to patrol the railway.**

RIGHT: **HMS Aniche is a Talbot armoured car. This is a modified version of the first Admiralty Pattern vehicle that was built for the RNAS in 1914–15. There are two spare tyres on the rear of the vehicle.** BELOW: **This bulldozer has been converted into an armoured vehicle by being covered with steel plate and having two machine-guns fitted to the front of the vehicle.**

a German attack. To put more rocket batteries into action the Americans mounted launch tubes on the back of "deuce and half" (GMC 2,540kg/2.5-ton) trucks. These trucks were also fitted with the M45 quad 12.7mm/50-caliber mounts to give supply convoys some protection from both air or ground attacks. In the island-hopping campaign of the Pacific war, the Jeep proved to be an excellent support AFV. Fitted with heavy machine-guns and rockets, it could go where other vehicles could not. During the Vietnam War, the Americans had a real shortage of armoured cars and other escort vehicles for their supply convoys which were constantly attacked. The men of the transport battalions started putting armour plate on some of their trucks, the favourite being the 5,080kg/5-ton M54A2. They then fitted them with a wide variety of weapons such as the M45 quad mount, mini guns. In a few cases, the complete hull of M113 APCs minus the tracks and running gear were placed on the back of the truck.

No matter where they are, troops will continue to adapt and convert their vehicles officially or unofficially to meet local circumstances, often with remarkable success.

ABOVE: **A line-up of three Austin vehicles. Two have been converted into AFVs by attaching steel plate around them. Each armoured car has an open roof so that a light machine-gun can be fitted on a pedestal mount. The middle vehicle is an ambulance.** BELOW: **An armoured 3,048kg/3-ton truck that has been converted into an APC using steel plate. The side-skirts covering the wheels are hinged to allow access to the tyres and fuel tank.**

The Cold War

World War II finished in 1945. The Cold War, which started in
1946 between the NATO countries (USA and most of Western
Europe) and those of the Soviet-led Warsaw Pact, would last for
some 45 years. The two sides never actually came to blows,
each no doubt deterred by the military might of their opponents.
The Cold War would see the greatest arms race in Man's history;
it would cover land, sea, air and space. Money for research and
development into better weapon systems was freely available at
first, but with crippling debts from World War II, most countries
had to drop out of the race leaving the Americans and the Soviet
Union as the front runners.

The Soviets placed large numbers of men in highly
mechanized units and machines along the border with Western
Europe – the infamous "Iron Curtain". The idea was that the
Soviets would launch an NBC (nuclear, biological or chemical)
attack first, then the mechanized forces would flood through in
a Blitzkrieg-style attack on the NATO forces.

The members of NATO decided to try for standardization
throughout their armed forces. A large number of members
could not afford to develop new weapons and so looked to

> "An iron curtain has descended across the Continent."
> Sir Winston Churchill, March 5, 1946

TOP: **An American cruise missile TEL system on exercise in Britain. The
vehicle had a MAN Cat I Al 8x8 tractor unit and a separate trailer which
carried four Tomahawk missiles. It had a crew of four.** ABOVE: **A Soviet
Scud B missile system being driven to a site. The launch vehicle was
known as the 9P117 and the MAZ-7310 LTM. It has a crew of four and
can only carry one missile at a time.**

America to act as the main weapon supplier. Ammunition was
standardized, and the same thing was done to vehicle types.
The idea was that you developed one engine and chassis and
then this basic vehicle filled many roles. In Britain, the 432
chassis was produced as a basic APC with 12 different models
and an SPG. The Land Rover became a multipurpose vehicle,
being produced in reconnaissance, anti-tank, signals and
ambulance roles. In America, the M113 was produced
and sold to over 40 different countries (not all members of
NATO), with some 40 different types being created due to local
modifications. Some models of both the 432 and the M113
were turned into anti-tank weapons. In the late 1950s and early
60s the guided missile started to make an appearance on the

ABOVE LEFT: **A German Leopard passing an M113 APC. The troops are riding on the outside of the vehicle, which is a very common practice of infantry using this type of carrier.** ABOVE RIGHT: **A Lance missile is about to be launched from an M752 TEL. This vehicle uses many of the parts of the M113 APC. It has a crew of four and is still in service with many countries.** LEFT: **A column of Soviet BMP-1 IFVs crossing a river, demonstrating that it is fully amphibious. When this vehicle first entered service it gave NATO a real fright. It has a crew of three and carries an infantry section of eight men in the rear of the vehicle.** BELOW: **A Berlin Brigade British FV 432 APC. On the top of the vehicle is a wire basket for additional storage. To the rear of the basket is a yellow flashing light which is carried on military tracked vehicles when travelling on public roads. British troops are no longer based in Berlin.**

battlefield. At the time this new lightweight weapon was supposed to sound the death knell of the Main Battle Tank (MBT). It could be mounted on just about any type of AFV and turn that vehicle into a tank killer. In the same way, the contemporary guided missile was expected to end the threat of fighter aircraft.

Vehicles and weapons were becoming very sophisticated and so required a higher degree of training for the troops who were to use the system in battle. In the West this weighted the balance in favour of professional volunteer armies. After World War II, America stopped conscription only to reintroduce it during the Vietnam War. Britain ceased conscription in 1962 and concentrated on developing a small but very professional army. This army would develop a very good reputation around the world and in 1982 would fight a war in the Falkland Islands that most of the world felt they could not win. Again during the Gulf War, Britain would demonstrate how professional and highly trained its armed forces were. The Soviet Union for the

most part stayed with a conscripted army, as it decided to make its weapons more basic and simpler to use. Consequently they were able to sell their weapons far and wide outside the Soviet Union and some of these have continued to be used long after becoming obsolete in the Cold War scenario.

Another major change in tactics and basic army doctrine was the introduction of the helicopter into service and its effect on military operations. The helicopter has changed the speed at which troops can be moved from one part of the battlefield to another. During the Vietnam War, the Americans fitted their transport helicopters with machine-guns and rockets, and this has now been taken one stage further with the development of the helicopter gunship. Heavy lift helicopters are also capable of moving artillery and light AFVs around the battlefield and newer vehicles are being developed to make the most of this capability.

With the collapse of the Soviet Union and the end of the Cold War in the early 1990s, some Warsaw Pact countries have joined NATO, and old enemies now work and train together.

The battlefield taxi with NBC and mine protection

Nuclear, Biological and Chemical (NBC) warfare is a new and terrifying type of war that has come to Man with the onset of the Cold War. Open-topped vehicles offered little protection for the crew from this new type of warfare. At the same time a lot of time and money was being spent on training these men because armies after World War II were becoming smaller and more professional. Here was a great incentive to develop protection for vehicle crews and infantry as quickly as possible.

The first modern APCs in the Soviet armed forces were open-topped such as the BTR-152. They gave the crew very little protection from incoming fire or the weather and were not very different from what the Allied forces had used during World War II. By the early 1960s this mistake had been rectified by the Soviet designers and new vehicles such as the BTR-60

and the BMP-1 came on to the scene. The BTR-60 was no danger to the NATO forces, but the BMP-1 was a very different matter and frightened the life out of NATO commanders. The BTR-60 and the BMP-1 are both fully amphibious and have a full NBC system fitted to protect the crew of the vehicle and the infantry section being carried. The Soviet NBC system first draws the outside air into a multi-filter that removes all the dangerous agents, then passes it through a heater if necessary and then into the crew compartment. The air pressure in the vehicle is also kept several atmospheres higher than the outside pressure, which ensures no chemicals or other agents can leak into the vehicle through the side gun-ports.

The first British APCs, such as the Humber "Pig" and the Saracen, did not have any form of NBC protection for the crew or the infantry section. This fault was put right when the 432 came into service. The vehicle was fully NBC protected just as other more modern vehicles have continued to be to this day. The Americans took a very different approach with the M113 and only protected the vehicle crew of the driver and commander and two others. The other nine men in the vehicle have to use their own respirators. Even in a more modern vehicle like the Bradley there is no protection for the infantry in the back of the vehicle. Crews for the open SPGs like the M110 had no NBC protection at all except for their own personnel NBC clothing.

LEFT: **Soviet BMP-1 MICV. This shows the back of the vehicle with the bulged rear doors, which is one of the major weaknesses of the vehicle as they contain fuel tanks. The low profile of the turret can be clearly seen and the very narrow tracks which give the vehicle a high ground pressure.**

LEFT: **Two American M113 APCs. The driver's hatch is in the open position, with the vehicle's 12.7mm/50cal machine-gun beside it. The commander's position is to the rear of the machine-gun. The M113 has been sold to nearly 50 countries around the world and will remain in service for many years.**
BELOW: **An American M2 Bradley halted and debussing its infantry section. The great height of the vehicle shows up clearly here and is a major weakness of the vehicle. The M2 has had several upgrades to help improve its performance and armoured protection.**

The anti-tank mine has always been a problem for wheeled and tracked vehicles. Designers have tried to give wheeled vehicles some form of survivability by making these vehicles bigger with six or eight wheels so if one is destroyed the vehicle can still get the crew to a place of safety. In Zimbabwe and South Africa between 1972 and 1980 there was a proliferation of armoured vehicles designed to protect the occupants from mines. The main body was shaped to direct the blast from the mine down and away from the vehicle, as with the 5-ton Crocodile which could carry up to 18 men in the troop compartment. Vehicles such as the Hippo were designed with the main body of the vehicle raised up off the chassis and again shaped to direct the blast away from it. A Land Rover-based product Ojay was produced for the domestic market. In Russia the BTR-80 and 90 have been designed to operate with several wheels damaged or blown off. The Germans have also developed this system for their heavy wheeled vehicles like the Luchs and the Fuchs. The American M113 has a very weak floor. During the Vietnam War, a large number of men were injured riding in the vehicle, so the floor was covered with sandbags and the men remained on top until fired upon. The Russians had the same problem in Afghanistan with the BMP-1 and 2, and their crews also rode on top until attacked.

> "The bullets entered our half-tracks and rattled around a little killing all inside."
> General Omar Bradley to General George Patton (Kasserine Pass), 1942

ABOVE: **Soviet troops climbing into the rear of a BMP-1. The eight-man infantry section sit back-to-back with the main fuel tank between them, and the rear doors also act as fuel tanks. As can be seen, Soviet mechanized infantry have very basic webbing and personal equipment.**

LEFT: **British FV 432 APC travelling in convoy and at speed through a forest. The vehicle commander is standing up in his position giving instructions to the driver, who has his seat in the fully raised position. The hatches above the mortar are also in the open position.**
BELOW: **French AMX VCI armed with a 20mm/0.79in cannon and coaxial 7.62mm/0.3in machine-gun. This was an optional extra that could be fitted to the vehicle. An infantry section of ten men is carried in the rear of the vehicle, each man having his own firing port.**

The birth of the Infantry Fighting Vehicle

Mechanized infantry tactics up till the late 1950s used the APC as a battlefield taxi, taking the infantry to the edge of the fighting. The infantry would then debus and go into action on foot. Both the British and the Americans were developing replacements for their ageing APCs, which resulted in 1960 with the Americans putting the M113 into production, followed in 1962 by the British with the 432, but these new vehicles would not herald any great change in tactics. The Soviets were also working on a new vehicle which would change infantry tactics for ever and which scared NATO commanders witless.

This new vehicle was the BMP-1 Infantry Fighting Vehicle (IFV). It was the first Soviet vehicle to be designed with the nuclear battlefield in mind from the start. The BMP-1 was one of the most significant innovations in AFV design in the latter half of the 20th century. Development started in the early 1960s, with trials commencing in 1964. In 1966, as the vehicle was about to be placed into production, the Soviet leader Nikita Khrushchev felt the vehicle was too expensive and that troops could be taken into battle far cheaper by the basic truck. Khrushchev was replaced as leader in the same year by Leonid Brezhnev who now rescinded the cancellation and allowed the BMP-1 to go into production. The BMP-1 was the first vehicle

that could take troops right into the engagement zone. The men inside could fire their weapons from the safety of the vehicle at first, and then when in a suitable position, the troops would debus and fight on foot with close support supplied by the BMP-1's gun. In a major change in tactics, only 8 men could be carried in the rear of the vehicle. They sat in two rows of four facing outwards, each man having a firing port for his own personal weapon. This vehicle was first seen by the Western powers at the Moscow May Day Parade in 1967.

NATO had to find away of combating this new threat. There was no way a new vehicle could be designed and developed from scratch, placed into production and then into service in the near future. The Germans were developing a multi-role chassis for a new family of vehicles including an IFV, the first prototypes of which were produced between 1961 and 1963. Eventually the vehicle went into production in 1970 and entered service with the German Army in 1971. Britain and America

> "The quickest and most effective way to exploit the success of the tank is by motorized infantry especially if the soldiers' vehicles are armoured and have complete cross country ability."
> General Heinz Guderian *Achtung – Panzer!*, 1937

were lagging far behind so they both went down the road of trying to turn the 432 and the M113 into IFVs from the APC. The Americans started development of the XM723 in 1972. In 1976, some changes were required to the basic vehicle out of which two vehicles would emerge: the XM2 IFV and the XM3 Cavalry Fighting Vehicle (CFV). The XM2 had a name change to the M2 Bradley and would enter service with the American Army in March 1983. In 1977, Britain started design and development of the MCV-80, which became the Warrior IFV, the idea being to replace most of the 3,000 432s in service with the Warrior. Orders were placed for 2,000 vehicles with the first entering service in 1987. With the ending of the Cold War in 1989 the order was cut back and the life span of the 432 has been extended by some 30 years, and the same has happened in America with the M2 Bradley and the M113.

The BMP and the Bradley both have amphibious capability, but the British Warrior does not as it was felt it was not required. The real problem with these vehicles is that they are too heavy to be transported by air except in the largest transports. The Bradley and the Warrior both proved to be very reliable during the Gulf War and Operation "Iraqi Freedom", and have even taken on the role of light tank in some areas. New smaller versions of the IFV are under development so that they can fit into the air-portable Rapid Reaction Force.

ABOVE: **Soviet BTR-70 APC. This particular vehicle is not a standard infantry vehicle as it has several side hatches down the length of the vehicle. The trim vane can be seen in the stowed position under the nose of the vehicle.**

ABOVE: **This British Warrior is stopped and is covering the infantry section that has debussed from the vehicle during an exercise. Only half of the infantry section can be seen.** LEFT: **A West German Marder MICV. The vehicle commander and driver have their hatches open. The turret is fitted with six smoke dischargers. The box on the side of the turret is a laser sight.** BELOW: **A column of M2 Bradley MICVs passing over a temporary pontoon bridge during an exercise in Germany. The vehicle commander and gunner are almost out of the turret helping to give the driver information on the vehicle's position. Each pontoon has a single crewman looking after the pontoon's station-keeping.**

Playing catch-up

Armies around the world have from time to time found themselves in the position of having to play catch-up against an enemy that out of the blue produces a new vehicle. There are two options open: either produce your own version of the new vehicle, or convert some of your existing stock into something similar to what the enemy has produced. The AFV seems to be capable of adjustments to meet almost any threat or need. These range from conversions done in the field to overcome a local problem, to production-line enhancements to fill the gap until more specialized vehicles become available. Its adaptability is truly amazing.

During World War II, the engineering officer of the German Panzerjager unit 653 converted a few of his unarmed Bergepanther recovery vehicles into armed vehicles by fixing Panzer IV turrets on them. The Germans took a number of old tank chassis like the Panzer II and placed the PaK40 anti-tank gun on some of these vehicles. They also did a large number of conversions on captured vehicles, turning them into mobile anti-tank guns or SPGs. The French Lorraine Schlepper chassis was used for two conversions, one to a 105mm/4.13in SPG and one armed with a PaK40 anti-tank gun.

The Israeli Defence Force have for many years been the masters of the vehicle conversion, turning old or captured vehicles into something new that they could use. The L33 SPG is a prime example of these conversions. They took the very old Sherman tank chassis and placed a 155mm/6.1in gun mounted in a very large box structure the size of a house on it. Another conversion was the Ambutank, also based on a

Sherman tank chassis but with the engine moved forward. It was developed so that the Israelis could evacuate their wounded while under fire – the rear area has been turned into an ambulance capable of taking stretcher cases.

A number of World War II vehicles were put into action during the recent troubles between Bosnian and Serbian forces in the former Yugoslavia. One of these was the M36 tank destroyer with "spaced armour". The M36 was never designed to withstand modern weapons like the RPG7 anti-tank rocket, so wooden batons were placed down the side of the vehicle and the space between them filled in with concrete. This was

ABOVE: **British FV 432 APC armed with a 30mm/1.18in RARDEN cannon. Each mechanized British infantry battalion had 17 of these vehicles. This is the same two-man turret as that fitted to the Fox armoured car.** BELOW: **A 90mm/3.54in turret developed by Israel Defence Industries in 2004 to give the M113 a greater punch and extend its service life. This two-man turret has also been used to upgrade Chile's M24 Chaffee tanks.**

then covered in heavy rubber sheeting that used to be conveyer belting in a factory. The other major change was in the engine. The old American engine was removed and with a little adaptation a Soviet T55 tank engine was dropped into the same space.

When the Soviets unveiled the BMP-1 at the May Day Parade in 1967, the British and Americans had only just brought the 432 and the M113 into service a few years previously and so had to make do with what they had until new vehicles like the IFV could be developed. The 432 and the M113 had a large number of conversions performed on them, both to improve the firepower of the basic vehicle and to give additional support to an infantry attack. Britain has done a number of conversions to the 432 by putting RARDEN 30mm/1.18in gun turrets on the top of the vehicle, and some 432s have been fitted with the Swingfire anti-tank missile to give the vehicle the ability to kill tanks. The Ferret armoured car was also fitted with two Swingfire missiles, one on each side

ABOVE LEFT: **British FV 432 APC fitted with a 120mm/4.72in Wombat Recoilless Rifle. The gun can be fired from the vehicle or dismounted, but the vehicle only carries 14 rounds of ammunition.** ABOVE: **American M113A2 Improved TOW Vehicle (ITV). This is a basic APC but fitted with the Raytheon TOW ATGW (Anti-Tank Guided Weapon). The vehicle carries ten missiles but no infantry.**

of the turret. Some 60,000 M113 vehicles have been produced since it went into production, a small number of which were converted on the production line, while others were converted by the different countries that bought them. The Australians at first placed old British Saladin armoured car turrets on some of their M113s and turned them into close-support vehicles. These have now been upgraded with the British Scorpion 76mm/2.99in turret. The RARDEN 30mm/1.18in turret and the British Fox armoured car turret is also capable of being fitted as an upgrade. The Swiss have fitted the 20mm/0.79in Hagglunds turret to some of their M113, and this conversion is also for sale to other M113 users.

LEFT: **A French AMX-30 chassis is used to mount the Euromissile Roland SAM system. The turret is in the raised position. The vehicle carries two missiles in the launcher and eight in the vehicle.** ABOVE: **American M163 Vulcan SPAAG. The vehicle has a crew of four but the turret is only a one-man operation. Developed by General Dynamics and entering service in 1965, the American Army had 671 of these vehicles in service by 1987.**

287

Peacekeeping around the world

In the last 35 years, armed forces around the world have found themselves having to undertake the role of riot-control forces and to do internal security operations that they have not been trained or equipped for. This has led to the development of many special vehicles that can protect the men using them and yet be non-confrontational.

Full tracked vehicles such as the British 432, Warrior and Challenger tank are not suitable for this job, as they are very expensive to operate and maintain compared to a wheeled vehicle. Tracked vehicles like tanks and IFVs have very poor manoeuvrability in built-up areas, poor observation for the driver and commander, and can cause headlines in newspapers and on TV of "tanks on the streets". AFVs have proved their adaptability in these situations, with some conversions. The vision blocks of the vehicle have to be fitted with wipers and a cleaning fluid dispenser for a form of paint remover. Diesel is the preferred fuel for internal security vehicles as it does not burn as easily as petrol, and diesel engines have more economic fuel consumption.

When the "Troubles" started in Northern Ireland in 1969, the British Army had disposed of almost all its Humber 1-ton 4x4 wheeled APCs which were being sold off for scrap, to vehicle collectors or to the Belgian Army. These were all bought back at an increased cost and put back into service, and some of the 6x6 Saracen APCs were also sent to Northern Ireland.

TOP: **British Warrior MICV armed with the 30mm/1.18in RARDEN cannon. All three of the crew can be seen. They have placed light blue UN covers over their helmets so they are easily visible and the vehicle has been painted white.**
ABOVE: **British Ferret Mk 2 in UN colours. The British Army has taken a full and active part in United Nations peacekeeping since World War II.**

The Humber 1-ton APC is better known as the "Pig" because it was a pig to drive. When in 1972 the IRA managed to acquire armour-piercing bullets, the Pig could not protect the troops from this new type of ammunition. All 500 Pigs were upgraded with better armour and armoured glass was put in the vision slits. Some Pigs were further converted with large gate-like structures covered in wire mesh that were attached to the

RIGHT: **The nickname for UN troops is the Blue Helmets, and their vehicles are always painted white so there can be no confusing the fact that these men and women are on peacekeeping duties.**
BELOW: **British Saxon Patrol. This vehicle was developed to replace ageing security vehicles such as the Humber "Pig" in Northern Ireland. The Saxon has been fitted with "wings" – riot-control screens that can be deployed from side of the vehicle.**

> "Our country is going to be what our people have proclaimed it must be – the Arsenal of Democracy."
> Franklin D. Roosevelt, April 1916

ABOVE: **Dutch Army AIFV in UN colours. The vehicle is an improved M113A1 and entered service in 1975 with the Dutch Army, who have bought 880. The AIFV has a crew of three and can carry an infantry section of seven men.**
BELOW: **British Warrior on sentry duty at the city boundary of Sarajevo in Bosnia. A large number of NATO forces were sent to the Balkans during the break-up of Yugoslavia to act as peacekeepers.**

sides of the vehicle and then swung out to give the troops protection from bottles, bricks and stones. This winged appearance gave rise to the name "Flying Pig".

South Africa has developed a special internal security vehicle in the Buffel. It has very high ground clearance, a V-shaped body to deflect the explosive force from mines, and a steel roof that can be folded down. The downside of this vehicle is that it has a very high centre of gravity and so can tip over when taking corners too fast or trying to cross rough ground. In Britain, the Saxon has been developed to be used in urban areas. Based on a Bedford truck chassis, the vehicle has a good ground clearance and has been sold to several other countries as an internal security vehicle.

The Shorts company of Northern Ireland has been building an internal security vehicle called the Shorland for many years. It is based on the Land Rover chassis and has been sold to some 40 countries, proving to be very cost effective and reliable. In America, the Cadillac company have produced the Commando III that is in use with most police departments in the USA and the National Guard.

In the former USSR, no special internal security vehicles were built. If there was a riot or demonstration then the police would work alongside the army, and standard armoured vehicles, including tanks, would be used against the unarmed public, as happened in Hungary in 1956 and later in Poland.

The East Germans did produce an armoured water cannon for the police and internal security forces. The vehicle was the SK-2, based on the G5 6x6 heavy truck, which was used in large numbers by the East German Army. The water cannon, with a range of 70m/230ft, was mounted on the roof in a small turret with a 360-degree traverse. It was reloaded by driving the vehicle over a water main, opening a trapdoor in the floor, and lowering a pipe to connect the vehicle to the water supply, taking 10 minutes to refill the water tanks in the vehicle.

Air mobility

In 1930 the Soviets formed the world's first parachute force and commanders have tried ever since to give airborne troops an armoured capability. Trying to fit a tank into a transport aircraft has always been very difficult, due to the weight and size of the vehicle. During World War II, the Allies used Horsa and Hamilcar gliders to move heavy equipment to the landing zone of the parachute troops. These gliders could only carry small light vehicles such as the Jeep and the Universal Carrier (which was used to tow 6-pound anti-tank guns) until the British developed a small light tank. This was called the Tetrarch and was armed with a 2-pound gun and capable of being carried by the Hamilcar. The Germans meanwhile concentrated on powered flight and built the largest transport aircraft of the war that could carry 3-ton trucks and light tanks such as the Panzer II. After World War II, larger transport aircraft with large rear loading doors came into service with other armies, but as tanks have grown in size and weight they could still not be carried. Even today the only aircraft capable of carrying a Main Battle Tank (MBT) are the American C5 Galaxy or the Soviet AN 124 and even these aircraft, the biggest in the world, can only carry two MBTs. Since the Vietnam War, the heavy lift types of helicopter have changed the way troops, guns, vehicles and supplies move around the battlefield.

With the ending of the Cold War and the break up of the Soviet Union, the type of warfare that modern armies are training to fight has changed. Long gone are the massed ranks of Warsaw Pact tanks facing the NATO forces on the ground,

TOP: **An American M551 Sheridan light tank being loaded on to a C130 transport aircraft. This was designed to equip the American airborne divisions, but withdrawn from service after only five years due to its vulnerability.** ABOVE: **A Willys Jeep being unloaded from a British Horsa glider in front of General Montgomery. The bumpers have been cut down and all the tie-downs and handles have been removed.**

and the battlefield of Western Europe has melted away to be replaced by the worldwide battlefield. Soldiers and their equipment have to be able to move very quickly and respond to a changing enemy with either low-technology weapons or good weapons but poorly trained operatives, or a mix of both. Troops used to be sent to the theatre of operations by aircraft with their heavy equipment following on in ships, but now soldiers and heavy equipment can be transported by air to theatre.

Vehicles like the British CVR(T) Scorpion can be airlifted to any part of the world and can then be slung under helicopters like the Chinook and delivered to the front line ready for battle. These fast light vehicles now carry a big punch and, being part of a fully integrated force, can respond to most situations that they come across. The sheer speed that commanders can now get troops into a theatre does not give the enemy time to construct defences or build up ground forces and supplies. Also, as the response time is now hours and not days, the local defence forces stand a better chance of holding the attackers at bay until reinforcements and AFVs arrive.

AFVs can also be delivered direct to the battlefield by heavy-lift aircraft from which the vehicles can be delivered by parachute or Low Altitude Parachute Extraction System (LAPSE). This technique allows an aircraft such as the Hercules to come in very low and fast and deliver the tanks that are tied on to special air drop sledges. The Soviet Union has experimented with this system and others. One system they tried out was fitting an airborne AFV like the BMD to an air landing platform, with rockets fitted to the underneath and the crew inside the vehicle. The platform would be steadied on leaving the aircraft by a small chute, and a weighted rope would hang down from the platform. On striking the ground the rope would set off the retro rockets which would slow the descent of the platform and give the crew and the AFV a safe landing. Perhaps not surprisingly, the Soviets lost a number of men in these trials.

With more and more armies turning to rapid deployment forces, the heavy MBT is being cut back in numbers and replaced by lighter, faster and more agile light tanks or AFVs. Could this be the end of the MBT?

TOP: **French Leclerc MBT being loaded on to a heavy transport C5 aircraft. The major problems with vehicles like this are the weight of the vehicle and the size of the transport aircraft required to move them by air.** ABOVE LEFT: **A Willys Jeep inside an American WACO glider. The front bumper has been shortened and only one headlight is fitted. The vehicle is shackled to the steel frame of the glider and only just fits inside.** ABOVE: **German Wiesel air-portable light tank inside a CH-53G heavy-lift helicopter. The crew of the vehicle varies between two and five, depending on its designated role. The German Army have some 400 of these vehicles in service.** LEFT: **Soviet BMD-1 airborne combat vehicle. The turret has been covered and the main parachute is fitted to the rear deck of the vehicle. Originally the crew were in the vehicle when it left the aircraft but they now drop separately.**

The multi-role family of vehicles

Long gone are the days of developing new vehicles from scratch, with new engines, chassis and weapons. These are very expensive, take a long time to come into service and require a lot of testing and training of new crews. World War II would see a new type of development where the vehicle "family" becomes more important. In Britain, the Churchill tank became the basic chassis for a number of new vehicles that would be known as the "Funnies". In the USA, several new vehicles such as the M10 and the M40, were based on the Sherman. The Germans turned the Panzer IV into a family of vehicles. Its well-tried and tested chassis gave rise to vehicles like the Hummel, Nashorn and Sturmgeschutz. The Soviets were a little behind on the idea of creating a basic chassis for several vehicles but the T-34 was used for several different vehicles including the SU100.

With the start of the Cold War and the birth of NATO with its ideas of standardization, the concept of a basic family of AFVs was born. In Britain the 432 was under development and would be produced in 19 variations, not including the SPG. In 1970

the CVR(T) Scorpion started its production run. This would lead to a new and revolutionary family of tracked vehicles that are capable of going were tanks cannot, and filling many of the MBT roles. Due to the very low ground pressure of the vehicle (less than an infantryman's foot in a size nine boot), this vehicle can even get to places on the battlefield where a soldier cannot. In the Falklands War of 1982, I watched a Scorpion come across a peat bog. The vehicle stopped and the commander jumped down, only to sink up to his knees while the CVR(T) sat on the top of the soft spongy ground. The CVR(T) is also the backbone of the Rapid Deployment Force as two can fit into a Hercules C-130 transport aircraft.

In the early 1960s, the Americans developed the M113 that would be produced in larger numbers than any other AFV since World War II with over 60,000 being built. It has been sold to 36 different countries around the world and there are 40 different variations on the basic vehicle chassis. These include bridge layers, flamethrowers, command, and anti-aircraft vehicles. The M113 has been in service for 40 years and it

> "The full power of an army can be exerted only when all its parts act in close combination."
> British Field Service Regulations, Part 1, 1909

ABOVE LEFT: **A line-up of British Spartan APCs. The cupola hatch opens to the rear and side and is the vehicle commander's position. The ambulance version of the Spartan family is called the Samaritan.** ABOVE: **British Spartan (FV 103) with Milan system on the rear of the vehicle. There are four of these vehicles per battalion. The vehicle has a narrow hull, blunt nose and a large sloping glacis plate. Two clusters of four smoke dischargers are mounted on the front.** LEFT: **Two British Spartan vehicles at speed in the desert during the Gulf War of 1991. All the personal kit of the crew and infantry in the vehicle has been stowed on the outside of the vehicle. Temporary storage boxes have also been fitted to the front of the vehicle.**

is expected to remain in service for many more years with the American Army and many of its customers. For most of its life, the US Marine Corps has had older and inferior equipment to the army. Now with the new Piranha Light Armoured Vehicle (LAV) they have a vehicle that will take them well into the future. The LAV has been developed into a family of vehicles that will remain at the forefront of future tactical development in both the US Army and Marine Corps for many years.

The French have produced several very good families of vehicles such as the AMX VCI. This is based on the very successful AMX-13 light tank chassis and has been in production since 1956. The early versions had an open machine-gun position on the top of the vehicle. By 1960, this had been replaced by a proper machine-gun turret and so could be regarded as the very first IFV. It has been sold to 10 different countries and produced in 12 different variations on the basic vehicle. The AMX VCI is now being replaced in the French Army by the AMX-10P that has so far been developed into ten variations on the basic IFV.

The former Soviet Union has in the past made several families of AFVs, which can be found in service all over the world. These vehicles, such as the BRDM, have been in service since 1960 but because of their basic design and simplicity of maintenance have been sold on to various Third World countries, and many remain in service today.

The AFV family of vehicles has proved an excellent idea and has given military commanders more options and a new flexibility in their tactical deployment of equipment and logistics on the battlefield.

TOP: **The Samaritan, like the other vehicles in the family, has no personal kit storage inside the vehicle, so in this case it is stored on the roof. The running gear can be clearly seen with the driving wheel at the front and the five large road wheels.**

ABOVE: **The British Striker SP ATGW (FV 102) launching a Swingfire missile. The rear launcher box is in the raised firing position, and holds five missiles. A further ten can be carried in the vehicle.**

LEFT: **The mother of the CVR(T) family is the Scorpion light tank. The three-man crew can be seen in their positions, with their personal kit stored on the outside of the vehicle. The turret is armed with a 76mm/2.99in main gun and coaxial 7.62mm/0.3in machine-gun.**

293

The future

It takes a very brave or very foolish person to predict the future. Time and time again such predictions have been proved wrong and the history of the development of AFVs has plenty of examples of such mistakes. In the 1950s the new guided anti-tank missile was going to make the battlefield a no-go area for the MBT yet the tank is still, at present, king of the battlefield in spite of this.

Armies around the world are undergoing major changes and restructuring at this time. There now seems to be no need for the old heavy tank formations that used to be lined up in Europe like great armoured juggernauts. In Britain, army units are being amalgamated to form bigger and more flexible units. The heavy tank regiments armed with the Challenger MBT are being cut back in number and replaced by the lighter CVR(T) type of vehicle. The British Army is one of the few in the world that has its light armoured fighting vehicles still mounted on full tracks, as most of the world's armies are going over to the cheaper all-wheeled vehicle.

In 1999 General Eric Shinseki, the United States Army Chief of Staff, outlined a plan to reorganize the army into new types of units that could deal with future deployments better. The new units will be called Objective Forces and will be in

TOP: **American Multiple Launch Rocket System (MLRS) firing a salvo of missiles. This system was first tried in battle during the Gulf War of 1991. The large back blast from the missile can clearly be seen, but with a range of 30km/ 18.6 miles, it is not a problem.** ABOVE: **The MOWAG Piranha has become a very successful vehicle, being built in several countries around the world and in service with many others. It is expected to remain in service for the next 30 years.**

place by 2010, equipped with new all-wheeled Future Combat Vehicles (FCV). These vehicles will be produced in prototype form by 2005; they must be able to fit into a Hercules C-130 transport aircraft and must not weigh more than 20 tons. The armoured protection has to be as good, if not better, than the M1 Abrams MBT with full NBC protection. Another part of the plan is to form an interim force that will use existing wheeled vehicles and will be of brigade size. The brigade will have to be fully air-portable and be able to deploy anywhere in the world within 96 hours. A full division will have 120 hours to do the same. The vehicle chosen to equip the interim force is the LAV III which will be built by General Motors and it has already been

> "Infantry is the arm which in the end wins battles. To enable it to do
> so the cooperation of the other arms is essential."
> British Field Service Regulations, 1924

LEFT: **Under development is the Stormer SPAAM which has the Rapier missile system fitted to the rear of the vehicle. The Stormer is just entering British service and is a larger version of the Spartan CVR(T).**
BELOW: **Soviet BTR-80 BREM. This is the engineers' support vehicle and the turret has been fitted with a 3,048kg/3-ton "A"-frame. Behind the crane is storage for spare wheels and other heavy equipment. The BTR-80 is expected to remain in service for many years to come.**

decided to create 10 variations of the basic vehicle. One of the reasons the LAV III has been selected is its top speed of 97kph/60mph, which means it can have a convoy speed of 64kph/40mph against tracked vehicles that have a convoy speed of 40kph/25mph. Over a century ago, Colonel Davidson suggested the formation of a cavalry unit using nothing but wheeled vehicles. Now the Americans feel the time is right for its formation.

Designers are looking at new propellants for munitions, as these at present take up a lot of space in the vehicle. If you can place more munitions in the vehicle then it can remain in action longer and logistic problems of rearming a vehicle decrease. One of the propellants the scientists are working on is liquid explosive, which would be injected into the breach of a gun once the warhead had been loaded. This will increase the space in the vehicle for more warheads and would make the use of automatic loaders a far better option. This will also either remove a crew member or free him for other duties in the vehicle. This offers new design possibilities.

Far more countries are beginning to develop their own wheeled AFVs, using basic truck chassis that can be bought "off the shelf" from many manufacturers. These might not have the sophistication of vehicles like the LAV III, but a high level of sophistication is not always required or desirable. Brazil used to be a major importer of AFVs but now it has started producing its own vehicles such as the EE-11 and is actively trying to sell them on the world market.

For the present the tank remains the king of the battlefield, but for how long? The AFV is now beginning to carry the punch of the Abrams MBT, can deliver a wide variety of munitions on to a target and get a high proportion of rounds on target first time to guarantee a kill.

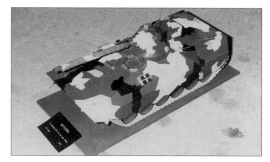

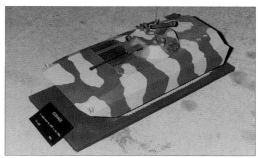

ABOVE MIDDLE: **A development model of a Wyvern which was intended to be a principle AFV in the late 1990s. As yet, it has not made a public appearance, but it does show the trend for smaller lighter vehicles that can be moved by air.**
ABOVE: **A possible development model for a future BMP-3 called Cossack. The body of the vehicle has cleaner lines for better performance in the water, but it still looks large and too heavy to be air-portable.**

A–Z of World War Armoured Fighting Vehicles 1914–45

With the invention of the compression engine in 1892, military weapons developers around the world tried to fit it to various horseless carriages, resulting in some wonderful but impractical machines that were unusable on a battlefield.

The earliest practicable designs were produced in 1914 when the Belgian Army fitted machine-guns to touring cars which had been covered in boiler plate. These performed very well and were copied and developed further by the RNAS who used them aggressively in several different theatres. In World War II, the armoured car became the eyes of the armoured division.

There were a number of unsuccessful attempts to produce SPGs in World War I but it was not until World War II that this vehicle was really developed. Initially these were very crude conversions but by 1945, they had been developed into purpose-built, sophisticated weapons systems and had proved their worth on the battlefield.

The infantry carrier was developed in the 1930s from the early German half-track, which gave the infantry only basic protection, to the Kangaroo in the 1940s, which would give troops the protection of tank armour and allow them to fight alongside the tanks.

LEFT: **A column of British Bren gun carriers passing over a bridge.**

LEFT: **An LVT (A) 1 climbing out of the water. The rear machine-gun position can be seen manned behind the turret. This was a weakness as it let water into the vehicle.** ABOVE: **75mm LVT (A) 4 from above showing the position of the turret. The deck of the vehicle is fully covered, while the top of the turret is open to the elements. The ring mount for the 12.7mm/50cal machine-gun can be seen at the rear of the turret.**

75mm LVT (A) 4 Close Support Vehicle

The LVT (Landing Vehicle Tracked) was used for the first time in August 1942 during the amphibious operation to capture Guadalcanal. After this operation it was felt that some form of close support for the assault troops was required, and so in the Bougainville and Tarawa operations the LVTs were equipped with a number of machine-guns, typically three or four per vehicle. Following the Tarawa landings it was decided that a heavier support weapon was required and so the LVT Assault vehicle was developed and placed into production at the end of 1943. The LVT 2 chassis was used as the basis for a new vehicle called LVT (A) 1, which was completed by constructing the hull out of armour instead of mild steel, plating over the hull compartment and mounting a

37mm/1.46in M3 light tank turret, with two machine-gun positions in the rear of the vehicle behind the turret.

The LVT (A) 1 first saw action during the ROI-Namur invasion in January 1943 when 75 of these vehicles were used. They proved to be very effective but an even heavier weapon was required to give the Marines better close support, so development started on the LVT (A) 4. Production commenced in March 1943 with its first combat mission being the invasion of Saipan in June 1944. The new vehicle had the complete turret from the M8 GMC; this was fitted with a 75mm/2.95in short-range howitzer and a single 12.7mm/50cal machine-gun. The LVT (A) 4 could carry 100 rounds of 75mm/2.95in ammunition and 400

rounds for the machine-gun. The Continental engine was mounted in the rear of the vehicle and used 4.55 litres/1 gallon of fuel per 1.6km/1 mile.

Total production for the LVT (A) 1 was 509 vehicles, and when production of the LVT (A) 4 ended in 1945, 1,890 of these vehicles had been built. A number of rocket launchers and flamethrowers were fitted to both the LVT (A) 1 and the LVT (A) 4. The LVT (A) 4 would take part in the Korean War and remained in service with the US Marine Corps until the late 1950s, when it was replaced by the LVTH-6 105mm Tracked Howitzer.

LEFT: **A 75mm/2.95in LVT (A) 4 on a beach with the crew on or beside the vehicle. The protruding track grousers can be clearly seen; these propel the vehicle through the water and help it to move across soft sand.**

LVT (A) 4 Close Support Vehicle

Country: USA
Entered service: 1943
Crew: 6
Weight: 18,140kg/17.9 tons
Dimensions: Length – 7.95m/26ft 1in
 Height – 3.1m/10ft 2in
 Width – 3.25m/10ft 8in
Armament: Main – 75mm/2.95in M2/M3 howitzer
 Secondary – 1 x 12.7mm/0.5in machine-gun
 and 1 x 7.62mm/0.3in machine-gun
Armour: Maximum – 44mm/1.73in
Powerplant: Continental W-670-9A 7-cylinder
 186kW/250hp air-cooled radial petrol engine
Performance: Speed – Land 32kph/20mph;
 Sea 12kph/7mph
 Range – 240km/150 miles

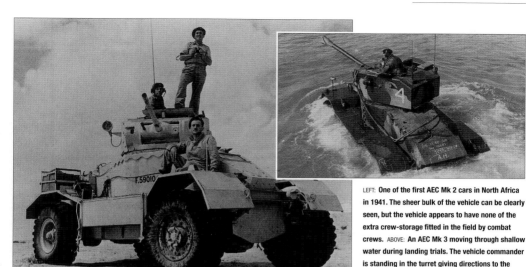

LEFT: **One of the first AEC Mk 2 cars in North Africa in 1941. The sheer bulk of the vehicle can be clearly seen, but the vehicle appears to have none of the extra crew-storage fitted in the field by combat crews.** ABOVE: **An AEC Mk 3 moving through shallow water during landing trials. The vehicle commander is standing in the turret giving directions to the driver, who has limited vision from his position.**

AEC Armoured Car

This was designed as a private venture by the Associated Equipment Company Ltd, which normally made London buses. Information sent back from North Africa indicated a need for a heavyweight armoured car. AEC were also producing the very successful Matador gun tractor and so from July 1941 they produced the AEC Mk 1 using many of the Matador chassis parts. The armoured hull was a simple design and had a 2pdr gun and coaxial Besa machine-gun in a turret, the same turret as that used for the Valentine tank. One hundred and twenty Mk 1s were produced before the improved Mk 2 came along. This had a 6pdr gun in the turret, a more powerful engine, and the crew was increased from three to four. This was a big improvement but the army still wanted a bigger punch and so the Mk 3 was developed.

The Mk 3 had an improved hull and the British copy of the American M3 tank gun fitted in a new turret that had improved ventilation. However, when the driver was hull-down his only view of the outside was through a periscope which gave him very poor visibility. The driver could select either two-wheel drive

RIGHT: **The improved frontal design to aid in obstacle clearing can be seen. The driver's hatch is large and opens towards the turret, so the gun barrel has to be offset to the left to allow him to enter or leave the vehicle. Mounted between the wheels are large storage panniers.**

to the front axial only, which was used for long road journeys to save fuel, or four-wheel drive for cross country or combat. In total, 629 of these heavy armoured cars were built.

Most of the Mk 1 and Mk 2 cars were sent to the 8th Army and saw action in North Africa, Sicily and Italy. The Mk 3 was at first issued to armoured car units that were destined to be used in north-west Europe as heavy support vehicles to the other armoured cars, as it had double the thickness in armour in comparison to these. A number of the Mk 3 armoured cars were used by the Belgian Army after the war and remained in service well into the 1950s.

AEC Mk 3 Armoured Car

Country: UK
Entered service: 1942
Crew: 4
Weight: 12,903.2kg/12.7 tons
Dimensions: Length – 5.61m/18ft 5in
Height – 2.69m/8ft 10in
Width – 2.69m/8ft 10in
Armament: Main – M3 75mm/2.95in tank gun
Secondary – Coaxial 7.7mm/0.303in Besa machine-gun
Armour: Maximum – 30mm/1.18in
Powerplant: AEC 6-cylinder diesel engine developing 116kW/155bhp
Performance: Speed – 66kph/41mph
Range – 402km/250 miles

Archer 17pdr Self-Propelled Gun

In May 1942 the 17pdr anti-tank gun was approved for service. In June it was decided to mount this new gun on a self-propelled chassis to produce a tank destroyer. The first vehicle considered was the Bishop 25pdr SPG but this proved impracticable. The next was the Crusader tank but this was discarded due to reliability problems. Finally, it was decided to convert the Valentine chassis as used for the Bishop but with a different superstructure. However, there were a number of problems due to the length of the gun. This was mounted facing the rear and over the top of the engine deck of the vehicle in an open-topped fighting compartment, and had a limited traverse. A light steel roof was added to some vehicles at a later date, mainly post-war. Despite the length of the gun, a very compact vehicle with a low silhouette was produced. The fighting compartment was small for the four-man crew and 39 rounds of ammunition. The driver's position was left in the same place as it had been in the Valentine tank, but he could not remain in position when the gun was firing. The upper hull was of all-welded construction, with the lower hull, engine, transmission, and running gear being the same as on later Valentines. Secondary armament was the Bren gun, but no permanent mounting was provided on the vehicle. A popular crew conversion was to fit a 7.62mm/30cal Browning machine-gun to the front of the vehicle.

Firing trials were carried out in April 1943 and proved successful apart from a few minor changes. The vehicle was placed into priority production with an order for 800, but only 665 were produced, the first vehicle being completed in March 1944. It was issued at first to the anti-tank units of armoured divisions fighting in north-west Europe from October 1944. Later some were sent out to the 8th Army in Italy. While at first it was called the S-P 17pdr Valentine Mk 1, this was quickly dropped in favour of Archer.

TOP: **An Archer fitted with deep-wading gear. The large ducting on the rear deck allows the vehicle to draw air into the engine from above the level of the water.**
ABOVE: **The front is to the right, the small fighting compartment is in the middle and the engine in the rear of the vehicle with the gun barrel passing over it.**

LEFT: **Some of the ammunition storage can be seen on the right beside the 17pdr gun breach inside the small and cramped fighting compartment. Between the front of the vehicle and the gun breach is the driver's position.**

Archer 17pdr SPG

Country: UK
Entered service: 1944
Crew: 4
Weight: 18,796kg/18.5 tons
Dimensions: Length – 6.68m/21ft 11in
Height – 2.24m/7ft 4in
Width – 2.64m/8ft 8in
Armament: Main – 17pdr OQF (ordnance quick-firing) (76.2mm/0.3in) gun
Secondary – 7.7mm/0.303in Bren machine-gun
Armour: Maximum – 60mm/2.36in
Powerplant: GMC M10 diesel 123kW/165hp
Performance: Speed – 24kph/15mph
Range – 145km/90 miles

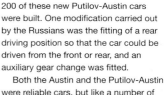

LEFT: **A pair of Austin cars travelling at speed. The large bulk of these vehicles and the twin offset turrets can be clearly seen. The Russians have placed armour plate next to the guns to protect the barrels.**

ABOVE: **An Austin armoured car in Russian service. The turret gunners are taking the opportunity to get some air as it is very cramped and stuffy inside the car. The driver has also dropped his visor for better vision and ventilation.**

Austin Armoured Car

Before the World War I, the Austin Motor Company Ltd was the largest supplier of cars and trucks to the Russian Imperial Army, and in 1913 won a contract to develop an armoured car for internal security duties in the large towns and cities. In 1914 an order was placed for 48 of these new armoured cars. The first armoured cars were built using the 22.4kW/30hp "Colonial" chassis, and had two machine-gun turrets mounted, one on each side of the rear of the vehicle. The wheels were all fitted with solid studded tyres. There were several problems with these early cars. Due to the height of the driver's cab, the machine-guns could not fire to

the front and were too close side by side for the gun crews to operate them efficiently. The Russians also wanted to increase the thickness of armour on the vehicle. Consequently, a number of improvements were put into place by the Russians and Austin. A 37.3kW/50hp engine was fitted to the vehicle to cope with the increased weight and the tyres were made pneumatic with the rear axle having dual wheels. The turrets were offset to improve the fighting efficiency and the driver's cab was lowered so the guns could fire to the front.

Austin also sent the Russians a large number of chassis which had their bodies fitted in the Putilov works in

Petrograd (now St Petersburg). About 200 of these new Putilov-Austin cars were built. One modification carried out by the Russians was the fitting of a rear driving position so that the car could be driven from the front or rear, and an auxiliary gear change was fitted.

Both the Austin and the Putilov-Austin were reliable cars, but like a number of early AFVs they suffered on the primitive Russian roads. In early 1917, all Austin production was switched to the Western Front and the 17th Battalion Tank Corps was equipped with these cars. The 17th Battalion with their Austins would lead the victorious British troops into Germany in November 1918.

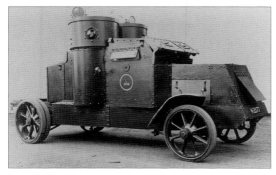

LEFT: **In 1919, Britain urgently required armoured cars for duties in India and Ireland, so Austin-designed bodies were placed on other chassis. Peerless used their truck chassis to produce the Peerless 1919 Pattern armoured car.**

Austin/Putilov-Austin Armoured Car

Country: UK
Entered service: 1914
Crew: 5
Weight: 5,384kg/5.3 tons
Dimensions: Length – 4.88m/16ft
　　　Height – 2.4m/7ft 10in
　　　Width – 1.95m/6ft 5in
Armament: Main – 2 x 7.7mm/0.303in
　　　machine-guns
　　　Secondary – None
Armour: Maximum – 8mm/0.315in
Powerplant: 37.3kW/50hp Austin petrol engine
Performance: Speed – 50kph/31mph
　　　Range – 200km/125 miles

LEFT: The rear driver's position visor is in the open position. Next to this is the rear-facing machine-gun. The hatch in the rear of the turret lifts up.
ABOVE: The AB 41 was an all-riveted construction. This could become lethal for the crew inside when the car was hit, as the rivets would burst loose and fly around the interior, wounding them.

Autoblinda AB 41 Armoured Car

In 1939, the Italian Colonial Police and the Italian cavalry had a requirement for a new armoured car, so both needs were combined and in 1940 production began with the Autoblinda 40. This had a four-man crew and was armed with twin machine-guns in a turret and one facing the rear of the vehicle. There was also a plan to build small numbers of a version armed with a 20mm/0.79in cannon as a support vehicle. It was quickly discovered that the cannon armament was far better in service than the machine-gun only armament, so production of the AB 40 was stopped and the AB 41 took over.

The AB 41 used a turret very similar to that of the L6/40 light tank, and had a very advanced design for its time but suffered from one recurring problem with the four-wheel steering. The main armament was a Breda 20mm/0.79in modello anti-aircraft cannon with a coaxial machine-gun specially designed for use in AFVs. These vehicles could be fitted with a number of different wheels and tyres. One type was an extra wide sand tyre that was used when operating in areas such as North Africa. Another special feature was that the car could be fitted with wheels that would allow it to run on railway tracks. These were carried in the spare wheel area on the car and could be changed by the crew in less than 30 minutes. The vehicle had six forward and four reverse gears and two driving positions, so two of the crew were designated drivers. The AB 41 was produced in larger numbers than any other Italian armoured car during World War II.

By the time of the Italian surrender to the Allies in September 1943, nearly 400 of these vehicles had been produced. When the Germans took over the campaign against the Allies in Italy, they captured 57 of these vehicles and also retained the car's production, managing to produce a further 120 AB 41 armoured cars for their own use.

RIGHT: The side entrance door to the crew compartment can be seen clearly in the rear of the raised body of the car. The armoured headlight covers are in the raised position exposing the large lights. The driver's vision slot is in between the lights and has a very limited field of vision.

Autoblinda AB 41 Armoured Car

Country: Italy
Entered service: 1940
Crew: 4
Weight: 7,518kg/7.4 tons
Dimensions: Length – 5.20m/17ft 2in
Height – 2.48m/8ft
Width – 1.92m/6ft 4in
Armament: Main – 20mm/0.79in Breda modello 35 cannon
Secondary – Coaxial 8mm/0.315in and rear 8mm/0.315in modello 38 air-cooled machine-guns
Armour: Maximum – 17mm/0.67in
Powerplant: 60kW/80bhp SAP Abn 6-cylinder water-cooled petrol engine
Performance: Speed – 78kph/49mph
Range – 400km/248 miles

Autoblindo Mitragliatrice Lancia Ansaldo IZ

The first Lancia Ansaldo IZ armoured car was not armed and was used as an artillery spotting vehicle but in 1915 the vehicle was dramatically redesigned and turned into an armoured car. The first version was armed with a single machine-gun mounted in a circular turret, but this was soon upgraded to a twin mounting for machine-guns. Another type of turret was tried on the vehicle and this had a second smaller turret mounted on top of the larger bottom turret and each had a single machine-gun mounted, each with a 360-degree traverse. Another unique feature of these cars was the twin steel rails that made up the wire cutter that extended from the top of the driver's cab forward and down and ended in front of the radiator. The wheels on later versions of the vehicle were protected by armoured shields. The rear wheels were dual and the tyres were all pneumatic. Armoured firing ports were placed around the top of the crew compartment to allow the extra men in the crew to fire small arms from the vehicle. There was also a mounting for a rear-firing machine-gun in the crew compartment. It had good ground clearance, and there was a rack for a bicycle on the rear of the vehicle.

For most of World War I, the Italian armoured car units played very little part in the fighting against the Austro-Hungarian forces in the mountains in northern Italy. However, a number of these cars were used to help stop the Austro-Hungarian and German forces breaking through in that area in 1917. Those captured by the Germans were used to equip armoured car units of their own. This vehicle was also used for training and equipping American troops in Italy. A large number of these cars were sent to North Africa on policing duties. They proved to be very durable and were used by the Italian Army in the Spanish Civil War between 1936–39. Total production was only 120 vehicles.

TOP: **Lancia armoured car fitted with the single large turret armed with twin machine-guns. The wire-cutter frame can be clearly seen fitted to the front of the vehicle. This structure was far from robust and easily damaged.** ABOVE: **A Lancia car fitted with two turrets, each armed with a single machine-gun. Both turrets can be operated independently and both can traverse through 360 degrees.**

LEFT: **A Lancia car in North Africa armed with three machine-guns, two in the large turret and one in the top turret. A large single headlight is mounted forward in the front of the vehicle. A number of these cars were still in service at the start of World War II.**

Autoblindo Mitragliatrice Lancia Ansaldo IZ

Country: Italy
Entered service: 1915
Crew: 6
Weight: 3,860kg/3.8 tons
Dimensions: Length – 5.40m/17ft 9in
 Height – 2.40m/7ft 11in
 Width – 1.82m/6ft
Armament: Main – 3 x Fiat machine-guns
 Secondary – Small arms
Armour: Maximum – 9mm/0.354in
Powerplant: 26/30kW/35/40hp petrol engine
Performance: Speed – 60kph/37mph
 Range – 300km/186 miles

LEFT: **The gun crew are sitting on the top of the turret behind the forward opening hatch. The driver's side door is open allowing better ventilation. Spare wheels are carried on each side of the vehicle. The radiator shutters are in the open position.** ABOVE: **The BA-6 armoured car used the GAZ AAA truck chassis. The turret of this armoured car was very large and sat over the rear axles of the vehicle.**

BA-6 Armoured Car

The BA-6 replaced the BA-3 on the production line in 1935 after only 160 BA-3s had been built. The main differences between them were that the BA-6 was 1,000kg/2,205lb lighter and had a strengthened rear suspension and a modified transmission.

The BA-6 was a mixture of riveted and welded construction and was built on a shortened GAZ AAA chassis. The armour was increased in several places to 9mm/0.354in and the vehicle had fair cross-country ability. Tracks could be fitted over the double pairs of wheels on the rear of the vehicle and turn it into a form of half-track, which improved the off-road ability of the car. The turret was

the same as that fitted to the T-26 light tank except that the rear machine-gun port was covered over, and there was storage for 60 rounds of 45mm/ 1.77in ammunition in the vehicle. The combat debut of the BA-6 was during the Spanish Civil War where it made a very good impression, and in 1937 it would be used as a basis for the Spanish Autometralladoro Blindado Medio Chevrolet.

In 1936 an improved version of the basic BA-6 was introduced – the BA-6M. This had the new GAZ M1 engine. The weight was further reduced and an all-welded turret was fitted to the new vehicle. The ammunition storage was

reduced to 50 rounds and the 71-TK-1 radio was fitted as standard. There was also a railway version of the BA-6, but these were a lot heavier than the road car as there were hydraulic jacks mounted to the front and the rear of the vehicle so that flanged railway wheels could be fitted over the normal road tyres. However, the wheel change took only 30 minutes. In total 386 BA-20 and BA-20M were built, of which only 20 were the new BA-20M. These cars remained in production until 1939.

A large number of these vehicles were stationed on the Russian–Chinese border having been used against the Japanese, so missed the initial slaughter of the Soviet Army by the Germans in 1941, but by 1945 none was left in service.

LEFT: **A BA-6 in rare pre-World War II camouflage markings. The spare wheels also act as additional unditching wheels and stop the car getting stuck in soft ground. The front machine-gun is not fitted on this vehicle and the armoured shutters for the radiator are closed.**

BA-6 Armoured Car

Country: USSR
Entered service: 1935
Crew: 4
Weight: 5,080kg/5 tons
Dimensions: Length – 4.9m/16ft 1in
   Height – 2.36m/7ft 9in
   Width – 2.07m/6ft 9in
Armament: Main – 1 x 45mm/1.77in M-1932 gun
   and 1 x coaxial 7.62mm/0.3in machine-gun
   Secondary – 7.62mm/0.3in DT machine-gun
Armour: Maximum – 9mm/0.354in
Powerplant: GAZ AA 4-cylinder 29kW/40hp
   petrol engine
Performance: Speed – 43kph/27mph
   Range – 200km/124 miles

BA-10 Armoured Car

By 1938, the Russians suspected that war with Germany was inevitable, despite political assurances to the contrary and the signing of the non-aggression pact between the Soviet Union and Germany. Consequently, a modernization of Soviet armoured vehicles was put in place. The BA-10 was already on the drawing board and would benefit from this acceleration in development. The vehicle used the GAZ AAA chassis, which was shortened and strengthened with the body being an all-welded construction. The main construction was done at the Izhorskiy plant where the body was built and then married to the GAZ chassis.

The BA-10 entered production in 1938 and would become the definitive as well as the most numerous form of the BA heavy armoured car. The layout was conventional with the engine at the front, driver and front gunner in the middle and a two-man turret at the rear. A modernized version of the BA-10 came into service in 1939, this improved design being called the BA-10M. The main improvements were an increase in armour for the vulnerable areas and a new 45mm/1.77in gun fitted in the turret – a simpler model with improved sights. The BA-10 and the BA-10M are often confused as there is very little difference between the two vehicles. The BA-10M has external fuel tanks mounted over the rear wheels and on both sides of the vehicle; these have often been mistaken for storage boxes. The BA-10 used the same turret as the BA-6 armoured car and was armed with the 45mm/1.77in M-1934 tank gun, together with a 7.62mm/0.3in DT machine-gun mounted

ABOVE: **Note the shelf on the rear of the BA-10 for the carriage of the "overall" tracks, which are used to improve its cross-country performance. The locking wires are still in place across the back of the vehicle.**

coaxially and another in the front of the car. The driver and front gunner sit side by side, with the vehicle commander and gunner in the two-man turret.

The BA-10/10M saw extensive service during the "Great Patriotic War" and large numbers of captured vehicles were put into service by the Finnish and German armies. Some 1,400 vehicles were produced of which 331 were the BA-10M version.

ABOVE: **A column of BA-10 cars. The crews are "buttoned up", but are not in a combat area as the radiator shutters are in the open position.**

ABOVE: **BA-10 cars in Poland in 1939, as Soviet crews show off their vehicles to German troops. Each car is carrying spare track-links on the side of the vehicle.**

BA-10 Armoured Car

Country: USSR
Entered service: 1938
Crew: 4
Weight: 5,080kg/5 tons
Dimensions: Length – 4.70m/15ft 5in
  Height – 2.42m/7ft 11in
  Width – 2.09m/6ft 7in
Armament: Main – 1 x 45mm/1.77in M-1934 tank gun and 1 x coaxial 7.62mm/0.3in DT machine-gun
  Secondary – 7.62mm/0.3in DT machine-gun
Armour: Maximum – 15mm/0.59in
Powerplant: GAZ M1 4-cylinder 38kW/52hp petrol engine
Performance: Speed – 55kph/34mph
  Range – 300km/186 miles

BA-20 Armoured Car

The BA-20 became the most numerous and popular armoured car in service with the Soviet Army in the late 1930s. Development for this car started at the GAZ factory in 1934 and under went trials in 1935. Once the vehicle had passed these trials it was accepted into service and placed into full production in late 1935.

The BA-20 used the GAZ M1 chassis which was built at the Novgorod factory, while the body was built at Vyksinskiy where the final assembly was also carried out. The original chassis had to be redesigned to accommodate the extra weight of the BA-20 body. The changes included a new differential and rear axle together with improvements to the suspension. The BA-20 normally carried

a crew of two but in the command version it had a crew of three. This was also the first Soviet armoured car to be fitted with an escape hatch in the floor of the vehicle. The BA-20 had an excellent cross-country performance and was especially good in soft going across marshy ground. The vehicle was also fitted with bullet-proof tyres and bullet-proof glass in the driver's vision block.

In 1938 the BA-20 was improved and became the BA-20M. It had a better turret and thicker armour and a three-man crew became standard. One interesting version of the BA-20 and the BA-20M was the ZhD. This car could change its road wheels for flanged steel railway wheels, which extended its range.

The BA-20 entered service in 1936 and remained in use until 1942, the BA-20M joining it from 1938 until 1942. The BA-20 first saw action in 1939 in the Battle of Khalkhin Gol against Japan, and later in the invasion of Poland and the Russo-Finnish war. The Finnish Army

LEFT: **Captured BA-20 ZhD Drezine rail scout car. The Germans captured a number of these vehicles and used them to patrol the rear areas. A rail tow-link could be fitted to the spare wheel spigot to allow the car to be towed by a train.**

TOP: **BA-20M armoured cars lined up in Moscow for the November Parade in 1940. The front row of cars are the command version as they have the radio aerial around the body of the vehicle.**
ABOVE: **The rear of the vehicle showing the single spare-wheel storage. This position was also used to store the rail-wheels.**

captured a number of these vehicles and put them back into service against the Russians. The Germans also captured a number of the BA-20M ZhD cars and used them for patrolling the rail network in an anti-partisan role. Both marks of the BA-20 proved to be very reliable and were well-liked by their crews.

BA-20 Armoured Car

Country: USSR
Entered service: 1936
Crew: 2 or 3
Weight: 2,341kg/2.3 tons
Dimensions: Length – 4.1m/13ft 5in
 Height – 2.3m/7ft 6in
 Width – 1.8m/5ft 9in
Armament: Main – 7.62mm/0.3in machine-gun
 Secondary – Small arms
Armour: Maximum – 6mm/0.24in
Powerplant: GAZ M1 4-cylinder 37kW/50hp
 petrol engine
Performance: Speed – 90kph/56mph
 Range – 350km/220 miles

BA-27 Armoured Car

Design work on the BA-27 started in 1924, with development models being produced in 1926. The first production model came out in 1927. The 1927 model was built on the 4x2 F-15 chassis and was very simple to maintain; it proved to be very reliable in service with the Soviet Army. There were several problems with the vehicle at first. When the armoured louvers were closed the engine would overheat very quickly, so a large fan was fitted behind the radiator that would draw air through slots cut in the armour and through the radiator to cool the engine. This helped but never really solved the cooling problems. The other big problem was the vehicle had large wheels with dual tyres on the rear axle, but the tyres were narrow and this caused the vehicle to bog down in any form of soft ground when the BA-27 went off-road.

Even when it went into production, the Russians did not stop development and in 1928 they produced the Model 1928 with the new Ford-AA chassis and a new engine, the GAZ four-cylinder 30kW/40hp. In the Model 1927 there

was a crew of four but this had proved to be cumbersome in the very small fighting compartment, so in the Model 1928 the crew was cut back to three. This became the definitive production model of the BA-27. The turret came from the T-18 light tank and was fitted with a Hotchkiss 37mm/1.46in gun and a 7.62mm/0.3in machine-gun. While in the West the BA-27 would be classified as a light to medium armoured car, the Soviet designation was heavy, due to its armament.

The BA-27 is significant in that it was the first series of heavy armoured car to be produced in the Soviet Union since Putilov. It was in production from 1927 to 1931, by which time over 100 of these heavy armoured cars had been produced. It would see a lot of action against the Japanese along the Chinese border in the 1930s and 1940s. The main production plant was Izhorskiy near Leningrad (now St Petersburg).

ABOVE: **The BA-27M was based on the Ford Timken chassis and was built by Remontbaza No.2 (Repair base No.2). The cross-country ability of the BA-27 was supposed to be improved by adding an extra axle, but it did not work.**

ABOVE: **A BA-27M abandoned at a ferry crossing in 1941. The car is carrying a set of overall tracks on the rear of the car. One of the outer rear wheels is missing.** LEFT: **BA-27s on parade in Moscow in 1931 during the November Parade. The offset armament clearly shows up with the 37mm/1.46in gun. Under the front of the vehicle is an air scoop that forces air into the radiator.**

BA-27 Model 1927

Country: USSR
Entered service: 1927
Crew: 3
Weight: 4,400kg/4.33 tons
Dimensions: Length – 4.62m/15ft 2in
    Height – 2.52m/8ft 3in
    Width – 1.7m/5ft 7in
Armament: Main – 37mm/1.46in Hotchkiss gun
    Secondary – 7.62mm/0.3in DT machine-gun
Armour: Maximum – 8mm/0.315in
Powerplant: AMO F-15 4-cylinder 26.1kW/35hp petrol engine
Performance: Speed – 35kph/22mph
    Range – 270km/168 miles

LEFT: **The rear of a BA-64B. Above the spare wheel is the rear pistol port. The origins of the vehicle can be clearly seen, as the vehicle is an armoured Jeep. One defect of the BA-64B was a lack of adequate armament, so in 1943 the improved BA-64D was produced with the 12.7mm/0.5in heavy machine-gun.**

BA-64B Armoured Car

The first new Soviet armoured car design of World War II was the BA-64, designed and developed at the GAZ works. Production was started at the end of 1941 and went on until early 1942. This vehicle was based on the GAZ 64 Jeep. The vehicle had a coffin shape and an open pulpit-style machine-gun position, but production was slow due to the demands for the GAZ Jeep. A troop carrier version was developed but never put into production as it was too small and could only carry six men.

In 1943 GAZ started to produce a new Jeep and the BA-64B armoured car was developed by using this new chassis. It was a better vehicle than its predecessor

as it was more reliable and had a wider chassis, giving it a better cross-country ability. It had an all-welded construction with steeply angled plates to give some form of deflection to incoming munitions. This design idea was copied from German vehicles such as the Sd Kfz 221 and Sd Kfz 222. The BA-64B also had a small one-man turret fitted to the top of the vehicle. These changes constituted a big improvement on the BA-64, but the greatest single improvement was four-wheel drive. Total production of both vehicles was 9,110 and while production would finish in 1945, it would remain in service with the Soviet Army until 1956 and later still with Soviet allies.

Various versions of the basic vehicle were built, one of these being a command car that was fitted with a radio and map boards fixed on special frames built on the top of the vehicle with the turret removed. This vehicle became very popular with all ranks of officer as a basic battlefield run-about and taxi. In another unusual version, the wheels were removed; the front wheels were replaced with two heavy-duty skis and the rear wheels were replaced by a Kegresse half-track. A large number of the basic armoured cars were upgunned in the field by their crews with the installation of the DShK 12.7mm/0.5in heavy machine-gun and captured German machine-guns and cannon. Its crews nicknamed the vehicle the "Bobik". Many of these cars saw action in the Korean War.

LEFT AND ABOVE: **Late production BA-64Bs: the vehicle above has all its pistol ports open, and the driver's periscope can be seen attached to the front hatch.**

BA-64B Armoured Car

Country: USSR
Entered service: 1943
Crew: 2
Weight: 2,359kg/2.3 tons
Dimensions: Length – 3.67m/12ft 4in
    Height – 1.88m/6ft 2in
    Width – 1.52m/4ft 10in
Armament: Main – 7.62mm/0.3in machine-gun
    Secondary – Small arms
Armour: Maximum – 15mm/0.59in
Powerplant: GAZ MM 4-cylinder 40kW/54hp petrol engine
Performance: Speed – 80kph/50mph
    Range – 560km/350 miles

Beaverette Light Reconnaissance Car

After the withdrawal of the British Expeditionary Force from France in 1940, there was a proliferation of AFVs but only two were officially placed into production, one of these being the Beaverette. The vehicle was named after Lord Beaverbrook, Minister of Aircraft Production, on whose instance it was designed and placed into production within a few months.

The Beaverette was built by the Standard Motor Company Ltd of Coventry and used the chassis of the Standard 14 saloon car. The vehicle was covered in 11mm/0.43in mild steel, and was open topped, backed by 76.2mm/3in oak planks but with no rear protection for the crew. The driver had a small vision slot to the front and side, which was covered by sliding steel shutters and gave a very restricted field of vision. The Mk I had only just entered production when the improved Mk II was introduced. As the restrictions on steel were being lifted extra armour could be fitted to the Beaverette giving the crew some rear protection, and the radiator grille changed from vertical, as in the Mk I, to horizontal.

In 1941, the Mk III came into service. This was a very different vehicle and gave the crew all-round protection. Armour plate was now being made available and although the thickness was reduced to 10mm/0.394in, the whole vehicle was now covered in it, which gave it a rear-end-down attitude while being driven. The only entrance to the vehicle was through the single large door at the rear. In front of the driver was a step in the armour which placed the driver a little further back in the vehicle than the turret. In the final version, the Mk IV, the step was done away with and the driver now sat in front of the turret so that the machine-gun crew had more room to operate. These cars remained in service for many years and some which had been used for airfield defence were handed over to the Americans in 1942.

LEFT: The Beaverette Mk III with the single light machine-gun turret. This gave the gunner far better protection, but very poor vision. The large door in the rear of the Beaverette is the only entrance and exit from the vehicle.

ABOVE LEFT: A Beaverette Mk III armed with twin Vickers K machine-guns. The gunner is very exposed in this early turret. As well as the large opening in the front of the turret, the top is also open.
ABOVE: A column of Beaverette Mk I and II cars moving in convoy. The open-topped fighting compartment can be clearly seen. Because of this, the crew have to wear their steel helmets.

Beaverette IV Light Reconnaissance Car

Country: UK
Entered service: 1940
Crew: 3
Weight: 2,540kg/2.5 tons
Dimensions: Length – 3.1m/10ft 2in
  Height – 2.03m/6ft 8in
  Width – 1.78m/5ft 10in
Armament: Main – 7.7mm/0.303in Bren light machine-gun
  Secondary – None
Armour: Maximum – 10mm/0.394in
Powerplant: Standard 14 4-cylinder 34kW/45bhp petrol engine
Performance: Speed – 65kph/40mph
  Range – Not known

Bedford Cockatrice

The Cockatrice was a mobile flame-thrower developed in 1940 by the Lagonda Company for airfield defence, using a Commer armoured truck as the prototype. The first production vehicles that came into service in early 1941 were built for the Royal Navy to act as airfield defence vehicles. Sixty of these vehicles were built using the Bedford QL 4x4 chassis. The armoured body was of a riveted construction, with the driver and engine at the front, the flame gun mounted in a small turret on the roof of the vehicle, and a machine-gun position at the rear with twin Vickers K guns. The flame projector used 36.4 litres/8 gallons of fuel per minute and had a range of 91.4m/300ft. The RAF were also looking at this type of vehicle but felt it was too small so asked for a vehicle to be developed based on the RAF's heavy fuel bowser which had an AEC 6x6 chassis. These were known as Heavy Cockatrice but only six of these vehicles were ever produced.

LEFT: **The Bedford Cockatrice has a very high ground clearance, with the flame gun mounted in the middle of the roof of the vehicle. The machine-gun position at the rear of the vehicle was open-topped.**

Bedford Cockatrice	

Country: UK
Entered service: 1941
Crew: 3
Weight: N/A
Dimensions: Length – 5.94m/19ft 6in
  Height – 2.59m/8ft 6in
  Width – 2.26m/7ft 5in
Armament: Main – Flame Gun
  Secondary – 2 x Vickers K machine-guns
Armour: Maximum – 11mm/0.43in
Powerplant: Bedford 6-cylinder 53.7kW/72hp petrol engine
Performance: Speed – 48kph/30mph
  Range – 370km/230 miles

Bison Concrete Armoured Vehicle

Designed by Concrete Ltd which developed and built the vehicle, the Bison was a solution to the shortage of armoured vehicles in Britain in 1940. No two vehicles were the same, as any truck that could be scavenged was converted.

Leyland Lynx Bison	

Country: UK
Entered service: 1940
Crew: 5–10 men
Weight: Variable
Dimensions: Length – 6.1m/20ft
  Height – 2.74m/9ft
  Width – 2.28m/7ft 6in
Armament: Main – Various small arms
  Secondary – None
Armour: Maximum – 152mm/6in reinforced concrete, backed by 25mm/1in timber
Powerplant: Leyland 6-cylinder 57kW/77hp petrol engine
Performance: Speed – Variable
  Range – Variable

The chassis were mainly pre-war civilian heavy trucks such as AEC, Dennis, Leyland, and Thornycroft. The vehicle was covered in wooden shuttering and fast-setting concrete was then poured over it to a depth of 152mm/6in, which made it bullet-proof and capable of withstanding hits from guns of up to 37mm/1.46in. There were two main variations. The first had a concrete-covered engine and cab with a separate pillbox mounted on the flatbed. The engine and cab were open-topped but protected by canvas covers as concrete tops would be too heavy. The second type had the whole flatbed and driver's cab covered in concrete, with no openings in the sides or top. Access was by a trapdoor under

ABOVE: **The Bison driver and vehicle commander have a very limited vision from the cab. The wheels and chassis were very exposed and there was no protection below the vehicle. As a result of this, these vehicles were mainly used as static armoured pillboxes.**

the vehicle. These vehicles carried a crew of between five and ten men and had a variety of armament, the heaviest being an LMG (light machine-gun).

LEFT: **One of the final type of Birch Gun. Only two of these turreted vehicles were made. The turret has a high front and is really a barbette. This affected the elevation and maximum range of the gun.**
BELOW: **The four Mk II Birch Guns of 20 Battery Royal Artillery during an exercise on Salisbury plain. The Birch Gun was the first genuine self-propelled artillery. However, the gun shield on the vehicle gives the crew very little protection.**

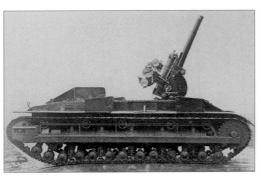

Birch Gun

The Birch Gun was named after the Master General of the Ordnance, General Sir Noel Birch. Officially known as the SP QF (quick-firing) 18pdr Mk I, this was the first self-propelled gun to go into production for the British Army. The vehicle used many of the parts from the Dragon Carrier and the Vickers Medium tank.

The first gun entered service in January 1925 and was attached to 28 Battery, 9th Field Brigade, but only one of this early type was built and it was used for trials. The vehicle was fitted with an Armstrong Siddeley air-cooled engine, which gave it a top speed of 24.1kph/15mph but when used cross-country the maximum speed of the vehicle fell to 16.1kph/10mph. The vehicle was open-topped and there was no protection for the crew from the weather or from small

arms fire. The gun was mounted on a pintle mount towards the front of the vehicle which gave it a 360-degree traverse and a maximum elevation of 90 degrees so it could be used in an anti-aircraft role. It had a very complex sighting system and the recuperator was fitted to the top of the barrel.

Late in 1925 an order was placed with Vickers for four more Birch Guns, but these had a number of improvements to both the gun and the sighting equipment. The recuperator was moved to underneath the gun barrel and a gun shield was mounted on the front of the gun to give the crew some protection. These vehicles were issued to the 20th Battery of the 9th Field Brigade.

The third and final type of Birch Gun was ordered in December 1927 and was finished a year later but never issued. This model was equipped with a turret to give the gun crew some form of protection but this limited the maximum elevation and the range of the weapon.

The Birch Guns were used in the Experimental Mechanised Force manoeuvres of 1928, but by 1931 they had all been removed from service and the British Army would not get an SPG for another 11 years.

Birch Gun	

Country: UK
Entered service: 1925
Crew: 6
Weight: 12,192kg/12 tons
Dimensions: Length – 5.8m/19ft
           Height – 2.3m/7ft 6in
           Width – 2.4m/7ft 9in
Armament: Main – QF (quick-firing) 8.17kg/18pdr
           Mk I gun
           Secondary – Small arms
Armour: None
Powerplant: Armstrong Siddeley 8-cylinder
           67kW/90hp petrol engine
Performance: Speed – 45kph/28mph
           Range – 192km/119 miles

LEFT: **The prototype Birch Gun showing the 18pdr at full elevation. The vehicle was given the designation of Mounting SP QF (quick-firing) 18pdr Mk I, but was better known as the Birch Gun.**

Bishop 25pdr Self-Propelled Gun Mk 1

The successful use of self-propelled artillery by the German Army in the Western Desert led to urgent calls from the British 8th Army for something similar. It was suggested that the 25pdr gun could be mounted on a tank chassis and the best one for the job at this time was the Valentine. The Birmingham Carriage and Wagon Company were given the task of making this idea work in June 1941. A pilot model was ready for trials by August and an order for 100 vehicles was placed in November 1941.

The chassis was a basic Valentine Mk II tank with the standard turret replaced by a very large fixed box turret mounting a 25pdr gun. This gave the vehicle a very high silhouette, which was a great disadvantage in the desert. The gun could not be used to its maximum

elevation or range and so the vehicle was confined to the close-support role. Two large doors were mounted in the rear of the turret, which had to be open when firing the gun to give the crew extra room. The vehicle would often pull a 25pdr limber behind it for increased ammunition supply as it could only carry 32 rounds internally.

In early 1942, the British Tank Mission to America had seen a demonstration of the M7 and placed orders for it that March. However, production continued on the Bishop (the Royal Artillery gave its SPGs ecclesiastical names) and by July 1942, 80 of the first order had been built and a number had been shipped to the 8th Army in North Africa. As the last 20 were under construction, a further order for 50 was placed with the promise of an

ABOVE LEFT: **The crew of a Bishop have come out of action. Before they can rest, they have to tend to the vehicle by refuelling, rearming, checking the engine and all the other parts that make up the Bishop.**

ABOVE: **A Bishop driving off a raised bank. These banks were dug to help increase the range of the gun, with the vehicle commander helping to direct the driver.**

order for 200 to follow, but this was cancelled in favour of the M7.

By July 1942 the M7 was entering service with the British and would be used alongside the Bishop for another year. The 8th Army used the Bishop until the end of the campaign in Sicily when it was replaced with the M7 and relegated to the training role. Compared to the M7, the Bishop was crude and unsophisticated.

LEFT: **A group of British officers having an "O" (Orders) group, issuing orders for the next attack. The Bishop has been parked close to the trees to help camouflage it but the height of the fixed turret can be clearly seen. The vehicle is covered in personal kit.**

Bishop 25pdr SPG Mk 1

Country: UK
Entered service: 1942
Crew: 4
Weight: 20,320kg/20 tons
Dimensions: Length – 5.62m/18ft 6in
    Height – 3.05m/10ft
    Width – 2.77m/9ft 1in
Armament: Main – 25pdr (87.6mm/3.45in)
    gun howitzer
    Secondary – Small arms
Armour: Maximum – 60mm/2.36in
Powerplant: AEC 6-cylinder 98kW/131hp
    diesel engine
Performance: Speed – 24kph/15mph
    Range – 177km/110 miles

LEFT: **The mantlet has been covered by a canvas cover to help keep dust out of the gun mechanism and the pistol port has been opened on the side of the fighting compartment. The side-skirts are still attached to this Brummbär.** ABOVE: **A knocked-out early Brummbär. The side skirt rails have been badly damaged. The vehicle is covered in *Zimmerit* paste to stop magnetic bombs being attached to the vehicle.**

Brummbär Sturmpanzer IV 15cm Self-Propelled Gun

As early as June 1941 a German Army paper suggested the idea of putting a 15cm/5.91in gun into an SP mount. In October 1942, Hitler was shown a plan drawn up by the firm Alkett for a close-support SPG using a 15cm short-barrelled gun mounted on the Panzer IV chassis. Hitler immediately insisted on the production of 40–60 of these vehicles, as he felt there would be a demand for them from the front-line troops, and on the development of a new high-explosive shell for the vehicle to use on buildings and other structures.

The first 60 vehicles were assembled by the Motor Vehicle Workshop in Vienna, the first 20 chassis being delivered in April 1943 with a further 32 in May. All were ready by June 1, 1943 and 50 were sent to Guderian on the Eastern Front, while 10 more were held back to be used at the Fuhrer's discretion. The Panzer IV Ausf F chassis required very little conversion: the turret was removed and a large box structure

was mounted on the top of the vehicle making it top-heavy. The frontal armour was increased to 100mm/3.94in and the driver's visor was at first the same as that in the Tiger 1, but later versions did away with this and replaced it with periscopes. At 28,651kg/28.2 tons, the vehicle was overloaded and the excessive weight caused suspension problems on the early vehicles, consequently the rubber-tyred wheels were replaced by steel-rimmed wheels on the first two bogie sets. Early service use showed that having no local defence machine-gun was a real handicap, so on later versions a machine-gun was mounted in the front of the hull above the driver. To increase the lower side protection for the vehicle, side plates called *Schürzen* (skirts) were hung from rails.

The Brummbär (Grizzly Bear) first saw action with *Sturmpanzerabteilung* 216 at Kursk, the largest tank battle of World War II, and later in Italy and in Normandy with units 217, 218 and 219.

ABOVE: **A late production Brummbär. The close-defence machine-gun port is mounted just above the driver's position on the front of the vehicle.**

Brummbär Sturmpanzer IV 15cm SPG

Country: Germany
Entered service: 1943
Crew: 5
Weight: 28,651kg/28.2 tons
Dimensions: Length – 5.93m/19ft 5in
Height – 2.52m/8ft 3in
Width – 2.88m/9ft 5in
Armament: Main – 1 x 15cm/5.91in StuH43 L/12
Secondary – 2 x 7.92mm/0.312in MG34 machine-gun
Armour: Maximum – 100mm/3.94in
Powerplant: Maybach HL 120 TRM 12-cylinder petrol engine 223.7kW/300hp
Performance: Speed – 40kph/24mph
Range – 210km/130 miles

Buffalo LVT Amphibious Assault Vehicle

When the US Marine Corps were looking for a vehicle capable of landing troops or supplies from the sea in 1940, they saw a vehicle designed and constructed by a Donald Roebling who wanted a vehicle to use in the Florida Everglades. He called it the "Alligator". They liked it, asked for a few changes, and then placed an order for 300.

The LVT 1 (Landing Vehicle Tracked) could carry 18 fully armed men ashore or 2,041kg/4,500lb of stores. The vehicle was propelled through the water by its tracks as these had special oblique shoes that also gave it good traction on land. The driver's position was in the front of the vehicle with the engines mounted in the side walls of the cargo compartment. A big drawback was that the men in the rear of the vehicle

had to climb up the side of the vehicle and then drop 2.1m/7ft over the side on to the ground with a full combat load on their backs. Development of the LVT 1 was frozen in 1941 but as the vehicle was needed urgently by the Marine Corps, 1,225 of these vehicles were built in 1942. They were first used in action in August 1942 during the invasion of Guadalcanal.

Early in 1943 production started on the LVT 2, an improved version of the LVT 1. The general hull of the vehicle was redesigned and given a better boat shape to improve its water handling. The engines were removed from the sides and placed in the rear of the vehicle. The tracks were fitted with new track grousers that were W-shaped which could be easily attached to the tracks of the vehicle. Troops still had to climb the sides

ABOVE: **The rear ramp of this Buffalo LVT 4 is in the down position with a Weasel coming down the ramp. The grousers on the track, which move this very large vehicle through the water, can be clearly seen.**
LEFT: **A column of British Buffalos moving through the smokescreen to cross the Rhine in 1945. Some of the vehicles are still loading their infantry while the gunners of the leading Buffalo are getting their guns ready for action.**

and drop down on to the beach, which was causing casualties among the Marines, so a better way of debussing had to be developed. Two thousand nine hundred and sixty three of these vehicles were built and their first operation was the invasion of Tarawa in November 1943.

Production of the LVT 4, basically an improved LVT 2, began in December 1943. The improvements were that the engine was moved from the rear to the front just behind the driver. A ramp was now fitted to the rear of the vehicle, a major change that would turn this vehicle into the most successful amphibious assault vehicle of the war with 8,348 being produced. The ramp was operated by hand-winch in normal conditions, but in combat the ramp would be released to fall under its own weight. The rear cargo area could now carry 35 fully armed men, an artillery gun or a Jeep. The driver's position was moved from the middle of the driver's compartment to the right-hand side and a bow machine-gun was fitted for the second crewman to use. The first American operation for this vehicle was the invasion of Saipan in June 1944.

The LVT 3 was due to go into production in early 1944 but due to a number of design faults this was delayed until late 1944. Like the LVT 4 it had a rear cargo ramp, and two engines were mounted in the vehicle, one in each side sponson. Apart from the twin engines the LVT 3's performance was the same as the LVT 4, but its water handling was better than the other marks of LVTs. The Americans named the vehicle the

"Bushmaster". Two thousand nine hundred and sixty three of these were produced and it was used by the Marine Corps and the US Army for many years, taking part in the Korean War and serving into the Vietnam War. The first combat operation for the LVT 3 was Okinawa in April 1945.

The Buffalo, as it was called in British service, was assigned to the 79th Armoured Division. Four hundred and twenty five vehicles from two marks, the LVT 2 and the LVT 4, were sent over from America and these would take part in several river crossings. The first British operation using it was the assault on the Breskens Pocket in October 1944, and it remained in service with the British Army until the late 1950s.

ABOVE: **British Buffalos landing on Walcheren island at the top of the Scheldt estuary in 1944. The Buffalo was one of the few vehicles that could cope with the sand and mud of the island.** LEFT: **An LVT 1 driving at speed over swampy ground. These vehicles were nicknamed the "Swamp Angel". The very large driver's window is in the raised position. It gave the driver excellent vision but in combat was a weakness.**

Buffalo Mk IV/LVT 4

Country: USA
Entered service: 1942
Crew: 2 plus 35 infantry
Weight: 12,428kg/12.2 tons
Dimensions: Length – 7.95m/26ft 1in
Height – 2.46m/8ft 1in
Width – 3.25m/10ft 8in
Armament: Main – 1 x 12.7mm/0.5in machine-gun
Secondary – 3 x 7.62mm/0.3in machine-guns
Armour: Maximum – 13mm/0.51in
Powerplant: Continental W670-9A 7-cylinder air-cooled radial engine 186kW/250hp
Performance: Speed – Land 32kph/20mph;
Water 12kph/7mph
Range – 240km/150 miles

Carriers – Machine-gun

A great deal of development was carried out by Vickers Armstrong during the early part of the 1930s using the Carden-Loyd light tank as the base vehicle. A new suspension system was developed consisting of a two-wheel Horstmann type unit with a large coiled spring each side and a single wheel unit behind. The idler wheel was at the front with the drive sprocket at the rear. The first vehicle was a machine-gun carrier. This had the driver on the right and the gunner on the left. Behind them there was room for four infantrymen to be

carried, though with very little protection. The first trials vehicle was produced in 1935 and a number of changes were made before 13 more were manufactured in 1936. A further order was placed later in 1936 for an extra 41 carriers. It was decided that three more types of carrier would be developed during 1936.

A carrier was developed to transport the 7.7mm/0.303in Bren light machine-gun forward under fire, as the gun was just coming into service. When that point was reached, this weapon could be used either from the carrier or dismounted. A number of these Bren Gun Carriers were still in service during World War II and saw action in the desert with the British 8th Army.

The Carrier Cavalry Mk 1 and the Scout Mk 1 were developed for the new

role that the mechanized cavalry units would carry out. The Carrier Cavalry had a driver and gunner in the front with seats on the rear for six cavalrymen, three each side sitting back-to-back. The first contract for 50 vehicles was placed in 1937. A large number of these carriers went with the BEF to France in 1940 but their original role was soon abandoned as it was too dangerous for the troops on the rear of the vehicle.

The Carrier Scout, of which 667 were built, carried various weapons and a radio mounted in the rear of the vehicle. Often confused with the Universal Carrier, it would see action with the BEF in France and in the desert.

MIDDLE LEFT: **A pair of Carriers, Scout Mk 1. These vehicles had a crew of three and were armed with a Boys anti-tank rifle and a Bren gun.**
LEFT: **A group of four Bren Gun Carriers. The crew positions can be clearly seen, especially the third crew position behind the gunner. The suspension on each side has two road wheels in a Horstmann-type bogie which is sprung on coiled springs, a single wheel in a similar unit and the idler at the front.**

Bren Gun Carrier	

Country: UK
Entered service: 1937
Crew: 3
Weight: 4,064kg/4 tons
Dimensions: Length – 3.66m/12ft
Height – 1.37m/4ft 6in
Width – 2.11m/6ft 11in
Armament: Main – Bren 7.7mm/0.303in
light machine-gun
Secondary – Small arms
Armour: Maximum – 12mm/0.47in
Powerplant: Ford 48kW/65hp petrol engine
Performance: Speed – 48kph/30mph
Range – 258km/160 miles

LEFT: **The heavy turret bolts stand out clearly on this Cromwell. The tank is covered in personal storage.**
ABOVE: **The crew of this vehicle have rigged up a rain shelter above their map boards. They are wearing the one-piece tank-suit, which was very warm.**

Cromwell Command/OP Tank

This was the simplest and yet one of the most important conversions of World War II. Due to the speed and danger of a modern mobile battlefield, forward commanders required an armoured vehicle that was capable of keeping up with the advance units, yet giving them some protection and the fullest possible access to communications relevant to their task. These vehicles were issued to formation commanders and forward observation officers of the Royal Artillery.

The Cromwell was chosen due to its good speed and reliability, although at first there were a number of problems with the engine. The speed and power was supplied by a Meteor V12 engine that was a development of the Rolls-Royce Merlin aircraft engine. The top speed was initially 61kph/38mph but this was too much for the vehicle chassis to take, so the engine had a governor placed on it that reduced the speed to 52kph/32mph. From the outside, the vehicle would look very much like a conventional tank except for two map stands mounted on the top and towards the front of the turret. Inside the turret the whole main gun and its controls were removed, along with all the ammunition storage. The main gun barrel was replaced with either an aluminium or wooden copy to disguise the true purpose and configuration of this tank. This gave a lot of additional space for the extra radios that the vehicle carried. Three radios were placed in the turret area, two No.19 sets and one T43 Command radio set. In some vehicles,

the Command radios were replaced by a ground-to-air radio set. In addition, two-man portable sets were carried for use by the Observation officers when away from the vehicle. The radios would be operated and maintained by members of the Royal Corps of Signals.

Three marks of Cromwell were converted to Command and OP tanks, these being the Mk IV, VI and VIII. These vehicles were to see service mainly in north-west Europe, and would remain in British Army service for many years after World War II.

LEFT: **Two Cromwell Command tanks lead a column of Sherman tanks along a road. The map boards can be clearly seen on both Command tanks. The vehicles are clear of any personal clutter as they are on exercise in Britain.**

Cromwell Command Tank

Country: UK
Entered service: 1944
Crew: 4/5
Weight: 26,416kg/26 tons
Dimensions: Length – 6.35m/20ft 10in
    Height – 2.5m/8ft 2in
    Width – 2.92m/9ft 7in
Armament: Main – None
    Secondary – 1 x Besa 7.92mm/0.312in
    machine-gun, and 1 x Bren 7.7mm/0.303in
    light machine-gun
Armour: Maximum – 76mm/2.99in
Powerplant: Rolls-Royce Meteor 12-cylinder
    447kW/600hp petrol engine
Performance: Speed – 52kph/32mph
    Range – 278km/173 miles

Crossley Armoured Car

In 1923, Crossley Motors of Manchester offered a new chassis that was very robust and cheaper than the Rolls-Royce, the main armoured car chassis used at this time. The Crossley six-wheeled chassis was used to produce a number of different armoured cars for the Royal Air Force (RAF) in the Middle East, the British Army in India, and a number of other governments in the 1930s.

The main contractor for building these vehicles was Vickers, which was able to build 100 six-wheeled armoured cars, most going to the British forces in India and Iraq. The first ones were based on the Crossley 30/70hp medium chassis and were over 6.1m/20ft long, so had a real problem with grounding in rough terrain. To overcome this problem Vickers mounted the spare wheels between the front and rear wheels so they hung below the chassis and could rotate freely, thus making it a four-axle vehicle which could withstand the rigours of less than perfect roads in the outlying

areas of India and Iraq. Another chassis was the 38/110hp Crossley IGA4 series with a six-cylinder engine. The body and turret were very similar to the Lanchester armoured car, but the turret was fitted with a single machine-gun. The Crossley 20/60hp light six-wheeled chassis was the basis for yet another armoured car. The first Crossleys were ordered from the Royal Ordnance Factory in 1928 and were armed with two machine-guns, one in a turret and one in the front hull. The turret was the same as a Vickers Mk 1 light tank.

Vickers produced a number of Crossley cars for export to several countries such as Argentina, Iraq and Japan. Most of these would see service for many years. The Iraqi cars were later commandeered by British forces and used by them in a training role until the

ABOVE LEFT: **Crossley armoured car on the 38/110hp chassis. This was known as the IGA4 series. The main customer for this car was the RAF.** ABOVE: **A Crossley 30/70hp chassis armoured car. The dome-shaped turret is very similar to the Indian Pattern armoured car and is armed with two Vickers guns.**

end of World War II. All Crossley cars in RAF service were equipped with ground-to-ground and ground-to-air radio sets. This proved very useful during combined operations in Iraq and India while trying to police the northern borders of these countries.

LEFT: **The pole frame above the vehicle carries the main aerial for the long-range radio, and for ground-to-air radio. The spare wheels were left free to rotate and so help the vehicle unditch itself.**

Crossley Mk 1 Armoured Car	

Country: UK
Entered service: 1931
Crew: 4
Weight: 5,516.88kg/5.43 tons
Dimensions: Length – 4.65m/15ft 3in
 Height – 2.64m/8ft 8in
 Width – 1.88m/6ft 2in
Armament: Main – 2 x Vickers 7.7mm/0.303in
 machine-guns
 Secondary – None
Armour: Maximum – 10mm/0.394in
Powerplant: Crossley 52kW/70hp
Performance: Speed – 80kph/50mph
 Range – 290km/180 miles

Daimler Armoured Car

The Daimler Dingo was such a success that it was suggested that it could be scaled up into a wheeled tank. Development started in 1939 but due to a number of technical problems the armoured car did not enter service (as the Daimler Mk 1) until 1941.

The Daimler had many unusual and very advanced features for its time. There was no chassis to the vehicle and all the suspension components were attached directly to the armoured lower hull. Instead of a normal clutch, a fluid flywheel torque converter was used and also a pre-selector gearbox was fitted. The car had two driving positions, one in the front for the vehicle driver and one in the rear, which the vehicle commander could use to drive the vehicle away in reverse. The vehicle could use all five forward gears in reverse and was also

fitted with disc brakes some 20 years before any commercial vehicle. The turret mounted a 2pdr (40mm) gun. This was the first time that this gun was mounted in a British armoured car and was the same as that fitted to the Tetrarch light tank. The three-man crew meant that the vehicle commander had to act as loader for this weapon. Smoke dischargers were often fitted to the sides of the turret and some of the Mk 1 cars had a Littlejohn Adaptor fitted to their main armament. This was a squeeze bore muzzle adaptor that allowed the Daimler to achieve better armour penetration of enemy vehicles.

The Mk 2 came into service in 1943 with a number of improvements, including an improved gun mounting. The radiator was given better protection

and improved to give better engine cooling, and the driver was given an escape hatch. Apart from these modifications, the Mk 2 was the same as the Mk 1. Total production was 2,694 vehicles of all marks.

The Daimler soon developed a very good reputation for performance and reliability with the 8th Army in North Africa and it went on to serve with British forces in northern Europe. It remained in service until well after the end of World War II.

Daimler Mk 1 Armoured Car

Country: UK
Entered service: 1941
Crew: 3
Weight: 7,620kg/7.5 tons
Dimensions: Length – 3.96m/13ft
    Height – 2.24m/7ft 4in
    Width – 2.44m/8ft
Armament: Main – 2pdr (40mm) gun
    Secondary – Besa 7.92mm/0.312in machine-gun
Armour: Maximum – 16mm/0.63in
Powerplant: Daimler 6-cylinder petrol engine, 71kW/95hp
Performance: Speed – 80.5kph/50mph
    Range – 330km/205 miles

RIGHT: A post-World War II Daimler Mk 1. A spare wheel has replaced the storage boxes on the side of the vehicle. This vehicle is shown in desert camouflage as used by the 7th Armoured Division in 1942.

Daimler Dingo Scout Car

One of the requirements for the new armoured force that was being developed in the late 1930s was for a light 4x4 scout car for general duties and reconnaissance. The design was originally put forward by the BSA motorcycle company, but they were taken over by the Daimler car company. An order for 172 vehicles was placed with the new company in 1939.

The Mk 1 was a 4x4 open-top vehicle which only had armoured protection for the crew at the front of the vehicle and proved to be under-powered. The Mk 1A incorporated all-round armoured protection for the crew and a bigger and more powerful engine. It also had a folding metal roof. These Mk 1 vehicles had four-wheel

steering and this proved to be a liability in the hands of unskilled drivers.

The steering was changed to be front wheels only in the Mk 2, which made it considerably easier to handle. The basic layout would hardly change during the course of the vehicle's production. The two crew members sat side by side in an open-topped armoured box, while the crew compartment had only a folding metal roof for protection. The engine was at the rear.

The Mk 3 was the heaviest version of the scout car but was still well within the limits of the vehicle. The metal roof was done away with as it was hardly ever used operationally by the crews. The engine was also given a waterproof ignition system.

ABOVE LEFT: **This Dingo Mk 1 is in the "buttoned down" mode with all the hatches closed. The rear view mirror is mounted on the top of the front plate but was rarely fitted.** ABOVE: **The frame on the back of the Daimler is to support the crew compartment hatch. The front part of the hatch folds back, and then both parts slide back and on to the frame.**

The vehicle was armed with a Bren gun for all of its service history although there were a number of local crew modifications on the armament. The Daimler scout car proved to be a very reliable and rugged vehicle and has the distinction of being one of the few vehicles to be in service at the start of the World War II and to remain in service well after the war had finished, with 6,626 of all marks being produced. This car could be found in most British and Commonwealth units, even in units that were not supposed to have it on strength.

ABOVE: **A Dingo Mk 3 in the North African desert. The roof hatch has gone on this mark. The crew have increased the firepower of the car by adding a Vickers gun.**

Daimler Dingo Mk 3 Scout Car	
Country: UK	
Entered service: 1939	
Crew: 2	
Weight: 3,215.2kg/3.2 tons	
Dimensions:	Length – 3.23m/10ft 5in
	Height – 1.5m/4ft 11in
	Width – 1.72m/5ft 8in
Armament:	Main – Bren 7.7mm/0.303in light machine-gun
	Secondary – None
Armour: Maximum – 30mm/1.18in	
Powerplant: Daimler 6-cylinder petrol engine 41kW/55hp	
Performance:	Speed – 88.5kph/55mph
	Range – 322km/200 miles

Dorchester Command Vehicle

The first command vehicle in British service was the Morris 762kg/15cwt. This came into service in 1937 but was far too small to be of any real use. The next vehicle was the 4x4 Guy Lizard which entered service in 1940 and most unusually had a Gardner diesel engine but again proved to be on the small side.

The Dorchester Command Vehicle was based on the AEC Matador chassis but with a few modifications. The fuel tank was moved and the winch was replaced with a generator for the radio sets that were carried in the vehicle. Two different marks of vehicle were produced, but there were no external differences between them – the changes were made to the internal fit

of the vehicle. The Mk 1 had a large single combined office and radio room, while in the Mk 2 there was a separate radio room. There were also two versions of each mark: the LP (Low Power) and HP (High Power) versions. The LP was fitted with No.19 radio LP and HP sets. The HP vehicle was fitted with an RCA (Radio Crystalline Amplifier) receiver and a No.19 set. The early versions of the vehicle were fitted with a canopy that, when unrolled, had side panels attached to form an extended working area. Later versions had a complete tent carried on the vehicle. There was normally a crew of seven with the vehicle, one driver, two radio operators and four officers.

Three Dorchesters were captured by the *Afrika Korps* in July 1941 and two

were given to Rommel to use as his own HQ vehicles. The official German designation for these vehicles was *Mammute* (Mammoths). The two vehicles used by Rommel were called "Max" and "Moritz" and were not recaptured by the British until the surrender of the German and Italian forces in Tunisia.

A new and larger vehicle did enter production towards the end of the war on the AEC 6x6 chassis. In all, 380 4x4 Dorchester command vehicles were produced from 1941–45. They would see service in North Africa, up through Italy and also in northern Europe.

LEFT: **The open side door of the vehicle has a blackout curtain on the inside, which was a standard fit. There is storage for several chairs on the back of the door. This door also gives access to the radio area and the driver's cab.**

Dorchester Armoured Command Vehicle

Country: UK
Entered service: 1941
Crew: 7
Weight: 10,500kg/10.33 tons
Dimensions: Length – 6.32m/20ft 9in
　　Height – 3.1m/10ft 2in
　　Width – 2.4m/7ft 10in
Armament: Main – Bren 7.7mm/0.303in light
　　machine-gun
　　Secondary – None
Armour: Maximum – 12mm/0.47in
Powerplant: AEC 6-cylinder 71kW/95hp
　　diesel engine
Performance: Speed – 58kph/36mph
　　Range – 579km/360 miles

LEFT: **Light Dragon Carrier Mk IIc.** This was an improved vehicle having a new suspension system designed by Horstmann. The vehicle exhaust on the rear of the body has been fitted with a shield. The external shields for the return rollers can also be clearly seen as can the canvas roof for the vehicle which is in the raised position.

Dragon Carrier Mk I

A number of experimental vehicles were designed at the Tank Design and Experimental Department commanded by Colonel P. H. Johnson. The origins of the Dragon lay in a number of experimental tropical tanks that were supply vehicles. The fourth vehicle of this series was sent to the 9th Field Brigade in 1922 for trials in gun-haulage. The army were not very impressed with these and so approached Vickers to produce three rival vehicles. One of these was built as a gun carrier for the 18pdr, the gun being carried on the top of the vehicle. It was hauled up ramps from the rear of the vehicle and positioned inside with the muzzle facing forward.

In 1922, the Royal Ordnance Factory at Woolwich produced two new vehicles called Artillery Transporters, which would be the prototypes for the Dragon Mk I. One was sent to India for trials and the other was sent to the 9th Field Brigade. An order was placed for 20 vehicles, 18 for the army and two for the RAF, and these entered service in 1923. The driver's compartment was down in the front of the vehicle next to the radiator. The vehicle commander sat next to the driver high up on the top of the vehicle and behind them was seating for a further 10 men who would man the gun. The crew compartment on the top of the vehicle was completely open to the elements, but a canvas tilt could be placed over the crew to protect them from rain. At the rear of the vehicle was storage for ammunition.

As soon as they were issued, the 9th Field Brigade began training with their new vehicles. In July 1923, they took part in a long-distance road march from Deepcut to Larkhill, a distance of 93km/58 miles. The march was completed in just 10 hours and all the crews arrived in good order. A horse-drawn battery would have been able to cover 20 miles in the same time. However, the Dragon had a number of mechanical problems and was withdrawn from service in 1926.

ABOVE MIDDLE AND ABOVE: **A Dragon Carrier with the roof folded to the rear of the vehicle, but it could also be collapsed and stored on one side. The carrier is shown with an 18pdr gun and limber, its normal load. Note that the gun and limber are still fitted with wooden wheels.**

Dragon Carrier Mk I	

Country: UK
Entered service: 1923
Crew: 2 plus 10 gun crew
Weight: 9,144kg/9 tons
Dimensions: Length – 5.03m/16ft 6in
  Height – 2.13m/7ft – with tilt 3.05m/10ft
  Width – 2.74m/9ft
Armament: Main – None
  Secondary – Small arms
Armour: None
Powerplant: Leyland 6-cylinder 45kW/60hp petrol engine
Performance: Speed – 19kph/12mph
  Range – 145km/90 miles

Ford Model T Scout Car

The Model T proved to be an outstanding scout and light armoured car, remaining in action long after other larger and more powerful armoured cars had broken down. There were two types of car built. The most numerous type used the basic Model T and was employed as a scout car. This was deployed mainly in the Middle East in countries such as Egypt and Palestine. The other type of car was a fully armoured version of the Model T and was used mostly in Russia and the Caucasus.

The scout car had a crew of two or three. In most of these, the machine-gun was mounted in the front of the car with the gunner sitting next to the driver. In some versions, a heavy machine-gun was mounted on the flatbed at the rear of the car. These vehicles had no armoured protection for the crew and no protection from the weather, while the machine-gun had very little traverse and none to the

rear. Nevertheless, due to its light weight and good reliability this vehicle proved to be well-liked by the men who used it. The American Army used several in Mexico and the Australians used them in Palestine and in Australia as they proved very good at covering large areas of dry, dusty ground.

The second car was developed by the British for the war in Russia, and designed by the Royal Navy, which had considerable experience with armoured cars. These vehicles were to replace a number of Lanchester armoured cars that had been damaged en route to Russia as they were all that was available at the time. Armour plate was placed around the engine and rear flatbed. The driver's cab was armoured except for the top which was canvas covered, and the Maxim machine-gun was mounted on a pintle mount on the rear flatbed with a 9mm/0.354in armoured shield fitted to it.

There was no forward field of fire for the machine-gun due to the driver's cab. These cars were ridiculed on arrival in Russia but soon proved far better than expected in service.

Ford Model T Scout Car

Country: USA
Entered service: 1914
Crew: 2
Weight: 508kg/10cwt
Dimensions: Length – 3.42m/11ft 3in
  Height – 1.54m/5ft 1in
  Width – 1.28m/4ft 4in
Armament: Main – 7.7mm/0.303in Vickers Maxim
  machine-gun
  Secondary – Small arms
Armour: Maximum – 5mm/0.2in
Powerplant: Ford 4-cylinder 16kW/22hp
  petrol engine
Performance: Speed – 50kph/31mph
  Range – 241km/150 miles

Grille 15cm Heavy Infantry Self-Propelled Gun Ausf M

LEFT: The rear doors of the vehicle are in the open position; this was a common practice as the rear of the vehicle was used to store extra equipment. The crude armour around the crew compartment is very clearly shown in this picture. It gave the crew very little protection. ABOVE: An overhead view of the vehicle showing the very cramped fighting compartment. The driver's position is on the left below the gun-control wheels.

By 1942 there was a growing demand for self-propelled artillery from the German Army so a number of chassis were considered for the task. The PzKpfw 38(t) was proving to be a very reliable and adaptable chassis and was used for a number of different gun platforms.

Development started in late 1942, and the prototype produced by Alkett using the 38(t) Ausf H chassis passed its acceptance trials. An order was placed for 200 units to be built on the Ausf K chassis, but this new chassis was not ready at that point, so construction started using the Ausf H. Production commenced in February 1943. After the initial production run was finished, it was agreed that all 38(t) chassis returned for

repair could also be converted into SPGs. Some of them were adapted to become the Grille, in which a 15cm/ 5.91in sIG 33 was mounted across the top of the body of the vehicle and bolted into place and an armoured superstructure was placed around the vehicle. This also covered the engine area to accommodate ammunition storage.

As soon as it became available, the Ausf M chassis was used for the bulk of the production of the Grille, which finished in September 1944. This new vehicle had a number of changes made to it. The rear engine in the H was moved forward to a mid position and the fighting compartment was moved to the rear of the vehicle. To protect the fighting

compartment, a large spring-loaded flap was used to cover the gun aperture when the gun was elevated.

Both versions of the Grille only carried 18 rounds of ammunition, so a further version was developed into an ammunition carrier using the Ausf M chassis. This was basically the same as the gun vehicle but without the gun, and consequently could be converted into the gun variant very quickly if needed. These vehicles were to see combat in Russia, Italy and northern Europe with many Panzer units of the German Army and the SS. In February 1945, there were still 173 Grille SPGs listed for combat.

Grille 15cm Heavy Infantry SPG Ausf M

Country: Germany
Entered service: 1943
Crew: 4
Weight: 12,192kg/12 tons
Dimensions: Length – 4.95m/16ft 3in
Height – 2.47m/8ft 1in
Width – 2.15m/7ft 1in
Armament: Main – 15cm/5.91in sIG 33/2
Secondary – 7.92mm/0.312in MG34
machine-gun
Armour: Maximum – 15mm/0.59in
Powerplant: Praga AC 6-cylinder 111kW/150hp
petrol engine
Performance: Speed – 42kph/26mph
Range – 190km/118 miles

LEFT: A battery of Grille 15cm SPGs. The vehicle in the front of the picture is a late production variant, with the fighting compartment in the rear. The gun is at maximum elevation. When the weapon is in this position, a spring-loaded flap closes the gap in the gun shield.

Guy Armoured Car Mk 1/1A

LEFT: **The driver's front hatch is in the open position, which improves the driver's vision. There are side hatches into the main fighting compartment just behind the front wheels on both sides. The very angular body and low ground clearance can be clearly seen.**

Following trials in 1938, the Guy Quad-Ant chassis was chosen to be the base for a "wheeled tank" as it was originally called. It was the first 4x4 vehicle to be specifically produced for the British Army. The engine was moved to the rear of the new vehicle, with a turret in the middle and the driver at the front. The other revolutionary thing about this vehicle is that it was of an all-welded construction for the hull and turret instead of riveted as specified for all other British AFVs at this time. An order was placed for 101 vehicles, one prototype and the remainder operational. The first 50 of these had one Vickers 12.7mm/0.5in and one 7.7mm/0.303in machine-gun. The next 50 vehicles had one Besa 15mm/0.59in gun and one 7.92mm/0.312in machine-gun. This configuration became the Mk 1A Guy Armoured Car. Only six of these went to France with the BEF and the rest remained in Britain with the Defence Force. All drawings were subsequently handed over to the Rootes Group.

Guy Armoured Car Mk 1/1A

Country: UK
Entered service: 1939
Crew: 3
Weight: 5,283kg/5.2 tons
Dimensions: Length – 4.12m/13ft 6in
Height – 2.29m/7ft 6in
Width – 2.06m/6ft 9in
Armament: Main – 12.7mm/0.5in Vickers machine-gun (Mk 1A 15mm/0.59in Besa machine-gun)
Secondary – 7.7mm/0.303in Vickers machine-gun (Mk 1A 7.92mm/0.312in Besa machine-gun)
Armour: Maximum – 15mm/0.59in
Powerplant: Meadows 40kW/53hp petrol engine
Performance: Speed – 64kph/40mph
Range – 338km/210 miles

Guy Lizard Command Vehicle

Britain appears to be the only country to develop and use the armoured command vehicle during World War II. There was a clear requirement for a 4x4 command vehicle equipped with radio for use as a mobile headquarters. The development programme was awarded to Guy in 1939, as they had finished the development of a heavy armoured car for the War Office.

Guy used the new Lizard 3,048kg/3-ton 4x4 chassis that the company had just developed. It was powered by the Gardner diesel engine which was most unusual for military vehicles at this time. The prototype was basically an open box with the driver's position accessible from the command area at the rear. This would be modified in the AEC Dorchester command vehicles in which the driver's compartment was separated from the rest of the vehicle. The original contract was for 30 of these but only 21 appear to have been built.

The majority of these vehicles remained in Britain but some were sent to join the 8th Army and at least one was captured by the Italians.

RIGHT: **Very few pictures of these command vehicles exist due to their security classification. This vehicle has been pictured in a base workshop. The large number of roof hatches can be seen. The canvas roll on the side of the vehicle is a tent that can be used as an office.**

Guy Lizard Command Vehicle

Country: UK
Entered service: 1940
Crew: 6
Weight: 10,668kg/10.5 tons
Dimensions: Length – 6.48m/21ft 3in
Height – 2.67m/8ft 9in
Width – 2.44m/8ft
Armament: Main – Small arms
Secondary – None
Armour: Maximum – 12mm/0.47in
Powerplant: Gardner 6-cylinder 71kW/95hp diesel engine
Performance: Speed – 56kph/35mph
Range – 563km/350 miles

LEFT: **Humber Mk 4 armoured car armed with the American 37mm/1.46in gun. These vehicles belong to the 49th Division, the "Polar Bears", and are taking part in an exercise in Britain during 1944.** ABOVE: **The angular design of the vehicle can be clearly seen along with its Guy heritage. The crew are leaving the vehicle by the turret hatches as these were easier to use than the hull doors.**

Humber Armoured Cars

The Humber was one of the most important British armoured cars of World War II, and the Rootes Group were to manufacture 5,400 of these, some 60 per cent of all British armoured cars used in that conflict. Rootes had taken over the design and development of the Guy Mk 1 and used the Karrier KT4 chassis, but Guy would continue to supply the turrets and hull as they had the special welding equipment. The new design was placed into production and renamed the Humber Mk 1, entering service with British forces in 1941.

The Humber had a short wheel base and even with this was not very manoeuvrable, which crews found frustrating at times. The Mk 1 was armed with one 15mm/0.59in and one 7.92mm/0.312in machine-gun and a total of 500

were built before it was replaced by the Mk 2. The improvements in the Mk 2 were confined to a better glacis plate at the front of the vehicle and improved radiator armour at the rear. The Mk 3 entered production in early 1942 and had a new type of turret that increased the crew to four men. A number of Mk 3 cars were converted into mobile artillery observation vehicles. The Mk 4 reverted to a crew of three and now mounted the American 37mm/1.46in gun in the turret as the main armament, becoming the first British armoured car to be fitted with this weapon. The driver was given a rear flap that he could open by a lever so that he could see when reversing or in an emergency.

The Canadians built 200 of these vehicles, calling them the Armoured Car

Mk 1 Fox 1, but the crews could not tell the difference except in armament. Another British version was the AA (anti-aircraft) Mk 1 armoured car, which came into service in 1943 but was decommissioned in 1944. The turret carried four 7.92mm/0.312in machine-guns.

The Humber began its service life in North Africa and then moved on up into Italy. The Mk 4 was to see extensive service in northern Europe. Some cars would remain in service with other countries until the early 1960s.

LEFT: **This Humber is leading a Dingo and a Jeep along a lane in northern France in 1944. The car is covered in additional personal storage and is armed with a 37mm/1.46in gun. The driver has fairly good forward vision when his front plate is raised.**

Humber Mk 2–4 Armoured Car

Country: UK
Entered service: 1941
Crew: 3 (Mk 3 – Crew 4)
Weight: 7,213kg/7.1 tons
Dimensions: Length – 4.57m/15ft
　　Height – 2.34m/7ft 10in
　　Width – 2.18m/7ft 2in
Armament: Main – 1 x Besa 15mm/0.59in, and
　　1 x coaxial Besa 7.92mm/0.312in machine-guns
　　Secondary – Bren 7.7mm/0.303in light
　　machine-gun
Armour: Maximum – 15mm/0.59in
Powerplant: Rootes 6-cylinder 67kW/95hp
　　petrol engine
Performance: Speed – 72kph/45mph
　　Range – 402km/250 miles

LEFT: **The eight wheels of the Panzer IV running gear can be clearly seen on this vehicle. It has the late production driver's position and radio operator's box structure, with improved forward vision.**

ABOVE: **The spacious fighting compartment can be seen here. The main gun is mounted on the top of the engine compartment. In action the crew have no protection from the weather.**

Hummel 15cm Heavy Self-Propelled Gun

Reports coming back from the Panzer Divisions showed a need for a heavy SPG on a fully tracked vehicle. It was originally intended to mount the 10.5cm/4.13in medium gun but experiments showed that the heavy sFH18 15cm/5.91in guns could be mounted on a tracked chassis. Development stated in July 1942 with Alkett doing the work, and by combining parts from the Panzer III and the Panzer IV a successful vehicle was developed. Nevertheless, as the Hummel had only limited traverse, this was an interim solution to the problem until an SPG with an all-round firing-arc such as the Waffenträger could be developed.

The prototype was shown to Hitler in October 1942 and was cleared for production, with the first 100 being ready by May 1943 and 666 built by late 1944. The vehicle was given the name of Hummel (Bumble Bee) and would remain in production for the rest of the war. The gun barrel on the early vehicle was fitted with a muzzle brake at first but this was soon discarded as unnecessary. Another early feature was the long finger of the driver's position protruding forward. To ease production this was changed to an enclosed cab going from side to side of the vehicle. The engine was moved from the rear of the chassis to just behind the driver. The box-shaped armoured fighting compartment was roomy but gave very little protection to the gun crew, being only 10mm/0.394in thick with no protection from the weather, so

a number of crews fitted canvas covers to improve their conditions. As it could only carry 18 rounds of ammunition, 157 Hummel vehicles were converted into ammunition carriers. With their gun apertures plated over, they could carry 40 rounds. The vehicle was popular with both its crews and the unit commanders as it gave them a mobile heavy punch against enemy targets.

The Hummel was first issued to units on the Eastern Front in early 1943 for the big push at Kursk which resulted in the largest tank battle in history and from then on would see action on every German front until the end of World War II.

RIGHT: **Due to the size of the vehicle, crews tried to camouflage them with netting which was tied to the sides of the fighting compartment. The rear doors are covered in personal kit that has been moved from under the gun.**

Hummel 15cm Heavy SPG

Country: Germany
Entered service: 1943
Crew: 6
Weight: 24,384kg/24 tons
Dimensions: Length – 7.17m/23ft 6in
  Height – 2.81m/9ft 3in
  Width – 2.87m/9ft 5in
Armament: Main – 15cm/5.91in sFH18/1 L/30
  Secondary – 1 x 7.92mm/0.312in machine-gun
Armour: Maximum – 30mm/1.18in
Powerplant: Maybach V-12 198kW/265hp
  petrol engine
Performance: Speed – 42kph/26mph
  Range – 215km/134 miles

Indian Pattern Armoured Cars

Shortly after the outbreak of World War I, arrangements were made in India to form an armoured car unit for internal security duties and for work on the North West Frontier. A number of these cars were built on any available chassis at the East Indian Railway Workshops at Lillooah. More vehicles were required as the Indian armoured car units expanded and chassis used included Minerva, Quad and even Fiat trucks. These were very basic armoured cars, even by the standards of the early RNAS vehicles.

Improved vehicles were sought in the 1920s. The first chassis used were the Rolls-Royce Silver Ghost but these were very expensive and Vickers looked for a cheaper alternative after only 18 vehicles. Crossley Motors of Manchester were able to provide a good strong chassis at half the price of Rolls-Royce and production of a 4x2 armoured car, using a Crossley truck chassis, started in 1923. The armoured car had the engine located in the front and the fighting compartment in the middle of the vehicle, topped by a domed turret which had four machine-gun mountings but only carried two guns. On the top of the turret was a small observation dome, and on some vehicles a searchlight was fitted to the top of this. The inside of the vehicle was covered in a thick layer of asbestos which helped insulate the crew from the heat of India. The insulation also

served to protect the crew from an electrical charge, as the crew could electrify the hull exterior when any enemy climbed on to the car. The footbrake acted directly on the propeller shaft of the vehicle and consequently made the car somewhat skittish on slippery roads. The vehicle was fitted with solid tyres and firm suspension, so the ride for the crew was very hard.

The chassis of these cars were worn out by 1939, but the bodies were still in good condition, so the Chevrolet truck chassis was used to refurbish the vehicle. These cars would remain in service until Indian independence in 1947. The new vehicle was also sent to Palestine and Syria in 1940.

TOP: **A pair of Vickers armoured cars built on the Crossley chassis outside the Erith plant in Kent. On the top of the turret is a fixed searchlight.**

ABOVE: **A group of three Crossley armoured cars, one of which has been unable to stop. These vehicles are fitted with solid tyres, so that they operate in the rough terrain of India.**

ABOVE: **An Indian Pattern Crossley car in Africa crossing a river by pontoon ferry. This armoured car has been fitted with aerials for a command radio set.**

Indian Pattern Crossley Armoured Car

Country: India
Entered service: 1923
Crew: 4
Weight: 5,080kg/5 tons
Dimensions: Length – 5.03m/16ft 6in
Height – 2.16m/7ft 1in
Width – 1.83m/6ft
Armament: Main – 2 x 7.7mm/0.303in machine-guns
Secondary – Small arms
Armour: Maximum – 8mm/0.315in
Powerplant: Crossley 6-cylinder 37kW/50hp petrol engine
Performance: Speed – 65kph/40mph
Range – 200km/125 miles

LEFT: **The IS II tank chassis can be clearly seen on this vehicle. The drums fitted to the rear are extended-range fuel tanks. The thickness of the gun mantlet is 160mm/ 6.3in. On the roof of the fighting compartment is the DShK 12.7mm/0.5in machine-gun mount. A number of these vehicles were captured and pressed into German service.**

ISU-152mm Heavy Assault Gun

The first chassis used for this vehicle was the KV-1S, at which point it was called the SU-152. It was developed and placed into production in just one month. The first vehicles were rushed to the Kursk salient as the Russians knew the Germans were going to attack at this point. The SU-152 used the 152mm/ 5.98in M-1937/43 howitzer mounted in a heavily armoured box on the front of the vehicle. At this stage of the war the Red Army made no difference between anti-tank and other SPGs, so the howitzer was used in the anti-tank role and relied on the weight of the shell to knock out the German tanks.

The new tank project called the IS (Josef Vissarionovich Stalin) was initiated and the gun tank developed from this was placed into production in December 1943,

followed very quickly by the ISU-152. The same chassis was also fitted with the 122mm/4.8in M-1931/44 gun and this became the ISU-122. No muzzle brake was fitted on the end of the barrel, which also had a screw breech. The vehicle could carry 30 rounds of main armament ammunition. A later model, the ISU-122A, was developed using the 122mm/4.8in 1943 model cannon (D-25-S) which was a tank destroyer of exceptional size and power. This had a large double-baffle muzzle brake and had a higher muzzle velocity than the 152mm/5.98in gun.

The ISU-152 had one weakness and this was that the vehicle could only carry 20 rounds of ammunition, but no armoured ammunition carrier was available. Extra ammunition was brought

up to the ISU-152 by basic open truck, but the risk involved in this was considered acceptable as the ISU was such an important vehicle to the Soviet infantry and armoured forces.

Each tank brigade would have 65 ISU-152s attached to it, which would take part in every major battle from Kursk to the fall of Berlin. These heavy assault guns would be in the vanguard of the Soviet Army entering Berlin in 1945 and would remain in service until early 1970 with the Soviet forces.

ISU-152mm Heavy Assault Gun

Country: USSR
Entered service: 1944
Crew: 5
Weight: 46,228kg/45.5 tons
Dimensions: Length – 9.05m/29ft 8in
　　　　Height – 2.48m/8ft 2in
　　　　Width – 3.07m/10ft 1in
Armament: Main – 152mm/5.98in M-1937/43 howitzer
　　　　Secondary – 12.7mm/0.5in DShK 1938/43 AA machine-gun
Armour: Maximum – 90mm/3.54in
Powerplant: 12-cylinder W-2-IS 388kW/520hp diesel engine
Performance: Speed – 37kph/23mph
　　　　Range – 180km/112 miles

LEFT: **This is one of the early SU-152 SPGs which has been knocked out by the Germans during the fighting at Kursk. The chassis is the KV heavy tank chassis.**

LEFT: **Developed in 1944 for operations behind the German lines in France by the Special Air Service (SAS), the driver and gunner have bullet-proof screens in front of them and extra large fuel tanks in the rear of the Jeep.** BELOW: **This is one of the last batch of Jeeps to be converted for the LRDG. It has been fitted with a twin and a single Vickers K guns plus a single 12.7mm/50cal heavy machine-gun. The vehicle is covered in extra fuel and water cans.**

Jeep Multi-Role Vehicle

The Jeep is the best known vehicle of World War II. Easily adapted into a light AFV, its reputation has gone from strength to strength and is as great today as it was in 1940. In the late 1930s, the US Army held a series of trials to find a new command and reconnaissance vehicle. The trials that were held in 1940 were won by the Bantam Car Company, their competitors being Willys Overland and the Ford Motor Company. All the companies were given small construction orders in 1940, but in July 1941 the contract for 16,000 vehicles was placed with Willys. It soon became very clear that Willys could not keep up with demand so the US Army insisted that they pass over the drawings and other details to Ford so they could also produce this vehicle. Between them, these two companies built 639,245 Jeeps between 1941 and 1945, but as the vehicle was developed in the post-World War II years, other companies would produce this remarkable little vehicle. By 1962, when American production finished, 800,000 of these ugly little vehicles had been built.

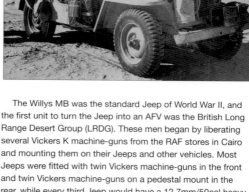

The Willys MB was the standard Jeep of World War II, and the first unit to turn the Jeep into an AFV was the British Long Range Desert Group (LRDG). These men began by liberating several Vickers K machine-guns from the RAF stores in Cairo and mounting them on their Jeeps and other vehicles. Most Jeeps were fitted with twin Vickers machine-guns in the front and twin Vickers machine-guns on a pedestal mount in the rear, while every third Jeep would have a 12.7mm/50cal heavy machine-gun fitted. The fuel tank was also doubled in size to 136 litres/30 gallons, and a condenser was fitted in the front of the radiator. The Jeep was often used by officers as a light reconnaissance vehicle in the desert campaign as it had a good turn of speed and was very small. The Jeep was still further modified by the men in the field and great assortments of weapons of various calibres were mounted on the vehicle during the war in the desert.

LEFT: **British paratroopers leaving the Horsa glider landing zone on D-Day, June 6, 1944. The Jeep is pulling a light trailer full of ammunition, and eight men have managed to get on the vehicle. The Jeep has no armament fitted to it.**

LEFT: **Lt Colonel David Stirling and some of the men from the LRDG. He found the Jeep ideal for long-range missions behind enemy lines. The vehicles are heavily overloaded with extra fuel, water and ammunition.** ABOVE: **This American Jeep is fitted with twelve 120mm/4.72in rockets. These vehicles had a crew of two. The man inside the vehicle is operating the elevation gear. The crew area has been protected by an armoured cover.**

Airborne forces were also looking at the Jeep as a light AFV that could be fitted into gliders and yet on landing could supply a fast moving, heavily armed vehicle to hit the enemy hard and to act as a reconnaissance unit, as the special Jeep squadrons did at Arnhem. The US 82nd Airborne trapped at Bastogne added armour plate to their Jeeps and mounted either one or two 12.7mm/50cal machine-guns on them. These vehicles had a crew of six men and acted as a mobile "fire brigade" that would move around the defensive perimeter from one hot spot to another. Other conversions produced in Europe were the mounting of twelve 114.3mm/4.5in rocket tubes on the back of the Jeep by the 7th US Army. The cab was covered with armour to protect the vehicle.

The US Marine Corps would also adapt the Jeep into a light AFV by placing 28 M8A2 rockets on the rear thus turning it into a rocket artillery support vehicle. However, the crew could not remain with the Jeep when firing as it was too dangerous. Others would have multiple machine-guns fitted as these

vehicles could get into the jungle better than heavier tanks and LVTs. In 1944 the Americans undertook a trial with the T19 105mm/4.13in recoilless rifle, turning the Jeep into an anti-tank weapons platform. This was a pointer to the future.

After World War II the Jeep was developed and became the Willys MC, and by 1950 the M38 was entering service and would be used alongside the Willys MB in Korea. In 1960 Ford started to produce the last version – the M151. This and the M38 would see extensive service in Vietnam and with the Israeli Defence Forces during the Arab-Israeli wars of the 1960s and 1970s. The M151, better known as the "Mutt", was withdrawn from service with the US forces due to its nasty habit of turning over. Now armed with TOW anti-tank guided missiles, the Jeep is very much a modern tank killer, but still carries a number of machine-guns for close support. The Jeep has proved over time to be a real multi-role vehicle but is now being replaced in service by the Humvee; however, it has attained cult status with private military vehicle collectors.

LEFT: **An American captain using the direct sighting device for the 120mm/4.72in rockets. This is the prototype vehicle and has only been fitted with six rockets. These vehicles carried no reload missiles, which were carried in a supply truck. These vehicles proved very popular as they could deliver a big punch close to the front line.**

Jeep MR LRDG Vehicle

Country: USA
Entered service: 1941
Crew: 3
Weight: 2,540kg/2.5 tons
Dimensions: Length – 3.33m/11ft
 Height – 1.14m/3ft 9in
 Width – 1.57m/5ft 2in
Armament: Main – 2 x twin Vickers K
 7.7mm/0.303in machine-guns
 Secondary – Bren 7.7mm/0.303in light
 machine-gun
Armour: None
Powerplant: Willys 441 or 442 Go Devil 4-cylinder
 45kW/60hp petrol engine
Performance: Speed – 104kph/65mph
 Range – 900km/559 miles

LEFT: **Side view of the Ram Kangaroo, clearly showing the forward storage boxes built into the hull of the vehicle. The running-gear on this vehicle is very similar to that on the Grant Mk 3 tank.**
ABOVE: **A Canadian Ram Kangaroo of the 79th Armoured Division. The driver's forward hatch is in the open position, and next to it is the close-defence machine-gun turret. There are storage boxes built into the front mudguards.**

Kangaroo Armoured Infantry Carrier

Just after D-Day, the Canadian II Corps deployed Priest SPGs with their guns removed as infantry carriers in Normandy. Each of these vehicles could carry 12 men, but there were problems with their height so the Canadians looked for a better alternative. They had been using the Ram tank as a training vehicle in Britain before being equipped with the Sherman, so some 500 tanks were sitting idle. The Canadians moved these to their base workshop in France, which was codenamed "Kangaroo", where they were converted into armoured infantry carriers. The turret, ammunition bins and any other unnecessary bits were removed and two bench seats fitted in the open turret space.

The Ram was built in Canada using many of the parts from the American M3 tank. The Ram Mk II versions had an auxiliary machine-gun turret in the front of the vehicle that would be retained in the Kangaroo for close support and self-defence. Some later versions did not have this turret but a standard Sherman hull machine-gun. These vehicles were standard British right-hand drive with either the auxiliary turret or bow machine-gun on the left. Debussing was a problem because the troops were exposed as they jumped down from the top of the vehicle. However, the worst problem was getting the men into the vehicle, so very quickly climbing rungs were welded to the sides as a field modification. The infantry could not use their weapons from the vehicle and there was no overhead protection for the troops once inside. In addition to its infantry carrier role, the Kangaroo was also used for bringing forward ammunition, fuel and other supplies to troops under fire.

The Ram Kangaroo entered service piecemeal with the Canadians in September 1944 but in December 1944, these minor units were combined to become the 1st Canadian Armoured Carrier Regiment, joining up with the British 49th Armoured Personnel Carrier Regiment, which came under the command of the 79th Armoured Division. The first operation for the Ram Kangaroo was the assault on Le Havre – the last one was taking the 7th Infantry Division into Hamburg on May 3, 1945.

Ram Kangaroo Armoured Personnel Carrier	
Country: Canada	
Entered service: 1944	
Crew: 2 plus 10 infantry	
Weight: 25,400kg/25 tons	
Dimensions: Length – 5.79m/19ft	
Height –1.91m/6ft 3in	
Width – 2.77m/9ft 1in	
Armament: Main – None	
Secondary – 7.7mm/0.303in Browning machine-gun	
Armour: Maximum – 60mm/2.36in	
Powerplant: Continental R-975 298kW/400hp petrol engine	
Performance: Speed – 40kph/25mph	
Range – 232km/144 miles	

LEFT: **A Ram Kangaroo loaded with troops, moving through the Low Countries, 1944. The rear of the vehicle is covered with personal kit. The lack of any climbing ladders on the curved cast hull shows why the Kangaroo was difficult to climb into in full kit.**

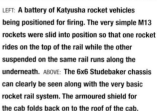

LEFT: **A battery of Katyusha rocket vehicles being positioned for firing. The very simple M13 rockets were slid into position so that one rocket rides on the top of the rail while the other suspended on the same rail runs along the underneath.** ABOVE: **The 6x6 Studebaker chassis can clearly be seen along with the very basic rocket rail system. The armoured shield for the cab folds back on to the roof of the cab.**

Katyusha BM-13 132mm Rocket Launcher

The BM-13 rocket launcher was the first self-propelled artillery weapon produced in quantity by the Soviet Union. This system was given a number of cover names, one being Kostikov Guns, but was officially designated the Guards' Mortars. The popular nickname for the vehicle was "Katyusha", a diminutive form of Katerina, which was the title of a popular piece of music at the time.

Development started on the M-132 in 1938 and at first was not very successful, mainly because the rockets were fired over the side of the vehicle. The first chassis used was the ZiS-5 truck, and with the rocket rails now mounted longitudinally, it proved to be very successful and was placed on test in August 1939. Production started in 1940 with the Soviet Army designating the vehicle BM-13-16.

Several different truck chassis were used as rocket launchers for the Katyusha system, most of them lend-lease vehicles from Canada and the United States. The most common mount was the 2,540kg/2.5-ton 6x6 Studebaker truck of which over 100,000 had been sent to the Soviet Union. This vehicle was selected for its superior cross-country performance and reliability, with nearly 10,000 being converted into Katyusha. The Soviets used the chassis, engine and cab of the Studebaker, leaving the rear for the rocket rail system. The cab was covered in anti-blast armour that covered the windscreen to protect it from the rocket motor blast. The Studebaker and its Hercules JXD engine would be copied and built after World War II by the Soviet Union.

These vehicles were at first issued to special units under the control of the NKVD (Soviet Secret Police) with the first combat action taking place at Orsha in July 1941. It had a devastating effect on the average German soldier and was given the German nickname of "Stalin's Organ". The Soviets would mount several other types of rocket on the basic vehicle, the largest of these, the M-30 300mm/11.8in, entering service in 1944. The battle for Berlin in 1945 would see over 400 Katyusha batteries bombarding the Germans. This system finally left Soviet service in 1980.

LEFT: **The rear of the BM-13 showing the rear supporting jacks that were lowered when firing. The launching platform had very little traverse so the whole vehicle was aimed at the target.**

Katyusha BM-13 132mm Rocket Launcher

Country: USSR
Entered service: 1941
Crew: 4
Weight: 6,096kg/6 tons
Dimensions: Length – 7.47m/24ft 6in
Height – 3.05m/10ft with rocket rails in the down position
Width – 2.21m/7ft 3in
Armament: Main – 16 x 132mm/5.2in rockets
Secondary – None
Armour: Maximum – 5mm/0.2in
Powerplant: Studebaker Hercules JXD 6-cylinder 65kW/87hp petrol engine
Performance: Speed – 72kph/45mph
Range – 370km/230 miles

Kfz 13/14 Medium Armoured Car

This was a medium 4x2 car based on the chassis of the Adler Standard 6 passenger car. In 1932 the German Army issued a requirement for this kind of vehicle, and after extensive trials it was placed into production in late 1933, entering service in 1934. Being inexpensive and simple to produce, it very quickly appeared in relatively large numbers, being issued to cavalry units as a reconnaissance vehicle.

The engine was mounted in the front with a 4-speed gear box which drove a conventional rear axle. The hull was box-shaped with an open top and all-welded construction. The Kfz 13 had the driver in the front, with the vehicle gunner and commander sitting in the rear. The machine-gun was pedestal mounted and had a limited traverse with the main field of fire to the front. There was no radio set in the vehicle, and consequently all communication was done by means of flags. The Kfz 14 was an unarmed radio car with a crew of three, with a large frame aerial mounted above the crew compartment that when not in use could be folded down flush with the top of the crew compartment. These vehicles were known popularly by their crews as "*badewannen*" (bath-tubs). Being two-wheel drive the vehicle had a poor cross-country ability, which was not helped by also having a high centre of gravity. The 8mm/0.315in armour plate also gave very little protection to the crew.

These vehicles were built as training and reconnaissance cars for the new German Army. Normally a section of Kfz 13 reconnaissance cars would operate alongside one Kfz 14 radio car. Both vehicles were due to be replaced by the Sd Kfz 221 by 1939, but war came too soon and a large number of both the Kfz 13 and the Kfz 14 were still in front-line service. They would see action in Poland, the invasion of the Low Countries and France during 1939–40. Some were still acting as reconnaissance vehicles for non-motorized infantry units during the invasion of Russia in 1941.

TOP: **A mixed column of Kfz 13 and 14 armoured cars moving along a road. The very high radio aerial frame can be clearly seen on the second car.**

ABOVE: **The very clean and simple design of the car is apparent, but the wheels of this vehicle were very easily damaged.**

Kfz 13/14 Medium Armoured Car

Country: Germany
Entered service: 1934
Crew: 2 (Kfz 13) and 3 (Kfz 14)
Weight: 2,235.2kg/2.2 tons
Dimensions: Length – 4.17m/13ft 8in
　　　　　　Height – 1.45m/4ft 9in
　　　　　　Width – 1.68m/5ft 6in
Armament: Main – 7.92mm/0.312in MG13
　　　　　　machine-gun (Kfz 13)
　　　　　　Secondary – Small arms
Armour: Maximum – 8mm/0.315in
Powerplant: Adler 6-cylinder 45kW/60hp
　　　　　　petrol engine
Performance: Speed – 70kph/44mph
　　　　　　Range – 300km/186 miles

LEFT: **The driver of this vehicle has his seat in the raised position so that he has good all-round vision. The gunner is in his normal position which is a little exposed.**

LEFT: **A Lanchester of the RNAS with all the hatches in the open position. Additional water storage for the radiator has been fitted to the side of the engine. The wire wheels were standard fit for this car.** ABOVE: **The rear of a Lanchester armoured car with the rear doors open; this was the main entrance and exit for all the crew. This vehicle is operating in Russia and has been fitted with additional armour to protect the gun barrel.**

Lanchester Armoured Car

After the Rolls-Royce, the Lanchester was the most numerous type of armoured car produced by the British in World War I. Designed by the Admiralty Air Department for the RNAS Armoured Car Section operating in France, the prototype was produced in December 1914, using the Lanchester Sporting Forty touring car chassis, with production following in early 1915. A number of changes were made to the basic chassis, the main ones being that the suspension and chassis were strengthened to take the extra weight of the armour plate, and dual wheels were fitted to the rear axle to improve the vehicle handling. The Lanchester had sloping armour over the front and bonnet of the car and the engine was mounted beside the driver. While the engine was powerful and very reliable, and also used an advanced epicyclic gearbox, the Lanchester could never get over the problem of the weak chassis that would be its Achilles' heel.

In 1915 the RNAS armoured cars were handed over to the army, which looked at the great variety of cars it had acquired and decided to standardize on the Rolls-Royce. This standardization would make resupply of spare parts much easier. The Lanchesters were all sent back to Britain for overhaul before being despatched to Russia with No.1 Squadron RNAS Armoured Car Division. The squadron arrived in Russia in 1916 and would remain there for a year fighting in Persia, Romania and Galicia, and operating in climates ranging from desert to near-Arctic conditions. During their time in Russia these cars covered 85,295km/53,000 miles. The cars were deployed in a manner that would become the standard for AFV warfare in the 20th century. Acting as scouts and armed raiders, they operated well forward of the infantry following in their armoured trucks. When operating alongside the infantry, they would act as fire-support vehicles. Their final operation was as part of the unsuccessful Russian Brusilov Offensive of mid-1917. After this Russia descended into civil war and the RNAS Armoured Car Division was withdrawn back to Britain.

LEFT: **A Lanchester 6x6 Mk 1 armoured car. This was a vast improvement over the early 4x2 Lanchester. The new vehicle was armed with three machine-guns, two in the turret and one in the hull next to the driver.**

Lanchester Armoured Car

Country: UK
Entered service: 1915
Crew: 4
Weight: 4,876.8kg/4.8 tons
Dimensions: Length – 4.88m/16ft
Height – 2.29m/7ft 6in
Width – 1.93m/6ft 4in
Armament: Main – Vickers 7.7mm/0.303in machine-gun
Secondary – 7.7mm/0.303in Lewis gun, and small arms
Armour: Maximum – 8mm/0.315in
Powerplant: Lanchester 6-cylinder 45kW/60hp petrol engine
Performance: Speed – 80kph/50mph
Range – 290km/180 miles

LEFT: A Loyd Carrier towing a 6pdr AT gun and carrying the whole crew waits to pass a German Panther tank. The vehicle is overloaded with ammunition and personal equipment. ABOVE: The drive-shaft of the vehicle is in a very exposed frontal position, but this made it easy to maintain. The front of the carrier is very clean and well sloped. This vehicle has the canvas weather protecting roof in the raised position.

Loyd Carrier

The Loyd Carrier was developed by Captain Vivian Loyd in 1939 as a simple cross-country tracked vehicle, using many existing components from various vehicle manufacturers. The basic vehicle was based on the 762kg/15cwt 4x2 Fordson truck, with tracks and suspension from Vickers light tanks.

The carrier used a basic Ford engine, radiator, gearbox and transmission, with the engine and radiator being mounted in the rear of the vehicle. The power from the engine was brought forward to the front sprockets, with brakes fitted to the front and rear sprockets. Steering was by means of steering levers that applied the front and rear brakes on one side of the vehicle or the other depending on the direction of turn, but care had to be taken as a track could be easily broken or shed. The vehicle was a simple open box with access either side of the engine in the rear, or over the side to get into the driver's position. An order was placed with Captain Loyd's firm in late 1939 for 200 carriers.

Originally intended as an infantry carrier with a capacity of between eight and ten men, the Loyd was very quickly adapted into various specialist roles. This included mechanical cable laying for the Royal Signals units or as a starting vehicle for tank units, as the Loyd was fitted out as a battery slave unit that was capable of starting tanks or charging batteries. There were also several trials using the carrier as an SPG mount for the 2pdr anti-tank gun and the 25pdr gun howitzer. However, the Loyd was mainly produced and used as a towing vehicle with infantry battalions for the 6pdr (57mm) anti-tank gun and the 107mm/ 4.2in mortar. These carriers were simple to maintain in the field and well-liked by their crews. They were built by the Vivian Loyd Company until 1941 but as demand increased during World War II, production was undertaken by five different companies in several different countries with Ford as the main manufacturer. Some 26,000 vehicles of this type were constructed during the war. A very adaptable vehicle, it was found in all British theatres of war.

RIGHT: The rear of a Loyd Carrier. The engine can be clearly seen in the middle of the vehicle and takes up most of the space. The carrier has a 6pdr gun attached to the hitch. The lack of storage space can also be seen, as four men were carried in this area.

Loyd Carrier

Country: UK
Entered service: 1940
Crew: Various
Weight: 4,064kg/4 tons
Dimensions: Length – 4.14m/13ft 7in
Height – 1.42m/4ft 8in
Width – 2.06m/6ft 9in
Armament: Main – None
Secondary – Small arms
Armour: None
Powerplant: Ford 8-cylinder 63kW/85hp petrol engine
Performance: Speed – 48kph/30mph
Range – 193km/120 miles

Lorraine Schlepper 15cm Self-Propelled Gun

After the fall of France, the Germans captured a large number of AFVs from the French Army and at first placed them in storage. Among these were the Lorraine tractor units. The French had originally built 387 of these. The driver sat in the front, with the engine just behind and a large cargo area in the rear. Converting these vehicles into an SPG carriage was not difficult: the rear cargo area and suspension were strengthened to take the gun mount. The exact number of captured chassis is not known but over 300 were repaired and converted into self-propelled mounts as either an anti-tank weapon or gun howitzer.

In May 1942 the vehicle, armed with the 15cm/5.9in FH13, was demonstrated to Hitler who passed it for further conversion. Initially 60 chassis with 10.5cm/4.13in le FH18, 40 chassis with 15cm/5.9in FH13 and 60 armed with the PaK40 7.5cm/2.95in were converted. Each vehicle was fitted with an open-topped fighting compartment with the main weapon filling most of this area. Most crews fitted a canvas cover over the top that could be quickly removed when necessary. The superstructures were made by Alkett and shipped to Paris where they were fixed to the chassis and issued to German units in France. It was standard practice for captured vehicles to remain in German service in the country where they were

captured. The 15cm/5.9in vehicle had a recoil spade fitted to the rear to help stabilize the vehicle during firing. The armour of the fighting area was very poor and was only just shell-splinter proof.

In July 1942, the first of these conversions arrived in North Africa. Ten were issued to the 21st Panzer Division and eleven to the 15th Panzer Division, and these would take part in the German attack on El Alamein. By November 1942, all the initial batch of vehicles had been destroyed or captured by the British. Large numbers of these vehicles were still available by D-Day, June 6, 1944, when 131 of the PaK40 conversion, 54 of the 15cm/5.9in FH13 and 37 of the FH18 with the 10.5cm/4.13in gun were serviceable.

TOP: A British Crusader tank towing a captured Lorraine Schlepper in the desert of North Africa. The small size of this SPG can be seen against the bulk of the tank. ABOVE: The rear of the Lorraine Schlepper showing the recoil spade in the raised position. When lowered into the ground, this helped to absorb some of the recoil from the gun.

LEFT: The diminutive size of the vehicle is clear in this picture. This allowed the vehicle to be easily hidden. The driver's position is below the gun barrel, with the engine immediately behind the driver.

Lorraine Schlepper 15cm FH13 SPG

Country: Germany
Entered service: 1942
Crew: 5
Weight: 8,636kg/8.5 tons
Dimensions: Length – 5.31m/17ft 5in
Height – 2.23m/7ft 4in
Width – 1.83m/6ft
Armament: Main – 15cm/5.91in sFH13/1
Secondary – 7.92mm/0.312in MG34 machine-gun
Armour: Maximum – 10mm/0.394in
Powerplant: Delahaye 6-cylinder 52kW/70hp petrol engine
Performance: Speed – 35kph/22mph
Range – 135km/84 miles

LEFT: **An M3 with the bad-weather roof-cover in place. This vehicle is fitted with a "pulpit" machine-gun mount over the vehicle commander's position. The armoured shutter for the windscreen is in the "up" position and has been used as a storage shelf for personal kit. The large whip aerial has been pulled over and attached to the front of the vehicle.**

M3 Half-Track Infantry Carrier

The Americans bought two French Citroen-Kegresse half-tracks during 1925 and purchased a further one in 1931. After a number of developments, they married the White Scout Car with the Kegresse suspension and came up with what would become the classic American half-track of World War II. The Car Half-Track M2 and the M3 Carrier Personnel Half-Track were two of the first half-track vehicles produced by the Americans in that conflict. The M2 was designed as a reconnaissance vehicle and as a prime mover for guns of up to 155mm/6.1in, while the M3 was designed as a personnel carrier for armoured divisions and motorized artillery. The distinction between the two vehicles very quickly disappeared once committed to action. These models were approved for production in October 1940 and entered service in 1941 with the American Army.

Under the competitive bidding system of the US Ordnance Department, the lowest bidder is awarded the construction contract. The Autocar company won the bid and secured the construction contract, but was very quickly joined by Diamond T and White. Total production would be 12,499 M3 vehicles of all marks, while 11,415 M2 carriers of all marks were built. It was agreed by the three manufacturers that as many parts as possible would be interchangeable between the M2 and M3.

The M3 could carry 13 men: the driver, commander and co-driver in the front with 10 infantry behind. The back of the vehicle had five seats on each side looking into the middle, with a large door in the rear. The armour on the rear crew compartment was only 7mm/0.28in thick, while that on the cab doors, windscreen shutter and radiator grill was 12.7mm/0.5in.

ABOVE: **The gunner's "pulpit" can be clearly seen on this vehicle, which is carrying four machine-guns. The vehicle exterior is covered with personal kit as there is no room inside to store the equipment of the ten-man crew.**

Armament was very varied and a lot depended on the crew of the vehicle. Officially there were to be two machine-guns, a 12.7mm/50cal in the front and a 7.62mm/30cal in the rear on a pintle mount. On the outside of the vehicle down each side of the rear compartment were two racks for carrying 24 anti-personnel mines.

In 1943 the M3A1 was developed and went into production in October of that year. The main improvement was to the armament of the vehicle. A M49 ring mount was fitted over the co-driver's position to take a single 12.7mm/50cal machine-gun. In the rear, three pintle sockets were installed each mounting a 7.62mm/30cal machine-gun. Diamond T was the main contractor and 2,862 of these vehicles were built before the contract was cancelled in January 1944. The last M2 was built in March 1944, and the last M3 was produced in February 1944 as sufficient of this type were stockpiled.

The M3A2 which was due to replace the M2, M2A1, M3, and M3A1 was going to be a universal carrier with movable storage lockers inside the vehicle. Depending on the role, it could be able to carry between 5 and 12 personnel with a great variety of weapons. The vehicle was passed by the Armoured Board in October 1943, but was never placed into serious production.

Production of brand new vehicles might have ceased in early 1944, but vehicle modification was still going strong with 2,270 M3 carriers upgraded to M3A1 standard. Personnel kit storage was very poor in the vehicle as it was never designed to act as a home-from-home for the section of men who lived and fought from their vehicle. The crews would personalize their vehicles by welding extra storage racks on the outside, in particular on either side of the door at the rear. The racks for mines on the side of the vehicle were converted to carry boxes of food and other important personal items.

One extremely important characteristic of these half-tracks was that the crew could fight from the inside of the vehicle in some safety. As more tracked gun tractors became available the half-track was passed over to the infantry. These vehicles could be found in every Allied army during World War II and on every front. In 1980 the M2/M3 could still be found in service with 22 different armed forces and some of these vehicles can still be found in service with the Israeli Defence Force reserve units.

TOP: **The driver's cab in the M3 is relatively spacious and has a very simple layout. The driver and vehicle commander have very good vision from the cab of the vehicle, but it is roofless.** ABOVE: **Access to the engine of the M3 was very good and it was simple to work on or maintain. The armoured louvers of the radiator grill can be open or closed from the driver's position.**

LEFT AND BELOW LEFT: **The front of these vehicles are fitted with a winch. The rack on the side of the crew compartment was originally intended for the storage of landmines. These vehicles are fitted with only a single machine-gun.**

M3A1 Carrier Personnel Half-Track

Country: USA
Entered service: 1943
Crew: 3 plus 10 infantry
Weight: 10,160kg/10 tons
Dimensions: Length – 6.14m/20ft 3in
Height – 2.69m/8ft 10in
Width – 2.22m/7ft 3in
Armament: Main – 12.7mm/0.5in Browning machine-gun
Secondary – 3 x 7.62mm/0.3in machine-guns
Armour: Maximum – 12.7mm/0.5in
Powerplant: White 160 AX 6-cylinder 95kW/128hp petrol engine
Performance: Speed – 64kph/45mph
Range – 280km/200 miles

LEFT: **This vehicle is fitted with a roller on the front that helps the vehicle climb over obstructions. The crew of the M3A1 vehicle were very exposed in the rear of the car.**

M3A1 Scout Car

The forerunner of this car was designed in 1933 by White and was based on a 4x4 van chassis produced by their subsidiary Indiana. The prototype (T7) was an open-topped scout car, armed with two 12.7mm/50cal and two 7.62mm/30cal machine-guns, which carried a crew of four men. The vehicle was placed into production and was given the designation M1, with a total production of 76 cars.

The M2 followed in 1935. It was bigger and more powerful and could carry a crew of seven, but only 20 of these vehicles were produced. White went on to produce the M3 version of this scout car and had delivered 64 to the US Army by 1938. Marmon-Herrington

also produced a number of these scout cars for Iran.

The M3A1 entered service in 1940 and would remain in production until 1944, by which time some 20,856 scout cars had been built. Fast and very reliable, it was well-liked by its crews, but its cross-country performance was poor and it was soon replaced by the half-track for many tasks. To help improve its off-road capability a roller was fitted to the front of the car. The open fighting compartment was a serious weakness – the men were very exposed and the rear was a grenade trap. However, it was fitted with the Tourelle skate rail that allowed the machine-guns to give all-round fire. General Patton used one as a command vehicle but had additional armour fitted and raised around the fighting compartment. The M3A1E1 was developed to increase the range and fuel economy of the vehicle. This model was fitted with the 58kW/78hp Buda-Lanova diesel engine and had a speed of

LEFT: **The driver's cab has a very simple layout. The dashboard has just two instrument dials and five switches, while the vehicle commander has a glove box. The wiper motors are mounted above the windscreen.**

ABOVE: **This British M3A1 Scout car belongs to the 11th Armoured Division and was photographed in Normandy in 1944. The front of the vehicle has been fitted with a wire-cutter pole, and has had its roller removed.**

87kph/54mph. All of these vehicles, the total production of which was 3,340, were sent to Russia.

Most of the M3 scout cars in British service were used in a secondary role, being issued to units like the engineers, signals and medical corps. Some of these vehicles were to remain in service with a number of countries after World War II, particularly the French.

M3A1 Scout Car

Country: USA
Entered service: 1940
Crew: 2 plus 6 infantry
Weight: 5,618kg/5.53 tons
Dimensions: Length – 5.62m/18ft 5in
Height – 2m/6ft 6in
Width – 2.03m/6ft 8in
Armament: Main – 12.7mm/0.5in Browning
machine-gun
Secondary – 2 x 7.62mm/0.3in Browning
machine-guns
Armour: Maximum – 12.7mm/0.5in
Powerplant: White Hercules JXD 6-cylinder
71kW/95hp petrol engine
Performance: Speed – 105kph/65mph
Range – 400km/250 miles

M3 75mm Gun Motor Carriage

The half-track served as the carrier for numerous self-propelled weapons, but relatively few of these would be standardized. The notable exception would be the anti-aircraft mounts that would remain in service for years after the end of World War II.

Development was started in June 1941 in response to a request from both the British and American armies for a mobile self-propelled anti-tank gun. The project was to mount the M1897 A4 75mm/2.95in gun in an M3 half-track. This gun was an American copy of the French 75mm/2.95in from World War I. The original gun mount was the M2A3, but there was a shortage of these and so the M2A2 was substituted on the M3A1 half-track conversion.

Autocar were given the first contract to convert these vehicles and built 86 in 1941. Fifty were sent to the Philippines to help bolster the forces there. Autocar produced a total of 2,202 of these conversions but due to a shortage of guns, 113 of these vehicles were converted back into personnel carriers.

A number of conversions were made to the basic carrier, these being the moving of the fuel tanks to the rear of the fighting compartment and adding a new sub-floor to the rear of the fighting compartment, along with storage for 59 rounds of 75mm/2.95in ammunition. Initially the vehicle crew was four but this was quickly increased to five. The gun shield at first allowed the gun crew to stand full height behind the gun but this gave the vehicle a high silhouette so it was made smaller. First used in the defence of the Philippines against the Japanese, the vehicle proved to be a very good gun platform. The next major operation it was used in was "Torch", the invasion of North Africa by the Allies in 1943. In British service, these vehicles were known as "75mm SP Autocar" and were used by HQ troops of armoured car reconnaissance units. Even after being declared obsolete in September 1944, they would remain in service with many units until the end of the war.

ABOVE: **A US Marine Corps vehicle is landed on a beach from an LCT (Landing Craft Tank). The vehicle has been fitted with three extra machine-guns. The front of the half-track has also been fitted with a winch, which proved very useful in the jungle fighting.**

ABOVE: **A battery of American half-tracks armed with 75mm/2.95in guns belonging to Patton's forces in Sicily. Most of the personal kit has been placed at the rear of the vehicle and on the ground.**
LEFT: **A line-up of five gun half-tracks at their training ground in the USA in 1942. All the vehicles have been fitted with the undirtching roller.**

M3 75mm Gun Motor Carriage

Country: USA
Entered service: 1941
Crew: 5
Weight: 10,160kg/10 tons
Dimensions: Length – 6.14m/20ft 3in
  Height – 2.26m/7ft 5in
  Width – 2.22m/7ft 3in
Armament: Main – 75mm/2.95in M1897 A4
  Secondary – 7.62mm/0.3in machine-gun
Armour: Maximum – 12.7mm/0.5in
Powerplant: White 160 AX 6-cylinder 95kW/128hp
  petrol engine
Performance: Speed – 64kph/45mph
  Range – 280km/200 miles

M5 Half-Track Personnel Carrier

Because demand was out-pacing production at the White Company factories building the M2 and M3, the M5 was built by the International Harvester Company (IHC). This new production facility started in April 1942 and produced 9,291 half-track carriers, most of them going to Lend-Lease. The M5 was similar in design to the M2 and M3 half-tracks, but their parts were not interchangeable as IHC used many of their own components in their vehicle. Obvious changes were the curved rear corners of the rear fighting compartment, the flat front mudguards and the use of homogeneous armour plate which increased the vehicle's weight.

The M5 entered service in December 1942 and remained in production until October 1943, when it was replaced by the M5A1. Like the M2A1 and the M3A1,

the improvement was in armament and the introduction of the M49 ring-mount. Between October and December 1943, 1,859 M5A1s were built, with a further extension to the contract of 1,100 vehicles with completion in March 1944. In April 1943 it was decided that IHC should produce a universal carrier to the same specification as the M2 and M3 carriers, but like these other universal carriers, the M5A2 was never put into production. The M5 itself would remain in production until June 1945.

The last version of this half-track was the M9A1 and this was the same as the M2A1. There was no basic version of the M9 as it was already fitted with the M49 ring-mount and the extra machine-gun mounts in the rear of the vehicle. Total production of the M9A1 was 3,433, with nearly all going into British service.

ABOVE LEFT AND ABOVE: **This M5 is covered in personal equipment, armed with three machine-guns and is fitted with a winch on the front of the vehicle. The shipping panel is still on this vehicle below the commander's door.**

Large numbers of M5 and M5A1 half-tracks were sent to the Soviet Union along with M17 anti-aircraft units. In British service, the M5 and the M9A1 were converted into several specialist roles such as radio and medical half-tracks. Other large users were the Royal Engineers (RE) and the Royal Electrical and Mechanical Engineers (REME). Large A-frames were fitted to the front so these vehicles could act as recovery vehicles in the field. They remained in British service until 1966.

LEFT: **Like the M3, the M5 was fitted with a storage rack for landmines but in combat it was never used for this purpose. The driver's side window is unglazed, having just a metal shutter with a very small vision slit cut in it.**

M5 Half-Track Personnel Carrier

Country: USA
Entered service: 1942
Crew: 3 plus 10 infantry
Weight: 10,668kg/10.5 tons
Dimensions: Length – 6.33m/20ft 9in
 Height – 2.31m/7ft 7in
 Width – 2.21m/7ft 3in
Armament: Main – 12.7mm/0.5in Browning machine-gun
 Secondary – 3 x 7.62mm/0.3in Browning machine-guns
Armour: Maximum – 10mm/0.394in
Powerplant: International Red 450B 6-cylinder 107kW/143hp petrol engine
Performance: Speed – 61kph/38mph
 Range – 201km/125 miles

M8 Greyhound Light Armoured Car

Armoured cars have acted as the armed reconnaissance vehicle of the American Army for a long time. During 1940–41, the Americans were able to observe the war in Europe and study the new operational trends, and so develop a number of new vehicles. Four companies entered the competition for the new heavy armoured car, and in 1941 the Ford T22 was chosen for this role. It went into production in late 1942 with the first vehicles entering service in early 1943, but the 37mm/1.46in main gun was considered to be too small by 1942 for a "heavy" designation, so the new car was given the revised designation of Light Armoured Car. The M8 remained in production until 1945, by which time 8,523 vehicles had been built.

The M8 was a 6x6 lightweight vehicle of all-welded construction, with the driving compartment in the front, turret in the middle and engine at the rear. The turret had an open roof and was hand-operated by a crew of two, while the other two crew members occupied the driver's position in the front of the vehicle. It had excellent cross-country ability, a low silhouette, and plenty of room for the crew. One weakness was its thin floor armour, so most crews covered the floor with sandbags to help protect themselves against the blast of a mine.

A variation on the M8 was the M20, which was basically the same vehicle except that the turret was removed. The fighting compartment was also cut away and fitted with a ring-mount for a 12.7mm/50cal machine-gun. The M20 was used as a reconnaissance and supply vehicle, and some 3,791 were built.

A few M8s were supplied to the British but it was not liked, as the armour was considered to be too thin. In 1973, the French demonstrated a new version of the M8 armed with the H90 90mm/3.54in turret. Some 22 countries still operated the M8 in 1976, and the Brazilian Army fitted their M8 cars with guided AT missiles.

ABOVE: **The clean lines of this vehicle are very apparent as is the two-man turret. It is one of the prototypes, and as such has no personal kit stored on the car.** LEFT: **The roof hatches above the driver's and co-driver's positions are open and folded to the side. The headlights have a protective frame over them and the turret has been fitted with a heavy machine-gun.**

RIGHT: **The wheels and chassis of the M8 are well protected from damage by angled covers. The driver's and co-driver's hatches are fully closed and, as can be seen, the vision slits are small and making forward vision very limited. A tie-down rail is fitted around the middle of the turret.**

M8 Greyhound Light Armoured Car

Country: USA
Entered service: 1943
Crew: 4
Weight: 8,128kg/8 tons
Dimensions: Length – 5m/16ft 5in
Height – 2.25m/7ft 5in
Width – 2.54m/8ft 4in
Armament: Main – 37mm/1.46in gun M6, and coaxial 7.62mm/0.3in machine-gun
Secondary – 12.7mm/0.5in machine-gun
Armour: Maximum – 19mm/0.75in
Powerplant: Hercules JXD 6-cylinder 82kW/110hp petrol engine
Performance: Speed – 89kph/55mph
Range – 563km/350 miles

M8 75mm Howitzer Motor Carriage

The American Army made repeated requests for a close-support howitzer and these were met in early 1942 by the appearance of the T30 half-track howitzer. This was developed as an expedient project in 1941 and entered production very quickly, with some 500 contracted to be built. However, only 320 were actually produced. The vehicle used the M1A1 75mm/2.95in pack howitzer, mounting the weapon on a new tracked chassis that was just becoming available.

This new chassis was the M5 and the first test vehicle built was the T41 Howitzer Motor Carriage, in which the howitzer was mounted on the hull centreline.

The vehicle existed only as a mock-up and was abandoned in favour of a new design – the T47. This new vehicle, now named the M8, still used the M5 chassis, but this time the weapon, the M2 or M3 75mm/2.95in howitzer, was mounted in a rotating turret. The 75mm/2.95in turret was much larger than the M5 turret and so the hull had to be altered to fit it, with the driver's hatches moved forward on to the glacis plate. The M8 was fitted with two V8 Cadillac engines, and proved to be a reliable vehicle. A mock-up was produced in April 1942 and was approved, with production starting in September 1942. The total number of vehicles built was 1,778 with production finishing in January 1944.

As the M7, a 105mm/4.13in howitzer mounted on the Sherman chassis, began to appear in greater numbers, the M8 was replaced in armoured formations and passed to reconnaissance units to replace half-track mounted close-support weapons. The M8 was also passed on to the Free French forces and other Allied nations. In the Pacific, the M8 was used in the close-support role by the Marine Corps and was well-liked,

ABOVE LEFT: **The large glacis plate on this vehicle is very striking, and has the driver's and co-driver's hatches recessed into it. Above these hatches each man has his own periscope.** ABOVE: **Two M8 SPGs are leading two half-tracks and a 2,540kg/2.5-ton truck down a road in Britain. In combat these vehicles would be covered in personal kit and tow an ammunition trailer.**

as it could bring a large weapon close to enemy positions to help extract them from caves and other dug-in positions. The M8 was often fitted with an ammunition trailer in the European theatre of operations as it only carried 46 rounds in the vehicle itself.

LEFT: **An M8 caught up in a traffic jam with a column of Jeeps. The turret of this vehicle is fitted with a manual traverse only, as it is an artillery vehicle and not a tank.**

M8 75mm Howitzer Motor Carriage

Country: USA
Entered service: 1942
Crew: 4
Weight: 15,605kg/15.45 tons
Dimensions: Length – 4.41m/14ft 6in
Height – 2.32m/7ft 7in
Width – 2.24m/7ft 4in
Armament: Main – 75mm/2.95in M2 howitzer
Secondary –12.7mm/0.5in Browning
machine-gun
Armour: Maximum – 44mm/1.73in
Powerplant: 2 x Cadillac V8 series 42 82kW/110hp
petrol engine
Performance: Speed – 56kph/35mph
Range – 210km/130 miles

M12 155mm Gun Motor Carriage

The M12 was one of the earliest self-propelled mounts to be designed, but was one of the last weapons to enter active service in World War II. Development started in June 1941 with a test model being ready in February 1942. The vehicle was based on the M3 chassis and mounted a 155mm/6.1in gun, the M1918, an old French weapon used as a towed field gun by the Americans during World War I and then placed into storage as obsolete.

Originally this vehicle was rejected by the army as they could see no need for such a powerful weapon on a self-propelled mount. The army had plenty of towed guns which it felt would more than meet any future requirement. The Ordnance Department disagreed, feeling there was a specific need for this kind of piece, and ordered 50 vehicles in March 1942. This order was overruled by the

Supply Board until the vehicle had been fully tested by the Artillery Department. The Artillery Department reported back in agreement with the Ordnance Department that there was a need for the M12 and recommending that it should be placed into production. This started in late 1943, but for 100 vehicles only, and was completed in March 1944.

The vehicle had a two-man compartment at the front for the driver and the vehicle commander. The engine was in the middle of the vehicle just behind the driver's compartment with an open gun area at the rear. There was only room for 10 rounds of ammunition and so the rest of the crew travelled on the M30 supply vehicle, which was an M12 without the gun and its mounting carrying an additional 40 rounds of ammunition and the other four men of the gun crew under a canvas cover.

ABOVE LEFT: **An American battery of M12 vehicles has been placed into the sustained fire position. The guns have been driven up and on to a raised ramp which helps increase the elevation of the gun.**
ABOVE: **The open nature of the fighting compartment of this vehicle can clearly be seen. The travel lock for the gun barrel is lying on the glacis plate between the driver's and co-driver's position.**

June 1944 saw 74 of these vehicles arrive in Europe and they made a big difference instantly. They were used as "door knockers" by the Americans during their attacks on the Siegfried Line. One of these guns would be brought forward and the Germans inside the defensive position were offered the options of surrender or having their bunker blown apart around them.

LEFT: **An American M12 being readied to fire. The target cannot be far away as the gunner is checking the visual sight and the barrel is flat. The gun might be about to be used as a "door knocker" on a fixed-defence structure.**

M12 155mm Gun Motor Carriage

Country: USA
Entered service: 1944
Crew: 6
Weight: 29,464kg/29 tons
Dimensions: Length – 6.73m/22ft 1in
Height – 2.69m/8ft 10in
Width – 2.67m/8ft 9in
Armament: Main – 155mm/6.1in M1918M1 gun
Secondary – 12.7mm/0.5in Browning machine-gun
Armour: Maximum – 50mm/1.97in
Powerplant: Continental R-975 Radial
263kW/353hp petrol engine
Performance: Speed – 39kph/24mph
Range – 225km/140 miles

M15 Multiple Gun Motor Carriage

The M15 was developed to provide an improved anti-aircraft capability for the American armoured formations as the M13 and M14 were not producing the desired results. Using the M3 chassis, the rear fighting compartment was removed and replaced by a flat bed on which the M42 multiple gun-mount was placed in a turret. The gun turret had a 360-degree traverse while its armament consisted of a fully automatic 37mm/1.46in gun and two 12.7mm/50cal machine-guns, with storage for 240 37mm/1.46in and 3,400 12.7mm/50cal rounds. It was designed to engage both ground and aerial targets, the 37mm/1.46in gun having a rate of fire of 40 rounds per minute and the 12.7mm/50cal 500 rounds per minute, giving the vehicle enough ammunition for six minutes firing. Autocar produced the

initial order of 600 vehicles between February and April 1943 and they entered service in May 1943. The M15 proved to be very effective in action and consequently a new order was placed for more vehicles, but this could not be fulfilled as there were no more M42 gun mounts and so a new mount was required for this development.

The new vehicle was the M15A1 which used the M54 gun mount. There was very little difference between the two vehicles except that in the M15, the 12.7mm/50cal machine-guns are mounted above the 37mm/1.46in gun, and in the M15A1 it is the other way round. Autocar again were the producers of the vehicle, with production starting in October 1943 and finishing in February 1944 during which time a total of 1,652 vehicles were built. To give the gun crew

ABOVE LEFT: **A prototype T28E1 vehicle dug in beside a fortress in Tunisia, North Africa, in 1943. These early vehicles had no crew protection and were fitted with water-cooled machine-guns.** ABOVE: **A M15A1 which has been fitted with a roller on the front of the vehicle. To give the gun crew some protection a three-sided turret was fitted around the gun mounting.**

more room to operate, the ammunition storage in the turret was reduced to enough for just five minutes firing time.

The M15 would see action in Sicily, Italy and northern Europe, while the M15A1 would only see service in Italy and northern Europe. These vehicles were greatly valued by the infantry as close-support guns, but one major weakness was the lack of protection for the crew. They would also see service in the Korean War and would remain in American service until late in the 1950s.

RIGHT: **A T28 prototype vehicle on test at the Aberdeen Proving Ground in 1942. The men standing beside the gun mount are the machine-gun magazine changers. The very exposed position of the crew can be clearly seen.**

M15 Multiple Gun Motor Carriage

Country: USA
Entered service: 1943
Crew: 7
Weight: 10,160kg/10 tons
Dimensions: Length – 6.14m/20ft 3in
　　　　Height – 2.44m/8ft
　　　　Width – 2.49m/8ft 2in
Armament: Main – 37mm/1.46in M1A2 automatic gun
　　Secondary – 2 x 12.7mm/0.5in Browning machine-guns
Armour: Maximum – 12.7mm/0.5in
Powerplant: White 160AX 6-cylinder 95kW/128hp petrol engine
Performance: Speed – 64kph/45mph
　　Range – 280km/200 miles

LEFT: **One of the prototype vehicles on test at the Aberdeen Proving Ground in the USA. When they were used in the ground-support role these vehicles were called "Meat Choppers".**
BELOW: **The gun mount for the M16 is the M45D. The low height of this mount required the sides and back of the rear compartment to be capable of folding down.**

M16 Multiple Gun Motor Carriage

Development started in December 1942 on a new vehicle as a replacement for the M13 which mounted the under-powered twin 12.7mm/50cal M33 gun. The improved version, known as the M16, carried the M45 gun mount.

The White Motor Company started production of the M16 in May 1943 and continued until March 1944, with a total production of 2,877 vehicles. The gun mount was placed in the rear fighting area which had been cleared of all the internal fittings. The rear area had no rear door and the tops of the sides were hinged so the guns could fire over the sides and rear of the vehicle. The new turret for the M16 was fitted with four 12.7mm/50cal machine-guns and had to be raised by 152mm/6in so that the guns could clear the sides of the vehicle. The

M16 could carry enough ammunition for eight minutes firing of the M45 gun mount. White were also given a contract to convert 677 M13 vehicles up to M16 standard, while a further 60 vehicles were converted by Diebold Incorporated, bringing total production of the M16 to 3,614 vehicles in all.

The M17 was similar to the M16, the only difference being the chassis, for while the M16 used the M3, the M17 used the M5. International Harvester produced a total of 1,000 M17s between December 1943 and March 1944, and all were sent to the Soviet Union under the Lend-Lease programme.

The M16 would see service on most fronts during World War II. They proved extremely valuable to the Marines in the Pacific as they could bring a large amount of firepower into a concentrated area. These vehicles would remain in service with the American Army until 1958 but the M45 gun mount would

LEFT: **The M16 had very little storage room for ammunition so most of these vehicles had a small ammunition trailer which was pulled behind the vehicle. Some of these systems would remain in active service for 40 years.**

remain in service until 1970. The chassis had changed but the M45 would find widespread use during the Vietnam War mounted on M54 5,080kg/5-ton supply trucks. In 1980 these vehicles were still in service with 12 different countries.

M16 Multiple Gun Motor Carriage

Country: USA
Entered service: 1943
Crew: 5
Weight: 10,160kg/10 tons
Dimensions: Length – 6.14m/20ft 3in
Height – 2.62m/8ft 7in
Width – 2m/6ft 6in
Armament: Main – 4 x 12.7mm/0.5in Browning machine-guns
Secondary – Small arms
Armour: Maximum – 12.7mm/0.5in
Powerplant: White 160AX 6-cylinder 95kW/128hp petrol engine
Performance: Speed – 64kph/45mph
Range – 280km/200 miles

M40 155mm Gun Motor Carriage

At the end of 1943, the American Army decided to standardize their AFV chassis into the Light Weight Combat Team based on the M24 light tank, and the Medium Weight Combat Team based on the M4A3 Sherman tank. The main idea behind this was to make production, the supply of spares and servicing quicker and easier for the troops in the field. Development of this new weapon started in January 1944, following the decision to send the M12 to Europe. The American Army Armoured Force Board still firmly believed that they did not require the M40 but the success of the M12 in active service forced them to change their minds.

The M40 fell into the Medium Weight Combat Team, as it was designed around the M4A3 chassis. This was widened and Horizontal Volute Spring Suspension (HVSS) was fitted. The general layout was the same as the M12 with the driver located in a crew compartment in the front of the vehicle, the engine in the middle and the gun in the rear area. An escape hatch was also fitted into the floor of the driver's compartment just behind the co-driver's position. The fighting compartment was open, as in the M12, because this vehicle was never intended to be deployed in the front line but several miles behind supporting the front-line troops. Like the M12 there was a recoil spade

ABOVE: **The M40 used the same chassis as the M4A3 Sherman tank, which helped to make the supply of spares easier. The gun is fitted with a shield but this gives the gun crew very little protection. The travel-lock for the gun barrel is in the raised position.**

attached to the rear of the vehicle and operated by a hand winch. The M40 would carry a new gun, as supplies of the M1918 had finished, and this would be the 155mm/6.1in M1 or the 203mm/8in howitzer, both very successful towed weapons that had proved themselves in combat. In March 1944, five pilot models were ordered from the Pressed Steel Car Company, with production starting in February 1945 and not finishing until late 1945. Total production for the M40 was 418 vehicles. The upper hull was made of 12.7mm/0.5in homogeneous armour plate, but gave the crew no protection at all as the sides were too low. Development of an armoured cover for the crew area of the M40 was under way but with the ending of World War II, the need for this shelter also ended. The vehicle could not carry a lot of ammunition in the fighting compartment so it was intended to convert some as cargo carriers. These would carry extra ammunition and also the other crew members for the gun. They were never developed because there was a shortage of vehicle chassis as they were urgently needed in northern Europe.

The Americans had problems in breaching the concrete bunkers during the fighting along the Siegfried Line as they had no AFV that could do this, unlike the British who had developed the Churchill AVRE. They got over this by bringing up the M12 to point-blank range (732m/2,400ft), calling on the German defenders inside to surrender and if they failed to do so, then blasting the bunker open. Due to the success of the M12 in breaching these bunkers, a larger weapon was developed to go on the M40 chassis to be used as a siege gun. This carried a 250mm/9.84in short-range mortar, but development was stopped in August 1945 as the war had finished.

The M43, the vehicle carrying the 203mm/8in howitzer, was developed at the same time as the M40, but was not put into production until August 1945. An order for 576 of these weapons had been placed but by the cessation of hostilities, only 48 had been built before the order was cancelled.

The M40s arrived in Europe in time to take part in the final battles in Germany, their first action being the bombardment of Cologne. They would remain in service with the American Army until the late 1950s, having proved their worth during the Korean War. The British Army bought a number of M40 and M43 vehicles from the Americans after the war and these would remain in service until the early 1960s. The M40 proved to be a very reliable and well-liked vehicle, and the men who manned this weapon were known as "long-range snipers" due to the accuracy of the gun.

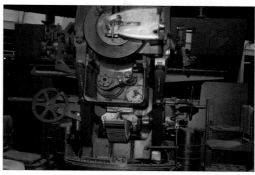

TOP AND ABOVE: **The driver's hatch was changed to an all-round vision cupola on the M40. There is a periscope through the top of the hatch. The lower picture shows the working end of the gun, the breach of which is an interrupted screw breach.**

ABOVE RIGHT: **Three fire extinguishers were attached to each side of the gun shield.**

ABOVE LEFT AND LEFT: **Inside the driver's position. The hand controls are in the middle of the picture with the foot pedals at the bottom. The recoil spade is in the lowered position and just requires the vehicle to reverse to push it into the ground.**

M40 155mm Gun Motor Carriage

Country: USA
Entered service: 1945
Crew: 8
Weight: 40,640kg/40 tons
Dimensions: Length – 9.04m/29ft 9in including gun barrel
 Height – 2.69m/8ft 10in
 Width – 3.15m/10ft 4in
Armament: Main – 155mm/6.1in M1A1 gun
 Secondary – Small arms
Armour: Maximum – 12mm/0.47in
Powerplant: Continental 9-cylinder 295kW/395hp radial petrol engine
Performance: Speed – 38.6kph/24mph
 Range – 161km/100 miles

LEFT: The first version of the Marder III was this vehicle, which is armed with the Soviet 76.2mm/3in gun. Both the high position of the gun and the very exposed crew position can be clearly seen. This was very much a makeshift vehicle with everything piled on top of the chassis. A total of 344 of these vehicles were produced between April and October 1942.

Marder III Self-Propelled Anti-Tank Gun

The Marder, the German name for the marten – a vicious little animal of the weasel family, was a series of three different vehicles built on several different chassis. Production of all three variants started in 1942 with three different manufacturers and in three different countries. They would remain in active service with the German Army until the end of World War II.

The Marder I was built on the captured French Lorraine Schlepper using the PaK40 anti-tank gun as main armament. The conversions were undertaken by a factory in Paris and all vehicles were to be issued to German units based in France. The Germans had captured over 300 of these old vehicles, most of which were converted into self-propelled artillery, but 84 were converted into Marder I anti-tank vehicles. The fighting compartment was at the rear and was surrounded by a sloped superstructure. The PaK40 retained its own gun-shield as a

form of mantle, but the main weakness was the open top to the fighting compartment which was a serious grenade trap.

The Marder II was built on the chassis of the Panzer II, but the German Army was by now questioning whether or not the Panzer II was still capable of combat. The driver's compartment was at the front, the fighting compartment in the middle and the engine at the rear. The main armament was again the excellent PaK40 anti-tank gun. Production started in 1942 and finished in June 1943, with a total of 671 Marder II vehicles being produced. As all Panzer II chassis were being switched to production of the Wespe SPG, production of the Marder II terminated prematurely. However, due to the success of the vehicle more were required, and so between July 1943 and March 1944 a further 73 were built. The fighting compartment was open-topped and open-backed but the

RIGHT: A mid-production Marder III in Italy in 1944. This vehicle has the gun and fighting compartment in the middle of the vehicle, but a much larger armoured shield has been placed around this compartment. The compact size of the Marder can be clearly seen.

LEFT: **The driver's position is forward and under the main gun, and has very limited vision. This vehicle has been hit in the engine and destroyed by fire.**
ABOVE: **The very open fighting compartment of this early Marder shows up well here. The basket on top of the engine deck was used to store personal kit and ammunition.**

front was closed by the gun-shield of the main armament. The Marder II was both very agile and very reliable, and proved to be a very useful combat vehicle. It would see service on all fronts and remained in active service until the end of the war.

The Marder III, based on the PzKpfw 38(t) tank chassis, was built in two versions. By late 1941, the 38(t) was considered both obsolete as a main battle tank and too slow for the reconnaissance role, so all production was changed to the SPG chassis. The first version was very much a makeshift temporary vehicle, using the captured Russian 76.2mm/3in gun. Production started in March 1942 with 24 units per month being built, moving up to 30 units per month by July 1942, with a total production of 344 vehicles. Most were sent to the Eastern Front, but 66 went to join the *Afrika Korps* in North Africa. The gun crew were very exposed in this vehicle and the Russian gun put considerable strain on the 38(t) tank chassis.

The Germans had realized that the first version of the Marder III was wasteful and unsatisfactory but now that the

initial pressing needs of the army had been dealt with, it could be redesigned and improved. The new vehicle was very different to the original with the successful PaK40 gun for its main armament. The driver's compartment in the front was improved with the engine moved to the middle of the vehicle behind the driver and the fighting compartment moved to the rear. These alterations made for a more balanced vehicle and gave the crew better protection, but it was still open-topped. It was built by BMM (*Böhmisch-Mährische Maschinenfabrik*). The original company designation had to be changed as it had a Jewish name in the title, but after the war the company reverted to its original name. Production stopped in May 1944 when the manufacturing facilities were switched to the Hetzer Tank Destroyer, by which time a total of 975 vehicles had been produced.

All the Marder vehicles performed well above their expected level and were a real problem to the Allied troops that came across them. They proved to be very reliable and by January 1945 some 300 were still in action in the German Army.

LEFT: **This is a late-production version of the Marder III. The gun position has been moved to the rear of the vehicle and the front has been completely redesigned. This Marder has a full load of ammunition in the gun position but has been damaged in an air raid.**

Marder III Self-Propelled Anti-Tank Gun

Country: Germany
Entered service: 1943
Crew: 4
Weight: 10,668kg/10.5 tons
Dimensions: Length – 4.95m/16ft 3in
 Height – 2.5m/8ft 2in
 Width – 2.15m/7ft 1in
Armament: Main – 7.5cm/2.95in PaK40/3 gun
 Secondary – 7.92mm/0.312in MG34 machine-gun
Armour: Maximum – 15mm/0.59in
Powerplant: Praga EPA 6-cylinder 112kW/150hp petrol engine
Performance: Speed – 42kph/26mph
 Range – 190km/120 miles

Marmon-Herrington Armoured Cars

South Africa had never produced an AFV until development started on the Marmon-Herrington armoured car. Progress was slow at first but once war was declared this speeded up dramatically. The chassis was made by Ford and imported from Canada, the four-wheel drive was imported from Marmon-Herrington in America and all the armament came from Britain. The armour plate was supplied by local factories and the assembly plants were old railway workshops.

The Mk 1 was only two-wheel drive and this was discovered to have poor cross-country ability. At first the vehicle had a riveted construction but this was quickly changed to an all-welded fabrication. Total production of the Mk 1 was 135 vehicles.

The Mk 2 was very similar in layout to the Mk 1 but was now fitted with four-wheel drive which improved its performance. The hull of the vehicle was quite spacious for the crew of four and had twin doors at the rear. The Mk 2 came in two variations: the Middle East (ME) and the Mobile Field Force (MFF). The ME had a Boys anti-tank rifle in the turret and two mounts on the turret for Bren guns, one being anti-aircraft. There were also flaps on each side of the vehicle for additional Bren guns. The MFF had a 7.7mm/0.303in Vickers machine-gun in the turret and another one in a ball mount on the near side of the vehicle. Total production of these vehicles was 549 MFF and 338 ME, and in the early days of the North African campaign they were the main armoured car used by British forces. A number of Mk 2s were converted with captured Italian and German weapons. The armour was a little thin so on the Mk 3 this was increased.

ABOVE LEFT: **This car has been fitted with a captured German 37mm/1.46in AT gun, which is mounted over the driver's position. A Vickers machine-gun is fitted in the rear.** ABOVE: **This column of cars is being prepared for a patrol in East Africa. Some of these cars have had additional Vickers machine-guns fitted to the rear of the turret.**

The Mk 2 was to see extensive service with British forces in several theatres of war. Some were even captured by the Japanese and used by them. Others were sent to East Africa and the West Indies. These cars were to prove surprisingly effective and easy to operate, with some remaining in service after the war.

LEFT: **These Marmon cars have been fitted with different turrets. The first vehicle has a heavy and a light machine-gun in the turret, while the following cars have been fitted with a single machine-gun.**

Marmon-Herrington Mk 2 ME Armoured Car

Country: South Africa
Entered service: 1941
Crew: 4
Weight: 6,096kg/6 tons
Dimensions: Length – 5.18m/17ft
Height – 2.67m/8ft 9in
Width – 2m/6ft 6in
Armament: Main – Boys 14mm/0.55in anti-tank rifle
Secondary – 2 x Bren 7.7mm/0.303in machine-guns
Armour: Maximum – 12mm/0.47in
Powerplant: Ford V8 63kW/85hp petrol engine
Performance: Speed – 80kph/50mph
Range – 322km/200 miles

LEFT: **A crew member is standing in the roof-mounted reloading hatch next to the 10-round Nebelwerfer. The elevation and rotation of the unit was done from inside the vehicle.** BELOW: **A design picture for the mounting of the 8cm R-Vielfachwerfer. This fired 24 fin-stabilized rockets and was adopted by the Waffen SS.**

Maultier Nebelwerfer 15cm Panzerwerfer

The Maultier (Mule) was developed following the German experiences in Russia when ordinary wheeled vehicles became immobilized by mud and snow. The original Maultier half-track was built by the SS Division *Das Reich*, who fitted a Carden-Loyd track system to a Ford V8 truck. This proved so very successful that an order came down from high command to develop the idea further. Some 20,000 of these vehicles were built by three manufacturers.

In late 1942 Opel were asked to develop a spacious armoured body for the Maultier. Some 289 of these were to be used as ammunition carriers and 300 others were to be fitted with the Nebelwerfer 15cm/5.91in rocket launcher. The body of the vehicle was

an all-welded construction and its simple design made mass production easy. The front wheels retained normal brakes operated by a foot pedal while the tracks were braked by two hand-operated leavers beside the driver. The engine was in the front of the vehicle with the driver's compartment behind. The driver and commander sat side by side with a third crew member behind them. The reload rocket storage was in the body of the vehicle, with a large hatch in the roof for the crew to reload the launch tubes in safety. When the Nebelwerfer fired it left great smoke trails behind pinpointing the battery position but by fitting the weapon to a half-track vehicle, the rockets could be fired then the vehicle could quickly move to a new position. The ten-

barrelled Nebelwerfer 42 was subsequently developed with five tubes layered in two rows mounted on a 360-degree mount fitted to the rear of the vehicle. To fire all ten rockets took just 10 seconds and a reload was completed in 90 seconds. These vehicles were organized into companies with each company having eight vehicles carrying 80 launch tubes.

The Nebelwerfer was nicknamed "Moaning Minnie" by Allied troops, due to the noise the rocket made in flight. These Panzerwerfer units were deployed mainly on the Eastern Front and in France.

RIGHT: **Under the rocket tubes can be seen the small sighting window, which has two manual sliding shutters. The large rear doors give access into the ammunition storage area which is at the rear. This half-track is well equipped with storage lockers down each side of the vehicle.**

Maultier 15cm Panzerwerfer

Country: Germany
Entered service: 1943
Crew: 3
Weight: 8,636kg/8.5 tons
Dimensions: Length – 6m/19ft 6in
    Height – 3.05m/10ft
    Width – 2.2m/7ft 3in
Armament: Main – 10 x 15cm/5.91in Nebelwerfer
    Secondary – 7.92mm/0.312in MG34
    machine-gun
Armour: Maximum – 10mm/0.394in
Powerplant: Opel 3.6-litre 6-cylinder 51kW/68hp petrol engine
Performance: Speed – 40kph/25mph
    Range – 130km/81 miles

Minerva Armoured Car

ABOVE LEFT: One of the early Minerva cars. The armoured doors in front of the radiator are half-open and the driver's visor is fully open. Extra storage boxes have been fitted to the car. ABOVE: The three-man crew of this car pose for a picture. The headlight has been moved on to the frontal plate of the vehicle next to the driver. The gun crew have very little protection when operating the gun.

The Belgians were the progenitors of armoured car warfare and would demonstrate to the world how flexible and useful the armoured car could be, yet in spite of this, Minerva armoured cars are not well known outside Belgium. Lieutenant Charles Henkart allowed two of his cars to be converted into armoured cars at the Cockerill Works in Hoboken and these cars were soon in action gathering intelligence and causing disruption among the German cavalry at the beginning of World War I.

The Minerva armoured car was based on the chassis of a 28kW/38hp touring car while the engine was a Knight-type four-cylinder double-sleeve valve which had proved itself in racing. The body of the car was covered in 4mm/0.16in armour plate, with the fighting compartment protected by two layers

of armour spaced 3mm/0.12in apart. However, this armour was only just about bullet- and shell-splash-proof. The fighting compartment was in the middle of the vehicle and was open-topped, with a large single light fitted to the front next to the driver. The normal armament was a single Hotchkiss machine-gun on a pintle mount with an armoured shield, but some vehicles had a single 37mm/1.46in Puteaux cannon fitted. In 1918 the Belgians modified the Minerva by placing a basic open-backed turret over the machine-gun to give the gunner better protection.

The Belgians converted several more cars in 1914 and used them very much in the guerrilla role, harassing the German advanced troops. They also gave a lot of support to local troops during the withdrawal of forces in front of the

German advance of 1914. By October 1914 the trench line had reached the coast and ended the mobile armoured car war. Like the British, the Belgians sent an armoured car section to help the Russians in their fight against the Germans, and these were shipped home in early 1918 and refurbished, following the Revolution and Russia's withdrawal from the war.

The Minerva armoured cars were to remain in service until the early 1930s. Some were even passed to the Gendarmerie and these would remain in police service until 1937.

ABOVE: A column of late-production Minerva cars. Some of the vehicles are carrying an extra crew member. The RNAS heard about these cars and very quickly copied the idea, and so the armoured car was born.

Minerva Armoured Car

Country: Belgium
Entered service: 1914
Crew: 3
Weight: 4,064kg/4 tons
Dimensions: Length – 4.9m/16ft 1in
  Height – 2.3m/7ft 6in
  Width – 1.75m/5ft 9in
Armament: Main – 8mm/0.315in Hotchkiss machine-gun
  Secondary – Small arms
Armour: Maximum – 11mm/0.43in
Powerplant: Minerva 4-cylinder sleeve valve 30kW/40hp petrol engine
Performance: Speed – 40kph/25mph
  Range – 240km/150 miles

Model 93 Sumida Armoured Car

The Sumida was designed by Japanese engineers to be able to run equally well on roads or railways, as it was intended to be used to police large areas. Development started in 1931; the vehicle went into production in 1933 and entered service in the same year.

It was a standard 6x4 chassis but with a few novel modifications to enable the car to carry out its dual role. The vehicle had one set of six wheels for road use and another for rails. These were easily interchangeable using four jacks built into the underside of the car, the spare set of six wheels being mounted in clips on the side of the fighting compartment. The driver and commander sat in the front of the vehicle with the other four crew members behind. There was a one-man turret mounted on the top of the fighting compartment with small arms firing slits in the sides. These vehicles were mainly operational in Manchuria, covering vast areas. These cars would always operate in pairs.

LEFT: **This Model 93 is being used as a railway patrol vehicle. It has its railway wheels fitted while its rubber road wheels are stored on the side of the vehicle. The radiator armoured doors are in the open position.**

Model 93 Sumida Armoured Car	

Country: Japan
Entered service: 1933
Crew: 6
Weight: 7,620kg/7.5 tons
Dimensions: Length – 6.55m/21ft 6in
Height – 2.97m/9ft 8in
Width – 1.9m/6ft 3in
Armament: Main – 6.5mm/0.256in machine-gun
Secondary – Small arms
Armour: Maximum – 16mm/0.63in
Powerplant: 6-cylinder 75kW/100hp petrol engine
Performance: Speed – 60kph/37mph
Range – 240km/150 miles

Morris CS9/LAC Armoured Car Reconnaissance

Between 1935 and 1936 the Royal Ordnance Factory at Woolwich built two prototype armoured cars using the Morris 762kg/15cwt as the chassis, but both were turned down by the British Army. The third one was much better as the chassis was lengthened by 457mm/18in, engine power was increased and the turret design was changed. The new turret was open-topped and was now armed with a Boys anti-tank rifle and a Bren gun, while between the two guns was a smoke discharger. The Morris CS9 entered service with the British Army in 1938 with a total production run of only 100 vehicles.

The BEF took 38 of these vehicles to France in 1939 and all were lost in the withdrawal to the Channel Ports. In North Africa the CS9 would remain in service until 1941, but by fitting a radio it became a troop leader's car, while some of these vehicles were converted to command cars. However, the steering and suspension did not hold up well over rough terrain or in the deserts of North Africa.

LEFT: **This is a troop commander's vehicle in the deserts of North Africa in 1942. The crew have found some additional shade. The Boys AT rifle is fitted in the front of the turret while the Bren gun is fitted to the rear.**

Morris CS9/LAC Armoured Car Reconnaissance	

Country: UK
Entered service: 1938
Crew: 4
Weight: 4,267kg/4.2 tons
Dimensions: Length – 4.78m/15ft 8in
Height – 2.21m/7ft 3in
Width – 2.06m/6ft 9in
Armament: Main – Boys 14mm/0.55in anti-tank rifle
Secondary – 1 x Bren 7.7mm/0.303 machine-gun, and 1 x 51mm/2in smoke discharger
Armour: Maximum – 7mm/0.27in
Powerplant: Morris Commercial 4-cylinder 52kW/70hp petrol engine
Performance: Speed – 72kph/45mph
Range – 386km/240 miles

LEFT AND BELOW: **This Morris armoured car seen here in Normandy has a cut-down turret, and the other gunner's hatches are in the open position. The car below has a full-size turret, but this afforded the gunner a very limited view, so in combat the crews cut the turret down as a field modification.**

Morris Mk 1 Light Reconnaissance Car

The Morris Mk 1 was one of the better British designs of a number of armoured cars produced during 1940 and 1941. Morris was subsequently given a contract to produce 1,000 of these Light Reconnaissance cars, with the first entering service in 1941.

The body of the car was a monocoque design of all-welded armour plate construction. The vehicle had a solid rear axle with independent suspension on the front wheels, but it was only two-wheel drive which would prove to be a problem in the cross-country role. The engine was mounted in the rear of the vehicle with the crew compartment in the front, while there were two large doors, one on each side, for the crew to enter and exit. The driver

sat in the middle of the crew compartment on the centreline of the vehicle with the turret gunner on the right side and the vehicle commander on the left. The vehicle commander would also operate the Boys anti-tank rifle, which could be fired to the front and rear only. The machine-gun turret had all-round traverse and a 51mm/2in smoke discharger mounted on its side.

Morris produced the Mk 2 version in 1942 and received an order for 1,050 of these new vehicles. The main improvements were that the vehicle was made into a 4x4 and the suspension was changed to leaf spring. The Boys anti-tank rifle was done away with and replaced with a second machine-gun. Large numbers of these armoured cars

were passed over to the RAF to be used as airfield defence vehicles. Some were also converted to turretless observation vehicles and a number of these would be taken to France by the RAF in 1944. When being used by the RAF as a Forward Observation Vehicle the gun turret was retained but the vehicle commander's position was converted to a radio position.

These armoured cars proved to be very serviceable and reliable and would remain in service in secondary roles until the end of the war.

LEFT: **The side door into the crew compartment is small, making access difficult. The crew compartment itself is compact with no space for the storage of personal kit. The turret on this vehicle has been fitted with a smoke discharger and is armed with a Bren gun.**

Morris Mk 1 Light Reconnaissance Car

Country: UK
Entered service: 1941
Crew: 3
Weight: 3,759kg/3.7 tons
Dimensions: Length – 4.06m/13ft 4in
　Height – 1.88m/6ft 2in
　Width – 2.03m/6ft 8in
Armament: Main – 14mm/0.55in Boys
　anti-tank rifle
　Secondary – Bren 7.7mm/0.303in machine-gun
Armour: Maximum – 14mm/0.55in
Powerplant: Morris 4-cylinder 53kW/71hp
　petrol engine
Performance: Speed – 72kph/45mph
　Range – 233km/145 miles

Ole Bill Bus

The name for this unusual AFV comes from a World War I cartoon character. The bus was a B-Type built by AEC for the London General Omnibus Company (LGOC) that had entered service on the streets of London in 1911. The LGOC allocated 300 B-Type buses to the British Army for use in France from October 1914 and they would remain on active service until 1918 when they helped bring the British Army home.

The first buses manned by volunteer crews arrived in France just in time to help move men forward during the First Battle of Ypres (October 19–November 22, 1914). They turned up painted in London red and cream livery with all the advertising still in place but were soon painted khaki and the windows were removed and boarded up. Wooden planking 51mm/2in thick was attached as armour but this was only effective against small shell splinters. Each bus could carry 25 fully armed men; the first unit carried being a London Scottish battalion. Some 900 buses would serve in France.

LEFT: **The first London buses sent out to France were required to enter service immediately so were seen moving behind the British lines in their full London livery.**

Ole Bill Bus B-Type	
Country: UK	
Entered service: 1914 Military service	
Crew: 2	
Weight: 4,064kg/4 tons	
Dimensions: Length – 6.86m/22ft 6in	
Height – 3.79m/12ft 5in	
Width – 2.11m/6ft 11in	
Armament: Main – None	
Secondary – None	
Armour: Maximum – 51mm/2in wooden planking	
Powerplant: AEC 4-cylinder 22kW/30hp petrol engine	
Performance: Speed – 32km/20mph	
Range – 241km/150 miles	

Otter Light Reconnaissance Car

The Otter, intended as a Canadian replacement for the British Humber Scout Car, was designed in early 1942 and went into production soon after. The vehicle turned out to be under-powered and had very poor visibility for the driver and crew, but despite these shortcomings, it was still placed into production. The vehicle had an all-welded construction with four-wheel drive and had a fair cross-country performance but, due to its height, a high centre of gravity. Total production of these vehicles was 1,761, with manufacturing finishing in 1943.

The Otter entered service with Canadian and British forces in late 1942, seeing action in Italy and northern Europe. The vehicle was very popular with its crews as it proved to be very reliable and was an easy vehicle to maintain in the field. The RAF regiment also used it as there was room in the body of the vehicle to carry extra radio equipment. The RAF increased the armament on its Otters including, among other weapons, an anti-aircraft machine-gun.

LEFT: **The Boys AT rifle has its own port in the front of the vehicle, while above this is a smoke discharger. This vehicle is covered in personal kit as there is no space for it inside the car.**

Otter Light Reconnaissance Car	
Country: Canada	
Entered service: 1942	
Crew: 3	
Weight: 4,877kg/4.8 tons	
Dimensions: Length – 4.5m/14ft 9in	
Height – 2.44m/8ft	
Width – 2.13m/7ft	
Armament: Main – 14mm/0.55in Boys anti-tank rifle	
Secondary – 1 x Bren 7.7mm/0.303in light machine-gun, and 1 x 101.6mm/4in smoke discharger	
Armour: Maximum – 12mm/0.47in	
Powerplant: GMC 6-cylinder 79kW/106hp petrol engine	
Performance: Speed – 72kph/45mph	
Range – 402km/250 miles	

PA-III Armoured Car

In the 1920s Czechoslovakia was a very poor country but was in need of modern armoured vehicles to bring its army up to date. Skoda started to develop the PA-III in 1924 while still manufacturing the PA-II. They kept the same chassis that had been used since the PA-I. This chassis was four-wheel drive and four-wheel steering and could be driven in both directions at the same speed as there were driving controls in both the front and the back of the vehicle's crew compartment.

The PA-III was a big improvement on the PA-II. The new car was lighter, smaller, more mobile and above all less expensive. The army kept changing its mind about what was required in the new car and this slowed up development. The original body was made up of beautifully curved armour plates, but these were replaced by short angled straight armour plates. This would speed up production and reduce costs, but would still give the same ballistic protection to the crew. In 1925 a single prototype was produced which immediately went for extensive testing by the army. In December 1927 the Czechoslovak Army accepted the PA-III as fit for service and placed an order for 12 cars with Skoda providing an extra three free of charge due to three

PA-II armoured cars being sold to the police in Vienna. Production started in 1929 and 16 cars were built. The engine was in the front of the vehicle with the fighting compartment in the middle, a turret fitted with two machine-guns mounted on the top and a single machine-gun in the rear.

The PA-III was easy to maintain, robust and well-liked by its crews, but by the time of the outbreak of World War II it was showing its age. The armoured cars were placed into three armoured regiments in 1937 to act as reconnaissance vehicles for the tanks and in 1938 they took part in the fighting for the Sudeten region. By 1939 nearly all of the cars had been captured by the German or Romanian forces, and only one survived the war.

LEFT: This is the rear of the PA-III and has a tow-hitch fitted to the lower body work. The turret has been rotated so the front machine-gun is facing the rear of the vehicle. The main doors into the vehicle are on either side below the turret.

PA-III Armoured Car ▶

Country: Czechoslovakia
Entered service: 1929
Crew: 5
Weight: 6,706kg/6.6 tons
Dimensions: Length – 5.35m/17ft 7in
Height – 2.66m/8ft 9in
Width – 1.95m/6ft 5in
Armament: Main – 2 x vz.7/24 7.92mm/0.312in machine-guns
Secondary – ZB vz.26 7.92mm/0.312in machine-gun
Armour: Maximum – 5.5mm/0.22in
Powerplant: Skoda 4-cylinder 44.3kW/60hp petrol engine
Performance: Speed – 35kph/22mph
Range – 250km/155 miles

FAR LEFT: **This car is in post-World War II service with the French Army. The driver's side hatch is in the open position. The coaxial machine-gun is not fitted to the turret of this car.**
LEFT: **This side view of the Panhard, in French camouflage colours,** shows the main entrance and exit door in the side of the vehicle below the turret. The design of this car would influence many designs in the 1950s.
TOP: **A French Panhard in German service in Russia, 1943. The extensive use of rivets in the construction of the vehicle can be clearly seen. The rear of the crew compartment below the turret can be raised to improve ventilation and give better vision.**

Panhard AMD Type 178 Armoured Car

The AMD (*Automitrailleuse de Découverte*) was conceived as a replacement for some of the ageing French armoured cars of World War I. The prototype appeared in 1933 but development was very slow as money was in short supply. It entered service with the French Army in 1935 and was issued to both infantry and cavalry units. The AMD 178 was a very good clean design, with the interior divided into fighting/driving and engine compartments. The armour was sloped and the construction was all riveted. The car was a 4x4 vehicle and had good cross-country performance due to the engine being mounted in the rear.

Only 360 were in service when the Germans invaded France in 1940 but the French had distributed these vehicles among so many units in "penny packets" that the Germans were able to capture over 200 of the AMD 178s intact and, as it performed well, they were taken into German service. However,

the French managed to rescue 46 of these cars and had them repaired after which they were then sent to the new unoccupied Vichy territory and hidden from the Germans.

The Germans replaced the 25mm/0.98in gun with their 37mm/1.46in anti-tank gun. Some were also modified to run on railway track by replacing the road wheels with railway wheels. A number of these cars were also converted into command radio cars by fitting a large frame aerial over the top of the vehicle. Many of these converted vehicles as well as standard AMD 178s were sent to the Eastern Front to support the anti-partisan war that was taking place behind the German lines. When the Germans overran Vichy they captured the remaining 46 AMD 178 cars that were in French hands. These were converted into a wheeled tank by installing a larger turret on the vehicle and arming it with a 50mm/1.97in gun. Most of these remained in France.

The AMD 178 was the most advanced medium armoured car in French service in 1940, and was soon back in production when the Renault factory was restored to French control in August 1944. It would remain in French service for many years after World War II.

Panhard AMD Type 178 Armoured Car

Country: France
Entered service: 1935
Crew: 3
Weight: 8,636kg/8.5 tons
Dimensions: Length – 4.79m/15ft 8in
Height – 2.31m/7ft 7in
Width – 2.01m/6ft 7in
Armament: Main – 1 x 25mm/0.98in gun, and
1 x 7.5mm/0.295in MG31 coaxial machine-gun
Secondary – None
Armour: Maximum – 26mm/1.02in
Powerplant: Panhard SK 6.33-litre 4-cylinder
78kW/105hp petrol engine
Performance: Speed – 72kph/45mph
Range – 300km/186 miles

LEFT: **An improved version of the Flakpanzer called the "Wirbelwind". This vehicle mounted the 2cm/0.79in Flakvierling 38 in an armoured rotating turret, and provided good crew protection. The slow rotational speed of this new turret was the one drawback of the design.** BELOW: **The first Flakpanzer to be issued to the Panzer formations was called the "Möbelwagen" (Furniture Van). To operate the gun you had to drop the sides of the vehicle.**

Panzer IV Flakpanzer

The problem of supplying the German Army with mobile anti-aircraft guns for protection from fighter bombers first came to light during the campaign in North Africa in 1942, when the RAF Desert Air Force destroyed large numbers of vehicles. To give the army convoys basic protection a number of very ad hoc conversions were made to allow some vehicles to carry a single 2cm/0.79in flak gun. However, this problem was passed back to the German High Command for a permanent solution to be found.

The first vehicle to based on the Panzer IV chassis was the Möbelwagen (Furniture Van) which was shown to Hitler on May 14, 1943, but he rejected it on the grounds that it was too expensive and that fighter bombers were not currently a great problem. The Möbelwagen was a basic Panzer IV chassis with

ABOVE: **The Flakpanzer Wirbelwind was seen as a stop-gap solution, allowing a quick conversion of the Panzer IV chassis. With this vehicle the driver could remain at his position for a fast response.**

the flak gun mounted in a box structure fixed to the top of the vehicle. When the gun went into action, the sides of the box were lowered exposing the gun and crew. The gun was the quadruple 2cm/0.79in Flakvierling 38, which had a high rate of fire but was magazine-fed. The vehicle was again shown to Hitler in October 1943 and was yet again rejected, this time due to its overall height being over 3m/9ft 10in and reservations that the crew had very little protection.

As the situation deteriorated on the Eastern Front and in Italy, an interim order was placed for the Möbelwagen, now armed with the 3.7cm/1.46in Flak 43. From February 1944, 20 of these vehicles were produced per month. The vehicle had a crew of seven, though in service this was often reduced to five, and could carry 416 rounds which gave three minutes firing time for the Flak 43. The first of these vehicles entered service in April 1944 and total production by the end of the war was 240 Möbelwagens.

The first true Flakpanzer was the Wirbelwind, which had been shown to General Guderian in May 1944. He requested that it be put into production straight away. These vehicles were built using old Panzer IV chassis returned from the front, with a total of 105 conversions being completed. There was a

LEFT: The "Ostwind" version of the Flakpanzer IV which mounted a single 3.7cm/1.46in Flak 36. This vehicle could also be used against ground targets.
ABOVE: Inside the driver's position of a Flakpanzer IV. The driver's vision block is top centre, the track control arms are in the middle, with the gear lever and other controls to the right of the seat.

crew of five; four were in the turret manning the gun, while the driver remained at his post. The turret was made from angled 16mm/0.63in armour plates welded into position, the angle of the plates helping to close the open top a little. The vehicle was armed with the quadruple 2cm/0.79in Flakvierling 38, which was enclosed in the armoured, but still open-topped, turret. The Wirbelwind entered production in July 1944, but the gun was not delivering the results required and so production stopped in November 1944.

The Ostwind was to replace the Wirbelwind, still using the Panzer IV chassis but with a new gun fitted. The new gun was the 3.7cm/1.46in Flak 43 as used on the Möbelwagen which was fitted into the same turret as had been used on the Wirbelwind. The Ostwind II had the same body and turret as the Ostwind, but with the armament changed to a twin 3cm/1.18in Flakzwilling 44 guns, with the twin barrels mounted side by side. This vehicle only reached the prototype stage before the war ended.

On April 20, 1944 Hitler ordered that the twin 3cm/1.18in Doppelflak 303 that was just going into production for the U-Boat service should be fitted to a Panzer IV chassis. This new vehicle would be called the Kugelblitz Anti-Aircraft Tank and would replace all the other flak vehicles in production. By February 1945 when production stopped only two full vehicles and five chassis had been built. Other chassis were also being considered for the new flak tanks and these included the PzKpfw 38(t) and the Panther.

In 1944 Flakpanzer Platoons were formed and were assigned to Panzer regiments. These were normally formed of 8 Möbelwagen or 4 Möbelwagen and 4 Wirbelwind per platoon. The vast majority of these Flak vehicles were sent to France in an attempt to protect the German tanks from the virtually unchallenged Allied air force. Most of these vehicles were either destroyed or captured in the Falaise Pocket in Normandy. The rest were abandoned during the retreat across the Seine.

LEFT: The Möbelwagen in the firing position. When the sides are dropped, the driver has very poor vision. When operating the weapon, the gun crew are very exposed. They have to travel in the open-topped box with the gun. This vehicle has a number of spare track links attached to the front of the hull to increase the armour.

Möbelwagen

Country: Germany
Entered service: 1944
Crew: 5
Weight: 24,384kg/24 tons
Dimensions: Length – 5.92m/19ft 5in
Height – 2.73m/8ft 11in
Width – 2.95m/9ft 8in
Armament: Main – 3.7cm/1.46in Flak 43
Secondary – 7.92mm/0.312in MG34 machine-gun
Armour: Maximum – 50mm/1.97in
Powerplant: Maybach HL 120 TRM 112 203kW/272hp 12-cylinder petrol engine
Performance: Speed – 38kph/24mph
Range – 200km/124 miles

LEFT: **This Priest of the 1st Armoured Division in North Africa is being readied for action. The lack of storage provision can be clearly seen as the vehicle is covered with personal kit, camouflage netting and bedding.** BELOW: **An American M7 on trial in America. When these vehicles went overseas, the large white star was made smaller. The crews very quickly found that the star was an aiming point for the Germans, so either painted it out or covered it in mud.**

Priest 105mm Self-Propelled Gun

Reports coming out of North Africa in 1940 had shown the Americans the urgent need for an SPG and as an interim solution the T19 half-track was introduced into service. In early 1941, an alternative solution of mounting the 105mm/4.13in howitzer on the M3 tank chassis was proposed. The weapon was mounted in an open fighting compartment and was offset to the right to give room for the driver. Trials of the vehicle proved to be very successful and reliable, and the British Tank Mission in America placed orders immediately it was shown to them. Known to the US Forces as the M7, the British named it the "Priest" as the AA machine-gun was mounted in what looked like a pulpit and all Royal Artillery SPGs were given ecclesiastical names.

American Loco started production in April 1942 and by the end of the year had produced 2,028 vehicles of a total M7 production of 3,490 vehicles. The first British order was for

2,500 in the first year and 3,000 by the end of 1943, but this was never met as the American forces were armed with the new weapon first. The Priest had identical chassis and automotive parts as the M3 tank but, just as the M4 Sherman tank was replacing the M3 Grant in service, so from late 1943 the M4 chassis replaced the M3 chassis in Priest production. In American service, this new vehicle using M4 chassis and automotive parts was known as the M7B1. The height of the fighting compartment sides was raised by the fitting of hinged plates to give the ammunition better protection as there was storage for 69 rounds in open bins. Nine hundred and fifty-three of these vehicles were built from March 1944 to March 1945.

LEFT: **This British Priest is being unloaded from an LCT (Landing Craft Tank). The driver's visor is in the open position but because of the poor vision, the "pulpit" gunner is helping direct the vehicle off the craft.**

LEFT: **The driver has good forward vision on his side of the main gun, but can see nothing on the machine-gunner's side of the vehicle. Here you can see the high driving position in the vehicle which has the effect of making the vehicle tall.** ABOVE: **The storage boxes on the front of the vehicle are for spare track links. The running gear and chassis for these vehicles came from the M4 Sherman. The machine-gun position has a circular swivel mount on the top of it.**

In September 1942, 90 Priest SPGs were sent to the British 8th Army in North Africa and took part in the second Battle of El Alamein. From this time onwards it became the standard issue to British medium SP batteries. The British units equipped with the Priest that landed in Normandy during June 1944 soon had their vehicles replaced by the Sexton SPG, but the Priest remained in service with the 8th Army for the remainder of the war as it fought all the way up Italy. One problem encountered there was that the howitzer could not be elevated enough to reach targets high up in the mountains, so the vehicle would be driven up on to a log ramp to increase the angle of elevation. This same problem would arise again during the Korean War and at first was solved in the same way as in Italy until a modification was made raising the gun by 155mm/6in, so creating the M7B2.

The Canadians, like the British, stopped using their M7 Priests soon after D-Day as they were replaced by the new 25pdr Sexton. However, General Simonds, commander of the Canadian II Corps, got permission to keep the M7 chassis for troop-carrying purposes, so at the end of July these chassis were sent to the Canadian field workshop codenamed "Kangaroo" for conversion. The main armament and all its internal fittings were removed and the aperture for the gun was plated over, but the "pulpit" with its machine-gun was kept to give covering fire to the troops as they debussed, and the side plates were raised to give the men more protection. These vehicles could carry 20 fully armed infantry and had a crew of two; they were a great success and would lead to a whole new type of infantry vehicle. The Canadians used a number of these "Unfrocked Priests" to drive their infantry through the German lines during Operation "Totalize". By August 6, 1944, 75 "Priest Kangaroos", as they were later named, were ready and the infantry had just one day to learn how to use them, the drivers for the new vehicle being taken from the artillery units that had used the Priest. This conversion proved very popular and more Priests were converted into Kangaroos in Italy. In addition, a number of redundant Priests were converted to artillery observation vehicles by removing the gun and putting extra radios, telephones and map tables into the resulting space.

LEFT: **A battery of Priest SPGs camouflaged up in Normandy on June 6, 1944. The sides of the vehicle have been increased in height by the fitting of the deep-water wading gear. The front of the vehicle is covered in spares for the running gear.**

Priest 105mm SPG

Country: USA
Entered service: 1942
Crew: 7
Weight: 26,010kg/25.6 tons
Dimensions: Length – 6.02m/19ft 9in
  Height – 2.54m/8ft 4in
  Width – 2.88m/9ft 5in
Armament: Main – 105mm/4.13in M1A2 howitzer
  Secondary – 12.7mm/0.5in machine-gun
Armour: Maximum – 62mm/2.44in
Powerplant: Continental 9-cylinder radial 280kW/375hp petrol engine
Performance: Speed – 41.8kph/26mph
  Range – 201km/125 miles

Renault and Peugeot Armoured Cars

The French formed their armoured car units in 1914. At first these used touring cars but they were soon replaced by rudimentary armoured cars such as the Renault and Peugeot. At the start of World War I, Renault was the largest car construction company in France. By November 1914 they had produced 100 AM Renault 20CV mod.E1 armoured cars which entered service in December 1914 crewed by French marines. At first the armour was poor but this was very quickly upgraded to 5mm/0.2in, while the famous Renault engine cover was retained and armoured. The vehicle was open-topped with an 8mm/0.315in Hotchkiss machine-gun mounted on a pintle mount. A heavier 37mm/1.46in Puteaux gun was carried by some Renault cars and these would be used in many actions as close-support vehicles especially during the retreat and advances of 1918.

The Peugeot 18CV was the other main French armoured car in 1914. They were designed by Captain Reynauld who made both the machine-gun car and the heavy gun car the same so armament could be interchangeable in these open-topped vehicles. The first ones were armed with an 8mm/0.315in machine-gun, but this was soon supplemented by fitting a 37mm/1.46in gun to some of the cars. These vehicles were built on the Peugeot 146 chassis at first and later the 148 chassis was used, giving a total production run of 150 of these armoured cars. The Peugeot cars initially saw active service in January 1915 when the first cars were sent to join the 7th Cavalry Division and formed the 6th and 7th Armoured Car Groups. There was a crew of three on the machine-gun car and four on the 37mm/1.46in heavy gun car. They could also carry five infantry if required and during the great German retreat of 1918 they were used to great effect in harassing the German infantry. By the end of World War I, the French had only 28 Peugeot armoured cars still fit for service. Poland bought 18 of these in 1918 and some were still in Polish service when the Germans invaded in 1939.

ABOVE: This Renault armoured car has a crew of four and is armed with a single 37mm/1.46in gun, which has an armoured shield around it. This car has its starting handle in place in the front of the vehicle between the wheels. LEFT: Five Peugeot machine-gun armed armoured cars at Magnicourt in May 1915. The third car in is armed with a 47mm/1.85in gun. The large single door is mounted in the side of the vehicle behind the driver and in front of the gun.

Peugeot 18CV Armoured Car

Country: France
Entered service: 1915
Crew: 3 plus 5 infantry
Weight: 5,000kg/4.9 tons
Dimensions: Length – 4.8m/16ft
　　　　Height – 2.8m/9ft 2in
　　　　Width – 1.8m/5ft 11in
Armament: Main – 8mm/0.315in Hotchkiss
　　　　Mle 14 machine-gun
　　　　Secondary – Small arms
Armour: Maximum – 5mm/0.2in
Powerplant: Peugeot 146 4-cylinder 34kW/45hp
　　　　petrol engine
Performance: Speed – 40kph/25mph
　　　　Range – 140km/87 miles

LEFT: **The driver is in his position and all his hatches are open. The hatch is split in two parts with the dome part folding backwards. The other crew position is all "buttoned up".** BELOW: **This UE is pulling a small four-wheel trailer, which has been fitted with cross-country tracks. Behind this is the Hotchkiss 25mm/0.98in AT gun.**

Renault UE Infantry Tractor

Production of these light tractors had started in 1931 at Renault and in 1936 at AMX, and by 1940 the French had some 6,000 in service. These vehicles were not designed for combat but to act as an armoured supply vehicle, the hardship of Verdun having shown the necessity for such a design. Some of these vehicles were produced with a machine-gun for the co-driver but these were far and few between.

Renault based these vehicles on the Carden-Loyd Mk VI carrier design. It was of a riveted construction, with a Renault engine. The crew were fully protected as they sat in the main body of the vehicle with the engine between them and only had their heads protruding. These were protected by armoured domes that were

hinged in the middle so that the front part could lift like a knight's visor. Behind the crew was a storage box for supplies but it was very small and could not carry more than 150kg/331lb. The vehicle was always designed to pull an armoured trailer, which was open-topped. These four-wheeled trailers were capable of carrying 500kg/1,102lb and for extreme conditions could be fitted with caterpillar tracks to improve their overall cross-country performance.

The Germans captured so many of these vehicles that they would see service in many areas and in many forms. A large number were converted into light Panzerjager, armed at first with a 37mm/1.46in PaK35/36, and many of these were used by garrison forces in

France. When Rommel took over the coastal defences in France, he instructed that a lot of the Renault UEs should be converted into rocket carriers. They were fitted with four Wurfrahmen 40 rockets mounted in either of two ways on the vehicle. One method was to put side-skirts on the vehicle with two rockets placed on each side, while the other means was a box structure built over the rear supply box and again capable of carrying and firing four rockets. These were first encounter by the Allies in Normandy, but later more widely throughout the European theatre.

Renault UE Infantry Tractor

Country: France
Entered service: 1931
Crew: 2
Weight: 2,032kg/2 tons
Dimensions: Length – 2.69m/8ft 10in
 Height – 1.03m/3ft 5in
 Width – 1.7m/5ft 7in
Armament: Main – None
 Secondary – Small arms
Armour: Maximum – 7mm/0.27in
Powerplant: Renault 4-cylinder 63kW/85hp petrol engine
Performance: Speed – 30kph/19mph
 Range – 180km/112 miles

LEFT: **This UE is being inspected by a group of British soldiers in France in 1944. The short exhaust can be seen. This was the cause of a few problems with fumes going into the crew compartments.**

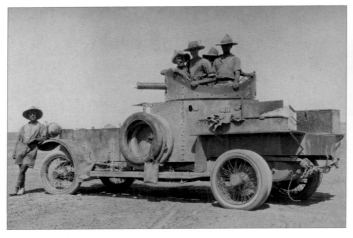

LEFT: Dominion troops in Palestine during World War I. The car has an open-topped turret allowing for much-needed additional ventilation in the hot climate. The desert was very hard on tyres, hence all the spares carried on the side of the car.
ABOVE: A column of Rolls-Royce cars stopped in a village behind the Western Front. The rear wheels have been fitted with chains to improve traction in the mud. The cars are covered in personal kit.

Rolls-Royce Armoured Car

When the Royal Naval Air Service (RNAS) was sent to France in 1914, it went with a very mixed array of aircraft and vehicles. After observing the Belgian Army using their armoured cars and how they were harassing the advancing German forces, the RNAS decided to join in, sending two Rolls-Royce Silver Ghost cars to a depot in Dunkirk for conversion into armoured cars. These were covered in boiler plate and armed with a machine-gun. This proved to be so successful that the Royal Navy agreed to develop the design into a proper armoured car using the Rolls-Royce Silver Ghost tourer as the chassis.

The chassis had its suspension strengthened and was fitted with 9mm/0.354in armour and a new large single turret. This turret was referred to as the "Admiralty Pattern" and would be fitted to all but the last model. It was shaped like a bishop's mitre and was fitted with a single heavy machine-gun, either a Vickers or a Maxim belt-fed 7.7mm/0.303in. In very hot weather the top could be removed to give better ventilation. The radiator had armoured doors and a large open space

was left behind the turret for the carriage of stores or another machine-gun. The first of these new cars arrived in France in late 1914 and were issued to the RNAS.

Once the "Race for the Sea" had reached the North Sea coast and the Western Front trench line was established, there was very little for the RNAS armoured cars to do. In 1915 the Navy handed over most of their cars to the British Army, which did not really want them initially as it had no idea how to use them. Some officers, like the Duke of Westminster and Colonel Lawrence (Lawrence of Arabia), took to these new weapons and, using them with dash and flair in the deserts of the Middle East, demonstrated to the army how to get the best from these machines. Seeing the potential but faced with several types of armoured car, the army decided to standardize on the Rolls-Royce and formed them into Light Armoured Motor (LAM) batteries of the Motor Machine-gun Corps. The Rolls-Royce armoured car was then sent to several other fronts during World War I, such as the North West Frontier in India, German South West Africa and Persia (later Iran). These 1914 Pattern

LEFT: A Rolls-Royce car bogged down in the mud of the Western Front. The car has been camouflaged in typical British World War I scheme. Note that the machine-gun has been removed. RIGHT: A Rolls-Royce 1924 Pattern Mk 1, with a modified turret, patrolling the border in Egypt in 1940.

LEFT: **This was originally a 1924 Pattern Rolls-Royce armoured car. By 1940 the chassis of these cars were worn out, so in August 1940 a number of Rolls-Royce cars were fitted with a Fordson chassis in Cairo, Egypt. These cars were armed with a Boys AT rifle, a Vickers machine-gun in the turret and a pair of Vickers K guns on the top of the turret.**

cars would remain in service officially until replaced by the Rolls-Royce 1920 Pattern.

This new car was placed into production after World War I and a number of the 1914 type were modernized to the 1920 Pattern. The wire-spoked wheels became disc-type, while the turret sides were made higher and louver doors were fitted to the radiator. The Air Ministry also produced these new 1920 Pattern cars for the RAF, but with wider tyres as they were operating in the deserts of Persia and Iraq. They would see service in many parts of the British Empire, being used to "police the Empire".

In 1924 a new pattern car went into production with a number of small changes and improvements. The body of the car was altered: a cupola for the vehicle commander was fitted to the turret and a new gun mounting was fitted to help close a weakness. A number of the 1920 cars were brought up to this

new pattern. Others were sold to various countries around the world and would see service in World War II.

There were a few problems with the Rolls-Royce, one being that there was a small fuel tank fitted in the dashboard and another that brakes were only fitted to the rear wheels, so stopping was a problem at times. These cars were still in active service with the British Army when war was declared in 1939 and in some parts of the Empire there were even a few 1914 Pattern cars in military use. In all, there was a total of 83 Rolls-Royce armoured cars remaining, most of them in Egypt. These were fitted with a new open-topped turret carrying a Boys anti-tank rifle instead of the machine-gun. A twin Lewis gun was mounted on a pintle mount on the back of the vehicle in an anti-aircraft role. These vehicles would, however, only remain in service for a few more years.

LEFT: **A Rolls-Royce Admiralty Pattern turreted car at a Forward Aid Station in France in 1915. The front of this car has been fitted with a pivoted hook to pull away barbed wire entanglements.**

Rolls-Royce 1920 Pattern Armoured Car

Country: UK
Entered service: 1920
Crew: 3
Weight: 3,861kg/3.8 tons
Dimensions: Length – 5.18m/17ft
  Height – 2.33m/7ft 5in
  Width – 1.9m/6ft 3in
Armament: Main – 7.7mm/0.303in Vickers machine-gun
  Secondary – Small arms
Armour: Maximum – 9mm/0.354in
Powerplant: Rolls-Royce 6-cylinder 60kW/80hp petrol engine
Performance: Speed – 80kph/50mph
  Range – 240km/150 miles

367

Sd Kfz 7/1 8-ton Half-Track

The design of these vehicles goes back to 1926 and was personally championed by Ernst Kniepkamp, head of the *Heereswaffenamt*. During 1932, it was decided to standardize the half-tracks into light (5,080kg/5-ton), medium (8,128kg/8-ton), and heavy (12,193kg/12-ton), while in 1934 two more half-tracks, a 1,016kg/1-ton and a 3,048kg/3-ton, were added to the list. The last one to be developed was the giant 18,289kg/18-ton half-track in 1936. The first of these vehicles to go into production and enter service with the German Army was the Sd Kfz 7 8-ton half-track. The army used the *Zugkraftwagen* (Towing Tractor) as their main artillery towing vehicle, but this half-track went on to be used for many other purposes for which it was never originally designed during World War II.

Development and design of the Sd Kfz 7 was undertaken by Krauss-Maffei (KM) based in Munich-Allach. They would be the largest single producer, building 6,129 of these vehicles with the remaining 5,880 being built by various other manufacturers. Production continued to the end of World War II. The vehicle had an 8-ton trailer-towing capacity, and the suspension was leaf-spring on the early models but by 1940 this had been changed to torsion bar which was much more satisfactory. The engine would not change from the original Maybach throughout the entire production run, but the horsepower it developed would increase from

89kW/120hp to 119kW/160hp. The tracks were made up of metal plates with rubber inserts, which had sealed lubricated needle-roller bearings in them. This helped to give the vehicle long track life and ensured low rolling resistance.

Some of the KM production run were converted into supply vehicles by removing the rear crew area and replacing this with a wooden flat bed. Another significant conversion of 442 units into Flakvierling vehicles started in late 1943. In this case the driver's bench seat was retained with a second one placed back to back and an anti-aircraft gun, either the quadruple 2cm/0.79in Flak 38 or the 3.7cm/1.46in Flak 36, mounted on the flat-bed. As the fighter bomber threat increased, armoured cabs were fitted to the vehicle to give the crew better protection while travelling, though not for the gun crew while the vehicle was in action.

TOP: **The first of the Flak half-tracks was the 1,016kg/1-ton Sd Kfz 10 which entered service in 1938. The single gun required a crew of seven men.** ABOVE: **The Sd Kfz 10 in action against a ground target. The exposed crew position can be clearly seen.**

LEFT: **The Sd Kfz 7 Flak half-track in action in Russia. These vehicles still had a very exposed crew position but with the introduction of the Flakvierling 38 the fire-power was quadrupled. These half-tracks proved to be deadly against both aircraft and ground targets.**

Sd Kfz 7/1 8-ton Half-Track

Country: Germany
Entered service: 1943
Crew: 10
Weight: 11,786kg/11.6 tons
Dimensions: Length – 6.85m/22ft 6in
　　　　Height – 2.62m/8ft 7in
　　　　Width – 2.4m/7ft 10in
Armament: Main – 4 x 2cm/0.79in Flak 38
　　　　Secondary – Small arms
Armour: Maximum – 8mm/0.315in
Powerplant: Maybach HL 62 6-cylinder TUK
　　　　104kW/140hp petrol engine
Performance: Speed – 50kph/31mph
　　　　Range – 250km/155 miles

Sd Kfz 8 and 9 Heavy Half-Tracks

These were two of the largest half-tracks produced by the Germans. In 1931, development was started by Daimler-Benz on the Sd Kfz 8, a 12,193kg/12-ton half-track. It was designed to be a heavy tractor for heavy artillery such as the 21cm/8.25in and the 10.5cm/4.13in Flak gun. The first 12-ton tractors were built by Krupp and Skoda from 1932 and between them they produced 315 of these vehicles. Daimler took over production from 1934, initially using the DB 7 chassis, and these vehicles would remain in production until late 1944 with the final mark of chassis used being the DB 11. In total, 3,973 of these half-tracks were built. In 1939, Krupp converted ten of these 12-ton half-tracks into self-propelled gun mounts by placing the 8.8cm/3.46in Flak 18 on the flat bed of the vehicle. The normal cab was done away with

and replaced with an armoured cupola for the driver, with ammunition stacked on the rear of the vehicle and the eight-man crew sitting unprotected under the gun. These weapons were built to destroy fortifications, as the gun had restricted movement and tended to destabilize the vehicle when fired.

The Sd Kfz 9 was an 18,289kg/18-ton heavy half-track; it was designed as a heavy tank recovery vehicle and as a prime mover for 24,385kg/24-ton recovery trailers. Four different models were built during the production run of 2,334 vehicles which would finish in late 1944. These vehicles were also used by the German engineers working for the bridging section. In 1940, 15 of these 18-ton half-tracks were converted into heavy self-propelled gun mounts for the 8.8cm/3.46in Flak 18. These guns were more manoeuvrable and stable on this

ABOVE: **The Sd Kfz 9 was the largest of the half-tracks produced by the Germans. These vehicles proved to be very good and stable firing platforms. The crew cab has been armoured, but when the crew operate the gun they have no protection. The wire-mesh sides of the vehicle have to be folded down before the gun can go into action.**

platform than on the Sd Kfz 8 and could be used for many tasks including anti-aircraft work. However, the main task of this vehicle, like the earlier 12-ton half-track version, was to destroy fortified positions. The engine and driver's position were covered in armour, with ammunition carried in a locker on the rear deck. There were also side-screens that were lowered when the gun was in action, increasing the rear deck area.

LEFT: **This version of the Sd Kfz 8 half-track was produced in 1939 and was designed to be a fortress-buster and heavy AT gun. The vehicles were very tall and the gun crew were very exposed on the rear of the vehicle.**

Sd Kfz 9 8.8cm SPG Half-Track

Country: Germany
Entered service: 1940
Crew: 9
Weight: 25,400kg/25 tons
Dimensions: Length – 9.32m/30ft 7in
   Height – 3.67m/12ft
   Width – 2.65m/8ft 8in
Armament: Main – 8.8cm/3.46in Flak 18
   Secondary – Small arms
Armour: Maximum – 14.5mm/0.57in
Powerplant: Maybach HL 108 TUKRM
   186kW/250hp 12-cylinder petrol engine
Performance: Speed – 50kph/31mph
   Range – 260km/162 miles

LEFT: **A 2.8cm/1.12in armed Sd Kfz 221 armoured car. The front of the turret has been cut away so the gun could be fitted on to the turret ring. The gunner has to stand high up in the turret to operate the gun.**
ABOVE: **An Sd Kfz 221 armoured car fitted with a 2.8cm/1.12in tapered-bore anti-tank gun. This vehicle has been fitted with wire-mesh anti-grenade screens. The gun was phased out of service due to the shortage of tungsten for the ammunition.**

Sd Kfz 221 Armoured Car

Development of this vehicle was started by the firm of Weserhütte in 1934 as a replacement for the Kfz 13. It entered service in 1936 with the reconnaissance forces of the German Army. Total production was 339 vehicles in two batches, the first of which comprised 143 vehicles.

The Sd Kfz 221 was built on the Horch 801 heavy passenger car chassis and had a crew of two. The driver sat in the front, while the turret was in the middle and the engine in the rear. The suspension was of independent coil spring type, with 4x4 drive and front-wheel steering. The construction was of rolled armour plate that was welded together at sharp angles, which made production slow and difficult. The armour

was little more than bullet-proof. The turret was a seven-sided truncated pyramid in which was mounted a single machine-gun. It had an open top but this could be covered by an anti-grenade screen. The first production run had very complicated vision ports that were cut from rolled armour plate but the second batch of vehicles had cast vision ports. No radio equipment was fitted to the vehicle as there was insufficient space in the main compartment and so communication was by semaphore flags.

In 1941 the PzB 39 anti-tank rifle was fitted in the turret alongside the machine-gun to improve the armament of the vehicle, but only a few of these conversions were carried out. In 1942 the machine-gun and the front of the turret

were removed so that a new larger gun, the 2.8cm/1.12in sPzB41 tapered-bore, light anti-tank gun, could be fitted. The gun was fixed above the driver's position forward of the turret and extended back into the modified turret as the new gun was breech-loaded.

The Sd Kfz 221 was used as a commander's vehicle and would be accompanied into action by radio cars and heavy armoured cars armed with a 2cm/0.79in gun. The combat life of this vehicle was extended to the end of World War II as a result of the 2.8cm/1.12in gun being fitted.

RIGHT: **The armoured body and turret were mounted on a standard German passenger car. Between the wheels is a large storage chest of vehicle tools. The turret is seven-sided and was normally fitted with wire-mesh anti-grenade screens.**

Sd Kfz 221 Armoured Car

Country: Germany
Entered service: 1936
Crew: 2
Weight: 4,064kg/4 tons
Dimensions: Length – 4.8m/14ft 7in
    Height – 1.7m/5ft 6in
    Width – 1.95m/6ft 4in
Armament: Main – 7.92mm/0.312in MG34
    machine-gun
    Secondary – Small arms
Armour: Maximum – 14mm/0.55in
Powerplant: Horch V8-108 8-cylinder 56kW/75hp
    petrol engine
Performance: Speed – 80kph/50mph
    Range – 320km/200 miles

Sd Kfz 222 Armoured Car

The Germans started developing a new armoured car in 1934 with several criteria in mind: that the vehicle was reliable, that it could run off various grades of fuel, that it was a simple construction and that it had a good cross-country ability. The first of these new cars was the Sd Kfz 221, but this proved to be too small and lightly armed, so in 1937 development started on the Sd Kfz 222. Two standard chassis for four-wheeled armoured cars had been developed during 1936–7, the first of which had the engine mounted in the rear while the second had the engine mounted in the front. The latter type was used in the Sd Kfz 222.

The Sd Kfz 222 would become the standard light armoured car of the German Army until the end of World War II. This car entered service in 1938 and had heavier armament and a larger turret than the Sd Kfz 221. However, the new turret was still very small and cramped. It was open-topped but included a wire mesh screen that could be pulled over to protect the crew. This screen was divided in the middle and would hang over each side of the turret when open. When the screen was in the closed position, use of the main armament was even more difficult. The Sd Kfz 222 mounted one 2cm/0.79in cannon and a coaxial machine-gun, both of which could be elevated to 87 degrees so that the car could engage enemy aircraft. The cannon was mounted on a pintle which

incorporated the elevation and traverse mechanism and had a firing button on the floor. At the rear of the vehicle the engine deck was sharply sloped to improve the driver's vision when reversing.

The Sd Kfz 222 suffered from a number of problems, particularly the poor cross-country performance and short range of the vehicle, which would lead to the car being removed from front-line service during the invasion of the Soviet Union in 1941. Production stopped in 1943 after 989 vehicles had been built.

TOP: **This Sd Kfz 222 armoured car has been caught in the open during an air attack. The turret has been removed from this vehicle and a larger wire mesh has been fitted.** ABOVE: **A mixed group of German armoured cars on exercise in 1938. The Sd Kfz 222 is on the right and has the turret-mounted screens in the raised position.**

Sd Kfz 222 Light Armoured Car

Country: Germany
Entered service: 1938
Crew: 3
Weight: 4,877kg/4.8 tons
Dimensions: Length – 4.8m/14ft 9in
Height – 2m/6ft 7in
Width – 1.95m/6ft 5in
Armament: Main – 2cm/0.79in KwK38
Secondary – 7.92mm/0.312in MG34 machine-gun
Armour: Maximum – 30mm/1.18in
Powerplant: Horch/Auto Union 108 8-cylinder 60kW/81hp petrol engine
Performance: Speed – 80kph/50mph
Range – 300km/187 miles

RIGHT: **This is the Sd Kfz 223 long-range radio car. This car uses the chassis, engine and the body of the Sd Kfz 222. The frame aerial folds back towards the rear of the vehicle and this aerial is in the down position.**

LEFT: **A standard Sd Kfz 231 coming down a slope. The long bonnet of the vehicle, which caused a number of problems for the driver, can clearly be seen. This car has the secondary hull machine-gun fitted.** ABOVE: **A heavy 6 Rad (six-wheeled) radio car. The frame aerial is fixed to the body of the vehicle at the rear and to two fixed uprights on the turret. The turret supports were quickly changed to a form that allowed the turret to rotate.**

Sd Kfz 231 Heavy Armoured Car 6 Rad

This German heavy armoured car was developed at the Kazan test centre in the Soviet Union in the 1920s. The first heavy car chassis to be developed were 8x8 and 10x10 but these were too expensive to be put into production. As a result the Germans decided to select a truck chassis already in production and fit an armoured body. The chassis selected was the Daimler-Benz 6x4, but other manufacturers' chassis were also used in production.

The Sd Kfz 231 had a front-mounted engine and the chassis was strengthened to take the extra weight of the armour. A second driving position was constructed in the rear of the fighting compartment so the vehicle could be driven in reverse. During trials it was discovered that the front axle needed strengthening and the radiators needed

to be improved. With these improvements, the car entered service with the German Army in 1932 and remained in production until 1935. Initially the armament was a single machine-gun in the turret, but this was quickly upgraded to a 2cm/0.79in KwK30 and coaxial MG34 machine-gun while there was provision for an anti-aircraft machine-gun on the roof of the turret. These vehicles did not perform particularly well as they were too heavy for the chassis, were underpowered, and had very poor cross-country ability. However, the car did provide the German Army with a very good training vehicle, as on hard roads the vehicle was as good as any of its contemporaries.

These armoured cars were used during the occupation of Austria in 1938 and of Czechoslovakia in 1939. They

would see combat during the invasion of Poland, and were used during the Blitzkrieg operations (the invasion of the Low Countries and France) in 1940. This vehicle looked very impressive in action and was used extensively in propaganda, receiving a lot of media coverage.

The Sd Kfz 232 was a long-range radio vehicle variant of the Sd Kfz 231. A basic Sd Kfz 231 was fitted with a large frame aerial fixed to the top of the vehicle and extra radio sets were installed in the fighting compartment.

Sd Kfz 231 Heavy Armoured Car 6 Rad

Country: Germany
Entered service: 1932
Crew: 4
Weight: 5,791kg/5.7 tons
Dimensions: Length – 5.61m/18ft 4in
Height – 2.24m/7ft 4in
Width – 1.85m/6ft 1in
Armament: Main – 2cm/0.79in KwK30 gun, and coaxial 7.92mm/0.312in MG34 machine-gun
Secondary – 7.92mm/0.312in MG34 machine-gun
Armour: Maximum – 8mm/0.315in
Powerplant: Daimler-Benz M09 6-cylinder 48kW/65hp petrol engine
Performance: Speed – 65kph/40mph
Range – 250km/150 miles

LEFT: **Behind the front wheel is an engine grill and beside that is a small hull hatch which gives access to the hull gunner's position. The spare wheel is carried on the rear of the car.**

Sd Kfz 231 Heavy Armoured Car 8 Rad

Almost as soon as the first six-wheeled armoured cars entered service, the expanding German Army realized that a better vehicle was needed and so development started in 1935. The new vehicle was to have eight wheels and a more powerful engine, based on the chassis of the Bussing-NAG 8x8 truck. The new car was given the same designation as the six-wheeled car except that 8 Rad (8-wheel) was added after the name.

This new armoured car was the most advanced cross-country vehicle at the time with a good road speed. However, the vehicle was very complex, the chassis was very complicated and the vehicle was very expensive and slow to produce. The eight-wheel drive and steering proved to be of great benefit in areas such as the Eastern Front and it was well able to cope with the Russian mud. In combat, the vehicle's most significant drawback was its height, which made it easier to observe from a distance. The engine was mounted in the rear of the vehicle and the rear deck was sloped to give a clear view from the rear driving position, allowing the car to be driven easily in reverse. Combat reports led to a number of changes to the design

in 1940, the main one being increased armour. Production started in 1937 and finished in 1942, by which time 1,235 had been built. It remained in service until the end of World War II.

The Sd Kfz 232 was the long-range radio version with extra radios fitted. A large frame aerial was fixed above the rear of the vehicle, while a small frame was fitted to the top of the turret with a pivot which allowed the turret freedom to traverse with the aerial attached.

The Sd Kfz 263 was a special command vehicle that had a fixed superstructure in place of the turret, extra radio sets and a large frame aerial, as in the Sd Kfz 232, attached to the top of the vehicle.

These vehicles came to prominence during the fighting in North Africa when they could range far and wide in the open expanses of the desert environment.

ABOVE: **A late production Sd Kfz 232 heavy radio car. This Sd Kfz 232 is fitted with a star aerial, which replaced the fixed frame aerial, attached to the rear of the car. The Sd Kfz 232 was fitted internally with extra radio equipment. The small rods at the front and rear of the vehicle help the driver judge the vehicle width.** BELOW: **A standard heavy Sd Kfz 231 armoured car. This car is fitted with an armoured shield on the front of the car, which had a secondary role as a storage bin. The hatch on the front of the vehicle gives access to the driver's controls.** BOTTOM LEFT: **This is a fixed-frame Sd Kfz 232 radio car on active service in Poland in 1939. The additional armoured shield has not as yet been fitted to the vehicle. The white cross has been smeared with mud.**

Sd Kfz 231 Heavy Armoured Car 8 Rad

Country: Germany
Entered service: 1937
Crew: 4
Weight: 8,433kg/8.3 tons
Dimensions: Length – 5.85m/19ft 2in
  Height – 2.34m/7ft 8in
  Width – 2.2m/7ft 3in
Armament: Main – 2cm/0.79in KwK38 gun and
  coaxial 7.92mm/0.312in MG34 machine-gun
  Secondary – Small arms
Armour: Maximum – 30mm/1.18in
Powerplant: Bussing-NAG L8V-GS 8-cylinder
  112kW/150hp petrol engine
Performance: Speed – 85kph/53mph
  Range – 150km/95 miles

LEFT AND ABOVE: **The main gun is offset to the right of the vehicle and there is a large cut-out next to the driver to allow the weapon to fire directly forwards. The gunsight periscope can be seen above the gun shield on the driver's side.**

Sd Kfz 233 7.5cm Heavy Armoured Car 8 Rad

The Sd Kfz 233 was manufactured by F. Schichau in Elbing from December 1942 to October 1943 with a total production run of 119 vehicles. These vehicles were issued to armoured reconnaissance units of the German Army to increase the offensive power of the unit and to act as a close-support weapon.

The basic chassis of this vehicle was the same as the Sd Kfz 231 8 Rad heavy armoured car, but otherwise there were substantial differences between the two. The Sd Kfz 233 had the turret removed while the roof of the fighting compartment was cut away to allow the gun crew to man the main weapon, but they were very exposed as the sides of the vehicle gave them little protection

when standing up. On later models the height of the side walls of the fighting compartment were raised by 20mm/ 0.79in which gave the crew better protection, but the interior of the fighting compartment was very cramped as, apart from the gun and mount, there were 55 rounds of ammunition for the main armament. The front right-hand side of the original Sd Kfz 231 design was cut away to make room for the 7.5cm/2.95in KwK37 short-barrelled, low-velocity tank gun. This weapon was salvaged from Panzer III and Panzer IV tanks when both types had their main armament upgraded to a longer gun. It had very limited traverse, an elevation of only 12 degrees in every plane, and could fire high-

explosive and armour-piercing ammunition. The driver remained in the front of the vehicle, but was offset to the left-hand side to create space for the gun mount while the rear driving position was retained as before. The frontal armour of the vehicle was upgraded to 30mm/1.18in as a result of feedback from combat reports of early operations with the basic armoured car.

These vehicles first saw action with the *Afrika Korps* during the campaign in North Africa and were well-liked by their crews for their reliability and ruggedness. The Sd Kfz 233 served on all fronts during World War II.

Sd Kfz 233 7.5cm Heavy Armoured Car 8 Rad

Country: Germany
Entered service: 1942
Crew: 3
Weight: 8,839kg/8.7 tons
Dimensions: Length – 5.85m/19ft 2in
 Height – 2.25m/7ft 5in
 Width – 2.2m/7ft 2in
Armament: Main – 7.5cm/2.95in KwK37
 low-velocity gun
 Secondary – 7.92mm/0.312in MG34
 machine-gun
Armour: Maximum – 30mm/1.18in
Powerplant: Bussing-NAG L8V-GS 8-cylinder
 134kW/180hp petrol engine
Performance: Speed – 85kph/53mph
 Range – 300km/190 miles

ABOVE: **The top of this vehicle has been covered with a canvas sheet, which is supported on two curved frames. This vehicle is also fitted front and back with width indicators.**

Sd Kfz 234/2 Puma Heavy Armoured Car

In August 1940, the German Army issued a requirement for a new heavy armoured car. This was to have a monocoque hull, i.e. no chassis, the wheels and suspension being attached directly to the hull of the vehicle. The car was also to be fitted with a Tatra diesel engine that would be both more powerful and more suited to operating in hot climates. The new vehicle would have increased armoured protection, increased internal fuel capacity, and in general better performance than previous armoured cars. The new body design was given the designation ARK and production lasted from September 1943 to September 1944. The original order was for 1,500 vehicles but this was reduced to 100 when the Sd Kfz 234/1 (earlier number but later into production) came into service. The first Puma cars had a range of 600km/373 miles but by improving the fuel capacity this was increased to 1,000km/621 miles. These changes would make this car the best all-round vehicle in its class during World War II.

The turret of the Puma was originally designed for the cancelled Leopard light tank. It was of an oval design with steeply sloping sides, giving it an excellent ballistic shape, and there were two hatches in the roof. The main armament was fitted with a semi-automatic sliding breach and a hydro-pneumatic recoil system mounted above the gun. The barrel was terminated with a muzzle brake and the mantlet was a single piece casting known as a *"Saukopf"* (Sow's Head). The Puma was very similar in design to the Sd Kfz 231 but it had large single-piece side fenders with four built in storage boxes on each side.

The 100 Pumas were divided up into four units of 25 cars and sent to join four armoured regiments, with which they would see service on both the Eastern and Western Fronts. The superb Sd Kfz 234 series of cars were the only reconnaissance vehicles kept in production after March 1945 with 100 of the various marks being produced each month until the end of the war.

ABOVE: **This is an Sd Kfz 234/1 armoured car and uses the same chassis as the 234/2. In 1943 an order was given that 50 per cent of Sd Kfz 234 production was to be armed with the 2cm/0.79in KwK38. The top of the turret has been fitted with the wire-mesh anti-grenade screen.**

ABOVE: **This vehicle is fitted with a Saukopf gun mantlet, and there are three smoke dischargers on each side of the turret. The side panniers are now made in one piece and give more storage space.**
LEFT: **The exhaust for the car is mounted on the rear of the side pannier, just above the rear wheel. This car belonged to a Panzer Grenadier regiment in Normandy.**

Sd Kfz 234/2 5cm Puma Heavy Armoured Car

Country: Germany
Entered service: 1943
Crew: 4
Weight: 11,928kg/11.74 tons
Dimensions: Length – 6.8m/22ft 4in
    Height – 2.28m/7ft 6in
    Width – 2.4m/7ft 10in
Armament: Main – 5cm/1.97in KwK39/1
    anti-tank gun and coaxial 7.92mm/0.312in
    MG42 machine-gun
    Secondary – Small arms
Armour: Maximum – 30mm/1.18in
Powerplant: Tatra 103 12-cylinder 164kW/220hp diesel engine
Performance: Speed – 85kph/53mph
    Range – 1,000km/621 miles

Sd Kfz 234 7.5cm Heavy Support Armoured Cars

ABOVE LEFT: **The driver's position is now in the middle of the front of the car and the gun is mounted above the driver. The height of the armour has been increased to give the crew better protection.** ABOVE: **An Sd Kfz 234/4 armoured car armed with the PaK40 AT gun which went into production in December 1944.**

In September 1943, half of all the new Sd Kfz 234 chassis produced were ordered to be converted into support vehicles for the reconnaissance forces. These cars were to mount the 7.5cm/2.95in KwK37 to enable them to act as close-support vehicles. The KwK37 had been removed from the Panzer IV in 1942 when the tank was upgunned and these weapons had been placed into store until required, so this seemed a quick and easy way to give the reconnaissance force some real hitting power on the new chassis.

From June 1944, it was decided that only one in four vehicles would be converted in this way. Then in November 1944, Hitler ordered that the PaK40 should be fitted to these vehicles, turning them into self-propelled anti-tank mounts. It was consequently often called the PaK-Wagen by the troops. In December 1944, production of the Sd Kfz 234/3 was stopped in favour of the new vehicle, the Sd Kfz 234/4, which would remain in production until March 1945. The Germans produced 88 of the Sd Kfz 234/3 and 89 of the Sd Kfz 234/4. The fighting compartment of both vehicles was open-topped but the sides were raised to give the crew some protection from small arms fire and shell splinters. The PaK40 was mounted on a pedestal mount and had limited traverse. It was raised up in the fighting compartment so that the driver could remain in his position under the gun in the centre of the front of the vehicle. One significant shortcoming with the Sd Kfz 234/4 was that it could only

carry 12 rounds of ammunition; the Sd Kfz 234/3 on the other hand carried 50 rounds of ammunition. The crew in both vehicles was increased from three to four, so that the driver was not necessary as part of the gun crew and could remain in position.

These heavy-support armoured cars were mainly issued to units in the West, but not always to the Panzer divisions. A number of these vehicles were sent to Normandy to help in attempting to stop the Allied invasion of France, but were easy prey for Allied aircraft.

LEFT: **The PaK40 takes up most of the room in the fighting compartment. It is mounted on a pedestal mount behind the driver and retains its original gun shield. The gun crew were very exposed when operating the gun.**

Sd Kfz 234/3 7.5cm Heavy Support Armoured Car

Country: Germany
Entered service: 1944
Crew: 4
Weight: 11,684kg/11.5 tons
Dimensions: Length – 6m/19ft 8in
  Height – 2.21m/7ft 3in
  Width – 2.4m/7ft 10in
Armament: Main – 7.5cm/2.95in KwK37 gun
  Secondary – 7.92mm/0.312in MG34 or
  MG42 machine-gun
Armour: Maximum – 30mm/1.2in
Powerplant: Tatra 103 12-cylinder 164kW/220hp
  diesel engine
Performance: Speed – 85kph/53mph
  Range – 1,000km/621 miles

Sd Kfz 250 Half-Track Armoured Personnel Carrier

This vehicle had its roots in the operational requirements of the German Army in the mid-1930s which led to the manufacture of the Sd Kfz 251 3,048kg/3-ton half-track. The Sd Kfz 250 was produced by two companies; the Demag AG Company of Wetter in the Ruhr built the chassis while Bussing-NAG built the body of the vehicle. There was a total production run of 5,930 of these carriers, which were designed to transport a half-section of infantry in support of the reconnaissance units. Trials started in 1939 and although delays held up production until 1940, a number of these vehicles were in service with the German Army by the time of the invasion of France.

The Sd Kfz 250 was an open-topped vehicle which could carry five men and a driver. In the rear of the vehicle was a single door, which made debussing slow. The front wheels were not powered and so made steering heavy. When a sharp turn was made using the steering wheel,

this action would automatically engage the required track-brake and so help the vehicle make the sharp turn. Two other variations were being built at the same time as the basic vehicle. The first was an ammunition carrier for the StuG batteries while the other vehicle was a signals car that could carry two large radios and had a large frame aerial over the top. In 1943, the Sd Kfz 250 was completely redesigned to make production simpler and faster. The angled sides of the crew compartment were now flattened and made from a single piece of armour plate.

These half-tracks were built in 15 official variants and many other modifications were carried out by vehicle crews in the field. In one variant, an armoured cover was fitted over the crew compartment and a turret placed on top. These vehicles replaced the 4x4 Sd Kfz 222 armoured car in front-line service. Among the other variants there were a mortar carrier, a telephone

exchange, an ammunition carrier, a command car and a self-propelled gun mount. These vehicles would remain in service until the end of World War II.

ABOVE: **This Sd Kfz 250 is "under new ownership" as it is being driven by British soldiers. Half the gun shield is missing along with the machine-gun. The half-track is passing over a pontoon bridge.**
LEFT: **This Sd Kfz 250 half-track is on active service in the desert of North Africa. It has had its forward firepower increased by the fitting of a PaK35/36.**

RIGHT: **This vehicle replaced the Sd Kfz 222 wheeled armoured car in service. The rear of the vehicle was roofed over and the turret from the armoured car was placed into the roof of the half-track. This vehicle has a crew of three and would remain in service until 1945.**

Sd Kfz 250/1 Half-Track Armoured Personnel Carrier

Country: Germany
Entered service: 1940
Crew: 1 plus 5 infantry
Weight: 5,893kg/5.8 tons
Dimensions: Length – 4.56m/15ft
 Height – 1.98m/6ft 6in
 Width – 1.95m/6ft 5in
Armament: Main – 2 x 7.92mm/0.312in MG34 machine-gun
 Secondary – Small arms
Armour: Maximum – 14.5mm/0.57in
Powerplant: Maybach HL42 6-cylinder 74.6kW/100hp petrol engine
Performance: Speed – 59.5kph/37mph
 Range – 299km/186 miles

LEFT AND ABOVE: **The Sd Kfz 251 on the left has the normal frontal armament of a single machine-gun, while the vehicle above has had the PaK35/36 fitted to increase the fire power of the half-track.**

Sd Kfz 251 Medium Half-Track

During the development of the Panzer Division in Germany throughout the 1930s it was very quickly realized that an armoured personnel carrier would be required and that this would have to have good cross-country ability to keep pace with the tanks. Development of a suitable vehicle started in 1937 with Hanomag producing the chassis and Bussing-NAG building the body. Production started in 1939 and initially three marks, A, B, and C, were built with 4,650 vehicles produced in total, but by far the largest production run was of the Ausf D of which 10,602 were built. This mark would remain in production until the end of World War II. General Guderian was unhappy with the original design as he anticipated that the Panzer Grenadiers would occasionally have to fight from inside their vehicles making the large open top a great weakness.

ABOVE: **This knocked-out Sd Kfz 251 Ausf D is a late version and has its engine covers in the open position.**

The chassis of the Sd Kfz 251 was very strong and well-protected and this gave the whole vehicle great strength. The body of the vehicle was bolted to the chassis in the early marks and was made in two sections with each section being bolted together just behind the driver's position. The body of Ausf A, B and C had a good ballistic shape but were very difficult and slow to produce. Hanomag and Bussing-NAG could not keep up with demand so other manufacturers were brought in to speed up production. The engine was at the front with the driver and commander's position behind and this area had an armoured roof on which a machine-gun was mounted. The platoon commander's vehicle would have a 3.7cm/1.46in anti-tank gun mounted on the roof instead of the machine-gun. The infantry section sat in the back on two benches running the length of the rear area with the men facing inwards. Two large doors giving easy accessibility for the infantry section were positioned at the rear, and above these was a mount for an anti-aircraft machine-gun. There were no brakes fitted to the front wheels; these were fitted instead to the driving sprockets of the track section. The tracks were light and lubricated, and each track shoe was fitted with a rubber pad which helped prolong the track life of the vehicle. Each road wheel had a rubber tyre and was grouped in a pair, being supported on a torsion bar type suspension system.

The last type of the Sd Kfz 251 was the Ausf D. This went into production in 1944 and was a major redesign of the basic vehicle. The Ausf D had a greatly simplified construction with the use of larger flat armour plates to build the body, which was now of an all-welded construction. The rear door was built with a reverse slope and the storage boxes along the sides had become part of the main body of the vehicle.

LEFT: **This German vehicle is symbolic of Blitzkrieg and would remain in service with other countries for many years after the war. The Sd Kfz 251 Ausf A has a large number of angled plates and this made production slow. Three storage bins are fitted on each side of the vehicle between the top of the tracks and the body of the vehicle.**

There were no less than 22 official variations of the basic half-track design. Many were simply changes in the armament fitted to the vehicle while others included command, communications, ambulance and observation types. The most powerful variant of these vehicles was the Sd Kfz 251/1 *Stuka zum Fuss* (Dive-bomber on Foot) which was more commonly known as the Infantry Stuka. Racks were fitted to the sides of the vehicle and three 28cm/11in or 32cm/12.6in rockets, which could be fitted with either high-explosive or incendiary warheads, could be mounted on each side. They were used to demolish strongpoints or large structures and also to give support to an attack on an enemy position. The last version was the Sd Kfz 251/22 which mounted the PaK40 7.5cm/2.95in anti-tank gun. However, the sheer weight of the weapon overloaded the half-track and firing the gun also put a great strain on the suspension of the vehicle.

Skoda in Czechoslovakia was one of the manufacturers of the Sd Kfz 251 and it was decided after World War II to keep it in production for the Czechoslovakian Army as the firm was tooled up to build this vehicle. With this second lease of life the vehicle would remain in service until 1980.

ABOVE: **This picture clearly shows the low profile of the Sd Kfz 251 Ausf A. To increase the frontal armour of the vehicle a common practice was to attach spare track-link to the front.** LEFT: **This is the post-war version of the Sd Kfz 251 that continued to be made in Czechoslovakia after World War II. This vehicle was known as the OT-810 and would remain in service for many years.**

Sd Kfz 251/1 Ausf A Medium Half-Track

Country: Germany
Entered service: 1939
Crew: 2 plus 10 infantry
Weight: 7,935kg/7.81 tons
Dimensions: Length – 5.8m/19ft
    Height – 1.75m/5ft 9in
    Width – 2.1m/6ft 10in
Armament: Main – 2 x 7.92mm/0.312in MG34
    machine-guns
    Secondary – Small arms
Armour: Maximum – 15mm/0.59in
Powerplant: Maybach HL42 TUKRM 6-cylinder
    89kW/120hp petrol engine
Performance: Speed – 53kph/33mph
    Range – 300km/185 miles

Sd Kfz 251 Support Vehicles

The Sd Kfz 251 went through many conversions into various close-support vehicles for the German Army and Luftwaffe. Some of these conversions were undertaken in a great hurry and proved less than satisfactory such as the Sd Kfz 251/17 Flak conversion, that was modified in the field and turned out to be of little use.

In March 1942 Bussing-NAG were instructed to develop a close-support version of their half-track, as the German infantry required better support in their attacks particularly if StuGs were unavailable. Two test vehicles were sent to the Eastern Front in June 1942 and proved to be very good, resulting in an order being placed that month for another 150 Sd Kfz 251/9s. These vehicles mounted the short 7.5cm/2.95in KwK40 gun from the old Panzer III and Panzer IV.

The co-driver's position was dispensed with as the weapon was mounted in this space and the roof and front vision port were removed so the gun could sit next to the driver. However, this was a very complicated conversion so the gun mount was redesigned in early 1944 so it could also be fitted to other vehicles such as the Sd Kfz 250. The new mount sat on top of the existing body of the vehicle and gave the crew extra protection.

The Sd Kfz 251/16 was a flamethrower vehicle. It was fitted with two flame guns and carried 700 litres/154 gallons of flame fuel. The rear door was fixed in the closed position as one of the fuel tanks was positioned in front of it. The vehicle carried enough fuel for 80 two-second bursts from the flame gun which had a range of 35m/115ft. These entered service in January 1943 and most were

ABOVE LEFT: **The exhaust system for the vehicle is mounted between the front wheel and the tracks. As there was only a crew of three, there was a lot of room for ammunition and equipment storage in the rear of the vehicle.** ABOVE: **Guns from old Panzer IV tanks were used to arm vehicles such as this. The vehicle commander's seat was removed and the armour was cut away.**

sent to the Eastern Front. They proved to be very useful in street fighting. Other conversions produced command, radio, ambulance, engineering and ammunition carriers. The Sd Kfz 251 was a vehicle that was well-liked by its crews and crucially was capable of being adapted to many uses on the battlefield.

LEFT: **This is the working end of the 7.5cm/2.95in KwK L/24 gun. The gun was taken from the PzKpfw IV when these tanks were upgunned. It was placed on a simple cradle in the half-track, making for a fast and easy conversion.**

Sd Kfz 251/9 Close Support Vehicle

Country: Germany
Entered service: 1942
Crew: 3
Weight: 8,738kg/8.6 tons
Dimensions: Length – 5.98m/19ft 7in
Height – 2.07m/6ft 9in
Width –2.1m/6ft 11in
Armament: Main – 7.5cm/2.95in KwK37 L/24 gun
Secondary – 2 x 7.92mm/0.312in MG34
machine-guns
Armour: Maximum – 15mm/0.59in
Powerplant: Maybach HL42 TUKRM 6-cylinder
89kW/120hp petrol engine
Performance: Speed – 53kph/33mph
Range – 300km/186 miles

LEFT: **This vehicle uses the M40 chassis which was the first type used. The main visual difference between the two chassis is that the track-guard does not run the length of the vehicle in the M40.** ABOVE: **This SPG uses the M42 chassis and was the final version of this vehicle. The gun has a very distinctive "pepper-pot" muzzle brake.**

Semovente M42 DA 75/18 Self-Propelled Gun

This was an excellent self-propelled gun/howitzer and was the first Italian vehicle to be produced as part of a series during World War II. The M42 was tested in early 1941 and went into production the same year with the first vehicles being issued to service units later that year. The first unit to receive these new vehicles was the Ariete Division who initially used it in North Africa in early 1942. Originally intended to fulfil a self-propelled artillery role within the armoured division, they were more often deployed in an anti-tank role. At this time, these vehicles were the best armed self-propelled guns in North Africa and could easily outgun any British or German tank.

The first vehicles in this series were built on the M13/40 tank chassis, but later the chassis of the M14/41 was used, with production being stopped in 1943. The first order was for 200 vehicles and this was met in full, with a further order for 500 being placed in 1943. These new vehicles were to be equipped with the 75/34, a longer gun. The M42 could carry 100 rounds of 75mm/2.95in

ammunition. However, delays in putting the new P40 tank into production resulted in the unused guns being fitted to the M42, which then became the M42M. None of these vehicles were issued to the Italian Army before Italy's surrender but they were captured and used by the Germans.

Each M42 battery was given a command vehicle built on the M13/40 chassis. This was basically a turretless tank chassis that was initially armed with twin 8mm/0.315in machine-guns mounted on the right-hand side of the vehicle. The twin guns were later replaced by a single 13.5mm/0.53in heavy machine-gun.

When Italy surrendered in 1943, the Germans took over the production facilities for the M42 as they had found this vehicle to be very good. They also took 292 of them into German service, common practice with captured weapons they admired. These vehicles would see constant service during 1944 in Italy and the Balkans and by January 1945 only 93 were left in action after months of heavy fighting.

ABOVE: **The driver's position in the Semovente M42. The side of the main armament sits beside the driver's head. The large lever in the picture is the firing handle.**

Semovente M42 DA 75/18 SPG

Country: Italy
Entered service: 1942
Crew: 3
Weight: 15,240kg/15 tons
Dimensions: Length – 5.04m/16ft 6in
Height – 1.85m/6ft 1in
Width – 2.23m/7ft 4in
Armament: Main – 75mm/2.95in model 35 gun/howitzer
Secondary – 8mm/0.315in Breda model 38
Armour: Maximum – 50mm/1.97in
Powerplant: Spa 15 TM41 8-cylinder 138kW/185hp petrol engine
Performance: Speed – 38kph/24mph
Range – 230km/143 miles

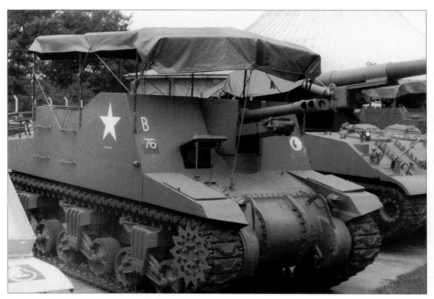

LEFT: **The Canadian Ram tank was used for this conversion. The Ram was a right-hand-drive vehicle and so the British crews took to it quickly. The driver's hatch on this vehicle is in the open position. The fighting compartment is covered with a canvas roof giving the crew some protection from the weather.**

Sexton 25pdr Self-Propelled Gun

In 1942, the Americans attempted to improve the M7 Priest by replacing the existing armament with a British 25pdr gun. The "pulpit" was retained to give the vehicle some close-quarter protection, and the gun was mounted well over on the right-hand side of the fighting compartment. There were a number of delays in the development programme when the first live-firing of the gun destroyed the gun mount. By the time the vehicle was ready for a second test firing, the Canadians had come up with the Sexton and so in March 1943 the British cancelled the American project in favour of the simpler Canadian vehicle.

The Canadian Department of National Defence selected the Ram tank to act as a chassis for the 25pdr gun to meet the British Army requirement for a self-propelled gun. The pilot model was finished in late 1942 and it proved to be very successful in tests. Production started at the Montreal Locomotive Works in early 1943 and continued until 1945, by which time 2,150 had been built. Originally designated the "25-pounder Ram Carrier", it was renamed following Royal Artillery tradition and given the religious name "Sexton". The 25pdr was mounted just off the centreline to the left-hand side of the fighting compartment. The driver's position was on the right-

LEFT AND RIGHT: **The driver's position in the vehicle is very cramped and yet very light, as it is open at the top into the fighting compartment. The dashboard has the minimum of gauges, and in the centre are the track control levers. The large doors on the rear of the vehicle give access to the radial engine.**

hand side of the fighting compartment down in the bottom of the tank chassis, the driver being below the level of the gun. The fighting compartment was constructed out of 12mm/0.47in armour plate, with an open back and low sides extending to just above waist height. It was also open-topped and exposed to the elements. However, a number of Sexton batteries had steel loops made in field workshops so that a canvas cover or tent could be placed over the fighting compartment. The front of the fighting compartment was protected by 25mm/0.98in armour plate with the final drive housing being in three pieces that were bolted together.

The 25pdr gun had a traverse of 25 degrees to the left and 15 degrees to the right, while the elevation range was plus 40 degrees to minus 9 degrees. The recoil of the gun was also restricted to 51cm/1ft 8in compared with 91cm/3ft of the standard 25pdr. The main ammunition storage was under the floor of the fighting compartment and held 112 rounds, but there was also one small ready-to-use locker on the rear wall of the fighting compartment. On a later version of the Sexton this housing was changed to a single casting and the running gear was modified. The suspension system was also changed on the Sexton II from an M3 style to an M4 trailing arm type, and the Canadian dry pin track was used. The rear deck of the vehicle carried box structures in each corner for batteries and an auxiliary generator.

The first 124 vehicles produced were designated Sexton I, but following a number of modifications the improved vehicle became the Sexton II. The Sexton I had no provision for anti-aircraft machine-guns on the vehicle and this was addressed with the Sexton II with the addition of two Bren light machine-guns. A number of Sextons also had a 12.7mm/50cal machine-gun fitted to the front left-hand corner of the fighting compartment as a field modification.

Some Sextons were converted to Gun Position Officers (GPO) vehicles with one of these being issued to each Sexton battery. This conversion involved the removal of the gun and most of the internal fittings to provide space for a map table, extra field telephones, and radios.

The Sexton would become the standard medium self-propelled gun used by the British and Canadian armies in World War II. It first saw action with the 8th Army in Italy and was used throughout the campaign in northern Europe. Some British units that were converted from the Priest to the Sexton had very few days to practise with their new equipment before going into action on June 6, 1944. A number of Sexton units were allocated "run-in shooting" missions (firing at shore targets from the landing craft bringing them in) as they landed on the D-Day beaches. This was intended to aid in the suppression of the German beach defences but, perhaps not surprisingly, was not very accurate.

ABOVE: **This Sexton has had an additional machine-gun fitted to the front of the fighting compartment above the driver. The front of the vehicle is three separate pieces bolted together. This gun has been assigned to the 11th Armoured Division.** BELOW: **The main weapon of the Sexton is the British 25pdr gun. The breach of this weapon slides vertically and the red wheels are the elevation and traverse controls.**

Sexton 25pdr SPG

Country: Canada
Entered service: 1942
Crew: 6
Weight: 25,908kg/25.5 tons
Dimensions: Length – 6.12m/20ft 1in
　　　　Height – 2.43m/8ft
　　　　Width – 2.71m/8ft 11in
Armament: Main – 11kg/25pdr C Mk II or III
　　　　Secondary – 2 x 7.7mm/0.303in Bren
　　　　light machine-gun
Armour: Maximum – 32mm/1.26in
Powerplant: Continental 9-cylinder 298kW/400hp
　　　　radial petrol engine
Performance: Speed – 38kph/24mph
　　　　Range – 200km/125 miles

LEFT: The height of this vehicle is very apparent and led to a number of problems during combat. The driver's position is on the left-hand side of the vehicle. These SPGs were issued to six Panzer divisions in 1940. BELOW: The gun and its unaltered carriage were placed on to the top of the Panzer I. The open rear and open top of the gun shield give the crew very little protection from either the weather or small-arms fire.

sIG33 15cm Infantry Support Self-Propelled Gun

This was the first self-propelled gun to see service in the German Army of World War II, and valuable experience was gained from its combat performance. It was an improvised vehicle manufactured to an army specification for a fully tracked vehicle that could give close support to the infantry. These vehicles were built by Alkett in 1939 and entered service in time to take part in the Blitzkrieg operation throughout northern France and the Low Countries in 1940. While it represented a great step forward for the military, it had significant faults and only 38 of these vehicles were built.

The chassis was that of the Panzer I Ausf B with the turret removed and the superstructure left in place. At this time,

the Panzer I was already being replaced by bigger and better tanks thus providing the chassis to mount the sIG33. A large box structure, 1.83m/6ft in height constructed of 10mm/0.394in armour was built on the vehicle. This box was open-topped, with two small doors on the rear which did not meet in the middle but only partially closed the opening. The gun, which retained its wheels and box trail, was mounted inside the box on the top of the tank superstructure.

This SPG could be brought into action very quickly and open fire instantly. It also proved to be very efficient in service. However, it is worth considering that all infantry guns were horse-drawn until this vehicle made its appearance, and so it did not have any equivalent competition.

The vehicle was not designated an Sd Kfz number and had a number of major faults. At over 2.74m/9ft high, the vehicle was very tall which gave it a high centre of gravity. It was also overloaded which placed a great strain on the suspension and contributed to the poor cross-country ability.

These guns were issued to Heavy Infantry Gun Companies 701–706, in early 1940. They would remain in service until 1943 when the last unit, the 704th of the 5th Panzer Division, was refitted.

sIG33 15cm Infantry Support SPG	

Country: Germany
Entered service: 1940
Crew: 4
Weight: 8,636kg/8.5 tons
Dimensions: Length – 4.42m/14ft 6in
  Height – 3.35m/11ft
  Width – 2.6m/8ft 6in
Armament: Main – 15cm/5.91in sIG33 L/11 gun
  Secondary – Small arms
Armour: Maximum – 13mm/0.51in
Powerplant: Maybach NL38 TKRM 6-cylinder
  75kW/100hp petrol engine
Performance: Speed – 40kph/25mph
  Range – 140km/87 miles

LEFT: An improved mount for the sIG 15cm was built using the Panzer II chassis. An extra road wheel had to be fitted to each side of the vehicle, which had been widened and lengthened. Only 12 of these vehicles were built and all were sent to the *Afrika Korps* in North Africa.

LEFT: This Staghound has both the driver's and hull gunner's front hatches in the open position. The side hatch behind the front wheel is also open and gives direct access to the driver's position. The large drum on the side of the vehicle is a fuel tank.
ABOVE: British Staghound armoured cars moving along an old railway line. The tyres of the cars have been fitted with "snow chains" to help them move across the soft ground in the winter. These cars remained in British service well after World War II.
BELOW LEFT: This is the close-support version of the Staghound and was armed with a short 76.2mm/3in howitzer.

Staghound Armoured Car

The Staghound was an American designed and built vehicle that was destined never to be used by the US Army. All the cars of this type that were produced were sent to the British and Commonwealth armies. The design had its origins in a US Army requirement for a heavy armoured car, which was developed in two forms – one with six wheels (T17) and one with four wheels (T17E1). The British Tank Mission to America saw the two cars, which had been heavily influenced by British experience in battle, selected the T17E1 and placed an initial order for 300 vehicles. Production started in early 1942 with the first vehicles entering service in later the same year. In British service, the vehicle was called the Staghound Mk I.

The Staghound was a large well-armoured vehicle having a 37mm/ 1.46in gun and coaxial 7.62mm/0.3in machine-gun in the turret. In combat it proved to be very reliable, easy to maintain and had good cross-country ability. It had a fully automatic hydraulic transmission with two engines mounted side by side in the rear of the vehicle, and two 173-litre/38-gallon jettison fuel tanks to increase the vehicle's range. The vehicle had no chassis with the suspension parts attaching directly to the hull. Two further machine-guns were fitted to the vehicle, one in the front next to the driver and one on a pintle mount on the rear of the turret for anti-aircraft use. However, the Staghound was found to be too large, heavy and unwieldy for fighting in northern Europe and Italy compared to the British Daimler armoured car and was not well-liked by its British and Commonwealth crews.

The British were to produce three more versions of the Staghound. The Mk II was a close-support version with a short 75mm/ 2.95in gun mounted in a new turret. The Mk III was an attempt to upgun the Staghound by fitting the Crusader III 75mm/2.95in gun turret to the vehicle, turning it into a wheeled tank. The last conversion was the Staghound AA vehicle, armed with two 12.7mm/0.5in machine-guns in a small open-topped turret. None of these conversions was produced in large numbers.

Staghound Mk I Armoured Car

Country: USA
Entered service: 1942
Crew: 5
Weight: 14,122kg/13.9 tons
Dimensions: Length – 5.49m/18ft
 Height – 2.36m/7ft 9in
 Width – 2.69m/8ft 10in
Armament: Main – 37mm/1.46in ATG,
 and coaxial 7.62mm/0.3in machine-gun
 Secondary – 2 x 7.62mm/0.3in machine-guns
Armour: Maximum – 22mm/0.866in
Powerplant: 2 x GMC 270 6-cylinder 72kW/97hp
 petrol engine
Performance: Speed – 89kph/55mph
 Range – 724km/450 miles

Sturmgeschutz III Self-Propelled Gun

The Sturmgeschutz III (StuG III) was an excellent vehicle performing well as a close-support weapon and, with its ability to take larger guns, would remain in service for most of World War II. It was relatively cheap and easy to produce when compared with a tank and this proved to be important in wartime Germany. Towards the end of the war, the StuG III would also have to fill gaps left by the shortage of tanks in the Panzer divisions – a role for which it was never designed – and was without doubt one of the most important vehicles the Germans produced in World War II.

The order to develop a close-support vehicle was given in June 1937 and by January 1940 the resulting vehicle was placed into production and given the designation of StuG III Ausf A. Two companies, Alkett and MIAG, undertook most of the production but these would be joined by MAN at times when extra output capacity was required. It used the same chassis, suspension and engine as the Panzer III Ausf F. The upper hull and turret were removed and replaced with a thick carapace of armour. A short 7.5cm/2.95in gun was mounted in the front of the vehicle and offset to the right providing space for the driver who sat on the left next to the main armament. These basic positions would not change throughout its career, even after a number of improvements. The Ausf B had improvements to the engine while Ausf C and D had improvements to the superstructure of the fighting compartment. The Ausf E was the last of the short-barrelled StuG IIIs and it was the first model to have a close-support machine-gun fitted to the upper hull. The standard gun up until then had been the 7.5cm/2.95in L/24 gun (the length of the barrel was 24 times the calibre).

TOP: **This was the most numerous StuG produced during World War II. The vehicle was made up of the Panzer III chassis and running gear. The superstructure was in two parts, with the main armament trunnioned between. The shield on the roof of the vehicle is for the close-support machine-gun.**
ABOVE: **The travel lock is mounted on the front of the vehicle under the gun barrel. When the vehicle was travelling any distance the barrel would be locked in place to save the gun mounting from damage.**

From April 1942 onwards when the Ausf F entered service, the gun length increased to L/43, and this was further improved in June when the gun was changed to the L/48. This gave the StuG III a very potent anti-tank capability that would serve the vehicle well for the remainder of the war.

The last version of the StuG III was the Ausf G that entered service in January 1943 and would remain in production and active service until the end of the war. The Ausf G had a number of improvements to the superstructure, such as the addition of a commander's cupola with periscopes and sloping of the side plates. Other modifications were the introduction of the *Saukopf* (Sow's Head) gun mantlet in late 1943, and the

LEFT: **The front of the fighting compartment had extra armour bolted to it, as on the left-hand side of the picture. In the middle is the gun mantlet and on the right is the driver's vision slit.** ABOVE: **This StuG III has had several bolt-on plates added to the front of the vehicle to increase its armour thickness.**

LEFT: **Two British soldiers are looking at the hits on this StuG III which has been struck four times on the lower front hull plate. The gun mantlet has collapsed into the vehicle.**

addition of a coaxial machine-gun in early 1944 as these vehicles were now engaging enemy infantry at close-quarters.

Variants of the StuG III included an assault howitzer which mounted a 10.5cm/4.13in gun for close-support duties. Alkett manufactured a total of 1,211 of these vehicles from October 1942 to March 1945.

From 1943 onwards, the StuG III was fitted with two further defensive measures. February 1943 saw the introduction of *Schürzen* (skirts). Made from wire mesh or metal plates, these helped stop anti-tank shells from penetrating the side of the vehicle where the armour was thin. However, the procurement of wire mesh proved difficult and so side-skirts of this type were not produced in great numbers. The second defensive measure was the introduction of *Zimmerit*. This was

a protective coating, 3–5mm/0.1–0.2in thick, that covered the hull and superstructure and was intended to prevent Russian troops from attaching magnetic mines or shaped charges to the hull of the vehicle. Initially this coating was to be made of tar but AFV crews rejected this due to the fire hazard, so a thin layer of cement paste was put on the vehicle instead, giving it a very distinctive finish.

During World War II, 74 StuG units were formed and these saw active service on all fronts. Total war production was 10,306 Sturmgeschutz III vehicles.

Sturmgeschutz III SPG Ausf G

Country: Germany
Entered service: January 1943
Crew: 4
Weight: 24,282kg/23.9 tons
Dimensions: Length – 6.77m/22ft 3in
    Height – 2.16m/7ft 1in
    Width – 2.95m/9ft 8in
Armament: Main – 7.5cm/2.95in StuK40
    L/48 gun
    Secondary – 2 x 7.92mm/0.312in MG42
    machine-guns
Armour: Maximum – 80mm/3.15in
Powerplant: Maybach HL 120 TRM 12-cylinder
    197.6kW/265hp petrol engine
Performance: Speed – 40kph/24.9mph
    Range – 165km/102 miles

ABOVE: **This is one of the first StuG III prototype vehicles to enter service and has an open-topped fighting compartment. The vehicle is armed with the short 75cm/2.95in gun.**

Sturmgeschutz IV Self-Propelled Gun

In February 1943, the Krupp company was asked to look at a proposal for mounting the StuG III superstructure on the Panzer IV chassis (8 BW). However, instead of using a basic Panzer IV chassis Krupp used a new development, the 9 BW chassis, which would have sloped frontal armour and much thicker side armour. These alterations would cause great disruption to StuG and Panzer IV production lines and resulted in no great saving in either the weight or the materials used in the new vehicle. These disruptions were deemed intolerable at this time, the spring of 1943, as the war was showing signs of turning against Germany.

In late November 1943, the Alkett factory was badly damaged during a bombing raid and production of the StuG III suffered. Hitler insisted that the shortfall must be made up and therefore some of the Panzer IV facilities at the Krupp factory in Magdeburg were reassigned to the production of a StuG IV using StuG III superstructures. The new StuG IV was shown to

ABOVE LEFT: **A column of StuG IVs stopped in the road. The vehicles are all fitted with the Saukopf mantle, and are carrying spare road wheels on the side of the vehicle.** ABOVE: **The front of this StuG has been covered with various lengths of spare track.**

Hitler on December 16, 1943, and he approved the vehicle, insisting that it was put into production immediately. An additional impetus was provided by combat reports stating that the Panzer IV was having a hard time on the battlefield, and the losses from battles such as Kursk also had to be made up as quickly as possible.

The Panzer IV chassis was combined with the super-structure of the StuG III G but due to the greater length of the tank, the driver's compartment was positioned forward of the superstructure and a special armoured cupola was built for the driver. This box-shaped structure was situated on the left-hand side at the front of the vehicle, with two periscopes

LEFT: **This vehicle has been fitted with rails for the side-skirt armour. The body of the SPG has been covered in anti-magnetic** *Zimmerit* **paste. On the roof of the vehicle is a remote-controlled close-support machine-gun which is operated from inside the vehicle by one of the gun crew. The rail on the hull front is for spare track.**

mounted on top of the cupola along with an escape hatch. The Panzer IV escape hatch was in the belly of the vehicle for use by the driver and radio operator, but in the StuG IV this was welded shut as it was not required. Ammunition storage was 87 rounds; an additional 12-round bin was planned for the engine bay utilizing vacant space left by the unfitted turret motors. However, this caused problems and at times great confusion at the chassis production plants so the idea was dropped. The StuG IV was also to be fitted with concrete armour. The concrete was to be applied some 100mm/3.9in thick, mainly to the driver's position and the flat front on the right-hand side of the superstructure, but tests revealed that this did not help deflect incoming munitions and it added considerable weight to the vehicle. The modification was therefore stopped by the manufacturers, who simply put a coat of *Zimmerit* on the vehicle. However, the troops in the field thought it was a good idea and so added the concrete and extra armour plate to what they felt were weak areas. The driver's seat was adjustable and the back rest could be folded down so that the driver could escape into the fighting compartment if necessary. A 2,032kg/2-ton crane could be attached to the hull of the vehicle to ease the removal of the gun and could also be used for basic engine maintenance. The StuG IV was also fitted with the new Rundum-Feuer machine-gun, which could be operated from inside the vehicle and give all-round defence against attacking enemy infantry. Like with the StuG III, the StuG IV was fitted with *Schürzen* (skirts). These had been inspected by Hitler in March 1943 and were placed in to production immediately with the first field modification kits going out in early June 1943 to be fitted by field workshops.

The Sturmgeschutz was intended to act as close support for the infantry, but this was one role that the StuG IV would not perform as the bulk of these vehicles went either to Panzerjager units to act as tank destroyers or to Panzer Divisions as replacements for knocked-out tanks. In total, 1,141 StuG IVs were built by Krupp.

ABOVE: **This StuG IV has the side-skirts fitted. These acted as a form of spaced armour. The driver's position on the StuG IV was moved forward of the superstructure.** BELOW: **A close-up of the driver's cupola: the driver's hatch is in the open position. The vehicle commander's hatch is also open and the cut-out for the commander's periscope can be seen. The front of the driver's position has a thick layer of concrete which acts as additional armour.**

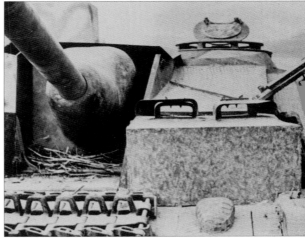

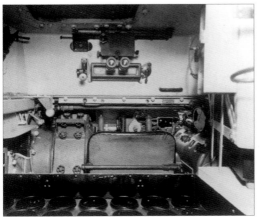

LEFT: **The driver's position inside a StuG IV. The periscope can be seen in front of the driver's seat. Above in the roof is the driver's hatch. The driving instruments are mounted on the right-hand side. In the front of the picture is one of the ammunition containers.**

Sturmgeschutz IV SPG

Country: Germany
Entered service: 1944
Crew: 4
Weight: 23,368kg/23 tons
Dimensions: Length – 6.7m/22ft
Height – 2.2m/7ft 3in
Width – 2.95m/9ft 8in
Armament: Main – 7.5cm/2.95in StuK40 L/48 gun
Secondary – 2 x 7.92mm/0.312in MG42
machine-guns
Armour: Maximum – 80mm/3.15in
Powerplant: Maybach HL 120 TRM 12-cylinder
198kW/265hp petrol engine
Performance: Speed – 38kph/24mph
Range – 210km/131 miles

LEFT: The hull of this Sturmmörser Tiger has been covered in *Zimmerit*, while the new superstructure and glacis are in painted bare metal. The crane on the rear of the fighting compartment is for loading the ammunition. ABOVE: Inside the rear of the fighting compartment is the ammunition storage. Six rounds were stored on each side of the loading tray. Due to the weight of the rounds, they were placed on the loading tray before being pushed up and into the weapon.

Sturmmörser Tiger Assault Rocket Mortar

The Sturm Tiger was the largest of the German heavy self-propelled guns produced during World War II. Officially these vehicles were known as *38cm Raketenwerfer 61 auf Sturmmörser Tiger* (38cm Rocket Launcher 61 on Assault Mortar Tiger). They were never issued with an Sd Kfz number and only 18 of them were built by their manufacturer, Alkett.

The project originally arose out of a requirement from Hitler in August 1943 to mount the 21cm heavy-support gun, but this was changed when the 38cm launcher became available and could be mounted on a Tiger 1 chassis. Hitler felt that there would be a great demand from the troops in the front line for these vehicles. The inspiration came from battle experience gained at Stalingrad and Leningrad, where there was a requirement for heavy close-support vehicles. Hitler and Guderian agreed for one prototype to be built, with, if successful, a production run of ten vehicles per month. The prototype was demonstrated to Hitler in October 1943, and in April 1944 it was decided to start a limited production run of a dozen vehicles, launchers and superstructures.

The vehicle conversions were carried out by Alkett at their Berlin/Spandau works. By September 1944, the first seven vehicles had been finished with the total rising to 18 vehicles by the end of the year. The monthly output of 38cm rockets was envisaged to be 300 rounds, this weapon having originally been developed for the German Navy as an anti-submarine warfare system. Two different warheads were available, one being high-explosive and the other being a hollow charge. The complete round which weighed 329kg/726lb was 1.5m/5ft long, and was loaded on to the vehicle using a hand-operated crane mounted on the rear of the superstructure. The ceiling of

ABOVE: **A German Bergepanther is being used to move this Sturmmörser Tiger. The enormous size of the vehicle can be seen from the two British officers standing next to the vehicle.**

the vehicle was fitted with an overhead hoist to move the ammunition from its racks and on to a loading tray, a ram was used to load the weapon and then the loading tray was folded away so the weapon could be fired. There was storage for 12 rounds in the fighting compartment and a thirteenth was carried loaded in the mortar.

The conversion of the vehicle consisted of removing the turret and hull top of the Tiger from the engine compartment forward. The new fighting compartment made from sloping armour plate was placed over the open space. The front glacis plate was sloped at 45 degrees and was 150mm/5.91in thick, with the driver's vision block on the left side with a sighting

LEFT: **On the left of the picture is the close-support machine-gun blister. Above the driver's vision slit is the sighting aperture for the main weapon.**
ABOVE: **Inside the fighting compartment. A round has been placed in the weapon and the breach is about to be closed. The circle of small holes on the rear of the round is the rocket motor exhausts.**

aperture above it and a close-support machine-gun on the right. The side and rear plates were made of 80mm/3.15in armour with a circular hatch in the rear wall of the fighting compartment and a large loading door for the ammunition in the roof.

The rocket launcher was the most interesting part of this vehicle. It was breech-loaded and the barrel was rifled with a right-hand twist to induce spin into the munitions as they left the weapon. As the munitions were rocket-propelled, a way had to be found of stopping the rockets' exhaust from entering the fighting compartment. The exhaust gases operated a bypass valve in the breech which allowed the gases to escape forwards as the round left the barrel. The vehicle had to carry out "shoot and scoot" operations as the exhaust from the

weapon was a give-away of the position of the vehicle even at the maximum range of 6km/3.7 miles.

As these vehicles could only carry a few rounds, each gun vehicle had to be supported by a tracked ammunition carrier built on Tiger 1 chassis that would carry an extra 40 rounds. Only one vehicle was ever produced before the Alkett factory was overrun by the Soviet Army.

Eighteen chassis were completed but only 12 of these vehicles were finished to be used in combat and these were formed into three companies of four vehicles each. The companies were 1001, 1002 and 1003, and were all used in the defence of the homeland, a task for which they were ill-suited. Some of them were used during the destruction of Warsaw and in fighting in other large cities.

ABOVE: **The small square blocks on the end of the barrel are for the attachment of a counterweight. On the top of the fighting compartment is a dome-shaped fume extractor.**

Sturmmörser Tiger Assault Rocket Mortar

Country: Germany
Entered service: 1944
Crew: 5
Weight: 66,040kg/65 tons
Dimensions: Length – 6.28m/20ft 7in
  Height – 2.85m/9ft 4in
  Width – 3.57m/11ft 9in
Armament: Main – 38cm/14.96in Stu M RW61
  L/5.4 rocket motar
  Secondary – 7.92mm/0.312in MG42
  machine-gun
Armour: Maximum – 150mm/5.91in
Powerplant: Maybach HL 230 P45 12-cylinder
  522kW/700hp petrol engine
Performance: Speed – 40kph/25mph
  Range – 120km/75 miles

LEFT: Several batteries of SU-76 vehicles drawn up for inspection. Part of the exhaust system can be seen below the vehicle number. This vehicle has had at least one tank kill, as it is painted on the side of the fighting compartment. BELOW: The very small fighting compartment can be clearly seen. The gunner is on the left, loader in the middle and vehicle commander on the right. The driver remained in his position in the front of the vehicle.

SU-76 Self-Propelled Gun

In 1942, the task of developing a new self-propelled gun was given to the Kolomenskiy Locomotive Works in Kirov. They were instructed to mount the ZiS 3 76.2mm/3in gun on a suitable chassis. Initially the T-60 was selected for this project but this proved to be far too small. In the spring of 1942 it was decided that the longer, T-70 chassis was more suitable for the ZiS 3, and the improved new vehicle was called the SU-76. The T-70 was becoming available at this time because it was being phased out as a tank as it was too lightly armoured and the twin-engine layout, one for each track, was not reliable.

Trials were conducted in the summer of 1942 and the new vehicle went into production in December, 26 of these being built in that month and issued to the army, who found it to be unusable.

In early 1943 the vehicle was passed to a new design bureau, which made several changes. They placed the engines in-line so that power from both was fed to both tracks and consequently if an engine broke down the vehicle would not simply go round in circles. The new engine layout also required the front of the vehicle to be redesigned, and the fighting compartment was improved. This new vehicle was called the SU-76M.

Even in its improved version the SU-76 was never liked by the crews who had to use the vehicle. The fighting compartment was open-topped and gave the gun crew very little protection from small arms fire and no protection from the weather. The driver had to sit with the engines as there was no bulkhead separating the two compartments and the noise was horrendous, added to

which the heat was very hard to work with in the summer. These SPGs were originally designed as anti-tank vehicles but were soon relegated to an infantry-support role. Nevertheless, they would serve on into the 1960s, seeing action on the Chinese side during the Korean War. The nickname of the vehicle was "Suka" meaning Bitch.

LEFT: This SU-76 has been painted up in a disruptive winter pattern with whitewash. The large driver's hatch in the centre of the glacis is in the open position. The exhaust system was inadequate on this vehicle and resulted in some of the fumes entering the fighting compartment.

SU-76 SPG

Country: USSR
Entered service: 1942
Crew: 4
Weight: 11,176kg/11 tons
Dimensions: Length – 5m/16ft 5in
  Height – 2.20m/7ft 3in
  Width – 2.74m/9ft
Armament: Main – 76.2mm/3in 1942 ZiS 3 gun
  Secondary – Small arms
Armour: Maximum – 35mm/1.38in
Powerplant: 2 x GAZ 6-cylinder 52.2kW/70hp
  petrol engine
Performance: Speed – 45kph/28mph
  Range – 450km/280 miles

LEFT: The short barrel of the SU-122 is clearly seen along with the very large gun mantle. These vehicles were copied from the German StuG III but never had the same success.

ABOVE: An SU-100 vehicle which replaced most of the SU-122 and SU-85 vehicles in combat. One problem the SU-100 had was that it was not as manoeuvrable in narrow lanes or woods due to the long gun barrel.

SU-122 Medium Self-Propelled Gun

This was the first self-propelled weapon to be mounted on the T-34 chassis and would lead the way to a whole family of guns based on this very famous tank.

The Soviet Army had been very impressed by the success of the German StuG vehicles, so in April 1942 the Main Artillery Directorate (GAU – *Glavniy Artilleriskoye Upravleniye*) issued a requirement for a self-propelled close-support gun. SPGs were a lot cheaper and quicker to produce than a tank mainly due to the tank's turret and turret-ring bearing race that were complicated to manufacture and required the use of specialist engineering equipment. Several vehicles were put forward by a

number of different design bureaux in consultation with the Commissariat for the Tank Industry (NKTP), but none of these passed the trials stage.

In October 1942 the State Defence Committee (GKO) ordered the design bureaux to have another look at an SPG design, but this time only using the T-34 chassis. The Uralmash plant in Sverdlovsk came up with the winning design. They removed the front and turret area of the T-34 chassis and mounted an all-welded box structure on the top of the opening. The glacis plate was made from one piece of sloped armour, and the sides of the fighting compartment were sloped as well. The new vehicle was designated the SU-35

and mounted the M-30 Model 1938 122mm/4.8in howitzer. On the successful completion of trials it was ordered into production in December 1942. GKO changed the name of the vehicle to SU-122 as it entered service in January 1943. Production finished in the summer of 1944, by which time 1,100 vehicles had been made.

It was intended to mix the SU-76 and the SU-122 in the same assault gun units, but due to the technical problems of the SU-76 this never worked. Each SU-122 regiment consisted of 16 vehicles divided into four batteries. These vehicles were slowly replaced by the SU-100, but some could still be found in service into the 1950s.

ABOVE: The extended range fuel tanks on the rear of the vehicle can be seen, as well as the very short barrel length. A two-man tree saw is fitted as standard to the hull of the vehicle: this item was fitted to all Soviet armoured vehicles.

SU-122 Medium SPG

Country: USSR
Entered service: 1943
Crew: 4
Weight: 30,480kg/30 tons
Dimensions: Length – 6.95m/22ft 10in
　　Height – 2.45m/8ft
　　Width – 3m/9ft 10in
Armament: Main – 122mm/4.8in M-30 howitzer
　　Secondary – 12.7mm/0.5in machine-gun
Armour: Maximum – 45mm/1.77in
Powerplant: V-2-34M 12-cylinder 375kW/500hp diesel engine
Performance: Speed – 55kph/34mph
　　Range – 271km/168 miles

Somua MCG Half-Track

LEFT: **This Somua has been fitted with an armoured roof on which an eight-tube Nebelwerfer rocket launcher has been mounted. One weakness of this vehicle was that the front wheels were very easily damaged.** ABOVE: **This U304 (f) half-track has been turned into an armoured ambulance by the Germans. The front of the vehicle is fitted with an unditching roller. This vehicle used the same chassis and track as the larger Somua.**

In the 1920s, the French led the world in the development of the half-track, especially using the Kegresse-type suspension. This system with its rubber tracks was even bought by the Germans and built under licence. In 1935, the Somua Company produced the MCG-type half-track, with production lasting until the invasion of France by the Germans in 1940. A year later they would produce an improved version, the MCL. In total 2,543 of both types of vehicle were built.

These vehicles were originally built for the French artillery as tractors for the 155mm/6.1in gun, and, using a heavy duty trailer, as general towing tractors for tank recovery. Most of these half-tracks were fitted with a jib with block and tackle for lifting the rear of the gun carriage up and on to the towing hook. They were not armoured and there was a standard wooden cargo bed behind the driver's cab.

The Germans captured over 2,000 of these vehicles and put them back into service with their own artillery units where they acted as tractors and supply vehicles. The MCL was redesignated the Le Zgkw S303 (f) while the MCG was given the designation of Le Zgkw S307 (f). In 1944, the Germans started to convert a number of these vehicles into self-propelled weapon carriers. All of these conversions were fitted with an armoured body and crew compartment, while 16 of them were converted into self-propelled anti-tank gun vehicles by the fitting of a

7.5cm/2.95in PaK40. Another conversion was the installation of sixteen 81mm/3.2in French mortars mounted in two rows of eight on the back of the half-track. The mortars would be preloaded and fired electrically from inside the armoured cab when the S307 had been driven to the desired position in the combat area. Other vehicles were fitted with various types of rocket launchers such as the Nebelwerfer.

These converted vehicles were issued to German units based in France, while some of the basic half-tracks remained in France and others were sent to Italy or the Eastern Front.

LEFT: **This Somua half-track has been converted to carry the German PaK40 AT gun. The gun and fighting compartment were placed at the rear of the vehicle. The driver's position was located in front of the gun.**

Somua MCG Half-Track

Country: France
Entered service: 1935
Crew: 3
Weight: 8,636kg/8.5 tons
Dimensions: Length – 5.3m/17ft 4in
    Height – 1.95m/6ft 4in
    Width – 1.88m/6ft 2in
Armament: Main – None
    Secondary – Small arms
Armour: None
Powerplant: Somua 4-cylinder 45kW/60hp
    petrol engine
Performance: Speed – 36kph/22mph
    Range – 170km/106 miles

LEFT AND BELOW: **This vehicle has been given the name of "Darlington" by its crew. The gun has been placed on a platform between the driver's and the brakeman's armoured cabins. The wheels for the gun have been stowed on the side of the vehicle, and the ammunition for the gun has been stored in the gap between the vehicle's brakeman's cabin and the engine compartment.**

The Gun Carrier

The Gun Carrier was a vehicle well ahead of its time and if it had been deployed more appropriately could have had a great impact on the outcome of World War I. These vehicles should have been able to take guns forward very quickly to help bolster the gains made by British infantry and help hold off the subsequent German counter-attack. They were ordered in October 1916 and were delivered to the army in France in July 1917.

The Gun Carrier used the engine and transmission of the Mk I tank, the basic vehicle being made up of six boxes. The tracks ran around two boxes 457mm/18in wide, 9.1m/30ft long and 1.5m/5ft high that made up the sides of the

vehicle. Above the tracks at the front of the vehicle were two one-man boxes; the one on the right was for the driver, the one on the left was for the brake man. Between the tracks was a platform open at one end while at the other was a box structure with a crew compartment, ammunition storage and the engine room. The open platform extended between the tracks and acted as a loading ramp which could be raised or lowered to mount a gun. A loading trolley which was housed on the platform could be run out in front of the vehicle and the gun would then be positioned over it. Its wheels were removed and the gun winched back on to the platform on the trolley. The wheels of the gun were then

placed on the side of the carrier. Guns such as the 152mm/5.98in howitzer could be fired from the carrier, making this vehicle the first true SPG.

These vehicles were first used at the Third Battle of Ypres in 1917, when they carried forward a number of 60pdr guns and several hundred tons of ammunition. They also carried out a limited number of night shoot missions on the German positions and some gas attacks. However, their main task was to carry supplies forward as each vehicle could do the work of 300 men. Well-suited to the conditions of the Western Front, they would remain in use as supply vehicles for the rest of the war.

The Gun Carrier	
Country: UK	
Entered service: 1917	
Crew: 4 plus gun crew	
Weight: 34,544kg/34 tons	
Dimensions: Length – 9.14m/30ft	
Height – 2.85m/9ft 4in	
Width – 2.49m/8ft 2in	
Armament: Main – None	
Secondary – Small arms	
Armour: Maximum – 8mm/0.315in	
Powerplant: Daimler 6-cylinder 78kW/105hp petrol engine	
Performance: Speed – 5.96kph/3.7mph	
Range – 56km/35 miles	

ABOVE: **The large box structure at the rear of the vehicle housed the engine in the front and a crew compartment in the rear. At the rear of the carrier are the Mk I steering wheels.**

Thornycroft "J" Type 13pdr Self-Propelled AA Gun

The Basingstoke firm of John Thornycroft had a long history of producing trucks to meet a military standard. The design and development of the "J" Type 3-ton General Service truck started in 1912 and it was ready and in production for the Government Subsidy Trials that were held during 1913–14. The British government introduced a subsidy scheme that allowed private companies to buy lorries suitable for military service and, in return for a grant of 110 pounds towards the purchase price of the vehicle, to place

them at the disposal of the government in times of national emergency. The "J" Type won most of its classes in the trials and it was also the lightest vehicle in the 3-ton class. The British Army were supplied with 5,000 of these vehicles between 1914–18, and by the end of World War I it would be the most highly mechanized force in the world. These vehicles would remain in production until 1926 and stay in service with the British Army until 1930. They were also used in a number of specialist roles providing the chassis for variants such as mobile anti-aircraft guns and mobile field workshops.

At the start of the World War I, the British Army had no anti-aircraft guns. This led to a stopgap solution where guns were mounted on vehicles to provide a mobile defensive capacity. Thornycroft built 183 of these vehicles between November 1915 and September 1916. The gun selected was the British

LEFT: The armament for the vehicle was the QF (quick-firing) 13pdr 9cwt Mk 1. The pedestal was kept to a very basic design and was fitted with an 18pdr mounting for the gun. A number of these guns remained in service in Canada until 1930.

13pdr, which was removed from its normal carriage and mounted on a high-angle pedestal on the rear of the vehicle to improve its elevation. The standard 13pdr munitions were not powerful enough to reach higher flying aircraft so the 13pdr shell was fitted to the 18pdr propellant cartridge. The new gun was called the 13pdr 9cwt anti-aircraft gun.

These vehicles were well-liked by their crews and were very reliable. They would see service on the Western Front until the end of the war even if they were originally intended as a stopgap weapon. The "J" Type did have one failing however and that was a very poor cross-country ability.

Thornycroft "J" Type 13pdr SPAAG	

Country: UK
Entered service: 1915
Crew: 8
Weight: 3,302kg /2.3 tons
Dimensions: Length – 6.7m/22ft 2in
  Height – 3.2m/10ft 5 in
  Width – 2.2m/7ft 2 in
Armament: Main – 5.9kg/13pdr, 457kg/9cwt
  Mk 1 AA gun
  Secondary – Small arms
Armour: None
Powerplant: Thornycroft 4-cylinder, side valve,
  30kW/40hp petrol engine
Performance: Speed – 27.4kph/14.5mph
  Range – 201km/125 miles

Troop Carrier/Supply Mk IX Tank

LEFT: **Next to the driver's visor is a ball-mounting for a machine-gun. The twin set of rails passing over the top of the vehicle is for an unditching beam that was carried by all British tanks.**
BELOW: **The screw-like device at the front of the track sponson is the track-tensioning device and was used to take up the slack in the track.**

The development of supply tanks was a major step towards the full mechanization of the British Army, these vehicles making their appearance in the summer of 1917. Two supply vehicles would appear at the same time: the Gun Carrier and a converted version of the Mk I gun tank, both having a large impact on the battlefield. In the case of the Mk I conversion, the gun sponsons were removed and replaced with 91cm/3ft mild steel sponsons that had a tendency to dig into the ground and slow the tank down. The handling was terrible on both vehicles. However, the significant issue was that these new vehicles could each free up 300 men from the job of moving supplies, and this meant that 300 trained infantry could be used in other

roles. The next tank to be converted was the Mk IV gun tank and some 200 of these were freed up from combat duties for conversion into supply tanks.

The Mk IX was the first purposed built supply tank to be designed from scratch rather than being converted from a combat tank. Designed by Lieutenant G. J. Rackham in September 1917, it would enter service in France in October 1918, but only 35 of these vehicles were built by the end of the war. To give extra space in the vehicle, the engine was located in a position just behind the driver, and two machine-guns were fitted, one in the front beside the driver and the other in the rear. This vehicle was designed to carry 30 fully armed men across No Man's Land and into the

German position, thus making it the first APC. The Mk IX could alternatively carry 10,160kg/10 tons of supplies, loading and unloading being carried out through four oval doors, two on each side of the vehicle and opposite to each other.

The load capacity of the vehicle was further increased by towing a specially designed sledge, which was developed by the tank workshop in France and allowed an additional 10,160kg/10 tons of supplies to be moved. Sadly, the Mk IX proved to be underpowered, slow, and very cumbersome to drive and handle.

Troop Carrier Mk IX

Country: UK
Entered service: 1918
Crew: 4
Weight: 37,592kg/37 tons
Dimensions: Length – 9.70m/31ft 10in
Height – 2.57m/8ft 5in
Width – 2.46m/8ft 1in
Armament: Main – 2 x Hotchkiss 8mm/0.315in
machine-guns
Secondary – None
Armour: Maximum – 10mm/0.394in
Powerplant: Ricardo 6-cylinder 112kW/150hp
petrol engine
Performance: Speed – 6kph/4mph
Range – 193km/120 miles

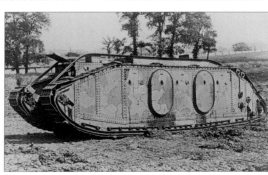

RIGHT: **This vehicle has been painted in a standard World War I camouflage pattern. The large entrance and exit oval doors can be clearly seen. Opposite these on the other side of the vehicle were two more doors.**

LEFT: **A Universal Carrier towing a 6pdr AT gun. The crew of the gun are perched on the top of the carrier as there is no room for them to sit inside. The carrier is also piled high with personal kit. The Germans captured a number of these and pressed them into service as Panzerjager Bren. This was just one amongst a wide variety of uses they made of them.**

Universal Carriers

The original role of an infantry carrier was as a fast, lightly armoured vehicle to transport a light machine-gun section into battle and to support an infantry section attack. Each infantry section would be issued with one carrier. By 1939 there were four different types of carrier in service with the British Army, but it was decided at this point that the cavalry carrier was no longer required and to simplify production by standardizing on one universal design for all purposes. The first production contract was issued in April 1939 and with a few modifications it would remain in production for the whole of World War II, with some 35,000 vehicles being produced in Britain alone.

The Universal Carrier No.1 Mk I was the first version to be placed into production and entered service in 1940. It had a riveted hull, which was made of armour plate and provided some protection for the bodies of the crew when sitting down, but none for their heads and shoulders. The engine, a Ford V8

48.5kW/65hp, had a large fan fitted to it to draw cooling air into the radiator and this made it extremely noisy. As it was mounted in the middle of the crew compartment, which was divided into two equal parts, conversation between the crew of the carrier was impossible. The driver was located on the right in the front of the carrier with the gunner, who manned the machine-gun, sitting next to him. Steering was controlled by a simple steering wheel that connected to the braking system on the tracks. When moved firmly left or right this would turn the vehicle sharply, but if it was only moved a few degrees the carrier used track-warp to turn the vehicle in a wide circle. This gave the carrier great manoeuvrability and good cross-country ability.

The Mk II had an improved engine, the Ford V8 63.4kW/85hp, and better stowage, while the Mk III was of all-welded construction and again had improvements to the engine and stowage.

ABOVE: **A Universal Carrier that has been converted into the amphibious flamethrower called the "Dragonfly". The flotation screen is in the folded-down position. When in the water, the screen comes above the height of the vehicle.**
RIGHT: **This Universal Carrier has got water in the engine and has stalled before reaching dry land. The vehicle is covered in personal equipment.**

A large number of infantry sections would carry out field modifications to their carrier by fitting more and heavier machine-guns such as the 7.62mm/30cal or the 12.7mm/50cal. In some cases, until the supply of tanks had improved, the carrier would act as a substitute in the jungles of the Far East.

The Carrier Armoured Observation Post, No.1 Mk II, was one of many conversions of the Universal Carrier. The OP Carrier was fitted with cable drums for field telephones and a No.19 radio set. This vehicle carried a crew of four. The machine-gun aperture in the gunner's position was covered over and the Bren gun was mounted on a pintle in the rear. Some 5,400 of these vehicles were produced, mainly for the artillery. Other conversions included the mounting of the 2pdr anti-tank gun on some 200 Carrier chassis. This proved to be very successful and would remain in British service until 1946. The Carrier was also used to tow the 6pdr (57mm) anti-tank gun. In 1942, a special Universal Carrier was designed to carry a 76.2mm/3in mortar and its crew, along with 30 rounds of ammunition. These were mainly produced by the Wolseley Motor Company, who had built some 14,000 of this type of carrier by the end of World War II.

One of the most successful conversions of the Universal Carrier carried a flamethrower and was known as the Wasp. Production of these vehicles started in 1942 and an order for 1,000 of them was placed in September that year. The Wasp Mk I had two large fuel tanks for the flame gun fitted in the crew compartments. The pipe work then passed over the top of the vehicle and down into the gunner's position in the front of the vehicle. The Mk I was deemed unsuitable for action by 1943 and was replaced by the Wasp Mk II. This carried 273 litres/60 gallons of fuel for the flame gun and had a range of 91.4m/300ft.

The Universal Carrier was inevitably used in many roles for which it was never originally intended, and would carry a great diversity of weapons. It was to serve on all fronts with British and Commonwealth troops throughout World War II. The Germans captured a number of British carriers and pressed them into service, calling them "Panzerjager Bren".

RIGHT: This Universal Carrier has been fitted with a Vickers machine-gun, and has a crew of four. The rear of the vehicle has extra jerry cans fitted to it, and canvas covers are rolled up and stored on the carrier.

Universal Carrier No.1 Mk II

Country: UK
Entered service: 1942
Crew: 3
Weight: 4,064kg/4 tons
Dimensions: Length – 3.76m/12ft 4in
Height – 1.63m/5ft 4in
Width – 2.11m/6ft 11in
Armament: Main – Bren 7.7mm/0.303in
light machine-gun
Secondary – Small arms
Armour: Maximum – 12mm/0.47in
Powerplant: Ford V8 8-cylinder 63.4kW/85hp petrol engine
Performance: Speed – 52kph/32mph
Range – 258km/160 miles

Wespe 10.5cm Self-Propelled Gun

LEFT: This is an ammunition carrier for the Wespe, basically a Wespe without the gun. The driver's top hatch and front visor are in the fully open position. This particular vehicle has been captured from the Germans by the French Maquis. ABOVE: This is one of the prototype Wespe vehicles and is being finished off by a small team of men from the manufacturer, FAMO. BELOW: The engine is mounted under the gun, with the air intakes built into the side of the fighting compartment. The crew area at the rear of the vehicle is very small.

When the Panzer II was withdrawn from front-line service in early 1942 and relegated to second-line duties, a number of these chassis were made available for conversion into SPG mounts. A design competition was run between the Panzer II, III and IV chassis to find a suitable mounting of the 10.5cm/ 4.13in le FH18/2 howitzer, and the Panzer II Alkett design was chosen.

The vehicle that won was the Wespe (Wasp) which was built on a modified Panzer II chassis. The first of these new vehicles were produced by Famo in March 1943 and entered service with the German Army in May 1943. The initial construction contract was for 1,000 vehicles but this was later reduced to 835, of which 150 were munitions carriers. The munitions carriers were the same specification as the gun vehicle except that the gun was not mounted; it could carry 90 rounds of ammunition. The Wespe had the main gun mounted in the rear of the vehicle in an open-topped fighting compartment. The

sides of this were made of 10mm/0.394in sloped armour and it had storage for 32 rounds of ammunition. The engine was placed in the middle of the vehicle, with the engine cooling-system louvers completely redesigned from the Panzer II and placed in the sides of the vehicle. The driver sat at the front in a separate compartment and the only contact he had with the rear of the vehicle was by intercom. The crew consisted of five men: the driver, commander, and three gun crew. The first versions of the Wespe were built on standard Panzer II chassis but this made the fighting compartment very small and cramped. The modified chassis was extended by 254mm/10in which resulted in an increased space between the road wheels and rear idler, but this did not improve the cramped conditions in the rear fighting compartment. The suspension system had to be strengthened to absorb the recoil of the gun, with bump-stop springs being added to the first, second and fifth road wheel. The production run was completed in August 1944 when it was intended to replace the vehicle with a Waffenträger (Weapon Carrier) with a turret-mounted 10.5cm/4.13in gun.

Several critical reports were written about the Wespe by the German units using it as it had several severe mechanical problems. The steering gear wore out very quickly in France and (especially) in Italy due to the narrow roads and tight turns. The brakes became covered in oil due to the leaking final drive, a fault that was never properly cured. It caused problems in convoy due to its slow speed and it did not cope well with the mud of the Russian spring and autumn, due to its narrow tracks which caused it to sink.

The combat debut for the Wespe was the great tank battle of Kursk, where it had been issued to six Panzer Divisions especially for the battle. The Wespe was intended to be deployed several miles behind the main action, rather than in the front line, but at Kursk this was not to be the case. However, due to its small size all but two of the Wespe managed to escape, having accounted for several Soviet tanks. Twelve Wespe were sent to the 17th Panzer Division on the Eastern Front where they fired off 18,000 rounds at the Soviet forces during the fighting around Orel and the withdrawal to the river Dnieper in August 1943. Another detachment of 12 Wespe vehicles was sent to Italy to join the 26th Panzer Division in November 1943, but in just four weeks none was left in service due to mechanical breakdowns. It had also been discovered that the vehicles could not be used in battery formations due to the nature of the Italian landscape and they were more often used on their own as single guns in the "shoot and scoot" role. It was therefore decided that the bulk of the Wespe production would be sent to the Eastern Front where its mechanical problems were not such a handicap.

The Wespe was disliked by its crews, as there was very little working space in the cramped crew compartment and nowhere for their personal kit. In addition, the vehicle was not reliable and there was no protection from the weather due to the low silhouette of the vehicle.

TOP: This Wespe is taking part in the Battle of the Bulge in the winter of 1944. Ammunition has been laid out on the rear door of the vehicle to keep it clean, ready for a bombardment. The small size of the fighting compartment is very clear in this picture. ABOVE: This Wespe has had the muzzle brake removed from the end of the barrel. The air intakes for the engine can be seen between the two American soldiers. The driver's top hatch is in the open position.

ABOVE: The Panzer II chassis and running gear can be clearly seen, but the vehicle is missing its exhaust. This should be mounted on the lower rear hull of the Wespe.

Wespe 10.5cm SPG

Country: Germany
Entered service: 1943
Crew: 5
Weight: 11,176kg/11 tons
Dimensions: Length – 4.82m/15ft 10in
 Height – 2.31m/7ft 7in
 Width – 2.28m/7ft 6in
Armament: Main – 10.5cm/4.13in le FH18 howitzer
 Secondary – 7.92mm/0.312in MG34 machine-gun
Armour: Maximum – 30mm/1.18in
Powerplant: Maybach HL62TR 6-cylinder 104kW/140hp petrol engine
Performance: Speed – 40kph/25mph
 Range – 140km/87 miles

A–Z of Modern Armoured Fighting Vehicles 1945 to the Present Day

With the beginning of the Cold War, an arms race started all around the world. Various weapons were rushed into development as military theory changed – such as the suggestion that the tank would become obsolete and would be replaced by the missile carrier. The armoured car remained a firm military favourite until 1970 when a number of armies replaced them with light tanks. Now, however, the armoured car has been revived and functions again as the eyes of armoured and infantry divisions. The self-propelled gun was developed further and has now become a very sophisticated weapons system with extremely long ranges that can reach far into the enemy's rear. Its modern mobility means the guns can use "shoot and scoot" tactics.

The infantry carrier has undergone the greatest metamorphosis of any vehicle type. In the early 1950s, carriers were open-topped vehicles with a single machine-gun. They then became "battlefield taxis" carrying the infantry to the battlefield in fully armoured vehicles with overhead protection. The latest infantry fighting vehicles take troops into the heart of the fighting while providing them with close support.

LEFT: **Fox armoured car.**

LEFT: A 2S1 in a two-tone camouflage scheme. The driver and vehicle commander are in their positions with their hatches open. The driver has no physical contact with the turret crew. On the barrel behind the muzzle brake is the fume extractor.
ABOVE: A battery of 2S1 SPGs taking part in a parade to commemorate the November Revolution. The 2S1 was given the name "Gvozdika" (Carnation) by the Soviet Army. When it entered service, the 2S1 was first issued to BMP-equipped units.

2S1 122mm Self-Propelled Gun

During the period when Khrushchev was in power in the Soviet Union from 1955–64, the armed forces were forced in the direction of nuclear weapons resulting in the demise of a number of basic weapon systems such as the SPG. When Leonid Brezhnev took over as the Soviet leader following Khrushchev's removal, it was realized that basic weapons development was lagging far behind those that NATO (the North Atlantic Treaty Organization) could deploy. In 1965, the GRAU (Gun Development Department) laid down a requirement for new conventionally tubed artillery, both towed and self-propelled. At this time NATO could field three main types of SPG, the M109, M110 and the Abbot, and had developed an excellent counter-battery fire technique based around these guns. With the development of improved artillery location radars the NATO guns could target the Soviet artillery very quickly, and with the new and improved ammunition at NATO's disposal, Soviet towed gun crews were very vulnerable.

The Soviet ground forces received several new guns in the 1960s. One was the D-30 122mm/4.8in towed gun and this was later mounted on a tracked chassis. Development of this vehicle started in the late 1960s and it was given the codename of "izdeliye 26". The chassis was developed by the GAVTU (Main Auto-transport Directorate) and was based on the MT-LB armoured transporter that was developed to replace the AT-P light artillery tractor. Production started in 1971 at the Karkov Tractor Plant, under the designation 2S1 Gvozdika (Carnation). The gun itself was a development of the 122mm/4.8in D-30, the main difference being the muzzle brake which on the 2S1 had a double baffle. The vehicle normally has a crew of four but when emplaced for a sustained fire role the crew is increased to six with the addition of two extra ammunition handlers. The gun can fire the full range of Soviet 122mm/4.8in ammunition to a maximum range of 15.2km/9.4 miles. The 2S1 carries 40 rounds of ammunition in the fighting compartment.

The 2S1 is fully amphibious and only takes a few minutes to be made ready to enter the water. The hull is boat-shaped and is very large, the bulky hull being necessary to provide enough buoyancy to allow the 2S1 to float. The vehicle uses its tracks to propel it through the water and a set of swim vanes are attached at the rear of the tracks to provide some form of steering. The driver is positioned right at the front of the vehicle on the left-hand side and his only contact with the fighting compartment is by internal intercom. The engine is placed alongside the driver, while the main air intake for the engine

LEFT: A group of 2S1 vehicles demonstrating its amphibious capability. The vehicle commander is acting as the eyes for the driver who can see nothing from his position.

LEFT: A 2S1 in an artillery scrape and under a camouflage net. The driver's front visor is in the open position. Next to the driver's position is the access hatch to the clutch and compressed air system. ABOVE: A cut-away view of the 2S1. In the front of the vehicle is the compressed air unit and clutch, next is the driver's compartment, then the engine, followed by the main turret area and finally ammunition storage.

is behind him. The gun is mounted in a turret at the rear of the vehicle and has a very low profile that has the appearance of an upside-down frying pan. The turret can be traversed through 360 degrees and is electrically powered or may be manually turned if necessary. The suspension is pneumatic and can be raised or lowered depending on the terrain that the vehicle is traversing. The vehicle is normally fitted with 400mm/15.7in wide tracks, but these can be replaced by 670mm/26.4in tracks to allow for better operation in snow or over soft ground.

The 2S1 chassis was used for a number of command vehicles, designated ACRV (Armoured Command and Reconnaissance Vehicle) and were attached to a number of SPG batteries. The ACRV-1 had a taller body, with the driver

at the front and the vehicle commander next to him and accommodation in the rear for four men. There was a fixed circular cupola on the roof with a single large hatch which was fitted with a 12.7mm/0.5in machine-gun. All versions of the 2S1 and the gun vehicle were equipped with a full NBC system.

The 2S1 was first seen in 1974 at a military parade in Poland, but had been in service for at least a year before this sighting. It was issued to Motor Rifle and Tank Divisions to replace the towed 122mm/4.8in guns. Each division had six 2S1 batteries attached to it, and each battalion had eighteen guns, divided between three batteries. Not surprisingly, given its adaptability and performance, it is still in service in many parts of the world today.

LEFT: The engine grill can be seen in front of the turret. The grill on the back of the turret is for the air filtration unit that is mounted in the rear of the turret.

2S1 122mm SPG

Country: USSR
Entered service: Approximately 1973
Crew: 4 plus 2 extra loaders
Weight: 15,951kg/15.7 tons
Dimensions: Length – 7.26m/23ft 10in
 Height – 2.73m/8ft 11in
 Width – 2.85m/9ft 4in
Armament: Main – 2A31 122mm/4.8in gun
 Secondary – Small arms
Armour: Maximum – 20mm/0.79in
Powerplant: YaMZ 238N V8 220kW/300hp
 diesel engine
Performance: Speed – Road 61kph/38mph;
 Water 4.5kph/2.8mph
 Range – 500km/311 miles

LEFT: **The muzzle brake has been covered by a canvas bag to stop dust and debris from entering the barrel while on the move. These vehicles belong to the East German Army, here seen in the Berlin area. This vehicle is fitted with an entrenching blade on the front of its hull.**

2S3 152mm Self-Propelled Gun

The development of this vehicle can be traced back to the end of World War II and the programmes of the Gorlitskiy design bureau based at the Uraltransmash plant at Sverdlovsk (now called Ekaterinberg) in 1949. Surprisingly, these designs were simply shelved and never went in to production. In 1965, some of the designs were resurrected and the first of these was the Obiekt 120 or SU-152. This was first modified in the early 1960s as the Obiekt 123 which became the SA-4 Ganef air defence missile system and was based on a 1949 chassis design. The Obiekt 120 was developed into a turreted self-propelled gun using the M-69 152mm/5.98in gun. This vehicle had a fully automatic loading system. A small number of these vehicles were built and put on trial but they were not accepted for service. In the late 1960s the Obiekt 303 was developed. This was another turreted self-propelled gun but used the 2A33 152mm/5.98in howitzer which was a development of the D-20 152mm/5.98in towed gun. In 1971 the Obiekt 303 was accepted for service in the Soviet Army and was renamed the 2S3 Akatsiya (Acacia).

The 2S3 is of an all-welded construction with thin armour that just about provides bullet and shrapnel protection to the crew (though not at close quarters) and is equipped with a dozer blade on the front for making its own field scrape. The driver has a compartment in the front of the vehicle with no direct contact with the rest of the crew in the fighting compartment. The engine is mounted next to the driver, and is a multi-fuel engine that normally uses diesel fuel but can in an emergency use other fuels for a short time. The vehicle is fitted with a full NBC system. Behind the engine and driver is the fighting compartment which takes up half the space in the vehicle. The turret can be traversed through 360 degrees,

ABOVE: **These 2S3 vehicles have just finished firing as evidenced by the dust created from the back-blast that is still settling. These vehicles were known as "Akatsiya" (Acacia) and they became the mainstay of Soviet mobile artillery.**

and the commander's cupola can be fitted with an anti-aircraft heavy machine-gun.

The gun was modernized twice in the 18 years of production. The first improvement, known as the 2S3M, came out in 1975 when the design of the autoloader was improved which increased the rate of fire of the vehicle. The second improvement, the 2S3M1, came out in 1987, with better communications and new sighting equipment for the gun. Normally there is a crew of four men on the 2S3, but in a sustained fire role two extra loaders can be placed outside the vehicle to load ammunition through two small hatches in the rear of the vehicle. The gun can fire all the Soviet types of 152mm/5.98in ammunition including nuclear shells, rocket-propelled shells (which give the gun a range of 30km/

18.6 miles) and precision-guided rounds such as the Krasnapol laser projectile. The normal rate of fire for this weapon is between three and four rounds per minute, but this cannot be sustained for long. The normal rate of fire in a sustained role is one round per minute, which means that the gun carries less than one hour's worth of ammunition, there being 46 rounds stored in the vehicle.

The 2S3 replaced the towed D-1 152mm/5.98in howitzer regiments in Motor Rifle Divisions. The new self-propelled 2S3 regiments consisted of eighteen vehicles divided into three batteries of six guns. In the tank regiments, the 2S3 replaced one battalion of 122mm/4.8in guns and gave the tank regiments greater firepower in the close-support role. This vehicle has also replaced a number of guns in the artillery divisions. The 2S3 is the second most common gun in the Soviet Army after the 2S1 and there were 2,012 in service in the western Soviet bloc in 1991, just prior to the break up of the Soviet Union. The 2S3 is now being replaced in the Russian Army by the new 2S19, but the 2S3 can still be found in service in 14 countries around the world. The Czechs were the only Soviet bloc country not to take the 2S3 as they had developed the wheeled 152mm/5.98in DANA self-propelled gun.

ABOVE: **Two East German 2S3 SPGs taking part in a November Parade in East Berlin. On the end of the barrel is a large double-baffle muzzle brake. There is also a fume extractor on the barrel.** BELOW LEFT: **When the 2S3 is being used in the sustained fire role then an ammunition vehicle can be parked at its rear and, using the two hatches in the lower rear hull, ammunition can be passed into the gun.**

ABOVE: **This vehicle has been painted up in a two-tone camouflage pattern. The commander's cupola has been fitted with a machine-gun.**
BELOW LEFT: **An entrenching blade is fitted under the front of the 2S3, which allows the vehicle to dig its own firing scrape. The driver and vehicle commander are in their positions.**

2S3 152mm SPG

Country: USSR
Entered service: 1972
Crew: 4 plus 2 extra loaders
Weight: 27,940kg/27.5 tons
Dimensions: Length – 8.4m/27ft 7in
　　　　　　　Height – 3.05m/10ft
　　　　　　　Width – 3.25m/10ft 8in
Armament: Main – 2A33 152mm/5.98in howitzer
　　　　　　Secondary – 7.62mm/0.3in PKT machine-gun
Armour: Maximum – 20mm/0.79in
Powerplant: V-59 12-cylinder 382kW/520hp multi-fuel engine
Performance: Speed – 60kph/37mph
　　　　　　　Range – 500km/311 miles

LEFT: **The 2S5 uses the same hull and chassis as the 2S3. The travel lock is mounted on the top of the driver's cupola. When operating the gun, the crew are very exposed. This vehicle was developed to improve the mobility of the towed 2A36.**

2S5 152mm Self-Propelled Gun

One of the last self-propelled guns of the first generation of mechanized artillery vehicles to enter service with the Soviet Army was the 2S5 Giatsint (Hyacinth). Development commenced in the early 1970s and the vehicle started life as the Obiekt 307, being a marriage of the Uraltransmash chassis as used for the 2S3 and the 2A36 towed 152mm/5.98in gun.

The 2S5 is of an all-welded construction, and the main body of the vehicle has just 15mm/0.59in of armour. The crew of five are very exposed when operating the weapon as they are out in the open behind the gun except for the gun layer, who is seated on the left, again in the open but with a small shield in front of him. The driver sits in the front on the left of the vehicle, while behind the driver is the vehicle and gun commander,

whose cupola is fitted with a machine-gun. Alongside them on the right of the vehicle is the compartment for the diesel and multi-fuel engine. The gun crew travel in a small compartment in the rear of the vehicle which is fitted with roof hatches for them. The gun is mounted on the roof at the rear of the vehicle, while to the left of the gun is storage for 30 warheads mounted on a carousel and on the other side of the vehicle are the 30 propellant charges. Crew fatigue is kept to a minimum by the use of a semi-automatic loading system. There is a large recoil spade on the rear of the vehicle and a small dozer blade is fitted to the front for removing small obstacles and making gun scrapes.

The 2S5 entered service in 1974, but was not identified by NATO until 1981. It

ABOVE: **The recoil spade on the rear of the 2S5 is in the raised position. The gun crew are entering the crew compartment in the middle of the vehicle, with the driver up front.**

replaced a number of towed guns in the heavy artillery brigades at army level. The 2S5 can be brought into action in just three minutes and a battery of six guns can put 40 rounds of ammunition in the air before the first one has landed. It is now being replaced by the 2S19.

RIGHT: **The entrenching spade can be seen under the front of the vehicle. The slotted muzzle brake of the gun can also be clearly seen. Mounted in the open like this, the gun is susceptible to damage.**

2S5 152mm SPG

Country: USSR
Entered service: 1974
Crew: 5 plus 2 extra loaders
Weight: 28,956kg/28.5 tons
Dimensions: Length – 8.33m/27ft 4in
　　　　　Height – 2.76m/9ft 1in
　　　　　Width – 3.25m/10ft 8in
Armament: Main – 2A37 152mm/5.98in gun
　　　　　Secondary – 7.62mm/0.3in PKT machine-gun
Armour: Maximum – 15mm/0.59in
Powerplant: V-59 12-cylinder 382kW/520hp
　　　　　multi-fuel diesel engine
Performance: Speed – 63kph/39mph
　　　　　Range – 500km/311 miles

2S19 152mm Self-Propelled Gun

In 1985 work started on a replacement weapon for the 2S3 and the 2S5 self-propelled guns. The new vehicle would use parts from both the T-72 and T-80 tanks, and a new gun was to be developed as the 2A33 had been in use since 1955. The 2S19 was accepted for service with the Soviet Army in 1989 and given the name of Msta-S. This was a departure from the previous practice of naming SPGs after flowers or plants as the Msta was a river in the Ilmen district of Russia.

The 2S19 uses the hull and suspension of the T-80 tank, but the tried and tested 12-cylinder diesel engine of the T-72. The first, second and sixth road wheels are equipped with regulated telescopic shock absorbers which are controlled when firing the gun so the vehicle does not require a recoil spade on the rear. The driver's compartment is the same as that in the T-80 and has no connection with the crew in the turret except by internal intercom. The turret sits on the top of the chassis and can traverse through 360 degrees. It is equipped with two loading systems: a fully automatic loader for the warheads, and a semi-automatic loader for the propulsion charges. These two systems allow the 2S19 to maintain a high rate of sustained accurate fire and it can hit 38 out of 40 targets at a range of 15km/9.3 miles. The auto-loaders can reload the gun at any angle so the gun does not have to return to the horizontal position

between rounds. The turret has an independent power supply from the main vehicle and this allows the diesel engine to be switched off during combat to suppress its heat signature. This is essential on the modern battlefield as the latest guided weapons can be targeted on to a heat source such as a hot engine or exhaust vents.

Like most Soviet weaponry, this vehicle is widely exported. In 2000, the basic export version of the 2S19 cost 1.6 million US dollars, and a special export version that will fire standard NATO ammunition has also been developed.

TOP: **This vehicle has an extremely long barrel, which shows up well in this picture. The very robust travel lock can be seen at the rear end of the barrel. On the front of the turret are six smoke dischargers and the vehicle commander's cupola has been fitted with a machine-gun.**

ABOVE: **The very large turret covers the top of the T-80 tank hull and chassis. On the end of the barrel is a double-baffle muzzle brake.**

LEFT: **A rear view of the 2S19. Under the rear of the turret are the engine grills. On the back of the turret is a large conveyor, which is used for resupplying ammunition into the turret. Towards the front of the turret on each side are large access hatches for the crew.**

2S19 152mm SPG

Country: USSR
Entered service: 1989
Crew: 5 plus 2 extra loaders
Weight: 41,961kg/41.3 tons
Dimensions: Length – 11.92m/39ft 1in
　　　　　Height – 2.99m/9ft 10in
　　　　　Width – 3.38m/11ft 1in
Armament: Main – 2A64 152mm/5.98in howitzer
　　　　　Secondary – 12.7mm/0.5in NSVT machine-gun
Armour: Classified
Powerplant: V-84A 12-cylinder 626kW/840hp
　　　　　multi-fuel diesel engine
Performance: Speed – 60kph/37mph
　　　　　Range – 500km/311 miles

LEFT: **This Abbot is on a live-firing exercise. The additional ammunition supply has been dropped at the rear of the vehicle; the rounds are delivered in plastic cases. The large rear door is used for passing ammunition through to the gun crew. The small hatch above the main door is for communication.** ABOVE: **The compact size of the Abbot can be clearly seen. The chassis is the same as the FV 432 armoured personnel carrier. Running along the side of the vehicle above the track is the exhaust system for the vehicle.**

Abbot 105mm Self-Propelled Gun

In the late 1950s NATO decided that the 105mm/4.13in calibre would be adopted as the standard close-support shell size. As a result, Britain had to retire the 25pdr gun and design a new weapon. The first Abbot prototype was produced in 1961, with the first vehicle being issued for service in 1965. It would remain in service until replaced by the AS90 in 1995.

The main production line was located at the Vickers Armstrong works in

LEFT: **The barrel of this Abbot is at maximum elevation. On the front of the turret are two clusters of smoke dischargers. There is a bank of four headlights on the hull front. The travel lock for the gun barrel is in the upright position.**

Newcastle-upon-Tyne. The Abbot was the field artillery version of the FV 432 family but the Abbot only used the engine and suspension of the FV 432. The vehicle was an all-welded construction. The driver was located on the right at the front of the vehicle with the engine next to him on the left. Mounted at the rear of the vehicle was a large spacious turret, which housed the three remaining members of the crew and had storage for 40 rounds of ammunition although only 38 were normally carried. The turret had a power-operated traverse but gun-elevation was performed by hand. A power rammer was installed to aid ramming the shells into the gun and a semi-automatic vertical sliding breach was also fitted. The gun had a maximum range of 17,000m/55,775ft and a maximum rate of fire of 12 rounds per minute, but this could not be sustained for long. Access to the fighting compartment was via a single large door in the rear of the vehicle and this was also used to pass

ammunition to the gun when tasked with a sustained fire mission. Six of the rounds carried in the turret were HESH (High-Explosive Squash-Head); this was an anti-tank round that was provided for use in the event of an engagement with enemy tanks. The Abbot was permanently fitted with a flotation screen to allow river-crossing and could be erected by the crew in 15 minutes.

Vickers also produced a simplified version for export but the only customer was India. An Abbot regiment consisted of three batteries, each with two troops of three guns supported in the field by the Stalwart 6x6 high-mobility load carrier.

Abbot 105mm SPG

Country: UK
Entered service: 1965
Crew: 4
Weight: 17,475kg/17.2 tons
Dimensions: Length – 5.84m/19ft 2in
    Height – 2.48m/8ft 2in
    Width – 2.64m/8ft 8in
Armament: Main – 105mm/4.13in L13A1 gun
    Secondary – 7.62mm/0.3in L4A4 machine-gun
Armour: Maximum – 12mm/0.47in
Powerplant: Rolls-Royce K60 6-cylinder
    179kW/240hp multi-fuel diesel engine
Performance: Speed – 50kph/30mph
    Range – 395km/245 miles

AMX-10P Mechanized Infantry Combat Vehicle

The AMX (*Atelier de Construction d'Issy les Moulineaux*) company started development on this vehicle in 1965 to meet a requirement from the French Army for a replacement for the AMX VCI infantry vehicle. The first prototype was finished in 1968 and proved to be unacceptable to the army, so major changes were made to the design, and new prototypes were produced. The resulting new vehicle was higher, wider and had a two-man 20mm/0.79in turret. The trials were completed successfully and the revised vehicle entered service with the French Army in 1973 as the AMX-10P.

The hull of the vehicle is made of all-welded construction with the driver's compartment at the front of the vehicle on the left-hand side. To the right of the driver is the main engine compartment which houses the Hispano-Suiza super-charged diesel engine. The engine compartment is fitted with aircraft engine-style fire-extinguishing equipment and the engine pack can be changed in just two hours. The AMX-10P is fully amphibious and has two water jets fitted to the rear of the vehicle to propel it when in the water. The two-man Toucan II turret is mounted in the centre of the vehicle, offset slightly to the left. The 20mm/0.79in cannon is mounted on the outside of the turret and has a dual-feed ammunition system which allows the gunner to select either HE (High-Explosive) or AP (Armour-Piercing)

ammunition. The turret carries 325 rounds which are made up of 260 rounds HE in one belt and 65 AP rounds in the other and the gunner can switch between belts while firing. The infantry compartment in the rear of the vehicle has accommodation for eight men, and is accessed via an electrically operated ramp at the back.

The basic AMX-10P has been developed into a complete family of vehicles numbering some 15 different types. A close-support version known as "Marine" has been produced for amphibious operations and is armed with a 90mm/3.54in gun.

The French Army has taken delivery of 2,500 of the AMX-10P, while the largest export order was for 300 vehicles for Saudi Arabia. Production of this vehicle has now finished.

TOP: **The 20mm/0.79in turret is mounted in the middle of the vehicle, while around the front of the turret is a bank of smoke dischargers. Down the side of this vehicle is a series of equipment attachment points.** ABOVE: **The large hydraulic ramp can clearly be seen. The men leaving the vehicle are carrying AT missiles. On each corner at the rear of the vehicle are two twin smoke dischargers. This vehicle is fitted with a MILAN AT system.**

LEFT: **The trim vane is in the down position on the front of the vehicle. Under the gun turret is a large cupola that is fitted with all-round vision blocks. The driver's periscopes are also clearly visible. The external equipment attachment points have been removed from this vehicle.**

AMX-10P MICV	

Country: France
Entered service: 1973
Crew: 3 plus 8 infantry
Weight: 13,818kg/13.6 tons
Dimensions: Length – 5.82m/18ft 1in
 Height – 2.54m/8ft 4in
 Width – 2.78m/9ft 2in
Armament: Main 1 x 20mm/0.79in M693 cannon,
 and 1 x coaxial 7.62mm/0.3in machine-gun
 Secondary – Small arms
Armour: Classified
Powerplant: Hispano-Suiza HS-115 8-cylinder
 194kW/260hp super-charged diesel engine
Performance: Speed – 65kph/40mph
 Range – 600km/370 miles

AMX-10RC Armoured Car

ABOVE: The boat-shaped hull of the AMX-10RC can be clearly seen in this picture. The gun barrel of this vehicle has a very long overhang. The wheels are in the raised position.

Development on the AMX-10RC started in September 1970 to meet a French Army requirement for a replacement for the Panhard EBR heavy armoured car. The first three prototypes were built in June 1971 and then a six-year trials and development period started which ended when the car was accepted for service in 1977. The AMX-10RC entered service in 1978 and by the time the production run was finished in 1987, the French Army had taken delivery of 207 cars, while the largest export contract (for 108 vehicles) was to Morocco, North Africa.

The all-welded aluminium hull and turret provide bullet and shell-splinter protection for the crew. The driver is positioned in the front of the vehicle on the left-hand side, with the main fighting compartment in the middle and the turret on the top. The engine is in the rear of the vehicle and is the same as that fitted to the AMX-10P MICV. The gearbox has two functions: one is to drive the vehicle in both directions using a pre-selection through four gears in both directions, and the other is to supply power to the two water-jets that are mounted on the rear of the car to propel it through the water. None of the wheels on the vehicle turns as the car uses the same skid-steering system as a tracked vehicle. The suspension is hydro-pneumatic and allows the vehicle to change its ride height depending on the terrain encountered. The vehicle is fitted with a full NBC system and night-fighting optics.

The AMX-10RC has a three-man turret with the commander and gunner on the right and the loader/radio operator on the left. The COTAC fire-control system is composed of a number of sensors that provide the computer with the following data: target range, speed, angle of cant and wind speed, while altitude and outside temperature are fed into the computer by the gunner. A laser is used for measuring the distance to the target and is effective from 400–10,000m/1,312–32,808ft. The vehicle commander can override the gunner and take over the aiming of the gun. This vehicle is currently in service with France and two other countries.

ABOVE: The grill behind the rear wheel is the intake for the water-jet propulsion system. The trim vane is folded down on the top of the glacis plate.

AMX-10RC Armoured Car

Country: France
Entered service: 1978
Crew: 4
Weight: 15,850kg/15.6 tons
Dimensions: Length – 9.15m/30ft
    Height – 2.69m/8ft 10in
    Width – 2.95m/9ft 8in
Armament: Main – 1 x 105mm/4.13in gun, and
    1 x 7.62mm/0.3in coaxial machine-gun
    Secondary – None
Armour: classified
Powerplant: Hispano-Suiza HS-115 8-cylinder
    194kW/260hp supercharged diesel engine
Performance: Speed – Road 85kph/53mph;
    Water 7.2kph/4.5mph
    Range – 1,000km/621 miles

AMX-13 DCA SPAAG

The first prototypes of the AMX DCA were completed in 1960, but were not fitted with the guidance radar as it was not yet ready. The first radar-equipped prototype was built in 1964 and was tested by the French Army until 1966, when an order was placed for 60 vehicles that were to be delivered and in service by 1969.

The AMX DCA system was mounted on the AMX-13 light tank chassis in a very similar way to that of the 105mm/4.13in SPG vehicle conversion. The driver was seated in the front of the vehicle on the left with the engine next to him on the right. The SAMM turret with positions for the other two members of the crew was mounted on the rear of the vehicle. The vehicle commander sat on the left with the gunner on the right, and between them were the twin 30mm/1.18in cannon, while mounted on the top rear of the turret was a pulse-Doppler DR-VC-1A radar dish. When the vehicle was moving, this was stowed in a lightly armoured box. Both the commander and gunner could traverse the turret. Each gun could be selected either independently of the other or both

together while the gunner could select single-shot, bursts of 5 or 15 rounds or fully automatic fire. The turret carried 600 rounds of belt-fed ammunition, 300 rounds per gun. The rate of fire of the guns per barrel was 600 rounds per minute, which gave the turret a 30-second supply of ammunition. The maximum range of the guns was 3,000m/9,842ft and all the empty cartridges and links were ejected to the outside of the turret. The turret also carried all the optical, electrical and hydraulic systems for the guns.

In the late 1960s the French took the DCA turret and mounted it on the AMX-30 tank chassis, but the improvement in mobility did not impress the French Army and so the project was dropped. In 1975, Saudi Arabia asked for the system but with an improved ammunition supply to 1,200 rounds, and subsequently placed an order for 56 vehicles.

ABOVE: **This is an early version of the AMX-13 DCA. The vehicle uses the chassis of the AMX-13 light tank. The guns are at 45 degrees of elevation. Two further 300-round belts of ammunition are carried below the turret in the body of the vehicle.**

ABOVE: **The vents for the exhaust system can be seen running down the side of the vehicle. On each side of the turret is a pair of smoke dischargers. The turret crew have remote gun-control boxes in front of them.** LEFT: **This is one of the prototype vehicles as it has no fittings on the turret. The three crew positions can be clearly seen on this vehicle.**

AMX-13 DCA SPAAG

Country: France
Entered service: 1968
Crew: 3
Weight: 15,037kg/14.8 tons
Dimensions: Length – 5.4m/17ft 9in
Height – 3.8m/12ft 6in (radar operating)
Width – 2.5m/8ft 2in
Armament: Main – 2 x 30mm/1.18in HSS-831A automatic cannon
Secondary – None
Armour: Maximum – 30mm/1.18in
Powerplant: SOFAM 8-cylinder 201kW/270hp petrol engine
Performance: Speed – 60kph/37mph
Range – 350km/215 miles

LEFT: **The extremely long gun barrel of this SPG is clearly visible. The GCT does not require any outriggers to stabilize the vehicle when firing due to the hydraulic shock absorbers. The extra long recuperators can be seen mounted under and over the gun barrel.**

AMX GCT 155mm Self-Propelled Gun

In the late 1960s, the French Army required a replacement for the ageing 105mm/4.13in Mk 61 and the 155mm/6.1in Mk F3 self-propelled guns, both of which used the AMX-13 light tank chassis. Development of the new vehicle started in 1969. The first prototype was completed in 1972 and went on public display the next year. Between 1974 and 1975 ten vehicles were built for trials with the French Army. The AMX GCT (*Grande Cadence de Tir*) finally entered production in 1977, with the first vehicles being sold to Saudi Arabia. It was accepted for service in the French Army in July 1979.

The chassis used was the AMX-30 MBT (Main Battle Tank). The engine and suspension were untouched in this conversion; the main area affected being the turret. This was removed together with all the ammunition storage in the body of the tank and was replaced by a generator and ventilator, which fed fresh air to the new 155mm/6.1in gun turret. The driver sits in the front of the vehicle on the left-hand side and has three periscopes in front of him, the central one of which can be

replaced by an infrared or image-intensifier periscope for night driving. The engine is at the rear of the vehicle and is a Hispano-Suiza HS 110 supercharged multi-fuel unit. The complete engine pack can be removed by a three-man team in as little as 45 minutes. The gearbox is mechanically operated and has just five gears for both forward and reverse, and is combined with the steering mechanism. The suspension system uses torsion bars and the first and last road wheels are fitted with hydraulic shock absorbers.

The turret is of all-welded construction with the commander and gunner stationed on the right of the turret and the loader on the left. The commander's cupola is fixed but has periscopes mounted all around it to give 360 degrees of sight. The loader has a hatch as he operates the anti-aircraft machine-gun that can be either a 7.62mm/0.3in or 12.7mm/0.5in weapon. The gun crew enter the turret through two side doors, the door on the left opening towards the front while the door on the right opens towards the rear. The turret and the breech are hydraulically operated. The breech is a vertically sliding wedge breech block which is hermetically sealed by a blanking plate. There are manual controls for use in the event of the vehicle losing hydraulic power. The gun takes just two minutes to bring into action and, in case of counter-battery fire, just one minute to take out of action and start to move the vehicle. The average rate of fire using the automatic loader is eight rounds per minute, while with manual loading the rate of fire falls to just three rounds per minute. The gun is capable of firing six rounds in just 45 seconds in what is called "burst firing". The ammunition is stored in the rear of the turret in two separate sections; in one box are

LEFT: **A night-firing exercise. The sheer size of the turret can be seen when compared to the hull of the AMX-30. This gives the vehicle a high centre of gravity.**

42 projectiles and in the other are 42 cartridge cases with propellant. A further 40 propellant charges can be stored in a fixed container under the turret. The turret is resupplied with ammunition through two large doors in the rear which fold down and form a platform for the reloading crew. The gun can be reloaded while still firing and a full reload will take a crew of four men 15 minutes or two men 20 minutes. The normal maximum range of the gun is 18,000m/59,055ft, but using rocket-assisted ammunition, this can be increased to 30,500m/100,065ft. Both the vehicle and the turret are fitted with a full NBC system and there is no recoil spade attached to the rear.

The turret can be adapted to fit many different MBT chassis including the German Leopard and the Russian T-72 and it is in service with three other countries in addition to France. In 2005, the French upgraded the engine to the Renault E9 diesel. The French Army have 190 AMX GCTs in service and so far, an additional 400 of these vehicles have been built for foreign customers.

ABOVE LEFT: **This GCT turret has been fitted to the T-72 hull and chassis. This is an Egyptian vehicle. The turret has also been developed to fit the German Leopard hull and chassis.** ABOVE: **The gun is at maximum elevation. The barrel is fitted with a large double-baffle muzzle brake. The lower front of the turret has two clusters of three smoke dischargers fitted.**

AMX 155mm GCT SPG

Country: France
Entered service: 1980
Crew: 4
Weight: 41,961kg/41.3 tons
Dimensions: Length – 10.4m/34ft 1in
 Height – 3.25m/10ft 8in
 Width – 3.15m/10ft 4in
Armament: Main – 155mm/6.1in howitzer
 Secondary – 1 x 7.62mm/0.3in or 1 x 12.7mm/
 0.5in machine-gun
Armour: Maximum – 30mm/1.18in (estimated)
Powerplant: Hispano-Suiza HS 110 537kW/720hp
 multi-fuel engine
Performance: Speed – 60kph/37mph
 Range – 450km/280 miles

ABOVE: **A GCT on exercise. This vehicle has been fitted with a 12.7mm/0.5in heavy machine-gun on the top of the turret.** RIGHT: **The rear of the turret opens downward and exposes the ammunition racks. The gun can continue to fire even with the back down. Full reloading takes the crew of the vehicle just 15 minutes.**

AMX VCI Infantry Combat Vehicle

The AMX VCI (*Véhicule de Combat d'Infanterie*) was developed in the early 1950s to meet a requirement for the French Army following the cancellation of the Hotchkiss TT6 and TT9 APCs. The first prototype was completed in 1955 with production starting in 1957.

The AMX VCI used the chassis and the front of the hull up to and including the driver's compartment of the AMX-13 tank. The hull behind the driver was increased in height to allow for troops to be seated in the rear of the vehicle. The infantry compartment in the rear held ten men seated back to back, five on each side. There were four firing ports in the side and two in the rear doors, which opened outwards. The vehicle had no NBC equipment at first but this was later fitted as an upgrade to all vehicles. The driver was in the front of the vehicle on the left, with the engine compartment on the right. Behind and above the driver was the vehicle gunner and the vehicle commander was next to him. When this vehicle originally came into service the gunner used a 7.5mm/0.295in machine-gun. This was quickly improved to a

ABOVE: **The hatches above the rear crew area are in the open position. The turret gunner is in his turret, with the vehicle commander next to him. The compact size of the vehicle can be seen clearly in this picture.**

12.7mm/0.5in heavy machine-gun, which was subsequently modified to a CAFL 38 turret armed with a 7.62mm/0.3in machine-gun which could be aimed and fired from inside the vehicle. The French then went on to develop a number of turrets that could be fitted to the vehicle ranging from a twin 7.62mm/0.3in Creusot-Loire TLiG to a CB20 20mm/0.79in turret. The AMX VCI was not amphibious but could ford shallow water and a splash board was

mounted on the glacis plate at the front of the vehicle to facilitate this.

The AMX VCI was developed into a family of vehicles with ten different variations. In total 15,000 of this family of vehicles were built of which 3,000 were the VCI version, and they are still in service with ten different countries. It was replaced in French service by the AMX-10P from 1977. The rest of the AMX family were phased out by 1982.

RIGHT: **The small square hatches in the top rear of the crew compartment are the firing ports. The dome under the turret is part of the air filter system.**

LEFT: **The turret of the AMX is armed with a single 12.7mm/0.5in machine-gun. The large driver's visor can be seen on the left of the vehicle. The gap between the tracks has been closed by a splash plate. The headlights are mounted halfway up the glacis plate.**

AMX VCI Infantry Combat Vehicle

Country: France
Entered service: 1958
Crew: 3 plus 10 infantry
Weight: 14,021kg/13.8 tons
Dimensions: Length – 5.54m/18ft 2in
  Height – 2.32m/7ft 7in
  Width – 2.51m/8ft 3in
Armament: Main 1 x 12.7mm/0.5in machine-gun
  or 1 x 7.62mm/0.3in machine-gun, basic fit
  Secondary – Small arms
Armour: Maximum – 30mm/1.18in
Powerplant: SOFAM 8 GXB, 8-cylinder
  186kW/250hp petrol engine
Performance: Speed – 65kph/40mph
  Range – 400km/250 miles

LEFT: **This is the six-wheeled Fuchs NBC vehicle. The commander's door is open, and a machine-gun has been mounted above his position. The rear of the vehicle is covered in personal kit.** BELOW: **This is the 4x4 version of the Fuchs. The exhaust system can be seen on the hull side; it exits the vehicle under the main armament and runs back along the length of the vehicle. This Fuchs is armed with a single 2cm/0.79in cannon.**

APC Transportpanzer 1 Fuchs

The development of this vehicle dates back to 1964, when the German Army were looking for a family of vehicles that would be capable of covering most of their future non-tank AFV requirements. This new generation of vehicles was to be developed using three new chassis, a 4x4, a 6x6 and an 8x8, for tactical trucks, reconnaissance vehicles and APCs. MAN won the contract to deliver the new trucks and Rheinmetall won the contract to supply the 6x6 armoured amphibious load carriers that became the Transportpanzer 1.

The Transportpanzer 1 is an all-welded steel construction and protects the crew from bullets and shell-splinters. The hull also has spaced armour in a number of critical places. The driver sits on the left in the front of the vehicle with the commander next to him on the right. Both the driver and the commander have their own access doors in the front of the vehicle and both doors have large windows that can be covered by an armoured shutter. The vehicle has a large single windscreen for both the driver and commander and gives an excellent field of vision. This is a bullet-proof screen but can be covered by an armoured shutter that folds down from the top of the vehicle. The engine compartment is behind the driver on the left of the vehicle with a small passageway linking the front to the rear crew compartment. The engine compartment is fitted with an automatic fire-extinguishing system and the complete engine pack can be removed in just ten minutes. The troop cargo area in the rear holds ten men in two rows of five sitting facing each other. The vehicle is fitted with a full NBC system and night-driving equipment.

The German Army started to take delivery of their vehicles in 1979 with the last batch being delivered in 1986; in total 996 were supplied. Britain, Holland and the USA have all bought a special contamination-measuring version that is fitted for NBC and electronic warfare. The vehicle is still in service with a number of armies around the world.

APC Transportpanzer 1 Fuchs

Country: Germany
Entered service: 1979
Crew: 2 plus 10 infantry
Weight: 16,967kg/16.7 tons
Dimensions: Length – 6.83m/22ft 5in
Height – 2.3m/7ft 7in
Width – 2.98m/9ft 9in
Armament: Main – None
Secondary – None
Armour: Classified
Powerplant: Mercedes-Benz V8 8-cylinder 239kW/320hp diesel engine
Performance: Speed – 105kph/65mph
Range – 800km/500 miles

LEFT: **The four-wheel steering can be clearly seen on this vehicle. The large trim vane is folded back on the front of the vehicle. The armoured shutter above the screen is half deployed.**

AS90 155mm Self-Propelled Gun

In the late 1960s, the British Army started to look for a replacement for the 105mm/4.13in Abbot and the American 155mm/6.1in M109. It was to be built by a consortium of firms from three countries: Britain, Germany and Italy. Britain was to produce the turret and sights, Germany would produce the engine, the hull and the main gun, and Italy would produce the recoil, fuel and loading systems. This new weapon system was due to go into service in 1980 but the project disintegrated with each of the participating countries going their own way, resulting in the joint venture being finally wound up in 1986. Vickers, the British firm in the consortium, decided to go it alone and produce a private venture vehicle using the FH70 gun that they had developed along with the German and Italian companies. The new vehicle they built was designated the GBT 155 and this

ABOVE: The soldier at the rear of the vehicle is standing under the auxiliary power unit which is fitted to the rear of the turret. A wire-mesh storage box has been fitted to the top of the turret for the storage of camouflage netting and tents. BELOW LEFT: The vehicle commander in his cupola is giving directions to the driver. The hatch in the side of the turret is folded back to give increased ventilation to the turret. BELOW: The gun barrel is locked into the travel lock, which when not in use folds back on to the glacis plate. On the front of the turret is one of the two clusters of smoke dischargers.

would become the prototype for the AS90. It was ready for testing in 1982, while the second prototype was ready to join the test programme in 1986. This new vehicle entered the competition for the replacement for the Abbot in 1989 and won, with the result that the army placed a fixed-price contract of

300 million pounds for 179 AS90 units. The first AS90 vehicles entered service in 1993 with the final deliveries to the British Army being made in 1995, replacing all its other self-propelled guns.

The AS90 uses a specially developed turret and chassis, but is otherwise constructed using a large number of standard parts from other vehicles in service with the British Army. It is of all-welded steel construction, which is bullet and shell-splinter proof. The driver sits in the front of the vehicle on the left-hand side, while alongside is the main power pack, consisting of a Cummins diesel engine. The turret houses the other four men in the crew, with the gunner and the vehicle commander, stationed on the right and the shell loader and the charge loader, on the left. Above the loaders is a hatch with an anti-aircraft 7.62mm/0.3in or 12.7mm/0.5in pintle-mounted machine-gun. The commander has a cupola with all-round vision. The turret houses all the targeting computers, direct sights and fully automatic gun-laying equipment, and also has an ammunition management system and a fully automatic loading system. Thirty-one warheads are stored in the turret bustle, with a further seventeen stored under the turret, which has a full 360-degree traverse. The normal maximum range of the FH70 155mm/6.1in 39-calibre gun is 24,700m/81,036ft but by using rocket-assisted ammunition the range can be extended

to 30,000m/98,425ft. The gun can elevate to maximum of 70 degrees, and has a minimum range of 2,500m/8,200ft. It can fire three rounds in less than 10 seconds and has a sustained rate of fire of two rounds per minute. The suspension is hydro-pneumatic which not only gives the vehicle excellent cross-country ability but also ensures a comfortable ride for the crew.

In 2005 the AS90 underwent an upgrade as it was quickly decided that the armour was too thin, the range of the gun needed increasing, and laser targeting was required. The upgrades have resulted in the vehicle now known as the AS90 Braveheart. The armour is fully bullet-proof and can even withstand a 14.55mm/0.57in anti-tank round. The roof of the turret has been fitted with a thermal shield to protect the crew from heat in desert conditions. BAE Systems have been awarded the contract to upgrade 96 of the basic AS90s to the new Braveheart standard. This also includes a new, longer 52-calibre gun barrel which increases the basic range of the gun to 40,000m/131,240ft. The new upgraded vehicles were due to be finished and back in service by 2003, but this was halted while further testing was being carried out. However, the new enhanced SPGs are expected to be in service by 2007. Poland has placed an order for 72 new AS90 vehicles to replace their ageing Soviet 2S3 self-propelled guns.

ABOVE: This AS90 has had a machine-gun fitted to the commander's position. Behind the fume extractor on the barrel of the gun is a rubber protective sleeve which helps keep dirt from entering the turret. BELOW: The crew of this AS90 are about to break camp. The vehicle would be placed in this type of hide each time it is stationary for long periods of time. Vehicles on the modern battlefield have to hide to survive.

ABOVE: The large storage boxes on the side of the turret can be clearly seen, along with the empty wire-mesh bin on the roof of the vehicle. The large door in the rear of the vehicle is in the open position; this is the main entrance and exit from the vehicle. The AS90 turret has also been fitted to the Indian T-72 MBT chassis for trials with the Indian Army.

AS90 155mm SPG

Country: UK
Entered service: 1993
Crew: 5
Weight: 45,000kg/44.3 tons
Dimensions: Length – 9.9m/32ft 6in
　Height – 3m/9ft 10in
　Width – 3.4m/11ft 4in
Armament: Main – FH70 155mm/6.1in howitzer
　Secondary – 7.62mm/0.3in machine-gun
Armour: Maximum – 17mm/0.67in
Powerplant: Cummins VTA 903T 660T-660
　8-cylinder 492kW/660hp diesel engine
Performance: Speed – 55kph/34mph
　Range – 370km/230 miles

LEFT: **This BMD is taking part in a November Parade in Moscow in 1981. The top of the commander's hatch has the badge of the Soviet Airborne Forces painted on it. The six men of the infantry section carried in the vehicle can be seen sitting on the rear of the BMD.** BELOW: **A side view of a BMD during a parade in Moscow. A Sagger AT missile is in place on its launcher on the top of the gun barrel.**

BMD Airborne Combat Vehicles

When the Soviet Union was forced into a humiliating climb down after the Cuban Missile Crisis in 1963, it was decided to expand and upgrade the Soviet Airborne Forces (VDV). It was very quickly realized that the paratroopers required some form of mechanization to combat anti-personnel weapons and to give them better mobility once on the ground. Development started on the BMD in about 1965. The first production vehicles were issued for service in 1969, and it was first seen by the West in 1970.

The BMD is the only airborne infantry vehicle in service anywhere in the world and it was initially thought by NATO to be an airborne tank. The driver/mechanic is seated in the centre-front of the vehicle with the gun barrel just above his head, while the vehicle commander and radio operator is to the left and slightly to the rear. To the right of the driver is the bow machine-gunner, and behind them is the turret with a single gunner in it. This is the same turret as fitted to the BMP and can fire Sagger wire-guided anti-tank missiles. Behind this is an infantry compartment that was originally designed to accommodate six men, but this has been reduced to five as the vehicle is very small and cramped for the crew. The vehicle is fully amphibious and has two water jets mounted on the rear for propulsion. A protective splash board is fitted on the glacis plate and this is raised when the vehicle enters the water. The turret is fitted with a low-pressure 73mm/2.87in gun fed by a 40-round magazine. The gun fires fin-stabilized HEAT (High-Explosive Anti-Tank) or HE-FRAG (High-Explosive Fragmentation) rounds. Once the round leaves the barrel,

a rocket motor fires in its rear and increases the speed of the round and its range to 1,300m/4,265ft, but this system is adversely affected by the weather and wind, reducing its accuracy greatly.

The Soviet Army realized that the three cargo parachutes that were required to drop the vehicle safely from an aircraft were very heavy, but that they could reduce this to a single parachute by fitting rockets to the PRSM-915 pallet used for air-launching the vehicle. As the pallet leaves the aircraft, four wires with ground contact sensors fitted to their ends are released under the pallet. When one of these sensors strikes the ground, the rockets are fired and these slow the vehicle down for a safe landing. They also realized that dropping the vehicle without its driver and gunner made it very vulnerable,

LEFT: This vehicle is the improved BMD-2. It is armed with a 30mm/1.18in cannon in the turret. The chassis has five road wheels, with the drive wheel at the rear of the vehicle. The air intake for the engine can be seen in the middle of the glacis. BELOW: These two BMDs are on exercise. When the driver is in his raised driving position then the gun barrel has to be at maximum elevation.

so at first the driver and gunner descended in the vehicle. The idea was that they could very quickly dispose of the parachutes, drive the vehicle off the pallet and go to find the rest of the crew. The vehicle would be dropped from a maximum height of 457.2m/1,500ft and the descent takes less than one minute. A great deal of courage was required by the crew to be in the vehicle when it leaves the aircraft especially as a number of accidents occurred in the development of this system, killing the crew. A new system has subsequently been developed where radio beacons are fitted to each vehicle, each one having a different signal, so that the crew can drop separately yet find their vehicle very quickly and move off into action.

Development of the BMD-2 was started in 1983 as an interim solution to combat reports from Afghanistan that showed a number of faults with the BMDs, which were the first vehicles into the country. In particular the 73mm/2.87in gun was shown to be very poor and so the turret was replaced in the BMD-2 with a new one armed with a 30mm/1.18in cannon.

Production started in 1985 and it entered service the same year. The BMD-3 was developed to overcome problems with the track and suspension, and the engine was also upgraded to a more powerful diesel. This new vehicle was due to go into service by 1990 but this was delayed by a year. Due to money problems in Russia this programme is still continuing, but very slowly. Russia is the only country to develop this kind of vehicle. Several specialist vehicles of the BMD-3 are under development at this time and the 125mm/4.92in 2S25 SPATG uses many of the components of the BMD-3.

RIGHT: This BMD-2 is taking part in an informal parade. The turret has an infrared light fitted to the side. At the rear of the turret is a pintle mount for a Spigot or Spandrel AT missile. This is the same turret as mounted on the BMP-2.

BMD-1 Airborne Combat Vehicle

Country: USSR
Entered service: 1969
Crew: 2 plus 5 infantry
Weight: 6,807kg/6.7 tons
Dimensions: Length – 5.4m/17ft 9in
Height – 1.77m/5ft 10in
Width –2.55m/8ft 4in
Armament: Main – 1 x 2A28 73mm/2.87in gun,
and 1 x coaxial 7.62mm/0.3in machine-gun
Secondary – 2 x 7.62mm/0.3in machine-guns,
and 1 x Sagger launch rail
Armour: Maximum – 23mm/0.91in
Powerplant: 5D20 6-cylinder 216kW/290hp
diesel engine
Performance: Speed – Road 80kph/50mph;
Water 10kph/6mph
Range – 320km/199 miles

LEFT: The low profile of the BMP-1 turret can be clearly seen. The chassis is made up of six road wheels with the driving wheel at the front. The upper part of the track is covered by a skirt. ABOVE: A BMP-1 leaving the water, with the trim vane in the raised position. The crew are in the closed-down position. The transition to amphibious vehicle only takes a few minutes.

BMP-1 Infantry Fighting Vehicle

The BMP (*Boevaya Mashina Pekhota*) was the world's first infantry combat vehicle and was the most significant innovation in infantry combat tactics of the late 20th century. It was also the first Soviet military vehicle to be designed with the needs of the nuclear battlefield in mind. This new vehicle provided the infantry with unprecedented firepower, mobility and protection that could be taken into the heart of the enemy position and the idea would be copied in vehicles such as the American Bradley, the German Marder and the British Warrior.

Development started in the 1960s and prototypes were ready for testing in 1964. In 1966 the BMP-1 was accepted for service and placed into production, but, due to a number of problems that subsequently came to light, mass production was not started until 1970. The BMP-1 is of an all-welded steel construction which offers protection from bullets and shell-splinters; the front is even proof against 12.7mm/0.5in anti-tank rounds. The glacis plate is distinctively ribbed with the driver located behind the ribbed area on the left-hand side of the vehicle and the commander seated behind. The engine is mounted on the right-hand side of the vehicle next to the driver and commander while the air intakes and outlets are on the top of the vehicle. Two forms of starting the main engine are fitted; either compressed air or battery. The compressed air system is normally used in very cold winter temperatures.

Behind the commander and the engine is a one-man turret which is equipped with the 73mm/2.87in smooth-bore low-pressure gun, fed from a 40-round magazine. On leaving the barrel, a rocket motor in the tail of each round is ignited, but these munitions are badly affected by the wind and the weather. The maximum rate of fire is eight rounds per minute.

RIGHT: The driver of this BMP-1 is standing in front of his vehicle in Afghanistan. The vehicle has been fitted with additional storage on the rear of the turret. The three pistol ports are open on the rear. The ribbed glacis plate can be clearly seen here. A large searchlight has been fitted in front of the commander's hatch but behind the driver's position.

Mounted coaxially to the main gun is a 7.62mm/0.3in PKT machine-gun which is fed by a 2,000-round belt housed in a box under the turret, while mounted over the main armament is a rail for a Sagger wire-guided anti-tank missile. The Sagger has a minimum range of 500m/1,640ft and a maximum of 3,000m/9,842ft. One missile is carried on the rail in the ready-to-use position, while two others are stored in the turret. Reloading takes 50 seconds. The missile controls are stored under the gunner's seat and these are pulled out and locked in position between his legs when required. After firing, the gunner watches the missile through a scope while controlling its flight using a joystick. This missile system can only be used in daylight as there is no other way of tracking it.

The BMP-1 has a full NBC air-filtration system. The troop compartment in the rear holds eight men, four down each side sitting back to back facing the outside of the vehicle. The main fuel tank is positioned between the backs of these men, while the rear doors of the vehicle are also fuel tanks, giving a total fuel capacity of 460 litres/101 gallons. This fuel storage system poses considerable risks to both vehicle and occupants on the battlefield. In the roof of the troop compartment are four hatches for the infantry to use and each man also has a firing port in front of his position in the rear of the vehicle. Apart from the men's own personal weapons an RPG-7 anti-tank grenade launcher is also carried. It has been found that the vehicle is very cramped under service conditions due to the low height of the roof and several countries using the BMP-1 have reduced the number of troops in the infantry section in the rear to six men. The vehicle also has a very poor ventilation system so the rear compartment becomes unbearably hot.

The BMP-1 is fully amphibious and is propelled through the water by the vehicle's own tracks. Just before entering the water, a trim vane is attached to the front of the vehicle, the bilge pumps are switched on and the splash plate is raised. When in the water the BMP-1 is driven in third gear when full and in second when it is empty.

TOP: The rear of a BMP-1 with all its doors and hatches open. The bulbous rear doors doubled as fuel tanks for the vehicle. The four large hatches are fully open, each hatch acting as an exit for two men. The pistol ports just above the track skirt are in the closed position. On the rear of the door is storage for two metal track chocks. ABOVE: The full complement of the vehicle can be clearly seen. On the left is the driver, behind him is the vehicle commander, in the turret is the gunner, and in the rear of the vehicle is the eight-man infantry section. LEFT: A close-up of the Sagger AT missile. The loading hatch is just large enough for the missile to be pushed up and on to its launching rail.

BMP-1 Infantry Fighting Vehicle

Country: USSR
Entered service: 1966
Crew: 3 plus 8 infantry
Weight: 12,802kg/12.6 tons
Dimensions: Length – 6.74m/22ft 1in
Height – 2.15m/7ft 1in
Width – 2.94m/9ft 8in
Armament: Main – 1 x 2A28 Grom 73mm/
2.87in gun, 1 x coaxial 7.62mm/0.3in
PKT machine-gun
Secondary – Sagger launch rail and small arms
Armour: Maximum – 33mm/1.3in
Powerplant: UTD-20 6-cylinder 224kW/300hp
diesel engine
Performance: Speed – Road 80kph/50mph;
Water 6–8kph/4–5mph
Range – 500km/311 miles

BMP-2 Infantry Fighting Vehicle

The BMP-2 was a development of the BMP-1 and was first seen by the NATO allies in the Moscow Parade of 1982. Several steps were taken to improve on the BMP-1. The new vehicle had a larger two-man turret, the infantry section in the rear was reduced from eight to six men and the vehicle commander was moved from behind the driver's position into the turret next to the gunner to give him better all-round vision.

The driver sits in the front on the left with the radio operator behind and the engine pack next to them. The two-man turret has the vehicle commander on the right and the gunner on the left. The main armament is the 30mm/1.18in 2A42 automatic cannon, which has two rates of fire: slow at 200 rounds per minute and fast at 550 rounds per minute. However, the turret can not remove the fumes from the gun when being fired at

the faster speed. A Spandrel anti-tank missile system is mounted on the roof. Twenty-two thousand BMP-2 vehicles were produced between 1990 and 1997.

LEFT: A BMP-2. The turret is fitted with two clusters of three smoke dischargers. On the rear of the vehicle is a snorkel tube in the stored position. The mounting for the Spandrel AT-5 ATGW is situated on the roof of the turret at the rear.

BMP-2 Infantry Fighting Vehicle

Country: USSR
Entered service: 1981
Crew: 3 plus 6 infantry
Weight: 14,224kg/14 tons
Dimensions: Length – 6.74m/22ft 1in
 Height – 2.45m/8ft
 Width – 3.15m/10ft 4in
Armament: Main – 2A42 30mm/1.18in cannon, and coaxial 7.62mm/0.3in machine-gun
 Secondary – Spandrel launcher and small arms
Armour: Classified
Powerplant: UTD-20 6-cylinder 224kW/300hp diesel engine
Performance: Speed – Road 65kph/40mph; Water 7kph/4mph
 Range – 600km/373 miles

BMP-3 Infantry Fighting Vehicle

LEFT: The rear of the BMP-3. The back of this vehicle has been redesigned and the fuel tanks have been removed from the doors and placed inside the vehicle under the floor of the troop compartment.

BMP-3 Infantry Fighting Vehicle

Country: USSR
Entered service: 1989
Crew: 3 plus 7 infantry
Weight: 19,304kg/19 tons
Dimensions: Length – 7.14m/23ft 5in
 Height – 2.3m/7ft 7in
 Width – 3.15m/10ft 4in
Armament: Main – 1 x 2A70 100mm/3.94in gun, 1 x 2A72 30mm/1.18in cannon, and 1 x 7.62mm/0.3in machine-gun
 Secondary – Small arms
Armour: Classified
Powerplant: UTD-29M 10-cylinder multi-fuel 373kW/500hp engine
Performance: Speed – Road 70kph/44mph; Water 10kph/6mph
 Range – 600km/373 miles

The BMP-3 is a radical new design and was first seen in 1990. In 2005, it represented the heaviest armed infantry fighting vehicle then in service but a number of ill-conceived improvements to the BMP concept have resulted in this vehicle having a very poor design. Experience has also shown that the vehicle has low battlefield survivability.

The driver is still seated in the front but is now located in the centre, under the main gun. The turret is fitted with three

weapons: a 100mm/3.94in 2A70 gun (a totally new design, not the same as the one fitted to the T-55), a 30mm/1.18in cannon and a 7.62mm/0.3in machine-gun. The BMP-3 has a new engine which is now positioned under the floor in the rear of the vehicle together with some of the fuel cells. It is propelled in the water by two water jets mounted at the rear of the vehicle.

The BMP-3 is in service with seven different countries and by 1997 Russia

had 200 BMP-3s on active service. However, the vehicle is not well-liked and this could explain why production has been so slow.

LEFT: **A Bradley at speed. The driver's hatch is in the half-open position to give improved vision. The large engine intake grills can be seen on the glacis plate.**
ABOVE: **The boxes on the side of the turret are for the twin TOW AT missile system. The upper part of the track and hull sides have been fitted with appliqué armour. The storage box on the rear of the vehicle is for camouflage netting.**

Bradley M2 Infantry Fighting Vehicle

In the mid 1960s the American Army required a new infantry vehicle, which they wanted to out-perform the Soviet BMP-1, to replace the M113. Until 1977 no development vehicle had been produced which proved to be adequate and so the projects were dropped. In that year, two new vehicles were developed – the XM2 (Bradley Infantry Fighting Vehicle) and the XM3 (Bradley Cavalry Vehicle). However, in 1978 both of these vehicles were condemned by the General Accounting Office as being too slow, too high, having a very poor engine and insufficient armour. Some of these problems, but not all, were rectified in further development and in 1981 the first production vehicles were handed over to the army.

Initially, the American Army had a requirement for 6,800 Bradley M2s, but this has since been reduced. The hull of the M2 is made of all-welded aluminium armour which is further protected with spaced laminated armour. The driver of the vehicle sits at the front on the left-hand side, with the engine on the right-hand side. The turret is mounted on the top of the vehicle in the middle with the commander on the right and the gunner on the left. The main armament is the 25mm/0.98in M242 chain gun with a coaxial M240 7.62mm/0.3in machine-gun. The gunner can select single shot or two different burst rates and, as it is fully stabilized in all plains, the gun can be laid and fired on the move. Two TOW missiles, with a range of 3,750m/12,300ft, are mounted on the outside of the turret. The Bradley has a swimming ability and this is effected by using a flotation screen that is permanently fitted to the vehicle. The rear of the vehicle holds six infantrymen, each with a firing port to the side or rear of the vehicle. The NBC system is limited to the three-man crew and does not provide protection for the infantry in the rear.

The Bradley is still very heavily criticized by the men who use it in the field, in spite of numerous upgrades since coming into service.

ABOVE: **The driver's hatch is in the fully open position on this vehicle. The large rear ramp is in the down position. The last appliqué armour plate is folded up; this allows access to the tracks without removing the armour.**

Bradley M2 Infantry Fighting Vehicle

Country: USA
Entered service: 1981
Crew: 3 plus 6 infantry
Weight: 22,260 kg/22 tons
Dimensions: Length – 6.47m/21ft 3in
    Height – 3m/9ft 10in
    Width – 3.28m/10ft 9in
Armament: Main – M242 25mm/0.98in cannon, and coaxial M240 7.62 mm/0.3in machine-gun
    Secondary – Small arms
Armour: Classified
Powerplant: Cummins VTA-903T turbocharged 8-cylinder 373kW/500hp diesel engine
Performance: Speed – Road 61kph/38mph; Water 6.4kph/4mph
    Range – 400km/249 miles

LEFT: **A radiological-chemical reconnaissance BRDM-2 car. The boxes at the rear of the car carry a number of pennants that are used to mark a safe lane through contaminated ground.**

BRDM-2 Armoured Car

The same team that designed the original BRDM armoured car were used to develop the BRDM-2. The process started in 1962, using their experience and the basic BRDM as a starting point. The new design had to incorporate several improvements such as better road and cross-country performance, full amphibious capability and heavier, turret-mounted armament. The new BRDM-2 entered production in 1963 and was first seen in a public parade in 1966. Production finished in 1989 but it is still in service with the Russian Army and the armed forces of some 55 other countries.

The BRDM-2 is an all-welded steel construction, with the driver and commander sitting side by side in the front of the vehicle. The turret, which is manually operated, is the same as that fitted to the BTR-60PB, BTR-70 and the OT-64 model 2A, and is armed with a 14.55mm/0.57in heavy machine-gun and a coaxial 7.62mm/0.3in machine-gun. The vehicle is equipped with a central tyre pressure system as fitted to all Soviet wheeled vehicles which allows the driver to increase or decrease the tyre pressure depending on the terrain encountered. Between the main wheels are a set of smaller chain-driven belly wheels which drop down when operating on soft ground. The engine is mounted in the rear of the vehicle to help improve the cross-country performance.

There are six variations of the basic vehicle, the most common being the BRDM-2 with Sagger ATGWs, which was first used in combat during the 1973

ABOVE LEFT: **A BRDM-1. The driver and commander sit in the front of this vehicle. The vehicle commander's position has been fitted with a single 12.7mm/0.5in machine-gun. The basic vehicle has a crew of five.**
LEFT: **A BRDM-2 armed with Sagger AT missiles. These missiles are in the raised ready-to-launch position. When not in use, the missiles are retracted into the vehicle.**

Middle East campaigns. In this variant the turret and the hull top are removed and replaced by a six-rail Sagger launcher in which the armoured cover, missile rails, missiles and firing mechanism are all one unit. When travelling the missiles are stored in the body of the vehicle but in action the entire unit is raised into the firing position. Other vehicle variants include a command version, radiological-chemical reconnaissance car, Swatter-B and Spandrel ATGW vehicles and the SA-9 Gaskin AA system.

The BRDM-2 has proved to be a very rugged and reliable design and is expected to be in service for many more years with a number of countries.

BRDM-2 Armoured Car

Country: USSR
Entered service: 1964
Crew: 4
Weight: 7,000kg/6.9 tons
Dimensions: Length – 5.75m/18ft 10in
　　　　Height – 2.31m/7ft 7in
　　　　Width – 2.35m/7ft 9in
Armament: Main – 14.55mm/0.57in KPVT machine-gun, and coaxial 7.62mm/0.3in PKT machine-gun
　　　　Secondary – Small arms
Armour: Maximum – 14mm/0.55in
Powerplant: GAZ 41 8-cylinder 105kw/140hp petrol engine
Performance: Speed – Road 100kph/62mph;
　　　　Water 10kph/6mph
　　　　Range – 750km/466 miles

BTR-60 Armoured Personnel Carrier

LEFT: **The first vehicle on the flat car is a BTR-60PU command car. This is a conversion of the basic BTR-60PB. The PU version is fitted with several radios and a 10m/32ft 10in aerial, which on this vehicle is folded down and stored on the top of the vehicle.** BELOW: **Two BTR-60PB vehicles being unloaded from tank landing craft during a Soviet exercise. The vehicle in front has one of the large hatches above the crew compartment open.**

The BTR-60 was developed in the late 1950s to replace the BTR-152. It entered service in 1960 with the Motorized Rifle Divisions and was first seen by the West during the Moscow Parade of November 1961. Each Rifle Division is equipped with 417 of these vehicles although some have since had their BTR-60s replaced by the BMP-1.

The BTR-60P, an open-topped vehicle, was the first model released. This was only in service for a few years and was quickly relegated to a training role. In 1961, the new BTR-60PA entered service. This had a covered armoured roof, but was quickly improved upon when the BTR-60PB entered service in 1965. The 60PB was the same as the PA except that it was fitted with the same turret as the BRDM and mounted a single 14.55mm/0.57in KPV machine-gun. This was the last improvement on the

basic Infantry Carrier, the other versions produced all being command vehicles.

The hull of the BTR-60 is an all-welded steel construction. The driver sits on the left and vehicle commander on the right in the front of the vehicle, while behind them is the one-man turret. Behind the turret area is the infantry accommodation which seats 14 men on bench seats. At the rear of the vehicle is the engine area, which houses the twin engines of the vehicle. The BTR-60 is an 8-wheel drive. The forward four wheels are steerable and each tyre is attached to a central tyre pressure system that is controlled by the driver. The vehicle has a good cross-country ability but debussing under fire is extremely exposed for the infantry, as they have to emerge from hatches in the top of the vehicle or through two small hatches, one on either side.

The BTR-60 was slowly phased out of service to be replaced by the BTR-70 from 1979 onwards. Total production was about 25,000 new vehicles, excluding the upgrades carried out on the early models to bring them up to BTR-60PB standard. These vehicles are still found in service with some countries of the former Soviet bloc.

RIGHT: **The driver's and vehicle commander's front hatches are open. The hatch halfway down the vehicle can be used as an exit point. The trim vane is in the stowed position under the nose of the vehicle.**

BTR-60PB APC

Country: USSR
Entered service: 1960
Crew: 2 plus 14 infantry
Weight: 10,300kg/10.1 tons
Dimensions: Length – 7.56m/24ft 10in
　　Height – 2.31m/7ft 7in
　　Width – 2.83m/9ft 3in
Armament: Main – 14.55mm/0.57in KPV
　　machine-gun
　　Secondary – Small arms
Armour: Maximum – 9mm/0.354in
Powerplant: 2 x GAZ 49B 6-cylinder 67kW/90hp
　　petrol engines
Performance: Speed – Road 80kph/50mph;
　　Water 10kph/6.2mph
　　Range – 500km/311 miles

427

BTR-70 Armoured Personnel Carrier

LEFT: **A column of BTR-70 APC vehicles out on exercise. The four large rubber wheels can clearly been seen on these vehicles. All the wheels are connected to a central tyre pressure system operated by the driver.** BELOW: **Between the second and third wheels is a small hatch which troops can use to exit the vehicle, but only when stopped. The pistol ports in the side of the crew compartment can also be seen.**

While the BMP was the most revolutionary armoured vehicle developed by the Soviet Union, the BTR-70 was the least radical as it was a straight evolution of the BTR-60. Development started in 1971 with production commencing in 1972. It entered service in 1976, but was not seen until 1980 when it was spotted in the November Moscow Parade. The delays in production were a result of a catastrophic fire at the engine factory.

The hull of the vehicle is longer than the BTR-60 while the front and rear were widened to give the wheels better protection. The hull was an all-welded steel construction, with the driver and commander in the front and behind them two infantrymen who could use the forward-facing pistol ports to cover the front of the vehicle and debussing infantry. Behind them was the turret area which was the same as that fitted to the BTR-60 and was operated by one infantryman. There were plans to fit the BMP turret to the vehicle but this proved to be too expensive and would have required a major redesign.

Behind the turret are two bench seats for six infantry who sit in two rows of three facing outwards so they could use the pistol ports in the side of the vehicle. Behind the infantry area is the engine compartment.

The BTR-70 retained the twin-engine layout of the BTR-60 except that one engine powered the first and third wheels while the other powered the second and fourth wheels, so that if the vehicle lost an engine at least it could limp off the battlefield unlike the BTR-60 which would go round in circles. Between the second and third wheels on each side is a small crew hatch for the infantry to debus, but the vehicle has to stop for

this to happen otherwise the soldiers would be crushed by the wheels.

During the fighting in Afghanistan the BTR-70 showed that it was very vulnerable to attack from the side by heavy machine-guns and rocket launchers such as the RPG7. A number of field modifications were carried out to increase the armour and extra weapons were fitted such as the AGS-17 grenade launcher.

ABOVE: **The boat shape of the hull shows up well on this vehicle. One of the two large exhausts can be seen at the rear of the vehicle.**

BTR-70 APC

Country: USSR
Entered service: 1976
Crew: 2 plus 9 infantry
Weight: 11,481kg/11.3 tons
Dimensions: Length – 7.54m/24ft 9in
   Height – 2.23m/7ft 4in
   Width – 2.8m/9ft 2in
Armament: Main – 14.55mm/0.57in KPVT
   machine-gun, and coaxial 7.62mm/0.3in
   PKT machine-gun
   Secondary – Small arms
Armour: Maximum – 10mm/0.394in
Powerplant: 2 x ZMZ-4905 6-cylinder
   172kW/230hp petrol engines
Performance: Speed – 80kph/50mph
   Range – 600km/370 miles

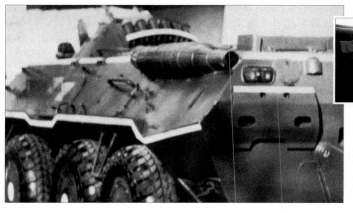

LEFT: The turret of this BTR-80 has a bank of six smoke dischargers fitted to the rear. Just in the picture is the hydro water-jet hatch which propels this type of vehicle in the water. The height of the rear of the vehicle has been raised. ABOVE: The new side door can be seen on this BTR-80. This allowed the crew to leave the vehicle while still on the move as they can jump clear of the wheels.

BTR-80 Armoured Personnel Carrier

The BTR-70 did not cure all the deficiencies of the BTR-60, which had become evident during the fighting in Afghanistan. It simply displayed the shortcomings of the reliance on the conservative development of armoured vehicles. The replacement for the BTR-70, initially called the GAZ 5903, started development in 1982. It passed its trials and was renamed the BTR-80, with production starting in 1984.

The three main differences to the BTR-70 were the engine, the crew exit doors and the turret. The twin-engine configuration was dropped in favour of a single large diesel engine, which simplified the automotive train and made maintenance easier. Clam-shell doors were fitted to the sides of the vehicle

instead of small hatches. When the doors are opened, the bottom one forms a step which drops down between the second and third road-wheels. The BTR-80 does not have to halt to allow the infantry to debus: the clam-shell doors are opened and the men leap off the step one at a time hoping to miss the wheels. It is consequently known as the "death step". The last major change was the turret. The gun was designed to allow elevation to 60 degrees, as it had been found in Afghanistan that the gun could not be elevated high enough to sweep the hills. This also gives the vehicle some anti-aircraft ability to deal with helicopters. The BTR-80 has two firing ports in the front and three down each side for the infantry to use, and is fully

amphibious with a single water jet mounted in the rear. The steering is applied to the front four wheels and the vehicle is fitted with a full NBC system and night-vision equipment. It is in service with some 20 countries.

One version of the BTR-80 is the BREM-80 (*Bronirovannaya Remontno-Evakuatsionnaya Mashina*) Armoured Recovery Vehicle, which was developed to recover damaged wheeled vehicles from the battlefield. There is a nose-mounted spade to secure the vehicle during winching operations, a small jib crane on the roof and a large "A" frame that can be fitted to the front of the BREM for engine changes.

RIGHT: The trim vane is in its new stored position lying flat on the glacis plate. The vehicle commander is standing in his position with his hatch opening to the front of the vehicle. The exhaust system on the BTR-80 now runs almost horizontal along the rear of the raised engine compartment.

BTR-80 APC

Country: USSR
Entered service: 1984
Crew: 3 plus 7 infantry
Weight: 13,614kg/13.4 tons
Dimensions: Length – 7.5m/24ft 7in
Height – 2.45m/8ft
Width – 2.9m/9ft 6in
Armament: Main – 14.55mm/0.57in KPVT
machine-gun, and coaxial 7.62mm/0.3in
PKT machine-gun
Secondary – Small arms
Armour: Maximum – 10mm/0.394in
Powerplant: KAMAZ 7403 8-cylinder 194kW/260hp
diesel engine
Performance: Speed – 80kph/50mph
Range – 600km/370 miles

BTR-152V1 Armoured Personnel Carrier

The BTR-152 was the first Soviet APC to be developed after World War II. The process started at the end of World War II and the vehicle entered service in 1950, but was first seen by the West during the Moscow Parade of 1951. Initially the BTR-152 was developed using the ZIL-151 2.5-ton truck but this was later changed to the ZIL-157 truck.

The BTR-152 has the engine located at the front of the vehicle and behind this is an open-topped compartment with accommodation for two crew and 17 infantry. The infantry in the rear of the vehicle sit on bench seats behind the crew compartment, while the driver and commander sit in the front with the driver on the left. There are eight firing ports, three down each side and one in each of the rear doors. The early vehicles had no NBC equipment, night-driving equipment or amphibious capability but some of the later variants such as the BTR-152V3

were fitted with a central tyre pressure system, and a night-driving infrared driving light.

The BTR-152K came into service from 1961. This has a full armoured roof with two large hatches, one in the front and one in the rear, each with a machine-gun mount. All the other improvements from the early versions were fitted to this mark, but still no NBC system. There were three machine-gun mounts in total, one over the driver and commander's position which would take a heavy 12.7mm/0.5in machine-gun and one 7.62mm/0.3in SGMB machine-gun mounted on each side of the vehicle. In addition to being used as an infantry carrier, the BTR-152 was also used as an artillery tractor, mortar carrier and a basic load carrier. One command vehicle version of the BTR-152 was produced as well as three anti-aircraft versions. The first of these mounted a

ABOVE: The truck origins of the vehicle chassis can be clearly seen. The driver is entering his position in the vehicle. The pistol ports in the side of the crew compartment are visible. The main 12.7mm/0.5in heavy machine-gun mount is sited above the driver's position.

twin 14.55mm/0.57in machine-gun turret, the second had a quadruple 12.7mm/0.5in machine-gun turret and the last version had twin 23mm/0.91in cannon. The Egyptians have fitted the Czechoslovak M53 turret to some of their BTR-152s.

The BTR-152 has been replaced in the Soviet Army but still remains in service with many countries.

BTR-152V1 APC

Country: USSR
Entered service: 1950
Crew: 2 plus 17 infantry
Weight: 8,738kg/8.6 tons
Dimensions: Length – 6.55m/21ft 6in
  Height – 2.36m/7ft 9in
  Width – 2.32m/7ft 7in
Armament: Main – 12.7mm/0.5in DShKM
  machine-gun, and 2 x 7.62mm/0.3in
  SGMB machine-guns
  Secondary – Small arms
Armour: Maximum – 14mm/0.55in
Powerplant: ZIL-123 6-cylinder 82kW/110hp
  petrol engine
Performance: Speed – 75kph/47mph
  Range – 600km/373 miles

LEFT: A BTR-40 APC. This was the second vehicle type to be built by the Soviet Union after World War II. It had a crew of two and could carry eight men in the back. There is a 12.7mm/0.5in machine-gun mount above the driver's cab.

Cascavel EE-9 Mk IV Armoured Car

The Cascavel was designed by ENGESA to meet the requirements of the Brazilian Army, with design work starting in July 1970. The first prototype was completed in 1970 and a pre-production order for ten vehicles was placed and delivered between 1972 and 1973. Production began in 1974 with the vehicle entering Brazilian Army service in the same year. These early vehicles (Mk I) were fitted with M3 37mm/1.46in turrets taken from the now-redundant American light tanks used by the Brazilian Army. The second version (Mk II) of the vehicle was fitted with the Hispano-Suiza H90 turret. The EE-9 and the EE-11 APC have many parts in common and a lot of these are standard commercial parts.

The hull of the vehicle is made from spaced armour with the outer layer having dual hardness. This outer layer is constructed of a hardened steel sheet

and a softer steel rolled together to form one single dual-hardened steel sheet. The driver sits in the front on the left-hand side with the two-man turret behind him and the engine in the rear. The rear wheels are mounted on an ENGESA Boomerang walking beam suspension arm that allows the vehicle to have all four wheels in contact with the ground at all times. The vehicle is a 6x6 and is fitted with run-flat tyres. Even after being fully deflated, the EE-9 can travel on them for 100km/62 miles before they have to be replaced.

Anticipating the finite supply of M3 turrets, ENGESA started to manufacture their own turrets and guns. These ENGESA ET-90 turrets and EC-90 guns were fitted to the EE-9 once the M3 turrets had run out, creating the Mk III. The Mk IV was the next version to enter production in 1979. This saw significant improvements over previous versions

ABOVE LEFT: **This is a Cascavel on parade in Venezuela. Both the vehicle commander and the turret gunner are standing in the top of their turret position. The commander's cupola is fitted with a machine-gun.**
ABOVE: **The Cascavel climbing a steep slope. The very flat rear of the vehicle and turret sides can be clearly seen. The rear of the turret on this Brazilian vehicle has been fitted with a storage basket.**

with the installation of a new engine and the fitting of a central tyre pressure system controlling all wheels similar to that on Soviet vehicles. The Mk V is the last variation and this is powered by a German Mercedes-Benz diesel rather than the American engine of the Mk IV.

Cascavel EE-9 Mk IV Armoured Car

Country: Brazil
Entered service: 1979
Crew: 3
Weight: 13,411kg/13.2 tons
Dimensions: Length – 6.2m/20ft 4in
　　　　　Height – 2.68m/9ft 9in
　　　　　Width – 2.64m/8ft 8in
Armament: Main – EC-90 90mm/3.54in gun,
　　　and coaxial 7.62mm/0.3in machine-gun
　　　Secondary – 12.7mm/0.5in anti-aircraft
　　　machine-gun
Armour: Maximum – 16mm/0.63in
Powerplant: Detroit Diesel model 6V-53N
　　　6-cylinder 158kW/212hp diesel engine
Performance: Speed – 100kph/62mph
　　　Range – 880km/547 miles

LEFT: **The vehicle commander's position has been fitted with a 7.62mm/0.3in machine-gun and the vehicle is fitted with two whip aerials. At the rear of the turret on each side is a cluster of smoke dischargers, one set of which is visible here.**

Commando V-150 Armoured Personnel Carrier

ABOVE: **This is one of the prototype development vehicles, and is fitted with a fixed turret. The large side door is in the open position with the top of the door folded back against the hull and the bottom of the door acting as a step.**

The Cadillac Gage Company started development of the Commando in 1962 as a private venture, with the first prototype being finished in March 1963. The first production vehicles entered service in 1964. The Commando saw extensive service with the American Army and with the American Air Force during the Vietnam War. It was deployed as a convoy escort for both services and also as an airfield defence vehicle.

The Commando is very much a mix-and-match vehicle: the customer can chose one of several bodies and one of about 14 different turrets. Its American designation is the M706. The first

type of vehicle was the V-100, which was followed very shortly by the V-200 and finally the V-150 which came into service in 1971 and replaced both the V-100 and V-200. The V-150S entered production in 1985. The V-100 is very similar to the V-150 except that the V-100 has a petrol engine while the V-150's engine is a diesel. The V-200 was a beefed-up version, much larger than either of the other two vehicles.

The V-150 is an all-welded steel construction and provides the crew with protection from up to 7.62mm/0.3in bullets and shrapnel. The driver sits at the front on the left-hand side and, depending on the version, the vehicle commander's seat is next to the driver. Behind them is the main crew compartment that can be fitted with a variety of turrets and can even have an open top. The one-man turrets have a single hatch in the top and are armed with a variety of machine-guns up to 20mm/0.79in, either mounted in pairs or singly. The two-man turret has two hatches and the armament ranges from 20mm/0.79in up to 90mm/3.54in guns. There are three doors in the main hull, one on each side and one in the rear. The top half of the door folds back flush with the vehicle while the bottom folds down and forms a step for the infantry to clear the vehicle and its wheels. There are eight pistol ports fitted to the vehicle, two in the front and three down each side. The maximum number of infantry that can be carried in the vehicle is 12 but

LEFT: **The rear of the Commando prototype vehicle showing the large rear exit door. The top of the door flips up and the bottom drops down to form a step.**

LEFT: **The good ground clearance can be clearly seen. This turret can be fitted with either a single or twin 7.62mm/0.3in machine-gun.** ABOVE: **This Commando is being used as a reconnaissance vehicle. It is armed with a single machine-gun. One of the men is operating from inside the vehicle but to have a better vision has opened the top half of the hull door.** BELOW: **A number of Commando vehicles have been sold to police forces around the world. They act as internal security or riot control vehicles.**

this does vary depending on the version. The engine is mounted in the rear of the V-150 on the left-hand side with a corridor on the right leading to the rear door. In this corridor are two seating positions while above the corridor is a small circular hatch that opens towards the front of the vehicle and has a pintle mount for a 7.62mm/0.3in machine-gun to cover the rear of the vehicle.

The mortar vehicle and the TOW missile vehicle have a raised section added to the roof in place of the turret. This is fitted with two folding hatches that run the length of the raised area and fold to the sides of the vehicle. The 81mm/3.19in mortar is mounted in the middle of the crew compartment on a turntable and can be traversed through 360 degrees. Its minimum range is 150m/492ft with a maximum range of 4,400m/14,435ft. There are also four pintle mounts for 7.62mm/0.3in machine-guns. The vehicle has a crew of five and also carries 62 mortar bombs. The hatches for the TOW vehicle open front and back; it can carry seven missiles and

has a crew of four. There is also a command version built using this basic type of hull and a police riot vehicle has also been developed for several American police departments. An armoured recovery version of the V-150 has also been developed and it is designed for the recovery of broken down or damaged light armoured vehicles. This is fitted with a heavy duty winch and "A" frame that is attached to the front of the vehicle and folds back across the top of the crew compartment when not required. A large number of these vehicles are still in service.

Some 4,000 of the V-150s have been built and are in service with 21 countries. The only country to purchase the V-200 was Singapore and the V-100 was only purchased by the USA.

RIGHT: **The driver's and vehicle commander's vision ports are protected by armoured covers. The vehicle also has a number of vision ports in the side of the vehicle. The open fixed turret of this vehicle has been improved and turned into a command turret.**

Commando V-150 APC

Country: USA
Entered service: 1971
Crew: 2 crew plus 10 infantry
Weight: 9,550kg/9.4 tons
Dimensions: Length – 5.68m/19ft 8in
　Height – 2.43m/8ft
　Width – 2.26m/7ft 5in
Armament: Main – Various
　Secondary – Small arms
Armour: Classified
Powerplant: Chrysler V-504 8-cylinder
　151kW/202hp diesel engine
Performance: Speed – 88kph/55mph
　Range – 950km/600 miles

LEFT: **The hatches over the troop compartment have been folded back against the hull of the vehicle, with the men sitting in the raised position. The vehicle commander is operating the machine-gun over his position.**

DAF YP-408 Armoured Personnel Carrier

DAF (*Van Doorne's Automobielfabrieken*) started development of the YP-408 carrier in 1956 to meet a Dutch Army requirement. The first prototypes were finished in 1958 and were powered by an American Hercules JXLD petrol engine, but this was changed in the production model. The vehicle went through a number of modifications and finally an order was placed for 750 vehicles with the first carriers being delivered to the

Dutch Army in 1964. By 1988, the YP-408 had been phased out of service with the Dutch being replaced by the YPR-765.

The hull is an all-welded construction with the engine, transmission and radiator in the front. The driver and the commander/gunner are placed side by side behind the engine with the driver on the left. The gunner's hatch cover is in two parts that only open to the vertical position and so provide some protection

when manning the machine-gun. The troop compartment is in the rear of the vehicle and holds ten men, who sit down the sides of the vehicle facing each other with their legs interlocking. Entry and exit from the crew compartment is by twin doors in the rear, each door having a single firing port in it.

The YP-408 uses many of the same components as the YP-328 (6x6) truck, but this vehicle is an 8x6 layout. It has power steering and steers using the front two axles, the second axle being unpowered. The YP-408 is fitted with dual air and hydraulic brakes, and the tyres can be driven on for 50km/31 miles when punctured. The vehicle is not fitted with an NBC system and is not amphibious, but it can be fitted with infrared night-driving equipment.

There were several variations on the basic vehicle. The two command versions had one row of seats removed and a map table in their place. Other variants include: an ambulance; an armoured supply carrier; a mortar tractor which had a total crew of seven, towed the 120mm/4.72in mortar and carried 50 mortar bombs; an anti-tank vehicle armed with TOW missiles; and a ground radar vehicle.

MIDDLE LEFT: **The gunner's hatch covers are fully open as they only open to this vertical position. The top of the troop compartment has six large hatches recessed into it.** LEFT: **The second axle from the front can be raised and locked into position clear of the ground. This is so the wheels can be used as spares for the other wheel positions.**

DAF YP-408 APC

Country: Netherlands
Entered service: 1964
Crew: 2 plus 10 infantry
Weight: 11,989kg/11.8 tons
Dimensions: Length – 6.2m/20ft 4in
  Height – 1.55m/5ft 11in
  Width – 2.4m/7ft 9in
Armament: Main – 12.7mm/0.5in heavy
  machine-gun
  Secondary – Small arms
Armour: Maximum – 15mm/0.59in
Powerplant: DAF Model DS-575 6-cylinder
  123kW/165hp diesel engine
Performance: Speed – 80kph/50mph
  Range – 500km/310 miles

LEFT: **This Ferret Mk 1 has a large storage basket fitted to the rear hull above the engine. Behind the storage bin between the wheels is an escape hatch. When opened, the hatch and storage bin drop away from the vehicle.** ABOVE: **The driver's position in this Ferret armoured car. The dashboard is split into two with the steering wheel in the middle. The handbrake is just in front of the driver's seat. The driver has one large vision block above the steering wheel with smaller ones to the side.**

Ferret Mk 1 Scout Car

In 1947, the British Army issued a requirement for a replacement for the Daimler Dingo scout car. Daimler consequently started development of the Mk 1 Ferret Scout Car in 1948 with the first prototype being produced in December 1949. The first production Mk 1 Ferrets were delivered in October 1952 and the type would remain in production for 20 years, the final Ferret being produced in 1971. Total production was 4,409 vehicles of which 1,200 were Mk 1s. The Ferret proved to be extremely popular with the men using it and could be found in almost every British Army unit, even units that were not issued with

them. It would remain in service with the British Army until 1994.

The Mk 1 Ferret is a monocoque design made from 30 separate flat plates and is an all-welded construction. The driver is seated in the front with the crew compartment in the middle and the engine in the rear. The crew compartment is open-topped but can be covered by a canvas tilt. The vehicle is a 4x4 layout with steering on the front axle which is not power-assisted. A spare wheel is carried on the left side of the vehicle with storage boxes on the right. The Daimler pre-selective gearbox has five forward and five reverse gears. The Ferret Mk 1

does not carry night-driving infrared lights or NBC system. It can be fitted with deep wading gear but this was a later development that appeared on the Mk 1/3.

The Ferret Mk 1 went through some modifications, the first being in 1959 when the Mk 1/1 came into service. This had increased armour protection, and the open top was covered by a fixed turret, which had a split hatch that folded towards the rear of the vehicle. The Mk 1/3 deep wading gear attaches over the top of the opening or turret area and is a canvas screen that can be raised like an inflated bellows, allowing the vehicle to be submerged (including the driver) with the commander standing in the top of the turret giving directions.

LEFT: **The last combat service for the Ferret was the Gulf War of 1991. This Mk 1 has had a fixed turret placed on the top of the crew area. On each side of the front of the vehicle is a cluster of three smoke dischargers. The storage basket on the rear of the vehicle has been raised.**

Ferret Mk 1 Scout Car

Country: UK
Entered service: 1952
Crew: 2–3
Weight: 4,369kg/4.3 tons
Dimensions: Length – 3.84m/12ft 9in
　　　　Height – 1.45m/4ft 9in
　　　　Width – 1.9m/6ft 3in
Armament: Main – 7.62mm/0.3in light
　　　　machine-gun
　　　　Secondary – Small arms
Armour: Maximum – 16mm/0.63in
Powerplant: Rolls-Royce B60 6-cylinder
　　　　87kW/116hp petrol engine
Performance: Speed – 93kph/58mph
　　　　Range – 300km/185 miles

LEFT: The Ferret Mk 2 is fitted with a fully rotating turret armed with a single machine-gun as standard. The exhaust system is fitted on the rear mudguard. BELOW: This Ferret Mk 2/6 has been fitted with the Vigilante AT missile system. This type of vehicle entered service in 1963. The missile boxes increase the overall width of the car. An additional storage box has also been fitted to the side of the vehicle.

Ferret Mk 2 Scout Car

The AFV offers an incredible variety of possibilities to the military. It is therefore not surprising that when the British Army issued a requirement for a replacement for the Daimler Dingo in 1947, Daimler developed two variants of the same basic type and both were adopted. Development of the Mk 2 Ferret Scout Car was started in 1948, the first prototype being produced in December 1949. The first production Mk 2 Ferrets were delivered in July 1952, entering service before the Mk 1 Ferrets. It remained in production for 20 years, the final Ferret being produced in 1971. Of the total production of 4,409 vehicles, 1,850 were Mk 2s.

The Mk 2 Ferret is a monocoque design made from 30 separate flat plates and is an all-welded construction. The driver is seated in the front with the turret in the middle and the engine in the rear. The driver has three hatches. The one to the front can be folded down so it lies on the glacis plate and can

then be replaced by a splinter-proof windscreen. There are also hatches on each side of his position, each fitted with a periscope. The turret is very small and cramped and was heavily modified during the trials as it was found that the gunner could accidentally catch his clothing in the trigger and fire the machine-gun. The turret is manually operated as it is small and light and so does not require power. It has two hatches; one in the top that opens forward and gives the gunner some protection as it does not fold flat, and one at the rear of the turret which also folds down to form a seat that the gunner can use. A sighting periscope is fitted in the top of the turret for the gunner to use when in the closed-down position. There are two escape hatches in the Ferret; one behind the spare wheel and the other behind the storage bin on the right-hand side of the vehicle.

LEFT: The rear vision visors are all open to give the driver a better rear view from the vehicle. Beside the jerry-can on the rear of the car is a fire extinguisher. The small compact size of the vehicle can be clearly seen.

LEFT: **This Ferret Mk 2/3 has two unditching channels fitted to the front of the car. The aerial on this car is mounted behind one of the clusters of smoke dischargers fitted to the vehicle. A large single searchlight has also been fitted to the side of the turret.** ABOVE: **The driver's and vehicle commander's positions inside the car. The steering wheel is set in a reversed–raked position. The gear selector box is under the steering wheel.**

The engine is fully waterproofed and drive is transmitted to all four wheels by a fluid coupling, five speed pre-selecting epicyclic gearbox and a transfer box, incorporating a forward and reverse mechanism, thus giving the vehicle five forward and five reverse gears and so allowing the vehicle to travel at the same speed in each direction. The Ferret is fully air-transportable and can be delivered by parachute cluster. As a result of this, a lightweight recovery vehicle had to be developed and a number of Ferrets were converted to the role. The Armoured Recovery Vehicle (ARV) conversion came as a kit and could be quickly fitted to a vehicle in the field. This was not an official conversion and remained classified as a local workshop conversion. Another modification that started off as a field modification was the introduction of a storage basket, which was mounted above the engine and was hinged so it could be tilted out of the way to give access to the engine. The basket was fitted to improve the storage of personal equipment which was always a problem.

The Ferret Mk 2 was produced in six different versions. The Mk 2/2 was a local conversion carried out on vehicles in the Far East and consisted of an extension collar fitted between the hull and the turret. The Mk 2/3 was an uparmoured version of the basic Mk 2 and was converted to carry the 7.62mm/0.3in GPMG (General Purpose Machine-Gun). The Mk 2/4 was an uparmoured version of the Mk 2/3 and was fitted with a new fire-fighting system in the crew compartment. The Mk 2/5 was the basic Mk 2 brought up to Mk 2/4 standard. The Ferret Mk 2/6 was fitted with two Vigilante anti-tank missiles, one on each side of the turret, with two spare missiles being carried instead of the spare wheel. The missiles were fired from inside the turret by the vehicle commander.

The Ferret proved to be extremely popular with the men using it and could be found in almost every British Army unit, including units that were not officially issued with them. It would remain in service with the British Army until 1994, some 20 years after it was supposed to retire.

LEFT: **The extra-large storage bin on the side of the vehicle carried two spare missiles. The vehicle commander guides the missiles from this position by a combined sight. The wire guidance box is situated on the top of the turret. Reloading of the missile launchers could be undertaken in less than five minutes.**

Ferret Mk 2 Scout Car

Country: UK
Entered service: 1952
Crew: 2
Weight: 4,369kg/4.3 tons
Dimensions: Length – 3.84m/12ft 9in
    Height – 1.88m/6ft 2in
    Width – 1.9m/6ft 3in
Armament: Main – 7.62mm/0.3in machine-gun
    Secondary – Small arms
Armour: Maximum – 16mm/0.63in
Powerplant: Rolls-Royce B60 6-cylinder 87kW/116hp petrol engine
Performance: Speed – 93kph/58mph
    Range – 300km/185 miles

LEFT: **This is the Ferret Mk 5 armed with two Swingfire AT missiles. Spare missiles are carried in storage bins fitted to the vehicle's sides under the turret. The missile boxes are in the maximum elevation firing position.** ABOVE: **This prototype Ferret Mk 4 has the flotation screen fixed in a box structure around the edge of the vehicle. The new water-tight glass-fibre storage box can be seen clearly.**

Ferret Mk 4 Big Wheeled Scout Car

In 1963 work began on improving the Ferret's automotive and amphibious capabilities, and on providing better storage facilities for the crew's personal equipment. The first six prototypes were converted from Mk 1 vehicles; the basic hull was unchanged but larger tyres were fitted and a flotation screen was carried around the top of the hull. The Mk 4 entered service with the British Army in 1967. None of these vehicles were brand new but were converted Mk 2/3 cars. The last of these conversions were carried out in 1976.

The Mk 4 Ferret is a monocoque design made from 30 separate flat plates and is an all-welded construction. The driver is seated in the front with the turret

in the middle and the engine in the rear. The driver's hatch is in the front of the vehicle and can be folded down so it lies on the glacis plate and can then be replaced by a splinter-proof windscreen. During development the larger wheels caused a number of problems with the steering due to the increased weight of the vehicle as the steering was not power-assisted. This would remain a problem with this mark of Ferret. Other improvements on the Mk 4 were enlarged disc brakes and improved suspension. The vehicle was also extended by 38cm/15in to incorporate the flotation screen.

The Mk 5 was a development of the Mk 4, the main difference being the

design of the turret. The Mk 5 was to have been built in large numbers but in fact only 50 of these vehicles were made. The new turret had a very flat design and carried four BAC Swingfire anti-tank missiles, two on each side of the centreline. The maximum range of the Swingfire was 4,000m/13,123ft and the missiles were wire-guided and controlled from inside the vehicle by the gunner using a combined sight and controller. Two spare missiles were carried on the vehicle. The turret was made from aluminium armour and could be traversed through 360 degrees but it was not power operated. A 7.62mm/0.3in machine-gun was mounted in the front of it for close protection.

LEFT: **The basic Mk 2/3 was used to produce the Mk 4. The 2/3 was fitted with new brakes, suspension and wheels which gave it a wider track. To make the Mk 5, the suspension changes were made to the 2/6 and a new turret was fitted.**

Ferret Mk 4 Scout Car

Country: UK
Entered service: 1967
Crew: 2
Weight: 5,400kg/5.3 tons
Dimensions: Length – 4.1m/13ft 5in
　　　　Height – 2.34m/7ft 8in
　　　　Width – 2.13m/7ft
Armament: Main – 7.62mm/0.3in light
　　　　machine-gun
　　　　Secondary – Small arms
Armour: Maximum – 16mm/0.63in
Powerplant: Rolls-Royce B60 6-cylinder
　　　　87kW/116hp petrol engine
Performance: Speed – 80kph/50mph
　　　　Range – 300km/185 miles

Fox Light Armoured Car

LEFT: The exhaust is mounted on the rear of the vehicle. There are two side hatches, one on each side of the vehicle below the large two-man turret. These vehicles had a high centre of gravity.

BELOW: When the flotation screen is raised, the driver has no vision from his position and so relies on the vehicle commander giving him directions. Transparent screens were fitted to the flotation screen on later models.

In the 1960s the Fighting Vehicles Research and Development Establishment (FVRDE) developed two vehicles; one was the Combat Vehicle Reconnaissance (Tracked) (CVR(T)) Scorpion and the other the CVR (Wheeled) Fox. Both used the same Jaguar engine. Development started in 1965 and a development contract for 15 prototypes was given to Daimler in 1966. The first vehicle was finished in November 1967 and the last in 1969. Production began in 1972 and the first vehicles entered service in 1973, but this was not to be a replacement for the Ferret. This was the projected role of the Vixen, which was cancelled in 1974.

The Fox was a further development of the late-production Ferret scout car. The vehicle has an-all welded aluminium hull and turret which gives the crew protection against light and heavy machine-guns and shell splinters. The driver sits in the front of the vehicle with his hatch opening to the right, while the two-man turret is positioned in the middle of the vehicle and is fitted with a 30mm/1.18in RARDEN cannon and a coaxial 7.62mm/0.3in machine-gun. The 4.2-litre Jaguar XK engine is positioned in the rear of the vehicle, where there are also two radiators, and a Ki-gas cold-weather starter is fitted. The Fox has the same fluid coupling, five speed pre-selecting epicyclic gearbox, and transfer box as the Ferret, giving the vehicle five forward gears and another five in reverse. It can ford to a depth of 1m/3ft 3in with no preparation. If the water is deeper, the flotation screen can be raised into position in just two minutes and then the vehicle becomes amphibious and is driven in the water by the wheels of the car. The Fox is fully air-transportable and three can be carried at once by a C130 Hercules transport aircraft. It can also be deployed by parachute. The vehicle is fitted with night-fighting and night-driving equipment, but no NBC system is installed.

The Fox was not a successful vehicle and did not remain in service for long. Its turrets were removed and fitted to the Scorpion and the FV 432.

Fox Light Armoured Car

Country: UK
Entered service: 1973
Crew: 3
Weight: 6,120kg/6 tons
Dimensions: Length – 5.08m/16ft 8in
    Height – 2.2m/7ft 3in
    Width – 2.13m/7ft
Armament: Main – 30mm/1.18in RARDEN cannon,
    and coaxial 7.62mm/0.3in machine-gun
    Secondary – Small arms
Armour: Classified
Powerplant: Jaguar XK 4.2-litre 6-cylinder
    142kW/190hp petrol engine
Performance: Speed – Road 104kph/65mph;
    Water 5.2kph/3mph
    Range – 434km/270 miles

RIGHT: The smoke dischargers have been moved from the hull and on to the front of the turret. The turret has a large overhang and so the driver's hatch was designed to fold to the side. The flotation screen is attached around the side of the hull of this vehicle.

LEFT: The large size of this vehicle can be seen from the crew member standing at the rear of the vehicle. The reloading crane can be seen under the missile launching rail. On the rear of the TEL are two stabilizers that have to be put in place before the missile can be elevated on its rail.

Frog-7 Battlefield Missile System

The Frog (Free Range Over Ground) missile system was designed and built to deliver nuclear warheads on to the battlefield, just like the American Honest John system. The first in the series was the Filin (Eagle Owl), which has the NATO codename Frog-1. This entered service in 1955 but was not seen by the Western allies until the Moscow November Parade in 1987. The launching vehicle for this system was the 2P4, which was based on the IS-2 heavy tank. Not very many of these rocket systems were deployed as the whole system was very large and unwieldy and the missile was powered by seven separate solid-fuel rockets which did not always fire at the same time, making it inherently unstable. The Frog-2 (NATO codename Mars), using the 2P2 modified PT-76 amphibious tank as its carrier, came into service in the same year as the

Frog-1, but only 25 of these vehicles were built and it was more of a propaganda tool than a useful battlefield system.

The Frog-3 used the Luna-1 (NATO codename Moon-1) rocket and appeared in 1957. This was the first true battlefield tactical missile system and was mounted on 2P16 vehicles, some 200 of these being produced for the Soviet Army and a further 100 for export. The vehicle was very similar to the 2P2 and was based on the PT-76 tank. It had a road speed of 44kph/27.3mph and could fire its first rocket within 15 minutes of parking, but reloading could take up to 60 minutes. The same vehicle was used for the Frog-3, Frog-4 and Frog-5 and remained in service for several years.

The final version of the Frog family was the Frog-7 which used the Luna-M rocket (NATO codename Moon-3) and the

RIGHT: This is a reload vehicle for the Frog-7 system. The same chassis as the TEL is used, except that the crane and launching rail have been removed and replaced with three fixed transport ramps. The official designation of this vehicle was 9T29.

LEFT: This Frog-7 system is ready for firing. Behind the TEL on the road is a column of tanks. Each Frog battery consisted of four TEL vehicles and 170 personnel. Each battery carries seven missiles for each TEL. ABOVE: The cab of the TEL has its blast screen folded down on to the glacis of the vehicle. The engine compartment is mounted behind the cab of the vehicle. The crews for the two TEL vehicles are being briefed by their officer.

9P113 TEL (Transporter, Erector and Launcher). This was based on the ZIL-135LM 8x8 heavy truck that was used for several rocket and transport duties. The ZIL-135LM was built at the Bryansk Automobile Plant near Moscow and was designated BAZ-135 but the Soviet Army still referred to the vehicle as the ZIL-135LM. The crew cab is at the front of the vehicle and holds four men. Before the missile is fired, an armoured cover which normally lies on the top of the front sub-nose of the vehicle is put in place by the crew to protect the windscreen from the rocket blast. Behind the cab is the engine bay. The engine area has two ZIL-135 8-cylinder petrol engines, with one engine for each side of the vehicle powering all four wheels on that side. Power steering was fitted on the front and rear axle and a central tyre pressure system was fitted as standard. Mounted behind the front axle and on the rear of the vehicle are four stabilizing jacks. In the middle of the vehicle are cable reels which are used for sending signals to the missile from a remote firing position some 25m/82ft away. On the right-hand side between the third and fourth axle is a 4,064kg/4-ton crane which is used for reloading. The hydraulically operated missile

erecting mechanism is at the rear of the vehicle, while the sighting and elevation controls are on the left-hand side. There is also a small platform that folds down to allow the operator to reach the sighting controls.

These vehicles were relatively cheap at just 25,000 US dollars when they came into service with the Soviet Army in 1965 and were the last unguided nuclear weapon in service with the Soviet Union and other Warsaw Pact members. The Bryansk plant produced 750 of these vehicles of which 380 have been exported and it is estimated that in 1999, Russia still had 1,450 nuclear warheads in stock for the Frog-7. The Frog has now been phased out of service with the Russian Army but is still in service with a number of Middle East countries.

The Luna-M missile is capable of carrying nuclear, high-explosive, chemical and sub munitions warheads. It has a minimum range of 15km/9.3 miles and a maximum of 65km/40.4 miles, but is not very accurate as it has a circular error of probability of between 500–700m/1,640–2,297ft, which means you could aim at an airfield and definitely hit it but not a target the size of a bridge.

ABOVE: These vehicles are taking part in a victory parade. Between the first and second wheels is the forward stabilizer, one on each side of the vehicle. The reload crane can be clearly seen in this picture.

Frog-7 Missile System

Country: USSR
Entered service: 1965
Crew: 4
Weight: 20,411kg/20.1 tons
Dimensions: Length – 10.69m/35ft 1in
Height – With missile 3.35m/11ft
Width – 2.8m/9ft 2in
Armament: Main – 1 x Luna-M missile
Secondary – Small arms
Armour: None
Powerplant: 2 x ZIL 135 8-cylinder 132kW/180hp petrol engine
Performance: Speed – 40kph/25mph
Range – 650km/400 miles

FV 432 Armoured Personnel Carrier

The first prototype for the FV 432 was completed in 1961, the first vehicle of this series being the earlier FV 431 which did not enter production as there was no need for an armoured load carrier. In 1962, GKN Sankey was given a contract to mass-produce the FV 432 or "Trojan" as it was called when it first entered service, but this name was dropped to avoid confusion with the Trojan car company. The first production vehicles were completed in 1963 and the FV 432 entered service with the British Army replacing the Humber "Pig" and Saracen APC over a period of time. The FV 432 was due to be replaced in the mid-1980s by the Warrior, but this has not happened due to defence cutbacks and the FV 432 is expected to remain in service for some years yet. These vehicles are currently undergoing a refurbishment programme to extend their service life.

The FV 432 is basically box-shaped and is an all-steel welded construction. The armour of the vehicle is proof against small arms fire and shell splinters. The driver sits in the front of the vehicle on the left-hand side and has a wide-angle periscope mounted in his hatch. The vehicle commander/gunner is situated behind the driver and has a cupola that can be rotated through 360 degrees with a mount for a single 7.62mm/0.3in GPMG mounted on the front of it. The driver's and commander's positions are open inside the vehicle and the commander can communicate with the driver by hitting him in

TOP: **This British FV 432 is on exercise in Germany. All the hatches on this vehicle are in the open position. The driver's and vehicle commander's positions are at the top of the picture. The large circular hatch above the crew compartment is in the open position, and a section of British troops are debussing.** ABOVE: **A side view of an FV 432 showing the exhaust system running the length of the vehicle. The exhaust stopped just by the rear exit, so at times when the vehicle was stopped, exhaust gases would enter the infantry compartment.**

the shoulders to indicate any desired changes of direction. Unfortunately this can be very painful after a while! Next to them on the right-hand side of the vehicle is the engine bay. Behind this is the infantry compartment which extends to the rear of the vehicle. This compartment can hold ten fully armed troops who sit on bench seats, five down each side of the vehicle facing each other. Above them is a large single circular hatch that is divided in the middle and, when opened, folds flush with the top of the vehicle on each side. Each half-hatch is hinged in the middle making opening easier. The bench seats can be folded up when not in use so the vehicle can then be used as a cargo carrier. At the rear of the vehicle is a single large door that opens outwards and to the right allowing the troops to debus very quickly, with the open rear door acting as a shield. The exhaust system is mounted on the left-hand side of the vehicle with the NBC system fitted to the right-hand side. All marks of the vehicle are fitted with a full NBC system.

The FV 432 was usually fitted with the Peak Engineering 7.62mm/0.3in turret, but the 30mm/1.18in turret from the Fox armoured car was mounted on a few vehicles of the Berlin Brigade. The turret was fitted behind the commander's position and into the upper hatch, which was now fixed in the closed position, and had a full 360-degree traverse, while behind the turret was a small circular hatch. The FV 432 is not amphibious but the Mk 1 was at first fitted with a flotation screen that could be raised in ten minutes, with the vehicle using its tracks to power it in the water. The flotation screen was not installed in the Mk 2 variant.

The FV 432 has been produced in three main marks. The Mk 1 was powered by a Rolls-Royce B81 8-cylinder 179kW/ 240hp petrol engine. The Mk 2 started to appear in 1966 and was fitted with a diesel engine that had a multi-fuel capability that

improved reliability and range. The last mark was the 2/1 and this had improvements to the exhaust system and the engine area. The vehicle commander is extremely vulnerable in the FV 432 and has no protection when manning the machine-gun with the hatch open. By 1967, many were slating the vehicle because it lacked heavy armament like that of the new Soviet BMP-1. However, no NATO APC could match the BMP for firepower.

ABOVE: **An FV 432 mine plough developed by the British Army but never seriously put into service. The glacis plate of the vehicle has several control boxes for the plough fitted to it. The plough blade is constructed in sections, so if one section is damaged it can be replaced quickly.** BELOW: **Another mine-clearing device fitted and tested on the FV 432 was the flail. The vehicle was called the Aardvark. The large box on the rear of the vehicle holds the lane-marking equipment. This device did not enter service with the British Army.**

MIDDLE LEFT: **The vehicle commander has a 7.62mm/0.3in machine-gun fitted to his cupola. The large boxes either side of the rear door are for storage. There**

was never enough storage space in or on the FV 432; many units fitted wire-mesh storage bins to the rear of the vehicle. LEFT: **A 432 Mk 1 fitted with a RARDEN turret from the cancelled Fox armoured car. This vehicle is also fitted with a flotation screen around the top of the FV 432. On the front of the vehicle is a trim vane. The 432 is moved through the water by its tracks.**

FV 432 Armoured Personnel Carrier

Country: UK
Entered service: 1963
Crew: 2 plus 10 infantry
Weight: 15,240kg/15.1 tons
Dimensions: Length – 5.25m/17ft 7in
    Height – 2.29m/7ft 6in
    Width – 2.8m/9ft 2in
Armament: Main – 7.62mm/0.3in General Purpose
    machine-gun
    Secondary – Small arms
Armour: Maximum – 12mm/0.47in
Powerplant: Rolls-Royce K60 No.4 Mk 4F
    6-cylinder 170kW/240hp diesel/multi-fuel engine
Performance: Speed – 52kph/32mph
    Range – 483km/300 miles

LEFT: **This German Gepard has the rear surveillance radar in the raised position. When the vehicle is moving, the surveillance radar folds back into the horizontal position. The vehicle commander is using a manual sight, attached to his cupola.** ABOVE: **Both radar dishes on this Gepard are in the raised active position. A bank of four smoke dischargers is fitted to each side of the bottom of the turret.**

Gepard Self-Propelled Anti-Aircraft Gun

In 1961, contracts were issued to two companies for the development of a new Self-Propelled Anti-Aircraft Gun (SPAAG) for the *Bundeswehr* (German Army) as a replacement for the American M42. However, the whole project was cancelled in 1964 as the projected main chassis was considered to be too small and the tracking radar was not fully developed. In 1965, it was decided that a new all-weather design based on the Leopard 1 MBT chassis was required. Two development contracts were issued in 1966 for two vehicles armed with 3cm/1.18in guns and two vehicles armed with 3.5cm/1.38in guns. In 1970, following the decision to concentrate on the 3.5cm/1.38in vehicle, an order for 420 Gepards was placed, with the first vehicles entering service in 1976. The Belgian Army placed a contract for 55 Gepards that was fulfilled between 1977 and 1980, while the Dutch Army order for 95 vehicles was completed over the same period. In 1998 the German Government donated 43 Gepard vehicles to the Romanian Army along with training and maintenance equipment. The first of these were delivered in 1999.

The all-welded hull of the Gepard is slightly longer than the Leopard MBT while the armour on the vehicle has been reduced in thickness. The driver is located in the front of the vehicle on the right-hand side due to the tracking radar being mounted on the front of the turret. Next to the driver is the auxiliary power unit which is a Daimler-Benz OM314 70.8kW/95hp engine. The exhaust pipe for this runs along the left-hand side of the hull to the rear of the vehicle. The vehicle is fitted with a full NBC system.

The two-man turret is positioned in the middle of the vehicle; the commander is on the left with the gunner on the right and both are provided with their own hatch which is mounted in the roof of the turret. Both the gunner and commander have a fully

ABOVE: **On the front of the turret is the tracking radar. Targets are acquired by the surveillance radar and then the most prominent threat is worked out by computer and the target information passed to the tracking radar, which then locks the guns on to the target.**

stabilized panoramic telescope sight which is mounted on the roof of the turret and is used for optically tracking aerial targets and for use against ground targets. The optical sights can be linked to the radar and computer, and a Siemens laser rangefinder is also fitted for engaging ground targets. Mounted on the rear of the turret is the pulse-Doppler search radar, which has a 360-degree traverse, a range of 15km/9.3 miles, and an IFF (Identification Friend or Foe) capability. Once a target has been acquired the information is passed to the tracking radar which is mounted at the front of the turret between the guns. The computer and radar systems are capable of dealing with several targets at once. The main

armament is two Oerlikon 35mm/1.38in KDA cannon. Each gun barrel has a firing rate of 550 rounds per minute and the vehicle carries 660 rounds in total, with 310 anti-aircraft shells and 20 rounds of armour-piercing ammunition for each barrel. A normal burst of fire lasts for a fraction of a second and can be up to a maximum of 40 rounds. The guns normally open fire when the target is at a distance of between 3,000m/9,842ft and 4,000m/13,123ft with the rounds reaching the target at a range of between 2,000m/6,561ft and 3,000m/9,842ft, the computer calculating the predicted position of the target. The guns are mounted externally on the sides of the turret with the ammunition being fed in on hermetically sealed chutes, which keeps the gun fumes away from the crew.

In 1996, the vehicle systems were upgraded so that the Gepard could remain in service for several more years. The Germans upgraded 147 of their vehicles while the Dutch upgraded 60, the main improvements being to the fire-control systems and the ammunition. As part of this project, the

ABOVE LEFT: **This is a Dutch Gepard. The Dutch fitted different surveillance radar to that installed by the Germans; it is shaped like a large letter "T" which rotates at 60 revolutions per minute. The Dutch also fitted banks of six smoke dischargers to each side of the bottom of the turret.** ABOVE: **The barrels of this Gepard have been covered in camouflage netting. The turret can complete a full rotation of 360 degrees in just 4 seconds. The fumes from the gun barrels and the empty cases are ejected directly to the outside of the vehicle.**

German and Dutch vehicles were data-linked so they can exchange information. The upgrade programme was finished in 2002 and should keep the vehicle in service until 2015. The German upgraded version is known as the Gepard Flakpanzer 1A2 while the Dutch vehicle is now known as the PRTL 35mm GWI. Since 1999, Krauss-Maffei Wegmann, who produced the upgrade package, have developed another upgrade which involves the fitting of four "fire and forget" Stinger SAMs, two being mounted externally on each 35mm/1.38in gun mount. This is not yet operational.

LEFT: **This Gepard is in travelling mode. The tracking radar dish has been folded forward to protect the dish from damage. With the surveillance radar folded down, the height of the vehicle is lowered by 1m/39in. Acquisition speed of the radar is 56 degrees per second, with a full traverse of the turret taking just four seconds.**

Gepard SPAAG

Country: West Germany
Entered service: 1976
Crew: 3
Weight: 45,009kg/44.3 tons
Dimensions: Length – 7.68m/25ft 2in
  Height – 3.01m/9ft 9in to top of turret
  Width – 3.27m/10ft 7in
Armament: Main – 2 x 35mm/1.38in Oerlikon
  KDA guns
  Secondary – None
Armour: Maximum – 70mm/2.76in
Powerplant: MTU MB 838 Ca M500 10-cylinder
  619kW/830hp multi-fuel engine
Performance: Speed – 64kph/40.5mph
  Range – 550km/340 miles

447

LEFT: The vehicle is fitted with three stabilizing jacks. One is mounted in front of the rear wheels on each side of the vehicle and a single jack is mounted at the rear of the vehicle in the centre.

ABOVE: A British Honest John during a live-firing exercise. The missile could be fitted with two 20 or 40 kiloton W31 nuclear warheads. It could also be fitted with a 680kg/1,500lb high-explosive or 564kg/1,243lb chemical warhead.

Honest John Missile System

Development of the M31 started at Redstone Arsenal, USA, in May 1950. The Douglas Aircraft Company was appointed to assist with development and later to carry out production, the first production contract being for 2,000 rockets. The M31 was deployed in Europe in June 1954 and it remained in service until 1961 when the improved M50 Honest John, which was lighter and had an increased range, replaced it. In July 1982, the Honest John system was declared obsolete as the Lance nuclear system came into service.

The rocket was a solid-fuel system and therefore required no countdown time and could remain in storage for several years with no maintenance. The M31 had a maximum range of 19.3km/ 12 miles, which meant that when firing a 20-kilotonne/19,684-ton nuclear warhead the fallout area would have been greater than the range of the missile, whereas the M50 missile, with its range of 48.3km/30 miles, would have been safer for the crew to use. The missile was unguided and required the whole vehicle to be pointed at the target area. The missile could be fitted with either a conventional high-explosive or a nuclear warhead and was never used in action.

The Transporter, Erector and Launcher (TEL) was built by the International Harvester Company and used the M139 5,080kg/5-ton truck, a stretched version of the M54 5,080kg/5-ton truck, as the base vehicle for the conversion. The TEL was designated M289 and was a 6x6 configuration which gave it excellent cross-country ability. The vehicle had the engine located at the front, the three-man soft-top crew cab behind it and the missile erector at the rear. The first version of the TEL had an "A" frame supporting the launch rail and this was pivoted in the middle of the vehicle above the two centrally mounted stabilizers while the launch rail protruded over the front of the TEL by 1.8m/6ft, restricting the driver's vision. The improved TEL had a much shorter launch rail, the front of which could be folded back on itself while travelling. The elevation controls were at the rear of the vehicle on the left-hand side.

ABOVE: A control wire is run from the vehicle to a command position a safe distance away from the back-blast of the missile. The three-man crew of this vehicle are getting instructions from an officer before firing the missile.

M289 TEL

Country: USA
Entered service: 1954
Crew: 3
Weight: 16,400kg/16.1 tons
Dimensions: Length – 9.89m/32ft 5in
    Height – 2.9m/9ft 5in
    Width – 2.67m/8ft 8in
Armament: Main – M31 Honest John Missile
    Secondary – Small arms
Armour: None
Powerplant: Continental R6602 6-cylinder 146kW/196hp petrol engine
Performance: Speed – 90kph/56mph
    Range – 480km/300 miles

LEFT: The launching arm on this vehicle is retracted for travelling and the driver's and vehicle commander/gunner's hatches are in the open position. Above the gunner's position is a domed armoured sight. ABOVE: The launching arm of this Hornet is in the raised firing position. This vehicle and missile system was specifically designed to be dropped by parachute.

Hornet Malkara Anti-Tank Missile System

The Hornet was developed from the Humber "Pig" 1-ton APC, and was originally designed to give the armoured divisions of the British Army a long-range anti-tank capability. This was intended to replace the Conqueror heavy tank with a guided missile system as it was felt that the tank no longer had a role on the modern battlefield.

The Hornet was based on the Humber 1,016kg/1-ton 4x4 vehicle and while it used the same chassis and engine as the standard vehicle, the crew compartment and the rear of the vehicle were modified to take the Malkara wire-guided missile system. The engine was located at the front, with the crew compartment behind and the missile launching arm fitted to the rear of the vehicle. The crew compartment was configured with the

driver on the right, the commander/ gunner on the left and the radio operator in the middle. The driver and radio operator also doubled as reload crew for the vehicle.

The superstructure at the rear of the 1,016kg/1-ton APC vehicle was removed and replaced by two storage boxes for two Malkara missiles and the launcher hydraulic arm. When travelling the launching arm was stowed in a lowered position below the top of the crew compartment. When the vehicle reached its firing location it halted and the launching arm was raised to the firing position, some 90cm/3ft above the crew compartment, so that the missiles had a clear flight to the target. The commander/ gunner had an optical sight that was mounted in the roof of the crew

compartment and controlled the missile using a joystick. Each missile had two flares attached at the rear which helped the gunner to track it to the target. The missile weighed 91kg/200lb of which the warhead was 27kg/60lb; this represented the largest warhead carried by any anti-tank missile at the time.

The Malkara missile was a joint British and Australian development, but was never very successful and the Hornet Malkara was replaced in service with the British Army from 1965 onwards by the Ferret Mk 2/6 armed with Vigilant ATGW missiles. The Hornet could rightly be described as a very expensive white elephant when compared with the economic Ferret.

LEFT: The rear storage area of the Hornet, where two reload missiles are carried. The rear hatch splits in two with the bottom part folding downwards to form a shelf, while the top half of the hatch folds flat on the top of the storage box. The wings are stored separately from the missiles in the rear of the vehicle.

Hornet Malkara ATGM

Country: UK
Entered service: 1958
Crew: 3
Weight: 5,893kg/5.8 tons
Dimensions: Length – 5.05m/16ft 7in
　Height – 2.34m/7ft 8in
　Width – 2.22m/7ft 3in
Armament: Main – 4 x Malkara ATGM
　Secondary – 7.62mm/0.3in General Purpose
　machine-gun
Armour: Maximum – 10mm/0.394in
Powerplant: Rolls-Royce B60 Mk 5A 6-cylinder
　89kW/120hp petrol engine
Performance: Speed – 64kph/40mph
　Range – 402km/250 miles

LEFT: This Humber Pig is fitted with a grill for pushing road blocks such as burning cars out of the way of the vehicle. An armoured plate has been fitted to the rear of the vehicle to stop fire-bombs or other objects being thrown under the vehicle.
ABOVE: The inside of the vehicle commander's door. Mounted in the door is an armoured vision port. The clear plastic tank in front of the commander's position is a screen-wash bottle. The bottle is filled with a chemical that can remove paint and other liquid that might be thrown at the vehicle.

Humber "Pig" 1-Ton Armoured Personnel Carrier

In the late 1940s and early 1950s, the Humber/Rootes Group developed a range of 1,016kg/1-ton armoured vehicles for the British Army. The Saracen APC was also under development at the same time but production proved to be slow and so the Humber "Pig" APC was developed as an interim solution. It was designed as a battlefield taxi and not as a combat vehicle; troops would debus away from the action and attack on foot. This interim vehicle entered production in 1954 and came into service in 1955. It was originally intended to produce only a few vehicles but the total quickly mounted to 1,700. This vehicle was so successful and adaptable that it is still in service with the British Army in 2005.

Humber took the basic 1,016kg/1-ton 4x4 cargo vehicle and added an armoured roof and rear doors to make a very basic APC for the army. The exact derivation of the vehicle's label

"Pig" is not known for certain, but it is certainly difficult to drive and lives up to its name.

The Pig is an all-welded construction with the engine at the front and the crew compartment behind. The driver and vehicle commander sit side by side in the front of the crew compartment behind the engine. Each of them has a windscreen to their front that can be covered when in action by an armoured shutter that folds down from the roof of the vehicle. Both also have an access door in the side of the vehicle and above them in the roof are two circular hatches. There are two firing ports in each side of the crew compartment with a further two mounted in the rear doors of the vehicle.

In the early 1960s it was thought that there were enough Saracen APCs in service and as the FV 432 was also just coming into service, it was decided to sell off the now-redundant Pigs. However, when the "Troubles" started in Northern Ireland in 1969, the army was asked to step in to help the police in maintaining the peace. The Pig was chosen to give the troops some mobility and protection without further arousing passions in a situation of civil unrest, being relatively small and innocuous and not having the aggressive appearance of a tank. Unfortunately, only a few of these vehicles had been kept in reserve, the majority having been scrapped or sold off to private collectors and the Belgian armed forces. These were bought back at an inflated price

LEFT: The driver's position inside the Humber Pig. The gear stick is between the seats with the handbrake next to the driver's seat. The dashboard is in the centre of the vehicle so both the driver and commander can see it.

LEFT: **This Humber Pig has been fitted with a six-barrel smoke and CS gas discharger. Under the rear of the vehicle, the armoured plate to stop bombs being thrown under the vehicle can be clearly seen.**
BELOW: **The inside of a Humber Pig command vehicle. One set of seats has been removed and replaced with a map table. Two wooden boards separate the driver and vehicle commander's cab from the troop compartment of the vehicle. The rear doors of the vehicle are held open by a simple metal hook and eye.**

and refurbished, and some 500 Pigs were sent to Northern Ireland. In 1972 it was discovered that the IRA had acquired armour-piercing ammunition that could damage the vehicle and cause casualties inside. As a result, Operation "Bracelet" was launched to upgrade the armour of the Pig and fit vision blocks to the open firing ports. The vehicle's suspension was also strengthened to accommodate the additional weight, and an extra armoured shutter was added to the rear of the vehicle which would fall into place when the rear doors were opened, protecting the legs of the men following the vehicle.

When the Saracen was withdrawn from Northern Ireland in 1984 the Pig had to take over its role and this led to a number of specialist conversions with exotic sounding names. The "Kremlin Pig" was covered with wire mesh as a protection against the Soviet RPG-7 rocket launcher. The "Flying Pig" has large side-mounted riot screens fitted to the vehicle. These fold back along the length of the crew compartment when not in use, but when in the open position have the appearance of wings and give troops protection from stones or other objects thrown at them. The "Holy Pig" has a Plexiglas fixed observation turret in the roof, the front of which can be folded down. Other Pig variants had smoke and CS gas launchers placed in the roof which can be fired from inside the vehicle, and large bull-bar bumpers have been fitted to the front.

The Pig proved to be a very reliable and "squaddy-proof" AFV especially given the "interim" nature of the design, and it continues to be an extremely valuable vehicle. The Saxon has replaced the Humber Pig in many roles.

ABOVE: **This is a "Flying Pig" in operation in Northern Ireland during the "Troubles" of the 1970s. The wire-mesh screens looked like a set of wings when deployed. Behind the wings of the vehicle are British troops. The soldier in the front is firing a baton-round gun, which could discharge either CS gas or rubber bullets.**

Humber "Pig" APC

Country: UK
Entered service: 1955
Crew: 2 plus 8 infantry
Weight: 6,909kg/6.8 tons
Dimensions: Length – 4.93m/16ft 2in
 Height – 2.12m/7ft
 Width – 2.04m/6ft 8in
Armament: Main – None
 Secondary – Small arms
Armour: Maximum – 10mm/0.394in
Powerplant: Rolls-Royce B60 Mk 5A 6-cylinder 89kW/120hp petrol engine
Performance: Speed – 64kph/40mph
 Range – 402km/250 miles

LEFT: **This HUMVEE has been fitted with an extended exhaust system, which allows the vehicle to wade through 1m/39in of water. The bonnet of the vehicle tilts forward to give access to the engine.** ABOVE: **The driver's position is on the left with the vehicle commander on the right. The large console in the middle of the vehicle has the communications equipment mounted in it. When the vehicle is fitted with a roof-mounted machine-gun, the turret gunner stands between the rear seats.**

Hummer Multi-Role Vehicle

Development of the High Mobility Multipurpose Wheeled Vehicle (HMMWV or HUMVEE) started in the 1970s. In 1983, the American armed forces signed a 1.2 billion-dollar production contract with the AM General Corporation under which AM General would produce 55,000 of these new vehicles for them between 1984 and 1989. Better known to the troops who use the vehicle as the "Hummer", it was given the official designation of M998. A further option was exercised by the US military for an additional 15,000 vehicles, while in 1989 another order was placed for 33,000 vehicles. More orders have since been placed for uparmoured variants, as a result of combat experience, which will bring the total production run to 125,000 vehicles so far.

The basic HMMWV has the engine in the front of the vehicle, the crew compartment in the middle and a load-carrying area in the rear. The vehicle is permanently in the 4x4 configuration and the bonnet tilts forward to allow easy access to the air-cooled 6.2-litre diesel engine. The crew compartment has a box frame steel roll-cage fitted to it, while the rest of the body is made from aluminium that is riveted and glued into position. This makes the replacement of damaged panels easier and quicker than if it were an all-welded construction. The four-man crew sit either side of the power transfer, two in the front and two in the rear of the compartment. There is a hatch in the roof above the crew compartment when the vehicle is fitted with a machine-gun or other weapon

system. The HMMWV can be fitted with a wide selection of armament ranging from a basic 7.62mm/0.3in machine-gun to a 30mm/1.18in cannon, Hellfire ATGMs or Starstreak AAGMs.

The HMMWV has been built in 18 different variations and development has continued with many improvements based on the results of combat reports. The engine has also been improved several times since coming into service. The original engine developed 97kW/130hp but this has now increased to 142kW/190hp. The latest version of the vehicle, designated the M1114, has increased armour and most HMMWVs will be brought up to this standard.

LEFT: **The front of the HUMVEE, with the recessed lights and a cow-catcher on the front of the vehicle. Increased cooling is supplied to the engine from the grill in the bonnet. The vehicle now carries the official American designation of M998.**

HMMWV M1114

Country: USA
Entered service: 1985
Crew: 1 plus 3 infantry
Weight: 5,489kg/5.4 tons
Dimensions: Length – 4.99m/16ft 4in
  Height – 1.9m/6ft 3in
  Width – 2.3m/7ft 7in
Armament: Main – 1 x 7.62mm/0.3in
  GP machine-gun (basic variant)
  Secondary – Small arms
Armour: Classified
Powerplant: General Motors 6.5-litre 8-cylinder 142kW/190hp diesel engine
Performance: Speed – 125kph/78mph
  Range – 443km/275 miles

LEFT: **A trio of long wheelbase reconnaissance Land Rover Defenders. The vehicles have been fitted with several heavy machine-guns, and smoke dischargers have been fixed to the top of the front bumper of the vehicle. The vehicles are all covered in extra equipment.** ABOVE: **The inside of "Dinky", the short wheelbase Land Rover Defender developed for the British Army. The vehicle is fitted with a roll-bar to protect the crew if the vehicle turns over. In the rear of the vehicle is a pintle mount for a machine-gun or MILAN AT missile system.**

Land Rover Defender Multi-Role Vehicles

The Land Rover has been in service with the British Army for over 45 years and has gone through many changes and improvements in that time. The latest series in service is the Defender which is produced in three chassis variations: 2.29m/90in, 2.79m/110in and 3.3m/130in. This is the distance between the wheel centres of the vehicle, known as the wheelbase. The Land Rover 90 and 110 are the core vehicles with the 130 being a special conversion vehicle, for example in the ambulance role. Development of the Defender started in 1983 when the then current range of Land Rover vehicles was beginning to show its age and in need of updating with modern technology. At first an order was placed for 950 of all types, followed by an order for 500 of the 90 version and 1,200 of the 110 version.

The Land Rover Defender uses the chassis and coil-spring suspension of the Range Rover and so is a stronger and more comfortable vehicle than the previous series of vehicles. In appearance, it is similar to other earlier models except that there are bulges over the wheel arches and there is a revised radiator grill. The windscreen is a one-piece unit and the vehicle is fitted with permanent four-wheel drive. The Defender is normally fitted with a diesel engine but an 8-cylinder petrol engine is also available. The roof is constructed from roll-bars and the gun-mounting. The weapons fit of the vehicle is very varied, but the basic configuration is three 7.62mm/0.3in GPMGs, one fitted in the front for use by the vehicle commander and two on a twin mount in the roof of the rear area. Other weapons available are a 30mm/1.18in cannon, TOW missiles, LAW 80 ATM or Browning 12.7mm/0.5in heavy machine-guns.

The Defender is available as a Special Operations Vehicle (SOV) and has been developed for the British SAS forces and the US Rangers. These vehicles are fitted with the 300Tdi direct injection intercooled diesel engine. The SOV is fully air-portable by heavy-lift aircraft such as the C-130 or can be under-slung from helicopters such as the Puma and Chinook.

ABOVE: **The famous SAS "Pink Panther"; this is a long wheelbase Land Rover. The vehicle has been fitted with several machine-guns and has smoke dischargers fixed to the top of the bodywork on the rear of the vehicle.**

Land Rover Defender 110 SOV

Country: UK
Entered service: 1990
Crew: 1 plus up to 5 infantry
Weight: 3,050kg/3 tons
Dimensions: Length – 4.67m/15ft 4in
   Height – 2.04m/6ft 8in
   Width – 1.79m/5ft 10in
Armament: Main – 3 x 7.62mm/0.3in GPMGs
   Secondary – Small arms
Armour: None
Powerplant: Rover 300Tdi 8-cylinder 100kW/134hp diesel engine
Performance: Speed – 90kph/56mph
   Range – 450km/280 miles

LAV-25 Light Armoured Vehicles

In September 1981 the Diesel Division of General Motors Defence, who also own MOWAG of Switzerland, was awarded a 3.1 million-dollar contract to build four 8x8 Piranha vehicles for a selection competition to provide a new Light Armoured Vehicle (LAV) for the US Marine Corps and the US Army. The first two vehicles were delivered in October 1981. One was fitted with an Arrowpointe two-man turret armed with a 25mm/0.98in chain gun, while the other vehicle had the same turret armed with a 90mm/3.54in Cockerill Mk III gun. Both turrets had an M240 coaxial machine-gun and eight smoke dischargers fitted as standard. In September 1982, the Diesel Division won the LAV competition and while the originally planned contract for 969 vehicles was not signed, annual orders were placed for the vehicle. The US Army pulled out of the programme in 1984 but 758 vehicles had been built for the US Marine Corps by 1985. The first production LAV-25 vehicles, similar to the 8x8 Piranha, were delivered in 1983 and the last one in 1987.

The all-welded steel hull of the LAV-25 protects the crew from small-arms fire and shell splinters. The driver sits in the front of the vehicle on the left-hand side, next to the engine which is on the right with the air-inlet and outlet louvers on the hull top. The exhaust outlet is mounted on the right-hand side of the vehicle. In the middle of the vehicle is the two-man turret and the infantry compartment is in the rear of the vehicle. Access to the rear compartment is by two doors that open outwards, each of which has a vision port fitted. The troop compartment is connected to a centralized NBC system, but the six men that sit in this area, three down each side facing

ABOVE: A LAV-25 armoured ambulance. This is a development of the logistics vehicle, which can be seen behind the ambulance. The ambulance is fitted with two clusters of four smoke dischargers on the rear roof of the vehicle.

inwards, are very cramped. Above the compartment are two hatches that can give access to the outside and there is also an escape hatch in the body of the vehicle. The Delco two-man turret has the commander on the right and the gunner on the left and is fitted with an M242 25mm/0.98in McDonnell Douglas Helicopter Company chain gun as the main armament. The vehicle commander can also have a 7.62mm/0.3in M240 machine-gun fitted on a pintle mount in front of the turret hatch, and on each side of the turret front are four smoke dischargers. The turret is fitted with laser range-finding and a full range of night-fighting optics. The driver also has night-driving optics fitted. When the vehicle is travelling cross-country full eight-wheel drive can be engaged, but in less demanding situations the vehicle is driven in the more economic mode which supplies power only to the rear four wheels. The steering controls the front four wheels, and the vehicle is fully amphibious. The LAV-25 is fitted with two propellers that propel the vehicle when in the water and steering is achieved using four rudders. A trim vane is fitted to the front of the vehicle and it takes just three minutes to make the LAV ready for the water.

The LAV has been built in a number of variants. The LAV Logistics Vehicle has a crew of two, a higher roof and a crane is fitted to the vehicle. The LAV Mortar Carrier has a crew of five, with the mortar fitted in the middle of the vehicle on a turntable where the turret would normally be. A large double-folding hatch covers the space left by the turret opening. The LAV-ARV has a crew of five and has a boom with a 265-degree traverse. An "A"-frame support is fitted to be used when lifting heavy loads. The LAV Anti-Tank Vehicle mounts a twin TOW launcher that can traverse through 360 degrees. Fourteen reload missiles are carried in the vehicle. The last version to enter service was the LAV Air Defence System, which is fitted with the General Electric Blazer system. This has two four-round Stinger missile pods on the side of a turret that is also fitted with the GAU-12/U 25mm/0.98in Gatling gun.

These vehicles have proved to very reliable in service, but suffer from lack of internal personal equipment storage space for the crew.

ABOVE: This LAV-25 is fitted with an Emerson twin TOW AT missile launcher. Two missiles are carried in the launcher, with a further 14 reloads carried inside the vehicle. This vehicle has a crew of three. The twin rear doors can be clearly seen in this picture.

ABOVE: A column of LAV-25 vehicles of the US Marine Corps in the Middle East. The large exhaust system on the side of the vehicle can be clearly seen. The front four wheels are used to steer the vehicle. These vehicles are not in a combat zone as they have no personal equipment stored on the outside.

ABOVE: This shows how cramped the command vehicle is when all the communication equipment is fitted. The vehicle has a crew of two but can carry five HQ staff in the rear.

LEFT: This mobile AA system was developed for the US Air Force. The one-man turret was armed with a 30mm/1.18in Gatling gun and four Stinger missiles. The project was dropped when the US Army took over airfield defence.

LAV-25 Light Armoured Vehicle

Country: Canada
Entered service: 1982
Crew: 3 plus 6 infantry
Weight: 12,792kg/12.6 tons
Dimensions: Length – 6.39m/21ft
Height – 2.69m/8ft 8in
Width – 2.5m/8ft 2in
Armament: Main – M242 25mm/0.98in chain gun, and coaxial M240 7.62mm/0.3in machine-gun
Secondary – Pintle mounted M240 7.62mm/0.3in machine-gun
Armour: Maximum – 10mm/0.394in (estimated)
Powerplant: Detroit 6V-53T 6-cylinder 205kW/275hp diesel engine
Performance: Speed – Road 100kph/62mph; Water 10kph/6mph
Range – 668km/415 miles

LVTP-7 Armoured Amphibious Assault Vehicle

ABOVE: **An LVTP-7 on a training exercise. The driver can be seen with his head just out of his cupola. Behind him is an instructor squatting next to the vehicle commander's cupola. The vehicle commander and gunner are beside the gun turret.**

The standard LVT of the US Marine Corps post World War II was the LVTP-5A1. This was an unsatisfactory vehicle as it had a very limited land and water range, was unreliable, and difficult to maintain. In 1964, the Marine Corps issued a requirement for a new LVTP and a development contract was awarded to the FMC Corporation. Development started in 1966 and the final 15 vehicles commissioned were delivered in 1967. Trials were completed in 1969 and in June 1970 a contract was signed with FMC to supply 942 LVTP-7 (Landing Vehicle Tracked Personnel Model 7). The first vehicles were delivered to the Marine Corps in August 1971 with the first unit being equipped in March 1972 and the final deliveries to the Marines being made in 1974.

The all-welded aluminium hull gives the crew protection from small-arms fire and shell splinters. The engine is in the front of the vehicle and is placed on the centreline. The driver's position is alongside the engine on the right-hand side and is fitted with all-round vision blocks. Behind the driver on the left-hand side is the vehicle commander's position which is also fitted with all-round vision blocks while a periscope in the front of the commander's cupola allows him to see over the driver's position. The turret is on the right-hand side of the vehicle beside the engine. The gunner has all-round vision from nine vision blocks fitted into the cupola and the turret is armed with a 12.7mm/0.5in M85 machine-gun with two rates of fire: either 1,050 or 480 rounds per minute. The vehicle carries 1,000 rounds of ammunition for this weapon. The turret traverse mechanism is electro-hydraulic and has a full 360-degree traverse in under five seconds.

The LVTP has no NBC system, but is fitted with infrared night-driving lights. The suspension consists of six dual rubber-shod road wheels on each side and the track is single pin type, fitted with replaceable rubber pads. The main troop compartment is situated behind the turret and extends to the rear of the vehicle providing accommodation for 25 men. There

LEFT: **This LVTP-7 is moving at speed in deep snow. The boat-shaped hull can be clearly seen along with the long track length, which gives the vehicle a low ground pressure.**

are three bench seats in the rear: one down each side and one in the middle, each seating eight men, while the other seating position is available behind the vehicle commander's position. The centre bench seat can be removed and stored on the left-hand side of the compartment and the other two bench seats can be folded up so the vehicle can be used for moving supplies or wounded.

The LVTP is fully amphibious and requires no preparation time when entering the water. It is propelled by two water jets mounted on the rear of the vehicle in the sponsons, each jet having a hinged water deflector fitted at the rear which acts as a protective cover when not in use. The tracks of the vehicle can also be used to provide additional propulsion when the vehicle is in the water. The Marines enter and leave the vehicle by a power-operated ramp. In the left-hand side of the ramp there is a small access door, and above the troop compartment two very large spring-balanced hatches are installed. These are used for loading the vehicle when it is waterborne while taking on supplies alongside a ship.

In March 1977, FMC was awarded a contract for the conversion of 14 LVTPs to a new configuration known as the LVTP-7A1. This upgrade included an improved engine, better night-driving equipment and fighting optics, improved radios, an improved fire-suppression system, better troop compartment ventilation, improved weapon stations and an ability to generate smoke. Subsequently, the Marine Corps decided to upgrade all of their LVTP-7 vehicles to the new

standard in 1982, and this was completed by 1986. These vehicles have also been fitted with a new turret that has an additional 40mm/1.58in grenade launcher installed along with the 12.7mm/0.3in machine-gun. RAFAEL appliqué armour has also been fitted to a large number of the new LVTP-7A1 vehicles since 1987. These vehicles are expected to remain in service for several more years as a result of this service life extension programme. They are currently operational in Iraq.

ABOVE: A column of LVTP-7 vehicles moving through the surf on the soft sand of a beach. The three-man crew are in their crew positions in the vehicle. The lights on the front of the vehicle are recessed into the hull to help protect them. LEFT: The three crew cupolas can be clearly seen. The driver's position is in the front on the left with the commander's behind. On the right of the vehicle is the gunner's turret.

LVTP-7A1 Armoured Amphibious Assault Vehicle

Country: USA
Entered service: 1977
Crew: 3 plus 25 infantry
Weight: 23,936kg/23.6 tons
Dimensions: Length – 7.94m/26ft 1in
 Height – 3.26m/10ft 8in
 Width – 3.27m/10ft 9in
Armament: Main – 12.7mm/0.5in M2 HB machine-gun, and 40mm/1.58in grenade launcher
 Secondary – Small arms
Armour: Maximum – 45mm/1.77in
Powerplant: Cummins VT400 8-cylinder 298kW/400hp turbocharged diesel engine
Performance: Speed – Road 72kph/45mph;
 Water 13kph/8mph
 Range – 482km/300 miles

RIGHT: The LVTP-7 has been in service for over 30 years. A new vehicle is required for the US Marines, and the AAAV is being developed by General Dynamics to fill this role. The first of the development vehicles were due out in 2004, but this has now been deferred for financial reasons.

M42 Duster Self-Propelled Anti-Aircraft Gun

In August 1951, the US Army authorized the development of a replacement vehicle for the M19A1 SPAAG and initially an interim design called the T-141 was developed. The final design was to be the T-141A1, and a fire control vehicle, the T-53, was also going to be developed but both were cancelled in 1952. However, the T-141 put into production and standardized as the M42. The first vehicle was produced in April 1952, with the last vehicle being handed over to the Army in December 1953. Total production was 3,700 vehicles.

The M42 used many of the same automotive components as the M41 light tank. The driver and radio operator/commander sat side by side in the front of the vehicle with the driver on the left. Behind them was the gun turret which was armed with twin 40mm/1.58in M2A1 cannon and had a crew of four, two gunners and two loaders. The turret had a power traverse and could complete a full 360-degree traverse in nine seconds. The guns could be fired in single shot or fully automatic modes and could discharge 120 rounds per minute when in the latter. When engaging ground targets the vehicle had a maximum range of 3,000m/9,842ft and a maximum ceiling of 3,962m/13,000ft. The Duster could carry 480 rounds of 40mm/1.58in ammunition in bins around the inside of the turret, which had a 7.62mm/0.3in machine-gun mount on the right-hand side. The engine and transmission was

in the rear of the vehicle and there were only had three gears – two forward and one reverse. The suspension was a torsion-bar type supporting five road wheels per side. The M42 had no NBC system and was not capable of any deep fording, but was fitted with infrared night-driving lights.

The Duster had a new engine fitted in 1956 which gave the vehicle an increased range and was redesignated the M42A1. The turrets of both vehicles could be manually operated and could track aircraft at up to 966kph/600mph, but they could only be used effectively during daylight.

TOP: The chassis of the Walker Bulldog M41 light tank was used for the development of this vehicle. The gun turret was very open and so gave the gun crew no protection. ABOVE: A column of American armoured vehicles being led by two M42 Dusters in the early 1950s. The driver and co-driver are in their positions in the front of the M42, while the rest of the gun crew are riding on the open gun turret.

LEFT: Two American M42 Dusters with a crewman standing between them. The small size of the vehicle can be seen by the size of the crewman. Some of the vehicles were improved upon by fitting anti-grenade screens to the top of the turret.

M42 Duster SPAAG	
Country: USA	
Entered service: 1952	
Crew: 6	
Weight: 22,452kg/22.1 tons	
Dimensions: Length – 6.36m/19ft 5in	
Height – 2.85m/9ft 4in	
Width – 3.22m/10ft 7in	
Armament: Main – 2 x 40mm/1.58in M2A1 cannon	
Secondary – 7.62mm/0.3in machine-gun	
Armour: Maximum – 25mm/0.98in	
Powerplant: Continental or Lycoming 6-cylinder 373kW/500hp petrol engine	
Performance: Speed – 72kph/45mph	
Range – 160km/100 miles	

ABOVE: This M44 has been fitted with a canvas roof which gives the crew some protection from the weather. The exhaust system is located on the right-hand side of the vehicle. The engine is mounted in the front of the vehicle, hence all the engine intake grills on the glacis.

M44 155mm Self-Propelled Gun

Development of this vehicle started in 1947 and two prototypes, given the designation T99, were built. The vehicle was to utilize as many automotive parts from the M41 light tank as possible to make maintenance and sourcing spare parts easier to manage. The vehicle was redesignated the T99E1 and a contract was issued in 1952 when production started. A number of changes were required due to problems with the pilot models, but by the time these had been finalized 250 of the production vehicles had been built. The new improved vehicle, now called the T194, was standardized in September 1953 as the M44, and all the service vehicles already produced were upgraded to the new T194 standard.

The hull of the M44 was an all-welded steel construction, with the engine and transmission in the front of the vehicle. The transmission was a General Motors Model CD-500-3 cross-drive unit which gave the vehicle two forward gears and one reverse. The suspension was a torsion-bar system and the rear idler was lowered to form a sixth road wheel. The crew compartment was mounted high up on the vehicle and included the vehicle driver who was positioned at the front on the right-hand side. The crew compartment was open-topped but could have a canvas cover fitted to protect the crew from the weather. The gun was an M45 howitzer which was installed on an M80 mount, while a close-defence 12.7mm/0.3in machine-gun was

fitted to the left-hand side of the vehicle behind the driver. At the rear of the vehicle a recoil spade was fitted and when this was lowered into position a platform could be folded down from the rear of the vehicle. This allowed the twin rear doors, which serve as ammunition storage, to open. The exhaust system was fitted to the top of the front track guards and was the source of a major problem as engine fumes travelled back into the crew compartment, gassing the crew.

The M44 later received an improved engine giving greater range and fuel economy and this new vehicle was standardized in 1956 as the M44A1. The British Army also used the M44.

LEFT: The driver's position was located in the turret of the vehicle on the left-hand side. In front of his position was a small windscreen, while behind the driver was the close-support machine-gun. A model with overhead armour was built and trialled, but was not adopted for service by any country.

M44 155mm SPG

Country:	USA
Entered service:	1953
Crew:	5
Weight:	28,346kg/27.9 tons
Dimensions:	Length – 6.16m/20ft 3in
	Height – 3.11m/10ft 3in
	Width – 3.24m/10ft 8in
Armament:	Main – 155mm/6.1in M45 howitzer
	Secondary – 12.7mm/0.5in machine-gun
Armour:	Maximum – 12.7mm/0.5in
Powerplant:	Continental AOS-895-3 6-cylinder 373kW/500hp petrol engine
Performance:	Speed – 56kph/35mph
	Range – 122km/76 miles

LEFT: **The crew compartment of the M52 is a covered armoured turret and gives the gun crew full protection from the weather and small-arms fire. The driver of the vehicle sits at the front of the turret. In this picture, he has his seat in the raised position, with the vehicle commander at the rear on the opposite side of the turret.** ABOVE: **The engine is positioned in the front of the vehicle with the exhaust systems on the front track guards. The front of the glacis is covered in air intake grills.**

M52 105mm Self-Propelled Gun

In February 1948, development was started on a replacement 105mm SPG for the M7 which was showing its age. Two prototypes, known as the T98E1, were built at the Detroit Tank Arsenal in 1950. They were to be constructed using as many parts from the M41 light tank as possible and the engine, transmission, tracks and suspension were all used. The T98E1 was standardized in 1953 as the M52 and entered service in 1954 with a total production run of 684 vehicles. In 1956 a new vehicle with an improved engine and fuel injection system was standardized as the M52A1.

The hull of the M52 was an all-welded steel construction, with the engine and transmission mounted at the front of the vehicle. The transmission was a General Motors Model CD-500-3 cross-drive unit which gave the vehicle two forward gears and one reverse. The suspension was a torsion-bar system and the rear idler was lowered to form a sixth road wheel. The large turret was mounted on the top of the hull towards the rear of the vehicle. All the crew were seated in the turret with the driver on the front left-hand side with a cupola above and a door in the side of the turret for access to the driving position. The gun layer was on the right-hand side of the turret at the front with the commander behind. The commander's cupola could be fitted with

a 12.7mm/0.3in machine-gun for close defence. On the rear, left-hand side of the turret a revolving drum was fitted which held 21 rounds of ready-to-use ammunition and a total of 102 rounds were carried in the vehicle. The turret had a 60-degree traverse to the left and right of the vehicle's centreline. No recoil spade was fitted to the rear of the vehicle, as it was not required.

The vehicle had no NBC system installed but was fitted with an over-pressurization system and infrared night-driving lights. It was the first NATO SPG to give the crew full protection on the modern nuclear battlefield.

RIGHT: **The compact size of the chassis can be seen, but the large turret takes up most of the space on the top of the vehicle. Driving the vehicle was not easy, but the crews did get used to it. Ammunition is stowed both in the turret and in the body of the vehicle.**

M52 105mm SPG	🇺🇸
Country: USA
Entered service: 1954
Crew: 5
Weight: 24,079kg/23.7 tons
Dimensions: Length – 5.8m/19ft
Height – 3.06m/10ft 1in
Width – 3.15m/10ft 4in
Armament: Main – 105mm/4.13in M49 howitzer
Secondary – 12.7mm/0.5in machine-gun
Armour: Maximum – 12.7mm/0.5in
Powerplant: Continental 6-cylinder 373kW/500hp petrol engine
Performance: Speed – 56kph/35mph
Range – 160km/100 miles

M107 175mm Self-Propelled Gun

All SPGs in service in the early 1950s were too large and heavy to be transported by air, but in 1956 the Pacific Car and Foundry Company was awarded a contract to build six prototype air-transportable SPG vehicles, two armed with the new 175mm/6.89in gun, three with the 203mm/8in howitzer and one with the 155mm/6.1in gun. Trials began in late 1958 but the engine was changed in 1959 when the American armed forces made a policy decision that all future vehicles would be fitted with diesel engines rather than petrol. Trials were completed in early 1961. The T235E1 (175mm) was standardized as the M107 and the T236E1 (203mm) as the M110, while the other vehicle was dropped. Production started in 1962 and was completed in 1980 by which time 524 vehicles had been built. After a short period of time in service, a large number of faults were discovered and these were rectified.

The M107 hull is an all-welded construction made from cast armour and high-tensile alloy steel. The driver is positioned in the front of the vehicle on the left-hand side with the engine on the right, while the main gun mount is at the rear of the vehicle. The driver is the only member of the crew to sit inside the vehicle and therefore be protected by armour. The torsion-bar suspension has five twin rubber tyre wheels per side with the drive sprocket at the front and the fifth road wheel acting as an idler. There is a shock absorber fitted to each road wheel and this helps transfer the recoil shock directly into the ground. In

ABOVE: **The M107 returned to the idea that artillery was not in the front line, so crew protection was not needed. The large full-width recoil spade can be seen in the raised position on the rear of this vehicle.**

LEFT: **The extremely long gun barrel stands out well in this picture. The driver and two of the crew can be seen in their travelling positions on the gun. The other two members of the gun crew were on the other side of the gun mount.**

addition there is a hydraulically operated recoil spade at the rear of the vehicle.

The M107 has a crew of 13; 4 of them – including the vehicle commander – travel on the vehicle with the driver inside, the other 8 are transported in an M548 ammunition vehicle. The M107 has internal storage space for only two ready-to-use 175mm/6.89in rounds

and the barrel of the 175mm/6.89in gun can be interchanged with the M110 203mm/8in barrel. This operation takes two hours and can be undertaken in the field.

LEFT: **Two M107 guns on exercise. The gun in the rear has just fired a round, while the vehicle in the foreground is on the move with the five-man crew at their travelling stations. The barrel of the gun has been covered in camouflage netting.**

M107 175mm SPG

Country: USA
Entered service: 1963
Crew: 4 plus 9 gunners
Weight: 28,143kg/27.7 tons
Dimensions: Length – 11.26m/36ft 11in
  Height – 3.67m/12ft
  Width – 3.15m/10ft 4in
Armament: Main – 175mm/6.89in M113 gun
  Secondary – Small arms
Armour: Classified
Powerplant: Detroit Diesel Motors 8V-71T
  8-cylinder 302kW/405hp diesel engine
Performance: Speed – 55kph/34mph
  Range – 725km/450 miles

M108 105mm Self-Propelled Gun

Take a 22,353kg/22-ton aluminium armoured vehicle and mount a relatively small 105mm/4.13in howitzer on it, and the result would appear to be a massively under-gunned self-propelled howitzer. A clean and simple design, the M108 represented a more sophisticated approach than the M52 but, not surprisingly, was only built in small numbers.

Development started in 1953 when it was decided to develop a 110mm/4.33in-armed SPG which was designated the T195. The first mock-up vehicle was built in 1954. Permission was subsequently given for prototype vehicles to be built and orders were placed for engines and transmissions. However, later that year it was decided to freeze the project, as there were doubts over the 110mm/4.33in gun. The engines and other parts were passed over to the T196/M109 project. It was

ABOVE: **The large size of the vehicle can be seen against the small size of the gun barrel. The 12.7mm/0.5in machine-gun can be seen on the roof of the turret.** BELOW LEFT: **This was the first turreted SPG to have the driver placed in the hull of the vehicle. The box on the rear of the turret is the air filtration system for the NBC system. These vehicles were produced for less than a year.** BELOW: **The M108 chassis was used for the American trials of the Roland Low-Altitude SAM system. It was converted in 1977 and the first firing trials were carried out in November 1977. The vehicle has a crew of four. From shut-down to fully operational takes under four minutes.**

finally decided to drop the 110mm/4.33in gun in favour of the 105mm/4.13in, as there was a plentiful supply of ammunition for this weapon. The first prototype was finally completed in 1958 but the suspension failed in its first firing trials. When the

American military ordered in 1959 that all vehicles were to have diesel engines fitted as standard from now on, the T195 had its petrol engine replaced by a diesel unit and was given the new designation T195E1. Trials started again, with suspension failures being repeated, but this time they were corrected, and in 1961 the T195E1 was finally standardized as the M108. Production started in October 1962 after a number of changes to the design including the addition of an idler wheel at the rear of the vehicle, the removal of the muzzle brake and changes to the turret shape. The very short production run finished in September 1963 with only a few vehicles completed, production being halted because the US military decided to concentrate on the T196/M109 155mm/6.1in SPG, a unit that is still in service today.

The hull and turret of the M108 is an all-welded aluminium construction. The transmission is located in the front of the vehicle with the driver behind this on the left-hand side and the engine on the right. The torsion-bar suspension system of the M108 is the same as that of the M113 with seven dual rubber-shod road wheels per side. The drive sprocket is at the front of the vehicle and an idler is at the rear. The top of the tracks can be covered with a rubber skirt but the crews rarely fit this.

At the rear of the vehicle is the manually operated turret which can rotate through 360 degrees and houses the rest of the crew and the gun. The gun-layer is on the left-hand side of this with the commander on the right, while the two ammunition handlers are positioned in the rear. In the roof of the turret above the commander is a cupola, and this can be traversed through 360 degrees and can be armed with a 12.7mm/0.5in local defence machine-gun. The gun-layer also has a hatch in the roof of the turret, and two side hatches which open towards the rear of the vehicle are also fitted. In the rear of the turret are two more hatches in the rotating top section, while in the lower fixed rear of the hull a large door is installed which is used for supplying ammunition to the gun. The M108 carries 87 rounds of ammunition. The vehicle is capable of firing three rounds per minute but this is only for a short period of time, the normal fire rate being one round per minute.

The M108 can be fitted with an NBC system but this is not fitted as standard, though infrared night-driving lights are. The vehicle can wade to a depth of 1.8m/5ft 11in but can also be fitted with nine flotation bags, one bag on the front and four down each side, which are inflated from the vehicle. However, these are not carried on the vehicle as standard. Propulsion in the water is supplied by the vehicle's tracks. Although an unmitigated failure in its original role and long out of service with the US Army, the Belgian Army has converted several of its M108 SPGs into command vehicles.

ABOVE LEFT: Only three other countries bought the M108: Belgium, Brazil and Spain. Belgium turned out to be the largest overseas customer. ABOVE: The very short length of the barrel can be clearly seen. The drive sprocket is at the front of the vehicle, which makes for a very compact drive train. The engine and drive train proved to be very reliable and were used in several vehicles. LEFT: The first vehicles had the headlight cluster mounted on the glacis plate, but on later production vehicles the headlights were moved to the front of the track guards.

M108 105mm SPG	
Country: USA	
Entered service: 1962	
Crew: 5	
Weight: 22,454kg/22.1 tons	
Dimensions: Length – 6.11m/20ft 9in	
Height – 3.15m/10ft 4in	
Width – 3.3m/10ft 10in	
Armament: Main – 105mm/4.13in M103 howitzer	
Secondary – 12.7mm/0.5in M2 machine-gun	
Armour: Classified	
Powerplant: Detroit Diesel Motors 8V-71T 8-cylinder 302kW/405hp diesel engine	
Performance: Speed – 55kph/34mph Range – 350km/220 miles	

LEFT: **The M109 had basically the same chassis and running gear as the M108. A few problems were experienced with the running gear but these have been fixed. It remains in service with a large number of countries to the present day.**
BELOW: **This vehicle is an improved M109A1. The new vehicle has an extended barrel, which now has a long overhang over the front of the vehicle. The travel lock for the gun barrel has been moved to the front edge of the glacis.**

M109 155mm Self-Propelled Gun

The first prototype M109, then designated the T196, was finally completed in 1959 but during its first firing trials the suspension failed. When in the same year the American military ordered that all future new vehicles were to have diesel engines fitted as standard, the petrol engine was replaced by a diesel and the vehicle was given the new designation T196E1. Trials started again and again there were suspension failures, as with the M108 which had the same chassis. These problems were corrected and the first vehicles were completed in October 1962 as Limited Production Vehicles. Finally, in 1963 the T196E1 was standardized as the M109. A number of changes were made to the design including the addition of an idler wheel at the rear of the vehicle and changes to the turret shape before the M109 entered service with the American Army in June 1963. It will remain in service until at least 2010, but the vehicle has gone through many changes and upgrades during its service life to keep it up-to-date.

The hull and turret of the M109 is an all-welded aluminium construction. The transmission is in the front of the vehicle with the driver located behind this on the left-hand side. The engine is next to the driver on the right, and the turret, which houses the rest of the crew and gun, is behind. The gun-layer is positioned on the left-hand side of the turret with the commander on the right. A cupola for the commander, which can be traversed through 360 degrees and can be armed with a 12.7mm/0.5in local defence machine-gun, is installed in the roof of the turret. The gun-layer also has a hatch in the roof of the turret, and two side hatches, which open towards the rear

of the vehicle, are also fitted. In the rear of the turret are two more hatches in the rotating top section, and there is a large door in the rear of the hull which is used for supplying ammunition to the gun. Mounted on the rear of the vehicle is a large recoil spade that is manually operated from within the turret. The main armament is the M126 155mm/6.1in gun on the M127 mount. The barrel is fitted with a double-baffle muzzle brake and a fume extractor two-thirds of the way up. The turret can traverse through 360 degrees and is power operated, but can be operated manually. The normal rate of fire is one round per minute but for short periods, three rounds per minute can be fired. The latest version of the vehicle, the M109A6 Paladin, is armed with the M284 L/39 155mm/6.1in howitzer and a new fire-control system.

LEFT: **A Swiss Army M109A2. On the roof of this vehicle is a new armoured hood for the optical fire-control system. This vehicle is known as the Pzhb 74 in the Swiss Army.** ABOVE: **A British M109A2 vehicle taking part in a live-firing exercise. The optical hood is on the front left of the turret. The turret of the M109A2 is fitted with a bustle that can hold an additional 22 rounds of ammunition. The gun has been heavily covered in camouflage netting and spare ammunition is laid out on a sheet behind the gun.**

The first improvements were made to the vehicle in 1972 and it was redesignated the M109A1. These were mainly to the gun that had a much longer and more slender barrel increasing the range to 18,288m/60,000ft. Further developments came in 1978 when the M109A2 went into production, with improvements to the ammunition storage, the rammer, and hull doors. A bustle was also fixed to the rear of the turret to take a further 22 rounds of ammunition. The M109A3 upgrade was M109A1s brought up to M109A2 standard. The vehicle became the M109A4 in 1990 with the fitting of an NBC kit as standard. The M109A5 designation was the upgrading of all the older marks to A4 standard, and the gun barrel was also changed to one that could fire rocket-assisted ammunition.

The latest version of the M109 is the A6 Paladin. Development of this started in 1990 and production began in 1992 with the new vehicle entering service with the American Army in 1993. The Paladin has the same chassis and hull as the basic M109 but everything else has been changed. The turret is bigger, the

rear doors in the upper part of the turret have been removed, as the bustle is now full width, and there is also a new muzzle brake. A new gun-control system has been fitted which is linked to a GPS (Global Positioning System), allowing the automatic gun controls to point the gun at the target with no human intervention.

ABOVE: **A line-up of American M109A6 vehicles. The M109A6 is better known as the "Paladin", and is the first vehicle in the series to be given a name. The large muzzle brake has a double baffle, and behind this on the barrel of the gun is the fume extractor.**

LEFT: **This vehicle is fording a stream at some speed. The M109 can ford water obstacles to a depth of 1m/39in. The vehicle commander can be seen standing in his cupola giving directions to the driver, who has very poor vision from his position.**

M109A6 155mm Paladin SPG

Country: USA
Entered service: 1993
Crew: 6
Weight: 28,753kg/28.3 tons
Dimensions: Length – 9.12m/29ft 11in
　　Height – 3.24m/10ft 7in
　　Width – 3.15m/10ft 4in
Armament: Main – 155mm/6.1in M284 L/39 howitzer
　　Secondary – 12.7mm/0.5in M2 machine-gun
Armour: classified
Powerplant: Detroit Diesel Motors 8V-71T 8-cylinder 302kW/405hp diesel engine
Performance: Speed – 56kph/35mph
　　Range – 405km/252 miles

LEFT: The gun crew of the M110 are very exposed when operating the gun, as can be seen with this vehicle. The recoil spade on this SPG is in the down position. BELOW: A line-up of three batteries of M110 vehicles. The gun has no muzzle brake or fume extractor. The vehicle can carry 5 of the 13-man crew; the rest travel in an M548 ammunition vehicle.

M110 203mm Self-Propelled Howitzer

In 1956 the Pacific Car and Foundry Company (PCF) was given a contract to build six prototype SPG vehicles for the US Army, two armed with the new 175mm/6.89in gun (T235), three with the 203mm/8in howitzer (T236) and one with the 155mm/6.1in gun (T245). The main design priority for these vehicles was that they all had to be air-portable to fill a requirement not met by the then available American SPGs, which were either too large or too heavy. The three prototype designs all used the same M17 lightweight gun mount and were all to have the ability for their gun barrels to be interchangeable. The T245 development was halted at the prototype stage as it was felt to be unnecessary. The T235 went on to become the M107, while the T236 became the M110. The M108, M109 and M110 all utilized the same transmission and engine.

Testing of the M110 prototype began in late 1958 but in 1959 the American military made a policy decision that all future vehicles would be fitted with diesel engines rather than petrol. The T236 with a diesel engine fitted was renamed the T236E1. Trials were completed in 1961 and the T236E1 was standardized as the M110. In June 1961, PCF was awarded a production contract for the new vehicle and the first production models were finished in 1962, entering service with the US Army in 1963. The original contract was for 750 vehicles, all built by PCF, which were completed by late 1969. Once the vehicle had entered service, it was found that improvements to the engine-cooling, electrical and hydraulic systems, the loader/rammer and the recoil spade were necessary. In March 1976, an improved vehicle incorporating these modifications was standardized as the M110A1. These vehicles included

RIGHT: The eight circular holes in the right-hand side of the vehicle are the exhaust outlets. This caused a lot of discomfort for the crew of the vehicle when it was stationary. The short, stubby gun barrel can be clearly seen on this SPG.

both M110s and some M107s, as a number of M107 vehicles were no longer required. A new longer gun barrel, the M201, was fitted to the vehicle so it could fire tactical nuclear shells as the M107 had done and which the M110A1 would eventually replace. In 1980, the last version of the M110 entered service, as the M110A2. This had an improved barrel and was fitted with a muzzle brake. Improvements were also made to the electrical and recoil systems. With this last upgrade the gun crew at long last had some protection from small-arms fire, shell splinters and the weather, as a Kevlar and aluminium shelter was built over the open gun area.

The M110 hull is an all-welded construction made from cast armour and high tensile alloy steel. The driver is located in the front of the vehicle on the left-hand side with the engine on the right, while the main gun mount is at the rear. The driver is the only member of the crew to sit inside the vehicle and therefore be protected by armour. The torsion-bar suspension has five twin rubber-tyred wheels per side with the drive sprocket at the front and the fifth road wheel acting as an idler. There is a shock absorber fitted to each road wheel and this helps transfer the recoil shock directly into the ground. There is also a hydraulically operated recoil spade at the rear. On the right-hand side of the vehicle are a series of holes in the sponson that act as exhaust outlets.

The vehicle commander and three members of the gun crew sit in the open, two either side, exposed to small-arms fire, shell splinters and above all the weather. The other eight crewmen are transported in an M548 ammunition vehicle along with all the personal kit of the gun crew. The main armament is fitted with a hydro-pneumatic recoil system and an automatic loader and rammer is located at the rear of the vehicle on the left-hand side. The M110 only has storage for two ready-to-use rounds, the remaining being carried in the ammunition vehicle. The normal rate of fire is one round every two minutes, but for short periods, two rounds per minute can be fired. The M110A2 is the only variation still in service and this is with a small number of countries.

TOP: An American M110 with the recoil spade in the raised position. One improvement the Americans made to this vehicle was the construction of a canvas tent around the exposed gun position on the rear of the vehicle. ABOVE: The M110 has five road wheels on each side and the drive sprocket is at the front. No return roller is fitted to the chassis. BELOW LEFT: These vehicles are the improved M110A1. They have much longer barrels but still no muzzle brake or fume extractor fitted; the M110A2 would have a large double-baffle muzzle brake. These M110A1 SPGs are at maximum elevation and the hoop frame of the canvas screen can be seen.

M110A2 203mm SPG

Country: USA
Entered service: 1980
Crew: 5 plus 8 gunners
Weight: 28,346kg/27.9 tons
Dimensions: Length – 7.5m/24ft 7in
Height – 3.15m/10ft 4in
Width – 3.15m/10ft 4in
Armament: Main – 203mm/8in M12A2 howitzer
Secondary – Small arms
Armour: Classified
Powerplant: Detroit Diesel Motors 8V-71T
8-cylinder 373kW/500hp diesel engine
Performance: Speed – 55kph/34mph
Range – 523km/325 miles

LEFT: **An American M113 fitted with a TOW AT missile launcher. The vehicle commander's hatch is open, but the position is empty. This APC has been fitted with rubber track guards.**
ABOVE: **A basic American M113 APC. The driver is in his position in the front of the vehicle on the left-hand side. The vehicle commander's position has been fitted with a 12.7mm/0.5in machine-gun.**

M113 Armoured Personnel Carrier

In January 1956 the Food Manufacturing Corporation (FMC) were awarded a contract to start development on the T113 and the T117 APCs. These new vehicles had to be fully air-portable, amphibious, lightweight and have a good cross-country performance. They had to be adaptable and be able to take modification kits with a long projected service life. Testing started and the steel-bodied T117 was quickly dropped in favour of the aluminium-constructed T113. The T113E1 was developed with a petrol engine and four prototypes were built, but the diesel-engined T113E2 was also developed following the US Army's 1959 requirement for diesel engines in all its new vehicles. Despite this, the T113E1 was standardized in 1960 as the M113 and FMC began production with an order for 900 vehicles, all with petrol engines. In 1963 the diesel-engined T113E2 was standardized as the M113A1 and entered production in 1964, replacing the basic M113.

The next version of the M113, the M113A2, entered production in 1978. This involved a number of improvements to the engine-cooling system, radiator, and suspension. All M113s and M113A1s were also to be brought up to the same standard, involving some 20,000 vehicles, and a further 2,660 new M113A2s were to be built. The whole programme had to be finished by 1989. In 1980 development started on a further improvement programme including a new engine, giving better performance, and improved cooling and suspension systems. Production of the new M113A3 began in 1987 and is still continuing today. It includes improvements such as external fuel tanks and the provision for the installation of external

ABOVE: **This Israeli M113 has been fitted with additional add-on armour. The crew of the vehicle are at action stations. The trim vane has been removed to allow the armour to be fitted.**

optional appliqué armour. Experience gained in the Gulf War of 1991 has influenced a number of these developments.

The hull of the M113 is an all-welded aluminium construction. The transmission, providing six forward and two reverse gears, is in the front of the vehicle. The driver sits behind this on the left-hand side, with the engine immediately on the right. The air inlet and outlet louvers for the engine are located on the roof of the hull. The commander's position is in the centre of the vehicle, and is provided with a cupola that can be traversed through 360 degrees and is fitted with a single

LEFT: This is an M113 armed with a TOW AT missile. The TOW is mounted on a pedestal mount, which when not in use is retracted inside the hull and covered by the large hatches on the roof of the vehicle. BELOW: An Israeli M113 in a combat area in the Middle East. The vehicle is armed with a TOW missile and two 12.5mm/50cal machine-guns. The front machine-gun is mounted over the commander's hatch. The M113 is covered in extra storage racks that have been added by the crew.

M2 12.7mm/0.5in machine-gun. In the rear of the vehicle is the troop compartment with accommodation for 11 men. These sit five down each side facing each other, with one single seat behind the vehicle commander. A large single hatch which opens to the rear of the vehicle covers the troop compartment. In the rear is the main entry and exit hatch that is a hydraulic ramp, with an integral door fitted to the left-hand side for use in the event of the ramp mechanism failing. The vehicle is fully amphibious and is ready to enter the water once the trim vane at the front of the vehicle has been raised. Propulsion in the water is provided by using its tracks.

In 2005 the M113A3 fleet had some 16 different models in service with the US Army and many others around the world. The vehicle has been modified into 40 specific variations with a further 40 unofficial variations and is the most widely produced, in-service vehicle in the Western World. The basic armament is a single 12.7mm/0.5in machine-gun, but after this, whatever is required seems to have been fitted to the vehicle. Cannon such as 20mm/0.79in and 30mm/1.18in and even up to a 90mm/3.54in-armed turret have been fitted, as well as various missile systems. The vehicle does possess one rather alarming fault which has not been eliminated despite numerous

improvements. If it loses a track or breaks a track shoe then extreme care must be taken when slowing the vehicle. Use of the foot brake or any other means of braking can cause the vehicle to pull to the side of the unbroken track and roll over.

The M113 family has been in production for a long time and some 80,000 of all types have been built. This vehicle is still a good basic reliable battlefield taxi and is well liked by its crews. In 2005, it was in service with 52 different countries and is expected to remain so for a further 10 to 15 years.

LEFT: This basic M113 is travelling across rough ground at speed. A number of countries have improved the armament of their basic M113 vehicles by adding various turrets. The largest of these is the 90mm/3.54in Cockerill Mk III turret.

M113A3 APC

Country: USA
Entered service: 1987
Crew: 2 plus 11 infantry
Weight: 12,339kg/12.1 tons
Dimensions: Length – 4.86m/15ft 11in
  Height – 2.52m/8ft 3in
  Width – 2.69m/8ft 10in
Armament: Main – 12.7mm/0.5in M2 HB
  machine-gun
  Secondary – Small arms
Armour: Maximum – 38mm/1.5in
Powerplant: Detroit Diesel model 6V53T
  6-cylinder 205kW/275hp
Performance: Speed – Road 65kph/41mph;
  Water 5.8kph/3.6mph
  Range – 497km/309 miles

LEFT: This M577 has had a wire-mesh storage basket fitted to the front of the vehicle next to the driver. Even with the increased height of the vehicle, the M577 retains its amphibious capability, hence this vehicle has its trim vane fitted to the front. ABOVE: An American M577 command vehicle, with an M60 MBT behind it. The driver has his hatch open and the vehicle commander is standing in his hatch in the roof of the vehicle.

M577 Command Vehicle

Once the basic M113 had entered production, FMC started development of the command post variant. Production commenced in 1962 and the first M577, the first true command post vehicle developed for the US Army, entered service in 1963. The M577 has gone through the same upgrades as the M113 APC with numerous improvements to the cooling and suspension systems, the driving controls and the engine. The M577A3 has also had the auxiliary petrol APU replaced with a 5kW/6.7hp diesel-powered unit. The first upgrade in 1964 produced the M577A1. In 2005, the vehicle in service was the M577A3 and this is expected to remain operational for 10 to 15 years. The US Army originally bought 944 M577 vehicles and they have purchased a further 2,693 M577A1 since 1964.

The hull of the M557 is an all-welded aluminium construction. The transmission is located in the front and provides the vehicle with six forward and two reverse gears. The driver sits behind the transmission at the front of the vehicle on the left-hand side, with the engine located on the right. Air inlet and outlet louvers for the engine are located on the roof of the hull. Behind the driver is the crew area, with a roof that is raised more than 91cm/3ft higher than the original hull top. This allows the command crew to work in the rear of the vehicle and provides the extra space required for the additional communication equipment. On the front of the raised crew area is the APU, and there is a cupola that can be fitted with an M2 12.7mm/0.5in machine-gun in the roof of the crew area for use by the vehicle commander.

In addition to its use as a command post, the M577A3 is used for several other tasks such as a fire-direction centre, field treatment centre and a communications vehicle. In 2005, the XM577A4 was under development, which is a stretched version of the M113. This lengthens the vehicle by 66cm/2ft 2in, and increases the payload to over 2,268kg/5,000lb. The vehicle's increased length means that an extra pair of road wheels had to be fitted to the vehicle.

LEFT: The increased height and bulk of the M577 can be clearly seen, compared to the original M113 APC. The top of this vehicle is covered in personal equipment. A number of these vehicles have been converted into mobile medical units.

M577A3 Command Vehicle	
Country: USA	
Entered service: 1987	
Crew: 4	
Weight: 14,424kg/14.2 tons	
Dimensions: Length – 4.86m/15ft 11in	
Height – 3.89m/12ft 9in	
Width – 2.69m/8ft 10in	
Armament: Main – 7.62mm/0.3in M60 machine-gun	
Secondary – Small arms	
Armour: Maximum – 38mm/1.5in	
Powerplant: Detroit Diesel model 6V53T 6-cylinder 205kW/275hp diesel engine	
Performance: Speed – Road 65kph/41mph; Water 5.8kph/3.6mph	
Range – 497km/309 miles	

M901 Improved TOW Vehicle

By 1979, the US Army had some 1,400 TOW-armed vehicles in service. These first TOW (Tube-launched, Optically-tracked, Wire-guided) vehicles were basic M113 APCs fitted with a pedestal-mounted weapon system that retracted into the troop compartment. However, development work was started in 1976 on a new and better Improved TOW Vehicle (ITV) system that could be fitted to the M113A2 vehicle; this would become the M901A1. The M901 would be developed in the same way as the M113 and went through the same upgrades of suspension, cooling, driving controls and engine. In 2005, the vehicle in service was the M901A3 and this has all the improvements of the M113A3 plus some additional improvements such as

M17 laser protection and enhanced armour protection. Production of the M901 started in 1979. The US Army had a requirement for 2,526 of these vehicles, and 1,100 of these vehicles were deployed in Europe by 1981.

The hull of the M901 is an all-welded aluminium construction. The transmission, giving six forward and two reverse gears, is located in the front of the vehicle. The driver sits behind the transmission at the front of the vehicle on the left-hand side, with the engine on the right. Behind the driver and engine position is an M27 cupola. This is fitted with an image-transfer system, armoured launcher, missile guidance equipment and an auxiliary back-up battery pack. Two

TOW missile tubes are fitted to the armoured launcher, the acquisition sight is mounted on the top and between the TOW tubes is the TOW sight. A further 10 TOW missiles are carried inside the vehicle. Behind the M27 cupola is a large hatch that provides access to the TOW launcher so that spent missile tubes can be removed and jettisoned over the side of the vehicle allowing reloading to take place. Once the vehicle comes to a halt the TOW launcher is raised to the firing height and the first target engaged. This takes 20 seconds and reloading can be completed in 40 seconds. When in the travelling mode the launcher is retracted and sits on the hull roof, making the vehicle more difficult to identify.

RIGHT: A US Marine Corps vehicle heading into the water. The launcher turret is built by Emerson. This is made up of the M27 cupola, image-transfer equipment, armoured launcher, missile guidance set and a battery back-up pack.

M901A3 ITV

Country: USA
Entered service: 1989
Crew: 3
Weight: 12,339kg/12.1 tons
Dimensions: Length – 4.86m/15ft 11in
　　Height – 3.36m/11ft
　　Width – 2.69m/8ft 10in
Armament: Main – TOW launcher
　　Secondary – 7.62mm/0.3in M60 machine-gun
Armour: Maximum – 38mm/1.5in
Powerplant: Detroit Diesel model 6V53T
　　6-cylinder 205kW/275hp diesel engine
Performance: Speed – Road 65kph/41mph;
　　Water 5.8kph/3.6mph
　　Range – 497km/309 miles

471

LEFT: **This German Marder 1 is armed with a 20mm/0.79in MK20 cannon, while above the rear exit of the vehicle is the remote-control 7.62mm/0.3in machine-gun. The Marder has a well-sloped glacis with the driver's position on the left-hand side of the vehicle.** BELOW: **This Marder 1 is taking part in an exercise in Germany. Some of the infantry section are standing up in the rear infantry compartment and are using their small arms from the safety of the vehicle.**

Marder 1 Infantry Combat Vehicle

In the late 1950s, development started on a chassis that could be used for a family of military vehicles for the Federal German Army. The first vehicles in the series required by the German Army were the tank destroyers – the Jagdpanzer Kanone and Jagdpanzer Rakete. The Kanone entered production in 1965 while the Rakete entered production in 1967, and both were still in service in 2005. The next vehicle to be developed was the Infantry Combat Vehicle (ICV). The contracts were issued in 1960 to three companies to be involved in prototype production; Rheinstahl-Hanomag, Henschel and MOWAG. Between 1961 and 1963, a second series of prototype vehicles were built and the final series of prototype vehicles were produced in 1967–68. In April 1969, the three companies were invited to tender for the production of the ICV. In May 1969, the new vehicle was given the name Marder, and Rheinstahl-Hanomag won the contract. The first production vehicles were completed in December 1970, but

did not officially enter service with the Federal German Army until May 1971. In total, 3,100 Marder 1 ICVs were produced.

The hull of the Marder is an all-welded aluminium construction, and provides protection from small-arms fire and shell splinters. The front of the Marder is proof against direct fire from 20mm/0.79in ammunition. The driver sits at the front of the vehicle on the left-hand side and has a single-piece hatch in front of which are three vision blocks. Next to the driver on the right-hand side is the engine; the radiators for this are mounted on the rear of the vehicle on either side of the ramp. Behind the driver is the squad commander who has a hatch in the roof of the vehicle.

The two-man turret is mounted on the centreline just behind the squad commander and engine. The vehicle commander sits in the turret on the right-hand side with the gunner on the left. Both have their own hatches in the turret and the

LEFT: **This overhead view of the Marder shows the vehicle driver in his position with his hatch open to the right. Most of the hatches above the rear infantry compartment are in the open position with men manning their positions.**

LEFT: **This Marder is taking part in a NATO exercise in Germany. The crew of the Marder are servicing their vehicle's armament, while the vehicle itself is covered in camouflage netting.** ABOVE: **Six smoke dischargers are fitted to the main support arm of the 20mm/0.79in cannon. In the side of the infantry compartment are two MOWAG ball mountings for the infantry to fire their weapons from inside the vehicle.**

commander has all-round vision from eight different vision blocks. The 20mm/0.79in Rheinmetall MK20 Rh202 cannon is mounted externally on the vehicle and can traverse through 360 degrees. The cannon is fed from two different ammunition belts which can be loaded with different types of ammunition and has a rate of fire of 800–1,000 rounds per minute. The vehicle carries 1,250 rounds of ammunition for this main gun. Mounted coaxially on the left hand side of the turret is a 7.62mm/0.3in machine-gun.

In the rear of the vehicle is the troop compartment with accommodation for six men sitting in the middle of the compartment, three on each side, facing outwards. There are also two firing ports on each side and four hatches in the roof. The main exit and entrance to the troop compartment is via a power-operated ramp that folds down from the top of the vehicle. A remote-controlled 7.62mm/0.3in machine-gun with a traverse of 180 degrees was originally fitted above the troop compartment at the rear of the vehicle, but this has now been removed on many vehicles. All Marder vehicles in German Army service have now been fitted with the MILAN anti-tank guided missile and a full NBC system.

In 1982 the Marder went through an upgrade programme which improved the main armament, night-vision lights, thermal pointer, and NBC system and gave better personal equipment stowage in the troop compartment. This vehicle became the Marder A1. The Marder A1A was also produced having all the same improvements the A1 except the improved night-vision equipment. The Germans brought 670 Marder vehicles up to A1 standard and 1,400 vehicles to the A1A standard. In 2005, the vehicle in service was the Marder 1A3, and all Marders have now been brought up to this standard, with improved armour and new improved roof hatches. A new vehicle, the Marder 2, was due to enter production in 1995, but with the demolition of the Berlin Wall and the unification of Germany, a large number of military projects have been cancelled due to a dramatic cutback in military budgets, among them the Marder 2. The Marder ICV is only in service with the German Army but the chassis has been used to mount the Roland Surface-to-Air Missile system which came into service in 2005 with several countries in the NATO Alliance.

LEFT: **The infantry section of this Marder are boarding their vehicle. The rear ramp is not fully lowered. A MILAN AT missile launcher has been fitted to the side of the main turret, which can traverse through 360 degrees and has a maximum elevation of 65 degrees.**

Marder 1 ICV

Country: West Germany
Entered service: 1971
Crew: 3 plus 6 infantry
Weight: 29,210kg/28.75 tons
Dimensions: Length – 6.79m/22ft 3in
 Height – 2.98m/9ft 9in
 Width – 3.24m/10ft 7in
Armament: Main – 20mm/0.79in MK20 Rh202
 cannon, and coaxial 7.62mm/0.3in machine-gun
 Secondary – Small arms
Armour: Classified
Powerplant: MTU MB 833 Ea-500 6-cylinder
 447kW/600hp diesel engine
Performance: Speed – 75kph/46mph
 Range – 520km/325 miles

LEFT: **This Marksman turret is fitted on a Chieftain chassis. The large adapter ring on which the turret sits has been designed to fit a number of tanks from other countries.**
BELOW: **The large ventilator grill is visible in the rear of the turret. The height and bulk of the turret can also be clearly seen.**

Marksman Self-Propelled Anti-Aircraft Gun

The Marksman twin 35mm/1.38in turret was developed by Marconi Command and Control Systems as a private venture and was very similar in concept to the German 35mm/1.38in Gepard. The Marksman system had to be able to function at any time of the day or night and in all weather conditions. Development started in 1983 and the first prototype was finished in time to go on display at the British Army Equipment Exhibition in 1984, where it was shown mounted on a Vickers Mk 3 MBT (Main Battle Tank) chassis. The second prototype was completed in 1986 and

was an all-welded steel construction; the turret was built by Vickers and the guns by Oerlikon.

The turret has been designed to be fitted to some 11 different MBT chassis, both NATO and ex-Warsaw Pact, and is easily fitted to this wide range of vehicles by using an adaptor ring where necessary. The only other part required is an electrical and communication interface so the turret crew can talk to the driver of the vehicle. The turret provides the crew with protection from bullets and shell splinters; the commander sits on the left-hand side with the gunner on the right. Both have all-round vision periscopes as well as a roof-mounted gyro-stabilized sight for optically acquired air or ground targets, while the gunner also has a laser range finder. In the rear of the turret is a diesel APU that is the main power supply to the turret.

The main armament is the Oerlikon 35mm/1.38in KDA cannon and one is mounted on each side of the turret. Each

gun is supplied with 250 rounds, 20 of them anti-tank. The ammunition is containerized and so reloading of the turret can be completed in 10 minutes. The guns are fully gyro-stabilized, allowing the Marksman to engage targets when the vehicle is on the move. To the rear of the turret roof is an ECM-resistant tracking and surveillance radar which has a range of 12km/7.5 miles. The only country to buy the Marksman is Finland which uses it on the T-55 MBT chassis.

LEFT: **The search radar is fitted to the rear of the turret, and stands 1m/39in above the top of this. Behind each gun barrel on both sides of the turret are a cluster of smoke dischargers.**

Marksman 35mm SPAAG on Chieftain Chassis

Country: UK
Entered service: 1987
Crew: 3
Weight: 54,864kg/54 tons
Dimensions: Length – 8.13m/26ft 8in
Height – 3.07m/10ft 1in
Width – 3.5m/11ft 6in
Armament: Main – 2 x 35mm/1.38in KDA cannon
Secondary – 7.62mm/0.3in machine-gun
Armour: Classified
Powerplant: Leyland 12-cylinder 559kW/750hp multi-fuel engine
Performance: Speed – 48kph/30mph
Range – 500km/310 miles

LEFT: **An MT-LB fitted with a SNAR 10 counter-battery radar. The SNAR 10 has the NATO codename of "Big Fred". The radar is fitted in a turret sited at the rear of the vehicle. The radar dish is in the raised position but when travelling the dish is folded down on top of the radar turret. The driver's and the vehicle commander/gunner's front visors are in the open position.** ABOVE: **A crew member is entering the front compartment of the vehicle. This compartment holds two: the driver and vehicle commander, while in the rear of the vehicle there is space for 11 men.**

MT–LB Infantry Carrier

In the late 1960s the Soviet Army required a replacement for the ageing AT-P armoured tracked artillery tractor, so a new vehicle based on the MT-L unarmoured tracked amphibious carrier was developed and called the MT-LB. Production started at the Kharkov Tractor Plant in the late 1969 and it was seen in public for the first time in 1970. The new vehicle can fill many roles including APC, prime mover for 100mm/3.94in AT guns and 122mm/4.8in howitzers, command and radio communication vehicles, and cargo carrier. It is also very good at crossing difficult terrain such as snow or swamp, and is still in service with 14 different countries.

The MT-LB is an all-welded steel construction, and gives the crew protection from small-arms fire and shell splinters. The crew compartment is in the front and occupies the full width of the vehicle with the driver on the left-hand side and the commander on the right. A manually operated turret, armed with a 7.62mm/0.3in PKT machine-gun is mounted in the roof above the commander's position. Next to the turret in the roof of the crew compartment is the commander's hatch and there is also a hatch above the driver's position. Both the driver and the commander have a windscreen to their front, and these are covered by an armoured flap when in action. The engine is mounted behind the driver, but does not run the full width of the vehicle. The air intake and outlet louvers for this are on the roof. Between the crew compartment and the troop compartment is an aisle which allows access to both compartments. The troops sit down each side of the vehicle facing inwards. There are two hatches in the roof and the main entrance and exit is via two doors in the rear of the vehicle which open outwards.

The MT-LB is fully amphibious and is propelled in the water by its tracks. A trim vane, mounted on the front of the vehicle, is raised before entering the water. This operation only takes a few minutes. The vehicle is fitted with a full NBC system and night-driving equipment.

LEFT: **This MT-LB is seen towing a T-12A 100mm/3.94in AT gun during a November Parade. The vehicle could carry the six-man gun crew and ammunition. The twin large hatches in the rear of the roof of the vehicle are visible.**

MT-LB Infantry Carrier

Country: USSR
Entered service: 1970
Crew: 2 plus 11 infantry
Weight: 11,887kg/11.7 tons
Dimensions: Length – 6.45m/21ft 2in
 Height – 1.86m/6ft 1in
 Width – 2.86m/9ft 5in
Armament: Main – 7.62mm/0.3in PKT
 machine-gun
 Secondary – Small arms
Armour: Maximum – 10mm/0.394in
Powerplant: YaMZ 238V 8-cylinder 179kW/240hp
 diesel engine
Performance: Speed – 62kph/38mph
 Range – 500km/320 miles

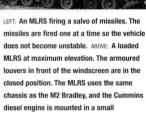

LEFT: **An MLRS firing a salvo of missiles. The missiles are fired one at a time so the vehicle does not become unstable.** ABOVE: **A loaded MLRS at maximum elevation. The armoured louvers in front of the windscreen are in the closed position. The MLRS uses the same chassis as the M2 Bradley, and the Cummins diesel engine is mounted in a small compartment behind the crew cab.**

Multiple Launch Rocket System

In 1972, the Americans started development on a new rocket system that would use a low-cost rocket and had to be as easy to use as a conventional artillery round. The two main companies involved in the project were Boeing and Vought; each company had to develop a Self-Propelled Launcher Loader (SPLL) and 150 rockets. In 1978 France, West Germany, Italy and the United Kingdom asked to join the project and some changes were made to the rockets. A larger rocket motor was to be fitted and the diameter of the rocket increased to 227mm/ 8.9in. In May 1980, Vought won the competition and were awarded the contract to manufacture the SPLL and rockets. The US Army ordered 491 SPLL and 480 reload vehicles together with 400 rockets, all to be delivered by 1990. These new vehicles would play a major part in the 1991 Gulf War (nicknamed "Steel Rain" by the Iraqi Army), and are expected to remain in service until 2020.

The vehicle uses many of the M2/M3 Bradley automotive components and running gear and is an all-welded aluminium construction. In the front of the vehicle is the three-man armoured cab, which houses the driver on the left, vehicle commander on the right and the gunner in the middle. Entry and exit to the cab is via two side doors, one on each side, and each man has a windscreen which is protected by armoured louvers. Only the vehicle commander has a roof hatch. Behind the armoured cab is the engine housing which is in an armoured box, on the top of which is the main air intake for the engine. Behind this is the main rocket pod, which is mounted on a turntable that allows a traverse of 180 degrees. The rocket pod houses 12 solid fuel rockets which are ripple-fired and can be reloaded in less than 10 minutes.

Various warheads can be fitted to the rockets: high-explosive sub-munitions, anti-tank mines and chemical warheads. The basic M77 rocket has a shelf life of 10 years and contains 644 pre-programmed shaped bomblets.

LEFT: **An MLRS in travelling mode. These vehicles are replacing long-range towed artillery in most modern NATO armies. They are expected to remain in service for the next 20 years.**

MLRS	
Country: USA	
Entered service: 1982	
Crew: 3	
Weight: 25,191kg/24.8 tons	
Dimensions: Length – 6.8m/22ft 4in	
Height – 2.6m/8ft 6in	
Width – 2.92m/9ft 7in	
Armament: Main – 12 x 227mm/8.9in M77 rockets	
Secondary – Small arms	
Armour: Classified	
Powerplant: Cummins VTA-903T turbocharged 8-cylinder 373kW/500hp diesel engine	
Performance: Speed – 64kph/40mph Range – 483km/302 miles	

OT-64 Armoured Personnel Carrier

The OT-64 (Obrneny Transporter) 8x8 was jointly developed by Czechoslovakia and Poland, the project starting in 1959. It uses many of the automotive parts of the Tatra 813 heavy truck series and entered service in 1964. The Czechoslovak company Tatra produced the chassis and automotive parts while the Polish firm FSC of Lubin produced the armoured body. The Polish designation for the vehicle was Sredni Kolowy Opancerzny Transporter; OT-64 being the Czech designation. It is still in service with 13 countries.

The hull of the OT-64 is an all-welded steel construction. The crew compartment is in the front of the vehicle, with the driver on the left-hand side and the vehicle commander on the right. Each has a large single door in the side of

the vehicle for access to the crew cab and also a hatch in the roof of the compartment. The driver has three vision blocks which provide views to the front and sides. The engine compartment is behind the crew cab and is mounted over the second axle with the air inlet and outlets on the roof and the exhaust pipes on either side of the vehicle. Behind the engine is an octagonal plinth on top of which sits the turret. The turret is operated by one man and has no hatch

ABOVE: **Three OT-64 APC vehicles taking part in a November Parade. The vehicle commanders are standing in their turrets. Half of the possible eight-man infantry sections are standing in the rear of the vehicles, and the doors of the rear roof hatches have been removed.** LEFT: **An OT-64 being guided around a tight corner. The front four wheels of the vehicle are used for steering, but the turning circle is very large. The exhaust system is fitted to each side of the hull of the vehicle. This APC does not have a turret fitted.**

in the top of it. To the rear of this is the troop compartment which runs to the rear of the vehicle and has room for eight men inside. At the rear are the main entry and exit doors, both of which are fitted with firing ports. There are four roof hatches above the troop compartment, all of which are also fitted with firing ports, which can be locked in the vertical position and used as shields when using the firing ports. There are also a further two ports in each side of the troop compartment.

The OT-64 is fitted with a basic NBC over-pressure system. Steering is on the front four wheels and the vehicle is fully amphibious, being propelled in the water by two propellers at the rear.

OT-64 Armoured Personnel Carrier

Country: Czechoslovakia
Entered service: 1964
Crew: 2 plus 8 infantry
Weight: 14,326kg/14.1 tons
Dimensions: Length – 7.44m/24ft 5in
  Height – 2m/6ft 6in
  Width – 2.5m/8ft 3in
Armament: Main – 14.5mm/0.57in KPVT machine-gun, and coaxial 7.62mm/0.3in PKT machine-gun
  Secondary – Small arms
Armour: Maximum – 14mm/0.55in
Powerplant: Tatra 928-14 8-cylinder 134kW/180hp diesel engine
Performance: Speed – 60kph/37mph
  Range – 500km/310 miles

ABOVE: **The trim vane on this vehicle is folded back against the glacis. The driver's side door is in the open position, folded back against the hull of the vehicle. Above the driver's position is the driver's cupola.**

OT-810 Armoured Personnel Carrier

During World War II, the Germans manufactured the Sd Kfz 251 half-track at the Skoda plant in Pilsen, Czechoslovakia. After the war had finished, the Czechoslovakian Army were desperate for vehicles and as the Skoda factory was tooled up for Sd Kfz production, they started to make the vehicle again. The first vehicles, unchanged from the basic German design, were delivered in 1948. The first major redesign occurred in the early 1950s when an armoured roof was placed over the troop compartment and the German engine was replaced with a Czech Tatra engine. When the OT-810 was replaced in 1964 on the introduction of the OT-64, a large number of the earlier carriers were converted to anti-tank vehicles. The rear of the vehicle was modified and the gun placed on to it. These variants would remain in service until the late 1980s.

The hull of the vehicle was an all-welded steel construction, with the engine in the front. Behind this was the joint crew and troop compartment. The driver sat in the front of the compartment on the left-hand side, with the vehicle commander, who also acted as the radio operator and gunner, on the right. The driver and commander had small vision

ports to their front and side, and the commander also had a hatch in the roof of the vehicle. The troop compartment held 10 men, five on each side facing each other. In the rear of the vehicle were two large doors that were the sole means of access for the troops and the crew. The OT-810 had neither night-driving equipment nor an NBC system.

The only variant of the OT-810 ever produced was the anti-tank conversion, which had a crew of just four men. This was armed with the M59A recoilless gun,

ABOVE: **The OT-810 was a copy of the World War II German Sd Kfz 251 half-track. The crew compartment has three pistol ports down each side of the hull. The frame above the vehicle commander's position was for a 12.7mm/0.5in heavy machine-gun.**

which was carried in the troop compartment and could be fired from inside the vehicle. Alternatively, it could be dismounted and fired from the ground. Forty rounds of ammunition for this weapon were carried in the vehicle. The twin doors at the rear were removed and replaced with a single hatch.

ABOVE: **The vehicle commander is standing up in his position with the roof hatch folded back. A number of these vehicles are being converted back into Sd Kfz 251s by collectors.**

OT-810 APC

Country: Czechoslovakia
Entered service: 1948
Crew: 2 plus 10 infantry
Weight: 8,534kg/8.4 tons
Dimensions: Length – 5.92m/19ft 1in
Height – 1.75m/5ft 8in
Width – 2.1m/6ft 9in
Armament: Main – 7.62mm/0.3in M59
machine-gun
Secondary – Small arms
Armour: Maximum – 12mm/0.47in
Powerplant: Tatra 6-cylinder 89kW/120hp
diesel engine
Performance: Speed – 52kph/32mph
Range – 320km/198 miles

LEFT: **This AML 90 car has two undtiching channels fitted to the front of the vehicle. On the each side at the rear of the turret are clusters of smoke dischargers. The commander's cupola has a 7.62mm/0.3in machine-gun fitted to the front edge.**

BELOW: **Venezuela is the only country to use this version of the AML. The turret is the S 530 armed with twin 20mm/0.79in cannon. On each side of the turret at the rear is a cluster of smoke dischargers. The large side hatch between the wheels of the vehicle can be clearly seen.**

Panhard AML 90H Armoured Car

In the late 1950s, the French Army issued a requirement for an armoured car similar to the British Ferret, which they had used in North Africa. Panhard produced the first prototype in 1959 as the Model 245. It passed the trials and was accepted into French Army service as the AML (*AutoMitrailleuse Légère*), the first production vehicle being delivered in 1961. The AML has been built in large numbers, and some 4,800 cars had been produced by 2002. In 2005, it was in service with 39 countries, including France, and production is still available for export customers.

The hull of the AML is an all-welded steel construction. The driver is in the centre front of the vehicle, and has a single hatch that opens to the right.

Behind and above the driver is the turret, which is manufactured by Hispano-Suiza and is armed with the 90mm/3.54in D 921 F1 gun. It also has a 7.62mm/0.3in coaxial machine-gun. The turret houses the vehicle commander on the left-hand side and the gunner on the right; both have hatches in the roof of the turret. There are two large hatches in the sides of the vehicle below the turret, which are the main method of access to the vehicle. The left-hand hatch has the spare wheel mounted on it and opens to the rear while the right-hand door opens towards the front of the vehicle. A 7.62mm/0.3in or 12.7mm/0.5in machine-gun can be mounted on the roof of the vehicle as an anti-aircraft weapon. The engine is in the rear and has two access hatches. Originally the

AML was fitted with a petrol engine but on late production vehicles this has been changed to a diesel unit.

The AML has been produced in many different variants. The body has remained the same but the turret has been changed and fitted with a variety of weapons. These include mountings for 60mm/2.36in mortars and a twin 20mm/0.79in anti-aircraft gun turret. The latest version has an open-topped turret and is known as the AML Scout Car.

Panhard AML 90H Armoured Car

Country: France
Entered service: 1961
Crew: 3
Weight: 5,486kg/5.4 tons
Dimensions: Length – 3.79m/12ft 5in
    Height – 2.07m/6ft 10in
    Width – 1.98m/6ft 6in
Armament: Main – 90mm/3.54in D 921 F1 gun,
    and coaxial 7.62mm/0.3in machine-gun
    Secondary – 7.62mm/0.3in machine-gun
Armour: Maximum – 12mm/0.47in
Powerplant: Panhard Model 4 HD 4-cylinder
    67kW/90hp petrol engine
Performance: Speed – 100kph/62mph
    Range – 600km/370 miles

LEFT: **The large double-baffle muzzle brake on the end of the barrel is very prominent. The driver has his hatch in the open position. The headlights are mounted under the undtiching channels on the front of the vehicle.**

Panhard ERC-90-F4 Sagaie

Panhard started development of the ERC (*Engin de Reconnaissance Cannon*) in 1975 as a private venture aimed at the export market. The first production vehicles were completed in 1979. The French Army carried out an evaluation between 1978 and 1980 and in December 1980, it was accepted for service. However, further trials were carried out until 1983, the first ERC cars entering French Army service in 1984. An order for 176 ERC-90-F4 Sagaie was placed with the final delivery being made in 1989.

The hull of the ERC is an all-welded steel construction which gives the crew protection from small arms and shell splinters. The hull bottom is made of two plates that are welded together, stiffening the floor and helping protect the vehicle from mines. The driver's position is in the front of the vehicle but is offset to the left-hand side. It can be fitted with night-driving equipment. The two-man turret, armed with a 90mm/3.54in Model 62 F1 gun, is behind and above the driver. The commander is on the left-hand side with the gunner on the right. The commander's cupola has periscopes all round providing a 360-degree field of vision and can also be fitted with a 7.62mm/0.3in or 12.7mm/0.5in machine-gun. The engine is in the rear of the vehicle and is a militarized Peugeot V-6 petrol engine, with six forward and one reverse gear. All six wheels are permanently driven, even the middle pair when raised. The central pair is raised off the ground when the car is driven on hard roads but lowered when traversing rough terrain cross-country.

The ERC range of vehicles use many of the same automotive parts as the VCR series of vehicles. The ERC-90-F4 has a full NBC system and is fully amphibious; normally it is propelled in the water by its wheels but it can be fitted with two water jets mounted at the rear of the vehicle. The vehicle can also be fitted with one of up to ten different turrets.

In 2005, the ERC and its variants were in service with seven different countries, and production can be restarted if necessary.

ABOVE LEFT: **This is the original version armed with the TTB 190 turret, but it is being replaced in service with the French Army by cars fitted with the Lynx turret.** ABOVE: **An ERC-90 fitted with the Lynx turret, which is the same as the one fitted to the AML. Steering is only available via the front wheels of the car. The centre wheels can be raised when travelling on roads.**

LEFT: **Two Lynx-armed vehicles training in the water. The trim vane folds into three and then folds back on to the glacis plate between the front wheels. When raised and unfolded, the trim vane is full vehicle width. It has clear panels in it so the driver has some forward vision when in the water.**

Panhard ERC-90-F4 Armoured Car

Country: France
Entered service: 1984
Crew: 3
Weight: 8,331kg/8.2 tons
Dimensions: Length – 5.27m/17ft 3in
  Height – 2.32m/7ft 7in
  Width – 2.5m/8ft 3in
Armament: Main – 90mm/3.54in Model 62 F1 gun, and coaxial 7.62mm/0.3in machine-gun
  Secondary – 7.62mm/0.3in machine-gun
Armour: Classified
Powerplant: Peugeot 6-cylinder 108kW/145hp petrol engine
Performance: Speed – 95kph/60mph
  Range – 700km/435 miles

LEFT: **This M3 is taking part in an exercise. This vehicle is fitted with an STB rotary support shield, which is armed with a 7.62mm/0.3in machine-gun.** ABOVE: **The large square rear of the M3, with two large doors for the infantry section to use. The vehicle is wider in the middle than at the end and also tapers down slightly towards the middle.**

Panhard M3 Armoured Personnel Carrier

Panhard started development of the M3 as a private venture for the export market. The first prototype was completed in 1969 and put through a series of trials. The design was subsequently changed, and in 1971 the first vehicle came off the production line. Some 1,500 M3 vehicles have been produced and exported to 26 countries and it was still in service with 12 of these countries in 2002. The M3 uses 95 per cent of the same automotive parts as the AML armoured car.

The hull of the M3 is an all-welded steel construction and gives the crew protection from small arms and shell splinters. The driver's position is on the centreline in the front of the vehicle and may be fitted with night-driving equipment. The engine compartment is behind this, with the air intake above and behind the driver. The air outlets are on either side of the roof along with one exhaust system tube per side. Behind the engine is the troop compartment with accommodation for ten men. There are

four doors in this compartment: two, both fitted with firing ports, mounted in the rear of the vehicle, and a large single door on each side of the M3. There are three firing ports down each side of the infantry compartment. Behind the engine in the roof of the vehicle is a forward hatch that can mount a wide range of turrets, cupolas and machine-gun mounts, which can in turn be armed with a variety of machine-guns and cannon. Anti-tank missiles such as MILAN can also be fitted to the M3. There is a second hatch in the rear of the roof of the troop compartment and this is normally fitted with a pintle mount for a 7.62mm/0.3in machine-gun. The M3 is fully amphibious and uses its wheels to propel itself through the water.

There are five variations on the basic vehicle; these are M3/VAT repair vehicle, M3/VPC command vehicle, M3/VLA engineering vehicle, M3/VTS ambulance and the M3 radar vehicle. In 1986 the Panhard Buffalo replaced the M3, on which it is based, in production.

ABOVE: **An M3 armed with an automatic 7.62mm/ 0.3in machine-gun. The vehicle has a cluster of two smoke dischargers on each side of the vehicle. The driver's hatch is open and swung out to the right of the vehicle.**

Panhard M3 Armoured Personnel Carrier

Country: France
Entered service: 1971
Crew: 2 plus 10 infantry
Weight: 6,096kg/6 tons
Dimensions: Length – 4.45m/14ft 6in
  Height – 2.48m/8ft 2in
  Width – 2.4m/7ft 9in
Armament: Main – 7.62mm/0.3in machine-gun
  Secondary – 7.62mm/0.3in machine-gun
Armour: Maximum – 12mm/0.47in
Powerplant: Panhard 4HD 4-cylinder 67kW/90hp petrol engine
Performance: Speed – 100kph/62mph
  Range – 600km/372 miles

Piranha Armoured Personnel Carrier

The MOWAG Piranha is a complete range of armoured vehicles and is available as 4x4, 6x6 and 8x8 chassis. This collection of vehicles started life as a private venture and was designed for the domestic and export market. Development started in 1972 and production started in 1976. The first customer was the Canadian Armed Forces and in February 1977 they placed an order for 350 6x6 vehicles which was very quickly increased to 491 6x6s.

The Piranha has an all-welded steel construction that protects the crew from small-arms fire and shell splinters. The driver sits at the front of the vehicle on the left-hand side and has a single-piece hatch with three periscopes in the front of it. The driver's position can also be fitted with night-driving equipment. The engine is next to the driver on the right-hand side of the vehicle with the air intake and outlet louvers on the top of the hull. The exhaust exit is on the right-hand side of the hull. The main armament is normally turret-mounted and this is positioned behind the driver on the centreline of the vehicle.

In the rear of the vehicle is the troop compartment that usually holds 11 men, although this number can be lower depending on the type of turret fitted to the vehicle. The main exit and entry to the compartment is via two large doors that open outwards. There are two hatches in the roof of the troop compartment and, depending on the customer's requirements, firing ports can be fitted into the sides of the vehicle and in the rear doors. Steering is on the front axle for the 4x4 and 6x6 vehicles, and on the front two axles on the 8x8. The fixed rear axles have torsion-bar suspension while the axles that can steer are fitted with coil springs. All the Piranha family are fully amphibious and are propelled in the water by two propellers. Once the trim vane, which is stowed under the nose of the APC, is raised, the vehicle is ready for the water in only a few minutes. The Piranha comes with an NBC kit fitted as standard and a full air-conditioning system.

ABOVE: **This Piranha prototype is fitted with a 90mm/3.54in Cockerill Mk III gun. On the front of the turret on each side is a cluster of three smoke dischargers. The vehicle commander's and gunner's hatches are open.**

LEFT: **This Piranha is fitted with a Blazer 25 air-defence gun turret. This is fitted with 25mm/0.98in GAU-12/U cannon, and four Stinger SAMs are fitted above the gun barrel. The gun is firing and the large number of empty shells can be seen being ejected from the weapon.**

All members of the Piranha family share many of the same components such as the front and rear hull sections, doors, hatches, wheel drives, wheels, differentials, suspension, steering and propellers, which makes maintenance of the vehicles easier and cheaper. The Piranha family has been designed to fill a wide variety of roles for both the military and internal security forces, for example ambulance, anti-tank, armoured personnel carrier, command, mortar carrier, recovery and reconnaissance. The most popular version of the Piranha family is the 6x6 which can be fitted with a wide array of armaments. This includes a remote-controlled 7.62mm/0.3in machine-gun, a 12.7mm/0.5in machine-gun turret, 20mm/0.79in GAD-AOA Oerlikon turret, 25mm/0.98in GBD series turret, a 30mm/1.18in turret and a two-man turret armed with a 90mm/3.54in Cockerill or Mecar gun. The Canadians and Australians have fitted the British Scorpion 76mm/2.99in L23A1 gun turret to a number of their vehicles.

The Swiss Army had a requirement for 400 6x6 Piranha anti-tank vehicles to replace the ageing 106mm/4.17in M40 recoilless rifle in Swiss Army service. Each Swiss infantry regiment has nine of these anti-tank vehicles in a tank-destroyer company. They are armed with the Norwegian Thune-Eureka twin TOW turret, which has a hatch in the rear for the gunner. In the forward part of the turret are the sight and guidance systems and these are the same as for the basic infantry version of the TOW. Within two seconds of the first

ABOVE: **This Piranha is fitted with a remote-controlled Oerlikon 25mm/0.98in GBD-COA turret. The gunner sits inside the vehicle and can select two different types of ammunition. The driver's hatch is at the front of the vehicle with the commander's hatch behind, while the engine intake grills are to the left.**

missile impacting, the turret can lock on to another target ready to fire again. Reloading is carried out from the rear of the turret and can be completed in 40 seconds for the two missiles.

The Piranha has been built under licence in a large number of countries and has proved to be very successful, reliable and well-liked by its crews. It is expected to remain in service until 2020. In 2005, the Piranha family of vehicles was in service with 14 different countries, and a new version of the family, the Piranha IV, is currently being developed.

RIGHT: **This is a Blazer 30 air-defence system fitted to a Piranha. The turret is armed with a 30mm/1.18in cannon, while above the cannon are four Javelin SAMs. The radar is mounted to the rear of the turret on a pintle mount.**

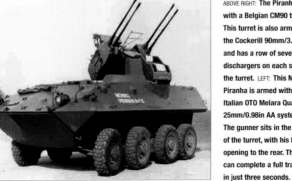

ABOVE RIGHT: **The Piranha armed with a Belgian CM90 turret. This turret is also armed with the Cockerill 90mm/3.45in gun and has a row of seven smoke dischargers on each side of the turret.** LEFT: **This MOWAG Piranha is armed with the Italian OTO Melara Quad 25mm/0.98in AA system. The gunner sits in the middle of the turret, with his hatch opening to the rear. The turret can complete a full traverse in just three seconds.**

Piranha 6x6 APC

Country: Switzerland
Entered service: 1977
Crew: 3 plus 11 infantry
Weight: 10,465kg/10.3 tons
Dimensions: Length – 5.97m/19ft 6in
　　　　　Height – 1.85m/6ft 1in
　　　　　Width – 2.5m/8ft 2in
Armament: Main – Variable
　　　　　Secondary – Small arms
Armour: Maximum – 10mm/0.394in
Powerplant: GM Detroit Diesel 6V-53T 6-cylinder
　　　　　261kW/350hp diesel engine
Performance: Speed – 100kph/62mph
　　　　　Range – 600km/370 miles

LEFT: The trim vane of the vehicle is folded back against the glacis plate. In the front of the hull are the headlights, and the commander's cupola is fitted with a 7.62mm/0.3in machine-gun. On each side of the turret is a row of four smoke dischargers.
ABOVE: This Luchs is negotiating a German driver-training course. The suspension is operating in several directions on all the wheels of the vehicle. The searchlight on the left-hand side of the turret is covered. The Luchs has developed a very good reputation for its cross-country ability.

Radspahpanzer Luchs Reconnaissance Vehicle

In 1964, the Federal German Army issued a requirement for a new family of vehicles, including an 8x8 armoured amphibious reconnaissance vehicle, to enter service in the 1970s. The prototypes were delivered for testing in 1968 and in 1971, the Daimler-Benz candidate was chosen, with a contract for 408 vehicles being placed in 1973. The first production vehicles were completed in May 1975 and the first vehicle was handed over to the army in September 1975. In service it is known as by the German Army as the Luchs. Production continued until 1978.

The hull of the Luchs is an all-welded steel construction which gives the crew protection from small-arms fire and shell splinters, while the front of the vehicle is proof against 2cm/0.79in cannon fire.

The driver is located in the front of the Luchs on the left-hand side and this position can be fitted with night-driving equipment. The two-man Rheinmetall TS-7 turret is situated to the rear of the driver, with the commander stationed on the right-hand side and the gunner on the left. This turret is fitted with spaced armour to improve protection. A searchlight is fitted to the left-hand side of the turret and is connected to the elevation controls of the gun. This can also be used in the infrared mode. Both the commander and the gunner are equipped with sights for the main gun.

The fourth man in the crew is the radio operator/rear driver, and they are seated behind the turret facing the rear of the vehicle on the left-hand side with the engine compartment on the right.

There is a large hatch that gives access to all crew positions in the left-hand side of the hull between the front four and rear four wheels. The Luchs is fully amphibious and is propelled through the water by two propellers mounted at the rear of the vehicle. Steering is on the front and rear axles which makes this vehicle very manoeuvrable.

The Luchs has developed a very good reputation for its cross-country ability, reliability and quietness.

LEFT: A Luchs leaving the water with its trim vane in the raised position. To give the driver some forward vision when in the water, the trim vane has several clear panels fitted in it.

Radspahpanzer Luchs Reconnaissance Vehicle

Country: West Germany
Entered service: 1975
Crew: 4
Weight: 19,507kg/19.2 tons
Dimensions: Length – 7.74m/25ft 5in
    Height – 2.9m/9ft 6in
    Width – 2.98m/9ft 9in
Armament: Main – 2cm/0.79in MK20 Rh202 cannon
    Secondary – 1 x 7.62mm/0.3in MG3 machine-gun
Armour: Classified
Powerplant: Daimler-Benz OM 403A 10-cylinder 291kW/390hp diesel engine
Performance: Speed – 90kph/56mph
    Range – 730km/455 miles

Rapier Tracked SAM Vehicle

LEFT: **A Rapier Tracked SAM Vehicle that has just launched a missile. The tracking radar on the rear of the turret can be seen in the raised position. The vehicle is divided into two clear parts: the crew and engine compartment to the front and the missile launcher/radar to the rear.**

Rapier Tracked SAM Vehicle

Country: UK
Entered service: 1984
Crew: 3
Weight: 14,010kg/13.8 tons
Dimensions: Length – 6.4m/21ft
Height – 2.5m/8ft 2in
Width – 2.78m/9ft 1in
Armament: Main – 8 x Rapier SAM
Secondary – Small arms
Armour: Classified
Powerplant: GMC 6-cylinder 186kW/250hp diesel engine
Performance: Speed – 80kph/50mph
Range – 300km/190 miles

Development of this vehicle commenced in 1974, initially using the chassis of the M548, but this was quickly changed for the RCM 748, part of the M113 APC family of vehicles. Originally developed for the Imperial Iranian Armed Forces, British Aerospace was left with a number of these vehicles and no customer following the overthrow of the Shah in 1979. Subsequently, the British Army agreed to conduct vehicle trials and in 1981 placed an order for 50 units. It entered service in 1984 with two Royal Artillery Regiments, each deploying 24 Rapier vehicles.

The hull is an all-welded aluminium construction, and is proof against small-arms fire and shell splinters. The driver, commander and gunner all share the very small and cramped cab in the front of the vehicle. The driver is on the left-hand side, while the engine is installed behind the crew compartment. The eight-round Rapier system is mounted on the rear of the vehicle. The time taken from the vehicle stopping to the first target being engaged is 15 seconds.

Rooikat 105mm Armoured Car

Development on this vehicle started in 1978. The first production vehicles were completed in 1989 and entered service in 1990, armed with a 76mm/2.99in fully stabilized gun.

Rooikat 105mm Armoured Car

Country: South Africa
Entered service: 1994
Crew: 4
Weight: 28,042kg/27.6 tons
Dimensions: Length – 7.09m/23ft 3in
Height – 2.8m/9ft 2in
Width – 2.9m/9ft 6in
Armament: Main – 105mm/4.13in GT7 gun, and coaxial 7.62mm/0.3in machine-gun
Secondary – 1 x 7.62mm/0.3in machine-gun
Armour: Classified
Powerplant: 10-cylinder 420kW/563hp diesel engine
Performance: Speed – 120kph/75mph
Range – 1,000km/620 miles

In 1994, further development resulted in a 105mm/4.13in version of the vehicle entering service with the South African National Defence Force. Total production so far has been 240 vehicles.

The hull is an all-welded steel construction, and is proof against small-arms fire, shell splinters and anti-tank mines. The front of the vehicle is proof against 24mm/0.94in cannon fire. The driver's position is located in the front on the centreline, while the other three members of the crew are situated in the turret. The commander and gunner are on the right-hand side of the turret with the loader on the left. The engine is in the rear of the vehicle, which can be driven in either 8x4 mode or 8x8 mode

ABOVE: **The driver's position is under the main gun, which has to be cantered off to one side to allow the driver to access the vehicle. There is a mount for a machine-gun at the rear of the commander's cupola.**

and accelerate from 0–30kph/0–18.6mph in under eight seconds.

The Rooikat is designed for the reconnaissance role but can also carry out "seek and destroy" missions.

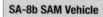

SA-8b SAM Vehicle

The SA-8 has the NATO designation "Gecko" and is an all-weather low-altitude Surface-to-Air Missile (SAM) system. The Gecko entered service in 1974 with the Soviet Armed Forces and was seen for the first time at the November Parade in Moscow in 1975. It was designed to fill the gap between the SA-7/SA-9 and the SA-6 and was developed in conjunction with the Soviet Navy SA-N-4 system. The Gecko is known in the Russian Army as the ZRK-SD Romb (*Zentniy Raketniy Komplex*) which indicates that the system is a complete SAM system. Each anti-aircraft division has 20 of these vehicles. This was the first anti-aircraft system to combine the surveillance, target-acquisition and missile launcher all-in-one vehicle.

The chassis of the Gecko, an all-welded steel construction, is based on the ZIL-167 6x6 truck and is not proof against small arms or shell splinters. The crew compartment is at the front of the vehicle where all three crew members sit in a row with the driver in the centre. In the roof above the driver is a small hatch which is the only access to and from the vehicle. The main missile control consoles, operated by all three crew members, are behind the crew. The vehicle is very spacious and the crew can even sleep in it. The engine is in the rear of the vehicle with the air intakes and outlets built into the top of the hull, while the exhaust is at the rear of the engine compartment.

The central radar dish is the main tracking system with the two smaller dishes acting as target-acquisition radar. On the top of the radar mount is a television camera which is used to acquire targets without having to switch on the radar. The SA-8b variant can carry

ABOVE LEFT: **The boat-shaped hull of the vehicle can be clearly seen, with the trim vane folded back in front of the windscreen. The missile turret sits high on the top of the vehicle.** ABOVE: **The main entry and exit hatch for the crew of the Gecko is in the roof of the vehicle immediately in front of the main radar dish and is seen here in the open position.**

six missiles (the SA-8a carries only four) and no reloads. The Gecko is fully amphibious, propelled in the water by two water jets built into the rear of the vehicle, and is also air-transportable. The vehicle has been used in combat and is very popular with several armies in the Middle East.

LEFT: **The main search radar of the Gecko is in the travel mode; it is folded down against the missile launching boxes. The water jet entry hatch is sited above the rear wheel with the exit in the rear of the vehicle.**

SA-8b SAM Vehicle

Country: USSR
Entered service: 1974
Crew: 3
Weight: 17,499kg/17.2 tons
Dimensions: Length – 9.14m/30ft
Height – 4.2m/13ft 10in
Width – 2.8m/9ft 2in
Armament: Main – 6 x SA-8b missiles
Secondary – Small arms
Armour: Classified
Powerplant: 5D20 B-300 223kW/299hp
diesel engine
Performance: Speed – 80kph/50mph
Range – 250km/155 miles

LEFT: **This Saladin armoured car has a machine-gun mounted in front of the commander's position. The external storage boxes can be seen mounted on the top of the wheels.**
BELOW: **A Saladin of the 3rd Royal Tank Regiment in Malaya. Behind are two Ferret armoured cars. The Saladin is covered in personal kit, which in combat was stored on the outside of the vehicle.**

Saladin Mk 2 Armoured Car

In 1947, a contract was issued to Alvis Ltd to develop a new 6x6 armoured car for the British Army. A mock-up was completed in 1948 and was given the designation of FV 601. This first vehicle was to be armed with a 2pdr gun (FV 601A) but this was quickly dropped in favour of a 76mm/2.99in gun (FV 601B). The first prototype vehicles were delivered in 1952–53 and were followed by six pre-production vehicles. Further modifications were made to these vehicles as a result of trials, in particular the turret was redesigned. In 1958 the FV 601C or Saladin Mk 2 entered production with the first vehicles being completed in 1959 and entering service the same year. Production continued until 1972, by which time 1,177 Saladins had been built.

The hull and turret of the vehicle were all-welded steel constructions and were proof against small-arms fire and shell splinters. The driver was located in the front of the vehicle on the centreline with a hatch in front that folded down on to the glacis plate. There was powered steering to the four front wheels. The steering wheel was rather oddly fitted sloping into the driver's chest, which took some getting used to. Behind and above the driver was the turret which housed the other two members of the crew. The commander was on the right-hand side of the turret with the gunner on the left. Both had hatches in the roof of the turret and the commander had a pintle mount for a 7.62mm/0.3in machine-gun. There was an escape hatch for the crew

below the turret in each side of the hull, while the engine and three fuel tanks were in the rear of the vehicle. The Saladin was not fitted with any form of NBC system, and did not carry night-driving or night-fighting equipment.

The CVR(T) 76mm/2.99in Scorpion replaced the Saladin in British Army service. Saladins would see service in many parts of the world, their last combat operation being in defence of Kuwait City during the 1991 Gulf War when they destroyed several T-55 MBTs.

Saladin Mk 2 Armoured Car

Country: UK
Entered service: 1959
Crew: 3
Weight: 11,582kg/11.4 tons
Dimensions: Length – 4.92m/16ft 2in
　　　　　Height – 2.92m/8ft 7in
　　　　　Width – 2.53m/8ft 4in
Armament: Main – 76mm/2.99in L5A1 gun,
　　　　　and coaxial 7.62mm/0.3in machine-gun
　　　　　Secondary – 7.62mm/0.3in machine-gun
Armour: Maximum – 16mm/0.63in
Powerplant: Rolls-Royce B80 Mk 6A 8-cylinder
　　　　　127kW/170hp petrol engine
Performance: Speed – 72kph/45mph
　　　　　Range – 400km/250 miles

RIGHT: **A detail of the front of a Saladin. On each side of the front of the turret are two clusters of six smoke dischargers. The driver's hatch has been pushed open; this makes a very useful shelf for a mug of tea.**

LEFT: **A Saracen command vehicle. The tube frame on the rear of the vehicle is for a tent extension to be fitted to increase the working space. This vehicle has been fitted with a turret with a cluster of four smoke dischargers on each side on the top of the vehicle,**
BELOW: **This vehicle has a light machine-gun fitted to the ring mount that is set in the rear of the roof. Most of the vision ports are in the open position; these are not fitted with any form of glass. A fire extinguisher is fitted to the rear mudguard of the Saracen, while camouflage netting has been stored above the centre road wheel.**

Saracen Armoured Personnel Carrier

After World War II, the British Army issued a requirement for a family of vehicles that were all 6x6 configurations. These were given the family designation FV 600. The family was made up of the FV 601 Saladin Armoured Car, the FV 602 Command Vehicle (which was cancelled but was later reincarnated as the FV 604) and the FV 603 Saracen Armoured Personnel Carrier. Development of the Saracen started in 1948 with the first prototype completed in 1952. The first production vehicle was completed in December 1952 and the type entered service in early 1953. The Saracen was rushed into production and given priority over the other vehicles in the family as a result of the emergency in Malaya. The Saracen would remain the main APC of the British Army throughout the 1950s and 1960s until replaced by the FV 432. Production continued until 1972, by which time 1,838 vehicles had been produced. Some of these vehicles are still in service with a few armed forces around the world. All vehicles in the family would share many of the same automotive parts and the unusual steering-wheel angle (see the Saladin). The last vehicle in the family was the Stalwart Amphibious Load Carrier (FV 620).

The hull of the Saracen is an all-welded steel construction, and is proof against small-arms fire and shell splinters. The radiator is in the front of the vehicle with the engine behind. The crew and troop compartments are all one in this vehicle, with the driver's position situated on the centreline in the front of the compartment directly behind the engine. There is no windscreen; the driver looks through a hatch that folds down and lays on the top of the engine in non-combat situations. The troop commander sits behind the driver facing forwards on the left-hand side of the vehicle, and also doubles as vehicle commander. The radio operator sits behind the driver on the right-hand side of the vehicle and also faces forwards. Between the commander and the radio operator is the machine-gun turret position. This is the same type of turret as that fitted to the Ferret Mk 2 armoured car and is un-powered.

LEFT: **This aerial view shows the front turret and the rear ring mount on the roof of the Saracen APC. The turret is fitted with a searchlight on the left-hand side, while two fixed steps at the rear make boarding quicker for the infantry.**

LEFT: **This Saracen has all the vision ports in the open position and the driver's hatch is in the half-open position. The Saracen has a cluster of three smoke dischargers on each front mudguard. The headlights proved to be very vulnerable to damage.**
ABOVE: **A Saracen on exercise in Britain. The driver has his hatch in the open position, while the vehicle commander is talking into the radio. The Saracen can continue to operate with a damaged wheel on each side of the vehicle.**

In the rear of the compartment is accommodation for eight troops, who sit four down each side facing inwards. There are two large doors in the rear of the vehicle, each of which has a firing port. These are the main entrance and exit from the vehicle for the crew and the troops. Below the doors are two steps and between them is a large towing hitch. In the rear of the roof behind the turret is a large sliding hatch which gives access to a ring-mounted anti-aircraft machine-gun which was initially an LMG, better known as the World War II Bren gun. Subsequently, this was replaced by a 7.62mm/0.3in machine-gun. There are also three firing ports in each side of the vehicle. The Saracen has no NBC system, night-driving or night-fighting equipment and is not amphibious, but can ford shallow water. Along with the other vehicles in the family, the Saracen can continue to operate on the battlefield even if it loses two wheels as a result of mine explosions, provided the wheels are lost one from each side.

The FV 603C was a tropical version of the Saracen. These were built mainly for Kuwait and had reverse-flow cooling. The air was sucked in at the rear of the engine, passed over the engine and out through the radiator. Libya also placed an order for these vehicles but they were never delivered due to the political situation, the Libyan vehicles being taken over by the British Army and sent to Northern Ireland. The FV 604 Command Vehicle was modified for the command role and had a crew of six, with map-boards and extra radios inside. The FV 610 was another command vehicle but was taller and wider than the FV 604 and saw service with the British Army in Northern Ireland. The FV 610 could also be fitted with FACE (Field Artillery Computer Equipment) and was trialled with the Robert Radar System but this progressed no further than a trials vehicle. The FV 611 was the ambulance version of the Saracen and could accommodate ten walking-wounded or three stretcher cases and medical personnel. Some of these vehicles remain in service around the world to this day.

BELOW: **This Saracen command vehicle has been fitted with an additional layer of armour. The cut-out around the driver's visors can be seen. The ring mount from the rear of the roof has been moved forward for the vehicle commander, as the turret has been removed.**

Saracen Armoured Personnel Carrier

Country: UK
Entered service: 1953
Crew: 2 plus 10 infantry
Weight: 10,160kg/10 tons
Dimensions: Length – 5.23m/17ft 2in
 Height – 2.46m/8ft 1in
 Width – 2.53m/8ft 4in
Armament: Main – 7.62mm/0.3in machine-gun
 Secondary –7.62mm/0.3in machine-gun
Armour: Maximum – 16mm/0.63in
Powerplant: Rolls-Royce B80 Mk 6A 8-cylinder
 127kW/170hp petrol engine
Performance: Speed – 72kph/45mph
 Range – 400km/250 miles

Saxon Armoured Personnel Carrier

In 1970, GKN Sankey started a private venture development of a wheeled personnel carrier for use in the internal security role. The development vehicle was known as the AT 104. It had the engine mounted at the front of the vehicle similar to the Saracen and although the armour around the engine was poor, the floor of the vehicle was redesigned to give better anti-mine protection. The first prototype vehicle of an improved design was produced in 1974, entering production in 1976 for the export market only with the designation AT 105. The name "Saxon" was not given to the vehicle officially until 1982. After further development, production would start for the British Army in 1983 and the Saxon entered service in 1984. Over 800 of these vehicles have been produced, with some 600 serving with the British Army.

The hull of the Saxon is an all-welded steel construction that gives the crew protection from small-arms fire and shell splinters. The floor of the vehicle is V-shaped, giving the crew and troops inside some protection from mines. The axles, however, are not protected. The chassis and automotive parts are taken from the Bedford MK design and these standard parts make logistics easier. However, to remove the engine the roof of the vehicle needs to be taken off which is time-consuming, requires heavy equipment, and makes maintenance in the field difficult.

The Saxon can be built in left- and right-hand drive versions. The driver's compartment is in the front of the vehicle on either the left- or right-hand side as required and can be accessed from the main troop compartment or from a large single hatch

in the roof of the driving compartment. The driver has three large bullet-proof vision blocks, one to the front and one in each side. The engine compartment is next to the driver, on either the right or the left of the vehicle depending on the configuration. The radiator grill is mounted in the front of the vehicle with the air outlet on the side of the vehicle, and again this is installed on one side or the other depending on the driving position.

Behind and above the driver's position is the vehicle commander's fixed cupola which is a four-sided box with all-round vision blocks and a large single hatch in the roof. There are machine-gun pintle mounts on each side of the cupola for a single 7.62mm/0.3in GPMG. As this cupola is only bolted to the roof of the vehicle, it can be replaced very quickly with a manually traversed machine-gun turret which can be armed with a single or twin 7.62mm/0.3in machine-gun. Alongside the commander's position in the hull of the vehicle is a single large door which in British service is normally fitted on the right-hand side of the vehicle, but again this door can be moved to the other side of the vehicle or two side doors can be fitted as required. The main troop compartment holds eight men, four down each side of the vehicle facing inwards. In the rear of the Saxon are two large doors that are the main exit and entrance for the infantry section using the vehicle. Each door is fitted with both a vision block and a firing port and there is another firing port in the front of the vehicle next to the driver. The British Army has fitted large storage boxes to the sides of the vehicle and a mesh rack to the roof behind the commander's cupola to improve personal equipment storage.

The Saxon recovery vehicle, designed to recover vehicles of its own type and soft-skin trucks, has been in service with the British Army for many years. This has a crew of four and a 5,080kg/5-ton hydraulic winch mounted on the left-hand side of the vehicle. A tent can be fitted to the vehicle to act as a covered workshop. In 2005, the Saxon was undergoing an upgrade programme and a Cummins diesel engine was being substituted for the original Bedford diesel engine. A command vehicle has also been developed for the British Army and the Royal Air Force for use with the Rapier missile batteries.

ABOVE: **This is a British Army Saxon recovery vehicle, which is fitted with a 5,080kg/5-ton hydraulic winch. The large side-mounted hull door was removed from these vehicles to allow for increased equipment storage.**

ABOVE: **The headlights of the Saxon are built into the front of the vehicle to give them better protection. The high ground-clearance of the body of the vehicle, which gives the infantry inside the Saxon some protection from land mines, can be clearly seen.** BELOW: **The turret of this Saxon has been fitted with a 7.62mm/0.3in GPMG. A hessian screen, which is rolled down when the vehicle is parked to help camouflage it, has been attached to the lower hull of the Saxon. The driver's hatch is open and folded forward. The spare wheel can be clearly seen attached to the underside of the vehicle.**

Saxon Armoured Personnel Carrier

Country: UK
Entered service: 1984
Crew: 2 plus 8 infantry
Weight: 11,684kg/11.5 tons
Dimensions: Length – 5.17m/17ft
    Height – 2.63m/8ft 7in
    Width – 2.49m/8ft 2in
Armament: Main – 7.62mm/0.3in GPMG
    Secondary – Small arms
Armour: Classified
Powerplant: Cummins 6BT 6-cylinder
    122kW/160hp diesel engine
Performance: Speed – 96kph/60mph
    Range – 510km/317 miles

Scud Missile System TEL

The Scud missile system was developed in response to the Soviet Army's requirement in the early 1950s for a tactical missile system that could deliver both conventional and nuclear warheads. This was to replace the Soviet-developed R-1 and R-2 missiles, which were based on the German V2 ballistic missile. These battery systems required 152 trucks, 70 trailers and over 500 men and could only fire 9 missiles per day. The new missile was called the R-11 (NATO codename Scud A). Its first test flight was in April 1953 and production began in 1955. The first TEL (Tractor, Erector and Launcher) was developed using the ISU-152 (Obiekt 218) tank chassis. These TEL vehicles, known as 8U218, entered service with the Soviet forces in 1955. They were deployed at the density of one regiment per army; each regiment being composed of three batteries, each of which had three TEL vehicles. These 9 TEL vehicles were supported by 200 trucks and 1,200 personnel and had an allocation of 27 missiles per day. It is believed that 100 TEL vehicles were built for the Soviet Army. In 1960 Khrushchev ordered that Soviet heavy tank production should be stopped and the decision was taken to develop a new TEL.

This new vehicle was based on the MAZ-543LTM 8x8 heavy truck, a standard Soviet heavy truck design. The wheeled chassis has many advantages over the tracked chassis. It provides a smoother ride which causes less vibration damage to the missile and the control and test equipment on the vehicle, and is a more reliable and cost-effective vehicle, with only a slight decrease in cross-country performance compared to the tracked chassis. The vehicle has a full set of power-assisted controls for the steering and gearbox which makes it easy to drive. All the wheels are connected to a central tyre pressure system that is regulated from the driver's position.

The vehicle was given the official designation of 9P117 TEL and the official name of "Uragan" (Hurricane) but was

TOP: **A Soviet Scud missile TEL about to take part in a November Parade. The compartment between the second and third wheels is the main fire control centre. The compartment on the other side of the vehicle holds the auxiliary power unit.** ABOVE: **A Soviet Scud B is halfway up to the vertical firing position, while the Scud behind is in the firing position. The six-man launch crew is attaching the control cables to the missile as it is being raised.**

popularly known as the "Kashalot" (Sperm Whale) by the Soviet Army because of its size. The driver is situated in the front of the left-hand crew compartment and has a very simple set of controls. Behind the driver is a member of the launch crew with a set of compressed air bottles between them which supply the power for the cold weather starter. The other crew compartment on the right side of the vehicle has the vehicle commander, the main communications equipment and the fourth crew member in it. Between the two crew compartments is the radiator and main engine, which is not shielded and can betray the vehicle's position with its heat signature. The exhaust from this comes out between the first and second wheels. Behind the crew cabins is an APU that is used when the main engine is shut down.

The missile and its erector are carried in a cavity down the centre of the vehicle when in the travelling mode. In the centre of the vehicle are two control cabins. The left-hand cabin houses the main selector switches and an auxiliary power unit. The right-hand cabin has accommodation for the targeting controls and missile testing equipment, along with seats for two crew members. The vehicle carries its own launching base-plate which is hydraulically operated and is folded up against the rear of the vehicle when in the travelling mode. Between this base-plate and the vehicle are two large stabilizing jacks that help support the weight of the missile when it is in the erect position. On the left-hand side at the rear of the vehicle is the main safety catch for the missile; this is a simple mechanical slide that is moved under the fuel pump switches.

The Scud B was first used in action during the war between Egypt and Israel in 1973. The next major use of the system was between 1986 and 1988 during the "War of the Cities" between Iran and Iraq. Long-range versions of the Scud were fired against Israel and Saudi Arabia during the 1991 Gulf War, but the largest number of missiles was fired by the Soviets during the Afghan War (1979–89) when 1,000 were fired against mountain villages.

TOP: **The two separate crew compartments with the radiator and missile warhead between them can be clearly seen. The driver's cab is on the left-hand side of the vehicle, while in the rear of the cab are a crew member and the compressed-air starting system for the vehicle.** ABOVE: **On the rear of the vehicle are two hydraulic jacks that are lowered into position before the missile is raised. The firing platform swings down with the missile resting on it. There are access ladders on the arms of the cradle.** MIDDLE LEFT: **A Scud TEL taking part in a parade. The front four wheels are used for steering the vehicle, with the exhaust system exiting between the first and second wheels. The large clamp just behind the warhead attaches the missile to the TEL.**

LEFT: **The red dot on the vehicle is a heavy canvas security blind covering the little window in the control cabin. The small ladder above the third wheel swings down to give access to the top of the TEL.**

MAZ 9P117 TEL

Country: USSR
Entered service: 1965
Crew: 4
Weight: 37,400kg/36.4 tons
Dimensions: Length – 13.36m/43ft 9in
Height – 3.33m/10ft 10in
Width – 3.02m/9ft 10in
Armament: Main – R300 missile
Secondary – None
Armour: None
Powerplant: D12A-525A 12-cylinder 391kW/525hp diesel engine
Performance: Speed – 45kph/28mph
Range – 450km/280 miles

Spartan Armoured Personnel Carrier

The Spartan was a development of the Scorpion CVR(T) and entered service with the British Army in 1978. It was designed to perform in a number of roles that the Saracen 6x6 APC had previously filled, but was not designed as a direct replacement for the FV 432 APC. Subsequently, this very adaptable vehicle has been deployed as a carrier for the Royal Artillery Blowpipe/Javelin surface-to-air missile teams, as a missile reload vehicle for the Striker and as a carrier for Royal Engineer assault teams. By 2001, 960 Spartan vehicles had been built. The late production vehicles have an improved suspension and a new fuel-efficient Cummins diesel engine fitted, and a large number of the early production vehicles have also now had these improvements fitted.

While officially the Spartan is designated as an APC, it can only carry four men in the rear of the vehicle. Its hull is an all-welded aluminium construction which is proof against small-arms fire and shell splinters. The driver is located in the front of the vehicle on the left-hand side and has a wide-angle periscope which can be replaced by passive night-driving equipment. Next to the driver on the right-hand side is the Jaguar 4.2-litre petrol engine, with air intakes and outlets on the glacis plate while the exhaust is on the roof on the right-hand side. The vehicle commander/gunner is behind the driver and is provided with a cupola mounted in the vehicle roof with eight periscopes, which provide all-round vision. Mounted on the right of the cupola is a 7.62mm/0.3in machine-gun

ABOVE LEFT: **A Spartan fitted with the Euromissile MILAN MCT turret. The launcher rails are empty on this vehicle. The long sloping glacis plate can clearly be seen.** ABOVE: **This Spartan has both the driver's and commander's hatches open. The driver's hatch opens towards the front of the vehicle. The Spartan has two clusters of three smoke dischargers fitted to the glacis plate.**

which can be aimed and fired from inside the vehicle. Next to the commander on the right of the vehicle is the troop commander/radio operator, who also has a hatch in the roof. In the rear of the vehicle is the troop compartment which holds four men, one seated behind the troop commander and three others on a bench seat on the left-hand side. Entry and exit from the vehicle is via a large single door in the rear.

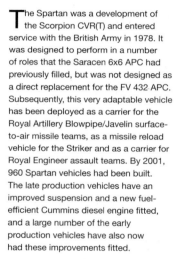

ABOVE: **A group of soldiers loading their sleeping bags into the back of the Spartan. The commander's cupola has its hatch in the open position.**

Spartan APC

Country: UK
Entered service: 1978
Crew: 2 plus 5 infantry
Weight: 8,128kg/8 tons
Dimensions: Length – 5.13m/16ft 11in
  Height – 2.26m/7ft 5in
  Width – 2.24m/7ft 4in
Armament: Main – 7.62mm/0.3in machine-gun
  Secondary – Small arms
Armour: Classified
Powerplant: Jaguar J60 No.1 Mk 100B 6-cylinder
  142kW/190hp petrol engine
Performance: Speed – 80kph/50mph
  Range – 483km/301 miles

LEFT: **An infantry section debussing from a Stormer IFV. The vehicle is armed with a Helio FVT 900 turret which is fitted with a 20mm/0.79in cannon. In the hull of the vehicle are firing ports for the infantry to use from inside the vehicle.** BELOW: **A Stormer fitted with a two-man turret, armed with a 30mm/1.18in cannon and coaxial 7.62mm/0.3in machine-gun. The vehicle can carry 165 rounds of ammunition for the main gun.**

Stormer Armoured Personnel Carrier

Development of the FV 4333 started at the Military Vehicle and Engineering Establishment in the 1970s and the first prototype was displayed in 1978. Alvis took over the development of the vehicle in June 1981, giving it the name "Stormer" and making it part of the CVR(T) family, as it uses many of the same automotive parts as the other members of this group. The Stormer is actually a stretched version of the Spartan with increased chassis length and an extra road wheel. Production began in 1982, for export orders only at first, with the first vehicles entering service with the Malaysian armed forces in 1983. In 1986 the British Army selected the Stormer for three roles: the Shielder anti-tank mine dispenser vehicle; a launch vehicle for the Starstreak SAM high-velocity missile

which entered service in 1989; and a reconnaissance vehicle for the Starstreak. Alvis have also produced a number of variations on the basic Stormer chassis but as yet none has been placed in production.

The hull of the Stormer is an all-welded aluminium construction and is proof against small-arms fire and shell splinters. The driver is located in the front of the vehicle on the left-hand side and has a single wide-angle periscope that can be replaced by passive night-driving equipment. The engine compartment is located next to the driver on the right. Behind the driver is the vehicle commander/gunner's position, which has a cupola in the roof with eight periscopes providing all-round vision and also mounts a 7.62mm/0.3in machine-gun. The radio operator/troop

commander's position is next to the vehicle commander, and behind this is the crew compartment, which accommodates eight infantry, four down each side on bench seats facing inwards. The main access point, a single large door with a vision block, is at the rear of the vehicle.

The Stormer and other members of the CVR family have a full NBC system and are air-portable. They can ford water to a depth of 1.1m/3ft 7in in their normal combat mode but, with a little preparation and the raising of a flotation screen, they become fully amphibious, propelling themselves in the water with their tracks.

LEFT: **A Stormer air defence vehicle armed with the Starstreak SAM system. The missiles are stored in their launch boxes, each box holding four missiles. A full reload is carried inside the vehicle. The flotation screen can be seen in its stored position around the edge of the vehicle.**

Stormer APC

Country: UK
Entered service: 1983
Crew: 3 plus 8 infantry
Weight: 12,700kg/12.5 tons
Dimensions: Length – 5.33m/17ft 6in
  Height – 2.27m/7ft 5in
  Width – 2.69m/8ft 10in
Armament: Main – 7.62mm/0.3in machine-gun
  Secondary – Small arms
Armour: Classified
Powerplant: Perkins T6/3544 6-cylinder
  186kW/250hp diesel engine
Performance: Speed – 80kph/50mph
  Range – 650km/400 miles

LEFT: **A Striker on a live-firing exercise. This vehicle has just launched one of the five Swingfire AT missiles that are carried in the launcher at the rear of the vehicle. The back-blast generated by the Swingfire on launching is small and so does not give away the position of the vehicle.**
BELOW: **The driver of this Striker is in his position with his hatch lying on the glacis plate. The exhaust system runs back down the right-hand side of the vehicle. At the end of the protective cover, the exhaust turns through 90 degrees and goes straight up for about 31cm/12in.**

Striker Self-Propelled Anti-Tank Guided Weapon Vehicle

The Striker (FV 102) is part of the Scorpion CVR(T) family. The first production vehicles entered service with the British Army in 1975. The Striker uses many of the same automotive parts as the other members of the CVR family and has been designed to be an air-portable anti-tank missile system capable of destroying MBTs. Having a similar performance to the Scorpion, the Striker can move in and out of unprepared positions very quickly and is well suited to "shoot and scoot" missions. During their service careers, both the Striker vehicle and the Swingfire missile system have been upgraded but are now being phased out, as the "Spartan" vehicles, armed with the

MILAN anti-tank guided missile, are entering service with the British Army.

The hull of the Striker is an all-welded aluminium construction, and is proof against small-arms fire and shell splinters. The driver is located in the front of the vehicle on the left-hand side, with the engine next to him on the right of the vehicle. The commander/gunner is situated behind the driver, and has a cupola above his position that has all-round vision and is armed with a 7.62mm/0.3in machine-gun. Next to the vehicle commander is the guided-weapons controller. He has a sight mounted above his position – as the Swingfire is a wire-guided system – the controller has to follow the flight of the missile, which can be guided on to the target by using a joystick. The missile system can operate either in daylight or in night-time conditions and can be fired from

inside or outside the vehicle. Behind the vehicle commander's cupola is a box structure holding five ready-to-use Swingfire missiles. To bring it into the firing position the box front is elevated to 35 degrees from the horizontal. Five further missiles, accessed through a large single door, are carried in the rear of the vehicle. Reloading is performed outside the vehicle.

The Striker is capable of fording 1.1m/3ft 7in of water without preparation, but the vehicle becomes fully amphibious by fitting a flotation screen, using its tracks to propel itself through the water.

LEFT: **On the front of the Striker are two clusters of three smoke dischargers. The headlights are attached to the front of the vehicle by simple brackets.**

Striker SP ATGW Vehicle	
Country: UK	
Entered service: 1975	
Crew: 3	
Weight: 8,331kg/8.2 tons	
Dimensions: Length – 4.83m/15ft 10in	
Height – 2.28m/7ft 6in	
Width – 2.28m/7ft 6in	
Armament: Main – 10 x Swingfire Wire-Guided Missiles	
Secondary – 7.62mm/0.3in machine-gun	
Armour: Classified	
Powerplant: Jaguar J60 No.1 Mk 100B 6-cylinder 142kW/190hp	
Performance: Speed – 80kph/50mph	
Range – 483km/301 miles	

LEFT: **Two of the driver's vision blocks have been covered to protect the vision port. The turret on the roof of the vehicle is a Creusot-Loire TLI 127, and is armed with a 12.7mm/0.5in heavy machine-gun and a coaxial 7.62/0.3in machine-gun.**
ABOVE: **A Belgian BDX APC used by the air force for airfield defence. A 7.62mm/0.3in machine-gun is mounted on the top of the shield on the vehicle roof. Just in front of the turret on each side of the hull is a bank of three smoke dischargers.**

Timoney Armoured Personnel Carrier

Due to the troubles in Northern Ireland, the Government of the Irish Republic decided to expand the army in the early 1970s, aiming for between 100 and 200 APC vehicles. In 1972 the Irish Army issued a requirement for a 4x4 armoured personnel carrier that could be used anywhere in the world operating under United Nations control. The Timoney brothers came up with a design, producing the first prototype in 1973. There were a large number of technical faults with this prototype vehicle, which were rectified to produce the Mk II in April 1974, and this was then put on trial with the Irish Army. After further improvements to the basic design, the Mk III was produced in 1976. Further development produced the Mk IV, of which only five vehicles were built. The final vehicle produced by Timoney in the series was the Mk VI, but again only five units were ever manufactured.

The hull of the Mk V was an all-welded steel construction, which was proof against small-arms fire and shell splinters. The vehicle could also withstand the blast from a 9kg/20lb mine. The driver was positioned in the front of the vehicle on the centreline, and had a windscreen to the front and one to each side. There were three doors in the vehicle, one in each side and one in the rear. The engine compartment was to the rear of the driver with the air louvers in the roof. There was a manual machine-gun turret armed with a single 7.62mm/0.3in machine-gun in the centre of the roof. The troop compartment in the rear had seats for ten men. The vehicle was fully amphibious, propelling itself through the water using its wheels.

The Belgian company Beherman Demoen negotiated a licence to produce the APC in 1976. Their vehicle, put into production in 1982, was called the BDX Armoured Personnel Carrier. In total 123 of these were produced, 43 for the Belgian Air Force and 80 for the Gendarmerie. The design was then bought by Vickers who developed the vehicle further and called it the "Valkyr", but no further vehicles were sold.

Timoney Mk V/BDX APC

Country: Eire (Republic of Ireland)
Entered service: 1982
Crew: 2 plus 10 infantry
Weight: 9,957kg/9.8 tons
Dimensions: Length – 4.95m/16ft 3in
Height – 2.75m/9ft
Width – 2.5m/8ft 3in
Armament: Main – 7.62mm/0.3in machine-gun
Secondary – Small arms
Armour: Maximum – 12.7mm/0.5in
Powerplant: Chrysler 8-cylinder 134kW/180hp petrol engine
Performance: Speed – 100kph/62mph
Range – 700km/430 miles

LEFT: A Warrior at speed during training in the Gulf. The driver and vehicle commander have their hatches open. Crews of AFVs had to be taught how to drive in the desert so as not to create a dust cloud. On the rear of the vehicle is a large storage bin for personal equipment. ABOVE: One of the Warrior development vehicles. The vehicle is fitted with several clusters of four infrared and smoke screening dischargers. On the turret are a further four smoke dischargers on each side. The driver's entry hatch is mounted on the sloped side of the vehicle hull.

Warrior Mechanised Combat Vehicle

The British Army's FV 432 entered service in the 1960s and was due for replacement by 1985. Development of the MCV-80 as the replacement vehicle started with various studies being carried out between 1967 and 1977, when the detailed design work started. By 1980, three prototype vehicles were being tested and these were followed by a further seven vehicles which were completed in 1984. In the same year development of MCV-80 variants and derivative vehicles started. In 1985 GKN Defence Operations were awarded three contracts for 1,048 MCV-80 vehicles, and it was given the name "Warrior" by the British Army. Production started in January 1986, the first vehicle being produced in December 1986. The first batch of vehicles numbered 290, consisting of 170 section vehicles and 120 of the specialized vehicles. Once production started the British Army would take delivery of 140 vehicles per year, and 70 per cent of the 1,048 Warriors ordered would be section vehicles. Vickers Defence Systems manufacture the turret in a modular form ready to drop into a vehicle on the production line, while Rolls-Royce do the same with the engine pack which is made up of the engine, the transmission and the cooling system. The first three variants under development, the Infantry Command Vehicle, the Artillery Observation Vehicle and a Repair and Recovery Vehicle, were all completed in 1985. Unfortunately, the cost of the Warrior has meant that by 2004 it had still not fully replaced the FV 432.

The hull of the Warrior is of an all-welded aluminium construction, and is proof against small-arms fire and shell splinters. The driver is located in the front of the vehicle on the left-hand side, with a single large hatch over his position that is fitted with a wide-angle periscope which can be changed for a passive night-sight. The engine is next to the driver on the right-hand side and is a Rolls-Royce Condor. This is linked to a

ABOVE: The RARDEN-armed turret is covered in camouflage netting. Modern camouflage netting helps hide the vehicle on the battlefield from infrared and other sensors that are now carried by modern reconnaissance aircraft. The headlight clusters are mounted on the leading edge of the glacis.

Detroit Diesel automatic transmission with four forward and two reverse gears made under licence by Rolls-Royce. The Warrior is fitted with a full NBC system and night-fighting equipment.

The two-man turret is a steel construction mounted in the centre of the vehicle but slightly offset to the left of the centreline. The vehicle commander sits on the right-hand side of the turret, with the gunner on the left. The vehicle commander can also double as the infantry section leader and can debus with the troops. The turret is armed with a 30mm/1.18in L21A1 cannon and a coaxial 7.62mm/0.3in machine-gun. The cannon can fire single rounds, a burst of six rounds or a high rate of 80 rounds per minute, all spent shell

LEFT: **All the crew of this Warrior have their hatches open. The driver's side hatch has gone and the main driver's hatch can now open fully to the left. A Spartan CVR(T) is following close behind.**
BELOW: **A pair of Warrior vehicles on a live-firing range. The low height of the turret can clearly be seen from the instructor standing on the rear of the vehicle. On each side of the rear door on the back of the Warrior are large equipment storage containers. A wire-mesh storage box has been fitted to one of the roof hatches in the rear of the Warrior.**

cases being expelled outside the turret. However, there have been a few problems with the main gun, in particular with accidental discharge.

The troop compartment is at the rear of the vehicle and holds seven men, four on the right and three on the left-hand side of the vehicle, each man having his own seat and seat belt. There is no provision for the infantry to fire their weapons from inside the Warrior. The main entrance and exit for the infantry section is a single power-operated door with a vision port in it in the rear of the vehicle, and above the troop compartment is a large double hatch which, when opened, lies flat on the top of the vehicle. There are storage baskets on the rear of the vehicle for personal kit as there is insufficient room for this inside.

There are three different command versions of the Warrior – Platoon, Company and Battalion, the main difference between these vehicles being the communications equipment fitted.

The Warrior Repair and Recovery Vehicle has a 6,502kg/6.4-ton crane and a 20,015kg/19.7-ton capstan winch, and also a hydraulically operated ground anchor which allows the vehicle to pull 38,000kg/37.4 tons. Other vehicles of the Warrior family serving with the British Army are the Artillery Observation Vehicle and the Battery Command Vehicle. A desert version of the Warrior has been developed for the export market and this has been bought by Kuwait as the Warrior proved to be a very reliable vehicle during the Gulf War of 1991.

ABOVE: **This Warrior is on active service with British forces in Bosnia. It has been fitted with appliqué armour to the sides and front of the vehicle. The Warrior has proved to be a reliable and strong vehicle in combat.**

Warrior Mechanised Combat Vehicle

Country: UK
Entered service: 1985
Crew: 3 plus 7 infantry
Weight: 24,486kg/24.1 tons
Dimensions: Length – 6.34m/20ft 10in
　　　Height – 2.79m/9ft 2in
　　　Width – 3.03m/9ft 11in
Armament: Main – 30mm/1.18in RARDEN cannon, and coaxial 7.62mm/0.3in machine-gun
　　　Secondary – Small arms
Armour: Classified
Powerplant: Perkins CV8 TCA 8-cylinder 141kW/190hp diesel engine
Performance: Speed – 75kph/47mph
　　　Range – 660km/412 miles

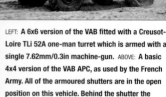

LEFT: **A 6x6 version of the VAB fitted with a Creusot-Loire TLi 52A one-man turret which is armed with a single 7.62mm/0.3in machine-gun.** ABOVE: **A basic 4x4 version of the VAB APC, as used by the French Army. All of the armoured shutters are in the open position on this vehicle. Behind the shutter the vision ports are protected by bullet-proof glass.**

VAB Armoured Personnel Carrier

In the late 1960s the French Army issued a requirement for a wheeled APC, as the tracked AMX-10 was proving to be too expensive and complex to fill all the roles required of it. This was further extended in 1970 when a requirement for a Forward Area Control Vehicle (*Véhicule de l'Avant Blinde*, VAB) was identified. The French Army tested 4x4 and 6x6 versions between 1972 and 1974, eventually selecting the Renault 4x4 vehicle to fulfil both roles. Production started in 1976 and the first vehicles entered service in 1977.

The basic vehicle used by the French is the VAB VTT (*Véhicule Transport de Troupe*). Its hull is an all-welded steel construction, proof against small-arms fire and shell splinters, with an NBC system. The driver sits at the front of the vehicle on the left-hand side, with the vehicle commander/gunner beside him on the right. In front of them is a bullet-proof windscreen. Both have access doors in the side of the cab opening towards the front of the vehicle and hatches above their positions. The commander also has a machine-gun mount, the Creusot-Loire type CB 52, armed with a 7.62mm/0.3in machine-gun. This can be replaced with a TLi 52A turret or CB 127 12.7mm/0.5in gun and shield.

The engine compartment is behind the driver with the air intake and outlet in the roof. On the right-hand side of the vehicle is a passageway between the crew compartment and the troop compartment in the rear. The ten men in here sit on bench seats, five down each side, while the main access to the vehicle is via two doors in the rear of the VAB. There are two firing ports in each side of the vehicle and one in each door. The VAB is fully amphibious and is propelled in the water by two water jets.

Renault developed a 6x6 vehicle for the export market and offered both for sale. By 1999 the French Army had taken delivery of over 4,000 vehicles and over 700 (6x6 and 4x4 vehicles) had been sold to the export market. There are 13 different variations on the basic vehicle with various types of armament.

LEFT: **Several 6x6 and 4x4 VAB APCs taking part in a French Army exercise. The VAB in the front of the picture has been fitted with a basic ring mount over the roof hatch for a 12.7mm/0.5in heavy machine-gun. The cylinder below the gunner is the exhaust system for the vehicle.**

VAB VTT

Country: France
Entered service: 1977
Crew: 2 plus 10 infantry
Weight: 13,614kg/13.4 tons
Dimensions: Length – 6.1m/20ft
    Height – 2.1m/6ft 11in
    Width – 2.5m/8ft 2in
Armament: Main – 7.62mm/0.3in machine-gun
    Secondary – Small arms
Armour: Classified
Powerplant: Renault MIDS 06.20.45 6-cylinder
    175kW/235hp diesel engine
Performance: Speed – 92kph/57mph
    Range – 1,000km/621 miles

LEFT: **This Shilka has the driver's hatch in the open position. In front of the driver's position is the splash board which helps to prevent water entering there. The main armament is at maximum elevation, and the Gun Dish radar is in the raised position at the rear of the turret.** BELOW: **A Shilka in travelling mode. The radar has been lowered and the guns brought down to the horizontal. To the left is a T-72 MBT and to the right is a BTR-60 PB, in the snow.**

ZSU-23-4 Self-Propelled Anti-Aircraft Gun

In 1960 development started in the Soviet Union on a replacement for the ageing ZSU-57-2, which was too slow, inaccurate and did not have an all-weather capability. The replacement unit carries the Soviet designation *Zenitnaia Samokhodnaia Ustanovka* (ZSU), which mounts a 23-calibre armament (23mm/ 0.91in) of which there are four, hence ZSU-23-4. They also called it "Shilka" after the Russian river of that name. First seen during the 1965 November Parade, having entered service in 1964, its NATO reporting name is "Awl" but it is more popularly known as "Zoo-23". Production finished in 1983 with more than 7,000 vehicles being produced.

The hull and turret are an all-welded steel construction. The glacis plate is proof against small arms and shell splinters, but the turret is susceptible to shell splinter damage. The driver is located at the front of the vehicle on the left-hand side in a small cramped position, with the cold weather starter and battery compartment next to him on the right. His position can be fitted with infrared night-driving equipment. The other three members of the crew are positioned in the rear of the turret, the commander on the left-hand side with the other two beside him, and the guns are separated from the crew by a gas-tight armoured bulkhead. Access to the guns is via two large hatches in the front roof of the turret. The gun barrels are water-cooled, although this is not always satisfactory and when the gunner releases the trigger the guns can still fire several more rounds. The gunner can select either single, twin or all four gun barrels to engage a target. At the rear of the turret is the Gun Dish Radar System which can be folded down into the travel mode when on the move. The engine is in the rear of the Shilka which is fitted with a full NBC system.

The Shilka proved to be a very effective system and during the Middle East War of 1973 it accounted for 31 out of 103 Israeli aircraft shot down. They normally operate in pairs placed 200m/656ft apart, and the vehicle can fire on the move but this decreases the accuracy by 50 per cent.

ZSU-23-4 Shilka SPAAG

Country: USSR
Entered service: 1964
Crew: 4
Weight: 14,021kg/13.8 tons
Dimensions: Length – 6.29m/20ft 8in
   Height – 2.25m/7ft 5in
   Width – 2.95m/9ft 8in
Armament: Main – 4 x AZP-23 23mm/0.91in
   cannon
   Secondary – None
Armour: Maximum – 15mm/0.59in
Powerplant: Model V6R 6-cylinder 179kW/240hp
Performance: Speed – 44kph/27mph
   Range – 260km/160 miles

RIGHT: **The large ammunition magazine running down the side of the turret can be clearly seen. Above the driver's hatch is the very small vision port. The driver has a very poor field of vision when the hatch is closed.**

Glossary

"A" vehicle An armoured vehicle, wheeled or tracked.

AA Anti-Aircraft.

AAGM Anti-Aircraft Guided Missile.

AEV Armoured Engineer Vehicle – AFV based upon an MBT chassis, crewed by engineers with the equipment to carry out engineering tasks.

AFV Armoured Fighting Vehicle – any armoured vehicle, whether tracked or wheeled, normally carrying an offensive weapon.

AP Armour-Piercing – ammunition that will penetrate armour plate rather than shatter or glance off on striking it.

APC Armoured Personnel Carrier – an AFV primarily designed to carry a number of fully equipped infantry soldiers.

APDS Armour-Piercing Discarding Sabot – a form of AP with a small, heavy core surrounded by a calibre-sized casing, which breaks up on leaving the gun muzzle. The core then flies on to the target with added velocity.

APFSDS Armour-Piercing Fin-Stabilized Discarding Sabot – the same as APDS but with a longer, finned core to give better penetration.

APU Auxiliary Power Unit.

ARV Armoured Recovery Vehicle – an AFV based on a tank chassis, crewed by fitters with the equipment to carry out the repair and recovery of most AFVs.

ATGM Anti-Tank Guided Missile.

ATGW Anti-Tank Guided Weapon.

Ausf *Ausführung* (German) – the word used to differentiate between various batches or models of the same type of AFV.

automatic gun A weapon that loads, fires, extracts, ejects and reloads continually while the firing mechanism is engaged and the feed mechanism supplies ammunition.

automatic loader A mechanism which, together with some form of magazine or dispenser, allows for automatic loading of a tank gun, thus dispensing with one crew member.

AVLB Armoured Vehicle Launched Bridge – an AFV based upon a tank chassis, normally crewed by engineers and carrying some type of vehicular bridge.

AVRE Armoured Vehicle Royal Engineers – British nomenclature for an AEV.

"B" vehicle Any unarmoured vehicle normally wheeled. Also known as a "soft-skinned" vehicle.

ball mount A spherical machine-gun mount permitting firing in various directions.

barbette An open-topped turret.

BARV Beach Armoured Recovery Vehicle – an ARV specially designed to recover "drowned" AFVs and keep exits from landing craft clear during assault landings.

bogie Units of a tank's suspension that help to distribute the sprung weight along the track.

BT *Bystrochodny Tankovy* (Russian) – Fast Tank.

bustle Rear storage container on a vehicle (named after the "bustle", the bulge on the back of a lady's skirt in the early 20th century).

"buttoned up" All hatches are shut with the crew inside.

calibre The diameter of the bore of a gun.

Carro Armato (Italian) – Tank.

central tyre pressure system Tyre pressures are controlled from a central position, normally the driver's, to match driving conditions.

chain gun Machine-gun.

Char (French) – Tank.

chassis That part of the vehicle that makes it mobile as opposed to the part for fighting.

closed-down All hatches are shut.

coaxial The mounting of two weapons in the same mount.

cradle The non-recoiling part of the gun mount that allows elevation of the gun about the trunnions, houses the recoil system and guides it in recoil.

Cruiser Tank British term used to describe the series of lighter, faster, less well armoured tanks in between the lights and the mediums. Their role was to attack or counterattack with speed and panache, while the heavier infantry tanks supported the foot soldiers in the main assault. They would be absorbed into the medium range of tanks by the end of World War II. The term is now no longer used.

cupola A small protuberance above the main turret, equipped with vision devices and a protective lid, mainly for use by the tank commander.

CV *Carro Veloce* (Italian) – Fast Vehicle.

CVR(T) Combat Reconnaissance Vehicle (Tracked).

double-baffle Muzzle brake with two holes.

DU Depleted Uranium – a very heavy metal used for the cores of certain types of AP ammunition to give better penetration.

ECM Electronic counter measures.

ERA Explosive Reactive Armour – explosive plates attached to the outside of a tank that explode outwards when struck, thus negating penetration.

fascine A large bundle of pieces of wood (or nowadays metal pipes) carried on an AFV to be dropped into a ditch or hole to enable the tank to cross.

fume extractor A device fitted to the barrel of a tank gun to enable the gases remaining behind after firing to be sucked out of the muzzle before the breech is opened, so that they do not enter the turret during reloading.

FV Fighting Vehicle, usually plus a number – British Defence Department nomenclature for British-built AFVs.

glacis plate The thick armour plate at the front of a tank, normally sloped at an angle so as to deflect enemy shot.

GPMG General Purpose Machine-Gun, typically 7.62mm/0.3in calibre.

hatch An opening complete with cover and often vision devices, giving access in and out by crew members.

HE High-Explosive – the standard bursting explosive.

HE-FRAG High-Explosive Fragmentation.

HEAT High-Explosive Anti-Tank – a type of projectile with a shaped charge that concentrates the explosion into a thin jet enabling it to penetrate armour plate.

Heavy Tank While the heavy tanks of World War I weighed only 28,449kg/ 28 tons, those of World War II were generally in the 50,802–60,963kg/ 50–60-ton bracket, or even heavier. Now they have been incorporated with the mediums under the general term MBT.

HESH High-Explosive Squash-Head – HE filled with plastic explosive that "squashes" on the armour plate before exploding, blowing a "scab" of metal off the inside surface rather than penetrating.

HMG Heavy Machine-Gun, typically 12.7mm/0.5in calibre.

hull The main body of the vehicle above the chassis.

idler The undriven guide wheel carrying the tank track.

IFV Infantry Fighting Vehicle.

Infantry Tank British term. These heavily armoured, relatively slow and, initially, cumbersome tanks were designed primarily to support dismounted infantry attacks, so speed was of little importance. However, infantry tanks like the Churchill would soon show their versatility as the British moved towards the universal tank.

KwK *Kampfwagen Kanone* (German) – Tank Gun.

Light Tank In the past this term was used to describe small, fast, lightly armoured tanks in the 5,080–15,241kg/ 5–15-ton range, used mainly for reconnaissance, liaison and similar tasks. They were also ideal for training purposes because they were cheap and relatively easy to manufacture. In World War II their main reconnaissance role was taken over by armoured cars, but now they are coming more into vogue again with the need for strategic air mobility and the advent of lighter, more powerful weapon systems.

LMG Light Machine-Gun, typically 7.62mm/0.3in calibre.

LVTP Landing Vehicle Tracked Personnel.

mantlet The moveable piece of armour plate that surrounds the hole into which the main armament is fitted into the turret. This hole has to be large enough to allow the gun to elevate and depress. It both protects and conceals this opening.

MBT Main Battle Tank – since World War II this term has been used to cover all types of modern medium and heavy tanks, from about 30,481kg/30 tons upwards to 60,963kg/60 tons and over. MBT is in essence the modern-day term for the British Universal Tank.

Medium Tank In the past this term was used to describe a tank of some 25,402–35,562kg/25–35 tons, reasonably well armoured and armed, with a good all-round performance. A perfect World War II example was the Russian T-34. Medium tanks have now been incorporated under the collective term of MBT.

MILAN *Missile d'Infanterie Léger Anti-Char*.

muzzle brake An attachment screwed on to the end of the gun barrel, deflecting the gases laterally so as to reduce recoil.

NATO North Atlantic Treaty Organization.

NBC Nuclear, Biological and Chemical.

over-pressurization system/over-pressure system Air pressure in a vehicle is raised by one or two atmospheres above outside atmospheric pressure as a crude form of NBC protection.

PAK *Panzer Abwehr Kanone* (German) – Anti-Tank Gun.

pdr Contraction of "pounder" – old British measurement for artillery pieces, which were measured by weight of their shell, e.g. "6pdr" – six-pounder.

pistol ports An opening in a vehicle allowing small arms to be used from inside.

portee Vehicle transporter for an artillery piece.

prime mover Dedicated tractor unit, for example one whose first job is to shift guns.

pulpit Slang term for a raised gunner's or driver's position.

PzKpfw *Panzerkampfwagen* (German) – Tank.

rifling The spiral grooves in the bore of the gun that impart accuracy and stability to a projectile in flight.

RNAS Royal Naval Air Service: the naval arm of the British military air forces between 1911 and 1918.

roadwheel One of the wheels in contact with the track, which supports the tank.

run-flat tyres These can be driven on even after punctures for around 30km/18 miles.

SAM Surface-to-Air Missile.

SAMM Surface-to-Air Mobile Missile.

Sd Kfz German abbreviation for *Sonderkraftfahrzeug*: Special Purpose Motor Vehicles.

section vehicle Either a platoon commander's vehicle or a vehicle which can carry an infantry section of 10 men.

"seek and destroy" missions Hunting missions.

semi-automatic gun A gun that requires the trigger to be pulled for each round fired.

separated ammunition Ammunition that requires separate loading of the projectile, propelling charge and primer.

"shoot and scoot" missions Ability to deliver approximately three rounds of fire on target and then speedily leave the area before the enemy can detect position and destroy.

skirting plates or side skirts Sheets of thin armour that hang in front of the upper run of the tracks and suspension. These cause HEAT projectiles to explode and thus dissipate their main force before reaching the hull.

SPAAG Self-Propelled Anti-Aircraft Gun.

spaced armour Armour built in two layers with a space in between.

SP ATGW Self-Propelled Anti-Tank Guided Weapon.

SPAT Self-Propelled Anti-Tank – an anti-tank gun mounted on either wheels or tracks with an engine, so that it does not need a towing vehicle.

SPG/H Self-Propelled Gun/Howitzer.

sponson A projection mounting a weapon, located upon a tank hull.

sprocket A toothed wheel which engages with the track to drive it, and is itself driven by the engine.

standardized (of US vehicles) Term used when a vehicle is accepted into service with the US Army and given a military designation.

suspension The wheels, tracks, rollers, roadwheels, bogies etc, on which the tank runs.

sustained rate of fire Rate of fire which a gun-crew can keep up over a period of time, not just for a short burst.

TD Tank Destroyer – a self-propelled anti-tank gun on a similar chassis to a tank but normally with lighter armour and an open top.

thermal sleeve An insulated cover to keep the gun barrel at an even temperature and reduce differential expansion, which otherwise causes barrel bend and inaccuracy.

TOW missile Tube-launched, Optically-tracked, Wire-guided missile.

track The part of a tank that is in contact with the ground and is guided by the idler, sprocket and top rollers.

track grousers Attachments to tracks for extra grip over soft ground or ice.

turret basket The floor attached to the rotating turret, so that the crew are rotated as the turret turns.

Universal Tank By 1945 British policy was moving towards the universal tank chassis, capable of mounting larger calibre guns and being continually improved. The Centurion is a perfect example, combining as it did the best qualities of the cruiser and infantry tanks, but with far superior firepower and performance.

uparmoured Increases in the original basic armour fitted to a vehicle.

vision slot/slit An opening in the hull or turret through which a crew member can get a limited view outside.

Warsaw Pact A military alliance of the USSR and its satellite countries set up in 1955 to offer mutual assistance against any attacks.

water jet Hydro-drive underwater propellant system.

weapon station Weapons firing position.

Key to flags

For the specification boxes, the national flag that was current at the time of the vehicle's use is shown.

Argentina

Australia

Austria

Belgium

Brazil

Canada

China

Croatia

Czechoslovakia

Eire (Republic of Ireland)

France

Germany: World War I

Germany: World War II

Germany

Hungary

India

Israel

Italy: World Wars I and II

Italy

Japan

Netherlands

Poland

Romania

Russia

South Africa (pre-democracy)

South Africa (post-democracy)

South Korea

Spain

Sweden

Switzerland

UK

Ukraine

USA

USSR

Acknowledgements

George Forty would like to thank the staff of the Tank Museum, Bovington, especially David Fletcher, Janice Tait and Roland Groom, for all their help.

Jack Livesey would also like to thank David Fletcher at the Tank Museum, Bovington, and his staff, the DAS MT Section, Duxford, and the Cambridge Branch of MAFVA, for all their help and advice. A special thank you to Bridget Pollard for all her encouragement and help, especially "de-jargoning".

The publisher would like to thank the following for the use of their pictures in the book (l=left, r=right, t=top, b=bottom, m=middle, um=upper middle, lm=lower middle). Every effort has been made to acknowledge the

pictures properly; however, we apologize if there are any unintentional omissions, which will be corrected in future editions.

After the Battle: 327tl.
© Crown Copyright/MOD. Reproduced with the permission of the Controller of Her Majesty's Stationery Office: 13tl; 13tr; 45b; 164bl; 175t; 175m; 176b; 177m.
Deutsche Panzermuseum Munster: 52t.
Simon Dunstan: 36t; 36b; 37t (US Army); 37m (US Army); 37b (US Marine Corps); 161tr; 170t; 188t; 188b; 189br; 195tl; 195m; 197t; 197m; 203ml.
David Eshel: 16t; 40t; 40b; 41tl; 41tr; 41b; 159m; 166b; 187t; 209t; 209b; 210t; 210b; 211t; 211m; 211b; 216t; 220t; 220m; 220b; 227t; 227m; 227b.

Bob Fleming: 230b.
George Forty: 18b; 26t; 26b; 27t; 27br; 28–9t; 30t; 30b; 32b; 33tr; 33b; 34t; 35bl; 35br; 38; 39tr; 42l; 42r; 44; 45tl; 45tr; 45mr; 48b; 57br; 80m; 85t; 108tr; 108b; 140b; 141m; 148b; 152tr; 164m; 165b; 168m; 173t; 194t; 201t; 201b; 207b; 208tr; 213t; 213m; 213b; 214t; 214b; 219b; 221t; 254b.
Christopher F. Foss: 162t; 162b; 163t; 163b; 164t; 170b (Indian MoD); 171m; 171b; 173b; 182b; 190t; 190m; 190b; 191t; 203tr; 205t; 205b; 218t; 218b; 223b; 228b; 236m; 240t; 240b; 241t; 241b; 243b; 244b; 245b; 247m; 247b; 248; 249t; 249b; 251t; 252bl; 252br.
General Dynamics Land Systems Division: 12b; 160t; 161m.
Richard P. Hunnicutt: 109tl (US Army); 199b; 204t

(US Army); 212m (US Army); 212b (US Army).
Imperial War Museum Photographic Archive: 60tr (TR 939); 260–1 (AP 61131); 263br (Q 72834); 267tl (Q 51506); 267m (HU 89293); 267b (Q 26825); 269tl (KID 51); 274tl (MA 6636); 274b (NXF 21959); 275tl (AP 61131); 275tr (NYF 18777); 275m (BU 3398); 275b (BU 4782); 276m (E 16517); 277umr (BU 4784); 277lmr (HU 91730); 290m (H 36442); 291ml (H 28755); 296–7 (K 685); 301tl (Q 7036); 302tr (STT 3222); 312tl (NA 5076); 312tr (NA 7259); 312b (NA 6815); 313tl (NA 15906); 314b; 315m (B 11628); 315b (IMD 4127); 316t (K 685); 316m (O 131); 316b (O 97); 317tl (BU 3341); 317tr (BU 2845); 317b (B 6011); 319t (E 21333); 320b (E 18530);

321tl (HU 87652); 322; 326tl (H 38157); 326b (NA 8429); 330tl (B 11921); 330m (NA 675); 330b (B 5205); 331tl (E 21338); 331tr (EA 56553); 331b (EA 56506); 332b (BU 1389); 336tl (B 6045); 337t (E 16522); 337m (E 16553); 337b (E 16519); 340m (BU 9267); 344b (NA 15330); 345tr (B 5413); 348 (DXP85/34/1); 350b (NA 15506); 351tl (NA 1960); 351tr (STT 4601); 351b (NA 15570); 352tr (NA 120); 353tl (MH 9046); 354b (Q 2957); 356b (MH 3755); 362t (E 18869); 362b (NA 6265); 363tl (NA 15051); 363b (B 5032); 365b (NA 15165); 366tl (Q 90301); 366br (E 378); 367b (Q 1222); 368t (E 7209); 368m (FLM 394); 369t (MH 9044); 371t (NA 4664); 371m (HU 75844); 371b (B 13254); 377t (NA 7750); 377bl (MH 6107); 377br (MH 10084); 378b (B 13737); 383t (B 9807); 387tr (HU 54177); 387m (NA 15178); 387b (PC 399); 398t (NA 4199); 398br (NA 4184); 399tl (K 7806); 399tr (B 5023); 448tl (BL/74/113/2/5); 448tr (BHQ/73/169/3/20); 448b (BHQ/73/169/3/14); 451b (HU 41939).

Jack Livesey Collection: 2; 3; 9r; 256–7; 258t; 259; 265; 273tr; 273br; 276t; 280; 282–3; 286b; 287tr; 287bl; 288–9; 290t; 291t; 291mr; 291b; 292mr; 293; 295tl; 295tr; 310b; 314t; 319m; 319b; 321tr; 321b; 327b; 329; 332tl; 332tr; 336tr; 336b; 338; 339t; 339um; 340t; 340b; 341–2; 343ml; 346b; 347; 349; 350t; 353b; 356tl; 356tr; 357; 362m; 363tr; 378tr; 380; 382; 383b; 386; 387tl; 391tl; 393tr; 396; 402–3; 404–5; 411–12; 414–34; 435tl; 435b; 436–7; 438t; 438m; 439; 440tl; 440tr; 441–7; 450; 451t; 451m; 452–81; 483t; 483mr; 483b; 484–8; 489tl; 489tr; 490–5; 496b; 498tr; 499m; 499b; 500–1; 510; 511.

Jim Osborne: 112b; 114b.
RTR Publications Trust: 12t; 13b; 47tr; 47b; 48t; 49tr; 174b; 175b; 176t; 177t; 177b.
The Tank Museum, Bovington: 1; 4; 5; 6t; 6b; 7; 8t; 8b; 9l; 10–11; 14–15; 16br; 17tl; 17tr; 17b; 18t; 19tl; 19tr; 19b; 20t; 20b; 21t; 21m; 21b; 22tl; 22tr; 22br; 23; 24t; 24b; 25tl; 25tr; 25b; 27bl; 28b; 29t; 29m; 29b; 30m; 31t; 31ml; 31mr; 31b; 32t; 33tl; 34b; 35t; 39tl; 39m; 39b; 43tl; 43tr; 43b; 46tl; 46–7t; 46b; 49tl; 49bl;

49br; 50–1; 52b; 53t; 53bl; 53br; 54t; 54b; 55t; 55b; 56t; 56b; 57t; 57bl; 58t; 58b; 59t; 59b; 60tl; 60b; 61t; 61b; 62; 63; 64t; 64b; 65t; 65b; 66t; 66b; 67t; 67b; 68t; 68b; 69t; 69bl; 69br; 70t; 70b; 71t; 71b; 72t; 73t; 73b; 74t; 74b; 75t; 75b; 76t; 76b; 77t; 77m; 77b; 78t; 79tl; 79tr; 79b; 80t; 80b; 81t; 81b; 82t; 82b; 83t; 83m; 83b; 84t; 84b; 86t; 86b; 87t; 87b; 88t; 88b; 89t; 89b; 90t; 90b; 91tl; 91tr; 91b; 92t; 92b; 93t; 93m; 93b; 94t; 94b; 95t; 95m; 95b; 96t; 96b; 97t; 97b; 98t; 98b; 99t; 99b; 100t; 100m; 100b; 101t; 101b; 102t; 102b; 103t; 103m; 103b; 104t; 104b; 105t; 105m; 105b; 106t; 106b; 107t; 107m; 107b; 108tl; 109tr; 109b; 110t; 110b; 111t; 111ml; 111mr; 111b; 112t; 113t; 114t; 116t; 116b; 119t; 119m; 119b; 120t; 120b; 121t; 121b; 122b; 123t; 123b; 124t; 124b; 125t; 125m; 125b; 126t; 126b; 127t; 127ml; 127b; 128t; 128b; 129t; 129b; 130t; 130b; 131t; 131b; 132t; 132b; 133t; 133ml; 133mr; 133b; 134t; 134m; 134b; 135t; 135b; 136t; 136m; 136b; 137t; 137b; 138t; 138b; 139t; 139b; 140tl; 141t; 141b; 142tl; 142tr; 142b; 143t; 143b; 144t; 144b; 145t; 145b; 146t; 146b; 147t; 147b; 149t; 149bl; 149br; 150t; 150m; 150b; 151t; 151b; 152tl; 152b; 153t; 154t; 154b; 155; 156–7; 158t; 158b; 159t; 159b; 161tl; 165t; 165m; 166t; 167t; 167m; 167b; 168t; 169t; 172t; 172b; 174t; 178t; 178b; 179t; 179m; 179b; 180t; 180b; 181t; 181b; 182t; 183t; 183m; 183t; 184t; 184b; 185t; 185b; 186t; 186m; 186b; 187m; 187b; 192t; 194b; 195tr; 195b; 196t; 196b; 197b; 198t; 198b; 199t; 199m; 200t; 200b; 201m; 202t; 202b; 203tl; 206t; 206b; 207t; 207ml; 207mr; 208tl;

208b; 212t; 216b; 217tl; 217tr; 217b; 219t; 221b; 223m; 224t; 224b; 225t; 225m; 225b; 226t; 226b; 228t; 228m; 229t; 229m; 229b; 230t; 231tl; 231tr; 231m; 231b; 232t; 232bl; 232br; 234t; 234b; 235ml; 235mr; 235b; 236t; 236b; 237t; 237b; 238t; 238b; 239t; 239m; 239b; 242t; 242m; 242b; 243t; 243m; 244t; 245t; 245m; 246t; 246b; 247t; 250t; 250b; 251b; 252t; 253t; 253bl; 253br; 254tl; 254tr; 255t; 255m; 255b; 258m; 262tl; 262m; 263tr; 263mr; 263ml; 264; 266; 267tr; 268; 269tr; 269m; 269br; 270–2; 273tl; 273ml; 273mr; 277t; 278–9; 286t; 287tl; 287br; 292ml; 292b; 294; 295mr; 295b; 298–300; 301tr; 301b; 302tl; 302b; 303–9; 310t; 311; 313tr; 313mr; 318; 320tl; 320tr; 323–5; 326tr; 327tr; 328; 333–5; 343t; 343b; 344tl; 344tr; 345tl; 345b; 346tl; 346tr; 352tl; 352b; 353tr; 354tl; 354tr; 355; 358–61; 364; 365tl; 365tr; 366tr; 366bl; 367t; 368b; 369b; 370; 372–6; 381; 384–5; 388–90; 391tr; 392b; 392; 393tl; 393b; 394–5; 397; 398bl; 399b; 400–1; 410; 413; 435tr; 438b; 440b; 449; 482; 483ml; 489b; 496tl; 496tr; 497; 502; 503; 505; 506; 508; 509; 510; 512; endpapers.

TRH Pictures: 72b; 78b; 85b; 115b; 115b; 117t; 117b; 118t; 118b; 122t; 140tr; 148t; 149m; 153b; 168b; 169m; 169b; 171t; 189t; 189bl; 191b; 192b; 193tl; 193tr; 193m; 193b; 204b; 215t; 215m; 215b; 222t; 222b; 223t; 233t; 233m; 233b; 339lm; 339b; 379b; 498tl; 498b; 499t.
US Army: 113b; 127mr; 160b; 161b; 203b; 235t.
US Marine Corps: 113m.
Victory Memorial Museum: 277b; 378tl; 379t; 379m; 507.

Index

Made in the USA
Monee, IL
17 March 2021

63022445R10215

THE PRINCESS ELECTRIC

DEREK SILVER

THE PRINCESS ELECTRIC

The Rememberist Saga
Book 1

PRAISE FOR *THE PRINCESS ELECTRIC*

"A kaleidoscopic neo-noir adventure packed with imaginative world building and gorgeous imagery, *The Princess Electric* is *Alice in Wonderland* meets *The Matrix* and *Dark City*, with dashes of *The Fifth Element* and *Jupiter Ascending* for good measure. A thrilling ode to the power of memory and the tragedy of forgetting, this book is a glittering fever dream that I won't soon forget."

—Claire Legrand, *New York Times* bestselling author of *Furyborn*

"Dark, edgy, and captivating, *The Princess Electric* swept me down the rabbit hole with its gripping tale of memory and madness."

—Morgan Rhodes, New York Times bestselling author of the *Falling Kingdoms* series

"Mixing epic action and out of this world fantasy, *The Princess Electric* is a heartfelt tale of sisterly love that defies being put down. This madly creative meditation on memory and the value of moments we hold dear is pulse pounding right to the last page."

—Frank Beddor, New York Times bestselling author of *The Looking Glass Wars* series

Cover design and interior illustrations by Joey Hi-Fi

Editorial Assistance by Alice Barker

Final proofing and formatting by LesCourt Author Services

––––––––––

Sign up for Derek Silver's newsletter to stay up to date on upcoming books, appearances, contests, sneak peeks, and more!

CONTENTS

PART D
ILLUMINATION

For Erika, who always believed in me, even when I didn't.
This one is for you.

PART A

NEWFALLEN

And she will light the way from tower high,
with moon-bright skin and fairy eyes,
memories end will start again,
Glitterglam breaking glass and sky.
PSALM OF ILLUMINATION, VERSES 7 AND 8

1/ TRIPPING DOWN THE KALEIDOSCOPE

THE CLOUDS above the psychiatric hospital were the color of wet mascara, smeared across the winter sky like tears.

"Wake up." Christine smacked her friend on the arm. "Your stop's coming up, Sunshine."

Violet Sinclair pulled her forehead from the bus's window. It wasn't easy being an albino and comments like that made it even harder. "I told you to stop calling me that." The sun had set on her high-spirited attitude when her older sister had been committed.

"Then take off your sunglasses."

Violet glared through her retro Ray-Ban cat eye shades. Christine knew she wore sunglasses pretty much non-stop, especially in winter. Violet was sun sensitive. Photophobic. And if she didn't wear sunglasses, she'd have a migraine before rolling out of bed.

Christine also knew Violet never took her sunglasses off when visiting her sister, even in the dim light of her hospital room. It wasn't because Violet's future was so bright—because it wasn't. Not since the accident. The reason was much simpler.

Violet didn't want her sister to see her crying.

"Don't you want to go shopping instead?" Christine added, trying to

change the topic. She twirled a strand of bubblegum pink hair with a freckled hand. Her fingers looked bruised, stained from the Manic Panic she'd used to dye Violet's hair the night before.

Violet hooked a lock of hair around her ear and pushed her sunglasses back up her nose. She loved Christine. They went to the same school, lived on the same street, and shared the same secrets— sometimes. After the accident, when all of Violet's so-called friends had abandoned her, Christine remained to hold Violet up, and for that she would always be thankful. Even if she never showed it.

"Obviously I want to go shopping," Violet said, "but you know I need to visit Karin today." She wasn't going to visit her tomorrow. Not on her birthday, and not on the anniversary of the accident that put her sister into a coma.

Memory loss had plagued Karin after she woke—couldn't remember the accident, couldn't remember how to tie her shoes. The doctors said it was normal for someone who had suffered such a high degree of trauma, that amnesia was nothing to be concerned about. Her sister had nearly died, and her body needed time to remember—time to recover.

But recovery never happened. Over the past year her sister's mental faculties steadily declined, her memories burning out like so many tired candles. The doctors gave her a blanket diagnosis and kicked her to a psychiatric hospital for monitoring. There, the bloom into dementia had begun to take its toll. Some days she was witty and beautiful and vibrant. But other days she struggled to speak, her sentences all staccato and broken, where her thoughts got lost from brain to mouth to air, where she'd change the topic of conversation mid-sentence without reason. Without knowing she'd done it.

"Message me when you're finished visiting and we'll grab the same bus home." Christine waved her phone in the air.

"Sure," Violet said, wrapping a scarf around her neck. It matched her black-and-white stockings and black wool peacoat. The only color in Violet's wardrobe came from the rainbow laces in her combat boots, and from her hair, a shocking bluish-purple cut in a wispy-fringed bob.

"Love the Lie Locks," Christine added. "Looks hot against that skin of yours. But watch your hair in the snow; it'll run if it gets too wet."

Violet nodded even though she knew how to protect her hair after a fresh dye job. She'd learned her lesson last year after getting caught in the rain on her way to school. By the time she arrived the dye had run across her face. She tried to wash it off in the washroom, but it had already stained her skin, making her porcelain face look as if it were covered in varicose veins.

But that was when her sister stepped in. Karin had found Violet crying in the washroom, and instead of laughing or brushing it off as bad luck, she used her cover-up to hide the stains as best she could. Karin wasn't an albino, but she was pale with marble green eyes, and so her own make-up lent well to Violet's complexion. After covering them up, she took her shopping for cosmetics and cupcakes.

And that was Karin. She'd always been there for Violet, through their parents' divorce and mother's remarriage. Through their father's heart attack and funeral. And for that Violet had promised to be there for her sister, right to the end, no matter how much it was going to hurt when the day came that Karin no longer knew her.

But today was so not going to be that day.

As the bus shuddered toward the hospital, Violet gazed through her reflection across the city. The road weaved along the edge of an escarpment that separated the sleepy upper suburbs with the grimy steel town below. Even with the countless smokestacks belching steam into the sky, the city looked snow globe gorgeous with its crosshatched streets of slush and crooked spires. Beyond the factories a large lake filled the horizon.

This was the only time Violet enjoyed the winter, when it was all postcard picturesque. But mostly she despised the season. She hated how the cold crept into her bones and turned her fingers into icicles. If only winter could freeze her soul maybe she'd like it more. In fact, if winter could make her forget the past year altogether, she'd love the season. But now it was at the top of her list of despised things—right alongside her mother.

Violet hammered the yellow bar above the window to let the driver know she needed off at the next stop, still pissed from the conversation with her mother that morning. She grabbed the top of the plastic seat in front of her and squeezed, her mother's voice echoing in her head.

There's a winter storm coming. It won't be safe to be out, you know. Snow squalls.

It was as if her mother were trying to trigger her; the accident that'd put Karin in the hospital happened during a snowstorm. And ever since then Violet had become invisible. She might as well be dead for all her mother and stepfather seemed to care. If her mother could check her into the hospital alongside Karin she would. She'd even made an appointment with a doctor because she insisted Violet wasn't quite right in the head, that the accident had knocked something loose in her brain. Violet had laughed in her mother's face when she'd told her, but each word was like a needle sticking into her pincushion heart.

When her mother was home, she only spoke to Violet when she had rules to put down or chores to give. So that morning when her mother had mentioned the incoming storm, Violet let the warning ghost right through her. Then she left to meet Christine, ignoring her stepfather yelling about listening to her mother or else. It didn't really matter what he said anyways; his threats were as empty as his head.

The city bus dropped Violet off at the base of the long driveway, leaving her in a cloud of snow and diesel exhaust as she waved goodbye to Christine.

The Weeping Willow Psychiatric Villa was perched atop the escarpment that horseshoed the city. The villa, with its century-old, whitewashed brick exterior and dark windows, hung over the city like a decrepit gargoyle. Violet had often wondered during her visits, as the winds whipped the building and it creaked and groaned in tandem with its residents, whether it was about to attempt flight.

She lowered her shoulders and tromped along the driveway as snakes of snow curled around her combat boots. An uncomfortable weight always settled on her when she approached the hospital. Her

counselor once said she manifested her guilt from the accident into physical symptoms, but Violet wasn't so sure the sense of foreboding she got from the hospital had anything to do with the accident. Nothing good in her life had ever happened in a hospital and she didn't expect that to change now.

The sliding glass doors shuddered open revealing two security guards flanking the entrance, positioned to worry about who was leaving the building, not entering. A familiar smell struck her as Violet stepped into the hot, dry air of the hospital's foyer. It wasn't a nausea-inducing smell, but one of unmistakable sadness. The redolence of sickness, of mental anguish and dissolving memory. Of urine and heat and antiseptics. Hospital food and depression. Of silent knowing and last visits. Final moments.

"Violet, dear, what are you doing here? You should've stayed home."

Alice was one of the head nurses in her sister's wing. She stood hunched over a trolley as she tried to jostle it through the medication room doorway, her long, over-peroxided hair a nest of numerous butterfly clips and scrunchies. A series of metallic Mardi Gras necklaces jangled over her chest, her shirt patterned like a shattered rainbow. Violet was surprised Alice hadn't been knifed by one of the patients yet.

"Hey Alice," Violet said, shuffling over with wet boots to hold open the door. "You know I can't make it during the week with school and all."

"But they're predicting a lot more snow tonight. It's already started." She pointed past the pair of security guards flanking the main doors.

"It's not that bad," Violet said, loosening her scarf. "If it gets any worse—"

"You'll be staying the night," Alice interjected. "And I'll be calling your mother. You're not risking your life in this weather."

Violet shrugged and signed the visitor logbook on the welcome desk. She wouldn't have to deal with tomorrow if something bad happened to her. Yet she appreciated Alice's concern. "How's Karin?"

"She's having a good day. Ate a lot at breakfast and lunch and

played bingo this afternoon." Alice pushed the trolley to a larger door to the left of the welcome desk, the wheels fluttering along polished concrete. She pressed a large green button and the door clicked, the magnetic security lock giving way. Violet stepped in and held the door open so Alice could enter. An elderly man with a hunchback and dirty track pants stood patiently along the wall, staring through thick glasses at the freedom beyond.

"Don't even think about it, Harold," Alice ordered. "I'm coming in and you're not going out. We don't need you setting off the proximity alarms again."

Harold grunted as Violet closed the door behind Alice. He didn't leave his spot, waiting for the next escape attempt.

Lethargic commotion filled the wing. The open concept lent well to seeing across the activity and dining areas. A nursing station sat off to one side where a pair of orderlies were having lunch, next to a television lounge and a security booth. Tables in the dining room had been pushed together to allow patients to play a game that involved pushing a ping pong ball around with paddles. Usually it deteriorated into yelling and someone getting hit. Beyond the game stood a small kitchen where cooks were preparing a less than appetizing meal. Violet crinkled her nose. The dinner smelled like wet dog food mixed with fresh baked bread, and she hated that her sister had to eat that sludge every day.

When Karin was first admitted, Violet found those in the Weeping Willow pathetically amusing. They weren't high-risk patients in her sister's wing, but those who needed assistance with the day-to-day tasks of life. Only those with brain injuries, or dementia and Alzheimer's, or those afflicted with minor deliriums, were housed in this wing. Those with more debilitating illnesses, some of whom had violent tendencies, were in the next wing over. Sometimes Violet could hear them screaming through the cinderblock, the moans of confusion and sorrow. Sometimes she could hear the silence.

But it wasn't until her sister's mind stuttered more often, like a car starting in the winter, that she realized the seriousness of the situation.

Everyone in the psychiatric hospital was dying a slow, painful death of memory loss, of physical and mental deterioration, their sense of self dissolving into a sort of vacuous infancy.

Violet didn't laugh after that. Instead, she struggled with the fact that her sister—who had just turned nineteen—was locked up in a psychiatric hospital, losing her memories right alongside seniors with dementia and Alzheimer's.

"She's in her room watching the snow fall," Alice said, parking her cart near the nurses' station. "It calms her."

Violet started down one of the hallways that led away from the living area. Outside each room was a plexiglass display cabinet set into the wall. There were a few knickknacks in her sister's cabinet: her favorite jewelry box, a pink iPod that she never let out of her sight, and a dried rose from their grandma's funeral a few years earlier. It lay in front of a picture of Karin and Violet. They both looked so happy, standing in front of Niagara Falls, rainbows and butterflies curling across the backdrop like a postcard. They were inseparable. Best friends. Sisters. At that moment in time, each believed they would share everything in their lives. Maid of Honor at each other's wedding. Sons and daughters; nieces and nephews. Summertime barbecues. Fairytales and ever afters. Now Violet knew just how fast a daydream could turn into a nightmare.

She knocked and pushed the door open. Her sister sat in a wheelchair, staring at the snow sifting over the city. The sun must have dipped below the lake, the sky inked into darkness. Lights were winking on in buildings, along the valley's streets. Distant headlights darted and sparked in the snowfall like fireflies wrapped in sheets of gauze. Their grandma's crocheted afghan covered her frail frame, hands folded over one another, twitching.

"Karin?" Violet whispered. "It's me. I'm here for our visit."

Her sister slowly turned her gaze from the window. When she saw Violet her eyes bloomed, her mouth stretching into a smile. Her hands shook with excitement as she tried to stand. Violet rushed to her side before she triggered the alarm that was clipped to her back. Karin some-

times forgot that she'd lost the use of her legs from the accident. She fell regularly from trying to stand, her body a checkerboard of bruises.

"No, no," Violet said, shushing her back into the wheelchair. "Don't stand up. I can hug you here."

"Why'd you take so long to visit me?"

"I was here last weekend," Violet said as she disengaged from her sister's grasp.

Karin's face twisted in puzzlement. "It's been months."

"Sure," Violet said. "Whatever you say."

"Take off your sunglasses."

Violet crouched down, leaning against the padded metal of the wheelchair. "You know I need to wear them. The bright light hurts my eyes."

"Then you should go to the doctors. Maybe you have a tumor."

Violet grinned. "I don't have a tumor."

Karin framed Violet's face with her cold hands. "I wish you wouldn't take so long between visits. It's so lonely on the island; nobody to talk to in the tower except the wind." Her hands fell onto her lap. She always referred to her loneliness as an island, her room as the tower, and the wind as the whispers of moments forgotten. Sometimes she scribbled notes describing her island and the tower on tiny pieces of paper, as if she were going to place them in a bottle and throw them out to sea.

There was no note today, only a crayoned piece of paper. It was colored blue with lines of black across it. Like bars.

Violet looked away, her eyes welling.

She was with Karin when their car was struck by a snowplow on a night very much like this one. She heard the crumple-twisting crash of metal and the shattering of glass, the screams of escaping life. She'd been covered in Karin's blood, watched it drizzle across the snow as they hung upside down from their seatbelts.

And then the silence—that awful, deadly silence.

Violet blinked hard, shook her head. She would not do this now. She would not remember it all again, not like this. Not here.

She glanced at her sister who sat quietly, staring out a window which had turned to mirror in the darkness. All Karin wanted was to remember, and all Violet wanted was to forget. Her eyes brimmed with tears as a sudden hollowness consumed her. Eyes twitched, and she felt warmth as tears rolled down, pooling where her sunglasses kissed her cheek.

"Let's get out of here and go for a walk." Violet sniffled and disengaged the wheelchair's brake. She pushed her sister out of the room and into the brightly lit hallway of polished concrete and fluorescent lighting.

"Thanks for visiting me," Karin said. "It's been so long since I've seen you."

———

After helping her sister with dinner, which consisted of some gross Salisbury steak slop that tasted like damp cardboard and old cafeteria gravy, Violet headed outside to get some fresh air. Even though she never had an appetite at the hospital, she always made herself try the food to remind herself just how bad Karin's new life was.

Alice stopped Violet by the nurse's station. "Honey, you should stay the night. It's really coming down. Accidents everywhere. Whiteouts."

"Nah, it's okay," Violet said, not wanting to spend any longer in the hospital than she had to. The uncomfortably warm urine-scented air was getting to her.

Alice reached out and grabbed Violet's shoulder. "I insist." She squeezed, her red and green press-on nails digging in.

"But—"

"I've already called your mom. She's more than happy for you to stay here."

I'm sure she is. Violet huffed. "Fine. Where can I sleep? In Karin's room?"

As much as she liked the nostalgic idea of staying with her sister, like

they used to do after watching horror movies when they were younger, or when they cried themselves to sleep after their parents' divorce, Violet didn't think it would be good for her own mental health to stay with her tonight. Not when tomorrow was the one-year anniversary of the crash that ruined Karin's life.

"No," Alice said, shaking her head. "We have a few recently vacated rooms. You can stay in 329."

"Alice," an orderly called from down the hall. "Harold soiled himself and is trying to fingerpaint again."

Alice rolled her eyes and took off after the orderly.

Recently vacated rooms? Violet shivered as she pulled her coat tight and went outside, hoping the previous inhabitants were simply discharged and not something worse. The snow continued to spill from the sky, drifts piling along the driveway, the cold air a welcome change against her cheeks. She unlocked her phone and called Christine.

Two rings. "Hey. Everything good?"

"I have to stay overnight at the Willow. They won't let me leave."

"What the hell? Can they do that?"

Violet shrugged, her breath clouding the night air. "Who knows? My mother is fine with it obviously. And they're having me stay in one of the empty rooms."

"Brutal. Well, it's getting nasty outside. Stay safe and have fun with the lunatics. Don't do anything I wouldn't do."

"You're funny," Violet said flatly.

"I'll message you in the morning. Happy birth—"

Violet ended the call and pretended she didn't hear that. She wasn't in the mood for pre-birthday wishes.

She just wanted to sleep.

Forever.

———

Room 329 was located not too far from the dining room, down a hall and around the corner. It appeared clean, fresh sheets wrapped around the mattress like a birthday present. But the room was blisteringly hot, like most of the hospital. Violet cracked the window to let the cold air rush in.

One day this'll be waiting for me, Violet thought as she threw her jacket on a chair and untied her boots. Maybe one day soon if her mother had any say—or the doctor she was supposed to meet next week.

Maybe she could share a room with her sister again.

Maybe she'd get her own tower.

Violet turned off the lights, placed her sunglasses on the nightstand, kicked her boots off and climbed under the covers. She quickly fell asleep with thoughts of tomorrow on her mind and how much she didn't want to wake up. That maybe if she slept long enough she'd forget the past altogether.

Forget that pulping snap of a body going all accordion.

That sleep would wipe her memory clean.

Violet's eyes fluttered open and she instinctively slipped on her sunglasses. Her breath fogged the air, the room dark with an ambient glow coming from under the door. Over the course of the night her room had become an icebox, the curtains swaying from a cold breeze blowing in from the open window. Snowflakes danced in the air until they found purchase on Violet's Joy Division t-shirt, along her forearms. She shivered and rubbed her tights to warm up her legs, the blankets in a clump at the foot of the bed.

She looked over at the illuminated red numerals flashing from a bedside clock.

1:11 A.M.

"Well happy-fucking-birthday to me. Sweet sixteen can kiss my ass."

Before she could contemplate just how sugar-free her birthday was going to be, heavy, distorted breathing filtered into her room from under the door. First she thought it was some perverted patient out for their late-night grope-stroll. But then the breathing turned into a slow slurping, as if someone had reached the end of an incredibly good milkshake.

Chills spidered across Violet's skin.

Viscous gurgles continued from another room, somewhere down the hallway.

Then it stopped.

Silence.

Violet's heart ricocheted in her chest, her breath filling the air in tight, short puffs of panic. Something wasn't right about that noise. It didn't sound like a patient getting off, or someone moaning from bed sores. It sounded like a dental hygienist's vacuum when it sucked the blood and spit from your mouth.

The deep-throated gurgle continued, then shuddering breaths and another slurp like the last bit of bathwater circling the drain. Violet slid off her bed and pulled on her combat boots. Slipped on her peacoat and scarf and walked toward the door.

The fluorescent hallway flashed in a spasmodic rhythm. Frost covered the polished concrete floors and white walls, air frigid. She peered further into the hazy hallway, straining to listen.

Quiet.

She shivered and stepped into the hallway, snuggling the collar of her coat about her. She slowly made her way toward the living area, hugging the frosted wall as she went. The lights continued to flicker. Another gurgle fluttered down the hallway followed by more breathing. The sounds started to filter into the hallway from multiple directions now, coming from other rooms, from other corridors. The hair on Violet's neck porcupined. Why were there no nurses about? No orderlies? Didn't patients need tending, even at night?

"Hello?" Violet said in more of a whisper than she intended. Her breath ghosted in the flashing light. She increased her walk and turned a corner, entering the dining space. From around the nursing station, a dark shadow fluttered and then disappeared down an adjacent hallway.

Alice was there, sitting in her nurse's chair with her back facing Violet.

"Alice?" Violet called out.

Nothing.

Violet walked toward her, looking cautiously down the other hallways as the lights continued to pulse. The security station was vacant except for the monitors displaying the blue screen of lost signals.

She placed her hand on Alice's shoulder and spun the chair around. Alice was staring straight ahead, eyes wide and her gaze as empty as the residents. Her face was frozen in shock while her chest continued to rise and fall.

"Alice, wake up, something's wrong." Violet grabbed the nurse's shoulders and shook her. Alice's hair moved aside revealing more of her face. There, against both of her temples, were small puncture marks. A syrupy, multicolored fluid oozed out. It glistened like liquid rainbow, like Alice's shirt, and continued to shift and swirl and glow in the dark.

Violet went to grab her phone to call the police when a scream from another hallway punctured the silence, followed closely by a slurping pop.

"Karin!" Violet yelled. She left Alice and ran down the hallway, dodging stray wheelchairs as she went. She slid to a stop on the icy floor, just outside her sister's room.

With her heart pounding, she flung the door open. Her sister was sitting in bed with a large metal device around her head like a bear trap. A network of glass tubes encircled the device with a series of spigots and valves spread throughout in erratic intervals. Needles were implanted in her temples which were extracting the same multicolored syrup Violet had seen on Alice. The tubes glowed and shifted from their contents.

Standing beside the bed were two men wearing black rubber gas

masks. But they weren't nurses or orderlies. They reminded Violet of the soldiers she'd seen in World War II movies, yet they were unnaturally tall, slender, limbs elongated.

Their willowy forms draped over Karin, trench coats curtaining about them like heavy fog. One of them adjusted spigots with mercurial movements while the other collected the rainbow liquid from the contraption, carefully draining the device into a series of tubes that snaked toward his head and connected to the black rubber mask. With each adjustment to the spigots came a siphoning slurp from the device—and another moan from Karin.

"What the hell are you doing?" Violet screamed.

The two men turned quickly. There were no eyes behind the masks' eyepieces, just rainbow-colored pinwheels spinning slowly as if caught in a breeze. Their scalps were glabrous and moonlight pale.

One of them quickly disengaged the device from Karin's head, her face wincing. The needles slid out of her temples with a suction-like pop. Liquid rainbow trailed down her jaw while the other man withdrew a cylinder from his trench coat pocket.

"Get away from her!" Violet yelled.

The man fumbled and dropped the cylinder as Violet charged further into the room. The other man flung the device onto his back and withdrew a similar cylinder. He twisted it and a sudden wash of green light filled the room. Within a heartbeat the two men were siphoned into the cylinder, their slender bodies narrowing and stretching even more until they disappeared. The cylinder hung in the air, folding in on itself. As Violet reached the bed the cylinder disappeared with a sparkle-flash of neon green light.

"Karin," Violet said. "Are you okay? What just happened?"

There was no answer. Violet's sister had already fallen back asleep, seemingly oblivious to the events of a moment ago. She brushed her sister's hair off her face. Violet took a deep breath, relieved to see the rise and fall of her sister's chest.

Then the chaos of what happened crashed into her.

Who were those guys? And what hell were they doing to Karin?

Violet had never seen anyone dressed like them before. Not in a movie or anime or comic, and not around the hospital. And how had they disappeared like that?

Maybe Mom was right? Maybe I do belong in here.

She crouched down and picked up the cylinder. It was pewter-dark and no longer than her forearm. Ornate etchings decorated the gunmetal in curlicues. She held it up and looked inside. It was filled with mirrors and multicolored beads and glass fragments.

A kaleidoscope?

Violet started to twist the tube, watching the beads and glass shards shuffle and merge and reflect along the inner mirrors. The patterns were hauntingly beautiful. They pulled at her. For a moment Violet thought of Alice and Karin, but her sister was no longer in danger and in a deep sleep. Maybe Alice was sleeping too? The whimsical images in the tube calmed her, making the recent events distant and foggy in her mind. Violet wanted to climb into the kaleidoscope to get a better view of the prismatic patterns, to get in close, to blend with them.

She felt buoyant, as if she were floating in a gigantic ocean, alone, drifting along the currents. The patterns began to change faster, and with each new blend of color Violet became more and more lethargic.

The shifting designs erupted into fireworks. Violet tried to look back, to remove the kaleidoscope, but all she saw was darkness. She wanted to continue into the fireworks, into the wash of rainbow light.

And as she drifted along the patterns of glass and mirror, she closed her eyes to their beauty and didn't open them again.

2/ SOMETIMES THINGS GET, WHATEVER

THE BEAUTY of the kaleidoscope's interior washed away into streaks of gray, as if Violet were nothing more than a raindrop falling from a cloud. Vertigo feathered her stomach and teased nausea up her throat. She landed softly on her feet on a patch of dead leaves. Static floated in the air like electric snowflakes. Trees encircled her, their naked branches corkscrewing into moonlight.

And the moon...Violet had never seen anything like it. It filled the sky, rotating slowly, its disco-ball surface refracting light into tiny spots of brightness that swam past her.

She spun around and around, trying to gain some bearing on reality, trying to make sure those strange men with the pinwheel eyes and gasmasks weren't about to jump her. They were nowhere to be seen.

Beyond the trees buildings stretched into the sky at odd angles, like piles of toppled dominoes. Rowhouses and office buildings were layered in front of larger riveted steel structures and bridgework and elevated platforms. The trees closest to Violet were shining brighter than the cityscape beyond, their paper-white trunks reflecting an ambient brightness that Violet traced back to her—to her skin.

She held up her hands in front of her face, palms turned skyward, fingers splayed. Pale skin shone all flashlight bright.

What. The. Fuck.

Violet put her hands back down and felt a bulge in her coat pocket. She reached in and pulled out the kaleidoscope. The etchings along the polished gunmetal shimmered in the light of her hands.

A sharp wail filled the air. Violet looked around, panic kicking her in the throat. Nothing good came from sirens. Its scream regurgitated images of blood-matted hair, of red and blue lights cardiac-flashing on icy snow. The scent of gasoline and burning plastic.

The hiss of escaping life.

A movement caught Violet's eye—a quick flash of black and gray. She spun and it was gone. Then it was there again, another streak of shadow. Violet continued to spin, trying to catch sight of whatever it was that happened to be working its way toward her.

Sirens blared louder and Violet's mouth went dry. Something was coming but she couldn't move, her legs heavy with fear, her body paralyzed as if caught in the web of a nightmare she couldn't control.

Wake up, she commanded herself. *Wake up, wake up!*

Shadowy wings fluttered, blotting out the moon. Arms encircled Violet's waist, pulling her backward. She screamed and tried to pry out of the grasp, but the arms locked together, hands over forearms.

As she raised her leg to kick backward, the arms gave a quick twist and Violet tumbled down a hill that dipped behind her, leaves spraying the air. She came to a stop on her side, her breath knocked from her lungs. As she sucked in the cool night air the sirens continued their banshee wail.

The person that tackled Violet unhinged his arms from her waist, then regained his feet cautiously. Violet hoisted herself onto her elbows and pulled her legs up to protect herself. He was her age, maybe a year or two older, and stood above her like an iron tower. Sweaty, wispy strands of pewter-dark hair framed his face. She couldn't see his eyes. They were hidden behind deep whorls of shadow that spanned his pale

cheeks, curving over his nose, along his lips and jaw. He wore a tight-fitting black leather jacket that zipped across his chest in numerous diagonal lines, merging into similar pants that disappeared into combat boots. Over the leather he wore a black trench coat that fluttered with his movements. Flowers hung around his neck in a knotted wreath like a Hawaiian lei. The heart of each flower was a spot of black rimmed by sun-kissed yellow, each petal all turbo blue and beautiful.

Violet dug her heels into the leaves, ready to push away.

He shifted his weight and glanced upward, toward the jagged rooftops. He cupped his fingers and pressed them to his eyes, then pulled back his hands to smear the shadows around his eyes away. When he looked back down the shadows had retreated to his temples. The whites of his eyes were not white but a vibrant blue, pupils black and dilated and ringed in sparks of yellow.

Like the flowers around his neck.

Violet pushed backwards to get some distance from him. He was way too close. Then again her depth perception was always a bit off due to the albinism. She was slightly cross eyed. Though it was minimal and few people picked up on it, it still lent to her misjudging depth.

"Don't move," he said, voice lyrical yet commanding. "Your safety depends on it."

"My safety?" Violet questioned, stopping. "Where am I?"

"Recollection City."

Violet shook her head. "What? No. Where the hell *am* I? Why am I glowing like this?" She raised her arms in front of her. Black metallic nail polish contrasted with her glowing white hands. He frowned and smacked them down.

"Are you trying to get us killed?" he whisper-yelled.

"Well, no, I—"

He grabbed the edges of his trench coat, snapped it high into the air, and pulled it back down quickly. The coat ballooned in the air, shifting in the moonlight to create a pocket of darkness that he brought down over them.

"Listen to me," he said through clenched teeth. "You hear that siren? They're coming for you."

Violet swallowed hard. "Who's coming?"

"Memjacks," he hissed. "Slurpers, clankers, everything."

"That doesn't help me," Violet said, squinting. "What are you even talking about?"

He bit his lip with pearl-white teeth. "There's too much to explain right now. I need to get you to safety. And to do that, I've got to dull your brightness. They're closing in on us already."

"I'm going to freaking scream in a minute."

"Listen, I can't say it in any way that won't make you panic. Understand?"

Violet clenched her fists into lightbulbs of anger. "In case you haven't noticed, I'm already starting to lose my shit. One minute I'm in my sister's hospital and I see these weird men hooking her up to this... this *machine*, and then I find this kaleidoscope-thingy and now I'm here. Oh, and did I forget the part that I'm *glowing?* Yeah, so what-ever-your-name-is, I'm sorry if I don't quite *understand*. Now tell me where the fuck I am!"

A moment passed in the enclosed space the guy had created with his trench coat. His eyes seemed to quiver, opening wide, the blue vibrant, the yellow all sparks of knowing. His mouth parted slightly as if to say something and then he paused.

He bit his lip again and said, "Dementia."

"What?" Violet said. "What are you talking about?"

"You're in *Dementia*."

"Dementia is not a place, it's a disease."

"I wish it were that simple...but it's not. Dementia is a *reality*."

Violet's mind raced as he reached into his trench coat and pulled out a silver can. He shook it vigorously, a marble inside clattering about its walls.

"I've got to take you to the others," he said. "Everything will be explained when we get there."

Others? Violet wondered. *Who's he talking about?*

He took the can and started to spray Violet's face with black paint. She screamed and put up her hands to protect herself. It felt cool and sticky against her skin as it spread out. It coated her cheeks, oozing across her mouth and sealing her lips.

Violet's breathing accelerated as she tried to wipe the paint away, but it just smeared like hot wax. When she tried to open her mouth, the tarry substance bubblegum-stretched until it snapped shut.

"Don't fight it," he said as he slowly faded into the darkness of the trench coat tent. "The liquid shadow won't hurt you. You'll be able to breathe through it. It's there for your protection while we travel. It'll cover up your light emissions."

Violet saw her illumination dull as the shadows snaked over her exposed flesh, curling over her nose, covering her sunglasses and eyes, her hands. Her stomach churned, nausea rising in her throat.

Once all light had been snuffed from within their tent, Violet felt him take one of her hands in his. He whispered, "The sniffers are almost here. We have to go now."

The sound of escaping air and cracking plastic filled the tent, and then the smell of antiseptic and lemon rinds. Something was placed over Violet's face, cold and wet like a wrung-out dishcloth. She tried to back away, but her head was held fast, a hand pressing against the back of her skull.

She kicked and struggled, her shadow-wet hands unable to find purchase.

"Forgive me," he said. "But you can't see the entrance to Pallium. Now relax and forget me not."

And then Violet's mind went dark.

3/ THE REMEMBERISTS

VIOLET'S HEAD thundered as she opened her eyes to a flood of light.

Sunglasses!

She didn't have them on. Blinded by brightness, her hand shot out to her side, instinctively looking for a bedtable, a chair, something. She felt the side of a mattress, jumbled sheets, then the hardness of a table edge. Trying not to panic, she ran her hand around the top of the table, carefully probing until she found her sunglasses. With a brief sigh, she slid them on and opened her eyes to the room beyond.

Across from the bed she found herself in, a steel table stood alone in the middle of a small room. On the table, a bouquet of flowers spilled out of a vase.

"Forget-me-nots."

Violet started from the butter-smooth voice that came from beside her. Her mouth was cotton dry, tongue thick against the back of her teeth.

"The flowers."

Violet sat up and turned to her right. It was the guy from earlier, sitting there in a wire-framed chair. He stood when their eyes locked.

He was dressed the same as before, all leather and zippers. Flowers still hung around his neck.

"They're wards," he said. "Protectors of memory." He plucked one of the flowers from his lei, its azure petals vibrant in the halogen light.

Violet thought she saw movement within the petals, like reflections in a window.

Without warning he pressed the flower against her forehead and she felt an electrical spark, a sizzle against skin. She fell back as an image perforated her mind.

A massive house sat in moonlight, tucked in a pocket of fir trees. A party raged within as high school students drank beer along the wraparound porch, smoking and dancing to music that spilled from the open windows. It was snowing, their breaths clouding the air around them. Violet's sister stumbled onto the porch from inside, her hair disheveled across her face. She was laughing, such a deep, innocent laugh, a laugh that charmed boys like pixie dust. She staggered toward Violet, tossing her hair back and calling her name.

Karin's eyes were wide open, the moon reflected mirror-perfect within. She called Violet again, words slurring as she took another swig from a bottle of cider. Karin reached into her pocket, fumbling around. She withdrew a pair of keys that hung in her grasp like miniature lightning bolts.

She licked her glossy lips and said, "Drive."

Violet sprang up from the bed, her heart racing to get out of her chest, her breathing nightmarishly heavy. She wanted to jump from the bed and run as fast as she could, away from this guy with his leather and zippers and summer sky eyes. She focused on slowing her breathing. There had to be a logical explanation for all of this. Surely, she would wake up at any moment in a cold sweat, screaming for her sister like she'd done so many times before.

Again, she willed herself to wake up but nothing happened. Instead, she simply sat there in a bed, surrounded by damp, black-stained sheets, her skin once again incandescent. The boy looked at her as if she were dying.

"The stains are from shadow runoff," he said. "Nothing to be alarmed about."

"Who are you?" Violet asked, hooking grape-bright hair around her ear.

Dark circles wreathed his eyes, though Violet couldn't tell if they were from tiredness or from the shadows that had once covered his face. The same shadows that now feathered his jaw and trailed down his neck into his leather jacket. He licked his lips before he spoke.

"I'm Declan Gloss, leader of the Rememberists. Well, I was—until a short while ago."

"Wait, what?" Violet scanned the room for the door. "Where am I? And who are the Rememberists?"

"You're safe," he said, adjusting a zipper on his jacket. "That's the most important thing right now."

"No, what's important is who's in charge?" Violet refocused on his lips, at how they glistened under the lights. "I need to speak with them immediately."

"Then you can speak with yourself while I go get the others. We've

been waiting for you to join us for a long time, Princess. An awfully long time."

————

Violet sat in stunned silence as Declan left the room to go fetch his friends. Her brain tried to process what she'd been told, but every time she landed on one thought another took over.

What was this talk about them *waiting* for her to join? Join what? Who?

And why did he call her princess? Princess was derogatory slang for a spoiled, prissy-assed bitch—and she was neither spoiled nor prissy. It was also a term of endearment and the last word her dad had said to her before he died.

There was no reason for Declan to call her that.

Violet swung her legs from the bed and stood, grabbing the edge of the bed to steady herself, her legs feeling all anxiety-heavy. There was too much to take in, too much to digest. Everything seemed to be sitting in her throat. She would wait until Declan returned and then get out of here.

Either that, or she'd puke.

Maybe both.

The door along the wall click-clacked open and in walked Declan, his trench coat dusting the floor. He led two guys and one girl into the room. One of the guys wore a ruffled white shirt, red vest, and matching knee-length overcoat embroidered with gold designs. The other was dressed in a similar ensemble as Declan. A rather fitting storm gray jacket clung to the girl and hung over a pair of puffy shorts that bloomed around her knees. They took a defensive stand around the table while Declan stood next to Violet.

"These are the Rememberists minus two," Declan said. He pointed to the guy standing to the right of the table in the white shirt. His teeth were fluorescent bright against his black skin. Dreadlocks spilled from

his head and squiggled in front of his face. A white patch covered his right eye.

"Violet, this is Morgan Foil," Declan said.

"Esquire," Morgan added. He bowed in Violet's direction.

"Uh, hi?" Violet said, not sure how to respond.

"Right," Declan said. "And the other bloke is Cheshire. We're the Brothers Gloss."

Violet shifted her gaze from Morgan to Cheshire. An overwhelming sense of awe consumed her, like the first time she'd looked out across New York City from the top of the Empire State Building.

Cheshire was freaking beautiful.

There were enough similarities between Declan and Cheshire that she could tell they were brothers, but there was an underlying confidence in Cheshire that wasn't there in his sibling. His eyes locked onto Violet's, sparking a quiver deep within her body. They were the same vibrant color as Declan's, yet when he blinked the lights cast a rainbow shimmer across them that disappeared as quickly as it came.

He smiled slowly, as if his mouth held a thousand secrets. "Pleasure's all mine," he said, bowing.

Declan cleared his throat and continued. "And the lovely lady hiding behind the flowers is the one and only Melody Maker."

"Welcome, Violet," Melody said, nodding her head slightly. Her voice was lilting, like the susurrant kiss of waves against sand. "I'm glad you were able to find your way." A fuchsia-and-emerald boa wrapped around her neck. Her hair was all porcelain-white ringlets.

"Together," Declan said, opening his arms wide, "we are the Rememberists."

"Well, that's great." Violet refocused her attention on the entire group. "But it doesn't help me understand what's going on, or why you fucking abducted me, now does it?"

The corners of Declan's mouth curled downward. "No, I guess it doesn't—and for that I must apologize. However, you weren't abducted. I saved your life."

"Oh yeah, how so?"

"You've transitioned into the middle of an age-old war."

"Really?" Violet scoffed. "You're joking, right? Between whom?"

"Between the Rememberists and the memjacks."

"Well that clears everything up." Annoyance flared under her skin from the repeated non-answers, as if she should know exactly what a memjack was. Or a Rememberist for that matter. Why couldn't Declan give her something straight-up? Mind you, if she was in her head, then nothing was ever straight-up; it was ninety different angles of crooked.

Declan looked at her, his face almost pitying—but not quite. "I understand your lack of sensibility to this matter," he said. "Trust me, I do. We've been there. Being thrust into a new reality can be a shock. It was to me, to Cheshire, to all of us when we had first transitioned."

Violet thought of the hospital and the men in gas masks, the kaleidoscope and bright lights and falling into this strange place and wondered if they'd all had similar experiences. If that was transitioning, then they must have some wild stories to tell.

Declan placed his hand on hers. It was warm and welcoming. She didn't pull away from his touch and noticed Cheshire watching. She didn't mind how his brother was staring at her with a devilish smile either. "But all of that doesn't change the fact that there's a war going on. A war we're about to lose."

Violet cleared the smile from her face. Regardless of how messed up this dream was, deep down she was enjoying the escape. Hell, she was even enjoying Declan's hand on hers. She hadn't had a boyfriend since the accident. Hadn't even been kissed. That was her old life. Her new one was all hospitals and regret.

Violet decided to play along for now. At least until she woke up.

"I can see in your eyes that you don't believe any of this," Declan said, pulling his hand away.

"No, I don't," Violet said, wanting to reach out and take his hand back. He was comforting in a morose, rainy Sunday kind of way. "You haven't given me anything to believe. I don't know who you people are,

or why you have me here. But that's okay. You know why? Because I'm going to crawl out of the rabbit hole eventually. I'm going to wake up and this will all disappear." She waved her hands around, her skin still bright and glowing.

"I wish that were the case," Declan said, sighing heavily. "But Dementia isn't going anywhere. Dementia is where memories go to die."

Violet shook her head, trying to understand what was being said. "What does any of this have to do with me? What am I here for?"

"To illuminate Recollection City," Cheshire said.

"What do you mean?" Violet asked. She took a deep breath. Things needed to slow down.

"Look at yourself," Melody added, her eyes bright behind the bouquet of flowers.

"You are the Princess Electric," Declan said. "The prophecy incarnate."

Violet's stomach twisted, skin turning to goose flesh. "I don't understand. My name's Violet. Why do you keep calling me princess?"

"Because you are the princess of prophecy," Declan said, the glow from Violet's skin flickering across his eyes.

"But that means nothing to me," Violet said, her voice rising with frustration. "You have to give me something."

"There's so much to explain," Declan said, sounding slightly defeated. "So much that I don't know how to say it without making us seem a bit ridiculous."

"Too late for that," Violet said dryly.

"What my brother is struggling to articulate," Cheshire said, casually running his finger along the table, "is that we have a lot to teach you. Until you learn the basics of Dementia, we can't make another move toward illuminating Recollection City and destroying the Queen of Glass."

"Who?" Violet's dream was derailing to a point well beyond confusion. She was getting the urge to punch herself awake. For as depressing

as her reality was, she at least knew where she stood in it—right alongside her sister in the Weeping Willow Psychiatric Villa.

"Queen Zamelerish rules Dementia," Cheshire said. "She oversees Recollection City from the Palace of Memories End. And—if I were to be forthright—I'd say she's a bitch."

Violet grinned. Cheshire, it appeared, had a way with words.

"Thanks for your forthrightness," Declan, shooting a glare toward his brother. "It's always appreciated."

Cheshire winked at his brother. "Anytime."

Declan turned his attention back to Violet. "You've seen some of the queen's minions. You've seen the slurpers."

"What are you talking about?" Violet said, refocusing on Declan.

"How else did you get this?" He held out the kaleidoscope. It rested in his palms, its cylindrical surface all gray and swirling in acid-etched beauty. *How did he get that?* Violet wondered. Did he go through her coat while she was drugged up? She added kleptomania to Declan's list of growing offences.

"I saw these men with gas masks and long coats of fog by my sister's bedside. They had this weird thing on her head, like a birdcage. It was screwed into her temples and—"

"They were siphoning," Morgan interrupted.

"Slurping your sister's memories," Declan added. "Liquid memory looks like rainbows. Did you see it?"

"Yes," Violet said, shuddering. She had tried to forget the way the machine gurgled and hissed. The way rainbow liquid curled through the glass tubes like a slushie through a silly straw. A shiver spilled down her spine. No luck in forgetting. That was a problem she had.

"Only those close to a psychotic break have the potential of seeing a slurper within the real," Melody said.

"What are you trying to say?" Violet asked. "That I've lost my grip on reality?"

"It's more like your definition of *reality* is starting to change, now that you've been exposed to Dementia," Cheshire said.

Violet wouldn't disagree. She'd almost convinced herself to check into the Weeping Willow a few months ago, but Christine had talked her out of it. Violet knew something wasn't firing on all cylinders in her brain. Even her mother believed that; the doctor was only going to confirm it next week.

"What Cheshire is saying," Declan interjected, snapping Violet back into the discussion, "is that doors open when we least expect them to. And one of those doors brought you to us. But before we can show you more you must agree to join the Rememberists... to join *us*."

"Why should I?" Violet said, looking around the room at each of the Rememberists. "Why would I join you when my sister needs me back in the real world? If this isn't all just a dream anyways." She felt out of place, like she didn't belong. Like when she ghosted down the hallway at school.

"Violet, please," Declan said, his voice stressed and quavering. His eyes pleaded with her, glassy and wet. "You saw the slurpers siphoning from your sister. That's how the queen is working her way into the real, how she gains her power. She preys on the elderly, the hospitalized, the mentally damaged. Did you see vials of liquid rainbow?"

"Yes," Violet said, remembering the small vials the strange men were filling from the device clamped around her sister's head. "There were a bunch of test tube things."

"Then the queen has your sister's memories. That's how they transport them, in those vials. And unless she's stopped, she will continue to take memories from you sister, from everyone. We can help you get them back. Somehow, someway, we'll track them down. But you must join us. Only you can destroy the Queen of Glass."

Violet closed her eyes and rubbed her temples, her jaw clenched. Why did she have to remove this queen from power? The Rememberists kept calling her princess. Was she related? And how would destroying the queen free these memories to illuminate the city? Violet wanted to climb back into the bed and pull the covers over her head. Maybe then she'd wake back up in the hospital and this craziness would stop.

"And with the queen gone," Declan continued. "Recollection City will shine with the power of unrestrained memory. Memories would be free to come and go from Dementia. People who had forgotten could remember once more."

"But I don't want to remember anything," Violet whispered. "I just want to forget."

The room fell silent. She looked up at Declan and found him staring at her, his face etched with shadows and sadness. Violet broke his gaze and looked at the vase on the table, at the bright blue flowers, at the forget-me-nots. She couldn't grasp everything that had been said to her. There was so much to take in that it didn't make any sense.

What did make sense was her sister and how much she struggled to remember the simplest of things. How she lost track of time, or how she could no longer lift a spoon to her mouth without spilling soup across her bib. Karin needed Violet more than ever. She would soon wake up and take her sister to breakfast in the dining hall of the psychiatric hospital, where she would spoon-feed her porridge and hold a glass of orange juice to her chapped lips.

That was Violet's reality now, not some dreamland adventure.

"You can think about it," Declan said calmly. He dragged his teeth along his lower lip, thinking. "It's a lot to take in—we all understand that." He walked over to the table and placed the kaleidoscope beside the forget-me-nots. "If you decide you don't want to join us, if you don't want to recover your sister's memories and protect your own in the process, then simply look through the kaleidoscope and you'll be transported back to the real, right back to where you left your sister."

Violet watched the kaleidoscope wobble as Declan removed his hand. It teetered, almost falling over. In that moment she thought about joining the Rememberists, that if the kaleidoscope fell she'd stay. She didn't really have anything to lose. What's the worst that could happen? She'd wake up back in the mental hospital, sixteen years old with a brain-damaged sister who was slowly forgetting herself—all because of one mistake.

She willed the kaleidoscope not to fall. She had to be there for Karin.

Relief filled Violet as the tube steadied and remained standing.

It's decided, Violet thought, the tension in her body dissipating. *I'm going home.*

Declan ushered the others out of the room. Violet could feel their eyes on her, staring, pleading, accusing. She didn't look up. Instead, she stared at the flowers beside the kaleidoscope, losing herself in the purity of their blueness. They reminded Violet of the car accident, the way the interior lighting shone on the snow in a wintry azure, the tempered glass shattered like so many diamonds on the wet asphalt.

"You know," Declan said, standing in the doorway, his body all silhouetted shadow. "We have a saying in Dementia when we depart. We say it to each other hoping that we'll meet again, that we'll not forget each other." Declan paused for a moment. "Forget me not," he said. "And then you should say remember me always."

But Violet didn't say anything. She simply sat there, staring at the kaleidoscope. Declan waited another moment, perhaps for as long as it takes to forget a name, and then he closed the door.

4/ UNLOCKING POSSIBILITY

THE MOMENT DECLAN closed the door Violet ran to the table and snatched up the kaleidoscope. The gray metal felt comforting in her hand, as if its sleek coolness could suck the anxiety from her veins. She'd made her decision to return home before Declan had even proposed any offer to stay, before she'd met the Rememberists, before she'd found herself sitting in a strange bed in some strange room.

This experience was obviously some kind of dreamland clusterfuck, brought on from the stress of seeing her sister's health degrade so quickly over the past year.

And from reading too many brochures on the diseases of the mind.

Pamphlets on Alzheimer's.

Books on dementia.

Not to mention the anniversary of the car accident.

Maybe that's why I'm in this strange place, Violet mused. Her brain launching off the anniversary and her birthday all rolled into one disaster of a day. She'd read enough fairytales to know strange things happened on significant dates.

Violet chewed on her bottom lip, frustration tensing her body. There

was only one thing worse than being trapped in your own head—and that was knowing about it. Why couldn't she wake up? Would the kaleidoscope really transport her back to her sister, like Declan said it would? Or would it throw her down a different track along this subconscious rollercoaster?

How can I trust someone who drugged me?

Violet tossed the kaleidoscope onto the bed. She needed a moment to think before acting. The last time she made an impulsive decision she put her sister in a coma. Maybe Christine would know what to do? Regardless it would be good to hear her voice. Violet pulled out her phone.

No signal.

Of course, Violet thought. *Why'd I expect the phone to work?*

She put the phone back in her coat pocket and ran her hand over the clumps of forget-me-nots sprouting from the vase on the table. They were frosted, an icy-cool haze hovering over the petals. Violet plucked a flower and held it up to the lights above. Anonymous imagery flickered in the windowpane petals. Scenes of cars on a busy downtown street, people out for dinner in restaurants, a couple stealing a kiss on a park bench under an umbrella, kids laughing while playing with a dog. Each image showed someone experiencing a moment in time, but she didn't recognize anyone.

Are these memories?

What if Declan had a point and he was telling the truth about Dementia, about the memory thieves and the Queen of Glass, about the power of remembering?

About Recollection City.

If this was Dementia and memories could be stolen from someone's head, who was the Queen of Glass and what did she want with them? And why Karin's?

Violet took the forget-me-not and kissed its sunspot heart, closed her eyes, and placed it on her forehead like Declan had done moments ago.

Nothing happened.

She pressed the forget-me-not harder into her forehead, her finger a makeshift pestle. After the snow plow had struck the car and flipped it casually in the air like some illusionist's trick, after the car came to a sliding stop, its metal frame grotesquely twisted, Karin had said something to Violet. Something comforting. Loving. But for as much as Violet tried to remember those words, all she ever saw was blood and smoke and flame. All she saw was her sister, hanging from the seatbelt like a discarded marionette.

Violet bit her cheek, fumbling with her memories. If there were any truth to Declan's words, she wanted to see it now. She wanted to hear those whispers.

Yet all she heard was silence, darkness swimming behind closed eyes.

She screamed, grinding the flower against her forehead. The petals melted like ice shavings on her skin. She removed the wilted flower and threw it onto the table. When it contacted the metal surface it sparked into a tiny bubble of sunlight.

The whit of light drifted into one of the bed posts and popped into smoke and ash.

Confusion and sadness filled her once again, those same racing emotions she'd felt after the car accident, after the firefighters cut through the car with saws and placed her on a stretcher, snow powdering her body. She remembered catching snowflakes on her tongue, their gelidness melting into the metallic taste of blood.

Violet had looked sideways as paramedics tried to secure her head between bright orange stabilizer blocks. Her sister lay on another stretcher, plastic tubes sprouting from her mouth. Tubes to make her breathe. Tubes to give her life.

And in that moment, under the emergency vehicle lights, she realized that she'd placed her sister on that stretcher. That she had inserted the tubes.

That she'd nearly killed her.

Violet knocked over the vase of forget-me-nots and rushed toward the bed. She snatched up the kaleidoscope as the flowers contacted the table. They crackled into a cloud of sun-yellow bubbles.

She held the kaleidoscope to her eye. As the bubbles contacted surfaces, colliding into walls, touching Violet's arms, her face and hair, they burst into smoke and soot.

Her sister was her priority. Not some strange guy. And not some make-believe war against a fairytale queen. She needed to get out of her head and back to the hospital.

Violet gazed into the kaleidoscope and the brightness of the room snuffed into ash—and disappeared.

The temperature within the kaleidoscope fluctuated once again as the shards of glass twisted and melded together into a patchwork quilt of color. Vertigo washed over Violet as the colors began to dissolve into a physical reality. But this time, instead of her stomach somersaulting, it pressed down, like when she rode the elevator in her counselor's building.

When the swirling color finally disappeared from Violet's vision, she found herself in her sister's room—holding the kaleidoscope. But something wasn't right.

Where's Karin?

Was she still dreaming? Or worse, stuck in some waking nightmare?

She tucked the cylinder into her coat pocket and looked around. Her sister's bed sat empty, sheets pristine and pressed. Outside the window, the sky was one entire canvas of cloud, dark and bruised. The red numerals on the bedside clock flashed 5:02PM. What was going on? Surely she hadn't slept the entire day away in the psychiatric hospital.

Violet cautiously walked into the hallway and turned toward the

dining area, listening for the sounds of slurping. Part of her still expected a slurper to jump out from a doorway like some cheesy horror film.

"What are you doing here on your birthday?"

Violet stopped as she entered the main room and looked toward the nurses' nook. Alice was sitting there, leafing through a clipboard and staring at Violet over her reading glasses.

"I didn't expect you today," she continued. "Especially with the roads the way they are after that snowstorm. When you didn't come in yesterday, I thought I wouldn't get to see you until next weekend."

Violet puzzled for a moment, not sure what to say.

"Anyways," Alice said, setting down the clipboard and getting up from her chair. "Happy sixteenth birthday, Sunshine." She sauntered over and gave her a hug.

"Thanks," Violet said, enveloped in a blanket of Alice's arms and peroxided hair. "But I was here yesterday. I slept in one of the vacant rooms...*remember?*"

Alice broke off her hug and held Violet back at arm's length. She cocked her head sideways, glancing up at a corner of the nurses' station as if her lost memory was hiding there. Alice plucked off her glasses and let them dangle against her multi-colored shirt by a lanyard.

"No way," Alice said, laughing to cover up her confusion. "I would remember you coming in yesterday. That was the worst snowstorm in years."

"But I did come in yesterday," Violet argued. "I stayed in Room 329."

Alice chortled. "Nice try, but we moved a new patient into that room this morning. Ms. Van Dyk. She's wonderfully charming—if not a bit eccentric. You should meet her."

Violet stood agape. How could Alice *not* remember? Sure, Violet's sister, being as dementia-riddled as she was, would forget her visits at times. But that was *expected*. Having Alice forget that Violet had been there yesterday, that she'd interacted with her, played cards with her, didn't make any sense.

In fact, it was downright freaky.

Violet continued into the dining hall with newfound haste, ignoring whatever Alice had started to babble on about. She scanned through the diners, past bibs splattered with gravy and pureed vegetables, past shouting and prattling residents, until she found her sister.

She was sitting at her usual table, in the far corner near the window, with three other women in various states of mental fragility.

"Hi, Karin," Violet said after negotiating the labyrinth of wheelchairs and tables. "How's dinner?"

Her sister backhanded a cup of milk. "Horrible. I can't believe you feed us this crap." The milk spilled across her neighbor's plate and splashed their bib. The other woman didn't notice—or didn't care.

"Well, I don't make the meals," Violet said, crouching down. "I just help you enjoy them."

Her sister glared at Violet, eyes smoldering with anger. Violet had seen Karin frustrated like this before, but usually Violet diffused the situation with lighthearted banter—or by bringing dessert.

"Do you want me to go see what's for dessert?" Violet asked. "I think they have pie. Strawberry-rhubarb, your favorite."

Her sister continued to stare at Violet, eyes narrowing into slits, jaw clenched. "Are you new?"

"New?"

"Where's my regular nurse? Where's the one with the rainbow shirt, or the one with those funny teeth? I don't like you."

"Karin," Violet said, taking her hand. "It's me, Violet."

Her sister pulled her hand back like a stubborn child. "Don't *touch me!* I don't know you. I want the other nurse. Nurse! Nurse, where are you?"

"I'm not a nurse," Violet said, stepping back. "I'm your sister." She had never seen Karin act this aggressively before. Violet felt sick. The doctors had warned her that this would happen.

"Get away from me," Karin yelled, food and spittle flecking the air. "Leave me alone. I want my regular nurse, you incompetent bitch."

Karin started shaking her wheelchair as if she were bound to a stretcher beyond her will. Her eyes were feral. Violet wanted to reach out and comfort Karin, but her arms were shaking and her legs weak. Violet fought the urge to crumple to the floor and cry. She had nearly lost her sister once before, and now it looked like she was going to lose her for real.

"What's the problem?" Alice said, running over from the other side of the dining room, a pair of orderlies flanking her.

"The problem is you keep getting these new nurses who don't have any respect," Karin said. "Look at that stupid look on her face. She knows nothing!"

Alice glanced at Violet, who could feel tears brimming in her eyes. If she was angry, her sister always picked out a hapless patient or one of the real nurses to blow off frustration—but never Violet.

"I'm sorry," Alice said, "but we get new nurses all the time, just like we get new residents. I know it can be hard to cope with, but you've got to calm down or I'll have to take you back to your room." The orderlies flanked Karin, restraining straps gripped in their hands.

"What's in my room?" Karin yelled. "More strangers to steal my wind?"

"You have to calm down," Alice said, her voice silken. She took out a small syringe from her pocket and stuck it into a vial of clear liquid. Tilting it upside down, she filled the syringe.

Violet hated needles. And she hated seeing her sister pricked with them even more, especially when they were filled with sedatives. She'd only witnessed Karin get combative once before and never wanted to see that again.

"I'm done with this shitty food," Karin continued. "And I'm done with her." She pointed at Violet with a shaking finger.

Alice glanced over her shoulder. "You should leave," she whispered to Violet. "You're making her worse."

Karin slammed her body against the wheelchair's backrest. "I don't want to see that bitch again!"

Violet trembled, backing away. Her sister's words were caustic, as if each one was a splash of acid. Karin continued to shake the wheelchair, smashing dishes on the table and throwing food. This wasn't her anymore. This wasn't Karin.

Violet wanted her old sister back so bad. The thought that this was Karin now, that this was because of Violet and her poor decision, sliced her apart like a million razorblades.

"You bitch," Karin chanted, rocking the wheelchair back and forth. "You bitch, you bitch, you bitch!"

Alice slid the needle into Karin's arm and compressed the syringe. Karin's eyes rolled back in her head, turning from jade to alabaster. Her body slumped.

She looked comatose.

Dead.

Like the day the doctors removed the tubes from her throat.

Alice didn't say anything as she and the orderlies wheeled her sister away. Silence spoke volumes. It always had.

A tear broke free and rolled down Violet's cheek. She lifted her sunglasses for a moment and wiped the tear away with a finger. As the rest of the patients went about their dinner completely oblivious to the outburst, Violet walked out of the room. She didn't feel like waiting for Alice to get back so she could be reassured that her sister's actions were normal for someone in her mental state, that she'd be fine in another day or so. She'd heard it countless times before. Besides, Violet wasn't certain she would be fine. Her memories were dissolving like sugar in water.

Violet stepped into a storage room and closed the door, the only illumination coming from a blue safety light above a shelf. She took a deep breath to collect her thoughts and placed her hands in the pockets of her peacoat.

Something cool and metallic grazed her hand.

She paused for a moment and then pulled out the kaleidoscope. Images of the prior night flooded her mind: flashes of frost, of cold hallways and that siphoning, slurping noise. Men in gas masks and fog-

covered trench coats. And that device on her sister's head, those tubes of glass and liquid rainbow. The same liquid rainbow she'd seen on Alice's temples.

Possibility clicked in Violet's mind like an unlocking door.

Was Declan right? Were there really creatures siphoning memories from the real world? Did Declan even exist, or were he and Dementia some weird subconscious byproduct of Violet's own depression?

Violet didn't know and didn't care. Her sister was deteriorating faster and faster, her mental landscape washing away like coastal erosion. There was nothing she could do about it. Unless—

It all sounded ludicrous, like some messed-up anime. Yet the possibility energized Violet. Hell, it even made sense in some weird, surrealistic kind of way. How else could Violet explain Alice forgetting about the prior night? If those creatures had preyed upon Alice before Karin, then that would account for her memory loss too.

And it would also explain her sister's behavior moments ago.

Violet spun the kaleidoscope in her hands, turning it around and around as the acid-etched patterns slithered.

Could there be possibility in this kaleidoscope?

If she looked back into the kaleidoscope and nothing happened, then she wouldn't go anywhere except back out of this closet the way she came in.

But if something did happen, if there was truth to what Declan had said about the Rememberists and the Queen of Glass, about the memory leeching and forgetting, then she would do everything she could to get her sister's memories back.

Excitement bloomed within her, pushing aside some of the sadness. She could almost see her spirit illuminating the darkness of the closet. There was only one way to find out if Declan was right.

Holding the kaleidoscope to her eye, Violet spun the cylinder, watching the melding colors suck her back into Dementia. Anticipation burbled in her stomach.

Her skin began to glow once again.

No regrets—not now. Not when there was the slightest sliver of possibility she could help her sister.

That she could reverse what she'd done.

5/ GLITTERGLAM

"I KNEW YOU'D RETURN."

Violet's feet settled on polished concrete. She tucked the kaleido-scope away. The words had come from behind her, and as she turned around she realized she was once again in the same room. Declan sat in the chair beside the bed.

The table was still wet from the spilled vase, the floor smeared with soot.

Declan rose when their eyes met, his trench coat swirling about in unnatural, syrupy movements. "I knew it."

"Well that's impressive since I didn't know I was coming back."

"Of course you knew. You're destined to illuminate Recollection City, and you can't do that from the real," Declan said rather assuredly. "I waited on the other side of the door when I left, listening. I heard you knock over the vase and by the time I convinced myself to come back into the room, you'd already departed." He broke their gaze and stared at the floor, his shoulders deflating. "I apologize for listening in, but we've been waiting so long for you to arrive, so long that I had to make sure you were indeed who I thought you were. And that you were going to stay."

"How long have you been waiting?"

"Me specifically?"

"No, in general," Violet said. "You keep saying you've all been waiting a long time. What's long? Like, a year?"

Declan's mouth waxed into a crescent smile. It was the first time Violet had seen him show any emotion other than a morose solicitude. And then, as quickly as the smile arrived, it waned.

"No, not a year," he said. "A *millennium*."

Violet scrunched up her face. She wasn't a kid anymore. With the car accident came reality and the letting go of fables and fantasy, of wiping her hands clean of fairytales. Then came the events of the past night. Karin had forgotten who Violet was, confusing her with being a nurse and freaking out to the point of being sedated like some out-of-control animal. The thought of something else out there, something that could make her sister remember, was emboldening. But a millennium? Seriously. She had taken a chance in believing that any of this was real, but waiting a thousand years for some girl to arrive was a bit much.

"Listen," Violet said. "I get this Dementia thing. At least I think I do. It makes some sense, sure, that maybe there's a place where memories disappear to, that they're not just forgotten. But waiting a *millennium* for me to arrive? Come on."

This time Declan didn't smile.

"I wish it were as simple as teaching you to ride a bicycle, but it's not. Look at your skin."

He reached out and took Violet's hand. His hand felt clammy, but there was a warmth, a caring touch—something she hadn't felt in a long time. Her skin glowed electric white. A blurring hazed the edges of her hand, as if she were vibrating beyond measure, like a filament ready to snap.

"See," Declan said, sandwiching Violet's hand between his, "there's raw power flowing in your veins. You're electric, Violet."

She didn't see the connection. She'd always been bright, being an albino and all. When she was younger she'd refused to play hide-and-

seek at night because she was always the first one caught. Even though her skin was cloud white she'd never *glowed*. Not like this.

"Okay, great," Violet said, "I'm a walking light bulb."

Realizing Declan was still holding her hand, she yanked it away—even though part of her didn't want to lose contact. His touch calmed her. "I don't see how that helps in any way," she added, somewhat embarrassed.

Declan looked toward the ceiling for a moment and then said, "Come with me. Although I can't officially show you Pallium until you're a member of the Rememberists, I can bring you to the roof. It'll help put things in perspective."

"What's Pallium?" Violet asked, following Declan to the door.

"You're in it." He opened the door and stepped into the hallway. "It's our stronghold. Our headquarters."

Violet wanted to ask how she could become a Rememberist but figured that question would be answered soon. She followed him into a hallway with glossy concrete floors and walls that seemed to corkscrew. She touched the wall for a moment to reclaim her balance. The twisting, funhouse-like hallway wasn't helping with her warped sense of perspective from her albinism.

Declan led her around a corner toward a large cage elevator. As she neared the elevator, her mouth fell open. The cage sat at the end of the hallway, away from the walls, its black art nouveau metalwork twisting into wrought iron ribbons and flowers and thorns. That alone wouldn't have surprised Violet, but that fact that there was no shaft above or below the elevator, just the cage, caused instant bewilderment.

"Oh," Declan said when he saw her face. "Right. You haven't met our transport system. This is Stem. It connects us to all of Pallium."

"But there's no shaft," Violet said, squinting. Even from a distance she could only see the ceiling above the elevator.

"Stem doesn't really work the way you'd expect, much like Dementia. It just gets us to where we need to be when we need to be there."

Violet rolled her eyes at his ridiculous explanation. For now she'd have to wait and see how far they'd get in an elevator with no place to go.

As they walked, the hallway reminded her of the Weeping Willow, with wide doors staggered intermittently and ceiling lights that didn't seem to work quite right.

Declan noticed her looking at the spasmodic lights. "We have the lighting set to flicker like that on purpose."

"Why?"

Declan opened the elevator cage doors. "Because," he said, waving a hand for her to enter the elevator first, "we all have certain powers that have manifested in Dementia that are unique to ourselves." Once he was inside, Declan slammed the cage door shut.

"Oh really," Violet said. "What's yours? Confusion?"

Declan pressed a button that read *Rooftop*. "No, I can fly."

Violet didn't know what to say to that. First she thought about making some smart-assed remark about Peter Pan, but that didn't seem appropriate. She just wanted to find her sister's memories without pissing off the one person who had offered to help her.

The elevator groaned and shook, puffs of steam filling the air outside the cage. The hallway faded from view beyond Stem's metalwork.

"And I manipulate shadow too," Declan continued. "I can ride it like a surfer, mold it like a potter, fold it, throw it, push it. The only thing I can't do is make it disappear."

The hallway had completely disappeared, replaced by thick fog. Jazz music started playing from blown glass flowers along Stem's ornate ceiling.

"And my power is to glow?" Violet guessed, assuming she'd have an ability in this strange world beyond constant bewilderment.

"Not exactly. Yours can be nurtured, like all of ours had to be. You'll need to work on it. And as for the lights—" He gestured to the flickering. "Cheshire's my polar-opposite. He manipulates light like I control shadow. That's why we have the lighting in Pallium set to flicker, to create pockets of shadow and light that we can control."

Violet assumed she looked confused because Declan was staring at her, as if the reason for the flashing lights was self-evident.

"It's in case we're attacked," Declan said finally, as if that answer was the most obvious thing in the world. "In case our defenses are breached. Pallium has been hidden from the queen for several centuries, and we want to keep it that way—but we also need to be prepared. This is our last refuge. If the queen finds out where we're hiding in Recollection City, we'll be wiped out before we can say forget-me-not."

"Umm, okay," Violet said. Besides seeing those fog-wearing creatures in the Weeping Willow, Violet didn't really know what being attacked meant. She didn't want to find out either. Every time she received an answer to one of her questions, it increased her curiosity tenfold and created more and more questions. To get Karin's memories back she was going to have to start getting concrete answers quickly.

If the Rememberists wanted her to be this prophetic princess of illumination or whatever they called it, then they had to cut out the sleight of hand answers and stop keeping her in the dark.

Or she'd just have to light her own path in Dementia.

The elevator vibrated as it ascended or descended—Violet couldn't tell—and suddenly pitched sideways, tossing her against the cage. She braced herself, a loud clang ringing out from above.

Hands appeared around her waist, steadying her.

"Easy," Declan said from behind Violet. His breath feathered her ear, sweet like the flowers around his neck. "Dementia is ever changing. You must always be ready for a twist, even within the walls of Pallium."

Violet turned around, breaking Declan's grasp. He was standing close enough that she could snatch one of the forget-me-nots wrapped around his neck with her teeth. This also meant she was staring right at his mouth, at his lips. Violet closed her eyes for a second and slithered to the side of the elevator. There was something magnetic about Declan—whether it was his disconsolate demeanor or his fortified good looks, she wasn't sure which. He pulled at her like the kaleidoscope without even saying a word.

The elevator shuddered once again, snapping Violet back to her current reality. "So, what do you mean, twist?" Violet said, weaving her fingers into the cage for balance.

"Dementia was built on the foundation of lost memory," Declan said, swaying to the elevator's movements. "From the buildings to the streets that join them together, the structures of Dementia are constantly being updated. As generations age and their memories settle in Dementia, the landscape shifts, like a constant, minor earthquake, molding Dementia to resemble their memories. Streets can change while you sleep. Entire buildings can disappear, only to be replaced by a new one. These are what we call twists, those aftershocks of dissipating memory."

Violet nodded, trying to follow along, trying to figure out how she could make a difference. She didn't know how any of this would help get her sister's memories back.

"I know it's a lot to take in," Declan said. "And there's lots more to learn, but don't worry, we're all here for you. We'll all help you get enlightened."

The elevator stopped vibrating and settled, the music fading. Outside the elevator the fog cleared, revealing a sprawling industrial rooftop illuminated by moonlight.

"Here we are," Declan said, pushing the cage door open. He motioned for Violet to walk out first.

———

Dementia bloomed in front of Violet in all directions, as if she were standing at the heart of a black-petaled daisy. Buildings of shadow fanned outward, stacked onto each other like so many discarded puzzle pieces. Neon reflected off windows and metal and polished concrete, colors amplified as if someone had applied a photo filter to everything, maximizing contrast and saturation. Yet for each burst of color, darkness snuffed out the spaces in-between trees and rowhouses, in the alleys

connecting old buildings and newfound skyscrapers. Glittering motes shifted in the sky, settling on the rooftop, on Violet's hair and skin. In the distance, a crooked clock tower tried to pierce the disco ball moon.

And then despair filled her. How was she ever to find her sister's memories in such a vast world? She didn't even know where to start.

"I remember the first time I looked out across its landscape," Declan said, standing beside Violet. "That feeling of impossibility is overwhelming."

"Yes," Violet whispered.

"But I joined the Rememberists and they showed me how to fold Dementia, how to manipulate it, and suddenly it didn't seem quite so impossible."

She'd come back to get Karin's memories, but now, looking out across the twisted world, she wasn't so sure how she'd be able to do that without the help of the Rememberists. And for that, it looked like she'd have to join them. If she didn't find Karin's memories, her sister would soon be dead, eventually forgetting the necessities of life, forgetting how to chew and swallow and would choke to death. Alone.

Feeling very much like how Violet felt right now.

"Why did you come here?" Violet asked, wondering what would make someone stay in Recollection City. "How long have you been in Dementia?"

Declan took a deep breath, his leather jacket swelling under his trench coat, zippers shimmering in the moonlight. After he exhaled, he said, "It's a painful story. I've been here for a while, both Cheshire and me. But now's not the time to get into that. What I can say is that I've learned a lot about Dementia, about the six boroughs that make up Recollection City. Things I've never thought possible are possible here."

He pointed toward the city encircling them, moving his arm through the glowing motes in the air. Bridges spanned rivers of milk-white water separating the boroughs.

"Each borough has its own uniqueness and dangers. They're all connected by rivers and bridges and tunnels, and each one is as equally

complex and deadly as its neighbor. I can help you navigate Recollection City and find your sister's memories, Violet. But—"

"I know," she interrupted. "I have to join the Rememberists."

Declan nodded, a lock of pewter hair falling across his face.

Violet adjusted her sunglasses and looked out across the city. It was massive and unlike anything she'd seen before, with buildings shifting and moving as if they were sprouting from a page in a pop-up book. She would need help navigating this strange world to find Karin's memories, but she wasn't quite ready to sign up with the Rememberists. They had to be more open with her first. Show her why it was so important she join them. She didn't even know what enlisting with them really entailed.

"What did you want to show me?" she asked.

"I want to show you where you fit in."

Finally, Violet thought, relief replacing some of the tension in her body.

Declan cleared his throat. "Although Cheshire can control light, he can't *generate* light. Just like I can't create shadow. I need to use what's around me."

"I'm not following you. So this glowing thing I've got going on, this is what I'm here for? That's why you've been waiting for me?"

"Sort of." Declan unzipped one of the twenty zippers lining his coat and reached inside. He pulled out a tiny black vial, stoppered by a cork. He zipped up his coat again and said, "Remember seeing these snowflakes floating around when you first arrived in the park?" He moved his hand around the air, the electric flakes swirling behind his movement.

"Yeah, sure," Violet said, nodding. "They look like dust."

"Well dust they are not. They're fragments of forgotten memory. Not a full memory, but an element of one. These are the things we naturally forget over time, our brains fading out the old to make room for the new. Insignificant events. Like what you did a few days ago, such as brushing your teeth. You might have remembered brushing

them later that day, but now, days later, do you remember the specifics?"

Violet tried to think back but came up empty. "No, but I know I did —I just can't remember *actually* doing it."

Declan popped the cork. "These are minor memories. They naturally break down and their essence sifts into Dementia, turning into the silt you see in the sky. We call it *glitter*."

He turned the vial upside down and shook his arm. Tiny motes of light spilled out, scattering and floating in the air until Declan was completely immersed in a shimmering cloud.

"These memory fragments are everywhere in Dementia," he said. "They're floating in the sky, dusting the streets, in every building and behind every door. But their potential power is minimal. There's no real benefit to collecting and distilling them down into raw essence—not like the liquid memory gained from siphoning. That stuff is a whole other story."

"Can we get my sister's memories from this glitter?" Violet asked. "Why are you showing me this?"

"Because to the right person, these memory fragments can be one of the biggest weapons ever. You can't extract memories from them. You need liquid memory for that. But the glitter can be the fuel to illuminate Recollection City. You can use it to defeat the queen."

"And you think I'm the right person?" Violet asked, even though she knew what he was going to say.

"I believe you are," Declan said, glitter swirling around him. His eyes were wide, glassy, radiating a sense of hope. "But there's only one way to be sure."

"And what would that be?" Violet asked. "Are you going to take my hand and make me jump off the roof to see if I can fly?"

"No," Declan said. "I just need you to concentrate." He took a few steps back until his legs bumped into the brick knee-wall that rimmed the roof. "Hold out your hands and focus your thoughts on them."

Violet held out her hands in front of her. She concentrated on the

chipped black nail polish decorating her fingertips, how it clashed with her white skin. She could see veins, like tiny filaments, spidering from her palms and into her wrists, disappearing into the cuffs of her peacoat. There was that vibration again, that tiny magnetic hum she'd noticed earlier. It feathered the edges of her hands, creating a permanent motion blur.

"Do you feel that?" Declan said. "That vibration? That's the undercurrents of Dementia. The power of twists, of memories forgotten. Tap into them. Concentrate. Ride the rush."

At first she didn't feel anything more than the vibration, like a build-up of static electricity in the winter from scuffing your socked feet on carpet.

Ride the rush? What does that even mean?

Then, slowly, she moved her hands in the cloud of glitter Declan had dispensed. The particles flowed around her hands like sand in water.

"Nothing's happening," Violet said. Then again, she wasn't sure what Declan was expecting of her, either.

"Concentrate on the vibration," he said. "Let the undercurrents of Dementia flow through you. Try to relax."

Violet glared through the cloud of memory fragments. How was she supposed to relax? As her anger and frustration increased, so did the vibrations coursing through her body. Her skin glowed more brightly. The glitter started to stick to her hands like ferrous dust to a magnet. She continued to swirl her hands in the particles, collecting them until her hands were completely covered.

"That's it," Declan said, his voice sounding distant against the thrum in Violet's ears. "Keep going."

Shocks crawled over Violet's skin like a million electric ants. In any other situation she would have screamed from the pain, but for some reason she easily pushed it aside, mesmerized by the glitter sticking to her. Glitter continued to zoom toward the mass until all the particles Declan had dispensed were swarming over her arms and hands, sun-

bright and hot. Objects became photo-negative in Violet's vision. Declan stood against the backdrop of Recollection City, as if he'd been sketched in phosphorescent white chalk on a blackboard.

"Funnel that energy into any object you can think of," Declan said. "Whatever comes to mind first."

Energy overwhelmed her. Adrenaline coursed through her veins. It reminded her of the car accident, that moment right before the snow-plow slammed into Karin's car. And then the anger of that night mixed with the energy, pain blending with the vibrations until Violet's arms began to shake. Flashes of snow penetrated her vision, of emergency lights and smoke, the blood rush of hanging upside down from her seat-belt, helpless as she'd watched her sister's life spill across the snow.

The sound of saws cutting into metal.

Violet screamed from the imagery, from the pain of the electricity washing over her. She forced her thoughts out and into her arms, away from her mind, away from the recollections, until glitter began shooting toward her, joining into the particles covering her arms. Glitter came from the air, from tiny drifts along the half-wall and from over the edge of the building. Violet forced out her anger, willed it out of her and into the glitter.

After the accident, her counselor had wanted Violet to find an outlet for the pain and guilt, something to channel her rage through, and so she had taken up kendo—Japanese fencing. She soon realized her depth perception problems caused more pain, though this time it was of a more physical variety. She'd refused to withdraw from training, even though her mother threatened to stop paying for the classes every time she saw new bruises. In some twisted, masochistic way, Violet liked the pain from training, from being struck. From striking out. If there was anything in the last year that'd helped ground her, it was her weekly kendo class. Her *shinai*—the bamboo sword used for training—hung on the wall above her bed.

And so Violet curled her hands into fists, placing them one on top of the other. Glitter shot from the swirling mass, ran down her arms to form

a solid shaft of particles that stretched upward from her fists like a sword of swarming fireflies.

Violet smiled, moving the sword around in a nova of light.

"Now that," Declan said with a grin, "is where you fit in. Say hello to the prophetic sword of the Princess Electric.

"Say hello to *Glitterglam*."

6/ THE FORGETTING

VIOLET OPENED HER EYES WIDE, staring at the sword in her hands, jagged and crackling like a bolt of lightning. "What the actual fu—"

"Disperse the sword," Declan barked, looking out across Dementia. His face crinkled with concern, illuminated by the light of the sword. "And be quick about it."

Before Violet had a chance to ask why, Declan sprayed shadow across the sword. The shadow fell from the blade like molasses. Declan cursed and stretched out his arms. He spun in a circle, raising his hands over his head. Curtains of shadow rose from the roof's brick half-wall, stretching high into the air until it felt as though Violet was standing at the bottom of a magician's top hat.

"What?" Violet said, distracted by the sudden wall of darkness encircling them.

"Glitterglam," Declan shouted. "Will it away."

Violet moved the blade around in the air. It sizzled like rain on coals. "How do I do that?"

"Think of it dissolving," Declan said, his arms still above his head. "Scatter the glitter in your mind. And hurry, I can't keep this shroud up

for much longer. I didn't think you'd illuminate the sword so much without formal training."

Sweat beaded on his forehead.

Violet snapped her arms back and forth, trying to disperse the glitter —but the sword remained. Her arms vibrated with electricity. She let go with one hand and shook the other but it was glued to her grip.

"I can't," she said. "It won't disappear."

Light beamed from the tip of the blade, casting a spotlight against the curtain of shadow.

"Hurry!" Declan's face twisted with fatigue. "When this curtain comes down Glitterglam has to be extinguished. You're like a star up here!"

"I don't even know what Glitterglam is!" Violet waved the sword around as if trying to remove something sticky from her hand.

"Glitterglam is the sword," he said, exasperated, his arms beginning to shake.

"Violet!"

She spun around to the sound of her name. Lights sparked, making her blink and squint against their brightness through her sunglasses. They torpedoed toward her, all shooting stars, until they whistled past her head and curled upward, bursting into golden fireworks. Violet brought up her hands to protect her eyes and in doing so the sword, Glitterglam, whatever, dissipated in a cloud of sparks.

Her chest rose and fell with rapid breathing. She rubbed her eyes behind her sunglasses and then opened them. A ghost-like figure drifted through the post-flash haze toward her, clapping and saying, "Well done, brother, well done. Kudos for being an idiot. Why don't you light a bonfire up here while you're at it? Maybe we can make s'mores and sing camp songs too."

Declan let his arms drop and the curtain fell. He hunched over, hands on his knees. When he straightened he said, "Watch your tongue, Cheshire. Especially in front of—"

"In front of who?" Cheshire interrupted. "In front of Violet?" He

pointed to her and Violet's stomach dropped. Cheshire's eyes were like Declan's, all cornflower and citrus, though their intensity differed. Declan's were haunted, sad, pleading. But Cheshire's...there was a beguiling deepness to them, like staring down a wishing well. When his eyes fell on Violet, she wanted nothing more than to be made of copper. Shiny and perfect and ready to fall.

"You don't seem very concerned about her safety," Cheshire said to his brother, eyes still locked on Violet.

"That's not true and you know it."

"Oh really?" Cheshire refocused on Declan. "Could have fooled me."

With Cheshire's gaze broken, Violet's stomach fluttered, breath all butterflies in her throat. For as much as she wanted him to look at her again, wanted him to shoot stars through her, the flirtations were distracting. She enjoyed the attention, sure, but she wasn't here to find a boyfriend—she was back in Dementia to find her sister's memories.

"You broke one of our cardinal rules bringing Violet up here," Cheshire continued. "Not to mention getting her to expose powers she has no control over yet."

Declan's body stiffened. "We can't wait for—"

"Besides," Cheshire interrupted, eyes narrowing, "Violet could be a memjack. But we'd know that if you'd inducted her first, instead of prancing her around Pallium."

"First of all," Violet said, stepping between the Brothers Gloss, "I'm not a horse. And second, do I look like a slurper? Last time I checked I wasn't wearing a gas mask and drinking memories."

"Of course you don't look like a slurper," Declan said, his cheeks tinting scarlet. "Or a clanker or sniffer. Or any of the other memjack agents. Trust me on this, you're much better-looking."

Violet's face warmed. "Then what's the problem? Believe it or not, I came back to join you."

"Violet," Cheshire said, putting his hand on her shoulder. Her knees

rubberized against the weight of his hand. His touch. "There are... concerns about newfallens. Years ago, people transitioned into Dementia all the time, but the queen has eliminated most of the portals, making it rare for someone to randomly fall into Recollection City. Which means newfallens like yourself are scrutinized more than ever."

"Because you think I came back for some other reason than my sister?" Violet asked, eyes narrowing.

"Yes." Cheshire waved his free hand through the sparkling motes in the air. "By summoning Glitterglam you've completed the first step in proving yourself as the Princess Electric. That is without question. But we can't discuss our concerns further until you're a member of the Rememberists. This is one of our core rules—a rule that has been in effect for close to a millennium. That rule will not be broken now. Not even for you."

Violet nodded and Cheshire removed his hand from her shoulder. She understood what he was saying. They didn't trust her yet, and really, they had no reason to. Just because she could somehow make a sword from glitter didn't mean she'd use it the way they wanted her to.

But she didn't trust them either.

"How do I join?" Violet asked, glancing sideways at Cheshire and Declan. "Do I need to sign something?"

Cheshire chuckled. "Not quite. It's a bit more involved than that. There's a bit of a ceremony. It's pretty painless."

Violet cast her gaze across Recollection City. Somewhere in the moving buildings and shadowy streets were Karin's memories. Without looking at either brother, she said, "I will join the Rememberists on one condition."

"Ultimatums," Declan added, "are not a form of currency in Dementia."

"Listen. If you want me to help you, then you need to help me."

"And what does this help entail?"

"You help me get my sister's memories back," Violet said, turning to

face Declan. "The ones the slurpers stole the other night. Once I get them to her and she remembers who I am, then and only then will I assist in illuminating Recollection City—or whatever it is you need me to do."

Declan bit his lip—a habit Violet had noticed from him before. Although it was cute, it also drew her attention to his lips. They were as dark as bruises, and Violet caught herself wondering just how deep they went.

"That sounds feasible to me," Cheshire said. "Though tracking specific memories through Dementia will prove difficult at best. And extremely dangerous. What do you think, brother?"

"I don't think we have a choice," Declan said, eyes glassy under the moonlight. "But Violet, please understand, tracking siphoned memories will lead us into some of the darkest parts of Dementia. Into places warped by the currents of time. Madness consumes fear in these places. You must understand what you're asking us to do."

Violet glanced into the sky for a moment, watched the glitter shift and sway like dying sparks. She looked at her hands, at how they glowed as bright as the moon. Her skin thrummed.

"I don't know where we need to go," she finally said. "But I do know I need to get my sister's memories back. Besides, Declan, you said I'm here to illuminate Recollection City, that I'm some sort of princess of prophecy. Can't we do that at the same time? Can't we go into these dark places and brighten them while getting the memories back?"

Declan closed his eyes and took a deep breath. When he opened them his face was calm, as if he'd washed away all emotion. Eyes distant, haunted. "I hope we can." He turned to look out across the cityscape. He shifted just enough so Violet could no longer see his face.

She knew he was hiding something because she did it all the time. When she was hurting, when she wanted to be left alone in a crowd of people, she turned away and hid her face. Declan was broken, though she had no idea why.

"Then it's decided," Cheshire said with unhindered enthusiasm. "I'll take Violet to the butterfly conservatory for the ceremony. Declan, go tell Parminder that she'll have a visitor shortly."

Cheshire grabbed Violet's hand before Declan could answer and started to pull her toward the elevator.

Who's Parminder? Violet wondered. *A Rememberist I haven't met yet?*

As they walked, she looked back, trying to make eye contact with Declan—but he just stared out across Recollection City, silent as a forgotten memory.

Cheshire and Violet rode Stem in silence. He stood with his back against one wall, eyeing her and running his tongue along perfect teeth. Violet stood on the opposite wall, fingers hooked into the cage mesh, trying her best not to make eye contact while listening to the chill muzak playing from the glass flowers.

She counted the number of black-and-white rings that spiraled down her stockings until they disappeared into scuffed boots. She toed the elevator floor and said, "Why are we going to a butterfly conservatory? I'm not a fan of things that flit. I'll scream if one comes near me, just so you know."

Cheshire smiled as the elevator came to a stop and opened the cage door. "It's an old conservatory that was attached to this building, or had twisted here at some point to be a part of it. Regardless, there are no butterflies per se."

"Then what's inside?"

"Memories," Cheshire said. He motioned for Violet to exit the

elevator into a large atrium. A lead-paned ceiling, filled with opaque glass, stretched above her. Glitter fell beyond the glass, diffused sparks dusting its surface like moths set to flame. A few panes were missing which allowed some of the glitter to ride the moonlight into the atrium proper.

"Whose memories?" Violet wondered if her sister's memories could be there.

"Ours," he said. "Rememberist memories."

As she stepped away from Stem, Violet pondered if part of the ceremony involved memories. Why else would Rememberist memories be in the conservatory? She glanced back at the elevator for a moment, its wrought-iron ornamentation shimmering in the glitter-dusted moonlight. For a moment she thought Stem groaned, like an old man standing up, joints creaking.

"How did we even get here?" Violet asked, still amazed there were no cables, no elevator shaft. Stem stood isolated like a garden statue in the middle of the atrium. "Isn't Pallium one building? Like the Empire State Building or something?"

"Not quite," Cheshire said, walking past Violet and motioning for her to follow. The forget-me-not lei left a sweetness on the air. "Pallium is made up of interconnected twists that we've secured. Twists are those random changes to the fabric of Recollection City from evaporating memory. Protecting Pallium from twists requires a bit of luck on our part, but so far any location we've hardwired into Stem seems to remain fastened to Pallium without changing much over time."

Violet rubbed her temples. "Okay, so Declan mentioned that Pallium is your headquarters. But it's hidden?"

"Right. Once a twist is part of Pallium, we seal it off from Recollection City. We use transcendence gates for secure travel between Pallium and Dementia. Unless someone finds a gate and knows how to use it, there's no getting in. Or out for that matter."

Violet shook her head, trying to process Cheshire's explanation. She felt as though she was trying to take a sip of water from a firehose.

Maybe at some point she'd understand everything better, but for now she'd be happy to catch her breath.

Cheshire led her along the atrium, dotted by randomly placed stands of halogen lighting which created pockets of shadow like in the hallway. As they neared a large glass door, he said, "Several of our secure twists branch off the atrium, including the Moulin Rouge, the greenhouse, and the conservatory. All of them can be reached by taking Stem to the atrium."

"The Moulin Rouge?" Violet asked, her interest perking. She'd learned about the famous Paris nightclub when studying Toulouse-Lautrec in art class. Really, she was more interested in reading about the parties he went to at the Moulin Rouge than his artwork.

"Yes. As in Oller and Zidler's famous cabaret of decadence and debauchery." Cheshire smiled when he said this, his voice beckoning. Violet's cheeks broiled under his gaze and she quickly looked away. "Supposedly it appeared as a twist about a hundred years ago."

Politely ignoring Violet's embarrassment, Cheshire swung open the large glass double-doors to the conservatory and stepped inside. The air was cold, and immediately tiny ghosts escaped his mouth. Violet welcomed the cool air on her cheeks and followed.

The conservatory spread out before her in a large circle about the size of a football field. An amphitheater, carved in stone, sat in the sunken center. Spread throughout were the remnants of foliage, now frozen and brittle and dead.

Cheshire walked her along a path toward the amphitheater. As they neared the steps down toward the stage, something multi-colored flitted past Violet's head. She screamed and ducked, swatting at the streak of color.

He grabbed her wrist and yelled, "Don't!"

"Why not? I told you I don't like butterflies! You said there weren't any in here."

"They're not butterflies." Cheshire slowly released Violet's wrist. "They're memories. Look."

Cheshire turned her around and stood behind her. Against her. And pointed over her shoulder. "There...see it? The flutter of rainbow... there, between those branches."

Violet followed the length of his arm and stared into a clump of dead trees. Sure enough, there, pirouetting through the trees, was a rainbow-colored butterfly.

"I see it," she said, "and it sure looks like a butterfly to me."

He tittered. "They're memories, Violet. Each of us plucked our most sacred memory from our minds and cast them into the conservatory during ordainment—as an oath to our fellow Rememberists, and as a promise to ourselves. It's called *The Forgetting*."

Violet saw another flutter to her right, and then a streak of color to her left. Each one was scintillating and beautiful and haunting. Ghosts of moments.

Seeing more butterflies made her wonder how many Rememberists there were in Dementia.

Cheshire shifted again and for the first time Violet truly registered his proximity. The forget-me-nots around his neck touched the back of hers, all icicle cool as her face warmed. She twisted out from his arms and straightened her peacoat, pretending nothing had happened even though the heat of her cheeks backstabbed any remaining innocence.

"Let me get this straight," Violet said, trying to adjust the focus away from her uneasiness. "Basically, from what you've told me, The Rememberists are sworn to protect memories, and in doing so, stop some evil queen from stealing them."

"More or less."

"Then why must I give up a cherished memory to join some organization sworn to protect them? Seems a bit backwards, no?"

"The Forgetting," Cheshire said, starting down the stairs of the amphitheater, "is our memory oath. It is the only step in becoming a Rememberist. There are no psalms to sing or scriptures to recite. There is only silence in the Forgetting, and only Forgetting in the silence."

Violet sighed heavily and stopped walking. "That doesn't answer my question. Stop talking in riddles and answer me."

Cheshire stopped and turned around. "It's so we all understand the emptiness one feels when you forget something dear to you. The feeling eats at your soul, that something is gone but you don't know what it is. You feel hollow. Haunted. And you never know why. That's why we sacrifice one of our most cherished memories. To remember what it is we're fighting for."

With that, he turned and continued down the stairs. Cheshire's explanation made sense, sure, but Violet thought about the painful memories packed into her head. Without hesitation she'd give up all the memories of the accident, or her father's funeral, or how the citrusy scent of his cologne faded from his jacket in the weeks after his death, rather than one cherished memory. Unfortunately, that would defeat the purpose of the memory oath.

Violet followed him until they reached the stage, then climbed up a secondary, smaller set of stairs. Sitting on the stage was a single chair, facing out into the amphitheater. Behind the chair sat a table with an assortment of chemistry paraphernalia. Glass tubing and metal clamps. Test tubes.

Cheshire motioned for her to sit.

"Should anyone else be here for this?" Violet asked. "I mean, like, witnesses or something?" Hadn't Cheshire said to Declan, *Go tell Parminder that she'll have a visitor?*

"No," he said, rummaging around the table. He blew dust off a jumbled mass of glass tubing wrapped with copper bands. "We generally do this ceremony quietly, with only one person. This is a quiet time of personal reflection and loss."

"Really? That seems kinda odd." Violet chewed on the inside of her cheek, unsure if she should press that nobody else was with them.

Screw it, she thought. *This doesn't feel right.*

"What about Parminder?" she blurted.

Cheshire walked in front of her carrying a contraption that looked

like the device that'd been strapped to her sister's head. "What about her?"

"Didn't you tell Declan she'd have a visitor? Who is she? Is she coming here for the ceremony?" Her heart two-stepped in her chest.

He shrugged, undoing leather straps along the opening of the brass contraption. "You'll see Parminder Honey soon enough. After you participate in the Forgetting." He dipped his chin into the lei around his neck, petals kissing his jaw. "One of her jobs is to grow these forget-me-nots. There's no point in making the apiarist's acquaintance until you become one of us."

Violet's body tensed as Cheshire placed the device on her head. He snaked the leather chin strap through a d-ring buckle and yanked it snug.

"Ow!" she yelled, reaching up to pull the strap away from her chin. "Do you need to be so rough?"

His eyes shimmer-flashed as they took her in. He paused for a breath. "I'm sorry. I didn't mean to pull the strap so hard. It's...been a while since I've done this."

Cheshire took her hand away from the strap and placed it on the arm of the chair. After loosening the strap, he straightened the contraption and continued to tweak the tubing.

Images of the slurpers flooded Violet's mind, the way they'd hunched over her sister, adjusting spigots as they siphoned her memories. The idea that Cheshire was going to do the same thing made her want to get up and run—but running wouldn't help her find Karin's memories. It would just send them farther away.

"This isn't going to hurt, is it?" Violet asked, steeling herself to the coldness and weight of the copper and glass. She bit her lip and instantly found herself thinking about Declan. Why wasn't he there to be her witness? To be her support. Though she didn't mind Cheshire's presence either. He had a different effect than Declan. There was no rainy Sunday demeanor with Cheshire, but one of sun-kissed beaches and crashing waves.

"You'll feel an itch on your temples, like a mosquito making its mark —but that's about it. Now, as I get this siphoner set up and calibrated, think of your most precious memory. One dearest to your heart. This is what you must sacrifice to be a Rememberist. The memory will be set to live within the confines of the conservatory until you no longer are a Rememberist."

"And when does that happen?"

"Either you leave Dementia after you've turned eighteen," Cheshire said, adjusting the siphoner, "after which you'll no longer be able to freely transition between the under-real and the real. Meaning you will be locked out of Dementia forever."

"Or?" Violet asked.

Cheshire knelt in front of Violet and placed his hands on her knees. Heat from his palms bled through her tights. His eyes were like an oasis amid this storm-gray world. "Or...you die."

Violet's stomach quavered. She'd never thought about death here; never thought of it as a possibility. Could people die in movies where they travelled to other worlds, other dimensions? What about all those science fiction and fantasy books she'd read to drown out reality? Did the main characters die in these alternate universes? She couldn't remember. Maybe that very memory was drifting along the glitter of Dementia, silently forgotten from her mind.

Considering she hadn't wanted to even wake up on her sixteenth birthday, dying in Dementia, where nobody would remember her if she died, felt peculiarly comforting.

"So what happens if you die here?"

"Well," Cheshire said, his hands still warm on her knees, "the conservatory used to house thousands of memories at one time. Our numbers for this borough of Recollection City used to be quite strong before the war against the Queen of Glass heated up. Now there are just the six of us. Six Rememberists against the countless."

"But are there other Rememberists?" Violet asked. "Other groups in different boroughs?"

"There *were* others. The conservatory was accessible from all boroughs, by all Rememberists. It used to be filled with butterflies. But that was a long time ago. Before the queen found a way to pinpoint the location of our transcendence gates. Once she figured that out, it didn't take long for her to ambush us and slaughter us like cattle."

The brightness of his eyes frosted for a moment, a flash freeze negating emotion. For the first time he seemed closed off to her, as if Violet were simply window shopping, all outside looking in. Wanting but not having. It was obvious Cheshire had disconnected from their conversation and was somewhere else. Lost in the remembrance of another time, another moment. And then he blinked and the frost melted away, his eyes bright and welcoming once more, a slight rainbow sheen playing across them.

Cheshire half-smiled, the corner of his mouth curling upward. He blinked, eyes ocean wet, mouth open slightly as if to say something. But he caught his breath with a slight inhalation and then closed his mouth.

He pulled back his hands and stood. Leaned over Violet to adjust the siphoner again, his forget-me-not lei brushing her face.

"What was up with Declan on the roof?" Violet asked, changing the topic. "He seemed so eager for me to join, that I'm this princess of prophecy or something, but when I gave my ultimatum on joining he got all weird and silent."

"Ask him about Oriana Palms," Cheshire said, walking back to the bench.

"Where's that?"

He shook his head. "Oriana is a girl."

"Seriously?"

Violet sat in silence for a moment, unsure of what to think. She'd just met Declan, Cheshire, and some of the other Rememberists a short time ago. But Violet felt there was a connection to Declan. That he was pure of intention and spoke from his soul—and she appreciated that. When he said he wanted to help get Karin's memories back, she believed

him. He was authentic and the first person she'd met upon arriving in this world.

Yet something about Cheshire rang sirens in Violet's mind. And not just police sirens, but holy shit air raid sirens. Everything in her told her to duck and cover. Find shelter and stay away. She had a bad feeling that if she dropped her protection, she'd be shot full of holes.

Cheshire returned with a series of empty vials and eyed the siphoner. "You ready?"

"No."

"What do you mean...no?" He took a step back and looked at her sideways.

"Something isn't right. We shouldn't be doing this alone." Violet reached up and shook the siphoner on her head, the glass vials and copper tubes jangling together. "I don't feel right about this thing on my head. I want Declan here. Somebody. I'm not doing this alone."

Her breathing quickened. Heat washed across her body, along the small of her back. Her face. She looked past Cheshire toward the stairs that led off the stage, to the aisles of the amphitheater, then toward the distant exit of the conservatory.

"Hey." Cheshire snapped his fingers, a tiny spark of light flashing between his thumb and middle finger. "Look at me."

Violet slowly turned her head toward him, narrowing her eyes.

"I already explained that this is a quiet ceremony of reflection. It's not some pep rally or award show. It's between two people trusting each other. Declan is busy with other preparations."

Violet huffed. "But I don't trust you. We just met." She pushed herself back against the chair, as if that would create more space between them.

Cheshire sniggered. "What, and you trust Declan? You just met him too." He took a breath, exhaled slowly as if to simmer his frustration. "Listen, your sister's memories were taken by slurpers. There's only a small window of opportunity to get them back, and for every second you

question our process, your sister's memories are getting farther and farther away from recovery. For all we know it could be too late as it is.

"So if you want our help, then you need to do your part and prove you're not some memjack spy by joining us. Whether or not you're the Princess Electric, we'll figure that out—but you need to partake in the Forgetting. Just like I did. Like Declan. Like every Rememberist before us, and those to come."

Cheshire wiped the corner of his mouth with the back of his hand. "Now I'm going to ask you one more time. Are you ready?"

Violet's jaw ached, her teeth compressing together like a vise. Cheshire had made a good point about Declan, that she'd only met him earlier in the day too and really had no grounds to trust him either. Regardless, having someone else there while she went through the ceremony would help put her at ease, Declan or not.

Yet she had to get Karin's memories. That was all that mattered right now. And if delaying this ceremony would jeopardize that possibility, then she'd have to take the risk.

"Fine." Violet took a deep breath. "Let's do it."

Cheshire nodded. "Very well. In a moment I'll need you to recall your most treasured memory. Something so dear to you that you'd feel lost without it, something that you pull strength from, something that soothes your soul in times of need. Something you'd feel empty without. When I tell you, you need to run through the memory as if it were happening all over again. As if you were there. While you're reminiscing, I'll siphon the memory from your mind. Do you have any questions before we start?"

"No," Violet said.

The quicker we do this, the quicker I can get Karin's memories back.

She placed her hands on the chair's armrests and squeezed.

"All right." He licked his lips. "Entering your temples in three, two, one..."

An itch formed just in front of Violet's ears. She went to scratch but her hands bumped off the siphoner, rattling the glass tubing.

"Just another second," he said. "Keep your hands down."

The itch continued to grow until it was nearly unbearable. She used every drop of willpower not to reach up and rip the siphoner from her head. And then, as fast as it had arrived, the itch was gone.

"How are you doing?" Cheshire asked.

"Fine."

"Okay, let's begin. Start replaying your memory, and I'll be done as soon as you are."

Violet didn't have to hunt for the memory dearest to her—the one she wanted floated to the surface of her mind faster than bubbles underwater. She had lots of memories that were important to her—memories of her grandma and grandpa, her parents from better times, childhood, friends, experiences.

But it was the memories of Karin that she held closest. Whether that was true because she had a direct hand in Karin's accident, she didn't know. Every memory of Karin was precious, each moment locked within her psyche, the key long since thrown away. Watching videos and looking at photos, well, those hurt like knives twisting into Violet's mind —but they weren't *moments*. These few fragments of time with her sister were more precious to Violet than any physical possession. Without them she'd feel hollow and haunted, as if someone had reached in and scooped out pieces of her soul.

Violet plucked her most favorite memory from her mind like a ripe piece of fruit and started to consume it. Tears welled. The siphoner shook on her head, clinked like windchimes, and then the unmistakable slurping noises began.

As Violet continued to consume the memory of her sister, of a time not too long ago, tears fell. Her cheeks grew wet, and tears collected where her sunglasses kissed cheek, along her jaw, her chin, and fell.

She noticed that the glass tubes snaking around her head began to glow with a multi-colored liquid, all rainbows against a slate sky. The liquid reflected in Cheshire's eyes as he adjusted the spigots and vials on the siphoner, his movements accelerating with each breath.

Fatigue filled Violet's body as she began to sob. Memories of her sister deluged her mind. Not just a single treasured moment anymore, but a steady stream of their life together. Birthdays, trips to the beach, camping and roasting marshmallows around the fire, laughing as they tried to blow them out when they caught fire. Tobogganing with their dad and ice skating with their mom. Sleepovers so they could share the same room, even though they shared the same house.

Moments upon moments fell from her mind, stacking on top of each other like a layered cake. The siphoner continued to leech memories while Cheshire filled vial after vial of syrupy liquid, his hands moving feverishly. His forehead crinkled as a rivulet of sweat trailed down the side of his face and curled along his jaw. As Violet slouched, exhausted and glassy-eyed, her surroundings smeared as if looking through rain on a windshield. The machine chugged and shook. A loud slurping noise filled the conservatory.

Then it went quiet.

"All done," Cheshire said, kneeling in front of Violet. Sweat dappled his brow. "How do you feel?"

"Tired," Violet said. "Empty. I just want to take a nap."

"You'll have time to rest later, after you see Parminder."

Cheshire removed the siphoner from Violet's head and placed it on the table. Her head felt like a fluffed pillow. She massaged her temples. When Cheshire came back he was carrying a beaker full of rainbow liquid.

He held up the container, staring at its contents. The liquid glowed, casting stained glass reflections across Cheshire's face. Violet couldn't tell whether he looked angelic or demonic or both.

"What is that?" Violet asked, puzzled by the amount of liquid in the beaker.

He slowly tilted the beaker and started to pour the liquid out, and as the rainbow syrup became free of the container it fluttered, as if a strong wind had caught it mid-stream. Wings formed and soon several butterflies appeared, flitting about Cheshire. He continued to pour

until the beaker was empty and hundreds of butterflies danced around him.

"These are all the good memories of your sister," Cheshire said, his voice emotionless.

Violet blanched, trying to count all the butterflies but losing track. "What do you mean?"

"When you grabbed the siphoner you must've banged something. Messed it up." Cheshire set the empty beaker on the ground, butterflies swirling around his head. "I tried to shut it off while you were recalling everything but the valve was jammed. There was...there was nothing I could do."

"How do I get them back?" she whispered, struggling to compute that more than one memory had been siphoned. That wasn't the plan. Wasn't what she agreed to. Nausea filled her stomach. Her throat felt full. She wanted to vomit. "How do I get them back inside my head?"

"It's not impossible," Cheshire said, running his hands through his hair. "This is only an inconvenience. But it'll take time to reinstall them, time we don't have if you want to find your sister's memories."

Violet sat there, silent and numb. Her body trembled, tiny vibrations running across her skin. Mouth dry. She knew that she had a sister, that she put her in a mental hospital and nearly killed her. All she could remember were memories of pain, of sadness and loss. All she could recall were the fights, the screaming and yelling and disagreements over boys or clothes or who missed their father more. But there was something else about her sister she couldn't remember, something that sat at the corner of her periphery like a sixth sense, like feeling as if someone's following you, yet when you spin around there's nothing but shadows and dead leaves.

She wanted to cry, but didn't know why.

Wanted to scream, but had forgotten the reason.

There was nothing happy left in her head.

Nothing that would part clouds.

"You're a Rememberist, Violet," Cheshire said. "How does it feel?"

She looked up at him, butterflies of memory flitting about. "I feel hollow."

"Good," he said, a slight frown tugging at his lips. "That's how you should feel."

"I didn't even feel anything when I forgot about my sister. Nothing."

"That is the most painful thing about forgetting," Cheshire said, raising his hands in the swarm of butterflies. "When you forget, you don't feel anything at all."

7/ APIARIST EXTRAORDINAIRE

VIOLET AND CHESHIRE once again found themselves in silence. As they walked through the conservatory toward the exit, she kept her head down, ignoring the butterflies flitting between the branches of dead trees. She tried to recall something about her sister, something beyond the arguments, but couldn't. It was as if every thought sat on the tip of her tongue, balancing precariously between remembrance and being forgotten.

Her head ached as she tried to remember her sister's smile, but all she remembered was how her eyes would turn to knives when angry, or when Violet would get her in trouble—whether intentional or not. Like the time Karin had thrown a bottle of nail polish at Violet's head for telling their mom about her smoking. It shattered against the bathroom wall, all plum and broken glass. A glittery bruise that never washed off, no matter how many times it'd been scrubbed with nail polish remover or painted over. Violet could never forget those darker moments.

Why do I only make bad decisions?

Even when I think I'm doing the right thing, it's wrong.

Like the accident.

Sirens filled Violet's mind. A wash of wintry air swept over her. The

crispness of the snow that night against the ice-blue chips of shattered windshield. Karin's blood drizzled over the snow like strawberry sundae topping. Upside-down, topsy-turvy. The seat belt, how it sawed into Violet's shoulder. Gasoline. The spark of flame.

Violet grabbed a railing and nearly heaved over the side. The memory was as vibrant as the night it'd happened. It always would be. She knew this. But when images of Karin in the twisted pretzel of a car permeated her thoughts she'd always counter with something good, something pleasant—but there was no sunshine in her head now. Just storm clouds and emptiness.

"Are you all right?" Cheshire asked.

She spun around. "Do I look like I'm all right?"

"Well—"

"What the fuck did you do to me, Cheshire?"

Cheshire stood in front of her, his eyes wide and glassy with a faint rainbow sheen. "There was—there was nothing I could do. The siphoner was jammed. Trust me. I would never—"

"I don't have to trust shit. I don't know you. I don't know *anything* about this place!" Violet's shoulders shuddered. She clenched her fists. They brightened, tiny wisps of electricity snaking around them. "What I do know is that you stole the good memories of my sister. All of them. You were supposed to only take one!"

Cheshire took a step forward, glancing toward her hands, their glow brightening his face. "I think accusing me of stealing is a bit much, but you're right, I did take them all. I'm guilty. And whether you believe there was an issue with the equipment or not, the fact is those memories are gone now. But I will get them back inside you. I promise."

"Promise? How can I ever trust you again?"

Violet laughed at his audacity. She wanted to turn the lump in her throat into nails and spit them at Cheshire. Instead she raised her hands, waved them around. They flashed against the walls of the conservatory like spotlights at a club.

"How can I believe anything you say? I can't remember a single good thing about my sister. She's the only reason I'm here!"

She started to walk away, pushing past Cheshire. He grabbed her wrist. Squeezed. Sparks crackled under his grasp, like water dropped onto a hot frying pan. His face twisted in pain, but he held on to her.

"*Don't. Fucking. Touch me*," Violet seethed, trying to pull her hand away.

"Listen to me." He held her wrist tightly, spinning her around to face him.

She shook her hand to dislodge his grasp but he grabbed her other wrist.

"We have all sacrificed beyond comprehension. Sacrificed in ways I cannot yet begin to explain to you."

Cheshire's face continued to show signs of discomfort as he held on to her wrists, tiny sparks dancing around his hands. His eyes narrowed and Violet wondered if that was from pain or from anger because she wasn't entertaining his excuses.

"Maybe that's part of the problem," she said, focusing on the oily swirls across his eyes. "Nobody really explains anything here. And when you do, it makes no sense."

"I get that, I do." Cheshire eased his grip on her wrists. "It's a lot to swallow. For everyone who transitions into Dementia. This frustration is not unique to you, Violet."

"Yeah, well, you didn't have a whole whack of memories dumped out of your head when you came here, did you?"

Cheshire let go of her wrists. She rubbed them as the glow waned.

"No, I didn't. And I'm sorry about that." His shoulders slumped. "But do know I will get the memories of your sister back in your head. This I swear to you."

She felt her anger diffusing as he spoke. But his words were empty and she doubted they'd ever hold weight again.

"I can live with knowing that my happy moments with my sister are safe in the conservatory. I can live with that for now." She glanced at the

butterflies flitting through the shadowy trees and pathways, then met his eyes once more. "They're safe here, right? At least tell me they're safe."

Cheshire stared at Violet for a moment. "They're safe." His eyes shimmered faintly like the inside of the kaleidoscope. "Why wouldn't they be?"

"I don't know. You tell me?"

"This," he said, nodding toward the conservatory proper, "has never been infiltrated by the queen's minions. Pallium is a bastion, a sanctuary, and there are no signs of that changing."

Violet wanted to believe Cheshire. There was a certain heartache to him, a kind of hollowness that matched her own—even before he'd taken her memories. And it was that deep-rooted pain that pulled at her, even though she knew she had to be careful.

She had to go along with the Rememberists and their strange prophecy. She didn't have a choice now that she'd lost the good memories of Karin. Before the Forgetting, Violet could have left Dementia and returned to an unchanged reality. But now that was not an option. Which reminded her...

"You'd mentioned that you can't leave Dementia after you're eighteen? What's up with that?"

Cheshire's brow furrowed. "That's not exactly what I said."

"Then what *did* you say?"

"I said that you can't *return* to Dementia after your eighteenth birthday. Once you turn eighteen, you stop aging in Dementia. Why? I have no idea. Just the way things work here. Time flows the same here as in the real. Anyone can leave at any time. For instance, you could leave right now if you wanted to, like you did before. But if you want to come back in ten years, it's not going to happen."

"Why?"

He shrugged. "Nobody really knows. Some think it has to do with the erosion of innocence, that once you turn eighteen you're no longer rooted to the wonder of childhood. Others think that your mind has already begun to

let go, that the protection younger people seem to have against the natural fade of memory starts to break down. You forget how to transition, forget about Dementia as a place and revert to thinking of it as nothing more than some sad disease. And some, well, some just think it's all a bad dream."

Violet looked around the conservatory, watching the memories dance about the dead trees. A butterfly waltzed around an empty bird-bath, and she caught herself wondering what happy moment of her sister could be locked within its iridescent wings. She glanced toward Cheshire. "And what do you think?"

He stood in silence for a moment, like a broken statue in a garden. "I think there's so much sadness in Dementia that if you leave your mind refuses to let you come back."

Violet searched his eyes. The rainbow sheen was gone, returning them to pure blue and yellow like the forget-me-nots on his lei. His statement reminded her that she didn't know when the Brothers Gloss had arrived in Dementia. Why were they even here?

The doors to the conservatory opened and Declan entered, silhouetted in light from the atrium. "Are you finished with the ceremony? We're all waiting in the greenhouse."

Cheshire glanced over his shoulder. "The Forgetting took longer than expected. We'll be there in a moment."

"You should be there now. We need to start Violet's training."

"I said we'll be there in a moment," Cheshire barked.

Declan looked at Violet, eyes moon wide. There was an underlying disappointment in them, a tarnish that shimmered in the floodlights. He opened his mouth to say something—then closed it. He turned and left, the conservatory doors whispering shut behind him.

"Let's go," Cheshire said, spinning around without another glimpse toward her. "We can't keep Parminder waiting. The last thing you want to do is meet her when she's pissed off."

Violet followed him out of the conservatory. She'd seen something in Cheshire and it wasn't all wishing wells and shiny coins. There was

something unpolished there, something raw and dark that she couldn't quite see.

Not even with her electric glow.

Cheshire led Violet into a large vestibule beyond the greenhouse entrance. Rows of rusty lockers ran across the room with benches in-between. The room was not well lit and smelled of dew-wet forests and campfires.

"I know it's a bit dingy in here," Cheshire said, as if reading her mind, "but we don't spend much time in transition to and from the greenhouse." He walked over to a series of bins along one of the walls.

"Can't we just go into the greenhouse?" Violet questioned, assuming Declan had gone straight there ahead of them. "I mean, it's just a green-house, right?"

"Like everything in Dementia," he said, riffling in the bins, "things are a bit different inside. This is Parminder's domain. We do what she says...and she says to wear these for our safety."

Cheshire handed Violet a pair of white coveralls. They were rather billowy—like pirate pantaloons—and about six sizes too big.

"Seriously?"

He passed Violet a mesh hood and a pair of white gloves. "Seriously. And you might want to take off your coat. It's hot inside."

"Believe it or not, I've been in a greenhouse before."

Violet snatched the clothes. As she slid her legs into the coveralls, she realized she'd seen these types of suits before. Last year Christine partnered with her for a science class project on the life cycle of the honeybee and how they've been domesticated for crop pollination and honey production.

Violet swallowed hard. "Bees?"

"Yeah," Cheshire said, sliding a mesh hood over his head. He looked like a fencer. "I thought you've been in a greenhouse before. It's full of flowers. Parminder Honey will explain."

"But I'm allergic to bees," Violet lied. She didn't like them. Not since she was six. She'd been running with a beach ball and yelling when a bee flew into her mouth. Instinctively she shut her mouth from surprise and the bee stung her tongue. When she screamed the bee flew out. Afterward, her mom made Violet suck on an ice cube for what seemed like an eternity, her tongue swollen. Not fun. Ever since then she simply told people she was allergic so she had a reason to run away from bees.

Thinking about her mother struck a pang of longing in her heart. Her mother had always been a loving and caring parent. Even a friend. But that all changed after the accident.

If only Violet could change the past.

But her mom had no interest in fixing the present.

She missed the way her family used to be.

Cheshire went to slide the hood over Violet's head, breaking her thoughts. "I've been meaning to ask you about your sunglasses. You haven't taken them off once since you came here."

"They're so I can see properly. In case you haven't noticed, I'm an albino. My eyesight isn't quite as good as yours. Bright lights hurt my eyes."

Cheshire huffed. "Well that's ironic, being that you *glow*."

"Yeah, well, what can I do? As long as I have my sunglasses I'll be fine."

He slid the mesh hood over Violet's head, careful not to knock her sunglasses off. "Anyway, don't worry about the bees. Parminder has a certain power over them. You'll be fine—as long as she likes you." He smiled.

Violet wasn't in the mood for his nonchalant attitude and his charming grin as if everything were all lollipops and unicorns, especially

after what had happened to her memories of Karin during the Forgetting.

She wasn't about to forget what he did—siphoner malfunction or not.

If she could smack that smile off his face she would.

Violet reefed the gloves on and secured their elastic cuffs in front of her elbows, unsure why it really mattered if Parminder liked her or not. That was just one more thing to amp her anxiety.

Cheshire walked to a table scattered with tarnished metal cylinders. Each cylinder had a spout on top and a black accordion-like contraption sticking out the side.

Bee smokers.

He unscrewed the top of a cylinder, sparked a match and dropped it into the opening.

"Can I get one of those smokers?" Violet asked. She'd never used one before but having one would make her feel better rather than relying only on a beekeeper suit.

"You won't need one." Pine-scented smoke curled out as he screwed the lid back on. "Just stay close to me and you'll be fine."

Cheshire walked past the rows of lockers toward a towering circular door at the back of the vestibule. He pulled down on a lever and a red light blinked from the top of the door. A dull siren whirred and smoke hissed out from around the door's seal. It shuddered and disengaged, rising open like something out of a science-fiction movie.

"Keeps the bees inside," Cheshire said, nodding toward the threshold of smoke. "You ready?"

He reached for Violet's hand but she pulled it back.

"I don't need you holding my hand. I'm ready."

She really wasn't ready, but if going into a greenhouse filled with bees would bring her closer to getting her sister's memories back, then she'd open a hive and harvest honey if she had to.

"Good, then let's go meet Parminder." He stepped through the wall of smoke.

As Violet broke the threshold, she made sure her mouth was firmly shut.

The heat and humidity of the greenhouse hit Violet like snapping awake from a fever dream covered in sweat. The chilled confines of the conservatory were much more to her liking than the tropical sultriness of the greenhouse—though Violet chalked that up to wearing a beekeeper's suit over a wool peacoat, scarf, tights, and combat boots rather than a bathing suit. There were no palm trees in the greenhouse either. And no cabana boys or piña coladas. Or any sign of Declan.

There were, however, forget-me-nots.

Millions of them.

Tiny blue flowers with cadmium yellow hearts spilled in floral waterfalls from planters and tables, almost flooding the walkways.

But it wasn't the intense humidity or abundance of flowers that caught Violet's attention—but a cacophonous drone, like some industrial factory working overtime. Violet squeezed Cheshire's hand as bees sparked in her vision, materializing above the sea of flowers. They swarmed over the forget-me-nots, dipping and darting like so many miniature hummingbirds.

She followed Cheshire as he weaved through the flowers, pressing the billows of the smoker. Clouds of smoke spilled from the contraption until they were walking in a fog. The bees that hovered around them slowed their movements, intoxicated.

It was then, as several bees came to rest on some flowers beside Violet, that she noticed a slight haze hovering over the forget-me-nots. As she passed, Violet placed a hand over them. They radiated with a refreshing coolness—even through her protective gloves.

"Look with your eyes and not your hands," Cheshire said without looking back at Violet.

Violet pulled her hand back.

"I'm only saving you from Parminder's wrath," he added. "She's the only person who can touch them before they've matured."

"Why?" Violet placed her hand back in the cool air over the flowers.

"Parminder makes the leis," Cheshire said, placing a hand near his neck. "You won't get one if you piss her off."

Every few steps he pressed the smoker's bellows and clouded the air as Violet followed close behind. Weaving through the circuitous pathways of the greenhouse she wondered why she'd need a lei beyond the fact that they were beautiful. She'd tried to use the flowers like Declan had when she'd first arrived but its petals simply melted like shaved ice. Maybe she'd figure out that trick one day.

Beyond the smoke spewing from Cheshire's canister, a tall hill rose sharply in front of them. The ocean of forget-me-nots ran ashore at the base of the hill, turning instead to tangles of grasses and wildflowers. The hill was stippled with large white boxes, bees swarming in and out of each box as they ascended.

A large tree decorated in lemony flowers stood at the peak of the hill. Around the tree circled a group of people wearing white beekeeper suits, each holding a smoker that trailed clouds.

As Violet climbed, she noticed the droning seemed to emanate from within the hill, the ground vibrating. A girl stood near the tree's trunk. Honeycomb-shaped holes encircled the base of the tree, reaching deep into the hill. Bees swarmed around the network of holes, spilling in and out of them.

Violet blanched. Knowing she stood on the top of a giant beehive warmed her legs to wax.

The girl standing below the tree was dressed in folds of black lace and petaled leather, face hidden behind a veil. Her arms were lackadaisically outstretched, palms facing up toward the dome. Shocks of lightning danced on her palms, bees swarming over them.

She looked as if she were attending a funeral, all melancholia and madness. The girl pulled back her veil, revealing a hauntingly beautiful face. Sepia brown skin, full lips, cheekbones as sharp as a horizon. Her eyes shone like suns.

"Welcome to Dementia," she said. "I'm Parminder Honey, apiarist extraordinaire. It appears that you've already proven yourself to the

Brothers Gloss." She tipped her head toward the group of white-clad people surrounding the crest of the hill, their smokers spilling plumes into the air. Although she couldn't make out what they were wearing under the beekeeper suits, she did recognize Declan's dreary face and shadow-wreathed eyes behind one of the mesh hoods. Relief filled her body like finding an umbrella as storm clouds open with a rain. Then she realized Cheshire was also with the group, leaving Violet to stand alone. The rest of the Rememberists were also there plus one more she didn't remember meeting.

Parminder raised her arms. Lightning leapt from bee-caked hands into the tree, weaving through the branches and into hundreds of beehives. The droning became deafening, as if Violet had fallen into the nest.

"And now," Parminder said, eyes narrowing into sunsets as she pulled the veil back over her face, "it's time to prove yourself to me."

Violet took a deep breath and steeled herself to whatever came from the apiarist, buoyed by the love for her sister, for the chance to make things right and recover Karin's memories.

She balled her hands into glowing orbs and matched Parminder's gaze.

"Consider it done."

8/ SMOKE AND MIRRORS

BEEHIVES FELL FROM THE TREE, cracking open on the ground like so many dropped eggs. Bees spilled out of each desecrated hive, incensed and taking to the air.

Parminder drew a pair of swords from behind her back. The blades were made of steel and smoke, bending and warping with each movement. Parminder whispered and the bees buzzed around her, covering the blades, her arms and head, her body. She stretched out an arm and pointed one of the swords at Violet who took a step back, startled at how fast Parminder went into attack mode.

Without hesitation, the bees shotgunned in a burst of black and yellow. "Swarm!" the apiarist yelled.

"Violet!"

Hearing her name snapped Violet out of her daze. She looked toward the source and caught Declan's eyes burrowing into her from behind his mesh hood, his arm up in the air. A metal tube somersaulted in the air like a gymnastic baton.

As the tube neared the height of its arc, Cheshire stepped forward, discharging a dart of light from an upturned hand. It cracked into the tube, shattering the container and sending a cloud of glitter into the air.

Instinctively, Violet placed a fist on top of the other and braced herself.

Oji waza.

Defense.

Even though she'd only trained for a year, her kendo techniques kicked in.

"Glitterglam," she shouted, willing the image of the sword into her mind. The glitter in the air streamed down toward her fists, stacking on top of them and forming a blade.

Everything slowed as she turned around, the first few bees pattering onto her back like raindrops on an umbrella. She stepped into the kamikaze swarm, bringing Glitterglam up and into the thick. Each bee hung in the air, as if stuck in an emulsion of honey and stingers, the beat of their wings slowing down to match the rolling thunder in Violet's chest.

Glitterglam cut into the first bee, severing the thorax. Cellophane wings carried the two halves into opposite spirals, slivers of fluid trailing. Violet continued to wade forward, Glitterglam dissecting each bee with shocking precision. She could feel the thoracic vibrations as her blade made contact, as it severed, as it killed, bee segments corkscrewing past her shoulders in slow motion.

Violet glanced toward Cheshire and Declan. They still stood with the other Rememberists, arms crossed, watching and...smiling. Seeing their approval energized her, and she refocused on reaching Parminder.

Glitterglam moved to its own rhythm, dicing hundreds of bees in the span of a moment, moving through each insect and then jumping to the next with lightning speed. Violet didn't understand how she was controlling a sword with such accuracy considering she'd only trained with a bamboo shinai. Not to mention her depth perception issues. Something else was at work here, but she wasn't about to question the mechanics, not now, not while she was facing an onslaught of potential bee stings.

Instead she allowed herself to embrace the moment, to let her move

in fluid motions, the thrum of Glitterglam guiding her through the funnel of bees. With each step a hundred bees were severed; with each swipe of her glimmering blade, a hundred more.

As she brought Glitterglam down and through the last bee, her sword crashed into a pair of crossed mirror-blades. Sparks shot into the surrounding smoke.

"Very impressive," Parminder said from behind her X of swords.

Violet shrugged as if she wielded a blade of electric dust every day.

Parminder kicked her in the stomach.

Violet launched backward, crashing onto her back and sending her gliding through bee carcasses.

She wasn't dreaming—that kick hurt.

Parminder took two quick steps and then jumped onto the trail of bee remains, sliding toward Violet, mirrored blades trailing smoke. Violet pushed the pain aside and raised her legs, then snapped them toward the ground, launching herself back onto her feet.

Parminder crashed into her seconds later, swords colliding. They stumbled, Violet bracing herself as Parminder pushed harder, their swords locking at the hilt. She needed to end this soon, her muscles burning with fatigue.

"Very impressive indeed." Parminder smiled behind her black veil, one of her eyeteeth crooked and cute. "But do realize, when I kill you," she leaned into Violet, their hips touching, swords up and vertical between their faces, "I'll just be proving that you're not the fabled Princess Electric."

Violet ground her teeth together, repeating Parminder's words in her head.

When. I. Kill. You.

On any other day since the accident Violet would have welcomed those words.

But not today.

She would not die.

She was the Princess Electric.

Violet had broken her sister, and in turn would put her back together again. She wasn't going to leave Karin's memories scattered across the ground like a shattered windshield, not when she knew how to pick them up—even though she might cut herself in the process.

When. I. Kill. You.

Those words reverberated in Violet's head again, and each time they echoed she grew more and more angry. Her hands clamped around Glitterglam's hilt, her jaw compressing. The fury of the past year burbled up from inside, filling her throat. The way her mother ignored her. How she blamed Violet for the accident. Cheshire taking her most coveted memories of Karin. Rage crackled in her veins. She wanted to blast it out. Wanted to discharge all her frustration in a violent scream.

A battle cry.

Then, as if he were right there, Violet could hear Declan instructing her on the rooftop. Remembered how he'd coached her into drawing on her anger to form Glitterglam.

To *electrify* herself.

Violet channeled the pain in her stomach up and out of her throat. But instead of a scream, she parted her mouth, willing the tension out. Her tongue buzzed as if touching the tip of a battery, her lips all pins and needles. She continued to push the anger out of her body, over her cheeks, her face, fanning outward to consume her head. The shocks traveled over her breasts and down her stomach, out across her limbs until she could see the illumination. Threads of light snaked along her arms like light bulb filaments cranked to an unsafe wattage.

Everything went photo-negative, all black and white reversal, like it had on the rooftop with Declan. Her entire body vibrated with energy. She stared holes through Parminder's veil. Eyes connected.

"If they say I'm the Princess Electric," Violet said taking a deep breath, "then I am. And you aren't going to get in the way of curing my sister."

She launched into Parminder, pushing her backward into the wet

trail of bee carcasses, swords still interlocked. Parminder braced her footing but couldn't stop sliding, her legs locked, body rigid.

As Violet continued to drive her back, she twisted Glitterglam free and, with one hand on the hilt, drove it up Parminder's bee-laced blade. The apiarist swung her other sword in a sweeping arc, coming in from the side. Everything was in slow motion, which allowed Violet time to bring Glitterglam back down, adjusting the angle for her inaccurate depth perception. She slammed it in front of Parminder's blade, parrying in a spray of sparks.

Before Parminder retaliated with the other mirror-blade, Violet took her free hand and grabbed the hilt, covering Parminder's hand with hers. She ignored the bloom of Parminder's eyes and instead watched the bees crawl over the smoking, sharpened mirror.

Violet continued to drive Parminder back. Was she supposed to kill her? She'd threatened Violet with death after all. But Parminder seemed important to Declan and Cheshire and she really wasn't down with killing someone as part of a foolish initiation.

Nobody said she couldn't rough up the apiarist.

Violet drew upon the electrical charge coursing through her veins with each step. She discharged a wave of power through her connected hand, illuminated threads leaping onto Parminder's blade.

Bees popped like popcorn.

The electrical charges continued to weave over Parminder's body. As the trail of bee guts came to an end, Parminder's foot found purchase on the dry grass and she lost her balance. Parminder flailed, her smoking blades drawing circles in the air. Violet let go of Parminder's hand and brought up her foot.

She kicked Parminder in the stomach.

Hard.

And with that connection, all the built up electrical current swirling over Violet's body cascaded into Parminder's. It detonated in a bright, crackling fire-light, launching the apiarist high into the air. She flew backward in a wide arc, crashing into the flowering tree. She slid down

the trunk, landing in a smoking lump of lace and leather. Lemony petals sashayed from the branches above, landing softly about her body.

Violet turned around to face the Rememberists, exhausted. They remained in a circle about the hilltop, their smokers still clouding the air. Cheshire was smiling behind his beekeeper hood, yet Declan's face was somber and whorled in shadow. Why did he look so...disappointed?

Her legs jellied. She wanted to lay down. Wanted to sleep. She was so tired from fighting she didn't even think to go see if Parminder was all right. Instead, she tossed Glitterglam onto the ground and willed the sword to dissipate. This time it did, dissolving into dust amongst the grass.

Violet took several deep breaths to slow her breathing down.

Blinked the sweat from her eyes.

"What are you going to do when you have no help?"

Violet's stomach depth-charged.

The honeyed voice had come from directly behind her.

Close. Too close.

Violet spun around.

Parminder stood a few paces away, her lace tattered, black leather ripped to expose strips of dark, smooth skin along her stomach. The veil was pulled back over her head and streaks of moon-bright hair curled out, hooking above her shoulders. Her eyes were wide and focused on Violet.

Parminder lowered her arms, the mirrored blades of smoke tipping toward the ground. She slowly raised them, as if lifting a heavy weight, her face straining under concentration.

Violet looked up, scanning the glass ceiling of the greenhouse, trying to find another container of glitter somersaulting through the air. But she found no canister, and she heard no call of her name. The Rememberists stood in silence behind her.

"What are you going to do when you are alone?"

Violet opened her mouth but no words came out.

As Parminder's hands surpassed her shoulders, a vibration started to

ripple the grass and wildflowers along the hill. The vibration penetrated Violet's boots, surging up into her body. A slight hum filled the air, like distant machinery. Parminder had her hands above her head now, her mirrored blades crossed, waterfalls of smoke spilling from them.

The hum of machinery turned into a drone that shook the hill. Violet glanced over her shoulder to Declan, to Cheshire, but cannister smoke had fully consumed them and the other Rememberists, each one an apparition, each one a replica of the other.

In a sudden panic, Violet reached her hand toward the ground, to the very spot she'd cast Glitterglam.

Nothing happened.

She concentrated, tried to summon the sword back to her hands, but all that came was a small crackle of light at her fingertips.

Nausea flared within Violet as the first bees came out of the hillside. They spilled out of the holes surrounding the tree, swarming in clouds of black and yellow. The drone was deafening, the bees blotting out the glass-paneled roof of the greenhouse.

"You're not the Princess Electric, Violet. So the answer is simple."

Parminder's dark lips curled upward.

"You die."

And with that Parminder snapped her arms down, pointing the swords toward Violet.

But I am the Princess Electric.

Clouds of bees hammered into her like machine gun fire, ripping off her mesh hood. Bees caked her face, her hair, crawling into her peacoat, covering her skin.

In her mouth.

Violet screamed when they started to sting.

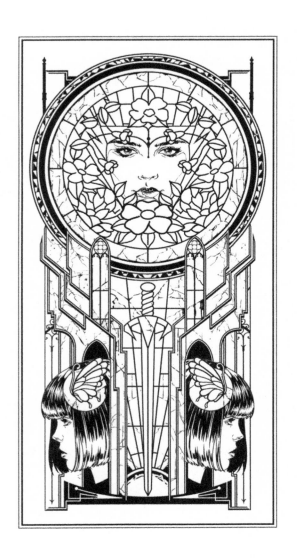

PART B

STAINED GLASS PROPHECY

"Burning away the darkness of forgetting will require the brightest of
filaments."
- Anonymous margin note translated from French, circa 1793
BOOK OF REMEMBRANCE

9/ DANDELION DREAMS

VIOLET AWOKE IN A FAMILIAR ROOM, on a familiar bed. But this time she wore her sunglasses. She was also naked. Her clothes were folded on the bedside chair, her boots nestled beside it. A thin tube coiled out of a catheter on her right hand, hooking into an intravenous drip bag that hung from a pole. A thin sheet covered her from the waist down. Her head swam with confusion.

Wait a minute. I'm naked?

Her cheeks burned. She wanted to yell. Something. Anything.

She closed her eyes to the halogen lighting. The brightness burned, her eyes puffy and raw as if she'd been crying for days. Maybe she had been. For all she knew, she could've been sleeping for years. Her skin shone in the lighting, pocked with hundreds of tiny welts and slick with a Vaseline-like substance.

What happened to me?

Her mind was like Times Square in New York City on New Year's Eve, a riot of lights and commotion and confetti. She couldn't distill one image from the next. Violet wanted to get out of bed and put on her clothes, but the slightest of movements sent the room spinning.

The door whispered open and in walked Parminder Honey.

Seeing the apiarist released a flood of toxic memory into Violet: the apiary, the circle of Rememberists, the duel with Parminder. And then there were the bees. Skin-piercing pain had consumed her body, the insides of her mouth—and then she had blacked out, throat clogged with bees.

Violet tugged the sheet securely about her neck and sat up. She dug her heels into the bed and pushed herself against the headboard, trying to gain distance from the apiarist. Was she here to finish the job? If she wanted her dead, why didn't she kill her in the greenhouse? She'd had the opportunity.

Parminder stopped alongside the bed. She pulled the black veil onto her head, exposing her ceramic-smooth face. A forget-me-not lei hung around her neck, something Violet didn't remember seeing before. She placed her hands on the bed's railing. "Don't worry, it was me who tended to your wounds."

"Wonderful." Violet tried to sound nonchalant. Even though she was glad it wasn't the Brothers Gloss, Parminder did just try to kill her. "Where am I and what do you want?"

Parminder leaned in, the scents of patchouli and sandalwood washing over Violet. "You are safe in Pallium but I want you to know that I don't like you."

"I think that's rather obvious." Violet held up her hand, the intravenous line shimmering in the halogen ambience.

"I'll be watching you." Parminder tapped Violet's forehead. "I don't trust *newfallen*."

"Well, that makes two of us," Violet spat. "I've no reason to trust any of you, either."

"See, there it is. That *I'm so innocent* routine may work on the guys, but I wasn't born yesterday. I'm nearly three hundred years old. I've seen a lot of people come and go through Dementia. I've seen a lot of pain and a lot of friends die. There's only a handful of us left and I will not sit idly by while some cute memjack spy infiltrates our ranks with a fake story of desperation and sadness."

Wait? Three hundred years old? What the actual fuck?

Violet recalibrated her thoughts and focused on the apiarist's accusation.

"Is that what you think I am—a spy?" Violet searched for something else to say, something with impact that she could defend herself with, but all she could muster was, "*Seriously?*"

"I don't know what or who you are. Not yet." Parminder hooked a dangling strand of platinum hair around her ear. "But I will. You may have fooled others that you're the Princess Electric, but you haven't fooled me. I'll be watching you, waiting for you to make a mistake. And when you do? My bees will be the least of your worries."

Violet perched onto her elbows. "Why don't you believe them? Did I do something to make you think otherwise?"

"*Do something?*" Parminder laughed. "Au contraire, Violet. You've done nothing. And that's the problem. Right now you're way too convenient."

Violet needed ammunition. If she wanted to recover her sister's memories, she needed Parminder's help. "What about that sword, Glitterglam?" she said, hoping the fabled blade would cut into Parminder's disbelief. "What about the prophecy? That must count for something."

Parminder stared at Violet for a moment, her lemon-drop eyes softening slightly. "Has anyone actually told you what the prophecy entails?"

"I was told you've been waiting for some princess to come illuminate Recollection City and kill the Queen of Glass. To do so, you need a magic sword called Glitterglam. Or something like that."

Parminder closed her eyes and stood in silence for a moment. She took one long, deep breath and then opened her eyes, slow as a sunrise.

"Can you walk?"

"I think so." Violet stretched her legs out across the bed. Her skin burned against the sheets. "I'm sore, but I can manage."

Where did she want to take her? The last thing Violet wanted to do

was go for a walk with Parminder. Yet the brothers held her in high regard, so maybe she could use the apiarist to find Karin's memories.

"Good," Parminder said, walking around to the other side of the bed. She grabbed the IV line, twisted it around her fingers, and snapped it out of Violet's hand.

"Ouch!" Violet yelled, rubbing where the catheter had been a second earlier. "What was that for?"

"You don't need any more sugar-water. You're hydrated enough." Parminder pointed to the chair as she walked toward the door. "Put on more antibiotic ointment. It'll help ease the swelling from the bee stings. Then get dressed and meet me at Stem. It's time to find out why I haven't killed you yet."

After Violet reapplied the ointment and dressed, she met Parminder at the ornate elevator. The apiarist pressed a button that read *Mausoleum*. It illuminated with a soft white light as Stem lurched into motion. Calming muzak started to play from the ceiling-mounted glass flowers as their surroundings outside the elevator cage faded.

Violet slid her hands into the peacoat's pockets to avoid itching her arms, the kaleidoscope brushing her hand. The touch of cold metal calmed her anxiety about going for a walk with Parminder. If things went sideways with the apiarist, she could use it to get away from her in short order.

"What do you want?" Parminder asked behind her charcoal-dark veil, her lips full and brushing the fabric.

"I wish I could forget the car crash, forget the accident I caused that put my sister in the hospital. And I want her memories back."

Parminder yawned. "So you say."

"Declan and Cheshire know why I'm here. I've explained every-thing to them."

"Yes, I know." Parminder's eyes sparkled. "But I don't think you've been totally honest either. You don't make sense. Nobody in their right mind comes back to Dementia after leaving. You came, you saw, you left." Parminder pointed an accusatory finger at Violet. "But then you *came back.*"

"I never said I was in my right mind."

"Obviously."

It seemed the apiarist enjoyed games of passive intimidation. Taunt and tease until her prey snapped. But she wouldn't give into Parmin-der's schoolyard tactics. According to Cheshire, she needed a forget-me-not lei, which meant she needed the apiarist. If she were to get on Parminder's good side, she was going to have to get on her level.

"Ask me *why* I came back," Violet said, her voice daring. "Or are you just a bitch?"

Parminder's bright yellow eyes smoldered behind the veil; then she launched across Stem. Violet screamed as her body slammed against the elevator's cage, skin still raw from the bee stings.

When Parminder spoke, her voice was calm yet commanding. "You know nothing of me, newfallen. You know nothing of Dementia. Other than what's been told to you by brothers who disagree more than the sun and moon, you know *nothing*. And who's to say they've been completely honest with you?"

Parminder slackened her grasp on Violet, adding a hand-span of space between them. "So, you took a bit of a tumble in the real and now you've got baggage. I get that. We've all got baggage or we wouldn't be here. I want to believe you're not a memjack. The other Rememberists have taken a liking to your brightness, but I can't believe in some glow-in-the-dark newfallen without proof of power. Just because you can summon Glitterglam with help from Declan doesn't mean you're the savior of memory. It just means you're a very lost, very gullible girl."

Violet slouched against the wall. The apiarist's words didn't cut or

burn but verified Violet's own thoughts that she knew nothing of Dementia or the prophecy. She'd convinced herself that Dementia was plausible based on what she'd seen and what the Brothers Gloss had explained to her. But to Parminder's point, she had no reason to trust them. Declan, maybe—he seemed genuinely concerned for her sister's memories and not just his own agenda. But Cheshire? Not after the Forgetting. Not after he'd drained more memories of her sister than he was supposed to.

Violet lowered her eyes to the floor as Stem shuddered and clanged, the elevator traversing the twists of Pallium. Without Parminder on her side, she'd have a hard time reclaiming her sister's memories. For a moment she thought about faking the whole prophecy thing like she'd faked the last year of her life. She could do it long enough to get what she needed and then get out.

But that wouldn't prove anything. She was tired of hating herself for one mistake. She balled her hands into fists, milk blue light pulsating through her skin. Things wouldn't change unless she changed.

"So what do you want from me so you'll help find my sister's memories?"

"It's rather simple." Parminder nodded toward Violet's glowing hands. "If, in fact, you are the Princess Electric, then you need to prove it—and not just to me, but to *yourself*. You need to earn that designation. And then I will train you to be hardened. Versatile. Deadly."

The only reason Violet had been so certain of being the Princess Electric was from all the hype. Both Declan and Cheshire championed her. They were convinced that she was the princess. But why? Maybe all the hype was simply hyperbole. Both times she'd summoned Glitter-glam, Declan had provided the catalyst—he'd given her the glitter.

Stem shook to a stop. Parminder slid open the cage door and motioned for Violet to exit as she continued, "But right now? I don't see you as the Princess Electric. You're like the image inside a kaleidoscope. A million possibilities of in-between."

Violet turned around, not quite sure how to feel. But then again,

maybe Parminder was right. She hadn't really done anything except get her ass kicked. Maybe she was blinded by her own overwhelming desire to reclaim Karin's memories.

Violet held up her hands and took in their glow, all halogen and bright.

There had to be something there. Something within her. All of this couldn't be for nothing.

A dream wasn't nothing.

Parminder breezed past her, stepping fully into the room. As Violet turned to follow she caught the full scope of where they were.

Stem opened into a massive coliseum. Rings upon concentric rings of seating spiraled up and away. Yet where there should have been spectators, there simply sat pedestals. Countless pedestals protruded from the seats, and on each pedestal sat a blown glass bust, its anonymous features smoothed over like a waxen mask.

Within each bust danced a butterfly of memory. Prismatic patterns swam across the coliseum like spotlights refracting off a disco ball.

"It's breathtaking." Violet's head spun and she placed her hand on Parminder's shoulder to steady herself; the sheer scale of the coliseum and the way the lights danced over the surfaces played with her depth perception.

"It's sad," the apiarist corrected. "This is the Mausoleum of Memory. This is death in Dementia."

"Death?" Violet questioned, removing her hand as her vision corrected and she swept her gaze across the busts.

"Yes. This is where we take the memory butterflies when someone passes away."

Parminder moved into the epicenter of the coliseum. She glanced over her shoulder for Violet to follow. "When a Rememberist dies, their bodies turn to glitter. But their extracted memory? That single, precious memory we gave to become a Rememberist is implanted into one of these anonymous busts. There are no personalized placards, no cere-

mony, nothing. Just silence in the remembrance of a life—and their memory everlasting."

Violet rejoined her, balls of reflected color sashaying across the floor as she walked. "And when someone leaves Dementia?" Violet said, watching one of the beams of light trail along the lower seats. "Is their butterfly returned to them? Do they get the memory they sacrificed in the Forgetting?"

"What do you mean?"

"Well, Cheshire alluded to—"

"That's your problem right there," Parminder said, interrupting. "One should never allow Cheshire to allude to anything."

"What are you saying, then?"

"I'm saying," Parminder said rather forcefully, "no one gets their memory back, regardless of what Cheshire said."

"But—" Violet stopped talking. Nausea tweaked her breathing into a state of paper bag hyperventilation. The coliseum spun again, her mind swimming along with the trail of lights.

"But?" Parminder coaxed impatiently.

"I lost all the good memories of my sister," Violet began, the words thick in her mouth. "Not one, not two, but all of them. Every single happy moment is gone from my head. All I can remember is the bad stuff, the fighting, the pain... the screams and death. The silence." Violet's voice trailed off.

"What? How could that have happened?" Parminder's voice rose with each word.

"I don't know...Cheshire said there was a calibration issue. Something wrong with the siphoner. He couldn't stop collecting. Said it would take time, but I could get them back. That I'd be able to remember the good times with Karin again. That I could close my eyes and picture her face smiling at me, talking to me. Laughing with me."

Violet was shaking, her legs ready to buckle.

"I'm sorry Cheshire said that," Parminder said, her voice filled with a sadness Violet hadn't heard before. "But there's no way to get them

back that I know of. Just realize that they're safe in the conservatory, and they'll be there when you want to feel your sister around you. But also know that you'll never have them inside your head again. That's reality."

Violet's heart fluttered like the butterflies in the glass busts. "But if that's the case, how can I get my sister's memories?"

"Those are different. Your memories were...converted. Poured into the air. If raw memory contacts air in Dementia it births into butterfly form. There's no recovery from that process. But your sister's memories were siphoned by memjack slurpers and stored in vials for transportation. Unless they've been compromised or processed at a facility, there shouldn't be any issue in recovering them. The issue is tracking them down before processing."

Violet stood in silence, covered in refracting rainbow light. Her mind raced as she unpacked what Parminder said. It was clear that she needed the apiarist if she had any hope in finding Karin's memories in Dementia.

"Do you dream, Violet?" Parminder asked, breaking her thoughts.

"If you're asking if I hope all of this is a dream, then yes, I do."

"This isn't a dream," Parminder said sadly. "There's no waking from Dementia."

"You would say that."

Parminder turned away from Violet and gazed at the thousands of illuminated busts. "Dementia is what makes adults scared of tomorrow. The uncertainty in the unknown. When you're in its grasp, there's no escaping Dementia. So, I'll ask you once again...do you dream of better futures?"

"I used to dream of tomorrow," Violet answered, wondering where these questions were headed. "But I don't anymore."

"That's most unfortunate. Dreams are like dandelions. From a distance, they look like flowers, bright and beautiful. But when you get up close? Unenlightened people think of them as nothing more than weeds that choke out possibility. Yet that couldn't be farther from the truth. When dandelions age they fertilize the wind. They send seeds in

a million different directions. Into a million different possibilities. Tomorrow can bloom brighter than today if you want it to, just like a dream," Parminder finished. "Besides, you can make a wonderful tea with them."

"Yeah, maybe," Violet said, "but the moment I almost killed my sister and permanently put her in the hospital, I killed any dreams of a better future—for her or me. Dandelions or not, I don't see the point in setting myself up for disappointment. Life is already full of that as it is."

"Then maybe you should leave Dementia," Parminder said, her voice terse and strained.

"I'm here to get my sister's memories back, and to help Declan with that prophecy thing. Then I will. Trust me on that."

"Well, that prophecy thing? That's the foundation of the Rememberists. Before you go spouting off, maybe you should check your facts. Without our dream to illuminate Recollection City and stop the memory leak into Dementia, there would be no Rememberists. And that means there'd be nobody to help fetch your precious sister's memories either. Now I suggest you pull yourself together and either truly join us, or get the hell out of Dementia for good."

Violet stood dumbfounded. Parminder's words rocked her. She couldn't risk alienating herself from the Rememberists. Without their help, she'd be lost. How was she supposed to navigate Dementia without a map or knowledgeable guide?

Violet would not let Parminder or anyone else get in the way of reclaiming Karin's memories. She'd already given up too much since arriving in this shithole world. Maybe she'd be able to find a way to get her own memories back inside her head at the same time.

But first things first.

"Tell me about the prophecy," Violet said, squaring up Parminder. "Tell me how to illuminate Recollection City so we can get on with tracking down my sister's memories.

"Oh, and while you're at it? Tell me why you haven't killed me yet."

10/ IN GLASS

"WHY HAVEN'T I KILLED YOU?" Parminder said. "That's easy. Look up."

Violet glanced up past the rows of illuminated busts, beyond the rings of colored light, until her eyes fell on a domed ceiling constructed entirely of stained glass that spanned the entire coliseum.

Her jaw opened wide. The ceiling ran riot with color, illuminated by the disco ball moon. Intricate veining divided each segment of glass until the entire piece formed leaves upon overlapping leaves of detail.

Reams of glass forget-me-nots rimmed the outer edges of the ceiling. They coiled inward, transitioning into swarms of multicolored butterflies that seemingly bloomed from the flowers. The butterflies swirled around jagged, black glass buildings. They fanned inward from the edges of the flowers, every rooftop stretching toward the center of the domed ceiling.

Spiraling around the lead-paned buildings were hundreds of apparitions etched in frosted glass, like the fog-shrouded slurpers Violet had seen in the Weeping Willow. Yet they had no discerning features. Each stained-glass silhouette was phosphorescent and locked in battle with another, arms entwined with illuminated glass. Some of the wraith-like

warriors wielded swords and Violet wondered if they represented the Rememberists.

The battle raged around a massive hourglass that dominated the apex of the dome. The bottom half of the hourglass contained glitter, the top half emptiness. Within the glitter stood a young woman, naked, her body and face consumed by rainbows of glass, beautiful and sharp and intricate. Her hair haloed her as if she were submerged in a pool, each strand a chain of golden glitter. One of her arms was outstretched, reaching into the other half of the hourglass.

Into the darkness.

The woman's gaze was locked onto a girl that filled the void; her enshrouded form was carved from clear glass that shone with moonlight. White glass surrounded her, pushing the blackness out against the walls of the top half of the hourglass. The same white glass that made up her arms, her hands and face. Her skin.

Violet took a step back, her jaw relaxing open. The similarities between her albino skin and the girl in the mosaic flip-flopped her stomach. She turned to Parminder who stood watching her from under her black veil, a slight smile playing across her lips.

Looking back at the stained-glass ceiling, Violet noticed that the girl was not entirely constructed of moon-bright glass. Her hair zigzagged from her head in fluorescent purple-blue locks.

In bolts of violet.

And in her outstretched arm she held a sword made of glitter. It reached into the space between the hemispheres of the hourglass, connecting with the hand of the other woman.

Yet the hand holding Glitterglam was not constructed by the same bright glass as the rest of her body, but of the same glass that decorated the other woman.

Glass forged from rainbows and shadow.

"Holy shit," Violet said, weak-kneed and refocusing on the illuminated girl. "That's me."

"Or someone who resembles you," Parminder said coldly. "Just

because someone dresses like a witch doesn't mean they're a witch. But regardless, you can see why I couldn't bring myself to kill you. I couldn't take a chance. You might be the Princess Electric or you might be a memjack. Who knows?"

Violet scanned the epic stained-glass mosaic above her. "What's going on in the picture? Who's the other person?"

"That would be Zamelerish, Queen of Glass and the Architect of Forgetting. And she's killing the Princess Electric."

"Killing her?" Violet took another step back, unsure of what she was seeing. "How's that possible? She's beautiful. I thought she was helping the princess."

Parminder shook her head, face devoid of amusement. "She's consuming her. Turning her into glass. Look at her arm."

"But what does that mean?" Violet stopped looking at the ceiling and turned toward Parminder. "You have to help me out here."

Parminder sighed, stepping toward her. "To paraphrase, the Luminous Prophecy states that a girl will fall from the real to illuminate Recollection City, dethroning the Queen of Glass in the process. And when I say dethrone, I really mean kill. End of story."

"Okay," Violet said. "That's pretty much what Declan had told me."

"But there's more," Parminder added, squaring up Violet and placing her hands on her shoulders. "Did Declan tell you that by retaking the throne of Dementia you would turn to glass in the process?"

"No, he missed that part," Violet said, uneasiness heavy against her chest.

"That's the crux of the prophecy. That by reclaiming the throne, you would officially become the *Filament of Recollection*. You'd rule by shining light into the depths of Recollection City." Parminder's breath breezed over Violet, scented like flowers and rain-wet soil. "Your light would create a haven for the forgotten moments that fall into Dementia so that they may one day be remembered. But if you do this, if you reset the balance of memory between the real and the under-real, then you'll never be able to return home. When Recollec-

tion City is fully illuminated, Dementia itself will become forgotten—along with you."

Parminder removed her hands from Violet's shoulders and took a step backward.

Violet stood in silence, processing Parminder's words. She focused on the apiarist's eyes, on their intensity, and knew that Parminder would sacrifice herself for this cause, that she believed in the illumination of Recollection City. That she *dreamed* of that moment.

And if Parminder thought for one second that Violet would prevent that from happening, that Violet was not the Princess Electric and instead an agent of the queen, then without a doubt Parminder would kill her—without hesitation, without remorse.

Without pity.

And that wasn't a bad thing. If Violet wasn't the princess of prophecy and she couldn't reclaim Karin's memories, then she may as well let Parminder kill her. She'd have nothing to go back to in the real world except a room in the mental hospital beside her dying sister.

The rest of her life would be nothing more than padded walls and paper gowns.

Violet was getting more and more frustrated with all the half-truths. Why hadn't Declan been completely honest with her? Would she have promised to help knowing the ramifications? He never said anything about not being able to return home if she illuminated Recollection City and dethroned the Queen of Glass. According to Cheshire, when she turned eighteen she'd still be able to return to the real regardless of sitting on the throne or not—she'd just never be able to come back to Dementia. But he also said he could get her own memories back, which according to Parminder was also a fallacy.

Who was she to believe? Violet wanted to crumple to the floor and let the weight of everything bury her. She pulled the collar of her coat around her head to shield herself from the mosaic of stained glass above her.

But its brightness was impossible to ignore. It shone on her like a

spotlight. The glitter called to her. She felt like the days after the accident, smothered by melancholia and shock. Overwhelmed and drowning.

Violet glanced toward the mosaic. There was comfort in the glitter, as if it charged her and brought clarity to her mind. She had to reclaim Karin's memories and then she'd honor any promise made. She'd illuminate Recollection City even though Declan hadn't been totally honest about the penalty for doing so. Besides, did anyone really know what would happen if the queen was killed? Thinking back to her history classes in high school, prophecies and doomsday predictions rarely came true anyway.

Violet looked at her hands. They glowed brighter, their wattage cranking up as she fortified herself to what needed to be done.

To what she needed to sacrifice.

"I promised Declan I would help illuminate Recollection City," Violet said finally, her voice firm. "But part of that agreement was to reclaim my sister's memories. So first we get her memories back, and then—and only then—will I assist in dethroning the Queen of Glass and rebalancing Dementia."

"Not so fast." Parminder raised her hand. "If we do in fact find your sister's memories, how are we supposed to trust you that you'll return to Dementia?"

"All I have is my word." She looked at her hands, watched how their brightness hazed the air like heat distortion on sunbaked asphalt. She held them up to Parminder. "I can offer my light."

"That's not enough." Parminder stuck her leg behind Violet and pushed her hard.

Violet lost her balance, twisting over the apiarist's shin and falling against the cold marble floor. "What the hell?" she blurted, rolling onto her back.

Before she could get up Parminder was on top of her, straddling Violet. "I need more."

"You have all the good memories of my sister." Violet squirmed,

freeing her hands from under Parminder's legs. "Cheshire took them. Maybe he took them as collateral. I don't know, but they're in the conservatory. What more do you want?"

"I want you to prove that you're the Princess Electric," Parminder said, voice calm yet commanding. "I want you to prove it beyond bright skin and sad stories."

"But that's all I have," Violet said, adjusting herself under Parminder. "I've wielded Glitterglam and you said that wasn't enough."

"Wrong," Parminder spat. "You didn't wield Glitterglam. The sword was presented to you. Faked. Declan wants to believe in the coming of the Filament so bad that he set you up. Don't you see that?"

Impossible, Violet thought. *I felt the electricity.*

"Everyone who comes from the real has some form of power in Dementia," Parminder continued. "Yours has not been fully realized, that's true. But Declan made you use whatever inherent power you do have to control the glitter he provided. All you had to do was direct some of your current into manifesting the sword and the glitter would react. That's it. Nothing more than a simple cantrip."

"But I felt it," Violet countered, desperate to find something, anything to sway Parminder into believing her. "I felt my body come alive when I held the sword. Whether Declan set me up or not, I felt something. I can wield Glitterglam."

"Then do it!" Parminder's eyes widened, bright and furious. "Summon the glitter above. Break the glass of the mausoleum and let the glitter rain down. Form Glitterglam without Declan being here, without tricks. Summon the sword of the Princess Electric and I will believe in you."

Violet tried to see past Parminder but she couldn't. All she could see was the curls of lace hanging from the apiarist's outfit, the reflection of light off her leather dress, the stained-glass branching outward from the hourglass above. The glitter was there. She could feel its electric hum above the dome, but she couldn't see it. She tried to stand.

"Summon the sword," Parminder said, pushing Violet back down.

"I'm trying!" Violet yelled. "But I can't see the glitter."

"You shouldn't have to. Know that it's there and bring it to you. It's everywhere in Dementia. Call it with your mind. Call it home."

Violet clenched her fists and closed her eyes. Glitter filled the darkness of her mind in great dunes of golden dust. She willed it toward her, envisioning Glitterglam forming from nothing more than her breath. She inhaled darkness and exhaled glitter. Her hands vibrated with electricity. Opening her eyes, she saw that her hands sparked like a pair of live wires.

"Summon the sword," Parminder said calmly. "Break the mausoleum."

Violet suddenly rolled sideways, forcing Parminder to jump off her. She slid on the smooth marble floor until she was on her back. Facing the stained-glass mosaic, Violet placed her hands together, fist on top of electric fist. The pull of the glitter tugged at her thoughts. She envisioned the sword cutting through the glass above and coming to her. The glitter stirred above the glass roof.

"*I don't believe in you*," Parminder mocked. "Look at you, floundering about like a fish out of water. If you were really the Princess Electric you would have shattered the mausoleum already."

Violet ignored Parminder's goading, focusing on the glitter instead. The sword blossomed in white gold within her mind. Her hands continued to spark, sending tiny motes of light to mix with the streaks of rainbow dancing around her. She reached toward the ceiling but nothing happened. The glass didn't break. It didn't even crack.

"You're nothing," Parminder said, standing over Violet. "You couldn't summon Glitterglam when your life depended on it." Parminder kneeled on her chest. "Why should we help you get your sister's memories back if you can't help us?"

Violet raised an arm to push Parminder aside, but the apiarist punched her wrist, knocking Violet's arm to the floor. Sparks scattered from the impact.

"How are we to get your sister's memories back," Parminder said,

leaning down until her veil brushed Violet's face, "if she doesn't even exist?"

Violet squirmed under Parminder's weight. "She's real!"

"How do we know that?" Parminder said, grabbing Violet's wrists. She leaned lower, pressing her veil-covered mouth against Violet's ear. "For all we know, you're a spy sent to infiltrate Pallium for the queen. Your memories are implants. You don't even question your own thoughts."

"That's bullshit and you know it!" Violet struggled to free her wrists from Parminder's grasp. Sparks continued to discharge into the ether, her energy shorting out against the apiarist's grasp.

"The accident, your sister, the memory siphoning? It could all be an elaborate ruse to bring down our guard."

"Don't talk about my sister like that, you bitch." Violet clenched her jaw and kicked out her feet, trying to throw Parminder off, but the apiarist countered by pushing her arms back down and locking her wrists against the marble floor. Ozone tinged the air. Out of the corners of her vision Violet could see her hands increasing in brightness.

Electricity danced about her body.

"Don't talk about your sister?" Parminder said, smiling under her veil. "Does that strike a nerve? Was the accident that hard on you? It's surprising that something which seems so real can be so fake."

Violet screamed, trying to raise her arms against Parminder's weight, but she couldn't move them more than an inch off the ground. Her energy fizzled, body limp. "My sister is real," Violet choked out. "Karin is real to me."

The current churning in her body began to evaporate. The air about Violet sizzled then went still. Brightness dimmed.

"Come on and fight me," Parminder said, lifting Violet's arms and smacking them down on the marble floor. "Get angry."

But Violet just lay there. Spent. Ambivalent. She let Parminder smash her wrists into the ground, letting the pain of her sister's missing

memories fill the void. The memories that now danced as butterflies in the conservatory. Memories of happier times.

"Enough, Parminder," shouted a voice from Violet's periphery. "Get off her."

"Stay out of this," Parminder huffed, cocking her head. "This is between me and Violet."

"I said *get off*!"

And then there were hands on Parminder's shoulders. She was flung to the side, rolling along the floor in a tangled mess of leather and lace. She sprang onto her feet and stood battle-ready. Reaching behind her back, Parminder unsheathed her blades of smoke and mirror. Bees darted out of the smoke, encircling the steel.

Violet looked up and saw Declan, pewter-streaked hair framing his face. He didn't look down, his sky-bright eyes locked on Parminder. He lifted his hands, palms out. Shadows congealed in the pockets of darkness around the busts. They spilled from the rows, over railings and down stairs, slithering along the ground until they coiled around Declan's fists.

"There are many ways to prove she's the Princess Electric," he said calmly. "This isn't one of them."

"You're the last person who should have any say in this," Parminder said. "If she's the Princess Electric, you've done a good job at jeopardizing her trust in us." Parminder smiled. "Old habits, eh, Declan?"

"Shut up," Declan said, straight-jawed. "Not now."

Parminder laughed, bees corkscrewing around her head. She sheathed her swords, the smoke dissipating in puffs behind her back. The bees flew out into the coliseum and disappeared. "That's fine, but when she brings about the fall of the Rememberists, I hope I get to say I told you so before we all turn to glitter."

The apiarist removed the forget-me-not lei from around her neck and walked over to Violet. "Here's your lei." Parminder tossed it onto Violet's chest. "You're going to need it more than you think."

Without another word, Parminder walked past Declan and entered

Stem. She closed the cage, pressed a button, and disappeared into the depths of Pallium.

Violet lay in stunned silence. Tears wet her cheeks. Her wrists throbbed. She cocooned her peacoat about her body and tried to remember her sister, tried to recall a good memory of Karin.

Instead, images of the car accident started to materialize. Streaks of wet snow on the windshield. The flash of headlights and how they scintillated before impact. Pristine white and winter blue. Nova bright.

Violet wept quietly, trying to push the images away.

She couldn't crash now, not again...not so soon.

Violet stared at the mosaic above her.

Stared at a crack in the glass.

Glitter dusting down.

11/ A FATE OF TWIST

EVEN THOUGH DECLAN stood a few paces away, Violet couldn't stop staring at the crack in the glass while she lay on the mausoleum's floor. It had to have been there already. There was no way she did that. But she hadn't noticed it before.

The crack was difficult to see, like spotting a blonde hair on a white blouse. But when the light from the butterflies caught the glitter at the right angle the hairline crack gleamed.

Suddenly the floor shuddered beneath Violet, the foundation of the Mausoleum of Memory quavering like a final breath. A sonorous drone filled the air from everywhere and nowhere at the same time. The sound of clanging, hemorrhaging pipes beat from beyond stone walls, from the very core of Pallium.

"What's happening?" Violet grabbed the lei of forget-me-nots that Parminder had tossed on her chest and sat up. She slipped them over her head, the flowers brushing away the tears that dappled her cheeks.

"It's a twist," Declan said. "Those memory aftershocks. They're coming more frequently now. The landscape of Dementia is always changing." He held out his hand to help her up.

"Don't," Violet said over the thrum. "Don't touch me. I can get up on

my own." She staggered to her feet, nearly falling over as the ground trembled.

Declan caught her, arms around her waist, his trench coat fluttering about them.

"I said *don't*." Violet gazed into his eyes, losing herself in the blue whorls for a breath. She blinked herself back into the moment and pushed him. "Don't fucking touch me, you liar."

For as much as she wanted to trust him, she couldn't. Not after he'd tricked her into thinking she summoned Glitterglam herself, into thinking she could go home.

There was no excuse for that.

Declan stumbled backward as if he'd been stabbed. "What are you talking about?"

The twist shook the mausoleum again. A sharp crack came from above. Violet looked and saw the fracture in the glasswork, bigger now. Glitter sifted into the mausoleum. She frowned, disappointed in the realization that she didn't cause the crack. Turning her attention back to Declan, she said, "You set me up. You made me believe I'm somebody I'm not."

"Why would you think—"

"The glitter," Violet said, pointing to the metallic dust flecking the air. "You manipulated whatever power I have to benefit you. You made me create Glitterglam because you wanted me to, because you have some weird idea of what I am. And don't try to deny that you set me up. Parminder told me everything."

Declan opened his mouth in protest but the twist stole his words in a huge, thunderous boom. The ground shook and he put his arms out to balance. Violet stumbled and fell. This time he didn't move to help her.

"I can explain. There's so much at stake."

"Enough to lie?" Violet stood, brushing off her peacoat. The kaleidoscope still sat in her pocket.

Declan sucked in a breath through his teeth. "Yes."

A bead of yellow light trailed over his shadow-covered face.

"Well that's pretty sad. I mean, come on, Declan, Dementia is hard enough to swallow without your bullshitting. I nearly killed my sister in a car accident. I put her in a coma only to have her wake up and forget who I am. And then to walk in and find some memjack whatevers sucking out the rest of her memories? I think I can handle the fucking truth."

The mausoleum stopped shivering as the drone of sirens faded like distant thunder. A stillness permeated throughout the room, leaving only the silent sparkle of rainbow butterflies encased in glass busts.

"I'm sorry about the accident," Declan said, his words pillow-talk quiet. "Nobody should have to go through that. And nobody should have to witness a loved one's memories being siphoned. But all of that has also made you stronger than me."

"What do you mean?" Violet's brow furrowed, touching the frame of her sunglasses.

"I mean that after all these years, I still struggle with the reality of Dementia. The truth of it is overwhelming. The Queen of Glass is growing in power and all we can do is hold on. We've run out of options." He paused for a moment and licked his lips. "That is, until you fell into Dementia."

Violet stared at him, but didn't say anything. He still seemed so sincere. So passionate. Shadows swirled along his pale skin, over the bridge of his slender nose, over wine-dark lips. She wanted to believe his words; he looked so helpless and broken, the light of the memory butterflies trailing over him in streaks of marigold and chartreuse, blueberry and vermillion.

But he'd tricked her.

Half-truths and incomplete details.

Just because her skin glowed did not mean she was the Princess Electric by default. It just meant she was a girl with albino skin that reflected moonlight.

"But you were a newfallen once," Violet said, surprised she remembered the word for recent arrivals in Dementia. "So was Cheshire, and

Parminder, and the others. Everyone had to figure things out. How long did it take you? You've never told me how long you've been here."

Declan shifted on his feet, teeth against his bottom lip. "Because it's always a lot to take in. We've learned over the years that it's easier to explain things to newfallens in small doses. Trying to give a kid a huge spoonful of medicine all at once is never a good idea. They tend to spit it out everywhere."

"Yeah, but I'm not a kid."

Declan nodded, a slight smile playing across his mouth. Shadows pooled under his eyes. "You're right. I transitioned during World War II. Cheshire and I both did. Plus our brother Cearul. And don't ask me how it all works, how I'm still young like you. We have ideas but that's it. I'm still trying to understand this bloody place. Some newfallens take longer than others to come to terms with Dementia, and some never do. But everyone has a reason for staying."

"And yours?" Violet asked, trying not to think about Declan's age. Or his other brother, Cearul, she'd yet to meet.

He looked at her, the shadows along his face trailing down his cheeks like tears. "It's...complicated. But it comes down to regret." Declan swallowed, a drop of shadow falling from his chin. He looked past Violet. "One day, I promise to tell you how I transitioned to Dementia and why I stayed, but not now. We don't have time for that."

Violet stepped into his gaze, waited for his eyes to fall on her again. "If all of that is true, then why not tell me everything right away? If you'd just been honest—"

"You would never have come back."

Violet screwed up her face as if sucking on a lemon. "Why do you say that? If I'm supposed to be this girl of prophecy, then I would've been fated to come back. Now you've gone and messed things up with your bullshit."

She'd always laughed at the whole prophecy thing. It never made sense to her in movies or books. That one person could be destined to change the future. Regular people doing extraordinary things was much

more real to her. Not because they were destined to, but because they *had* to.

"Prophecies are what desperate people tell themselves to create hope about tomorrow. And we've been desperate for a long time." Declan stepped toward Violet. He placed his hands on her arms. Gently. "If you're indeed the Princess Electric—and I do believe that— then I need you to believe in yourself as quickly as possible, regardless of consequence. We've lost touch with the other Rememberist groups. The other boroughs have grown dark to us. The twists are happening more often, rupturing the very foundation of Dementia. Recollection City will be nothing more than an afterthought if we don't act now. And if that happens, there won't be any chance of getting your sister's memories back."

Violet stared into the wide, rocking sea of Declan's eyes. Although she'd been learning the truth about Dementia in fits and starts, if she'd been bombarded with that information right after arriving, she would've left Dementia the first chance she got.

"So I guess we have an agreement then." She shrugged Declan's hands from her arms. "I'd promised to help you illuminate Recollection City and take out the Queen of Glass if you'd help me retrieve my sister's memories first. I still intend to honor that promise, even if you weren't completely honest with me about the prophecy."

"What do you mean?" Declan asked, eyes narrowing.

"Well, let's see." Violet looked at the stained glass mosaic above. "You left out the part about me turning to glass. Oh, and the part about me not being able to return home after I take the throne. Yeah, those are big points to leave out, don't you think?"

Declan's cheeks darkened. "Yes, but I was going to tell you..."

"When? After I take the throne and wonder why my arms have turned to glass? Or when I try to go back home and realize I can't?"

Declan stood in silence.

"How about we make another promise right here, right now?"

He sighed. "Fine. What's the deal?"

"Honesty."

Declan looked away for a moment. "How so?"

"It means that you're honest with me in all things, and I'll be honest with you."

"Have you been dishonest?" he asked, cocking his head sideways, eyes locked on her.

"Not yet."

Declan chewed on his lip for a second. "Fine, I'll be honest with you from now on. That I promise."

"And I promise to be honest with you," Violet said, nodding. "No matter what."

"No matter what."

"So now that we agree to be honest with each other," she said, dipping her head toward him, "who's Oriana Palms?"

Declan's face blanched, the shadows fading along his cheeks. "Who," he stuttered, "who told you about her?"

"Cheshire," Violet said, regretting having mentioned Oriana. It was evident by Declan's shift in demeanor that she'd struck a rather painful nerve. Was Oriana the reason he was still in Dementia? His source of regret?

"And what else did my sieve of a brother say?"

"That's all. You don't have to tell me. Not if you don't want to."

Declan's eyes were wide and ocean-wet. "Thank you."

Feeling as if she had to change the topic from Oriana or else Declan would melt into a puddle of emotion, Violet blurted, "Cheshire siphoned all the happy memories of my sister."

"What?" The glassiness of Declan's eyes frosted to ice. "What do you mean?"

"He said there was a calibration issue and couldn't stop the machine. That it was broken or something. He also said there was a way for me to get them back."

"But that's—"

"Impossible," finished Violet. "I know. Parminder said the same thing. But Cheshire said there was a way."

Declan shook his head. "No, there isn't. And there aren't things like calibration issues either. That's never happened before."

Violet took a step back. "Cheshire made it sound like it was just a mistake, that it can happen from time to time."

Declan stepped forward, right up close to Violet. He smelled of rainwater and lavender and copper.

"I'll get to the bottom of what happened. And I'm so sorry, Violet. We're only supposed to sacrifice one cherished memory—not all of them." He cupped Violet's chin in his palm. "I'm so, so very sorry."

"It is what it is," Violet said, taking a step back and letting his hand fall from her chin. "We'll get them back, I'm sure of it. Cheshire said he could. I want to believe him."

"Don't we all," Declan whispered.

"Not that I'm not grateful for the help with Parminder, but why did you come to the mausoleum?"

"Because," he said. "I figured out how to track down your sister's memories.

"I know how to get them back."

12/ CAFETERIA BLUES

PROPELLED by the news that he knew how to find Karin's memories, Violet kissed Declan firmly against his cheek. The finest of stubble sent a tickle over her lips, the swirl of pigment cool to the heat of her breath. Shadow followed her as she broke contact, strung between her mouth and his cheek like thin strands of gum.

She smiled as he swatted them away, the strands sticking to his hand. He wiped them onto his trench coat.

"I can't believe you found a way to get my sister's memories back," Violet said, a smile playing across her face. "Where are they? How do we do it?"

"It's complicated but straightforward at the same time." He glanced toward Stem, the ornate metal enclosure that housed the elevator cage sitting empty in the middle of the mausoleum. "I'd rather fill you in with the other Rememberists." He paused for a moment, looked back at Violet and said, "if you don't mind, of course."

"Oh, that's fine." Violet scuffed the toe of her combat boot along the marble floor, the light emanating from the glass-encased butterflies trailing over her black-and-white striped stockings.

"It's not that I don't want to," Declan said, reassuringly. "But it's

dangerous and I want to make sure we all discuss it together before committing to anything."

"So what now?"

Declan hiked up the collar of his trench coat. He plucked out a pocket watch from one of the zippered pockets of his jacket, checked the time, and then dropped it back in. "In an hour we're going to have a meeting with all of the Rememberists in the Moulin Rouge." Declan turned on his heels and started walking toward Stem. "But first, I need to have a word with my brother."

"Cheshire or Cearul?" Violet asked, remembering that he mentioned the other brother earlier.

Without looking back, Declan said, "Cearul's not in Pallium."

Violet followed him to the elevator, assuming that Declan was going to confront his brother about siphoning her good memories. Clearly he didn't want to discuss Cearul, but she was curious where he was if not in Pallium—and why they hadn't mentioned him before.

"And what about me?"

Declan pressed the elevator's call button. A soft chime dinged. "What about you?"

"Am I coming with you?"

Declan cocked his head slightly. "Violet...as much as I want to spend time with you, I need to have a word with Cheshire in private."

"Where should I go until then? It's not like I really know my way around."

Stem arrived in a cloud of steam that hissed into the mausoleum and surrounded Declan and Violet. It smelled like diesel exhaust.

"Are you hungry?" Declan pulled open the cage doors. "I don't think you've eaten since falling."

He was right. She hadn't thought about food since arriving in Dementia. And now that he mentioned food, her stomach suddenly felt empty.

"Yeah, I could eat."

Declan stepped into Stem. He motioned for Violet to follow, closing

the cage doors behind her. "Here," he said, pressing a button labeled *Cafeteria*. It bloomed with a soft white light, exposing other words underneath that had been covered over by masking tape. "Take Stem to the cafeteria. Grab anything you want and then meet me at the Moulin Rouge. Remember how to get there?"

"Through the atrium," Violet said.

"Right. Don't go anywhere else. Stem can lead to some dangerous places. Even though they might be connected to Pallium, it's better to not take chances."

"But...you have a *cafeteria* here?" Waves of hunger swept over her. Images of onion rings and burgers and fries with gravy so loaded with monosodium glutamate that you'd need to chug water just from looking at them.

"Of course. We all have to eat."

Declan pressed another button that read *Gapstow*. The word had also been printed overtop of masking tape and other faded letters like the Cafeteria button. From what she'd been told, Violet assumed that it was more than likely due to the different locations that had twisted into Pallium over the years, replacing others. There were only so many spots on the panel for new buttons.

"We may not age here, but we still need to nourish our bodies," Declan continued as Stem shuddered and filled the area around the cage with fog. Muzak started to play from the blown glass flowers in the ceiling, a smooth jazz number. "The cafeteria appeared about fifty years ago, evicting an old Italian restaurant we used to eat at. It had checkered tablecloths and the best veal parmigiana this side of Dementia. The cafeteria doesn't compare."

"Where's the cafeteria from?"

Declan screwed up his face. "A hospital."

Violet shuddered. She remembered eating food from the hospital after the car accident, all dried rawhide that was passed off as Salisbury steak, trays of cold oatmeal, bruised fruit, and desserts that stuck to the

roof of her mouth like bad vegan brownies. Not to mention the slop they fed her sister at the mental hospital. "You're kidding, right?"

Declan shook his head. "That's our food reality until another restaurant twists into Pallium. It's depressing."

Stem vibrated and then stopped in the usual patch of fog, a squeal filling the air like the wet brakes of a train. Beyond the cage door was a winding pathway that led to the distant, shadowy form of an old stone bridge, lit by rain streaked with glitter and moonlight. Cheshire was nowhere in sight, so Declan didn't open the cage and instead pressed another button that read *Cadogan*.

"You're not getting off?" Violet asked as Stem jolted and sank into darkness again.

"I should check Cheshire's room first. If he's not there, I'll hit up a few of his favorite brooding spots."

Stem stopped again. Declan opened the cage door and slipped out into a dark hallway lined with curlicued wallpaper and flickering, wall-mounted lights.

"Go get some food," Declan said, turning around. "Then meet me at the Moulin Rouge in an hour. Don't worry, time passes the same way here as in the real. There's a clock in the cafeteria in case you don't have a watch. We'll set out for your sister's memories after we discuss the plan with the others."

Violet stepped forward. She wanted to hug Declan, wanted to squeeze a thank you into him. Kiss his syrupy, shadow-covered cheek again. But Declan slid the cage closed before Violet could cross the threshold.

Stem chugged and started to rise. Beyond the elevator cage, Declan disappeared in Stem's exhaust, and suddenly Violet's stomach was no longer empty. There was a weight that filled it now. A heaviness that sated nothing, like the dark core of a spoiled peach.

The cafeteria was a large, white dining hall with matching Formica tables and peach-colored plastic chairs. Banks of fluorescent tubes lined the ceiling with only the odd light illuminated, which created pockets of shadow like other areas within Pallium. Moonlight streamed in from a long set of windows that ran along one wall, glitter shifting outside like golden snow.

Violet stepped into the cafeteria from the elevator and noticed a few empty vending machines with old-style pull dispensers flanking Stem. The smell of deep-fried food mixed with the scent of popcorn and fresh-baked cookies assaulted her—a collision of carnival aromas, all corn dogs and cotton candy.

If this cafeteria was indeed from a hospital, Violet knew those delicious scents were nothing more than a mirage that would turn water cracker bland the moment she started eating.

She didn't care at this point if the food was prepared by a Michelin star chef or fell out of a can. Her stomach rumbled. A long counter shielded by glass sat in front of an open kitchen. Behind the glass were warming basins loaded with food: fries and onion rings, steamed vegetables and mashed potatoes, hamburger patties, and macaroni and cheese. A hot dog roller grill turned wieners beside a popcorn machine, its door open and welcoming. Even the salad station looked encouraging with multiple salad dressing options and more condiments than Violet knew what to do with.

This was buffet heaven. She grabbed a tray, slipped behind the counter, and started heaping food onto a plate. Before leaving the area she snagged a carton of chocolate milk from a refrigerated bunker.

It wasn't until she sat down, ready to dive into her plate of food, that she took a second to think about what was before her. Though it all smelled a million times more appetizing than any of the food she'd had

in the hospital, it lacked a certain vibrancy. The hot dog wiener didn't have the usual oily sheen and the fries didn't glisten in the light.

Besides, where did the food come from anyway? Nobody was working in the kitchen preparing things. She took her fork and prodded the salad. It seemed legit if not a bit wilted. The ranch dressing smelled tangy enough to make her mouth salivate.

Violet opened the milk carton. The chocolate milk looked fresh enough, so she took a sip and immediately spit it out.

What the hell? This has no taste. Ugh.

She grabbed the utensils and started eating. The texture of the food was accurate, but the flavor was far from it. Everything was bland, like the overcooked porridge her mom used to make before the accident, back when she cared enough to have family breakfasts.

Violet moved onto the salad, hoping for something, *anything*, to have more flavor than a pizza box. The salad disappointed just the same. Regardless of the lackluster taste, she felt sated after a few bites. Her stomach no longer growled from hunger. She couldn't imagine a lifetime of eating the same unappetizing food.

No wonder everyone in Dementia was depressed.

Violet sat in the quiet of the cafeteria and gazed through the windows, watching the mesmerizing sway of the sifting glitter. As she looked around the cafeteria she realized that for the first time since falling into Dementia, nobody was around. Sure, she'd been alone in that small room, either passed out or hooked up to intravenous drips— but that was it. Did they trust her now? Did they trust her enough to grant free rein within Pallium?

Within Dementia?

Are they watching me?

She didn't see any security cameras. Maybe one of the Rememberists had a crystal ball to track her movements? She wouldn't be surprised.

Violet pushed her plate away and stood, the kaleidoscope in her pocket clanking against the table's edge. She pulled it out. The acid etch-

ings swirled around its surface as she ran her hands over the smooth exterior. She knew how easy it would be to leave Dementia. All she'd have to do was look inside the kaleidoscope and she'd be back home.

Declan had said everyone had a reason to stay in this messed-up place and to Violet, hers was clear. She put the kaleidoscope back in her pocket to remove temptation. The only way she'd go home would be with Karin's memories. Besides, if she were to go back now she'd never have a chance at getting her own memories back.

The memories Cheshire had siphoned.

As Violet walked to the windows, she wondered why Cheshire hadn't come to see if she was okay after the incident. Was he that self-absorbed? Did he not care about what had happened? Every time she tried to recall what he'd taken she came up empty. It was like scanning a beach with a metal detector, trying to find something hidden in the sand. She knew that she loved her sister, but didn't know the reason for the emotion. It was the most confusing, vacuous feeling she'd ever felt.

Loving someone but having no idea why.

Violet placed her hands against the cool glass, glitter dusting down from the moon-filled sky. The city swept outward from the elevated cafeteria. Traffic lights flashed. Cars drove about the streets, fading into each other, into buildings, into corners. People scurried along sidewalks. Bridges spanned rivers of milk-blue water. In the distance, neon flickered in mesmerizing, cathartic rhythms. The heartbeat of a city forged from noir and shadow and loss.

Recollection City.

It wasn't until Violet stood in front of its vastness that she felt the full weight of the sadness permeating Dementia. Buildings randomly caved into themselves. Sirens in the distance whirred as storefronts melted. Brownstone frontages fluttered like butterflies, vibrating and shimmering until they formed industrial lofts.

As Violet watched, the city continually twisted within the glitter, changing like the shore of a beach, each wave molding the sand, each tide wiping away the history. She gazed beyond the bridges, beyond the

rivers that severed the various boroughs of Recollection City, until her eyes fell on a massive fortress of riveted metal and black glass. It bloomed from a towering cliff, perched above the city like a crow ready to feast on carrion. Rainbow-colored waterfalls shot through with lightning poured from the citadel, terminating in clouds of luminescent foam along the base of the cliff.

Without a doubt, Violet knew the queen lived there.

That was the Palace of Memories End.

Haunting and beautiful and impossible.

And then the realization of what was being asked of her slammed into Violet like a tsunami. How was she supposed to dethrone the Queen of Glass in an impenetrable fortress high above the city when she couldn't even use her powers properly—whatever they were supposed to be? Not to mention, before she could even think about doing that, she had to find Karin's memories out in the vastness of Dementia. With people she couldn't trust.

It all seemed futile.

She pressed her forehead against the window, tears welling in her eyes. Her hands glowed, each breath coming faster, shallower. The walls of the cafeteria seemed to close in on her, the glitter beyond the glass swirling in the air outside.

Violet missed her sister so much. The way things used to be.

Or how she thought they were.

Did they curl up on Karin's bed and talk about random shit?

About stupid videos on social media?

About guys?

Did they bitch about school, or their mom? Or just life?

I just want to remember something good about Karin.

Tears fell along her cheeks, her body humming.

Anything.

Violet couldn't catch her breath.

Couldn't remember how to breathe.

Sobs wracked her body. She wanted to scream.

If only she had good memories of Karin to temper the panic.

But all she had was pain and heartache and emptiness.

Even talking to her mom again would help calm her thoughts.

But they were broken too. The foundation of their family was shattered.

Everything was so upside down.

All because of me.

She turned around, put her back against the window, and collapsed on the floor.

I can't breathe, I can't breathe, I can't...

Tears covered Violet's face. Her body shook. Heart thundered.

Every cell in her vibrating body felt like a spring door stop that had been kicked.

She tried to suck in a breath but her body pushed it out.

Wanted to lie on the cold floor forever.

Let the weight of everything crush her into oblivion.

Her vision blurred. She wiped her eyes under her sunglasses and saw a spark of brightness about her. Blinking away tears she noticed her hands glowing more than before. Pulsating.

Violet forced in a breath, then another. Her body calmed, the trembling in her chest, her legs, slowly waning as she stared at her hands. Blinked again and she saw the clock in the distance.

The meeting at the Moulin Rouge.

Violet vaulted up. She wasn't late, but the clock reminded her that Declan had found a way to track down Karin's memories. And they would be leaving to get them soon after discussing the plan.

She looked at her hands again, how they pulsated with light. Something was going on with her body in Dementia; she could feel it like a scratch at the back of her throat that no amount of water could fix. Everyone said it would take time to realize her potential. To nurture her powers.

Maybe time was all she needed?

Or maybe she just had to believe?

Regardless, she wasn't going to take shit from anyone else again. Not Declan, nor Cheshire or Parminder. Nobody. The realization that her good memories of Karin could be gone forever was hard to come to terms with, but she had to compartmentalize that, had to pack it away. That was her reality and she would deal with it when the time came. But right now, nothing was more important than getting Karin's memories back.

And if she had to go into Recollection City herself to find them, she would.

She squeezed her fists, which intensified the light emissions.

The sound of cracking glass filled the cafeteria.

Violet spun around.

Her jaw dropped.

The entire window running the length of the cafeteria was coated in glitter obscuring the city beyond.

It swirled in curlicues along the glass, shifting toward Violet. She placed her hands against the cool window. Veins of platinum dust shot through the glitter like lightning bolts, terminating at her hands.

And there, right in front of her, was the crack. Like the hairline fissure in the stained glass ceiling of the Mausoleum of Memory, it was difficult to see. She focused on the window, her reflection incandescent, and the glass spider-cracked outward from her hands.

A smile played across Violet's face as she moved her glowing hands around, trails of glitter following her movements like static-charged dust.

"Nobody will tell me I'm not the Princess Electric."

Violet stepped away from the window, the glitter continuing to swirl like pinwheels where her hands had last touched. She glanced at the clock. Still a bit of time until the meeting, but she didn't want to wait for things to happen. If there was a plan to get Karin's memories back, maybe there was a way to get her own memories back inside her head at the same time?

Her conversation with Cheshire about the calibration issue, or lack thereof, was not over. He owed her more details on how he was going to fix what he'd done.

With newfound determination she hustled toward Stem and pressed the call button. The elevator thundered into the row of vending machines in a cloud of steam. Violet opened the cage doors and slipped inside, closing the cage behind her. She didn't know where Cheshire's room was, so she pressed the button Declan had pressed earlier.

Gapstow illuminated with her touch. Stem clanged and groaned as the elevator lurched into motion, and Violet set off into the depths of Pallium.

Alone.

13/ MIDNIGHT ON THE BRIDGE OF GOLDEN RAIN

VIOLET STOOD in the metal confines of Stem, gazing out into the golden rain. Gaslights sprouted at odd intervals along the edge of a winding pathway. They illuminated the rain, turning each streaking droplet into threads of light. Puddles shimmered with slicks of rainbow. There was no glitter sifting from the sky, only the wet wash of metallic rainwater.

A large pond filled the area immediately in front of the elevator, the pathway skirting around the pond and disappearing into the dark arms of trees. Across the pond, framed between trees and gaslights, spanned an old stone bridge covered in ivy.

The bridge looked familiar, yet had such a fairytale quality that Violet wasn't sure where she'd seen it before. Years ago, she'd gone to Central Park on a school trip to New York City. This area certainly looked like somewhere in the park, but she'd never heard the name *Gapstow*.

She shrugged and opened the cage, stepping into the rain. A bucket of umbrellas sat beside Stem, but Violet liked the coldness of the rain and decided to leave the umbrellas. She didn't mind getting wet. Like her sister watching the falling snow, walking in the rain calmed her,

made her feel more alive. She had walked the entire way home from school the day she found out about her dad having a heart attack at work. It was a cold, April rain, and by the time she made it home, she'd calmed herself enough to understand what had happened—and that things were never going to be the same again.

The pathway broke out in two directions. One led toward the trees and bridge, the other into darkness. She was nervous about walking into the dark, Declan's words about her safety echoed in her mind. *Don't go anywhere else. Stem can lead to some dangerous places.* She pulled up the collar of her coat and made her way along the pathway. Rain dappled the pond. Lightning sparked across the sky, illuminating a distant backdrop of shadowy buildings and skyscrapers. Was she outside the safety of Pallium? She thought Cheshire had said the Rememberists used transcendence gates for travel into Dementia from the protection of their stronghold.

Either way, she had to be careful here.

Gaslights perched on the top of large black poles continued under the overhanging branches, providing enough light to see, and enough shadows for Violet to feel uneasy. She was alone and had no idea how to protect herself, how to summon Glitterglam. If she couldn't create Glitterglam from glitter, she sure wasn't going to build it from rainwater.

And she felt bad about ignoring Declan's warning. Was he trying to protect her? Did he genuinely care for her? If she was the princess then she had to figure some things out for herself.

She rounded a bend, the rain not quite as intense under the canopy of trees. Leaves nodded with an incessant pitter-patter. Hairs on Violet's neck prickled as rainwater snaked down her back.

The bridge now stood before her. Gaslights flanked either side and created pockets of shadow off the pathway. It wasn't a large bridge, but one of age and grace and strength, built by blocks of stone that created a perfectly rounded arch. Violet walked out from the trees, stopping at the bridge's apex. She placed her hands on the stonework, its surface cold and wet.

What is this place? She looked back along the pathway that hugged the pond until she found Stem. The elevator was gone, leaving a hollow shaft of metal framework. Why had Declan wanted to come here? Was this one of Cheshire's brooding spots?

Violet huffed, her breath ghosting in the cool night air. She cupped her hand and turned it to the sky, catching rainwater. Golden water puddled in her palm. She took her other hand and placed a finger in the water, stirring it about. A tickle climbed up her finger, a slight electrical pulse.

"How can I use this glitter?" Violet asked herself in frustration. "How can I make a sword without Declan doing all the work for me?"

Violet looked around and saw no sign of Cheshire, Declan, or any of the other Rememberists. She was about to continue along the pathway when Stem slid into the metal framework.

The cage opened and out stepped Cheshire into the swirls of steam created by the elevator's arrival. Violet's heart accelerated, and she gripped the wet stone of the bridge and stepped back out of the gas lamp's illumination. Before closing the cage, Cheshire reached inside and pressed enough buttons to make the interior of Stem glow like daylight. He slammed the cage door shut and Stem sunk into the ground. He glanced around the pond and plucked an umbrella from the basket. He hadn't seen her. With a flick of his wrist the umbrella expanded into a large black canopy. He started to walk along the path toward the bridge, his head down, rainwater sliding over the umbrella in golden runnels.

Violet was about to yell out, her hand suspended in mid-wave, when Cheshire stopped beside a wrought-iron bench that overlooked the pond. He reached into his trench coat and pulled out a kaleidoscope. Without looking into it, he twisted it in several different directions, as if he were spinning a dial on a combination lock. Green light shot out from both ends of the kaleidoscope. He tossed it into the pond.

At first nothing happened. Then bubbles slowly began to dot the surface where the kaleidoscope had broken the water. More bubbles

until the area frothed like a hot tub. Beams of rainbow-colored light shot out, disappearing into the trees and sky.

Ever so slowly, a man emerged from the bubbles, rising like a phoenix from the ashes of itself. His hair stuck out in angular spikes of rainbow. A heavy coat of white feathers hung from his shoulders, trailing down into the foaming pond water and ending with feathers shot through with silver and purple. Fog clung to him.

Violet sucked in a quick breath.

He glided ghostlike toward Cheshire, who immediately bowed as the man came to rest before him. And he was beautiful, almost angelic, with rose-colored lips and shimmering skin brushed with a hundred shades of gold. His eyes burned molten red as he looked around the pond and pathway, his movements herky-jerky like a bird, neck tilting in odd, spasmodic angles.

Then he looked at the bridge.

Violet ducked below the wall, hoping he didn't see her. She felt like a voyeur, that if she were to make herself known there would be consequences. She didn't know what was going on, but Violet knew it would be best if she didn't announce herself. Not yet anyway.

She slowly pulled herself up and peered over the edge. The pair were gone. She scanned the area. Nothing. Her heart thundered. Chest tight. How could they have moved so fast and so noiselessly? And were they coming to the bridge?

Voices broke through the din of rain. She glimpsed and saw they were under the canopy of trees, masked in gaslight shadows, just rounding the final bend that would lead them toward the bridge. In a few heartbeats they'd be in direct line of sight to where Violet stood.

She forced herself to concentrate, not knowing why she had to hide, but the feeling overwhelmed her. She looked over the edge of the bridge, down toward the pond. Not a viable option. Even if she jumped before they saw her, they'd hear the splash and wait for her to surface.

She clenched her fists, noticing how bright they were. If she didn't hide, they'd see her glow in a second. The voices grew louder. She

chanced a quick glance and saw the outline of white feathers. The outline of an umbrella. They were almost to the bridge.

Violet thought about running down the opposite side of the bridge, but if it looped around like the cafeteria hallways did, then she'd come out near Stem. That could be a good thing, but if Cheshire and the Feather Man were on the bridge where she was standing now, they'd see her.

She pushed herself from the stone railing and ran away from the voices. She tossed herself over the stone wall near the bottom of the walkway where she knew there was ground below and not water. Violet fell more than she'd expected, crashing against a slight embankment slick with wet grass. Her lungs punched her breath into the night air. As she gasped to regain it, she slid further, stopping in a patch of white daffodils.

She lay still for a moment, lungs rasping, trying to listen for the voices, half-expecting Cheshire and the Feather Man to peer over the bridge.

They never came.

Violet sat up, rubbing the small of her back. Her coat was soaked, the water glistening on the wool of her coat, on her hands. She hooked wet hair behind her ears.

Voices floated down from the bridge as she regained her feet but she couldn't make out the words. The two men were on the bridge, though it appeared she had escaped without them noticing. The pond broke into a stream under the bridge, and a few feet downstream stood a large tree, its trunk forking at shoulder height.

Glancing toward the bridge, she made her way to the tree. Cheshire and the Feather Man were facing each other. The natural forking of the trunk gave her an optimal view, and, with a bit of concentration, Violet could now decipher the words that drifted down through the shush of rain.

"...and continuing to dwell on such insignificant details is a waste of time," Cheshire said, annoyed.

"A single detail can turn insignificance into a rhyme or reason," said the feather-coated man, his voice haunting and lyrical and all melancholy. "Therefore, dwelling on minutia is significant, and time well spent."

"But time is something we don't have a lot of. Not right now. Stem will be back at any moment. I'm sure my brother's trying to find me as we speak."

"Hmmm...then why don't you bring your brother into the fold?" Wisps of fog puffed from the Feather Man's mouth with each word. They swirled about his head in a thick cloud. The fog drifted over the edge of the bridge, fanning over the water toward Violet. It was then that Violet realized it was not fog, but smoke. Perfumed, like jasmine incense.

"Which brother?" Cheshire questioned, laughing. "Declan? You must be joking, Mister Cinder. His will is forged of hope and steel. There's no breaking it."

"I'm sure you can get creative." Mister Cinder's neck continued to snap at odd angles, as if it were broken, or on hinges, never quite settling on one gradient.

"Maybe," Cheshire said. "But knowing Declan, he'd rather die than dine with Queen Zamelerish. Let alone swear fealty to her throne."

Mister Cinder's head snapped down, then sharply to the right. "If that is what it takes, hmmm, then that is what it takes." He shook his shoulders, jostling the feathered coat into a spray of glittering rainwater. It gently resettled about him. "What about your other brother? What about Cearul?"

Cheshire tensed. "You should know."

"I do know, hmmm, but do you?"

"I haven't heard anything from Cearul since he left." Cheshire flexed his free hand. "Not a word since he crossed over into the Borough of Pons. What do you know, Cinder? Is he reuniting the other Rememberists? Is he becoming the hero he so desperately wanted to be?"

"That is *Mister* Cinder, hmmm, boy," the feather-coated man said,

tongue clacking with annoyance. "I have several millennia on you, so best show respect where it's due, or I'll make our arrangements disappear." He cracked his neck in several different spots. "Is that understood?"

"Yes." Cheshire lowered his head.

"Good," Mister Cinder said lackadaisically. "Now, I know Cearul's planning to come back to rally the troops. Are you ready to rally around your good brother?"

Cheshire spat over the bridge. "Cearul is dead to me."

So Cearul is looking for other Rememberists? Violet thought. *Why's that so bad?*

Mister Cinder rubbed his hands together, fingernails black metallic and curled like talons. "You'll have your chance to settle any qualms with Cearul soon. I've left enough breadcrumbs that a blind man could find his way back here. Perhaps I can orchestrate a reunion. What say you?"

Cheshire nodded under the umbrella, the moonlight catching the slant of his jaw. "A reunion would be wonderful."

"I will have my agents dangle the lure, hmmm, but they'll only set it if you can bring me something."

Cheshire glanced out across the pond. "What?"

"Oh, I think you know."

Cheshire nodded, somewhat reluctantly. "Everything's in place. When the time is nigh, your memjacks will be notified."

Violet found herself gulping for air. Cheshire was working with memjacks. He was a traitor. And he had stolen more than one of her memories. She felt sick.

"Very well," Mister Cinder said, smoke spilling from his mouth in white-blue curlicues. "And the newfallen?"

Violet leaned into the crook of the tree, straining to listen. The rain had started to fall harder.

"What about her?" Cheshire said defensively.

"Memjacks already tried to apprehend her, but she was—"

"Taken?" Cheshire interrupted. "Yes, I know."

Was he referring to Declan grabbing her when she'd first arrived?

"And?" Mister Cinder said, that single word laced with such an eagerness Violet thought the man would pounce on Cheshire to get the answer faster.

"And..."

The words faded in the rain. Violet squinted as if that would help her hear better, but all she could make out was rain on the leafy canopy above. She couldn't make out what Cheshire was saying. She huffed in frustration, then caught herself. The last thing she needed was to be discovered now.

Violet knew siblings had disagreements, or even nasty, bloody fights. But something terrible must have happened for him to not even mention Cearul. And Declan had only brought him up in passing. What did he do that was so horrible? She leaned further into the crook of tree, pressing herself against the wet bark.

Mister Cinder stepped toward the edge of the umbrella, his back severely hunched under the coat of feathers. "Are you sure about that, young Gloss?" He leaned forward, eyes razor-narrow. "You said that about the other girls, hmmm—and they all burned out, each and every one."

Other girls? What are they talking about?

Mister Cinder made a popping noise with his lips, sending out a halo of smoke. Violet shivered; partly due to being wet with rain, partly due to being freaked right the hell out. There was something ancient and malevolent and just plain wrong about Mister Cinder. But she couldn't place her unease. Besides Halloween, she'd never really seen anyone with gold skin. It was as if his face had been exquisitely carved from gold bars, his features sculpted perfectly.

"I know what I'm talking about," Cheshire said. He placed a finger in the hoop of smoke and sliced it in half. "There's a light that wasn't present in the others. A power."

Violet stared for a moment at the raindrops dancing along the pond. So Cheshire believed she was the princess?

"What's your proof, hmmm?"

Cheshire swallowed, hesitating. He twirled the umbrella, as if calculating what to say next. Violet leaned further and almost lost her balance, straining to hear every word.

"You'll see when the filament is ignited," Cheshire said. "But I need certain assurances too, Mister Cinder. I need to know that your end of the bargain will be granted. I need to know you can restore the memories I had siphoned. That you can put them back in someone's head."

So he's trying to figure out a way to help me?

"Hmmm," Mister Cinder said, and then he turned toward the pond, the feathers of his coat swirling behind him in a flutter of white. "I don't see—"

Violet could no longer hear the conversation again. She stepped away from the protection of the tree, not thinking, and right onto a twig. It snapped like a wishbone. The sharp crack carried up into the trees and toward the bridge. Cheshire whirled. Mister Cinder squawked in alarm, his eyes flaring into halos of red. Feathers blurred in the rain. Smoke folded like a white sheet around him.

Violet threw herself behind the tree, back to bark, and she slid down until she crouched. Her head swirled with vertigo, chest heavy against the crashing of her heart. She concentrated on her breathing, *in and out, in and out*, like she'd learned from her counselor to help control panic attacks, *in and out, in and out.*

Silence, then the crash of footsteps behind the tree. Violet closed her eyes. *In and out, in and out.* Clangs erupted, loud and penetrating. The sound of steel grating on steel. Sparks crackled. Violet gulped. Someone was coming.

"Quick! Into the river," Cheshire barked.

The sound of a huge splash. The whoosh of air—then silence once more.

Violet wanted to peek around the tree to see if the feather-coated man still stood on the bridge. But she knew Mister Cinder was gone.

Relief washed through her, yet it left her veins as quickly as it arrived. Cheshire was still unaccounted for. Violet pressed her back against the tree, half expecting Cheshire to jump out from behind it. But he didn't. The only sound was rain tapping on leaves, on the bridge, on the water. Violet took a deep breath and turned to her left, leaning out slowly.

Nothing.

Where are you, Cheshire? she thought.

"Violet?"

She screamed, collapsing against the sodden ground as she twisted around. Cheshire stood over her, his trench coat wet with gold rainwater, the umbrella tilted back over his head.

"What are you doing here?" he said quickly, his voice low, words rushed. "Did you hear anything?"

"I went for a walk," Violet said, talking fast, as if she had to explain herself before she lost the opportunity. "To find you."

"Well you found me." Cheshire glanced under the bridge and beyond the pond toward Stem. "But my brother will be here any moment. He wants to chat." He reached out his hand. "He can't see you here, okay?"

She clambered to her feet ignoring his offer. "Why?"

"Dealing with the Delirium Directorate is a delicate ordeal. There's so much to explain," Cheshire said, looking at the pathway, his summery eyes darting in the shadows that spilled from the gaslight. "And I will, but not here. Not at Gapstow."

"What's going on? The Delirium Directorate?" Violet asked, her voice firm. She wasn't going to ask about Mister Cinder, not yet. Cheshire didn't know how long she was there or what she'd heard.

"Do you want the memories of your sister back? The ones I took in the conservatory?"

"Of course I do."

"Then you have to trust me." Cheshire moved a strand of hair from her cheek. She pulled back, but he leaned forward, leaving them under the shelter of the umbrella. He smelled of woodsmoke and cloves.

"Fine," she lied, staring at how Cheshire's lips dripped liquid gold. She wasn't about to trust someone who was a traitor to his friends, to his brother. Yet he'd asked the birdman about restoring her memories. Was he trying to help her while backstabbing the Rememberists? This wasn't making sense. Something else had to be at play.

"Now stay here and don't say a word while I talk to Declan. No matter what. I'll explain everything later." He tugged up Violet's collar, shielding her neck from the rain. Then he held the umbrella up and flew across the air and settled down on the bridge in a shimmer of gaslight.

Cheshire glanced down to where Violet stood between the tree's forking trunk. He grinned, and in that moment she felt uncomfortably warm and weak-kneed. Though he was working against Declan and had stolen her memories, he had a captivating pull that was hard for her to ignore. Was that part of his power? Some form of beguiling charm? The rainwater cooled the heat of her body, her coat hot against her skin, the wool scratchy against the bee stings. She refused to return his smile as he walked toward the pathway leading up to the bridge.

Then Declan was there, walking up the bridge with a matching umbrella, his face determined under whorls of shadow. The gaslights hissed as the brothers met at the center of the bridge.

"Evening, brother," Cheshire said sardonically. "Funny meeting you here."

"Let's cut the bullshit." Declan's umbrella pressed against Cheshire's. "What happened in the conservatory?"

"What do you mean? I completed the Forgetting with Violet."

"No, you stripped her of more than just one memory. That's not the Forgetting, that's *erasing*. That's what a memjack does, not a Rememberist," Declan seethed. "We sacrifice *one* memory, Cheshire... *one* moment in honor of those who have forgotten before us. Not an entire lifetime."

Violet's stomach dropped. She hadn't thought of that. Was Cheshire a memjack? Or just working with them?

Cheshire stared at Declan, his eyes focused and dialed down into tight sparks of yellow. When he finally spoke his voice was calm yet calculated. "There was a calibration issue. Do you think I *wanted* to strip her of those memories? Do you think I *planned* to do that? If you have something to say, then don't hide behind your mask of shadow—come out and say it."

Why didn't Cheshire just say she'd bumped the siphoner and messed something up? Violet wondered. Unless that was a weak excuse and he really did take her memories on purpose.

Declan clenched his fist. Shadow leapt from dark corners of the bridge, swirling around his hand. "There's no such thing as a calibration issue and you know it. Why are you trying to bullshit your way through this? What are you up to? Do you think the other Rememberists are going to just shrug this off like it was an accident?" His voice was growing in fervor, shadow roiling about his fist. "Your actions were *calculated*."

"I made a *mistake*," Cheshire yelled, creating a fist with his free hand. Light from the gaslights streamed toward his hand in bright threads, coiling about it like a lit up ball of yarn. "I lost track of what I was doing. They were coming out of her fast, and by the time I realized my error—"

"But," Declan said, the shadow spinning around his fist in black corkscrews, "she will *never* get those memories back. She will never remember her sister the way she should. All she has are the dark moments now."

No, Declan was wrong. Cheshire said he would help her. He'd even asked the birdman about it. Who was she supposed to believe?

Silence filled the space between the brothers. Gold rain spilled from the black sky above, the buildings of Recollection City jigsawing in the background. They stood under their umbrellas, fists illuminated in light and shadow.

"I can get them back," Cheshire said, breaking the tension. "I can get her memories back inside her head."

"That's impossible," Declan spat. "They're not liquid anymore. They've transformed into the butterflies of memory. They're lost to her forever."

"Not so," Cheshire said. "There is a way."

"How?"

"I can't elaborate on that—not yet."

Declan laughed. "You play me for a fool."

"You must believe me," Cheshire said, pleading.

"I've heard that before. We've all heard that before. Not this time."

"Have faith, Declan."

"Faith is reserved for the religious and the dying, and I'm neither. I believe in hope and reality. Restoring Violet's memories are not a part of either hemisphere. But I *can* get her sister's memories back. I know how to track them down—and that, Cheshire, *is* a reality."

Cheshire flicked his hand and the light fell from it in a waterfall of sparks. "Very well. We'll recover her sister's memories according to your plans—whatever they are. But I took Violet's memories, and I will get them back. I'll find a way to travel the six boroughs of Dementia if I must. I'll do whatever it takes. Violet deserves that."

Declan scowled. "Violet deserves honesty; something I haven't participated much in myself. And I have vowed to remedy that. If she's to destroy the Queen of Glass and illuminate Recollection City, then we need to be honest with her. Telling her pipe dreams of remembering her sister is not going to help." Declan flicked his hand and shadow fell from it, dripping like warm toffee.

"Whatever you say. You always know what's best."

"Get over yourself, Cheshire. I believe in unlocking Dementia. I believe in Violet. What do *you* believe in?"

Cheshire glared at Declan but didn't say a word.

"Exactly," Declan said. "Now let's go to Moulin Rouge so I can

explain how we're going to track down those memories to the others. Violet will be there waiting for me."

Cheshire nodded and followed his brother off the bridge. Before he disappeared along the path, he looked back over his shoulder but his face was masked by the umbrella.

Violet waited until she heard Stem leave with the brothers before walking out from the protection of the tree. So much had happened, her brain heavy with the weight of processing it all. She scrambled up to the path and walked along the bridge toward the elevator. She'd have to unpack what she'd heard later.

She had to get to the Moulin Rouge fast.

14/ IN PREPARATION FOR MADNESS

STEAM HISSED into the Atrium as the elevator slowed its ascent. It clanged to a stop and Violet stepped out of the elevator into the airy room. She'd been through the Atrium twice before with Cheshire but didn't recall seeing the entrance to the Moulin Rouge. Chewing on her bottom lip, she looked around for signs. One direction led to the conservatory, and the other led to the greenhouse, which she could see in the distance. Violet shuddered and rubbed her sore arms, thinking about the bees stinging her body, filling her mouth with their crackling buzz.

I don't need to go back to the greenhouse anytime soon, thank you very much.

She spun around and nearly smacked into a metal signpost topped by a burning gaslight. How she'd missed the signpost the other times she walked through the atrium she didn't know, as it towered above her and had numerous labeled arrows pointing in different directions. Clearly she was too focused on her conversations with Cheshire to notice.

It took her a moment to scan the signpost and find the Moulin Rouge arrow, which pointed back behind her. Violet walked quickly toward a cobblestone pathway that snaked away from the atrium proper.

It led to a large oak door filled with leaded windows which obscured the warm light beyond.

The doors opened onto a street lit by gaslight. An old street sign, balanced precariously on an iron post, read *Boulevard de Clichy*. Beyond the sign, the street was cast in alternating patches of shadow and light, like a chess board. Rain spilled in the squares of shadow creating puddles of mirrored reflections, yet the areas under the gaslights were dry. The buildings lining the gutters were translucent and undulating. At the end of the street stood a building draped in velvety red light. A large windmill churned above, each blade covered in twinkling lights like the boughs of a Christmas tree. Mounted below the windmill was a sign in illuminated white letters that read *MOULIN ROUGE*. The sounds of music and chatter and clinking glasses spilled from the cabaret. It was just how Violet had imagined it when she'd studied Toulouse-Lautrec.

Violet stepped onto the wet boulevard, glad to see the pockets of rain. Her hair and peacoat were still damp from Gapstow. Only Cheshire knew she was there and she didn't feel like having to explain why she was wet to Declan.

She made her way along the street toward the cabaret, with its grandiose doors set in brass and glass. The giant windmill creaked above as she entered.

The first thing she noticed was the sudden silence. All the raucous shouting, the merriment and hollering, the music and clinking glasses, were gone. Instead everything was eerily quiet.

"Hello?"

Violet broke the threshold. The doors slammed shut behind her. She jumped, heart racing. Something wasn't right.

As she made her way into the cabaret, a riot of color greeted her. Boas of chartreuse and raspberry, feathers of lemon and tangerine, snaked around the necks of women dressed in form-fitting petticoats. Skirts ribboned from their waists in waves of white fabric. And from those waves stretched legs covered in black stockings. Men in tuxedos

balanced themselves on canes. A few sported monocles under bowlers; some had their hair combed back with grease and confidence.

Yet they were all still, as if someone had pressed pause. The entire scene was a snapshot in time. The women were locked in dance around tables decorated with electric lamps that breathed red light. Pillars dotted the room, reaching high into the ceiling and rimmed with oil lamps. Cigars and pipes trailed pewter smoke. Fountains of glass spilled liquid onto slotted spoons held by patrons.

Chills crept up Violet's back. And then she heard the giggle.

She couldn't pinpoint its location, but it came from deeper within Moulin Rouge. It was a childish, impish giggle that made the hairs on the nape of her neck thistle. She glanced at the wooden bar, at the hundreds of multicolored bottles lining the shelves. She thought of absinthe, Toulouse-Lautrec's drink of choice. A great mirror filled the wall behind the bar, reflecting the cabaret.

Another giggle. Near the back of the club. Violet spun around and saw a series of velvet-covered booths, each populated by paused patrons in various acts of drinking or flirting or both.

A sharp double-clap rang out.

And the entire room came to life, slow at first, but then sweeping to full motion like a merry-go-round. Women danced, legs kicking in streaks of black. Gentlemen milled about, drinking and saluting the dancers. Some twirled their canes; some smoked pipes that spilled cherry-scented smoke.

All were drunk on desire.

Violet navigated the flailing limbs toward the row of booths. Everyone appeared in their own world, unaware of her walking by. Music pounded into the cabaret from a band that graced a small stage, the beats quick and focused and full of energy. As she neared the booths another double-clap cut the music. Everything paused again.

"Okay, seriously, this isn't funny anymore." Violet tried to spy Declan or Cheshire through the smoke. Her confusion made way for a

sudden jolt of anger. Violet needed to be hunting for her sister's memories, not playing hide and seek in the Moulin Rouge.

Leaning against the edge of the booth stood a guy Violet hadn't seen before. His hair was impeccable, combed sharply and parted to the side. His cheekbones were angled under the glare of lamplight, eyes sharp and green. He was draped in a long trench coat under which he had on a double-breasted suit jacket and high collared shirt. There was no lei around his neck.

Another giggle broke the silence of the Moulin Rouge. This time it came from directly behind her. She whirled.

"Joke's over," Violet said. But there was nothing. No movement.

Then Violet spied Melody Maker. She hadn't seen her since arriving in Dementia, but she recognized her immediately with her porcelain-colored hair cascading over her shoulders in corkscrew curls. She was encased in swirls of color, her boa a blur of fuchsia and emerald, a leg covered in black striking high in the air. A large grin played across her face, her eyes twinkling as if she were the only one in on a practical joke. Violet took a few steps toward her and stared into her eyes, into the flecks of lemon rinds and hazy indigo. Nothing. Not even a blink.

Violet turned around, trying to find the other Rememberists, and as she did so a double-clap rang out from behind her. She whirled again, hoping to catch whoever it was. Patrons drank and laughed in the cabaret once more. Melody danced past her, twirling and spinning in a pinwheel of color. She trailed her boa over Violet, snaking it around her neck, over the forget-me-not lei, and the boa smelled of sex and perfume, of vanilla and lavender and heat.

Melody giggled and sashayed around Violet, continuing in quicker, more dizzying circles. She moved faster and faster until the colors blended into each other, Melody's skirt a continuous ripple of white and peach, her boa a hula hoop around them. Violet lost her bearings, vertigo kicking in, her depth perception off kilter. And then Melody double-clapped and all went still.

Violet nearly toppled over at the sudden pause, her feet tangled and

tripping over each other. She took a few steps sideways to get away from Melody and bumped into someone.

Click.

Something hard pressed against the back of her head.

Click.

Another point of pressure.

She whirled.

And found herself staring down the barrels of a pair of handguns.

Beyond them stood the guy in the double-breasted suit jacket who had been leaning against the booth.

He smiled, green eyes focused yet full of whimsy.

Then he spat and said, "Boom."

––––––––

Violet blanched but the guy never pulled the triggers. He stood there, smiling with an electric glint in his eyes. He tapped one of the barrels against Violet's forehead, hard and cold, then pulled the guns back, blew on the ends of the barrels as if blowing out candles, spun them a few times on his fingers and holstered them. "You really ought to be more careful around here."

"I was told to meet everyone in the Moulin Rouge." Violet glanced at Melody Maker. "Besides, we're still in Pallium right? It's your safe house, so it should be, um, *safe* in here."

The guy laughed, shaking his head. His slicked hair didn't budge. "Just because we're in Pallium doesn't mean the queen's agents aren't amidst us. Spies are everywhere. They could be in this cabaret. They could be sitting in the booth behind me. Hell, for all you know, I could be a memjack. Mind you, if that were the case, I'd be a ridiculously good-looking one." The guy paused for a moment, as if expecting Melody to say something. "Maybe I'm just buttering you up to make you feel comfortable so that the next time I have my darlings pressed against your forehead, you won't be expecting me to pull the triggers.

But I *cancan*...and I will. I'll blow your brains across the cabaret if I have to."

Laughter erupted behind Violet. A hand touched her shoulder, grabbing the boa and unwrapping it from her neck. "Dillinger, you and your cancan jokes. They're bad, you know." Melody Maker sidestepped into view, giving him a hug and a kiss on the cheek. She turned around. "Never mind him. He likes to scare newfallens for kicks."

"Yes, I can see that." Violet glared. "Don't ever point a gun at my face again."

"I wouldn't dream of it." He bowed, his trench coat pooling on the wooden floor. "I'm Dillinger Smith, robber of hearts and slinger of guns."

Violet stared him down, pissed off that they thought it was a good time to play a joke. Where was everyone else? They were supposed to be here. Her blood rushed through her body, face warming. She looked through the crowd and saw the rest of the Rememberists walking toward them.

About time, she thought.

"What's going on?" Declan asked, concern rippling the shadows across his forehead. He led Cheshire and Parminder toward the booths. Morgan Foil followed, his dreadlocks bouncing with each step.

"I don't know," Violet said, her words terse with annoyance. "Melody and Dillinger thought it would be funny to play some prank on me."

Parminder laughed behind her black veil. Cheshire smirked. Morgan stayed silent.

Declan shot Melody a glare, his eyes narrowing into slivers of blue horizon. "Really, Melody? You can't help yourself, can you?"

Her joyous expression faded. "You know I like do that to all the newfallens," Melody said, snaking her boa around her arm. "I love to make everyone's first experience in the Moulin Rouge memorable with a *tableaux vivant.*"

"What are you talking about?" Violet asked, watching the patrons

talking and smoking and carrying on behind her. "The pausing of everything?"

"Well, yes." Melody flicked her wrist flamboyantly. "It's one of my abilities in Dementia. It's like painting with people. I can pause figments and fallens at will, though I can't do it indefinitely and I have to pause everyone in the area at once—except for me of course. No picking and choosing. A few quick stops like I just did aren't a big deal, but if I were to do it for ten minutes, I'd be exhausted. Double clap on, double clap off. It's fun."

Violet looked to the Rememberists standing around. Nobody was volunteering an explanation. "So, let me get this straight. You can pause figments...but we're not figments. We're fallens?"

"That's right. Anyone that transitions into Dementia is a fallen." Melody dipped her head, ringlets bouncing. "Figments are different. So you know what glitter is by now, obviously. The essence of minor memories; things people did thousands of times that were inconsequential and forgotten just as fast as the action itself—like washing dishes. Well, figments are a more concentrated version of a replicated memory. Sometimes they involve multiple experiences folded into each other. Things folks did regularly that brought joy or pain to their lives, or something completely mundane like going to work every day. Those frequent motions form figments in Dementia, distilled constructs from repeated experiences. Look around the Moulin Rouge. All these people having a dandy time, well, they're figments. They may seem like you and me, but they're far from it." She took a breath and eyed Violet. "Just don't tell them they're not real. Figments tend to get a bit agitated when you say that."

Violet stood for a moment, eyeing Melody, then taking in the Rememberists. The explanation made sense. But she had a big problem. She could feel the anger coming to a slow boil in her veins; she balled her glowing hands. "It must have been fun watching me."

"Well, it's all in good fun," Melody said, slightly taken aback. "We

certainly didn't mean anything by it. It's kind of a tradition in a way. Things are pretty gloomy around here without a laugh."

Violet was so mad she could spit nails. She'd shoot them into Melody's saccharine grin if she could.

Cheshire stepped between Melody and Violet. "I apologize for the tableaux vivant on behalf of the Rememberists."

"Yes," Declan interjected. "It was uncalled for, regardless of tradition. We have things to discuss more pressing than talking about figments." He swept his arm out toward the booths. "Shall we sit?"

The anger boiling within Violet settled into a slow simmer as the Rememberists piled into a large horseshoe-shaped booth. Parminder went in first, taking the back and sitting funeral-silent in her black apiarist's garb of leather and lace. Everyone else slid in where they could. Violet sat beside Melody. She could smell her perfume, a mix of lavender and tangerine that helped take a bit of the edge off.

Cancan music thundered about the cabaret. Figments caroused. Danced. Kissed.

"So, can we get on with things?" Violet glanced around the table.

"Agreed," Declan said. "Let's get this meeting underway. As you've been made aware, Violet has offered to stay in Dementia to help us illuminate Recollection City and dethrone Queen Zamelerish if—and only if—we recover the memories that were siphoned from her sister. To fulfill this agreement, she must be allowed to return them to her in the real."

A heartbeat of silence and then Parminder said, "And you trust this newfallen to come back to Dementia? We're going to risk our lives getting a few memories back for a person who's halfway in the grave. If tracking down raw memory is even possible, that is."

Violet stretched her neck to either side, defusing the sudden irritation that Parminder's words ignited within. She knew the apiarist was goading her, trying to illicit a violent response so she could attack Violet with just cause. But Violet wasn't going to give her the satisfaction.

"If you so much as say anything like that about my sister again,"

Violet said, each word delivered slowly, "I will illuminate Recollection City by shoving Glitterglam so far up your ass you'll glow like a Christmas tree."

Nobody said anything at the table—not even Parminder, who sat in smoldering smugness—until Cheshire burst out laughing.

"And yes," Declan said, interrupting the laughter and drawing the conversation back, "I do trust Violet. She has already come back once before; she will come back again."

"Yeah," Morgan said, leaning forward, "but she came back before you inundated her with the hocus pocus realities of Dementia. Now she's probably itching to get back to the real."

"We all have to believe in her," Declan said. "I believe she's the prophecy incarnate. And so should you. If she is indeed the Princess Electric, then she will return to Dementia to illuminate Recollection City as promised."

Finally, Violet thought. *He is sticking up for me.*

"And if she doesn't?" Dillinger questioned, his bottle green eyes bright and cracked in the cabaret's lamplight.

"Listen," Violet said, "I'm not going anywhere. I know there's nothing else I can offer, that you just have to believe me. But isn't that all you've ever had? Isn't that all you've ever relied on to keep you going? *Belief.* You must believe that I'll come back to Dementia. All I have is my word and my desire to come back to help you—if you help me."

Violet pulled out the kaleidoscope from her pocket and set it on the table. The kaleidoscope's etchings seemed to glow in the lamplight. "I've had this since returning to Dementia. And I've had it since the good memories of my sister were drained from my head."

Cheshire focused on the lamp in the middle of the table, refusing to make eye contact with Violet.

"Here." She pushed the kaleidoscope toward the center of the table. "Take it. That way I can't go anywhere until we've at least recovered my sister's memories. When we have them, give it back to me. I'll deliver the memories to my sister and then come right back." She turned up her

empty hands, their skin bleach white and just as bright. "That's all I've got. If that's not enough to convince you, then I give up. There's nothing else I can give."

"You've already given enough," Declan said with resolve. "Cheshire took the good memories of your sister. All of them. And that is more than any of us have ever given."

"Agreed," Parminder said. She plucked the kaleidoscope from the table, spun it in her hands like a baton, and then slipped it into the folds of her apiarist clothes. "But I still accept the offer of the kaleidoscope. We can't have you running off unexpectedly, now can we?" She said this while staring at Violet.

Violet glared in retaliation.

"Good." Dillinger glanced about the table. "Now that we have our newest inmate, what's next?"

Violet leaned forward, looking at Declan beyond Melody. "How do you plan on tracking down my sister's memories?"

"Well," he said, "it would need to be done in two phases. The first would be to find out what processing facility in Medulla they are in transport to."

Violet looked around questioningly. "Medulla?"

"My apologies," Declan said, dipping his head, "but Dementia is broken up into six boroughs, Medulla being one of them. The others are Diencephalon, Mesencephalon, Cerebellum, and Pons. Each borough surrounds the central borough of Cerebrum, where the queen resides in the Palace of Memories End. Within each borough there are numerous districts."

Violet's shoulders slumped. This confirmed her fears about the size of Dementia from what she'd seen from the cafeteria and the rooftop. How were they going to track down her sister's memories? Even if they limited their search to one borough, the task was beyond daunting.

"And the second phase," Declan continued, addressing the rest of the table again, "would be to either intercept the memories in transport,

which would be the preferred method, or we infiltrate the processing plant and take them by force before they're destroyed."

Morgan adjusted his white eye patch, his teeth luminous against midnight black skin. "You're joking, right?"

"It could be fun." Dillinger smoothed his wet-slicked hair with a steady hand. "But I agree with Morgan—it sounds a bit delusional. Besides breaking into a processing plant, how do you plan on finding out which facility the memories are being shuttled to? Trying to infiltrate one plant is a suicide mission. We can't really guess which one they're at."

Declan smiled, and for the first time Violet could see without a doubt the family resemblance to his brother. His smile was striking, with devious little dimples that creased the shadows along his cheeks. He obviously knew something the others didn't and was dying to spill it.

"There are three processing plants in Medulla, and they're located in the Cuneate District, the Gracile District, and in the Tract of Goll."

"Well that's wonderful," Cheshire said. He was still staring at the lamp, the light dancing across his eyes. "So that narrows it down to most of Medulla. You're only missing the District of Metacoel."

"And there's no processing plant in Metacoel," Declan said, "so we can easily scratch that off the list."

"Okay, so that still leaves us with three districts," Dillinger clarified. "How do you plan on narrowing it down?"

"Easy," Declan said, leaning over the table. Lamplight and shadows flickered over his face like a distant lightning storm. "The Accountant."

"Okay, now I really know he's gone mad." Morgan shook his head, dreadlocks swaying like pendulums. "Even if the Accountant would entertain a visit, why would he help us?"

"Because he's neutral," Declan said, shrugging. "And he owes me a favor."

"Excuse me," Violet interjected, "but who is the Accountant?"

Morgan sighed. "He's a memory broker of sorts. Untrustworthy as

shit. But Declan has a good point. If anyone is going to know how to track those memories down, it'd be him."

"Great, let's go," Violet said, putting her hands on the table to slide out of the booth.

"Hold on," Melody said, raising a finger up. "The Accountant owes Declan Gloss a favor? How did that happen? Sure, he might be neutral to the whims of Dementia, but he's also paid by the queen."

"How he is indebted to me is of no concern to you," Declan said, deflecting Melody's question. "What's important is that he is."

"That's all well and good," Melody said, curling the tip of her boa around her fingers, "but how do we even know that the slurpers returned to Dementia via the Medulla channel? Really, they could have entered any of the boroughs."

"That was one of the first things I wondered about," Declan said. "Violet fell into Dementia by using a kaleidoscope and not by stumbling into some random memory perforation. And that kaleidoscope—the one Parminder has now—had been dropped by a slurper. Which, incidentally, means that it was programmed to attach back to a specific channel. The slurpers originated from the Borough of Medulla, and thus returned from whence they came."

"Makes sense." Cheshire stroked his chin. He looked at Violet for the briefest of moments. Long enough for their eyes to lock. Then he looked back at Declan. "What if you're wrong?"

Declan glanced sideways at Violet, then up into the haze of smoke that filled the rafters. "Then her sister's memories will be in another borough, but I don't believe that's the case."

"So we can get them there if we have to," Violet said, more to assure herself than the others. "We can check with a different accountant and see where they're being shipped to?"

"No," Declan said, his voice heavy, as if weighted by a stone and thrown overboard. "We've lost the way into other boroughs. The inter-borough channels have been sealed off with strange shadow vortexes and our transcendence gates are being scrambled somehow. We're

locked within Medulla until we can find a way to burn away the shadows."

Violet's hope started to wane, her body deflating of energy. She slumped against the padded seat of the booth. Didn't Cheshire and the birdman talk about his brother, Cearul, looking for other Rememberists in different boroughs? Maybe he could help get them into those other areas. She perked up. "How about—"

"We get our asses moving," Cheshire said, talking over Violet. "Let's pay the Accountant a visit. It's the only way we'll know for sure. If Declan's right, we'll be one step closer to finding her sister's memories."

"And if he's wrong?" Violet said softly. She didn't mind being interrupted. Maybe she should see where this goes before asking questions about Cearul.

"I'm not wrong." Declan reached past Melody and put his hand on Violet's. His fingers wrapped around hers, their touch warm and comforting. He squeezed and then let go. Violet didn't have to look up to know Cheshire was glaring at his brother.

"So I assume Violet is going to stay back with the operator?" Parminder asked. "She hasn't been trained in combat. Nor have we properly taught her the ins and outs of Dementia—what to do and not to do, what to touch and not to touch."

"It's probably best if she stays back in Pallium with the operator," Dillinger agreed. "It's safe here."

"I'm not staying," Violet pleaded. "It's not my fault you haven't bothered to train me. Actually, Parminder, you said you'd train me and you haven't. We're going after *my* sister's memories, so that means I'm going. End of discussion."

"But—" Declan tried to say.

"But nothing," Violet added. "I'm coming."

"I think everyone should go see the Accountant," Cheshire said. "We need to cover each other, and watch out for the newfallen at the same time. Leaving a Rememberist back here to guard Pallium is pointless and a misdirection of resources."

"We always keep someone back in Pallium," Parminder said. "Regardless of Violet tagging along or not, we need to have coverage here."

"Sorry, Cheshire," Morgan said, tossing a few dreads over his shoulder, "but I agree with Parminder. We need someone to stay. What happens if there's a problem or a breach? If there's nobody here, we're not going to be notified while we're out in the field. We would never get back in time to defend Pallium."

The rest of the Rememberists agreed.

"All right," Cheshire said reluctantly. "Then let's give Violet the rundown."

"Okay," Parminder said. "It's rather simple. If we say don't touch, you don't touch. If we say jump, you fucking jump. We've lost a lot of friends out there and none of us want to lose another, you got that?"

"Yes." Violet swallowed, nervousness leeching the moisture from her mouth. "And to think I thought Recollection City looked so peaceful when I first arrived."

"Dementia is anything but peaceful," Cheshire said. "It's like every thought, every emotion that anyone has ever had curled into a spring. It gains tension and then pops when you're least expecting it. Be careful. Even if we're all around you, at any moment something can go off. Something could separate us. If that happens, hold your position. Find a landmark and don't move. Someone will come for you. Just don't panic."

"Not panicking seems to be the theme here," Violet said, trying to sound lighthearted.

"It's a good theme," Dillinger said. "Especially when you run into *maremons*."

"Maremons?" Violet questioned.

"They're like memjacks, like the slurpers you ran into," Morgan said, toying with a dreadlock. "Where most memjacks are the husks of those who have accidentally fallen into Dementia and have been stripped of memory, maremons are an amalgamation of nightmares and demons personified. They can be anything from regurgitated ancient history to a

fusion of make-believe and reality. But once they've been created by the queen, they can't change form. A dragon is a dragon is a dragon."

"So let me understand this correctly." Violet edged closer to the table. "Maremons can be anything from history or fantasy? Or both? Like they could literally be Medusa crossed with the statue of David by Michelangelo?"

"Yes," Morgan said.

"That would actually be kind of hot," Melody added with a smile.

Everyone at the table took a moment to ponder that reality.

"Anyway," Cheshire said. "Traditional methods to kill a maremon work okay. Like silver against werewolves, iron against fairies. But you can also use your forget-me-not leis. The flowers are wards. You can use them like silver, like holy wafers, however you want. The touch of a forget-me-not to an agent of the queen is like dousing a traditional vampire with holy water. It burns like napalm. Though don't touch one of your lei's flowers to one of us, or you'll kick start a memory walk—and that's a whole other world of shit."

"Okay," Violet said, delicately touching a petal on one of the forget-me-nots around her neck. She had tried using one before but it simply melted at her touch. Declan had used one on her when she first arrived and Violet wondered if there was something else she had to do to use them properly. It was beginning to seem like anything in the human psyche could manifest into some twisted reality in Dementia.

"Before we can leave Pallium," Declan said, "we need to gear up."

"What do you mean?" Violet looked at each Rememberist. "You've already got your powers. All of you do."

Dillinger stood up and pushed the table back. "Powers are one thing." He smiled and slid open his trench coat, hooking the folds of it on his holsters. "But you need more than powers to survive in Dementia." He drew his pistols, spinning them in a blur of metal on his trigger fingers. "You need guns, too. A shitload of guns."

15/ TRANSCENDENCE

DILLINGER LED the Rememberists from Moulin Rouge to Stem, which had been waiting along Boulevard de Clichy. They packed into the elevator like sardines. Violet couldn't believe they all fit. It was a quick ride, the only sound coming from the smooth jazz playing from the blown glass flowers in the ceiling. Stem vibrated to a stop, puffing out steam into a narrow hallway. The air was cool and dank, the walls carved from rock. Lightbulbs dangled from electrical cords every few dozen feet, leaving nimbuses of light in the distance.

"Where are we?" Violet asked.

"We're in The Ravelin," Dillinger bumped a bulb and turned around. The lightbulb swayed, elongating shadows along the walls. "It's an underground bunker that dates to somewhere around the American Civil War. Down the hall's the magazine. Traditionally they used to store just ammunition in there, but we keep all our weapons inside as well. Blades. Guns. Grenades. Whatever you need is stockpiled in there. It's a bloody smorgasbord of weapons."

"Okay," Cheshire said, clapping his hands together, "let's gear up and trance out."

They followed a stairway chiseled out of the bedrock, its surface

rough and jagged. It wound downward, around corners shielded by shadow. Violet wasn't claustrophobic but the more the stairway narrowed, the more she became uneasy, guiding herself by dragging her hand along the damp stones. The lack of light played tricks with her depth perception and she almost missed a step, catching herself at the last moment with Declan's shoulder. Eventually they came to an iron gate that sat open on rusty hinges, the room beyond illuminated with more of the halogen light stands that dotted Pallium's darker areas.

"This is the magazine," Dillinger said, stopping at the gate and waving the Rememberists inside. Declan and Morgan disappeared into the Ravelin.

"You don't keep it locked up?" Violet stopped beside Dillinger, looking inside with curiosity. She'd never seen a gun in the real before.

"There's no point," Cheshire said, breezing past Violet. "If someone's infiltrated Pallium and they've made it this far, then we've got bigger problems than simply needing a few weapons."

"I get that," Violet said. "But shouldn't you lock it up just in case? Better safe than sorry, right? If someone got into Pallium, you wouldn't want them coming here first and destroying your weapons, would you?"

Violet had seen enough war movies with her grandpa that she knew leaving your cache of weapons unlocked and unguarded was a bad idea. And from what she could see from the limited light, there were a lot of weapons. Racks of guns reached deep into the shadows.

"She has a point," Melody said, twirling her boa as she walked past Violet and into the magazine proper. "A point I've been trying to make for a century. But nobody listens to me. I'm just the courtesan after all."

"Courtesan?" Violet asked.

"A paramour," Melody said with panache. "A lover of fine gentlemen."

"You mean prostitute," Cheshire added.

"Don't be crude," Melody countered. "You never complained."

Violet glanced at Cheshire with raised eyebrows. His cheeks

warmed as the edge of his mouth curled upward. He then walked into the magazine.

"Anyways," Violet continued. "I don't see how that matters. Whether you're a courtesan or not, you have an opinion. You have an opinion as a Rememberist, don't you?"

Melody turned back in a ruffled swirl. "It doesn't matter if you're a bloody maharajah. The Gloss brothers are going to do what they want, when they want. They don't like when you call them on it, but it's true. You'll see."

"But Declan said I'm the leader now." She kept her voice low, unsure how Melody or anyone in earshot would take that statement. "I'm the Princess Electric."

Melody sighed. "Honey, that's what he says to all the glowers."

Violet stared at Melody, turning her words over in her head. Was Declan being dishonest with her still, even after they'd promised to tell the truth?

"What are you talking about?" Declan glided out of the shadows of the magazine like a ship breaking fog, the collar of his trench coat curled up around his head.

"Nothing," Melody said, tossing her ringlets back nonchalantly. "Just discussing why the magazine isn't locked up, that's all."

"Come on," Dillinger said to Violet, grabbing her by the arm and dragging her inside. "Time to get you geared up."

Violet followed his lead, Melody circling in behind her. She glanced back at Declan, who stood statuesque near the gate in a curve of shadow. His face was emotionless, yet his eyes were dull and brooding, like the sky just before it rains.

Did he overhear us? Violet thought. *Maybe that's a good thing.*

"Okay," Dillinger said. "You need a gun." There was something in his voice that said to forget what'd just happened and to move on. But Violet couldn't. She wanted to look back at Declan, wanted to see if he was still watching her with those whirlpool eyes. Violet turned to look but Melody was blocking her line of sight.

"Wait a minute," Melody said. "We don't know who's staying back to guard Pallium. I'm not going to gear up if I'm staying put."

"Right." Morgan walked over from a rack of swords that hung on the wall. "Guess we should figure that out before we get too carried away."

"I'll stay," Parminder said, leaning against one of the walls, arms crossed and hands hidden in folds of lace and leather. She looked as if she had a million things she'd rather be doing.

"We're going to need your firepower on this trip." Cheshire walked over, setting a massive rifle-like gun on the table. "I still think we should all go."

"And we already said that someone has to stay to alert us in case there's a breach in Pallium," Declan said.

"I'll stay back," Melody said. "I don't mind."

"Are you sure?" Cheshire asked.

"I'm more comfortable with the operator controls than any of you." Melody looked around at the Rememberists. "Really, it's all good. You folks load up."

"Looks like we've got our operator." Morgan walked over to Melody and placed a hand on her shoulder.

"Really?" Cheshire said.

"She said she'd stay, so let her stay." Violet didn't know what Cheshire's deal was trying to get Melody to join them, but time was ticking. She was eager to go see the Accountant—her sister's memories were still out in Dementia.

Cheshire glared at Violet.

"The sooner we gear up the sooner we can trance and get back," Dillinger said. "I don't like leaving Melody alone."

Melody curtsied. "Why thanks, Dill. Always the gentleman."

Dillinger smirked, redirecting his attention toward Violet. "You need a gun."

He adjusted several lights so they illuminated the room better. For the first time Violet saw just how many guns were in the magazine. Hundreds. Maybe thousands. Racks and tables of guns filled every area

of the room. Violet was no expert on firearms, her only education being from Hollywood movies and anime. Which, really, formed a rather broad and probably inaccurate knowledge base. But there were so many here that counting them would take days or weeks or even months. Hallways branched off the main room like spokes of a bicycle wheel. The glint of oiled gunmetal shined from within each hallway.

And that was just the firearms. Racks of swords hung from each wall, with every type of blade imaginable.

"I know this is a bit overwhelming," Dillinger said, smiling like a boy in a toy shop, "but you only need to pick one gun to supplement Glitterglam. So look around. See what feels good in your hand. What feels comfortable."

"Oh I know what I want," Violet said, eyeing one of the tables.

"That was fast." Dillinger followed her gaze as Violet walked over to the table and picked up the gun. It was small, compact, and shined bruise-black. "A Mini Uzi?" Dillinger laughed. "I don't think you could have picked anything more fitting."

"I'm not done," Violet said.

Puzzled, Dillinger asked, "What else do you need?"

Violet smiled. "I need two."

———

It didn't take Dillinger long to find another Mini Uzi for Violet while the rest of the Rememberists geared up with their favorite items. He then helped her fasten a pair of gun harnesses under her peacoat. Luckily, the coat wasn't tailored under her arms, which allowed for the guns to rest against her torso without too much discomfort. They crisscrossed over her white Joy Division t-shirt like zebra stripes.

"So why don't you wear a lei?" Violet asked Dillinger as he cinched up the harnesses.

"I don't believe in them."

"What do you mean?"

"Bullets and butterflies, baby. That's all. Bullets and butterflies."

"But if a memjack or whatever they're called, those mare—*mare-mons*, get close to you, it'd help wouldn't it, having a lei?"

Dillinger stopped tightening a harness and looked up at Violet. The light from behind her head caught his face, and it lit up like sunlight catching silver. He handed Violet her coat.

"I can bend bullets with a thought, or make them bounce across water like skipping stones. I can break locks, smash vaults, and infiltrate hardened areas like no other. It's what I do and I don't need flowers to do it. This is me." Dillinger removed his guns from the holsters and spun them around. He pressed them to his chest. "And I love it."

Violet nodded, buttoning up her coat over the Mini Uzis. "So why are you in Dementia?"

Dillinger holstered his guns and swept his hair back, pressing it to his scalp. A single oiled lock fell, framing one of his bottle green eyes. He took a breath and said, "I don't remember."

He turned and started talking to Morgan about one of the swords he was holding. Violet didn't want to push him on his answer—or lack thereof—but she didn't believe him either. Who doesn't remember their reason for staying here?

Unless he lost more than one memory? Violet surmised. *Just like me.*

Within a few minutes everyone stood near the doorway. Cheshire had a rather large assault rifle strapped to his back. Morgan played with an old-looking pistol that was gilt with brass, while Declan had a full-sized Uzi slung over his shoulder. He greeted Violet with a sly grin when he saw her eyes on his gun. She returned the smile, tucking her arms down to feel the press of metal against her sides. Dillinger didn't add any company to his darlings. And Parminder had no firearms—or none that Violet could readily see anyway. She just carried a large duffel bag.

"Aren't we forgetting something?" Violet asked. "Don't we need ammo? I can't fire my guns without bullets."

"Ah, my mistake for not explaining this to you earlier," Dillinger

said. "My darlings are unique in that their clips don't expire. But for the rest of you? Your clips hold about ten times their actual capacity due to some weird compartmental fluctuations between the real and Dementia. So you either toss your weapons and grab guns from fallen memjacks. Or you *channel*."

Violet raised an eyebrow. "Channel?"

"Pushing your powers through your firearms," Dillinger said through a grin. "It's exhausting, but it's also pretty powerful. Wait till you see Cheshire turn that assault rifle into a fireworks cannon."

"True, I tend to go a little pyro with it," Cheshire said matter-of-factly. "But you've got to be careful. Using your abilities is tiring enough, but channeling can make you vulnerable. You know how tired you get when you lose blood? Multiply that by a thousand. And when the shit's flying, the last thing you want to do is channel-crash."

Even with this newfound knowledge about channeling, Violet wasn't sure how to do it. She couldn't even summon Glitterglam without help from Declan, so how was she supposed to shoot glitter through her guns? Maybe the heat of battle would kickstart her powers.

"Are we good?" Violet asked, keen to get out of Pallium.

"I think so," Declan confirmed. "Let's go trance."

———

The transcendence gates were marked in Stem by a button that read *T-Gates*. Stem opened into a large chamber, the floors covered in thick, red carpeting. Massive chandeliers hung from the coffered ceiling; each depicted cherubs dancing amongst forests of crystal. Huge mirrors, their frames gilded in gold and topped by matching cherubs, covered the crimson carpeted walls. Between each mirror stood a bronzed statue, locked in poses of admiration or dance. At the end of the room, four golden lions resting on marble balls guarded the dais. Two velvet-cushioned chairs sat at the top of the dais, paired behind a massive table littered with electronic paraphernalia, lights, and clumps of wiring.

"Welcome to the throne room of the Royal Palace of Madrid," Declan said to Violet as they exited Stem. "We're not sure how or why this ended up being the main transcendence gate location, but supposedly one of Charles III's thirteen children entered Dementia and twisted the throne room into Pallium. It was later converted into the primary portal room about a century ago when the previous one collapsed under an attack."

"So there are other transcendence gates?" Violet asked, looking around the throne room and admiring the sheer opulence in every detail, including the frescoed ceiling of cherubs and blue sky.

"Well, these are all the T-gates in Pallium now," Declan explained. "Every mirror is a programmable gateway into Recollection City. Once we step through a T-gate, we transcend into Dementia proper and say goodbye to all the protection Pallium provides. The other T-gates in Pallium have been destroyed over the centuries."

Violet walked toward one of the mirrors. A slight haze drifted over the surface. It radiated a dry ice chill, her reflection distorted and transparent as if she were a ghost. In front of the mirror, resting on an ornate table, sat a box lit up with numerous glass tubes and tiny lights. Copper wiring stretched from the box in each direction, connecting to similar boxes in front of the dozen or so mirrors rimming the throne room. The wiring all led to the table on the dais.

"That's where Melody, our operator, sits," Morgan said. "She'll monitor our progress through Dementia and can open up a portal back to Pallium if things get too ramped. But she'd have to find a safe zone first. She won't be able to open a portal within line of sight to a memjack or maremon so they can't hijack our T-gate. Of course, we always have preordained extraction points that we can navigate to."

Violet headed toward the table. Several computer screens sat there, but they were extremely dated. The table looked more like a DJ set-up than anything to do with managing portals into Dementia.

"And if the operator is alerted to something odd within Pallium, like an attempted breach," Melody said walking toward the operator station,

"they can jack a location and open up something for the Rememberists to jump into."

"The operator's job used to be way more stressful," Dillinger said. "Back when numerous tangles—that's our term for a deployment team—would trance in parallel, it was the operator's job to guide them and keep them safe."

"Like an air traffic controller," Violet said, nodding.

"Exactly," Cheshire affirmed.

Melody stepped onto the dais and sat down in one of the plush chairs. With a slight pull the table swung in front of her, boxing Melody in like a cockpit. She put on a pair of goggles that were rimmed with tiny lights. A small microphone sat in front of her mouth. She placed black over-the-ear headphones on her head, keeping one ear exposed.

She started to press a series of buttons, and a low hum filled the room, like an electric guitar amp powering up. Violet leaned over one of the banks of glass tubes to get a better look. "Stand away from the thermionic valves," Melody quickly said. "They consume a lot of current and I don't want you to jolt yourself into glitter."

Violet stepped back as the hum continued to escalate. "Who built all of this?"

"Rememberists who are no longer with us," Parminder said. "Though trancing has always been around, it was much more random and much more risky centuries ago, before there was a way for the operator to deep-dive into Dementia and proactively monitor."

"But what if it breaks?" Violet asked, concern starting to bud in her mind. "What if these tubes blow out like lightbulbs?"

"We have replacements," Dillinger said. "But the operator could be offline for a bit."

"Luckily," Morgan added, "the thermionic valves rarely blow, which means the operator is never offline." He grabbed a box on the operator's table and started handing out earphone headsets to each Rememberist. A blue LED glowed on each one.

Violet stared at the hundreds of tubes lining the cabinets around the

operator's desk. She didn't want to think about all the tubes she'd seen in each box under the mirrors—there were just too many of them.

"I've got a bead on a safe drop zone," Melody said. "Low activity. Alley near 4th and Williams; District of Metacoel. Get yourselves ready to trance in one."

"Do I get a headset?" Violet asked as Morgan placed the box back on the table.

"Not on this trance," he answered. "It'd be too distracting hearing the operator and trying to listen to us at the same time. Just make sure you stay close to us."

"Okay," Declan said, standing in front of Violet. He placed his hands on her shoulders. "The first few times you trance are going to be disorienting. Like the first time you held your breath underwater for longer than you should have."

Violet gave an affirming nod. "How do we trance? Do we all hold hands in a circle like a séance? Or what?"

Declan shook his head. "We walk through the mirrors."

Violet laughed. "How does that work?"

"You'll see in a minute."

"We're locked and jacked in," Melody said from behind her mess of copper wiring and vacuum tubes. The lights of the monitors reflected against her skin, her eyes all bright and liquid cobalt behind the goggle's lenses. She punched her voice above the hum. "Hit the power on mirror six."

A flurry of activity erupted around Violet as the Rememberists moved to one of the mirrors. A number 6 was painted on the box of lights and tubes below the frame. Morgan grabbed a lever attached to the side of the box and slammed it down. Another secondary hum filled the room, sparks jumping from the box. The mirror's frame lit up like Christmas garland.

"Ready in five seconds," Morgan called back to Melody.

Violet's stomach fluttered with a jumble of trepidation and excitement. She couldn't believe they were actually going to get Karin's memo-

ries. The reality of it all quickened her breathing, her hands glowing brighter.

The surface of the mirror splashed, as if a thousand stones were simultaneously cast into a still pond. It frothed and began to swirl. At first the swirls were tiny, concentrated in different spots of the mirror, and then one of them took over, consuming others until the center of the mirror was a whirlpool of activity. Quicksilver bloomed in the center of the whirlpool until it touched the edges of the frame, sending out curls of steam.

"We're good," Morgan said, stepping onto a small stool that was sitting in front of the table. He continued onto the table and turned around. "Trancing now."

Melody said, "Forget-me-not."

Morgan answered with, "Remember me always." Then he stepped into the swirling mirror and disappeared, leaving only a few ripples in his wake.

Violet sucked in a quick breath. The shock of seeing Morgan dissolve into the mirror caused the fluttering in her stomach to fly up her throat.

Parminder followed, her black dress fluttering behind her. Melody once again said, "Forget-me-not," and Parminder replied with the same words as Morgan.

Declan and Cheshire both reached for Violet's hand at the same time. "It's okay," Violet said without taking either hand, noticing their surprise. "If I transitioned into Dementia twice, I think I can handle transcendence."

"As you wish," Declan said. He stepped up onto the table, answered Melody's goodbye, and stepped into the mirror.

"After you," Cheshire said, sweeping his hand in front of him toward the table. "Don't forget to breathe."

Violet stepped onto the footstool and then onto the table. A damp coldness spilled from the mirror, but there was no breeze, no other

element of energy or power. The table vibrated from the power box that sat beside her foot, a hundred tiny tubes thrumming inside.

She was no longer nervous, her stomach settling into a slight vibration of excitement. Lights flashed. Violet glanced back at Cheshire and he smiled, as if telling her it was okay. Excitement burned in Violet's veins, filling her with a magical energy. She was finally going to get Karin's memories back.

"Forget-me-not," Melody said to Violet, breaking her daze. Violet turned, looking at Melody over her shoulder. Light flickered across her face, lips full and glossy.

"Remember me always," Violet replied. She then took a deep breath, held it for a moment, and stepped into the haze of mirror.

PART C
INTO DEMEMTIA

"Dining on memories is the most rapturous of feasts."
- Queen Zamelerish, Architect of Forgetting

16/ THE ACCOUNTANT

DON'T PANIC.

Violet couldn't breathe. An invisible pressure fell over her, as if she were at the bottom of a pile-on. Wavering light filled her vision. She pushed forward through the gelatinous morass of the portal. A desire to kick to the surface overwhelmed her, even though she was standing on some form of ground. She moved her hands, trying to part the jelly-like substance, tried to walk faster instead of a slow-motion crawl. Black spots danced along her eyes. She needed to breathe.

Then she punched through whatever had been holding her and she fell. Hit the ground; rolled and splayed. She sucked air in ravenous gulps. Coughed. After a few deep breaths, the sharpness of her senses came flooding back. She stood up, the asphalted ground cold and dirty and littered with trash. It was night, and dark walls of brick rose high on either side of her. She could smell rotting vegetables. Urine. Garbage dumpsters lined the alley she found herself in.

Violet turned around to look for the Rememberists who had already crossed over when someone grabbed her shoulder and flung her backward. She crunched against the wall.

"Stay back and hang in the shadows." It was Morgan's voice, calm and direct. "Don't move until we pinpoint our location and assess risk."

The t-gate she had come through hung in the air a few feet above the ground, its surface matching the tumult of the mirror from the portal room, including the gaudy, gold leaf covered frame. From her angle, Violet could see that the portal was paper-thin. Fog wisped along its surface, waterfalling and trailing over the ground.

"You all right?" Declan asked. He stood beside Morgan, looking up into the night sky. Glitter filtered downward in tiny sparks of static.

"Fine," Violet said, trying to regulate her breathing. Before she could say anything else, Cheshire jumped from the mirror, landing cat-like. He looked around, seemingly assessing the area. Once he saw the rest of the group along the wall, he joined them. Cheshire looked at Violet, spying the accelerated rise and fall of her chest. He smiled. "You forgot to breathe didn't you?"

"Obviously." She shook her head, frustrated with herself for not listening. Learning to breathe while walking through Jell-O might take some getting used to.

"Don't worry," he comforted, "you'll be a pro after a few more T-gate jumps."

Dillinger jumped out of the portal next, his guns drawn and held out to the side. He quickly scanned the area. Holstering his pistols, he made his way to the group. "We're good?"

"Yeah," Morgan said. He placed his hand against the earphone. "We're clear. Disengage the portal."

A moment later the hum surrounding the portal intensified. The surface frothed; then the frame began to origami-twist, bending and folding in on itself until it became smaller and smaller. It disappeared with a puff of smoke.

"Did Melody drop us where we need to be?" Dillinger looked down to the mouth of the alley. Car headlights flashed by. Neon shimmered.

Parminder held a small black device in the palm of her hand, its

screen a flutter of activity that cast a spectral glow against her veil. "Bullseye."

"Okay," Cheshire said more to Violet than anyone else. "The District of Metacoel is like any megacity core you may be used to. Lots of traffic, lots of figments. This is about as congested as you want to get. So keep your eyes and ears open. Listen to us. If things go bad, they'll go bad fast. But don't worry, I've got your back."

"I'm sure you do," Parminder said without looking up from the device.

"I'm serious." Cheshire placed a hand on Violet's shoulder. Squeezed it. "Stay close to me."

"Or me," Declan interjected. He seemed to catch his over-insistence and added, "Or any of us for that matter. Don't leave our sides."

"You guys are doing a pretty good job of freaking me out," said Violet. She understood that things would be different in Dementia, that things operated at a different frequency than normal. She'd figured that out a few minutes after falling the first time, when Declan played with shadow and flew around. But all these warnings of how fast things could turn bad, or how dangerous Dementia was, were getting tiresome. Violet just wanted to get in, find her sister's memories, and get the hell out.

"We don't mean to," Declan said, slightly above a whisper.

"Then how about you stop babying me and we go see this friend of yours."

"The Accountant is *not* my friend. He's neutral to everyone. All he cares about is himself."

"Getting out of this alley would be a good start," Morgan said. "Sniffers will be on our scent soon. Melody's already picking up heat a few blocks away."

That was fast, Violet thought. She patted her peacoat to make sure the Mini Uzis were still there.

"Confirmed," Parminder said, adjusting a dial on the side of the device. It made the sound of an old radio being tuned on, like the one

Violet's grandpa had listened to in his garage. "I'm seeing activity north of Lexington."

"That's not good." Declan looked down the alley. "We need to hit Lexington and 42nd to see the Accountant. He operates out of the Chrysler Building."

"Scanner says we're south of Lexington." Parminder looked up from the device for the first time. "We should be able to make it there and enter the Chrysler before we encounter any opposition."

The scanner started making loud beeping noises.

"Scratch that," Parminder said, flicking the device toward the end of the alley. "Heat coming in from Fleet Street to the west. We're going to get boxed in real fast unless we double-time it." Her eyes flared like sunspots under her veil. "The alley empties out onto 42nd. Let's go north and follow it direct. I think if we try and get fancy with our approach we're going to lose time and the sniffers will hit us."

"Everyone ready?" Morgan said, checking that his antique pistol was loaded to his liking. He slid the gun into his knee-length jacket as the Rememberists chimed in with their approval. "All right, conceal it, people."

At Morgan's command, anyone who had a weapon exposed made certain that it was hidden. Violet remembered what Parminder had said about figments and how they believe that they're alive. They spooked just as easily as a living human would if they saw a group of people walking down the street with guns exposed and swords flashing. Tucking them away made sense.

As the Rememberists walked down the alley toward 42nd, Violet pressed her elbows against her ribs and felt the hard metal of her twin Mini Uzis. The idea that she could pull them out and shoot something, even if that *something* was a figment of memory, or an agent of the queen, still made her nervous and exhilarated at the same time. She had all these romanticized images in her head of anime heroines and deadly shōjo manga girls where they rocked out with their guns out, Uzis blazing, pigtails waving. Nothing stopped them. Nobody got in the way of

their goal, even if it were only to buy a pack of bubblegum. They were made of awesome. And Violet, deep in the core of herself, wanted to be awesome too.

After the accident, she didn't think that would ever be possible.

But now, looking at her glowing skin, at how she had moved glitter outside the cafeteria windows and stood her ground against Parminder in the greenhouse, she felt empowered to change her trajectory for the first time in a year.

To help Karin remember.

And that was pretty awesome.

————

42nd was a madhouse of activity.

Cars jammed six lanes of traffic. Horns blared. People cursed. Glitter danced in the lights of buildings as it settled to the ground. The sidewalks were clotted with figments rushing to work or shopping. Some bought flowers from sidewalk vendors, while others talked on phones, hailed cabs or read books while nearly walking into light posts.

So many of the sights and sounds reminded her of New York City— but it wasn't. It was some twisted parallel, an amalgamation of metropolises merged into each other.

Ambulance crews rushed to buildings, their vehicles blurring through taxis or other vehicles without so much as a honking horn or break of siren. Cars crashed with the crushing metal of sudden impacts. Violet jolted at that unmistakable sound of machines colliding, of lives ending. The screams of the figments ignited her own memories of how Karin's car twisted like licorice, up and around the snowplow's blade. She shook her head, demanding that the memories of the accident would flee forever—but they never listened. They just hid, waiting for the next trigger for recollection.

Figments were struck by cars in front of Violet, their bodies broken and splayed out across the road. Bodies fell from the sky, smacking side-

walks with the sick crack-thump of pulping flesh and breaking bones. Though for every catastrophe or emergency, countless figments passed by without notice, entranced within their own repeating memories of what had been, all to the sashay of glittering moments, lost to those still alive in the real.

"You okay?" Declan said, walking beside Violet.

She glanced up at him, and even though his face was masked in shadow, his eyes attested to his concern. Violet looked ahead, staring at the back of Parminder, who navigated the sidewalk with Cheshire. Dillinger and Morgan took up the rear.

"Yes," she said. "But thanks for asking. It's a lot to take in."

"It always is."

They came to an intersection. Parminder held up a fist and checked the scanner. "I'm seeing exhaust signatures coming from the east now, just beyond Arbat Street. And the sigs from the west are closing in on our position. They could just be preliminary sniffers, but I don't really care to find out. We need to get into the Chrysler Building or lose them by twisthopping."

"No," Cheshire said. "I don't want to take a chance twisthopping, not with Violet on her first trance run. We could lose her in a bad hop and she wouldn't know how to find an escape portal."

"I agree," Declan added.

Violet hadn't heard that term before. "What's twisthopping?"

"That's when we go into one twist and come out another," Declan said, running a hand through his pewter hair.

"You mean you guys walk into a twist on purpose?" Even in her short amount of time in Dementia, Violet knew that it wasn't a good idea to be in a twist when it's happening.

"Yes," Declan confirmed. "We use them to travel a lot of distance in a short amount of time, or to lose maremons on our tail. They're extremely hard to navigate. We've lost a lot of good Rememberists while twisthopping."

"Well let's not lose any more, okay?" Violet said to Declan.

"We never intend to."

Hopefully, they could get through their meeting with the Accountant and get back to Pallium without twisthopping. For all their quirks and colorful personalities, Violet was starting to like the group and didn't want to lose someone because of her.

Declan looked across the intersection and pointed. "Let's pick up our pace. We're only two blocks away. I can see the silver crown between those two buildings."

Parminder and Cheshire led them across the intersection. The traffic lights flashed in hues of white and black, none of the colors doing an adequate job of directing traffic flow. Declan directed Violet into the intersection with his hand once again on her back. "Just like you're aware of the figments and their ability to manipulate physical objects," he said, "so must you be aware of the physical objects. Cars will break you if they make contact. Taxis can be hailed. Bullets puncture. There are a million ways to die in Dementia."

"Do you really think the Accountant will know where my sister's memories are?" Violet asked as she stepped onto the sidewalk.

"Of course," Declan said, looking down the cross street. "I wouldn't be risking our safety by coming here if I didn't. He'll know exactly where they are. The question is whether he'll honor the favor he owes me."

The ground shook, nearly knocking Violet into a passing figment carrying a dog in a purse. Across the street, one of the office buildings shimmered and began to fade, growing increasingly transparent with each rumble. "Twist," said Declan, as the building's façade started to peel away. Great chunks of concrete crashed into parked cars or slammed into figments who were desperately trying to scramble out of its way. Windows popped and rained glass. A second building, its façade more contemporary with windows that nestled into each other, blended into the old building. Figments screamed within, their memory replays cut short by the twisting buildings. Dust exploded outward from the bottom of the building, curling toward the Rememberists on the oppo-

site side of the street. And then the new building stood complete, with lights on in the windows and new figments going about work or making dinner.

"Those twists are the ones we worry about when twisthopping through buildings," Declan said once the dust had settled and they were back to their march along the sidewalk. "They hit fast and they leave little room for composing exit strategies."

"I can see that," said Violet, still eyeing the newly formed building. She couldn't imagine being in the epicenter of a twist when it was happening.

No wonder they've lost Rememberists in them.

"The operator said there's a signature bloom behind us," Dillinger said, hustling up between Declan and Violet. "Maremon exhaust signatures are flaring up on the operator's monitors. Hey, Parminder, are you reading that?"

Parminder had already stopped and was turning a few dials on the scanner. "Yeah, I see it. Nothing we haven't seen before and evaded successfully."

"Though not without serious twisthopping," Cheshire said, looking beyond Morgan and Dillinger to where they had just walked. "And we already decided that wasn't an option. We're only half a block away from Lexington." He spun around. "I can see it from here. And the Chrysler Building's right there. Let's see the Accountant and decide on a course of egress afterward."

Parminder started walking without waiting for a consensus, glitter swirling behind her. She constantly twisted dials, the scanner bobbing with each hurried step. "Activity is picking up to the north, right where we're walking. I think they're just sniffers though."

"Regardless," Dillinger said, "I don't want them running interference so that whatever's behind us can catch up."

"East and west heat streams are converging on our point," Parminder said, almost turning her hastened gait into a jog. "Something's not right. I haven't seen heat like this since—"

"It's almost like the memjacks knew we were coming," Morgan added. "Operator said the thermionic valves are running hot too, but none of them have blown yet."

"Operator, how long until convergence?" Cheshire asked, trench coat waving behind him. His hand cupped the side of his ear.

"Less than a minute?" Parminder questioned. "This is going to be close. *Run.*"

Violet's heart fluttered. Things were getting real. She ran beside Declan, following Parminder's lead along 42nd and pushing aside figments.

"Keep those weapons concealed until we need them," Morgan yelled.

Violet wove around figments as if she'd done it a million times before. Cheshire followed in her wake, though not quite as gracefully. He knocked a few figments down, sidestepping when he could. Violet's breathing raced. Adrenaline pumped in her veins. She didn't know what they were running from, but if a Rememberist said *run*...she ran. Violet didn't want to turn to glitter. Not yet.

They stopped outside the Chrysler Building, its multi-storied entranceway arched in black metal and glass. The doorway was flanked by a pair of revolving doors. Standing in front of each revolving door were a pair of large men impeccably dressed in tailored suits and black ties. They stood with their arms crossed, coats bulging with firearms and juiced-up muscle. Declan started talking to them.

"Sniffers," Parminder said, pointing further down 42nd. "We've been spotted. Declan, get us in and fast. We don't need them skunking us."

Violet followed Parminder's arm to where she was pointing. She couldn't make out anything different, just figments and cars and glitter. Declan walked up to one of the guards, and as he began to talk, she saw what Parminder was pointing at. Several men were barreling through figments, one on either side of the sidewalk, and one in the middle of the street, jumping onto passing cars, oblivious to their horns or screeching brakes. They weren't completely upright either, scurrying on hands and

feet. They wore flowing black coats that shimmered in the streetlights like garbage bags, a single white stripe running down their chests. A breather mask covered their mouths and nose, only leaving their neon green eyes exposed. Glittering exhaust spilled out of their backpacks in corkscrewing funnels. They motioned as if sniffing the air, all animalistic, then continued toward Violet and the rest of the Rememberists.

Violet swallowed hard. She placed her hands inside her peacoat, ready to pop the straps that held her Mini Uzis in place. Her mouth went dry.

"Hurry up," Dillinger said to Declan, resting his hands on his guns. "You've got ten seconds to get us inside or I'm going to give these sniffers a blow hole."

"Need another minute," Declan said over his shoulder, still talking to the guards outside the revolving doors.

"We don't have a minute." Dillinger drew out his darlings and aimed them down the street. A few nearby figments screamed and ran for cover.

"Five seconds," Dillinger said, steadying his aim. The guards didn't move behind him, locked in heavy conversation with Declan.

In the distance, beyond the sniffers, Violet saw the unmistakable sight of the trench coated slurpers. Her mind catapulted back to the room in the Weeping Willow and how they had towered over Karin, sucking out her memories with that horrible slurping noise. This time they weren't walking, but gliding along the sidewalk, frost emanating from around their bodies. The lenses of the slurpers' gasmasks spun with the hypnotic pinwheels Violet remembered seeing in the nursing home. Figments parted out of their way without question. Nausea filled her. She unfastened the Mini Uzis and placed her hands on their rubberized grips.

"Out of time," Dillinger said. He unloaded his pistols, their recoil kicking his hands back with each shot. Firelight flashed out of the muzzles. Violet was surprised how loud they sounded, but she didn't cover her ears. Bullets slammed into the lead sniffer, its body snapping

backward. It fluttered then skidded along the sidewalk in a slick of smoking white liquid.

Declan spun around. "We're in," he said, motioning toward the revolving door. He grabbed Violet's hand and pulled her past the guards and into the spinning doorway. They stumbled into the lobby of the Chrysler Building, almost tripping over each other.

Outside, Dillinger was screaming obscenities as he continued to unload round after round down the street. When everyone was in the lobby, Dillinger ran into the revolving door. He kept firing until his arm was almost jammed between the frame and glass door.

"Did you have to do that?" Morgan asked as Dillinger entered the lobby, the ends of his pistols smoking.

"Of course," he said. "They were coming pretty fast. I took two of them out."

"Yeah, but they saw us," Parminder said. "Which means they'll be waiting for us to leave."

The remaining sniffer skidded to a stop beyond the guards, just outside the doors. It sat there awkwardly, the breather intakes on its mask whirring as it sniffed the air, its chest heaving. The sniffer stared at the Rememberists through the glass. A moment later a dozen slurpers glided in behind the sniffer. They hovered over the sidewalk, pinwheels spinning on their gasmasks, skulls tonsured. Their trench coats shimmered from the light of the Chrysler Building lobby.

"Why aren't they coming in?" asked Violet.

"The Accountant is a neutral party in Dementia, remember?" Declan said. "He has a contract with the queen. They cannot enter unless he allows them to do so."

"And will he?"

"If we spend more time than I just bargained for, yes. I told the guards that the Accountant owed me a favor. They confirmed and gave us a small window to meet with him. Once the time expires, he'll allow the queen's agents inside."

"Great," Cheshire said. "How much time do we have?"

Declan smoothed a swirl of shadow along his forehead, as if wiping away sweat.

"Ten minutes."

———

The Rememberists rode one of the elevators to the 77th floor.

"Is there no security inside this building?" Violet asked from the back corner of the elevator. It was humid, and muzak played over the speakers, which reminded her of riding in Stem. "Do they usually let people with guns stroll in like that?"

"There used to be metal detectors in the lobby," Morgan said, staring at the row of numbers above the elevator door. A light illuminated each floor as they passed by. "The Accountant had them removed, keeping guards stationed throughout the building instead."

"He's actually in every borough at the same time." Dillinger looked over his shoulder at Violet.

"How's that possible?"

"His body is connected to some kind of network. He sees everything that comes into Dementia from all boroughs, all districts, all the time. So if he's taken out here, it's nothing more than an inconvenience. They'd just bring in another body and jack in. Nothing comes into Dementia without the Accountant knowing about it. He's a contracted monitoring service for the queen."

"And she can't do that herself? Seems like she owns Dementia."

"Not without considerable effort and cost to her. The Accountant used to be a Rememberist who got tainted by her power. Went rogue half a millennia ago. By the time the queen realized what was happening, he was so networked into Dementia it was easier for her to make a deal with him rather than wipe him out. He exchanges knowledge for power, and he's not going anywhere anytime soon."

The elevator dinged and the doors slid open. The Rememberists emptied into a lush foyer with high-end chandeliers made of LED-

infused crystal and illuminated pillars that reached into a coffered ceiling. Glitter dusted a series of triangular skylights, sending golden rays of light into the room. Several guards stood before the entrance to a long hallway, each dressed in a similar suit and tie combination as the men outside. A pair of cushioned sofas flanked either side of the foyer.

"Seven minutes, fourteen seconds," Parminder said, adjusting the scanner.

Morgan, Dillinger, and Declan stepped forward. One of the guards put up his hand motioning for them to stop. He cupped the earpiece that corkscrewed out of his ear, a thin white wire trailing into his suit jacket. "Only two may enter."

"Get in there and get your information Declan," Morgan said. "Operator said she's getting heat sweats."

"I'm going in too." There was no way Violet was going to let Declan in there alone. She had to start getting some answers herself.

"But—"

The guard stepped forward. "She may enter."

Declan narrowed his eyes but didn't object. A pair of guards led them down a long, marble hallway. Paintings from various modern art movements lined the walls between interspersed doors: Rothkos, Warhols, Pollocks. Art History was one of the few classes Violet enjoyed attending at school. A large set of ornately carved double-doors greeted them at the end of the corridor. Declan held his hand to his earpiece. He looked at Violet and said, "Several vacuum tubes have blown. The operator needs to replace them."

"What? I thought that's rare. How long will it take?"

"I know," Declan said. He bit his lip, trying to hide his concern and failing. "She'll be offline for two minutes."

"I know it's Melody," Violet said. "So why don't you stop referring to her as the operator?"

"Protocol. Minimizes confusion when things turn sour."

"Like now?"

"Yeah."

One of the guards scanned a security card and the doors hissed inward. Crisp white light poured out of the room, and Violet had to shield her eyes from its painful sharpness. Once they were fully in the room, the doors closed and the clacking sound of numerous deadbolts locking into position filled the air. The room was illuminated from the ceiling, walls, and floor. There were no shadows anywhere. And no glitter.

They were powerless.

Declan held his hand against the earpiece again, scrunched his eyebrows together, and concentrated. He shook his head and said, "Operator says she's fixed the burned-out tubes, but several alarms have been tripped in Pallium."

Violet was surprised.

"Don't worry, alarms usually short when thermionic valves burn out."

"Do we go back?" Violet asked, concerned about Melody's wellbeing —but at the same time afraid she wouldn't be able to ask the Accountant about her sister's memories if she left.

"No," Declan said reassuringly. "She's gone to check them out. The main alarm in Gapstow has alerted. We wait until she reports back before changing plans."

The wall opposite the entrance suddenly broke apart in segments and sunk into the floor, exposing a thick sheet of glass that separated the room. Banks of monitors filled the alcove beyond, their intrinsic glow matching the brightness surrounding Declan and Violet. Thousands of multicolored wires spilled into the room from the ceiling, from the walls and floor and monitors, surrounding a central recliner in a spider web of copper conduit.

A gentleman slowly swiveled around in the recliner. The wires surrounding him were clumped and twisted into an electrical top-knot that jacked into his skull. His eyes were television bright and just as mesmerizing.

"Back so soon, Mr. Gloss? You have two minutes, forty-seven

seconds until I release the queen's hounds. You know I don't like crowds in my offices." His voice was monotone and drawn out, all crackle-static.

Declan leaned toward Violet and whispered, "No matter what you hear, know that I believe in you."

She nodded, even though she thought it was a rather odd statement, especially with the Accountant sitting right there.

"I know we've agreed to be honest, but I haven't had the opportunity to explain everything yet," Declan whispered through clenched teeth. He bit his lip again, hard, and Violet thought she saw his skin break. "Promise that you'll look at me the same way." His eyes shimmered like waterfall mist. "Please."

"Yes, fine, I promise." Violet didn't want to agree without thinking it through, but she had no choice—they were running out of time with the one person who could tell them where Karin's memories were.

He sucked in a sharp breath, as if in relief, then raised his head toward the Accountant. "I'm here to exercise my favor."

"Which favor are you referring to? We've had numerous arrangements in the past." Light flashed from the Accountant's mouth when he spoke.

Declan's lips parted slightly. He glanced at Violet for a moment, then focused his attention back on the Accountant. "During our last meeting, I supplied you with two butterflies; one as requested, one not. It's that last transaction you owe me a favor for. Check your books."

The Accountant stared at Declan. His eyes shifted in their imagery, as if changing channels a thousand times between each blink. Finally he said, "You are correct, Mr. Gloss. You delivered the requested butterflies for processing. One was scanned, liquefied, and the results discharged to Queen Zamelerish. The other butterfly was also processed and the results were delivered to you. I believe that concluded our arrangement."

Declan swallowed, trying not to look at Violet. "That contract was multifaceted. It stipulated that, beyond delivery of the results, I would be allowed a secondary information request at a time of my choosing."

"Confirmed," the Accountant said, body rigor mortis rigid. He unnerved Violet, how he sat zombie-like, skin semi-translucent and illuminated from within. His veins matched the multicolored wiring that fed into his head. "But you must learn to read the fine print, Mr. Gloss. That secondary request has already expired. It was only good for twenty-four hours. And now you have one minute, forty-six seconds until meeting adjournment."

Declan blanched, shadow beading on his forehead. "What are my options?"

"Provide another butterfly, and I will provide information."

Declan closed his eyes. When he opened them, he reached into his coat and pulled out a miniature cage the size of an apple. Inside flitted a single rainbow butterfly, its wings luminescent under the room's intense lighting.

"No!" Violet yelled, placing a hand on his arm. "I have hundreds of butterflies in the conservatory from when Cheshire siphoned them. Take one of them instead."

Declan shook his head, the corners of his eyes quivering. "I already have."

"What do you mean?" Violet said confused.

"The two butterflies the Accountant's referring to were yours."

Violet stared at Declan, not sure what to say, a cocktail of shock and disappointment shaking within. She watched Declan's eyes glaze with regret or guilt or both. "How could you do that? You're just as bad as your brother, taking things without asking!"

Declan frowned, head tilting toward the floor. "I'm worse. Cheshire made a mistake. I did not. And for that I'm terribly sorry. But there are other things at play here. I had to confirm that you are indeed the Princess Electric, and in doing so I also confirmed this to the queen. You must understand I had no choice."

"We all have choices," Violet said. "Some of us just make the wrong ones more than others."

"Tick tock," the Accountant interrupted, steepling boney fingers below his chin.

"I have a butterfly that you can take for payment," Declan said, turning away from Violet. "It is my own, and the only memory I have willingly forgotten."

A tile on the floor slid aside and a narrow white pedestal rose in front of Declan.

"Place the cage on the pedestal," the Accountant said emotionless.

"I'm sorry, Violet—for everything." Declan placed the birdcage onto the pedestal. "I'd give up a thousand memories if it would renew your trust in me." The pedestal sunk back into the floor, the tile sliding into place with a soft tap. "Unfortunately, all I have is one."

"Declan," Violet started, then stopped. She didn't know what to say anymore. In fact, she didn't know if she wanted to say anything at all.

"What information do you seek?" the Accountant asked. "Fifty-four seconds until meeting adjournment."

"I'm requesting the whereabouts of memories siphoned three days ago. Where are they and what processing plant is scheduled to receive them?"

"Details are required to cross-reference all transactions over the last few days. Provide the location where the memories were siphoned in the real. Name, age, sex of subject."

Violet provided the details.

As the Accountant processed the information, she looked over at Declan. He continued to stare ahead, his gaze locked on the Accountant and the monitors that flashed behind him, no doubt showcasing the memories that streamed into Dementia from transitioning memjacks. Tears trailed down his cheeks in the hard shimmer of monitor light. It didn't make sense to her. Both Declan and Cheshire seemed to have the same goals but different methods, and both were doing a good job of pulling her in different directions. They kept doing things that made her question their sincerity. For as much as they believed in her, she had to

believe in them. If she didn't, then her sister's memories would be lost forever.

Violet had to trust—something she hadn't done since the car accident. Declan had just given up his most cherished memory for her. For Karin. And that had to mean *something*. There had to be something inherently genuine in that sacrifice. Maybe he really was trying?

She reached out and brushed her hand against his. She didn't know what memory had been wrapped up in his butterfly, but it must have been something special, for he took her fingers without looking at her, wrapped them in the warmth of his grasp...and squeezed.

———

"I have located the memories you requested," the Accountant said.

"And?"

Violet squeezed Declan's hand.

"They're in a vial labeled serial number **DM-FGJf98f45gg**, and are in transport to the Gracile processing facility."

"How long until they're received?" Declan asked.

"Six hours."

"That doesn't give us a lot of time to intercept the supply train." Declan's brow furrowed, shadows curling around his eyes. "How long until processing?"

"Twenty-two hours."

"Wonderful."

"And that concludes our meeting," the Accountant said nonchalantly, as if the previous conversation hadn't happened. "Pleasure doing business with you. The queen's agents have been granted full access to the building."

With that the armor-shielded wall clanked up from the floor sealing off the Accountant's room. Deadbolts disengaged and the door behind them swung open.

"Remember when we talked about things going bad fast?" Declan asked, still holding Violet's hand.

"Yes."

"Well here we go." Declan ran out of the door, pulling her along like a rag doll. They navigated the long hallway back to the waiting Rememberists as the Accountant's guards went into various side rooms.

"Where're they going?" Violet asked running behind Declan.

"They've no interest in our squabbles, just protecting the Accountant. They know things are going to get hot, so they're backing off."

Get hot? Violet thought. She undid her peacoat and pulled it open, exposing her twin Mini Uzis. *Too late for that.*

She had already started sweating.

17/ IT'S CALLED A MINIGUN

DECLAN AND VIOLET stumbled into the foyer where the rest of the Rememberists were waiting on the couches. "Company's coming," Declan huffed.

"Nice of you to join us," Dillinger said, slowly spinning his darlings on his trigger fingers. He was leaning against a wall instead of sitting with the rest of the Rememberists.

"Did you get your information?" Morgan asked, rising.

"Six hours until delivery," Declan confirmed. "Twenty-two hours until processing. Gracile facility."

"That's tight," Cheshire said, jumping up. "But doable."

"Has the operator come back online yet?"

"No," Dillinger said, pushing himself from the wall. "She's been offline for a while now."

"It doesn't take long to check and reset a tripped alarm." Parminder stood and looked at the scanner. "Something's not right. My scanner's dead."

"What do you mean dead?" asked Morgan.

"Dead as in morgue dead. No juice. Defunct. Hard offline." Parminder shook the device as if that would pick up a signal again.

"Then something's definitely not right in Pallium," Cheshire said, his brow crinkling with concern.

"That's what I've been saying." Morgan tried to contact Melody again without any luck.

Cheshire pointed to the bank of elevators. "Company's coming fast. We've got to move."

There were two elevators in the bank and each one had a set of numbers above the doors. Their lights flashed as the elevators rose in tandem. They were currently on the 57th floor and climbing.

"Stairs?" Dillinger asked.

"Not yet," Cheshire said, shaking his head. "We need to purge these elevators first so the memjacks won't follow us down the stairwell and sandwich us."

"Can't we take an elevator once it's emptied?" Violet asked.

"No," Morgan said quickly. "You don't want to trap yourself in an elevator. Outside Pallium the queen controls certain mechanics within Dementia. She could have the elevator shut down or stopped at a floor where memjacks are waiting. It's too risky. We don't even take them when twisthopping. When in flight, always take the stairs."

"But we already took the elevator up." Violet continued to sweat and she hadn't taken a single step down the stairs yet. She was really going to have to evaluate her peacoat in Dementia.

"We were here with permission from the Accountant, so he kept things locked down. He's now opened the building to the queen's minions to get us out. So no elevator."

"Okay, let's reveal and get ready to drop some lead," Dillinger said, walking in front of an elevator. He crouched down and raised his guns, aiming toward the elevator door. He glanced up at the numbers. "69th floor and counting. Get in position."

The Rememberists assembled in front of the elevators, pulling out their various firearms. Violet unfastened her Mini Uzis. Their rubberized grips felt cool in her hands, the weight of the guns heavier now that she had to use them.

"Crouch down," Cheshire said to Violet as he uncovered his assault rifle and aimed at the elevator, just over her shoulder. Violet went on one knee as Declan readied his Uzis to her left. Morgan unsheathed his foil in one hand, its blade glimmering in the chandelier LED ambience. He held an ancient pistol in his other hand.

Parminder stood beside Morgan. She unstrapped the duffel bag from her shoulders, set it on the ground, and unzipped it. Inside a massive six-barrel gun gleamed. She hoisted it out of the bag with a huff, slinging a support strap over her head and across her chest.

"Shit," Violet said. "What the hell is that?"

Parminder flipped back her veil, eyes bright and focused as sunbeams. "It's called a minigun." She reefed on the side of it, smacking a long belt of bullets into the gun's feed intake. Parminder's face was mannequin calm. "And it means stay the fuck out of my way."

Cheshire leaned forward, his head near her shoulder. She could feel the coolness emanating from his cheek as it brushed hers. "When the doors open, don't worry about aiming those babies. Just squeeze and spray. Let the guns do the rest."

Violet swallowed. "Sure," she said, trying to sound as cavalier as she could. She figured that the only good thing about the rapid ascent of the elevators was that she didn't have time to get nervous. Well, not enough to make her puke anyways. Sweat collected between her palms and the grips, making her hold on her guns slick.

Squeeze and spray, she thought as she adjusted her grip. *Squeeze and spray.*

"One more floor," Dillinger called out.

The barrels of Parminder's gun began to spin, slowly at first and then whirring into a high-pitched wail.

"Ready," Dillinger continued, his voice much calmer than Violet would have expected. "Ready..."

Ding!

The elevator doors opened.

Before Violet could make out the various hunched and twisted

forms within the elevators, guns erupted with all the fury of Fourth of July fireworks. Flames licked out from the barrels as they discharged. Bullets rained into the elevators.

Violet compressed the triggers and her Mini Uzis bucked to life. The kickback surprised her, spraying bullets across the elevator and into the illuminated numeric panels above. Glass and plaster rained down. She eased off the triggers and her guns came to a smoking rest as Cheshire continued to discharge his assault rifle in controlled bursts. Everyone was silent as they shredded the contents of the elevators. Parminder's minigun chewed through ammo, smoke and fire spilling from the spinning barrels. Empty shells waterfalled out of the gun, tinkling on the marble floor in a sea of brass casings.

Violet aimed and fired again, this time expecting the kickback and keeping her bullets to around the elevator entrance. Inside, dark-jacketed bodies popped like water balloons filled with milk. She could make out the hunched shapes of sniffers dancing as bullets tore into them. They wailed as they ruptured, crumpling to the floor of the elevator. A few fell out into the foyer, bullet holes smoking.

"Cease fire," Declan yelled. "They're down."

The Rememberists slowly stopped discharging their weapons, the minigun coming to a slow-whir stop, its barrels red hot and warping the air with heat dissipation. Corpses gurgled.

"Not bad for a first timer," Cheshire said, glancing down at Violet. "You managed to not hit the ceiling." He winked.

"Ha-ha," she said, trembling. Adrenaline surged in her veins. Her grip felt tight and weak all at once. She wanted to shoot more memjacks.

"Don't worry," Morgan said as if reading her mind. "There'll be more where those came from." He turned to Parminder. "Are we back online?"

She let the minigun hang from the support strap as she pulled out the scanner. Her face gave the answer.

"Dammit," Morgan cursed. "Operator, come in?" He pressed the butt of his pistol against his earpiece. "Operator?"

"She's hard offline," Cheshire said. "We have to move it or we'll be joining her."

"Cheshire's right," Declan agreed. "We've got to get out of this building before we're overwhelmed." He pointed one of his Uzis to a door at the end of a short hallway. "Stairs. Now."

There was no discussion. Cheshire directed Violet in front of him, following Dillinger and Declan. Morgan and Parminder fell in behind. When they got to the stairwell, Dillinger stopped and held his ear to the door. He shook his head and opened the door.

Bullets rang out from the stairwell, missing Dillinger and Declan and almost hitting Violet.

"Whoa," Violet yelled, stepping back into Cheshire.

The bullets pulverized the doorway and ceiling beyond. Tiling broke and fell, dusting down. Dillinger returned fire.

"You're okay," Cheshire said. "Just breathe."

She didn't reply, instead doing what she was told, taking a slow, deep breath to reset her nerves. She'd never been shot at before and didn't care for the experience.

"They're in the stairwell already?" Morgan called from behind. "How did they get up so quickly?"

"They obviously knew we were coming," Parminder said.

Declan cursed. "There's only one way down." He sent a wave of bullets blindly into the stairwell.

"There are elevators," Parminder said.

"No," Cheshire added between breaks of gunfire. "No elevators."

"Then down we go," Declan said.

Violet watched him kick open the door and unload his Uzis for cover-fire. Dillinger stepped in behind him, firing over his shoulder. Declan tossed aside one of his guns. He formed a fist and drew in shadow from the stairwell's dark corners. He threw a glob of shadow between the downward spiral of railings, and a second later the building rumbled below. "Shadow cover is set. We hit this floor by floor. Alternate covering fire."

Dillinger snaked around the stairs, back against the wall, guns scoping around each corner. Cheshire led Violet into the stairwell, following Declan. They made it down to the next floor, stopping at the doorway.

Excitement burbled in Violet's stomach. Things were intense, but knowing that they had the information to get Karin's memories back once they got out of the building made the danger easier to swallow. She hadn't felt this alive since before the accident.

"Let those in the back rotate to the forward positions on each floor," Cheshire said to Violet, pressing her against the steel door. "We've got a long way to go."

Violet tried to look beyond Cheshire but he masked her view. Shots rang out, punching into the concrete walls. Morgan and Parminder moved past Violet and Cheshire, crowding the stairwell until they were beyond Dillinger's position.

Declan drew in more shadow from the recesses, curling it around his free hand. Before Parminder slithered past Declan as best she could with the bulky minigun, he threw it down the inner spiral of railings. The building rumbled again as the shadow grenade discharged.

Parminder revved up her minigun and proceeded down, spewing rounds as she went. Smoke filled the stairwell as Declan followed the apiarist.

Cheshire looked up and swore. "Get back," he yelled, pushing Violet hard against the door. Her chest compressed, and the breath she'd been inhaling kicked out of her lungs. Bullets tore into the wall above her head. Concrete ruptured into dust. Cheshire let go of his assault rifle and pointed toward a set of lights above, his other arm falling across Violet in protection. Light leeched from the bulbs, arcing to his hand. The light intensified until the bulbs exploded in a crackle of lightning. Dark, trench-coated shapes above ignited into flame. They crackled and popped like twisted bubble wrap as they discharged their guns in random directions.

"Protect the princess!" Declan shouted, running back up the stairs

and pushing Cheshire against the stairwell door. He summoned more shadow, throwing balls of it into the above stairwell. Night descended as bullets and fire continued to rain down.

Violet watched Declan with admiration, though she wanted to help protect the group as much as they were guarding her back.

Dillinger sidestepped past Violet, firing his pistols into the cloud of darkness. "We've been set up. There's no way they should be above us already."

Declan looked at Cheshire, his eyes burrowing, as if something unspoken was being said between them. "Stairs to street level and then we're going to twisthop back to Pallium. Got that?"

Bullets ripped into Dillinger's arm from above as dark shapes poured through the shadow and muzzle flash. Blood sprayed the wall. Declan turned and screamed in anger, sending a barrage of shadow-cased bullets from his Uzi. Darkness exploded as each bullet connected with memjack or wall or rail.

Cheshire pointed to another bank of lights above. He flicked his wrist and they exploded in a nova-bright flash of light and white smoke. Turning in a swath of trench coat, he twisted the doorknob and opened the stairwell door. He pushed Violet over the threshold and she tumbled into the hallway.

"What's going on?" she said, regaining her feet. "Was Dill shot?"

Cheshire didn't say anything. He closed the door and grabbed her wrists.

"What are you doing? You're hurting me." She dropped the Mini Uzis.

Cheshire kicked the guns aside and pulled her along the hallway. Smoke wafted along the floor. Gunfire and screams continued from the stairwell. He stopped in front of the elevators and pressed the call button.

"What the hell, Cheshire?"

"Do you want the good memories of your sister back?" His eyes were a storm, dark and flecked with rainbow-bright chaos.

"Yes, but—"

"Good." The elevator doors opened. Cheshire shoved Violet into the elevator and followed her inside. "You have someone to meet."

Violet slammed against something rigid yet soft. The smell of woodsmoke and ash greeted her, a hint of cloves. That scent. The same one she smelled on Cheshire. Then the click-clacking sound of a wood-pecker on metal filled her ears. She turned around and found herself staring into the lava-red eyes of the birdman from the bridge.

"Hello princess," he hissed, smoke puffing from his golden lips. "I'm Mister Cinder, emissary to the Queen of Glass. She requests the honor of your presence."

18/ OFFLINE

"WHAT THE *FUCK* IS GOING ON?" Violet yelled.

She spun around to confront Cheshire, not expecting to be forced into an elevator with the strange gold-skinned man from Gapstow Bridge.

Cheshire's hand fell on her shoulder. "We're offline. Invisible." He looked at her as if he needed to add something further, to soothe her uncertainty as to what was happening. "I'm sorry, but this is the only way. We don't have a lot of time."

"The only way for what?" She shrugged Cheshire's hand from her shoulder. "You could have told me."

"Told you what? That the only way for you to regain the memories I siphoned was to meet the Queen of Glass? You would've laughed in my face."

"Time to fly," Mister Cinder said from behind Violet, his voice syrupy and lyrical like a lullaby. Curlicues of smoke wafted over her shoulders. "The diversion will only last so long."

"Diversion?" Violet stared darts into Cheshire's eyes. "So this was all planned? Dammit, Cheshire, Dill was *shot!*"

"You don't know that."

"Don't you even try to bullshit me now," she seethed. "I saw the blood. Saw his face. I haven't seen pain like that since—"

"Violet," Cheshire pleaded, her name lilting off his tongue like cotton on the wind. His eyes rainbow-sparkled. "This is your opportunity. We only have until the Rememberists reach the ground floor to travel to and from the Palace of Memories End. We don't have long. What's it going to be?"

Violet squeezed her fists, wanting to punch him in the face. She didn't like being put in a bad spot and forced to make a decision like this. She had two options: either accept Cheshire's offer and visit the queen to see what she had to say, or leave the elevator and rejoin Declan and the others in their fight. But if she did that, she may never know what her options were. Maybe it had to do with her memories that Cheshire stole? She could feel the compression of time around her, the urgency. The disturbing chirp of Mister Cinder behind her, with his gold skin and aromatic breath, wasn't helping her remain calm or decide any quicker.

It was that single possibility of regaining the happy memories of Karin which made her say, "Yes." She almost choked on the word, knowing full well what was happening outside the elevator. That the other Rememberists were fighting for their lives.

For *her*.

"Yes," Violet said again, almost to reassure herself that it was the right decision, to push away the sudden flood of guilt. "I'll see the queen —but on one condition."

"Which is?" Cheshire asked.

"You give me back my kaleidoscope. If for one second I don't feel safe, I'm out of here." There was no way Violet was going to march into the queen's palace without an escape plan. She had no reason to trust Cheshire. Especially after what she'd heard on the bridge. And she sure as hell didn't trust the feather-coated man. But if there was a way to get her own memories back at the same time as Karin's, then it was at least

worth talking to the queen. If that was even what this side meeting was about.

Cheshire smiled that Cheshire grin, and Violet wondered if there was something else behind that smirk, something she didn't want to see. But he agreed, and handed her a kaleidoscope. "This isn't the one Parminder took from you, but it'll take you back to the real just the same."

Violet grabbed the kaleidoscope and pocketed it, unsure if she should believe Cheshire. She felt only slightly protected knowing she had a way to flee in an emergency—if it even worked. "So, how do we see this queen?"

"We fold Dementia," Cheshire said as if he'd done it a thousand times before. "Much like we fold the real with a kaleidoscope. Only this time we'll do it wrapped in the wings of a phoenix."

"I'm not sure what—"

Before Violet could finish her sentence, the white feathers of Mister Cinder's coat unfurled to either side of her. Smoke and ash swirled until Cheshire's face became hazy. Violet turned around.

Mister Cinder towered in the elevator, his arms outstretched in glorious, angelic wings. The broken-neck movements she'd witnessed on the bridge were amplified as he hunched over, his chest and neck compressing into the ceiling. His body was gaunt and birdcage boney, yet there was an underlying strength to his frame. Bright, purplish feathers covered his torso, his waist disappearing into milk-blue smoke. His eyes smoldered like liquid lava rock, gold skin a hundred shades of brilliant.

Mister Cinder curled his wings around Violet and Cheshire, and her world turned to ash.

———

Violet left the ground for only a moment, the sensation of vertigo coming and going faster than the quick drop of an elevator. The smoke covering

her vision cleared, slow like a choking fire. Cheshire stood beside her, Mister Cinder's wings falling from their shoulders. They were standing on a dock made from white marble. Milk-blue water surrounded the dock, its surface glass smooth. Beside the dock rested a gondola, and behind them a massive set of gold doors towered above, easily three or four stories high.

"Those doors lead to the palace proper," Mister Cinder puffed. "To the vulgarity of courtiers and sycophants and their fawning ways. But we have bypassed its hallways and formalities. You are now in Cerebrum, the inner sanctum of the Palace of Memories End. Please, step into the gondola, Princess."

Before she could take in the rest of her surroundings, Violet was taken aback by all the butterflies. Unlike the conservatory, where there had only been a few flitting about, there were tens of thousands in Cerebrum. Perhaps millions. Countless really. They danced through alabaster-colored trees, wings of illuminated rainbow waltzing over the water. A butterfly curlicued in front of her face, and she wondered how many memories called Cerebrum home. What were they all doing in here? What purpose did they serve?

Cheshire stepped into the gondola first and held out a hand. Violet ignored it and stepped into the boat. The gondola didn't move when Mister Cinder glided in. A gondolier stood at the back, mummified in white robes and a veil so thick that Violet couldn't make out their face. After they all found a seat, he pushed off from the dock, paddling in slow, haunting movements. At school, Violet had been learning about Greek mythology in her history class, and she wasn't keen on how the gondolier reminded her of Charon shuttling souls across Acheron.

Violet focused on where they were headed. Trees upon twisted trees stood statuesque in the milky water, their bark and branches and leaves papier-mâché white and just as delicate. Their only color bloomed from cherry blossoms, butterflies pirouetting amongst the petals as they sashayed in the air. They rested on the surface of the blue-

tinted water like paper boats. A light mist hugged the water, and high above the treetops a ceiling of pastel blue and pink stained glass shimmered.

How is such a place of sadness so beautiful, she thought.

Tiny stabbing pains filled Violet's stomach as she realized meeting the Queen of Glass was about to become her reality. This moment of quiet serenity would not last. Slight waves of nausea filled her body to its core, rippling through her arms and legs, up her throat. The beauty of Cerebrum was countered by an eerie silence, the only sounds emanating from the flitting butterflies and the boat drifting through the water. Knowing that so many countless, precious memories were in one location, locked away from their owners through time and space, was an almost unbearable, crushing thought.

Violet recalled her feeling of complete emptiness when Cheshire had removed her memories of Karin. It made her touch the kaleidoscope in her pocket. She never wanted to experience that sense of loss and betrayal again. If there was anything she could do to prevent someone from ever feeling so hollow, she would do it. And now it appeared that the first part of making that happen was meeting the queen. She removed her hand from the kaleidoscope and focused on their destination.

The gondola moved into a large clearing rimmed by trees. High above, the glass ceiling opened to the night sky, framing the disco ball moon amidst the delicate glitter that sifted down amongst the butterflies. A white marble dais floated on the water in the center of the clearing. A narrow pole sprouted from the dais, and atop the pole rested a single, high back chair of black glass.

A throne.

And on the chair sat a woman forged from stained glass, each cheek or brow or freckle an exquisitely cut pane. A lace ruff hugged her neck, merging into a pearlescent white dress that shimmered like fish scales. Her hair spiked in every direction in long shocks of glitter, as if she wore a crown of lightning bolts.

The woman's hands were folded neatly on her lap, a gold scepter tucked under an arm. A miniature disco ball sat on top of it.

But it wasn't the clothes or wild hair that reminded Violet of the ceiling in the Mausoleum of Memory. It was the rainbows. They beamed from her glass skin in every direction, arching into the water, into the trees, and curling toward the moon. It was as if she were a prism, refracting and bending light.

"She's beautiful," Violet mouthed, rising to her feet in the gondola.

"May I present Zamelerish, Queen of Glass, Architect of Forgetting," Mister Cinder said from behind Violet. "Matron Mother of Recollection, Consumer of Memory, Forger of—"

The queen wiggled her glass fingers—they sounded like tinkling bells—and Mister Cinder immediately stopped talking. Cheshire bowed and motioned for Violet to do the same. She curtsied in her peacoat to the best of her ability, though she felt awkward doing it. For one, she didn't owe the queen shit. And two, the queen owed her Karin's memories. That was it. So she'd appease Cheshire for now and go through the formalities—if only to get information. Then she'd leave, with or without him and his feathered friend.

"Welcome, dearest Violet," the queen said, each word echoing like clinking crystal. "Thank you for gracing me with your presence."

"Okay," Violet said with a shrug. "I appreciate you wanting to meet me, but once you're finished saying what you need to say, I'm gone."

Cheshire's mouth opened in shock. "Violet."

"It's okay," the queen said, raising her hand in a dismissive gesture. "Her candor does not offend. In fact it does the opposite." The queen stared at her for a moment. Her eyes were mesmerizing, a thousand rainbows refracting within. "Why are you here?"

"Because Cheshire said you wanted to see me."

"Yes," Queen Zamelerish said, leaning forward. "But why are you in Dementia?"

"To get my sister's memories back."

"Well," the queen said, brushing a butterfly away from her face, "all

you had to do was ask. You didn't need to see the Accountant. They'll be waiting for you at the processing facility in the Gracile District, unharmed and untouched, for when you want them."

Violet looked at the queen askance. "You're just giving them to me?"

"Yes."

There had to be a catch. Nothing was free in the real, and so far, nothing had been free in Dementia either. "There has to be more to it than that."

"As a matter of fact, there is." The queen pressed a lever beside her chair and it began to descend, stopping on the dais. "How much do you know about the mechanics of memory?"

"Not much, since I have no idea what you're talking about."

"What about the Delirium Directorate?"

"I've heard of that," Violet said, staring off at one of the distant trees. "I think Cheshire had mentioned them."

Queen Zamelerish beamed, light refracting from her glass skin. "The Delirium Directorate operates on memories like a surgeon, transplanting them, tweaking them, slurping them. They orchestrate attacks into the real, siphoning memories from those who no longer require them. Ripping them away from people who don't deserve the luxury of remembrance. The Rememberists call them slurpers or sniffers or clankers or what have you. But they are all memjack soldiers. And they can be *saviors*." She paused for a moment, eyes glittering and locked on Violet. "They can restore your memories of your sister."

Violet's legs weakened and she nearly tumbled overboard. She took a deep breath and calmed her thundering heart. So there was a way for her memories to be replanted. Cheshire hadn't been lying. Was that part of the arrangement he had discussed with Mister Cinder on the bridge? Is that what all of this was about? Violet pushed the thought aside. She'd deal with that later. For now, she had to figure out what the consequences of doing so would be. Surely the Queen of Glass, the very being the Rememberists had pledged to destroy, had ulterior motives. She

wasn't going to hand over the services of her memjacks without getting something in return.

"But you don't even have them," Violet said.

"Yes...I do." The queen tinkled her fingers again and Mister Cinder opened his feathered coat. He pulled out a pair of golden birdcages from under his wings. Hundreds of butterflies flitted inside. He gave them a shake and the doors to the cages popped open. A stream of butterflies flew out, corkscrewing in the air toward the queen. They seemed to be more vibrant than the other butterflies in Cerebrum, their colors darker. Reds like blood, purples like bruises.

Violet gawked, horrified. "How did you get those?"

"While you were all visiting the Accountant," Mister Cinder said, "Cheshire had left the backdoor to Pallium open. I simply walked into the conservatory and collected them. All of them."

"Cheshire?" Violet mouthed, turning to him. "But what about Melody?" Then things started to snap into place. The alarms. Melody going offline. The sudden attack in the Chrysler Building after speaking with the Accountant. Everything had been orchestrated to swipe Violet's memories from Pallium and create a diversion so she could meet the queen without any of the Rememberists knowing.

Except for Cheshire, of course.

"Don't worry about your operator," Mister Cinder said. "I left her a present in the conservatory. She's remembering what it's like to be real."

"What have you done?" Violet asked Cheshire, pawing at his arm. She grabbed the crook of his elbow and twisted him toward her. His eyes were rainbow-glassy, the corners quivering where tiny diamond-tears bloomed. Cheshire blinked and the tears disappeared, his face hardening. "It was the only way."

"Only way for what?" Violet blurted. "For you to backstab your friends? Your brother? Melody might be dead for all you know!"

Cheshire sucked in a breath. "My brother has a different viewpoint. And as for Melody? She can take care of herself. This was the only way for you to see the queen and hear her offer."

"Cheshire, no," Violet breathed. "No, this isn't right."

He took Violet's hands in his. She wanted to pull her hands away so bad, but didn't, her body paralyzed from shock. "It's not about right and wrong," Cheshire said. "It's about possibility. It's about believing in something so much your heart wants to explode from your chest when you think about it. Like how I believe in you. How I *think* about you." He squeezed her hands, sending electric ripples through her body. "You *are* the Princess Electric. I know this. And once you understand that yourself, you'll recognize that this is not about remembering, but forgetting. Memory is nothing but pain and sadness. There is no pain in forgetting. There is only serenity in letting go."

Vertigo dropkicked Violet, confusion setting her mind aflutter. She let go of Cheshire's hands, trying to steady herself. Total overload, like when she'd first arrived in Dementia. That same bright lights big city feeling that hit her when she saw Times Square at midnight for the first time.

"How does this involve me? What are you talking about?"

"How much do you know of the Luminous Prophecy?" the queen asked.

Violet swallowed, remembering her talk with Parminder in the Mausoleum of Memory. She turned to the queen, her legs wobbling as she balanced in the gondola. "I know enough."

"Like?"

"I know that I'm supposed to kill you."

The queen's laugh sounded like wind chimes. "Is that what the Rememberists are preaching to newfallens nowadays? Cheshire, surely your friends can do better than that."

Cheshire shrugged.

"You've seen the stained glass ceiling of the Mausoleum of Memory, correct?" the queen asked Violet. "The one depicting the prophecy?"

Violet nodded.

"There are two interpretations of that ceiling. In the mosaic, I'm reaching out to the Princess Electric—and vice versa. Over the millen-

nia, Rememberists have concocted an ornate tale around this gesture, saying that we're locked in an epic battle to the death, fighting over the future of Recollection City, Dementia, humanity." The queen smirked, butterflies flitting about her head. "I don't believe in such fanciful tales."

"So what do you believe then?" Violet asked curiously.

"That you're reaching out to me."

"That's it?" Violet asked. *There must be more to it than that.*

"Not everything needs to be complex. You're reaching out to join me. Not to take my throne, but to share it. To sit beside me so that we can break into the real together."

"But why do you need me?" Violet asked. "You can send memjacks into the real world already. Why not just send yourself if you want to go there so bad?"

"I do not wish to enter the real, but to merge the real with Dementia," the queen said. "And I'm close. With every memory that is siphoned and consumed, I tip the balance even more in my favor, slowly opening more and more holes between our worlds. Once that happens, the balance will flip like the hourglass in the mausoleum's ceiling. And by joining with you, we can consume more memories than ever before."

Violet shook her head, trying to understand. "But why would I want to help you?"

Mister Cinder stepped forward, holding a feather-coated arm in front of Violet. Queen Zamelerish plucked one of Violet's memories from the air and curled the butterfly around her fingers. "You have no control of your powers yet. Cheshire tells me you can't even summon Glitterglam on your own, so you certainly pose no threat to me. And I have all the good memories of your sister. These mean something to you, yes?"

"Yes," Violet whispered. She still held Cheshire's hand, and squeezed it as the queen continued to wrap the butterfly around her finger.

"So," the queen continued, "if you don't join me, I will slowly consume each memory of your sister until you do." She paused for a

moment, staring at the butterfly that squiggled between her fingers. "Tell me, Violet. Have you ever consumed?"

"No," Violet breathed. She watched the queen play with the hapless butterfly.

"It's the most brilliant feeling. It makes everything sharp in your eyes, crisp and bright. And the sensation is orgasmic. It fills your body with bursts of pleasure beyond your imagination. One taste and you'll be obsessed with trying to duplicate it. Hasn't Cheshire told you about chasing the butterfly yet?"

She placed the butterfly into her mouth. It struggled to escape, shaking in an epileptic seizure. She closed her jaw around the butterfly, rainbows of light streaming out. The queen chewed slowly and swallowed. Beams of light bled from her skin, bright and powerful. She leaned back in unadulterated bliss, as if she were about to melt.

"No!" Violet screamed.

"So. Very. Tasty." The queen licked her lips with a bejeweled tongue.

"Why are you doing this?" Violet stuttered between sudden sobs. A moment of time with her sister had just been consumed in front of her like candy. A memory that she would never know again.

A memory that may explain why she loved her sister so much.

"Because, my brilliant Violet," Zamelerish said, "I want you to join my side." She held out the scepter and waved it in the air. The two birdcages flew from Mister Cinder and hooked themselves onto a pair of iron stakes that appeared on either side of the queen's throne. The dark-colored butterflies danced into the cages. "Beyond the golden doors of Cerebrum lie the corridors and chambers of the Palace of Memories End. Within each room are uncountable pleasures. The deliriums and diseases you fear now will become your most beloved companions. Like the taste of memory.

"Like Dementia."

Nausea coiled up Violet's throat. The weight of the queen's words was nearly unbearable. Cheshire placed an arm around Violet to help

her weakening legs. She wanted to push him overboard, but she couldn't think beyond the queen's penetrating gaze.

"Think about it," the Queen of Glass said. "You're free to go back, but know that I have a voracious appetite and these butterflies are the most intoxicating delights." She tapped one of the cages with her wand. It swung gently, the butterflies shimmering inside.

Mister Cinder signaled for the gondolier to turn the craft around. As he started to push the gondola in the water, Zamelerish clacked her tongue and the gondolier stopped. "One more thing," the queen said. "I heard that you had a rather nasty accident a little while ago."

The nausea burbling in Violet's throat plunged down into her stomach. Knees faltered. She braced herself on the edge of the gondola. "Yes," Violet said weakly.

"Those horrific memories? The ones that make you wake up in feverish sweats, screaming? The ones that drown you in depression. The ones that make you want to die?"

"Yes?" Violet whispered.

The queen waved a glass hand in the air. "I can make those all go away. I can pluck the pain and hurt out of you like candy from a dish."

"What?" Violet said, her voice choked with a sudden rush of images and emotion. The pop-crash of metal. The screams. The blood. The soft hiss of Karin's breath. "How?"

"If you join me," Zamelerish said, her kaleidoscope eyes spinning and sparking in the rainbow-hued light, "I will have them removed from your mind. And, as a token of my gratitude, I will personally reinstate these butterflies into your head. Yes, Violet, you *can* remember your sister again in the light of laughter and love. Anything is possible."

Violet collapsed in the gondola and began to cry.

"Now go back and think about my offer. But don't take too long in deciding," Zamelerish said, tapping one of the cages. "I've got quite the sweet tooth."

19/ BULLETS AND BEES

THE GONDOLA RIDE BACK to the Gates of Cerebrum was a blur of butterflies and cherry blossoms. Before Violet had realized what was happening, she was back in the Chrysler Building elevator, Mister Cinder's wings brushing her shoulders.

Violet couldn't snap out of the daze, her body completely numb. The image of Queen Zamelerish consuming the butterfly replayed in her mind in a nightmarish feedback loop. Her skin hummed from stress. Not since the accident had she felt this traumatized. And the fact that Cheshire had put her in that position made it even worse. She was pissed and horrified in the same breath, but the idea that the queen could make the memories of the car crash, of Karin bleeding out across the snow, disappear from her head overwhelmed Violet with hope.

"Is it true?" she asked Mister Cinder as he straightened out his feathered coat, pulling it taut like a suit jacket. "Can the queen make me forget everything about the accident? About the coma and mental hospital...and my sister forgetting who I am?"

"Of course." Mister Cinder puffed out a chortle. His neck crick-cracked to the side. "It's what she does."

Violet closed her eyes to the possibility.

"But don't take long in your decision," Mister Cinder added. "The queen also lacks restraint when it comes to savoring certain delicacies." The illuminated numerals above the elevator door were reflected in the shiny, gold-bright skin of the phoenix. "And with that, our time has come to an end. Cheshire Gloss, do be in touch."

"Of course," Cheshire said, eyeing Violet. "I know where to find you."

Fog whorled upward from the floor of the elevator, filling the small space as Mister Cinder flung out his arms. Great wings crunched against the elevator's walls; then he dipped forward in a stationary somersault, curling in on himself and disappearing in a puff of cinder and smoke.

Cheshire pressed her against the wall. "We're going to be in the lobby in about two seconds. You can't say a word about any of this, do you understand?"

"Yeah," Violet said, more to get Cheshire to back down than in agreement.

"No," Cheshire snapped, his breath sweet and hot against her face. "I don't think you do. If you say anything, even a word that we were anywhere else than this elevator, they will kill me—especially if they know we met with the queen. I did this for you, Violet. I gave you this opportunity because I believe in you. Don't make the wrong decision. You'll regret it."

Violet slapped Cheshire. Hard.

Cheshire yelled out in pain or surprise or both. "What was that for?" He massaged his jaw.

"You don't get to say that word," Violet yelled, her hand throbbing. It pulsed with anger and brightness. "You don't get to tell me what I can or cannot regret, Cheshire. You don't have that right. You don't know me. You don't know what I've been through. Those memories? The ones the queen has in those cages. The one she fucking ate. Those are mine. *My memories*. Happy memories. And they're there because you stole them from me."

"Violet—" Cheshire whispered.

"No!" she said, cutting him off. She pointed at him, her hand illuminating his face. "You don't get to talk. Not now. Not until I'm finished."

He nodded.

"You know, Declan lied to me when I arrived. He told me mistruths because he thought it'd help me see the light. That was wrong and he knows it. But he's also trying to make up for his mistakes. He sacrificed his butterfly to the Accountant so that we could track down my sister's memories."

Cheshire stared at her, his eyes all blue fire.

"But you?" she continued. "I don't trust you. You say all this shit about how you want to help me, how you believe in me, but then you take everything that's important from me and give it all to the queen? What the fuck, Cheshire? Who does that to someone they supposedly care about? Or believe in?"

She stood on her tiptoes, leaning into Cheshire. The brightness emanating from her skin reflected off Cheshire's face.

"So no," Violet said, her jaw tight, "you don't get to talk to me about regret. I bleed regret. I regret ruining my sister's life. I regret ever coming here. I regret trusting you. And most of all, I regret ever meeting you."

Cheshire's face dropped, shoulders sagging.

"So until you figure your shit out and can be honest, I don't want to hear one more thing about what you can do for me. Until you can explain how you even know the queen, or that freaky birdman thing, I don't want to hear anything at all. I'll figure things out with those who do believe in me. Like Declan."

Cheshire stood agape. "Violet," he pleaded. "I believe in you too. But there's so much you don't understand. So much you don't see." His eyes rainbow-glistened as he tongued the back of his teeth, as if he wanted to talk but something was preventing him. "You're not ready for me to explain it to you."

"Yeah, I've heard that before. And that's the problem." Violet pointed her glowing finger at him, pushing it into his chest. "You don't

tell me anything. I have to find things out when I stumble into your conversations. Like on the bridge."

Cheshire's eyes widened.

"That's right. I heard you and Mister Cinder. So you let me know when you're ready to talk, and I will listen. Until then, I won't say anything about meeting the queen or your rendezvous with the birdman on the Gapstow Bridge, but you better get us back to Melody right away or I'll spill. And if for one second I think that the other Rememberists are in danger because of you, then I'm opening the floodgate."

"Understood," Cheshire said, dipping his head in a slight nod.

The elevator's descent slowed, then stopped. A chime echoed, doors sliding open. Sounds of gunfire and kamikaze screaming flooded the elevator.

Violet peered out into the hallway, pushing against Cheshire's attempt to hold her back. Her mouth fell open.

The lobby of the Chrysler Building was swarming with bees.

———

"Oh, look who decided to join the parade," Parminder hissed from across a hallway, bullets and bees flying like horizontal hail. She was standing in another elevator, feeding in a new chain of ammunition into her minigun.

The bodies of perforated memjacks littered the elevator bank hallway, their milky blood covering the marble floor in puddles. Even though their bodies were shredded by bullets, Violet could make out similarities to the slurpers and sniffers that had chased them outside of the Chrysler Building and attacked them in the stairwell. A cloud of darkness filled the end of the hallway, sealing off the main lobby.

"What were you thinking?" Declan yelled between spraying bursts of cover fire into the wall of shadow. He was crouched on one knee in an adjacent elevator to Parminder's. "You know you're not supposed to take the elevators."

"We got cornered wondering where you'd disappeared to," Morgan said. He was in an elevator beside Declan, the last one in a row of four.

"Well, we got separated," Cheshire said. "It was either the elevator or you guys illuminating our busts in the mausoleum."

Declan stopped firing and tipped his head toward Cheshire. He didn't say anything. Didn't need to. His eyes were focused, cold and icepick sharp. Violet could tell he didn't believe a word his brother said.

"It's true," Violet stammered, trying to sound sure of herself over the crackle-pop of gunfire and droning bees. "I got knocked out of the stairwell and didn't know what was going on. We had to take a different set of stairs for a bit. The elevator was the only way to catch up to you."

Declan broke his staring contest with Cheshire and refocused on Violet. "Well, I'm glad you're safe."

"Where we at?" Cheshire poked his head out of the elevator, peeking down the hallway. He quickly pulled his head back inside.

Dillinger was standing in the elevator closest to the lobby, continually firing into the wall of shadow blocking the lobby proper. A bloody bandage was wrapped around his right arm. He stopped to swat at the bees. "Did you have to channel in the building, Parminder?"

She slid into the hallway and glanced over at the gunslinger, staring icicles into his back. "If you ask something so mundanely stupid again, I will shoot you myself."

"So let me ask again," Cheshire said, interrupting, "where are we at? Looks like the operator is still offline; nothing but static since we separated." Bullets ripped into the marble wall at the end of the hallway, chipping away at the finish and making tiny clouds of dust.

Morgan nodded. He was holding a black assault rifle. "That's correct."

"Where'd you get that AK-47?" Cheshire took a step back inside the elevator.

"Lifted it from a shocktrooper." Morgan leaned out of his elevator and fired a few bursts into the shadow. The deflating, screeching noise of rupturing memjacks came in answer as some tumbled out of the dark-

ness and into the hallway, wet and smoking. He slid back inside the elevator.

"Dammit," Cheshire spat. "Shocktroopers already?"

"Yeah," Declan yelled over the din of gunfire. "We need to get out of this building. And then we'll need to get to a nearby T-gate. Melody could be in serious trouble."

Violet grabbed Cheshire's arm and gave it a tug, reminding him that they needed to get back to the courtesan as soon as possible. He looked down at her, and she could see deep concern in his eyes. He looked back to Declan and said, "I need a firearm. So does Violet. We lost our guns upstairs."

Parminder hooked the duffel bag strap around her foot and kicked it across the hallway. It slid into the elevator. "That's all we've got until you can lift something."

Cheshire dug around the duffel bag and pulled out a pistol. He quickly checked the clip and chamber, slammed the clip back in, and passed it to Violet. "Point and shoot," he said, digging back into the bag.

"Like a camera?" Violet balanced the pistol in her hand. It felt heavier than it looked. Solid.

"Sure," Cheshire said. He pulled out a pair of Uzis, clacking them together to get accustomed to their weight. "So what's the story?"

Violet couldn't see the targets, the swirling cloud of shadow obscuring the enemy. Declan fired a dozen rounds until his rifle clicked. He slid back into the elevator, his trench coat curling about his legs. Return fire spray-painted his elevator frame and the adjacent wall, marble crumbling alongside ribbons of dust.

"I'll negate the shadow wall so we can see clearly into the lobby," Declan said, reloading his rifle. "I'll petal anything that's there with my lei. Then you guys sweep in. Use the pillars for cover."

"And after that?" Cheshire leaned out of the elevator and fired a tight burst. Shell casings tinkled on the floor.

"The Dog and Duck." Parminder was adjusting dials on the scan-

ner. It cast a slight glow across her veil making her look like more of an apparition than she already did.

"Seriously? A British pub?" Dillinger had his back pressed against the elevator wall as bullets riddled the inside. "That's the closest T-Gate? That's a hike."

"We're going to have to twisthop, *obviously.*" Parminder's words were laced with razorblades. She took out her frustration by slamming the scanner on the elevator wall. Violet could see that the pressure of being offline in Dementia turned Parminder into an even bigger bitch than she usually was.

"I don't like the idea of twisthopping with Violet," Declan said. "It'll be too easy to lose her."

"We don't have much of a choice," Morgan said.

Declan huffed with reluctance. "I know, but I don't like it." He turned to the apiarist. "What's the quickest route from the Chrysler Building to The Dog and Duck?"

Parminder checked the scanner. "42nd to Bryant Park, across to Arbat Street, and then into the first twist we see. We should be able to traverse twists from that point to come out in Soho."

"And all the while we'll be getting hammered by memjacks," Morgan said. "Lovely."

Cheshire shrugged. "Soho or bust, baby." He kicked the duffel bag back across the hallway of gunfire to the apiarist.

"Mausoleum bust, you mean," Parminder said, sliding the duffel bag onto her back. "An empty one will be waiting for each of us if we don't get our asses moving."

"Point taken," Cheshire said. "Ready to run the gauntlet?"

"Yes," Violet said, her hand sweating, the pistol getting heavier with each heartbeat. She wanted to get out of the Chrysler Building as fast as possible. The sooner they were outside, the sooner they could get back to Melody and the safety of Pallium.

The rest of the Rememberists chimed in with their approvals, cycling through the elevator bank like clockwork. Without further

discussion, Declan leaned out into the hail of gunfire, pointed to the wall of shadow and flung his hand toward the ground. The wall of shadow sloshed downward, thick and syrupy. It coated the bodies of the memjacks like molasses.

A sudden silence rang louder than gunfire as everyone stopped shooting. Beyond the slick mess of shadow on the floor, a hundred memjacks stood in the lobby. Violet hadn't seen these memjacks before, though they looked like slurpers. *Shocktroopers,* Violet quickly realized. Their heads were helmeted. Gasmasks with long breather hoses snaked into their trench coats. Emblazoned DD logos were wrapped around their biceps in large white letters. Unlike the rainbow pinwheels of the slurpers, black and white pinwheels spun in their goggles. They were all armed with shiny, gunmetal-black assault rifles. And each rifle was pointed at the bank of elevators the Rememberists had holed themselves in.

Before Violet could say a word, she heard a click.

––––––––––

The click was from Parminder setting her minigun barrels in motion. As the barrels revved, Declan stepped into the hallway and launched into the air, flying into the lobby. When he reached the apex of the lobby, he slid off the forget-me-not lei and whipped it around as if he were about to lasso a steer.

Declan had moved so quickly that the shocktroopers paused in assessing the sudden attack. Slowly, they raised their rifles toward Declan, who hovered above them in a swirl of shadow. He snapped his arm down and the forget-me-not lei disintegrated, scattering flowers across the entire lobby. They flitted toward the shocktroopers as if a thousand blue butterflies had been cast down from the marble-veined sky of the Chrysler Building lobby. They found purchase on helmets and gasmasks, trench coats and rifles. Sizzles emanated from each point of contact, sending curls of smoke into the air. Shocktroopers recoiled

from the burning touch of the forget-me-not flowers. Some tried to brush off the petals. Others deflated, milky liquid shooting out in long gouts where the petals had burned holes.

"Churn and burn!" Parminder stepped out from her elevator and screamed an obscenity. Bullets erupted from the barrels of the minigun, sending out streams of superheated bullets. Streaks of light hammered into the shocktroopers.

Declan darted above the massacre, corkscrewing to avoid the few shots the shocktroopers were getting off. As Parminder let her barrels slow down, Morgan and Dillinger stepped out and joined her side. The three of them quickly rushed forward, twisting around and putting their backs to one of the large columns in the lobby.

"Stay on my ass," Cheshire said to Violet as he moved into the hallway. He fired his twin Uzis with each step toward a second column, expertly aiming controlled bursts toward the helmeted heads of the shocktroopers. A dozen heads exploded like dropped pumpkins.

Bullets peppered the other side of the column, making Violet flinch.

"Okay, we need to get out of here via the 42nd Street doors, which are blocked by about a dozen shocktroopers." Parminder checked the scanner, giving it a smack in the process. "The scanner is working again, though barely. Lobby is clear except for a few half-deflated memjacks, but the other two entrances are showing activity outside. We've got to hit the 42nd doors now or we're going to get pinched."

"Agreed," Morgan said, picking up another AK-47 from a downed shocktrooper. "On my count. Three—"

Cheshire reached out, pointing to a sign above the small information booth that sat dead-center between the four hallways of elevators. "Diversion," he whispered to the team. The sign grew in brightness.

"Two—"

The sign exploded in a shower of sparks, which was quickly greeted by return gunfire. Bullets chiseled the wall around the information booth, breaking the marble down into pock-marked bits of concrete and dust.

"Screw it," Violet said, stepping out from the column. She raised the pistol and squeezed the trigger. The gun kicked, a bullet slamming into the shoulder of a shocktrooper that was shooting at the information booth. She continued to fire, laying fire into the crowd.

"Dammit," Morgan called out. Moving around to the opposite side of the pillar, he lit up his AK-47, muzzle flash reflecting off the marmalade-colored walls. Bullets tore into the group of shocktroopers that stood in several ranks near the revolving doors out to 42nd, their rifles still firing at the information booth.

The back of Violet's peacoat was yanked and she tumbled backward, firing into the ceiling. She was pushed behind the column where Cheshire and Declan glared at her. "What were you thinking?" they said in tandem.

"I can help."

"Help by staying put," Declan said, his sea-storm eyes wide with concern. "We don't want you dead."

Cheshire and Declan nodded to each other and then spun out from the column in opposite directions, their twin Uzis prattling rounds into the shocktroopers. Cheshire aimed a bit higher and let a few rounds shatter the ribbed, yellow glass above the revolving doors, sending down shards of glass. The shards ripped into the shocktroopers, spilling milky fluid and sending more steam into the air. Dillinger joined in, his darlings crackling over the more subdued Uzi fire. When the Rememberists stopped firing, there was nothing more than a steaming pile of trench coats at the end of the 42nd Street hallway.

Cheshire came back and grabbed Violet's hand, pulling her down the hallway. The Rememberists moved with smooth automation, as if they'd done this a thousand times before, each checking over each other's shoulder, each rotating who was guarding the back.

As they reached the revolving doors, Morgan's rifle erupted from the rear. "Shocktroopers are coming in from the other entrances."

Dillinger swung around and popped off a few rounds, covering for Morgan, whose rifle jammed. He snatched up another from the ground.

Declan threw himself into the revolving door and out onto the street. Violet followed, pulling Cheshire into the same space, sandwiching each other between the panes. Then they were outside.

Parminder came through the door that sat between the two revolving doors, her minigun leading the way. Dillinger came out next, followed by Morgan, the barrels of their guns trailing smoke.

"Why's it so quiet out here?" Violet asked, suddenly alert to the stillness. The streets were dead. Abandoned cars, abandoned street-meat stands. And no figments.

"The queen," Morgan said, somewhat out of breath. "She's playing with us. The shocktroopers inside stopped attacking and left out the other doors. As if they were being called back."

"Why would she do that?" Violet wondered.

"Something's not right," Declan said, staring at Violet. She wanted to confess right there, wanted to tell them all about her visit with the queen. With each beat of her heart, Violet's mouth opened more. With each blink of Declan's sorrowful eyes, the words burbled up, balancing precariously on the tip of her tongue.

"Regardless of what games the queen is or is not playing," Cheshire chimed in, "we have a lull and no operator. Melody's a strong girl, but if she's outnumbered she'll only be able to survive for so long, even if she makes it to the panic room."

Violet couldn't believe what she was hearing from Cheshire. She stared at him, knowing full well that it was his diversion so Mister Cinder could steal her memories from the conservatory. That was the only reason Melody was offline. Violet was close to telling Declan and the other Rememberists, but that wouldn't help them get back any faster. If anything it would slow them down as they'd start to fight amongst themselves. She bit her tongue.

Cheshire didn't make eye contact with Violet and continued. "I say we make up as much ground as we can before the queen decides to throw something else our way."

Morgan agreed. So did Dillinger. Parminder yawned.

"Fine," Declan said, his eyes slowly going back and forth between Cheshire and Violet as if he was watching a slow-motion ping-pong game, trying to figure out their secret but not getting it. "Let's go then."

"Next stop Bryant Park, Arbat Street, and then twisting to Soho." Parminder checked the scanner and frowned.

"What is it?" Morgan asked.

"We've got company," Parminder said. "Quick, across the street." She started to run, the duffel bag shaking and clinking on her back. Violet ran after her without hesitation, as if she were getting used to the constant state of danger. The Rememberists followed her. "Don't look back," Parminder yelled over the clomp of footsteps, her veil curling about her head.

Violet ran as fast as she could. It was difficult keeping up with Parminder, which was impressive considering she was carrying a minigun and duffel bag full of ammunition and who knew what else.

"Faster," Parminder yelled over her shoulder as they ran past the New York Public Library, its massive stone facade shimmering and hazy in the falling glitter.

Adrenaline pulsed in Violet's veins. She wanted to turn around, to see what they were running from, but that never worked out well for people in movies so she decided against it.

They reached the steps of Bryant Park, taking two at a time until they staggered onto the stone patio. Umbrella-covered tables and chairs sat vacant under the towering, light-spackled skyscrapers. Violet bent over, hands on her knees as she sucked in air to catch her breath, the wool of her peacoat itching her neck and her healing bee stings. Parminder continued toward the expanse of grass that made up most of the park, its surface illuminated in a sickly green glow.

"Come on," Parminder ordered. "Everyone across the lawn."

As Violet hustled along the flagstone patio of Bryant Park, she looked back toward the Chrysler Building. Its silver-domed top glowed brightly against the glitter-dark sky. Around the building's peak circled a pair of large creatures, glinting against the light of the moon. At first

Violet didn't know what they were. She squinted against the glitter sifting down, trying to make out more details. And then she saw why they were running.

One of the metal-headed gargoyles of the Chrysler Building broke free with a thunderous crack. Brickwork folded outward into great, voluminous wings that somehow caught air as it plummeted. And then another severed from the building's stone facade. And another, until all eight of the Chrysler Building's gargoyles swarmed around the silver-pleated roof like monolithic vultures.

Then they banked, and dove straight for Bryant Park and the Rememberists.

Violet gulped.

And started to run.

20/ MAREMONS

VIOLET FOLLOWED BEHIND PARMINDER, who was streaking across the verdant lawn of Bryant Park faster than a vampire fleeing sunlight. The strength of the apiarist impressed Violet, the minigun still slung over her shoulder and swaying with each step. Violet hurdled a narrow bench at the edge of the lawn. Her boots hit grass and she stumbled. As she regained her balance, she looked over her shoulder and quickly regretted it.

Cheshire and Declan were right behind her, their eyes wide as they spread out onto the lawn, trench coats snapping behind them. Dillinger and Morgan were on their heels, matching steps while yelling, "Move, move, move!" Beyond them, the metallic heads of the plummeting gargoyles.

Violet twisted around, refocusing on following Parminder across the park. If they could make it to the street, maybe they'd be able to lose them. Even in the hazy moonlight of Dementia, shadows quickly washed over Violet as she ran, covering the lawn in great pools of blackness.

"*Get down!*" someone yelled from behind.

Violet dove head first, sliding across the damp grass. One of the

gargoyles flew over her, so close it brushed her back while letting out a deafening jet-engine howl. A moment later, a pair of hands hoisted her to her feet before she could think about how close she had almost come to being headless. The New York Public Library behind Bryant Park wavered and shimmered, her head feeling like a cotton ball. The quick down and up motion had thrown her depth perception off and kicked in a shot of vertigo.

"Come on," Cheshire said, breathing hard. "No time to dawdle."

"Parminder!" shouted Morgan.

Violet spun around, almost falling over. She steadied herself with Cheshire's shoulder and noticed Parminder standing alone. Three gargoyles slammed into the lawn in front of her like comets, the ground shaking and cratering under them. The gargoyles screamed at Parminder, their massive metal jaws open wide.

"What the hell are those?" Violet gasped.

Liquid shadow snaked over Declan's face. "Maremons."

"Shouldn't we help her?" For as much as Violet had issues with Parminder, she didn't want to see her destroyed. She could see her jostling with the minigun, the barrels spinning. The maremons started to move toward her. Parminder swore and pulled the trigger. Electric-bright fire shot across the park, bullets pounding into the lead gargoyle, sparking against its silver head. The maremon screamed again, snapping its head back and forth in rage.

Violet fired her pistol at the maremon, the bullets sailing wide. She was too far away to help. The maremon continued forward against Parminder's bullets, hunkered low to the ground, as if walking into heavy rain and hail. It took another step and fell apart, wings crumbling across the lawn.

Parminder was swinging the minigun toward one of the other maremons when the barrels suddenly whirred in silence.

"Dammit," said Morgan. "She's out of ammo."

Declan started running, firing his Uzis at the maremons.

"Those aren't going to do anything!" said Dillinger. "We need a

diversion!"

The two gargoyles were moving toward the apiarist. One of them heaved, releasing a funnel of flame.

"Parminder," Violet hollered.

The apiarist jumped straight up in the air, minigun and all, levitating high above the swath of fire. As the flames extinguished, she dropped to the ground, landing firmly in a scorched patch of grass.

Declan was nearly to Parminder. The apiarist smacked the side of her minigun and yelled something less than pleasant at the maremons. She revved up the barrels again. Smoke swirled around her, spilling out of her clothes and veil. Flashes of electrical energy wove across her body.

A droning sound filled the park, as if they were all standing on the beehive hill again in the greenhouse.

The pair of gargoyles were nearly within striking distance when they both inhaled, their great torsos of concrete and brick expanding and cracking outward.

"Cheshire," Violet whispered, knowing that the maremons were about to release another blast of fire.

As Declan and Morgan stopped firing and slowed their approach, the first few bees flew out of Parminder's barrels. At first they appeared drowsy, as if they'd been smoked. Then more and more bees came out of the gun, shooting toward the maremons and packing their gullets, preventing them from breathing flame.

Parminder screamed, then staggered sideways, exhausted from channeling.

Violet took off toward the apiarist, Cheshire yelling after her. She fired her pistol at the maremons, bullets pelting their sides with puffs of dust. The Rememberists were risking their lives to help Violet find her sister's memories, and she wasn't about to let one of them fall. Not if she could do something about it. She balled her free hand into a fist, squeezing tightly until it glowed brighter, and waved it in the glitter.

I will summon Glitterglam, she thought. *I'll create this sword on my own.*

Sparks popped around her fist as it touched glitter, like a wire short circuiting.

Dammit.

Someone tackled Violet from behind and they collapsed across the dew-wet lawn. It was Cheshire, all woodsmoke and cloves. Violet looked up, and as Parminder fell to the ground, so did the gargoyles. They exploded in massive fireballs of brick and metal, mushrooming up and over the prone apiarist and into the glittering sky. Declan and Morgan were knocked to the ground from the explosion. Violet covered her head, avoiding pieces of flying brick and shrapnel.

Violet pushed away from Cheshire, clambering to her feet. She stumbled into the cloud of ash and ruin, searching for Parminder, and found her under a blanket of metal shards and stone, covered in dust. She was completely still.

"Oh my god," Violet gasped, looking for movement along her chest. "She's fucking dead."

"No," Cheshire said. "You'll know when someone dies in Dementia."

Relief spilled into Violet. The last thing she needed right now was a death on her conscience—whether it was Parminder or not.

"She's just exhausted." He scooped her up.

"Put me down," Parminder barked, eyes half closed.

"Change that to exhausted and cranky," Cheshire said. "And no."

Parminder huffed. "Grab my minigun."

"I don't think so." Morgan shook his head, dreadlocks dusting the air with glitter.

Violet picked up the duffel bag. "I've got the bag," she said, straining to throw it over her back.

"Let's get to the road," Declan said, wiping dust from his mouth with the back of his hand. "Arbat Street is right behind those trees."

Violet ran with the Rememberists to the edge of the park, keeping an eye on the remaining gargoyles that circled overhead. They spilled out onto a street which ran alongside the tree line. Another street ran

perpendicular, lined by ornate gaslights that illuminated the heavy snow sifting down from the night sky.

"There's the Arbat," Morgan said, pointing to the snowy street.

"Wait, what?" Violet questioned, squinting at the snow falling at the edge of Bryant Park, as if a pane of glass separated the two worlds. Beyond the snow, rustic, turn-of-the-century shops were illuminated by neon and gaslight. "Is that really—"

"Snow?" Cheshire said, shifting Parminder in his arms. "Yes."

"How's that possible?"

Declan started toward the street, glancing skyward. "There's a higher concentration of Arbat Street memories with snow than without, so we get snow."

"I don't even know where the Arbat is," Violet admitted, running after Declan.

"It's in Russia," Morgan said. "Moscow."

Violet didn't even know how to respond. Dementia was obviously an amalgamation of places from around the world, though there seemed to be no reason why they mixed the way they did. She looked both ways as she crossed 6th Avenue to where West 41st Street should have been.

Cheshire ran up beside Violet as they crossed the snowy threshold, Parminder's legs bobbing. The temperature change was shockingly abrupt. Violet's breath ghosted as she pulled her coat tight.

"Let's follow the gaslights toward Arbatskaya Square," Declan called over his shoulder. Snow kicked up in powdery puffs as he wove past the first light post. The street was lined on both sides by brick and mortar apartment buildings, most four to six stories high. They wavered like seaweed in a current, the colored brick fading from white to peach to blue. "And keep an eye out for an oncoming twist. We need to hit the first one we see if we're going to lose these maremons."

Almost as if the maremons were waiting for someone to call attention to them again, they jetliner-roared behind the Rememberists. Violet caught a flash from over her shoulder and instinctively ducked as a gargoyle sailed overhead, slamming down in the middle of the street. A

second one followed close behind, passing the Rememberists and crashing into a row of gaslights. Pools of shadow bled out across the street. Snow blossomed around the gargoyle's bulk, cascading in waves of white powder as it slid and turned, coming to rest right beside the other gargoyle. They roared in unison, thunderous like the passing of two freight trains.

"This is *not* working out in our favor," Declan said. "Though we should be thankful they're not all attacking at once."

"Maybe the queen just wants to bang us up?" Morgan said, tossing his AK-47 into the snow. "It's like she's playing with us. I don't get it either." He pulled out his silver foil, its needle-thin blade scintillating in the gaslight glow.

"If this is playing," Violet said, moving a lock of snow-wet hair out of her face, "I'd hate to see her angry." And she knew the anger would come the longer she took to decide. She shifted the duffel bag from one shoulder to the other.

"If she got angry," Cheshire said, shrugging Parminder up into his arms for a better grip, "half of us would be dead by now."

Violet tried to make eye contact with Cheshire, knowing full well that he knew what the queen was doing, but he just continued to stare at the gargoyles blocking their path.

"A Starbucks is about to twist," Declan said, pointing.

"In Moscow?" Violet asked.

"They're everywhere, even in Dementia."

Beyond the gargoyles, the green and white siren sign glowed above the street-level storefront of an apartment building, snow and glitter falling in front of the sign.

"Good," Cheshire said, nodding toward the coffee shop. "I can grab a latte while we pass through."

Morgan cleared his throat. "There's one problem with that logic." He pointed to the pair of metal-faced gargoyles standing between the Rememberists and the Starbucks. Flames flickered from within their stainless steel gullets.

Cheshire shrugged. "Minor inconvenience."

A massive crash sounded behind Violet. And then another, and another, like cannons going off. Violet wheeled to see the remaining three gargoyles.

"Make that a major inconvenience," Dillinger said.

"We can either go back-to-back and fight." Morgan held out his foil, pointing it toward the gargoyles. "Or we run."

"We run," Parminder whispered.

Cheshire swore and took off toward the two gargoyles in front of the Starbucks, one arm holding the apiarist, the other arm holding an outstretched Uzi that he unloaded. Bullets sparked against its steel head. Dillinger ran in a random direction, kicking up snow and firing his darlings to no real effect. Morgan tipped his head and spun backward, running toward the three gargoyles near Bryant Park.

Violet was about to follow Cheshire when Declan grabbed her and took to the sky. Her stomach lurched. She didn't really care to be plucked from the ground and flown about. If she was going to fly, she'd rather be in a plane.

"Hold on," Declan yelled as he corkscrewed higher and higher. The air and snow felt cold against her cheeks, yet the glitter was warm, creating an odd feeling as if her face had fallen asleep. Declan cut back toward the Arbat.

That was when Violet saw they weren't alone.

A pair of gargoyles were on a collision course with them, their wings flapping in great curls of brickwork. Violet screamed. Right before impact Declan twisted to the side, avoiding the maremons. Somehow they flew right between the gargoyles without a scratch.

They landed, the Starbucks sign casting a nimbus of green light across them. The building was flickering; the twist was near.

"Stay here and don't move." Declan stepped onto the street and stretched out his arms. He pulled pockets of shadow from around the gaslights, creating a sphere of darkness around Violet. She could see out of it, as if looking through tinted glass. "This will keep you hidden from

the maremons," Declan said. He smiled and then rocketed toward the descending gargoyles.

Violet looked out of the shadow bubble, trying to locate the rest of the Rememberists. Dillinger was running around a series of light posts, taking shots with his pistols. He was threading his way closer to the Starbucks while a maremon followed, spewing steam and flame. Fireballs crashed into storefronts, shattering windows and igniting the interior.

She glanced to her right, the vibrant green glow of Bryant Park lighting up the distance. Her eyes widened. Cheshire was running toward her, Parminder slung over his shoulder like a sack of potatoes.

Before Violet could yell out a warning, the gargoyle slammed into Cheshire, lifting him off the ground like a bull spearing a matador. He flew through the air, Parminder's body twisting and separating from Cheshire. They both crashed onto the street at the same time, their bodies sliding across the snow. When they stopped, neither Parminder nor Cheshire moved.

"Get up!" Violet yelled, panicking that they weren't breathing, that they were dead. Even though Cheshire had said she'd know if someone died in Dementia, she couldn't see the rise and fall of their chests. Couldn't see their breath fog the air. She felt sick.

Violet balled her hands into fists and raised them in front of her, concentrating on her intrinsic glow. *Come on*, she thought. *Let's do this.* She willed the glitter to her hands. Tiny swirls of glitter snaked toward her, wrapping around her hands. But instead of forming Glitterglam, they ignited like birthday cake sparklers.

The gargoyle landed, turning to face the motionless bodies. It reared, inhaling the crisp night air. Steam vented from its hawk-head, the polished and pleated steel shining. A second maremon landed on the other side of them, snorting and huffing. Cheshire and Parminder were trapped between the gargoyles.

"Somebody help!" she screamed, smashing her sparking fists against the orb of shadow. Then she saw Morgan, a streak of dreadlocks and steel, running toward the gargoyle that stood menacingly over the limp

body of the apiarist, her duffel bag laying on top of her. Morgan sprinted up its tail. He somersaulted, then landed on its corrugated neck.

Morgan cursed, holding the foil high over his head. It sparked in the gaslight glow as he brought it down. The gargoyle bucked again as Morgan slid the foil in and out, over and over again. It reared, drawing in oxygen. Morgan backflipped off the maremon, landing eloquently in the snow. He dove on top of Parminder as the gargoyle's head ignited into a giant fireball. It fell backwards, exploding into a cloud of brick and metal.

Up above, streaks of shadow trailed off Declan, the gargoyles chasing him as best they could, barrel-rolling and banking around the glittering sky. He led them apart, working them farther and farther away from each other. Then, he flew to a central point between the two, hovering over Arbat Street. The maremons flew toward him with incredible speed, their wings driving them forward. Right before they would have collided with Declan, he burst upward. The gargoyles collided, a sonic boom rupturing the sky in a flash of white lightning.

Violet turned her attention back to Cheshire, relieved that Declan was safe. He was lying face down, arms tucked underneath. A bright glow emanated from under his body, melting the snow around him. Gaslight was traveling toward him in runnels of light. The gargoyle clambered over him, sweeping its head toward Cheshire. Steam feathered the air from its nostrils.

"Cheshire!" Violet yelled from within her bubble of shadow. She pounded her fists against the glass-smooth wall of shadow as the gargoyle started to inhale, sparks cascading from her hands and sizzling on the snow.

Cheshire suddenly rolled over, his arms completely consumed with liquid light. "Suck on this, big boy." He discharged every drop of power into the gargoyle's head, blowing it clean off. The metal head spun high into the air, exploding in a giant flower of silver and red fire. The gargoyle collapsed, bricks tumbling in on itself until it was nothing more than a pile of rubble.

Declan swooped down and landed between Cheshire and Parminder. "You okay?"

"Never mind me." Cheshire grimaced as he regained his feet. "Where's Violet?"

"She's over by the Starbucks," Declan said, nodding toward Violet. "Under the sign in a shadow fortification bubble."

BANG!

Violet's shadow bubble shuddered, knocking her down. Dillinger was standing on one side of it, between Violet and the coffee shop, which was flickering and growing semi-translucent. On the other side was a maremon. It smashed its head against the orb, shadow-glass spidering. Violet backed up to the other side of the small compartment. Her hands were no longer sparking, having returned to their usual glow.

"Get me out of here!" Violet yelled in panic, dropping the duffel bag.

"Not much I can do," Dillinger answered from behind her. "You're safer in there."

The gargoyle slammed its metal head against the orb again. More veining appeared in the glass.

"I doubt that," Violet said, sweat beading on her forehead.

BANG!

The gargoyle smashed into the orb again. Glass shattered, sending shards of shadow down on Violet. They liquefied on impact, melting over her like syrup. Right before Violet screamed, Declan stepped in front of her and held an Uzi to the gargoyle's torso. "Move back," Declan ordered. Violet complied, shuttling backward along the inky snow.

Declan unloaded into the gargoyle as it reared back, ready to swipe down at the Rememberist. As he fired, he stepped back toward the flicker-fading Starbucks. Bells clanged from behind them, the ground shaking. The twist was coming.

Morgan ran from one side of the gargoyle. "Inside the coffee shop. Now." He opened the door, motioning for them to get in.

"Where's Cheshire and Parminder?" Violet asked as Dillinger

pulled her inside, the sweet sharpness of ground coffee greeting her.

"Here!" Cheshire called from the other side of the maremon. The maremon roared, confused and seemingly frustrated with so many moving targets in front of it. It inhaled deeply and launched a blast of fire at Cheshire, who nimbly jumped to the side while still carrying Parminder.

Violet watched Declan scramble into the Starbucks, followed by Morgan brandishing his foil. Violet pressed herself against one of the Starbucks's windows and watched Cheshire dance around the gargoyle's fireballs.

Cheshire bent down and let Parminder pick up the duffel bag as he swept around the maremon, making it twist in odd ways as it tried to keep track of the Rememberists. He made it halfway into the coffee shop when he suddenly stopped and his grin disappeared. The gargoyle had clamped onto Parminder's duffel bag. Cheshire turned around in the middle of the doorway, knocking the apiarist into the doorframe.

"Just drop the bag," Morgan yelled, grabbing Cheshire to pull him into the coffee shop.

"No!" Parminder unzipped the duffel bag and reached inside, the gargoyle's jaw firmly locked around the material. She twisted around on Cheshire's shoulder, moving into a sitting position. Cheshire reached out and took Morgan's extended hand, and he began to pull him into the Starbucks. Declan grabbed Cheshire's other hand and joined the tug of war.

Violet left the window and went in front of Cheshire. She knotted Cheshire's trench coat in her hand, helping to pull him into the Starbucks. The apiarist sat on Cheshire's shoulder, one hand gripping the top of the doorframe, the other holding a double-barreled shotgun. She placed the gun inside the gargoyle's mouth, and for the first time since arriving in Dementia, Violet thought she saw Parminder smirk under her charcoal-dark veil.

"Hey, bitch," Parminder said. "Eat bees and die."

Then she pulled the trigger.

21/ TWISTHOP

THE GARGOYLE'S head exploded in curls of metal and buckshot and flame.

Parminder's chest and arm snapped backward from the shotgun's kickback. She fell into Morgan and Declan, who both failed to catch her. They tumbled into a heap of arms and legs. Cheshire joined the pile, stumbling into the Starbucks from the sudden weightlessness of the maremon losing its grip.

"That's all eight," Dillinger said, helping the Rememberists untangle themselves.

Morgan stood, brushing off his jacket as if it were dusty. "And nobody died."

"We still need to get back to Pallium," Violet said, reaching out a hand to Declan. He took it and hoisted himself up. "Melody's in trouble."

"I'm sure she's fine," Parminder whispered. She groaned as she stood slowly, the channeling having fatigued her. "We've never had a breach in Pallium before."

"Doesn't mean there can't be a first," Cheshire said, wiping a line of

blood from the corner of his mouth. Violet shot him a glare, knowing full well that Cheshire knew Melody was in trouble.

She hated playing both sides. Having knowledge of what was going on behind the scenes made her stomach sour, especially when everyone was completely clueless. Well, everyone but Cheshire. He knew. And maybe Declan did too. He was staring at Violet, trying to read her. When Violet matched his gaze, he didn't turn away. He just stood there, eyes penetrating. Violet could feel them burrowing into her. He knew something, and that made her nervous.

The Starbucks rattled. Clangs rang from deep within the foundation, brick walls cracking, mortar popping. For the first time Violet took a quick glance around. It was a small coffee shop, with only a few tables and a cramped espresso bar that stretched along one wall. At the back, a narrow hallway disappeared into darkness. And there were figments inside—the first she'd seen since entering the Chrysler Building. They sat around tables and stood in corners and along the bar, drinking and smoking and all of them staring at the Rememberists.

The coffee shop shuddered again. Pieces of ceiling plaster crumbling and pattering down. Floorboards popped, splintering upward. Deep, thunderous clangs filtered through the building.

"Put these on," Cheshire said, holding out a pair of velvet-lined handcuffs. "I don't want to lose you when we twisthop. Things are going to get upside down."

"Where the hell did you get those from?" Violet was certain her eyes almost popped out of her head.

"I always come prepared."

Her face warmed, and as she glanced down at the handcuffs, she knew that the red velvet matched her current complexion.

"Besides," Cheshire added, his voice all velveteen, "it's for your own protection."

"Of course it is." She took the handcuffs and slid one of the cuffs around her left wrist, the velvet soft and welcoming.

The handcuff ratcheted closed as the coffee shop vibrated, sending glasses and mugs tumbling to the floor. Bottles of flavored syrup along the back of the espresso bar fell in a crescendo of shattering glass. Cheshire grabbed the other handcuff and expertly slipped it around his right wrist.

Violet noticed that Declan was staring at her again, though this time there was a newfound sadness in his eyes; a disappointment that hadn't been there before, like knowing you have an important train to catch and no matter what you do, you'll never make it on time. She felt the sadness traverse the tension between them, and as she moved her cuffed hand to touch her hair, she realized why. She was attached to Cheshire—by velvet-lined handcuffs no less—and not Declan. And there was nothing she could do about it.

She softened her face and mouthed the word "*sorry.*" She knew how bad this must look to Declan. His face hardened, shadows clouding over his eyes until she could no longer see them. He turned his back to her.

"Can you walk on your own?" Cheshire asked Parminder. "Because I'm kind of tied up at the moment."

Before Parminder could reply, the room tilted sideways like a funhouse. Violet staggered, yet before she fell Cheshire pulled on her handcuff and she steadied. A continuous clash of gongs rolled through the Starbucks. The Rememberists adjusted to the sudden flux. Violet noticed that after a moment, the twisting occurred around her, and not directly to the floor she was standing on. Walls tilted inward and flexed outward, pictures or stairs or hallways warping more than they did in Pallium or the Chrysler Building. The usual soft-focus that permeated objects in Dementia intensified.

"Here we go!" Morgan yelled over the cacophony of clangs, the very foundation of the coffee shop cracking away from Dementia. "Stay close. We've all done this before, so if you get separated, find your way to the Dog and Duck and trance back to Pallium. Forget me not."

"Remember me always," Violet answered along with the rest of the Rememberists.

"Now follow me the best you can," Parminder added, holding the scanner above her, its nimbus of lemony light a beacon in the twisthop haze. She moved toward the black hole at the back of the coffee shop's hallway.

Figments ignored the chaos of the twist, continuing with their regularly scheduled programming. A wall slammed down on a group of them drinking espresso. They never screamed when the wall collided with their semi-transparent bodies. They exploded in glitter.

The Rememberists reached the hallway, Cheshire tugging Violet along. Parminder waved her hand for them to stop. Even though she was only a few feet away, it looked as if she were standing in thick fog. "Wait for the collapse," she said over the din of the twist, inching forward. "Wait for it and then jump."

Violet didn't know what she was waiting for. She stood beside Cheshire as the walls of the Starbucks pinwheeled, spinning around them. Yet, something was off. There was no wind. Nothing. Just the collapse of structure, the crack-tear of plaster and brick, the kindle-snap of wooden beams. And it was then that Violet realized that she'd never felt a breeze brush her cheeks since being in Dementia. No wind. No rustling of tree branches. Just a sad, stagnant stillness that permeated everything.

The coffee shop exploded.

Cheshire grabbed Violet's head and tucked it toward his chest. The musky sweetness of cloves and woodsmoke spilled off him, and she inhaled his scent deeply. A scent that smelled of mystery and of possibility. It was a scent that made her feel safer than she'd ever felt. But it also scared her senseless. She had no idea who this trench-coated guy really was—and she wondered if she'd ever trust him.

He suddenly pushed her away, hard and fast and with more force than she ever thought possible. Her arm extended and she snapped against the handcuffs, the velvet compressing as the metal tore into her flesh. Her shoulder threatened separation. The floor went topsy-turvy, the ceiling of the coffee shop spinning up and around them as it cracked

open exposing upside-down apartments above. Weightlessness sucker-punched Violet in the stomach and she quickly realized that Cheshire hadn't shoved her away, but the floor had disappeared below. She made out the sudden exhalation of breath around her as the other Rememberists screamed in surprise.

Impact. Violet landed on something soft and hard. Cheshire swore. "This isn't how I envisioned you on top of me for the first time," he huffed.

"Me neither," Violet said. She quickly regretted saying that and scrambled off him, a sharp pain erupting in her shoulder, the handcuff tugging at her arm awkwardly as she maneuvered to her feet.

The rest of the Rememberists were regaining their feet, albeit slowly. Walls continued to fold and shift around them. "What happened to the coffee shop?" Violet yelled, realizing that they were no longer in the brick-walled Starbucks. They were high above the ground. Maybe in a penthouse. A cityscape of fog and jigsaw-crooked buildings spread out beyond a series of windows.

"I don't know," Morgan said, looking toward Parminder for guidance.

The apiarist stared at the scanner as one of the far walls fell away exposing a lavish apartment, full of marble and mahogany. "We've twisthopped about a dozen blocks," she said over the clanging. She shook the scanner. "We're at the top of the Beresford."

"As in the Central Park Beresford?" Violet questioned. She remembered driving past it on her tour of New York City. The guide had explained that it was one of the most desirable apartment buildings in Manhattan. Old money.

Parminder nodded. "Yes, but there's no Central Park in the Metacoel District. It's currently in the Tract of Goll. Well, except for the Gapstow Bridge which is anchored in Pallium of course. Anyway, we're farther from Soho than we need to be. We've gone the wrong way."

"But the Beresford hasn't changed in forever," Violet added. "It's iconic. Why's it twisting?"

"The concentrated memories of a place do not equal permanence," Declan said, his trench coat sculpted around his legs. He tugged at it to unwind the material. "It's probably breaking down and twisting into a new district. Maybe even a different borough. There's no common sense or predictability to the twists of Dementia. This world is in permanent flux."

"So what's outside these windows then?" Violet started toward them when the handcuff chain grew taut. She looked back at Cheshire who was shaking his head no. "We don't go near windows during twisthops," he said firmly as the plaster ceiling broke away, spiraling up into the hazy, glittery sky. "They're too unstable."

"Dill, get back!" Morgan yelled.

Dillinger stood near a window, looking out across the district. The entire window shattered, blowing shards of glass into the building. Before a single piece touched the floor, they were suctioned back out, as if a vacuum nozzle had been placed against the window's opening. The concrete surrounding the window cracked, large chunks of stone and rebar pulling away. Soon the entire wall caved outward, opening the building to the cityscape below.

Dillinger stumbled back from the missing wall, looking queasy and pale in the moonlight.

"Can I help you?"

Violet turned back into the room. A butler was standing in a doorway, his hair slicked to the side. He was impeccably dressed, his face ghostly transparent, cheekbones hard against the misty light.

"There, beyond the figment." Parminder pointed with her free hand, the scanner held close to her face. "Twist-tunnel opening. Scanner says that one should take us to Soho. Move!"

As Declan launched toward the doorway the wall collapsed inward, crushing the butler. He burst in a cloud of glitter, the floor warping beneath him. Declan staggered to the side, then ran full-tilt toward the hole left by the collapsed wall. He jumped through to the other side. "Quick!" he yelled, extending a hand. Violet squinted to

make out more details, but everything shifted, all soft-focused and bleary.

Rain started to fall. Lightning veined the sky. Thunder cracked.

Parminder went next, jumping the chasm as more of the floor whirlpooled downward. Declan grabbed her, his movements fluid as shadow. "Don't look down," Parminder called to Morgan as he neared the edge. "The building is caving into itself!"

Morgan took a few steps back, then charged. As he jumped a piece of the opposite floor crumbled and he smacked his chest hard against the disintegrating concrete, missing his mark by a few feet. He scrambled to grab a hold of something. One hand latched onto a piece of twisted rebar that protruded from the floor. Declan grabbed Morgan by the forearm and hoisted him up.

"Hurry!" Parminder yelled, quickly glancing at the wall of shadow and glitter that swirled behind her. "You've got two seconds to jump or we're hitting this twist-tunnel without you."

Cheshire took Violet's handcuffed hand in his and squeezed. The floor bucked, and another wall disintegrated, blowing out into the fog-heavy sky. Violet could see across the entire top floor of the Beresford, though her view was out of focus, as if she were looking through a soapy window.

"It's a long jump to make," Cheshire said. "We have to do it together."

Violet nodded. She wanted to puke.

"Three, two, one, run!" Cheshire said and then started to bolt toward the gap. She matched him, step for step. As they approached the hole she glanced downward. She couldn't see anything except swirling glitter and fog, threads of lighting crackling around in an electric whirlpool.

As Cheshire leapt, Violet stumbled, her foot catching on a piece of debris. The chain between them snapped taut and she pulled Cheshire back against his momentum. He hung suspended over the twisting churn of the under-real for a moment, and she thought in that single

heartbeat she could pull him back to her, or that Declan would grab his brother's free arm and prevent him from falling. But none of those things happened. Instead, Cheshire fell like an anvil, his bodyweight viciously tugging Violet over the edge.

And they both tumbled down the twist hole.

22/SMELLS LIKE LONDON

VIOLET CORKSCREWED in the electrical fog, her hand clasped tightly within Cheshire's. Raindrops streaked alongside her, their descent seemingly paused in flight. Yet, for all the falling she thought she was doing, her stomach remained where it was supposed to be and didn't try climbing out of her mouth. She braced for an impact that never came.

A dark streak flashed above and then below. Trails of phosphorescent ink blazed throughout the vapor. Then Declan was there, snaking between Violet and Cheshire. He wove his arms around them, the collar of his trench coat hiding most of his face.

"Got you," Declan breathed.

"You should've let us fall," Cheshire yelled from the other side. "You know you can't channel in a twist. You're burning up!"

Declan's face scrunched up as he fought the invisible currents of the twist. Liquid shadow ran across his face in runnels, dripping and trailing off him. His arm felt hot across Violet's back. "I can't leave you both to chance," he said, straining to fly with two bodies of dead weight under his arms.

His grip seemed to weaken, albeit slightly, but enough that Violet

took notice. She glanced at Declan and saw the concentration in his face. He *believed* in her. Violet knew that. And that was why she couldn't get the image of his disappointment out of her mind. The way he'd looked so defeated in the Starbucks shredded her heart. But for every pull toward Declan, there were two thoughts of his brother. They were so different and yet so very much the same. But something in Cheshire hypnotized her, something carnal. Yet she knew there was another facet to him, something dark and fragile and all glass-hearted.

Shadow spilled from Declan's eyes like tears, his head cocked back, fighting against failure. Energy burned, fatigue furrowing his brow. His gaze was locked on a pinpoint of lemony light above. Parminder's scanner, Violet realized.

"You're fading," Cheshire yelled to his brother. "Take Violet."

"No!" Declan swore, fighting against the currents. The exhaust that spewed from his trench coat was growing darker, the color of deoxygenated blood.

Cheshire leaned forward and looked at Violet. He winked.

"What are you doing?" Violet asked, though somewhere inside she knew the answer.

He just smiled and whispered, "Miss me." He reached in front of Declan and slid something small and shiny into the keyhole of the handcuffs. With a quick twist it unlatched, and before Violet could scream, Cheshire was caught in the lightning-streaked currents of the under-real and whisked away.

————

Declan accelerated with Cheshire gone, powering toward Parminder's scanner and the Beresford penthouse. Violet held on, trying to look for Cheshire in the swirling darkness below.

Nothing.

Declan swooped up, set Violet down on the floor and then collapsed from exhaustion. The room was in complete breakdown. Only a single,

perforated wall remained of the top floor, leaving the rest of the pent-house exposed to Recollection City. The cityscape wavered in the distance, buildings folding in on themselves like dying flowers. New structures bloomed in their remains.

"What were you thinking?" Parminder yelled at Declan.

Morgan hoisted him up. "I had to get Violet," he said, coughing. Blood-dark shadow oozed from his mouth, teeth blackened. He looked concussed, pupils dilated, eyes unable to lock onto an object. "Had to—"

Parminder wheeled on Violet. "You're becoming a lot more trouble than you're worth, which isn't much. I suggest you plug yourself in and do something soon, Princess Electric, or I'm going to—"

"Where's Cheshire?" Violet asked in a daze, ignoring the apiarist's ramblings. "Is he..."

"No," Morgan said, shaking his head. "He'll land somewhere in the district and make his way back to Pallium. We've all been stranded in the under-real before and had to find breadcrumbs."

Violet appreciated Morgan's reassurances, but she was pissed off. Probably more mad than concerned. Mad that Cheshire could just *leave* her like that. Was this another one of his ploys to meet with Mister Cinder again? Or someone else?

Declan would never dream of leaving her—*ever*. She grabbed his arms and held him steady, glitter dusting his shadow-wet cheeks. He tilted along with the floor, punch-drunk. "Thank you," she whispered, staring into his distant eyes. He simply nodded as Parminder stepped alongside them. "You can thank him for saving your ass later. We have to hit that twist-tunnel before the entire building implodes."

Morgan swung one of Declan's arms over his shoulder and they started shuffling toward the twist-tunnel, its composition of shadow and swirling glitter breaking down at its edges, disintegrating into black mist. Violet followed on the heels of Parminder. Unlike Cheshire, she had no breadcrumb skills. If she were to become separated and alone, she'd starve before figuring out what a breadcrumb even looked like in Dementia.

A sudden, crushing roar cut through the rain and thunder. It sounded like a hundred maremon gargoyles releasing all their anger in one shot. The thump of wings reverberated across the Beresford. Violet looked back hesitantly. There, hovering beyond the penthouse was what looked like a dragon, its crenulated skull sweeping back in jagged undulations, eyes gigantic teardrops of smoky jade. Lightning flashed, illuminating the electric ruby skin that spanned its wings.

Violet blanched. "What the hell is that?"

"A dragon," Parminder chimed.

"Really? I think I know that," Violet quipped, shooting a rabid glare toward Parminder. "But is it real?"

"That's Vermillion," Morgan said. "A member of the queen's retinue. She has a bad habit of sneaking up on you even though she's the size of a building."

"Does she breathe fire?" Violet asked, eyeing the brimstone-laced fumes spilling from the dragon's mouth.

"No," Morgan said, inching backward. "She sprays liquid nightmare." He twisted around, pushing Declan toward the twist-tunnel, who was oblivious to the dragon hovering beside the Beresford penthouse.

"I guess that means—"

Parminder glanced at Violet and then back to the dragon. "We run."

Vermillion roared again, then banked to circle the disintegrating building. The flap of her wings shook the penthouse, causing Violet to stutter-step as she ran toward the twist-tunnel. Morgan limped ahead, dragging Declan with him. Parminder ran alongside them, her duffel bag clasped tightly in hand. The dragon passed overhead, casting a foreboding shadow over the fleeing Rememberists—but she never attacked. Instead she circled, spying their movements. Was the queen gathering intelligence by watching them through Vermillion, even in these twists? Violet glanced up and thought she saw the dragon smile at her the way a dog does. It was as if the queen was toying with her. Showing her what she had in her pocket. And there seemed to be a lot in there. The shocktrooper attacks in the Chrysler Building, the

maremons, the twisthops, and now a freaking dragon circling the Beresford.

Violet wasn't too keen on finding out what the queen's next trick would be.

They hit the twist-tunnel, its cool air washing over them in welcomed relief. Violet broke the threshold and spilled over as if she'd stepped into an exposed manhole, tumbling blindly downward. Legs splayed wildly, arms waving. Violet yelled and then splashed into darkness. Cold, grimy water soaked her, the air heavy with the stench of sewage and oil. As she stood, Violet wiped her hands on her coat, as if the damp wool would help dry them. But instead of drying them, it drew attention to them.

They were glowing, bright and phosphorescent. The light emanating from her skin illuminated the curved brick walls and wide trough of water that she now found herself standing in. Fog clung to the ceiling, cascading onto the water and spreading out in either direction. Bricks shifted around the tunnel, popping in and out of the wall on their own.

"Where are we?" Morgan asked as he helped a choking Declan stand.

"Looks like a sewer to me," Dillinger said, checking to make sure his darlings were still in their holsters.

"Smells like London." Declan flopped his dripping hair back, the pale light from Violet ghosting softly against him. Violet's body shiver-tingled—and not from the cold water she was standing in either. Declan looked wet, vulnerable, and his forget-me-not eyes glowed in the darkness of the tunnel in the way blue sky cuts through the canopy of a forest. Declan glanced at her and she answered with a sigh, then turned away.

"London it is," Parminder said, adjusting dials on the scanner. Her veil was suctioned to her face, features sharp in the ambient light. "Which means we're right near our extraction point. The Dog and Duck should be right above us."

Violet wanted to ask how the apiarist navigated the twists, whether she had any control over where they landed, but thought better of it. Now wasn't the time—unless she wanted to get a rather nasty response.

"There's a ladder over here." Morgan pointed down the tunnel, sloshing toward it. He held up an arm against the bricks that click-clacked in and out of the wall, though none of them actually made contact. He climbed the ladder, disappearing into the darkness above. He swore and a brick fell into the water.

Violet walked over and stood underneath, raising her hands to illuminate the well above. He was at the top of the ladder, straining against a manhole cover.

"Move," Dillinger said, standing beside the ladder.

Morgan climbed down. "All yours."

Dillinger hustled up the ladder, dark water falling from his trench coat. He placed his hands on the manhole cover, then traced around its diameter. A silver light glowed where he traced until he completed the circle. He took a deep breath and then punched the steel cover. It exploded out of the well with a lightning-bright flash, spinning high into the air. He stuck his head out of the manhole and looked around. "All clear," he yelled down, then climbed out. "We're in Soho."

Parminder went next, then Violet. They were suddenly standing in the middle of a busy but tight intersection. There were only a few cars driving by as figments filled most of the street, carrying bags, laughing, shouting. Rustic buildings shimmered along the streets, jagged and dark against the falling glitter. Declan came next, then Morgan.

"The Dog and Duck is there, on the corner." Parminder pointed across the street.

Violet followed her finger to a pale brick building with white-framed windows. Along the street, dark granite and wood merged with a narrow sidewalk.

The Dog and Duck was packed. The smell of sweat, stale beer, and deep-fried food permeated the Victorian-flavored establishment. Etched glass panes separated various areas, while the polished wood bar shone

under the ornate lights hanging from the ceiling. Figments filled every available space, laughing with their pints. Dillinger pushed his way through the crowd, straight down a tightly winding stairwell to the men's room.

Parminder followed as if she did that all the time.

"Come on," Declan said to Violet. "Mirror's in here."

"Seriously?" Violet stopped outside the door.

"Seriously," Morgan said as he walked past. He grabbed her hand and pulled her inside. The sudden stench of concentrated beer and piss made Violet screw up her nose. Parminder was at a small, cracked mirror that hung over an abused sink surrounded by black tile. She held up her hands to the mirror, wiping it down as if cleaning it. The mirror began to fog up under her hands. Condensation soon covered the entire surface.

"Join hands," Parminder said, facing the mirror. She reached back with one of her hands, the other still pressed against the mirror. Declan took her hand, then reached out for Violet's. She took it, the handcuff banging against Declan's arm. He glanced down, but didn't say anything. Morgan took Violet's other hand, and Dillinger locked up with Morgan.

Parminder pushed her hand into the mirror. Her arm slowly disappeared as she was pulled into the wet surface. She climbed onto the sink and pushed herself into the mirror.

"Remember to breathe this time," Declan said to Violet as he hoisted himself onto the sink, his combat boot scuffing the porcelain. He glanced back, squeezed her hand, then followed Parminder into the mirror.

Violet took a deep breath, trying not to be unnerved that she was holding onto what appeared to be a dismembered arm as the rest of Declan's body was in the mirror from the elbow down. The mirror was cold and wet as she let her hand follow Declan's. She looked over her shoulder toward Morgan, who simply nodded.

Violet closed her eyes, and fell into quicksilver.

PART D

ILLUMINATION

"There is no greater sorrow than forgotten love; and no greater joy than embracing love anew."
- Memory Archivist Cillian Grey in a letter to Rememberist Oskar Brandt, 1917

23/ FORGET ME

VIOLET FELL out of the mirror, tripping over wiring and skipping off a table, cracking several glass tubes in the process. She landed on the plush carpet of the Royal Palace of Madrid.

Morgan jumped down from the small table below the mirror. "Very elegant." He tossed his AK-47 onto the table.

"At least I remembered to breathe this time."

"That's a good thing," Dillinger said, stepping from the mirror. He looked around the throne room, eyeing each mirror, each box of thermionic valves. He raised an eyebrow. "Any sign of Melody?"

"No," Parminder said. She was standing at the operator station. Monitors flashed overhead like strobe lights. "Everything's offline still. From what I can tell, alarms were tripped in Gapstow. They were reset a short time later, but she obviously never made it back here to light up the system. I'm still reporting vacuum tubes blown on board seventeen, there by Mirror 5. Oh, and the valves Violet crushed when she got out of Mirror 7 of course."

Morgan and Dillinger grabbed a box of valves and started replacing them, blowing out fragments of shattered glass before snapping in the new tubes. Within a minute they were done. The apiarist flicked a few

switches and a low hum filled the room. Monitors flickered and reset. Mirrors began to fog over once more.

"There we go," Parminder said from under her veil. "Online."

If it took more than a few seconds to find Melody, Violet would tell them about the meeting with the queen. And about Cheshire. They had to find the courtesan fast. For everyone's sake.

Declan walked over and checked the operator station with Parminder. "Where's Stem right now? That should give us an idea of Melody's location."

Parminder sat down, adjusting a few dials. She moved a slider down and a deep-bass sound filled the room. "One more second," she said, typing furiously on the keyboard. Monochrome lighting washed over Declan as he looked over the apiarist's shoulder, his face a tiger stripe of tangerine shadows.

Violet felt hopeless as the Rememberists worked on tracking down Melody. She tried to think where Melody could be in Pallium.

Then it hit her like a flash of oncoming headlights.

It was something Mister Cinder had said. *I left her a present in the—*

"I've found Stem," Parminder shouted, jumping up from the console. "It's in the—"

"Conservatory," Violet whispered. She grabbed Morgan's AK-47 from the table and ran toward Stem's empty cage, pressing the call button. Her sudden elation dissipated when she turned around. The Rememberists were all staring at her.

"How did you know that?" Parminder asked, her voice ripping through the electromagnetic hum. She leapt onto the console, took two steps, and dropped down to the carpet. Morgan and Dillinger joined her as she started to walk toward Violet.

"I don't know?" Violet lied. "Good guess?" She backed up against the cage door.

Parminder shook her head. "I don't think so."

The three Rememberists walked closer. Sweat dappled Violet's forehead. She wasn't sure what they were going to do when they reached

her and she sure didn't want to find out. If she admitted to meeting the queen incommunicado, then they'd stop listening to her and know of Cheshire's betrayal. She didn't think they'd harm her, but they'd lock her up until things got straightened out, limiting the amount of time they had to recover her sister's memories—if the queen was even telling the truth.

On second thought, it was good that Violet hadn't said anything without Cheshire here to explain himself.

Stem clanged to a stop in the cage behind Violet. She spun around, pulling open the cage door in one smooth motion. Slipping inside, she reversed her spin, slamming the cage closed.

"Open the door," Morgan ordered.

"Sorry," Violet said, slipping to the back of the elevator. "But that's not an option right now. You guys look like you want to tear me apart."

"Au contraire," Parminder said ardently. "We just want some answers."

"Don't we all," Violet murmured, pressing the button that read *Atrium*.

———

Violet felt like a rat in a cage the entire way to the atrium. When Stem stopped, she flung open the cage door and ran toward the conservatory entrance. Glitter shimmered on the rails of moonlight that penetrated the broken panes of ceiling glass. When she heard Stem leave with a whooshing clang, she didn't look back. It would only be a few minutes before the Rememberists arrived behind her.

Violet had to get to Melody first, had to make sure she was okay.

Had to explain herself.

If Melody was dead, her blood would be on Violet's hands.

Just like the accident. Like her sister's.

Violet threw open the double glass doors of the conservatory and vaulted inside. An eerie, troubling silence greeted her along with the

familiar chill air. She stopped for a moment to listen and heard nothing. Running along one of the stone pathways toward the amphitheater, she realized that something was off. None of the butterflies were flitting about the trees. She knew that hers were stolen by Mister Cinder and now sat in two tiny birdcages beside Queen Zamelerish in Cerebrum. But the other butterflies—the cherished memories of the Rememberists —should be there still. The birdman never said he'd taken them as well.

Then again, he never said he didn't either.

Her head lanced with pain. The realization that they were gone floored her like an aneurysm. All the memory butterflies had been stolen and taken to the queen. There were no wings of rainbow dancing in the trees.

Violet rounded the final corner toward the amphitheater and stopped at the stairs. Melody was sitting on the stage, arms limp at her side. The stage and table were still riddled with illuminated lamps in varying styles. A small stool stood beside Melody. Something glinted in her hand; something shiny sparked on the stool.

"No!" Violet yelled as she ran down the stairs, two at a time. Did Mister Cinder slurp all the courtesan's good memories like Cheshire had done to her? Or worse, had he stripped her of everything? Was she brain dead?

Violet ran up the rickety stage stairs and hustled over to Melody, weaving around the lamps. The girl's head was tilted back, mouth agape and eyes staring toward the heavens. Her platinum ringlets spilled over her shoulders and down the back of the chair, body limp like a discarded marionette.

She leaned over Melody, brushing a lock of hair off her face. Her eyes were glassy and transparent with wavy streaks of milky rainbow, like the toothpaste marbles Violet used to play with as a little girl. She snapped her fingers above Melody's face. Her eyes didn't move, glistening under the lamp light.

A small, ornate box sat on the stool, its outside decorated in kaleidoscopic glass. The inside was lined with crushed velvet, black and dusted

with glitter. Beside the box sat a single white feather. Violet recognized the birdman's plumage, her heart thundering in her chest. She took a step back, eyeing the courtesan. A pink and black boa was tied around her left arm like a tourniquet. A single dot of blackened blood in the crook of her elbow marked her otherwise porcelain-perfect skin.

And there, dangling in her right hand, rested a syringe. Violet plucked it carefully from her fingers. Blood and congealed rainbow smeared the inside of the glass chamber, the needle glinting in the moonlight.

A small tag was attached to the syringe.

Violet turned the tag over. Two words were written in beautifully ornate letters, all black ink on silver foil.

Forget Me

Violet stared at the script, how the letters swam across the foil like spilled ink. They tugged at her, and Violet wondered how much pain Melody had been in to want to be forgotten. What was so horrific to her that she'd inject a mysterious liquid into her body, into her *mind*, just to forget? Violet felt the allure. Deep within her soul, she knew that she'd have done the same. She'd have risked everything just to forget the accident—to forget how she maimed her sister.

Unless she could fix her.

Unless there was hope.

She threw the syringe onto the stage and stomped down on it, grinding the syringe into the stage floor. Anger and concern coursed thought her. Violet felt for a pulse. Her fingers pressed into the soft flesh under Melody's jaw. She felt a slight heartbeat, faint and fading. A slight hit of relief filled her. Then it was gone, replaced by sadness.

It was the same sadness Violet had felt when her sister hung from the seatbelt, eyes glazed with the numbness of shock and escaping life.

That same sadness when you know someone was about to die.

Violet's shoulders slumped. Head bowed. Cheshire's empty hand-cuff banged against her knee.

"What have I done?" she whispered to herself.

"I'm not sure it's a question of what you've done," Parminder said sardonically, "but more a question of what you've done again?"

Violet whirled, locking eyes with Parminder. The apiarist stood amidst the forest of lamps, warm light encircling her. "What are you talking about?"

Parminder took a step forward and stopped. "You know."

"Enlighten me."

"Well, people seem to either die or disappear around you," Parminder said in a monotone voice that made the hairs on Violet's neck porcupine.

"Nobody has died." Violet nodded toward Melody. "Or disappeared for that matter."

Parminder laughed. "Cheshire disappeared in the twisthop."

"And he's going to be fine," Violet snapped back. She could feel Parminder jostling for position. The apiarist was setting her up for a reveal.

"You don't know that." Parminder shrugged nonchalantly. "And even if he is, Melody's well on her way to the Mausoleum of Memory."

"And you don't know that," Violet countered.

"True," Parminder said. Under the veil, a slight smile curled across her lips. "But I do know that you killed your sister."

Violet's knees jellied. "She's not dead."

"She may as well be. She's dead inside."

It was one thing to know a fact, to live with a certain reality, but it was a completely different thing to hear it recited back to you with such pompous certainty. But Parminder was right and there was nothing Violet could say except, "You fucking bitch. Don't. Even. Think. About going there!"

"I just did." Parminder reached behind her and pulled out her two blades of smoke and bees. They hummed in the tense silence.

Morgan and Dillinger joined Parminder on the stage. Morgan continued to Melody, checking her pulse. "We need to get her to the medical room. She needs isolation to work through the nightmares."

"Nightmares?" Violet questioned, trying to look at Morgan and Parminder at the same time. "What are you talking about? What did she take?"

"Looks like she mainlined crystalMem." Morgan touched the bruise that was starting to bloom along the crook of Melody's elbow. It had an oil on water sheen about it.

"CrystalMem?" Violet asked, trying to ignore the drone of Parminder's bee swords.

"Yeah," Dillinger said. "It's concentrated memory, cooked into crystals. You know, chasing the butterfly? Breaking wings? Whatever you want to call it, the queen manufactures it for her memjacks. She distributes it as a reward. But when a human takes a hit? It's a rapid flood of memory—and then a rush of forgetting. Looks like Melody's hit was cut with the essence of delirium too."

Dillinger walked over to the crushed syringe and touched his fingers to the wetness. He raised them to his nose. "Yeah, I can smell the nightmares. She's either going to fall into madness—or she'll die." The gunslinger shook his head and sighed. "Hopefully, she'll die, because if she doesn't? She's never going to be the same girl again. We might as well lock her up in a straitjacket and throw away the key."

Morgan ran his hand through Melody's hair, the porcelain-pale tresses contrasting against his dark skin. "All the butterflies are gone too," he said sadly, dipping his dreadlocks toward the conservatory proper. "Did you notice? Every single one. Our most cherished memories."

"I noticed." Parminder took another step toward Violet, her swords smoking around her like oiled torches. "But regardless, what I want to know is how—"

"...you knew to come to the Conservatory."

The voice came from the other side of the stage. Violet turned around. There, standing beside a tall Tiffany lamp that cast multicolored light against his shadowed face, was Declan. His hair was still damp from the London tunnel, hanging in straggly curls.

"I didn't know anything. I just guessed." *Where are you, Cheshire?* Violet thought.

Declan slouched slightly in obvious disappointment. He looked beyond Violet to Parminder and said, "Put those away. She's not going to open up with you pointing your smoking sticks at her."

Parminder huffed and put her swords away.

"Thank you," Declan said. He balled his fists repeatedly, as if he were squeezing a stress reliever toy. "Now, Violet, let's chalk the conservatory guess up to just that—a guess. And let's say you had no idea Melody would be in here with a tourniquet around her arm and bad dreams in her blood."

"I didn't," Violet started to say, but Declan raised a finger, silencing her.

"Let's forget all about that," he continued, "and go back to the Chrysler Building."

Here we go. Violet bit her lip, remembering the way Declan had looked at her when they exited the elevator after her visit to the queen.

Declan walked over to Melody and placed his hand on her forehead. He smoothed his hand over her face, closing her eyes. She murmured against his touch. Declan looked back to Violet. "We got separated in the stairwell."

"Right," Violet said, trying to sound as obvious as possible.

"So how is it," Declan asked, rubbing his chin, "that you came down in that specific bank of elevators?"

Violet looked toward the rafters, as if the answer would be hidden in the tracks of defunct lighting. Sweat bloomed on her forehead, her armpits uncomfortably hot. What was Declan getting at? They got separated and went into an elevator, tranced to the queen via Mister Cinder,

and then back again. What did Declan see that she didn't? "I don't know what you mean. I was only following Cheshire."

Declan took in a deep breath, then licked his lips and exhaled. "I mean, the bank of elevators you came down only service the lower floors of the Chrysler Building. They do not go to the upper floors. That's an entirely different bank. So, let me ask again...how is it that you came down in that specific elevator?"

The heat from the lamps burned into Violet; the glare from their shades shining into her eyes like a hundred spotlights. Declan seemed to blur and she held up her hand to shield her face, handcuffs swaying. The bile of sudden panic rose in her throat. She didn't know Dementia, didn't understand what made it tick-tock. Could she blame the twists that shudder through the under-real, or would that make her look like more of a cuckoo than she already did?

She looked at Melody sitting slumped on the chair, her feather boa still wrapped around her arm. Rainbow-dark veins spider-webbed across her skin, and for a moment Violet thought she saw the shimmer of glass between them. Morgan stood beside her, hand on her shoulder and concern etched across his forehead. Dillinger was between them and Parminder, the cloth around his bicep dark crimson from the bullet wound. His face was calm yet his brows were knotted, as if he were gauging the situation to see where the cards fell. Parminder's arms hung at her sides, slightly tense and ready to pull out her swords again in a moment's notice. Under her veil, her face was focused. She knew Parminder had questioned her allegiance from the start, so anything to derail the trust Violet thought she'd created didn't help matters. If she said anything about seeing the queen, Violet knew Parminder would not hesitate to split her open.

Violet turned to look at Declan again, and melted when her eyes met his. They were summer-sky bright, though dark around the corners, as if rain clouds were threatening to storm. His sun-flecked corneas were dim, even under the lamplight. He was fighting with himself. He'd given up his most cherished memory to the Accountant for Violet so she could

get her sister's memories back, and here she was, spilling doubt into his mind. And the sad thing about it all was that he was right. Whatever Declan was thinking, whatever bad thoughts he was churning around about Violet, *he was right.* And that made her want to divulge everything.

It also made her want to puke right there on the stage.

Without Cheshire she had no choice but to fess up. She had to be honest with Declan. She had promised him that in the Mausoleum—*no matter what.* Those three words rung in her head. She'd let herself get into this situation, and now she had to own it.

Violet opened her mouth to speak when someone else's voice cut across the stage.

"You know, she's not going to answer that question—and neither am I."

Violet spun around and looked out into the amphitheater. There, walking down the central stairs, was Cheshire. His trench coat trailed off him in shreds, the leather underneath dusty and cut open in places. Zippers glinted from the light of the stage, glitter scintillating around him from a slight crack in the conservatory's ceiling. His hair was ratty, clumped together, and blood caked one side of his face. But his eyes, they were still as bright and tropical as ever.

"Cheshire," she said, relief flooding over her. "Are you all right?"

He held up a bloody hand as he neared the last step. "I'm fine," he said, coughing. He weakly smiled, as if it were forced. "Ran into a few memjacks as I was following breadcrumbs back to Pallium. For some reason I landed in the middle of Bourbon Street during Mardi Gras."

"How convenient for you," Parminder chided.

"Or not," Cheshire said, stopping on the last step. "It's hard to navigate through a sea of drunk figments with no scanner and memjacks on your ass." He coughed again, blood flecking the air.

"You need to rest," Morgan said.

"You need to answer our questions," Declan added, staring down at his brother.

Cheshire tensed, wavering on the spot like a tree ready to fall. "I told you, I'm not answering. If you have something to say, then fucking say it. That goes for you too, Parminder. What about you, Dill? Morgan?"

Parminder pulled her veil back and narrowed her eyes at Cheshire. "We want answers. Too many things are not adding up. You and Violet disappeared in the Chrysler Building and came down in a completely different bank of elevators—elevators which don't service the upper floors. While we were trancing, Pallium was breached and our memories netted from the conservatory. The so-called Princess Electric here somehow knew Melody was in the conservatory when we got back to Pallium. And, conveniently, the only person who knows any details on how the breach transpired is sitting in that chair, jacked on crystalMem. Now, I can't speak for the others, but I find it rather odd that you were the only person wanting to break protocol so that we could all trance into Dementia and leave Pallium unguarded. Seems a little fishy, don't you think?"

Cheshire's gaze flitted to Declan. "And you, brother? Do you have the same concerns?"

Declan took a deep breath and said, "Yes."

Cheshire stood in silence, his eyes locking onto each Rememberist for a moment, then moving on to the next. When he finally spoke, his voice was granite-hard. "It appears you've already found us guilty. I've done nothing but aid Violet in her quest to recover her sister's memories. When we get the memories back, she'll deliver them to her sister. Once done, she'll come back and honor her part of the prophecy by joining the Rememberists so that we can illuminate Recollection City. If you feel that I've wronged you, or that I'm in league with the queen, then say so. Strike me down right now. Turn me to glitter and forget me forevermore."

Cheshire held out his hands to the side. Violet's breath caught in her throat. The amphitheater was silent except for the hum of the lamps. Nobody moved.

Then Declan walked over to Violet. "There will be no striking down

of anyone. Not now. Nobody has slept in ages, so first, Morgan, please move Melody into one of the medical rooms for monitoring. Let us rest and regroup in the morning. We can meet in the throne room before transcendence into Gracile. Are we good?"

Everyone agreed, though with some hesitation. Parminder swore.

"Come with me Violet," Cheshire said, swaying. "I'll take you to your room. You can rest there."

"No," Declan said, taking Violet's hand in his. "She's coming with me. I'd like to talk to her—alone."

Cheshire swallowed hard, but did not object. Morgan carefully lifted Melody from the chair and carried her off with Dillinger and Parminder.

Violet took her hand back from Declan. She didn't need to be led, uneasiness of what he wanted to talk to her about rippling through her stomach. They walked through the forest of lamps and down from the stage. As she passed Cheshire, she could see the concern in his eyes, how they were all glassy twilight. The brothers said nothing to each other as they passed. As she reached the top of the amphitheater, Violet looked back and saw Cheshire sitting in the quiet lamplight of the stage, on the same chair Melody had sat in moments earlier.

Cheshire held the white feather that had sat beside the box in his blood-dark fingers. He slumped back and dropped the feather. And it sashayed to the stage floor, silent.

24/ CLOCK TOWER SONATA

VIOLET AND DECLAN walked to Stem through the Conservatory with nary a word between them. He pressed a button that read *Clock Tower* inside the elevator. When the elevator stopped in its usual cloud of steam, he led her into a corridor and through a small wooden door. Dirty white limestone stairs with iron railings corkscrewed up for as far as Violet could see.

"Come," Declan said, walking toward the first stair.

"Where are we going?" Violet asked, hesitant to follow, dizziness washing over her as she stared up the spiraling staircase. She adjusted her sunglasses.

"To my room. I want you to see something."

"Do we really have time for this?" Violet questioned. She couldn't imagine what he wanted her to see, not when Melody was fighting for her life and Karin's memories were scheduled for processing.

"This is something important. We'll leave tomorrow morning to reclaim your sister's memories. We still have a small window of time to rest and recharge. The last thing we want to do is make a push into Dementia when everyone is drained. That's a good way to not come back."

After about fifty steps, Violet asked, "How many stairs are there?"

"Three hundred and thirty-four."

"Wonderful," Violet huffed. "Is that how you stay so trim?"

Declan sniggered. "Yes, between the stairs and the cafeteria food I find it hard to put on weight."

The climb continued in exasperated silence, her breathing the only real sound in the stairway. Declan didn't seem to be breaking a sweat as he lithely took stairs two at a time. The stairwell was no different than any other corridor or room in Pallium, the walls slightly bending inward and outward at times, a surreal sheen to their texture. A few times the stairs went out at wide angles, where Violet would have to walk a good four or five steps across a single stair before the next step up.

"What's with the messed-up stairs?" Violet asked, her breath short, legs burning. The number 182 was stamped on the corner of a stair.

"Remember that crooked clock tower you saw from the rooftop when you first arrived? That's the famous clock tower of the Palace of Westminster." Declan said this as if Violet should know what he was referring to. "In London," he finally added.

"Big Ben?" It was the only clock tower she knew in the real.

"Well, that's the nickname for the giant bell inside, but yes. Dementia has warped the structure of the clock tower, twisting it like a coat hanger."

When they reached the top, Violet nearly toppled over from exhaustion, her legs burning. When she caught her breath, she followed Declan through a doorway and into a tall-ceilinged room filled with steel girders and high, open-air windows that were covered with metal mesh. Beyond the screening she could see the shifting buildings of Recollection City fanning outward. A massive bell hung in the center of the room, surrounded by a fence. A hairline crack snaked up one side. Four smaller bells hung around the room, nestled between girders.

"Is this your bedroom?" Violet asked, looking around.

"Not quite," Declan said, motioning for Violet to follow him. "I sleep below, in the mechanism room. The tick-tock of the timekeeping

machinery lulls me to sleep. This is the belfry." A metal staircase stood in front of them, and beside that, a narrow walkway ran alongside the giant bell fence. "And that's Big Ben." Declan nodded toward the massive bell.

"Well, it definitely is big," Violet said, not sure what else to say about a giant bell.

"The Westminster Chimes only play in Dementia for one reason."

"And that would be?"

Violet was familiar with the Westminster Chimes; the doorbell to her grandma's home had played them. Every time she went over to visit as a little girl, she couldn't help but press the doorbell over and over again just to hear their familiar tune.

"The chimes only play when a Rememberist is illuminated in the Mausoleum of Memory."

"Oh," Violet said, suddenly embarrassed, as if she'd just asked why someone was absent from school, not knowing they were at a funeral.

"Luckily, they haven't played in a while," Declan said, heading up the metal staircase in front of them.

"How high are we going?" Violet looked through the wire-meshed, cathedral-like windows to the glittering cityscape beyond. Buildings continued to twist into each other in pockets of metal and shadow and brickwork.

"All the way to the top, to the lantern."

Violet sighed with the prospect of more climbing.

They continued up the staircase until it opened into a large, high-ceilinged chamber. Small windows rimmed the room, letting in slivers of moonlight. A catwalk surrounded a pair of large steel girders cross-hatched above the belfry. Big Ben was suspended from the center of the girders, with the quarter bells flanking the sides. Declan didn't stop in this room, instead leading Violet to a spiral staircase of dark metal that corkscrewed up from the catwalk. His boots clunked on the metal stairs as she followed him up.

The stairs spiraled a few times and then they were standing on a

narrow walkway, a massive metal and glass lantern filling the center of the platform. Tall, narrow windows encircled the platform, though the wire-mesh that had covered the lower-level windows had been removed. The only thing that prevented them from tumbling out was an ornate railing that looked more for aesthetics than safety.

Violet closed her eyes for a moment. A cool, rejuvenating breeze drifted over her, the first one she'd felt since being in Dementia, and she wondered if the breeze had twisted here with the clock tower. When she opened her eyes again, Declan was standing in front of her, glitter swirling around him, his hair and trench coat fluttering in the wind.

"This is the Ayrton Light," Declan said, pointing toward the central glass structure. "It's foretold that the illumination of Recollection City will start from here."

Violet couldn't believe what she was hearing. Anger bloomed in her body. "Are you kidding me? This is why you brought me up here? Why are you doing this now? You don't even know if the prophecy refers to me! I can't wield Glitterglam without you helping. I tried to summon it when you were battling the maremons and all I got were sparks." Violet paused, looking Declan straight in the eyes. "I'm nothing more than a girl trying to get her sister's memories back. That's it. I don't know why any of you stay in this fucked-up world when you can just leave."

"We can't just leave," Declan said. "We've been here too long. It'd be a death wish."

"What do you mean?"

"Look at me," he said, arms outstretched. "You know that when you turn eighteen, you stop getting older in Dementia. But if any of us were to go back to the real, we'd rapidly age to however old we're supposed to be, all in the span of a few heartbeats. So for all of us that have been here beyond our natural lifespans..."

"You'd die," Violet surmised. "Understood. But you haven't even told me why you're here. You should have left a long time ago. This place is shit."

Declan bit his lip. Behind him, the mirror-glass moon filled the

horizon beyond the Palace of Memories End. Glitter sparkle-dusted the sky. Shadows swirled around Declan's face, curling over his blood-dark lips, and for the briefest of moments Violet thought she saw his lower lip quiver. His eyes glazed, and he said, "I killed her."

"What?" Violet asked, taken aback from such a sudden confession.

"Oriana Palms," Declan breathed. "I killed her by believing in her, and I don't want the same thing to happen to you."

"I don't know what to say."

So there were other girls, Violet thought. *Others that glowed.*

"There's nothing to say." Declan took a deep breath and shook his head as if clearing cobwebs. His whole body shuddered. "It is what it is."

He wavered for a moment, shifting on the spot like one of the walls in Pallium, threatening collapse. Their eyes locked, and there was such an exquisite pain imprinted on them, haunted and distant, that her own eyes welled at the sight.

"It's okay," he said, half-smiling. "I lost my love a lifetime ago, and have grown to understand that I may not experience love like that again. All I ask is that you allow me to show you why I'm still in Dementia. And why I believe that you're the Princess Electric."

She breathed him in, all metal and rainfall, and said, "Tell me what happened. Tell me about Oriana Palms."

He tensed for a moment and then looked down at her, a lock of pewter hair slicing his face in half. "In order for me to tell you what happened to her, I need to explain how I transitioned here...and why I stayed in Dementia."

"Okay," Violet said. "Why did you stay here?"

Declan swallowed. "The same reason we all stay in Dementia at the beginning. I wanted to forget."

"I understand that," she said.

"Will you dance with me first?" he asked.

"Of course," Violet said, still tracing the pain along his eyes.

Declan walked behind the lantern. He came back carrying a square box roughly the size of a briefcase. He knelt and opened it. Inside sat a

record, a small lever, and a weird-shaped silver tube. He fastened the tube beside the record and attached the lever to the side of the box. He cranked the lever a few times and adjusted a switch, setting the record in motion. He lowered the tube assembly and a sudden static-crackle burst through it.

"What's that?" Violet asked, not having seen a record player since her grandpa had showed off his vinyl collection to her when she was around seven or eight years old. The entire collection was sold in a garage sale for a few dollars.

"A portable phonograph," Declan said. "I listen to music up here to center myself. To keep memories fresh in my mind." Music filtered up from the phonograph, crackling with each note. "I was a fan of jazz before I transitioned."

Declan stepped forward and took Violet's hand in his, placing his other arm around the small of her back. He pulled her close to his body but remained somewhat rigid even though the beats of the music begged for more movement. The scent of oil, of machinery and time, emanated from his body. He smelled of comfort, and it reminded her of her grandpa's garage, the way it had always smelled of oil and turpentine and cherry-scented tobacco. Declan made her calm, and that in itself was magic in such a dark world. He was the kind of boy she could curl up with on a rainy day and stare at the water running down the windowpanes, lost in a tumble of blankets and unknown tomorrows.

And now, dancing to an old phonograph recording, Violet wanted that comfort more than anything. She wanted to be pulled closer, tighter to Declan's body. She wanted to close her eyes to the sweeping churn of buildings and nightmare, knowing that tomorrow they would be going back into the wilds of Dementia to fetch her sister's memories. And after seeing how difficult it had been to return to Pallium from the Accountant's office, she knew that this moment with Declan, this tiny fragment of time they were sharing, would never happen again.

25/ FLASHBACK FIDELITY

"I FIRST TRANSITIONED to Dementia on the evening of November 14, 1940, along with my brothers, Cearul and Cheshire. We lived in a flat in downtown Coventry, an English city north of London. It was the height of World War II, and Nazi Germany had started its bombing Blitz against Britain a few months earlier. We were all at home, along with our parents and our other brothers and sisters. We had three sisters and two more brothers, all varying ages from one to seventeen. There were eight of us children in total."

Declan's voice was reflective, as if talking about something he hadn't discussed in a long time. The record on the phonograph skipped for a second and restarted from the beginning of the jazz number. Declan rolled his eyes and continued.

"The air raid sirens had been going on for some time, but we all quietly ate our dinner as if nothing out of the ordinary was happening. We didn't have anywhere to go, and Father didn't want us all crammed into a makeshift bomb shelter like sardines. He didn't want to run the risk of losing one of us in the crowds, so we stayed in our flat and ate dinner and listened to the radio like any other night. After dinner, Mum put on one of her Billie Holiday records. I remember this moment as

clear as yesterday; my parents dancing in the center of the living room, laughing and twirling as the bombs began to fall."

Violet squeezed Declan's hand as they danced in the clock tower, his voice turning more sober as he spoke.

"From a distance bombs sounded like toy guns," Declan continued. "My parents continued to dance as bombs fell closer. There was nothing they could do. I remember them pulling us all together, my mum holding our infant brother Albert in her arms. Even though people screamed outside our windows, we still danced.

"Fires raged outside. Buildings were being destroyed and yet our flat stood sound. We danced and danced. As Coventry fell, we danced. We held our arms around each other, my father's eyes gleaming from the firelight outside, and we danced.

"Then the first bomb struck our flat.

"It shook the building like an earthquake. It sheered the entire side of our flat right off. The ceiling collapsed on top of us, crushing my sister Aoife to death. Rubble had crashed into my shoulder and cut me deep, but Cheshire was there, blood streaming from a gash in his forehead. He pulled me aside as the floor caved in.

"Father was slumped over, tiny arms and legs sticking out from under him. Rubble and dust covered his body. I remember Cearul turning him over. My father's head was caved in, completely crushed on one side. I vomited. I'd never seen anything like that before. Underneath him were Maeve and Nellie, and my brother Patrick. They were covered in blood and dust, their eyes staring open and lifeless. Dead.

"Another bomb slammed into our building. Cheshire lost his balance from the explosion and nearly tumbled down into the flat below, but I grabbed his shoulder and pulled him back. There was crying, the sound of a baby, and I spun around to see Mum crumpled in the corner, covered in pieces of plaster and metal. Blood covered her dress and face, her hand still clutching onto Albert. She was dead too, but my baby brother wasn't. I snatched him up and made my way to Cearul and Cheshire. Cearul had found a way down into the flat below.

And I remember as we left our home that the record was still playing on the phonograph in the corner even though nobody was dancing anymore.

"We continued down. The building was nearing collapse. Bodies lay in heaps. Those who were not dead were begging for us to help them, but we were children. I was no more than twelve at the time and there was nothing I could do but leave them. Bombs continued to fall on Coventry. When we thought we could go no further, Cheshire found a hole in a wall that led into the adjacent building's basement.

"If I remember correctly, it was an antiques store. The entire room was filled with mirrors. They were covered with dust. A few lay broken in shards on the dirt floor, but most were still whole and not cracked.

"More bombs shook the building and mirrors toppled. We were going to wait out the shelling in that small room until Cearul noticed that one of the mirrors was smoking. He walked over to investigate when the ceiling caved in on one side of the room, nearly trapping Cheshire under debris. Cearul put his hand to the mirror and it passed through. He looked up and saw that unmistakable glow of fire above, the wooden floor lit and burning. He yelled for us to follow as he plunged into the mirror.

"Cheshire followed immediately behind Cearul, and then I jumped through as the ceiling disintegrated. You know what happened next."

"You transitioned into Dementia," Violet said, her words quiet with emotion.

"Yes."

"And what happened to Albert? I haven't seen him."

Declan sighed, twirling Violet to the music. "He was already dead before I even made it to Dementia. The blood, it wasn't my mother's. It was his."

"Declan," Violet said, staring into his eyes, "I'm so sorry."

He nodded. "It's okay. That all happened a long time ago. But I still come here and listen to the music so I don't forget what happened, even though I stayed in Dementia to do just that."

"Why didn't you force yourself to forget it? Or give that memory to the Accountant? That's horrific, to see your family die like that."

He breathed slowly, as if collecting his thoughts. "Because there's more to learn in remembering than in forgetting. There's a certain flash-back fidelity to it all. And I hope you learn that soon. Your true powers won't manifest until you do."

"You don't know that."

"You're right," Declan agreed. "But it worked for me, and I think it will for you too. It's all I have to hope for. If that isn't enough to trigger the prophecy in you, then I've got nothing else to give."

"But I don't see how repeatedly replaying the accident in my head will lead to understanding more than I already do. I know I caused my sister's brain damage. I put her in the hospital and exposed her to the slurpers. I'm the reason she's forgotten me. There's so much pain in those memories that I don't want to remember it anymore. I just want to forget them. Forever."

"And if you do that," Declan said, all energy slipping from him like a dying breath, "then Recollection City will forever remain in the dark, and Dementia will continue to spread like a cancer into the real."

Violet bit her lip. She didn't know which way was up anymore. To remember or to forget, that was the question of the moment. And right now, she so desperately wanted to forget the car crash, wanted to strike that memory of Karin bleeding out across the snow, that she was tempted to let Dementia perforate into reality a little bit more just to ease her pain.

Just to forget her own mistake.

"So," Violet said, trying to derail the current topic, "how did Oriana Palms fit into all of this?"

"Well," Declan said, tilting his head so Violet couldn't see his eyes. "She was the love of my life. And I'm the reason she's dead."

———

"Oriana transitioned from Sorrento, a small Italian town on the coast, a dozen years or so after we did. She was a newfallen and had skin so luminescent you'd think the sun rode on her back. You know that glow you get from tanning?"

"No, I don't, actually." Violet looked askance at Declan. "But I know of it."

"Right, my apologies. Of course." His cheeks flared between the whorls of shadow. "Anyway, that was Oriana Palms. Bright and beautiful, with tiny sun freckles that peppered her cheeks. We fell for each other immediately. I'm not sure why she was so drawn to me, because there were a lot more Rememberists around in those days, and a lot of them were vying for Oriana's affections—including Cearul and Cheshire. But she gravitated to me nonetheless.

"I was convinced she was the Princess Electric. She glowed in the dimmest of light, and her smile sparked a room. I was still relatively new to Dementia and the Rememberists and the history of this place, but to me, she was the electric girl the prophecy referred to."

"Does the prophecy mention the princess being an albino?" Violet asked. "Or did she just glow?"

Declan shook his head. "Oriana wasn't an albino, if that's what you're asking. Not that it would matter—there's no mention of that in the prophecy. And we've seen no pattern or reason why some newfallens glow, whereas most do not. It's a mystery." He shrugged. "Anyway, over time I convinced Oriana that she was indeed the princess by spiking the glitter around her so that she could summon Glitterglam, and by putting her in situations where she was guaranteed to come out on top."

"Like what you've been doing with me," Violet said, deflated. She still held Declan's hand, her other hand on his waist, dancing.

"Yes and no," Declan said with a rise of his shoulders. "Yes, regarding you summoning Glitterglam without you actually doing it. I just used simple cantrips and magician games using my own powers and the abundance of glitter. And no, in that I haven't put you in any posi-

tion that you were guaranteed to win. Although you handled yourself well in the battle with Parminder, you would never have won that. With Oriana? She beat Parminder. But it was rigged, and in the end, my entire wish for her to be the Princess Electric failed."

"So what happened?" Violet asked as Declan twirled her.

"We had intelligence on a secret entrance into the Palace of Memories End, somewhere in the Hippocampus sprawl between the Borough of Diencephalon and the palace proper. We went in with two tangles—our term for deployment teams. They were our best Rememberists, but things went sour. The intelligence was bad, and our tangles lost communication with each other, and back to the operator. We were running blind in one of the most dangerous areas of Dementia. Eventually my tangle was separated from each other. Each Rememberist was picked off silently, as if snatched up in the middle of the night by the Gestapo. Soon it was only Oriana and me. We were ambushed by memjacks, led by the queen's dragon, Vermillion."

"The dragon we saw while twisthopping?"

"That would be her," he said, nodding in agreement as they danced to the music. "I was pinned in an alley by memjacks, across the street from Oriana. She was so sure of herself that she stood and confronted Vermillion. She stood there in the electric light from the sprawl, oblivious to the fact that she'd never actually summoned Glitterglam on her own. The dragon toyed with her, and when she finally blew out a stream of liquid nightmare, Oriana threw her arms out to pull the glitter toward her, to defend herself. Nothing happened. The liquid nightmare slammed into Oriana, knocking her to the ground. She grabbed her head, screaming. Her hands desperately tried to corral the glitter, but it just hung in the air.

"Then Vermillion pounced. She snatched Oriana Palms up in her maw and flew back to the palace. I've never seen nor heard from her again."

Violet didn't say anything. She just let Declan lead their dance.

"I was so enraged, I destroyed those memjacks barricading the alley,

found a twist and hopped back to Pallium bloody and barely alive."

"I'm sorry."

Declan shook his head. "There's nothing for you to apologize for. I caused her to believe something that wasn't, because I was selfish, because I desperately wanted to believe. And I know that in a way I haven't changed, that I was going down the same road with you. But I've made adjustments. The rest of the Rememberists understand what we were trying to do by only feeding you pieces of information, by allowing you to only see what you needed to see. And I'm sorry for that, Violet." He took her arms in his hands and held her out so that he could fully look at her. "I'm truly sorry for not being forthright with you from the start, but you have to believe that this is everything. There's nothing more for me to hide. No more smoke and mirrors. You know how I came here, and you know what happened to Oriana Palms."

Violet stared into Declan's eyes. "You haven't told me why you wanted to remember."

Declan let a breath shudder from his lips. "Before I turned eighteen, I went back to Coventry numerous times. And every time I stood at the very spot where our flat had once stood, where I had danced to my mum's records and laughed and cried with my family. It was there that I realized this was who I am. That this catastrophic event had shaped me, and without it, I would not be who I am today. I had no life left in the real, and so I came back to Dementia to let my brothers know about what I'd learned of myself.

"But it wasn't until years after Oriana's death that I came up to this very spot, high atop the clock tower, and replayed every memory that I could remember from childhood onward. I stepped through the imprints of my life again, focusing on the moments of pain and of loss, and analyzed how they affected me—how they *shaped* me. It was only then that I fully learned how to fly and manipulate shadow in all the ways I can now."

"From here?" Violet asked, looking across Recollection City.

"Yes." He took Violet's hand and led her to the edge of the lookout.

"However, my realization did not come easily. Even though I understood the power of memory, I had also looked deep within and didn't like what I saw. I was so depressed over what I had done to Oriana. Years of regret and hating myself. Keeping the pain bottled inside only to fester and rot. Up until this point my powers had only shown themselves in fits and starts. I could only do simple cantrips to manipulate glitter and shadow, fooling people like Oriana into thinking they were someone they weren't. Like I'd been doing to myself. So I walked to this very spot and stepped off the edge. I figured either my powers would kick in, or I'd turn to glitter and be done with everything."

"And you flew?"

"I flew," Declan said, the corners of his mouth curling upward. "Like a bird, I caught air and sailed above the rooftops of Recollection City. I flew so quick and furious that I felt the wind again. I flew so fast that the glitter brushed my cheeks and made me feel as if the winds were whistling through the West Midlands again. It wasn't until I made my way back to the clock tower that I realized what had happened—that I had seen the true power of memory."

"Which is what?" Violet asked.

"Clarity."

Violet shook her head in disagreement. She wasn't sure what to believe anymore, especially after Declan had openly admitted to fixing the glitter she'd used to summon the fabled sword. There was too much pain wrapped up in the car accident for her to easily brush it aside. She hated herself for putting her sister in the mental hospital. For exposing her to the slurpers.

As if having one more nightmare would make me a better person for what I've done. Forgetting the whole thing would be so much easier. So painless.

"I don't know," Violet said. "You went through all of that with your family, with Oriana, and in the end, what did you learn from it? You ended up doing the same thing to me. You tried to trick me into thinking I'm someone I'm not. That's not cool."

"Violet," Declan said reaching out and taking her by the wrist. "You're not seeing the whole picture. *You must remember to forget the pain.*"

"I think I'd rather forget altogether."

"No," Declan said, pleading, his grip on her wrist more vise-like. He was pulling her toward the edge of the balcony. "Come fly with me. You'll see."

"We don't have the time for that," Violet said, tugging him back toward the glass lantern. "I have to see Cheshire."

"I'm right here," came a voice from behind Violet. She glanced sideways, and saw Cheshire standing in the stairwell, the moonlight silver against his skin. "Leave her alone, Declan. You've had your chat and she clearly doesn't want to be entertained any further. It's my turn."

"Fine," Declan said through clenched teeth.

"Melody is in the hospital and stable. Only time will tell if she can shake the nightmares. I spoke to the others and we're leaving first thing tomorrow morning to get Violet's sister's memories from the Gracile processing facility. Rest up, good brother. You will need all of your energy tomorrow."

"Violet, please listen to what I said." Declan stared at her, ignoring his brother's words. "You must remember to forget. Don't think it'll be so easy to just forget and move on. The only person that works for is the Queen of Glass." Declan let go of Violet's wrist and she stumbled backward, landing in Cheshire's arms.

"And it works for me," Cheshire said, looking past Violet to his brother.

"I know," Declan said. "And that scares me more than the Queen of Glass herself."

There was a brief silence and then the snap of a trench coat caught in the wind. Violet turned around to see emptiness where Declan had stood a moment before. He was framed within the disco ball moon, a streak of black against the moonlight shimmer, and then he was gone, the phonograph skipping static through the silence of the clock tower.

26/ CHASING THE BUTTERFLY

THE ELEVATOR WAS WAITING for Cheshire and Violet as they reached the bottom of the clock tower. Thankfully, it only took a fraction of the time to descend all the stairs than it did to climb to the Ayrton Light. Inside the elevator, Cheshire pressed a button that read *Cadogan*.

Violet remembered stopping there when Declan had been trying to find his brother.

Violet fidgeted with the kaleidoscope in her pocket. There was a lot to take in from her conversation with Declan, most notably that Declan had not been completely honest with her for a second time, even though he promised to do so a day earlier. It wasn't like she had any idea what he was hiding. Nor did she know that he was trying to manipulate her into thinking she was the Princess Electric. He should have volunteered that information way earlier. Not now. Not on the final night before trancing back into Recollection City to steal her sister's memories from the one person who had been the most honest with her—the Queen of Glass.

What in the world were you thinking, Declan?

"He means well," Cheshire said leaning against Stem's interior,

hands in his pockets. He was staring at Violet, analyzing the confusion that etched her face.

"I'm not sure about that," Violet said, trying not to make eye contact behind her sunglasses. "I'm not sure anyone around here means well—especially you. Why didn't you tell me that Declan was setting me up all these times?" She looked at Cheshire. "You even helped with faking Glitterglam. You *knew* that I wasn't summoning the sword, and yet you didn't tell me. Why?"

Cheshire shrugged. "Simple. You didn't need to know. Not then. Not even now, really. I believe in you, and now you need to believe in yourself. Being told about the prophecy in detail wasn't going to accelerate the process."

"That's easy for you to say. Taking me to the queen behind everyone's back is hardly proof that you believe in me. Why didn't you tell me about how you fell to Dementia, about the Blitz and bombs and room of mirrors? Why did I have to hear all of that from your brother?"

"Because I don't remember it all," Cheshire said distantly. "Every year, on the anniversary of our transition into Dementia, Declan recounts the story to me in the clock tower. And every year, as time progresses, I forget each moment."

"Why?" Violet asked, puzzled.

"Because," Cheshire said as the elevator clanged to a stop, "I chase the butterflies away."

————

Violet followed Cheshire along a hallway of paisley wallpaper and sconces. He stopped in front of a small door, a tarnished plate reading Room 118. He dug in his trench coat pocket, pulled out a small brass key and opened the door. Cheshire motioned for her to enter with a sweep of his arm.

Wide, wood planks made for a rather warm floor, and an antique desk sat off to the side with an emerald green reading lamp. A large and

neatly made bed filled most of the room with a white duvet that looked as fluffy as whipped meringue, and dark chocolate brown throw pillows —with matching velvet headboard. She was so tired she wanted to climb onto the bed immediately, but thought better of it.

Beyond the bed stood three ceiling-high windows, with the central window cut into a small alcove. Silk curtains framed the windows, hanging like curls of chocolate fondant. In the central window stood a table with a glorious glass vase with a series of small tubes and spigots sticking out of it. Instead of flowers, water filled the vase, ice cubes refracting the warm light that spilled from the lamps scattered about the room.

"Your room makes me hungry," Violet said, looking for someplace to sit other than the bed. "Who lived here?"

"Well," Cheshire said, pulling out the desk's chair for Violet to sit in, "nobody really lived here. It's a room in the Cadogan Hotel, in London. Oscar Wilde was arrested while staying in this room."

"And you stay here because?" Violet asked, pushing the chair back under the desk's frame.

"It's got a certain charm that I haven't found in any of the other places that have twisted into Pallium. Everyone has their taste, like Declan with the clock tower, or Melody with Moulin Rouge. This is mine." Cheshire swept his arm in front of him. "Room 118 at the Cadogan Hotel. It reminds me of the flat we had in Coventry."

"So," Violet said, unbuttoning her peacoat, "are you ready to talk to me now? I want to know about Cearul. The birdman. Everything. I meant what I said in the elevator, that I don't want to hear anything more from you unless you're explaining yourself."

Cheshire walked past her and went to one of the large windows beside the alcove. He brushed the curtain aside and stared out into the glitter-black night. He whispered, "Yes."

"Good," Violet said. "You can start by telling me about Cearul. I heard you on Gapstow Bridge talking to Mister Cinder. Heard a lot more than I wanted to."

"I had a feeling," Cheshire said, still staring out the window. "Why didn't you tell the others?"

"Because I didn't know anyone. Didn't know what they'd do. To you or me. But I came close a couple times because your actions weren't making you look good—and they still aren't."

"Story of my life." Cheshire chuckled. "Listen, about Cearul. Let's just say he's rather self-centered and cavalier and doesn't give a shit about anyone else."

"But the birdman said he's out trying to find other Rememberists in Dementia. Is that true?"

Cheshire nodded, the light from outside the windows playing along the curtains. "Unfortunately yes."

Violet twisted up her face. "Then how is that such a bad thing?"

"Because he left us. He rallied up a few Rememberists here in Pallium and took off into Dementia alone and offline, breaking protocol. Had to try and be the bloody hero. But in the end he left me. Left Declan. Left all of us."

Cheshire's words were spiked with emotion, a mixture of anger and betrayal.

"We had made a promise to each other," he said, smacking his fist against the window frame. Panes rattled. "The three of us had vowed to never be alone again after the rest of our family had perished in the Blitz, right in front of our eyes. In our arms. That if we were going to die, we would die together. If we left Pallium and went into Dementia, we went together. Everything was to be done together. Like the Three fucking Musketeers."

"How is that different than you galivanting around Dementia yourself?" Violet asked, puzzled at how Cheshire could make different rules for himself. "You've been meeting with the queen and the birdman and who knows who else."

"Good question," he said, playing with a fold of curtain between his fingers. "And the answer is there's no difference. Was I going out and

meeting the birdman before Cearul took off? Yes, but rarely. It wasn't until he left us that I really fell apart."

Cheshire paused for a moment and Violet sensed that he wasn't finished talking so she waited, watching him continue to pleat the curtain.

"Our parents were gone," he finally continued. "We were young boys when we fell into Dementia. Declan was twelve. Cearul was four-teen. And I was only eleven. I looked up to them, but mostly Cearul. The promise was his idea. Those first few years here were a living night-mare, one that I still feel I'm trapped in. So it was Cearul's idea to make the promise that we would always be together. And he was the one to break it."

"I'm sorry, Cheshire, but it sounds like he means well. He's trying to find other Rememberists," Violet said, not sure how to navigate the conversation. She couldn't imagine losing her sister and her parents all at once and being alone in Dementia at such a young age. Tears welled in her eyes as she pictured herself in that situation. It was difficult at seventeen trying to understand Dementia, let alone at eleven. And she still had her mother and sister.

Once she got Karin's memories back inside her sister's head, Violet promised herself she'd go talk to her mom. Figure out their shit. Both Declan and Cheshire's stories proved that you never know when your last moment with someone could be.

"He only cares about being the hero," Cheshire said, his voice wavering. "I have nothing to say to him. The Brothers Gloss are only me and Declan now. In my eyes, he died the moment he tranced out of here ten years ago."

Violet couldn't believe it had been so long since Cearul left. Had he really been gone for a decade? They must have been very tight for him to be this upset still. Even Declan didn't discuss Cearul when prodded. Family issues cut deep.

She needed to change the topic. "So what about chasing butterflies. Are you talking about consuming? Like what the queen did to one of my

memories?" She took her coat off and hung it on the back of the desk chair, hoping he would say no.

"Yes," Cheshire said, still looking out the window. "Chasing the butterfly. Breaking wings. *CrystalMem*. It means," Cheshire ran a finger down a windowpane, tracing a bead of condensation with a squeaky vibration, "that I'm addicted to forgetting."

"Great," Violet scoffed. "You're a druggie."

"It's not like that," Cheshire said. Pain laced each word. She had never felt such rawness from him before.

"Then tell me what it's like."

Cheshire shuddered out a sigh. After a moment of hesitation, he finally said, "Fine. I will tell you what I can remember. And I will tell you what I know. But the in-betweens? The small details that fall through the cracks between the remembering and the forgetting? Those are lost."

Violet wanted to walk over to him, to put her hand on his shoulder, but instead she just said, "Okay."

Cheshire replied with a slight hesitation, not leaving the window. "After Oriana Palms's death, Declan came to an understanding with the way the universe works. Or at least Dementia. Through his grief and guilt, he found a certain enlightenment. I've never developed that understanding. And I've certainly never found enlightenment. What I found was an insight of a different sort."

"Which was?" Violet eyed Cheshire's silhouette against the gauze of inner curtain.

"That sometimes it's okay to forget. That for as much as my brother and the other Rememberists preach about the power of memory, there's just as much to learn from forgetting. And it's so much more painless."

"How's that possible?" Violet asked. "How did you develop your powers then? Declan says I need to believe in myself and the power of remembrance to release them."

"There are two methods of madness, Violet. Two schools of thinking: that of the Rememberists, and that of the Delirium Directorate.

One believes in the power of recollection, and one in the power of forgetting."

"And you went down the path of forgetting and still opened up your powers? And you hid that from the Rememberists? From Declan? You betrayed him."

"Yes, but for good reason," Cheshire said, running his pale fingers along a stretch of silk curtain, a slight glow washing across the window-panes. "Before turning eighteen and being shut out of the real, I also went back several times. But I didn't see the same things as Declan. I saw death and destruction. I saw every moment of our lives being burned away by firestorms, by buildings collapsing. Our family being crushed to death in front of us. But Declan kept preaching the power of remembrance, of what we could learn from these painful memories. Other Rememberists revealed powers beyond their wildest dreams by doing just that—by replaying key, defining moments of their lives. Yet others, like myself, couldn't unlock anything—and those Rememberists either died trying, left Dementia altogether, or joined the queen. In my mind I kept going back to the real, standing there in the ruins of Coventry and envisioning every torturous memory, trying with all my might to unlock my powers, whatever they were.

"Yet I could never process the horrific images I'd bottled up inside like Declan could. They haunted me, tormented me, like your car crash visions. One day I left Pallium to get away from the headache this culture of remembrance was setting on me. I was approached by a man in a feather coat who said he could help with the pain that was inside my mind."

"So Mister Cinder got to you early on," mused Violet.

Cheshire nodded. "He took me to see the Queen of Glass, and there she made me a similar offer as she did to you. She would help me forget the pain if I would help her when called upon. At first I was repulsed by her offer. I would never switch allegiances and betray my friends or my brothers. And so I left her courtroom swearing that I'd return with the Rememberists to kill her. She let me go without hesitation. In hindsight,

I think she knew I'd be back to accept her offer. She had seen something in me that I hadn't seen yet myself."

"What was that?" Violet asked, although Cheshire didn't seem to hear.

"When I returned to Pallium, my powers still never manifested. Frustrated, I couldn't stop thinking about the queen's offer. Not because I wanted to join her, but that I could have the pain of the Blitz removed from my head and still be a Rememberist, as ironic as that sounds. I mean, really, what was the queen going to have me do? I wasn't part of the prophecy. I was just a fallen soul, lost and without direction.

"As I thought about it more and more, I realized I could give myself purpose if I accepted the queen's offer. She'd erase my pain, but in doing so, I would have access to her. I'd be closer to her than any Rememberist had ever been. I could learn about her methods of operation and gather intelligence for the Rememberists, without her or them knowing."

"You're a double agent?" asked Violet. She had not considered this before and suddenly she trusted Cheshire a bit more. He was fighting for and against the Queen of Glass and the Rememberists, which somehow felt like less of a full betrayal.

"If that's what you call it. It would've been the best of both worlds. The queen could help me forget, and I could learn how to bring about her downfall at the same time. So I accepted her offer.

"And, Violet, having my bad memories erased was everything I thought it would be. It was heaven. Euphoric. I had every horrific memory scraped from my head. I felt a sudden weightlessness, and with that came unimaginable powers. I could bend and shape light like a god. I could take the slightest flicker of a candle and illuminate the entire sky. Light became both a weapon and an object of beauty. I created stars in the palm of my hand and made them dance in the heavens.

"I was stronger and faster than Cearul and Declan combined, or any other Rememberist for that matter. But then my powers slowly waned. Over a few days I grew weak and gaunt and so I visited the queen. She refused to see me. The golden doors of Cerebrum were closed, the

Palace of Memories End sealed off from my admittance. I could barely walk and thought I was going to die—until the man in the feather coat came to my side once again. He offered me a packet of crystalMem and a syringe. I crawled into a derelict building and found a room that was in a quasi-solid state. It was there I took my first hit of crystalMem. Once again I felt euphoric. I felt alive. Powerful. I sparked stars and found my way out of the sprawl, back to Pallium.

"But something wasn't right. My powers only lasted a few days before they stated to fade again. There was such a potent pull to consume more crystalMem that I hunted for the feather-coated man. I didn't have to look far. He was waiting for me against a lamppost in Medulla, as if he were expecting me. He took me to the queen, where she taught me how to scrub memories like a memjack slurper. Taught me how to leach my own memories and cut them with liquid delirium, how to cook them down into crystalMem.

"And so every year I welcomed Declan's recanting of our fall. I allowed those memories to fill up my head. I fermented their pain until I could no longer take their horror. Slowly, over days and weeks and months I'd scrub them from my head, creating more crystalMem so that I could chase the butterflies, to live and forget and live again. To power the stars in my eyes.

"And I was shown all of this knowledge, all of this power, for one simple return of a favor."

"Which is?" Violet asked, walking toward him. His haunting story reverberated in Violet, his pain a beacon to her. She understood wanting to forget, wanting to erase grief from your mind.

Cheshire turned around. Tears trailed down his cheeks, glinting in the lamplight like silver threads. "The favor is that I bring any newfallen who exhibits a certain brightness to the Queen of Glass when asked."

Violet took Cheshire's hands. They were cold and clammy in her luminescent palms. "But you did that and I survived to see another day. Besides, you also brought me there so I could have the good memories of my sister reinstated, right?"

"Memories that I siphoned from you."

She looked into Cheshire's eyes, their usual cerulean crispness broken like a kaleidoscopic rainbow. Like Queen Zamelerish's. "But that was an accident. I damaged the siphoner when I bumped it."

"I'm so sorry," he said, the tears on his cheeks illuminated like quicksilver. "I'm so addicted to chasing butterflies that I took those memories from you on purpose. In the heat of the moment I lost myself and didn't stop you from opening the floodgates."

"What?" Violet said, dropping Cheshire's hands and stepping back from him. "How could you?"

He raised his hands up. "I'm sick, Violet. Consumed with hunger for more butterflies. I'm sorry." He wiped tears away with the back of his hand. "Once I came to terms with what happened, I set up the meeting with the queen to have them returned. I had to fix what I'd done. Any negative memory can be reinserted into someone's mind with little effort, but to replace happy ones, well, the queen is the only one who can do that."

Violet kept shaking her head. She couldn't believe what she was hearing. Cheshire was an addict and he was using her memories to barter with his dealer. He was more broken than Declan.

"Decades have passed and I've yet to see a chink in her armor," Cheshire continued. "So I thought by having her reinstate your memories I'd expose her in ways I've never seen. That maybe, just maybe, I'd learn how to bring her down."

Violet took her hand and wiped a tear from Cheshire's face, its wetness cool against her glowing albino skin. The Queen of Glass could erase memories. She could take away Violet's pain. And then they could figure out a way to break her.

"Cheshire, it's okay," Violet said, her voice calm. "I want to forget the car accident and what I've done to my sister. I've wished it, but never knew it could happen for real."

Cheshire shuddered as he sucked in a breath. "You don't know what you're saying. I'm not telling you all of this so you'll want to forget. I'm

telling you this so you'll want to remember. You must reject the queen's offer."

"But why?" Violet asked, confused. "You're the one that brought me to her."

"I know, and I shouldn't have. There's something you must see, but if I show you, you must promise me something."

Violet looked up into Cheshire's fractured kaleidoscope eyes and nodded. "Okay."

"You must promise not to look at me any differently. And you must not share what you've heard or are about to see with anyone. Not even Declan. Do you promise?"

Cheshire was so deadpan serious Violet couldn't help but wonder what was so horrific to warrant such a promise, but she agreed.

He reached up and started to unzip his jacket, one zipper and then another.

Violet wasn't sure what he was hiding under his jacket. She watched his hands move with hesitation, almost shaking.

"No, it's not like that," he said, as if to mollify any concern she may have that he was looking for something else.

Violet exhaled and placed her fingers on one of the remaining zippers. "Let me help."

He relaxed slightly as she took over, his hands dropping to his sides. When she undid the last zipper, Violet peeled his coat back and let it crumple to the floor. Underneath he wore a simple cotton shirt, which he let Violet unbutton. She undid the final button and his body tensed. He reached up and held the two halves of the shirt tight together, as if he were standing in a windstorm.

"It's okay," Violet said, overlaying his hands with hers. They were winter-cold. "Whatever you're hiding will not change anything."

"Please look at me with your own eyes," he said.

"What? These are my—"

"No, take off your sunglasses. Let me see your eyes."

Violet swallowed. Hesitated for a moment. She never took her

sunglasses off, not for anyone. She felt naked without them, exposed and vulnerable. The room was not well lit, and so her eyes would be able to process the light.

Exhaling slowly, she reached up and slid them off, setting the sunglasses on the table beside her.

She looked up and Cheshire smiled, his eyes warm in the soft lamplight.

"You're beautiful," he said, running his hand along her face.

"Thank you," was all Violet could say, her body relaxing against his touch.

Cheshire let go of his shirt and nodded. Violet pulled it back in one movement, letting the shirt slide off his arms and tumble to the floor. What she saw made her want to gasp, to cover her mouth and scream and cry, but she did none of those things.

Instead she placed her hand on his chest and felt its coldness.

She ran her fingers along the ribs of lead.

Along the panes of stained glass.

She brought her fingers to his chest and trailed them across the ruby panes illuminated by her soft glow. Layers upon layers of glass filled his torso, melding into the flesh of his stomach and shoulders and neck. Each vein, each organ an exact replica in exquisite blown glass. And there, deep inside his chest, Violet saw his stained glass heart, shimmering like a setting sun.

"This," Cheshire said, pulling Violet's gaze up toward him with a soft touch under her chin, "is why you must not accept the queen's proposal. This is the price I have paid for my power, for the forgetting. With every hit, the crystalMem is slowly turning me into a prince of forgetting. And if there is no way to reverse this, I will soon be at the queen's side in Cerebrum forever. But you have the choice now, Violet. If you want to forget the accident and its aftershocks, I won't begrudge you that pleasure. We'll find a way to strike those memories from your mind. But no matter what happens, no matter what the queen offers you, you can't accept it. She will find a way inside you, and when she

does, you will cease to exist the way you do now. Your light will be snuffed out.

"You will no longer be electric."

"But Cheshire," Violet said, trailing her fingers on the panes of glass that constructed his chest, "there must be a way to stop this. I want to help you."

"There is no way that I know of," Cheshire said, coddling Violet's head against him. "For now, let us enjoy our time together and rest. Tomorrow morning we depart to get your sister's memories."

Cheshire laid down on the bed and Violet followed, resting her head against his windowpane chest. She felt the rise and fall of his breathing, listened to the fragile clink-thrum of his stained glass heart. And as she drifted into sleep, all she could think about was how she would never forget this moment.

27/ PICTURES AND PILLS

VIOLET AWOKE to the hotel room door closing.

Her heart kickstarted in her chest, immediately thinking about Karin.

Today is the day.

She swung herself out of the bed and walked across to the writing desk tucked against the wall. On the desk was a note from Cheshire:

V,
Make use of the shower and anything else you want. Swing by the
Ravelin to arm yourself, and then meet us at the Royal Palace of Madrid.
Don't dawdle.
C

A silver tray of fresh fruit, coffee, and a croissant sat beside the note. Violet wanted to throw on her clothes and go meet the Rememberists to not waste any time, but thought it best to eat and shower first. She'd need her energy to deal with another outing into Recollection City.

Violet ate voraciously, the food tasting so much better than what she'd had in the cafeteria the day before. In the shower, memories of the

previous night washed over her. Images of Cheshire glinted in her mind, of his sun shower eyes, of the layers of blown glass that covered his chest and the stained glass heart beating within.

She quickly got dressed after the shower, energized and refreshed. As she slipped on her peacoat, something glinted on the small table in the alcove. There, sitting beside a crystal water fountain and tin of sugar cubes was an ornate box, covered with crushed glass and beads—a box like the one found beside Melody. This one was darker and heart-shaped, with chips of onyx and jade and tiny shadows that swirled over the contours of crushed glass.

A used syringe sat beside the silver tray, tiny droplets of rainbow and blood oozing out of the needle's tip. The box was unlocked. Inside were more syringes and needles and vials of crystallized rainbow, all perfectly placed within midnight velvet. All perfectly haunting.

Cheshire had forgotten to put away his box of forgetting.

A small piece of paper stuck out from a fold of velvet. Violet took the paper, turning it over. It was an old black-and-white photograph of a large family. They were posed in front of a Christmas tree, smiles smeared across their sugarplum faces. Violet traced each one with her finger. *The Glosses.* They looked beautiful and happy and oblivious to their fate. Even Declan, who Violet picked out immediately, was smiling, standing beside his mother with his token wisp of hair and sunken eyes.

Two of the boys in the family were scribbled out. One boy stood off to the side, his face etched over with black ink. His face was drawn on so much that the paper was nearly transparent. As if he'd been erased.

The other, slightly taller than the others and standing beside his father, also had his face covered with the same black ink. Violet assumed that was Cearul.

She placed the picture back into the heart-shaped box of paraphernalia and closed the lid. It would be so easy to let go of the pain; so easy to forget the car accident altogether. The queen's offer danced around her thoughts, teasing her to reach out and grab it. But first she had one

thing left to do. She left Room 118 and went to arm herself in the Ravelin.

Things were about to get sideways.

————

Violet entered the Royal Palace of Madrid so weighed down with ammunition her coat didn't move as she walked. Nobody was in the Ravelin when she was there, so Violet selected another pair of Mini Uzis and wrapped numerous clip-belts around her torso. She also crammed as many clips as she could into her pockets.

"So she *is* alive," Parminder said, standing in the middle of the room. Her black leather dress coiled about her like licorice, silver zippers shining. A duffel bag lay at her feet.

Violet looked around the room, ignoring the apiarist. "Where's Cheshire and Declan?"

"Right here," Cheshire said, standing up from behind the operator's station. "Just making some final adjustments to the thermionic valves. We can't have things break while we're trancing this time."

Seeing Cheshire again made Violet's heart flutter. She looked at Cheshire in a different light now, one of abstract secrets and colored glass. Deep under the folds of his trench coat beat a heart of glass, and she would do what she could to help prevent it from cracking. Although she didn't agree with a lot of the things he'd done, she had a deeper understanding of why. If only he could give up the crystalMem.

"Where's Declan?" Violet asked, taking a second quick look around the throne room. Dillinger and Morgan were also making final adjustments to equipment, but there was no sign of the other brother.

"He tranced into the Gracile District about thirty minutes ago," Morgan said, turning around from the box of vacuum tubes in front of Mirror 3. "He was adamant about scouting ahead to make sure we could trance closer to our target. He didn't want you exposed to the mental corruption of Gracile for too long while we advanced on the factory."

Violet wished Declan hadn't gone into Dementia without the Rememberists to back him up—or without her for that matter. She wanted to speak with him before they made their move on the factory. Violet didn't like how they'd parted on the clock tower; how he had jumped into the sky and disappeared before she had a chance to say goodbye.

She wanted to share a moment with him alone before she accepted the queen's offer.

Before I betray him.

"Gracile itself is no worse than any of the other districts within Medulla," Morgan said.

"Then why did he have to scout ahead?" Violet asked, concern making her mouth dry.

"Because," Parminder said, lugging her duffel bag toward Morgan and Mirror 3, "as you get closer to a processing facility, you are more exposed to rifts in the fabric of Dementia."

"The rifts play on you like a nightmare after waking," Morgan added, adjusting his eye patch. "You may not notice it, but the pollution generated from the processing of memories will seep into your psyche. It may make you look at things differently. Emotional drivers may be slightly...exaggerated. The glitter is more concentrated in these areas, which can weigh negatively on your emotions."

"We're only telling you this because you're going to have to take a pill before we trance." Parminder dropped her duffel bag in front of the mirror. "We all will."

"What kind of pill?" Violet asked.

"It's a mood stabilizer," Dillinger clarified. "Takes the edge off. It's called Chill. Because—"

"It mutes our emotions against the processing rifts," Cheshire said. "Without it, threats might look like a joke. A gun to your face may make you laugh. A laugh might make you hostile. Without dropping Chill before trancing, you'd be as emotional as a lit stick of dynamite in a nitroglycerin factory."

Dillinger stood up quickly, placing a hand against one of the headphones. He spoke feverishly into the small microphone beside the control deck, the monitors above flickering like mistuned televisions. "Declan has cleared his position for portal creation," Dillinger said, taking off the headphones. He adjusted numerous dials and pressed a few buttons. "He's just on the outskirts of the Packard Factory, northside. I'm setting the portal to open in Mirror 3 now."

Dillinger walked down from the operator station to where the rest of the Rememberists were standing. He handed a glass of water to Parminder and deposited a small pink pill into her hand. She pulled her veil back, popped the pill in her mouth and washed it down with a sip of water. Dillinger continued to distribute pills to Morgan and Cheshire. When he reached Violet, he plucked another pill from his pocket and handed it to her. She placed the pill on her tongue and rolled it around her mouth. It tasted like bubblegum. She took the glass from Cheshire and swallowed the pill with a quick drink.

While everyone popped Chill, the mirror behind Morgan had begun to froth and sweat, mist spilling down and across the thermionic valves and onto the plush red carpeting like a slow-motion waterfall. Dillinger took the glass from Violet, popped a pill, and took a swig of water.

"Wait," Violet said, taken aback, "aren't you staying here? We need an operator."

Dillinger shook his head. "Not this time."

"What do you mean?" Violet asked, confused. "I thought it was strict protocol to have an operator?" Violet turned to Cheshire.

"After the last time it appears so," Cheshire answered, nodding. "But there are so few of us left. We're entering a high-risk area of the Gracile district and can't afford to leave someone back this time. We need all the support we can get to even hope at succeeding in recovering your sister's memories, let alone getting out of there alive."

"So we're going in blind?" Violet asked, turning on her heels to

Morgan. Her head felt tingly and buoyant, as if she were drifting alone in the ocean. "What about Melody? We're leaving her alone?"

Mist swirled around the Morgan. "She's still in a coma and locked up in an isolation chamber. She'll be secure, even if Pallium is breached again."

"I'm not sure—"

"That's how it's going to be," Parminder said, walking toward the smoking mirror. "Take it or leave it."

Violet didn't say anything. There was no point. Parminder didn't trust Violet now, not after yesterday's stage show. No matter what she suggested, the apiarist would laugh at her face until Violet proved herself to Parminder.

"Now let's trance and meet up with Declan before he gets in a jam," Parminder continued.

"You heard the beekeeper," Dillinger said, hopping onto the mirror's table. "Time to hit the Packard Factory before the Chill hits."

"Where's the Packard Factory located?" Violet asked. "I mean, where is it in the real?"

Dillinger turned around, one leg in the mirror, hands holding on to its ornate frame for balance. "Where else would a massive, dilapidated factory reside?"

"I don't know," Violet said. "You tell me."

Dillinger smiled, his broken-bottle eyes flashing.

"Detroit, of course."

28/ ALL THAT GLITTERS

THE FIRST THING Violet noticed after trancing into Gracile was the amount of glitter-snow. It covered everything in swathes of white-gold, drifting up against the concrete and razor-wire wall that stood beside her. And it was cold, her breath spilling from her mouth in plumes.

The second thing she noticed was Declan. He was leaning with his back against the concrete wall, one foot against the wall for balance, trench coat collar up and hands in his pockets. His pewter-black hair was powdered with snow.

"Hello, Violet," he said.

Violet left the portal and walked toward him. "Declan, about last night—"

He took his hand out of his pocket and made a brushing away movement, as if not wanting to hear what she had to say. "Not everything can go the way we want in life, whether that life is in the real or in Dementia." He said that so matter-of-factly that Violet's heart trembled. "I just hope that when it comes time to make a decision, that you make it with your heart. I will continue to dream of an illuminated Recollection City, no matter what happens here. And that dream will always have you in it, even if you decide never to be in mine."

Violet melted. Her skin thrummed as if her body was statically charged, each snowflake, each mote of glitter sizzling against her skin. She wanted to step up to Declan and tell him that she'd always be there. *You will always be in my dreams.* And then she realized how false those words sounded as they reverberated in her mind. One day soon she would forget him, along with this moment.

Glitter drew Violet's eyes away from Declan, each flake smearing into the next. Her emotions felt raw and sharp. She wanted to yell and cry all at the same time. Was the Chill even working yet? Or was this what it's supposed to be like around a processing facility, emotions swirling around like a tornado?

Her head felt as if it had been pumped full of helium and then rubbed against carpet.

"Where's Dillinger?" Cheshire asked, stepping beside Violet. He had his assault rifle out.

"He went to scout ahead. Things are quiet at the factory. Something's off." Declan replied without looking at Cheshire. Instead, he continued to stare at Violet, as if she owed him a response. She answered by unholstering her Mini Uzis.

"They're expecting us, aren't they?" Parminder said, joining the group.

"If the Accountant sold our information to the queen as I'd expect him to do," Cheshire said, stepping up to a broken area of the wall. "Then yes, they're expecting us." He carefully stuck his head out to view the factory beyond. Violet knew that her sister's memories would be waiting for them inside. For some strange, inexplicable reason, she knew the queen would honor her offer and leave them to sweeten the already saccharine deal.

"We wouldn't have it any other way, would we?" Morgan said, exiting the portal. As he walked toward the group, the mirrored panel's hum increased in intensity. The frame twisted until it disappeared with a wisp of smoke and a boiling kettle hiss.

"No we wouldn't," Cheshire said. He leaned back from the crack in the wall, his lei sashaying around his neck. "Here comes Dill."

A moment later Dillinger ran through the crack, glitter and snow kicking up around his boots.

"So what's the story?" Morgan asked, tightening his embroidered coat for warmth.

"The factory's dead," the gunslinger said, sliding up against the wall. "Shut down. There's no sign of anybody."

That comment sobered Violet up. She refocused on Dillinger instead of watching the glitter sparkle in the factory's exterior lighting. "What do you mean no sign of anybody? Are my sister's memories inside? Are we at the right place?" An odd mix of anger and anticipation swashed inside her.

"Yes and yes." Dillinger unholstered his darlings. "We're at the right place, that's for sure. Your sister's memories are inside the northern building."

"How do you know that?" Violet asked. Her grip tightened on her guns.

"Because I saw them." Dillinger locked his bottle green eyes onto Violet. "They're in a vial on a table in the center of the main building. There's a thousand spotlights pointing right at the vial."

Violet ran over to Dillinger. She could feel herself crackling with hope, her skin bright under the glitter-snow. The idea that her sister's memories were inside the factory made her overflow with eagerness. Soon she'd be able to gift her sister with the ability to remember again. No longer would Violet be nameless. She would be *Violet*, Karin's sister. Emotion welled inside. Her hands shook, fluorescent bright. Tears bristled at the corners of her eyes. "But how do you know they're my sister's?"

"I walked right up to them," Dillinger said, his voice dead calm.

Declan stepped away from the wall. "All that glitters—"

"What was the serial number?" Violet said, cutting off Declan as if he wasn't even there.

Dillinger looked up to the sky and then back to Violet. "It matched."

"Should I go double-check?" Morgan offered.

"I think we'll be all right," Parminder said, looking at her scanner. "Let's move forward with caution."

The Packard Plant loomed before them like a toppled house of cards. Buildings shimmered and shifted under shadows cast by numerous floodlights. The sky above the factory swirled in a slow-motion vortex of rainbow clouds. The moon hung low within the rift, threatening to swallow the factory and setting the glitter-snow into a cosmic twinkle.

Something was otherworldly about the sky; about the air and how charged it was with random hits of naked emotion.

The Rememberists moved through a dilapidated cemetery, up and over train tracks, and across a field iced with snow-bright glitter. Violet's mind was crisp and focused, the large northern building her target. She stopped at a long ramp that led into the building proper, her breathing harsh and hot in the cold air. After confirming with Parminder's scanner that things looked okay, they continued into the factory.

The main room was the size of an aircraft hangar, filled with a spiderweb of glass tubes, some empty, some filled with liquid rainbow. The siphoned memories lit up the room like the Las Vegas strip, glitter-snow sashaying through the perforated ceiling. Multiple levels of catwalks rimmed the periphery, intermixed with conveyor belts and machinery.

The ramp continued down until it opened onto a wide floor. More machinery filled the sides of the building, dead quiet even though she could feel heat emanating from them. Wires were strung between machines and glass tubes, each wire suspending thousands of tiny glass vials. Some vials were empty. Others, however, were filled with liquid memory, refracting light like patio lanterns. And within some of those vials stretched the wings of butterflies, ready to shed their glass cocoons and take to the air.

Yet no butterflies flew in the building.

Instead they were trapped within larger cages, stacked like shipping crates. As Violet moved to the bottom of the ramp, she noticed other machines. Small machines. Machines that resembled clocks and bells and chemistry paraphernalia. Organs were spread throughout the machinery, their interconnected pipes twisting up through the ceiling. Tiny spigots were attached to each organ, and near each spigot sat metal tins filled with rainbow-colored sugar cubes that glowed gem-bright.

The entire building was an electric wonderland of moments.

A meth lab of memory.

And there, in the very center of the room lit by a thousand spotlights, sat a small table. But it wasn't the table that caught Violet's attention, nor the stillness of the factory. It was the flower that stood alone on the table. A vial of liquid rainbow bloomed from the top of a wire stem, delicately balanced as if the slightest of movements would make it wither and fall and break.

Violet ran to the glass flower, stopping just short of bumping into the table. Her chest heaved as she stared at the vial so precariously balanced on the wire stem. She read the serial number etched along the glass: DM-FGJf98f45gg. It matched what the Accountant had given her, letter for letter, number for number.

Tears began to stream down her cheeks, plunking softly on the metal table. A tidal wave of extreme joy and bitter sadness washed over her, crashing together within the core of her body. *My sister's memories...* Then she looked around and saw the millions of memories that had been siphoned, how they glittered in the filtered moonlight. So many lost moments, so many hollow minds.

Violet's stomach burbled with so much raw emotion that she wanted to puke. She couldn't focus. Sadness enveloped her and she nearly crumpled from its sudden weight. The liquid memories around her seemed to vibrate, as if calling to her, as if begging for release. CrystalMem sugar cubes sparkled under a million cocooned memories, each one precious to countless someone's, each one ready to be consumed.

As Violet glanced upward, a crystalMem sugar cube glinted turbo

blue in the distance. A sudden flash of car crash images ruptured her thoughts. The blue light of the snow plow. The red flash of emergency vehicles. The impact of the plow's blade, and how it cut through the car like a can opener.

The silent folding of a body between metal.

Violet shuddered from the imagery and pain. She swayed, confusion evaporating and replaced by an assurance of decision.

The possibility of being able to forget outweighed any benefit to remember.

She dropped her guns and reached out, ever so slowly, her moon-bright hand shaking.

Karin's memories...

Then she felt the pressure of a gun barrel against her back.

———

"You've got a decision to make before you touch that vial."

Violet raised her hands slowly and turned around. She wasn't surprised to be staring into the barrel of a gun.

"Dillinger?" Parminder added. "What the hell are you doing?"

"Shut your hole, bee bitch," Dillinger snapped. "If any of you so much as move I'll turn Violet's head into honeycomb."

A flutter of trench coat in the corner of her eye and Cheshire blitzed forward. But Dillinger was fast. Way fast. He had his other darling pointed at Cheshire's head before he could tackle the gunslinger.

"Do that again, and you can make Glitterglam out of your girl-friend," Dillinger said to Cheshire, waving the pistol in his face.

Movement flashed in Violet's periphery, but it only took a moment for her to realize it wasn't coming from the other Rememberists.

Vials tinkled together as countless shocktroopers filled the labyrinthine catwalks above, pointing their assault rifles down upon the Rememberists. Walls began to unfold, curling outward in great swathes of metal and exhaust. The sound of escaping steam filled the air, the

thrum of pistons coming to life. A pair of mechanized machines stomped out of the shadows, each step pulverizing the ground, each flanked by more shocktroopers. Their clanking gearwork whirred as they towered above the Rememberists. One arm consisted of a sledgehammer, the other a minigun twenty times the size of Parminder's.

"Clankers," Declan said under his breath.

Perched above the catwalks walked the birdman. When he was immediately overhead, he stepped onto the catwalk's railing and walked off the edge. As he fell, he snapped open his coat and extended his arms. The air caught and he drifted down, feather-soft, until he landed beside Violet without a sound.

His head snapped toward her in an inhuman angle, neck crackle-popping. Golden skin refracted the rainbow hue that encompassed the interior of the Packard Plant, his coat pulled tightly about his body once more. "Good evening, princess," the birdman said, smoke puffing from his lips with each word. "We've been expecting you."

Violet tilted her head toward him in acknowledgement. "Mister Cinder."

"Wait," Declan said. "How do you know the Feather Man?"

Violet avoided Declan's eyes and said, "We were introduced by a mutual friend."

"Introduced?" Morgan said. He jostled his AK-47 which triggered numerous shocktroopers to do the same. "What the hell is going on here? Dillinger?"

"The gunslinger had nothing to do with your fabled Princess Electric meeting me," Mister Cinder said while he inhaled deeply, as if drawing on a cigar. "Or the queen for that matter. He's simply here to make sure you all made it without issue, and that you all behave yourselves. We can avoid bloodshed."

"You met the queen?" Declan whispered, more to himself than Violet.

"Does your brother not tell you anything?" Dillinger said, smirking as he drew his broken bottle eyes to Declan. "He took her. Remember

when I got shot in the stairwell? What a perfect diversion. Even Cheshire didn't know I was helping him backstab you all."

Declan looked as though he'd been shot, as if his life were oozing out between bloody fingers. "Cheshire," he said, his brother's name stone-heavy. "Is that true?"

Cheshire didn't say anything, his eyebrows crinkling with emotional pain. He looked like a boy who'd just been told his dog had to be put down.

What little color Declan had left in his cheeks drained from his face. He stood there, swaying, as if he'd been told he had only a few moments left to live.

Violet smirked.

"What's so funny?" Parminder asked.

Violet laughed.

"Violet?" Morgan said from beside the apiarist. "Are you okay?"

"She's just fine," Dillinger said. "Placebos can be wonderful things."

"Why did you do that to her?" Cheshire asked, pushing forward slightly. "She should've been protected from the processing residue like the rest of us."

Dillinger lowered the gun so it pressed into Cheshire's chest. "I gave her a placebo so she can make an informed decision. Letting the memory rifts perforate her psyche will let her pick what she really wants to do—without you or me or anyone else influencing her. The queen is confident that Violet will make the right decision."

"Well at least we know who the spy is," Parminder said. Behind her veil, Violet knew the apiarist was gritting her teeth, ready to tear into Dillinger and Cheshire with her smoking bee swords at the earliest convenience.

"Spy has such negative connotations," Dillinger said, smiling.

Violet couldn't stop laughing at the absurdity of the situation. She understood that Dillinger had given her a placebo, and that she was naked to the memory processing toxins in the air—which was pretty humorous. But it was even more funny that nobody knew he was a spy.

Everyone seemed so surprised. Cheshire was the double-whammy. She guffawed.

"I like to look at myself as more of an entrepreneur," Dillinger said, ignoring Violet's laughter. "I simply exchanged a few things with the queen."

"Like your morals?" Declan said.

"No." Dillinger smirked. "I joined the Delirium Directorate and they provided me an opportunity. I have limitless freedoms. I can cross over into the real and back again without your pathetic age restrictions. I have guns that never expire. I have unlimited access to the pleasures and corruptions within the Palace of Memories End. And to think all I had to do was give up a few token memories. A small price to pay for power."

Violet laughed again, this time loud and forced. She looked around the Packard Plant, at the hundreds of memjack shocktroopers, and at the two dreadnaught behemoths spewing exhaust into the crystalline air. The number of memjacks around them was disconcerting at best. If things went sour, then the Rememberists would be mowed down like weeds. Even with their powers, there were so many memjacks that they wouldn't even have a chance to spark a lightning storm or hide behind a shield of shadow before bullets would rain.

Not to mention the two clankers. One clanker looked like it could destroy Pallium, let alone two.

Violet stopped laughing. Mister Cinder jerked his head around, smoke wreathed around his feathered-coat. He narrowed his lava-bright eyes on Violet. "Have you made a decision?"

"Yes," Violet said, trying not to look at Cheshire or Declan. "I have."

"And what is it?" Mister Cinder said as smoke twirled from his mouth.

Violet took a deep breath. She glanced at Cheshire and let herself soak in the sea of his eyes. They were no longer looking at Dillinger or the gun pointed at his face, but at her. She didn't want to turn away. Violet could almost feel the coldness of his chest, the soft palpitations of

her hand against glass, and the way his stained glass heart sunset-shimmered within.

She turned her gaze toward Declan, and as their eyes met she wanted to turn away. But she didn't. There was such an unconditional love in them, such profound sadness, such *disappointment*, that Violet nearly broke down. Tears welled, matching shimmer for shimmer with Declan's. He slowly shook his head, as if he already knew what she was going to say. Declan closed his eyes for a moment, the compression of eyelids pressing out a single tear that snaked down the shadows which clung to his face. As the tear sparkled like a diamond within the dimple of his chin, Violet turned away, not wanting to see it fall.

One day soon she would forget this very moment; forget the way Declan had believed in her.

One day she would forget *him*.

"What do I need to do to accept the queen's offer?" Violet said amidst several gasps from the Rememberists.

"You simply need to accept my hand," Mister Cinder said, unfurling his feathered coat and extending a white-gloved hand.

As Violet reached out to take it, Cheshire yelled. Declan ran forward in a streak of shadow. In one fluid motion he took off his forget-me-not lei and tossed it around Violet like a lasso. He wrapped his hands within the lei. Forget-me-nots popped like bubble wrap, instantly melting and soaking Violet with their ice-cold wash.

Gunshots exploded from Dillinger's darlings. And as the edges of Violet's vision blurred into electric azure, bullets perforated Declan's body.

And he fell into her arms.

INTERLUDE/ TWINKLE, TWINKLE

VIOLET IS STANDING beside her sister's white car. She has a snow-brush in her hand, and she's in the middle of clearing a carpet of powder from the windshield. Her breath clouds with each sweep of the brush. The car's running, headlights cutting into the wintry darkness. Music thumps from a house in the distance, its windows lantern-yellow and inviting. People are loud in their shouting and laughing, amplified by alcohol and naivety.

Snow falls.

She finishes brushing off the car when the déjà vu slams into her. *I've been here before.* She smacks the brush against one of the tires. *I've been to this house party.* Violet looks around, trying to recall a moment or a clue, anything to ease her mind away from the uncomfortable feeling of having done something the same before. She shrugs, not able to pin the recollection to the moment.

Violet opens the driver-side door and slips into the car, tossing the brush onto the passenger side floor. Karin is sitting in the passenger seat, her head lolling as she turns to face Violet. Karin's hair is slightly matted from the melting snow, but it still shimmers from the car's interior light. She's hammered. Violet can smell the wine coolers on her breath and

she hasn't even spoken yet. The alcohol is seeping out of her pores. The car smells like strawberries and sugar.

"Take me home before I freeze my ass off some more," Karin slurs, her head bobble-heading about as she tries to sit still.

Karin?

This isn't right.

Something's not right.

"What?" Karin says, knocking her head against the window. "Can we go, or what? I have to work first—" She pauses and places a hand delicately on her chest. Concentration waxes across her face, and then almost as quickly fades. Hard, deep swallow and then she says, "I have to work first thing in the morning. So let's go!" She lightly punch-pushes Violet in the arm.

Violet feels foreign sitting in the driver's seat. Luckily, nobody is parked in front of her. She effortlessly pulls out of the parking spot and onto the driveway. Snow crunches under the tires. Windshield wipers sweep.

Snow falls.

She checks her mirrors as she drives toward the road, snowflakes bright as stars in the headlight beams. Karin groans, but ignores Violet and continues to lean against the cold glass of the window.

Violet screams.

In the rearview mirror are a pair of shadow-ringed eyes staring back at her.

She doesn't need to ask who it is. She knows.

Declan.

"What are you doing back there?" Violet questions as the sudden reasoning for the déjà vu smacks into her. This is not some strange dream, or some alternate reality. This is a replay.

"I'm here to show you something," he says calmly. "I'm here to walk along this memory with you."

He looks paler than usual in the back seat of the car, sitting in shadow. Alone.

"There is nothing to see," Violet says as she stops at the end of the driveway, the car sliding slightly. "We both know what's going to happen."

"Do we?" he says. "I don't think we do."

Declan's face twists in pain. He coughs. When he pulls his hand away, there is a streak of red across the corner of his mouth. Violet is about to ask if he is okay when she remembers the Packard Plant and her sister's memories. Dementia and Mister Cinder. She remembers Declan looking so lost and hurt at her decision to join the Queen of Glass. She remembers how he ran and broke his lei over her to initiate this memory walk. Remembers the muzzle-flash that lit up Declan's face like a campfire.

Dillinger.

Gunfire.

Bullets.

Snow falls.

"You should never have done this, Declan," Violet says, pulling onto the country road. The shoulders of the road are invisible against the snow. A car goes by too fast, fishtailing. "You should have just let me go. The queen would have erased this memory from my mind. I could have forgotten all of this!"

Declan takes a pained breath. "And for what cost? An eternity in the Palace of Memories End?" He coughs again, blood spackling the air. "An eternity of forgetting what makes you the Princess Electric?"

"At what cost?" Violet says, gripping the steering wheel as the car slides into the other lane and back again. "You could die. You could die right there in the factory and then what? All of that sacrifice, the forgetting, would have been worth it just for you to be alive. For you to continue to *remember*. Remembrance is what makes you, you, Declan. You have learned so much more from your memories than I ever will. Continue to fight the Delirium Directorate, and one day, when you cut me down alongside the queen, be assured that I will not remember how wonderful you are. I will have forgotten how you had believed in me.

"I will have forgotten myself."

Declan leans forward, wincing in pain. "No," he says, shaking his head, "no. You must see this memory through. Open your eyes, Violet. Open them to the possibility that you've been wrong all this time; that true power is within the memories we hold closest to our hearts, no matter how painful they are. Forgetting is easy and painless. But remembrance," he says, staring at her through the rearview mirror. "Remembrance is illuminating."

She glances over at Karin, her stomach in knots. Her sister is passed out against the window, oblivious to the conversation around her. In a few moments she will put her in a coma again. Unless, that is, she pulls the car off the road. Violet tries to turn the steering wheel, tries to tap the brakes but she can't. Something unseen is preventing her from doing so, as if she's on rails.

"Let me stop this," she says, trying to force the car to stop. "I can't do this again."

"There's no stopping the memory walk once it's begun," Declan says, sitting back in the shadows. "It is what it is and will be again."

"Dammit, Declan!" Violet shakes the steering wheel, her hands slick with sweat. "This isn't worth it." Tears bristle across Violet's eyes. Her gut clenches. "This isn't worth the pain."

Violet drives down a small hill toward a four-way stop. The car slows and then skids to a stop at the intersection. The road to her right goes up a hill, steep and snow-covered. To her left there is nothing but flat, open road lined by naked trees, just like in front of her. The stop sign has a flashing red light that pulses like a heart.

Snow falls.

This is the intersection. She takes her foot off the break. *This is where it starts.* She places her foot lightly on the gas. She glances at Karin once more, drunk and quiet and beautiful beside her. Violet goes to open her mouth to wake her, but she can't. Not because she's prevented by some invisible force, but because she doesn't want Karin to see what is about to happen. Not again.

Violet pulls the car slowly into the intersection, but the asphalt is coated in a thick sheet of ice and snow. Tires spin. The car inches forward and then stops. She sees headlights.

Snow falls.

Flashing blue maintenance lights.

A snowplow crests the top of the hill to Violet's right, barreling down toward the car. It's going fast, recklessly fast, and the headlight beams cut through the car like lasers. Violet instinctively presses the gas pedal. Tires spin. She slams her foot back down on the gas pedal, and the tires spin more, but the car's not moving. The plow's blade is curling snow off the road like vanilla fondant. The plow starts to slide slowly sideways, brakes squealing.

Snow falls.

Violet screams.

Her foot is pressed so hard against the gas pedal her leg is locked. Tires whir against the snow and ice. Karin groggily wakes, peeling herself from the illuminated window. She looks at Violet, and in that moment, Violet knows that her eyes are betraying her guilt. Karin sobers instantly and turns toward the oncoming plow.

Impact.

The blade slams into the car, curling and compressing the metal like a trash compactor. Everything slows down, and Violet sees how Karin's head snaps toward her, how her body is squeezed against the seatbelt. Her hair floats in the air as if immersed in water, angelic in the headlight glow. The car is picked up by the speed of the plow, coddled and flipped over in the arms of the blade and deposited on its roof.

Glass explodes and ricochets in the interior. The sound of grinding metal fills the cabin. The sound of metal on asphalt.

Then there is nothing but silence.

The escaping of breath.

Violet is upside down, hanging from her seatbelt. Even though her body is exploding with pain, she looks toward Karin. Screams after Karin. Her sister is suspended, arm limp at her side. Her other arm,

along with the other side of her body, is compressed into the frame of the car in a mangled, misshapen mess. Blood is spilling from her injuries, drizzling through the fractured windshield and onto the snowy road. The ambient light from the snowplow flashes turbo blue across the snow. Violet counts the flashes, times them with her sister's rampant breathing. Karin's breath is fluttering in and out in the sudden rush of cold air, in and out, like the flit of a butterfly.

Violet twists around to look in the back of the car. Declan is there, hanging upside down. He is covered in so much blood that his trench coat glistens wetly in the snowplow's lights, zippers metallic crimson. About a dozen small holes riddle his coat, tiny wisps of smoke licking the air from them. Blood runs out of his coat and down his neck in bright rivulets, over his jaw and along his cheeks, pooling around his eyes and continuing into his hair. Liquid shadow drips from his skin, his placid face cracking into a slight smile as he says, "See, Violet. I told you it was an accident. I told you to just believe." With that his body turns limp, his arms fall, resting on the roof of the car. A final breath shudders from his wheezing chest.

Declan's eyes focus on everything and nothing at the same time.

Then he fades away.

Before Violet can yell at Declan, Karin slowly turns her head toward her. Her hair is thick with blood, her face peaceful and calm, the pain long since replaced by shock and inevitability. She reaches out and Violet takes her hand. It's cold and syrupy with blood, but Violet squeezes it.

"Remember me always," Karin says, her eyes wide and tired. "Twinkle, twinkle, my little star." And with that, Karin's hand grows limp in Violet's.

The brightness within her eyes dissipates like dying stars.

And Violet is left alone in the silence of falling snow.

29/ THE PRINCESS ELECTRIC

THE ACCIDENT SCENE SHIMMERED, the flashing blue and red lights of emergency vehicles reflecting off the snow. Violet was still holding her sister's hand when the car blurred. Then she was back in the Packard Plant, her vision adjusting to the countless spotlights that were directed on her. She was still holding a hand, though it no longer belonged to her sister.

Declan.

She was on her knees in a large pool of blood, his head coddled within her lap. Bullet holes continued to smoke as blood drained from his chest, spreading out in a pool across the floor. She squeezed his hand to let him know that she was still there, that she was with him for whatever happened.

"What have you done, Dill?" Parminder whispered from somewhere outside the ring of light.

"He moved so fast," Dillinger said. "I had no choice. It didn't have to be this way."

Violet didn't give the gunslinger the satisfaction of a look. Instead, she took her free hand and swept Declan's disheveled hair away from his face. The liquid shadow had dripped away, leaving his face clear and

exposed and pristine, like freshly carved marble. It was the first time she'd ever seen Declan without shadow masking his face, and he was angelic under the spotlights. Blood stippled his lips. "Come close to me," he wheezed.

She leaned closer, resting her ear against his lips.

"Do you believe now?" he breathed. "Do you believe that you're the one?"

"Declan," she answered, trailing a finger along his face. "I'm nobody. Just a girl who got lost."

"No," he said, straining to breathe. He coughed weakly, fluid heavy on his lungs. "You're the Princess Electric. Look at yourself."

She looked at her hand within Declan's, at how bright it was glowing. It had never shone so intensely before—not even with Cheshire. Same with her other hand. She looked around and quickly realized that the circle of light she was kneeling in was not from the spotlights directed down at the table, but was emanating from her.

Her skin crackled. She could feel the power coursing through her body. Maybe the crash wasn't her fault. Maybe everything that had happened because of it was coincidence from something she couldn't control. She looked at Declan, tears sliding down her face. He had given his life to show her the power of memory. He had believed in her so much that he sacrificed himself just so that she could see the light.

She placed her head next to his, his breathing shallow and slow. "I do believe," she whispered. "I do."

And with that her light intensified even more, sending out streaks of luminescence into the factory. A wave of relief seemed to blanket Declan and his body tensed, and then relaxed. "I know," he sighed. He squeezed her hand once more, his eyes sea-dark and filled with a knowing satisfaction.

Violet hovered over his lips.

"Forget-me-not," he said, his voice as distant as yesterday.

"I will remember you always," Violet lowered her lips onto his and

she kissed him delicately. His lips responded for a moment, pressing against hers.

Then the pressure began to fade, his mouth growing unresponsive. Violet pressed against his mouth again, but her efforts weren't returned. She felt a brush of coldness. Declan's body began to shimmer, his skin sparking under her. She pulled away from his lips, slowly, and brushed her hand across her mouth. Glitter. She could taste its metallic tincture and the inherent traces of memory.

Violet pressed against his body, tears spilling from her face, but he caved away, as if she were hugging sand on the beach. His body shimmered star-bright and dissolved under her, spilling out across the pool of blood.

Declan was gone.

He had turned to glitter.

———

Violet ran her hands through the glitter, trying desperately to scoop it up and hold it close to her, but it slipped through her fingers—fingers that glowed electric bright.

She paused for a moment to feel the power surging through her hands and the way the glitter reacted to her touch. It crackled under her hands like sparklers. She stood up, and as her hands pulled away from the pile of glitter surrounding her, it followed her lead, spiraling up into her hands and swirling about her in coils of gold.

The Rememberists stood motionless, staring agog as she rose. Cheshire's face was streaked with tears, his eyes wet and well-wide and staring at the glitter circling about Violet. Dillinger had his darlings still trained on her, but his face was a mixture of shock and fear. Mister Cinder stood beside Dillinger, his perfect gold face emotionless except for the curlicues of smoke that leaked from his mouth.

"I take it you are reneging on the offer," the phoenix said.

"No," Violet said as glitter swirled about her. "I'm changing the offer."

Mister Cinder chortled, his boney body shaking under his coat of feathers. "Nobody changes offers."

"I do," Violet said, eyes focused. "And my change is this: I will accept the queen's offer if she agrees to stop all memory siphoning from the real while I share her throne."

"Don't be ridiculous," Mister Cinder snapped. "She would never accept that."

"Then it looks like we don't have an agreement."

"Indeed it does." Mister Cinder cracked his head in an odd angle of acceptance. "Be aware that this was a one-time offer. Queen Zamelerish will not take the news favorably."

"I'm not concerned with how the queen takes anything."

Mister Cinder stared at Violet with his magma-bright eyes and unfurled his abnormally long arms. Underneath his feather coat he wore an impeccable suit, tailored and pinstriped in the myriad colors of the rainbow. "Cheshire, come along now."

He glanced at Mister Cinder, then back to Violet. Inner turmoil furrowed his brow. He took a few long, drawn out breaths and said, "No. My place is with the Rememberists. My place is alongside the Princess Electric."

Mister Cinder puffed out a long stream of smoke. "Then you can die with them too." He snapped his arms down and flew high into the air.

The briefest pause followed. Violet could hear the hearts of the Rememberists beating in their chests and the clink-clack of Cheshire's stained glass core. The sound of distant wind chimes. The sand-on-concrete brush of glitter. Sweat dappled Dillinger's forehead. He licked his lips.

The swirling glitter around Violet increased its intensity, her skin florescent-bright within the golden cyclone. Time had grown still. She could see each individual grain of glitter encircling her, the slow blink of

Dillinger's eyes, the slight increase of pressure as he began to squeeze the triggers.

Violet splayed her fingers. She willed the remaining glitter off the floor, the glitter which had once been Declan. It rose, joining the rest of the glitter flying around her. She placed her hands together, fist upon fist, and envisioned the fabled sword.

This time when her hands made contact a larger globe of light burst forth. The glitter funneled toward her hands, stacking up and compressing into a hardened blade. It continued to accumulate until a towering blade of gold-red glitter stretched from her hands.

"Glitterglam," Cheshire whispered. "You did it."

Violet turned to face Dillinger as he squeezed the triggers. The pistols kicked, muzzles flashing repeatedly. Violet held up the sword and watched the bullets leave the guns, watched them spiral toward her. Effortlessly, she moved the blade into their path, smacking them out of the air like bees drunk on winter.

She moved toward Dillinger as she batted down bullets. He continued to fire, faster and faster, until the barrels of his darlings began to glow red. Violet walked toward him, redirecting bullets up into the catwalk. Shocktroopers tumbled, their suits rupturing. They slammed into the ground, bodies bursting in gouts of white fluid and escaping steam.

When Violet reached Dillinger she swiped the sword across the barrels of his guns, severing them at the cylinder yoke. His mouth opened in horror, and he dropped his darlings at her feet. He raised his hands in surrender and took a step backward.

Cheshire dropped his assault rifle and removed his lei as he walked up to him. He tossed it around Dillinger's head, twisting it like a noose. "Don't forget this," Cheshire said as he kicked him. Dillinger's green eyes opened wide as he stumbled backward, falling onto the concrete floor.

Smoke began to emanate from the lei as the forget-me-nots burned into his flesh. Sizzling and boiling, they cooked into him, slowly

dissolving his body. Steam and screams filled the air until Dillinger was no more.

Hovering above, Mister Cinder's feathered coat stretched wide in the ambient light. His head twisted down as his body elongated, the suit tearing as multicolored feathers burst through. "Wipe. Them. Out." And with those words, he tumbled into himself, the wings cracking and folding until he dissolved in a cloud of smoke and ash.

Chaos erupted.

Shocktroopers opened fire as the Rememberists scattered. Loud, monotonous whirs sounded from the clangers, their massive miniguns spinning. Bullets spewed from the miniguns, sending streaks of fire throughout the factory.

Morgan huddled behind one of the large organs. "What do we do now?" he yelled while shooting at targets along the catwalks.

Parminder opened her duffel bag and removed her minigun. "We need to take at least one of the clangers down as fast as we can or our cover will be disintegrated."

Violet crouched down as bullets slammed into the machine in front of her. "I'll create a diversion if you can channel into one of the clangers from behind."

"A diversion? Like this?" The voice came from behind Morgan. Violet turned in time to see Mister Cinder towering over him, almost doubling Morgan's height. The birdman flicked out his clawed hand. Numerous obsidian-black talons grew outward like horrifically long needles. He took his arm and slammed it into the back of Morgan, lifting him up and throwing him across the factory. Morgan crashed into stacks of crystalMem, sending rainbow sugar cubes flying.

Parminder screamed and lit up her minigun, but Mister Cinder was too fast. He burst into a cloud of smoke.

Clangers moved forward, clomping as they went, servos whirring. Plumes of exhaust floated upward and clouded the catwalks.

"That might be an advantage we can use," Cheshire said, pointing toward the smoke.

"And I see movement over there from Morgan," Parminder said. "He's not dead."

"Or at least, not yet," Cheshire added under his breath.

"Okay," Violet said, holding Glitterglam beside her. "Parminder, get ready to take one of those tanks down. Cheshire, light up those catwalks. And both of you, watch out for the birdman."

Cheshire nodded as he held out his hands. Small sparks of light formed in his palms. He closed his hands around the sparks, pulling in more light and drawing attention to his position. He stood stoically as thousands of bullets hammered his position. When he gathered enough light to form two spheres the size of basketballs, he stepped out into the line of fire and threw one at a clanger. The light ball hit its target, knocking the clanger back and short-circuiting it for a moment. Lightning crackled over its metal body. The other ball he tossed up into the air. It flew into the clouds of clanger exhaust and exploded, blinding the memjacks and opening the floor for safe movement.

"Now!" Cheshire yelled.

Violet ran out from cover and toward the operational clanger. A few shocktroopers were standing around it, firing on her as she ran. She knocked away bullets, redirecting some of them back to their source. Shocktroopers hissed as bullets tore into their armor, white splashes of memory-striped fluid leaking out. She ran under the clanger's legs, dragging her sword across its underbelly. Sparks exploded as electrical wires were severed. It stumbled but regained its composure, slamming the sledgehammer down on Violet. She had forgotten about the hammer, and didn't realize how fast these mechanized machines could move. Violet dodged at the last moment, the sledgehammer cratering the concrete.

Parminder stepped out of the shadows, her minigun revving. Bees and bullets shot out of the minigun, smoke spilling from each barrel. They darted toward the clanger's back as it aimed its minigun at Violet. Bees slammed into the dreadnaught. It staggered, the bees drilling into its internal components. Smoke began to pour out of its back.

The apiarist continued to scream obscenities as she channeled her powers into her minigun, unleashing more and more bees that took to the air and attacked the shocktroopers along the catwalks. Soon memjacks began to drop like dead flies from above, hitting and bursting along the concrete floor.

The clanger went limp and short-circuited. It grew quiet for a moment, then exploded in a great ball of fire and metal, sending out pieces of shrapnel that trailed through the air.

Violet had run up the minigun and now stood atop the second clanger. She raised Glitterglam, ready to stab it down into the dreadnaught's core when it re-engaged, nearly bucking her off. She quickly found her balance and grabbed a maintenance railing to hold on to. The dreadnaught raised its sledgehammer and tried to sweep her off, smashing itself and damaging its armor in the process. She held her breath and raised her sword one more time.

She slammed the sword down into the dreadnaught, pushing Glitterglam as deep as she could. Electrical cording burst out, sparking. Fire ignited. She pulled out the sword and pointed to the interior of the clanger. Glitter snaked up from the floor of the factory and into the clanger. As the chemical fire increased, she unhooked her boot and back-flipped off, somersaulting through the air and perfectly landing catlike on the ground.

The clanger shook, raising its sledgehammer. Violet pointed toward the dreadnaught and splayed her fingers. It exploded in a flash of neon fire and electric glitter, taking out the catwalks above. The remaining shocktroopers fell, some landing within the burning inferno, their bodies hissing and steaming as they ignited.

Violet turned around. Parminder was on the other side of the factory, exhausted and sitting beside her minigun, her eyes bright behind her veil. Across the way was Morgan. He was severely injured, but somehow standing and leaning against one of the factory machines, holding his stomach.

"Where's Cheshire?" Violet asked.

"Right here," he said from behind her. Violet spun around, her heart skittering. Mister Cinder had his arm around Cheshire.

"Very impressive," the phoenix said, smoke trailing from his words. "But we have something to discuss before I leave."

"And what's that?" Violet asked cautiously.

"Cheshire has decided that he no longer wants to be loyal to the Queen of Glass, and that he would much rather be in your company. Well, that's well and lovely, but you see, he is not just a member of the queen's retinue. He is a *part* of her. His heart belongs to Queen Zamelerish. Not you."

Violet tensed. She was the only one outside of the queen and her minions that knew of his stained glass heart, and she wanted to keep it that way. If the phoenix was going to take Cheshire, she'd have to take him out.

"So," Mister Cinder continued, "he can stay here, but remember, *newfallen*, that Dementia is the queen's domain. She controls everything —including Cheshire. There will come a time that she'll call on him. And he'll come home like a good dog, right after you wake up with a shard of glass in your stomach."

Violet stared at Mister Cinder, then looked over at Cheshire. He was calm, his eyes reflecting the light of the chemical fire behind her. He winked.

"Thanks for the advice," Violet said, turning back to Mister Cinder. "Tell the queen that I hope she chokes on my memories."

Mister Cinder chortled, smoke shooting out of his mouth as his head pinioned. He shoved Cheshire toward her and disappeared in a cloud of smoke, leaving only a few white feathers behind.

30/ ILLUMINATION

VIOLET STILL HELD Glitterglam in her hands, its gold-red blade scintillating in the fires that burned throughout the factory. She didn't want to discard it. It contained the final traces of Declan Gloss, his essence compacted into each tiny spark of glitter that made up the blade. She realized that when she dismantled Glitterglam, Declan would disperse into the folds and shadows of Dementia, erased like footprints along a shore. But then again, now that Violet had refused the queen's offer, she would have his memory locked within her mind, forever able to replay their moments together—and that made a smile curl upon her lips.

Then her stomach plummeted.

Memories!

Violet spun around, trying to locate the table that held her sister's memories. She spotted it, upturned with its broken legs splayed in the air. "No!" she yelled, running over to the table. She scoured the ground, pushing the table aside and frantically sifting through the battle's detritus.

They must be here!

Panic overwhelmed her. Her sister's memories were the reason she'd come back to Dementia in the first place. Her heart ricocheted within her ribcage. Cheshire was beside her, rummaging through deflated memjack bodies. Morgan was limping toward them.

"Is this what you're looking for?"

Violet stopped scrounging. That voice was the last one she'd expect to hear. She turned around to see Parminder slouching from the weight of her minigun, its barrels still drawing white trails of smoke in the air. Her veil was stuck to her face with sweat, eyes dim from exhaustion. She held a vial that swirled with liquid rainbow.

"Yes!" Violet said, running over to the apiarist. Parminder shrugged off the minigun and it clanged to the ground. Violet took the vial and held it up to the light. Her eyes widened as the serial number read true, the contents purling against her touch.

"I could hug you," Violet said unabashedly.

"Please don—"

Careful of Glitterglam, Violet wrapped her arms around Parminder. The apiarist tensed for a moment and then relaxed. Parminder hugged her back, albeit weakly. When Violet backed away, Parminder said, "Be careful. If you do that again I may like it."

Violet smiled, tucking the vial into her peacoat. An explosion shook the building as a fire moved through the crystalMem lab equipment. "Take Morgan back to Pallium," Violet said, looking around the factory. "I have one more thing left to do here."

"You should leave now," Cheshire said as another explosion rippled through the factory. "Who knows how safe it is? The queen could send reinforcements at any time."

"No," Violet said, shaking her head. "She'll be waiting for us to make our next move. She won't strike before that."

"How do you know?" Morgan asked, coughing and wincing in pain. Blood soaked his vest and coat. Blood spackled his pillowy shirt. He took Parminder's shoulder for support.

"Because," Violet said, smirking. "We embarrassed the Queen of Glass in her own backyard. She won't let that happen again so easily. Now get out of here. Head back to the portal while I finish up. I'll meet you back at Pallium."

"What are you going to do?" Cheshire asked with concern as he took the other side of Morgan. They started walking toward the ramp with Parminder.

"Oh, nothing much." Violet held up Glitterglam, watching it refract the firelight. "I just have a factory to destroy."

————

Violet watched the Rememberists walk out into the glitter-snow and disappear. The heat from the fires warmed her face. It was a welcome relief from the cool confines of Dementia and the perpetual chill that seemed to permeate everything. She watched the crystalMem sugar cubes ignite and burn in chemical-rainbow brightness. Those were a lost cause. There was no way that she knew of to reengineer the memories that had been cooked down and cut with diamorphine and other narcotics to form crystalMem.

But the vials of memories were another story. Countless stories in fact. It appeared that the lower level of the factory created the sugar cubes, and the upper levels housed the premium essence—the raw, liquid memory that would be birthed into butterflies for consumption by the queen and her prized retinue.

"This is where the ending starts," Violet said, eyeing a series of vials that hung from a severed cord above. She walked over and took a swing. Glitterglam ruptured the vials. Memory sprayed the air in a fan of multi-colored grume. As the congealed liquid fell it started to flutter, wings taking shape from clots of green and orange and blue. They pirouetted in flashes of yellow and purple, red and violet, until there were so many butterflies they sounded as if they were speaking to her in whispers of forgotten moments.

Violet pointed to the tumult outside and said, "Go home." As if by command, the butterflies began to disperse, funneling away from her. She smashed more vials until she could no longer reach them, her heart beating fast with the excitement of freeing so many memories. There was no way she could ever find the rightful owners to the memories. But simply knowing that they would no longer be captured and consumed by the queen filled her with overwhelming purpose.

She held out her arms and Glitterglam separated, forming two blades, one in each hand. Violet focused on the glitter-snow outside, focused on the stream of butterflies and how they coiled and danced with newfound freedom. She closed her eyes, imaging the glitter reacting to her thoughts, flowing around her, through her.

When she opened her eyes, the butterflies appeared to be surfing a stream of liquid gold as the glitter flew into the factory from the outside, separating from the snow. Glitter spilled in from the perforated ceiling, past the organ chimneys and burning catwalks, past the conveyor belts and processing machinery and storage cages. It merged with the glitter from outside, spinning around Violet in a whirlwind of gold dust.

She felt electric. Her skin glowed nova-bright, illuminating the entire factory in an angelic incandescence. Glitter continued to spill into the factory in chains, until a vortex of glitter surrounded her, throwing debris and memjack bodies against the exterior walls. Violet inhaled deeply, a sudden sense of calm focus falling upon her. She raised her arms, directing the dust with Glitterglam into the upper levels of the factory.

The glitter reacted, bursting out in every direction like a million shooting stars. It smashed into vials and storage cages, ruptured machinery and containment crates. New fires burst forth, catwalks and conveyor belts collapsing under the weight of so much glitter.

Liquid memory began to pour from the rafters like syrup as Violet began to walk outside. Behind her, waterfalls of memory cascaded down, fluttering and bursting into butterflies. She continued walking until she reached the concrete fence. Turning around in the snow, she

watched the myriad of butterflies flit about the factory, which burned brightly against the winter landscape.

Violet held out the pair of swords. She let go, and they hovered in front of her. With a sweep of her hand, Glitterglam broke down, shifting back to red-gold glitter. She reached out and grabbed a handful, placing it inside her inner peacoat pocket. It burned against her breast, and she knew that feeling would never leave her for as long as she lived.

For as long as she could remember.

Violet pointed toward the burning factory and the red-gold glitter shot toward it like a rocket. The entire structure exploded in a chemical mushroom cloud of butterflies and glitter. The moon shimmered beyond the firelight, reflecting the scene below, and the rift in the firmament irised into itself until it disappeared.

A rainbow arched from the center of the destroyed factory, stretching far into the distance, illuminating Dementia as it cut across the sky and landed somewhere in the adjacent district. The clouds and darkness cleared at that moment, allowing Violet to see where the rainbow had touched down.

It connected to a crooked clock tower.

Violet smiled at this, watching the millions of butterflies dance along the multicolored pathway, traversing the rainbow toward the clock tower.

Toward the Ayrton Light.

Violet took a deep breath as she watched the clock tower start to glow like a high-powered lantern. It refracted the rainbow into a single concentrated light that swept through the Borough of Medulla like a lighthouse beam. It melted the darkness from the sky, replacing it with an orangey-blue canvas filled with rainbow-tinted clouds. The buildings in the illuminated areas stabilized, their facades more solid, more vibrant. And the glitter continued to sift down across the borough, but it was luminous and golden compared to the silvery motes she'd become accustomed to in Dementia.

She placed her hand on her peacoat and felt the warmth of the glitter, of her sister's memories. Excitement filled her body and she allowed her mouth to curl into a slight smile, knowing that she could finally deliver Karin's memories to her. Violet's sister would remember her once again.

"I can see clearly now, Declan," she said, a warm tear trailing across her cheek.

Then she turned around, and walked into the portal.

Cheshire was waiting for Violet when she stepped out of the mirror and into the throne room of the Royal Palace of Madrid.

"What did you do?"

"I took care of something."

"We can see that," he said, helping Violet down from the mirror. "Everyone can. The clock tower is illuminating Medulla."

"Good," Violet said. "And to think we're just getting started." She stopped outside of Stem. "Is Parminder okay?"

"Parminder is fine, just a few bruises here and there. I think she's most damaged from the hug you gave her."

"I'm sure. And Morgan and Melody?"

"Morgan is in pretty bad shape, but Parminder is tending to him with salves and some sort of disgusting honey and dandelion tincture. He's going to be okay once he recovers from the shit Parminder's pouring down his throat. Melody is still in a coma. She goes into these fits of delirium, so we have her in a padded room and locked down in restraints. I don't know if she'll ever come out of it."

Violet bit her lip, suddenly thinking of Declan. "And you,

Cheshire?" she asked, taking her hand and placing it on his chest. Even through his trench coat she could feel the coldness of the glass, the clack-thrum of his glass heart beating within ribs of pewter. "How are you doing, my stained glass prince?"

Cheshire grinned sadly. He placed his hand on top of hers and pressed it firmly against his chest. "I miss my brother already," he said, his summer-bright eyes flooding. "I don't want to forget him, Violet. I don't. But I'm afraid my memory is damaged from chasing so many butterflies. I fear I've already forgotten things, like how he'd look at me when I'd say something he disagreed with. I think I'm already forgetting his voice. I can't remember what Declan's laugh sounded like."

"That's because he never laughed," Violet said, smiling.

That evoked a chuckle from him, and a few tears fell along his cheeks. "That," he said, sniffling, "I do remember."

"Don't worry," Violet said, her voice soft. "I'm not going anywhere. I'm going to be right here with you, in Dementia, and I'll make sure you don't forget anything again."

"Promise?"

Violet leaned forward and kissed him, soft as a butterfly. "I promise."

Cheshire smiled then, curling a lock of Violet's hair around her ear.

"Now I need to go do one last thing," Violet said, tracing a tear along Cheshire's cheek.

"Want company?"

"No," Violet said, stepping away from Cheshire's embrace and into Stem. She closed the cage door. "This is something that needs to be done alone."

Realization spread across Cheshire's face. "Right. Then I will see you soon?"

"Forget-me-not," Violet said, pressing a button with a wink.

"I will remember you always."

Violet smiled at that. Then Stem descended into Pallium in a cloud of steam.

———

Violet walked into the Mausoleum of Memory alone.

The concentric rings of illuminated busts spiraled up into the domed ceiling where the prophecy was still etched in glass. So much had happened since Violet had stood here with Parminder. So many illuminations. So much pain and death.

Violet looked up into the rings of glass and found an empty bust, devoid of butterflies. She realized that tradition stipulated the memory that was sacrificed upon joining the Rememberists should be used. But Declan had bartered his memories with the Accountant to help Violet track down her sister's memories. Declan's butterflies were gone.

She walked up to the anonymous bust and placed her hand on its cool glass surface, her fingers breathing light into the head. Violet reached into her pocket and pulled out a handful of the red-gold dust. She knelt in front of the bust, cupping the glitter tightly in her hand. Leaning forward, she placed her hand next to the small opening in the bust's lips that would have been used to deposit the butterfly.

She thought back to all the moments she had spent with Declan, from her first arrival to his ultimate sacrifice. For only knowing him for such a short time, he had shown her more than anyone else about love and life and the power of looking back, of remembering those moments, no matter how small and insignificant they may be. For as much as her heart lay with Cheshire, she owed Declan her life—and she would never forget that.

Violet took a deep breath, leaned forward, and slowly blew the glitter into the bust as she recalled every touch, every look, every comment Declan had given her, every dance. He had believed in her unconditionally, and she would continue to let him illuminate her way in Dementia with his memory.

As the glitter swirled within the bust, it caught light from Violet's breath, scintillating inside like a snow globe. Violet softly kissed the forehead of the bust and said goodbye to Declan Gloss.

"I will remember you always, shadow boy."

As Violet turned to walk back to Stem, the sound of bells filled the mausoleum.

They were the Westminster chimes, ringing from the clock tower.

A Rememberist had been laid to rest in the Mausoleum of Memory.

And another was ready to set Dementia on fire.

EPILOGUE/

THE MENTAL HOSPITAL was exactly as Violet had left it. The storage closet still smelled of bleach and cleaning products, and the hallways reeked of frailty and hopelessness. She couldn't tell what time it was, or the date, but due to the darkness of the hallway she figured it must be after midnight.

Violet navigated the various wings of the Weeping Willow Psychiatric Villa, passing a few nurses in their various stations, talking and laughing about residents, or sitting quietly drinking coffee and planning dosages for the following day.

Eventually she found her sister's room, though instead of going in right away, she paused outside her door. This was where everything had started, where she had surprised those slurpers into dropping a kaleidoscope. It was scary to think where she'd be if that hadn't happened. More than likely she'd be in this very psychiatric hospital hooked up to a lithium drip, biding her days till the end.

She cracked her sister's door.

Shadows played across the room from the moonlight, the curtains parted. It was snowing outside, soft, billowy flakes that floated down like cotton balls. She slipped inside and closed the door.

Her sister lay there, sleeping soundly, peacefully, her sheets held tightly to her chin. A sudden flood of emotion hit Violet, her stomach nauseous, tears rimming her eyes. What if this didn't work? What if these memories went back in and she still freaked out?

But then Violet remembered Declan, and what he had sacrificed so she could retrieve that small vial of possibility. She remembered what all the Rememberists had given. What Melody had given. And with that, she walked up alongside the bed and gently pulled down the sheets to her sister's shoulders.

Violet reached into her peacoat and removed the vial. It glinted in the moonlight, the liquid memory shifting and swirling within. She tilted Karin's head back, opening her mouth in the process, and unstoppered the vial. Tiny wisps of rainbow-colored light danced along the vial's opening. She took a breath and poured the liquid memory into Karin's mouth.

When Violet finished pouring the vial, Karin vaulted awake, sitting straight up and coughing. Her eyes were wild and kaleidoscopic, shimmering in the moonlight from the window.

"Shhh," Violet said. "It's okay, Karin, I'm here." She reached down and took her hand. It was warm to the touch, Violet's skin as bright as the moonlight streaming through the window.

Her sister turned to her, eyes fading back to a marbled green. Confusion furrowed her brow. Surprise filled her face.

"What time is it?" she said, more awake than groggy.

"I don't know, but it's early in the morning," Violet said cautiously, somewhat waiting for her sister to start yelling obscenities and calling for the nurse.

Karin blinked. Refocused.

Then smiled.

"Violet," she said, laughing. "It's a bit early for a visit, isn't it?"

"Never," Violet said, beaming. Relief flooded her body. "It's never too early or too late for a visit."

"I agree," Karin said. "Now are you going to give me a hug or do I have to wait?"

"You never have to wait for a hug. Ever."

Violet gave her sister the biggest hug she could muster.

And then another one.

Violet spent the entire day at the Weeping Willow, visiting with Karin. Even Alice seemed more like herself and was happy to see her visiting once again. At the end of the day, Violet said her goodbyes, though she knew she'd be back soon. She wasn't eighteen yet and could come and go from Dementia without restriction. Besides, she'd have to keep an eye on Karin. Until the Queen of Glass was destroyed, Karin wouldn't be safe, though the queen had other things to worry about after losing a processing plant and the illumination of an entire borough.

Before using the kaleidoscope to transition back to Dementia and rejoin the Rememberists, Violet had a final stop to make.

She had to see her mom.

Violet took the bus home, the weather not nearly as bad as when she'd left. On the bus she tried calling Christine. Surely her friend would be worried sick about her and where she'd been for the last few days. Violet left her a voicemail, making up some story about how she had a hard time dealing with her birthday and the anniversary of the accident, and that she needed some time. She knew Christine would call bullshit on that explanation, but really, now wasn't the time to explain Dementia—or the prophecy. She hoped to come back soon and explain everything.

When the bus dropped Violet off, she walked up to the front door,

then realized she didn't have her house keys on her. The door was locked, so she went around back.

From the backyard, a large window provided a great view into the kitchen. Her mom was making dinner—which she never did. Violet moved down to the sliding door and looked inside. Her stepfather was watching television with a beer and a giant bowl of chips resting on his gut.

Home sweet home.

She slid open the sliding door and stepped inside, kicking snow from her boots. Her stepfather didn't move; he just stared at the television like a zombie. Violet's mother was stirring something on the stove, her back turned toward the sliding door. The house smelled like pasta sauce and garlic bread.

Violet's stomach gurgled with hunger.

"Hey," Violet said, sounding bored. "I'm home."

Nothing.

"Guys?" Violet said a bit louder.

Silence.

Violet walked over to her stepfather and then she stopped dead. There, from one of his temples, dripped a trail of liquid rainbow. Violet's heart rocketed. She looked around. Besides the football game, the house looked untouched and quiet. She turned around and faced her mother. "Mom?" Violet said. "Mom, what's going on?"

Her mother stopped stirring. She set the spoon down beside the stove.

"Mom, it's Violet. Answer me."

Her mom turned around slowly, her apron smeared with tomato sauce. Her eyes were distant, glazed over and lost.

"Who are you?" she asked, her voice harsh and angry. "And what the hell are you doing in my house?"

Golden rain continued to fall around Gapstow Bridge, illuminated by the gaslights marking the pathway. The large tree near the bridge sat quietly in the still air, white daffodils nodding to the raindrops that slipped off the boughs above.

The rain intensified in a small area of the pond, no more than the width of a hula hoop. The drops continued to hammer the water until the splashes turned into tiny waves. They rose in the compact area, sluicing against an invisible barrier. The water began to froth.

And then a man shot out of the circular patch of crashing waves and foam, high into the air. He hovered for a moment in the rain, a long white trench coat hanging off his lithe form. Underneath, a crisp white shirt and black tie.

He glided toward the bridge and set down with an effortless grace, his body perfectly erect. The man took out a comb and fixed his hair while taking in the surroundings.

His gaze fell on Stem, sitting in the distance.

"You'd think after ten years away they could at least roll out a red carpet for me." He shook his head and walked toward the elevator, the surface of the pond quiet once more except for the patter of rain.

THE END

ACKNOWLEDGMENTS

Since I avoid clichés while writing, I'm going to use one (or more) in the acknowledgments: it takes a village to develop a book from the tiniest spark of an idea to the completed work before you. And this feat would not have been possible without the love and support of the following:

My wife, Erika, for your constant, unwavering support over the years. You have been there from the very beginning, cheering me on through countless ups and downs as I rode the rollercoaster of publishing life. When I've needed to bury myself in writing, or revisions, or numerous other book-related tasks, you've been there to handle everything else and keep our family afloat. Even now, as I write this acknowledgment, you are helping our kids with their homework. I am forever grateful. And I love you.

My daughters, Charlotte, Claire, and Maddy, for your excitement about the book and for always spreading the word that your dad is a "cool" writer. You are the ultimate street team. Thank you for understanding when I've had to disappear into my writing cave. Your enthusiastic questions of "How's it going?" while dropping off drinks and snacks propelled me to the finish line. Thanks for being my biggest fans. <3

My brother, Paul Mann, for always checking in to make sure I'm

still living in reality, and that I haven't decided to move into my worlds full-time.

My in-laws, Bob and Karin Tiefenbach, Bobby and Anita Grottoli, and Jennee Mann, for taking a genuine interest in how things are going with "the writing." Your support is beyond appreciated. And Karin, thank you for the constant food deliveries—I'll never say no to rouladen or freshly baked muffins. They are the ultimate writing fuel.

Karin Lowachee, for tirelessly reading multiple drafts of pretty much everything I write including emails (I send a lot), for every conversation over sushi, or late night coffee in Tim Hortons because Starbucks closes way too early. For the countless texts to bounce ideas around, and for being one of my earliest supporters. Thank you for being such an amazing friend. I appreciate you.

Amber Van Dyk, for being at the ready to read new material, fun competitions on who can make the best "joiny" words, and for whipping me with the Buddha noodle when I need it—which is often!

Hailey Turner, for being my ride or die foodie and always being up for hitting the best restaurants (gimme meat!) and watering holes (omg those pearl onions!). I could not have done this without your always-there-to-help support and encouragement, even when I'm messaging you with ridiculous questions at weird hours because I'm panicking about something trivial. Next dinner is on me! (You so know where we're going. :))

John Klima, for listening to me prattle on at 3am about the trials and tribulations of writing while we're on the verge of passing out. You are a consummate roomie at conventions, my BarCon partner and Taco Bell champion. I will share a bathroom counter with you always.

Adrienne Kress and Maureen McGowan, for the long conversations on summertime patios or inside toasty pubs. This thing called life can be a challenge at the best of times, and it's downright ludicrous once you add word wrangling into the mix. Thank you for your shoulders when I've needed them; you'll always have access to mine.

Claire Legrand, for being my movie soundtrack sister. It seems like

eons ago that we discussed this book over questionable pizza at Book Expo America, and your excitement has never waned. Thanks for all the fun conversations about film scores, life, the universe, and everything.

Susan Dennard, for your friendship and laughter. Distance and life have made it difficult to hang out in person lately, but your support and enthusiasm for this book means a lot to me. Thank you.

Morgan Rhodes, Eve Silver, and Juliana Stone, for sharing your wisdom and welcoming a new soul into your world. The hilarity around the table when we're together is intoxicating. Let's get out of this pandemic and straight to a restaurant or patio soon!

Frank Beddor, for sharing your zest for imagination and creating exciting worlds. It's always a blast to talk world building and I look forward to the next time we can do it in person. You first read this book during its infancy—thank you for your continued enthusiasm about Violet and her adventure.

Rae Carson, for the laughter, friendship, and for reading some early drafts of the opening and providing feedback when the book was starting to bloom. The journey to bring this book to life has been extremely long and I'm thankful you've been a part of it since the beginning.

Marcy Pedersen, for devouring an early draft and sharing your thoughts. You've read more books than anyone I know and your insight is very much appreciated. Sending you another first draft. Check your inbox. Just kidding. Or am I?

Torkidlit (Toronto Area MG & YA Author Group), for countless get-togethers to celebrate success and talk shop, providing enough inspiration to last a lifetime. Thank you to: Claudia Osmond, Debbie Ridpath Ohi, Megan Crewe, Leah Bobet, Lesley Livingston, Ian Keeling, Bev Katz Rosenbaum, Lena Coakley, Danielle Younge Ullman, Karen Krossing, Kate Blair, Joanne Levy, Helaine Becker, Robert Paul Weston, Ishta Mercurio, and Jo Karaplis.

To the rest of my author and publishing family: Michael R. Underwood, C.C. Finlay, S.K.S. Perry, Kelly Morisseau, Carolina M. Valdez,

Lee Harris, Tobias S. Buckell, Peter Darbyshire, Miriam Kriss, Jenni Gaynor, Holly McDowell, Suzie Townsend, Courtney Moulton, Julie Particka, Bradley P. Beaulieu, Kelly Swails, Chris Szego, and Jamie Lee Moyer, thank you so much! You have all supported me in a multitude of different ways, and I am extremely thankful.

And finally, to Betty Tyman. You were the best grandma a boy could have and this story would not exist without you. I will remember you always.

As I said at the beginning of the acknowledgments, it takes a village.

I hope you enjoy THE PRINCESS ELECTRIC.

Forget-me-not,
Derek Silver
January 2021

CONNECT WITH DEREK

Want to find out when the next book is being released? Sign up for Derek Silver's newsletter to stay up to date on his upcoming books, appearances, contests, sneak peeks, and more! He promises to only send exciting news items. No spam.

You can find Derek at his website dereksilver.com, or at the following places:

Facebook Author Page
Instagram
Twitter
Goodreads

Honest reviews are always welcome.

Thank you!

f facebook.com/dsilverbooks
twitter.com/dsilverbooks
instagram.com/dsilverbooks
goodreads.com/dsilverbooks